PENGUIN  CLASSICS

WAR AND PEACE

COUNT LEO NIKOLAYEVICH TOLSTOY was born in 1828 at Yasnaya Polyana in the Tula province, and educated privately. He studied Oriental languages and law at the University of Kazan, then led a life of pleasure until 1851 when he joined an artillery regiment in the Caucasus. He took part in the Crimean war and after the defence of Sevastopol he wrote *The Sevastopol Stories*, which established his reputation. After a period in St Petersburg and abroad, where he studied educational methods for use in his school for peasant children in Yasnaya Polyana, he married Sophie Andreyevna Behrs in 1862. The next fifteen years was a period of great happiness; they had thirteen children, and Tolstoy managed his vast estates in the Volga Steppes, continued his educational projects, cared for his peasants and wrote *War and Peace* (1865–68) and *Anna Karenin* (1874–76). *A Confession* (1879–82) marked an outward change in his life and works; he became an extreme rationalist and moralist, and in a series of pamphlets after 1880 he expressed theories such as rejection of the state and church, indictment of the demands of the flesh, and denunciation of private property. His teaching earned him numerous followers in Russia and abroad, but also much opposition, and in 1901 he was excommunicated by the Russian holy synod. He died in 1910, in the course of a dramatic flight from home, at the small railway station of Astapovo.

ROSEMARY EDMONDS was born in London and studied English, Russian, French, Italian and Old Church Slavonic at universities in England, France and Italy. During the war she was translator to General de Gaulle at Fighting France Headquarters in London and after the liberation, in Paris. She went on to study Russian Orthodox Spirituality, and has translated Archimandrite Sophrony's *The Undistorted Image* (now published in two volumes as *The Monk of Mount Athos* and *The Wisdom from Mount Athos*) and *His Life is Mine*. She has also translated Tolstoy's *Anna Karenin*, *The Cossacks*, *Resurrection*, *Childhood, Boyhood, Youth*, Turgenev's *Fathers and Sons* and Pushkin's *Queen of Spades*. Her other translations include works by Gogol and Leskov. She is at present researching into Old Church Slavonic texts.

L · N · TOLSTOY

WAR AND PEACE

TRANSLATED AND

WITH AN INTRODUCTION

BY

ROSEMARY EDMONDS

PENGUIN BOOKS

PENGUIN BOOKS

Published by the Penguin Group
27 Wrights Lane, London W8 5TZ, England
Viking Penguin Inc., 40 West 23rd Street, New York, New York 10010, USA
Penguin Books Australia Ltd, Ringwood, Victoria, Australia
Penguin Books Canada Ltd, 2801 John Street, Markham, Ontario, Canada L3R 1B4
Penguin Books (NZ) Ltd, 182–190 Wairau Road, Auckland 10, New Zealand

Penguin Books Ltd, Registered Offices: Harmondsworth, Middlesex, England

First published 1869
This translation first published in Penguin Classics in two volumes 1957
Reprinted with revisions 1978
Reissued in one volume 1982
10

Copyright © Rosemary Edmonds 1957, 1978
All rights reserved

Made and printed in Great Britain by
BPCC Hazell Books Ltd
Member of BPCC Ltd
Aylesbury, Bucks, England
Set in Monotype Bembo

CONTENTS

Introduction   vii
Note on the 1978 Revisions   xiv
Four Notes   xv
Biographical Note   xvii
Principal Characters   xix

Book One

    Part 1: July 1805 (old style)   3
    Part 2: October 1805   125
    Part 3: November 1805   231

Book Two

    Part 1: 1806   345
    Part 2: 1807   406
    Part 3: 1808–10   490
    Part 4: 1810–11   574
    Part 5: 1811–12   632

Book Three

    Part 1: May, June, July 1812   715
    Part 2: August 1812   810
    Part 3: September 1812   974

Book Four

    Part 1: August 1812   1107
    Part 2: October 1812   1168
    Part 3: October–November 1812   1220
    Part 4: November–December 1812   1273

Epilogue

    Part 1: 1813–20   1339
    Part 2   1400

INTRODUCTION

*'There is no greatness where simplicity, goodness and
truth are absent.'*

*In the year 1861 Tolstoy organized a school on his estate, where he taught
the children of his unlettered serfs. At the same time he was publishing a
magazine to 'educate the educated'. At first the twofold self-imposed task
seemed to progress well; but gradually the desire to teach and the necessity
for hiding the fact that he did not know what to teach brought him very near
despair, from which only the thought of marriage saved him. He had tried
everything but family life, and although in January 1862 he noted in his
Journal: 'All my teeth are coming out and I am still unmarried; it is likely
that I shall remain a bachelor for ever,' and the thought of a single life no
longer 'terrified' him, he decided to test the one remaining promise of happiness. Spiritually exhausted, discouraged, and worn down with a cough which
he was unable to throw off, at the age of thirty-four, in the autumn of 1862,
he married a girl sixteen years younger than himself.*

*In a letter to his cousin a year later Tolstoy writes: 'Never before have I
felt my intellectual and even all my moral faculties so unimpeded, so fit for
work. And I have work – a novel of the period 1810–1820, which has completely absorbed me since the beginning of the autumn.... Now I am an
author with all the powers of my soul, and I write and reflect as I have never
written or reflected before.' The novel was War and Peace, and Tolstoy
had entered on the third period of his life, the eighteen years during which he
lived what he called a 'sound, upright, family life.'*

*Tolstoy had read 'with relish' the history of Napoleon and Alexander I
of Russia, and immediately found himself 'enveloped in a cloud of joy. My
mind was filled with the possibility of doing a great thing – of writing a
psychological novel of Alexander and Napoleon, and of all the baseness, all
the empty phrases, the foolishness and the inconsistencies of their entourage
and of the pair themselves'. Eager and exhaustive research into his subject –
il lungo studio e il grande amore – and the writing of War and Peace
occupied him to the exclusion of all else for the next five years, until the
final proof sheets were corrected and the book appeared, first serially and*

then in six volumes in 1869. Emerging from his study after a day when the work of creation had gone well, Tolstoy would tell his family that a little more of his life-blood had gone into the inkwell. From beginning to end the Countess acted as his amanuensis, struggling with the often barely decipherable manuscript, parts of which Tolstoy drafted seven times before being satisfied. (The entry in her Journal for 12 November 1866 reads: 'I spend my whole time copying out Liova's novel. This is a great delight to me. As I copy, I live through a whole world of new ideas and impressions. Nothing has such an effect upon me as his ideas and his genius.' And two months later: 'All this winter L. has kept on writing, wrought up, the tears starting to his eyes and his heart swelling. I believe his novel is going to be wonderful.')

Tolstoy's subject is humanity – people moving in the strange delirium of war and war's chaos. The historic scenes are used as a foil and background for the personal dramas of those who took part in them. Interest is mainly concentrated in two households – the Rostovs, impoverished country squires, and the Bolkonskys, standing outside and higher than 'high' society – and Pierre Bezuhov. In the way Tolstoy has of walking through all his books, in War and Peace he may be identified with the two heroes, Pierre and Prince Andrei, in their passionate, unremitting strivings towards 'the infinite, the eternal and the absolute'. (He even anticipates his own maturer views when Pierre comes to the conclusion that 'to live with the sole object of avoiding doing evil so as not to have to repent is not enough. I used to do that – I lived for myself and I spoilt my life. And only now, when I am living for others – or at least trying to – only now do I realize all the happiness life holds.')

'The one thing necessary, in life as in art, is to tell the truth' was Tolstoy's doctrine, and his life was bound up with this anxiety, this search for the inward truthfulness which is reality. Tolstoy does not contrive: he records, recoiling from nothing and 'in the gutter seeing the image of the sky'. With him we watch his characters grow – Natasha running into the drawing-room with her doll in 1805 and Natasha going to church in 1812 is one and the same person at two different ages – not two ages fitted on to one person. We are conscious of family resemblances: Prince Andrei and his father are alike, only one is young and the other old. The Rostovs have in common some intangible quality which makes one conscious that Vera is a true Rostov while Sonya comes of different stock. In Pierre we can recognize his father, although old Prince Bezuhov appears only to die, and never utters a word.

Tolstoy knows *his characters inside out – even to the way they walk.* (*Prince Vasili 'did not know how to walk on tiptoe and jerked his whole body awkwardly at each step'.*) *Revealing psychological pictures are conveyed with no less economy:* 'Prince Andrei always showed particular energy when the chance occurred of taking a young man under his wing and furthering his ambitions. Under cover of obtaining assistance of this kind for another, which his pride would never let him accept for himself, he kept in touch with the circle which confers success and which attracted him.' Here is Julie Karagin, *the wealthy heiress who succeeds in bringing Boris Drubetskoy to the point of proposing:* 'There was no need to say more: Julie's face beamed with triumph and self-satisfaction; but she forced Boris to say all that is usually said on such occasions – to say that he loved her and had never loved any woman more. She knew that for her Penza estates and the Nizhni Novgorod forests she could demand that, and she received what she demanded.' And *the French general Davoust who could have claimed better conditions than a peasant's hut with a tub for a seat:* 'Better quarters could have been found for him, but Marshal Davoust was one of those men who purposely make the conditions of life as uncomfortable for themselves as possible in order to have an excuse for being gloomy. For the same reason they are always hard at work and in a hurry. "How can I think of the bright side of existence when, as you see, I sit perched on a barrel in a dirty shed, hard at work?" the expression of his face seemed to say.'

This penetrating observation is equally sure when applied to nations. 'A Frenchman's conceit springs from his belief that mentally and physically he is irresistibly fascinating both to men and women. The Englishman's self-assurance comes from being a citizen of the best-organized kingdom in the world, and because as an Englishman he always knows what is the correct thing to do, and that everything he does as an Englishman is undoubtedly right. An Italian is conceited because he is excitable and easily forgets himself and other people. A Russian is conceited because he knows nothing and does not want to know anything, since he does not believe that it is possible to know anything completely. A conceited German is the worst of them all, the most stubborn and unattractive, because he imagines that he possesses the truth in science – a thing of his own invention but which for him is absolute truth.'

Nothing could be simpler than the mass of incidents described in War and Peace. *All the everyday happenings of family life – conversations between brother and sister, between mother and daughter, partings and reunions, hunting, Christmas holidays, dancing, card-playing* (*all the 'superbly ren-*

dered domesticity' over which Arnold Bennett was so enthusiastic) – are threaded on to the necklace with as much care as the account of the battle of Borodino. Each incident is vividly portrayed, each circumstance is real, as seen through the eyes of the various protagonists. An oak-tree standing by the highway, a moonlit night are choses vues, not by the author but by Prince Andrei driving by, and Natasha who cannot sleep. In the same way we live the battle of Austerlitz with Nikolai Rostov, share Petya's excitement over the Emperor Alexander's arrival in Moscow, and are one with Natasha as she interprets the solemn prayer for deliverance from the invader. It is never events themselves, however important and far-reaching, which interest Tolstoy, but the effect of the event on the individual and the latter's contribution to the event. In following the life of the spirit Tolstoy would have us seek out the spark of heroism, discover the poetry and dignity lying hidden in the human soul on its long progress in quest of the Kingdom of Heaven. But in his preoccupation with the ethical domain Tolstoy never loses sight of his aim as an artist, which, as he said in a letter to a friend, 'is not to resolve a question irrefutably but to compel one to love life in all its manifestations, and these are inexhaustible. If I were told that I could write a novel in which I could indisputably establish as true my point of view on all social questions, I would not dedicate two hours to such a work; but if I were told that what I wrote would be read twenty years from now by those who are children today, and that they would weep and laugh over it and fall in love with the life in it, then I would dedicate all my existence and all my powers to it.'

War and Peace is a hymn to life. It is the Iliad and the Odyssey of Russia. Its message is that the only fundamental obligation of man is to be in tune with life. In the words of a contemporary critic it is 'a complete picture of human life; a complete picture of the Russia of that day; a complete picture of everything in which people place their happiness and greatness, their grief and humiliation. That is War and Peace.... When the Russian Empire ceases to exist, new generations will turn to War and Peace to find out what sort of people were the Russians.' All the historians' accounts of the fateful year of 1812 ring hollow in comparison with the vitality, the actuality of Tolstoy's tableau of Russia during the great Napoleonic wars. And since Tolstoy's approach is always sub specie aeternitatis, he has created human beings working out their destiny in accordance with the eternal implacable laws of humanity. (In one place he even comments ironically: 'People of limited intelligence are fond of talking about "these days", imagining that they have discovered and appraised the peculiarities of "these days" and that human nature changes with the times.') He is deeply aware of the continuity of life. 'Life – actual everyday life,' he writes, 'with its essential concerns of health and sickness, work and recreation, and its intellectual preoccupations with philosophy, science, poetry, music, love, friendship, hatred, passion – ran its regular course, independent and heedless of political alliance or enmity with Napoleon Bonaparte and of all potential reforms.' And when the long chronicle draws to its end, nothing is finished. The last words are given to Prince Andrei's son, a child of fifteen, on the threshold of life. For Tolstoy, as for Pierre Bezuhov, 'Life is everything. Life is God. Everything changes and moves to and fro, and that movement is God. And while there is life there is joy in consciousness of the Godhead. To love life is to love God.' It is a pantheist philosophy, and Tolstoy is obsessed by the thought of man's greatest efforts and best hopes being defeated by death. (His own private tragedy was that having got to the gates of the Optinsky monastery, in his final flight, he could go no farther, and died.)

Tolstoy is a moralist, not a mystic. Christianity for him was a moral teaching, not a revelation. He loved the empirical, hated the transcendental. In his rationalism, in his luminous cleverness, he is a typical child of what Léon Daudet called 'le dix-neuvième siècle stupide'. His greatness lies in his extraordinary gift for psychological analysis and introspection – in his ability to capture and portray the flavour, the intimate quality of physical sensations (the little girl climbing down from the stove and feeling with her toes for the crevices between the bricks), and atmosphere (the feverish gaiety of Moscow in the weeks before the city fell to the French): this is not transient, this is immortal.

Tolstoy's realism drove him to strip war of its panache. 'Not to take prisoners ... that by itself would transform the whole aspect of war and make it less cruel. As it is we play at being magnanimous and all the rest of it. Such magnanimity and sensibility are like the magnanimity and sensibility of the lady who faints at the sight of a calf being killed: she is so tender-hearted that she can't look at blood – but fricassée of veal she will eat with gusto.... If there were none of this magnanimity-business in warfare, we should never go to war, except for something worth facing certain death for. ... And when there was a war ... it would be war! And then the spirit and determination of the fighting men would be something quite different.... War is not a polite recreation but the vilest thing in life, and we ought to understand that and not play at war. Our attitude towards the fearful necessity of war ought to be stern and serious. It boils down to this: we should have done with humbug, and let war be war and not a game. Otherwise, war is a favourite pastime of the idle and frivolous ... there is no profession held in higher esteem than the military.'

His attitude to history is the exact opposite of Carlyle's hero-worship. He sees the unconscious urges of mankind as the only agents of history, and applies to events the law of necessity that he observes operating in the lives of individuals. The note of philosophical fatalism sounds again and again. ('Hamlet should have been a Russian, not a Dane,' exclaimed William Morris after reading War and Peace in which every personage, every incident may echo Luther's cry, 'Ich kann nicht anders'.)

The second part of the famous Epilogue is entirely devoted to the problem of freewill versus this driving force of necessity. Tolstoy shows us what lay behind the epic conflict between Napoleon and the Russian people. For the first time since the beginning of history the Russian ideal manifested itself, and, confronted with this dynamic, the whole might of Napoleon and Napoleonic France crumbled and was eclipsed. The automatic interaction of cause and effect screened the awakening of forces which had not had to be reckoned with before: the spirit of simplicity, goodness, and truth – simplicity, the supreme beauty of man; goodness and truth, the supreme aims for which man should live and work. In 1812 simplicity, goodness, and truth overcame power, which ignored simplicity and was rooted in evil and falsity. This is the meaning of War and Peace. Tolstoy describes Kutuzov, the symbol of the Russian people (whose personal motto was 'Patience and Time'), as 'a simple, modest and therefore truly great figure who could not be cast in the lying mould invented by history'; and with Prince Andrei sees his importance in the fact that he 'will not introduce anything of his own. He will not scheme or start anything, but will listen, bear in mind all that he hears, put everything in its rightful place. He will not stand in the way of anything expedient or permit what might be injurious. He knows that there is something stronger and more important than his own will – the inevitable march of events, and he has the brains to see them and grasp their significance, and seeing that significance can abstain from meddling, from following his personal desires and aiming at something else.'

Kutuzov is complemented by Karatayev, the old soldier, 'qui accepte sa place dans la vie et dans la mort', and is the incarnation of the wisdom Pierre gropes for. 'Karatayev had no attachments, friendships, or loves, as Pierre understood them; but he felt affection for and lived on sympathetic terms with every creature with whom life brought him in contact, and especially with man – not any particular man but those with whom he *happened to be.... His life, as he looked at it, held no meaning as a separate entity. It had meaning only as part of a whole of which he was at all times conscious.' In Karatayev, 'the unfathomable, rounded-off, eternal personification of the spirit of simplicity and truth', we have the whole Russian people – the real heroes of the tremendous* épopée *of* War and Peace.

R. E.

NOTE ON THE 1978 REVISIONS

For this reprint of my translation of *War and Peace* (first published in the Penguin Classics series in 1957) I have made some slight amendments in order to conform to the definitive Russian text prepared by E. E. Zaïdenshnure of the L. N. Tolstoy State Museum for the Belles Lettres edition of the *Collected Works of L. N. Tolstoy*, Moscow 1962–3.

In his absolute moral awareness and total moral engagement with the fate of his characters Tolstoy often neglected literary style. His handwriting was close and all but indecipherable. Most pages of his manuscript present an intricate maze of superimposed drafts, marginal insertions and substitutions. Small wonder that in her nightly copying of her husband's output during the day the Countess misread words, mistook word order, even missed out whole phrases occurring between two identical words. Printers and proof readers succeeded no better, and the first (1868–9) Russian publication of *War and Peace* contained 1,885 errors which automatically reappeared in all subsequent editions during the following ninety-four years.

The textual analysis undertaken by Madame Zaïdenshnure and her fellow scholars involved disciplined and intelligent checking and comparing of Tolstoy's MSS., the copies made by his wife and other collaborators, proofs corrected (often rather half-heartedly) by the author or one of his disciples, and so on – in all, some 5,500 pages of manuscript and print. Corrections concerning the aspect of Russian verbs, word order and the like often do not affect the English translation; but misreadings and omissions which distort or entirely fail to convey Tolstoy's original version have been rectified in the present reprint.

R.E.

FOUR NOTES

1. *Proper Names*. To ease the path of the Western reader I have often dispensed with the Russian patronymic, retaining only the first name and surname. To the same end the feminine termination of proper names has not been rendered into English.

2. *Passages in French*. French, the study of which was first encouraged in Russia by Catherine the Great, eventually became the language in which the educated classes thought and expressed themselves. In several of the various versions of *War and Peace* long passages appeared in French, but when Tolstoy undertook some revision in connexion with an edition of his collected works early in 1873 he excluded the French language. As there is no final, definitive, 'canonical' text of the novel, all but short remarks have been translated, though I have indicated where the original reads in French.

3. *Dates*. Apparent discrepancies in dates – for the French, for instance, the battle of Borodino occurred on 7 September, which for the Russians was 26 August – are explained by the fact that Russia, and Eastern Europe, generally, held to the old Julian calendar, and only adopted the new Gregorian calendar at the beginning of the present century.

4. *Sun-spots*. Tolstoy is guilty of various inaccuracies, of trifling importance in themselves but troubling to the translator. In 1805 Natasha appears as a child of thirteen; in 1809 she is sixteen. Her sister is seventeen in 1805 and twenty-four in 1809. Nikolai Rostov joined the army in September 1805 and returned in February 1806 – after an absence, that is, of five months. But in the memorable description of his home-coming we are told that he had been away 'a year and a half'.

Kutuzov is mentioned as having only one eye – but this does not prevent Tolstoy from referring to Kutuzov's 'eyes'.

When Prince Andrei left for the front his sister hung round his neck an antique silver icon on a finely wrought silver chain. But when he is picked up wounded on the battlefield the French remove from his neck the 'gold icon with its delicate gold chain' which had been put there by Princess Maria.

Old Prince Bolkonsky was well on 5 August, the day of the bombardment of Smolensk. He died on the 15th, after lying paralysed 'for three weeks'.

But where the spirit of life is concerned the alembic of Tolstoy's art is sure and unfailing.

R. E.

L. N. TOLSTOY

Born in 1828 (28 August, old style = 9 September,
  new style)
Married in 1862

Began to write *War and Peace* in 1863
First part published in 1865
Last part published in 1869

Began to write *Anna Karenin* in 1873
Final parts published in 1877

Died in 1910 (7 November, old style = 20 November,
  new style)

PRINCIPAL CHARACTERS

PIERRE (PIOTR KIRILLOVICH) BEZUHOV

COUNT ILYA ROSTOV
COUNTESS NATALIA ROSTOV
NIKOLAI (NICOLAS), their elder son
PIOTR (PETYA), their younger son
VERA, their elder daughter (*m.* Lieutenant Berg)
NATALIA (NATASHA), their younger daughter

SONYA, a niece of the Rostovs

PRINCE NIKOLAI ANDREYEVICH BOLKONSKY
ANDREI (ANDRÉ), his son
MARIA (MARIE), his daughter
LISA (LISE), Prince Andrei's wife
NIKOLAI, their son

MADEMOISELLE BOURIENNE, Princess Maria's French companion

PRINCE VASILI KURAGIN
HIPPOLYTE, his older son
ANATOLE, his younger son
HÉLÈNE, his daughter

OTHER CHARACTERS

ALEXANDER I, Tsar of Russia
BAZDEYEV, OSIP ALEXEYEVICH, a prominent
   Freemason
DENISOV, VASSKA, friend of Nikolai Rostov
PRINCESS ANNA MIHALOVNA DRUBETSKOY, friend of the
   Rostovs
BORIS DRUBETSKOY, her son (*m.* Julie Karagin)
KUTUZOV, Commander-in-Chief of the Russian army
NAPOLEON
ROSTOPCHIN, Governor-General of Moscow

WAR AND PEACE

*

BOOK ONE

PART ONE

I

'*Eh bien, mon prince*, so Genoa and Lucca are now no more than private
estates of the Bonaparte family. No, I warn you – if you are not telling me that this means war, if you again allow yourself to condone all
the infamies and atrocities perpetrated by that Antichrist (upon my
word I believe he is Antichrist), I don't know you in future. You will
no longer be a friend of mine, or my "faithful slave", as you call
yourself! But how do you do, how do you do? I see I'm scaring you.
Sit down and talk to me.'

It was on a July evening in 1805 and the speaker was the well-
known Anna Pavlovna Scherer, maid of honour and confidante of
the Empress Maria Fiodorovna. With these words she greeted the
influential statesman Prince Vasili, who was the first to arrive at her
soirée.

Anna Pavlovna had been coughing for some days. She was suffering from an attack of *la grippe* as she said – *grippe* being then a new
word only used by a few people. That morning a footman in scarlet
livery had delivered a number of little notes all written in French and
couched in the same terms:

If you have nothing better to do, count (or prince), and if the prospect of spending an evening with a poor invalid is not too alarming, I
shall be charmed to see you at my house between 7 and 10.

ANNETTE SCHERER.

'Mercy on us, what a violent attack!' replied the prince, as he came
forward in his embroidered court uniform with silk stockings and
buckled shoes. He wore orders on his breast and an expression of
serenity on his flat face; he was not in the least disconcerted by such a
reception. He spoke in the elegant French in which our forefathers
not only spoke but also thought, and his voice had the quiet, patronizing intonations of a distinguished man who has spent a long life in

3

society and at court. He went up to Anna Pavlovna, kissed her hand, presenting to her view his perfumed, shining, bald head, and complacently seated himself on the sofa.

'First of all, *chère amie*, tell me how you are. Set my mind at rest,' said he, with no change of voice and tone, in which indifference and even irony were perceptible beneath the conventional sympathy.

'How can one feel well when one's moral sensibilities are suffering? Can anyone possessed of any feeling remain tranquil in these days?' said Anna Pavlovna. 'You are staying the whole evening, I hope?'

'What about the party at the English ambassador's? Today is Wednesday. I must put in an appearance there,' said the prince. 'My daughter is coming to fetch me.'

'I thought it had been put off. I must say, all these fêtes and firework displays are beginning to pall.'

'If they had known that it was your wish, the party would have been put off,' replied the prince mechanically, like a watch that has been wound up, saying things he did not even wish to be believed.

'Don't tease me! Well, and what has been decided in regard to Novosiltsov's dispatch? You know everything.'

'What is there to tell?' said the prince in a cold, listless tone. 'What has been decided? It has been decided that Bonaparte has burnt his boats, and it's my opinion that we are in the act of burning ours.'

Prince Vasili always spoke languidly, like an actor repeating his part in an old play. Anna Pavlovna Scherer, on the contrary, in spite of her forty years, was brimming over with vivacity and impulsiveness. To be enthusiastic had become her pose in society, and at times, even when she did not feel very like it, she worked herself up to the proper pitch of enthusiasm in order not to disappoint the expectations of those who knew her. The affected smile which constantly played round her lips, though it did not suit her faded looks, expressed her consciousness of having an amiable weakness which, like a spoilt child, she neither wished, nor could, nor considered it necessary to correct.

In the middle of a conversation about politics Anna Pavlovna burst out:

'Oh, don't speak to me of Austria. Of course I may know nothing about it, but Austria has never wanted, and doesn't want war. She is betraying us. Russia alone must save Europe. Our gracious benefactor realizes his lofty destiny and will be true to it. That is the one thing I have faith in. The noblest rôle on earth awaits our good and wonder-

4

ful sovereign, and he is so virtuous and fine that God will not desert him. He will fulfil his mission and crush the hydra of revolution, which is more horrible than ever now in the person of this murderer and scoundrel. We alone must avenge the blood of the righteous one. On whom can we rely, I ask you? ... England with her commercial spirit will not and cannot comprehend all the loftiness of soul of the Emperor Alexander. She has refused to evacuate Malta. She wants to see – she looks for – some hidden motive in our actions. What answer did Novosiltsov get? None. The English have not understood, they're incapable of understanding the self-sacrifice of our Emperor, who desires nothing for himself and everything for the good of humanity. And what have they promised? Nothing! And what little they did promise they will not perform! Prussia has already intimated that Bonaparte is invincible and that all Europe is powerless before him. ... And I don't believe a word that Hardenberg says, or Haugwitz either. This famous Prussian neutrality is nothing but a snare. I have faith only in God and the high destiny of our beloved Emperor. He will save Europe!'

She broke off suddenly, with a smile of amusement at her own vehemence.

'I think,' said the prince, smiling, 'that if you had been sent instead of our dear Wintzingerode you would have captured the king of Prussia's consent by assault. You are so eloquent. Will you give me some tea?'

'In a moment. A propos,' she added, becoming calm again, 'I am expecting two very interesting men tonight, the vicomte de Morte-mart, who is connected with the Montmorencys through the Ro-hans, one of the best families in France. He is one of the good *emigrés*, the genuine sort. And the Abbé Morio. You know that profound thinker? He has been received by the Emperor. Had you heard?'

'I shall be delighted to meet them,' said the prince. 'But tell me,' he went on with studied carelessness as if the matter had just occurred to him, whereas in fact the question he was about to put was the chief object of his visit, 'is it true that the Dowager Empress wants Baron Funke appointed first secretary at Vienna? The baron is a poor creature, by all accounts.'

Prince Vasili coveted for his son the post which others were trying to secure for the baron through the influence of the Empress Maria Fiodorovna.

Anna Pavlovna almost closed her eyes to signify that neither she nor anyone else could pass judgement on what the Empress might be pleased or see fit to do.

'Baron Funke was recommended to the Dowager-Empress by her sister,' was all she said, in a dry, mournful tone. As she named the Empress, Anna Pavlovna's face suddenly assumed an expression of profound and sincere devotion and respect, tinged with melancholy, and this happened whenever she mentioned her exalted patroness. She added that her Majesty had deigned to show Baron Funke *beaucoup d'estime*, and again her face clouded over with melancholy.

The prince preserved an indifferent silence. Having given him a rap for daring to refer in such terms to someone who had been recommended to the Empress, Anna Pavlovna, with the adroitness and quick tact natural in a woman brought up at court, now wished to console him, so she said:

'But *à propos* of your family – do you know that since your daughter came out she has won everyone's heart? People say she is as lovely as the day.'

The prince bowed in token of his respect and gratitude.

'I often think,' pursued Anna Pavlovna after a short pause, drawing a little closer to the prince and giving him an affable smile, as if to imply that nothing more was to be said about politics and social topics and that the time had come for a confidential chat – 'I often think how unfairly the good things of life are sometimes distributed. Why should fate have given you two such splendid children? I don't include Anatole, your youngest. I don't like him,' she added in a tone admitting of no rejoinder, and raising her eyebrows. 'Two such charming children. And really you appreciate them less than anyone – you don't deserve to have them.'

And she smiled her ecstatic smile.

'*Que voulez-vous?* Lavater would have said I lack the bump of paternity,' said the prince.

'Don't keep on joking. I mean to talk to you seriously. Do you know, I am displeased with your younger son. Between ourselves,' (and her face assumed its melancholy expression) 'they were talking about him in her Majesty's presence the other day and everyone was sorry for you …'

The prince made no reply, but she was silent, looking at him significantly and waiting for him to answer. Prince Vasili frowned.

'What can I do about it?' he said at last. 'You know I did everything in a father's power for their education, and they have both turned out *des imbéciles*. Hippolyte is at least a quiet fool, but Anatole's a fool that won't keep quiet. That is the only difference between them,' he said, smiling in a more unnatural and animated way than usual, which brought out with peculiar prominence something surprisingly coarse and disagreeable in the lines about his mouth.

'And why is it that children are born to men like you? If you were not a father I could find no fault with you,' said Anna Pavlovna, looking up pensively.

'I am your faithful slave and to you alone I can confess that my children are the bane of my existence. They are the cross I have to bear. That is how I explain it to myself. *Que voulez-vous?*' He broke off with a gesture expressing his resignation to a cruel fate.

Anna Pavlovna meditated.

'Have you never thought of finding a wife for your prodigal son Anatole?' she asked. 'They say old maids have a mania for matchmaking. I am not yet conscious of that weakness in myself, but I know a little person who is very unhappy with her father. She is a relation of ours, the young Princess Bolkonsky.'

Prince Vasili said nothing, but with the rapidity of reflection and the memory characteristic of a man of the world he signified by a motion of the head that he had taken in and was considering this information.

'Do you know that that boy Anatole is costing me forty thousand roubles a year?' he said, evidently unable to restrain the gloomy current of his thoughts. He paused. 'And what will it be in five years' time, if he continues at this rate? These are the advantages of being a father. Is she wealthy, this princess of yours?'

'Her father is very rich and miserly. He lives in the country. You know, he is the famous Prince Bolkonsky who was retired from the army when the late Emperor was still alive, and nicknamed the "king of Prussia". He is a very clever man but eccentric and difficult. The poor girl is as miserable as can be. She has a brother who recently married Lisa Meinen. He is an aide-de-camp of Kutuzov's. He'll be here this evening.'

'Listen, *chère* Annette,' said the prince, suddenly taking his companion's hand and for some reason bending it downwards. 'Arrange this affair for me and I am your most devoted slave – *slafe* with an f, as a bailiff of mine writes in his reports – for ever and ever. She is of good family and rich. That's all I want.'

And with the free and easy grace which distinguished him he raised the maid of honour's hand to his lips, kissed it, and having kissed it swung it to and fro as he sank back in his armchair and looked away.

'*Attendez*,' said Anna Pavlovna, reflectively. 'I will speak to Lisa, young Bolkonsky's wife, this very evening, and perhaps it can be arranged. It shall be in your family that I serve my apprenticeship as old maid.'

2

ANNA PAVLOVNA'S drawing-room was gradually filling. The cream of Petersburg arrived, people differing widely in age and character but alike in that they all belonged to the same class of society. Prince Vasili's daughter, the beautiful Hélène, came to take her father to the ambassador's party. She was wearing a ball dress and her maid of honour's badge. Then there was the youthful little Princess Bolkonsky, known as *la femme la plus séduisante de Pétersbourg*. She had been married during the previous winter, and now, owing to her condition, had ceased to appear at large functions but still went to small receptions. Prince Vasili's son, Prince Hippolyte, arrived with Mortemart, whom he introduced. The Abbé Morio and many others also came.

'You have not seen my aunt yet,' or 'You do not know my aunt?' Anna Pavlovna was saying to each new-comer, whom she then gravely conducted to a little old lady with tall stiff bows of ribbon in her cap, who had come sailing in from another room as soon as the guests began to arrive. Slowly switching her eyes from the visitor to her aunt, Anna Pavlovna presented them by name and then withdrew.

Everyone had to go through the same ceremony of greeting this old aunt whom not one of them knew or wanted to know or was interested in, while Anna Pavlovna in pensive silence solemnly observed and approved the exchange of formalities. *Ma tante* repeated the same words to each, asking after the visitor's health and reporting on her own and on that of her Majesty, 'who was better today, thank God'. Politely trying to betray no undue haste, her victims made their escape with a sense of relief at having performed a tiresome duty, and took care not to go near her again for the rest of the evening.

The young Princess Bolkonsky had brought some work in a gold-embroidered velvet bag. Her bewitching little upper lip, shaded with the faintest trace of down, was rather short and showed her teeth prettily, and was prettier still when she occasionally drew it down to meet the lower lip. As is the case with a very charming woman, this little imperfection – the shortness of the upper lip and her half-open mouth – seemed to be a special form of beauty peculiarly her own. Everyone enjoyed seeing this lovely young creature so full of life and gaiety, soon to become a mother and bearing her burden so lightly. Old men and dull and dispirited young men felt as though they had caught some of her vitality after being in her company and talking to her for a little while. Whoever spoke to her and saw the bright little smile accompanying every word and the constant gleam of her white teeth was sure to go away thinking that he had been unusually amiable that day. And it happened the same with everyone.

Swaying slightly, the little princess tripped round the table, her work-bag on her arm, and gaily arranging the folds of her gown seated herself on a sofa near the silver samovar, as if all that she was doing was a *partie de plaisir* for herself and everyone around her.

'I have brought my work,' she said in French, opening her reticule and addressing the company generally. 'Mind you don't let me down, Annette,' she turned to her hostess. 'You wrote that it was to be an informal little evening, so you see what I have got on.'

And she spread out her arms to display her elegant grey dress trimmed with lace and girdled with a wide ribbon just below the bosom.

'*Soyez tranquille, Lise*, you will always be prettier than anyone else,' replied Anna Pavlovna.

'You know,' Lisa went on in French and in the same tone of voice, addressing a general, 'my husband is deserting me. He is going to get himself killed. Tell me what this nasty war is about,' she said, this time to Prince Vasili, and without waiting for an answer she turned to speak to his daughter, the beautiful Hélène.

'What an adorable creature the little princess is!' whispered Prince Vasili to Anna Pavlovna.

Shortly after the little princess, a stout, burly young man with close-cropped hair and spectacles appeared. He wore the light trousers then in fashion, a high starched jabot and a cinnamon-coloured jacket. This stout young man was the natural son of the celebrated grandee of Catherine's reign, Count Bezuhov, who now lay dying in Moscow.

The young man had not as yet entered any branch of the service, having only just returned from abroad, where he had been educated, and this was his first appearance in society. Anna Pavlovna greeted him with the nod she reserved for the lowest in the hierarchy of her drawing-room. But in spite of this welcome of the lowest grade a look of anxiety and dismay, as at the sight of something too huge and out of place, came over her face when she saw Pierre enter. He was indeed rather bigger than the other men in the room, but her dismay could only have reference to the clever, though diffident and at the same time observant and natural expression which distinguished him from everyone else in that drawing-room.

'It is very good of you, Monsieur Pierre, to come and visit a poor invalid,' said Anna Pavlovna, exchanging uneasy glances with her aunt to whom she conducted him.

Pierre muttered an unintelligible reply and continued to let his eyes wander round as if in search of something. He bowed to the little princess with a pleased and happy smile, as though she were an intimate acquaintance, and went up to the aunt. Anna Pavlovna's dismay was not unjustified, for Pierre turned away without waiting to hear the end of the old lady's speech about her Majesty's health. Anna Pavlovna stopped him in alarm with the words:

'Do you know the Abbé Morio? He is a most interesting man ...'

'Yes, I have heard of his scheme for permanent peace, and it is very interesting but hardly practical ...'

'You think not?' said Anna Pavlovna for the sake of saying something and in order to get back to her duties as hostess. But Pierre now committed a blunder in the reverse direction. First he had left a lady before she had finished speaking, and now he detained another who was wishing to get away from him. With head bent and long legs planted wide apart, he proceeded to explain to Anna Pavlovna why he considered the *abbé*'s plan an idle dream.

'We will discuss it by and by,' said Anna Pavlovna with a smile.

And having freed herself from the young man who did not know how to behave, she resumed her duties as mistress of the house and continued to listen and look on, ready to lend her aid wherever the conversation might happen to flag. Like the foreman of a spinning-mill who after settling his men to work walks up and down among the machinery noting here a stopped spindle or there one that squeaks or makes more noise than it should, and hastens to slow down the machine or set it running properly, so Anna Pavlovna moved about her drawing-room, approached some group that had fallen silent, or was talking too excitedly, and by a word or a slight rearrangement kept the conversational machine in smooth running order. But her singular apprehensions about Pierre were apparent all the time that she was occupied with these labours. She kept an anxious watch on him when he went to listen to what was being said in the circle around Mortemart, and then joined another group where the *abbé* was discoursing.

For Pierre, who had been educated abroad, this party at Anna Pavlovna's was the first he had attended in Russia. He knew that all the intellectual lights of St Petersburg were assembled there, and like a child in a toy-shop he did not know which way to look first, so fearful was he of missing any clever discussion that was to be heard. As he looked at the assured and refined expressions on the faces of all those present, he kept expecting something very profound. At last he came up to Morio. Here the talk seemed interesting and he stood waiting for a chance to air his own views, as young men are fond of doing.

3

ANNA PAVLOVNA's *soirée* was in full swing. On all sides the spindles hummed steadily and without pause. With the exception of *ma tante*, beside whom sat only an elderly lady with a thin, careworn face who looked rather out of her element in this brilliant society, the company had settled into three groups. In one, composed chiefly of men, the *abbé* formed the centre. In another, young people were gathered round the beautiful Princess Hélène, Prince Vasili's daughter, and the very pretty, rosy-cheeked little Princess Bolkonsky, who was rather too plump for her years. In the third circle were Mortemart and Anna Pavlovna.

The *vicomte* was a pleasant-faced young man with soft features and nice manners who evidently considered himself a celebrity, though out of good breeding he modestly placed himself at the disposal of the company in which he found himself. Anna Pavlovna was obviously serving him up as a treat to her guests. Just as a clever *maître d'hôtel* offers as a particularly choice dish some piece of meat which no one who had seen it in the dirty kitchen would care to eat, so

Anna Pavlovna that evening served up to her guests first the *vicomte* and then the *abbé*, as peculiar delicacies. The circle round Mortemart immediately began discussing the execution of the duc d'Enghien. The *vicomte* said that the duc d'Enghien had fallen a victim to his own magnanimity, and that there were personal reasons for Bonaparte's resentment.

'Ah, yes! Do tell us all about it, *vicomte*,' said Anna Pavlovna, with a pleasant feeling that *Contez-nous cela, vicomte* had a Louis Quinze air.

The *vicomte* bowed and smiled urbanely, in token of his willingness to comply. Anna Pavlovna arranged a circle round him, inviting everyone to listen to his account.

'The *vicomte* knew the *duc* personally,' she whispered to one of the guests. 'The *vicomte* is a wonderful *raconteur*,' she said to another. 'How one sees the man of quality,' she exclaimed to a third; and the *vicomte* was handed round to the company in the most exquisite and advantageous light, like a well-garnished joint of roast beef on a hot platter.

The *vicomte* was ready to begin his story and a faint smile played about his lips.

'Come over here, *chère Hélène*,' said Anna Pavlovna to the lovely young princess who was sitting a little way off, the centre of another group.

The princess smiled. She rose with the same unchanging smile with which she had first entered the room – the smile of an acknowledged beauty. With a slight rustle of her white ball-dress trimmed with ivy lichen, with a gleam of white shoulders, glossy hair and sparkling diamonds, she made her way between the men who stood back to let her pass; and not looking at any one in particular but smiling on all, as it were graciously vouchsafing to each the privilege of admiring her beautiful figure, the shapely shoulders, back and bosom – which the fashionable low gown fully displayed – she crossed to Anna Pavlovna's side, the living symbol of festivity. Hélène was so lovely that not only was there no trace of coquetry in her, but on the contrary she even appeared a little apologetic for her unquestionable, all too conquering beauty. She seemed to wish but to be unable to tone down its effect.

'What a lovely creature!' remarked everyone who saw her. The *vicomte* lifted his shoulders and his eyes fell, as though he were overwhelmed by something quite out of the ordinary, when she took her seat opposite him and turned upon him the radiance of that un-changing smile.

'Madame, I doubt my ability in the face of such an audience,' said he, inclining his head with a smile.

The princess leaned her bare round arm on a little table and did not think it incumbent on her to say anything. She smiled and waited. All the time that he was telling his story she sat upright, glancing occasionally now at her beautiful rounded arm elegantly resting on the table, now at her still more beautiful bosom on which she re-adjusted a diamond necklace. Once or twice she smoothed the folds of her gown, and whenever the story was particularly exciting she would glance round at Anna Pavlovna and at once assume the very same expression that was on the maid of honour's face, and then relapse again into her radiant smile.

The little Princess Bolkonsky had also left the tea-table and fol-lowed Hélène.

'Wait a moment till I get out my work,' she exclaimed. 'Come, what are you thinking of?' she went on, turning to Prince Hippolyte. 'Fetch me my reticule, please.'

There was a general stir as the princess, smiling and having a word for everyone, sat down and gaily smoothed out her skirts.

'Now I am all right,' she said, and begging the *vicomte* to begin she took up her work.

Prince Hippolyte, having brought her the reticule, joined the circle, moving an armchair close to hers and seating himself beside her.

Le charmant Hippolyte struck one by his extraordinary likeness to his beautiful sister, and still more by the fact that in spite of this resemblance he was astoundingly ugly. His features were like his sister's, but in her case everything was illumined by the joyous, con-tented, unfailing smile of life and youth, and by the uncommonly classic proportions of her figure, while the same features in the brother were dulled by imbecility and looked conceited and sulky, and his body was thin and feeble. Eyes, nose, and mouth were all twisted into a vacant, bored grimace, while his arms and legs always fell into grotesque attitudes.

'It isn't a ghost story?' he said, sitting down beside the princess and hurriedly fixing his eye-glass in his eye, as though without this instrument he could not say a word.

'Why no, my dear fellow,' said the astonished *vicomte*, with a shrug.

13

'Because I detest ghost stories,' said Prince Hippolyte, in a tone which showed that he only understood the meaning of his words after he had uttered them.

He spoke with such self-confidence that no one could be sure whether his remark was very witty or very stupid. He wore a dark green frock-coat, knee-breeches of a shade that he called *cuisse de nymphe effrayée*, silk stockings and buckled shoes.

With much grace the *vicomte* recounted an anecdote then going the rounds, to the effect that the duc d'Enghien had secretly gone to Paris to visit Mademoiselle Georges, and there he came upon Bonaparte, who also enjoyed the favours of the famous actress, and that Napoleon, meeting the *duc*, had fallen into one of the swoons to which he was subject, and was thus at the *duc*'s mercy. The latter had taken no advantage of his position, and Bonaparte subsequently revenged himself for this magnanimous behaviour by having the *duc* executed.

The story was very neat and interesting, especially at the point where the rivals suddenly recognize each other, and the ladies appeared to be greatly excited by it.

'Charming!' said Anna Pavlovna with an inquiring glance at the little princess.

'Charming!' whispered the little princess, sticking her needle into her work as an indication that the interest and fascination of the tale prevented her from going on with her sewing.

The *vicomte* appreciated this silent homage and with a gratified smile was about to resume, but just then Anna Pavlovna, who had been keeping an eye on that dreadful young man, noticed that he was talking too loudly and heatedly with the *abbé*, and hurried to the rescue. Pierre had managed to start a conversation with the *abbé* about the balance of power, and the *abbé*, evidently interested by the young man's ingenuous fervour, was dilating at length on his pet theory. Both of them were talking and listening too eagerly and too naturally, and Anna Pavlovna did not like it.

'The means? The means are the balance of power in Europe and the rights of the people,' the *abbé* was saying. 'It is only necessary for one powerful nation like Russia – with all her reputation for barbarism – to place herself disinterestedly at the head of an alliance having for its object the maintenance of the balance of power in Europe – and the world would be saved!'

'But how would you establish that balance?' Pierre was beginning;

but at that moment Anna Pavlovna came up and, giving Pierre a stern glance, asked the Italian how he stood the Russian climate. The *abbé*'s face instantly changed and took on an offensively affected, sugary expression, evidently habitual to him when conversing with women.

'I am so enchanted by the wit and culture of the society – especially of the feminine members – into which I have had the honour to be received that there has been no time yet to think of the climate,' said he.

Making sure of the *abbé* and Pierre, Anna Pavlovna, the more conveniently to keep them under observation, brought them into the general circle.

At this point a new actor appeared on the scene: the young Prince Andrei Bolkonsky, husband of the little princess. Prince Bolkonsky was a very handsome youth of medium height, with firm, clearcut features. Everything about him, from the weary, bored expression of his eyes to the measured deliberation of his step, presented the most striking contrast to his lively little wife. It was clear that he was not only acquainted with everyone in the room but found them so tedious that even to look at them and hear their voices was too much for him. And of all the faces of which he was so tired the face of his pretty little wife was apparently the one that bored him most. With a grimace that distorted his handsome countenance he turned away from her, kissed Anna Pavlovna's hand and screwing up his eyes scanned the whole company.

'Are you enlisting for the war, prince?' said Anna Pavlovna.

'General Kutuzov has been kind enough to make me his aide-de-camp.'

He spoke in French and stressed the last syllable of Kutuzov's name like a Frenchman.

'And what about Lise, your wife?'

'She is going into the country.'

'Don't you think it too bad of you to rob us of your charming wife?'

'*André*,' said the little princess, addressing her husband in the same coquettish tone which she employed with other men, 'you should have heard the story the *vicomte* has been telling us about Mademoiselle Georges and Bonaparte!'

Prince Andrei frowned and turned away. Pierre, who had been

15

watching him with glad, affectionate eyes ever since he came in, went up and took his arm. Without looking round, Prince Andrei twisted his face into a grimace of annoyance at being touched, but when he saw Pierre's beaming countenance he gave a smile that was unexpectedly cordial and pleasant.

'What, you here! You in gay society too!' he said to Pierre.

'I knew I should find you here,' Pierre answered. 'I'm coming to supper with you. May I?' he added in an undertone, not to disturb the *vicomte* who was proceeding with his story.

'No, impossible!' said Prince Andrei, laughing and pressing Pierre's hand to show that there was no need to ask. He was about to say something more but at that instant Prince Vasili and his daughter got up and the two young men rose to let them pass.

'You will excuse me, my dear *vicomte*,' said Prince Vasili to the Frenchman, affectionately holding him down by the sleeve to prevent him from rising. 'This wretched reception at the ambassador's deprives me of a pleasure and obliges us to interrupt you. I am very sorry to leave your delightful party,' said he, turning to Anna Pavlovna.

Lightly holding the folds of her gown, his daughter, Princess Hélène, made her way between the chairs, the smile on her lovely face more radiant than ever. Pierre gazed with rapturous, almost frightened eyes at this beautiful creature as she passed him.

'Very pretty,' said Prince Andrei.

'Very,' said Pierre.

As he went by, Prince Vasili seized Pierre by the arm and turned to Anna Pavlovna.

'Get this bear into shape for me!' he said. 'Here he's been staying with me a whole month and this is the first time I have seen him in society. Nothing is so necessary for a young man as the society of clever women.'

4

ANNA PAVLOVNA smiled and promised to take Pierre in hand. She knew that on his father's side he was related to Prince Vasili. The elderly lady who had been sitting with *ma tante* jumped up hastily and overtook Prince Vasili in the ante-room. The look of interest which her kindly, careworn face had affected till now had vanished, leaving nothing but anxiety and alarm.

'What have you to tell me, prince, concerning my Boris?' she said, hurrying after him into the ante-room. (She pronounced the name Boris with the accent on the *o*.) 'I cannot stay in Petersburg any longer. Tell me what news am I to take back to my poor boy.'

Although Prince Vasili's manner as he listened to the old lady was reluctant and almost uncivil, showing impatience even, she gave him an ingratiating, appealing smile and clung to his hand to detain him.

'It is nothing for you to say a word to the Emperor, and then he would be transferred to the Guards at once,' she implored.

'Princess, I am ready to do all I can,' answered Prince Vasili; 'but there are difficulties in the way of my proffering such a request to the Emperor. I should advise you to approach Rumyantsev, through Prince Golitsyn. That would be the wiser course.'

The elderly lady was a Princess Drubetskoy, belonging to one of the best families in Russia, but she was poor, and having long been living in retirement had lost touch with her former influential connexions. She had now come to Petersburg to get her only son into the Imperial Guards. It was, in fact, solely in order to see Prince Vasili that she had invited herself to Anna Pavlovna's party and sat listening to the *vicomte*'s story. She was dismayed at Prince Vasili's words, and her once handsome face expressed vexation, but only for a moment. She smiled again and clutched Prince Vasili's arm more tightly.

'Listen, prince,' she said. 'I have never asked you for anything before, and I never will again, nor have I ever reminded you of the friendship my father felt for you. But now I entreat you in God's name, do this for my son, and I shall always regard you as our benefactor,' she added hastily. 'No, don't be angry but promise me! I asked Golitsyn and he refused. Be the kind-hearted man you always were,' she said, trying to smile though tears were in her eyes.

'Papa, we shall be late,' said Princess Hélène, turning her beautiful head and looking over her statuesque shoulders as she waited at the door.

Influence in the world, however, is a capital which has to be used with economy if it is to last. Prince Vasili knew this and, having once realized that if he were to ask favours for everybody who petitioned him he would soon be unable to ask anything for himself, he rarely exerted his influence. But in Princess Drubetskoy's case, after her new appeal, he felt something like a qualm of conscience. She had re-minded him of what was quite true: that he owed to her father his early advancement in his career. Moreover, he could see by her man-ner that she was one of those women – mostly mothers – who once having taken a notion into their heads will not rest until they have attained the desired object, and if opposed are ready to go on insisting day after day and hour after hour, even to the point of making scenes. This last reflection made him waver.

'My dear Anna Mihalovna,' he said with his habitual familiarity and the note of boredom in his voice, 'it is next to impossible for me to do what you ask; but to show how fond I am of you and how much I honour your father's memory I will do the impossible: your son shall be transferred to the Guards. Here is my hand on it. Now are you satisfied?'

'My dear friend, my dear benefactor! This is what I expected from you – I know how good you are.' He turned to go. 'Wait – one word more! When he has been transferred to the Guards ...' she hesitated. 'You are on good terms with Mihail Ilarionovich Kutuzov ... recom-mend Boris to him as adjutant. Then I shall be content, and never again ...'

Prince Vasili smiled.

'That I do not promise. You have no idea how Kutuzov has been besieged since his appointment as commander-in-chief. He told me himself that all the ladies in Moscow have conspired to surrender all their sons to him as adjutants.'

'No, no, you must promise! I will not let you go, my dear bene-factor ...'

'Papa,' said his beautiful daughter again in the same tone as before, 'we shall be late.'

'Well, *au revoir*! Good-bye, you see how it is ...'

'Tomorrow then you will speak to the Emperor?'

'Without fail; but I make no promises about Kutuzov.'

'Yes promise, do promise, *Basile*,' Anna Mihalovna called after him with a coquettish smile which in days long gone by, when she was a young girl, might have been becoming but which now ill suited her haggard face.

She had evidently forgotten her age and from habit was employing all the old feminine arts. But as soon as the prince had gone her face resumed its former cold, artificial expression. She returned to the

18

group where the *vicomte* was still telling stories, and again pretended to listen, watching for the time when she could leave, now that her purpose was accomplished.

'And what do you think of this latest farce, the coronation at Milan?' asked Anna Pavlovna. 'And the new comedy of the people of Genoa and Lucca laying their petitions before Monsieur Bonaparte, and Monsieur Bonaparte sitting on a throne and granting the petitions of the nations! Delicious! No, but it's enough to turn one's brain! You would think the whole world had gone mad.'

Prince Andrei smiled ironically, looking straight into Anna Pavlovna's face.

' "*Dieu me la donne, gare à qui la touche,*" ' he said, (repeating Bonaparte's words at his coronation). 'They say he was very impressive when he pronounced that,' he remarked and he now repeated it in Italian: ' "*Dio mi la dona, guai a chi la tocca.*" '

'I only hope that this will be the last drop that overflows the glass,' continued Anna Pavlovna. 'Really the sovereigns of Europe cannot continue to endure this man who is a living threat to them all.'

'The sovereigns?' echoed the *vicomte* in a polite but hopeless tone. 'The sovereigns, madame – I do not refer to Russia ... What did they do for Louis XVI, for the queen or Madame Elisabeth? Nothing!' and he became more animated. 'And believe me, they are reaping their rewards for having betrayed the cause of the Bourbons. The sovereigns! Why, they send ambassadors to present their compliments to the usurper!' And with an exclamation of contempt he again shifted his position.

Prince Hippolyte, who had been staring at the *vicomte* for some time through his eye-glass, at these words suddenly turned his whole body round to the little princess and asked her for a needle, with which he began tracing the arms of the Condé family on the table, expounding them to her with the utmost gravity, as if she had requested him to do so.

'*Bâton de gueules, engrêlé de gueules d'azur* – house of Condé,' he said.

The princess listened with a smile.

'If Bonaparte remains on the throne another year,' resumed the *vicomte* with the air of a man who, in a matter with which he is better acquainted than anyone else, is accustomed to pursue his own train of thought without heeding the reflections of others, 'things will have gone too far. By intrigue, violence, exile and executions French society – I mean good society – will have been destroyed for ever, and then …'

He shrugged his shoulders and spread out his hands. Pierre was about to put in a word, for the conversation interested him, but Anna Pavlovna, who had a watchful eye on him, interrupted.

'The Emperor Alexander,' said she, with the pathetic note which accompanied all her references to the Imperial family, 'has declared that he will leave it to the French people themselves to choose their own form of government. And I imagine it is certain that the whole nation, once delivered from the usurper, would throw itself into the arms of its rightful king,' she concluded, trying to be amiable to the royalist *émigré*.

'That is doubtful,' said Prince Andrei. '*Monsieur le vicomte* is quite right in thinking that matters have gone too far by now. In my opinion it would be difficult to return to the old régime.'

'From what I have heard,' remarked Pierre, blushing and again breaking into the conversation, 'almost all the aristocracy have already gone over to Bonaparte.'

'That is what the Bonapartists say,' replied the *vicomte* without looking at Pierre. 'At the present time it is not easy to find out what the public opinion of France really is.'

'Bonaparte has said so,' observed Prince Andrei with a sarcastic smile. (It was evident that he did not like the *vicomte* and was directing his remarks against him, though he did not look at him.)

'"I showed them the path of glory and they would have none of it,"' he continued, after a short silence, again quoting Napoleon's words. '"I opened my antechambers and they crowded in." I do not know what justification he had for saying that.'

'None,' retorted the *vicomte*. 'After the murder of the duc d'Enghien even his most partial supporters ceased to regard him as a hero. If indeed some people made a hero of him,' he went on, turning to Anna Pavlovna, 'since the murder of the *duc* there has been one martyr more in heaven and one hero less on earth.'

Before Anna Pavlovna and the others had time to smile their appreciation of the *vicomte*'s epigram Pierre again burst into the conversation, and though Anna Pavlovna had a presentiment that he would say something unseemly she was unable to stop him.

'The execution of the duc d'Enghien,' declared Pierre, 'was a political necessity, and I consider that Napoleon showed nobility of soul in not hesitating to assume full responsibility for it.'

'*Dieu! Mon Dieu!*' murmured Anna Pavlovna in dismay.

'What, Monsieur Pierre ... do you think murder a proof of nobility of soul?' said the little princess, smiling and drawing her work nearer to her.

'Oh! Oh!' exclaimed different voices.

'Capital!' said Prince Hippolyte in English, and began slapping his knee with the palm of his hand. The *vicomte* merely shrugged his shoulders.

Pierre looked solemnly at his audience over his spectacles.

'I say so,' he went on desperately, 'because the Bourbons fled from the Revolution, leaving the people to anarchy; and Napoleon alone was capable of understanding the Revolution, of quelling it, and so for the general good he could not stop short at the life of one man.'

'Won't you come over to the other table?' suggested Anna Pavlovna. But Pierre continued without heeding her.

'Yes,' he cried, growing more and more excited, 'Napoleon is great because he towered above the Revolution, suppressed its abuses, preserving all that was good in it – equality of citizenship and freedom of speech and of the press – and that was the only reason he possessed himself of power.'

'Yes, if when he had obtained power he had restored it to the lawful king, instead of taking advantage of it to commit murder,' said the *vicomte*, 'then I might have called him a great man.'

'He could not have done that. The people gave him power simply for him to rid them of the Bourbons and because they believed him to be a great man. The Revolution was a grand fact,' continued Monsieur Pierre, betraying by this desperate and challenging statement his extreme youth and desire to give full expression to whatever was in his mind.

'Revolution and regicide a grand fact! ... What next? ... But won't you come over to this table?' repeated Anna Pavlovna.

'Rousseau's *Contrat social*,' said the *vicomte* with a bland smile.

'I am not speaking of regicide, I am speaking of the idea.'

'Yes, the idea of plunder, murder, and regicide,' an ironical voice interjected again.

'Those were extremes, of course; but the whole meaning of the

Revolution did not lie in them but in the rights of man, in emancipation from prejudice, in equality; and all these principles Napoleon has preserved in all their integrity.'

'Liberty and equality,' exclaimed the *vicomte* scornfully, as though he had at last made up his mind to prove seriously to this young man how foolish his arguments were. 'All high-sounding words which have long been debased. Who does not love liberty and equality? Our Saviour Himself long ago preached liberty and equality. Have people been any happier since the Revolution? On the contrary. We wanted freedom, but Bonaparte has destroyed it.'

Prince Andrei with a smile on his face looked from Pierre to the *vicomte* and from the *vicomte* to the mistress of the house. In the first moment of Pierre's outburst Anna Pavlovna, in spite of her experience as a hostess, was appalled. However, when she saw that Pierre's sacrilegious utterances did not incense the *vicomte*, and had convinced herself that it was impossible to suppress them, she rallied her forces and joined the *vicomte* in falling on the orator.

'But, my dear Monsieur Pierre,' said Anna Pavlovna, 'what have you to say for a great man who was capable of executing a duke – or a commoner, for that matter – without cause and without trial?'

'I should like to ask how Monsieur explains the 18th Brumaire,' said the *vicomte*. 'Was not that a piece of trickery? It was chicanery in no way resembling the conduct of a great man.'

'And the prisoners he massacred in Africa?' said the little princess. 'That was horrible!' and she shrugged her shoulders.

'He's an upstart, whatever anyone says,' Prince Hippolyte threw in.

Monsieur Pierre, not knowing which to answer, gazed at them all and smiled. His smile was not like the half-smile of other people. When he smiled his serious and indeed rather morose look vanished in a flash and in its place appeared another – childlike, kindly, even rather foolish – which seemed to plead for indulgence.

The *vicomte*, who was meeting him for the first time, saw quite clearly that this young Jacobin was not nearly so terrible as his words suggested. Everyone was silent.

'How do you expect him to answer you all at once?' said Prince Andrei. 'Besides, in considering the actions of a statesman one has to distinguish between what he does as a private individual and as a general or an emperor. So it seems to me.'

'Yes, yes, of course!' caught up Pierre, delighted at the arrival of this reinforcement.

'One must admit,' continued Prince Andrei, 'that Napoleon on the bridge at Arcola, or in the hospital at Jaffa shaking hands with the plague-stricken, is great as a man; but ... but there are other things it would be difficult to justify.'

Prince Andrei, who had evidently wished to smooth over the awkwardness of Pierre's remarks, rose, making a sign to his wife that it was time to go.

Suddenly Prince Hippolyte started up and detaining the company with a wave of his hand and begging them to be seated began:

'Oh, I heard a delightful Moscow story today – I really must entertain you with it. You will excuse me, *vicomte* – I shall have to tell it in Russian, or the point will be lost.' And Prince Hippolyte began in Russian, speaking with the sort of accent a Frenchman has after spending some twelve months in Russia. Everyone stopped to listen, so eagerly and insistently did he demand their attention for his story.

'In Moscow there lives a lady, *une dame*. And she is very stingy. She must drive with two footmen behind her carriage. And very tall footmen. That was her style. And she had a lady's maid, also very tall. She said ...'

Here Prince Hippolyte paused and pondered, apparently having difficulty in collecting his thoughts.

'She said ... Oh yes! "Girl," she said to the maid, "put on livery and get up behind the carriage, and come with me while I make some calls."'

Prince Hippolyte burst into a loud guffaw, laughing long before any of his audience, which showed the narrator to disadvantage. A few persons, among them the elderly lady and Anna Pavlovna, did smile, however.

'They drove off. Suddenly there was a violent gust of wind. The girl lost her hat, and her long hair fell down ...' At this point he could contain himself no longer and between gasps of laughter concluded:

'And the whole town heard about it.'

This was the end of the anecdote. Although it was incomprehensible why he had told it, or why it had to be told in Russian, still Anna Pavlovna and the others appreciated Prince Hippolyte's good breeding in so agreeably putting a close to the unpleasant and ill-bred harangue of Monsieur Pierre. After the anecdote the conversation broke up into small talk of no import concerning balls past and to come, theatricals and when and where they should meet again.

5

THANKING Anna Pavlovna for her *charmante soirée*, the guests began to depart.

Pierre was ungainly, stout and uncommonly tall, with exceptionally large red hands; as the saying is, he had no idea how to enter a drawing-room and still less of how to get out of one. In other words, he did not know how to make some especially agreeable remark to his hostess before leaving. Moreover, he was absent-minded. He got up and, instead of his own, seized the plumed three-cornered hat of a general and stood holding it, pulling at the plume, until the general claimed it from him. But all his absent-mindedness and inability to enter a drawing-room and converse in it were redeemed by his kindly expression of modest simplicity. Anna Pavlovna turned to him, with an air of Christian meekness signifying her forgiveness for his misbehaviour, nodded and said:

'I hope to see you again, but I also hope you will change your opinions, my dear Monsieur Pierre.'

When she said this he made no reply but simply bowed and once more displayed to them all his smile, which said plainly as words: 'Opinions or no opinions, you see what a capital, good-hearted fellow I am.' And everyone, Anna Pavlovna included, could not help feeling this was so.

Prince Andrei had gone out into the hall, and presenting his shoulders to the footman for his cloak to be thrown over them was listening indifferently to the chatter of his wife and Prince Hippolyte, who had also come into the hall. Prince Hippolyte stood close to the pretty, pregnant princess and stared straight at her through his eyeglass.

'Go in, Annette, you will catch cold,' exclaimed the little princess, saying good-bye to Anna Pavlovna. 'It is settled,' she added in an undertone.

Anna Pavlovna had already managed to have a word with Lisa about the match she was plotting between Anatole and the little princess's sister-in-law.

'I rely on you, my dear,' said Anna Pavlovna, also in a low tone. 'You write to her and let me know how the father will view the

24

matter. *Au revoir!*' and she went back out of the hall.

Prince Hippolyte approached the little princess and bending his face down close to her began saying something in a half whisper.

Two footmen, one the princess's, holding her shawl, the other his, with his *redingote*, stood waiting for them to finish talking. They listened to the unintelligible conversation in French with an air of understanding but not wishing to appear to do so. As usual, the little princess was smiling as she spoke, and she laughed as she listened.

'I am very glad I did not go to the ambassador's,' said Prince Hippolyte. 'So boring. It has been a delightful evening. Hasn't it, delightful!'

'They say the ball is to be a splendid one,' replied the princess, curling her downy lip. 'All the pretty women in society will be there.'

'Not all, since you won't be there; not all,' said Prince Hippolyte, tittering gleefully; and snatching the shawl from the footman, shoving him aside as he did so, he began to wrap it round the princess. Either from awkwardness or intentionally (no one could have said which), even after the shawl had been adjusted it was some time before he removed his arms: he almost seemed to be embracing the young woman.

Gracefully, but still smiling, she drew back and turning round glanced at her husband. Prince Andrei's eyes were closed; he appeared to be drowsy and tired.

'Are you ready ?' he asked, looking past his wife.

Prince Hippolyte hastily flung on his cloak, which being in the latest fashion fell below his heels, and stumbling over it rushed out on to the steps after the princess, whom the footman was helping into the carriage.

'*Princesse, au revoir!*' he cried, his tongue as badly entangled as his feet.

Picking up her gown, the princess was taking her seat in the darkness of the carriage, her husband was arranging his sword; Prince Hippolyte, on the pretence of assisting, was in everyone's way.

'Ex-cuse me, sir,' said Prince Andrei drily and disagreeably in Russian to Prince Hippolyte, who was blocking his path.

'I shall expect you, Pierre,' the same voice called in warm affectionate tones.

The postilion whipped up the horses and the carriage rumbled away. Prince Hippolyte gave vent to a short, jerky guffaw as he stood on the steps waiting for the *vicomte* whom he had promised to take home.

*

'Well, *mon cher*, your little princess is very nice, very nice,' said the *vicomte*, seating himself in the carriage beside Hippolyte. 'Very nice indeed, quite French,' and he kissed the tips of his fingers.

Hippolyte burst into a laugh.

'And do you know, you are a terrible fellow for all that little innocent way of yours,' pursued the *vicomte*. 'I am sorry for the poor husband, that officer boy who gives himself the airs of a reigning monarch.'

Hippolyte spluttered again and through his laughter articulated:

'And you said that Russian ladies were not up to Frenchwomen. One must know how to set about things, that is all.'

Pierre, arriving first, went straight to Prince Andrei's study like one thoroughly at home, and at once, from habit, stretched himself out on a sofa, took from the shelf the first book that came to hand (it was Caesar's *Commentaries*) and leaning on his elbow began reading it in the middle.

'What have you done to Mademoiselle Scherer? She will be quite ill now,' said Prince Andrei, as he came into the study rubbing his small white hands together.

Pierre rolled his whole person over so that the sofa creaked, lifted his eager face to Prince Andrei, smiled and waved his hand.

'That *abbé* was very interesting, only he has got hold of the wrong end of the stick. To my thinking, permanent peace is possible but – I don't know how to put it … Not by means of a political balance of power.'

Prince Andrei was obviously not interested in such abstract conversation.

'My dear fellow, one can't everywhere and at all times say all one thinks. Come, tell me, have you made up your mind at last? Is it to be the cavalry or the diplomatic service?' he asked after a momentary silence.

Pierre sat up on the sofa with his legs crossed under him.

'Can you imagine it, I still don't know! Neither prospect smiles on me.'

'But you must decide on something! Your father's expecting it.'

At the age of ten Pierre had been sent abroad with an *abbé* as tutor, and had remained away till he was twenty. On his return to Moscow, his father had dismissed the *abbé* and said to the young man, 'Now you go to Petersburg, look round and make your choice. I agree to anything. Here is a letter to Prince Vasili, and here is money. Write and tell me all about everything, and I will help you in every way.' Pierre had already been three months trying to choose a career and had come to no decision. It was in regard to this choice of a career that Prince Andrei spoke to him now. Pierre rubbed his forehead.

'But he must be a freemason,' said he, meaning the *abbé* he had met at the party.

'That is all nonsense.' Prince Andrei pulled him up again. 'We'd better talk business. Have you been to the Horse Guards?'

'No, not yet, but here is an idea that occurred to me which I wanted to tell you. This war now is against Napoleon. If it were a war for freedom, I could have understood it, and I should have been the first to join the army; but to help England and Austria against the greatest man in the world – that is not right. ...'

Prince Andrei merely shrugged his shoulders at Pierre's childish talk. He assumed the air of one who really finds it impossible to reply to such nonsense; but it would in fact have been difficult to answer this naïve querying in any other way than Prince Andrei did answer it.

'If everyone would only fight for his own convictions, there would be no wars,' he said.

'And a very good thing that would be,' said Pierre.

Prince Andrei laughed.

'Very likely it would be a good thing, but it will never happen.'

'Well, what are *you* going to the war for?' asked Pierre.

'What for? I don't know. Because I have to. Besides, I am going ...' He stopped. 'I am going because the life I lead here – is not to my taste!'

6

THE rustle of a woman's dress was heard in the adjoining room. Prince Andrei gave a start, as though to pull himself together, and his face assumed the expression it had worn in Anna Pavlovna's drawing-room. Pierre removed his feet from the sofa. The princess came in. She had now changed her dress for another, a house gown to be sure but equally fresh and elegant. Prince Andrei rose and courteously pushed forward an easy-chair.

'I often wonder,' she began, speaking in French as usual and briskly and fussily settling herself in the arm-chair, 'how it is Annette never married. You are very foolish, all you men, not to have married her! Forgive me for saying so, but you really have no sense where women are concerned. What a contentious person you are, Monsieur Pierre!'

'Your husband and I were just at this moment having an argument: I can't make out why he wants to go to the war,' said Pierre, addressing the princess without any of the constraint so common between a young man and a young woman.

The princess jumped. Evidently Pierre's words touched her to the quick.

'Ah, that is exactly what I say. I don't understand – I simply do not understand why men cannot get on without war. Why is it we women want nothing of the kind? We don't care for it. Come, you shall be the judge. As I am always telling him: here he is uncle's adjutant, a most brilliant position. Everyone knows and esteems him. Only the other day at the Apraksins' I heard a lady asking, "Is that the famous Prince Andrei?" I did really!' She laughed. 'And it is the same wherever he goes. He might easily become aide-de-camp to the Sovereign. You know the Emperor spoke to him most graciously. Annette and I were saying it would be quite easy to arrange. What do you think?'

Pierre glanced at Prince Andrei and seeing that his friend did not like the conversation made no reply.

'When do you leave?' he asked.

'Oh, don't talk about his going, don't talk about it! I don't want to hear a word on the subject,' exclaimed the princess in the same capriciously playful tone that she had used to Hippolyte at the *soirée* and which was so obviously out of place in her own home circle, where Pierre was like one of the family. 'Today when I remembered that it would be the end of all these pleasant associations ... And then you know, André ...' (she gave her husband a meaning look) 'I am afraid, I am afraid,' she whispered, and a shudder ran down her back.

Her husband looked at her as though he were surprised to observe someone else in the room besides himself and Pierre. With frigid courtesy, however, he addressed an inquiry to his wife:

'What is it you are afraid of, Lise? I don't understand.'

'There, what egoists men are! Egoists, every one of you. Just for a whim of his own, goodness knows why, he deserts me and shuts me up alone in the country.'

'With my father and sister, don't forget that,' said Prince Andrei quietly.

'It comes to the same thing: I shall be alone, without *my* friends. ... And he expects me not to be afraid.'

Her tone was querulous now and her drawn-up lip no longer suggested a smile but gave her face the look of a vicious little squirrel. She paused as though feeling it indecorous to speak of her condition before Pierre, though in that lay the whole gist of the matter.

'I still cannot imagine why you are afraid,' said Prince Andrei slowly, not taking his eyes off his wife.

The princess blushed and lifted her arms in a gesture of despair.

'No, André, I must say you have changed. Changed terribly. ...'

'Your doctor said that you were to go to bed earlier,' said Prince Andrei. 'It's time you were asleep.'

The princess said nothing and suddenly her short downy lip began to quiver. With a shrug of his shoulders Prince Andrei got up and walked about the room.

Pierre looked through his spectacles in naïve wonder from him to the princess, and made a movement as if he too would rise, but then thought better of it.

'Why should I mind if Monsieur Pierre is here!' suddenly exclaimed the little princess, and her pretty face contorted into a tearful grimace. 'I have been wanting to ask you for a long time, André, why you have changed towards me so? What have I done? You are going off to the war, you don't feel for me. Why is it?'

'Lise!' was all Prince Andrei said. But this one word conveyed entreaty and menace, and, most of all, conviction that she would herself regret her words; but she went on hurriedly:

'You treat me as though I were an invalid or a child. I see it all. You weren't like this six months ago, were you?'

'Lise, I beg you to stop,' said Prince Andrei, still more emphatically.

Pierre, who had been growing more and more agitated as this conversation proceeded, got up and went to the princess. He seemed unable to bear the sight of tears, and looked ready to weep himself.

'Please don't upset yourself, princess. All this is only your fancy

29

because, I assure you, I know myself ... and so ... because ... No, excuse me, an outsider has no business ... No, don't distress yourself ... Good-bye.'

Prince Andrei caught him by the arm.

'No, wait, Pierre. The princess is so kind, she would not wish to deprive me of the pleasure of your company for an evening.'

'Yes, he only thinks of himself,' muttered the princess, not attempting to restrain her tears of vexation.

'Lise!' said Prince Andrei coldly, raising his voice to a pitch which showed that he had come to the end of his patience.

All at once the angry squirrel-like expression on the princess's pretty little face changed to a moving and piteous look of fear. Her beautiful eyes gave a sidelong glance at her husband and her face assumed the timid, deprecating expression of a dog when it rapidly but feebly wags its drooping tail.

'*Mon Dieu, mon Dieu!*' she muttered and gathering the skirt of her dress with one hand she went up to her husband and kissed him on the forehead.

'*Bonsoir*, Lise,' said he, rising and courteously kissing her hand, as though she were a stranger.

The friends were silent. Neither felt inclined to be the first to speak. Pierre kept glancing at Prince Andrei; Prince Andrei rubbed his forehead with his small hand.

'Let us go and have supper,' he said with a sigh, getting up and walking to the door.

They went into the elegant newly-decorated, luxurious diningroom. Everything, from the table-napkins to the silver, china and glass, wore the peculiar stamp of newness characteristic of the establishments of newly-married couples. Half-way through supper Prince Andrei lent his elbow on the table and like a man who has had something on his mind for a long time and suddenly determines to speak out he began talking with a nervous irritation which was new to Pierre.

'Never, never marry, my dear fellow. That is my advice to you – don't marry until you can say to yourself that you have done all you are capable of doing, and until you cease to love the woman of your choice and see her plainly, as she really is; or else you will be making a cruel and irreparable mistake. Marry when you are old and good for nothing. Otherwise everything that is fine and noble in you will be thrown away. It will all be wasted on trifles. Yes, yes, yes! Don't look at me with such surprise. If you marry while you still have any hopes of yourself you will be made to feel at every step that for you all is over, every door closed but that of the drawing-room, where you will stand on the same level as the court lackey and the idiot. ... But what is the good? ...'

He made a vigorous gesture with his arm.

Pierre took off his spectacles, which altered his face, making it look even more good-natured, and gazed wonderingly at his friend.

'My wife,' pursued Prince Andrei, 'is an excellent woman – one of those rare women with whom a man's honour is safe but, great heavens, what wouldn't I give not to be married! You are the first and only person I say this to, because I hold an affection for you.'

As he said this, Prince Andrei was less than ever like the Bolkonsky who had lolled in Anna Pavlovna's easy-chairs with half-closed eye-lids filtering French phrases through his teeth. Every muscle of his spare face now quivered with feverish excitement; his eyes, which had seemed lustreless and without life, now flashed with a fierce brilliancy. It was evident that however apathetic he might appear at ordinary times he more than made up for it by his vehemence in moments of irritation.

'You don't understand why I say this,' he went on, 'but it is the whole story of life. You talk of Bonaparte and his career,' said he (though Pierre had not mentioned Bonaparte). 'You talk of Bonaparte, but Bonaparte while he was working his way step by step towards his goal – he was free; there was nothing for him but his goal, and he reached it. But tie yourself up with a woman and like a convict in irons you lose all freedom! And all your aspirations, all the ability you feel within you is only a drag on you, torturing you with regret. Drawing-rooms, tittle-tattle, balls, idle conceits and futility – such is the enchanted circle that encloses me. I am setting off now to take part in the war, the greatest war there ever was, and I know nothing and am fit for nothing. I am an amiable fellow with a caustic wit,' continued Prince Andrei, 'and at Anna Pavlovna's they hang upon my words. And then think of that stupid set without which my wife cannot exist, and those women. ... If you only knew what all these fine ladies, indeed women in general, amount to! My father is right. Selfish, vain, humdrum, trivial in everything – that's what women

31

are when they show themselves in their true colours! When you see them in society, you might fancy they had something in them, but there is nothing, nothing, nothing! No, don't marry, my dear chap, don't marry!' concluded Prince Andrei.

'It seems odd to me,' said Pierre, 'that you – you of all people – should consider yourself a failure, your life wrecked. You have everything before you, everything. And you ...'

He did not finish but his tone made it clear how highly he thought of his friend and how much he expected of him in the future.

'How can he talk like that?' thought Pierre, who considered the prince a model of perfection for the very reason that Bolkonsky possessed to the highest degree all those qualities that Pierre lacked, and which might best be summed up as will power. Pierre always admired Prince Andrei's easy demeanour with people in every walk of life, his extraordinary memory, his erudition (he had read everything, knew everything, had ideas on every subject), but above all he admired his capacity for work and study. And if Pierre was often struck by Andrei's lack of capacity for speculative philosophy (to which Pierre was particularly addicted), he regarded even this not as a defect but as a sign of strength.

Even in the best, most friendly and simple relations of life, praise and commendation are as indispensable as the oil which greases the wheels of a machine to keep them running smoothly.

'My day is done,' said Prince Andrei. 'What is there to say about me? Let us talk about you,' he added after a short silence, smiling at his own reassuring thoughts.

The smile was instantly reflected on Pierre's face.

'Why, what is there to say about me?' asked Pierre, his face relaxing into an easy-going, happy smile. 'What am I? Illegitimate!' He suddenly blushed purple. Obviously it cost him a great effort to bring out the word. 'Without name and without fortune ... and yet it is true....' But he did not say what was true. 'For the present I am free, and enjoying it. Only I haven't the least idea what to take up. I wanted to consult you seriously about it.'

Prince Andrei looked at him with kindly eyes. But his glance, friendly and affectionate as it was, still betrayed a consciousness of his own superiority.

'You are dear to me especially because you are the one live soul in all our circle of acquaintances. You are lucky. Choose as you will, the choice matters little. You will be all right anywhere. But look here: do break with the Kuragins and their kind of life. That sort of thing – all that junketing, dissipation and the rest of it so ill becomes you!'

'Can it be helped, my dear fellow?' said Pierre, shrugging his shoulders. 'Women, my dear fellow, women!'

'I don't understand it,' replied Prince Andrei. 'Women who are *comme il faut*, that is a different matter; but Kuragin's women – "women and wine" – I can't understand!'

Pierre was staying at Prince Vasili Kuragin's and taking part in the dissipated life of his son Anatole, the very young man whom his father and Anna Pavlovna were proposing to marry to Prince Andrei's sister in the hope of reforming him.

'Do you know what?' said Pierre, as if he had suddenly had a happy inspiration. 'Seriously, I have been thinking of it for a long time. ... Leading this sort of existence I can't decide or think properly about anything. One's head aches and one spends all one's money. He invited me this evening, but I won't go.'

'Give me your word of honour not to?'

'Word of honour.'

*

It was past one o'clock when Pierre left his friend. It was a luminous Petersburg midsummer night. Pierre took an open cab intending to drive straight home. But the nearer he got to the house the less he felt like sleep on such a night, which was more like evening or early morning. It was light enough to see far down the empty streets. On the way Pierre remembered that the usual set were to meet for cards at Anatole Kuragin's that evening, after which there was generally a drinking bout, finishing off with one of Pierre's favourite pastimes.

'It would be nice to go to Kuragin's,' he thought, but immediately recalled his promise to Prince Andrei not to go there again. Then, as happens to people with no strength of character, such a passionate desire came over him for one last taste of the familiar dissipation that he decided to go. And the thought immediately occurred to him that his word to Prince Andrei was not binding because before he had given it he had already promised Prince Anatole to come. 'Besides,' he reasoned, 'all these "words of honour" are mere convention and have no precise significance, especially if one considers that by tomorrow one may be dead, or some extraordinary accident may happen to sweep away all distinctions between honour and dishonour.' Arguments of this kind often occurred to Pierre, nullifying all his resolutions and intentions. He went to Kuragin's.

Driving up to the large house near the Horse Guards' barracks, where Anatole lived, Pierre ran up the lighted steps and went in at the open door. There was no one in the ante-room; empty bottles, cloaks and overshoes were scattered about; there was a smell of wine, and in the distance he heard talking and shouting.

Cards and supper were over but the company had not yet dispersed. Pierre threw off his cloak and entered the first room in which were the remains of supper, and a single footman, thinking himself unobserved, was surreptitiously drinking what was left in the glasses. From the third room came sounds of scuffling, laughter, familiar voices shouting, and the growl of a bear. Some eight or nine young men were crowding eagerly round an open window. Three others were romping with a bear cub, which one of their number was dragging by its chain and trying to set at his companions.

'I bet a hundred on Stevens!' shouted one.

'Mind, no holding on!' cried another.

'I back Dolohov!' cried a third. 'Kuragin, you come and see to the bets.'

'Let Bruin go now, here's a wager.'

'At one draught, or he loses!' shouted a fourth.

'Jacob, bring a bottle!' ordered the host, a tall, handsome fellow, standing in the midst of the group. He had taken off his coat and his fine cambric shirt was open over his chest. 'Wait a minute, gentlemen ... Here is our old Pierre! Good lad!' he cried, turning to Pierre.

A man of medium height, with clear blue eyes, whose voice was particularly striking among all those drunken voices for its tone of sobriety, called from the window:

'Come over here and look after the bets!'

This was Dolohov, an officer of the Semeonovsk regiment, a notorious gambler and dare-devil, who was making his home with Anatole. Pierre smiled, looking about him gaily.

'I don't understand. What's it all about?'

'Stop, he's not drunk! A bottle here!' cried Anatole; and taking a glass from the table he went up to Pierre.

'First of all, you must drink.'

Pierre proceeded to drain glass after glass, surveying from under his eyebrows the tipsy guests who were crowding round the window again, and lending an ear to their chatter. Anatole kept his glass filled while he explained that Dolohov had laid a wager with Stevens, an English sailor who was there, backing himself to drink a bottle of rum sitting on the sill of the third-floor window with his legs hanging down outside.

'Come on now, empty the bottle,' said Anatole, handing Pierre the last glass, 'or I shan't let you go!'

'No, I don't want any more,' said Pierre, pushing Anatole aside and going up to the window.

Dolohov was holding the Englishman's hand and clearly and ex-plicitly repeating the terms of the wager, addressing himself more particularly to Anatole and Pierre.

Dolohov was a man of medium height, with curly hair and bright blue eyes. He was about five and twenty years old. Like all infantry officers he wore no moustache, so that his mouth, the most striking feature in his face, was not concealed. The lines of the mouth were remarkably finely drawn. The upper lip curved sharply in the middle and closed firmly over the strong lower one, and something in the nature of two smiles played continually, one on each side, round either corner of his mouth; and altogether, especially with the steady, insolent intelligence of his eyes, produced an effect which made it impossible to overlook his face. Dolohov had little fortune and no connexions. And yet through Anatole got through tens of thousands of roubles. Dolohov lived with him and had succeeded in so regula-ting the position that Anatole and all who knew them had a higher regard for him than for Anatole. Dolohov played every kind of game and almost always won. However much he drank he never lost his head. Both Kuragin and Dolohov were at that time notorious among the rakes and spendthrifts of Petersburg.

The bottle of rum was brought. Two footmen, evidently rather flustered and made nervous by the orders and shouts from all sides, were pulling at the sash-frame which prevented anyone from sitting on the outer sill.

Anatole with his swaggering air strode up to the window. He was longing to smash something. Pushing the footmen aside he tugged at the frame but it would not yield. He broke a pane.

'Now you have a try, Hercules,' said he, addressing Pierre.

Pierre seized hold of the cross bar, gave it a wrench and the oak frame came away with a crash.

'Take it right out, or they'll think I'm holding on,' said Dolohov.

'Is the Englishman bragging? ... Eh? ... Is it all right?' said Anatole.

'All right,' said Pierre, watching Dolohov, who had taken the bottle of rum and was going to the window through which the light of the sky was visible, the afterglow of sunset fading into dawn.

With the bottle of rum in his hand Dolohov jumped on to the window-sill.

'Listen!' he cried, standing there and speaking to those in the room. All were silent.

'I wager' – he spoke French so that the Englishman might understand him, and spoke it none too well – 'I wager fifty imperials ... or do you wish to make it a hundred?' he added, addressing the Englishman.

'No, fifty,' said the Englishman.

'Very well, fifty it is – that I will drink this whole bottle of rum without taking it from my lips, drink it sitting outside the window on this spot' (he stooped and pointed to the sloping ledge outside the window), 'and not holding on to anything. Is that understood?'

'Very well,' said Stevens.

Anatole turned to the Englishman and taking him by one of his coat buttons and looking down at him – the Englishman was short – began to repeat the terms of the wager in English.

'Wait!' cried Dolohov, knocking on the window-sill with the bottle to attract attention. 'Wait a minute, Kuragin, listen! If anyone else does the same thing I'll pay him a hundred imperials. Is that clear?'

The sailor nodded without making it plain whether he intended to take this new bet or not. Anatole still held him by the coat button and, though the Englishman kept nodding to show that he understood, went on translating Dolohov's words into English. A thin young hussar of the Life Guards, who had been out of luck all the evening, climbed up on to the window-sill, poked his head out and looked down.

'Oh-h-h!' he exclaimed, looking out of the window at the paving stones below.

'Shut up!' cried Dolohov, pulling him back so that the lad got his feet entangled in his spurs and jumped awkwardly into the room.

Placing the bottle on the window-sill so as to have it within reach, Dolohov climbed slowly and carefully through the casement and lowered his legs. Pressing with both hands against the sides of the frame he settled himself in a sitting position, let go his hands, shifted a little to the right, then to the left, and took up the bottle. Anatole brought a pair of candles and set them on the window-sill, although it was now quite light. Dolohov's back in his white shirt, and his curly head, were lighted up from both sides. Everyone crowded to the window, the Englishman in front. Pierre was smiling and silent. One of the party, rather older than the others, suddenly moved forward with a scared and angry face, and tried to clutch Dolohov by the shirt.

'Gentlemen, this is madness! He'll be killed!' said this man, less foolhardy than the rest.

Anatole stopped him.

'Don't touch him. You'll startle him and he'll fall and be killed. Eh? ... And what then, eh?'

Dolohov looked back, and again holding on with both hands arranged himself on his seat.

'If any one touches me again,' said he, articulating the words one by one through his thin compressed lips, 'I'll send him flying below. Now! ...'

Saying this he turned round again, let his hands drop, took the bottle and lifted it to his lips, threw his head back and raised his free hand to balance himself. One of the footmen who was stooping to pick up some broken glass remained in a half-bent attitude, his eyes fixed on the window and Dolohov's back. Anatole stood erect with staring eyes. The Englishman watched from one side, pursing his lips. The man who had tried to stop the proceedings ran to a corner of the room and flung himself on a sofa with his face to the wall. Pierre covered his eyes. A faint forgotten smile still hovered over his lips though horror and apprehension were written on his face. All were silent. Pierre took his hands from his eyes. Dolohov was still sitting in the same position, only his head was thrown farther back till the curly hair at the nape of his neck touched his shirt collar, and the hand holding the bottle was lifted higher and higher, trembling with the effort. The bottle was emptying visibly, rising almost perpendicularly over his head. 'Why does it take so long?' thought Pierre. It seemed to him as though more than half an hour had elapsed. Suddenly

Dolohov made a backward movement of the spine and his arm trembled nervously; this was sufficient to cause his whole body to slide as he sat on the sloping ledge. As he slipped, his head and arm wavered still more violently with the strain. One hand moved as if to clutch the window-sill but he brought it back. Pierre shut his eyes once more and declared to himself that he would never open them again. Suddenly he was conscious of a general stir. He looked up: Dolohov was standing on the window-sill, his face pale but triumphant.

'Empty!'

He tossed the bottle to the Englishman, who caught it neatly. Dolohov jumped down from the window. He smelt powerfully of rum.

'Capital! ... Bravo! ... That's something like a bet! You're a devil of a fellow!' rang the shouts from all sides.

The Englishman produced his purse and began counting out the money. Dolohov stood frowning and silent. Pierre dashed up to the window.

'Gentlemen, who wants to make a bet with me? I'll do the same!' he shouted suddenly. 'Or even without a bet, there! Give me a bottle. I'll do it ... bring a bottle!'

'Let him – let him!' said Dolohov, smiling.

'Are you mad? Who do you think would let you? Why, you turn giddy going downstairs,' protested several voices from various sides.

'I'll drink it! Let's have a bottle of rum!' shouted Pierre, pounding on a chair with drunken vehemence, and climbing out of the window.

They seized his arms; but he was so strong that everyone who touched him was sent flying.

'No, you'll never dissuade him like that,' said Anatole. 'Wait, let me fool him ... Listen! I'll take your bet, but for tomorrow; for now we are all going to —'s.'

'Come along then,' cried Pierre. 'Come along ... And we'll take Bruin with us.'

And he caught the bear up in his arms and began waltzing round the room with it.

7

PRINCE VASILI fulfilled the promise he had made to Princess Drubetskoy on the evening of Anna Pavlovna's *soirée*, when she had pleaded with him to help her only son Boris. A request had been preferred to the Emperor, an exception made, and Boris transferred to the Semeonovsk regiment of the Guards as ensign. But he was not appointed aide-de-camp, or attached to Kutuzov's staff, in spite of all Anna Mihalovna's endeavours and stratagems. Shortly after Anna Pavlovna's reception, Anna Mihalovna returned to Moscow and went straight to her rich relations, the Rostovs, with whom she always stayed when in Moscow. It was with these relations that her darling Bory, who had only recently entered a regiment of the line and was now being transferred to the Guards as ensign, had been brought up from childhood and lived for years at a time. The Guards had already left Petersburg on the 10th of August, and her son, delayed in Moscow for his equipment, was to overtake them on the march to Radzivilov.

The Rostovs were celebrating the *fête* day of the mother and the younger daughter, both called Natalia. Since morning an unceasing stream of six-horse carriages had been coming and going with visitors bringing their congratulations to the Countess Rostov's great mansion in Povarsky street, which all Moscow knew. The countess and her handsome elder daughter were in the drawing-room with the visitors, who were constantly followed by new arrivals.

The countess was a woman of about five and forty, with a thin oriental type of countenance, evidently worn out with child-bearing – she was the mother of a dozen children. Her languid movements and slow speech due to her frail health gave her an air of dignity which inspired respect. Princess Anna Mihalovna Drubetskoy, as an intimate friend of the family, also sat in the drawing-room, helping to receive and entertain the company. The young people were in the rooms behind the drawing-room, not considering it incumbent upon them to take part in receiving the visitors. The count met the guests and escorted them to the door again, inviting them all to dinner.

'Much obliged to you, much obliged, my dears' (he called everyone 'my dear' without exception, making not the slightest distinction between persons of higher or lower standing than his own). 'Much obliged for myself and my two dear ones whose name-day we are celebrating. Mind you come to dinner now, or I shall be offended. On behalf of the whole family I beg you to come, my dear.' This formula he repeated to all alike, without exception or variation, and with the same expression on his round jolly clean-shaven face, the same firm grip of the hand and repeated short bows. As soon as he had seen one visitor off, the count would return to one or another of those still in the drawing-room, pull forward a chair, and jauntily spreading out his legs and putting his hands on his knees with the air of a man who enjoys life and knows how to live, he would shake his head significantly and offer conjectures concerning the weather, or exchange confidences about health, sometimes in Russian and sometimes in execrable though self-confident French; and then again, looking weary but unflinching in the performance of duty, he would go to the door with still another departing guest, smoothing the scanty grey hairs over his bald patch and repeating his invitations to dinner. Now and then on his way back from the ante-room he would pass through the conservatory and the butler's pantry into the large marble dining-hall where covers were being laid for eighty people, and looking at the footmen who were bringing in the silver and china, moving tables and unfolding damask table-linen, he would call up Dmitri Vasilyevich, a man of good family who had charge of all his affairs, and say:

'Well, Mitenka, mind everything is all right. That's nice!' he would add, glancing with satisfaction at the enormous table extended to its full length. 'The great thing is the serving, you understand that.' And with a complacent smile he would return to the drawing-room.

'Maria Lvovna Karagin and her daughter!' announced the countess's colossal footman in his bass voice at the drawing-room door. The countess reflected for a second and took a pinch of snuff from a gold snuff-box with her husband's portrait on it.

'I'm worn out with callers,' she said. 'Well, this is the last one I'll see. She is so affected. Show her up,' she added to the footman in a dejected tone, as though she were saying, 'Finish me off and have done with it.'

A tall, stout woman with a haughty air, followed by a smiling round-faced girl, rustled into the drawing-room.

'Dear Countess, what an age ... She has been laid up, poor child ... at the Razumovskys' ball ... and Countess Apraksin ... I was so delighted ...' The fragmentary phrases spoken by animated feminine voices broke in on one another and mingled with the hiss of silks and the scraping of chairs. The sort of conversation had begun which can be interrupted at the first pause for the visitor to rise and with a swish of her skirt murmur: 'I am so charmed ... Mamma's health ... and Countess Apraksin ...' and then rustling again, make her way into the ante-room to put on pelisse or mantle and drive away.

The conversation touched on the chief topic of the day – the illness of the famous old Count Bezuhov, one of the richest and handsomest men of Catherine's time, and his illegitimate son Pierre, the young man who had behaved in such an unseemly manner at a *soirée* at Anna Pavlovna's.

'I am very sorry for the poor count,' declared the visitor. 'His health is so wretched, and now to have to suffer this anxiety about his son – it will be the death of him!'

'What is that?' asked the countess, pretending ignorance though she had already heard about the cause of Count Bezuhov's distress at least fifteen times.

'There's modern education for you!' continued the visitor. 'Even when he was abroad as a child he was allowed to do as he liked, and now, so I hear, he has been behaving so atrociously in Petersburg that the police have ordered him out of the city.'

'You don't say so!' replied the countess.

'He got into bad company,' interposed Princess Anna Mihalovna. 'Prince Vasili's son, this Pierre and a certain young man named Dolohov, they say, have been up to heaven only knows what! And two of them have had to suffer for it – Dolohov has been reduced to the ranks, and Bezuhov's son sent back to Moscow. Anatole Kuragin's part in the affair, his father managed to hush up, but even so he has been ordered out of Petersburg.'

'But what did they do?' asked the countess.

'They are regular bandits, Dolohov especially,' replied the visitor. 'He is the son of Maria Ivanovna Dolohov, such a worthy woman, but there! Can you imagine it – the three of them somehow got hold of a bear, took it in a carriage with them and set off to visit some actresses. The police hurried to interfere, and they seized a police officer, tied him back to back to the bear and then threw the bear into the Moyka. And there was the bear swimming about with the police-man on his back!'

'What a figure the officer must have cut, my dear!' cried the count, helpless with laughter.

'Oh, how dreadful! What can you find to laugh at, count?'
But the ladies had to laugh in spite of themselves.

'It was all they could do to rescue the poor man,' pursued the visitor. 'And to think it is Kirill Vladimirovich Bezuhov's son who amuses himself in such a clever fashion! And he supposed to be so well-educated and intelligent! That shows what comes of educating young men abroad. I hope no one here in Moscow will receive him, in spite of his money. They wanted to bring him to my house but I absolutely declined: I have my daughters to consider.'

'What makes you say this young man is so rich?' asked the countess, leaning away from the girls, who immediately pretended not to be listening. 'Aren't all his children illegitimate, Pierre too?'

The visitor waved her hand.

'There are a score of them, I believe.'

Princess Anna Mihalovna intervened in the conversation, evidently burning to show her connexions and air her knowledge of what went on in society.

'The fact of the matter is,' said she significantly, speaking in a half-whisper, 'Count Kirill Vladimirovich's reputation is notorious.... He has lost count of the number of his children, but this Pierre was his favourite.'

'How handsome the old man was,' said the countess, 'only last year. I never saw a finer-looking man.'

'He is very much altered now,' said Anna Mihalovna. 'As I was saying, Prince Vasili is the next heir through his wife, but the count is very fond of Pierre: he took great pains with his education and has written to the Emperor about him, so that no one can tell, in the event of his death – and he is so ill that he may die at any moment, and Dr Lorrain has come from Petersburg – no one can tell, I say, who will come into his enormous fortune, Pierre or Prince Vasili. Forty thousand serfs and millions of roubles! I know it for a fact, Prince Vasili told me so himself. Besides, Kirill Vladimirovich is my mother's second cousin. He's also my Bory's godfather,' she added, as if she attached no importance to this circumstance.

'Prince Vasili arrived in Moscow yesterday. On some inspection business, I am told,' remarked the visitor.

'Yes, but between ourselves,' said the princess, 'that is a pretext. He has really come to see Count Kirill Vladimirovich, having heard how ill he is.'

'At all events, my dear, that was a capital joke,' said the count, and perceiving that the elder visitor was not listening he turned to the young ladies. 'I can just imagine how funny that policeman must have looked!'

And as he waved his arms in imitation of the police officer his portly form again shook with a deep ringing laugh, the laugh of one who always eats well and, in particular, drinks well. 'So, do come and dine with us,' he said.

8

A SILENCE ensued. The countess looked at her visitor, smiling affably but making no attempt to conceal the fact that she would not be in the least sorry if the guest were to get up and go. The visitor's daughter was already smoothing her dress and looking inquiringly at her mother, when suddenly from the next room came the sound of boys and girls running to the door and the noise of a chair falling over, and a girl of thirteen, holding something in the folds of her short muslin frock, darted in and stopped in the middle of the drawing-room. It was plain that her headlong flight had brought her farther than she had intended. Behind her in the doorway appeared a student with a crimson collar to his coat, a Guards officer, a girl of fifteen and a plump, rosy-cheeked little boy in a child's smock.

The count jumped up and opening his arms threw them round the little girl who had come running in.

'Ah, here she is!' he exclaimed, laughing. 'My little pet, whose name-day it is!'

'My dear child, there is a time for everything,' said the countess with feigned severity. 'You always spoil her, Ilya,' she added, addressing her husband.

'How do you do, my dear? Many happy returns of the day,' said the visitor. 'What a charming child,' she went on, turning to the mother.

The little girl with her black eyes and wide mouth was not pretty but she was full of life. In the wild dash her bodice had slipped from the bare childish shoulders and the black curls were tossed back in confusion. She had thin bare arms, little legs in lace-frilled drawers, and low shoes upon her feet. She was at the delightful age when a girl is no longer a child, though the child is not yet a young woman. Escaping from her father she ran to hide her flushed face in the lace of her mother's mantilla – paying no attention to her severe remarks and going into fits of laughter. Laughing and incoherent, she tried to

43

explain something about a doll which she produced from the folds of her frock.

'Do you see? ... It's my doll – Mimi.... You see ...'

And Natasha could not go on, it still seemed to her so funny. She leaned against her mother and burst into such loud, ringing laughter that even the prim visitor could not help joining in.

'Now run along and take that horrid object with you,' admonished her mother, pushing away her daughter with pretended sternness. 'She is my younger girl,' she added, turning to the visitor.

Natasha, raising her face for a moment from her mother's lace mantilla, glanced up through tears of laughter and hid her face again.

Obliged to contemplate this family scene, the visitor felt it incumbent upon her to take part in it.

'Tell me, my dear,' said she to Natasha, 'how did you come by Mimi? Is she your little girl?'

Natasha did not like the condescending tone, and looked at the visitor gravely, without speaking.

Meanwhile all the younger generation: Boris, the officer, Princess Anna Mihalovna's son; Nikolai, the undergraduate, the count's elder son; Sonya, the count's fifteen-year-old niece; and little Petya, his younger boy, had all settled down in the drawing-room, making conspicuous efforts to restrain within the bounds of decorum the glee and excitement which convulsed their faces. Evidently in the back part of the house, from which they had dashed out so impetuously, they had been engaged in much more entertaining conversation than town gossip, the weather and Countess Apraksin. Now and then they would glance at one another, hardly able to suppress their laughter.

The two young men, the student and the officer, friends from childhood, were of the same age and both good-looking, though not alike. Boris was tall and fair, and his calm, handsome face had regular, delicate features. Nikolai was a short, curly-haired young man with an open expression. The first dark down was already showing on his upper lip, and his whole face was expressive of impetuosity and enthusiasm. Nikolai had flushed crimson as soon as he entered the drawing-room, and could not find a word to say. Boris, on the contrary, at once found his footing and related quietly and humorously how he had known that doll Mimi before her nose had lost its beauty; how she had aged during the five years of their acquaintance, and how she was cracked right across the skull. As he said this he glanced at

44

Natasha, but Natasha turned away from him and looked at her little brother, who was screwing up his eyes and shaking with noiseless merriment, until, feeling she could control herself no longer, she jumped down and darted from the room as fast as her nimble little feet would carry her. Boris preserved his composure.

'You were meaning to go out, weren't you, mamma? Shall I order the carriage?' he smilingly asked his mother.

'Yes, yes, go and tell them, please,' she answered, returning his smile.

Boris quietly left the room and went in pursuit of Natasha. The plump little boy trotted crossly after them, as if vexed that their programme had been upset.

9

THE only young people remaining in the drawing-room – not counting the Karagin girl and the countess's elder daughter (who was four years older than her sister and already regarded herself as grown up) – were Nikolai and Sonya the niece. Sonya was a slender, tiny brunette with soft eyes shaded by long lashes, a thick braid of black hair coiled twice round her head, and a tawny tint to her skin especially noticeable on her neck and her bare, thin but shapely, muscular arms. The smooth grace of her movements, the soft elasticity of her small limbs and a certain wary artfulness in her manner suggested a beautiful, half-grown kitten which promises to develop into a lovely cat. She evidently considered it proper to show an interest in the general conversation and smile; but in spite of herself her eyes under their long thick lashes watched her cousin, who was soon to be off to his regiment, with such passionate girlish adoration that her smile could not for a single instant deceive anyone, and it was plain to see that the kitten had only crouched down the more energetically to spring up and play with her cousin the moment they, too, like Boris and Natasha could escape from the drawing-room.

'Yes, my dear,' said the old count, addressing the visitor and pointing to Nikolai, 'his friend Boris here has been given his commission, so for friendship's sake my Nikolai throws up the University and deserts his old father to go into the army. And to think there was a place and everything waiting for him in the Archives! There's friendship for you, eh?' said the count inquiringly.

'Yes, they say war has been declared,' remarked the visitor.

'They have been saying so for a long while,' replied the count, 'and they will say so again, and again after that, and that will be the end of it. My dear, there's friendship for you,' he repeated. 'He is going to join the Hussars.'

The visitor, not knowing what reply to make, shook her head.

'It is not out of friendship at all,' declared Nikolai, flaring up and spurning the accusation as though it were a shameful aspersion. 'It is not from friendship at all but simply because I feel that the army is my vocation.'

He glanced at his cousin and at the visitor's daughter, who were both looking at him with smiles of approbation.

'Colonel Schubert of the Pavlograd Hussars is dining with us today. He has been here on leave and is taking Nikolai back with him. What am I to say?' asked the count, shrugging his shoulders and speaking jestingly of a matter that had evidently occasioned him no little pain.

'I have already told you, papa,' said his son, 'that if you do not wish to let me go, I'll stay. But I know I am no use anywhere except in the army. I am not a diplomatist, or a government clerk – I'm not clever at disguising my feelings,' and as he spoke he kept glancing with the flirtatiousness of a handsome youth at Sonya and the young visitor.

The little kitten, feasting her eyes on him, seemed ready at a moment's notice to start her gambolling and display her kittenish nature.

'Well, well, very well!' said the old count. 'How he flares up at once! This Bonaparte has turned all their heads. They are all thinking of how he rose from ensign to emperor. Well, good luck to them,' he added, not noticing his visitor's amused expression.

While their elders began discussing Bonaparte, Julie Karagin turned to young Rostov.

'What a pity you weren't at the Arharovs' on Thursday. I missed you,' she said, smiling softly at him.

Flattered, the young man drew his chair closer to her with a flirtatious look and engaged the smiling Julie in a confidential conversation, entirely oblivious that his unconscious smile had stabbed the heart of Sonya, who flushed and tried to force a smile. In the midst of talking he glanced round at her. She gave him a passionate angry look and, scarcely able to hold back her tears and maintain the artificial smile on her lips, she got up and left the room. All Nikolai's animation vanished. He waited for the first pause in the conversation and then with a distressed face walked out of the room to find Sonya.

'How all these young people wear their hearts on their sleeves!' remarked Anna Mihalovna, nodding in the direction of the departing Nikolai. 'Cousinhood's a dangerous relationship,' she added.

'Yes,' said the countess, when the sunshine the young people had brought into the room with them had disappeared. And then, as though she were answering a question which no one had put but which was constantly in her mind: 'How much suffering, how much worry we go through before we can at last rejoice in them. And even now there is really more anxiety than joy. One is apprehensive the whole time, always apprehensive! This is the most perilous age for girls as well as for boys.'

'It all depends on their upbringing,' said the visitor.

'Yes, you are right,' continued the countess. 'So far I have always, thank God, been my children's friend and enjoyed their full confidence,' she declared, repeating the mistake of so many parents who imagine that their children have no secrets from them. 'I know I shall always be first in my daughters' confidence, and that if my dear Nikolai with his impetuous nature does get into mischief (boys will be boys), at any rate he will not behave like those Petersburg young gentlemen.'

'Yes, they are splendid children, splendid,' confirmed the count, who always settled all perplexing questions by finding everything splendid. 'Just fancy – insisting on getting into the Hussars! What's one to do, my dear?'

'What a charming creature your younger girl is!' said the visitor. 'Like a little bit of quicksilver!'

'Yes, that she is,' said the count. 'Takes after me! And what a voice she has! Though she's my daughter, I dare to say that she'll be a singer, a second Salomoni. We have engaged an Italian master to teach her.'

'Isn't she too young still? I have heard it spoils the voice to train it at that age.'

'Oh no, why should it be too soon!' replied the count. 'Didn't our mothers get married at twelve or thirteen?'

'And she's in love with Boris already! What do you think of that!' said the countess, looking at Boris's mother with a gentle smile, and

47

continued, evidently concerned with a thought that was always in her mind, 'Now you see, if I were to be too strict with her and forbid her … goodness knows what they might get up to behind my back' (the countess meant that they might kiss in secret), 'but as it is I know every word she utters. She will come running to me of her own accord in the evening and tell me everything. Perhaps I spoil her, but really I believe it's the best way. I was stricter with her sister.'

'Yes, I was brought up quite differently,' remarked the elder daughter, the handsome Countess Vera, with a smile.

But the smile did not enhance Vera's beauty as smiles generally do: on the contrary it gave her face an unnatural and therefore unpleasing expression. Vera was good-looking, far from stupid, quick at learning, was well bred and had a pleasant voice. What she said was right and proper enough, yet, strange to say, everyone – countess and visitors alike – turned to look at her as if wondering why she had said it, and they all felt awkward.

'People are always too clever with their elder children: they try to make something exceptional of them,' said the visitor.

'What's the good of denying it, *ma chère*? Our dear countess tried to be too clever with Vera,' said the count. 'Well, what of that? She has turned out splendidly all the same,' he added, with a wink of approval to Vera.

The guests got up and took their leave, promising to return to dinner.

'What manners! I thought they were never going,' said the countess, when she had seen her visitors to the door.

10

When Natasha ran out of the room she only went as far as the conservatory. There she paused and stood listening to the conversation in the drawing-room, waiting for Boris to come out. She was already beginning to grow impatient, and stamped her foot, on the verge of crying because he did not come at once, when she heard the young man's discreet steps, approaching neither too slowly nor too quickly. Natasha hastily flung herself among the flower-tubs and hid.

Boris paused in the middle of the conservatory, looked round, flicked a speck of dust from the sleeve of his uniform and going up to a mirror examined his handsome face. Natasha, not moving, peered out from her hiding-place, waiting to see what he would do. He stood for a little while in front of the glass, smiled and walked towards the opposite door. Natasha was on the point of calling to him but changed her mind. 'Let him look for me,' she said to herself. Boris had hardly left the conservatory before Sonya, flushed and in tears, came in at the other door, talking angrily to herself. Natasha restrained her first impulse to run out to her, and stayed in her hiding-place, watching (as though she wore a cap that made her invisible) what went on in the world. She was experiencing a novel and peculiar sort of enjoyment. Sonya, still murmuring to herself, kept looking round towards the door of the drawing-room. It opened and Nikolai made his appearance.

'Sonya, what is the matter? How can you?' said Nikolai, running up to her.

'Nothing, nothing; leave me alone!' sobbed Sonya.

'No, I know what it is.'

'Well, if you do, so much the better, and you can go back to her!'

'So-o-onya! Listen! How can you torture me and yourself like that over a mere fancy?' said Nikolai, taking her hand.

Sonya did not pull her hand away, and she left off crying.

Natasha, not stirring and scarcely breathing, watched from her hiding-place with sparkling eyes. 'What will happen now?' she wondered.

'Sonya, the whole world is nothing to me. You are my all,' said Nikolai. 'I'll prove it to you.'

'I don't like it when you talk like that.'

'Well then, I won't. Only forgive me, Sonya!' He drew her to him and kissed her.

'Oh, how nice,' thought Natasha; and when Sonya and Nikolai had left the conservatory she followed and called Boris to her.

'Boris, come here,' said she, with her face full of mischievous meaning. 'I want to tell you something. Here, come here!' and she led him into the conservatory, to the place among the tubs where she had been hiding.

Boris followed, smiling.

'What is the *something*?' he asked.

She grew confused, glanced round and seeing the doll she had thrown on one of the tubs picked it up.

'Kiss the doll,' said she.

49

Boris looked down with an attentive, friendly expression into her eager face, and made no reply.

'Don't you want to? Well, then, come here,' she said, and went deeper among the plants, tossing away the doll. 'Closer, closer!' she whispered. She seized the young officer by his cuffs, and a solemn, scared look appeared on her face.

'Then would you like to kiss me?' she whispered almost inaudibly, peeping up at him from under her brows, smiling and almost crying with agitation.

Boris reddened.

'How absurd you are!' he said, bending down to her and blushing still more but waiting and making no advance.

Suddenly she jumped up on to a tub, so that she stood taller than he, flung her thin little bare arms round him above his neck and, tossing back her curls, kissed him full on the lips.

Then she slipped down among the flower-pots on the other side of the tubs and stood, hanging her head.

'Natasha,' he said, 'you know that I love you, but ...'

'Are you in love with me?' Natasha interrupted him.

'Yes, I am, but please don't let us do this again. ... In another four years ... Then I shall ask for your hand.'

Natasha considered.

'Thirteen, fourteen, fifteen, sixteen,' she counted on her slender little fingers. 'All right! Then it's settled?' And her excited face beamed with a smile of delight and relief.

'Settled!' replied Boris.

'For ever and ever?' said the little girl. 'Till we die?'

And taking his arm, and with a happy face, she walked quietly beside him into the adjoining sitting-room.

II

THE countess was now so tired after receiving visitors that she gave orders not to admit anyone else, but the hall-porter was told to ask all further callers to be sure and return to dinner. The countess was longing for a *tête-à-tête* with the friend of her childhood, Princess Anna Mihalovna, whom she had not seen properly since her return from Petersburg. Anna Mihalovna, with her tear-worn, pleasant face, drew her chair nearer to the countess's.

'With you I will be quite frank,' said Anna Mihalovna. 'There are not many of us old friends left! That is why I value your friendship so.'

Anna Mihalovna looked at Vera and paused. The countess pressed her friend's hand.

'Vera,' she said to her elder and obviously not her favourite daughter, 'how is it you have no notion about anything? Can't you see that you are not wanted? Go and join your sister, or ...'

The handsome Vera smiled disdainfully, evidently not in the least mortified.

'If you had told me sooner, mamma, I should have gone immediately,' she replied as she rose to go to her own room.

But as she was passing through the sitting-room she noticed the two couples, a pair in each window-seat, and stopped to smile satirically. Sonya was sitting close up to Nikolai, who was copying out some verses for her, the first he had ever written. Boris and Natasha were at the other window and ceased talking when Vera came in. Sonya and Natasha looked up at Vera with guilty, happy faces.

It was both amusing and touching to see these two little girls so head over ears in love, but apparently the sight of them roused no pleasant feelings in Vera.

'How many times have I asked you not to touch my things,' she said. 'You have a room of your own,' and she took the inkstand from Nikolai.

'Just a minute, just a minute,' said he, dipping his pen in.

'You always succeed in doing things at the wrong time,' continued Vera. 'Just now you came tearing into the drawing-room so that everyone was ashamed of you.'

In spite or perhaps in consequence of the truth of her remark no one replied, and the four simply looked at one another. She lingered in the room with the inkstand in her hand.

'And what secrets can you have at your age, Natasha and Boris, or you two? It's all nonsense!'

'Now what does it matter to you, Vera?' said Natasha in defence, speaking very gently.

She was evidently even more than usually sweet and well-disposed to everyone that day.

'It is very silly,' said Vera. 'I am ashamed of you. Secrets indeed! ...'

'Everyone has secrets. We don't interfere with you and Berg,' answered Natasha, beginning to get angry.

51

'I should think not,' said Vera, 'because there could never be any harm in anything I do. But I shall tell Mamma how you behave with Boris.'

'Natalia Ilyinishna behaves very well with me,' said Boris. 'I have nothing to complain of.'

'Stop, Boris, you are such a diplomat' – the word 'diplomat' was much in vogue among the children, who attached a special meaning to it – 'it is really tedious,' said Natasha in a hurt, trembling voice. 'Why is she always at me? You'll never understand, because you've never loved anyone,' she added, turning to Vera. 'You have no heart! You are just a Madame de Genlis,' (this nickname, which was considered very offensive, had been bestowed on Vera by Nikolai) 'and your greatest satisfaction is to make things unpleasant for people! Go and flirt with Berg as much as you like,' she finished quickly.

'Well, at all events, you won't see me running after a young man in the presence of visitors.'

'There now, she has gained her object!' interrupted Nikolai. 'Said something nasty to everyone and upset us all. Let's go to the nursery.'

All four rose like a flock of frightened birds and left the room.

'You said nasty things to me!' cried Vera. 'I never said a thing to anyone!'

'Madame de Genlis! Madame de Genlis!' shouted laughing voices through the door.

The handsome Vera, who had such an exasperating, unpleasant effect on everyone, smiled and, evidently unmoved by what had been said to her, went up to the glass and rearranged her sash and hair. Looking at her own handsome face she seemed to become colder and more composed than ever.

*

In the drawing-room the conversation continued.

'Ah, my dear,' said the countess, 'my life is not all roses either. Don't I see that if we go on at this rate our means can't last long? It's this club, and his easy-going nature. Even when we live in the country do we get any rest, with all the theatricals, hunting, shooting and heaven knows what else! But don't let us talk about me. Come, tell me how you managed it all? I often marvel at you, Annette – the way at your time of life you post off alone in a carriage, going to Moscow, to Petersburg, seeing all those ministers and important people and knowing how to deal with them all! I marvel at you! How in the world did you do it? I could never have managed it.'

'Ah, my love,' replied Princess Anna Mihalovna. 'God grant that you never know what it is to be left a helpless widow with a son you love to distraction! One learns a great many things then,' she went on with some pride. 'That lawsuit taught me much. When I wish to see one of the big-wigs I write a note: *Princess So-and-so desires an interview with Monsieur Un Tel*, and then I hire a cab and go two, three or four times, until I get what I want. I don't care what they think of me.'

'Well, tell me, whom did you interview for Boris?' asked the countess. 'Here's your boy an officer in the Guards, while my Nikolai is going as a cadet. There was no one to do anything for him. Whose help did you ask?'

'Prince Vasili's. He was most kind. Agreed to everything at once, and put the matter before the Emperor,' said Princess Anna Mihalovna enthusiastically, quite forgetting all the humiliation she had endured to gain her end.

'Prince Vasili, has he aged much?' inquired the countess. 'I have not seen him since we acted together in theatricals at the Rumyant-sevs', and I dare say he has forgotten me. He used to pay court to me in those days,' the countess recalled with a smile.

'He is just the same as ever,' replied Anna Mihalovna, 'amiable and overflowing with compliments. His head has not been turned at all. "I am only sorry that it is such a small thing to do for you, dear Princess. I am at your command," he said to me. Yes, he is a fine fellow and an extremely nice relation to have. But Nathalie, you know my love for my boy: there is nothing I would not do for his happiness. But my affairs are in such a bad way,' continued Anna Mihalovna sadly, lowering her voice, ' – such a bad way that I am in the most dreadful position. That wretched lawsuit is eating up my all, and making no progress. Would you believe it, I literally haven't a penny, and I don't know how I am going to get Boris his uniform.' She took out her handkerchief and began to cry. 'I must have five hundred roubles, and all I have is one twenty-five rouble note. I am in such straits. ... My only hope now is Count Kirill Vladimirovich Bezuhov. If he will not come forward to help his godson – he is Bory's godfather, you know – and make him some sort of allowance for his support, all my trouble will be thrown away. ... I shall not be able to equip him.'

The countess's eyes filled with tears and she pondered in silence.

'I often think,' said the princess, 'maybe it's a sin but I often think: There's Count Kirill Vladimirovich Bezuhov all alone ... that enormous fortune ... and what is he living for? Life's a burden to him, while Bory's life is just beginning.'

'Surely he will leave something to Boris,' said the countess.

'Heaven only knows, my dear! These rich grandees are such egoists. However, I shall take Boris and go and see him this minute and tell him straight out how things are. People may think what they choose of me, it is really all the same to me when my son's fate depends on it.' The princess rose. 'It is now two o'clock and you dine at four. I shall just have time.'

And in the manner of a practical Petersburg lady who knows how to make the best use of her time Anna Mihalovna sent for her son and with him went out into the ante-room.

'Good-bye, dearest,' said she to the countess, who accompanied her to the door, and added in a whisper so that her son should not hear, 'Wish me luck.'

'Are you going to Count Kirill Vladimirovich, my dear?' said the count coming out of the dining-room into the hall. 'If he is better, ask Pierre to come and dine with us. He used to come here and dance with the children, you know. Be sure to invite him, my dear. We will see how Tarass distinguishes himself today. He tells me Count Orlov never gave such a dinner as we are having today.'

12

'MY dear Boris,' said Princess Anna Mihalovna to her son as Countess Rostov's carriage in which they were seated drove along the straw-covered street and turned into the wide courtyard of Count Kirill Vladimirovich Bezuhov's house. 'My dear Boris,' said the mother, drawing her hand from beneath her old mantle and laying it timidly and tenderly on her son's arm, 'be affectionate and attentive to him. Count Kirill Vladimirovich is your godfather, after all, and your future depends on him. Remember that, my dear, and be nice to him, as you so well know how ...'

'If only I knew that anything would come of this except humiliation ...' replied her son coldly. 'However, I promised you, and I will do it for your sake.'

Though there was a visiting carriage standing at the steps, the hall-porter, after scrutinizing mother and son (who without asking to be announced had walked straight through the glass vestibule between the two rows of statues in niches) and eyeing the lady's threadbare mantle, asked whether they wished to see the princesses or the count, and hearing that they wanted the count he told them that his Excellency was worse and was not receiving anyone that day.

'We may as well go back,' said the son in French.

'My dear!' exclaimed his mother imploringly, again laying her hand on his arm, as if the touch might pacify or inspire him.

Boris said no more and looked inquiringly at his mother, without taking off his cloak.

'My good man,' said Anna Mihalovna ingratiatingly, addressing the hall-porter, 'I know Count Kirill Vladimirovich is very ill ... that is why I have come ... I am a relative of his ... I shall not disturb him, my good man ... I need only see Prince Vasili Sergeyevich: he is staying here, is he not ? Kindly announce us.'

The hall-porter sullenly pulled the cord of a bell that rang upstairs, and turned away.

'Princess Drubetskoy to see Prince Vasili Sergeyevich,' he called to a footman in knee-breeches, slippers and a swallow-tail coat who ran to the head of the stairs and looked over from above.

The mother smoothed the folds of her dyed silk gown, glanced at herself in the massive Venetian mirror on the wall and briskly mounted the carpeted staircase in her down-at heel shoes.

'My dear, you promised me,' she said to her son again, encouraging him with a touch of her hand.

The son, with eyes lowered, followed submissively after her.

They entered the large hall, one of the doors of which led to the apartments that had been assigned to Prince Vasili.

Just as the mother and son reached the middle of the hall and were about to ask the way of an elderly footman who had sprung to his feet at their approach, the bronze doorknob of one of the doors turned, and Prince Vasili, dressed in a velvet house jacket with a single star on his breast, came out, accompanying a handsome man with black hair. This was the celebrated Petersburg Doctor Lorrain.

'There is no doubt, then ?' the prince was saying.

'Prince, *errare humanum est* – to err is human – but ...' replied the doctor, rolling his r's and pronouncing the Latin words with a French accent.

'Very well, very well. ...'

Seeing Anna Mihalovna and her son, Prince Vasili dismissed the physician with a bow and silently but with a look of inquiry came forward to meet them. The son noticed that an expression of profound grief suddenly appeared in his mother's eyes, and he smiled slightly.

'Ah, prince, in what melancholy circumstances we meet again! Well, how is our dear invalid?' said she, as though unaware of the frigid, offensive look fixed on her.

Prince Vasili stared at her, then at Boris with a look of inquiry that amounted to perplexity. Boris bowed politely. Ignoring the bow, Prince Vasili turned to Anna Mihalovna, replying to her question by a movement of his head and lips indicating very little hope for the patient.

'Is it possible?' cried Anna Mihalovna. 'Oh, how terrible! It is dreadful to think. ... This is my son,' she added, introducing Boris. 'He was anxious to thank you in person.'

Boris again bowed politely.

'Believe me, prince, a mother's heart will never forget what you have done for us.'

'I am glad I was able to be of service to you, my dear Anna Mihalovna,' said Prince Vasili, adjusting his shirt frill, and in tone and manner portraying here in Moscow before Anna Mihalovna who was under an obligation to him an even more consequential air than he had at Petersburg at Anna Pavlovna's *soirée*.

'Try to do your duty in the service, and prove yourself worthy of it,' he added, addressing Boris with severity. 'I am delighted. ... Here on leave, are you?' he asked indifferently.

'I am awaiting orders to join my new regiment, your Excellency,' replied Boris, betraying neither resentment at the prince's disagreeable manner nor any desire to pursue the conversation, but speaking so quietly and respectfully that the prince fixed an appraising glance on him.

'Are you living with your mother?'

'I am living at Countess Rostov's,' said Boris, again adding, 'your Excellency.'

'That is, with Ilya Rostov, who married Nathalie Shinshin,' said Anna Mihalovna.

'I know, I know,' returned Prince Vasili in his monotonous voice.

'I have never been able to understand how Nathalie could make up her mind to marry that raw cub! A completely stupid, ridiculous fellow, and a gambler into the bargain, so they say.'

'But a very good sort, Prince,' observed Anna Mihalovna with an affecting smile, as though she too knew that Count Rostov merited this view of himself but would ask him not to be too hard on the poor old man.

'What do the doctors say?' inquired the princess after a pause, her careworn face again assuming an expression of deep distress.

'They give very little hope,' said the prince.

'And I should so much have liked to thank *Uncle* once more for all his kindness to me and to Boris. Boris is his godson,' she added, her tone suggesting that this piece of information ought to give Prince Vasili extreme satisfaction.

Prince Vasili thought this over and frowned. Anna Mihalovna saw that he was afraid of finding in her a rival for Count Bezuhov's fortune, and hastened to reassure him.

'If it were not for my genuine love and devotion to *Uncle*' – she let the word drop with peculiar assurance and unconcern – 'I know his character – noble, upright ... but with only the young princesses about him ... they are still young....' She inclined her head and continued in a whisper: 'Has he performed his final duties, prince? These last moments are so precious. He is as bad as he could be, it seems; it is absolutely necessary to prepare him, if he is so ill. We women, prince,' she smiled sweetly, 'always know how to put these things. I absolutely must see him, however painful it may be for me; but then I am accustomed to suffering.'

Evidently the prince understood, and saw too, just as he had at Annette Scherer's, that he would have no little difficulty in getting rid of Anna Mihalovna.

'Would not such an interview be too much of an ordeal *chère* Anna Mihalovna?' said he. 'Let us wait till this evening. The doctors are expecting the crisis.'

'But one cannot delay, prince, at such a moment! Just think, his soul's salvation is at stake.... Oh, the duties of a Christian are a terrible thing....'

The door from the inner rooms opened, and one of the princesses, the count's nieces, entered. She had a cold, forbidding face and a long body strikingly out of proportion to her short legs.

Prince Vasili turned to her.

'Well, how is he?'

'Still the same. And what can you expect, with this noise? ...' said the princess, surveying Anna Mihalovna as though she were a stranger.

'Ah, my dear, I hardly recognized you,' exclaimed Anna Mihalovna with a happy smile, ambling lightly up to the count's niece. 'I have just arrived, and am at your service to help in nursing *mon oncle*. I can imagine what you must have gone through,' she continued, speaking in French and sympathetically turning up her eyes.

The count's niece made no reply, nor did she even smile, but immediately left the room. Anna Mihalovna drew off her gloves and, entrenched as it were in an arm-chair, beckoned Prince Vasili to sit down beside her.

'Boris,' she said to her son with a smile, 'I shall go in to see the count, to poor uncle, but meanwhile you, my dear, had better go and find Pierre, and don't forget to give him the Rostovs' invitation. They ask him to dinner. I suppose he won't go?' she continued, turning to the prince.

'On the contrary,' replied the latter, plainly cast down, 'I should be only too glad if you would relieve me of that young man. He sticks on here. The count has not once asked for him.'

He shrugged his shoulders. A footman conducted Boris down one flight of stairs and up another to Pierre's room.

13

PIERRE had not had time to choose a career for himself in Petersburg before being banished and sent back to Moscow for disorderly conduct. The story told about him at the Rostovs' was true. Pierre had assisted in tying a policeman on to the back of a bear. He had now been in Moscow for some days and was staying as usual at his father's house. Though he expected, of course, that his escapade would already be known in Moscow and that the ladies surrounding his father – who were never favourably disposed towards him – would have taken advantage of it to put the count against him, he still on the day of his arrival went to his father's part of the house. Entering the drawing-room, where the princesses spent most of their time, he greeted the ladies, two of whom were sitting at their embroidery-frames, while the third read aloud from a book. It was the eldest – the one who had come out to Anna Mihalovna – who was reading: a neat, prim, long-waisted maiden lady. The two younger ones, both rosy-cheeked pretty little creatures exactly alike except that one had a little mole on her lip which made her much prettier, were busy with embroidery. Pierre was received like a man risen from the dead or stricken with the plague. The eldest princess paused in her reading and stared at him in silence with eyes of dismay; the younger one without the mole assumed precisely the same expression; while the youngest – with the mole – who had a gay and lively disposition bent over her frame to hide a smile evoked, no doubt, by the amusing scene she saw coming. She drew her embroidery wool down through the canvas and lent over, pretending to be studying the pattern, scarcely able to suppress her laughter.

'How do you do, cousin?' said Pierre. 'Don't you recognize me?'

'I recognize you only too well, far too well.'

'How is the count? Can I see him?' asked Pierre awkwardly as usual but unabashed.

'The count is suffering both physically and morally, and your only anxiety, it seems, has been to increase his sufferings.'

'Can I see the count?' repeated Pierre.

'H'm!... If you want to be the death of him, to kill him outright, of course you can. Olga, go and see whether uncle's beef-tea is ready – it is almost time,' she added, thus giving Pierre to understand that they were busy, and busy seeing after his father's comfort, while he was evidently only busy upsetting him.

Olga left the room. Pierre stood still a moment, looked at the sisters and said with a bow:

'Then I will go to my rooms. You will let me know when I can see him.'

He went out, followed by the low but ringing laugh of the sister with the mole.

Next day Prince Vasili had arrived and taken up his quarters in the count's house. He sent for Pierre and said to him:

'My dear fellow, if you behave here as you did in Petersburg, you will come to a bad end. That is all I have to say to you. The count is very, very ill: you really must not go near him.'

After that Pierre had been left alone, and he spent his days in solitude in his apartments upstairs.

When Boris appeared at his door Pierre was pacing up and down the room, stopping occasionally in the corners to make threatening gestures at the wall, as if running a sword through an invisible enemy, and glaring savagely over his spectacles, before resuming his promenade, muttering indistinct words, shrugging his shoulders and gesticulating.

'England's day is over,' said he, scowling and pointing his finger at some imaginary auditor. 'Mr Pitt, as a traitor to his country and the rights of man, is sentenced ...' But before Pierre – who at that moment was imagining himself to be his hero Napoleon, in whose person he had already effected the dangerous crossing of the Channel and captured London – could pronounce Pitt's sentence, he saw a well-built and handsome young officer entering his room. Pierre stopped short. Boris was a lad of fourteen when he had last seen him, and Pierre did not recognize him at all, but in spite of that, in his usual impulsive, cordial way, he took Boris by the hand and smiled affably.

'Do you remember me?' asked Boris quietly with a pleasant smile. 'I have come with my mother to see the count but it appears he is not well.'

'Yes, he is ill, so it seems. They do not give him a minute's peace,' answered Pierre, trying to think who this young man might be.

Boris perceived that Pierre failed to recognize him but he did not consider it necessary to introduce himself, and without the slightest embarrassment looked Pierre full in the face.

'Count Rostov begs you to come and dine today,' said he after rather a long silence which made Pierre feel uncomfortable.

'Ah, Count Rostov!' exclaimed Pierre joyfully. 'Then you are his son, Ilya? Fancy, I didn't recognize you at first! Do you remember how we used to drive to Sparrow Hills with Madame Jacquot? ... Ages ago.'

'You are mistaken,' said Boris in leisurely fashion with an assured and slightly derisive smile. 'I am Boris, Princess Anna Mihalovna Drubetskoy's son. It is Count Rostov, the father, who is called Ilya, and his son's name is Nikolai. And I never knew any Madame Jacquot.'

Pierre shook his head and waved his arms as if a swarm of mosquitoes or bees had attacked him.

'Oh dear, what am I thinking about? I have got everything mixed up. One has so many relatives in Moscow! You are Boris ... to be

60

sure. Well, now we know where we are. And what do you think of the Boulogne expedition? It will go pretty hard with the English if Napoleon gets across the Channel. I think the expedition quite possible. So long as Villeneuve doesn't make a mess of things!'

Boris knew nothing about the Boulogne expedition; he did not read the papers and this was the first time he had ever heard of Villeneuve.

'Here in Moscow we are more occupied with dinner-parties and scandal than with politics,' he said in his quiet, ironical tone. 'I know nothing about it and have not given it a thought. Moscow is mainly busy with tittle-tattle,' he continued. 'Just now they are talking about you and the count.'

Pierre smiled his good-natured smile, as if afraid for his companion's sake that the latter might say something he would afterwards regret. But Boris spoke with circumspection, clearly and drily, looking straight into Pierre's eyes.

'Moscow has nothing else to do but gossip,' he went on. 'Everybody is wondering to whom the count will leave his fortune, though who can say, he may outlive the lot of us, as I sincerely hope he will ...'

'Yes, it is all very sad,' interrupted Pierre, 'very sad.'

Pierre was still apprehensive lest this young officer should inadvertently let fall some remark disconcerting to himself.

'And it must seem to you,' said Boris, flushing slightly but not changing his tone or attitude, 'it must seem to you that everybody's one idea is to get something from the rich man.'

'Exactly,' thought Pierre.

'And that's just what I want to tell you, to prevent misunderstandings, that you will be greatly mistaken if you reckon me and my mother among such people. We are very poor but, anyhow as far as I am concerned, just because your father is rich I don't regard myself as his relation, and neither I nor my mother would ever ask anything or take anything from him.'

For a long time Pierre did not understand, but when he did he jumped up from the sofa, seized Boris under the elbow with characteristic impetuosity and clumsiness, and, blushing far more than Boris, began to speak with a mixture of shame and vexation.

'Well, this is strange! Do you suppose I ... indeed who could think? ... I know very well ...'

But Boris again interrupted him.

'I am glad to have spoken freely. Perhaps you dislike it. You must forgive me,' said he, trying to put Pierre at ease instead of being put at ease by him, 'but I hope I have not offended you. It is a principle with me to speak out. ... Well, what message am I to take? Will you come to dinner at the Rostovs'?'

And Boris, with an obvious sense of relief at having discharged an onerous duty, extricating himself from an awkward situation and placing somebody else in one, became completely charming again.

'No, but I say,' said Pierre, regaining his composure, 'you are an amazing fellow! What you have just said is first-rate, first-rate. Of course you don't know me. We haven't seen each other for such a long time ... not since we were children. You might have thought I ... I understand you, understand you perfectly. I should never have done it, I should not have had the courage, but it's splendid. I am very glad to know you. A queer idea,' he added after a short pause, and smiling – 'a queer idea you must have had of me.' He began to laugh. 'Well, what of it! We must get better acquainted, I beg of you.' He pressed Boris's hand. 'Do you know, I have not once been in to the count. He has not asked for me ... I am sorry for him, as a man, but what can one do?'

'So you think Napoleon will succeed in getting his army across?' asked Boris with a smile.

Pierre saw that Boris wanted to change the subject and being of the same mind began to expound the advantages and disadvantages of the Boulogne expedition.

A footman came in to summon Boris to his mother – the princess was going. Pierre, in order to see more of Boris, promised to come to dinner and shook hands warmly, looking affectionately through his spectacles into Boris's eyes.

After Boris had gone, Pierre continued to walk up and down the room for some time, no longer piercing an imaginary foe with his sword but smiling at the recollection of that likeable, intelligent and resolute young man.

As often happens with young people, especially if they are leading a lonely existence, he felt an unaccountable affection for this youth and promised himself that they should become good friends.

Prince Vasili escorted the princess to the door. She was holding a handkerchief to her eyes, and her face was tearful.

'It is dreadful, dreadful!' she was saying. 'But whatever the cost, I shall do my duty. I will come back tonight and sit up with him. He can't be left like this. Every minute is precious. I can't think what the princesses are waiting for. God willing, I may perhaps find a way of preparing him! ... Adieu, prince! May God support you. ...'

'Good-bye, my dear,' replied Prince Vasili, turning away from her.

'Oh, he is in a dreadful state,' said the mother to her son when they were back in the carriage. 'He scarcely recognizes anyone.'

'I can't make out, mamma – what are his feelings towards Pierre?' asked the son.

'The will will make everything clear, my dear; our fate, too, hangs upon it ...'

'But what makes you think he will leave us anything?'

'Ah, my dear! He is so rich, and we are so poor!'

'Well, that's hardly a sufficient reason, mamma.'

'Oh, Heaven, how ill he is, how ill he is!' exclaimed the mother.

14

AFTER Anna Mihalovna had driven off with her son to visit Count Kirill Vladimirovich Bezuhov, Countess Rostov sat for a long time all alone, applying her handkerchief to her eyes. At last she rang.

'What is the matter with you, my dear?' she demanded crossly of the maid, who had kept her waiting a few minutes. 'Don't you care for attending on me, eh? I'll put you to other work, if that is the case.'

Her friend's anxieties and humiliating poverty had upset the countess and so she felt out of temper, a state of mind which always found expression in such remarks to her maid.

'I am very sorry, ma'am,' the girl apologized.

'Ask the count to come here.'

The count came waddling in to see his wife, looking, as usual, rather guilty.

'Well, my little countess! What a *sauté* of a game *au madère* we are going to have, *ma chère*! I've tried it; Tarass is well worth the thousand roubles I gave for him. It was money well spent.'

He sat down by his wife, jauntily planting his elbows on his knees, and ruffling up his grey hair.

'What are your commands, my little countess?'

'It's this, my dear – How did you get that stain there?' she said, pointing to his waistcoat. 'It's some of your *sauté*, no doubt,' she added with a smile. 'Well, you see, count, I want some money.'

Her face grew mournful.

'Oh, little countess!' ... And the count began fiddling to get out his pocket-book.

'I want a good deal, count! I want five hundred roubles.' And taking her cambric handkerchief she began to rub at her husband's waistcoat.

'You shall have it at once. Hey, there!' he shouted, as men only shout who are certain that those they summon will rush headlong to obey. 'Send Mitenka to me!'

Mitenka, a man of good family who had been brought up in the count's house and now had charge of all his affairs, stepped softly into the room.

'Listen, my dear boy,' said the count to the young man who came up respectfully. 'Bring me ' – he thought for a moment – 'yes, bring me seven hundred roubles, yes. But mind, not tattered, dirty notes like last time but nice clean ones, for the countess.'

'Yes, Mitenka, clean ones, please,' said the countess, sighing deeply.

'When does your Excellency desire me to get them ?' asked Mitenka. 'I must inform your Excellency ... However, do not be uneasy,' he added, perceiving that the count was already beginning to breathe heavily and rapidly, which was an unfailing sign of approaching wrath. 'I was forgetting ... Do you wish to have the money at once ?'

'Yes, yes, that's right, bring it now. Give it to the countess.'

'What a treasure that Mitenka is,' added the count with a smile, when the young man had left the room. 'He doesn't know the meaning of the word "impossible". That's a thing I cannot stand. Everything is possible.'

'Ah, money, count, money! How much sorrow it causes in the world!' said the countess. 'But I am in great need of this sum.'

'You, my little countess, are a notorious spendthrift,' said the count, and having kissed his wife's hand he went back to his study.

When Anna Mihalovna returned from her visit to Bezuhov the money, all in crisp new notes, was lying ready under a handkerchief on the countess's little table, and Anna Mihalovna noticed that something was agitating the countess.

'Well, my dear ?' asked the countess.

'Oh, what a terrible state he is in! One would not recognize him,

64

he is so bad, so ill. I only stayed a minute, and did not say two words.'

'Annette, for heaven's sake don't refuse me,' the countess began suddenly, with a blush that looked strangely incongruous on her thin, dignified, elderly face, as she took the money out from under the handkerchief.

Anna Mihalovna instantly guessed what was coming and stooped to be ready to embrace the countess gracefully at the appropriate moment.

'This is for Boris from me, for his equipment. ...'

Anna Mihalovna was already embracing her and weeping. The countess wept too. They wept because they were friends, and because they were warm-hearted, and because they – friends from childhood – should have to think about anything so sordid as money, and because their youth was over. ... But the tears of both were sweet to them.

15

COUNTESS ROSTOV, with her daughters and already a considerable number of guests, was sitting in the drawing-room. The count had taken the gentlemen into his study and was showing them his choice collection of Turkish pipes. From time to time he would go out to inquire: 'Hasn't she come yet?' They were waiting for Maria Dmitrievna Ahrosimov, known in society as *le terrible dragon*, a lady distinguished not for her fortune or rank but for her direct mind and frank, unconventional behaviour. Maria Dmitrievna was known to the Imperial family as well as to all Moscow and Petersburg, and both capitals, while they marvelled at her, laughed up their sleeves at her brusqueness and told good stories about her; but at the same time everyone respected and feared her.

In the count's room, full of tobacco-smoke, the conversation turned on the war, which had just been announced by a manifesto, and on the subject of recruiting. As yet no one had read the manifesto, though all were aware of its appearance. The count was sitting on an ottoman couch with two of his guests smoking and talking on either side of him. He himself was neither smoking nor talking but with his head cocked first one way and then the other watched the smokers with evident satisfaction and listened to the arguments of his two neighbours, whom he had egged on against each other.

One of them was a sallow, clean-shaven civilian with a thin, wrinkled face, already advanced in years though dressed like a young man in the height of fashion. He sat with his legs up on the ottoman, as though he were at home, and having stuck the amber stem of his pipe far into the side of his mouth was spasmodically inhaling smoke and screwing up his eyes. This was an old bachelor, Shinshin, a cousin of the countess, famed in Moscow drawing-rooms for his biting tongue. He seemed supercilious as he talked to his companion, a fresh, rosy officer of the Guards, irreproachably groomed and buttoned, who held his amber mouth-piece in the middle of his handsome mouth, gently inhaling the smoke and letting it escape through his red lips in rings. This was Lieutenant Berg, an officer in the Semeonovsk regiment with whom Boris was to travel to join the army and concerning whom Natasha had teased her elder sister Vera, calling him her 'intended'. The count was sitting between these two, listening closely. His favourite occupation, next to playing boston, a card game of which he was very fond, was that of listener, especially when he succeeded in starting two good talkers on the opposite sides of an argument.

'Well then, old chap, *mon très honorable* Alphonse Karlovich,' said Shinshin, laughing ironically and mixing the most colloquial Russian expressions with exquisite French phrases (which lent peculiarity to his speech), 'you reckon you'll get an income from the Government, and your idea is to make a little something out of your company too?'

'Not at all, Piotr Nikolayevich, I only want to prove that the advantages of serving in the cavalry are few as compared with the infantry. Just consider my own position now, Piotr Nikolayevich.'

Berg always spoke quietly, politely and with extreme precision. His conversation invariably related entirely to himself: he always preserved a serene silence when a topic arose which was of no direct personal interest. He could remain silent for hours without feeling or causing others to feel the slightest embarrassment. But as soon as the conversation touched him personally he would begin to talk at length and with visible satisfaction.

'Consider my position, Piotr Nikolayevich: if I were in the cavalry I should not get more than a couple of hundred roubles every four months, even with the rank of lieutenant; while as it is I get two hundred and thirty,' said he, beaming happily at Shinshin and the count as though he had no doubt that his success must always be the chief desire of everyone else.

'Moreover, Piotr Nikolayevich, by transferring to the Guards I shall be to the fore,' pursued Berg. 'Vacancies occur so much more frequently in the Foot Guards. Then just think what can be done with two hundred and thirty roubles. I can even put a little aside, as well as sending to my father,' he went on, puffing out a smoke ring.

'True ... A German knows how to skin a flint, as the proverb says,' remarked Shinshin, shifting his pipe to the other side of his mouth and winking at the count.

The count chuckled. The other guests, seeing that Shinshin was in the vein, gathered round to listen. Berg, oblivious of irony or indifference, proceeded to explain how by transferring into the Guards he had already gained a step on his old comrades of the Cadet Corps; how in time of war the captain might get killed and he, as senior in the company, might easily succeed to the command; how popular he was with everyone in the regiment and how pleased his father was with him. Berg was evidently enjoying himself, and did not seem to suspect that other people also had their own interests. But all that he said was so prettily sedate, the naïveté of his youthful egotism so obvious, that he disarmed his hearers.

'Ah well, my boy, you will get on whether you are in the infantry or cavalry – that I'll warrant,' said Shinshin, patting him on the shoulder, and taking his feet off the ottoman.

Berg smiled with self-satisfaction. The count, followed by his guests, went into th e drawing-room.

*

It was that interval just before dinner when the assembled guests, expecting the summons to the dining-room, avoid embarking on any lengthy conversation; while they feel it incumbent on them to move about and say something, in order to show that they are in no wise impatient to sit down to table. The host and hostess look towards the door, and now and then exchange glances, while the visitors try to guess from these glances whom or what they are waiting for – is it some belated influential connexion, or a dish that is not quite done?

Pierre arrived just before the hour for dinner and awkwardly sat down in the middle of the drawing-room, on the first chair he came across, blocking the way for everyone. The countess tried to make him talk but he went on naïvely looking about through his spectacles, as though in search of somebody, answering all her inquiries in monosyllables. He was being very difficult, and he was the only person who did not notice the fact. Most of the guests, knowing of the affair with the bear, turned curious eyes on this big, stout, quiet-looking man, wondering how such an indolent, unassuming creature could have played such a prank on a policeman.

'You have only lately arrived in Moscow?' the countess asked him.

'*Oui, madame,*' replied he, glancing round.

'You have not seen my husband yet?'

'*Non, madame.*' He smiled quite inappropriately.

'You have been in Paris recently, I believe? It must have been very interesting.'

'Very interesting.'

The countess exchanged glances with Anna Mihalovna, who realized that she was being asked to take charge of the young man, and crossing to a seat by his side she began to speak about his father; but, just as with the countess, he answered only in monosyllables. The other guests were all busily talking among themselves.

'The Razumovskys ... It was delightful ... You are very kind ... Countess Apraksin ...' were the broken phrases heard on all sides. The countess rose and went into the ante-room.

'Maria Dmitrievna?' she was heard to ask there.

'Herself,' came the answer in a harsh female voice, and Maria Dmitrievna entered the room.

All the unmarried ladies and even the married ones, with the exception of the very oldest, rose. Maria Dmitrievna paused at the door. A woman of fifty, tall and stout, she wore her grey hair in ringlets and held her head erect. Under the pretext of turning back and adjusting the wide sleeves of her dress, she stood surveying the guests. Maria Dmitrievna always spoke in Russian.

'Health and happiness to our dear one whose name-day it is, and to her children,' she said in her loud, deep voice which drowned all other sounds. 'Well, you old sinner,' she went on, addressing the count who was kissing her hand, 'bored to tears in Moscow, I dare-say? No chance to go shooting with the dogs? But what is to be done, old friend, these nestlings will grow up,' and she waved a hand towards the girls. 'You must look for husbands for them, whether you like it or not.

'Well, and how's my Cossack?' she went on. (Maria Dmitrievna always called Natasha a Cossack.) And she stroked the child's hair as

Natasha came up, gaily and not at all shy, to kiss her hand. 'I know she's a scamp of a girl but I'm fond of her all the same.'

She got out of her huge reticule a pair of ear-rings of pear-shaped precious stones and giving them to the blushing Natasha, beaming with birthday happiness, turned away at once and addressed herself to Pierre.

'Ho, ho, sir! Come here to me,' said she, assuming a soft, gentle voice. 'Come here, sir ...' and she tucked her sleeve up higher in an ominous manner.

Pierre approached, ingenuously looking at her through his spectacles.

'Come along, come along, sir! I was the only person to tell your father the truth when he was in high favour, and in your case it's a sacred duty.'

She paused. All held their breath, waiting for what was to come, feeling that this was but the prologue.

'A pretty fellow, I must say! A pretty fellow! ... His father lies on his death-bed and he amuses himself setting a policeman astride a bear! For shame, sir, for shame! It would be better if you went to the war.'

She turned away and gave her hand to the count, who could scarcely keep from laughing.

'Well, I suppose it is time we were at table, eh?' said Maria Dmitrievna.

The count led the way with Maria Dmitrievna, followed by the countess on the arm of a colonel of hussars, a man to be made much of since Nikolai was to travel in his company to join the regiment. Then came Anna Mihalovna with Shinshin. Berg offered his arm to Vera. The smiling Julie Karagin walked in with Nikolai. A string of other couples followed, stretching the length of the dining-hall, and last of all, one by one, came the children with their tutors and governesses. The footmen bustled about, chairs scraped, the orchestra in the gallery struck up, and the guests took their places. The strains of the count's household band were succeeded by the clatter of knives and forks, the voices of the company and the subdued tread of the waiters. At one end of the table the countess presided, with Maria Dmitrievna on her right and Anna Mihalovna on her left, and the other ladies of the party. At the opposite end sat the count with the hussar colonel on his left and Shinshin and the other male guests on his right. On one side midway down the long table were the young people: Vera next to Berg, Pierre and Boris together; and on the other side the children with their tutors and governesses. From behind the crystal decanters and fruit-epergnes the count peeped across at his wife and her tall cap with its pale blue ribbons, and zealously filled his neighbours' glasses, not forgetting his own. The countess in turn, without neglecting her duties as hostess, threw significant glances from behind the pine-apples at her husband, whose rubicund face and bald forehead struck her as all the more conspicuous against his grey hair. At the ladies' end there was a rhythmic murmur of conversation; at the men's end the voices grew louder and louder, and loudest of all was the colonel of hussars who ate and drank so much, growing more and more flushed, that the count was already holding him up as an example to the rest. Berg with a tender smile was telling Vera that love was an emotion not of earth but of heaven. Boris was informing his new friend Pierre of the names of the guests, while he exchanged glances with Natasha, who was sitting opposite. Pierre spoke little, examined the new faces and ate with a will. Of the two soups he chose *à la tortue*, and from the savoury patties to the game he did not let a single dish pass or refuse any of the wines which the butler offered him, mysteriously poking a bottle wrapped in a napkin over his neighbour's shoulder and murmuring: 'Dry Madeira' ... 'Hungarian' ... or 'Rhine wine'. Pierre held up a wine-glass at random out of the four crystal glasses engraved with the count's monogram that stood before each guest, and drank with relish, gazing with ever-increasing amiability at the company. Natasha, who sat opposite, was looking at Boris as girls of thirteen gaze at the boy they have just kissed for the first time and are in love with. Sometimes she let this same look fall on Pierre, and the funny lively little girl's expression made him want to laugh, he could not tell why.

Nikolai was seated at some distance from Sonya, beside Julie Karagin, and was talking to her again with the same involuntary smile. Sonya wore a company smile on her lips but she was obviously in agonies of jealousy; first she turned pale, then blushed, and strained her ears to hear what Nikolai and Julie were saying. The governess kept looking round uneasily, as if preparing to resent any slight to the children. The German tutor was trying to fix in his memory all the different courses, desserts, and wines, in order to write a detailed description of the dinner to his folks in Germany; and he was greatly

70

mortified when the butler with the bottle wrapped in a napkin passed him over. He frowned, trying to make it appear that he did not want any of that wine but was affronted because no one would believe that he did not want it to quench his thirst, or out of greediness, but simply from a conscientious desire for knowledge.

16

A T the men's end of the table the talk was growing more and more animated. The colonel was telling them that the manifesto on the declaration of war had already appeared in Petersburg, and that he had seen a copy of it which had that day been delivered by courier to the commander-in-chief.

'And why the deuce should we have to fight Bonaparte?' exclaimed Shinshin. 'He has already stopped Austria's cackle. I fear it may be our turn next.'

The colonel was a stout, tall German of sanguinary temperament, evidently devoted to the service and patriotically Russian. He resented Shinshin's remark.

'For ze reason, my goot sir,' said he, mispronouncing every word, 'for ze reason zat ze Emperor knows zat. He says in ze manifesto zat he cannot fiew wiz indeeference ze danger treatening Russia and zat ze safety and dignity of ze Empire as vell as ze sanctity of her *alliances...*' he spoke this last word with particular emphasis as though it contained the whole essence of the matter. Then with the infallible memory for official matters that was characteristic of him he quoted from the preamble to the manifesto:

'... and the desire which constitutes the Emperor's sole and immutable aim – to establish peace in Europe on lasting foundations – have now decided him to move part of his army across the frontier in a fresh effort towards the attainment of that purpose.'

'Zat, my dear sir, is ze reason,' he concluded, emptying his glass of wine with dignity and looking round at the count for encouragement.

'Do you know the saying, "Cobbler, cobbler, stick to your last!"?' returned Shinshin, knitting his brows and smiling. 'It fits us to a T. Even Suvorov was hacked to pieces, and where are we to find a Suvorov nowadays, may I ask?' said he, continually dropping from Russian to French and back again.

'Ve must fight to ze last tr-r-op of our plood!' said the colonel, thumping the table; 'und ve must be villing to tie for our Emperor, and zen all vill be vell. And ve must argue as leedle as po-o-ossible ...' (he lingered particularly on the word *possible*), 'as leedle as po-o-oss-ible,' he finished up, again turning to the count. 'Zat is ze vay ve old hussars look at it. But vat is your opinion, young man and young hussar?' he added, addressing Nikolai, who forsook his fair companion when he heard the talk on the war, and was eyes and ears intent on the colonel.

'I entirely agree with you,' replied Nikolai, colouring as red as a poppy, twisting his plate round and moving his wine-glasses about with a face as desperate and determined as though he were exposed to great danger at that actual moment. 'I am convinced that we Russians must die or conquer,' said he, feeling as soon as the words were out of his mouth, as did the others, that they were too impassioned and vehement for the occasion and therefore embarrassing.

'What you just said was splendid,' sighed Julie, who was sitting next to him. Sonya trembled all over and blushed to the ears and behind her ears and down her neck and shoulders while Nikolai was speaking.

Pierre listened to the colonel's speech and nodded approvingly.

'That is well spoken,' said he.

'You're a true hussar, young man!' cried the colonel, thumping the table again.

'What are you making such a noise about over there?' Maria Dmitrievna's deep voice suddenly inquired from the opposite end. 'Why do you pound the table?' she demanded of the hussar. 'What are you getting so heated about, pray? Do you imagine you have got the French here?'

'I am speaking the truth,' replied the hussar with a smile.

'We are talking about the war,' cried the count down the table. 'My son's going, you see, Maria Dmitrievna, my son's going.'

'Well, I have four sons in the army but still I don't fret. It is all in God's hands. You may die in your bed, or God may bring you safely out of a battle,' said Maria Dmitrievna, her deep voice easily carrying the whole length of the room.

'That is so.'

And the conversation was confined once more, among the ladies at one end and the men at the other.

'You wouldn't dare ask,' said her little brother to Natasha. 'I know you won't.'

'Yes, I will,' replied Natasha.

Her face suddenly glowed with a gay and desperate resolution. She half rose from her chair, with a glance inviting Pierre, who sat opposite, to listen to what was coming, and turned to her mother.

'Mamma!' rang the clear childish voice down the length of the table.

'What is it?' asked the countess in dismay; but seeing by her daughter's face that it was only mischief she shook a finger at her sternly and nodded her head in warning.

There was a sudden silence.

'Mamma, what sweets are we going to have?' cried Natasha's voice even more clearly and deliberately.

The countess tried to look severe but could not. Maria Dmitrievna shook a fat finger at the child.

'Cossack!' she said threateningly.

Most of the guests, uncertain what to make of this sally, looked at the parents.

'You will see what I'll do to you!' said the countess.

'Mamma, tell me what sweets we are going to have?' repeated Natasha boldly, with saucy gaiety, confident that her prank would not be taken amiss.

Sonya and fat little Petya were doubled up with laughter.

'There, you see, I did ask,' whispered Natasha to her little brother and to Pierre, glancing at him again.

'Ice-cream, only you will not be allowed any,' said Maria Dmitrievna.

Natasha saw there was nothing to be afraid of and so she braved even Maria Dmitrievna.

'Maria Dmitrievna! What sort of ice-cream? I don't like ice-cream.'

'Carrot-ices.'

'No, what kind, Maria Dmitrievna? What kind?' she almost shrieked. 'I want to know!'

Maria Dmitrievna and the countess burst out laughing, and all the guests joined in. They all laughed, not at Maria Dmitrievna's repartee but at the incredible audacity and smartness of this little girl who had the pluck and wit to tackle Maria Dmitrievna in this fashion.

Natasha only desisted when she was told that there would be pine-apple ice. Before the ices champagne was served. The orchestra struck up again, the count kissed his 'little countess' and the guests rose to drink her health, clinking glasses across the table with the count, the children, and one another. Again the footmen bustled about, chairs scraped, and in the same order in which they had entered, but with faces a little more flushed, the company returned to the drawing-room and to the host's study.

17

THE card-tables were brought out, partners selected for boston, and the count's guests distributed themselves about the two drawing-rooms, the sitting-room and the library.

Having spread his cards out fanwise, the count with difficulty kept himself from dropping into his usual after-dinner nap, and laughed at everything. The young people, at the countess's suggestion, gathered round the clavier and the harp. Julie first, by general request, played a little air with variations on the harp, and then joined the other young ladies in begging Natasha and Nikolai, who were noted for their musical talent, to sing something. Natasha, though much flattered at being treated like a grown-up person, at the same time felt shy.

'What are we to sing?' she asked.

'*The Fountain*,' suggested Nikolai.

'Well, then, let's be quick. Boris, come over here,' said Natasha. 'But where is Sonya?'

She looked round and seeing that her cousin was not there flew off in search of her.

Running into Sonya's room and not finding her, Natasha made for the nursery but Sonya was not there either. Natasha concluded that she must be on the chest in the passage. The chest in the passage was the spot consecrated to the woes of the younger female generation in the Rostov household. And there in fact was Sonya, lying face down-wards on Nanny's dirty striped feather-bed on top of the chest, crumpling her gauzy pink dress beneath her. Hiding her face in her slender fingers, she was sobbing so convulsively that her bare little shoulders shook. Natasha's face, which had been so radiant all through her name-day, changed at once: her eyes grew fixed, then her throat contracted and the corners of her mouth drooped.

'Sonya! What is the matter ? ... What has happened ? ... Oo-oo! ...'

And Natasha's large mouth widened, making her look quite ugly, and she began to wail like a baby, without knowing why except that Sonya was crying. Sonya tried to lift her head to answer but could not and buried her face still deeper in the bed. Natasha wept, sitting on the blue-striped feather-bed and hugging her friend. With an effort Sonya sat up and began to wipe away her tears and explain.

'Nikolai is going away in a week, his ... papers ... have come ... he told me himself ... But I should not have cried for that ...' (she showed Natasha a sheet of paper she was holding in her hand; on it were verses written by Nikolai), 'I should not have cried for that but you can't ... no one can understand ... how good and noble he is!'

And she began to cry again at the thought of how good and noble he was.

'It's all right for you ... I'm not envious ... I love you, and Boris, too,' she went on, gaining a little composure. 'He is a dear fellow ... there are no obstacles in your way. But Nikolai is my cousin ... the archbishop himself would have to ... else it would be impossible. And then if Mamma's told ...' (Sonya looked on the countess as her mother, and called her so) ... 'she'll say that I am spoiling Nikolai's career, that I am heartless and ungrateful, while truly ... God is my witness ... '(she crossed herself) 'I love her so much, too, and all of you, only Vera ... Why is she like that ? What have I done to her ? I am so grateful to you all that I would gladly make any sacrifice, only I have nothing to sacrifice. ...'

Sonya could say no more and again she buried her face in her hands and the feather-bed. Natasha set about consoling her but it was clear from her expression that she understood the full seriousness of her friend's trouble.

'Sonya!' she exclaimed suddenly, as though she had surmised the true reason for her cousin's misery. 'I'm sure Vera said something to you after dinner ? She did, didn't she ?'

'Yes, Nikolai wrote these verses himself, and I copied some others, and she found them on my table and said she'd show them to Mamma, and she says I am ungrateful and that Mamma will never let him marry me, but that he'll marry Julie. You saw how he devoted himself to her the whole day. ... Oh, Natasha, why is it ? ...'

And she started to sob again, more bitterly than ever. Natasha lifted her up, hugged her and smiling through her tears began to comfort her.

'Sonya, don't you believe her, darling! Don't believe her! Remember what we were saying, you and I and Nikolai, after supper in the sitting-room the other evening? We settled the way it should all be: I forget now exactly how it was, but you know it all came out right and quite possible to arrange. Why, Uncle Shinshin's brother is married to his first cousin, and we are only second cousins. And Boris said there would be no difficulty at all. You know I told him all about it. And he is so clever and so good!' said Natasha. 'Don't cry, Sonya, my pet, my darling!' and she kissed her, laughing. 'Vera's spiteful, never mind her! And it will all come right and she won't say anything to Mamma. Nikolai will tell her himself, and he's never thought of Julie.'

And Natasha kissed her head. Sonya sat up, and the little kitten revived; its eyes danced and it seemed ready to lift its tail, drop down on its soft paws and begin playing with the ball of wool again as a kitten should.

'Do you think so? ... Really and truly?' she asked, quickly smoothing her frock and hair.

'Really and truly,' answered Natasha, tucking back a crisp lock that had strayed from under her cousin's plaits.

And they both laughed.

'Well, let's go and sing *The Fountain.*'

'Come along then.'

'You know, that fat Pierre who sat opposite me is so funny,' said Natasha, stopping suddenly. 'I feel so happy!'

And Natasha set off at a run along the passage.

Sonya, shaking off some down that clung to her dress and slipping the verses inside her bodice next to her bony little chest, speeded after Natasha down the passage into the sitting-room with light, joyous steps and face aglow. At the company's request the young people sang the quartette *The Fountain,* which charmed everyone. Then Nikolai sang a new song he had just learnt.

> On a soft night beneath the moon,
> How joyous to feel and to know
> *That in this world there is someone*
> *Whose thoughts are thinking of thee!*

Her lovely fingers are straying
O'er the golden strings of the harp
Making passionate harmonies
Call and call to thee!
A day or two, then Paradise ...
But thy love on her death bed lies!

He was hardly at the end before the young people began to get ready for dancing in the large hall, and the musicians were heard clearing their throats and shuffling in the gallery.

*

Pierre was sitting in the drawing-room, where Shinshin had engaged him, as a man recently returned from abroad, in a political discussion in which others joined but which bored Pierre. When the music struck up, Natasha came into the drawing-room and walking straight up to Pierre said, eyes laughing, and blushing:

'Mamma told me to ask you to come and dance.'

'I am afraid of upsetting the figures,' Pierre replied, 'but if you will be my teacher ...' And he offered his large arm to the slender little girl, bending down to her level.

While the couples were arranging themselves and the musicians tuning up, Pierre sat down with his little partner. Natasha was blissful: she was dancing with a *grown-up* man come from *abroad*. She was sitting in view of everyone and talking to him like a grown-up lady. In her hand was a fan which one of the ladies had given her to hold, and assuming quite the air of a society woman (heaven knows when and where she had learnt it), she talked to her partner, fanning herself and smiling over the fan.

'Dear, dear! Look at her now!' exclaimed the countess as she crossed the ballroom, pointing to Natasha.

Natasha coloured and laughed.

'What do you mean, mamma? Why do you say that? It's quite natural – why shouldn't I?'

*

In the midst of the third *écossaise* there was the sound of chairs being pushed back in the sitting-room, where the count and Maria Dmitrievna had been playing cards with the majority of the more distinguished and older guests. Stretching their limbs which were cramped after sitting still so long, and putting away purses and pocket-books, they entered the ballroom. First came Maria Dmitrievna and the count, both in high good humour. With playful ceremony the count curved his arm after the style of a ballet dancer, and gave it to Maria Dmitrievna. He drew himself up, his face brightened into a debonair smile, and as soon as they had danced the last figure of the *écossaise* he clapped his hands to the musicians and called up to the first violin:

'Simeon! Do you know the *Daniel Cooper*?'

This was the count's favourite dance that he had danced in his youth. (*Daniel Cooper* was really one of the figures in the *anglaise*.)

'Look at papa!' cried Natasha at the top of her voice, quite forgetting that she was dancing with a grown-up partner. She bent her curly head over her knees and made the whole room ring with her laughter.

Everyone present was, in fact, looking with a smile of pleasure at the jolly little old gentleman beside the stately Maria Dmitrievna, who was taller than her partner. Arms beating time to the music, shoulders back, toes turned out and tapping gently, and a broad smile on his round face, he prepared the onlookers for what was to follow. As soon as the gay irresistible strains of *Daniel Cooper* were heard (with a swift rhythm like that of a peasant dance) every door of the ballroom was suddenly filled with men on one side and women on the other beaming all over their faces – the servants had come to watch their master making merry.

'Just look at the master! Soaring about like an eagle!' an old nurse said out loud in one of the doorways.

The count danced well and knew that he did, but his partner could not dance at all and had no wish to excel at it. She held her portly figure erect, with her sturdy arms hanging by her sides (she had handed her reticule to the countess). It was only her stern but comely face that entered into the dance. What was expressed by the whole rotund person of the count, in Maria Dmitrievna found expression only in her increasingly radiant smile and the puckering of her nose. But if the count, getting more and more into his stride, captivated the spectators by his light-footed agility and unexpectedly graceful capers, Maria Dmitrievna with the slightest of exertions in moving her shoulders or curving her arms, when they turned or marked time with their feet, excited no less enthusiasm because of the contrast, which everyone appreciated, with her size and usual severity of demeanour. The dance grew livelier and livelier. The other couples could not attract a moment's attention to themselves, and did not even try to. All eyes were fastened on the count and Maria Dmitrievna. Natasha kept pulling everyone by the sleeve or dress urging them to *look at papa!* though as it was they needed no telling. They never took their eyes off the couple. In the intervals of the dance the count, stopping for breath, waved and shouted to the musicians to play faster. Faster, faster, and faster, lightly, more lightly, and ever more lightly whirled the count, flying round Maria Dmitrievna, now on his toes now on his heels, until at last he swung his partner back to her place, executed the final *pas*, lifting one fat leg in the air behind, bowing his perspiring head, smiling and making a wide sweep with his right arm amid a thunder of applause and laughter led by Natasha. Both partners stood still, out of breath and wiping their faces with cambric handkerchiefs.

'That's the way we used to dance in our time, *ma chère*,' said the count.

'That *was* a *Daniel Cooper*!' exclaimed Maria Dmitrievna, drawing a long breath and tucking back her sleeves.

18

A T the same time as the sixth *anglaise* was being danced in the Rostovs' ballroom, and while the musicians were playing out of tune from sheer tiredness, and the weary servants, footmen and cooks were getting the supper, Count Bezuhov had his sixth stroke. The doctors pronounced him past all hope. The form of confession was read over the dying man, the sacrament administered and preparations made for the final anointing, and the house was full of the bustle and thrill of suspense usual in such circumstances. Outside, a crowd of undertakers waited at the gates, eagerly anticipating a good order for the count's funeral and dodging behind the carriages that drove up. The military governor of Moscow, who had been assiduous in sending aides-de-camp to inquire after the count, this evening came himself to bid a last farewell to the renowned grandee of Catherine's court, Count Bezuhov.

The magnificent reception-room was crowded. Everyone stood up respectfully when the governor, after half an hour alone with the dying man, came out, bowing slightly in acknowledgement of their salutations and endeavouring to escape as quickly as possible from the glances fixed on him by doctors, clergy and relatives of the family. Prince Vasili, who had grown thinner and paler during the last few days, accompanied him to the door, repeating something several times in an undertone.

Having escorted the governor, Prince Vasili sat down on a chair alone in the ball-room, crossing one leg high over the other, leaning his elbow on his knee and covering his eyes with his hand. After sitting like this for some time he rose, looking about him with frightened eyes, and made his way with unwonted hurry down the long corridor leading to the back of the house, to the apartments of the eldest princess.

Those who remained in the dimly-lighted reception-room talked among themselves in jerky whispers and relapsed into silence, looking round inquiringly or expectantly whenever the door that led into the sick-room creaked as someone went in or came out.

'The limits of human life,' said a little old man, an ecclesiastic of some sort, to a lady who had taken a seat beside him and was listening naïvely to his words, 'the limits of human life are determined, one may not live beyond them.'

'I wonder, is it not too late for the last anointing?' inquired the lady, adding his clerical title, and apparently having no opinion of her own on the point.

'Ah, madam, it is a great sacrament,' replied the priest, passing a hand over the thin grizzled strands of hair combed across his bald head.

'Who was that? Was it the military governor himself?' someone asked at the other end of the room. 'What a youthful-looking man!'

'Yes, and he's well over sixty. I hear the count no longer recognizes anyone. Were they going to give him the final anointing?'

'I knew someone who received the last sacrament seven times.'

The second niece came out of the sick-room, her eyes red from weeping, and sat down by Doctor Lorrain, who had arranged himself gracefully under a portrait of the Empress Catherine, leaning his elbow on a table.

'Beautiful!' said the doctor in answer to a remark about the weather. 'Beautiful weather, princess; besides, in Moscow it is like being in the country.'

'It is, indeed,' replied the princess with a sigh. 'So he may have something to drink?'

Lorrain considered.

'He has taken his medicine?'

'Yes.'

The doctor glanced at his watch.

'Then give him a glass of boiled water containing a pinch of cream of tartar.' With his slender fingers he indicated what was meant by a pinch.

'Dere has neffer been a gase,' a German doctor was saying to an aide-de-camp, 'vere a mahn liffed after de dird sdroke.'

'What a constitution he had!' remarked the aide-de-camp. 'And who will inherit his fortune?' he added in a whisper.

'It vill not go begging,' replied the German with a smile.

They all looked round again at the door, which creaked as the second princess went in with the drink which Lorrain had prescribed for the sick man. The German doctor went over to Lorrain.

'Do you t'ink he can last till morning?' he asked in French which he pronounced vilely.

Lorrain, pursing his lips, waved a severely negative finger in front of his nose.

'Tonight, at latest,' said he in a low voice, and moved away with a decorous smile of self-satisfaction at being able so clearly to diagnose and state the patient's condition.

Meanwhile Prince Vasíli had opened the door into the princess's apartment.

It was almost dark in the room; only two tiny lamps burned before the icons and there was a pleasant scent of flowers and burnt pastilles. Small articles of furniture, chiffoniers, cabinets and little tables, filled the room. The white quilt of a high feather-bed was visible behind a screen. A small dog began to bark.

'Ah, is that you, *mon cousin?*'

She rose and smoothed her hair which was, as usual, so extraordinarily smooth that it might have been made of one piece with her skull, and varnished.

'What is it, has anything happened?' she asked. 'I live in continual dread.'

'No, there is no change. I only came to have a little talk with you, Katishe – about business,' said the prince, wearily sinking into the

chair she had just vacated. 'I say, how warm you have got the room!'
he remarked. 'Well, come and sit here: let us have a talk.'

'I thought perhaps something had happened?' said the princess, and
sitting down opposite the prince she prepared to listen, her face stony
and obdurate as ever. 'I was trying to get a nap, *mon cousin*, but it's
no good.'

'Well, my dear?' said Prince Vasili, taking her hand and bending it
downwards, a habit of his.

It was plain that this 'well?' referred to a number of things which
they both understood without naming them.

The princess, who had a thin erect body quite incongruously long
for her legs, looked straight at the prince with no sign of emotion in
her prominent grey eyes. Then she shook her head and glanced up
at the icons with a sigh. The gesture might convey grief and devotion,
or it might imply weariness and hope of a speedy respite. Prince
Vasili interpreted it as an expression of weariness.

'And what about me?' he said. 'Do you suppose it's any easier for
me? I am as played out as a post-horse, but still I must have a talk
with you, Katishe, and a very serious one.'

Prince Vasili paused, and his cheeks began to twitch nervously, first
on one side, then on the other, giving his face an unpleasant expression such as it never had when he was in company. His eyes, too, were
different from usual: at one moment they gleamed impudently sly,
at the next they looked round furtively.

The princess, holding the little dog on her lap with her thin bony
hands, gazed intently into Prince Vasili's eyes, but it was plain that
she was resolved not to be the first to break the silence, even though
she sat till morning.

'Don't you see, my dear princess and cousin, Katerina Semeonovna,'
pursued Prince Vasili, evidently having to brace himself to go on with
what he wanted to say, 'at such a moment as the present, one must
think of everything. One must think of the future, of all of you. ...
I love the three of you as if you were my own children; you know
that.'

The princess continued to regard him with the same dull unwavering eye.

'And then of course my family also has to be considered,' Prince
Vasili resumed, testily pushing back a little table and not looking at
her. 'You know, Katishe, that you three Mamontov sisters and my

wife are the count's only direct heirs. I know – I quite understand how painful it is for you to talk or think about such things. And it is no easier for me; but, my dear, I am getting on for sixty, I must be ready for anything. You know that I have sent for Pierre ? The count pointed directly to his portrait, signifying that he wanted to see him.'

Prince Vasili looked inquiringly at the princess but could not make out whether she was considering what he had just said or merely staring at him.

'One thing, cousin, I never cease praying God to be merciful to him, and grant his noble soul a peaceful passage from this …'

'Yes, yes of course,' interrupted Prince Vasili impatiently, rubbing his bald forehead and angrily pulling towards him the little table that he had just pushed away. 'But … in short the fact is … you yourself are aware that last winter the count made a will passing over his direct heirs and us, and bequeathing all his property to Pierre.'

'He has made many a will!' remarked the princess placidly. 'But Pierre can't be his heir. Pierre is illegitimate.'

'*Ma chère,*' said Prince Vasili suddenly, clutching the little table in his excitement and speaking more rapidly, 'but what if a letter has been written to the Emperor begging him to have Pierre declared legitimate ? You understand that the count's services would make his petition carry weight ?'

The princess smiled as people smile when they think they know more about the subject under discussion than those with whom they are talking.

'I will tell you another thing,' Prince Vasili went on, clasping her hand. 'That letter was written, though it was not despatched, and the Emperor has heard about it. The only question is – has it been destroyed or not ? If not, then as soon as *all is over,*' and the prince sighed, thereby intimating what he meant by the words *all is over,* 'and the count's papers are opened, the will and the letter will be delivered to the Emperor, and the petition will certainly be granted. Pierre, as the legitimate son, will get everything.'

'What about our share ?' demanded the princess, smiling ironically, as if anything were possible except that.

'Why, my poor Katishe, it is as clear as daylight! He will be the sole legal heir to everything and you won't get a penny. You must know, my dear, whether the will and letter were written, and whether they have been destroyed or not. And if they have somehow

83

been overlooked, you must know where they are and ought to find them because ...'

'What next!' interrupted the princess, smiling sardonically, with no change in the expression of her eyes. 'I am a woman and according to you all women are idiots, but I do know that an illegitimate son cannot inherit ... *un bâtard!*' she added, as if the word *bastard* would effectively prove to Prince Vasili the invalidity of his argument.

'Well, really, Katishe, can't you understand? You are so intelligent, how is it you don't see that if the count has written a letter to the Emperor begging him to recognize Pierre as legitimate, it follows that Pierre will not be Pierre any longer but Count Bezuhov, and will then inherit everything under the will? And if the will and the letter are not destroyed, all you will have will be the consolation of knowing that you were dutiful and the rest of it. That's certain.'

'I know the will was made, but I also know that it is invalid; and it seems to me, *mon cousin*, that you take me for a perfect fool,' said the princess with the air women assume when they suppose they have said something clever and stinging.

'My dear Princess Katerina Semeonovna!' began Prince Vasili impatiently. 'I came here not to squabble with you but to talk about your own interests as with a kinswoman, a kind, good, true kinswoman. I tell you for the tenth time that if this letter and the will in Pierre's favour are among the count's papers, then you, my dear little friend, are not an heiress, nor are your sisters. If you don't believe me then believe an expert. I have just been talking to Dmitri Onufrich' (this was the family solicitor), 'and he says the same.'

At this a sudden alteration evidently took place in the princess's ideas; her thin lips grew white (though her eyes did not change) and her voice when she began to speak came in jerks which obviously surprised even her.

'That would be a fine thing!' said she. 'I never wanted anything and I don't now.'

She pushed the little dog off her lap and smoothed the folds of her dress.

'That's his gratitude – that's the recognition people get who have sacrificed everything for him!' she cried. 'Very nice! Excellent! I want nothing, prince.'

'Yes, but you are not alone. There are your sisters,' replied Prince Vasili. But the princess did not heed him.

'Yes, I have known it for a long time but I had forgotten ... I knew I had nothing to expect in this house except meanness, deceit, envy, intrigue, and ingratitude – the blackest ingratitude ...'

'Do you or do you not know where that will is?' asked Prince Vasili, his cheeks twitching more than ever.

'Yes, I was a fool! I still believed in people, cared for them and sacrificed myself. But only the base, the vile succeed! I know whose work this is!'

The princess started to her feet but the prince stayed her. She looked like one who has suddenly lost faith in the whole human race. She gave her relative a vicious glance.

'There is still time, my dear. You must remember, Katishe, that it was all done without thinking, in a moment of anger, of illness, and afterwards forgotten. Our duty, my dear, is to rectify his mistake, to ease his last moments by not letting him commit this injustice. We must not let him die feeling that he was making unhappy those who ...'

'Those who have sacrificed everything for him,' caught up the princess, who would have risen again but the prince still held her fast, 'though he never had the good sense to appreciate it. No, *mon cousin*,' she added with a sigh, 'I shall live to learn that in this world one can expect no reward, that in this world there is no such thing as honour or justice. In this world one has to be cunning and wicked.'

'Come, come now! Calm yourself. I know your good heart.'

'No, I have a wicked heart.'

'I know your heart,' repeated the prince. 'I prize your friendship and I could wish that you had as high an opinion of me. Don't upset yourself, and let us talk sensibly while there is still time – be it a day or be it but an hour. ... Tell me all you know about the will, and above all where it is: you must know. We will take it at once and show it to the count. No doubt he has forgotten all about it and will wish it to be destroyed. You understand that my sole desire is to carry out his wishes religiously; that is my only reason for being here – I came simply to be of use to him and you.'

'Now I see it all! I know who has been intriguing – I know who it is!' cried the princess.

'That is not the point, my dear.'

'It's that protégée of yours, that precious Princess Drubetskoy, that

Anna Mihalovna of yours whom I would not take for my housemaid – the infamous, vile creature!'

'Let us not lose time,' said the prince in French.

'Ah, don't talk to me! Last winter she wormed her way in here and told the count such a pack of nasty, mean tales about all of us, especially Sophie – I can't repeat them – that it made the count really ill and for two whole weeks he would not see any of us. It was then, I know, that he wrote that horrid, vile document, but I thought it was of no consequence.'

'We've got to it at last – why ever did you not tell me about it sooner?'

'It's in the inlaid portfolio which he keeps under his pillow,' said the princess, ignoring his question. 'Now I know! Yes, if I have a sin, a heavy sin on my conscience, it is hatred of that horrible woman!' the princess almost shrieked, altogether different now. 'And what does she come worming herself in here for? But I will give her a piece of my mind! The time will come!'

19

WHILE all these various conversations were taking place in the reception-room and in the princess's apartment the carriage with Pierre (who had been sent for) and Anna Mihalovna (who found it necessary to accompany him) was driving into the courtyard of Count Bezuhov's house. As the wheels rolled softly over the straw spread beneath the windows Anna Mihalovna turned to her companion with words of consolation, discovered that he was asleep in his corner, and roused him. Waking up, Pierre followed Anna Mihalovna out of the carriage, and began to think for the first time of the interview before him with his dying father. He noticed that they had drawn up not at the main entrance but at a back door As he was leaving the carriage two men who looked like tradespeople shrank back from the doorway into the shadow of the wall. Pausing for a moment, Pierre observed several other similar figures in the shadow on both sides of the house. But neither Anna Mihalovna nor the footman nor the coachman, who could not have helped seeing these people, paid any attention to them. 'So I suppose it must be all right,' Pierre argued to himself, and he followed Anna Mihalovna.

With hurried steps Anna Mihalovna tripped up the narrow dimly-lit stone staircase, calling to Pierre, who was loitering behind. Though he could not see why he had to go to the count at all, and still less why he had to go by the back stairs, yet judging by Anna Mihalovna's air of assurance and haste Pierre concluded that it was all absolutely necessary. Half-way up the stairs they were almost knocked over by some men, who came running down carrying pails, their boots clattering. These men pressed close to the wall to let Pierre and Anna Mihalovna pass, and showed not the slightest surprise at seeing them there.

'Is this the way to the princesses' apartments?' inquired Anna Mihalovna of one of them.

'Yes,' replied the footman in a loud, bold voice, as if anything were permissible now. 'The door on the left, ma'am.'

'Perhaps the count did not ask for me,' said Pierre, when he reached the landing. 'I had better go to my own room.'

Anna Mihalovna waited till Pierre came up.

'Ah, my friend!' she said, laying her hand on his arm just as she had done earlier in the day to her son. 'Believe me, I suffer no less than you do, but be a man!'

'Really, hadn't I better go to my own room?' asked Pierre, looking benignly at her through his spectacles.

'Ah, my dear friend, forget the wrongs that may have been done you. Remember only that he is your father ... and in his death agony, perhaps.' She sighed. 'I have loved you like a son from the very first. Trust in me, Pierre. I shall not forget your interests.'

Pierre did not understand a word but it came over him with even more force that all this had to be, and so he meekly followed Anna Mihalovna, who was already opening a door.

The door led into the ante-room of the rear apartments. In one corner sat an old manservant of the princesses, knitting a stocking. Pierre had never been in this part of the house and had no idea of the existence of these rooms. Addressing a maid who was hurrying by with a carafe of water on a tray, and calling her 'my dear' and 'my good girl', Anna Mihalovna inquired after the princesses' health, and beckoned Pierre to follow her along the stone passage. The first door on the left led into the princesses' apartments. In her haste the maid with the carafe had not closed the door (at this time everything in the house was done in haste), and as Pierre and Anna Mihalovna passed by they involuntarily glanced into the room where the eldest niece was sitting in close conference with Prince Vasili. Seeing them pass, Prince Vasili made a movement of annoyance and drew back, while the princess sprang to her feet and, exasperated, slammed the door with all her might.

This action was so unlike the princess's habitual composure, and the dismay depicted on Prince Vasili's face so out of keeping with his usual air of importance, that Pierre stopped short and looked inquiringly through his spectacles at his guide. Anna Mihalovna manifested no surprise; she merely smiled faintly and sighed, as much as to say that all this was no more than she had expected.

'Be a man, my friend. I am here to watch over your interests,' said she in reply to his glance, and went tripping along the passage even faster than before.

Pierre could not make out what it was all about, and still less what 'watching over his interests' meant, but he decided that all these things had to be. From the passage they went into a large dimly-lit chamber adjoining the count's reception-room. It was one of those cold sumptuous apartments which Pierre had previously only entered from the front. But even in this room, right in the middle, there now stood an empty bath tub, and water had been spilt on the carpet. They were met by a servant coming towards them on tiptoe, and a deacon carrying a censer, neither of whom paid any attention to Pierre and Anna Mihalovna, who went into the reception-room familiar to Pierre, with its two Italian windows opening into the conservatory and the large bust and full-length portrait of Catherine. The same people were still sitting here in almost the same attitudes as before, whispering to one another. As Anna Mihalovna entered they all fell silent and turned to look at her pale, careworn face and at the stout, burly Pierre who followed her submissively, hanging his head.

Anna Mihalovna's face expressed consciousness that the critical moment was at hand. With the bearing of a Petersburg lady of experience, keeping Pierre close at her side, she marched into the room even more boldly than she had that afternoon. She felt that as she was bringing the person whom the dying man wished to see her own admission was assured. Casting a rapid glance at all those in the room and noticing the count's spiritual adviser there, she glided up to him with a mincing gait, not exactly bowing but suddenly diminishing her stature, and respectfully received the blessing first of the one and then of another ecclesiastic.

'Thank God we are in time,' said she to one of the priests. 'All of us, his kinsfolk, have been so anxious. This young man is the count's son,' she added in a lower tone. 'What a terrible moment!'

After this she went over to the doctor.

'My dear doctor,' she said to him, speaking in French. 'This young man is the count's son. ... Is there any hope?'

The doctor cast his eyes upwards and silently shrugged his shoulders. With just the same gesture Anna Mihalovna raised her shoulders and eyes, almost closing her eyelids, gave a sigh and moved away from the doctor to Pierre. She addressed Pierre with peculiar deference and a tender melancholy.

'Have faith in His mercy,' and pointing out a small sofa where he should sit and wait for her, she noiselessly directed her steps towards the door which was the centre of attention and which creaked faintly as it closed behind her.

Pierre, having made up his mind to obey his monitress in all things, moved towards the little sofa she had indicated. As soon as Anna Mihalovna had disappeared he noticed that the eyes of everyone in the room were fastened on him with something more than curiosity and sympathy. He noticed that they whispered together, casting significant looks at him with a kind of awe and even obsequiousness. He was shown a degree of respect such as he had never been shown before. A lady whom he did not know, the one who had been talking to the priests, rose and offered him her place; an aide-de-camp picked up and handed to him a glove Pierre had dropped; the doctors became respectfully silent as he passed by them, and moved to make way for him. Pierre's first impulse was to sit somewhere else so as not to disturb the lady, to pick up his own glove and to walk round the doctors who were not really at all in his way; but all at once he felt that this would not do, that tonight he was a person obliged to go through some terrible ceremony which everyone expected of him, and that he was bound to accept their services. He took the glove from the aide-de-camp in silence, and sat down in the lady's chair, placing his large hands on his squarely planted knees in the naïve attitude of an Egyptian statue, fully decided in his own mind that all was as it should be, and that in order not to lose his head and commit some folly he must not follow his own notions but must yield himself up entirely to the will of those who had assumed direction of him.

Two minutes had not elapsed before Prince Vasili entered, carrying his head high and wearing his long frock-coat with three stars on his breast. He seemed to have grown thinner since the morning; his eyes looked larger than usual when he glanced round the room and caught sight of Pierre. He went up to him, took his hand (a thing he had never done before) and drew it downwards as if wishing to test whether it were firmly fixed on.

'*Courage, courage, mon ami*. He has asked to see you. *C'est bien …*' and he turned to go.

But Pierre thought it necessary to ask: 'How is …' He hesitated, not knowing whether it would be proper to call the dying man 'the count', yet blushing to call him 'father'.

'He had another stroke half an hour ago. Another stroke. *Courage, mon ami …*'

Pierre was in such a confused state of mind that at the word 'stroke' he imagined a blow of some kind. He stared at Prince Vasili in perplexity, and only later grasped that a stroke meant an attack of illness. Prince Vasili said a few words to Lorrain in passing and went through the door on tiptoe. He did not know how to walk on tiptoe and jerked his whole body awkwardly at each step. The eldest princess followed him, and after them went the priests and deacons, and some of the servants of the house. Through the door was heard a stir of movement, and finally Anna Mihalovna, still with the same expression – pale but resolute in the discharge of duty – came running out and touching Pierre on the arm said:

'The goodness of God is inexhaustible. The office of the last anointing is about to begin. Come.'

Pierre went through the door, treading on the soft carpet, and noticed that the aide-de-camp, and the lady he did not know, and some more of the servants all followed him in, as though it were now no longer necessary to ask permission to enter that room.

20

PIERRE well knew this vast room divided by columns and an arch, its walls hung with Persian tapestries. The part of the room behind the columns, where on one side stood a tall mahogany bedstead with silken hangings and on the other a huge case containing icons, was brightly illuminated with a red light like a church for evening service. Under the shining icons Pierre saw a long invalid chair, and in this chair, propped up by smooth, snowy-white pillows, the slips obviously just changed, lay the majestic form of his father, Count Bezuhov, covered to the waist by a bright green quilt, with the familiar mane of grey hair above his lofty forehead, reminding one of a lion, and the deep typically aristocratic wrinkles on his handsome brick-coloured face. He was lying directly under the icons, both his great stout arms outside the quilt. A wax taper had been thrust between the forefinger and thumb of his right hand which lay palm downwards, and an old servant was bending over from behind the chair to hold the candle in position. Around the chair stood the clergy, their long hair falling over their magnificent glittering vestments, with lighted tapers in their hands, performing their office with slow solemnity. A little behind them stood the two younger princesses holding handkerchiefs to their eyes, and just in front of them their eldest sister, Katishe, fixing a vicious and determined look on the icons, as though declaring to all that she would not answer for herself if she were to look round. Anna Mihalovna, with a meek and mournful all-forgiving expression on her face, stood by the door with the unknown lady. Prince Vasili, on the other side of the door, near the invalid chair, was leaning his left arm on the carved back of a velvet chair which he had turned round for the purpose. He held a wax taper in his left hand and was crossing himself with his right, raising his eyes each time his fingers touched his forehead. His face wore a calm look of piety and resignation to the will of God. 'If you cannot comprehend such sentiments, so much the worse for you,' he seemed to be saying.

Behind him stood the aide-de-camp, the doctors and the men-servants: just as in church, the men and women had separated to opposite sides. All were silently crossing themselves; the only sounds were the reading of the Scriptures, the subdued chanting of deep bass voices and during the intervals of silence profound sighing and the restless movement of feet. Anna Mihalovna, with an air of importance to show that she knew what she was about, walked right across the room to where Pierre was standing and gave him a taper. He lit it, and then, confused under the glances of those around him, began to cross himself with the hand that held the candle.

The youngest of the sisters, the rosy, fun-loving Princess Sophie, the one with the mole, was watching him. She smiled, hid her face in her handkerchief and remained with it hidden for some time; but looking up and seeing Pierre she began to laugh again. She was evidently unable to look at him without laughing but could not resist looking at him, so to be out of temptation she crept away behind one of the columns. In the middle of the service the voices of the clergy suddenly ceased; the priests whispered together and the old servant who was holding the candle in the count's hand straightened himself and turned to the ladies. Anna Mihalovna stepped forward and bending over the sick man beckoned behind her back to Lorrain. The French doctor had been standing without a candle, leaning against one of the pillars in the respectful attitude of a foreigner conveying that in spite of belonging to a different faith he appreciates all the solemnity of the rite being performed and even approves of it. He now approached the sick man with the noiseless step of one in the prime of life, with his delicate white fingers lifted the hand that lay on the green quilt and turning sideways began to feel the pulse, considering for a moment. The sick man was given something to drink, there was a stir around him, then once more they all resumed their places and the service continued. During this interval Pierre noticed that Prince Vasili left his position behind the carved chair and, with an air which intimated that he knew what he was doing and if others failed to understand it was so much the worse for them, went not to the dying man but past him to the eldest princess, and together they retired to the depths of the alcove where the high bedstead stood with its silken hangings. From there both the prince and the princess disappeared through the farther door, but before the end of the service returned, one after the other, to their places. Pierre paid no more attention to this occurrence than to the rest of what went on, having made up his mind once for all that everything he saw happening around him that evening was in some manner essential.

The chanting ceased, and the voice of the priest was heard respectfully felicitating the sick man on having received the sacrament. The dying man lay as lifeless and immobile as before. Around him there was a general stir: footsteps were audible and whispers, of which Anna Mihalovna's was the most distinct.

Pierre heard her say:

'He positively must be carried to the bed; here it would be impossible. ...'

The sick man was so surrounded by doctors, princesses and servants that Pierre could no longer see the reddish-yellow face with the mane

92

of grey hair which, though he saw other faces as well, he had not lost sight of for an instant throughout the whole service. He surmised by the cautious movements of those who crowded round the invalid chair that they had lifted the dying man and were carrying him across to the bed.

'Catch hold of my arm or you'll drop him,' he heard one of the servants say in a frightened whisper. 'Lower down ... once more,' exclaimed other voices, and the laboured breathing and shuffling steps of the bearers grew more hurried, as if the weight they carried was beyond their strength.

As the bearers, among their number Anna Mihalovna, passed the young man he caught a momentary glimpse over their heads and backs of the dying man's high, fleshy bare chest and powerful shoulders, raised by those who were holding him under the armpits, and of his leonine head with the mane of grey curls. This head, with its extraordinarily wide brow and cheekbones, its fine handsome voluptuous mouth and cold, majestic expression, was not disfigured by the approach of death. It was just the same as Pierre remembered it three months previously, when the count had sent him to Petersburg. But now this head was rolling helplessly with the uneven steps of the bearers, and the cold listless eyes gazed unseeing.

After a few minutes' bustle around the high bedstead the little party who had been carrying the sick man broke up. Anna Mihalovna touched Pierre on the arm and said, 'Come.' Pierre went with her over to the bed on which the sick man had been arranged, limbs piously disposed in keeping with the rites which had just been performed. He lay with his head propped high on the pillows. His hands had been symmetrically placed on the green silk quilt, palms downwards. When Pierre approached, the count was looking straight at him but with a gaze the intent and significance of which no mortal man could fathom. Either this look had simply nothing to say and merely fastened upon him because those eyes must needs look at something, or it had too much to say. Pierre hesitated, not knowing what to do, and glanced inquiringly at his guide. Anna Mihalovna made a hurried sign with her eyes towards the sick man's hand and moved her lips as though sending it a kiss. Carefully craning his neck to avoid disturbing the quilt, Pierre did as he was bid, and pressed his lips to the broad-boned fleshy hand. Neither the hand nor a single muscle of the count's face quivered. Once more Pierre looked questioningly at Anna Mihalovna to see what he was to do now. She indicated with her eyes a chair that stood beside the bed. Pierre obediently sat down in the chair, his eyes inquiring whether he had done the right thing. Anna Mihalovna nodded approvingly. Pierre again assumed the naïvely symmetrical pose of an Egyptian statue, obviously troubled that his ungainly person took up so much room, and doing his utmost to appear as small as possible. He looked at the count. The count was still gazing at the spot where Pierre's face had been before he sat down. Anna Mihalovna's expression conveyed that she appreciated the affecting solemnity of this last meeting between father and son. Two minutes went by, which seemed like an hour to Pierre. Suddenly the powerful muscles and lines of the count's face began to twitch. The twitching increased, the handsome mouth was drawn to one side (only now did Pierre realize how near death his father was), and from the distorted mouth issued an unintelligible, hoarse sound. Anna Mihalovna looked intently into the sick man's eyes, trying to make out what he wanted, pointing first at Pierre, then at the tumbler; then she said Prince Vasili's name in an inquiring whisper, then pointed to the quilt. The eyes and face of the sick man showed impatience. With an effort he looked at the servant who never left his master's bedside.

'Wants to be turned over on the other side, the master does,' whispered the servant, and got up to turn the count's heavy body towards the wall.

Pierre rose to help the man.

While the count was being turned over, one of his arms fell back helplessly and he in vain endeavoured to pull it after him. Perhaps he noticed the look of horror on Pierre's face at the sight of that lifeless arm, or some other thought may have flitted across his dying brain at that moment, in any case he glanced at the refractory arm, at Pierre's horror-stricken face and at the arm again, and on his lips a feeble piteous smile appeared, quite out of character with his features, seeming to deride his own helplessness. Suddenly, at the sight of that smile, Pierre felt a lump in his throat and a tickling in his nose, and tears dimmed his eyes. The sick man was turned on to his side with his face to the wall. He gave a sigh.

'He is dozing,' said Anna Mihalovna, observing one of the nieces approaching to take her turn by the bedside. 'Come …'

Pierre left the room.

21

THERE was no one in the reception-room now except Prince Vasili and the eldest princess, who were sitting under the portrait of Catherine the Great in eager conversation together. As soon as Pierre and his companion appeared they fell silent, and Pierre fancied he saw the princess hide something as she whispered:

'I cannot abide that woman.'

'Katishe has had tea served in the small drawing-room,' said Prince Vasili to Anna Mihalovna. 'Go and have something to eat, my poor Anna Mihalovna, or you will collapse.'

To Pierre he said nothing, merely giving his arm a sympathetic squeeze just below the shoulder. Pierre and Anna Mihalovna went into the small drawing-room.

'There is nothing so refreshing after a night without sleep as a cup of this excellent Russian tea,' Lorrain was saying with an air of restrained briskness as he sipped tea from a delicate Chinese cup without a handle. He was standing before a table on which tea and a cold supper had been laid in the small circular room. Around the table all who were at Count Bezuhov's house that night had gathered with a view to fortifying themselves. Pierre well remembered this little circular drawing room with its mirrors and tiny tables. In the days when balls were held at the house, Pierre, who did not dance, had liked to sit in this little room of mirrors and watch the ladies as they passed through in their ball dresses with diamonds and pearls on their bare shoulders glance at themselves in the brilliantly lighted glasses with their repeating reflections. Now this same room was dimly lighted by a pair of candles and, in the middle of the night, on one small table stood a disorderly array of tea things and supper dishes, and a motley crowd of people who were anything but festive sat talking in whispers, every gesture, every word betraying that not one of them was oblivious to what was happening and what was about to happen in the bedroom. Pierre did not eat anything, though he very much wanted to. He looked round inquiringly at his monitress, and saw that she was tiptoeing back to the reception-room, where they had left Prince Vasili and the eldest princess. Pierre supposed this also was as it should be, and after a short interval followed her. Anna Mihalovna was standing beside the princess, and both were speaking at once in angry undertones.

'Allow me, madam, to know what is and what is not to be done,' the Princess Katishe was saying, evidently in the same angry temper as when she had slammed the door of her room.

'But, my dear princess,' answered Anna Mihalovna in a bland persuasive manner, barring the way to the bedroom and preventing the other from passing, 'would this not be too great a tax on our poor uncle at such a moment, when he needs quiet? To discuss worldly matters when his soul has already been prepared. ...'

Prince Vasili was seated in an easy chair, one leg crossed high above the other, in his familiar posture. His cheeks, which were so flabby that they seemed to hang in pouches, were twitching violently; but he wore the air of a man little concerned with what the two ladies were saying.

'Come, my dear Anna Mihalovna, let Katishe have her way. You know how fond the count is of her.'

'I have no idea what is in this document even,' said the younger of the two ladies, turning to Prince Vasili and pointing to the inlaid portfolio which she held in her hand. 'I only know that the real will is in his writing-table, and this is a paper that has been forgotten. ...'

She tried to pass Anna Mihalovna, but the latter sprang forward to bar her way again.

'I know, my dear, good princess,' said Anna Mihalovna, grabbing the portfolio so firmly that it was plain she would not readily let go of it again. 'Dear princess, I beg of you, I implore you, spare him! I implore you!'

The princess did not reply. All that was heard was the sound of a scuffle for possession of the portfolio, but there could be no doubt that if the princess did open her mouth to speak what she said would not be flattering for Anna Mihalovna. Though the latter clung on tightly, her voice lost none of its soft firmness.

'Pierre, my dear, come here. I imagine he will not be one too many in this family council, eh, prince?'

'Why don't you speak, cousin?' suddenly shrieked Katishe, so loud that those in the drawing-room heard her and were startled. 'Why do you keep silent while heaven knows who takes upon herself to interfere and make a scene on the very threshold of a dying man's room? Scheming creature, you!' she hissed viciously, and tugged with all her might at the portfolio, but Anna Mihalovna took two or three steps forward to keep her hold on it, and succeeded in changing her grip.

Prince Vasili rose. 'Oh!' said he with reproach and surprise. 'This is preposterous. Come, let go, I tell you.'

The Princess Katishe let go.

'You too!'

But Anna Mihalovna paid no heed.

'Let go, I tell you. I will assume the whole responsibility. I will go and ask him myself. I ... will that satisfy you?'

'But, prince,' said Anna Mihalovna, 'after such a solemn sacrament, let him have a moment's peace. Here, Pierre, tell us your opinion,' said she, turning to the young man who had come close to them and was looking with astonishment at the princess's angry face, which had lost all dignity, and at Prince Vasili's twitching cheeks.

'Remember that you will answer for all the consequences,' said Prince Vasili severely. 'You don't know what you are doing.'

'You vile woman!' screamed the princess, darting unexpectedly at Anna Mihalovna and snatching the portfolio from her.

Prince Vasili bowed his head and spread out his hands.

At this point the door, the dreadful door which Pierre had watched so long and which usually opened so gently, burst open noisily, banging back against the wall, and the second of the three sisters rushed out wringing her hands.

'What are you thinking of?' she cried frantically. 'He is dying and you leave me alone!'

Her sister dropped the portfolio. Anna Mihalovna swiftly stooped and, snatching up the object of contention, ran into the bedroom. The eldest princess and Prince Vasili, recovering themselves, followed her. A few minutes later the eldest sister emerged again with a pale, hard face, biting her underlip. At the sight of Pierre her face expressed uncontrollable dislike.

'Yes, now you can rejoice!' said she. 'This is what you have been waiting for.'

And breaking into sobs she hid her face in her handkerchief and ran from the room.

The next to come out was Prince Vasili. Reeling slightly, he dropped down on to the sofa where Pierre was sitting, and covered his face with his hand. Pierre noticed that he was pale, and that his lower jaw trembled and shook as though he had an attack of ague.

'Ah, my friend,' said he, taking Pierre by the elbow, and there was a sincerity and softness in his voice which Pierre had never heard before. 'We sin and we deceive, and all for what? I am getting on for sixty, my dear boy … I too … Everything ends in death, everything! Death is awful …' and he burst into tears.

Anna Mihalovna was the last to come out. She went up to Pierre with slow, quiet steps.

'Pierre!' she said.

Pierre looked at her inquiringly. She kissed the young man on the forehead, wetting him with her tears. Then after a pause she said:

'He is no more. …'

Pierre gazed at her through his spectacles.

'Come, I will take you away. Try to weep. Nothing relieves like tears.'

She led him into the dark drawing-room and Pierre was glad that no one was there to see his face. Anna Mihalovna left him, and when she returned he was fast asleep with his head on his arm.

Next morning Anna Mihalovna said to Pierre:

'Yes, my dear, it is a great loss for us all. I do not speak of you. But God will uphold you, you are young and now, I hope, in command of an immense fortune. The will has not been opened yet. I know you well enough to rest assured that this will not turn your head, but it will impose new duties on you, and you must be a man.'

Pierre was silent.

'Perhaps later on I will tell you, my dear boy, that if I had not been here, God only knows what might have happened. You know, uncle promised me only the day before yesterday not to forget Boris. But he did not have time. I hope, my dear friend, that you will carry out your father's wish.'

Pierre did not understand a word of all this and colouring shyly looked dumbly at Princess Anna Mihalovna. After this talk with Pierre Anna Mihalovna returned to the Rostovs' and went to bed. On waking later in the morning she began to tell the Rostovs and all her acquaintances the details of Count Bezuhov's death. She declared that the count had died as she would wish to die herself, that his end had been not simply affecting but edifying; that the last meeting between father and son had been so touching that she could not recall it without tears, and that she did not know which had borne himself the more admirably in those awful moments – the father who had had a thought for everything and everybody during those last hours, and had spoken such moving words to his son, or Pierre, whom it had been pitiful to see, so stricken was he though he struggled to control his grief so as not to distress his dying father. 'Such scenes are painful, but they do one good. It uplifts the soul to see such men as the old count and his worthy son,' said she. The behaviour of the eldest princess and Prince Vasili she also reported, in disapproving terms but under the seal of secrecy and in a whisper.

22

AT Bald Hills, Prince Nikolai Andreyevich Bolkonsky's estate, the arrival of the young Prince Andrei and his wife was expected daily, but this did not upset the ordered routine which regulated life in the old prince's household. General-in-chief Prince Nikolai Andreyevich (nicknamed in society 'the king of Prussia'), having been banished to his country estates in the reign of the Emperor Paul, had remained at Bald Hills ever since, with his daughter Princess Maria and her companion, Mademoiselle Bourienne. Though in the new reign he was free to return to the capitals he still continued to live in the country, saying that anyone who wanted to see him could come the hundred miles from Moscow to Bald Hills, while so far as he himself was concerned he needed nothing and nobody. He was in the habit of remarking that there are only two sources of human vice, idleness and superstition; and only two virtues, energy and intelligence. He had personally undertaken his daughter's education, and to develop in her these two cardinal virtues gave her lessons in algebra and geometry up to her twentieth year, and mapped out her life into an uninterrupted schedule of occupations. He himself was constantly engaged in writing his memoirs, solving problems in higher mathematics, turning snuff-boxes on his lathe or working in the garden and superintending the building ever in progress on his estate. As the prime condition of successful activity is order, order in his household was exacted to the utmost. He always appeared at meals in precisely the same circumstances, and not only at the same hour but at the same minute. With those about him, from his daughter to his serfs, the prince was sharp and inflexible, so that without being a cruel man he inspired a degree of fear and respect such as a really brutal man would have found difficult to obtain. Although he was living in retirement and now had no influence in matters of state, every high official in the province where the prince's estates lay felt obliged to pay his respects, and waited in the lofty antechamber just like the architect, the gardener or Princess Maria, till the prince made his appearance punctually at the regular hour. And everyone waiting in this antechamber knew the same feeling of deference and even awe when the enormously high door of the study swung open and the figure of the little old man appeared, in his powdered wig, with his small dry hands and bushy grey eyebrows, which sometimes when he frowned hid the gleam of his shrewd, youthfully bright eyes.

On the day when the young couple were to arrive, Princess Maria as usual came down into the antechamber at the hour appointed to wish her father good morning, crossing herself in trepidation and repeating a silent prayer. This happened every morning, and every morning she prayed that the daily interview might pass off felicitously.

An old manservant in a powdered wig who was sitting in the antechamber got up quietly and greeted her in a whisper.

Through the door came the steady hum of a lathe. The princess timidly opened the door, which moved easily and noiselessly on its hinges, and stood still on the threshold. The prince was working at his lathe, and after glancing round went on with what he was doing.

The great room was full of objects evidently in constant use. The huge table covered with books and plans, the tall, glass-fronted bookcases with keys in the locks, the high desk for the prince to write at while standing up, on which was an open manuscript-book, and the carpenter's lathe with tools laid ready to hand and shavings scattered around – all suggested continuous, varied, and regulated activity. The motion of the small foot shod in a Tartar boot embroidered in silver, and the firm pressure of the lean sinewy hand showed that the prince still possessed the tenacious strength and vigour of a green old age. After a few more turns of the lathe he removed his foot from the treadle, wiped his chisel, dropped it into a leather pouch attached to the lathe, and going to the table called his daughter to him. He never wasted blessings on his children, so he simply held out his bristly cheek (as yet unshaven for the day) and said, with a severe and at the same time tenderly attentive look:

'Quite well? All right then, sit down.'

He took the exercise-book containing lessons in geometry which he had written out himself, and drew up a chair with his foot.

'For tomorrow!' said he, briskly finding the page and marking from one paragraph to another with his horny nail.

The princess leaned over the table towards the exercise-book.

'Wait, here's a letter for you,' said the old man abruptly, pulling out from a pocket fastened to the table an envelope addressed in a feminine hand and tossing it on to the table.

The princess's face coloured in blotches at the sight of the letter. She hastily picked it up and bent her head over it.

'From your Héloise?' asked the prince with a cold smile that showed his still sound but yellowing teeth.

'Yes, it's from Julie,' replied the princess with a timid glance and a timid smile.

'I shall allow two more letters to pass, but the third I shall read,' said the prince sternly. 'You write much nonsense, I'll be bound. I shall read the third.'

'Read this one if you like, father,' replied the princess, flushing still more and holding out the letter.

'The third, I said, the third,' cried the prince shortly, pushing the letter away; then, leaning his elbows on the table, he drew towards him the exercise-book with the geometrical figures.

'Well, madam,' began the old man, stooping over the book close to his daughter and laying one arm on the back of her chair, so that she felt herself surrounded on all sides by the acrid odour of tobacco and old age which she had so long associated with her father. 'Now, madam, these triangles are equal; if you will observe the angle a-b-c...'

The princess glanced up in dismay into her father's eyes glittering so close to her. The red patches on her face came and went, and it was plain that she understood nothing and was so frightened that her fear would prevent her understanding any of her father's explanations, however clear they might be. Whether it was the teacher's fault or the pupil's, the same thing recurred every day: the princess's eyes grew dim, she could not see or hear anything and was only conscious of her father's stern withered face close to her, his breath and the smell of him, and her one thought was to get away as quickly as possible to work out the problem in peace in her own room. The old man would lose all patience, noisily push back the chair on which he was sitting and then draw it forward again, make efforts to control himself and not fly into a rage, but he almost always did break out into a fury, storming and sometimes flinging down the exercise-book.

The princess made a wrong answer.

'What an idiot the girl is!' roared the prince, pushing the book aside and turning away sharply; but rising immediately he paced up and down, touched his daughter's hair and seated himself again.

He drew up his chair and proceeded to explain.

'This won't do, young lady. It won't do,' said he, as the princess took and closed the exercise-book with the next day's lessons and made to leave. 'Mathematics are a most important subject, madam. And I don't want you to be like all the other silly women. Persevere and you will get to like it.' He patted her on the cheek. 'Mathematics will drive all the nonsense out of your head.'

She turned to go but he stopped her by a gesture and took a book with pages uncut from the high desk.

'Here, your Héloise has sent you something else: some *Key to the Mystery*. A religious book. I don't interfere with anyone's belief. ... I have glanced at it. Take it. Now, be off, be off.'

He patted her on the shoulder, closing the door after her himself.

Princess Maria returned to her room with the sad, scared expression that rarely left her and made her plain, sickly face still less attractive. She sat down at her writing-table on which were some miniatures and a litter of books and papers. The princess was as untidy as her father was tidy. She put down the geometry book and eagerly broke the seal of her letter. It was from the most intimate of her childhood friends, none other than Julie Karagin, who had been at the Rostovs' name-day party.

Julie wrote entirely in French:

Chère et excellente amie,

How terrible and frightful a thing separation is! Though I tell myself that half my life and half my happiness are bound up in you, that in spite of the distance separating us our hearts are united by indissoluble bonds, mine rebels against fate and in spite of all the pleasures and distractions that surround me I cannot overcome a certain secret sorrow which has lurked in the depths of my heart ever since we parted. Why are we not together as we were last summer, in your big study, on the blue sofa – the confidences sofa? Why can I not, as I did three months ago, draw fresh moral strength from your eyes, so sweet, so calm, so

penetrating, the eyes which I loved so much and seem to see before me
as I write.

Having read thus far, Princess Maria sighed and glanced into the
pier-glass which stood on her right. It reflected a slight, homely figure
and thin features. Her eyes, always melancholy, now looked with
particular hopelessness at her reflection in the mirror. 'She flatters me,'
thought the princess, turning away and continuing to read. Julie,
however, had not flattered her friend: indeed, the princess's eyes –
large, deep and luminous (it sometimes seemed as if whole shafts of
warm light radiated from them) – were so lovely that very often in
spite of the plainness of her face they gave her a charm that was more
attractive than beauty. But the princess never saw the beautiful expression of her own eyes – the expression they had when she was not
thinking of herself. Like most people's, her face assumed an affected,
unnatural expression as soon as she looked in a glass. She went on with
the letter:

All Moscow talks of nothing but war. One of my two brothers is
already abroad, the other is with the Guards, just about to march for the
frontier. Our beloved Emperor has left Petersburg and intends, they say,
to expose his precious person to the hazards of war. God grant that the
Corsican monster who is destroying the peace of Europe may be
brought low by the angelic being whom the Almighty in His mercy
has sent to rule over us. To say nothing of my brothers, this war has
deprived me of one most dear to my heart: I mean young Nikolai
Rostov, whose ardour could not endure inaction and who has left the
University to go and join the army. Yes, my dear Marie, I will own to
you that notwithstanding his extreme youth his departure for the army
has been a great grief to me. This young man – I told you about him
last summer – has so much nobility, so much of that genuine youthfulness which we meet with so rarely in this age of ours, when every lad of
twenty is an old man. Above all he has so much candour and heart. He
is so pure and poetic that my acquaintance with him, transient as it was,
must be counted one of the sweetest enjoyments of my poor heart,
which has already suffered so deeply. Some day I will tell you about our
parting and what passed between us. All that is still too recent. Ah, dear
friend, how happy you are not to know these poignant joys and sorrows! You are fortunate, because the keenest are usually the latter! I
know very well that Count Nikolai is too young ever to be anything
more than a friend, but this sweet friendship, this intimacy, so poetic and
pure, were what my heart needed. But enough of this. The chief news

of the day, and the talk of all Moscow, is the death of old Count Bezuhov, and his will. Just fancy – the three princesses get very little, Prince Vasili nothing, and it is Monsieur Pierre who inherits all. He has, into the bargain, been recognized as legitimate, and is therefore Count Bezuhov and possessor of the finest fortune in Russia. They say Prince Vasili played a very ugly part in the whole affair and has gone back to Petersburg quite out of countenance.

I confess I understand very little to do with bequests and wills; but I do know that since the young man whom we all knew as plain Monsieur Pierre has become Count Bezuhov and master of one of the largest fortunes in Russia, I am greatly amused to observe the change in tone and behaviour of mammas burdened with daughters to marry – and of the young ladies themselves – towards this individual, who, between you and me, has always seemed to be a poor specimen. As people have amused themselves for the past two years by marrying me off (generally to men I don't even know), the matrimonial gossip of Moscow now speaks of me as the future Countess Bezuhov. But I need not tell you that I have no ambition for the post. *A propos* of marriages, do you know that quite recently that *universal aunt*, Anna Mihalovna, confided to me, under seal of strictest secrecy, a marriage project for you – neither more nor less than with Prince Vasili's son, Anatole, whom they want to reform by marrying him to someone rich and *distinguée*, and it is on you that his relations' choice has fallen. I don't know what you will think of it, but I felt it my duty to warn you. He is said to be very handsome and very wild. That is all I have been able to find out about him.

But enough of this gossip. I am at the end of my second sheet of paper, and mamma has sent for me to go and dine at the Apraksins'. Read the mystical book I am sending you: it is all the rage here. Although there are things in it difficult for the feeble mind of man to fathom, it is an admirable book which soothes and elevates the soul. Adieu! Give my respects to your father and my compliments to Mademoiselle Bourienne.

Fond love,   JULIE

P.S. Let me have news of your brother and his charming little wife.

The princess sat thinking, a pensive smile playing over her lips; her face, lighted up by her luminous eyes, was completely transformed. Then suddenly jumping up she walked over to the table, treading heavily. She got out a sheet of paper and her hand began to fly rapidly over it. This is the reply she wrote, also in French:

Chère et excellente amie,

Your letter of the 13th was a great joy to me. So you still love me, my romantic Julie? And separation, of which you say such hard things, has not had its usual effect upon you. You complain of our separation – what should I have to say if I ventured to complain, bereft as I am of all who are dear to me? Ah, if we had not religion to console us life would be very sad. Why should you suspect me of looking stern when you speak of your affection for that young man? In such matters, I am only severe with myself. I understand such feelings in others, and if I cannot actually approve them, never having experienced them, neither do I condemn them. Only it seems to me that Christian love, love of one's neighbour, love of one's enemies, is more meritorious, sweeter and more beautiful than the feelings inspired in a romantic and affectionate young girl like you by a young man's beautiful eyes.

The news of Count Bezuhov's death reached us before your letter, and affected my father deeply. He says that the count was the last representative but one of the *grand siècle*, and that now it is his turn, but that he will do his best to put it off as long as possible. God preserve us from that terrible misfortune! I cannot agree with you about Pierre, whom I knew when he was a boy. He always seemed to me to have an excellent heart, and that is the quality I value most in people. As to his inheritance and the *rôle* played by Prince Vasili, it is very sad for both of them. Ah, my dear friend, our divine Saviour's words, that it is easier for a camel to go through the eye of a needle than for a rich man to enter into the kingdom of God, are terribly true; I pity Prince Vasili but I am sorrier still for Pierre. So young, and burdened with such riches – what temptations he will be exposed to! If I were asked what I wished most in the world it would be to be poorer than the poorest beggar. A thousand thanks, dear friend, for the volume you sent me and which is all the rage with you in Moscow. Yet since you tell me that along with many good things it contains others which the weak intellect of man cannot fathom, it seems to me rather useless to spend time in reading what is unintelligible and can therefore bear no good fruit. I have never been able to understand the mania some people have for confusing their judgement by devoting themselves to mystical books which only arouse their doubts and excite their imaginations, giving them a bent for exaggeration utterly contrary to Christian simplicity. Let us rather read the Epistles and the Gospels. Let us not seek to penetrate the mysteries they contain, for how should we, miserable sinners that we are, presume to inquire into the awful and holy secrets of Providence so long as we wear the garment of this mortal flesh which forms an impenetrable veil between us and the Eternal? Let us rather confine ourselves to studying the sublime principles which our divine Saviour has left for our guidance here below; let us seek to conform to them and follow them, and let us be persuaded that the less we allow our feeble human minds to roam, the more pleasing it will be to God, Who rejects all knowledge that does not proceed from Him; and the less we strive to search out what He has been pleased to conceal from us, the sooner will He discover it to us through His divine Spirit.

My father has said nothing to me of any suitor: he only told me that he had received a letter and is expecting a visit from Prince Vasili. In regard to this project of marriage for me, I may say to you, *chère et excellente amie*, that I regard marriage as a divine institution to which we are bound to conform. However painful it may be, should the Almighty ever impose upon me the duties of wife and mother I shall endeavour to fulfil them as faithfully as I am able, without disquieting myself by inquiring into the nature of my feelings towards him whom He may bestow on me for husband.

I have had a letter from my brother, announcing his speedy arrival at Bald Hills with his wife. This pleasure will be of brief duration, for he is leaving us again to take part in this unhappy war into which we have been drawn, God knows how or why. Not only where you are – at the heart of affairs and of the world – is the talk all of war: even here amid the labours of the countryside and nature's peace – which townsfolk consider typical of the country – rumours of war are heard and make themselves painfully felt. My father can talk of nothing but marches and countermarches, things of which I understand nothing; and the day before yesterday during my usual walk through the village I witnessed a heartrending scene … a convoy of recruits conscripted from our estate and on their way to the army. You should have seen the state of the mothers, wives and children of the men who were going, and heard them sobbing. It seems as though humanity has forgotten the precepts of its divine Saviour, Who preached love and forgiveness of injuries, and that men ascribe the greatest merit to the art of killing one another.

Adieu, chère et bonne amie. May our divine Saviour and His most holy Mother keep you in their holy and all-powerful care!

MARIE

'Ah, you are finishing a letter, princess. I have already sent mine. I wrote to my poor mother,' said the smiling Mademoiselle Bourienne in her full sweet voice, speaking rapidly and rolling her *r*'s, and altogether bringing into Princess Maria's intense, melancholy and overcast atmosphere what seemed like the breath of another world, carefree, gay, and self-sufficient.

'Princess, I must warn you,' she added, lowering her voice and listening to herself with pleasure as she rolled her *r*'s, 'the prince has been rating Mihail Ivanov. He is in a very bad humour, very morose. Be prepared, you know ...'

'Ah, *chère amie*,' replied Princess Maria. 'I have asked you never to call my attention to the humour in which my father happens to be. I do not allow myself to criticize him, and would not have others do so either.'

The princess glanced at her watch and seeing that already she was five minutes late in starting her practice on the clavier hurried into the sitting-room, a look of alarm on her face. Between noon and two o'clock, in accordance with the time-table mapped out for each day, the prince took his siesta while the princess practised the clavier.

23

THE grey-haired valet was sitting in the study dozing and listening to the snoring of the prince, who was in his large study. From a distant part of the house, through the closed doors, came the sound of difficult passages – twenty times repeated – of a Dussek sonata.

Just then a carriage and a gig drove up to the porch. Prince Andrei got out of the carriage, helped his little wife to alight and stood back for her to pass in front of him. Old Tikhon in his wig, popping his head out of the door of the ante-room, reported in a whisper that the prince was asleep and then hastily closed the door. Tikhon knew that not even the arrival of the son of the house, nor any other unusual event, must be allowed to disturb the appointed order of the day. Prince Andrei apparently knew this as well as Tikhon; he looked at his watch as if to ascertain whether his father's habits had changed since he had last seen him and having satisfied himself that they had not he turned to his wife.

'Twenty minutes and he will get up. Let us go along to Princess Maria's room,' he said.

The little princess had grown stouter during this time but her eyes and her short downy smiling lip lifted just as gaily and prettily as ever when she began to speak.

'Why, this is a palace,' she said to her husband, looking around with the expression with which people compliment their host at a ball. 'Come along, quick – quick!' And she glanced with a smile at Tikhon and her husband and the footman who was leading the way.

'Is that Marie practising? Let's go quietly and take her by surprise.'

Prince Andrei followed her with a courteous but melancholy expression.

'You're looking older, Tikhon,' he said in passing to the old man-servant, who kissed his hand.

Just as they reached the room from which the sounds of the clavi-chord were coming, the pretty, fair-haired Frenchwoman tripped out from another door. Mademoiselle Bourienne seemed overwhelmed with delight.

'Oh, what happiness for the princess!' she cried. 'I must go and tell her.'

'No, no, please.... You are Mademoiselle Bourienne,' said the little princess, kissing her. 'I know of you already as my sister-in-law's friend. She is not expecting us!'

They went up to the door of the sitting-room, from which came the notes of the oft-repeated passage of the sonata. Prince Andrei stopped and made a grimace, as if expecting something disagreeable. The little princess entered the room. The passage broke off in the middle, a cry was heard, then Princess Maria's heavy tread and the sound of kissing. When Prince Andrei went in the two princesses, who had only met once before for a short time at his wedding, were clasped in each other's arms, warmly pressing their lips to whatever place they happened to touch. Mademoiselle Bourienne stood near them pressing her hand to her heart, with a beatific smile and appar-ently as ready to cry as to laugh. Prince Andrei shrugged his shoulders and frowned just as lovers of music do when they hear a wrong note. The two women let go of one another; then once again, as though time were precious, seized each other's hands and began kissing them and pulling them away, and took to kissing each other's face again, and to Prince Andrei's complete surprise they both burst into tears and began to kiss again. Mademoiselle Bourienne started to cry, too. Prince Andrei obviously felt uncomfortable but to the two women it seemed perfectly natural that they should weep: it evidently never entered their heads that it could have been otherwise at this meeting.

'Ah, chère! ...' 'Ah! Marie ...' both suddenly exclaimed and then laughed. 'I dreamed last night ...' 'Weren't you expecting us? ... Ah, Marie, you have got thinner! ...' 'And you have grown stouter! ...'

'I recognized the princess at once,' put in Mademoiselle Bourienne.

'And I had no idea! ...' exclaimed Princess Maria. 'Ah, André, I did not see you.'

Prince Andrei kissed his sister, took her hand in his, and told her that she was as great a cry-baby as ever. Princess Maria had turned towards her brother and through her tears her large eyes, now beautiful and luminous, rested on him with a fond expression, gentle and sweet.

The little princess chattered incessantly. Her short downy upper lip danced up and down, lightly touching the rosy lower one then curling into a smile that showed off her glistening teeth and sparkling eyes. She was describing an accident that had occurred to them on Spassky hill and might have been serious for her in her condition, and immediately went on to tell them that she had left all her clothes in Petersburg and heaven knew what she would have to wear here, and that Andrei had quite changed, and that Kitty Odyntsov had married an old man, and that she had a suitor for Princess Maria, who was in earnest but that they would talk about that by-and-by. Princess Maria was still looking silently at her brother, and her beautiful eyes were full of love and melancholy. It was clear her thoughts were following a train of her own, regardless of her sister-in-law's prattle. In the middle of the latter's description of the latest fête at Petersburg she addressed her brother:

'And are you really going to the war, André?' she asked with a sigh.

Lisa sighed too.

'Yes, and I must be off tomorrow,' he replied.

'He abandons me here, and the Lord knows why, when he might have had promotion ...'

Princess Maria did not listen to the end of this remark but following the thread of her thoughts turned to her sister-in-law with a tender glance at her figure.

'Is it certain?' she asked.

The little princess's face altered. She sighed.

'Quite,' said she. 'Oh, I am so frightened....'

Her lip went down. She brought her face close to her sister-in-law's, and unexpectedly again burst into tears.

'She needs rest,' said Prince Andrei with a frown. 'Don't you, Lise? Take her to your room, while I go to father. How is he? The same as ever?'

'Yes, just the same. But perhaps your eyes will see some change,' replied the princess cheerfully.

'The same regular time-table, the same walks in the garden, the lathe?' asked Prince Andrei with a scarcely perceptible smile, showing that in spite of all his love and respect for his father he was not blind to his foibles.

'Yes, the same time-table, and the lathe, and mathematics and my geometry lessons,' replied the princess merrily, as though her geometry lessons were among the greatest delights of her life.

When the twenty minutes had elapsed and the time had come for the old prince to get up, Tikhon appeared to summon the young prince to his father. The old man made a departure from his usual routine in honour of his son's arrival: he gave orders to admit him to his apartments while he dressed before dinner. The prince kept to the old fashion and wore a caftan and powdered hair. And when Prince Andrei entered his father's room (not with the peevish face and manners which he assumed in society but with the lively expression he had when talking with Pierre), the old man was sitting in a large leather-covered arm-chair, wrapped in a powdering mantle, while he entrusted his head to Tikhon.

'Ah, here's the warrior! Out to conquer Bonaparte, are you?' cried the old man, shaking his powdered head as far as the pigtail which Tikhon was busy plaiting would allow. 'Mind you set about him good and true, or as things are he'll soon be putting us on the list of his subjects! How are you?' and he held out his cheek.

The old man was in a good humour after his nap before dinner. (He was accustomed to say that a nap after dinner was silver but one before dinner was gold.) He cast happy, sidelong glances at his son from under his thick beetling brows. Prince Andrei went up and kissed his father on the spot indicated to him. He made no reply on his father's favourite topic – quizzing the military men of the day and Bonaparte in particular.

'Yes, here I am, father, and I have brought my wife who is with child,' said Prince Andrei, watching every movement of his father's features with eager and respectful eyes. 'How is your health?'

'Only fools and rakes ever need to be ill, my boy, and you know me – abstemious, and busy from morning till night, so of course I am well.'

'Thank God for that,' said his son smiling.

'God has nothing to do with it. Come now.' he continued, going back to his favourite hobby, 'tell us how the Germans have taught you to fight Bonaparte according to this new science you call "strategy"?'

Prince Andrei smiled.

'Give me time to collect my wits, father,' said he with a smile which showed that his father's foibles did not prevent his honouring and loving him. 'Why, I haven't had time to settle down yet!'

'Nonsense, nonsense!' cried the old man, pulling at his pigtail to assure himself that it was firmly plaited, and grasping his son by the arm. 'The quarters for your wife are all ready. Princess Maria will take her over and show her round, and they'll chatter nineteen to the dozen. That's the way of all women! I am glad to have her here. Sit down and talk to me. Mikhelson's army I understand, and Tolstoy's too ... a simultaneous attack.... But what's the southern army going to do? Prussia remains neutral, I know that. How about Austria?' said he, rising from his chair and pacing up and down the room with Tikhon running behind to hand him various articles of clothing. 'What's Sweden going to do? How will they get across Pomerania?'

Seeing that his father insisted, Prince Andrei – at first reluctantly but gradually warming up and from force of habit unconsciously dropping from Russian into French – began to expound the plan of operation for the coming campaign. He explained how an army, ninety thousand strong, was to threaten Prussia and force her to abandon her neutrality and take part in the war; how a portion of this army was to go to Stralsund and unite with some Swedish forces; how two hundred and twenty thousand Austrians with a hundred thousand Russians were to operate in Italy and on the Rhine; how fifty thousand Russians and as many English were to land at Naples; and how this total force of some five hundred thousand men was to attack the French from different sides. The old prince did not manifest the slightest interest in this description – in fact he might not have been listening: he continued to dress as he walked about, and three times unexpectedly interrupted. Once he held up the story by shouting: 'The white one, the white one!'

This meant that Tikhon was not handing him the waistcoat he wanted. Another time he stopped to ask:

'And is she to be confined soon?' and reproachfully shaking his head said, 'That's too bad! Go on, go on!'

The third interruption came when Prince Andrei was nearing the end of his discourse. The old man began to sing in a cracked old voice: *'Malbrook s'en va-t-en guerre. Dieu sait quand reviendra.'*

His son merely smiled.

'I'm not saying it's a plan I approve of,' he remarked. 'I was just stating it. Napoleon has certainly one of his own by now, which is probably as good as ours.'

'Well, you've told me nothing new.' And meditatively the old man repeated to himself quickly: *'Dieu sait quand reviendra.* Now go to the dining-room.'

24

AT the appointed hour the prince, powdered and shaven, entered the dining-room where his daughter-in-law, Princess Maria and Mademoiselle Bourienne were awaiting him together with his architect, who by a strange caprice of his employer's was allowed at table though his subordinate position gave him no claim to that honour. The prince, who was a great stickler for distinctions of rank and rarely admitted even the local bigwigs to his table, had suddenly selected Mihail Ivanovich (who always went into a corner to blow his nose on a checked pocket handkerchief) to illustrate the theory that all men are equal, and had more than once impressed on his daughter that the architect was every whit as good as themselves. At table the prince was wont to address his conversation mainly to the tongue-tied Mihail Ivanovich.

In the dining-room, which like all the other rooms in the house was tremendously lofty, the members of the household, and the footmen – one behind each chair – stood waiting for the prince to enter. The head butler, napkin on arm, was scanning the table to see that it was properly set, beckoning the waiters and anxiously glancing from the clock on the wall to the door through which the prince was to appear. Prince Andrei was staring at a huge gilt frame, new to him, containing the genealogical tree of the princes Bolkonsky, opposite which was a similar frame with a badly-executed portrait (evidently painted by an artist belonging to the estate) of a ruling prince in a crown – an alleged descendant of Rurik and ancestor of the Bolkonskys. Prince Andrei was looking at this genealogical tree, and shaking his head and laughing, as a man laughs at a portrait so like the original as to be comical.

'That's father all over!' he said to Princess Maria as she came up to him.

Princess Maria looked at her brother in surprise. She did not understand what he was laughing at. Everything her father did inspired her with a reverence that did not admit of criticism.

'To everyone his Achilles' heel,' continued Prince Andrei. 'Fancy, with *his* tremendous intellect, indulging in such nonsense!'

Princess Maria could not understand how her brother could be so audacious, and was about to object when the awaited footsteps were heard coming from the study. The prince walked in briskly, jauntily, in his usual manner, as though he meant his precipitate movements to contrast with the strict formality of the house. Just at that moment the great clock struck two, and was echoed in shriller tones by another clock in the drawing-room. The prince paused. His keen, flashing eyes from under their thick, overhanging brows sternly scanned all present and came to rest on the little princess. As courtiers do when the Tsar enters, she experienced the sensation of fear and respect which the old man inspired in all around him. He stroked her hair and then patted her awkwardly on the back of the neck.

'I am glad, glad to see you,' he said, looking her steadily in the eyes again, and quickly turned away to take his seat. 'Sit down, sit down! Mihail Ivanovich, sit down!'

He pointed his daughter-in-law to a place beside him. A footman pushed the chair forward for her.

'Oho!' said the old man, casting an eye on her rounded figure. 'You've been in a hurry. Too bad!'

He laughed a dry, cold, disagreeable laugh, laughing as he always did, with his lips but not with his eyes.

'You must take plenty of exercise – walk as much as possible, as much as possible,' he said.

The little princess did not, or did not wish to, hear his words. She sat silent and appeared agitated. The prince asked after her father, and she began to smile and talk. He asked about mutual acquaintances, and she grew still more animated and chattered away, giving him greetings from various people and retailing the gossip of the town.

'Countess Apraksin, poor thing, has lost her husband. She cried her eyes out,' said she, growing more and more lively.

The livelier she became the more sternly the prince looked at her, and suddenly, as though he had studied her sufficiently and had

113

formed a clear idea of her, he turned away and addressed Mihail Ivanovich.

'Well, Mihail Ivanovich, our friend Bonaparte is in for a bad time. Prince Andrei' (he always spoke of his son in the third person) 'has been telling me of the forces being massed against him! And to think that you and I have always considered him a man of straw!'

Mihail Ivanovich did not at all know when 'you and I' had ever said any such thing about Bonaparte, but realizing that he was wanted as a peg on which to hang his employer's favourite topic he glanced wonderingly at the young prince, not quite sure what was coming next.

'He is a capital tactician!' said the prince to his son, indicating the architect.

And the conversation turned again on the war, on Bonaparte, and the generals and statesmen of the day. The old prince seemed convinced not only that all these men were mere schoolboys ignorant of the a b c of war and politics, and that Bonaparte was a trumpery little Frenchy successful only because there were no longer any Potemkins or Suvorovs to stand up to him; but he was also persuaded that no political complications existed in Europe, and that the war did not amount to anything but was merely a sort of puppet-show at which the authorities were playing while pretending to be doing something serious. Prince Andrei gaily bore with his father's sarcasm at the expense of the new men, and drew him on and listened to him with obvious pleasure.

'The past always seems good,' said he, 'but did not Suvorov himself fall into the trap Moreau laid for him, and not know how to get out?'

'Who told you that? Who said so?' cried the prince. 'Suvorov!' And he flung away his plate, which Tikhon caught very neatly. 'Suvorov!... Consider, Prince Andrei! Frederick and Suvorov were a pair.... Moreau! – Moreau would have been taken prisoner if Suvorov's hands had been free; but he was saddled with the Hofs-kriegs-wurst-schnapps-rath. The devil himself could not have done anything. You'll see – you'll find out what those Hof-kriegs-wurst-raths are like! Suvorov was no match for them, so what chance do you suppose Mihail Kutuzov will have? No, my dear young friend,' he continued, 'you and your generals won't make any progress against Bonaparte: you'll have to call in Frenchmen – set a thief to catch a thief! The German, Pahlen, has been sent to New York in America to fetch the Frenchman Moreau,' he said, referring to the overtures that had been made that year to Moreau to enter the Russian service. 'It's marvellous! Were the Potemkins, Suvorovs and Orlovs Germans, pray? No, my lad, either you fellows have all lost your wits, or I have outlived mine. May God help you, but we shall see. They call Bonaparte a great general now! Ha!'

'I don't at all say that our plans are perfect,' remarked Prince Andrei. 'Only I can't understand how you can have such an opinion of Bonaparte. Laugh as much as you please, but all the same Bonaparte is a great general!'

'Mihail Ivanovich!' cried the old prince to the architect, who was giving his attention to the roast and hoping that they had forgotten him. 'Didn't I tell you Bonaparte was a great tactician? And here he says the same thing.'

'To be sure, your Excellency,' replied the architect.

The prince again laughed his chilling laugh.

'Bonaparte was born with a silver spoon in his mouth. His soldiers are first-rate. Besides, he began by attacking Germans and one would have to be half asleep not to beat the Germans. From the very beginning of the world everyone has beaten the Germans. They never beat anyone – except one another. He made his reputation fighting against them.'

And the prince began to expatiate on all the blunders which in his opinion Bonaparte had committed in his wars, and even in politics. His son made no rejoinder, but it was evident that whatever arguments were advanced he was as little able as his father to change his opinion. Prince Andrei listened, refraining from reply and involuntarily wondering how a solitary old man having for so long lived in retirement in the country could know and discuss in such detail and so acutely all the military and political events in Europe of recent years.

'You think, do you, that I am too old to understand the present state of affairs?' concluded his father. 'But my mind's full of them. I can't sleep of a night. Tell me now, this great commander of yours – where and how has he proved his skill?'

'That would be a long story,' answered his son.

'Well, then, you go along to your Bonaparte! Mademoiselle Bourienne, here is another admirer of your powder-monkey of an emperor!' he cried in excellent French.

'You know I am no Bonapartist, prince.'

'*Dieu sait quand reviendra ...*' hummed the prince out of tune, and with a still more discordant laugh he quitted the table.

The little princess had sat silent all through the discussion and the rest of the meal, looking in alarm now at Princess Maria, now at her father-in-law. When they left the table she took her sister-in-law's arm and drew her into another room.

'What a clever man your father is,' said she. 'Perhaps that is why I am afraid of him.'

'Oh, he is so kind!' answered Princess Maria.

25

PRINCE ANDREI was to leave the following evening. The old prince, not making any alteration in his habits, retired as usual after dinner. The little princess was with her sister-in-law. Prince Andrei in a travelling coat without epaulets was in his suite packing with the help of his valet. After inspecting the carriage himself and seeing the trunks put in, he ordered the horses to be harnessed. Only the things he always carried with him remained in his room: a dressing-case, a large canteen fitted with silver plate, two Turkish pistols, and a sabre – a present from his father who had brought it from the siege of Ochakov. All these travelling effects of Prince Andrei's were in the most perfect order: everything was new and clean, in cloth covers carefully tied with tapes.

People who are given to deliberating on their actions generally find themselves in a serious frame of mind when it comes to embarking on a journey or changing their mode of life. At such moments one reviews the past and forms plans for the future. Prince Andrei looked very thoughtful and tender. With his hands behind his back he paced briskly from corner to corner of the room, looking straight before him and meditatively shaking his head. Did he dread going to the war, or was he sad at leaving his wife ? Both perhaps, but evidently he had no wish to be seen in such a mood, for catching the sound of footsteps in the passage he hurriedly unclasped his hands, stopped at the table as if fastening the cover of the dressing-case, and assumed his usual serene and impenetrable expression. It was the heavy tread of Princess Maria that he heard.

'They told me you had ordered the carriage to be brought round,' she cried, panting (she had apparently been running), 'and I did so want to have another little talk alone with you. God knows how long we may be parted again. You are not vexed with me for coming? You have changed so, Andrusha,' she added, as though to explain the question.

She smiled as she called him by his pet name. It was obviously strange to her to think that this stern, handsome man should be the same Andrusha, the slender mischievous boy who had been the play-mate of her childhood.

'And where is Lise?' he asked, answering her question only by a smile.

'She was so tired that she fell asleep on the couch in my room. Oh, Andrei, what a treasure of a wife you have,' she said, sitting down on the sofa facing her brother. 'She is quite a child: such a sweet, merry-hearted child. I have grown so fond of her.'

Prince Andrei was silent, but the princess noticed the ironical, con-temptuous expression which appeared on his face.

'But one must be indulgent to little weaknesses – who is free from them, Andrei? She was brought up and has grown up in society, don't forget. And then her position now is not a rosy one. We ought to put ourselves in other people's places. *Tout comprendre, c'est tout pardonner.* Just think what it must be like for her, poor little thing, after the life she has been used to, to part from her husband and be left alone in the country, and in her condition too! It's very hard.'

Prince Andrei smiled as he looked at his sister, in the way we smile at those we fancy we can see through.

'You live in the country and don't find the life so terrible,' said he.

'I? – but that's different. Why speak of me? I have no desire for any other life – I couldn't have because I have never known any other. But you think, Andrei: for a young society woman to be buried in the country during the best years of her life, all alone too, for papa is always busy and I ... well, you know what poor company I am for a woman accustomed to the best society. There is only Mademoiselle Bourienne ...'

'I don't like your Mademoiselle Bourienne at all,' said Prince Andrei.

'Oh no! She is very kind and good, and, what is more, much to be pitied. She has nobody, nobody at all. To tell you the truth, I don't need her – she's even in my way. I have always been rather a solitary creature, you know, and now I am more so than ever. I like to be alone. ... Father likes her very much. She and Mihail Ivanovich are the two people to whom he is always gentle and kind, because both of them are under an obligation to him. As Sterne says: "We don't love men so much for the good they have done us as for the good we have done them." *Mon père* took her in when she was a homeless orphan, and she is very good-natured. And father likes her way of reading. She reads to him in the evenings. She reads aloud beautifully.'

'Tell me the truth, Marie. I expect father's temper must make things trying for you sometimes, doesn't it?' Prince Andrei asked suddenly.

Princess Maria was first surprised, then aghast at this question.

'For me? ... Me? ... Trying for me?' she stammered.

'He has always been harsh; and now I should think he's getting very difficult,' said Prince Andrei, speaking slightingly of their father either in order to disconcert his sister or to see what she would say.

'You are a good man, André, except for a sort of intellectual pride,' said the princess, following her own train of thought rather than the thread of the conversation – 'and that is a great sin. Have we any right to judge father? And even if it were possible, what feeling but *vénération* could such a man as my father inspire? And I am so contented and happy with him. I only wish that you were all as happy as I am.'

Her brother shook his head incredulously.

'The only thing that worries me – I will tell you the truth, André – is father's attitude to religion. I cannot understand how a man of his tremendous intellect can fail to see what is as clear as daylight, and can go so far astray. That is the only thing that makes me unhappy. But even in this I have begun to notice a shade of improvement. His satire has been a little less biting of late, and there was a monk whom he received and had a long talk with.'

'Ah, my dear, I am afraid you and your monk are wasting your powder,' said Prince Andrei banteringly but affectionately.

'Ah, *mon ami*, I can only pray and hope that God will hear me. André,' she said timidly, after a moment's silence, 'I have a great favour to ask of you.'

'What is it, my dear?'

'No – promise you won't refuse. It will be no trouble to you, and there is nothing beneath you in it. Only it will be a comfort to me. Promise, Andrusha,' said she, thrusting her hand in her reticule and taking hold of something but not bringing it out, as if what she held were the subject of her request and must not be shown until she were assured of his promise to do what she desired.

She looked at her brother with a humble, beseeching glance.

'Even if it cost me a great sacrifice ...' answered Prince Andrei, as if guessing what it was about.

'Think whatever you will! I know you are just like father. Think as you choose, but do this for my sake! Please do! Father's father, our grandfather, wore it in all the battles he fought.' (She still did not take out what she was holding in the reticule.) 'So you promise?'

'Of course, what is it?'

'André, I will bless you with this icon and you must promise me you will never take it off. ... Do you promise?'

'If it does not weigh half a hundredweight and won't break my neck. ..., To please you ...' said Prince Andrei, but immediately seeing the pained expression that came over his sister's face at this jest he repented and added: 'I shall be very glad to, my dear – really very glad.'

'He will save you in spite of yourself, and have mercy on you and bring you to Himself, for in Him alone is truth and peace,' she said in a voice trembling with emotion, solemnly holding up in both hands before her brother a small old-fashioned oval icon of the Saviour with a dark face in a silver setting, on a little silver chain of delicate workmanship.

She crossed herself, kissed the icon and handed it to Andrei.

'Please, André, for my sake ...'

Her large timid eyes shone with kindly light. Those eyes lighted up the whole of her thin, sickly face and made it beautiful. Her brother put out his hand for the icon but she stopped him. Andrei understood, crossed himself and kissed the icon. His face was both tender (for he was touched) and at the same time ironical.

'Thank you, my dear.'

She kissed him on the brow and sat down again on the sofa. Both were silent.

'As I was saying to you, André, be kind and generous-hearted as you always used to be. Don't judge Lise harshly,' she began. 'She is so sweet, so good, and her position just now is a very hard one.'

'Come, Masha, I don't think I have complained of my wife to you, or found fault with her. Why do you say all this to me ?'

Red patches appeared on Princess Maria's face and she was dumb as though she felt guilty.

'I have said nothing to you, but you have been *talked to*. And that makes me sad.'

The red patches flamed still deeper on her forehead, neck and cheeks. She tried to say something but could not get a word out. Her brother had guessed right: the little princess had cried after dinner, and spoken of her forebodings about her confinement, and of how she dreaded it, and had complained of her lot, of her father-in-law and her husband. After her tears she had fallen asleep. Prince Andrei felt sorry for his sister.

'Let me tell you one thing, Masha, I have no fault to find with *my wife*, I never had and never shall have, nor have I any cause for self-reproach in regard to her; and this will always be so in whatever circumstances I find myself. But if you want to know the truth ... if you want to know whether I am happy ? The answer is No. Is she happy ? No. Why is this so ? I do not know. ...'

As he said this he got up, went over to his sister and, stooping, kissed her forehead. His fine eyes shone with a thoughtful, kindly, unwonted gleam though he was not looking at his sister but over her head towards the dark aperture of the open door.

'Let us go to her, it is time to say good-bye. No, you go ahead and wake her, and I will follow. Petrushka !' he called to his valet. 'Come here and take these things. That goes under the seat, and this on the right.'

Princess Maria rose and started towards the door. Then she stopped and said in French:

'André, if you had faith you would have turned to God and implored Him to give you the love you do not feel, and your prayer would have been granted.'

'Well, maybe !' said Prince Andrei. 'Go on, Masha, I'll come immediately.'

On the way to his sister's room, in the gallery which connected one house with the other, Prince Andrei encountered Mademoiselle Bourienne smiling sweetly. It was the third time that day that she had thrown herself in his path in a secluded corridor, with the same ecstatic and artless smile.

'Oh, I thought you were in your room,' said she, for some reason blushing and casting down her eyes.

Prince Andrei looked at her severely, and his face suddenly showed irritation. He did not speak but stared at her forehead and hair, not looking at her eyes, with such contempt that the Frenchwoman flushed scarlet and turned away without a word. When he reached his sister's room his wife was awake and her blithe voice could be heard through the open door babbling away. She was chattering on in French, as though anxious to make up for lost time after long repression.

'No, but imagine the old Countess Zubov with her false curls and a mouth full of false teeth, as though she would defy the years. ... Ha, ha, ha, Marie!'

It was at least the fifth time that Prince Andrei had heard his wife tell the same story about Countess Zubov, with the same laugh. He entered the room quietly. The little princess, plump and rosy was sitting in an easy-chair with her work in her hands, pouring out Petersburg reminiscences and even the catch-phrases of Petersburg. Prince Andrei went up to her, stroked her hair and asked if she felt rested after the journey. She answered him and continued with her chatter.

The coach with six horses was waiting at the porch. It was an autumn night, so dark that the coachman could not see the pole of the carriage. Servants with lanterns bustled about on the steps. The great mansion was brilliant with lights shining through the lofty windows. The domestic serfs crowded in the outer hall, waiting to say good-bye to the young prince. The members of the household were collected in the big hall: Mihail Ivanovich, Mademoiselle Bourienne, Princess Maria and the little princess. Prince Andrei had been summoned to his father's study, where the old prince wished to bid him a private farewell. All were waiting for them to come out.

When Prince Andrei went into the study the old man, the spectacles of old age on his nose and wearing a white dressing-gown in which he never received anyone except his son, was sitting at the table writing. He glanced round.

'Are you off?' And he went on writing.

'I have come to say good-bye.'

'Kiss me here,' and he indicated his cheek. 'Thank you, thank you!'

'Why do you thank me?'

'Because you don't dilly-dally, because you aren't tied to your wife's apron-strings. The service before everything. Thank you, thank you!' And he went on writing so vigorously that his quill spluttered and squeaked. 'If you have anything to say, say it. I can attend to these two things at once,' he added.

'About my wife, ... I am so sorry to leave her on your hands ...'

'Why talk nonsense? Say what it is you want.'

'When the time comes, send to Moscow for an *accoucheur*. ... Get him here.'

The old prince stopped writing and pretending not to understand fixed his son with stern eyes.

'I know that if nature does not do her work no one can help,' said Prince Andrei, obviously embarrassed. 'I know that not more than one in a million cases goes amiss, but this is her whim and mine. People have been telling her things, she has had a dream, and she's frightened.'

'H'm ... H'm ...' growled the old man, taking up his pen again. 'I'll see to it.'

He signed his name with a flourish, and suddenly turned to his son with a laugh.

'It's a bad business, eh?'

'What is. father?'

'Your wife!' said the old prince with blunt significance.

'I don't understand,' said Prince Andrei.

'Yes, there's nothing to be done about it, my young friend,' said the prince. 'They're all alike; and there's no getting unmarried again. Never fear, I won't tell anyone; but you know yourself it's the truth.'

He grasped his son's hand with his small bony fingers, shook it, looked him straight in the face with keen eyes which seemed to see through a person, and again laughed his chilly laugh.

The son sighed, thereby admitting that his father had read him correctly. The old man continued to fold and seal his letters, snatching up and throwing down wax, seal and paper with his habitual rapidity.

'What can you do? She's a beauty. I'll see to everything. Make your mind easy,' said he abruptly, as he sealed the last letter.

Andrei was silent. It was both pleasant and painful that his father understood him. The old man got up and handed the letter to his son.

'Come,' said he, 'don't worry about your wife. Whatever can be done shall be done. Now listen. Give this letter to Mihail Ilarionovich.'

(This was Kutuzov.) 'I have asked him to make use of you in proper places, and not keep you too long as an adjutant: it's a nasty job! Tell him that I remember him with affection. Write and let me know how he receives you. If he gives you a proper welcome, stay with him. The son of Nikolai Andreich Bolkonsky need serve no one on sufferance. Now come here.'

He spoke so rapidly that half his words were left unfinished, but his son was used to understanding him. He led him to a desk, threw back the lid, pulled open a drawer and drew out a manuscript-book filled with his own bold, angular, close handwriting.

'I am sure to die before you. So remember, these are my memoirs to be given to the Emperor after my death. Now here is a bank-note and a letter: it is a prize for anyone who writes a history of Suvorov's campaigns. Send it to the Academy. Here are some jottings for you to read after I am gone. You will find them worth your while.'

Andrei did not tell his father that he would no doubt live a long time yet. He felt it better not to say that.

'I shall carry out your wishes, father,' he said.

'Well, now, good-bye.' He gave his hand to be kissed, and embraced his son. 'Remember one thing, Prince Andrei: if you get killed, it will be a grief to me in my old age ...' He paused abruptly and then in a scolding voice suddenly cried: 'But if I were to hear that you had not behaved like the son of Nikolai Bolkonsky, I should be – ashamed!'

'You need not have said that to me, father,' replied the son with a smile.

The old man did not speak.

'There's another thing I wanted to ask you,' continued Prince Andrei. 'If I am killed and if I have a son, keep him here with you, as I was saying yesterday. Let him grow up under your roof.... Please.'

'Not let your wife have him?' said the old man, and he laughed.

They stood in silence, facing one another. The old man's keen eyes gazed straight into his son's. There was a tremor in the lower part of the old prince's face.

'We have said good-bye ... now go!' said he suddenly. 'Go!' he shouted in a loud, angry voice, opening the study door.

'What is it? What has happened?' asked Prince Andrei's wife and sister as Prince Andrei came out and they caught a momentary glimpse of the old man in his white dressing-gown, without his wig and wearing his spectacles, as he appeared at the door shouting irately.

Prince Andrei sighed and made no reply.

'Well!' said he, turning to his wife. And this 'Well!' sounded like a cold sneer, as though he were saying: 'Now go through your little performance.'

'André, already?' said the little princess, turning pale and fixing terror-stricken eyes on her husband.

He embraced her. She shrieked and fell swooning on his shoulder.

He warily released the shoulder she leant on, glanced into her face and carefully laid her in an armchair.

'Adieu, Marie,' said he gently to his sister, taking her by the hand and kissing her, and hastened out of the room.

The little princess lay in the armchair, Mademoiselle Bourienne chafing her temples. Princess Maria, supporting her sister-in-law, continued to look with her beautiful eyes dim with tears at the door through which Prince Andrei had disappeared, and she made the sign of the cross after him. From the study came the sounds of the old man blowing his nose with sharp angry reports like pistol shots. Hardly had Prince Andrei left the room before the study door was flung open and the stern figure of the old man in his white dressing-gown looked out.

'Gone, has he? Well, and a good thing too!' said he, and looking furiously at the fainting little princess he shook his head reprovingly and slammed the door.

124

PART TWO

I

In the October of 1805 a Russian army was cantoned in the villages and towns of the Archduchy of Austria, and fresh regiments kept arriving from Russia and encamping about the fortress of Braunau, making a heavy burden for the inhabitants on whom they were billeted. Braunau was the headquarters of the commander-in-chief, Kutuzov.

On the 11th of October 1805 one of the infantry regiments that had just reached Braunau halted about half a mile from the city, waiting to be reviewed by the commander-in-chief. Despite the un-Russian appearance of the locality and surrounding landscape – orchards, stone walls, tiled roofs and distant hills – and the fact that the peasants gazing with curiosity at the soldiers were not Russians, the regiment looked exactly like every Russian regiment when it is getting ready for an inspection anywhere in the heart of Russia.

In the evening, on the last stage of the march, an order had been received that the commander-in-chief would review the regiment on the march. Though the wording of the order had not seemed altogether clear to the commanding officer, and the question arose whether the troops were to be in marching order or not, it was decided at a consultation between the battalion commanders to present the regiment in parade formation, on the principle that it is always better 'to bow too low than not bow low enough'. So the soldiers, after a twenty-mile march, did not get a wink of sleep but were up all night cleaning and polishing, while the adjutants and company commanders calculated and reckoned; and by morning the regiment – instead of the straggling disorderly mob it had been on the last stage of its march the day before – presented a compact array of two thousand men, each of whom knew his place and his duty, and had every button and strap shining and in position. Not only externally was all correct – if the commander-in-chief should think fit to look beneath the uniforms he would see on every man alike a clean shirt, and in every knapsack he would find the regulation number of articles, 'awl, soap and all' as the soldiers put it. There was only one detail concerning which no one could be at ease. This was their footgear. The boots of more than half the men were worn out. But this was not the fault of the commanding officer since, notwithstanding his repeated demands, supplies had not been issued by the Austrian commissariat, and the men had marched some seven hundred miles.

The commander of the regiment was a florid-looking general past middle age, with grizzled eyebrows and whiskers, stout, and thick-set: the depth of his chest was greater than the breadth of his shoulders. Wearing a brand-new uniform showing the creases where it had been folded, and heavy gold epaulets which seemed to stand up rather than lie on his massive shoulders, he had the air of a man happily performing one of the most solemn functions in life. He walked up and down in front of the line, throwing his leg out at every step and slightly arching his back. It was plain that the commander was proud of his regiment, delighted in it and was heart and soul wrapped up in it. His pompous gait, however, seemed to suggest that his military interests left plenty of room in his thoughts for the attractions of society and the fair sex.

'Well, my dear Mihail Mitrich,' said he, addressing one of the battalion commanders, who stepped forward with a smile (it was clear that both were in excellent spirits), 'we had a tough night of it, didn't we? However, everything seems all right. The regiment doesn't look at all bad, eh?'

The battalion commander understood the jovial irony and laughed.

'No, we shouldn't even be turned off the Petersburg Parade Ground.'

'What's that?' asked the commander.

At that moment two figures on horseback appeared on the road from the town, along which signallers had been posted. They were an aide-de-camp and a Cossack riding behind him.

The aide-de-camp had been sent from headquarters to confirm the order not clearly worded the day before, and make it plain that the commander-in-chief wished to inspect the regiment in exactly the condition in which it had arrived – wearing greatcoats and carrying packs, and without any polishing up.

A member of the Hofkriegsrath from Vienna had been with

Kutuzov the previous day, with proposals and demands for Kutuzov to join up in all haste with the allied armies under the Archduke Ferdinand and General Mack; and Kutuzov, not considering this junction advisable, intended, as one of the arguments in support of his view, to show the Austrian general the pitiable state in which the troops from Russia had arrived. With this object he was anxious to go out to meet the regiment, so that the worse the condition of the men the better pleased the commander-in-chief would be. Though the aide-de-camp did not know these ins-and-outs, he nevertheless delivered the urgent order that the men should be in their greatcoats and carrying packs, and insisted that if it were otherwise the com-mander-in-chief would be ill pleased.

On hearing this the commanding officer's head sank; he shrugged his shoulders in silence and testily spread out his arms.

'A fine mess!' he cried. 'Didn't I tell you, Mihail Mitrich, that "marching order" meant greatcoats?' said he, turning reproachfully to the battalion commander. 'Oh, my God!' he added, stepping resolutely forward. 'Company commanders!' he shouted in a voice accustomed to giving orders. 'Sergeant-majors! ... How soon will his Excellency be here?' he asked the aide-de-camp with respectful deference evidently proportioned to the dignity of the personage to whom he was referring.

'In about an hour, I fancy.'

'Shall we have time to make the change?'

'I can't say, general ...'

The commanding officer, hastening among the ranks himself, ar-ranged for the men to change back into their greatcoats. The com-pany commanders ran off to their companies, the sergeant-majors began bustling about (the greatcoats were not quite up to the mark), and in an instant the solid squares which till then had been standing silent and motionless, stirred, stretched out and began to hum with talk. Soldiers ran this way and that, throwing up their knapsacks with a jerk of their shoulders and pulling the straps over their heads, un-fastening their greatcoats and lifting their arms high in the air, trying to get them into the sleeves.

Half an hour later everything was in the same good order as before, only the square had been transformed from black to grey. The general strutted out to the front of the regiment again and examined it from a distance.

'Whatever does this mean? What is that?' he shouted, stopping short. 'Captain of the 3rd company!'

'Captain of the 3rd company wanted by the general! ... captain to the general ... 3rd company to the captain! ...' the command passed along the lines and an adjutant ran to look for the missing officer.

When the eagerly but wrongly-repeated summons reached its destination in a cry of: 'The general to the 3rd company!' the missing officer emerged from behind his men and, though well on in years and not in the habit of running, came towards the general, trotting awkwardly on his toes. The captain's face showed the uneasiness of a schoolboy called upon to repeat a lesson he has not learnt. Patches of deeper colour appeared on his red face (the redness of which was obviously due to intemperance), and his mouth twitched nervously. The general looked the captain up and down as he approached panting, slackening pace as he drew nearer.

'You'll soon be dressing your men in petticoats! What does that mean?' shouted the commanding officer, thrusting out his lower jaw and pointing to a soldier in the ranks of the 3rd company who wore a greatcoat a different colour from the other greatcoats. 'And where have you been? The commander-in-chief is expected and you leave your post? Eh? I'll teach you to rig your men out in dressing-gowns for inspection! ... Eh? ...'

The captain, never taking his eyes off his superior, pressed two fingers more and more rigidly to his cap, as if in this pressure lay his only hope of salvation.

'Well, why don't you speak? Who's that you've got dressed up there like a Hungarian?' demanded the commander with grim facetiousness.

'Your Excellency ...'

'Well, "your Excellency" what? Your Excellency! Your Excellency! What about your Excellency? ... Nobody knows.'

'Your Excellency, it's the officer Dolohov, who was reduced to the ranks,' the captain said softly.

'Well? Degraded into a field-marshal was he, or into the ranks? If he's a soldier, then he must be dressed like the others, in regulation uniform.'

'Your Excellency, you yourself authorized him to wear that, on the march.'

'Authorized? Authorized? That's just like you young men,' said the commanding officer, cooling down a little. 'Authorized indeed ... We give you an inch, and you take ...' The general paused. 'We give you an inch, and you – Well!' said he with a fresh access of temper. 'Be good enough to dress your men properly....'

And the general glanced at the adjutant and directed his jerky steps towards the regiment. It was obvious that he was pleased with his display of anger and hoped to find a further pretext for wrath as he progressed along the ranks. Having berated one officer for an un-polished badge and another because his line was not straight, he reached company three.

'Ho-o-o-w are you standing ? Where's your leg ? Your leg – where is it ?' shouted the commanding officer with a note of anguish in his voice, while there were still half a dozen men between him and Dolohov in his bluish greatcoat.

Dolohov slowly straightened his bent knee staring the general in the face with his bright, insolent eyes.

'Why that blue coat ? Off with it! ... Sergeant-major! Strip this man ... the rasc ...' He did not have time to finish.

'General, I am bound to obey orders, but I am not bound to put up with ...' said Dolohov quickly.

'No talking in the ranks! ... No talking, no talking!'

'Not bound to put up with insults,' Dolohov concluded in a loud, ringing voice.

The eyes of the general and the private met. The general stopped silent, angrily pulling down his tight muffler.

'Have the goodness to change your coat, I beg of you,' said he as he turned away.

2

'He's coming!' shouted one of the signalmen at that moment.

The commanding officer, flushing, ran to his horse, seized the stir-rup with trembling hands, threw his body across the saddle, righted himself, drew his sabre and with a radiant, resolute face, opening his mouth sideways, prepared to shout the word of command. The regi-ment fluttered like a bird preening its wings, and became still.

'Atten – tion!' roared the general in a soul-shaking voice, express-ing at once gladness on his own account, severity towards the regi-ment and welcome as regards the approaching chief.

Along the broad country road, shaded with trees on both sides, came a high Viennese calèche painted light blue, slightly creaking on its springs and drawn by six horses at a brisk trot. Behind the calèche galloped the suite and an escort of Croats. Beside Kutuzov sat an Austrian general in a white uniform which made a strange contrast with the Russian black. The calèche drew up in front of the regiment. Kutuzov and the Austrian general were talking in low voices and Kutuzov smiled slightly as, treading heavily, he stepped down from the carriage, exactly as though the two thousand men breathlessly gazing at him and at their general did not exist.

The word of command rang out, and again the regiment quivered and with a jingling sound presented arms. The dead silence was broken by the feeble voice of the commander-in-chief, and the regiment roared 'Long life to your Ex ... len ... len ... lency!' And again all was still. At first Kutuzov stood where he was, while the regiment moved; then he and the general in white, accompanied by the suite, started to walk down the line.

From the way the general in command of the regiment saluted the commander-in-chief, drawing himself up obsequiously and devouring him with his eyes, and from the way he followed the two generals through the ranks, bending forward and hardly able to restrain his jerky gait, and from the way he darted forward at Kutuzov's every word or gesture, it was plain that he performed his duties as a subordinate with even greater enjoyment than he did those of a commander. The regiment, thanks to the stern discipline and strenuous endeavours of its general, was in splendid condition compared to others that had reached Braunau at the same time. The number of sick and stragglers left behind was only two hundred and seventeen. And everything was in excellent order, with the exception of the soldiers' boots.

Kutuzov proceeded down the ranks, stopping now and then to say a few friendly words to officers or even privates whom he had known in the war against Turkey. Glancing at their boots he more than once shook his head mournfully, pointing them out to the Austrian general with an expression implying that he blamed no one but could not help noticing what a bad state of things it was. Each time this happened the commanding officer ran forward, afraid of missing a single word the commander-in-chief might utter in regard to the regiment. Behind Kutuzov, at a distance that allowed every softly-spoken word to be heard, followed some twenty personages of his suite. These gentlemen were talking among themselves and occasionally laughing. Nearest of all to the commander-in-chief walked a handsome adjutant. This was Prince Bolkonsky. Beside him was his comrade Nesvitsky, a tall, excessively stout staff-officer with a kind, smiling, handsome face and liquid eyes. Nesvitsky could hardly keep from laughing at the antics of a swarthy officer of the Hussars walking near him. This hussar, with a grave face and without a smile or a change in the fixed expression of his eyes, watched the commanding officer's back and mimicked his every movement. Each time the commander tottered and leaned forward, the hussar officer would totter and lean forward in precisely the same manner. Nesvitsky was laughing and nudging the others to look at the wag.

Kutuzov walked slowly and languidly past thousands of eyes that were almost falling out of their heads in the effort to watch him. On reaching the third company he suddenly stopped. His suite, not anticipating this halt, involuntarily crowded up close to him.

'Ah, Timohin!' said the commander-in-chief, recognizing the red-nosed captain who had been in trouble over the blue greatcoat.

Timohin, who, one would have said, had drawn himself up to his fullest height when he was reprimanded by his commanding officer, now when addressed by the commander-in-chief stood so rigidly erect that it seemed the strain must prove too much should the commander-in-chief continue looking at him; and accordingly Kutuzov, evidently realizing the position and wishing the captain nothing but good, quickly turned away, a scarcely perceptible smile flitting over his puffy, scarred face.

'Another Ismail comrade,' said he. 'A brave soldier! Are you satisfied with him?' he asked of the commanding officer.

And the latter – unconscious that he was being reflected in the hussar as in a looking-glass – started, stepped forward and replied:

'Highly satisfied, your Excellency!'

'We all have our little weaknesses,' said Kutuzov, smiling and walking away. 'He used to have a predilection for Bacchus.'

The commanding officer was afraid that he might be held responsible for this, and did not answer. The hussar at that moment noticed the face of the red-nosed captain with his stomach drawn in, and imitated his expression and attitude so exactly that Nesvitsky laughed outright. Kutuzov turned round. The officer evidently possessed perfect control of his features: while Kutuzov was turning round he managed to replace the grimace by the most serious, deferential and innocent of expressions.

The third company was the last and Kutuzov paused, apparently trying to remember something. Prince Andrei moved forward from the suite and said in an undertone, in French:

'You ordered me to remind you of the officer Dolohov, reduced to the ranks in this regiment.'

'Where is Dolohov?' asked Kutuzov.

Dolohov, attired by now in the grey greatcoat of an ordinary soldier, did not wait to be summoned. The well-proportioned figure of the fair-haired soldier with clear blue eyes stepped forward from the ranks, went up to the commander-in-chief and presented arms.

'A complaint to make?' Kutuzov asked with a slight frown.

'This is Dolohov,' said Prince Andrei.

'Ah!' said Kutuzov. 'I hope you will profit by this lesson. Do your duty. The Emperor is gracious. And I shan't forget you if you deserve well.'

The bright blue eyes looked at the commander-in-chief just as boldly as they had looked at the general of his regiment, their expression seeming to rend the veil of convention that so widely separates commander-in-chief from private.

'I only beg one favour, your most high Excellency,' said Dolohov in his firm, ringing, deliberate voice. 'I ask for an opportunity to atone for my offence, and prove my devotion to his Majesty the Emperor and to Russia!'

Kutuzov turned away. For a second there was a gleam in his eyes of the same smile with which he had turned from Captain Timohin. He frowned, as though to declare that everything Dolohov had said to him, and everything he could possibly say, he had known long ago and was weary of, and that it was all so much wasted breath. He moved away and went back to the carriage.

The regiment broke up into companies and set off for their appointed quarters not far from Braunau, where they hoped to find boots and clothes, and to rest after their hard marches.

'Don't bear me a grudge, will you, Prohor Ignatich?' said the commanding officer, overtaking the third company and riding up to Captain Timohin who was marching in front. The commanding officer's face now that the inspection was successfully over beamed with delight he could not suppress. 'In the Emperor's service ... one can't help ... one sometimes flies off the handle on parade. ... I am the first to apologize, you know me! ... He was very pleased!' And he held out his hand to the captain.

'Upon my word, general, as if I'd make so bold! ...' answered the captain, his nose growing plum-colour as he gave a smile which showed where two front teeth were missing that had been knocked out by the butt-end of a gun at Ismail.

'And assure Dolohov that I shall not forget him – he may rest easy on that score. By the way, tell me, pray, how is he behaving himself? I've been meaning to inquire. ...'

'He's most punctilious in the discharge of his duties, your Excellency; but his temper ...' said Timohin.

'What about his temper?' asked the general.

'It varies with the day, your Excellency.' said the captain. 'One day he is sensible, intelligent and quiet. And the next he's like a wild beast. In Poland, if you please, he all but killed a Jew.'

'Yes, yes,' remarked the commanding officer. 'Still, one must be easy on a young man in misfortune. He has influential connexions, you know. ... So you would be wise to ...'

'Exactly so, your Excellency,' said Timohin, showing with a smile that he understood his chief's wishes.

'Quite, quite.'

The commanding officer sought out Dolohov in the ranks and reining in his horse said to him:

'The first engagement may bring you your epaulets!'

Dolohov looked round and said nothing. There was no change in the ironical smile that curled his lips.

'Well, that's all right then,' continued the commanding officer. 'A round of vodka for the men from me,' he added loud enough to be heard by the soldiers. 'I thank you all! God be praised!' And he rode past that company and overtook the next one.

'After all, he's really a good fellow and not difficult to serve under,' said Timohin to the subaltern beside him.

'"King of hearts", in fact,' said the subaltern, laughing. (The commanding officer was nicknamed the 'king of hearts'.)

The happy mood of their officers after the inspection infected the men. The company marched along cheerfully. Soldiers' voices could be heard on all sides chatting away.

'Who invented the story that Kutuzov's blind in one eye?'

'Well so he is! Quite blind.'

'Nay, lad, he can see better than what you can. Boots and leg-bands ... he didn't miss a thing.'

'I say, mate, when he looked at my feet ... well, thinks I ...'

'And that other one with him, that there Austrian – looked as if 'e was smeared with chalk – white as flour, 'e was. I bet they polish 'im up like us rubs the guns!'

'Hey, Fedeshou! ... Did he say when the fighting would start? You were near him. They did say Bonaparte himself was at Braunau.'

'Bonaparte here! ... That's fool talk! What won't you know next! The Prussians are up in arms now. The Austrians, you see, are laying theirs down. When they're out of it, then the war will begin with Bonaparte. And here you go saying Bonaparte's in Braunau! Shows you're a fool! Why not keep your ears open?'

'Plague take these quartermasters! See, there's the fifth company turning off into the village already. ... They'll have their buckwheat cooked before we get in.'

'Give us a biscuit, old man.'

'And yesterday did you give me a plug of baccy? Not a bit of it. Still, all right, here you are.'

'They might call a halt here – the idea of another four miles on an empty stomach!'

'Wasn't it fine when those Germans gave us carts? Sitting easy and going alone – that was something like!'

'But hereabouts, my friend, the folk look half daft. Back there the Poles at any rate were our Emperor's people, but here they're all regular Germans.'

'Singers to the front!' shouted an officer.

And a score of men broke from different ranks and ran to the head of the column. The drummer, who led the singing, faced about, flourished his arm and struck up an interminable soldier's song beginning: *Morning dawned, the sun was rising* and ending *On then, boys, on to glory, led by old Father Kamensky*. This song had been composed in Turkey and now was sung in Austria, the only variation being the words *Father Kutuzov* in place of *Father Kamensky*.

Jerking out the last words in military style and waving his arms as if he were hurling something to the ground, the drummer, a lean, handsome soldier of about forty, looked sternly at the singers and screwed up his face. Then, satisfied that all eyes were fixed on him, he raised both arms as though he were carefully lifting some invisible but precious object above his head and, holding it there for several seconds, suddenly flung it down with a despairing gesture:

'Oh, my bower, oh, my bower! ...'

'Oh, my bower new! ...' chimed in twenty voices, and the kitchen orderly, disregarding the weight of his equipment, frisked out in front and walking backwards before the company twitched his shoulders and made gestures of defiance with his ladles. The soldiers, swinging their arms in time with the music, marched with long steps, involuntarily keeping to the beat. Behind the company was heard the rattle of wheels with the creaking of springs and the tramp of horses. Kutuzov and his suite were returning to town. The commander-in-chief made a sign for the men to continue marching at ease, and he and all his staff showed pleasure at the singing and the spectacle of the dancing soldier and the gay and lively appearance of troops as they marched. Conspicuous in the second file of the right flank, the side on which the carriage was passing the company, was Dolohov, the blue-eyed private, who was jauntily swinging along with particular grace, keeping time to the song and looking into the faces of those driving by with an expression that seemed to smack of pity for all who were not at that moment marching with the company. The hussar cornet in Kutuzov's suite who had mimicked the commanding officer fell behind the carriage and rode up to Dolohov.

Hussar cornet Zherkov had at one time belonged to the same wild set in Petersburg of which Dolohov had been the leader. Meeting Dolohov abroad as a common soldier, Zherkov had not found it expedient to recognize him. But now that Kutuzov had spoken to the gentleman-ranker he addressed him with the cordiality of an old friend.

'My dear fellow, how are you?' said he through the singing, walking his horse abreast of the company.

'How am I?' Dolohov repeated coldly. 'As you see.'

The lively song gave a special flavour to the tone of easy good fellowship in which Zherkov spoke and to the studied coolness of Dolohov's reply.

'And how do you get on with your officers?' inquired Zherkov.

'All right. They are good fellows. How did you manage to wriggle on to the staff?'

'I was attached: I'm on duty.'

Neither spoke.

She let the hawk fly upward from out of her right sleeve, rang out the song, the very sound of it inspiring a bold, blithe sensation. Their conversation would probably have been different but for the influence of the song.

'Is it true that the Austrians have been beaten?' asked Dolohov.

'The devil only knows. They say so.'

'I'm glad,' answered Dolohov briefly and clearly, as the song demanded.

'I say, come round one evening. We'll have a game of faro,' said Zherkov.

'Why, have you too much money?'

'Do come.'

'Can't. I've sworn off. I'm neither drinking nor playing cards till I get reinstated.'

'Well, that's only till after the first engagement.'

'We shall see.'

They were silent again.

'Look in if you need anything. One can at least be of use on the staff ...' said Zherkov.

Dolohov grinned.

'Don't worry yourself. If I want anything, I shan't beg for it – I'll take it myself.'

'Well, I only meant ...'

'And I only meant ...'

'Good-bye.'

'Good-bye to you. ...'

And high in the air, and far away,
The hawk flew off to her native land.

Zherkov put spurs to his horse, which pranced excitedly from foot to foot uncertain which to move first, then steadied itself and galloped forward, outstripping the company and catching up with the carriage, all in time to the song.

3

On his return from the review Kutuzov took the Austrian general into his private room and calling his adjutant asked for certain papers relating to the state of the troops on their arrival, and the letters that had been received from the Archduke Ferdinand, who was in command of the advanced army. Prince Andrei Bolkonsky came in with the required documents. Kutuzov and the Austrian member of the Hofkriegsrath were sitting over a map which was spread on the table.

'Ah! ...' said Kutuzov, glancing at Bolkonsky and by this exclamation as it were inviting his adjutant to wait while he went on with the conversation in French.

'All I can say, general,' proceeded Kutuzov with a pleasing elegance of expression and intonation which constrained one to listen to each deliberately uttered word. It was evident that Kutuzov took pleasure in listening to himself. 'All I can say, general, is that if the matter depended on my personal wishes the desire of his Majesty the Emperor Francis would have been fulfilled long ago. I should long since have joined the Archduke. And upon my honour I assure you that for me personally it would be a relief to hand over the supreme command of the army to a general better informed than myself, and more expert – of whom Austria possesses an abundance – and so throw off all this weighty responsibility. But circumstances are sometimes too strong for us, general.'

And Kutuzov smiled in a way that seemed to say: 'You are quite at liberty not to believe me, and indeed I don't care whether you believe me or not, but you have no grounds for telling me so. And that is the whole point.'

The Austrian general looked dissatisfied, but had no choice but to reply in the same tone.

'On the contrary,' said he, in a querulous, irritated manner that contrasted with the flattering intention of the words he uttered, 'on the contrary, his Majesty highly appreciates the part that your Excellency has played in the common cause; but we consider that the present delay robs the glorious Russian troops and their generals of the laurels which they are accustomed to win in their battles,' he concluded, with a phrase evidently prepared beforehand.

Kutuzov bowed, still with the same smile.

'That is my conviction, however, and judging by the last letter with which his Highness the Archduke Ferdinand has honoured me, I have no doubt that the Austrian troops, under the direction of so skilful a leader as General Mack, have by now already gained a decisive victory and no longer need our aid,' said Kutuzov.

The general frowned. Though there was no definite news of an Austrian defeat, there was too much circumstantial evidence confirming the unfavourable rumours that were rife; and so Kutuzov's assumption of an Austrian victory sounded very much like a sneer. But Kutuzov continued to smile blandly with the same expression, which seemed to say that he had a right to make this assumption. And in fact the last letter he had received from General Mack informed him of a victory and of the very favourable strategic position of the army.

'Let me have that letter,' said Kutuzov turning to Prince Andrei. 'Here, listen to this' – and Kutuzov with an ironical smile hovering about the corners of his mouth read out to the Austrian general the following passage in German from the Archduke Ferdinand's letter:

'We have fully concentrated forces of nearly seventy thousand men with which to attack and defeat the enemy should he cross the Lech. Since we are already masters of Ulm, we cannot be deprived of the advantage of commanding both banks of the Danube, and therefore should the enemy not cross the Lech we can at any moment cross the Danube, throw ourselves on his line of communication, recross the river lower down and frustrate his intention should he think of turning the main body of his forces against our faithful ally. We shall wait confidently therefore until the Imperial Russian army is ready to join us, when we shall easily find an opportunity in common to prepare for the enemy the fate he deserves.'

Kutuzov drew a long breath on coming to the end of this paragraph, and looked with an attentive, affable expression at the member of the Hofkriegsrath.

'But you know the wise maxim, your Excellency, which bids us be prepared for the worst,' said the Austrian general, evidently anxious to have done with jests and to get to business.

He cast a displeased glance at the adjutant.

'Excuse me, general,' interrupted Kutuzov, also turning to Prince Andrei. 'Look here, my dear fellow, get from Kozlovsky all the reports from our scouts. Here are two letters from Count Nostitz, and here's one from his Highness the Archduke Ferdinand – and these,' he said, handing him several papers. 'Make out a neat memorandum in French showing all the information we have had of the movements of the Austrian army. When you have finished, give it to his Excellency.'

Prince Andrei inclined his head in token of having understood from the first not only what had been said but also what Kutuzov would have liked to tell him. He gathered up the papers and with a bow to include both men stepped softly over the carpet and went out into the waiting-room.

Though not much time had elapsed since Prince Andrei had left Russia, he had changed greatly during that period. In the expression of his face, in his movements, in his gait, scarcely a trace was left of his former affected languor and indolence. He now looked like a man who has no time to think of the impression he is making on others, and is absorbed in work, both agreeable and interesting. His face showed more satisfaction with himself and those around him; his smile and glance were brighter and more attractive.

Kutuzov, whom he had joined in Poland, had received him very kindly and promised not to forget him. He had singled him out from among the other adjutants, taken him with him to Vienna and entrusted him with the more important duties. From Vienna Kutuzov had written to his old comrade, Prince Andrei's father:

'Your son', he wrote, 'bids fair to become an officer distinguished by his learning, energy and ability. I count myself fortunate to have such a subaltern.'

On Kutuzov's staff, among his fellow-officers and in the army generally, Prince Andrei had, as he had had in Petersburg society, two diametrically opposed reputations. Some, a minority, recognized Prince Andrei as being in a way different from themselves and everyone else, expected great things of him, listened to him, admired and imitated him; and with them Prince Andrei was natural and pleasant. Others, the majority, disliked him and considered him conceited, cold and disagreeable. But Prince Andrei had known what line to take with them too, so that they respected and were even afraid of him.

Coming out of Kutuzov's room into the waiting-room with the papers in his hand Prince Andrei went up to his comrade, the aide-de-camp on duty, Kozlovsky, who was sitting at the window with a book.

'Well, prince?' asked Kozlovsky.

'We are to draw up a memorandum to account for our not moving forward.'

'And why is it?'

Prince Andrei shrugged his shoulders.

'Any news from Mack?' asked Kozlovsky.

'No.'

'If it were true that he has been defeated news would have come.'

'Probably,' said Prince Andrei moving towards the outer door. But at that instant a tall Austrian general in a greatcoat with a black bandage round his head and the order of Maria Theresa on his collar, who had evidently just arrived, hurried into the room, slamming the door behind him. Prince Andrei stopped short.

'Commander-in-chief Kutuzov?' demanded the newly-arrived general, speaking quickly with a harsh German accent. He looked about him, and then made straight for the door of the private room.

'The commander-in-chief is engaged,' said Kozlovsky, hurrying towards the unknown general and barring his way to the door. 'Whom shall I announce?'

The unknown general looked down disdainfully at the short figure of Kozlovsky, as if surprised that anyone should not know him.

'The commander-in-chief is engaged,' repeated Kozlovsky calmly.

The general's face contracted, his lips twitched and trembled. He took out a notebook, hurriedly scribbled something in pencil, tore out the leaf, handed it to Kozlovsky, stepped quickly over to the window and threw himself into a chair, surveying those in the room as if asking what they were looking at him for. Then he lifted his head, stretched his neck as though intending to say something but immediately, with affected indifference, began to hum to himself, producing a strange sound which he instantly broke off. The door of the private room opened and Kutuzov appeared on the threshold. The general with the bandaged head bent forward as though running away from some danger, and with long, swift strides of his thin legs hastened up to Kutuzov.

'You see before you the unfortunate Mack,' he articulated in a broken voice.

Kutuzov's face as he stood in the open doorway remained perfectly immobile for several seconds. Then a frown ran over it, like a wave, leaving his forehead smooth again. He bowed his head respectfully, shut his eyes, ushered Mack in before him without a word, and himself closed the study door behind them.

The report which had already circulated of the defeat of the Austrians and the surrender of their entire army at Ulm proved to be correct. Within half an hour adjutants had been despatched in various directions with orders to the effect that the Russian troops, who had hitherto been inactive, would soon have to meet the enemy.

Prince Andrei was one of those rare staff-officers whose chief interest was centred on the general progress of the war. When he saw Mack and heard the details of the disaster he realized that half the campaign was lost, appreciated to the full the difficult situation of the Russian army, and vividly imagined what awaited it and the part he would have to play. He could not help feeling a thrill of delight at the thought of arrogant Austria's humiliation, and that perhaps within a week he would have a chance to witness and take part in the first Russian encounter with the French since the days of Suvorov. But he feared that Bonaparte's genius might outweigh all the valour of the Russian troops, and at the same time he could not bear to entertain the idea of his hero suffering disgrace.

Agitated and upset by these thoughts, Prince Andrei started for his room to write to his father, to whom he wrote every day. In the corridor he fell in with Nesvitsky, the comrade who shared quarters with him, and Zherkov, the comic man. They were, as usual, laughing at some joke.

'Why are you looking so glum?' asked Nesvitsky, noticing Prince Andrei's pale face and glittering eyes.

'There's nothing to be cheerful about,' answered Bolkonsky.

Just as Prince Andrei met Nesvitsky and Zherkov there came towards them from the other end of the corridor Strauch, an Austrian general who was attached to Kutuzov's staff to look after the provisioning of the Russian army. He was with the member of the Hofkriegsrath who had arrived the previous evening. There was plenty of room in the wide corridor for the generals to pass the three officers but Zherkov, giving Nesvitsky a push, exclaimed in a breathless voice:

'They're coming! ... they're coming! ... Stand aside, make way! Make way, please!'

The generals came along, looking as if they wished to avoid embarrassing demonstrations of respect. A silly smile of glee which he seemed unable to suppress spread over the face of Zherkov, the comic man.

'Your Excellency,' said he in German, stepping forward and addressing the Austrian general, 'I have the honour to congratulate you.'

He bowed, and awkwardly, like a child at a dancing lesson, scraped first with one foot and then with the other.

The member of the Hofkriegsrath looked at him severely; but seeing the earnestness of his silly smile could not refuse him a moment's attention. He screwed up his eyes and showed that he was listening.

'I have the honour to congratulate you. General Mack has arrived, quite safe and sound but for a slight bruise just here,' he added, pointing with a beaming smile to his head.

The general frowned, turned and went on his way.

'Good God, what a fool!' said he angrily, when he was a few steps away.

Nesvitsky with a chuckle threw his arms round Prince Andrei, but Bolkonsky, paler than ever and with an angry look on his face, pushed him aside and turned to Zherkov. The nervous irritability induced by the appearance of Mack, the news of his defeat and the thought of what lay before the Russian army found vent in wrath at Zherkov's untimely jest.

'If you, sir,' he began cuttingly, with a slight trembling of his lower jaw, 'choose to set up as a clown, I can't prevent you; but I warn you, if you dare a second time to play the fool in my presence I'll teach you how to behave.'

Nesvitsky and Zherkov were so astounded at this outburst that they gazed at Bolkonsky in silence, with wide-open eyes.

'Why, I only congratulated them,' said Zherkov.

'I am not trifling with you; be good enough to hold your tongue!' cried Bolkonsky, and taking Nesvitsky by the arm he walked off, leaving Zherkov who could find nothing to say.

'Come, what's the matter, old fellow?' said Nesvitsky soothingly.

'What's the matter?' exclaimed Prince Andrei, standing still in his excitement. 'Don't you understand, either we are officers serving our Tsar and our country, rejoicing in the successes and grieving at the misfortunes of our common cause, or we're hirelings caring nothing for our master's concerns! Forty thousand men massacred and the army of our allies destroyed, and you find it something to laugh at!'

he said in French, as if the use of this language added to the effect of what he was saying. 'It's all very well for a twopenny-halfpenny individual like that young man of whom you have made a friend, but not for you, not for you. Only a *whipper-snapper* could amuse himself in this fashion,' added Prince Andrei in Russian but pronouncing the word *whipper-snapper* with a French accent, when he noticed that Zherkov was still within hearing.

He waited to see if the cornet had any answer to make. But Zherkov turned on his heel and walked out of the corridor.

4

THE Pavlograd Hussars were encamped two miles outside Braunau. The squadron in which Nikolai Rostov was serving as a cadet was quartered in the German village of Zalzeneck, and the best billet in the village had been assigned to the squadron-commander, Cavalry-Captain Denisov, known to the entire cavalry division as 'Vasska' Denisov. Ensign Rostov had been sharing the squadron-commander's quarters ever since he had joined the regiment in Poland.

On October the 8th, the very same day when the news of Mack's defeat had raised a stir at headquarters, the camp life of the officers of the squadron was quietly proceeding as usual. Denisov, who had been losing at cards all night, had not yet come in when Rostov returned early in the morning from a foraging expedition. Rostov in his cadet uniform rode up to the porch, checked his horse, swung his leg over the saddle with the supple dexterity of youth, paused a moment in the stirrup as though sorry to dismount and at last sprang down and called to his orderly.

'Ah, Bondarenko, my dear fellow,' he cried to the hussar who rushed forward to attend to the horse. 'Walk him up and down for a bit, my friend,' he continued with that fraternal cordiality with which handsome young men are apt to treat everybody when they are happy.

'Right, your Excellency,' answered the Ukrainian with a gay toss of his head.

'Mind now, walk him up and down properly!'

Another hussar also rushed towards the horse but Bondarenko had already thrown the reins of the snaffle over the horse's head. It was evident that the ensign was liberal with his tips and that it paid to serve him. Rostov stroked the animal's neck and then its flank, and lingered for a moment on the step.

'Splendid! He'll make a fine charger!' he said to himself with a smile, and lifting his sabre he ran up the steps, his spurs rattling. The German on whom they were billeted, wearing a jerkin and a pointed cap, looked out from the cowshed where he was clearing manure with a pitchfork. At the sight of Rostov the German's face immediately lit up with a jolly smile.

'*Schön gut Morgen! Schön gut Morgen!*' he repeated, giving a wink, evidently pleased to greet the young man.

'Busy already?' said Rostov with the same gay brotherly smile that was constantly on his face. 'Hurrah for the Austrians! Hurrah for the Russians! Hurrah for the Emperor Alexander!' he went on, quoting the German's often repeated cry.

The German laughed, came right out of the cowshed, pulled off his cap and waving it over his head cried:

'And hurrah for the whole world!'

Rostov, following the German's example, waved his cap above his head and with a laugh shouted: 'And hurrah for the whole world!' Though neither the German cleaning his cowshed nor Rostov back with his platoon from foraging for hay had any reason for rejoicing, both looked at each other with happy enthusiasm and brotherly love, wagged their heads in token of mutual affection, and parted with smiles, the German returning to his cowshed and Rostov going into the cottage which he occupied with Denisov.

'Where's your master?' he asked Lavrushka, Denisov's orderly, whom the whole regiment knew for a rogue.

'He hasn't been in since last night. He must have been losing,' answered Lavrushka. 'I know by now, if he wins he comes home early, blowing his own trumpet; but if he's not back before morning it means he's lost and will come in in a rage. Will you have some coffee?'

'Yes, make haste.'

Ten minutes later Lavrushka brought the coffee.

'Here he comes!' said he. 'Now for trouble!'

Rostov glanced out of the window and saw Denisov returning home. Denisov was a little man with a red face, sparkling black eyes, and tousled black moustache and hair. He wore a hussar's cloak, which was unfastened, wide, sagging pantaloons, and a crumpled shako on the back of his head. He came up to the porch gloomily hanging his head.

'Lavwuska!' he shouted loudly and angrily. 'Take this off, idiot!'

'I *am* taking it off,' replied Lavrushka's voice.

'Ah, you're up already,' said Denisov, entering the room.

'Long ago,' replied Rostov. 'I have already been after the hay, and seen Fraülein Mathilde.'

'Oho! And I've been losing, bwother, losing all night like a son of a dog!' cried Denisov, not pronouncing his r's. 'Such howid bad luck! Such howid bad luck! The moment you left, so it began. Hey there! Tea!'

Puckering up his face in a sort of smile and showing his short strong teeth, he began to run the stubby fingers of both hands through his thick black hair which stood up like a forest.

'The devil himself must have dwiven me to that wat' (an officer nicknamed 'the rat'), he said, rubbing his forehead and face with both hands. 'Just fancy! He didn't give me a single cahd, not one, not a single one!'

Denisov took the lighted pipe that was offered to him, gripped it in his fist and tapped it on the floor, making the sparks fly, while he continued to shout.

'Gives you the singles but collahs the doubles!'

He scattered the burning tobacco, smashed the pipe and threw it down. Then, after a short silence, he suddenly looked up at Rostov, his glittering black eyes full of merriment.

'If only we had some women here. But there's nothing for one to do but dwink. If only we could soon start the fighting. Hey, who's there?' he called, turning to the door as he heard the tread of heavy boots and the clatter of spurs followed by a respectful cough.

'The quartermaster!' said Lavrushka.

Denisov scowled even more.

'W'etched business!' he exclaimed, flinging down a purse containing a few gold pieces. 'Wostov, deah fellow, see how much is left, and shove the purse undah the pillow,' said he, and went out to see the quartermaster.

Rostov took the money and mechanically arranging the old and new coins in separate piles began counting them.

'Ah, Telyanin! How d'ye do? I got a dwubbing last night,' Denisov was heard saying in the next room.

'Where was that? At Bykov's, at the rat's? ... I heard about it,' said a second piping voice, and thereupon Lieutenant Telyanin, a small man, an officer of the same squadron, entered the room.

Rostov thrust the purse under the pillow and shook the damp little hand that was held out to him. Telyanin had for some reason been transferred from the Guards shortly before the present campaign. He conducted himself very properly in the regiment but was not liked, and Rostov especially could neither conquer nor conceal his ground-less aversion for the man.

'Well, my young horseman, how do you like my Rook?' he asked. (Rook was a saddle horse that Telyanin had sold Rostov.)

The lieutenant never looked the person he was speaking to in the face: his eyes were continually flitting from one object to another. 'I saw you out riding this morning ...'

'Oh, he's all right, a good horse,' replied Rostov, though the animal for which he had given seven hundred roubles was not worth half that sum. 'He's begun to go a bit lame on the left foreleg,' he added.

'Cracked hoof! That's nothing. I'll tell you what to do, and show you what kind of a rivet to put on.'

'Yes, please do,' said Rostov.

'I'll show you, I'll show you! There's no secret about it. And you'll be thanking me for that horse.'

'Then I'll have him brought round,' said Rostov, anxious to get away from Telyanin, and he went out to give the order.

In the passage Denisov with a pipe in his mouth was squatting on the threshold facing the quartermaster who was reporting to him. When he saw Rostov, Denisov screwed up his face and, pointing with his thumb over his shoulder to the room where Telyanin was sitting, frowned and shuddered with loathing.

'Ugh, I don't like that fellow!' said he, regardless of the quarter-master's presence.

Rostov shrugged his shoulders as much as to say: 'Nor do I, but what's to be done about it?' And having given his order, he returned to Telyanin.

Telyanin was still sitting in the same indolent attitude in which Rostov had left him, rubbing his small white hands.

'There certainly are disgusting people about,' thought Rostov as he went into the room.

'Well, have you told them to bring the horse round?' asked Tely-anin, getting up and looking carelessly about him.

'I have.'

'Let's go ourselves. I only came over to ask Denisov about today's orders. Have you got them, Denisov?'

'Not yet. Where are you off to?'

'I want to teach this young man how to shoe a horse,' said Telyanin.

They went out down the front steps to the stable. The lieutenant explained how to rivet the hoof and went away to his own quarters.

When Rostov returned there was a bottle of vodka and a sausage on the table. Denisov was sitting at the table scratching with his pen on a sheet of paper. He looked gloomily into Rostov's face and said:

'I am w'iting to her.'

He leaned his elbows on the table, with the pen in his hand, and evidently delighted at the chance of saying what he had in mind faster than he could put it on paper he related to Rostov the contents of his letter.

'Don't you see, my fwiend,' said he, 'we are asleep until we love. We are childwen of dust ... but when we fall in love we are gods, puah again as the day we were cweated. ... Who's that now? Send him to the devil! I'm busy!' he shouted to Lavrushka who, not in the least daunted, came up to him.

'Who should it be? You told him to come yourself. It's the quarter-master for the money.'

Denisov scowled, opened his mouth to shout something but stopped.

'W'etched business,' he muttered to himself. 'I say, Wostov, how much is left in the puhse?' he asked, turning to Rostov.

'Seven new, three old.'

'Oh, w'etched! Well, what are you standing there foh, you sca'-cwow? Fetch in the quahtehmasteh!' he shouted to Lavrushka.

'Please, Denisov, let me lend you some money. I've got plenty, you know,' said Rostov, reddening.

'I don't like bowowing fwom my own fellows, I don't like it,' growled Denisov.

'But if you won't let me lend you some like a comrade I shall be offended. Really I've got it,' repeated Rostov.

'No, I tell you.'

And Denisov went over to the bed to get the purse from under the pillow.

'Where did you put it, Wostov?'

'Under the bottom pillow.'

'It isn't here.'

Denisov flung both pillows on the floor. There was no purse.

'That's stwange.'

'Hold on, didn't you throw it out?' said Rostov, picking up the pillows one at a time and shaking them.

He pulled off the quilt and shook it. There was no purse.

'I couldn't have forgotten, could I? No, I remember thinking how you kept it under your pillow like a secret treasure,' said Rostov. 'I put it just here. Where is it?' he demanded, turning to Lavrushka.

'I haven't been in the room. It must be where you put it.'

'But it isn't!'

'That's just like you. You throw a thing down anywhere and forget all about it. Look in your pockets.'

'No, if I hadn't thought about treasure,' said Rostov, 'but I remember putting it there.'

Lavrushka tore the whole bed apart, looked under it and under the table, searched everywhere and then stood still in the middle of the room. Denisov watched him in silence, and when Lavrushka spread out his hands in amazement, saying that the purse was nowhere to be found, he glanced at Rostov.

'Wostov, none of your schoolboy twicks ...'

Rostov, conscious of Denisov's gaze fixed upon him, raised his eyes and instantly dropped them again. All the blood which had seemed congested somewhere below his throat rushed to his face and eyes. He could hardly draw his breath.

'And no one's been in the room 'cept the lieutenant and yourselves. It must be here somewhere,' said Lavrushka.

'Now then, you devil's puppet, fly awound, hunt for it!' shouted Denisov suddenly, turning purple and starting towards the valet with a threatening gesture. 'Find that puhse or I'll horsewhip you. I'll horsewhip the lot of you!'

Rostov, avoiding Denisov's glance, began buttoning up his jacket, buckled on his sabre and put on his cap.

'I must have that puhse, I tell you,' roared Denisov, shaking the orderly by the shoulders and knocking him against the wall.

'Denisov, let him be; I know who has taken it,' said Rostov, going towards the door without raising his eyes.

Denisov paused, considered a moment and evidently understanding the meaning of Rostov's remark clutched him by the arm.

'Wubbish!' he cried, and the veins on his forehead and neck stood out like cords. 'I tell you, you're mad; I won't allow it. The puhse is here. I'll have the hide off this wascal, and it'll be found.'

'I know who has taken it,' repeated Rostov in an unsteady voice, and went to the door.

'And I tell you, don't you dahe to do it!' shouted Denisov, rushing at the cadet to hold him back.

But Rostov wrenched his arm free and with as much fury as though Denisov were his worst enemy fixed his eyes firmly and directly on his face.

'Do you realize what you are saying?' he said in a trembling voice. 'Except for myself no one else has been in the room. So that if it was not he, then ...'

He could not finish and ran from the room.

'Oh, may the devil take you and evewybody else!' were the last words Rostov caught.

Rostov made for Telyanin's quarters.

'The master is not in, he's gone to the staff,' Telyanin's orderly told him. 'Has something happened?' he added, wondering at the cadet's agitated face.

'No, nothing.'

'You've only just missed him,' said the orderly.

The staff quarters were some two miles from Zalzeneck, and Rostov, without returning home, mounted his horse and headed in that direction. In the village was an inn which the officers frequented. Rostov rode up to this inn and at the porch saw Telyanin's horse.

In the second room of the tavern the lieutenant was sitting over a dish of sausages and a bottle of wine.

'Ah, so you've come here too, young man!' said he, smiling and raising his eyebrows.

'Yes,' said Rostov, as if it cost him a great effort to utter this mono-syllable: and he sat down at the next table.

Both were silent. There were two Germans and a Russian officer in the room. No one spoke and the only sounds were the clatter of knives against plates and the lieutenant's munching. When Telyanin had finished his lunch he pulled out of his pocket a double purse and, pushing the rings apart with his small white, curved-up fingers, drew out a gold piece and with a lift of his eyebrows gave it to the waiter.

'Make haste, please,' he said.

The coin was a new one. Rostov stood up and went over to Telyanin.

'Allow me to look at your purse,' he said in a low, almost inaudible voice.

With shifting eyes but eyebrows still raised, Telyanin handed him the purse.

'Yes, it's a pretty little purse, isn't it ? ... Yes ... yes ...' said he, and suddenly turned pale. 'Look at it, young man,' he added.

Rostov took the purse in his hand and examined it, and the money in it, and looked at Telyanin. The lieutenant was glancing around in his usual way and seemed suddenly to have grown very good-humoured.

'If we ever get to Vienna, I shall leave it all there, but here in these rubbishy little towns there's nowhere to spend it,' said he. 'Well, let me have it, young man, I must be going.'

Rostov said nothing.

'What about you ? Going to have lunch too ? They feed one quite decently here,' continued Telyanin. 'Give it to me now.'

He stretched out his hand and took hold of the purse. Rostov let go of it. Telyanin took the purse and began slipping it into the pocket of his riding breeches, while his eyebrows lifted carelessly and his mouth half opened, as much as to say, 'Yes, yes, I am putting my purse in my pocket, and that's a very simple matter and no one else's business.'

'Well, young man ?' he said, sighing and glancing into Rostov's eyes from under his raised brows. A flash darted with the swiftness of an electric spark from Telyanin's eyes into Rostov's, and was shot back again, and again and again, all in a single instant.

'Come over here,' said Rostov, catching hold of Telyanin by the arm and almost dragging him to the window. 'That money is Denisov's ! You took it ...' he whispered just above Telyanin's ear.

'What ? ... What ? ... How dare you ? What ? ...' exclaimed Telyanin.

But the words sounded like a piteous cry of despair and an appeal for forgiveness. As soon as Rostov heard this note in his voice a great weight of suspense fell from him. He was rejoiced and in the very same instant began to feel sorry for the miserable creature standing before him; but he had to carry the thing through to the end.

'There are people here, heaven knows what they will think,' muttered Telyanin, snatching up his forage-cap and moving towards a small empty room. 'We must clear this up ...'

'I know it, and I shall prove it,' said Rostov.

'I ...'

Every muscle of Telyanin's pale terrified face began to twitch, his eyes still shifted from side to side though they looked down and never once rose to Rostov's face, and his sobs were audible.

'Count! ... Don't ruin a young man ... here's the wretched money, take it ...' He threw it on the table. 'I have an old father, a mother!'

Rostov took the money, avoiding Telyanin's gaze and without a word made to leave the room. But at the door he paused and turned back.

'My God,' he said, with tears in his eyes, 'how could you have done it?'

'Count ...' said Telyanin, moving towards the cadet.

'Don't touch me,' cried Rostov, drawing back. 'If you are in need, take the money.'

He flung the purse at him and ran out of the inn.

5

In the evening of the same day an animated discussion was taking place in Denisov's quarters between some of the officers of the squadron.

'And I tell you, Rostov, that it's your business to apologize to the commanding officer,' a tall grizzly-haired staff-captain with enormous moustaches and a large-featured furrowed face was saying to Rostov, who was crimson with excitement.

This staff-captain Kirsten had twice been reduced to the ranks for affairs of honour and had twice regained his commission.

'I will not allow anyone to call me a liar!' cried Rostov. 'He told me I was lying and I told him he was lying. And there the matter will rest. He can put me on duty every day, or place me under arrest, but no one can force me to apologize, because if he, as the colonel, thinks it beneath his dignity to give me satisfaction, then ...'

'Yes, but wait a bit, old man, and listen to me,' interrupted the staff-captain in his deep bass, calmly stroking his long moustaches.

'In the presence of other officers you tell the colonel that an officer has stolen ...'

'It wasn't my fault that the conversation took place in the presence of other officers. Maybe I ought not to have spoken before them, but I am not a diplomat. That's why I went into the Hussars – I thought that here I should have no need of such finicky considerations – and he tells me I am lying – so let him give me satisfaction ...'

'That's all very fine, no one imagines you're a coward; but that isn't the point. Ask Denisov if it isn't out of the question for a subaltern to demand satisfaction of his commanding officer ?'

Denisov sat gloomily chewing his moustache and listening to the conversation, evidently with no desire to take part in it. In reply to the staff-captain's question he shook his head.

'In the presence of other officers you speak to the colonel about this unsavoury business, and Bogdanich' (Bogdanich was the colonel) 'shuts you up.'

'He did not shut me up, he said I was lying.'

'Well, have it your own way, but you talked a lot of rubbish to him and you ought to apologize.'

'Not on your life!' shouted Rostov.

'I did not expect this of you,' said the staff-captain gravely and sternly. 'You don't want to apologize, but, man, you're in the wrong all round – not only with him but with the whole regiment and all of us. Look here: if only you'd thought the matter over, and taken advice before acting – but no, you go and blurt it all out before the officers. What was the colonel to do ? Have the officer court-martialled and disgrace the whole regiment ? Bring shame on the whole regiment on account of one scoundrel ? Is that your idea ? Well, it isn't ours ! And Bogdanich was a brick: he told you you were telling an untruth. It's not pleasant, but what's to be done, my dear fellow ? You brought it on yourself. And now, when we want to smooth things over, you're so high and mighty you won't apologize, and insist on making the whole affair public. You're huffy at being put on extra duty but why can't you apologize to an old and honourable officer ? Whatever Bogdanich may be, he's an honourable and gallant old colonel. You're quick at taking offence but you don't mind disgracing the whole regiment !' The staff-captain's voice began to tremble. 'You have been in the regiment next to no time, my lad, you're here today and gone tomorrow, transferred somewhere as adjutant. Much you'll care if it's said there are thieves among the Pavlograd officers! But we do care. Am I not right, Denisov? We do care!'

Denisov had kept silent all this time, and did not move though he occasionally glanced at Rostov with his glittering black eyes.

'Your pride is so dear to you that you aren't willing to apologize,' continued the staff-captain, 'but we old fellows who have grown up and, God willing, hope to die in the regiment – we have the honour of the regiment at heart, and Bogdanich knows it. Oh yes, we have its honour at heart all right! And this is wrong, wrong, I tell you! You may take offence if you choose, but I shall never mince words. It's all wrong!'

And the staff-captain got up and turned away from Rostov.

'That's twue, devil take it!' shouted Denisov, jumping up. 'Now then, Wostov, now then!'

Rostov, alternately flushing and growing pale, looked first at one officer and then at the other.

'No, gentlemen, no ... you mustn't think ... I see, you are quite mistaken to think that of me ... I ... for me ... for the honour of the regiment I'd ... Ah well, I'll prove that in action, and for me the honour of the flag.... Well, never mind, you're right, I am to blame!' The tears stood in his eyes. 'I was to blame, to blame all round. Now what more do you want?'

'Well done, count,' cried the staff-captain, turning round and clapping Rostov on the shoulder with his large hand.

'I tell you,' shouted Denisov, 'he's a capital fellow.'

'That's better, count,' repeated the staff-captain, beginning to address Rostov by his title, as though in acknowledgement of his confession. 'Go and apologize, your Excellency, yes, sir, go and apologize!'

'Gentlemen, I'll do anything. No one shall hear another word from me,' Rostov protested in an imploring voice, 'but I cannot apologize. By God I can't, say what you will! How can I go and apologize, like a little boy begging pardon?'

Denisov burst out laughing.

'It'll be the worse for you, if you don't. Bogdanich is vindictive: he'll make you pay for your obstinacy,' said Kirsten.

'No, on my word it's not obstinacy! I can't describe my feeling. I can't ...'

153

'Well, it's as you like,' said the staff-captain. 'By the way, where has the scoundrel hidden himself?' he asked Denisov.

'He weported sick. He's to be stwuck off the list tomowow,' muttered Denisov.

'It is an illness, there's no other way of explaining it,' said the staff-captain.

'Illness or not, he'd better not cwoss my path – I'd kill him!' cried Denisov in a bloodthirsty tone.

At this point Zherkov came into the room.

'What brings you here?' demanded the officers turning to the new-comer.

'We're going into action, gentlemen! Mack and his whole army have surrendered.'

'What a story!'

'I've seen him myself.'

'What, seen Mack alive, in the flesh?'

'Into action! We're going into action! He must have a good drink for such news. But how is it you're here?'

'I've been sent back to my regiment again, on account of that devil Mack. An Austrian general complained of me. I congratulated him on Mack's arrival.... What's the matter, Rostov? You look as if you'd just come out of a hot bath.'

'Oh, my dear fellow, we've been in such a mess here the last couple of days.'

The regimental adjutant came in and confirmed the news brought by Zherkov. They were under orders to march next day.

'Active service, gentlemen!'

'Well, thank God! We've been sitting here too long!'

6

KUTUZOV fell back towards Vienna, destroying behind him the bridges over the rivers Inn (at Braunau) and Traun (near Linz). On October the 23rd the Russian army was crossing the river Enns. At noon the Russian baggage-wagons, the artillery and columns of troops stretched through the town of Enns on both sides of the bridge.

It was a warm, showery autumnal day. The wide view that opened out from the heights where the Russian batteries stood guarding the bridge was at times narrowed by a diaphanous curtain of slanting rain, then suddenly widened out so that distant objects shone distinct in the sunlight, as though they were varnished. Down below, the little town could be seen with its white, red-roofed houses, its cathedral, and the bridge, on both sides of which jostling masses of Russian troops poured past. At the bend of the Danube, vessels, an island and a castle with a park surrounded by the waters of the two rivers, where the Enns flowed into the Danube, all became visible, as well as the rocky left bank of the Danube covered with pine forests, with a mysterious background of green summits and bluish gorges. The turrets of a convent rose up beyond a wild apparently virgin pine forest, and far away on the other side of the Enns could be discerned the mounted patrols of the enemy.

Among the field-guns on the brow of the hill the general in command of the rearguard stood with an officer of his staff scanning the countryside through field-glasses. A little behind them Nesvitsky, who had been sent to the rearguard by the commander-in-chief, was sitting on the tail of a gun-carriage. His Cossack who accompanied him had handed him over a knapsack and a flask, and Nesvitsky was treating some officers to little pies with genuine *doppel-kümmel* to wash them down. The officers were gathered round him, in a delighted circle, some on their knees, some squatting Turkish fashion on the wet grass.

'Yes, the Austrian prince who built that castle over there was no fool. It's a magnificent spot! You are not eating anything, gentlemen!' Nesvitsky was saying.

'Thank you very much, prince,' answered one of the officers, pleased to be talking to such an important member of the staff. 'Yes, it's a lovely spot. We passed close to the park and saw a couple of deer … and what a wonderful house!'

'Look, prince,' said another, who would dearly have liked to take a further pie but felt shy, and therefore affected to be examining the landscape. 'Look over there, our infantry have gone in already. Over there, do you see, in the meadow behind the village, three of our men are dragging something along. They'll ransack that little palace quick enough!' he remarked with evident approval.

'That they will,' said Nesvitsky. 'Ah, but what I should like,' he added, munching a pie in his handsome mouth with its dewy lips, '– would be to slip in yonder!'

He pointed to the turreted convent which could be seen on the mountain-side. He smiled, and his eyes narrowed and gleamed. 'That would be something like, gentlemen!'

The officers laughed.

'Just to flutter the little nuns a bit. Italians, they say, and some of them young and pretty. Upon my word, I'd give five years of my life for it!'

'They must be bored to death, too,' laughed an officer bolder than the rest.

Meanwhile the staff-officer standing on the brow of the hill was pointing out something to the general, who looked through his field-glasses.

'Yes, so it is, so it is,' said the general angrily, lowering the glasses and shrugging his shoulders. 'So it is, they'll be fired on at the crossing. And why are they dawdling so?'

On the opposite side the enemy could be seen by the naked eye, and a milk-white puff of smoke arose from their battery, followed immediately by a distant report, and our troops could be seen hurrying to get across the river.

Nesvitsky dismounted from the cannon with a grunt and went up to the general, smiling.

'Wouldn't your Excellency like to eat something?' he asked.

'It's a bad business,' said the general, without answering him. 'Our men were too slow.'

'Shall I ride down to them, your Excellency?' asked Nesvitsky.

'Yes, please do,' said the general, and he repeated the orders that had already once before been given in detail. 'And tell the hussars that they are to cross last and set fire to the bridge, as I ordered; and check over the inflammable material on the bridge.'

'Very good,' replied Nesvitsky.

He called the Cossack to bring up his horse, told him to put away the knapsack and flask, and lightly swung his heavy body into the saddle.

'I'm away to pay a visit to those little nuns,' said he to the officers who were watching him with smiles, and he rode off by the path that wound down the hill.

'Now then, captain, let's try the range,' said the general, turning to an artillery officer. 'Have a little fun to relieve the monotony!'

'To the guns!' commanded the officer, and in a moment the gunners came running cheerfully from their camp fires and began to load.

'One!' rang the command.

Number one recoiled nimbly. There was a deafening metallic roar from the cannon and a shell whistled over the heads of our men under the hillside and fell a long way short of the enemy, a little spurt of smoke showing where it burst.

The faces of officers and men lit up at the sound. They leaped to their feet and began busily watching the movements of our troops below and, farther off, of the approaching enemy – all of which could be seen as in the hollow of a hand. At the same instant the sun came out fully from behind the clouds and the fine note of the solitary cannon-shot and the brilliance of the bright sunshine merged into a single inspiriting impression of light-hearted gaiety.

7

Two of the enemy's shots had already flown over the bridge, where there was a crush of men. Half-way across stood Prince Nesvitsky, who had dismounted from his horse and whose stout person was jammed against the parapet. He looked laughingly back at his Cossack who was a few steps behind, holding the two horses by their bridles. Each time Prince Nesvitsky tried to move forward, soldiers and baggage-wagons forced him back, crowding him against the side of the bridge, and all he could do was to smile.

'Look out there, my boy!' cried the Cossack to a convoy soldier who was driving his wagon into the press of infantrymen round his wheels and almost under the horses' hooves. 'Look out there! No, you wait a tick! Can't you see the general wants to pass?'

But the convoyman, paying no heed to the title of general, shouted at the soldiers who blocked his way. 'Hi there, boys! Keep to your left! Wait now!'

But the 'boys', shoulder to shoulder with their bayonets interlocking, pushed on over the bridge in one dense mass. Looking down from the parapet, Prince Nesvitsky saw the rapid, noisy little ripples of the Enns chasing each other along as they bubbled and eddied around the piles of the bridge. Looking along the bridge, he saw equally lively waves of soldiery, shoulder-knots, covered shakos, knapsacks, bayonets, long muskets, and under the shakos faces with broad cheek-bones, sunken cheeks, and listless tired expressions, and feet moving through the sticky mud that coated the planks of the bridge. Sometimes among the monotonous waves of infantry, like a fleck of white foam on the ripples of the Enns, an officer in a riding-cloak, with a different type of face from the men's, squeezed his way through; sometimes, like a chip of wood whirling along in the river, a hussar on foot, an orderly or a civilian would be carried across the bridge by the tide of troops; and sometimes, like a log floating downstream, an officers' or company's baggage-wagon, loaded high and covered with leather, would roll across the bridge, hemmed in on all sides.

'Why, it's like a burst dam,' said the Cossack, hopelessly blocked. 'Are there many more of you to come?'

'A million minus one!' replied a cheerful soldier in a torn greatcoat, winking as he passed out of sight. After him came an old soldier.

'If *he*' (*he* was the enemy) 'begins popping at the bridge now,' said the old soldier glumly to a comrade, 'you won't stop to scratch yourself.'

And the soldier passed on. Following him came another, riding on a cart.

'Where the devil did you put the leg-bands?' said an orderly, running behind the cart and rummaging in the back of it.

And he in turn was borne past with the wagon.

Then came some hilarious soldiers who had evidently been drinking.

'And then, my old chum, he ups with the butt of his gun and hits him one in the teeth ...' one of the soldiers was saying gaily, with a wide swing of his arm. He wore his greatcoat tucked up round his waist.

'Yes – that ham was a bit of all right,' answered another with a loud laugh.

And they, too, passed on, so that Nesvitsky did not find out who had been struck in the teeth, or what the ham had to do with it.

'Bah! How they scurry! *He's* only got to fire a blank, and one would think they were all in danger of being killed,' said a sergeant in an angry, reproachful tone.

'When it flew past me – that round shot, I mean,' said a young soldier with an enormous mouth, 'I thought I was done for. It's a fact, 'pon my word, I was that scared!' he added, almost laughing, as if he were proud of having been frightened.

And he, too, tramped by. Next followed a cart unlike any that had gone before. It was a German *Vorspann* drawn by a pair of horses driven by a German, and was loaded with what appeared to be the effects of an entire household. A fine brindled cow with an enormous udder was fastened to the cart behind. On a pile of feather beds sat a woman with a baby at the breast, an old granny, and a healthy young German girl with bright red cheeks. The little party of refugees had no doubt obtained a special permit to pass. The eyes of all the soldiers turned towards the women, and as the cart moved forward at walking pace their remarks were all related to the two young women. Every face wore a practically identical smile born of unseemly thoughts concerning the pair.

'Look, the German sausage is making tracks, too!'

'Sell us the missis,' cried another soldier, addressing the German, who strode along with downcast eyes, angry and frightened.

'See how smart she's made herself! Oh, the little hussies!'

'There now, Fedotov, you ought to be billeted on them!'

'No such luck, old fellow!'

'Where are you off to?' asked an infantry officer who was eating an apple, also half smiling as he looked at the handsome girl.

The German shut his eyes, signifying that he did not understand.

'Have one if you like,' said the officer, giving the girl an apple. She accepted it with a smile.

Nesvitsky, like the rest of the men on the bridge, did not take his eyes off the women till they had passed. When they had gone by, the same stream of soldiers followed, with the same interchange of repartee, until at last they all came to a halt. As often happens, the horses attached to some company's baggage-wagon became restive at the end of the bridge, and the whole crowd was obliged to wait.

'What are we stopping for? There's no proper order!' said the soldiers. 'Where are you shoving to? What the devil! Have patience, can't you? It'll be worse than this when the bridge is set fire to. Look, there's an officer hemmed in too,' different voices were saying in the crowd, as the men looked about them and kept trying to press forward to get off the bridge.

Looking down under the bridge at the waters of the Enns, Nesvitsky suddenly heard a sound that was new to his ears – the sound of something swiftly approaching ... something that splashed into the water.

'I say, look where that one went!' a soldier near by observed gravely, looking round at the sound.

'Encouraging us to get along quicker!' said another uneasily.

The crowd moved on again. Nesvitsky realized it had been a cannon-ball.

'Hey, Cossack, my horse!' he said. 'Now then, you there! Out of the way! Make way there!'

With great difficulty he managed to get to his horse. Shouting continually, he moved forward. The soldiers squeezed back to let him pass, but immediately after pressed on him again so that his leg was jammed, and those nearest him could not help themselves for they were pushed on still more violently from behind.

'Nesvitsky! Nesvitsky! you old fwight!' cried a hoarse voice from the rear.

Nesvitsky looked round and saw, some fifteen paces away but separated from him by the living mass of moving infantry, Vasska Denisov, red, black and shaggy, with his cap on the back of his head and his hussar's cloak jauntily flung over his shoulder.

'Tell these devils, these demons, to give us woom,' shouted Denisov, evidently in a paroxysm of excitement, his coal-black eyes with their bloodshot whites flashing and rolling while he brandished his sheathed sabre in a small bare hand as red as his face.

'Ah, Vasska!' replied Nesvitsky, delighted, 'but what are you doing here?'

'The squadwon can't get thwough!' roared Vasska Denisov, showing his white teeth fiercely and spurring his raven thoroughbred Bedouin. The horse twitched his ears as he brushed against bayonets, and snorted, spurting white foam from his bit, pawing the planks of the bridge with his hooves, and apparently ready to leap over the parapet, if his rider would let him.

'What is this? They're like sheep! Just like sheep! Out of the way! … Make woom! Stop there, you devil with the cart! I'll cut you to pieces!' he shouted, actually drawing his sword from its scabbard and beginning to flourish it.

The soldiers crowded closer together with terrified faces, and Denisov joined Nesvitsky.

'How's it you're not drunk today?' said Nesvitsky when Denisov had ridden up to him.

'They don't give us time to get dwunk,' replied Vasska Denisov. 'The wegiment is dwagged to and fwo all day long. If they mean us to fight, let's fight. But as it is, the devil only knows what we're doing!'

'What a beau you are these days!' said Nesvitsky, looking at Denisov's new cloak and saddle-cloth.

Denisov smiled, pulled out of his sabretache a handkerchief that diffused a smell of scent and thrust it under Nesvitsky's nose.

'Of course! I'm going into action! I've shaved, bwushed my teeth and scented myself!'

Nesvitsky's imposing figure, with his Cossack in attendance, and Denisov's determination as he flourished his sword and shouted at the top of his voice, enabled them to squeeze through to the farther end of the bridge and halt the infantry. At the end of the bridge Nesvitsky found the colonel to whom he had to deliver the command and his errand accomplished he rode back.

Having cleared the way, Denisov reined in his horse at the end of the bridge. Carelessly holding in his stallion who was neighing and pawing the ground, anxious to join his fellows, he watched the squadron approaching him. The hooves rang hollow on the planks of the bridge, sounding like several horses galloping, and the squadron, with the officers riding in front and the men four abreast, spread across the bridge and began to pour off at the other end.

The infantry who had been halted, packed together, in the trampled mud gazed with that peculiar aloof feeling of ill-will and derision with which troops of different arms usually encounter one another at the neat jaunty hussars riding by in regular order.

'Smart, tidy lads! Only fit for a circus!'

'What's the use of them? They're led about just for show!' remarked another.

'Don't kick up the dust, you infantry!' jested a hussar whose prancing horse had spattered a foot soldier with mud.

'I'd like to put you on a two-days' march with a knapsack! Your gold lace would soon get a bit tarnished,' said the infantryman, wiping the mud off his face with his sleeve. 'Perched up there, you're more like a bird than a man.'

'There now, Zikin, they ought to put you on a horse. You'd look fine,' said a corporal, chaffing a thin little soldier stooping under the weight of his knapsack.

'Put a broomstick between your legs and ride-a-cock-horse,' the hussar shouted back.

8

THE rest of the infantry hurriedly crossed the bridge, squeezing together into a funnel at the end. At last all the baggage-wagons were across, the crush became less and the last battalion marched on to the bridge. Only Denisov's squadron of hussars were left on the farther side of the river facing the enemy. The enemy, though plainly visible from the heights opposite, could not as yet be seen from the level of the bridge, since from the valley through which the river flowed the horizon was bounded by rising ground only half a mile away. At the foot of the hill lay waste land dotted here and there with bands of Cossack patrols. Suddenly, on the road at the top of the high ground troops appeared in blue uniform, accompanied by artillery. It was the French. The Cossack patrol retired down the hill at a trot. All the officers and men of Denisov's squadron, though they tried to talk of other things and to look in other directions, thought only of what was there on the hill-top and their eyes constantly turned to the patches coming into sight on the skyline, which they knew to be the enemy's troops. The weather had cleared again since noon, and a brilliant sun was moving westward over the Danube and the dark surrounding hills. There was no wind, and at intervals from that hill-top floated the sound of bugle-calls and the shouts of the enemy. Except for a few scattered skirmishers there was no one now between the squadron and the enemy. An open space of some seven hundred yards was all that separated them. The enemy had ceased firing, and that rigid, ominous gap, unapproachable and intangible, which divides two hostile armies was all the more keenly felt.

'One step beyond that line, which is like the bourne dividing the living from the dead, lies the Unknown of suffering and death. And what is there? Who is there? There beyond that field, beyond that tree, that roof gleaming in the sun? No one knows, but who does not long to know? You fear to cross that line, yet you long to cross it; and you know that sooner or later it will have to be crossed and you will find out what lies there on the other side of the line, just as you will inevitably have to learn what lies the other side of death. But you are strong, healthy, cheerful and excited, and surrounded by other men just as full of health and exuberant spirits.' Such are the sensations, if not the actual thoughts of every man who finds himself confronted by the enemy, and these feelings lend a singular vividness and happy distinctness of impression to everything that takes place at such moments.

A puff of smoke rose from the high ground occupied by the enemy, and a cannon-ball whistled over the heads of the squadron of hussars. The officers, who had been standing together, scattered to their posts. The hussars began carefully aligning their horses. The whole squadron subsided into silence. All looked intently at the enemy in front and at the squadron commander, awaiting the word of command. Another cannon-ball flew by them, and a third. There was no doubt that the enemy was aiming at the hussars but the balls whizzing regularly and rapidly passed over the heads of the horsemen and struck the ground somewhere in the rear. The hussars never looked round but every time they heard the whizz of a ball as though at the word of command the whole squadron with its rows of faces so alike yet so different, holding its breath until the cannon-shot had passed over, rose in the stirrups and sank back again. Without turning their heads the soldiers glanced at one another out of the corners of their eyes, curious to see the effect on their comrades. Every face, from Denisov's to the bugler's, showed around lips and chin one common expression of conflict, excitement and agitation. The quartermaster frowned, and glared at the men as though meditating punishment for them. Cadet Mironov ducked every time a ball flew over. On the left flank Rostov on his Rook, a handsome beast despite its unsound legs – had the happy air of a schoolboy called up before a large audience for an examination in which he feels sure he will distinguish himself. He was glancing round at everyone with a serene, radiant expression, as if asking them to notice how calmly he sat under fire. But into his face too there crept, against his will, that line about the mouth that betrayed something novel and stern.

'Who's bobbing up and down there? Cadet Miwonov? That's not wight! Look at me!' cried Denisov who could not keep still in one place and kept riding to and fro before the squadron.

Vasska Denisov, with his snub nose and black hair, his short stocky figure, his sinewy hands with the stumpy, hairy fingers grasping the hilt of his drawn sword, looked just the same as always, or rather, as he was apt to look especially towards evening after he had emptied his second bottle. He was only a trifle redder in the face than usual, and tossing back his shaggy head, as birds do when they drink, his little legs pitilessly plunging the spurs into the sides of his good Bedouin, he galloped to the other flank of the squadron, sitting as though he were falling backwards in the saddle, and shouted to the men in a husky voice to look to their pistols. He rode up to Kirsten. The staff-captain, on his sedate, broad-backed charger, came at a walking-pace to meet him. The staff-captain's face with its long whiskers was as grave as ever, only his eyes flashed with unwonted brilliance.

'Well,' said he to Denisov, 'it won't come to a fight. You'll see – we shall retire.'

'The deuce knows what they're about!' muttered Denisov. 'Ah, Wostov!' he cried, noticing the cadet's beaming face, 'you've not had long to wait.'

And he smiled approvingly, unmistakably pleased at the sight of the cadet. Rostov felt perfectly happy. Just then the colonel appeared on the bridge. Denisov galloped up to him.

'Your Excellency! Let us attack 'em. I'll dwive them back!'

'Attack indeed!' said the colonel in a peevish voice, puckering up his face as if to shake off a persistent fly. 'And why are you delaying here? Don't you see the scouts are withdrawing? Lead your squadron back.'

The squadron crossed the bridge and passed out of range of the enemy's guns without losing a single man. The second squadron that had been in the line followed them across and the last Cossacks quitted the farther side of the river.

The two squadrons of the Pavlograd regiment after crossing the bridge rode one after the other up the hill. Their colonel, Karl Bogdanich Schubert, had joined Denisov's squadron and was riding at a foot-pace not far from Rostov but without taking the slightest notice of him, though this was the first time they had met since the incident in connexion with Telyanin. Rostov, feeling himself at the front in the power of the man with whom he now admitted that he had been to blame, did not lift his eyes from the colonel's athletic shoulders, the light hair at the back of his head, and his red neck. It seemed to Rostov that Bogdanich was only pretending not to notice him, and that his whole aim now was to test the cadet's courage, so he drew himself up and looked around gaily. Then he fancied that Bogdanich was riding close to him in order to display his own valour.

Next it occurred to him that his opponent would send the squadron into some desperate attack on purpose to punish him, Rostov. And then again, he imagined how after the attack Bogdanich would come up to him as he lay wounded, and magnanimously extend the hand of reconciliation.

Zherkov, whose high shoulders were well known to the Pavlograd Hussars as he had not long left their regiment, rode up to the colonel. After his dismissal from the general staff Zherkov had not remained in the regiment, saying that he was not such a fool as to slave at the front when he could get more pay for doing nothing on the staff, and had succeeded in attaching himself as an orderly-officer to Prince Bagration. He now came to his former chief with a message from the commander of the rearguard.

'Colonel,' said he, with his melancholy air of gravity, addressing Rostov's enemy and glancing round at his comrades, 'there's an order to halt and fire the bridge.'

'An order, *who to*?' asked the colonel grimly.

'Well, I don't know, colonel, *who to*,' replied the cadet gravely, 'only the prince told me to "go and tell the colonel that the hussars are to make haste back and burn the bridge".'

Zherkov was followed by an officer of the suite, who rode up to the colonel of the hussars with the same order. After the officer of the suite Nesvitsky came galloping up on a Cossack horse that could scarcely carry his weight.

'How's this, colonel?' he shouted, while still at a distance. 'I told you to fire the bridge, and now someone has gone and blundered. They're all out of their minds over there, and one can't make head or tail of anything.'

The colonel took his time in halting the regiment, and turned to Nesvitsky.

'You spoke to me about inflammable material,' said he, 'but you never said a word about firing it.'

'But, my dear sir,' exclaimed Nesvitsky as he reined in his horse, taking off his forage-cap and passing his plump hand over his hair which was wet with perspiration, 'wasn't I telling you to fire the bridge when the inflammable material had been put in position?'

'I am not your "dear sir", Mr Staff-officer, and you did not tell me to burn the bridge! I know my duty, and it is my habit orders strictly to obey.' (Bogdanich was a Russo-German who spoke very poor

Russian.) 'You said the bridge would be burnt, but who would burn it, by the Holy Ghost I could not tell ...'

'Ah, that's always the way!' cried Nesvitsky with a wave of the hand. 'What are you doing here?' he asked, turning to Zherkov.

'I am on the same errand. But you *are* wet! Let me give you a wipe.'

'You were saying, Mr Staff-officer ...' pursued the colonel in an aggrieved tone.

'Colonel,' interrupted the officer of the suite, 'there is need of haste, or the enemy will be pouring grape-shot into us.'

The colonel looked dumbly at the officer of the suite, at the stout staff-officer, at Zherkov, and scowled.

'I will the bridge fire,' said he in a solemn voice, as if to announce that in spite of everything they might do to annoy him he would still do his duty.

Spurring his horse with his long, muscular legs, as though the animal were to blame for it all, the colonel moved forward and ordered the second squadron, the one in which Rostov was serving under Denisov, to return to the bridge.

'There, it's just as I thought,' said Rostov to himself. 'He wants to test me!' His heart contracted and the blood rushed to his face. 'Let him see whether I am a coward!' he thought.

Once more, over all the light-hearted faces of the men in the squadron the same serious expression appeared that they had worn when under fire. Rostov, not taking his eyes from his enemy, the colonel, tried to discover in his face confirmation of his conjectures; but the colonel never once glanced at Rostov but gazed ahead solemn and stern as he always was at the front. The word of command rang out.

'Lively now, lively!' several voices repeated around him.

Their sabres catching in the bridles and their spurs jingling, the hussars hastily dismounted, not knowing what they were to do. The soldiers crossed themselves. Rostov no longer looked at the colonel: he had no time for that. He was afraid of falling behind the hussars, so much afraid that his heart stood still. His hand trembled as he turned his horse over to an orderly, and he felt the blood rushing back to his heart with a thud. Denisov rode past him, leaning back and shouting something. Rostov saw nothing save the hussars running by his side, their spurs catching and their sabres clattering.

'Stretchers!' shouted a voice behind him.

Rostov did not think what this call for stretchers meant; he ran on, striving only to be ahead of the others; but just at the bridge, not looking where he was going, he came on some slimy, trodden mud, stumbled, and fell on his hands. The others outstripped him.

'On boss zides, captain,' he heard the voice of the colonel who, having ridden ahead, had reined in his horse not far from the bridge and sat looking on with a triumphant, cheerful face.

Rostov, wiping his muddy hands on his breeches, glanced at his enemy and was about to run on, imagining that the farther forward he went the better. But Bogdanich, though without looking at him, or recognizing that it was Rostov, shouted to him:

'Who is that in the middle of the bridge? Get to the right! Cadet, come back!' he cried angrily, and turned to Denisov, who with swaggering bravado had ridden on to the planks of the bridge.

'Why you run risks, captain? You had better dismount,' said the colonel.

'Oh, every bullet finds its billet,' replied Denisov, turning in his saddle.

*

Meanwhile, Nesvitsky, Zherkov and the officer of the suite were standing together out of range of the enemy's fire, watching now the little band of hussars in yellow shakos, dark green jackets braided with gold lace, and blue riding-breeches, who were swarming about the bridge, and then what was approaching in the distance from the opposite side – the blue uniforms and the groups with horses, easily recognizable as artillery.

'Will they be able to burn the bridge or not? Who'll get there first? Will they be in time to fire the bridge, or will the French train their grape-shot on them and wipe them out?'

These were the questions every man in the main body of troops on the high ground above the bridge involuntarily asked himself with sinking heart, as he watched the bridge and the hussars in the bright evening light, and the blue tunics advancing from the other side with their bayonets and guns.

'Ugh! The hussars will catch it hot!' exclaimed Nesvitsky. 'They're within grape-shot range now.'

'He shouldn't have taken so many men,' said the officer of the suite.

'That's true,' said Nesvitsky. 'Two smart young fellows would have done the job just as well.'

'Ah, your Excellency,' put in Zherkov, his eyes fixed on the hussars though he still spoke with that naïve air of his that made it impossible to guess whether he was in jest or in earnest. 'Ah, your Excellency! What an idea! Send two men? And then who would give us the Vladimir medal and ribbon? But now, even if they do get a peppering, the squadron may be recommended for honours and the colonel receive a ribbon for himself. Our Bogdanich knows a thing or two.'

'There now,' said the officer of the suite. 'Here comes the grape-shot.'

He pointed to the French field-pieces, which were being unlimbered and hurriedly brought into action.

On the French side, amid the groups with cannon, a puff of smoke arose, then a second and a third, almost simultaneously; and by the time the report of the first had reached their ears, the smoke of a fourth was seen. Then two reports, one after another, and a third.

'Oh! Oh!' moaned Nesvitsky, as if in excruciating pain, clutching at the staff-officer's arm. 'Look, a man has fallen! One is down, one fallen!'

'Two, I think?'

'If I were Tsar I would never make war,' said Nesvitsky, turning away.

The French guns were speedily reloaded. The infantry in their blue uniforms advanced towards the bridge at a run. Smoke appeared again, but at irregular intervals, and grape-shot pattered and rattled on the bridge. But this time Nesvitsky could not see what was happening there. A dense cloud of smoke poured from the bridge. The hussars had succeeded in setting fire to it, and the French batteries were now firing at them, no longer to hinder them but because the guns were trained and there was someone to shoot at.

The French had time to send three charges of grape-shot before the hussars got back to their horses. Two were misdirected and the shot went high, but the last round fell in the midst of the group of hussars and hit three of them.

Rostov, preoccupied by his relations with Bogdanich, had paused on the bridge, not knowing what to do. There was no one to hew down (which had always been his idea of a battle), nor could he help to fire the bridge, because he had not provided himself with burning straw like the other soldiers. He was standing there looking about him when suddenly he heard a rattling on the bridge as though someone were scattering hazel nuts, and the hussar nearest him fell against the parapet with a groan. Rostov ran up to him with the others. Again there was a cry of 'Stretchers!' Four men seized the hussar and began lifting him.

'O-o-o-h! For Christ's sake let me be!' shrieked the wounded man, but nevertheless he was lifted and laid on a stretcher.

Nikolai Rostov turned away and, as if searching for something, started to gaze into the distance, at the waters of the Danube, at the sky, at the sun. How beautiful the sky looked, how blue and calm and deep! How brilliant and majestic was the setting sun! How tenderly shone the distant waters of the Danube! And fairer still were the purpling mountains stretching far away beyond the river, the convent, the mysterious gorges, the pine forests veiled in mist to their summits. ... There all was peace and happiness. 'I should wish for nothing, wish for nothing, for nothing in the world, if only I were there,' thought Rostov. 'In myself alone and in that sunshine there is so much happiness, while here ... it is groans, suffering and confusion, hurry. ... Now they are shouting again, and all running back somewhere, and I shall run with the rest, while death, death is all above me and around me. ... A moment more and I shall never see this sun, this river, that gorge again. ...'

At that instant the sun began to hide behind the clouds, and more stretchers came into view ahead of Rostov. And the fear of death and of the stretchers, and love of the sun and of life all merged into one sickening agitation.

'O Lord God! Thou Who art in this heaven, save, forgive and protect me!' Rostov whispered.

The hussars ran back to the men holding their horses. Their voices grew louder and more confident; the stretchers disappeared from sight.

'Well, fwiend? So you've smelt powdah?' shouted Vasska Denisov just above his ear.

'It's all over; but I am a coward – yes, I am a coward,' thought Rostov, and with a heavy sigh he took Rook, who was standing resting one foot, from the orderly and prepared to mount.

'Was that grape-shot?' he asked Denisov.

'It was, and no mistake!' cried Denisov. 'You worked like hewoes.

But it is wascally work! An attack is ware sport, you hew down the dogs! But this sort of thing is the vewy devil, being shot at like a tahget.'

And Denisov rode up to a group that had stopped near Rostov, composed of the colonel, Nesvitsky, Zherkov and the staff-officer.

'I believe no one noticed,' thought Rostov. And this was true: no one had noticed anything, for everyone was familiar with the sensation which the cadet under fire for the first time experienced.

'This will make a fine despatch to send in!' said Zherkov. 'They'll be promoting me sub-lieutenant before I know where I am, eh?'

'Inform the prince that I the bridge fired!' said the colonel triumphantly and gaily.

'And if he inquires about the losses?'

'Not worth mentioning,' growled the colonel in his bass voice. 'A couple of hussars wounded, and one knocked out on the spot,' he added with undisguised cheerfulness, unable to restrain a smile of satisfaction as he sonorously enunciated the words *knocked out*.

9

PURSUED by the French army of a hundred thousand men under the command of Bonaparte, encountering a population that was unfriendly to it, losing confidence in its allies, suffering from shortness of supplies, and forced into action under conditions of war unlike anything that had been foreseen, the Russian army of thirty-five thousand men commanded by Kutuzov was hurriedly retiring along the Danube, stopping when overtaken by the enemy, and fighting rearguard skirmishes only so far as was necessary to ensure their retreat without the loss of their heavy equipment. There had been actions at Lambach, Amstetten and Melk; but despite the courage and endurance – which even the enemy acknowledged – with which the Russians fought, the only consequence of these engagements was a yet more rapid retreat. Austrian troops that had escaped capture at Ulm and had joined Kutuzov at Braunau, now parted from the Russian army, and Kutuzov was left with only his own weak and exhausted forces. It was no longer possible to think of defending Vienna. Instead of an offensive, the plan of which, carefully elaborated in accordance with the new science of strategics, had been communicated to Kutuzov by the Austrian Hofkriegsrath when he was in Vienna, the only thing that remained to him now, unless he were to sacrifice his army as Mack had done at Ulm, was to effect a junction with the fresh troops arriving from Russia, and even this was almost an impossibility.

On the 28th of October Kutuzov and his army crossed to the left bank of the Danube and, for the first time, halted, having now put the river between himself and the main body of the French. On the 30th he attacked and defeated the division under Mortier, which was stationed on the left bank. In this engagement for the first time some trophies were captured: a standard, some cannon, and two enemy generals. For the first time, after retreating for a fortnight, the Russians had halted and at the end of the battle not only held the field but had driven off the French. Though the troops were exhausted and in rags, and the dead, the wounded and sick, and stragglers had reduced their numbers by a third; though some of the sick and wounded had been abandoned on the other side of the Danube with a letter from Kutuzov commending them to the humanity of the enemy; though the big hospitals and the houses of Krems which had been converted into *lazaretti* were unable to accommodate all the sick and wounded remaining – still, in spite of all this, the stand made at Krems and the victory over Mortier raised the spirits of the troops considerably. Throughout the whole army and at headquarters the most gratifying though erroneous reports were rife of the imaginary approach of columns from Russia, of some victory won by the Austrians, and of the panic retreat of Bonaparte.

Prince Andrei during the battle had been in attendance on the Austrian general Schmidt, who was killed in action. He himself had had his horse wounded under him and his hand slightly grazed by a bullet. As a mark of especial favour the commander-in-chief sent him with news of this victory to the Austrian court, now no longer at Vienna (which was threatened by the French) but at Brünn. In spite of his apparently delicate constitution Prince Andrei could endure physical fatigue far better than many very strong men, and on the night of the battle, having arrived at Krems, excited but not weary, with despatches from Dokhturov to Kutuzov, he was sent on immediately with a special despatch to Brünn. Such an errand not only ensured a decoration for the courier but was an important step towards promotion.

The night was dark and starry: the road made a black line across the snow that had fallen the previous day – the day of the engagement.

171

Now reviewing his impressions of the recent battle, now picturing pleasantly the effect he would create with his news of the victory, or recalling the farewells of the commander-in-chief and his fellow-officers, Prince Andrei drove swiftly along in his post-chaise, enjoying the feelings of a man who has at last attained the first instalment of some long-coveted happiness. As soon as he closed his eyes the roar of musketry and cannon filled his ears, mingling with the rumble of wheels and the sensation of victory. He began to dream that the Russians were flying and that he himself was slain. Then he would awake with a start, happy in the realization that nothing of the sort had happened and that, on the contrary, it was the French who had run away. He would again recall all the details of the victory and his own calm courage during the battle and, reassured, doze off again. ... The bright, starlit night was followed by a bright, cheerful morning. The snow was melting in the sunshine, the horses sped swiftly along past varying forests, fields and villages on both sides of the road.

At one of the post-houses he overtook a convoy of Russian wounded. The Russian officer in charge of the transport was lolling in the foremost cart, shouting and berating a soldier with coarse abuse. Six or more white-faced, bandaged, dirty men were being jolted over the stony road in each of the long German wagons. Some of them were talking (Prince Andrei caught the sound of their Russian speech), others were eating their bread, while the more severely wounded gazed dumbly, with the languid interest of sick children, at the courier hurrying past them.

Prince Andrei ordered his driver to stop, and asked one of the soldiers in what action they had been wounded.

'Day before yesterday, on the Danube,' answered the soldier. Prince Andrei took out his purse and gave the man three gold pieces.

'That's for them all,' he said to the officer who came up. 'Get well soon, lads!' he continued, turning to the soldiers. 'There's plenty to do still.'

'What news, sir?' asked the officer, evidently anxious to start a conversation.

'Good news! ... Forward!' he cried to his driver, and they galloped on.

It was quite dark when Prince Andrei reached Brünn and found himself surrounded by lofty buildings, the lighted windows of shops and houses, by street lamps, by fine carriages rumbling over the cobbled streets and all that atmosphere of a large and lively city which is always so fascinating to a soldier after camp life. Despite his hurried journey and sleepless night. Prince Andrei drove up to the palace feeling even more excited and alert than he had the evening before. Only his eyes glittered feverishly, and his thoughts followed one another with extraordinary clearness and rapidity. Vividly, all the details of the battle came into his mind, no longer confused but in due sequence, word for word, as he saw himself stating them to the Emperor Francis. Vividly he imagined the casual questions that might be put to him and the answers he would give. He expected to be presented immediately to the Emperor. But at the principal entrance to the palace an official came running out to meet him and, learning that he was a courier, conducted him to another door.

'To the right at the end of the corridor, your Excellency! There you will find the adjutant on duty,' said the official. 'He will take you to the minister of war.'

The adjutant on duty came to meet Prince Andrei and asked him to wait, and went on to the minister of war. Five minutes later he returned and, bowing with marked courtesy, ushered Prince Andrei before him along a corridor into the room where the minister of war was at work. The adjutant by his extravagant politeness appeared to wish to ward off any attempt at familiarity on the part of the Russian courier. Prince Andrei's exultant feelings were considerably impaired by the time he approached the door of the minister's room. He felt affronted, and this sense of wounded pride instantly and without his noticing it changed into one of disdain for which there was no foundation. His fertile brain at the same moment suggested to him a point of view which gave him the right to despise both the adjutant and the minister of war. 'Gaining victories probably seems easy to them, when they don't know the smell of gunpowder!' he said to himself. His eyes narrowed contemptuously, and he walked into the minister's office with deliberately slow steps. His feeling was still further intensified when he caught sight of the minister of war seated at a large table and for the first two minutes taking no notice of his arrival. The minister's bald head with its fringe of grey hair was bent over some papers which he was reading and marking with a lead pencil. There was a wax candle on each side of the papers, which he finished reading without raising his eyes at the opening of the door and the sound of footsteps.

'Take this and deliver it,' said the minister to his adjutant, handing him the papers and still taking no notice of the courier.

Prince Andrei felt that of all the matters that preoccupied the minister of war the feats of Kutuzov's army either interested him the least, or else he felt obliged to give this impression to the Russian courier. 'Well, it's all the same to me,' he thought. The minister pushed the remaining papers aside, arranged them neatly and looked up. He had an intelligent head full of character but the instant he turned to Prince Andrei the firm, intelligent expression of the minister's face changed in a manner which was evidently habitual and deliberate, and took on the stupid, artificial smile – which does not even attempt to hide its artificiality – of a man who is continually receiving many petitioners one after another.

'From General Field-Marshal Kutuzov?' he queried. 'I hope it is good news? There has been an encounter with Mortier? A victory? It is high time.'

He took the despatch, which was addressed to him, and began to read it with a melancholy expression.

'Ach, my God, my God! Schmidt!' he exclaimed in German. 'What a misfortune! What a misfortune!'

Having skimmed through the despatch he laid it on the table and raised his eyes to Prince Andrei, evidently meditating something.

'Ach, what a misfortune! The affair, you say, was decisive? But Mortier was not taken.' He pondered. 'I am very glad you have brought good news, though the death of Schmidt is a heavy price to pay for the victory. His Majesty will no doubt wish to see you, but not today. I thank you. Go and get rested. Be at the levée tomorrow after the review. However, I will have you informed.'

The stupid smile, which had disappeared while he was speaking, reappeared on the minister's face.

'Au revoir. I thank you indeed. His Majesty will probably wish to see you,' he repeated, and inclined his head.

Prince Andrei left the palace feeling that he had abandoned all the interest and happiness afforded him by the victory into the indifferent hands of the minister of war and the polite adjutant. The whole tenor of his thoughts changed instantaneously: the battle figured in his mind as a remote, far-away memory.

PRINCE ANDREI put up at Brünn with a Russian acquaintance of his, Bilibin, the diplomat.

'Ah, my dear prince! I could not have a more welcome visitor,' said Bilibin, as he came out to greet Prince Andrei. 'Franz, put the prince's things in my bedroom,' said he to the servant who was ushering Bolkonsky in. 'So you're the messenger of victory, eh? Splendid! For my part, I am kept indoors ill, as you see.'

Having washed and changed, Prince Andrei walked into the diplomat's luxurious study and sat down to the dinner which had been prepared for him. Bilibin settled himself comfortably beside the fire.

After his journey and the whole campaign during which he had been deprived of all the conveniences of cleanliness and all the refinements of life, Prince Andrei experienced an agreeable feeling of repose among luxurious surroundings such as he had been accustomed to from childhood. Moreover, it was pleasant after his reception by the Austrians to talk, not indeed in Russian, for they were speaking French, but at least with a Russian who would, he supposed, share the general Russian aversion (which was then particularly strong) for the Austrians.

Bilibin was a man of five and thirty, a bachelor, who belonged to the same set as Prince Andrei. They had known each other previously in Petersburg, but had become more intimate during Prince Andrei's last stay in Vienna with Kutuzov. Just as Prince Andrei was a young man who gave promise of rising high in the military profession, so Bilibin promised to do even better in the diplomatic service. He was still a young man but no longer a young diplomat, since he had begun his career at the age of sixteen, had served in Paris and Copenhagen, and now held a fairly important post in Vienna. Both the chancellor and our ambassador in Vienna knew him and prized him highly. He was not one of that great multitude of diplomats whose merits are limited to the possession of negative qualities, who have only to avoid doing certain things, and to speak French in order to be considered good diplomats. He was one of those who like and know how to work, and notwithstanding his natural indolence would sometimes spend the whole night at his writing-table. He put in equally good work whatever the nature of the matter in hand. It was the question

'How?' that interested him, not the question 'What for?' He did not care what the diplomatic business was about, but found the greatest satisfaction in preparing a circular, memorandum or report skilfully, pointedly and elegantly. Bilibin's services were valued not only for the labours of his pen but also for his talent for dealing and conversing with those in the highest spheres.

Bilibin enjoyed conversation, just as he enjoyed work, only when it could be made elegantly witty. In society he was always on the watch for an opportunity to say something striking, and took part in a conversation only when this was possible. His talk was always plentifully sprinkled with amusingly original and polished phrases of general interest. These sayings were elaborated beforehand in the alembic of his mind as if intentionally in a portable form easy for even the dullest member of society to remember and carry from salon to salon. And in fact Bilibin's witticisms were hawked round the Viennese drawing-rooms and were often not without influence on matters that were considered important.

His thin, worn, sallow face was covered with deep wrinkles, which always looked as clean and well-washed as the tips of one's fingers after a bath. The movement of these wrinkles made up the principal play of expression of his countenance. Sometimes it was his forehead that would pucker into deep folds and his eyebrows lift, sometimes his eyebrows would drop and heavy furrows crease his cheeks. His deep-set little eyes always looked out frankly and twinkled.

'Well, now, tell us about your exploits,' said he.

Bolkonsky, very modestly and without once mentioning himself, described the engagement and his reception by the minister of war.

'I got as much welcome as a dog in a game of skittles,' he said in conclusion.

Bilibin smiled and the wrinkles on his face relaxed.

'However, my dear fellow,' he remarked, examining his nails at a distance and wrinkling the skin above his left eye, 'with all my respect for the *Orthodox Russian army*, I must say that your victory was not particularly victorious.'

He continued in this fashion, talking in French and introducing Russian words only when he wished to give scornful emphasis

'Come now! With all your weight of numbers you fell on the unfortunate Mortier and his one division, and even then Mortier slips through your fingers! Where's the victory?'

'No, but seriously,' said Prince Andrei, 'at least we may say without boasting that it was rather better than at Ulm ...'

'Why didn't you capture one, just one, marshal for us?'

'Because things don't always turn out as forecast or go with the smoothness of a parade. We had expected, as I told you, to be at their rear by seven o'clock in the morning, but we did not arrive there until five of the afternoon.'

'And why didn't you reach them at seven in the morning? You ought to have reached them at seven in the morning,' said Bilibin, smiling. 'You ought to have been there at seven in the morning.'

'Why didn't you succeed in impressing on Bonaparte through diplomatic channels that he had better leave Genoa alone?' retorted Prince Andrei in the same tone.

'I know,' interrupted Bilibin, 'you're thinking that it's very easy to capture marshals, sitting on a sofa by one's fireside. That is true, but still why didn't you take him? And don't be surprised if not only the minister of war but also the most august Emperor and King Francis is not particularly jubilant over your victory. Why, even I, a poor secretary of the Russian Embassy, feel no especial joy ...'

He looked straight at Prince Andrei and suddenly the wrinkled skin on his forehead smoothed out.

'Now it is my turn to ask "why?", *mon cher*,' said Bolkonsky. 'I confess I cannot understand – perhaps there are diplomatic subtleties here beyond my feeble intellect, but I can't make it out: Mack loses a whole army, while the Archduke Ferdinand and the Archduke Karl give no sign of life and make one blunder after another. Kutuzov alone at last gains a real victory and breaks the French spell, and the minister of war is not even interested enough to inquire after the details!'

'That's just it, my dear fellow! Don't you see – it's hurrah for the Tsar, for Russia, for the Faith! All very fine and good, but what do we, the Austrian court, I mean, care for your victories? Bring us nice news of a victory by the Archduke Karl or Ferdinand – one archduke's as good as another, as you know – if it's only a victory over a fire-brigade of Bonaparte's, and it will be quite another story, to be proclaimed by a salute of guns! But this sort of thing can only annoy. The Archduke Karl does nothing, the Archduke Ferdinand covers himself with disgrace; you abandon Vienna, give up its defence, as much as to say, God is on our side and the devil take you and your capital! The one general we all loved – Schmidt – you put in the way of a bullet, and then expect compliments on a victory! ... Confess that more exasperating news than yours could not have been conceived. It's as if it had been done on purpose, on purpose. Besides, even if you had won the most brilliant victory, supposing even the Archduke Karl had won a victory, what difference would it make to the general course of events ? It's too late now, with Vienna occupied by the French army.'

'What ? Occupied ? Vienna occupied ?'

'Not only occupied, but Bonaparte is at Schönbrunn, and the count, our dear Count Vrbna, goes to him for orders.'

After the fatigues and impressions of his journey, after his reception and especially after having dined, Bolkonsky felt that he could not take in the full significance of the words he heard.

'This morning Count Lichtenfels was here,' continued Bilibin, 'and showed me a letter containing a circumstantial account of the parade of the French in Vienna, with Prince Murat and the whole bag of tricks. ... So you see, your victory is not such a great matter for rejoicing, and you can't be received as a saviour ...'

'Really I don't care about that, I don't care at all!' said Prince Andrei, beginning to understand that his news of the battle before Krems was in fact of small importance in view of such events as the fall of Austria's capital. 'However did Vienna come to be taken ? What of the bridge and the famous bridge-head, and Prince Auersperg? We heard reports that Prince Auersperg was defending Vienna,' said he.

'Prince Auersperg is on this, on our side of the Danube, and is defending us – doing it pretty badly, I think, but still defending us. But Vienna is on the other side. No, the bridge has not yet been taken, and I hope it will not be, for it is mined and orders have been given to blow it up. Otherwise, we should long ago have been in the mountains of Bohemia, and you and your army would have spent an unpleasant quarter of an hour between two fires.'

'But still this does not mean that the campaign is over,' said Prince Andrei.

'Well, I believe it is. And so do the bigwigs here, though they dare not say so. It will be just as I foretold at the beginning of the campaign: your skirmish at Dürenstein will not settle the affair, nor will gunpowder decide the matter, but those who invented it,' said Bilibin, quoting one of his own *mots*, releasing the wrinkles on his forehead and pausing. 'The only question is what the meeting in Berlin between the Emperor Alexander and the King of Prussia may bring forth. If Prussia joins the alliance, Austria's hand will be forced and there will be war. But if not, it will merely be a matter of settling where the preliminaries of a second Campo Formio are to be drawn up.'

'But what an extraordinary genius!' Prince Andrei suddenly exclaimed, clenching his small fist and pounding the table with it. 'And what luck the man has!'

'Buonaparte?' said Bilibin inquiringly, knitting his brow to indicate that he was about to say something witty. 'Buonaparte?' he repeated, accentuating the *u*. 'I certainly think now that he is laying down laws for Austria from Schönbrunn we must relieve him of that *u*. I am firmly resolved on an innovation, and call him simply Bonaparte!'

'No, joking apart,' said Prince Andrei. 'Do you really think the campaign is over?'

'This is what I think. Austria has been made a fool of, and she is not used to that. And she will retaliate. And she has been fooled in the first place because her provinces have been pillaged – they say the *Orthodox Russian troops* are terrible looters – her army is beaten, her capital taken, and all this for the beautiful eyes of his Sardinian majesty. And therefore – this is between ourselves, *mon cher* – my instinct tells me that we are being deceived; my instinct tells me of negotiations with France and projects for peace, a secret peace, concluded separately.'

'Impossible!' cried Prince Andrei. 'That would be too base.'

'Time will show,' said Bilibin, letting the creases run off his forehead again as a sign that the conversation was at an end.

When Prince Andrei went to the room prepared for him and stretched himself in a clean nightshirt on the feather bed with its warmed and fragrant pillows he began to feel that the battle of which he had brought tidings was far, far away. The alliance with Prussia, Austria's treachery, Bonaparte's new triumph, tomorrow's parade and levée, and his audience with the Emperor Francis occupied his mind.

He closed his eyes, but instantly the roar of cannon, of musketry, and the rattling of carriage wheels sounded in his ears, and now once more the musketeers were descending the hill-side in a thin line, and the French were firing, and he felt his heart palpitating as he rode forward beside Schmidt with the bullets merrily whistling all around, and he experienced tenfold the joy of living, as he had not done since childhood.

He woke up. ...

'Yes, that all happened!' he said, and smiling happily to himself like a child he fell into a deep, youthful slumber.

II

NEXT morning he woke late. Recalling his recent impressions, the first thought that came into his mind was that today he was to be presented to the Emperor Francis; he remembered the minister of war, the extravagantly polite Austrian adjutant, Bilibin, and last night's conversation. Having dressed for his attendance at court in full parade uniform, which he had not worn for a long time, he went down to Bilibin's study fresh, full of spirits and handsome, with his arm in a sling. In the study were four gentlemen of the diplomatic corps. With Prince Hippolyte Kuragin, who was a secretary at the embassy, Bolkonsky was already acquainted. Bilibin introduced him to the others.

The gentlemen assembled at Bilibin's were wealthy, gay young society men, who here, as in Vienna, formed an exclusive circle which Bilibin, their leader, called *les nôtres*. This set, consisting almost without exception of diplomats, evidently had its own interests having nothing to do with war or politics but related to the doings of society, their intimacies with certain women, and to the official side of the service. These gentlemen received Prince Andrei as one of themselves, (an honour they did not extend to many). Out of politeness and to break the ice, they asked him a few questions about the army and the battle, and then the conversation quickly drifted back into inconsequential, merry sallies of wit and gossip.

'But the best of it was,' said one, relating a disaster that had befallen a fellow diplomat, 'the best of it was that the chancellor told him flatly that his appointment to London was a promotion, and that he was to regard it so. Can you imagine his face at that?'

'Worse than that, gentlemen – I am giving Kuragin away to you – here is this Don Juan going to profit by his misfortune: he's a shocking fellow!'

Prince Hippolyte was lolling in an easy chair, his legs thrown over the arm. He laughed.

'Come, come!' said he.

'Oh, you Don Juan! Oh, you serpent!' cried various voices.

'You don't know, Bolkonsky,' said Bilibin turning to Prince Andrei, 'that all the atrocities committed by the French army (I almost said the Russian army) are nothing compared to what this man has been doing among the women!'

'Woman is the companion of man,' announced Prince Hippolyte, and began staring through his eyeglass at his raised legs.

Bilibin and *les nôtres* roared with laughter as they looked in Hippolyte's eyes. Prince Andrei saw that this Hippolyte, of whom – he could not disguise it from himself – he had so nearly been jealous on his wife's account, was the butt of the circle.

'Oh, I must give you a treat with Kuragin,' Bilibin whispered to Bolkonsky. 'He's exquisite when he discusses politics – you should see his gravity!'

He sat down beside Hippolyte and wrinkling his forehead began talking about politics. Prince Andrei and the others gathered round the pair.

'The Berlin cabinet cannot express its opinion concerning an alliance,' began Hippolyte, gazing round with importance from one to the other, 'without expressing ... as in its last note ... you understand ... you understand ... and then if his Majesty the Emperor does not waive the principle of our alliance ...

'Wait, I have not finished ...' said he to Prince Andrei, seizing him by the arm. 'I believe that intervention will be stronger than nonintervention. And ...' he paused. 'The non-receipt of our despatch of November the 28th cannot be counted conclusive. That is how it will all end.'

And he let go of Bolkonsky's arm to indicate that he had now quite finished.

'Demosthenes, I know thee by the pebble thou secretest in thy golden mouth!' said Bilibin, his thick thatch of hair moving forward on his head with satisfaction.

Everybody laughed, and Hippolyte louder than any of them. He was visibly distressed, and breathed painfully, but could not restrain the wild laughter that convulsed his usually impassive features.

'Now then, gentlemen,' said Bilibin. 'Bolkonsky is my guest here in Brünn, and I want to entertain him, to the best of my ability, with all the attractions of our life here. If we were in Vienna it would be easy enough, but in this beastly Moravian hole it is more difficult, and I beg you all to help me. We must do him the honours of Brünn. You can undertake the theatre, I will introduce him to society, and you, Hippolyte, the women, of course.'

'We ought to let him see Amélie, she's a charmer!' said one of *les nôtres*, kissing his finger-tips.

'Altogether, this bloodthirsty soldier must have his attention turned to more humane interests,' said Bilibin.

'I shall scarcely be able to avail myself of your hospitality, gentlemen: it is already time I was off,' replied Bolkonsky, glancing at his watch.

'Where to?'

'To the Emperor.'

'Oh! Oh! Oh!'

'Well, *au revoir*, Bolkonsky! *Au revoir*, prince! Come back early to dinner,' cried several voices. 'We are taking you in hand.'

'Try to extol the work of the commissariat and the planning of routes when you are speaking to the Emperor,' said Bilibin, accompanying Bolkonsky as far as the hall.

'I should like to say flattering things of them, but as far as I know the facts I can't,' replied Bolkonsky with a smile.

'Well, do as much of the talking as you can, anyway. Audiences are his passion but he doesn't like talking himself and never has a word to say, as you will find out.'

12

AT the levée the Emperor Francis merely looked intently into Prince Andrei's face and nodded his long head to him as he stood in the place assigned to him among the Austrian officers. But after the levée the adjutant he had seen the previous day ceremoniously informed Bolkonsky of the Emperor's desire to grant him an audience. The Emperor Francis received him standing in the middle of the room. Prince Andrei was struck by the fact that before beginning the conversation the Emperor seemed embarrassed and did not know what to say, and was blushing.

182

'Tell me, when did the battle begin?' he asked hurriedly.

Prince Andrei told him. This question was followed by others no less simple: 'Was Kutuzov well? How long was it since he left Krems?' and so on. The Emperor spoke as though his sole aim were to put a given number of questions – the answers to which, as was only too evident, could have no interest for him.

'At what o'clock did the engagement begin?' asked the Emperor.

'I cannot inform your Majesty at which o'clock the fighting began in the front lines, but at Dürenstein, where I happened to be, our army made the first attack after five in the afternoon,' replied Bolkonsky, growing more animated and supposing that now he would have a chance to enter into the accurate account, which he had ready in his mind, of all he knew and had seen. But the Emperor smiled and interrupted him.

'How many miles is it?'

'From where to where, your Majesty?'

'From Dürenstein to Krems.'

'Three and a half miles, your Majesty.'

'The French abandoned the left bank?'

'According to our scouts, the last of them crossed on rafts during the night.'

'Have you enough forage at Krems?'

'Forage had not been supplied to the extent ...'

The Emperor interrupted him.

'At what o'clock was General Schmidt killed?'

'At seven o'clock, I believe.'

'At seven o'clock? Very sad! Very sad!'

The Emperor said that he thanked him, and bowed. Prince Andrei withdrew and was immediately surrounded by courtiers on all sides. Everywhere he saw friendly eyes gazing at him and heard friendly voices addressing him. Yesterday's adjutant reproached him for not having stayed at the palace, and offered him his own house. The minister of war came up and congratulated him on the Maria Theresa Order of the third class, with which the Emperor was presenting him. The Empress's chamberlain invited him to wait upon her Majesty. The Archduchess, too, wished to see him. He did not know whom to answer and it took him several seconds to collect his wits. The Russian ambassador put a hand on his shoulder, drew him to the window and began to talk to him.

Contrary to Bilibin's prognostications, the news brought by Bolkonsky was hailed with rejoicing. A thanksgiving service was arranged, the Grand Cross of Maria Theresa was conferred on Kutuzov, and the whole army received awards. Bolkonsky was overwhelmed with invitations and had to spend the whole morning calling on the principal dignitaries of Austria. Between four and five in the afternoon, having paid all his visits, he was returning homewards to Bilibin's mentally composing a letter to his father about the battle and his reception at Brünn. On his way back to Bilibin's Prince Andrei had stepped into a bookshop to provide himself with some books for the campaign, and had spent some time there. At the steps of Bilibin's house stood a vehicle half full of luggage, and Franz, Bilibin's man, with some difficulty dragging a travelling-trunk was coming out of the door.

'What's this?' asked Bolkonsky.

'Ach, your Excellency!' said Franz, struggling to tumble the trunk into the cart. 'We are to move on. The scoundrel is at our heels again!'

'Eh? What?' queried Prince Andrei.

Bilibin came out to meet Bolkonsky. His ordinarily composed face betrayed excitement.

'There now, you must confess that this is a pretty business,' said he. 'This affair of the Tabor bridge – the bridge at Vienna. They are across, and not a shot fired!'

Prince Andrei could not understand.

'But where have you been that you don't know what every coachman in town has heard by now?'

'I come from the Archduchess. I heard nothing there.'

'And didn't you see that people are packing up everywhere?'

'No, I didn't. ... What is it all about?' inquired Prince Andrei impatiently.

'What is it all about? Why, the French have crossed the bridge that Auersperg was defending, and the bridge was not blown up: so Murat is at this moment rushing along the road to Brünn, and today or tomorrow they'll be here.'

'What do you mean – here? And how is it the bridge wasn't blown up, since it was mined?'

'That's what I ask you. No one – not Bonaparte himself – knows why.'

Bolkonsky shrugged his shoulders.

'But if the bridge is crossed it means it's all over with the army: it will be cut off,' said he.

'That's just it,' replied Bilibin. 'Listen! The French enter Vienna, as I told you. Very well. Next day, which was yesterday, *messieurs les maréchaux* Murat, Lannes, and Belliard get on their horses and ride down to the bridge. (Observe that all three are Gascons.) "Gentlemen," says one, "you are aware that the Tabor bridge is mined and counter-mined, and is protected by formidable fortifications and fifteen thousand troops with orders to blow up the bridge and not let us cross? But our Sovereign Emperor Napoleon will be pleased if we take this bridge. So let the three of us go and take the bridge." "Yes, let's!" say the others. And off they go and take the bridge, cross it and now with their whole army are on this side of the Danube, marching on us, on you, and on your lines of communication.'

'Stop jesting,' said Prince Andrei sadly and gravely.

The news grieved him and yet it gave him pleasure. As soon as he heard that the Russian army was in such a hopeless situation, the idea occurred to him that it was he who was destined to extricate it from that situation – that this was his Toulon that would lift him from the ranks of obscure officers and open to him the path to glory! As he listened to Bilibin he was already picturing himself arriving at the camp, and there, at a council of war, giving an opinion that alone could save the army, and how he would be entrusted personally to execute the plan.

'Stop jesting,' said he.

'I am not jesting,' Bilibin went on. 'Nothing could be truer or more melancholy. These gentlemen ride on to the bridge without escort, and wave white handkerchiefs. They assure the officer on duty that it's a truce and that they, the marshals, are come for a parley with Prince Auersperg. The officer on duty lets them enter the *tête de pont*. They spin him a thousand Gascon absurdities, saying that the war is over, that the Emperor Francis has arranged a meeting with Bona-parte, that they desire to see Prince Auersperg, and so on. The officer sends for Auersperg; these gentlemen embrace the officers, crack jokes, sit about on the cannons, while a French battalion meantime advances unnoticed on to the bridge, flings the bags with the incen-diary material into the river, and marches up to the fortifications. Finally the lieutenant-general, our dear Prince Auersperg von Mau-tern himself, appears on the scene. "My dear enemy! Flower of

Austrian chivalry, hero of the Turkish wars! Hostilities are at an end, we can take each other's hands. ... The Emperor Napoleon burns with impatience to make Prince Auersperg's acquaintance." In short, these gentlemen, who are not Gascons for nothing, so bewilder Auersperg with fair words – he is so flattered by this speedy intimacy with French marshals, so dazzled by the spectacle of their cloaks and Murat's ostrich plumes – that their fire gets into his eyes and he quite forgets that he ought to be firing away at the enemy.' (In spite of the *élan* of his remarks, Bilibin did not omit to pause after this witticism, to allow Bolkonsky time to appreciate it.) 'The French battalion rushes to the bridge-head, spikes the guns and the bridge is taken! But this is the best of all,' he went on, his excitement subsiding under the fascination of his own story, '– the sergeant in charge of the cannon which was to give the signal for firing the mines and blowing up the bridge, this sergeant seeing the French troops running on to the bridge was on the point of firing when Lannes pulled his arm away. The sergeant, who seems to have had more sense than his general, goes up to Auersperg and says: "Prince, you are being deceived, here are the French!" Murat sees the game is up if the sergeant is allowed to have his say. With feigned astonishment (he is a true Gascon) he turns to Auersperg and observes: "Is this your world-famous Austrian discipline – do you permit a man from the ranks to address you like that?" It was a stroke of genius. Prince Auersperg feels his dignity at stake and has the sergeant put under arrest. Come, you must own that all this story of the Tabor bridge is sheer delight. It was not exactly stupidity, nor was it dastardly ...'

'Perhaps it is treason, though,' said Prince Andrei, vividly seeing in his imagination the grey greatcoats, the wounds, the smoke of gunpowder, the sounds of firing and the glory that awaited him.

'Not that either. This puts the court into a sorry pickle,' continued Bilibin. 'It's not treason, or dastardliness, or stupidity: it's the same as at Ulm ... it is ...' – he seemed to be trying to find a suitable expression. 'It's ... *c'est du Mack*. We've been Macked,' he concluded, feeling that he had coined a word, a new word that would be repeated. His hitherto puckered brow became smooth in token of his satisfaction, and with a faint smile on his lips he fell to contemplating his finger-nails.

'Where are you going?' he said, suddenly turning to Prince Andrei, who had risen and was making for his room.

'I'm off.'

'Where to?'

'To the army.'

'But you meant to stay another couple of days, didn't you?'

'Yes, but now I am off at once.'

And Prince Andrei, after giving directions about his departure, went to his room.

'Do you know, my dear fellow,' said Bilibin, coming into his room, 'I have been thinking about you. What are you going for?'

And in support of the irrefutability of his argument all the creases ran off his face.

Prince Andrei looked inquiringly at him and made no reply.

'Why are you going? I know you think it is your duty to gallop back to the army now that the army is in danger. I understand that, my dear fellow, it's heroic.'

'Nothing of the kind,' said Prince Andrei.

'But you are *un philosophe*, so be a complete one: look at things from the other side, and you will see that your duty, on the contrary, is to take care of yourself. Leave it to others who are not fit for anything else. ... You have had no orders to return and you have not been dismissed from here; therefore you can stay and go with us wherever our unhappy lot carries us. They say we are going to Olmütz. And Olmütz is a very decent little town. And you and I can make the journey very comfortably in my calèche.'

'Do stop jesting, Bilibin,' cried Bolkonsky.

'I am speaking to you sincerely, as a friend. Consider. Where and why are you going, when you might remain here? One of two things will happen' (here he puckered the skin over his left temple): 'either peace will be concluded before you can reach your regiment, or else defeat and disgrace await you with the rest of Kutuzov's army.'

And Bilibin let his brow go smooth again, feeling that his logic was incontestable.

'I cannot argue about it,' replied Prince Andrei coldly, but he was thinking: 'I am going to save the army.'

'My dear fellow, you are a hero!' said Bilibin.

THAT same night, after taking leave of the minister of war, Bolkonsky set off to rejoin the army, though he did not know where he would find it and was fearful of being captured by the French on the way to Krems.

In Brünn everybody attached to the court was packing up, and the heavy baggage was already being despatched to Olmütz. Near Etzelsdorf Prince Andrei struck the high road along which the Russian army was moving with the utmost haste and in the greatest disorder. The road was so encumbered with carts that progress by carriage was impossible. Prince Andrei procured a horse and a Cossack from the officer in command of the Cossacks, and hungry and weary, threading his way past the baggage-wagons, rode in search of the commander-in-chief and of his own luggage. He heard the most sinister reports of the position of the army as he went along, and the appearance of the troops fleeing in disorder confirmed these rumours.

'As for that Russian army which English gold has brought from the ends of the universe – we shall see that it meets the same fate as met the army at Ulm.' He remembered these words from Bonaparte's address to his army at the opening of the campaign, and they inspired in him admiration for the man's genius, together with a feeling of wounded pride and a hope of glory. 'And should there be nothing left but to die?' he said to himself. 'Well, I shall know how to die, and no worse than the next man, if I must.'

Prince Andrei looked disdainfully at the endless confusion of detachments, baggage-wagons, field-pieces, artillery, baggage-wagons again, and still more baggage-wagons and carts of every possible description, overtaking one another and jamming the muddy road, three and four abreast. On every side, behind and before, as far as the ear could hear there was the creaking of wheels, the rumble of wagons, carts, and gun-carriages, the tramp of hooves, the cracking of whips, the shouts of drivers urging on their horses, the cursing of soldiers, orderlies and officers. Lying by the sides of the road were the carcases of dead horses, some flayed, some not, and broken-down carts beside which solitary soldiers sat waiting for something; then again he saw soldiers straying from the main column and hastening in bands to the neighbouring villages or returning from them dragging fowls, sheep, hay or bulging sacks. At each slope, up or down, of the road the crowds packed closer and the din of shouting was more incessant. Soldiers floundering knee-deep in mud pulled at the guns and wagons themselves. Whips cracked, hooves slipped, traces gave way and lungs were split with yelling. The officers directing the retreat rode back and forth among the wagons. Their voices were but feebly audible amid the general uproar and their faces betrayed their despair of being able to check the chaos.

'*Voilà* our precious Orthodox Russian army,' thought Bolkonsky, remembering Bilibin's words.

Wishing to find out where the commander-in-chief was, he rode up to a convoy. Directly opposite him came a strange one-horse vehicle, evidently rigged up by soldiers out of any available materials and looking like a cross between a cart, a cabriolet and a calèche. A soldier was driving it, and a woman enveloped in shawls sat behind the apron under the leather hood of the conveyance. Prince Andrei rode up and was just putting his question to the soldier when his attention was diverted by the desperate shrieks of the woman sitting in the vehicle. An officer in charge of the convoy was beating her driver for trying to pass ahead of the others, and the blows of his whip lashed the apron of the equipage. The woman screamed piercingly. Seeing Prince Andrei she leaned out from behind the apron, and waving her thin arms from under the woollen shawls cried:

'Aide-de-camp. Mr Aide-de-camp! ... For God's sake. ... Protect me. ... Whatever will become of us? ... I am the doctor's wife – the doctor of the 7th Chasseurs. ... They won't let us through: we have been left behind and have lost our party ...'

'I'll flatten you flatter than a pancake!' shouted the angry officer to the soldier. 'Turn back with your slut!'

'Mr Aide-de-camp, help me! What are they going to do with us?' screamed the doctor's wife.

'Kindly let this cart pass. Don't you see there's a woman in it?' said Prince Andrei riding up to the officer.

The officer glanced at him and without replying addressed the soldier again. 'I'll teach you. ... Back!'

'Let them pass, I tell you!' repeated Prince Andrei, compressing his lips.

'And who are you?' cried the officer, suddenly turning upon him in a drunken fury. 'Who do you think *you* are? Are *you*' (he put a

peculiarly offensive intonation into the word) 'in command, pray?
I am commander here, not you! Back there, or I'll flatten you
flatter'n a pancake,' he repeated, the expression having evidently
taken his fancy.

'A proper snub for the little adjutant,' said a voice behind.

Prince Andrei saw that the officer was in one of those paroxysms of
drunken fury in which a man does not recollect what he says. He
realized that his championship of the doctor's wife in her odd trap
might expose him to what he dreaded more than anything in the
world – ridicule – but instinct urged him on. Before the officer had
time to finish what he was saying, Prince Andrei, his face distorted
with rage, rode up to him and raised his riding-whip.

'Kind – ly – let – them – pass!'

The officer flourished his arm in an angry gesture and hastily rode
away.

'It's all because of these staff-officers that there's all this disorder,' he
muttered. 'Have it your own way.'

Prince Andrei, without lifting his eyes, made haste to escape from
the doctor's wife, who was hailing him as her deliverer, and dwelling
with disgust on the minutest details of this humiliating scene he can-
tered on towards the village where he was told that he would find
his commander-in-chief.

On reaching the village he dismounted and went to the nearest
house, intending to rest, if only for a minute, eat something, and try
to sort out the mortifying thoughts that tormented his mind. 'This
is a mob of scoundrels, not an army,' he thought, going up to the
window of the first house, when a familiar voice called him by name.

Looking round, he saw Nesvitsky's handsome face thrust out of a
little window. Nesvitsky, chewing something between his moist lips,
was waving and calling him in.

'Bolkonsky! Bolkonsky! Can't you hear? Come on in quickly!'
he shouted.

Entering the house, Prince Andrei found Nesvitsky and another
adjutant having a meal. They turned round eagerly asking if he had
any news. He read agitation and alarm on their familiar features, particularly on Nesvitsky's usually laughing face.

'Where is the commander-in-chief?' asked Bolkonsky.

'Here, in that house over there,' answered the adjutant.

'Tell us, is it true about the peace and capitulation?' asked Nesvitsky.

'I was going to ask you that. I know nothing except that it was all I could do to get here.'

'And look at the plight we're in! Awful! I own it was wrong – we laughed at Mack, but here we are doing even worse,' said Nesvitsky. 'But sit down and have some food.'

'You won't find your baggage or anything else now, prince. And God only knows what has become of your man Piotr,' said the other adjutant.

'Where are headquarters?'

'We are to spend the night in Znaim.'

'Well, I've got all I need into packs for two horses,' said Nesvitsky; 'and capital packs they made for me – I could cross the mountains of Bohemia with them. We're in a bad way, brother. But, I say, you must be ill, shivering like that,' he added, noticing Prince Andrei wince violently.

'It's nothing,' replied Prince Andrei. He had just remembered his recent encounter with the doctor's wife and the convoy officer.

'What is the commander-in-chief doing here?' he asked.

'I haven't the least idea,' said Nesvitsky.

'Well, all I can make out is that everything is abominable, absolutely abominable,' said Prince Andrei, and started for the house where the commander-in-chief was.

Passing by Kutuzov's carriage and the exhausted saddle-horses of his suite, with their Cossacks vociferating loudly together, Prince Andrei entered the passage. Kutuzov himself, he was told, was inside with Prince Bagration and Weierother. Weierother was the Austrian general who had succeeded Schmidt. In the passage little Kozlovsky was squatting on his heels in front of a copying-clerk. The clerk, with cuffs rolled back, was writing rapidly, using a tub turned bottom upwards as a table. Kozlovsky's face looked worn – he too had evidently not slept all night. He cast a glance at Prince Andrei and did not even nod to him.

'Second line.... Have you written that?' he continued dictating to the clerk. 'The Kiev Grenadiers, the Podolian ...'

'Not so fast, your Honour,' said the clerk, glancing up at Kozlovsky in a rude, surly fashion.

Through the door came the sound of Kutuzov's voice, excited and impatient, interrupted by another, an unfamiliar voice. The sound of these two voices, the preoccupied way in which Kozlovsky had glanced at him, the disrespectful manner of the harassed clerk, the fact that the clerk and Kozlovsky were sitting round a tub on the floor at so little distance from the commander-in-chief, and the noisy laughter of the Cossacks holding the horses outside the window – all made Prince Andrei feel that some grave calamity was hanging over them.

He turned to Kozlovsky with urgent questions.

'In a moment, prince,' said Kozlovsky. 'These are the dispositions for Bagration.'

'But the capitulation?'

'There is no such thing. Orders are issued for a battle.'

Prince Andrei moved towards the door of the room from which the voices were heard. But just as he was going to open it there was silence, the door opened and Kutuzov with his aquiline nose and puffy face appeared on the threshold. Prince Andrei was standing directly in front of Kutuzov but the expression of the commander-in-chief's one sound eye showed him to be so absorbed by his thoughts and anxieties that he did not see anything at all. He looked straight into his adjutant's face without recognizing him.

'Well, have you finished?' he inquired of Kozlovsky.

'In one second, your Excellency.'

Bagration, a gaunt middle-aged man of medium height with firm impassive features like an oriental, came out after the commander-in-chief.

'I have the honour to present myself,' repeated Prince Andrei rather loudly, holding out an envelope to Kutuzov.

'Ah, from Vienna? Very good. Presently, presently!'

Kutuzov went out into the porch with Bagration.

'Well, good-bye, prince,' said he to Bagration. 'Christ be with you. My blessing on you in your great endeavour.'

Kutuzov's face suddenly softened, and tears came into his eyes. With his left hand he drew Bagration to him, while with his right, on which he wore a ring, he made the sign of the cross over him with a gesture evidently habitual, and offered him his podgy cheek, but Bagration kissed him on the neck instead.

'Christ be with you!' repeated Kutuzov, and went towards his carriage. 'Get in with me,' said he to Bolkonsky.

'Your Excellency, I could wish to be of use here. Allow me to remain in Prince Bagration's division.'

'Get in,' said Kutuzov, and noticing that Bolkonsky hesitated he added: 'I have need of good officers myself, need them myself.'

They took their seats in the carriage and drove for some minutes in silence.

'There is still much, much before us,' said he as though with an old man's keenness of perception he understood all that was passing in Bolkonsky's mind. 'If a tenth part of his division returns tomorrow, I shall thank God,' he went on, as if speaking to himself.

Prince Andrei glanced at Kutuzov and his eyes were involuntarily attracted by the deep scar with its clear-cut edges on Kutuzov's temple, where a bullet had pierced his skull at Ismail, and the empty eye-socket, less than eighteen inches from him. 'Yes, he has a right to speak so calmly of the death of so many men,' thought Bolkonsky.

'That is why I beg to be sent to that division,' he said.

Kutuzov made no reply. He seemed to have forgotten what he had just said, and sat plunged in thought. Five minutes later, gently swaying on the easy springs of the carriage, he turned to Prince Andrei. There was no trace of emotion on his face. With delicate irony he began to question Prince Andrei on the details of his interview with the Emperor, on the remarks he had heard at court concerning the Krems affair, and about certain ladies they both knew.

14

On November the 1st Kutuzov had received information from one of his spies that showed the army he commanded to be in an almost hopeless position. The spy reported that the French, after crossing the bridge at Vienna, were advancing in considerable strength upon Kutuzov's line of communication with the troops arriving from Russia. If Kutuzov decided to remain at Krems, Napoleon's army of a hundred and fifty thousand men would cut him off completely and surround his exhausted army of forty thousand, and he would find himself in the same predicament as Mack at Ulm. If Kutuzov decided to abandon the road connecting him with the reinforcements arriving from Russia, he would have to march into the unknown and pathless regions of the Bohemian mountains, defending himself against superior forces and giving up all hope of effecting a junction with Buxhöwden. If Kutuzov decided to retreat along the road from Krems to Olmütz, to unite with the troops from Russia, he ran the risk of finding himself forestalled on that road by the French who had crossed the Danube at Vienna, and having to accept battle while on the march, encumbered by his baggage and transport, against an enemy three times as numerous and hemming him in from both sides.

Kutuzov chose this last course.

The French, the spy reported, having crossed the bridge at Vienna, were advancing by forced marches towards Znaim, which lay about sixty-six miles away on the line of Kutuzov's retreat. To reach Znaim before the French offered the best hopes of saving the army. To let the French get to Znaim first would mean exposing his entire army to a disgrace like that of the Austrians at Ulm, or to total destruction. But to forestall the French with his whole army was impossible. The road for the French from Vienna to Znaim was shorter and better than the road for the Russians from Krems to Znaim.

On the night he received this information Kutuzov despatched Bagration's vanguard, four thousand strong, to the right across the hills from the Krems-Znaim to the Vienna-Znaim road. Bagration was to effect this march without resting, and to halt facing Vienna with Znaim to his rear, and if he succeeded in arriving before the French he was to delay them as long as he could. Kutuzov himself with all his transport took the road to Znaim.

Marching thirty miles that stormy night across the roadless hills, with his famished, ill-shod soldiers, and losing a third of his men in stragglers by the way, Bagration came out at Hollabrünn on the Vienna-Znaim road a few hours ahead of the French who were approaching Hollabrünn from Vienna. It would take Kutuzov with all the transport fully another twenty-four hours to reach Znaim, and so to save the army Bagration with his four thousand hungry exhausted men would have to engage the entire force of the enemy confronting him at Hollabrünn for four-and-twenty hours, which was manifestly impossible. But a freak of fate made the impossible possible. The success of the trick that had placed the bridge at Vienna in the hands of the French without a blow inspired Murat to try to trick Kutuzov too. Meeting Bagration's feeble detachment on the Znaim road he supposed it to be Kutuzov's whole army. In order to make sure of crushing this army absolutely he decided to await the arrival of all the forces that had started out from Vienna, and with this end in view he proposed a three days' truce, on condition that both armies should remain where they were without moving. Murat declared that negotiations for peace were already proceeding and that therefore, to avoid unnecessary bloodshed, he proposed this truce. The Austrian general, Count Nostitz, occupying the advanced posts, believed Murat's emissary and retired, leaving Bagration's division exposed. Another emissary rode to the Russian line to make the same assurances about peace negotiations and to offer the Russian army the three days' truce. Bagration replied that he was not authorized either to accept or decline a truce, and sent his adjutant to Kutuzov to report the proposition he had received.

A truce was Kutuzov's sole chance of gaining time, of giving Bagration's exhausted troops some rest, and letting the transport and heavy convoys (the movements of which were concealed from the French) advance if but one stage nearer Znaim. The offer of a truce gave the only – and quite unexpected – opportunity of saving the army. On the receipt of the news Kutuzov promptly despatched Adjutant-General Wintzingerode, who was in attendance on him, to the enemy camp. Wintzingerode was instructed not merely to agree to the truce but to propose terms of capitulation, and meanwhile Kutuzov sent his aides back to hasten to the utmost the movements of the baggage-trains of the entire army along the road from Krems to Znaim. Bagration's weary, famished contingent, alone covering this operation of the baggage-trains and of the whole army, was to remain stationary in face of an enemy numerically eight times as strong.

Kutuzov's anticipations that the proposals of capitulation, which bound him to nothing, would give time for part of the transport to come up, and also that Murat's blunder would very soon be discovered, proved correct. As soon as Bonaparte, who was at Schönbrunn, sixteen miles from Hollabrünn, received Murat's despatch and the proposal for a truce and capitulation he detected a ruse and wrote the following letter to Murat:

Schönbrunn, 25th Brumaire, 1805,
at eight o'clock in the morning.

To Prince Murat.

I cannot find words to express to you my displeasure. You only command my advance-guard and have no right to arrange an armistice without my orders. You are causing me to lose the fruits of a campaign. End the armistice immediately and march up on the enemy. Inform him that the general who signed this capitulation had no right to do so – that no one but the Emperor of Russia has that right.

If, however, the Emperor of Russia should ratify the said convention, I will ratify it; but it is only a trick. Advance, destroy the Russian army. ... You are in a position to capture their baggage and artillery.

The Russian Emperor's aide-de-camp is an impostor. Officers are of no account when they have no powers. This one had none. The Austrians let themselves be tricked about the crossing of the bridge at Vienna; you are letting yourself be tricked by one of the Emperor's aides-de-camp.

NAPOLEON

Bonaparte's adjutant dashed off at full gallop with this menacing letter to Murat. Bonaparte himself, not trusting to his generals, with all the Guards moved towards the field of battle, afraid of being cheated of his prey, while Bagration's four thousand men merrily lighted camp fires, dried and warmed themselves, cooked their porridge for the first time in three days, and not one of them knew or dreamed of what was in store for him.

15

BETWEEN three and four o'clock in the afternoon Prince Andrei, who had persisted in his request to Kutuzov, arrived at Grunth and reported to Bagration. Bonaparte's adjutant had not yet reached Murat's detachment and the battle had not yet begun. In Bagration's division nothing was known of the general course of events: some talked of a peace but did not believe in its possibility; others of a battle, but neither did they believe in the imminence of an engagement.

Knowing Bolkonsky to be a favourite and trusted adjutant, Bagration received him with distinction and special marks of favour, explaining to him that that day or the next would probably see action, and giving him full liberty to be present with him during the battle or to join the rearguard and superintend the retreat, 'which is also very important'.

'However, I hardly think there will be an engagement today,' said Bagration, as if to reassure Prince Andrei. At the same time he thought, 'If this is one of the common run of little staff dandies out to win a medal, he will get it just as well by staying in the rear; but if he wants to be with me, let him. ... He will be useful if he is a brave officer.'

Making no reply, Prince Andrei asked permission to reconnoitre the position and learn the disposition of the forces, so as to know his bearings should he be sent to execute an order. The officer on duty, a handsome, elegantly-attired man with a diamond ring on his fore-finger, who was fond of speaking French though he spoke it badly, offered to be Prince Andrei's guide.

On all sides they saw rain-soaked officers with dejected faces, who appeared to be looking for something, and soldiers dragging doors, benches and fencing from the village.

'See that, prince! We can't stop those fellows,' said the staff-officer pointing to the soldiers. 'The officers let them get out of hand. And look there,' he pointed to a sutler's tent, 'there they gather and there they sit. This morning I drove them all out and now look, it's full again. I must go and scare them a bit, prince. One moment.'

'Let us go together, and I'll get myself some cheese and a loaf of bread,' said Prince Andrei, who had not yet had time for a meal.

'Whyever didn't you mention it, prince? I would have offered you something.'

They got off their horses and went into the sutler's tent, where several officers with flushed and weary faces were sitting at a table eating and drinking.

'Now what does this mean, gentlemen?' said the staff-officer in the reproachful tones of a man who has repeated the same thing more than once. 'You know it won't do to leave your posts like this. The prince gave orders forbidding this sort of thing. Really, captain,' and he turned to a thin, muddy little artillery officer who without boots (he had given them to the sutler to dry) stood up in his stockinged feet as they entered, smiling not altogether comfortably.

'Now, aren't you ashamed of yourself, Captain Tushin?' pursued the staff-officer. 'One would think that you as an artillery officer would set a good example, yet here you are with your boots off! If the alarm sounded, you'd cut a pretty figure without boots!' (The staff-officer smiled.) 'Have the goodness to return to your posts, gentlemen, all of you, all!' he added in a tone of authority.

Prince Andrei could not help smiling as he looked at Captain Tushin, who, silent and grinning, shifted from one stockinged foot to the other, and looked inquiringly with his large, intelligent, good-natured eyes from Prince Andrei to the staff-officer.

'The soldiers say it's easier barefoot,' said Captain Tushin smiling shyly, evidently anxious to carry off his awkward predicament by assuming a jocular tone. But before he had uttered the words he sensed that his jest was not appreciated and would not be a success. He grew confused.

'Kindly go to your posts,' said the staff-officer, trying to preserve his gravity.

Prince Andrei glanced again at the diminutive figure of the artillery officer. There was something peculiar about it, quite unsoldierly, rather comical but extraordinarily attractive.

The staff-officer and Prince Andrei mounted their horses and rode on.

Riding out beyond the village, continually overtaking or meeting soldiers and officers of various divisions, they came in sight on their left of some new entrenchments being thrown up, the freshly-dug clay showing red. Several battalions of soldiers, in their shirt-sleeves despite the cold wind, swarmed in these earthworks like white ants; unseen arms kept tossing up shovelsful of red clay, behind the breast-works. Prince Andrei and his guide rode up to the entrenchment, examined it and went on. Just behind it they came upon some dozens of soldiers all running to and fro to take their turns in the entrenchment. They were obliged to hold their noses and put their horses to a trot to escape the pestilential atmosphere.

'The pleasures of camp life, prince,' remarked the staff-officer.

They rode up the opposite hill. From the top of it they could see the French. Prince Andrei reined in his horse and began to look around.

'That's where our battery stands,' said the staff-officer, indicating the highest point. 'It's commanded by that queer fellow we saw without his boots. You can see everything from over there: shall we go, prince?'

'A thousand thanks, I can find my way alone now,' said Prince Andrei, to be rid of his escort. 'Please do not trouble yourself further.'

The staff-officer turned back, and Prince Andrei rode on alone.

The farther forward and nearer the enemy he went, the more orderly and cheerful he found the men. The greatest disorder and despondency had been in the baggage-train he had passed that morning on the road to Znaim and seven miles from the French. In Grunth too a certain apprehension and alarm could be felt. But the nearer Prince

Andrei rode to the French lines the more confident was the appearance of our troops. The soldiers in their greatcoats stood drawn up in line, and a sergeant-major and a captain were calling over the men, poking the last man in each section in the chest and telling him to hold up his hand. Soldiers were dotted all over the plain, dragging logs and brushwood, and constructing rude huts, laughing good-humouredly and chatting together; around the bivouac fires sat others, some dressed, some stripped, drying their shirts and leg-bands, or mending boots or greatcoats, and crowding round the cauldrons and porridge pots. In one company dinner was ready and the soldiers gazed with eager eyes at the steaming boiler, waiting while the quartermaster-sergeant carried a wooden bowful to be tasted by an officer who sat on a log in front of his shanty.

In another company – a fortunate one since not all were provided with vodka – the men stood in a group round a pock-marked, broad-shouldered sergeant-major who was tilting a keg and filling one after another the canteen-lids held out to him. The soldiers with reverent faces lifted the canteen-lids to their mouths, drained them, and licking their lips and wiping them on the sleeves of their greatcoats walked away from the sergeant-major with brightened expressions. Every face was as serene as if all this were happening at some quiet halting-place at home in Russia, instead of within sight of the enemy on the eve of an action in which at least half of the detachment must be left on the field. After riding past a regiment of chasseurs Prince Andrei reached the lines of the Kiev Grenadiers – stalwart fellows engaged in similar peaceful pursuits – and not far from the regimental commander's hut, distinguished by its height from the others, came out in front of a platoon of grenadiers before whom a man was stretched, naked, on the ground. Two soldiers held him down while two others were flourishing their switches and bringing them down at measured intervals on his bare back. The victim shrieked unnaturally. A stout major was pacing up and down the line and regardless of the screams kept repeating:

'It's a disgrace for a soldier to steal. A soldier should be honest, honourable and brave, but if he robs his comrades there is no honour in him, he's a scoundrel. Go on! Go on!'

So the swishing of the canes and the despairing but exaggerated screaming continued.

'Go on, go on!' repeated the major.

A young officer with a bewildered expression of compassion on his face stepped away from the scene of punishment and looked round inquiringly at the aide-de-camp as he rode by.

Prince Andrei, having reached the front line, rode along by the outposts. Our line and that of the enemy were separated by a considerable distance at both flanks but in the centre where the truce envoys had crossed that morning the lines came so close that the pickets of the two armies could see each other's faces and exchange remarks. Besides the soldiers who formed the picket line many inquisitive onlookers had gathered from both sides who laughed and jested as they scrutinized their strange foreign enemies.

Since early morning, in spite of orders not to approach the picket line, the officers had been unable to keep off the local townspeople. The soldiers whose post was in that part of the line, like showmen exhibiting something unusual, no longer paid any attention to the French but made observations on the sightseers while they wearily waited to be relieved. Prince Andrei pulled up to study the French.

'Look – look there!' one soldier was saying to his comrade, pointing to a Russian musketeer who had gone up to the lines with an officer and was talking rapidly and excitedly to a French grenadier. 'Hark at him jabbering away! The Frenchie can't get a word in! What d'ye say to that, Sidorov?'

'Wait – listen. Ah, that's good, that is!' answered Sidorov, who considered himself a scholar at French.

The soldier they were laughing about was Dolohov. Prince Andrei recognized him and stopped to hear what he was saying. Dolohov together with his captain had come from the left flank where his regiment was stationed.

'Now then, go on, go on!' urged the captain, leaning forward and trying not to miss a word, though it was all unintelligible to him. 'Go on, keep it up! What's he saying?'

Dolohov did not answer his captain: he had been drawn into a heated dispute with the French grenadier. They were talking, as was to be expected, about the campaign. The Frenchman, confusing the Austrians with the Russians, contended that it was the Russians who had surrendered and fled from Ulm, while Dolohov maintained that the Russians had never been defeated but had beaten the French.

'Our orders are to clear you out of here, and we shall too,' said Dolohov.

200

'Better mind you aren't taken prisoner and all your Cossacks with you!' retorted the French grenadier.

Spectators and listeners on the French side laughed.

'We'll make you dance, the way Suvorov did ... *on vous fera danser*,' said Dolohov.

'What's he prating about?' asked a Frenchman.

'Ancient history,' said another, guessing that Dolohov was referring to a former war. 'The Emperor will show your Suvara, the same as he did the others ...'

'Bonaparte ...' Dolohov was beginning, but the Frenchman interrupted him.

'Not Bonaparte. He is the Emperor! *Sacré nom* ...!' he cried angrily.

'The devil skin your Emperor!' And Dolohov swore coarse soldier's oaths at him in Russian, and shouldering his musket walked away.

'Let us be going, Ivan Lukich,' he said to his captain.

'Ah, that's how they talk French-language,' said the picket soldiers. 'Now you have a try, Sidorov!'

Sidorov winked and turning to the French began to gabble a stream of meaningless syllables as fast as his tongue would move:

'*Kari – mala – tafa – safi – muter – kaska*,' he rattled out, trying to throw expression into his voice.

'Ho! ho! ho! Ha! ha! ha! ha! Ouh! ouh!' Peals of such hearty, jovial laughter rang out from the soldiers, in which the French across the line could not help joining, that it seemed as though after that they could only fire off their muskets in the air, explode the ammunition and all hurry back to their homes as fast as possible.

But the guns remained loaded, the loop-holes in blockhouses and entrenchments looked out as threateningly as ever, and the unlimbered cannon confronted one another as before.

16

HAVING ridden along the entire line, from the right flank to the left, Prince Andrei made his way to the battery from which, according to the staff-officer, he could get a view of the whole field. Here he dismounted, and leaned against the end one of the four field-pieces, which had been taken off their platforms. An artilleryman on sentinel duty in front of the guns was about to stand to attention before the officer but at a sign from Prince Andrei resumed his measured, mono-tonous pacing. Behind the cannon were their limbers, and still farther back picket-ropes and the gunners' bivouac fires. To the left at a short distance from the farthest piece was a new little hut made of wattles, from which came the sound of officers' voices in lively conversation.

It was in fact true that a view over the whole Russian disposition and the greater part of the enemy's opened out from this battery. Directly facing it, on the crest of the opposite hill, could be seen the village of Schön Graben and in three places, farther to the left and to the right, Prince Andrei could distinguish through the smoke of their camp-fires the mass of the French troops, of whom the greater num-ber were undoubtedly in the village itself and behind the hill. To the left of the houses something resembling a battery was discernible in the smoke but it was impossible to see it clearly with the naked eye. Our right flank was distributed along a rather steep incline which dominated the French position. Our infantry were here, with the dragoons at the very ridge. In the centre, where Tushin's battery stood and from which Prince Andrei was surveying the position, there was a sharp drop towards the brook separating us from Schön Graben. On the left our troops were close to a copse where bonfires smoked and the infantry were felling wood. The French line was wider than ours and it was plain that they could easily outflank us on both sides. To our rear was a steep and precipitous ravine which would make it difficult for artillery and cavalry to retire. Prince Andrei took out his pocket-book and, leaning an elbow on the can-non, sketched a plan of the disposition of the armies. In two places he pencilled certain observations to which he intended to draw Bagra-tion's attention. His idea was firstly to concentrate all the artillery in the centre, and secondly to remove the cavalry back to the other side of the ravine. Prince Andrei, who was constantly in attendance on the commander-in-chief, concerned with the movements of masses of men and organization in general, and always studying historical ac-counts of battles, now found himself involuntarily trying to imagine in broad outline the course of the coming action. He pictured even-tualities somewhat as follows: 'If the enemy makes the right flank the point of attack,' he said to himself, 'the Kiev Grenadiers and the Podolsky Chasseurs must hold their position till reserves from the centre come up. In that case the dragoons could make a successful flank counter-attack. If they attack our centre we place the centre battery on this high ground and under its cover withdraw the left flank and retire to the ravine by echelons.' So he reasoned. ...

All this time while he stood beside the cannon he could hear the voices of the officers talking in the hut but, as often happens, he had not taken in a single word of what they were saying. Suddenly, however, he was so struck by the earnestness of their tones that he began to listen.

'No, my dear friend,' said a pleasant voice which Prince Andrei seemed to recognize, 'what I say is – if one could know what will happen after death, then not one of us would be afraid of death. That is true, my dear fellow.'

Another and younger voice interrupted.

'Well, afraid or not, it's all the same, there's no escaping it.'

'It makes no difference, one's afraid! Oh you clever people who know all about it!' said a third lusty voice, breaking in upon them both. 'You artillerymen are so cocksure because you can carry everything along with you – you have your tipples of vodka and snacks wherever you go.'

And the owner of the lusty voice, evidently an infantry officer, laughed.

'Yes, one is afraid,' pursued the first speaker, the one with the familiar voice. 'One's afraid of the unknown, that's what it is. It is all very well saying the soul goes up to heaven ... don't we know that up yonder it's not heaven but just space.'

Again the manly voice interrupted.

'Well, give us a taste of your herb-vodka, Tushin,' it said.

'Why, that's the captain who stood in the sutler's hut with his boots off,' thought Prince Andrei, pleased to recognize the agreeable philosophizing voice.

'Some herb-vodka? Certainly!' said Tushin. 'But now, about understanding the life to come ...' He did not finish. At that instant there was a hiss in the air: nearer and nearer, swifter and louder, louder and swifter, and a cannon-ball, as though it had not completed all it wanted to say, smacked into the ground not far from the hut, tearing up the soil with superhuman violence. The ground seemed to groan with the terrible impact.

Little Tushin immediately rushed out of the hut ahead of the rest, his stumpy pipe stuck in the corner of his mouth and his kind intelligent face looking rather pale. He was followed by the owner of the lusty voice, a dashing infantry officer who hurried off to his company, buttoning his jacket as he ran.

17

MOUNTING his horse Prince Andrei lingered to watch the puff of smoke from the cannon that had fired the ball. His eyes rapidly scanned the wide landscape but all he could see was that the hitherto motionless masses of the French were beginning to stir, and that there really was a battery to the left. The smoke still clung about it. Two Frenchmen on horseback, adjutants probably, were galloping on the hill. A small but clearly distinguishable enemy column was moving downhill, apparently for the purpose of strengthening the front line. Before the smoke of the first shot had drifted away a fresh puff appeared, followed by a report. The battle had begun. Prince Andrei turned his horse and spurred back to Grunth to look for Prince Bagration. Behind him he heard the cannonade growing louder and more frequent. Evidently our guns were beginning to reply. From the bottom of the slope, where the lines were closest, came the crack of musketry.

Lemarrois had just arrived at a gallop with Bonaparte's angry letter, and Murat, humiliated and anxious to retrieve his blunder, had immediately moved his forces to attack the centre and outflank both the Russian wings, hoping before nightfall and the arrival of the Emperor to demolish the insignificant division that stood opposite.

'It has begun! Here it is!' thought Prince Andrei, feeling the blood rush to his heart. 'But where – what form will my Toulon take?'

Passing between the companies that only a quarter of an hour before had been eating kasha-gruel and drinking vodka, he saw soldiers hastily moving about everywhere, falling into line and getting their muskets ready, and on every face he recognized the same eagerness that filled his own heart. 'It has begun! Here it is! Terrible but glorious!' said the face of every private and officer.

Before he reached the earthworks still in process of construction, he saw in the twilight of the dull autumn evening mounted men coming towards him. The foremost, wearing a Cossack cloak and lambskin cap and riding a white horse, was Prince Bagration. Prince Andrei stopped and waited for him to come up. Prince Bagration reined in his horse and recognizing Prince Andrei nodded to him. He continued to gaze ahead while Prince Andrei reported what he had seen.

The thought, *It has begun! Here it is!* could be read even on Prince Bagration's strong brown face with its half-closed dim, sleepy eyes. Prince Andrei glanced with uneasy curiosity at that impassive countenance and wished he could tell what, if anything, the man was thinking and feeling at this moment. 'Is there anything at all behind those dispassionate features?' Prince Andrei wondered. Prince Bagration nodded his head in approval of what Prince Andrei told him, and said, 'Good!' in a tone seeming to mply that all that was taking place and all that was reported to him was exactly what he had anticipated. Prince Andrei, out of breath from galloping, spoke rapidly. Prince Bagration pronounced his words with an oriental accent, letting them drop very slowly, as if to impress that there was no need for haste. However, he put his horse to the trot in the direction of Tushin's battery. Prince Andrei followed with the suite. The party consisted of an officer of the suite, Bagration's personal adjutant, Zherkov, an orderly officer, the staff-officer on duty riding a fine bobtailed horse, and a civilian official – an auditor who had asked out of curiosity to be present at the battle. The auditor, a fat man with a fat face, kept looking about him with a naïve smile of delight, cutting a queer figure among the hussars, Cossacks and adjutants, in his camlet coat as he jolted along on his horse with a convoy-officer's saddle.

'He wants to see a battle,' said Zherkov to Bolkonsky, pointing to the auditor, 'but the pit of his stomach's turning already.'

'Come, that's enough!' exclaimed the auditor with a beaming smile that was at once artless and artful, as if he were flattered at being made the butt of Zherkov's jokes and was purposely trying to appear more stupid than he really was.

'It's very amusing, *mon monsieur prince*,' said the staff-officer. (He remembered that in French there was some peculiar way of addressing a prince, but could not get it quite right.)

By this time they were all nearing Tushin's battery, and a ball struck the ground in front of them.

'What was that that fell?' asked the auditor with his naïve smile.

'A French pancake,' said Zherkov.

'So that's what they send over?' asked the accountant. 'How awful!' And he seemed to swell with enjoyment. The words were hardly out of his mouth when there was another sudden violent whistling

205

noise which ended abruptly in a thud into something soft ... f-f-flop!
and a Cossack, riding a little behind and to the right of the auditor,
crashed off his horse to the ground. Zherkov and the staff-officer
crouched down in their saddles and turned their horses away. The
auditor stopped, facing the Cossack, and examined him with curiosity.
The Cossack was dead but the horse was still struggling.

Prince Bagration screwed up his eyes, glanced back over his shoulder and seeing the cause of the confusion turned his head again
indifferently, as much as to say: 'Is it worth while bothering with
trifles?' He reined in his horse with the ease of a good rider, and
slightly bending over disengaged his sabre which had caught in his
cloak. It was an old-fashioned one, of a kind no longer in general use.
Prince Andrei remembered the story of how Suvorov had presented
his sabre to Bagration in Italy, and the recollection was particularly
agreeable to him at this moment. They reached the battery from
which Prince Andrei had surveyed the field of battle.

'Whose company?' asked Prince Bagration of an artilleryman
standing by the ammunition-wagon.

He asked, 'Whose company?' but really he meant: 'Got cold feet
here, haven't you?' and the gunner understood him.

'Captain Tushin's, your Excellency!' shouted the freckled, red-
headed artilleryman in a cheerful voice, standing to attention.

'Good, good,' muttered Bagration absent-mindedly, and he rode
past the limbers to the end cannon.

As he approached, a shot boomed from the cannon, deafening him
and his suite, and in the smoke that suddenly enveloped the gun they
could see the artillerymen seizing and straining to get it quickly back
into position. A huge broad-shouldered soldier, Gunner Number
One, holding the sponge, his legs wide apart, sprang to the wheel;
while Number Two with a shaking hand rammed the charge into the
cannon's mouth. The short, round-shouldered Captain Tushin, stumbling over the tail of the gun-carriage, hastened forward without
noticing the general and gazed into the distance, shading his eyes with
his small hand.

'Two points up and that'll do it,' he cried in a thin little voice to
which he tried to impart a swaggering note that did not go with his
appearance. 'Number Two!' he piped. 'Let 'em have it, Medvedev!'

Bagration called to him, and Tushin, raising three fingers to his
cap with a shy awkward gesture more like a priest giving a benedic-

tion than a soldier saluting, came up to the general. Though it had been intended for Tushin's field-pieces to sweep the valley, he was throwing fire-balls at the village of Schön Graben, visible just opposite, in front of which large masses of the French were concentrating.

No one had given Tushin any orders where to fire and what ammunition to use, and so, having consulted his sergeant-major Zaharchenko, for whom he had great respect, he had decided that it would be a good thing to set fire to the village. 'Very well!' said Bagration when he had listened to the officer's report, and he began to scan the battlefield extended before him, as if he were deliberating something. The French had advanced closest on our right. Below the height on which the Kiev regiment was stationed, in the hollow where the brook flowed, could be heard the soul-shaking roll and rattle of musketry, and much farther to the right, behind the dragoons, the officer of the suite pointed out to Bagration a column of French that was outflanking us. To the left the horizon was bounded by the adjacent wood. Prince Bagration ordered two battalions from the centre to go to the right to reinforce the flank. The officer of the suite ventured to remark to the prince that if these battalions were withdrawn the artillery would be exposed. Prince Bagration turned to the officer and with his lifeless eyes looked at him in silence. It seemed to Prince Andrei that the officer's observation was a very true one, and was, in fact, irrefutable. But at that moment an adjutant galloped up with a message from the colonel of the regiment in the hollow reporting that enormous masses of the French were marching down upon them, that his regiment was in disorder and was falling back upon the Kiev Grenadiers. Prince Bagration inclined his head in token of assent and approval. He rode off at walking pace to the right and sent an adjutant to the dragoons with orders to attack the French. But the adjutant returned half an hour later to say that the commander of the dragoons had already retired beyond the ravine to escape heavy fire and useless loss of life, and had hurried his sharpshooters into the wood.

'Very good!' said Bagration.

As he was leaving the battery, firing was also heard to the left in the wood. It was too far for him to reach the left flank in time so Prince Bagration despatched Zherkov to tell the senior general (the one who had paraded his regiment before Kutuzov at Braunau) to retreat as quickly as possible beyond the ravine, as the right flank would probably not be able to hold the enemy for long. Tushin and the battalion that had been covering his battery were forgotten. Prince Andrei listened carefully to Bagration's colloquies with the commanding officers and to the orders he gave them and remarked to his astonishment that in reality no orders were given but that Prince Bagration merely tried to make it appear as though everything that was being done of necessity, by accident or at the will of individual commanders, was performed if not exactly by his orders at least in accordance with his design. Prince Andrei noticed, however, that though what happened was due to chance and independent of the general's will, the tact shown by Bagration made his presence extremely valuable. Officers who rode up to him with distracted faces regained their composure; soldiers and officers saluted him gaily, recovered their spirits in his presence, and unmistakably took pride in displaying their courage before him.

18

HAVING ridden up to the highest point of our right flank, Prince Bagration began to make the descent to the spot where there was a continual racket of musketry and nothing could be seen for the smoke. The nearer they got to the hollow the less they could see but the more they felt the proximity of the actual battlefield. They began to meet wounded men. One man with a bleeding head and no cap was being dragged along by two soldiers who supported him under the arms. There was a rattle in his throat and he vomited blood: the bullet must have hit him in the mouth or throat. Another whom they met was walking sturdily along by himself, without his musket, groaning aloud and shaking his arm which had just been injured, while the blood streamed down over his greatcoat as from a bottle. He looked more scared than hurt: he had been wounded only a moment ago. Crossing a road they descended a steep incline and saw a number of men lying on the ground; they also met a crowd of soldiers, some of whom were not wounded. The soldiers were climbing the hill, breathing heavily and, despite the general's presence, talking loudly and gesticulating. Farther forward in the smoke rows of grey cloaks were now visible, and an officer catching sight of Bagration rushed after the retreating throng of men shouting to them to come back.

Bagration rode up to the ranks along which shots crackled out swiftly, now here, now there, drowning the sound of voices and the shouts of command. The whole atmosphere reeked with burnt explosives. The men's excited faces were black with powder. Some were using their ramrods, others putting powder on the touch-pans or taking charges from their pouches, while still others were firing, though what they were firing at could not be seen for the fog which there was no wind to carry away. Quite often there was a pleasant buzz and whistle. 'What is going on here?' wondered Prince Andrei, riding up to the crowd of soldiers. 'It can't be the line, for they are all crowded together. It can't be a charge because they are not moving. It cannot be a square for they are not drawn up for that.'

The commander of the regiment, a rather thin, frail-looking old man with an amiable smile and eyelids that drooped more than half-way over his old eyes, giving him a mild expression, rode up to Bagration and welcomed him as a host welcomes an honoured guest. He explained to Prince Bagration that his regiment had had to face a cavalry attack of the French, that though the attack had been repulsed he had lost more than half his men. The colonel said that the attack had been repulsed, supposing this to be the proper military term for what had happened; though in point of fact he did not know himself what had taken place during that half-hour to the forces entrusted to his command, and was unable to say with certainty whether the attack had been thrown back or whether his regiment had been worsted. All he knew was that at the beginning of the engagement balls and shells began flying all about his regiment and hitting his men, then someone had shouted 'Cavalry!' and our side had started to fire. And they were still firing, not now at the cavalry which had disappeared, but at the French infantry who had shown themselves in the hollow and were shooting at our men. Prince Bagration inclined his head, to signify that this was all he could wish and just what he had foreseen. Turning to his adjutant he ordered him to bring down the two battalions of the 6th Chasseurs whom they had just passed. Prince Andrei was struck at that instant by the change that had come over Bagration's face, which now wore the concentrated, happy look of determination of a man taking a final run before plunging into the water on a hot day. The dull lethargic expression was gone, together with the affectation of profound thought: the round, steady, hawk's eyes looked before him eagerly and somewhat disdainfully, apparently not resting anywhere although his movements were as slow and deliberate as before.

The regimental commander turned to Prince Bagration urging him to go back as it was too dangerous where they were. 'Please, your Excellency, for God's sake!' he kept repeating, glancing for support to the officer of the suite, who looked away from him. 'There, you see!' and he drew attention to the bullets perpetually buzzing, singing, and whistling around them. He spoke in a tone of entreaty and protest such as a joiner might use to a gentleman picking up an axe: 'We're used to it, sir, but you'd blister your fine hands.' He spoke as if those bullets could not kill him, and his half-closed eyes lent still more persuasiveness to his words. The staff-officer joined his entreaties to those of the colonel but Prince Bagration made no reply and merely gave an order to cease firing and re-form, so as to give room for the two battalions approaching to join them. While he was speaking a breeze sprang up and like an invisible hand drew the curtain of smoke hiding the hollow from right to left, and the hill opposite with the French moving about on it opened out before them. All eyes instinctively fastened on this French column advancing against them and winding down over the rough ground. Already the soldiers' shaggy caps could be seen; already the officers could be distinguished from the men, and the standard flapping in folds against the staff.

'They march well,' remarked someone in Bagration's suite.

The head of the column had already descended into the hollow. The clash then would take place on this side of the dip. ...

The remains of our regiment which had already been in action hastily re-formed and moved to the right; from behind it, dispersing the laggards, came the two battalions of the 6th Chasseurs in fine order. They had not yet reached Bagration but the heavy measured tread could be heard of a whole body of men marching in step. On their left flank, nearest to Bagration, marched the captain, a stately figure with a foolish happy expression on his round face – the same man who had followed Tushin when they rushed out of the wattle-hut. It was clear that his one idea at this moment was to march past the commander with a swagger.

With the self-complacency of a man in the front line on parade he stepped springily by on his muscular legs, almost sailing along, stretching himself to his full height without the smallest effort, his ease contrasting with the heavy tread of the soldiers who were keeping step with him. He wore hanging by his leg a slender unsheathed sword (it was small and curved, and not like a real weapon), and looked round now at the superior officers now back at his men, not once losing step, with supple turns of his powerful body. It seemed as though his whole soul was concentrated on marching past the commander in the best possible style, and feeling that he was doing it well he was happy. 'Left … left … left …' he seemed to repeat to himself at each alternate step; and in time with him, every face different but every face grave, the moving wall of soldiers marched by, burdened with knapsacks and muskets, as though each one of these hundreds of soldiers was repeating to himself at every other step: 'Left … left … left. …' A stout major, puffing and falling out of step, skirted a bush in his path; a straggler, out of breath and frightened at his defection, ran at the double to catch up with his company. A cannon-ball cleaving the air flew over the heads of Bagration and his suite and fell into the column to the accompaniment of 'Left … left!'

'Close the ranks!' rang out the jaunty voice of the captain. The soldiers passed in a semicircle round something on the spot where the ball had fallen, and an old trooper on the flank, a warrant-officer who had lingered behind near the dead regained his line, skipped into step, and looked sternly about him. *Left! left! left!* seemed to resound from the ominous silence and the regular monotonous tramp of feet beating the ground in unison.

'Well done, lads!' said Prince Bagration.

'For your your Ex … slen … slen – slency!' came a confused shout from the ranks. A surly-looking soldier marching on the left looked up at Bagration as he shouted, with an expression that seemed to say: 'We know that without telling!' Another, opening his mouth wide, shouted and marched on without looking round, as though fearful of letting his attention stray.

The order was given to halt and down knapsacks.

Bagration rode round the ranks that had just marched past him, and dismounted. He gave the reins to a Cossack, took off and handed over his cloak, stretched his legs and set his cap straight. The head of the French column, with its officers leading, appeared at the foot of the hill.

'Forward, and God with us!' cried Bagration in a firm, ringing voice, turning for a moment to the front line, and swinging his arms a little went forward himself, almost stumbling over the rough field, with the awkward gait of a man always on horseback. Prince Andrei felt that some irresistible power was impelling him on, and he knew a great happiness.*

Already the French were at hand: Prince Andrei, walking beside Bagration, could distinguish without difficulty their bandoliers, the red epaulets, even the faces of the French. (He saw quite clearly one bandy-legged old French officer wearing Hessian boots who was struggling up the hill, catching hold of the bushes.) Prince Bagration gave no further orders, and continued to march in silence at the head of his forces. Suddenly one shot, then another, then a third snapped out from among the French, smoke appeared all along their uneven ranks and there was the rattle of musketry. Several of our men fell, among them the round-faced officer who had marched so gaily and diligently. But at the very instant the first report was heard Bagration turned round and shouted: 'Hurrah!'

'Hurrah-ah-ah!' rang a long-drawn shout from our ranks, and outstripping Bagration and one another our men dashed down the slope in a broken but joyous eager crowd on to the disordered foe.

19

THE charge of the 6th Chasseurs secured the retreat of our right flank. In the centre Tushin's forgotten battery, which had succeeded in setting fire to the village of Schön Graben, held up the French advance. The French stopped to put out the fire, which the wind was spreading, and thus gave us time to retreat. The withdrawal of the centre through the hollow to the other side was effected with much haste and noise, though in good order. But the left flank, which consisted of the Azov and Podolsky infantry and the Pavlograd Hussars, was simultaneously attacked and outflanked by the cream of the French forces under Lannes, and was thrown into confusion. Bagration had sent Zherkov to the general commanding that left flank with orders to retreat immediately.

Zherkov, not removing his hand from his cap, dug his spurs into his horse and dashed off. But no sooner had he left Bagration than his

---

*This was the attack of which Thiers says : 'The Russians behaved valiantly and, a rare occurrence in war, two bodies of infantry were seen to march resolutely upon each other, neither giving way until they met in head-on collision.' And Napoleon said at St Helena: 'Some of the Russian battalions showed complete fearlessness.'

courage failed. He was seized with panic and could not persuade himself to go to where there was danger.

Having reached the left flank, instead of continuing to the front where the firing was, he began to look for the general and his staff where they could not possibly be, and so it was he did not deliver the message.

The command of the left wing belonged by right of seniority to the general of the regiment Kutuzov had reviewed at Braunau and in which Dolohov was serving as a private. But the command of the extreme left flank had been assigned to the colonel of the Pavlograd Hussars in which Rostov was serving, and this led to a misunderstanding. The two commanders were exceedingly irritated with one another and, long after the right flank had gone into action and the French were already advancing, the pair were engaged in discussions having the sole object of giving offence to one another. Both regiments, cavalry and infantry alike, were by no means in readiness for the work before them. No one, from private to general, expected a battle and they were all calmly engaged in peaceful pursuits – the cavalry feeding their horses and the infantry collecting fire-wood.

'He higher dan I in rank iss,' said the German colonel of the hussars, flushing and addressing an adjutant who had ridden up, 'so let him do vhat he vill, but I my hussars cannot sacrifice. ... Bugler, sount ze retreat!'

But matters were becoming urgent. Cannon and musketry roared and rattled in unison on the right and in the centre, while the capotes of Lannes' sharpshooters were already seen crossing the mill-dam and forming up on this side hardly out of range. The infantry general walked over to his horse with his jerky step, clambered into the saddle and, drawing himself up very erect and tall, rode to the Pavlograd colonel. The two commanders met with polite bows and secret malevolence in their hearts.

'Once again, colonel,' said the general, 'I cannot leave half my men in the wood. I *beg* of you, I *beg* of you,' he repeated, 'to occupy the *position* and prepare for an attack.'

'And I peg of you not to mix in vot iss not your pusiness!' replied the colonel heatedly. 'If you vere a cavalryman ...'

'I am not a cavalryman, colonel, but I am a Russian general, and if you are unaware of the fact ...'

'I am quite avare, your Excellency,' suddenly shouted the colonel, touching up his horse and turning purple with rage. 'Vill you be so goot to come to ze front and you vill see dat dis position iss no goot. I haf no vish to massacre my men for your gratification.'

'You forget yourself, colonel. I am not considering my own satisfaction and I will not permit such a thing to be said.'

Accepting the colonel's invitation as a challenge to his courage, the general squared his chest and, frowning, rode forward beside him to the front line, as if all their differences were to be settled there among the bullets. They reached the outposts, a few shots flew over them, and they halted in silence. There was nothing fresh to be seen from the line, for the impossibility of cavalry manoeuvring among the bushes and gullies was equally obvious from the spot where they had been standing before, as was the fact that the French were outflanking our left. The general and the colonel glared sternly and significantly at one another like two game-cocks about to fight, each seeking in vain for signs of cowardice in the other. Both stood the test. As there was nothing for them to say, and neither wished to give occasion for it to be alleged that he had been the first to retire from the range of fire, they might have remained there indefinitely, mutually testing each other's courage, if just then they had not heard the snap of musketry and a muffled shout in the wood almost behind them. The French had fallen on the men gathering fire-wood in the copse. It was no longer possible for the hussars to withdraw along with the infantry. They were cut off from the line of retreat on the left by the French. Now, however inconvenient the position, they would have to attack in order to force their way through.

The squadron in which Rostov was serving had scarcely time to mount before they found themselves face to face with the enemy. Again, as on the bridge at Enns, there was no one between the squadron and the enemy, and once more that terrible dividing line of uncertainty and fear – like a line separating the living from the dead – lay between them. All were conscious of this invisible line, and the question whether they would cross it or not, and how they would cross it, filled them with excitement.

The colonel rode up to the front, angrily gave some reply to questions put to him by his officers, and like a man desperately insisting on his own rights thundered out an order. No one said anything definite but the rumour of an attack spread through the squadron. The command to fall in was given, and there was the scrape of sabres being drawn from scabbards. But still no one stirred. The troops of the left flank, infantry and hussars alike, felt that the command itself did not know what to do, and this hesitation communicated itself to the men.

'If only they would be quick,' thought Rostov, feeling that at last the time had come to experience the intoxication of a charge, of which he had heard so much from his fellow hussars.

'Fo'ard, and God be with you, lads!' rang out Denisov's voice. 'At a twot, fo'ward!'

The horses' rumps in the front rank began to sway. Rook pulled at the reins and started of his own accord.

On the right Rostov could see the foremost rows of his own hussars and still farther ahead there was a dark streak which he could not make out distinctly but assumed to be the enemy. Shots were heard, but in the distance.

'Charge!' came the word of command, and Rostov felt the droop of Rook's hindquarters as he broke into a gallop.

Anticipating his horse's movements, Rostov became more and more elated. He had noticed a solitary tree ahead. At first this tree had been in the very centre of the line that had seemed so terrible. But now they had crossed that line and not only had nothing terrible happened but on the contrary it was all jollier and more exciting every moment. 'Oh, won't I slash at them!' thought Rostov, gripping the hilt of his sabre.

'Hurr-a-a-ah!' roared cheering voices.

'Let anyone come my way now,' thought Rostov, driving his spurs into Rook and allowing him to go at full gallop so that they outstripped the others. Ahead the enemy were already visible. Suddenly something like a wide birch-broom seemed to sweep over the squadron. Rostov lifted his sabre ready to strike, but at that instant Nikitenko, the trooper who was riding in front of him, veered aside, and Rostov felt himself as in a dream being carried forward at an unnatural pace yet not moving from the spot. A hussar he knew, Bandarchuk, bumped into him and looked at him angrily. Bandarchuk's horse swerved and dashed past.

'What's the matter? I am not moving? Have I fallen? Am I dead? ...' Rostov asked and answered himself all in one breath. He was alone in the middle of a field. Instead of galloping horses and hussars' backs he saw around him nothing but the still earth and the stubble. There was warm blood under him. 'No, I am wounded and my horse is killed.' Rook tried to rise on his forelegs but fell back, pinning his rider's leg. Blood was flowing from the horse's head. Rook struggled but could not rise. Rostov tried to get to his feet but he too fell back: his sabretache had caught in the saddle. Where our men were, where the French were, he did not know. There was not a soul to be seen.

Having disentangled his leg, he stood up. 'Where, in which direction now was the line that had so sharply divided the two armies?' he asked himself and could not answer. 'Can something have gone wrong with me? Is this the regular way of things, and what do I do?' he wondered as he scrambled to his feet; and at that moment he began to feel as though there were something unusual about his benumbed left arm. The wrist felt as if it did not belong to it. He examined his hand carefully but could find no sign of blood. 'Ah, here's someone coming,' he thought joyfully, seeing men running towards him. 'They will help me!' The foremost was wearing a strange shako and a blue cloak. He was dark and sunburnt, and had a hooked nose. Two others were running at his heels and there were many more behind. One of them said something in a strange language that was not Russian. Surrounded by similar figures in the same sort of shakos, behind the others, stood a lone Russian hussar. They were holding him by the arms, and his horse was being led behind him.

'It must be one of our men, taken prisoner. ... Yes, that's it. Surely they couldn't take me prisoner too. Who are these men?' thought Rostov, unable to believe his own eyes. 'Can they be the French?' He looked at the approaching Frenchmen, and in spite of the fact that only a moment before he had been dashing forward solely for the purpose of getting at these same Frenchmen to hack them to pieces their proximity now seemed so awful that he could not believe his eyes. 'Who are they? Are they coming at me? Can they be running at me? And why? To kill me? Me whom everyone is so fond of?' He thought of his mother's love for him, of his family's and his friends', and the enemy's intention of killing him seemed impossible. 'But perhaps they will!' For over ten seconds he stood rooted to the spot, not realizing the situation. The foremost Frenchman, the one with the hook nose, was already so close that he could see the expression on his face. And the excited, alien features of the man who was bearing so swiftly down on him with fixed bayonet and bated breath terrified Rostov. He snatched up his pistol and instead of firing flung

it at the Frenchman and tore with all his might towards the bushes.
He did not now run with the feeling of doubt and conflict with which
he had trodden the Enns bridge but like a hare fleeing from the
hounds. A single unmixed instinct of fear for his young and happy
life possessed his whole being. Leaping over the furrows, he fled
across the field with the urgency with which he used to run when
playing tag in his boyhood, now and then turning his pale, kindly,
youthful face to look back, while a chill of horror shivered down his
spine. 'No, better not look,' he thought, but as he got near the bushes
he glanced round once more. The Frenchmen had slackened their
pace and just as he looked round the first man slowed down to a walk
and turned to shout something in a loud voice to a comrade farther
back. Rostov paused. 'No, there's some mistake,' thought he. 'They
can't have meant to kill me.' But meanwhile his left arm felt as heavy
as though it weighed an extra half hundredweight. He could not run
another step. The Frenchman stopped too and took aim. Rostov shut
his eyes and ducked. One bullet, then another whistled past his head.
He mustered his last remaining strength, and carrying his left wrist
in his right hand he reached the bushes. In the bushes there were
Russian sharpshooters.

20

THE infantry regiments that had been caught unawares in the wood
rushed out, men from different companies getting mixed up, and
retired in a disorderly mob. One soldier in his panic shouted the
meaningless words 'Cut off!' that are so terrible to hear in battle, and
the cry infected the whole throng.

'Surrounded! Cut off! We're lost!' shouted the fugitives.

The moment he heard the firing and the cry from behind, the
general realized that something dreadful was happening to his regiment, and the thought that he, an exemplary officer of many years'
service, never guilty of any breach, might now be accused of negligence or inefficiency, so staggered him that, forgetting the recalcitrant
cavalry colonel, his own dignity as a general, and, above all, quite
forgetting the danger and all regard for self-preservation, he clutched
the saddle-bow and spurring his horse galloped to the regiment under
a hail of bullets falling all around but fortunately missing him. His
one desire was to find out what was wrong and at any cost remedy
or correct the blunder, if he had made one, so that he, an exemplary

officer with twenty-two years' service who had never incurred a reprimand, should not be held to blame.

Having galloped unharmed between the French, he reached a field behind the wood through which our men were running, deaf to orders, and scattering down the hill. This was the critical moment of moral vacillation which decides the fate of battles: would this disorderly mob of soldiers heed the voice of their commander, or would they merely look at him and continue their flight? Despite his despairing yells – and hitherto their general had always been such a redoubtable figure – despite his infuriated, purple countenance distorted out of all likeness to itself, and despite his brandished sword, the soldiers all continued to run, shouting, shooting into the air and not listening to the word of command. The moral see-saw which decides the fate of battles was evidently coming down on the side of panic.

The general coughed and nearly choked with shouting and powder-smoke, and stood still in despair. All seemed lost. But at that moment the French, who had been attacking, suddenly and for no apparent reason turned and fled, disappearing from the outskirts of the wood, and in the wood, Russian sharpshooters showed themselves. It was Timohin's company, the only one to have maintained its order in the wood, and having lain in ambush in a ditch they now attacked the French unexpectedly. Timohin, armed only with his short sword, had dashed at the enemy with such a frantic cry and such mad drunken determination that the French, unable to collect their wits, had thrown down their muskets and run. Dolohov, running beside Timohin, shot and killed one Frenchman at close quarters, and was the first to seize a surrendering French officer by his collar. Those who were running away returned, battalions re-formed, and the French, who had been on the verge of splitting our left flank in half, were for the moment repulsed. Our reserve units were able to reunite and men stopped deserting. The general was standing at the bridge with Major Ekonomov, letting the retreating companies file past them, when a soldier came up, caught hold of his stirrup and almost leaned against him. The soldier was wearing a bluish coat of broadcloth, he had no knapsack or cap, his head was bandaged, and over his shoulder was slung a French cartridge pouch. In his hand he held an officer's sword. The soldier was pale, his blue eyes looked impudently into the general's face while a smile parted his lips. Although the general was engaged in giving orders to Major Ekonomov, he could not help noticing this soldier.

'Your Excellency, here are two trophies,' said Dolohov, pointing to the French sword and cartridge pouch. 'An officer was taken prisoner by me. I stopped the company.' Dolohov breathed hard from exhaustion and spoke in broken sentences. 'The whole company can bear me witness. I beg you will remember this, your Excellency!'

'Very good, very good,' replied the general, and he turned to Major Ekonomov.

But Dolohov did not go away; he untied the handkerchief round his head, pulled it off and called attention to the blood congealed on his hair.

'A bayonet wound. I kept in the front. Please remember, your Excellency!'

＊

Tushin's battery had been forgotten, and it was only at the very end of the action that Prince Bagration, still hearing the cannonade in the centre, sent a staff-officer, and later Prince Andrei, to order the battery to retire as speedily as possible. The supporting columns attached to Tushin's battery had been withdrawn in the middle of the engagement, in obedience to someone's order, but the battery continued to blaze away, and was not taken by the French simply because the enemy could not conceive of the temerity of firing from four quite unprotected guns. On the contrary, the energetic activity of this battery led the French to suppose that the main Russian forces must be concentrated here in the centre. Twice they had attempted to storm this point but on each occasion had been driven back by grape-shot from the four isolated guns on the hillock.

Shortly after Prince Bagration's departure Tushin had succeeded in setting fire to Schön Graben.

'Look at them scattering! It's burning! Just look at the smoke! A fine job! My word! See that smoke – there's smoke for you!' exclaimed the artillerymen, their spirits reviving.

All the cannon, without waiting for orders, were directed on the conflagration. Every shot was hailed with shouts of 'Bravo! That's the way to do it! Look there! Capital!', as if the soldiers were urging each other on. The fire, fanned by the breeze, was spreading rapidly. The French columns that had marched out beyond the village went back, but as though in revenge for this reverse the enemy mounted ten guns to the right of the village to return Tushin's fire.

In their childlike glee at the conflagration of the village and at their success in cannonading the French our gunners did not notice this battery until two balls, followed immediately by four more, fell among our guns, one knocking over two horses and another tearing off the leg of the powder-wagon driver. The men's ardour once roused was not cooled, however, but only changed character. The horses were replaced by others from a reserve gun-carriage, the wounded were carried away, and the four cannon were turned against the ten-gun battery. Tushin's companion officer had been killed at the beginning of the engagement and within an hour seventeen of the forty men making up the crew had been disabled, but the gunners were still as cheerful and as eager as ever. Twice they noticed the French appearing down below, close to them, and they sent volleys of grape-shot at them.

Little Tushin, with his soft, awkward movements, kept calling on his orderly to 'refill my pipe for that one!' and then, scattering sparks from it, sprang forward shading his eyes under his small hand to look at the French.

'Smack at 'em, lads!' he would exclaim, and seizing the cannon by the wheel would work the screws himself.

In the smoke, deafened by the incessant discharges which made him shudder every time, Tushin ran from one gun to another with his pipe between his teeth, adjusting the aim here, counting the charges there, seeing to the replacing of dead or wounded horses, and shouting orders in his shrill, high-pitched, undecided voice. His face grew more and more excited. Only when a man was killed or wounded did he frown and turn away from the sight, calling out angrily to the others who, as is always the case, hesitated about lifting the injured or dead. The soldiers, for the most part handsome fellows (and, as they always are in the artillery, a head and shoulders taller than their officer and twice as broad in the chest), all looked at their commander with the inquiring look of children in trouble, and the expression which happened to be on his face was invariably reflected on theirs.

Owing to the terrible din and uproar, and the necessity for concentration and diligence, Tushin did not experience the slightest qualm of fear, and the idea that he might be killed or badly wounded never entered his head. On the contrary, he grew more and more elated. It seemed to him that it was a very long time ago – almost as far back as the day before – when he had first caught sight of the enemy and fired the first shot, and that the little scrap of field where he stood was well-known, familiar ground. Though he forgot nothing, thought of everything, did everything the best of officers could have done in his position, he was in a state akin to feverish delirium or intoxication.

The deafening roars of his own guns on every side, the whistle and thud of the enemy's cannon-balls, the sight of the flushed, perspiring faces of the crews bustling round the guns, the sight of the blood of men and horses, of the little puffs of smoke on the enemy's side (always followed by a ball flying over to hit the earth, a man, a cannon or a horse) – all these sights and sounds formed into a fantastic world which took possession of his brain and at this moment afforded him sheer delight. The enemy's guns were in his imagination not guns but pipes from which an invisible smoker occasionally puffed out wreaths of smoke.

'There, he's having another puff,' muttered Tushin to himself as a curling cloud of smoke leaped from the hill and was borne off to the left in a ribbon by the wind. 'Now look out for the ball – we'll toss it back!'

'What is it, your Honour?' asked an artilleryman who stood near him and heard him muttering.

'Nothing ... a shell ...' he replied.

'Come along now, our Matvevna,' he said to himself. 'Matvevna' was the name his fancy gave to the large, old-fashioned gun at the far end. The French swarming round their artillery reminded him of ants. In his dream-world the Number One gunner of the second field-piece, a handsome fellow too much given to drink, was 'uncle'; Tushin looked at him oftener than at the others, and delighted in his every movement. The noise of musketry at the foot of the hill, now dying away now quickening again, seemed like someone's breathing. He listened intently to the ebb and flow of these sounds.

'Ah, she's taking another breath again!' he soliloquized.

He imagined himself as a powerful giant of monstrous stature hurling cannon balls at the French with both hands.

'Now then, Matvevna, my little one, don't disappoint me!' he was saying as he moved away from the gun when a strange unfamiliar voice called above his head:

'Captain Tushin! Captain!'

Tushin looked round in alarm. It was the staff-officer who had turned him out of the hut at Grundth. He was shouting and out of breath.

'I say, are you mad? Twice you've been ordered to retreat, and you ...'

'Now what are they pitching into me for?' Tushin wondered, looking with apprehension at his superior.

'I ... I don't ...' he stammered, putting two fingers to the peak of his cap. 'I ...'

But the staff-officer did not finish all he meant to say. A cannon-ball flying close made him duck down over his horse. He paused and just as he was about to continue another ball stopped him. He wheeled the animal round and galloped off.

'Retire! Everyone is to retire!' he shouted back from a distance.

The soldiers laughed. A moment later an adjutant arrived with the same order.

This was Prince Andrei. The first thing he saw as he rode up to the space occupied by Tushin's guns was an unharnessed horse with a broken leg, that lay screaming beside the harnessed horses. Blood was gushing from its leg as from a fountain. Among the limbers a number of the killed were lying. One cannon-ball after another flew over as he approached, and he was conscious of a nervous tremor running down his spine. But the mere thought of being afraid roused his courage again. 'I cannot be afraid,' he said to himself, and dismounted slowly among the guns. He delivered his message but did not leave the battery. He decided to have the guns removed from their positions and withdrawn in his presence. Together with Tushin, stepping over dead bodies, and under terrible fire from the French, he attended to the limbering of the guns.

'A staff-officer was here a minute ago, but he soon made himself scarce,' remarked an artilleryman to Prince Andrei. 'Not like your Honour.'

Prince Andrei said nothing to Tushin. They were both so busy that they hardly seemed to see each other. When they had limbered up two of the four field-pieces and were moving downhill (one gun that had been smashed and a howitzer were left behind) Prince Andrei went up to Tushin.

'Well, good-bye till we meet again ...' he said, holding out his hand.

'Good-bye, my dear fellow,' said Tushin. 'Dear, good soul! Farewell, my dear fellow,' said Tushin, and for some unknown reason tears suddenly filled his eyes.

21

THE wind had dropped and black clouds hung low over the field of battle, mingling on the horizon with the smoke of gunpowder. It was growing dark and the glow of conflagrations showed all the more distinctly in two places. The cannonade was dying down but the rattle of musketry in the rear and on the right sounded oftener and nearer. As soon as Tushin with his field-pieces, continually driving round or coming upon wounded men, was out of range of fire, and had descended into the ravine, he was met by some of the staff, among them the officer and Zherkov, who had twice been sent to Tushin's battery but had never reached it. Interrupting one another they all gave orders and counter-orders as to how and where to proceed, loading him with blame and criticism. In silence Tushin rode behind on his artillery nag, fearing to open his mouth because at every word he felt, he could not have said why, ready to burst into tears. Though the orders were to abandon the wounded, many of them dragged themselves after the troops and begged for a seat on the gun-carriages. The jaunty infantry officer – the one who had darted out from Tushin's hut just before the battle lay stretched on 'Matvevna's' carriage with a bullet in his stomach. At the foot of the hill a pale hussar cadet supporting one hand with the other came up to Tushin and pleaded for a place.

'Captain, for God's sake, I've hurt my arm,' he said timidly. 'For God's sake ... I can't walk. For God's sake!'

It was plain that this cadet had more than once repeated the request for a lift and been refused. He asked in a hesitating, piteous voice.

'Tell them to let me get on, for God's sake.'

'Give him a place,' said Tushin. 'Put a coat under him, you, uncle,' he said, addressing his favourite soldier. 'But where is the wounded officer?'

'We set him down. He was dead,' replied someone.

'Help him up. Sit there, sit there, my dear fellow. Spread out the cloak, Antonov.'

The cadet was Rostov. With one hand he supported the other; he was pale and his lower jaw trembled and his teeth chattered with fever. He was helped on to 'Matvevna', the gun from which they had removed the dead officer. There was blood on the cloak they spread out which stained his breeches and hands.

'What, you wounded, lad?' said Tushin, going up to the gun on which Rostov sat.

'No, only a sprain.'

'But this blood on the gun-carriage?' asked Tushin.

'That was the officer, your Honour, stained it,' replied a gunner, wiping away the blood with his coat-sleeve as if apologizing for the state of his cannon.

By main force and with the help of the infantry the guns were dragged up the rise, and having reached the village of Guntersdorf they halted. By this time it was so dark that it was impossible to distinguish the soldiers' uniforms ten paces away, and the firing had begun to subside. Suddenly shouts and the rattle of shots were heard again near by on the right. The darkness was lit by flashes. This was the last attack on the part of the French, and the soldiers were replying to it as they entrenched themselves in the houses of the village. Once more they all rushed out but Tushin's guns were stuck, and the artillerymen, Tushin and the cadet exchanged silent glances, awaiting their fate. The firing began to die down, and soldiers talking eagerly streamed out of a side street.

'Safe and sound, Petrov?' asked one.

'We gave it 'em hot, mate! They won't stick their noses out again now,' said another.

'It's too dark to see a thing. How they shot up their own fellows! It's as dark as pitch, mate! I say, isn't there something to drink?'

The French had been driven back for the last time. And once more through the impenetrable darkness Tushin's field-pieces moved forward, surrounded by the rumbling infantry as by a frame.

In the dark it seemed as though a sombre invisible river flowed on and on in one direction, murmuring with whispers and the droning of voices, the sound of hooves and wheels. Amid the general hum, clearer than all the other noises in the blackness of the night, rose the groans of the wounded. The gloom that enveloped the army was filled with their cries. Their groaning was one with the blackness of the night. A little later a wave of excitement ran through the moving mass. Someone followed by a suite had ridden by on a white horse, and had said something in passing.

'What did he say? Where do we go now? Is it a halt? Thanked us, what?' were the eager questions heard on all sides, and the whole moving mass compressed into itself (evidently those in front had stopped) and a report spread that there were orders to halt. All stood still where they were, in the middle of the muddy road.

Fires were lighted, and voices were heard more audibly. Captain Tushin, after giving orders to his battery, sent one of his men to look for a dressing-station or a surgeon for the cadet, and sat down by the bonfire his soldiers had kindled by the roadside. Rostov too dragged himself to the fire. Feverish shivering caused by pain, cold and damp shook his whole body. Sleep almost overpowered him but he was kept awake by the agony of his arm for which he could find no satisfactory position. Sometimes he closed his eyes for a moment or two, then he would gaze at the fire which seemed to him a burning glare, or turn and look at the weedy round-shouldered figure of Tushin sitting cross-legged like a Turk beside him. Tushin's large, kindly, intelligent eyes were fastened upon him with sympathy and commiseration. Rostov saw that Tushin wished with all his soul to help him but could not.

On all sides they could hear the footsteps and chatter of the infantry moving about, driving by and settling down around them. The sounds of voices, of tramping feet, of horses' hooves stamping in the mud, the crackling of wood fires far and near – all merged into one pulsating uproar.

Now it was no longer an invisible river rolling on in the darkness but the swell of a glowering sea, subsiding and still agitated after a storm. Rostov in a dazed fashion saw and heard what was going on around him. A foot-soldier came up to the fire, squatted on his heels, held his hands to the blaze and turned his face.

'No objection, your Honour?' he asked Tushin. 'I've got lost from my company, your Honour. I don't know where I am. It's the devil!'

At the same time as the soldier an infantry officer with a bandaged cheek came up to the fire, and addressing Tushin requested to have the guns moved a trifle to let a baggage-wagon go past. The company commander was followed by a couple of soldiers, quarrelling and fighting desperately over a boot each was trying to snatch from the other.

225

'What, you picked it up? I should say so! A smart one, you are!' one of them was shouting hoarsely.

Then a thin, pale soldier, his neck bandaged with a bloodstained leg-band, came up and angrily asked the artillerymen for water.

'Must one be left to die like a dog?' said he.

Tushin told them to give the man some water. Then a cheery soldier ran up to beg for some red-hot embers for the infantry.

'Fire, fire all hot for the infantry! Good luck to you, lads, and thanks for the fire. We'll pay it back with interest,' said he, bearing the flaming brand away into the darkness.

Next came four soldiers carrying something heavy on a cloak, and passed by the blaze. One of them stumbled.

'Oh the devils, they've spilled logs on the road,' snarled he.

'He's dead, what's the use of dragging him along?' said another of the four.

'Shut up!'

And they disappeared into the darkness with their burden.

'I say, does it hurt?' Tushin asked Rostov in a whisper.

'Yes, it does ache.'

'Your Honour, the general wants you. He's in the hut here,' said a gunner, coming up to Tushin.

'Right, my boy.'

Tushin rose and walked away from the fire, buttoning his greatcoat and setting himself straight.

Not far from the artillery camp-fire, in a hut that had been made ready for him, Prince Bagration sat at dinner, talking with a number of high officers who had gathered at his quarters. The little old colonel with the half-closed eyes was there, greedily gnawing at a muttonbone, and the general of twenty-two years' irreproachable service, his face flushed with a glass of vodka and dinner, and the staff-officer with the signet-ring, and Zherkov stealing uneasy glances at them all, and Prince Andrei, pale, with compressed lips and feverishly glittering eyes.

In a corner of the hut stood a standard captured from the French, and the auditor with the naïve face was fingering the stuff it was made of and shaking his head doubtfully, possibly because the banner really interested him, possibly because it was hard to look on at a dinner where no place had been laid for him when he was so hungry. In the next hut there was the French colonel who had been taken prisoner

226

by the dragoons. Our officers were flocking round to have a look at him. Prince Bagration was thanking the commanders of the various divisions and inquiring into details of the engagements and our losses. The general whose regiment had been inspected at Braunau was telling the prince that as soon as the action began he had withdrawn from the woods, mustered the men engaged in felling trees and, allowing the French to go by, had then made a bayonet charge with two battalions and routed them.

'As soon as I saw that their first battalion was disorganized, your Excellency, I stood in the road and said to myself: "I'll let them get through and then open fire on them"; and that's what I did.'

The general had so longed to do this, and was so regretful that he had not succeeded in doing it, that it seemed to him now that this was what had happened. Indeed, might it not actually have been so? How could anyone tell in all that confusion what did or did not happen?

'By the way, your Excellency, I ought to inform you,' he continued, remembering Dolohov's conversation with Kutuzov, and his own late interview with the gentleman-ranker, 'that Private Dolohov, who was reduced to the ranks, took a French officer prisoner before my eyes and notably distinguished himself.'

'It was there I saw the charge of the Pavlograd Hussars, your Excellency,' chimed in Zherkov, looking around uneasily. He had not seen a single hussar the whole day, and had only heard about them from an infantry officer. 'They broke up two squares, your Excellency.'

Hearing Zherkov, several of those present smiled, expecting one of his usual sallies, but perceiving that what he was saying also redounded to the glory of our arms and of the day's work they looked grave again, though many of them were very well aware that what Zherkov was saying had no foundation in fact. Prince Bagration turned to the elderly colonel.

'I thank you all, gentlemen. All branches of the service behaved heroically: infantry, cavalry, and artillery. How was it two field-pieces were abandoned in the centre?' he inquired, searching with his eyes for someone. (Prince Bagration did not ask about the cannon on the left flank: he knew that all the cannon there had been abandoned at the very beginning of the action.) 'I believe I sent you, didn't I?' he said, turning to the staff-officer on duty.

'One was damaged,' answered the staff-officer, 'but the other I can't explain. I was there all the time myself, giving orders, and had only just left. … It was pretty hot, it's true,' he added modestly.

Someone remarked that Captain Tushin was bivouacking close by in the village and had already been sent for.

'Ah, but you were there, were you not?' said Prince Bagration, addressing Prince Andrei.

'Yes, indeed, we just missed each other,' said the staff-officer, giving Bolkonsky an affable smile.

'I had not the pleasure of seeing you,' declared Prince Andrei, coolly and abruptly.

Everyone was silent. Tushin appeared in the doorway, timidly edging in behind the backs of the generals. Making his way past the high-ranking officers in the crowded hut, abashed as he always was before his superiors, he did not notice the staff of the banner and stumbled over it. Several of those present laughed.

'How is it that a gun was abandoned?' asked Bagration, frowning not so much at the captain as at those who were laughing, among whom Zherkov's voice was distinguished above the rest.

Only now, when confronted by stern authority, did Tushin realize the full horror of his crime and the disgrace of still being alive after having lost two guns. He had been so wrought up that until that moment he had not thought about it. The officers' laughter confused him still more. He stood before Bagration, his lower jaw trembling, and was hardly able to stammer out:

'I … I don't know … your Excellency … I hadn't the men … your Excellency.'

'You could have got them from the covering troops.'

Tushin did not say that there had been no covering troops, although actually this was the truth. He was afraid of getting some other officer into trouble, so he stood in silence with his eyes fixed on Bagration in the way a bewildered schoolboy stares at the face of an examiner.

The silence lasted some time. Prince Bagration, evidently not wishing to be severe, found nothing to say, and the others did not venture to intervene. Prince Andrei looked at Tushin from under his brows and his fingers twitched nervously.

'Your Excellency!' Prince Andrei broke the silence in his curt voice. 'You were pleased to send me to Captain Tushin's battery. I went there and found two-thirds of his men and horses knocked out, two guns disabled, and no covering forces whatever.'

Prince Bagration and Tushin now looked with equal intensity at Bolkonsky who spoke with suppressed emotion.

'And if your Excellency will permit me to express my opinion,' he went on, 'we owe today's success mainly to the action of this battery and the heroic endurance of Captain Tushin and his company.' And without waiting for a reply Prince Andrei rose and walked away from the table.

Prince Bagration looked at Tushin and, apparently reluctant to evince any mistrust of Bolkonsky's outspoken judgement yet unable to put complete faith in it, inclined his head and told Tushin that he could go. Prince Andrei followed him out.

'Thanks, my dear fellow, you got me out of a scrape,' said Tushin.

Prince Andrei gave him a look but said nothing, and went away. His heart was heavy and full of melancholy. It was all so strange, so unlike what he had hoped.

*

'Who are they? Why are they here? What do they want? And when will all this end?' Rostov asked himself, as he watched the changing shadows. The pain in his arm grew steadily worse. He ached with sleep, crimson circles danced before his eyes, and the impression of those voices and faces and a sense of loneliness merged with the physical pain. It was they, those soldiers, wounded, not wounded – it was they who were pressing upon him, crushing him, twisting the sinews and scorching the flesh of his shattered arm and shoulder. To get rid of them he closed his eyes.

For a moment he dozed off but in that brief interval of oblivion he dreamed of innumerable things: he saw his mother and her large white hand, Sonya's thin shoulders, Natasha's eyes and her laugh, Denisov with his voice and his whiskers, and Telyanin, and all the affair with Telyanin and Bogdanich. All that affair was inextricably mixed up with this soldier with the harsh voice, and it was that affair and this soldier that were so agonizingly, so ruthlessly pulling and squeezing his arm and dragging it always in the same direction. He was trying to free himself but they would not let go of his shoulder for a single second, or relax their hold a hair's breadth. It would not have hurt, it would have been all right, if only they would stop pulling at it; but there was no escape from them.

He opened his eyes and looked up. The black canopy of night hung less than a yard above the glow of the charcoal fire. Powdery snow fluttered down through the glow. Tushin had not returned, the surgeon did not come. He was alone except for some poor soldier sitting naked at the other side of the fire, warming his thin, sallow body.

'Nobody cares about me!' thought Rostov. 'There is no one to help me or take pity on me. Yet once I was at home, strong, happy and loved.' He sighed, and the sigh unconsciously became a groan.

'In pain, eh?' asked the little soldier, shaking his shirt out over the fire, and not waiting for an answer he gave a grunt and added: 'Shocking number of fellows done for today!'

Rostov did not heed the soldier. He gazed at the snowflakes fluttering above the fire and thought of winter at home in Russia, the warm, bright house, his soft fur coat, the swiftly-gliding sledge, his healthy body, and all the love and affection of his family. 'And what did I come here for?' he wondered.

Next day the French did not renew their attack and the remnant of Bagration's division was reunited with Kutuzov's army.

PART THREE

I

PRINCE VASILI was not a man to plan and look ahead. Still less did he ever plot evil with a view to his own advantage. He was merely a man of the world who had got on and to whom success had become a matter of habit. Circumstances and the people he encountered were allowed to shape his various schemes and devices, which he never examined very closely though they constituted his whole interest in life. Of such plans he had not just one or two but dozens in train at once, some at their initial stage, others nearing achievement, still others in course of disintegration. He never said to himself, for instance: 'So-and-so now has influence, I must gain his confidence and friendship and through him secure a special grant'; or 'There's Pierre, a rich fellow: I must entice him to marry my daughter and lend me the forty thousand I need.' But when he came across a man of position instinct immediately whispered to him that this person might be useful, and Prince Vasili would strike up an acquaintance and at the first opportunity, without any premeditation, led by instinct, would flatter him, treat him with easy familiarity, and finally make his request.

He had Pierre ready at hand in Moscow and procured for him an appointment as gentleman of the bedchamber, which at that time conferred the same status as the rank of privy councillor, and insisted on the young man's travelling with him to Petersburg and staying at his house. With an absent-minded air, yet at the same time taking it absolutely for granted that it was the right thing, Prince Vasili was doing everything to get Pierre to marry his daughter. Had he thought out his ideas beforehand he could not have been so natural in his behaviour, and so simple and unaffected in his relations with everybody, both above and below him in social standing. Something always drew him to men richer or more powerful than himself, and he was endowed with the rare art of being able to hit on exactly the right moment for making use of people.

Pierre, on unexpectedly becoming Count Bezuhov and a wealthy man, after his recent life of loneliness and inaction found himself so busy and beset that only when he was in bed could he have a moment to himself. He had to sign papers, to appear at Government offices for reasons which were not clear to him, to catechize his chief steward, to visit his estate near Moscow and to receive a great number of persons who had hitherto not cared even to be aware of his existence but now would be offended and hurt if he refused to see them. All these various individuals – business men, relations and acquaintances alike – were with one accord disposed to treat the young heir in the most kindly, friendly manner: they were all evidently firmly persuaded of Pierre's noble qualities. He was continually hearing such phrases as: 'With your extraordinary kindness,' or 'Thanks to your generous heart,' or 'You who are so upright, count ...' or 'If he were as clever as you are,' and so on, until he actually began to believe in his exceptional kindness and remarkable intelligence, the more so as at the bottom of his heart it had always seemed to him that he really was very good-natured and very intelligent. Even people who before had been spiteful and openly hostile now became gentle and affectionate. The cross-grained eldest princess with the long waist and the hair plastered down like a doll's had come into Pierre's room after the funeral. With lowered eyes and crimson cheeks she told him how sincerely she regretted the misunderstandings that had arisen between them in the past, and asked him – she felt that that was all she had the right to ask – to be allowed, after the blow that had befallen her, to remain for a few weeks longer in the house she was so fond of and where she had made such sacrifices. She could not restrain her tears and wept freely at these words. Touched by such a change in this statue-like princess, Pierre took her hand and begged forgiveness, though he did not know for what. Later that day the princess began to knit Pierre a striped comforter, and from that time was quite different to him.

'Do this for her, *mon cher*. After all, she had to put up with a great deal from the deceased,' said Prince Vasili, handing him some deed to sign for the princess's benefit.

Prince Vasili had decided that this bone – a note of hand for thirty thousand – had better be thrown to the poor princess lest it enter her head to gossip about the part he had played in the matter of the inlaid portfolio.

Pierre signed the deed, and after that the princess became even more amiable. The other sisters became equally affectionate, especially the youngest, the pretty one with the mole, who often embarrassed him with her smiles and her confusion at the sight of him.

It seemed so natural to Pierre that everyone should like him, it would have seemed so unnatural had anybody disliked him, that he could not help believing in the sincerity of those around him. Besides, he had no time to ask himself whether these people were sincere or not. He never had a moment of leisure: he felt as if he were living in a constant state of mild and agreeable intoxication. He was the centre of some important social mechanism and something was for ever expected of him, which he must perform or people would be grieved and disappointed; but if he did this and that all would be well; and he did whatever was required of him, but still the happy result remained in the future.

More than anyone else in these early days Prince Vasili took control of Pierre's affairs and of Pierre himself. On the death of Count Bezuhov he did not let Pierre slip out of his hands. He went about with the air of a man weighed down by affairs, weary, worn out, but too tender-hearted to abandon this helpless youth, who after all was the son of his old friend, and the possessor of such an enormous fortune, to the vagaries of fate and the designs of scoundrels. During the few days he stayed on in Moscow after Count Bezuhov's death he would invite Pierre, or go to him himself, and advise him on what ought to be done in a tone of such weariness and assurance as to imply each time: 'You know that I am overwhelmed with business and that it is out of pure charity that I concern myself with you; and of course you realize too that the suggestions I make are the only possible ones.'

'Well, my dear fellow, tomorrow we are off at last,' said Prince Vasili one day, closing his eyes and drumming his fingers on Pierre's elbow, speaking as if he were saying something that had long since been decided and could not now be altered. 'We start tomorrow and I'm giving you a place in my carriage. I am very glad. We have got through everything that was pressing here, and I ought to have been back long ago. Here, I received this from the chancellor. I put in an application for you, and you have been entered in the diplomatic corps and made a gentleman of the bedchamber. Now a diplomatic career lies open to you.'

Notwithstanding the effect produced on him by the tired, confident tone with which these words were pronounced, Pierre, who had thought long about his career, tried to protest. But Prince Vasili broke in on his protest in a cooing bass which precluded all possibility of interrupting the flow of his words and which he employed in cases where extreme measures of persuasion were needed.

'*Mais, mon cher*, I did it for my own sake, to satisfy my conscience, and there is no need to thank me. No one ever yet complained of being too well loved; and besides, you are not tied down, you could throw it up tomorrow. You'll see for yourself in Petersburg. And it is high time you got away from these painful associations.' Prince Vasili sighed. 'So that's all arranged, my dear boy. And my valet can go in your carriage. Ah, yes, I was almost forgetting,' he added. 'You know, *mon cher*, your father had a little account to settle with me, so as I have received some monies from the Ryazan estate I'll keep them; you don't want them. We'll make it all square by and by.'

What Prince Vasili called 'some monies from the Ryazan estate' meant several thousand roubles quit-rent from Pierre's peasants, which sum he retained for himself.

In Petersburg Pierre found himself surrounded by the same atmosphere of tenderness and affection as in Moscow. He could not decline the post, or rather the dignity (for he did nothing), that Prince Vasili had procured for him, and acquaintances, invitations and social obligations were so numerous that he felt even more conscious than he had in Moscow of a sense of bewilderment, bustle and continual expectation of some future good which was always near but never attained.

Of his old circle of bachelor friends many were no longer in Petersburg. The guards had gone on active service. Dolohov had been reduced to the ranks, Anatole was in the army somewhere in the provinces, Prince Andrei was abroad, and so Pierre had no opportunity of spending his nights in the way he used to enjoy them, or of opening his mind in intimate talks with some friend older than himself and whose opinions he respected. His whole time went in dinners and balls, or, more often than all, at Prince Vasili's in the company of the elderly, portly princess, his wife, and his beautiful daughter Hélène.

Like everyone else, Anna Pavlovna Scherer made Pierre aware of the change that had taken place in society's attitude towards him.

In Anna Pavlovna's presence of old, Pierre had always felt that what he was saying was unseemly, tactless and not the right thing, that remarks which were sensible while they were forming in his mind became idiotic as soon as he spoke them aloud, whereas Hippolyte's feeblest utterances had the effect of being clever and endearing. Now everything that Pierre said was *charmant*. Even if Anna Pavlovna did not say so he could see that she was longing to and only refrained out of regard for his modesty.

At the beginning of the winter in this year 1805 Pierre received one of Anna Pavlovna's customary pink notes of invitation to which was added the postscript: '*La belle Hélène* will be here, whom one is never tired of feasting one's eyes on.'

As he read this it struck Pierre for the first time that a certain link which other people recognized had been formed between himself and Hélène, and the thought both alarmed him as though an obligation were being laid on him which he could not fulfil, and at the same time pleased him as an entertaining idea.

Anna Pavlovna's party was exactly like the former one, except that the novelty she offered her guests on this occasion was not Mortemart but a diplomat newly arrived from Berlin and bringing the very latest details of the Emperor Alexander's visit to Potsdam, and of how the two august friends had there pledged themselves in an indissoluble alliance to uphold the cause of justice against the enemy of the human race. Pierre was welcomed by Anna Pavlovna with a shade of melancholy, evidently relating to the recent loss which the young man had sustained in the death of Count Bezuhov. (Everyone constantly felt it their duty to assure Pierre that he was greatly afflicted by the passing away of the father he had hardly known.) Her melancholy was of precisely the same kind as the exalted melancholy she always manifested at any allusion to Her Most August Majesty the Empress Maria Fiodorovna. Pierre was flattered. Anna Pavlovna had arranged the groups in her drawing-room with her habitual skill. The large circle, in which Prince Vasili and some generals were conspicuous, were enjoying the benefit of the diplomat. Another group was gathered about the tea-table. Pierre would have liked to join the former but Anna Pavlovna – who was in the state of nervous excitement of a commander on the battlefield whose head is full of a thousand new and brilliant ideas which he has hardly time to put into execution – on seeing Pierre laid a finger on his coat-sleeve and said:

'Wait, I have designs on you for this evening.' She glanced at Hélène and smiled at her. 'My dear Hélène, be charitable to *ma pauvre tante* who adores you. Go and keep her company for ten minutes. And that you may not find it too tiresome, here is our dear count who certainly won't refuse to escort you.'

The beauty moved away towards *ma tante*, but Anna Pavlovna detained Pierre, with the air of still having some last and indispensable arrangement to complete with him.

'Isn't she exquisite?' she said to Pierre, indicating the stately beauty as she glided away. 'And how she carries herself! For such a young girl what tact, what finished perfection of manner! It comes from the heart. Happy the man who wins her! With her the most unworldly of men could not fail to occupy a brilliant position in society, and with no effort. Don't you think so? I only wanted to know your opinion,' said Anna Pavlovna, and released Pierre.

Pierre was perfectly sincere when he agreed with Anna Pavlovna as to Hélène's perfection of manner. If he ever thought of Hélène it was of her loveliness and of this extraordinary ability of hers to appear silently serene and dignified in society.

The old aunt received the two young people in her corner but seemed desirous of hiding her adoration for Hélène and more inclined to show her fear of Anna Pavlovna. She looked at her niece as though to inquire what she was to do with the pair. As Anna Pavlovna turned away, she again laid a finger on Pierre's sleeve, remarking:

'I hope you will never say in future that people find it dull in my house,' and she glanced at Hélène.

Hélène smiled in a way which implied that she could not admit the possibility of anyone seeing her and not feeling enchanted. The aunt coughed, swallowed the phlegm, and said in French that she was very glad to see Hélène; then she addressed Pierre with the same greeting and the same grimace. In the middle of a halting and tedious conversation Hélène looked at Pierre and smiled with the beautiful radiant smile she gave to everyone. Pierre was so used to this smile, and it had so little meaning for him, that he paid no attention to it. The aunt was just speaking of a collection of snuff-boxes that had belonged to Pierre's father, Count Bezuhov, and she showed them her own box. Princess Hélène asked to see the portrait of the aunt's husband on the lid.

'The work of Vines, probably,' said Pierre, alluding to a celebrated miniature-painter, and he leant over the table to take the snuff-box, all the time trying to hear what was being said at the other table.

He half rose, meaning to go round, but the aunt handed him the snuff-box, passing it across Hélène's back. Hélène bent forward to make room, and looked round with a smile. She was, as she always did for evening parties, wearing a gown cut in the fashion of the day, very low back and front. Her bosom, which always reminded Pierre of marble, was so close to him that his short-sighted eyes could not but perceive the living charm of her neck and shoulders, so near to his lips that he need only stoop a little to have touched them. He was conscious of the warmth of her body, of the smell of perfume, and heard the slight creak of her corset as she breathed. He saw not her marble beauty forming a single whole with her gown, but all the fascination of her body, which was only veiled by her clothes. And once having seen this, his eyes refused to see her in any other way, just as we cannot reinstate an illusion that has been explained.

She looked up, straight at him, her dark eyes sparkling, and smiled. 'So you have never noticed before how beautiful I am?' Hélène seemed to say. 'You had not noticed that I am a woman? Yes, I am a woman, who might belong to anyone – might even belong to you,' said her eyes. And at that moment Pierre was conscious that Hélène not only could but must become his wife, and that it must be so.

He was aware of this at that moment as surely as if he were standing at the altar with her. How and when it would be, he could not tell. He did not even know if it would be a good thing (indeed, he had a feeling that for some reason it would not), but he knew that it was to be.

Pierre dropped his eyes, then lifted them, and tried to see her again as a distant beauty removed from him, the way he had seen her every day until then, but found it no longer possible. He could not do it any more than a man who has been staring through the mist at a tuft of steppe grass and taking it for a tree can see it as a tree once he has recognized it for a tuft of grass. She was terribly close to him. Already she had power over him. And between him and her there existed no barrier now save the barrier of his own will.

'Well, I will leave you in your little corner,' came Anna Pavlovna's voice. 'I can see you are very comfortable here.'

And Pierre, frantically trying to think whether he had been guilty of anything reprehensible, crimsoned and looked about him, it seemed to him that everyone knew as well as he did what had happened to him.

After a little while, when he had joined the large circle, Anna Pavlovna said to him: 'I hear you are having your Petersburg house redecorated.'

This was true. The architect had told him it was necessary, and Pierre, without knowing why, was having the huge Petersburg mansion done up.

'That is an excellent idea, but don't give up your quarters at Prince Vasili's. It is good to have a friend like the prince,' said she, smiling at Prince Vasili. 'I know something about that, do I not? And you are still so young. You need someone to advise you. You mustn't be angry with me for exercising an old woman's privilege.'

She paused, as women always do after talking about their age, expecting some comment. 'If you marry, it's a different matter,' she continued, uniting the pair in one glance. Pierre did not look at Hélène, nor she at him. But she was still as terribly close to him. He stammered something and coloured.

Back at home Pierre could not get to sleep for a long while for thinking of what had happened. What had happened? Nothing. He had merely discovered that a woman he had known as a child, a woman of whom he had been able to say indifferently, 'Yes, she's nice-looking' when anyone told him that Hélène was a beauty, might be his.

'But she's brainless, I have always said so,' he thought. 'No, this isn't love. On the contrary, there's something nasty, something not right in the feeling she excites in me. Didn't I hear that her own brother Anatole was in love with her and she with him, that there was a regular scandal and that was the reason he was sent away? Her brother is – Hippolyte. Her father – Prince Vasili. That's not good,' he reflected, but while he was thus musing (the reflections were not followed to their conclusion) he caught himself smiling and was conscious that another line of thought had sprung up and while meditating on her worthlessness he was also dreaming of how she would be his wife, how she would love him, how she might become quite different, and how all he had heard and thought about her might be untrue. And he again saw her not as Prince Vasili's daughter but visualized her whole body only veiled by her grey gown. 'But no, why did this idea never enter my mind before?' and again he told himself that it was impossible, that there would be something

nasty and unnatural in this marriage, something which seemed dishonourable. He recalled past words and glances of hers, and the
words and looks of people who had seen them together. He remembered Anna Pavlovna's words and looks when she had spoken about
his house, recalled a hundred similar hints on the part of Prince Vasili
and others, and was seized with terror lest he had already in some
way bound himself to do a thing which was obviously wrong and
not what he ought to do. But at the very time he was expressing this
conviction to himself, in another part of his mind her image rose in
all its womanly beauty.

2

IN November 1805 Prince Vasili was obliged to go on a tour of
inspection through four provinces. He had secured this commission
for himself so as to call in on his neglected estates at the same time.
He intended to pick up his son Anatole on the way (where his regiment was stationed) and take him to visit Prince Nikolai Andreyevich
Bolkonsky, in the hope of marrying him to the rich old man's daughter. But before setting out on these new ventures Prince Vasili wanted
to settle matters with Pierre, who had, it was true, of late spent whole
days at home, that is in Prince Vasili's house where he was staying,
and was absurd, agitated and foolish in Hélène's presence (the proper
condition of a man in love), but still had not made his declaration.

'This is all very fine, but matters must come to a head,' said Prince
Vasili to himself with a melancholy sigh one morning, feeling that
Pierre, who was under such obligations to him ('but never mind that'),
was not behaving very well in the circumstances. 'Youth ... frivolity
... well, God bless him,' thought he, relishing his own goodness of
heart. 'Mais il faut que ça finisse. The day after tomorrow is my little
Hélène's name-day. I will invite a few friends in and then, if he does
not see what he ought to do, it will be my affair. Yes, my affair. I'm
her father.'

Six weeks after Anna Pavlovna's 'At Home' and the sleepless agitated night when he had decided that to marry Hélène would be a
calamity and that he must escape her and go away, Pierre, in spite of
this decision, had not moved from Prince Vasili's and felt with horror that in people's eyes he was committing himself more every day,
that he could not go back to his former ideas of her, that he could not

break away from her even, and though it would be an awful thing he would have to unite his life to hers. Perhaps he might have been able to hold back, but not a day passed without a party at Prince Vasili's (where parties had hitherto been the exception), and Pierre had to be present unless he wished to spoil the general pleasure and disappoint everyone. Prince Vasili in the rare moments when he was at home would take Pierre's hand in passing and, drawing him down absent-mindedly, present his wrinkled, clean-shaven cheek for a kiss, saying: 'Till tomorrow,' or 'Be in to dinner or I shan't see you,' or 'I am staying in on your account,' and the like. But though when Prince Vasili did stay at home for Pierre (as he said) he barely exchanged a couple of words with him, Pierre did not feel equal to disappointing him. Every day he repeated one and the same thing to himself: 'It is time I understood her and made up my mind what she really is. Was I mistaken before, or am I mistaken now? No, she is not stupid. No, she's a fine girl!' he would say to himself sometimes. 'She never does the wrong thing, never makes silly remarks. She does not talk much but what she does say is always clear and simple, so she cannot be stupid. She has never been disconcerted and is never out of countenance, so she cannot be a bad woman!' It often happened that he began to argue or think aloud in her company and every time she had replied either by some brief but appropriate remark that showed she was not interested, or by a mute smile and glance which to Pierre proved her superiority more palpably than anything else. She was right in regarding all reflections as nonsense in comparison with that smile.

She always turned to him now with a radiantly confiding smile meant for him alone, in which there was something more significant than in the smile which she wore for the world in general. Pierre knew that everyone was waiting for him to speak the one word needful, to cross a certain boundary, and he knew that sooner or later he would cross it; but an unaccountable horror seized him at the mere thought of this fearful step. A thousand times in the course of those six weeks, during which he felt himself being drawn nearer and nearer to that dreadful abyss, Pierre said to himself: 'What am I doing? I must act with determination. Can it be that I haven't any?'

He was anxious to come to a decision but felt with dismay that in this matter he lacked the strength of will which he had known in himself and really did possess. Pierre belonged to the category of people who are strong only when their consciences are absolutely clean. But since that day when he had been overpowered by a feeling of desire while stooping over the snuff-box at Anna Pavlovna's an unacknowledged sense of the sinfulness of that impulse paralysed his will.

On Hélène's name-day a small party of friends and relatives – 'Our nearest and dearest,' as his wife called them – met for supper at Prince Vasili's. All these friends and relatives had been given to understand that the evening was to be a momentous one for the young girl's future. The guests were seated at supper. Princess Kuragin, a portly, imposing woman who had once been handsome, was sitting at the head of the table. On either side of her were the most honoured guests – an old general and his wife, and Anna Pavlovna Scherer. At the other end of the table sat the younger and less important guests, and there too were placed as members of the family Pierre and Hélène, side by side. Prince Vasili was not having supper: he walked round in high good humour, sitting down beside one friend after another. He had a light-hearted pleasant word for everybody, except Pierre and Hélène, whose presence he seemed to ignore. He was the life of the whole party. The wax candles burned brightly, the silver and crystal gleamed, as did the ladies' finery and the gold and silver of the men's epaulets; footmen in scarlet livery moved round the table; and the clatter of plates mingled with the clink of knives and glasses and the hum of various animated conversations. At one end of the assembly an old chamberlain was heard assuring an aged baroness of his ardent love for her, while she laughed; at the other someone was relating the misfortunes of a certain Maria Viktorovna. In the centre Prince Vasili focused attention on himself. With a playful smile on his lips he was telling the ladies about the previous Wednesday's session of the privy council at which Sergei Kuzmich Vyazmitinov, the new military governor-general of Petersburg, had received and read a rescript – much talked of at the time – from the Emperor Alexander Pavlovich. The Emperor, writing from the army to Sergei Kuzmich, had said that he was the recipient of declarations of loyalty from all sides, that the testimony from Petersburg afforded him particular pleasure, that he was proud to be at the head of such a nation and would endeavour to prove himself worthy. This rescript began with the words: 'Sergei Kuzmich, From all sides reports reach me,' etc.

'So he never got further with it than "Sergei Kuzmich" ?' asked one of the ladies.

'No, no, not a syllable,' answered Prince Vasili, laughing. '"Sergei Kuzmich ... From all sides." "From all sides ... Sergei Kuzmich ..." Poor Vyazmitinov could not get any further. He started again and again but no sooner did he utter *"Sergei"* – than a sniff ... *"Kuz-mi-ch"* – tears ... and *"From all sides"* is smothered in sobs, and he could not go on. And out came the handkerchief again, and again we heard "Sergei Kuzmich, From all sides," ... and more tears, until at last somebody else was asked to read it for him.'

'"Kuzmich ... From all sides" ... and tears,' someone repeated, laughing.

'Don't be unkind,' cried Anna Pavlovna from her end of the table, holding up a threatening finger. 'He is such a worthy, excellent man, our good Vyazmitinov....'

All the company laughed heartily. At the head of the table, in the places of honour, everyone seemed to be in high spirits and under the influence of various enlivening tendencies. Only Pierre and Hélène sat mutely side by side almost at the bottom of the table, a radiant smile hovering on both their faces, a smile which had nothing to do with Sergei Kuzmich – a smile of bashfulness at their own feelings. But gaily as the others all talked, laughed and joked, much as they enjoyed their Rhine wine, the *sauté* and the ice cream, carefully as they avoided glancing at the young couple, and heedless and un-observant as they seemed of them, yet it was somehow perceptible from the occasional glances they gave that the anecdote about Sergei Kuzmich, the laughter and the food were all affectation, and that the whole attention of all the party was in reality concentrated on the two young people, Pierre and Hélène. Prince Vasili mimicked the sniffs of Sergei Kuzmich and at the same time ran a searching eye over his daughter, and while he laughed the expression on his face said: 'Yes, yes, it's going on all right, it will be settled this evening.' Anna Pavlovna shook her finger at him for laughing at 'our good Vyaz-mitinov' and in her eyes which flashed for a moment in Pierre's direction Prince Vasili read congratulation on his future son-in-law and his daughter's felicity. Old Princess Kuragin, offering her neigh-bour some wine with a melancholy sigh, looked resentfully at her daughter, her sigh seeming to say: 'Yes, there is nothing left for you and me but to sip sweet wine, my dear, now that it is the turn of the young ones to be so flauntingly, clamorously happy.' 'And what stupid stuff it all is that I am saying, as though it interests me,' thought a diplomat, glimpsing the glad faces of the lovers. 'That's happiness!'

Into the petty trivialities, the conventional interests that united the company, there had entered the simple feeling of attraction felt by handsome and healthy young creatures for each other. And this human emotion dominated everything else and triumphed over all their artificial chatter. Jests fell flat, news was not interesting, the animation was unmistakably forced. Not only the guests but the very footmen waiting at table appeared to feel the same and they forgot their duties as they looked at the beautiful Hélène with her radiant face and at Pierre's broad, red, happy and uneasy countenance. Even the light from the candles seemed to focus on those two happy faces.

Pierre was conscious that he was the centre of all this, and his position both pleased and embarrassed him. He was like a man absorbed in some occupation. He had no clear sight nor hearing; no understanding of anything. Only now and then disconnected ideas and impressions from the world of reality flashed through his mind.

'So it is all over,' he thought. 'How on earth did it all happen? And so quickly! Now I know that not for her sake alone, nor for my own sake, but for everyone it must inevitably come to pass. They are all expecting it, they are so sure that it will happen that I cannot, I cannot, disappoint them. But how will it be? I do not know; but it certainly will happen!' thought Pierre, glancing at those dazzling shoulders so close to his eyes.

Or he would suddenly feel a vague shame. It made him uncomfortable to be the object of general attention and considered a lucky man and with his homely face to be looked on as a sort of Paris in possession of his Helen of Troy. 'But no doubt it's always like this, and must be so,' he tried to console himself. 'And yet what have I done to bring it about? When did it begin? I travelled from Moscow with Prince Vasili. That was nothing. Next, I stayed in his house, and why not? Then I played cards with her and picked up her reticule and drove out with her. When did it begin, how had it all come about?' And here he was sitting by her side as her betrothed, hearing, seeing, feeling her nearness, her breathing, her movements, her beauty. Then all at once it would seem to him that it was not she but he who was so extraordinarily beautiful that they all had to look at him; and made happy by this universal admiration he would expand his chest, raise his head high and rejoice at his good fortune. Suddenly he heard a familiar voice addressing him for the second time. But

Pierre was so absorbed that he did not take in what was said to him.

'I'm asking you when you last heard from Bolkonsky,' repeated Prince Vasili a third time. 'How absent-minded you are, my dear boy.'

Prince Vasili smiled, and Pierre noticed that everyone in the room was smiling at him and Hélène. 'Well, what of it, since you all know?' said Pierre to himself. 'What of it? It's the truth,' and he himself smiled his gentle, childlike smile, and Hélène smiled too.

'When did you get the letter? Was it from Olmütz?' repeated Prince Vasili, who pretended that he wanted to know in order to settle some argument.

'How can people consider or talk of such trifles?' thought Pierre. 'Yes, from Olmütz,' he answered with a sigh.

After supper Pierre led his partner into the drawing-room in the wake of the others. The guests began to disperse, some without taking leave of Hélène. Others as if unwilling to distract her from serious concerns came up for a minute and then hurried away, refusing to let her see them off. The diplomat preserved a mournful silence as he left the drawing-room. What was his futile career compared with Pierre's happiness? The old general snapped at his wife when she asked him how his leg was. 'Oh, the old fool,' he thought. 'That Hélène now will be just as much of a beauty when she's fifty.'

'I believe I may congratulate you,' whispered Anna Pavlovna to Hélène's mother and kissed her warmly. 'But for this sick headache I would stay longer.'

The princess made no reply: she was tormented by jealousy of her daughter's happiness.

While the guests were taking their leave Pierre was left for a long while alone with Hélène in the little drawing-room where they were sitting. Often before during the past six weeks he had been alone with her, but he had never spoken to her of love. Now he felt that it was inevitable but he could not make up his mind to the final step. He felt ashamed: it seemed to him that he was occupying some other man's place at Hélène's side. 'This happiness is not for you,' whispered a voice within him. 'This happiness is for those who have not in them what you have within you.'

But he had to say something and so he began by asking whether she had enjoyed the evening. She replied with customary directness that this name-day had been one of the pleasantest she had ever had.

One or two of the nearest relatives were still lingering on. They were sitting in the big drawing-room. Prince Vasili walked up to Pierre with languid steps. Pierre rose and observed that it was getting late. Prince Vasili levelled upon him a look of stern inquiry, implying that Pierre's remark was so strange that he could not believe his ears. But the expression of severity was immediately replaced by another, and taking Pierre's hand Prince Vasili drew him down into a seat and smiled affectionately.

'Well, my little girl ?' he said at once, addressing his daughter in the careless tone of consistent tenderness which comes natural to parents who have petted their children from babyhood, but which Prince Vasili had only acquired through imitating other parents.

And he turned to Pierre again.

'"*Sergei Kuzmich From all sides* –"' he began, unbuttoning the top button of his waistcoat.

Pierre smiled, but his smile showed that he knew it was not the anecdote about Sergei Kuzmich that interested Prince Vasili at that moment, and Prince Vasili knew that Pierre knew it. He suddenly muttered something and went away It seemed to Pierre that even Prince Vasili was embarrassed, and this elderly man of the world's discomfiture touched Pierre: he glanced at Hélène and fancied that she too was disconcerted, and her look seemed to say: 'Well, it's your own fault.'

'It is inevitable – the step must be taken – but I can't, I can't!' thought Pierre, and once more he began to talk about irrelevant matters, of Sergei Kuzmich, inquiring what was the point of the story, as he had not heard it properly. Hélène with a smile answered that she did not know either.

When Prince Vasili returned to the drawing-room his wife was talking in low tones to an elderly lady about Pierre.

'Of course it is a very brilliant match, but happiness, my dear …'

'Marriages are made in heaven,' responded the elderly lady.

Prince Vasili walked over and sat down on a sofa in the far corner of the room, pretending not to have heard the ladies. He closed his eyes and appeared to be dozing. His head began to droop and he roused himself.

'Aline,' he said to his wife, 'go and see what they are doing.'

The princess went up to the door, walked past it with a dignified, nonchalant air and glanced into the little drawing-room. Pierre and Hélène still sat talking as before.

'Just the same,' she said in reply to her husband.

Prince Vasili frowned, twisting his mouth to one side, and his cheeks began to twitch with the disagreeable, brutal expression characteristic of him. He shook himself, got up, threw back his head and with resolute steps walked past the ladies into the little drawing-room. Swiftly and with an assumption of delight he went up to Pierre. His face was so extraordinarily solemn that Pierre rose in alarm.

'Thank God!' said Prince Vasili. 'My wife has told me!' He put one arm round Pierre, the other round his daughter. 'My dear boy. ... My little girl.... I am very, very pleased.' His voice trembled. 'I loved your father ... and she will make you a good wife.... God bless you both!'

He embraced his daughter, then Pierre again, and kissed him with his malodorous mouth. Real tears moistened his cheeks.

'Princess, come here!' he called.

The princess came in, and she too wept. The elderly lady also put her handkerchief to her eye. Pierre was kissed, and several times he kissed the hand of the lovely Hélène. After a while they were left alone again.

'All this had to be and could not have been otherwise,' thought Pierre, 'so it's no use wondering whether it is a good thing or not. It is good at least in that it's definite and I am no longer tortured by doubts.' Pierre held his betrothed's hand in silence, watching her beautiful bosom as it rose and fell.

'Hélène!' he said aloud, and stopped.

'Something special is said on these occasions,' he thought, but could not for the life of him remember what it was. He glanced into her face. She bent forward closer to him. Her face flushed rosy-red.

'Oh, take off those ... those ...' she said, pointing to his spectacles.

Pierre took them off, and his eyes, besides the strange look people's eyes have when they remove their spectacles, held a look of dismay and inquiry. He was about to bend over her hand and kiss it, but with a quick, rough movement of her head she intercepted his lips and pressed them with her own. Pierre was struck by the transformed, unpleasantly distorted expression of her face.

'Now it's too late, it's all over; and besides I love her,' thought Pierre.

'*Je vous aime!*' he said, remembering what had to be said on these occasions; but the words sounded so thin that he felt ashamed for himself.

Six weeks later he was married and settled in the enormous newly-decorated Petersburg mansion of the Counts Bezuhov, the fortunate possessor, as people said, of a beautiful wife and millions of money.

3

IN the December of 1805 old Prince Nikolai Bolkonsky received a letter from Prince Vasili, announcing that he intended to visit him with his son. ('I am setting out on a journey of inspection and of course seventy miles is only a step out of the way for me to come and see you, my honoured benefactor,' wrote Prince Vasili. 'My son Anatole is accompanying me, *en route* for the army, and I hope you will allow him the opportunity of expressing in person the deep respect that, following his father's example, he entertains for you.')

'Well, there's no need to bring Marie out, it seems, if suitors come to us of their own accord,' incautiously remarked the little princess when she heard about this.

Prince Nikolai frowned and said nothing.

A fortnight after the letter Prince Vasili's servants arrived in advance of him one evening, and on the next day he and his son appeared.

Old Bolkonsky had never had much of an opinion of Prince Vasili's character, and the high position and honours to which Kuragin had risen of late, in the new reigns of Paul and Alexander, had increased his distrust. And now from the letter and the little princess's hints he saw what was in the wind, and his poor opinion altered into a feeling of contemptuous ill-will. He snorted whenever he mentioned him, and on the day that Prince Vasili was expected was particularly testy and bad-tempered. Whether he was out of humour because Prince Vasili was coming or particularly annoyed at Prince Vasili's visit because he was out of humour did not alter the fact that he was in a bad temper, and early in the morning Tikhon was already advising the architect not to go to the prince with his report.

'Listen to him tramping up and down,' said he, drawing the architect's attention to the sound of the prince's footsteps. 'Stepping flat on his heels, and we all know what that means. ...'

However, at nine o'clock the prince went out for his usual walk, wearing his velvet fur-lined coat with the sable collar and a sable cap.

There had been a fall of snow on the previous evening. The path to the orangery which the prince was in the habit of taking had been swept clear: the marks of a broom were still visible in the snow and a spade had been left sticking in one of the banks of loose snow that bordered the path on both sides. The prince continued on through the conservatories, the serfs' quarters and the out-buildings, frowning and silent.

'Could one get through in a sleigh?' he asked his overseer, a venerable man resembling his master in looks and manner, who was escorting him back to the house.

'The snow is deep, your Excellency. I am having the avenue swept.'

The prince nodded and went up to the porch. 'God be praised,' thought the overseer, 'the cloud has blown over!'

'It would have been difficult to drive up, your Honour,' he added. 'So I hear, your Honour, there's a minister coming to visit your Honour?'

The prince turned round to the overseer and fixed him with scowling eyes.

'What's that? A minister? What minister? Who gave you orders?' he began in his shrill, harsh voice. 'For the princess, for my daughter, you don't sweep the road, but for a minister –! I don't recognize ministers!'

'Your Honour, I thought ...'

'You thought!' shouted the prince, his words tumbling out with more and more haste and incoherence. 'You thought! ... Brigands! Blackguards! ... I'll teach you to think!' and raising his stick he swung it and would have hit the overseer had not Alpatych instinctively avoided the blow. 'You thought! ... Blackguards! ...' shouted the prince rapidly. But although Alpatych, shocked at his own temerity in dodging the blow, moved closer to the prince and bowed his bald head submissively, or perhaps for that very reason, the prince, while he continued to shout: 'Blackguards! ... Shovel the snow back again!' did not lift his stick a second time but hurried into the house.

Princess Maria and Mademoiselle Bourienne stood waiting for the old prince before dinner, well aware that he was in a bad temper – Mademoiselle Bourienne with a radiant face that said: 'I am aware of nothing, I am just the same as usual,' Princess Maria, pale and terrified, with downcast eyes. What made it harder for Princess Maria was that she knew she ought to act like Mademoiselle Bourienne at such times, but she could not manage it. 'If I pretend not to notice his ill-humour he will think I have no sympathy with him,' she would think to herself. 'If I appear depressed and out of spirits myself, he will accuse me (as he has done before) of being sulky,' and so on.

The prince glanced at his daughter's scared face and snorted.

'Little idiot!' he muttered under his breath. 'And the other one not here! So they've been tittle-tattling to her already,' he thought, when he saw that the little princess was not in the dining-room.

'And where is the princess?' he asked. 'In hiding?'

'She is not very well,' answered Mademoiselle Bourienne with a bright smile. 'She won't come down. It is natural in her condition.'

'H'm! H'm! Kh! Kh!' grunted the prince, and sat down to table. His plate seemed to him not quite clean; he pointed to a spot and flung it away. Tikhon caught it and handed it to the butler. The little princess was not ill but she went in such overwhelming terror of the prince that on hearing he was in a bad temper she decided not to appear.

'I am afraid for the baby,' she said to Mademoiselle Bourienne. 'Heaven knows what a fright might do.'

The little princess, in fact, lived at Bald Hills in a continual state of fear of her father-in-law, for whom she also felt an antipathy, though she did not realize it because the fear was so much the stronger feeling. The prince reciprocated this antipathy but in his case it was swallowed up in contempt. As she settled down at Bald Hills the little princess took a special fancy to Mademoiselle Bourienne, spent her days with her, sometimes begged her to sleep in her room, and often talked about the old prince with her, criticized him.

'So we are to have company, *mon prince?*' remarked Mademoiselle Bourienne, as she unfolded her white napkin with her rosy fingers. '*Son excellence* Prince Kuragin and his son, I hear?' she said in a tone of inquiry.

'H'm! His *excellence* is a young puppy.... I got him his appointment in the service,' said the prince disdainfully. 'And why the son should come is more than I can make out. Perhaps Princess Lisa and Princess Maria can tell us. I don't know what he's bringing his son here for. I don't want him.' And he looked at his daughter who had blushed crimson. 'Aren't you well? Eh? In awe of the "minister", I suppose, as that blockhead Alpatych called him this morning?'

'No, *mon père.*'

Unsuccessful as Mademoiselle Bourienne had been in her choice of a topic she did not desist but prattled on about the conservatories and the beauty of some flower that had just opened, and after the soup the prince became more genial.

Dinner over, he went to see his daughter-in-law. The little princess was sitting at a small table gossiping with Masha, her maid. She turned pale on seeing her father-in-law.

The little princess had altered very much. She was now more plain than pretty. Her cheeks were sunken, her lip was drawn up and there were sagging folds of skin under her eyes.

'Yes, I feel a sort of heaviness,' she replied to the prince's inquiry as to how she was.

'Is there anything you want?'

'No, merci, mon père.'

'Very well then, very well.'

He went out and into the butler's pantry, where Alpatych stood with downcast head.

'Filled up the road again?'

'Yes, your Honour. Forgive me for heaven's sake. ... It was only my stupidity.'

'All right, all right,' the prince interrupted him, and laughing in his unnatural way he stretched out his hand for Alpatych to kiss, and then proceeded to the study.

In the evening Prince Vasili arrived. He was met in the avenue by coachmen and footmen, who with much shouting dragged his carriages and sledges up to one wing of the house, over snow which had purposely been shovelled back on the driveway.

Prince Vasili and Anatole were conducted to separate apartments.

Taking off his tunic, Anatole sat with his arms akimbo before a table on a corner of which he fixed his large, handsome eyes, smiling absent-mindedly. His whole life he regarded as one unbroken round of gaiety which someone or other was for some reason bound to provide for him. So now he looked on this visit to a churlish old man and a rich and ugly heiress in just the same way. It might all, he thought, turn out very jolly and amusing. 'And why not marry her if she really has such a lot of money? Money never comes amiss,' reflected Anatole.

He shaved and scented himself with the care and elegance which had become habitual to him, and with his characteristic air of all-conquering good humour walked into his father's room, holding his head high. Two valets were busily engaged in dressing Prince Vasili, who was looking about him with lively interest. He gave his son a cheerful nod as the latter entered, as much as to say: 'Good, that's how I want to see you looking.'

'I say, father, joking apart, is she very hideous? Eh?' he asked in French, as though reverting to a subject more than once discussed in the course of their journey.

'That'll do. What nonsense! The great thing is for you to try and be respectful and cautious with the old prince.'

'If he gets nasty, I'm off,' said Anatole. 'I can't stand these old gentlemen. What?'

'Remember that for you everything depends on this.'

Meanwhile, in the feminine part of the household not only was it known that the minister and his son had arrived but every detail of their personal appearance had been inventoried. Princess Maria was sitting alone in her room vainly trying to master her agitation.

'Why did they write? Why did Lise tell me about it? Of course it can never be!' she said aloud, looking at herself in the glass. 'How am I to go into the drawing-room? Even if I like him I could never be natural with him now.' The mere thought of her father's look filled her with terror.

The little princess and Mademoiselle Bourienne had by this time received all the intelligence they needed from Masha, the lady's maid, who told them what a handsome young man the minister's son was, with his rosy cheeks and black eyebrows; how his papa had dragged his legs upstairs with difficulty while the son had flown up like an eagle, three steps at a time. With these items of information the little princess and Mademoiselle Bourienne hastened to Princess Maria's room, the lively sound of their chatter preceding them along the corridor.

'You know they've come, Marie?' said the little princess, waddling in and sinking heavily into an arm-chair.

She was no longer in the loose gown she generally wore in the mornings but had put on one of her best dresses. Her hair had been carefully arranged and her face was full of animation, which did not, however, conceal its flabby, pasty contours. In the finery in which she was accustomed to appear in Petersburg society it was still more noticeable how much plainer she had become. Mademoiselle Bourienne, too, had taken pains to add some subtle finishing touches which rendered her fresh, pretty face still more attractive.

'What! Aren't you going to change, *chère princesse* ?' she exclaimed. 'They'll be coming in a minute to tell us the gentlemen are in the drawing-room and we shall have to go down, and you aren't doing a thing to smarten yourself up!'

The little princess got up from the arm-chair, rang for the maid, and hastily and merrily began to think out what her sister-in-law should wear and to put her ideas into effect. Princess Maria's self-respect was wounded by the fact that the arrival of a suitor could perturb her, and it was still more mortifying that both her friends took her agitation as a matter of course. To tell them that she felt ashamed for herself and for them would be to betray her agitation, while to decline to dress up as they suggested would prolong their banter and insistence. She flushed, her lovely eyes lost their brilliance, red blotches appeared on her face, which took on the unbeautiful victimized expression it so often wore, as she surrendered herself to Mademoiselle Bourienne and Lisa. Both women laboured with *perfect sincerity* to make her look pretty. She was so homely that it could never have entered the head of either of them to think of her as a rival. Consequently it was with perfect sincerity, in the naïve, unhesitating conviction women have that dress can make a face pretty, that they set to work to attire her.

'No, really, *ma bonne amie*, that dress is not becoming,' said Lisa, looking sideways at Princess Maria from a distance. 'Tell her to bring out your maroon velvet. Yes, really! Why, you know, this may be the turning-point of your life. That one's too light, it doesn't suit you. No, it's all wrong!'

It was not the dress that was wrong, but the face and whole figure of the Princess Maria, but neither Mademoiselle Bourienne nor the little princess realized this: they still fancied that if they put a blue ribbon in her hair and combed it up high, and arranged the blue sash lower on the maroon velvet, and so on, all would be well. They forgot that the frightened face and the figure could not be altered, and therefore, however much they might vary the setting and adornment, the face itself would remain pitiful and plain. After two or three changes to which Princess Maria submitted meekly, when her hair had been arranged on the top of her head (a style which quite altered and spoilt her looks) and she had put on the maroon velvet with the blue sash, the little princess walked round her twice, with her small hand smoothing out a fold here and pulling down the sash there, and then gazed at her with head first on one side and then on the other.

'No, it won't do,' she said decidedly, clasping her hands. 'No, Marie, this dress really does not suit you at all. I like you better in your little grey everyday frock. Please, for my sake. Katya,' she said to the maid, 'bring the princess her grey dress, and you'll see, Mademoiselle Bourienne, how I'll arrange it,' she added, smiling in anticipation of artistic enjoyment.

But when Katya brought the required garment Princess Maria still sat motionless before the glass looking at her face, and in the mirror she saw that there were tears in her eyes and her mouth was quivering and she was on the point of breaking into sobs.

'Come, *chère princesse*,' said Mademoiselle Bourienne, 'just one more little effort.'

The little princess, taking the dress from the maid, went up to Princess Maria.

'Now, we'll try something simple and nice,' she said.

The three voices – hers, Mademoiselle Bourienne's and Katya's, who was laughing at something – blended into a sort of gay twitter like the chirping of birds.

'No, leave me alone,' said Princess Maria.

And there was such seriousness and such suffering in her tone that the twitter of the birds was silenced at once. They looked at the great beautiful eyes, full of tears and brooding, turned on them imploringly, and realized that it would be useless and even cruel to insist.

'At least alter your coiffure,' said the little princess. 'Didn't I tell you,' she added reproachfully to Mademoiselle Bourienne, 'Marie has one of those faces which that style never suits. Never. Do please re-arrange it.'

'Leave me alone, leave me alone. I don't care in the least,' answered a voice scarcely able to keep back the tears.

Mademoiselle Bourienne and the little princess were obliged to acknowledge to themselves that Princess Maria in this guise looked very plain, far more so than usual, but it was too late. She was staring at them with an expression they both knew, thoughtful and sad. It did not frighten them (Princess Maria never inspired fear in anyone). But they knew that when this expression appeared on her face she became mute and inflexible.

'You will alter it, won't you?' said Lisa, and when Princess Maria made no answer Lisa went out of the room.

Princess Maria was left alone. She did not comply with Lisa's request, and not only did not rearrange her hair but did not even look at herself in the glass. Letting her arms drop helplessly, she sat with downcast eyes, and day-dreamed. She imagined a husband, a man, a strong, commanding and mysteriously attractive being, suddenly carrying her off into a totally different happy world that was his. She pictured a child, *her own* – like the baby she had seen the day before in the arms of her old nurse's daughter – at her own breast, with her husband standing by and gazing fondly at her and the child. 'But no, it can never be, I am too ugly,' she thought.

'Tea is served. The prince will be out in a moment,' said the maid's voice at the door.

She started up and was horrified at what she had been thinking. And before going downstairs she went into the little prayer-room hung with icons, and fixing her eyes on the blackened countenance of a large icon of the Saviour, in front of which burned a lamp, stood before it for several moments with folded hands. Princess Maria's soul was full of an agonizing doubt. Could the joy of love, of earthly love for a man, be for her? In her reveries of marriage Princess Maria dreamed of happiness with a home and children of her own, but her strongest and most secret craving was for earthly love. The more she tried to conceal this feeling from others and even from herself, the stronger it grew. 'O God,' she cried, 'how am I to stifle in my heart these temptings of the devil? How am I to renounce for ever these vile fancies, so as to fulfil Thy will in peace?' And scarcely had she put this question than God's answer came to her, in her own heart: 'Desire nothing for thyself, seek nothing, be not anxious or envious. Man's future and thy destiny too must remain hidden from thee, but live to be ready for whatever may come. If it be God's will to prove thee in the duties of marriage, be ready to obey His will.' With this consoling thought (though still she hoped for the fulfilment of that forbidden earthly longing) Princess Maria sighed, crossed herself and went downstairs, without thinking of her gown or her hair, or of how she would make her entrance or of what she would say. What could all that signify in comparison with God's ordering for her, without Whose will not one hair falls from the head of man?

4

WHEN Princess Maria came down, Prince Vasili and his son were already in the drawing-room talking to the little princess and Mademoiselle Bourienne. When she walked in with her heavy step, treading on her heels, the gentlemen and Mademoiselle Bourienne stood up and the little princess, with a gesture indicating her to the gentlemen, said: '*Voilà, Marie!*' Princess Maria saw them all and saw them in detail. She saw Prince Vasili's face look grave for a second at the sight of her but instantly smile again, and the little princess watching with curiosity to see the impression 'Marie' produced on the visitors. She saw Mademoiselle Bourienne too, with her ribbon and pretty face more eager than she had ever noticed it turned towards *him*. But *him* she could not see, she only saw something large, brilliant and handsome moving towards her as she entered the room. Prince Vasili was the first to greet her, and she kissed the bald forehead bent over her hand and in reply to his words said that, on the contrary, she remembered him very well. Then Anatole came up to her. She still could not see him. She was only conscious of a soft hand taking hers firmly, while she lightly brushed with her lips a white forehead beneath beautiful fair hair smelling of pomade. When she looked at him she was dazzled by his beauty. Anatole stood with the thumb of his right hand hooked round a button of his uniform, chest thrust out and spine drawn in, slightly swinging one foot which rested on his heel, as with head a little on one side he looked blithely at the princess without speaking and obviously not thinking at all about her. Anatole was not quick-witted, nor ready or eloquent in conversation, but he had the faculty, so invaluable for social purposes, of composure and imperturbable assurance. If a man lacking in self-confidence remains dumb on being introduced, and betrays a consciousness of the impropriety of such dumbness and an anxiety to find something to say, the effect will be bad. But Anatole was dumb and swung his foot as he cheerfully observed the princess's coiffure. It was clear that he could be silent in this way for any length of time. 'If anyone finds this silence awkward, let him talk, but I have no desire to,' his demeanour suggested. Moreover, in Anatole's manner with women there was that air of supercilious consciousness of his own superiority which does more than anything else to excite curiosity, awe and even love. His manner made it seem as if he were saying to them: 'I know you, yes; but why should I let you bother me? You'd be only too pleased, of course.' Perhaps he did not really think this when he met women (it is probable, indeed, that he did not, for he thought very little at any time), but that was the effect conveyed by his look and manner. The princess felt it and as though to show him that she did not venture to expect to interest him she turned to his father. The conversation was general and animated, thanks to Lisa's voice and the little downy lip that flew up and down over her white teeth. She met Prince Vasili with that playful tone so often adopted by voluble lively people, which consists in the assumption that between the person so addressed and oneself there are some semi-private long-established jokes and amusing reminiscences, even where no such reminiscences really exist – just as none existed in the present case. Prince Vasili readily fell in with this tone and the little princess drew Anatole too, whom she hardly knew, into these recollections of ridiculous incidents that had never happened. Mademoiselle Bourienne also joined in, and Princess Maria was pleased to find that even she was being made to share in their gaiety.

'Well, anyway, here we shall have your company all to ourselves, dear prince,' said the little princess (in French, of course) to Prince Vasili. 'Not like at Anna Pavlovna's receptions, where you always escape. Do you remember, *cette chère Annette?*'

'Ah, but you don't talk politics to me like Annette!'

'And our little tea-table?'

'Oh yes!'

'Why were you never at Annette's?' the little princess asked Anatole. 'Ah, I know, I know,' she said with a sly glance. 'Your brother Hippolyte has told me fine tales of your doings. Oh!' and she shook her finger at him. 'I know about your pranks in Paris too.'

'But Hippolyte didn't tell you, did he –' said Prince Vasili, addressing his son and seizing the little princess's arm as though she would have run away and he were just in time to catch her, '– he didn't tell you how he himself was breaking his heart over our sweet princess and how she showed him the door? Oh, she is a pearl among women,' he added, turning to Princess Maria.

For her part, Mademoiselle Bourienne, at the mention of Paris, did not let the chance slip to join in the general stream of recollections. She ventured to inquire if it were long since Anatole had left Paris and how he had liked that city. Anatole answered the Frenchwoman very readily, and smiling and staring at her he talked to her about her native land. When he saw the pretty little Bourienne Anatole decided that it would not be so very dull at Bald Hills after all. 'Not half bad-looking!' he thought, watching her. 'Not half bad-looking, this *demoiselle de compagnie*. I hope she'll bring her along when we're married,' he mused. '*La petite est gentille.*'

The old prince in his room was taking his time about dressing, frowning and ruminating on what course to adopt. The visit annoyed him. 'What are Prince Vasili and that son of his to me? The father is an old windbag and the son must be a fine specimen,' he growled to himself. What angered him was that the visit revived in his mind an unresolved and constantly avoided question, concerning which the old prince was never honest with himself. The problem was whether he could ever decide to part with his daughter and let her marry. The prince could never make up his mind to put this squarely to himself, knowing beforehand that if he did he would have to answer it truthfully, and truth conflicted not only with his feelings but with the whole possibility of existence for him. Life without Princess Maria, little as he appeared to care for her, was unthinkable. 'And why should she get married?' he thought. 'No doubt to be un-happy. Look at Lisa with Andrei – a better husband one would fancy could hardly be found nowadays – but is she contented with her lot? And who would marry Maria for love? She's plain, ungraceful. They'd take her for her connexions, her money. And don't old maids get on well enough? They are happier really.' So mused Prince Bol-konsky while he dressed, yet the question he was always putting off demanded immediate attention. Prince Vasili had brought his son obviously with the intention of making an offer and probably that day or the next would ask for a definite reply. His name and position in society were quite all right. 'Well, I've no objection,' the prince kept saying to himself. 'Only he must be worthy of her. And that is what we shall see. Yes, that is what we shall see, that is what we shall see,' he repeated aloud, and with his habitual alert step he walked into the drawing-room, taking in the whole company at a rapid glance. He noticed that the little princess had changed her dress, noticed Mademoiselle Bourienne's ribbon and the hideous way in which Princess Maria's hair was done, noticed the smiles that Mademoiselle Bourienne and Anatole were exchanging and his daughter's isolation amid the general conversation. 'She's decked herself out like a fool!' he thought, looking vindictively at Princess Maria. 'No shame in her; and he ignores her!'

He went up to Prince Vasili.

'Well, how d'ye do, how d'ye do, glad to see you.'

'Friendship laughs at distance,' began Prince Vasili rapidly, speaking in his accustomed self-confident, familiar tone. 'This is my younger son. I beg you to favour him with your friendship.'

Prince Bolkonsky surveyed Anatole.

'A fine young fellow, a fine young fellow!' he said. 'Well, come and give me a kiss,' and he offered his cheek.

Anatole kissed the old man and looked at him curiously and with perfect composure, waiting for some instance of the eccentricity his father had told him to expect.

Prince Bolkonsky sat down in his usual place in the corner of the sofa, drew up an arm-chair for Prince Vasili, pointed to it and began inquiring about political affairs and news. He listened with apparent attention to what Prince Vasili had to say but he glanced continually at Princess Maria.

'So they are writing from Potsdam already, are they?' he said, repeating Prince Vasili's last words. Then he suddenly got up and went over to his daughter.

'Was it for our guests that you got yourself up like that, eh?' he said. 'Nice of you, very nice! You have done your hair in some new fashion for visitors, and before visitors I tell you, never dare in future to change your style of dressing without my consent.'

'It was my fault, *mon père*,' interceded the little princess, flushing.

'*You* may do as you please,' said Prince Bolkonsky, with an exaggerated bow to his daughter-in-law, 'but she need not make a guy of herself, she's plain enough without that.'

And he sat down on the sofa again, paying no further attention to his daughter, whom he had reduced to tears.

'On the contrary, that coiffure suits the princess very well,' said Prince Vasili.

'Well, my young prince, and what's your name?' said Prince Bolkonsky, turning to Anatole. 'Come here and talk to me, let us get acquainted.'

'Now the fun begins,' thought Anatole, and with a smile he took a seat by the old prince.

'Well, my dear boy, I hear you've been educated abroad, not taught to read and write by the parish clerk like your father and myself. Tell me, my dear boy, you are serving in the Horse Guards now, are you not?' asked the old man, scrutinizing Anatole intently.

'No, I have transferred into the line,' replied Anatole, scarcely able to keep from laughing.

'Ah, excellent! So you want to serve your Tsar and country, do you? These are times of war. A fine young fellow like you ought to see service. Ordered to the front, eh?'

'No, prince, our regiment has gone to the front but I am attached ... what is it I am attached to, papa?' asked Anatole, turning to his father with a laugh.

'A credit to the service, I must say. "What is it I am attached to!" Ha-ha-ha!' laughed the old prince, and Anatole laughed still louder. Suddenly the old prince frowned.

'Well, you may go,' he said to Anatole.

With a smile Anatole rejoined the ladies.

'So you had him educated abroad, eh, Prince Vasili?' said the old prince to Kuragin.

'I did what I could, and I assure you the education there is far better than ours.'

'Yes, everything is different nowadays, everything is newfangled. The lad's a fine fellow, a fine fellow! Well, come along to my room.'

He took Prince Vasili's arm and led him away to the study. As soon so they were alone Prince Vasili promptly made known his hopes and desires.

'Do you suppose I keep her chained up, that I can't part with her?' said the old prince indignantly. 'What an idea! It can be tomorrow as far as I'm concerned. Only let me tell you I shall want to be better acquainted with my future son-in-law. You know my principles – everything above-board! Tomorrow I will ask her in your presence: if she wants it, then he can stay on. He can stay on and I'll see.' The old prince snorted. 'Let her marry, it's all the same to me,' he screamed in the piercing voice in which he had said good-bye to his son Andrei.

'I will be frank with you,' said Prince Vasili in the tone of a crafty man convinced of the futility of being crafty with so sharp-eyed a sparring partner. 'I know you see through people. Anatole is no

259

genius, but he is an honourable, good-hearted lad; an excellent son and kinsman.'

'Very well, very well, we shall see.'

As is always the case with women who have led secluded lives without masculine society for any length of time, with Anatole's appearance all three of the women in Prince Bolkonsky's household felt that life had not been life till this moment. Their powers of thinking, of feeling, of observation immediately increased tenfold, so that their existence which till now had been passed as it were in darkness was suddenly lit by a new light that was full of significance.

Princess Maria did not give another thought to her face and coiffure. The frank handsome countenance of the man who might perhaps become her husband absorbed all her attention. He seemed to her good, brave, resolute, manly and high-minded. She was convinced of this. A thousand dreams of a future family life continually rose in her imagination. She did her best to drive them away and strove to conceal them.

'But am I not too cold with him?' wondered the princess. 'I try to hold myself in check because in my heart of hearts I feel too close to him already; but then of course he cannot be aware of what I think of him, and may imagine I don't like him.'

And Princess Maria endeavoured and yet did not know how to be cordial to her new guest.

'Poor girl, she's devilish plain!' was what Anatole was thinking.

Mademoiselle Bourienne's reflections – she too had been thrown into a great state of excitement by Anatole's arrival – were of a different nature. Naturally, a pretty young woman with no stated position in society, no relations or friends and far from her native land did not intend to devote her life to waiting on Prince Bolkonsky, to reading aloud to him and playing the part of companion to Princess Maria. Mademoiselle Bourienne had long been looking out for the Russian prince who would immediately appreciate how superior she was to the ugly, badly dressed, ungainly Russian princesses, would fall in love with her and carry her off. And now this Russian prince was here at last. Mademoiselle Bourienne knew a little story her aunt had told her and to which her fancy supplied a sequel. The story, which she loved to go over in her imagination, was about a young girl who had been seduced, and her poor mother (*sa pauvre mère*) had appeared to her and reproached her for yielding to a man without being married. Mademoiselle Bourienne was often touched to tears as in imagination she told *him*, her seducer, this tale. Now this *he*, a real Russian prince, had arrived. He would elope with her, then *ma pauvre mère* would come on the scene, and he would marry her. This was how her future shaped itself in Mademoiselle Bourienne's brain all the while she was talking to him about Paris. Not that Mademoiselle Bourienne was calculating (not for a moment did she think out beforehand what she should do) but it had all been ready within her long ago and now simply fell into place round Anatole, whom she was anxious and determined to please as much as possible.

The little princess, like an old war-horse that hears the trumpet, instinctively and quite oblivious of her condition prepared for the familiar flirtatious gallop, without any *arrière-pensée* or particular effort, but with a naïve and light-hearted gaiety.

Although in feminine society Anatole generally affected the attitude of a man weary of being run after by women his vanity was flattered by the spectacle of the effect he produced on these three ladies. Moreover, he was beginning to feel for the pretty and provocative Mademoiselle Bourienne that passionate animal attraction which was apt to come upon him with extreme rapidity and prompt him to the coarsest and most reckless actions.

After tea the company moved into the sitting-room and Princess Maria was invited to play on the clavichord. Anatole leaned on his elbows facing her, near Mademoiselle Bourienne, and fixed his sparkling, laughing eyes on Princess Maria, who with painful and joyous agitation felt his gaze resting on her. Her favourite sonata bore her away into the most intimate of poetic worlds, and the feeling of his eyes upon her added still more poetry to that world. In reality, however, though he was gazing in her direction, Anatole was not thinking of her but was occupied with the movements of Mademoiselle Bourienne's little foot, which he was at that moment touching with his own under the clavichord. Mademoiselle Bourienne, too, was looking at Princess Maria, and in her fine eyes there was an expression of uneasy joy and hope, also new to the princess.

'How fond she is of me!' thought Princess Maria. 'How happy I am now, and how happy I may be with such a friend and such a husband! Husband? Can it be possible?' she asked herself, not daring to look at his face but still feeling his eyes fastened upon her.

When the party broke up after supper to retire for the night Anatole kissed Princess Maria's hand. She did not know how she found the courage but she looked straight into his handsome face as it came near her short-sighted eyes. After the princess he bent over the hand of Mademoiselle Bourienne (this was not etiquette but then he did everything with such assurance and simplicity) and Mademoiselle Bourienne flushed and glanced in dismay at the princess.

'*Quelle délicatesse* – how considerate of him,' thought the princess. 'Can Amélie' (this was Mademoiselle Bourienne's name) 'suppose I could be jealous of her, and fail to appreciate her tenderness and devotion to me?' She went up to Mademoiselle Bourienne and kissed her warmly. Anatole made to kiss the little princess's hand.

'No, no, no! When your father writes and tells me that you are behaving well, I will give you my hand to kiss. Not before!' And smiling and shaking a finger at him she left the room.

5

THEY all went to their apartments and, except Anatole who fell asleep the moment he got into bed, all lay awake a long time that night.

'Is he really to be my husband, this handsome stranger who is so kind? Yes, above all, kind,' thought Princess Maria, and a feeling of terror such as she had almost never experienced before came upon her. She was afraid to look round: it seemed to her that there was someone standing there behind the screen in the dark corner. And this someone was *he* – the devil – and *he* was this man with the white forehead, black eyebrows and red lips.

She rang for her maid and asked her to come and sleep in her room.

Mademoiselle Bourienne walked up and down the winter garden for a long while that evening in vain expectation of someone, now smiling at that someone, now working herself up to tears by imagining her *pauvre mère*'s reproaches after her fall.

The little princess scolded her maid because her bed was not comfortable. She could neither lie on her side nor on her face. Every position was awkward and unrestful. Her burden oppressed her – oppressed her now more than ever because Anatole's presence had so vividly recalled the time when she was not like that and had felt light and gay. She sat in a low chair, in dressing-jacket and night-cap, while Katya, sleepy and dishevelled, beat and turned the heavy feather-bed for the third time, muttering to herself.

'I told you it was all humps and hollows,' repeated the little princess. 'I should be glad enough to go to sleep, so it's not my fault.' And her voice quivered like a child's about to cry.

The old prince was awake too. Tikhon, half asleep, heard him stamping angrily up and down and snorting. The old prince felt as though he had been affronted through his daughter. The affront was the more bitter because it concerned not himself but another, his daughter, whom he loved better than himself. He told himself that he would think the whole matter over thoroughly and decide what was right and what must be done, but instead of doing so he only further worked up his irritation.

'The first man that turns up – and she forgets her father and everything else. Flies upstairs, combs her hair and twists her tail and makes herself generally unrecognizable! She's glad to throw over her father! And she knew I should notice it. Frr … frr … frr … And don't I see that young tomfool had no eyes for anyone but the little Bourienne (must get rid of her)! And where is her pride that she doesn't realize for herself? If not for her own sake she might at least show some for mine. I must make her see that this fool doesn't give her a thought but only gapes at Bourienne. No, she has no pride, but I'll make her see. …'

The old prince knew that if he were to tell his daughter she was labouring under a delusion, that Anatole was bent on a flirtation with Mademoiselle Bourienne, he would wound her self-respect and his case (not to part with her) would be won. Pacifying himself with this reflection he summoned Tikhon and began to undress.

'What devil brought them here?' he thought while Tikhon was slipping the night-shirt over his master's shrivelled old body and the chest furred with grey hairs. 'I never invited 'em. They come and upset my life. And there's not much of it left.'

'Damn them!' he muttered, while his head was still hidden in the night-shirt.

Tikhon was used to the prince's habit of expressing his thoughts aloud, and so it was with unmoved countenance that he met the wrathful inquiring face that emerged from the shirt.

'Have they gone to bed?' asked the prince.

Tikhon, like all good valets, knew by instinct the direction of his master's thoughts. He guessed that the inquiry referred to Prince Vasili and his son.

'Their Honours have gone to bed and put out their lights, your Excellency.'

'Never mind, never mind ...' exclaimed the prince briskly, and thrusting his feet into his slippers and his arms into the sleeves of his dressing-gown he went to the couch on which he always slept.

Although nothing had been said between Anatole and Mademoiselle Bourienne they understood one another perfectly so far as the first part of their romance was concerned, up to the appearance on the scene of the *pauvre mère*. They felt that they had a great deal to say to each other in private, and so from early morning both sought an opportunity of meeting alone. While Princess Maria went to her father's room at the usual hour, Mademoiselle Bourienne and Anatole met in the winter garden.

On this particular day Princess Maria made her way to the study door with more trepidation than ever. It seemed to her that not only was everyone aware that her fate was about to be decided but they also knew what she was feeling about it. She read it in Tikhon's face, and in that of Prince Vasili's valet who made her a low bow when she encountered him in the passage carrying hot water.

The old prince's manner to his daughter was extremely affectionate and careful that morning. That expression of restraint Princess Maria knew very well: it was the look her father's face wore while his withered hands clenched with vexation because she could not grasp a problem in arithmetic, and he would get up and walk away from her repeating the same words in a low voice several times over.

He came to the point at once, speaking formally.

'A proposal has been made to me on your behalf,' he said with an unnatural smile. 'You guessed, I presume, that Prince Vasili did not come here and bring his *protégé*' (for some unknown reason Prince Bolkonsky elected to refer thus to Anatole) 'for the sake of my charms. Last night a proposition was made to me on your account. And as you know my principles, I refer the matter to you.'

'How am I to understand you, *mon père*?' said the princess, turning pale and then blushing.

'How understand me!' cried her father angrily. 'Prince Vasili finds you to his taste as a daughter-in-law and makes you a proposal for his *protégé.* That is how and what you are to understand! And I am asking you.'

'I do not know what you think, *mon père,*' the princess articulated in a whisper.

'I? I? What have I to do with it? Leave me out of the question. *I* am not going to be married. What is *your* opinion? That is what I should be glad to learn.'

The princess saw that her father regarded the project with disfavour but at the same instant the thought occurred to her that now or never the destiny of her whole life hung in the balance. She lowered her eyes so as to avoid his gaze which she felt would deprive her of all power of thought and make her incapable of anything but her habitual compliance.

'I only want to carry out your wishes,' she said, 'but if I had to express my own desire ...'

She had not time to finish. The old prince interrupted her.

'Admirable!' he shouted. 'He will take you with your dowry and hook on Mademoiselle Bourienne into the bargain. She'll be the wife, while you ...'

The prince stopped. He noticed the effect of these words on his daughter. She bowed her head and was ready to burst into tears.

'There, there, I was joking, I was joking,' he said. 'Remember one thing, princess: I hold to the principle that a girl has a perfect right to choose for herself. I give you complete freedom. But remember one thing: your life's happiness depends on your decision. Never mind about me.'

'But I don't know ... father.'

'There's no need for discussion. He will do as he's told, whether it's to marry you or anyone else, but you are at liberty to choose. ... Go to your room, think it over and come back to me in an hour's time and in his presence tell me your decision, yea or nay. You will pray over it, I know. Well, pray if you like, only you'd do better to exercise your judgement. Now go.

'Yea or nay, yea or nay!' he still shouted, after the princess, reeling as if in a trance, had left the study.

Her fate was decided, and decided for happiness. But what her father had said about Mademoiselle Bourienne – that insinuation was horrible. It was not true, of course, but still it was horrible and she could not get it out of her mind. She walked on straight through the

265

winter garden, neither seeing nor hearing, when all of a sudden she was roused by the familiar voice of Mademoiselle Bourienne. She lifted her eyes and two steps away saw Anatole clasping the French-woman in his arms and whispering something in her ear. With a horrified expression on his handsome face Anatole looked round at Princess Maria but did not immediately let go of Mademoiselle Bourienne's waist, who had not yet seen her.

'Who's there? What do you want? Wait a moment!' was what Anatole's face seemed to say. Princess Maria gazed blankly at them. She could not believe her eyes. At last Mademoiselle Bourienne uttered a scream and fled. Anatole bowed to Princess Maria with an amused smile, as though inviting her to join in a laugh at this peculiar incident, and then shrugging his shoulders went to the door that led to his apartment.

An hour later Tikhon came to summon Princess Maria to the old prince, and added that Prince Vasili was with him. When Tikhon came for her, Princess Maria was sitting on a sofa in her room holding the weeping Mademoiselle Bourienne in her arms and gently stroking her hair. The princess's beautiful eyes had regained their serenity and radiance, and were directed with fond and tender pity on Mademoiselle Bourienne's pretty little face.

'Oh, princess, I must have lost your affection for ever!' said Mademoiselle Bourienne.

'Why? I love you more than before,' replied Princess Maria, 'and I will try to do everything in my power for your happiness.'

'But you despise me. You who are so pure – you could never under-stand being carried away by passion. Oh, if only my poor mother ...'

'I understand everything,' answered Princess Maria, smiling mourn-fully. 'Calm yourself, my dear. I am going to my father,' she said, and went out.

Prince Vasili was sitting with one leg crossed high over the other and a snuff-box in his hand. There was a smile of emotion on his face, as if he were so deeply moved that he could only regret and laugh at his own sensibility. When Princess Maria entered, he took a hasty pinch of snuff.

'Ah, my dear, my dear!' he began, getting up and taking her by both hands. He heaved a sigh and went on: 'My son's fate is in your hands. Decide, my good, dear, sweet Marie, whom I have always loved like a daughter.'

He drew back. A real tear appeared in his eye.

'Huh!... Huh!...' snorted Prince Bolkonsky.

'The prince on behalf of his *protégé* – I mean his son – makes you a proposal. Are you or are you not willing to be the wife of Prince Anatole Kuragin? Say Yes or No!' he shouted. 'And then I reserve for myself the right to state my opinion too. Yes, my opinion, and merely my opinion,' added the old prince in response to Prince Vasili's beseeching expression. 'Yes or no? Well?'

'My desire, *mon père*, is never to leave you, never to part my life from yours. I do not wish to marry,' she said firmly, glancing with her beautiful eyes at Prince Vasili and at her father.

'Nonsense! Fiddlesticks! Stuff and nonsense!' cried Prince Bolkonsky, frowning. He took his daughter's hand and drawing her towards him did not kiss her but only leaned his forehead to hers, just touched it, and squeezed the hand he held, so violently that she winced and uttered a cry.

Prince Vasili rose.

'My dear, let me tell you that this is a moment I shall never forget, never; but my dear, can you give us no hope, however small, of touching this heart of yours, which is so kind and generous? Say that perhaps ... The future is so vast. Say "Perhaps".'

'Prince, what I have told you is all that my heart can say. I thank you for the honour, but I shall never be your son's wife.'

'Well, there's an end of it, my dear fellow. Very glad to have seen you, very glad! Go back to your rooms, princess, go along now,' said the old prince. 'Most glad to have seen you,' he reiterated, embracing Prince Vasili.

'My vocation is a different one,' Princess Maria was thinking to herself. 'My vocation is to be happy in the happiness of others, in the happiness of love and self-sacrifice. And cost what it may, I will make poor Amélie happy. She loves him so passionately. She is so passionately penitent. I will do all I can to bring about a match between them. If he is not rich I will give her means, I will beg my father, I will ask Andrei. I shall be so happy when she is his wife. She is so unfortunate, a stranger, alone and helpless. And, oh God, how passionately she must love him if she could so far forget herself! Perhaps I might have done the same! ...' thought Princess Maria.

6

THE Rostovs had received no news of their Nikolai for a long time when one day in the middle of winter the count was handed a letter addressed in his son's handwriting. Anxious and in haste to escape notice, he ran off on tiptoe to his study, shut himself in a . began to read. Anna Mihalovna, hearing of the arrival of a letter – she always knew everything that happened in the house – went softly into the room and found the count with the missive in his hand, sobbing and laughing at once. Though her circumstances had improved, Anna Mihalovna was still living at the Rostovs'.

'My dear friend?' she brought out with a note of melancholy inquiry in her voice prepared to sympathize in any direction.

The count sobbed more violently.

'Our little Nikolai ... letter ... wa ... a ... s ... wounded, *ma chère* ... wounded ... my darling boy ... the little countess ... promoted to be an officer ... thank God ... how are we to tell the little countess?'

Anna Mihalovna sat down beside him, with her own handkerchief wiped the tears from his eyes and from the page, then having dried her own eyes read the letter, soothed the count and decided that during dinner and before tea she would prepare the countess, and then, after tea, with God's help break the news to her.

All during dinner Anna Mihalovna talked about the war and dear Nikolai, inquired twice when his last letter had been received, though she knew already, and remarked that they might well be getting a letter from him this very day. Every time the countess began to look uneasy under these hints, and glance in trepidation from the count to Anna Mihalovna, the latter adroitly turned the conversation to insignificant topics. Natasha, who of the whole family was the one most keenly alive to shades of intonation, look and expression, pricked up her ears from the beginning of the meal and was certain that there was some secret between her father and Anna Mihalovna, that it had something to do with her brother and that Anna Mihalovna was paving the way for it. For all her recklessness she did not venture to ask any questions at dinner (she knew how sensitive her mother was where news of Nikolai was concerned); but she was too excited to eat anything and wriggled about on her chair regardless of the protests of her governess. As soon as dinner was over she rushed headlong after Anna Mihalovna and catching up with her in the sitting-room flung herself on her neck.

'Auntie darling, do tell me what it is!'

'Nothing, my dear.'

'Yes, there is, you darling sweet precious pet, I won't leave off – I am sure you know something.'

Anna Mihalovna shook her head.

'You are a sly puss, *mon enfant*,' she said.

'Is it a letter from Nikolai? It is!' cried Natasha, reading confirmation in Anna Mihalovna's face.

'But for heaven's sake be careful: you know what a shock it may be to your mamma.'

'It will be, it will be, only tell me about it. You won't? Then I shall go right away and tell her this minute.'

Anna Mihalovna gave her a brief account of what was in the letter, on condition that she did not breathe a syllable to anyone.

'No, I won't, word of honour,' promised Natasha, crossing herself, 'I won't tell a soul!' and she ran off at once to Sonya.

'Nikolai ... wounded ... a letter,' she proclaimed in gleeful triumph.

'*Nicolas!*' was all Sonya could articulate, instantly turning white. Natasha, seeing the effect the tidings of her brother's wound produced on Sonya, felt for the first time the distressing aspect of the news.

She rushed over to Sonya, hugged her and began to cry.

'It's only a little wound, but he has been made an officer; he's all right now, he wrote himself,' she said through her tears.

'One can see what regular cry-babies all you women are,' said Petya, stalking up and down the room with determined strides. 'Now I'm very glad, very glad indeed that my brother has distinguished himself so. You're all of you blubberers! You don't understand a thing.'

Natasha smiled through her tears.

'You haven't seen the letter?' asked Sonya.

'No, but she said it was all over, and that he's an officer now.'

'Thank God!' said Sonya, crossing herself. 'But perhaps she didn't tell you the truth. Let us go to *maman*.'

Petya had been strutting up and down in silence.

'If I'd been in Nikolai's place I would have killed a lot more of

269

those Frenchman,' he said 'They're such beasts! I'd have killed so many there would have been a pile of them.'

'Be quiet, Petya, what a silly you are!'

'I'm not a silly – you're sillies to cry about nothing,' retorted Petya.

'Do you remember him?' Natasha asked suddenly, after a moment's silence.

Sonya smiled. 'Do I remember *Nicolas*?'

'I mean, Sonya, do you remember him properly so that you can recall every single detail about him?' said Natasha with an emphatic gesture, evidently trying to put into her words the most earnest meaning. 'I do Nikolai, I remember him,' she said. 'But not Boris. I don't remember him a bit.'

'What? You don't remember Boris!' exclaimed Sonya in amazement.

'It's not that I don't remember – I know what he's like, but it's not the way it is with Nikolai: if I shut my eyes I can see *him*. But not Boris' (she shut her eyes), 'no, there's nothing there.'

'Oh, Natasha!' said Sonya, solemnly and earnestly, not looking at her friend, as though she considered her unworthy to hear what she had in mind to say, and was saying it to someone else with whom joking was out of the question. 'I fell in love with your brother once and for all, and whatever may happen to him, and to me, I shall never cease to love him – as long as I live.'

Natasha gazed at Sonya with wondering inquisitive eyes, and did not speak. She felt that what Sonya had said was true, that there was love such as Sonya was speaking of. But Natasha had never experienced anything like it. She believed that it could exist but she did not understand it.

'Shall you write to him?' she asked.

Sonya was thoughtful. The question of how to write to *Nicolas*, and whether she ought to write, was one that worried her. Now that he was an officer and a wounded hero, would it be nice on her part to remind him of herself and, as it were, of the obligations he had taken on himself in regard to her?

'I don't know. I suppose if he writes to me I shall write back,' she said, blushing.

'And you wouldn't feel shy to write to him?'

Sonya smiled. 'No.'

'Well, I should blush to write to Boris. I'm not going to.'

'But what is there to blush about?'

'Oh, I don't know. I just feel awkward, ashamed.'

'Well, I know why she'd be ashamed,' said Petya, who had been offended by Natasha's remark to him. 'It's because she was in love with that fat man in glasses' (this was how Petya described his namesake, the new Count Bezuhov); 'and now she's in love with that singing fellow' (he meant Natasha's Italian singing-master), 'that's why she's ashamed.'

'Petya, you are a stupid,' said Natasha.

'No stupider than you are, madam,' said the nine-year-old Petya with the air of an elderly brigadier.

The countess had been prepared by Anna Mihalovna's hints during dinner. Retiring to her room, she sat down in a low chair and riveted her gaze on a miniature of her son painted on the lid of a snuff-box, while the tears kept coming into her eyes. Anna Mihalovna, with the letter in her hand, tiptoed to the countess's door and paused.

'Don't come in,' she said to the old count who was following her; 'later,' and she closed the door behind her.

The count put his ear to the keyhole and listened.

At first he heard the sound of vague conversation, then Anna Mihalovna's voice alone, uttering a long speech, then a shriek, then silence, then both voices talking at once with joyful intonations, and finally footsteps and Anna Mihalovna opened the door. Her face wore the proud expression of a surgeon who has performed a difficult amputation and invites the public in to admire his skill.

'It is done!' she said to the count, pointing triumphantly to the countess, who sat holding in one hand the snuff-box with the portrait and in the other the letter, and pressing her lips first to one and then to the other.

When she saw the count she held out her arms to him, embraced his bald head, looking over the top of it at the letter and the portrait again, and in order to press them to her lips once more she gently pushed the bald head away. Vera, Natasha, Sonya and Petya came into the room, and the reading of the letter began. After a brief description of the march and the two engagements in which Nikolai had taken part, and his promotion to officer's rank, Nikolai said that he kissed the hands of *maman* and papa, begging their blessing, and sent kisses to Vera, Natasha and Petya. Then he sent greetings to Monsieur Schelling and Madame Schoss and to his old nurse, and finally asked them to kiss for him his dear Sonya, whom he still loved and thought of the same as ever. When she heard this Sonya blushed so that the tears came into her eyes, and unable to bear the looks turned upon her she ran into the ballroom, whirled and spun round till her skirts puffed out like a balloon, and, flushing and smiling, she plumped down on the floor. The countess was crying.

'What are you crying about, *maman*?' asked Vera. 'From all he writes you ought to be glad instead of crying.'

This was perfectly true, but the count and the countess and Natasha all looked at her reproachfully. 'Who is it that she takes after?' thought the countess.

Nikolai's letter was read over a hundred times, and those who were considered worthy to hear it had to come to the countess, for she would not let it out of her hands. The tutors went in, the nurses, Mitenka, and several acquaintances, and the countess read the letter each time with new delight and each time discovered in it fresh proofs of Nikolai's virtues. How strange, how extraordinary and joyful it was to her to think that her son – the little son whose tiny limbs had faintly stirred within her twenty years ago, the son over whom she had so often quarrelled with the count who would spoil him, the son who had learnt to say 'pear' before he could say 'nanny' – should now be away in a foreign land, in strange surroundings, a gallant warrior, alone, without help or guidance, busy doing his proper work. All the universal experience of the ages, showing that imperceptibly children do grow from the cradle to manhood, did not exist for the countess. Her son's progress towards manhood at each of its stages had seemed as extraordinary as though there had not been millions upon millions of human beings who had gone through exactly the same process. Just as twenty years before she could not believe that the little creature that was lying somewhere under her heart would one day wail and suck her breast and begin to talk, so now it was incredible that that little creature could be this strong, brave man, the paragon of sons and of men, that judging by this letter he was now.

'What *style*, how charmingly he describes everything!' said she, reading over the descriptive parts of the letter. 'And what nobility of soul! Not a word about himself ... not a word! He mentions some Denisov or other, though he himself, I dare say, was braver than any of them. Nothing at all about his sufferings. What a heart! How like him it is! And how he has remembered everybody! No one forgotten. I always said – I said when he was only so high, I used to say ...'

For over a week they were all hard at work preparing a letter to Nikolai from the entire household, writing out rough drafts and making fair copies; while under the watchful eye of the countess and the fussy solicitude of the count all sorts of necessaries were collected into a parcel, together with money for the new uniform and equipment of the recently commissioned officer. Anna Mihalovna, a practical woman, had succeeded in obtaining special patronage for herself and her son among the army authorities that even extended to their correspondence. She had opportunities of sending her letters to the Grand Duke Konstantin Pavlovich, who commanded the Guards. The Rostovs assumed that 'The Russian Guards Abroad' was quite a sufficiently definite address, and that if a letter reached the Grand Duke in command of the Guards there was no reason why it should not reach the Pavlograd regiment which was no doubt in the immediate vicinity. And so it was decided to send the letters and the money by the Grand Duke's courier to Boris, and Boris must see that they were forwarded to Nikolai. The letters were from the old count, the countess, Petya, Vera, Natasha and Sonya, and finally there was a sum of six thousand roubles for his equipment, and various other things which the count was sending to his son.

7

On the 12th of November Kutuzov's campaigning army, encamped near Olmütz, was preparing to be reviewed on the following day by the two Emperors – the Russian and the Austrian. The Guards, who had only just arrived from Russia, spent the night ten miles from Olmütz and next morning were to proceed straight to the review, reaching the parade-ground at Olmütz by ten o'clock.

That day Nikolai Rostov had received a note from Boris telling him that the Ismailov regiment was quartered for the night ten miles from Olmütz, and that he wanted to see him to give him a letter and some money. The money Rostov was particularly in need of now that the troops, after their active service, were stationed near Olmütz and the camp swarmed with well-provisioned canteen-keepers and Austrian Jews offering all kinds of attractions. The Pavlograds held banquet after banquet to celebrate honours won in the field, and made expeditions into town to a certain Caroline the Hungarian who had recently opened a restaurant there with girls as waiters. Rostov, who had just celebrated his promotion to cornet and had bought Denisov's horse Bedouin, was in debt all round, to his comrades and the sutlers. On receipt of the note from Boris, Rostov rode into Olmütz with a fellow-officer, dined there, drank a bottle of wine, and then set off alone to the Guards' camp to find the companion of his childhood. Rostov had not yet had time to get his new uniform. He was wearing a shabby cadet's jacket with a private's cross, equally shabby riding-breeches with the leather seat all worn, and an officer's sabre with a sword-knot. The Don horse he was riding was one he had bought from a Cossack during the campaign. A crumpled hussar's cap was stuck jauntily back on one side of his head. As he rode up to the camp of the Ismailov regiment he was thinking of how he would impress Boris and all his comrades in the Guards by looking so thoroughly a hussar who has been under fire and suffered the rigours of the front.

The Guards had made their whole march as though it were a pleasure excursion, showing off their smartness and discipline. They had come by easy stages, their knapsacks transported on baggage-wagons, and at every halt the Austrian authorities had provided excellent dinners for the officers. The regiments had made their entry into towns and their exit from them with bands playing, and, by the Grand Duke's orders, the men had marched all the way in step (a point on which the Guards prided themselves), the officers on foot and in their proper places.

Boris had marched and shared quarters throughout with Berg, who was already in command of a company. Berg, who had received his captaincy during the march, had succeeded in gaining the confidence of his superiors by his zeal and exactitude, and had established his financial affairs on a very satisfactory basis. Boris during the same period had made the acquaintance of many persons who might prove useful to him, and among their number, through a letter of introduction from Pierre, was Prince Andrei Bolkonsky, through whom he had hopes of obtaining an appointment on the staff of the commander-in-chief. Berg and Boris, both as neat and smart as new pins and quite recovered from the fatigues of the previous day's march, were playing chess at a round table in the clean quarters that had been assigned to them. Berg held a smoking pipe between his knees. Boris in the precise manner characteristic of him was piling draughts into a little pyramid with his slim white fingers while he waited for Berg's move, watching his opponent's face and obviously thinking only of the game, his attention concentrated, as it always was, on what he was engaged on.

'Well, how are you going to get out of that?' he remarked.

'We'll do our best,' replied Berg, touching his pawn and taking his hand away again.

At that moment the door opened.

'Here he is at last!' shouted Rostov. 'And Berg too! *Ah, petisong-fong, allay cushay dormir!*' he cried, imitating the French of his old Russian nurse which he and Boris used once upon a time to make fun of.

'Goodness, how you have altered!' Boris got up to greet Rostov, not forgetting as he did so to hold on to the board and replace some falling pieces. He was about to embrace his friend but Nikolai drew back. With the dread of beaten tracks peculiar to youth, the desire to avoid imitation and express one's feelings in some new and original way, and shun the conventional forms employed by one's elders, Nikolai wanted to do something singular on meeting his friend. He wanted to pinch Boris, or give him a shove – anything rather than the customary kiss, which was what everybody did. Boris, on the contrary, embraced Rostov in a composed and friendly fashion and kissed him three times.

They had not met for nearly six months, and being at the age when young men take their first steps along life's road each saw immense changes in the other, quite new reflections of the different circumstances in which those first steps had been taken. Both had changed greatly since they were last together, and both were in a hurry to show the changes they had undergone.

'Ah, you damned dandies! Cool and trim as if you'd just come in from a stroll! Not like us poor devils from the line,' exclaimed Rostov, with martial swagger and baritone notes in his voice that were new to Boris, pointing to his own mud-stained riding-breeches.

The German landlady popped her head out of a door at Rostov's loud voice.

'Rather pretty, what?' cried Nikolai with a wink.

'Why do you shout so? You'll scare the wits out of them,' said Boris. 'I wasn't expecting you today,' he added. 'I only sent the note

275

off to you yesterday – through Bolkonsky, an adjutant of Kutuzov's, who's a friend of mine. I didn't think he would get it to you so quickly. . . . Well, how are you ? Been under fire already ?' asked Boris.

Without answering, Rostov fidgeted with the soldier's cross of St George suspended from the gold lace of his uniform and indicating his bandaged arm glanced smiling at Berg.

'As you see,' he said.

'So you have, to be sure!' said Boris with a smile. 'And we had a capital march here too. You know his Imperial Highness kept all the while with our regiment, so that we had every convenience and comfort. In Poland the receptions, the dinners, the balls! I can't tell you. And the Tsarevich was very gracious to all our officers.'

And the two friends related their experiences: the one describing gay revels with the hussars and life in the fighting line, the other the charms and advantages of service under the command of royalty.

'Oh, you Guards!' said Rostov. 'But I say, send for some wine.'

Boris made a grimace.

'If you really think so,' he said.

And going to his bed he took a purse from under the clean pillows and ordered wine to be brought.

'Oh, and I have your money and a letter to give you,' he added.

Rostov took the letter and tossing the money on the sofa put both elbows on the table and began to read. He read a few lines and then looked daggers at Berg. Meeting Berg's eyes, he hid his face behind the letter.

'Well, they've sent you a tidy sum,' said Berg, looking at the heavy purse that sank into the sofa. 'And here are we, count, having to scrape along on our pay. I can tell you in my own case ...'

'I say, Berg, my dear fellow,' began Rostov, 'when you get a letter from home and meet one of your own people whom you want to talk everything over with, and I'm on the scene, I'll clear out at once so as not to be in your way. Do you hear, be off, please, anywhere, anywhere ... to the devil!' he cried, and immediately seizing him by the shoulder and looking amiably into his face, evidently anxious to mitigate the rudeness of his words, he added, 'Don't be angry, my dear fellow. You know I speak straight from the heart to an old friend like you.'

'Why, of course, count, I quite understand,' said Berg, getting up and speaking in a muffled throaty voice.

'You might go and see the people of the house: they did invite you,' suggested Boris.

Berg put on the cleanest of coats, without a spot or speck of dust, stood in front of a mirror and brushed his lovelocks upwards, after the style of the Emperor Alexander Pavlovich, and having assured himself from Rostov's expression that his coat had been observed left the room with a bland smile.

'Oh dear, what a beast I am, though!' muttered Rostov, as he read the letter.

'Why is that?'

'Oh dear, what a brute I've been not once to have written and to have given them such a fright! Oh, what a brute I am!' he repeated, flushing suddenly. 'Well, did you send Gabriel for some wine? All right, let's have a drink!'

Among the letters from home was enclosed a note of recommendation to Prince Bagration which the old countess, on Anna Mihalovna's advice, had obtained through acquaintances and sent to her son, urging him to present and make use of it.

'What nonsense! What do I want with that?' exclaimed Rostov, flinging the letter under the table.

'What did you throw that away for?' asked Boris.

'It's some letter of recommendation ... what the deuce do I want with a letter like that!'

'What the deuce do you want with it?' said Boris, picking it up and reading the inscription. 'This letter might be very useful to you.'

'I'm not in need of anything, and I won't be adjutant to anybody.'

'Why not?' inquired Boris.

'It's a lackey's job.'

'You are still the same old idealist, I see,' remarked Boris, shaking his head.

'And you're still the same diplomatist. But that's not the point.... Well, tell me, how are you?' asked Rostov.

'Just as you see. So far everything's all right; but I don't mind confessing I should be glad, very, to be made an adjutant and not always have to stick in the line.'

'Why?'

'Why, because once a man goes in for a military career he ought to try to make it as brilliant a career as he can.'

'Oh, so that's it!' said Rostov, clearly thinking of something else.

He looked intently and inquiringly into his friend's eyes, searching vainly, it seemed, for the solution to some question.

Old Gabriel brought in the wine.

'Shouldn't we send for Berg now?' suggested Boris. 'He'll drink with you, but I can't.'

'Send for him, do! Well, and how do you get on with the Hun?'

'He's an extremely nice, straightforward, pleasant fellow,' said Boris.

Again Rostov looked narrowly into Boris's eyes and sighed. Berg returned, and over the bottle of wine conversation between the three officers grew lively. The Guardsmen told Rostov about their march and how they had been fêted in Russia, in Poland, and abroad. They recounted the sayings and doings of their commander, the Grand Duke, together with anecdotes of his kind-heartedness and his irascibility. Berg, as usual, kept silent when the subject did not concern him personally, but à propos of the Grand Duke's quick temper he related with gusto how in Galicia he had been successful in speaking to him when His Highness had inspected the regiments and had flown into a rage over some irregularity in the way the men marched. With a satisfied smile on his face he described how the Grand Duke had ridden up to him in a violent passion shouting: 'Pack of mercenaries!' (mercenary was the Tsarevich's favourite term of abuse when he was in a rage), and called for the company commander.

'Would you believe it, count, I wasn't in the least alarmed, because I knew I was right. Without boasting, you know, count, I may say I know the regimental drill-book by heart, and the standing orders, too, as well as I know the Lord's Prayer. So you see, count, there's never the slightest detail neglected in my company, and so my conscience was easy. I came forward.' (Berg stood up and showed how he had come forward with his hand to the peak of his cap. It would certainly have been difficult for a face to express more respectfulness and self-complacency than his did.) 'Well, he boiled over, as you might say, and stormed and stormed at me until it was more a matter of death than life, as the saying is, shouted "Mercenary!" and threatened me with the devil and Siberia,' proceeded Berg with a knowing smile. 'I was certain I was right, so I held my tongue – wasn't that best, count? ... "You dumb, are you?" he shouted. Still I held my tongue. And what do you think, count? Next day it was not mentioned even in the order of the day! That's the result of keeping one's head. Yes, indeed, count,' said Berg, lighting his pipe and sending up smoke rings.

'Yes, that was capital,' said Rostov smiling.

But Boris saw that Rostov was preparing to make fun of Berg, so he skilfully changed the subject, begging Rostov to tell them how and where he got his wound. This pleased Rostov, and he began a circumstantial account, growing more and more animated as he went on. He described the Schön Graben affair exactly as men who have taken part in battles always do describe them – that is, as they would like them to have been, as they have heard them described by others, and as sounds well, but not in the least as they really had been. Rostov was a truthful young man and would never had told a deliberate lie. He began his story with the intention of telling everything exactly as it happened, but imperceptibly, unconsciously and inevitably he passed into falsehood. If he had told the truth to his listeners who, like himself, had heard numerous descriptions of cavalry charges and had formed a definite idea of what a charge was like and were expecting a precisely similar account from him, either they would not have believed him or, worse still, would have thought Rostov himself to blame if what generally happens to those who describe cavalry charges had not happened to him. He could not tell them simply that they had all set out at a trot, that he had fallen off his horse, sprained his arm and then run from the Frenchmen into the woods as fast as his legs would carry him. Besides, to tell everything exactly as it had been would have meant the exercise of considerable self-control to confine himself to the facts. It is very difficult to tell the truth and young people are rarely capable of it. His listeners expected to hear how, forgetful of himself and all on fire with excitement, he had rushed down like a hurricane on the enemy's square, hacked his way in, slashing the French right and left; how his sabre had tasted flesh, and he had fallen exhausted, and so on. And that was what he told them.

In the middle of his tale, just as he was saying: 'You can't imagine the strange frenzy one experiences during a charge,' Prince Andrei Bolkonsky, whom Boris was expecting, walked into the room. Prince Andrei, who liked playing patron to young men and was flattered at being applied to for his influence, had taken a fancy to Boris (who had succeeded in making a favourable impression on him the day before), and was disposed to do for the young man what he desired. Having been sent with papers from Kutuzov to the Tsarevich, he had looked up his young *protégé*, hoping to find him alone. When he came in and saw a hussar of the line recounting his military exploits (Prince Andrei could not endure that type of person), he smiled cordially to Boris but scowled and dropped his eyelids as he made Rostov a slight bow before wearily and languidly sitting down on the sofa, disgusted at finding himself in such uncongenial society. Perceiving this, Rostov seethed. But he did not care, the man was nothing to him. Glancing, however, at Boris he saw that he too seemed ashamed of the valiant hussar. In spite of Prince Andrei's disagreeable, ironical manner, in spite of the disdain with which Rostov from his point of view as a *fighting* soldier, regarded all these little staff-adjutants in general, of whom the new-comer was evidently one, Rostov felt uncomfortable; he reddened and subsided into silence. Boris inquired what news there was at headquarters, and what, without indiscretion, one might ask about our plans.

'We shall probably advance,' replied Bolkonsky, obviously reluctant to say more in the presence of a stranger.

Berg seized the opportunity to inquire with great deference whether the report was true that the allowance of forage-money to captains of companies was to be doubled? To this Prince Andrei replied with a smile that he could not presume to offer an opinion on state questions of such gravity, and Berg laughed with delight.

'In regard to that business of yours,' Prince Andrei continued, addressing Boris again, 'we will have a word about it later,' and he looked round at Rostov. 'Come to me after the review and we'll do what we can.'

And having glanced about the room, Prince Andrei turned to Rostov, whose childish, uncontrollable embarrassment, now changing to anger, he did not condescend to notice, and said: 'You were talking, I believe, of the Schön Graben affair? Were you there?'

'I was,' said Rostov in a curt tone apparently intended as an insult to the adjutant.

Bolkonsky observed the hussar's temper, and it amused him. With a faintly contemptuous smile he said:

'Ah, there are a great many stories now about that affair!'

'Yes, stories!' exclaimed Rostov loudly, looking from Boris to Bolkonsky with eyes full of sudden fury. 'A great many stories, I dare say, but the stories we tell are the accounts of men who have been under the enemy's fire. *Our* stories carry some weight, they're not the tales of little staff upstarts who get decorations for doing nothing.'

'The race to which you assume I belong?' said Prince Andrei with a quiet and particularly amiable smile.

A strange feeling of exasperation was mingled in Rostov's heart at that moment with respect for this man's self-possession.

'I am not talking about you,' he said. 'I don't know you, and frankly I don't want to. I'm speaking of staff-officers in general.'

'And I will tell you this much,' Prince Andrei interrupted in a tone of quiet authority, 'you are bent on insulting me, and I am ready to agree that it would be very easy to do so if you haven't sufficient respect for yourself; but you must admit that the time and place are ill chosen for this squabble. In a day or two we shall all have to take part in a great and more serious duel, and besides, Drubetskoy here, who tells me he is an old friend of yours, is in no way to blame that my physiognomy has the misfortune to displease you. However,' he added as he got up, 'you know my name and where to find me; but remember, I do not regard either myself or you as having been insulted, and my advice, as an older man, is to let the matter drop. Well, Drubetskoy, I shall expect you on Friday after the review. Good-bye till then,' he concluded, and with a bow to them both he went out.

Only when Prince Andrei was gone did Rostov bethink him of the answer he ought to have given, and not having thought of it in time made him more furious still. He ordered his horse at once and, coldly taking leave of Boris, rode home. Should he go to headquarters tomorrow and challenge that conceited adjutant, or in fact let the matter drop, was the question that worried him all the way back. At one moment he pictured vindictively how he would enjoy seeing the fright the feeble, bumptious little fellow would be in, facing his pistol; at the next he was feeling with surprise that of all the men he knew there was none he would be more glad to have for his friend than that detestable little adjutant.

8

THE day after Rostov's visit to Boris the review took place of the Austrian and Russian troops, including the reinforcements freshly arrived from Russia as well as those who had been campaigning with Kutuzov. Both Emperors, the Russian with his heir the Tsarevich and the Austrian with the Archduke, were to inspect the allied forces which together made up an army of eighty thousand men.

From early morning the troops, scoured and polished, had been shifting about the plain, lining up in front of the fortress. Thousands of legs and bayonets moved and halted at the word of command, turned with banners flying, formed up in detachments, and wheeled round other similar masses of infantry in different uniforms. Farther off, with measured hoof beats and the jingling of trappings, rode the cavalry, elegant in blue, red and green laced uniforms, mounted on black, roan or grey horses, bandsmen in front, their jackets covered with lace. Yonder, the artillery was crawling slowly into place between infantry and cavalry, the long line of polished shining cannon quivering on the gun-carriages, which made a heavy, brazen din and left behind the smell of linstocks. Not only the generals in full-dress uniform, wearing scarves and all their decorations, with slender waists or thick waists pinched in to the uttermost, and red necks squeezed into stiff collars; not only the flamboyant pomaded officers, but every soldier with face newly washed and shaven and weapons clean and rubbed up to the final glitter, every horse groomed till its coat shone like satin and every hair of its mane had been damped to lie smoothly – all alike felt that something grave, important, and solemn was happening. From general to private, every man was conscious of his own insignificance, aware that he was but a grain of sand in that ocean of humanity, and yet at the same time had a sense of power as a part of that vast whole.

By dint of strenuous exertion and bustle since early morning, by ten o'clock everything was in the required order. The ranks were drawn up on the huge parade-ground. The whole army was arranged in three lines: the cavalry in front, next the artillery, and behind them the infantry.

A lane was left between the different branches of soldiery. The army was sharply divided into three sections: Kutuzov's veterans (with the Pavlograd Hussars on the right flank in front), the Guards and regiments of the line recently arrived from Russia, and the Austrian troops. But they all stood in line, under one command and in similar order.

Like wind rustling through leaves ran an excited whisper: 'They're coming! They're coming!' Alarmed voices were heard, and a stir of final preparation swept through the troops.

From the direction of Olmütz in front of them, a group of horsemen came into sight. And at that moment, though the air was still, a gentle breeze blew overhead, fluttering the streamers on the lances and worrying at the unfurled standards which flapped against their staffs. It seemed as though by this slight tremor the army itself was expressing its joy at the advent of the Emperors. A single voice was heard shouting: 'Eyes front!' Then, like cocks at sunrise, other voices at different extremities of the plain caught up and repeated the command. And all fell silent.

In the deathlike stillness the only sound was the tramp of horses' hooves. It was the Emperors' suites. The two monarchs rode towards the flank, and the trumpets of the first cavalry regiment began to play the assembly march. But it seemed less as though the notes came from the buglers than as if the entire army, in its delight at the Emperors' approach, had spontaneously burst into music. Through the flourish of trumpets the youthful gracious voice of the Emperor Alexander was distinctly heard, uttering some words of greeting, and the first regiment's roar of 'Hurrah' was so deafening, so prolonged, so joyful that the men themselves felt awestruck at the multitude of their numbers and the immense strength they constituted.

Rostov, standing in the foremost ranks of Kutuzov's army, which the Tsar approached first, was possessed by the same feeling as every other man there present – a feeling of self-forgetfulness, a proud consciousness of might, and passionate devotion to the man round whom this solemn ceremony was centred.

One word, he thought, from this man and this vast mass (myself, an insignificant atom, with it) would plunge through fire and water, ready to commit crime, to face death or perform the loftiest deeds of heroism. And so he could not but tremble and feel his heart stand still at the imminence of the Emperor who was the embodiment of that word.

'Hurrah! hurrah! hurrah!' thundered from all sides, one regiment after another greeting the Tsar with the strains of the march, and then 'Hurrah!...' and the assembly march again, followed by 'Hurrah! hurrah!' swelling louder and louder and merging into one deafening roar.

Until the Sovereign reached it each waiting regiment in its silent immobility appeared like a lifeless body; but as soon as the Sovereign came abreast of it the particular regiment woke to life and its thunder joined the roar extending down the whole line past which he had ridden. In the terrible overwhelming tumult of those voices, amid the square masses of troops standing as if turned to stone, a few hundred men on horseback, the suites, moved with careless ease, yet symmetrically and above all freely, and in front of them two figures – the Emperors. Upon them was concentrated the undivided raptly-passionate attention of all that mass of soldiery.

The handsome, youthful Emperor Alexander, in the uniform of the Horse Guards, in a cocked hat worn point forward, with his pleasant face and low resonant voice, was the focus of all eyes.

Rostov was not far from the trumpeters, and with his keen sight he recognized the Tsar from a distance and watched him approaching. When the Emperor had come to within twenty paces of him and Nikolai could distinguish quite clearly every detail of his handsome, happy young face, he experienced a feeling of tenderness and ecstasy such as he had never known before. Everything about the Sovereign – every trait, every movement – seemed to him entrancing.

Pausing in front of the Pavlograd regiment, the Tsar said something in French to the Austrian Emperor and smiled.

Seeing that smile, Rostov unconsciously began to smile himself and felt a still stronger surge of love for his Sovereign. He longed to express this love in some way, and knowing that this was impossible was ready to weep. The Tsar called the colonel of the regiment to him and said a few words.

'Oh God, what would happen if the Emperor were to speak to me!' thought Rostov. 'I should die of happiness!'

The Tsar also addressed the officers.

'I thank you all, gentlemen (to Rostov every word sounded like a voice from heaven). 'I thank you from the bottom of my heart.'

How gladly would Rostov have died there and then for his Tsar!

'You have earned the standards of St George and will be worthy of them.'

'Oh, to die, to die for him!' thought Rostov.

The Tsar said something more which Rostov did not catch, and the soldiers, bursting their lungs, roared 'Hurrah!'

Rostov cheered too, leaning forward in his saddle and cheering with all his might, beside himself with enthusiasm and willing to do himself any injury to express it.

The Tsar stopped for several seconds facing the hussars, as if he were undecided.

'How could the Emperor be undecided?' wondered Rostov, but immediately even this hesitation appeared to him majestic and captivating, like everything else the Tsar did.

The Sovereign's hesitation lasted only an instant. The Tsar's foot, in the narrow pointed boot of the day, touched the belly of the bob-tailed bay mare he was riding; the Tsar's hand in a white glove gathered up the reins, and he moved off accompanied by an irregularly swaying sea of aides-de-camp. Farther and farther he rode away, stopping in front of other regiments, until at last all that Rostov could see of him was the white plume of his cocked hat waving above the heads of the suite that encircled the Emperors.

Among the gentlemen of the suite Rostov noticed Bolkonsky, sitting his horse in an indolent careless fashion. Rostov recalled their quarrel of the previous day, and the question presented itself whether he ought or ought not to challenge Bolkonsky. 'Of course not!' he now thought. 'Is it worth thinking or speaking of it at a moment like this? At a time of such devotion, such rapture, such self-sacrifice, what do any of our squabbles and affronts matter? I love all men now, and forgive everyone.'

When the Emperor had inspected almost all the regiments, the ceremonial march past began, and Rostov on Bedouin, recently purchased from Denisov, brought up the rear of his squadron – that is, he rode alone and in full view of the Emperor.

Before he reached the Tsar, Rostov, who was a splendid horseman, twice dug his spurs into Bedouin's flanks and succeeded in forcing him into the spectacular trot to which the animal had recourse when excited. Bending his foaming muzzle to his chest, arching his tail, and seeming to fly along without touching the ground, Bedouin, as if he, too, were conscious of the Emperor's eye upon him, passed by in superb style, daintily lifting his feet high in the air.

Rostov himself, legs well back and stomach drawn in, feeling all of a piece with his horse, rode past the Emperor with a frowning but blissful face 'like a vewy devil', as Denisov expressed it.

'Bravo Pavlograds!' exclaimed the Tsar.

'Oh God, shouldn't I be happy if he bade me fling myself into fire this instant!' thought Rostov.

When the review was over the officers fresh from Russia and those of Kutuzov's army collected into groups and began to discuss the honours that had been conferred, the Austrians and their uniforms, the front line, Bonaparte and the bad time in store for him now, especially when the Essen corps arrived and Prussia took our side.

But the main topic of conversation everywhere was the Emperor Alexander. His every word and gesture were expatiated upon with ecstasy.

Each had but one and the same desire: under the Emperor's command to advance with all speed against the enemy. Led by the Emperor himself, none could deny them victory: so thought Rostov and most of the officers after the inspection.

The occasion produced in them all more confidence of success than the winning of a couple of decisive engagements would have done.

9

THE day after the review Boris put on his best uniform and, armed with his comrade Berg's good wishes, rode off to Olmütz to see Bolkonsky, in the hope of profiting by his friendliness to obtain for himself the best possible post – preferably that of adjutant to some important personage, a position in the service which seemed to him particularly alluring. 'It's all very well for Rostov, whose father sends him ten thousand roubles at a time, to talk about not caring to cringe or be anyone's lackey, but I have nothing except my own brains so I must pursue my career and not let opportunities slip but must make the most of them.'

He did not find Prince Andrei in Olmütz that day. But the sight of the town where the headquarters and the diplomatic corps were established, and the two Emperors were living with their suites, their households and their courts only strengthened his desire to belong to this upper world.

He knew no one, and in spite of his dashing Guardsman's uniform all these exalted beings driving about the streets in their elegant carriages, with their plumes, ribbons and decorations, courtiers and military alike, seemed so immeasurably above him, a little officer in the Guards, that they not only would not but could not recognize his existence. At the quarters of the commander-in-chief Kutuzov, where he inquired for Bolkonsky, all the adjutants and even the orderlies looked at him as though they wished to impress the fact that there were a great many officers of his sort hanging about the place and they were heartily sick of seeing them. In spite of this, or rather because of it, he went to Olmütz again on the following day, the 15th, after dinner, and going into the house occupied by Kutuzov asked for Bolkonsky. Prince Andrei was in and Boris was shown into a large room, probably at some time used for dancing but which now held five bedsteads and various pieces of furniture: tables, chairs and a clavier. One adjutant was sitting in a Persian smoking-jacket writing at a table near the door. Another, the stout, red-faced Nesvitsky, lay on a bed with his arms clasped behind his head, laughing with an officer who had sat down beside him. A third was playing a Viennese waltz on the clavier, while a fourth, leaning on the instrument, hummed the tune. Bolkonsky was not there. None of these gentlemen made any move on seeing Boris. The one who was writing, in reply to Boris's inquiry turned round crossly, saying that Bolkonsky was on duty and that he should go through the door on the left, into the reception-room, if he wanted to see him. Boris thanked him and went to the reception-room, where he found some ten officers and generals.

When Boris entered, Prince Andrei, his eyelids drooping disdainfully (with that peculiar air of polite weariness which says as plainly as words: 'If it were not my duty I should not think of wasting a minute talking to you'), was listening to an old Russian general with many decorations, who stood rigidly erect, almost on the tips of his toes, reporting some matter to Prince Andrei with the obsequious expression of a common soldier on his purple face.

'Very well, then, be so kind as to wait a while,' said Prince Andrei to the general in Russian with the French accent he affected when he wanted to speak contemptuously, and noticing Boris, Prince Andrei paid no further heed to the general (who ran after him begging to be allowed to say one thing more), but nodded to Boris and turned to him with a bright smile.

At that moment Boris realized clearly something of which he had already had an inkling – that in the army, quite apart from the subordination and discipline prescribed in the military code and recognized by him and the others in his regiment, there existed another and more actual form of subordinancy, one which compelled this tight-laced, purple-faced general to wait respectfully while Captain Prince Andrei chose to chat with Lieutenant Drubetskoy. More than ever was Boris determined to follow in future the guidance not of the written code laid down in regulations but of this unwritten code. He felt now that simply by having been recommended to Prince Andrei he immediately took precedence over the general, who in other circumstances, at the front, had the power to annihilate a mere lieutenant in the Guards. Prince Andrei came up to him and shook hands.

'Very sorry you did not find me in yesterday. I was fussing about with Germans the entire day. Went with Weierother to look over the dispositions. When a German starts being accurate there's no end to it!'

Boris smiled, as though he understood as a matter of common knowledge what Prince Andrei was referring to. But it was the first time he had heard the name of Weierother, or even the term 'dispositions'.

'Well now, my dear fellow, so you still want to be an adjutant? I have been thinking about you since I saw you.'

'Yes, I was considering' – for some reason Boris could not help blushing – 'asking the commander-in-chief. He has had a letter about me from Prince Kuragin. I only wanted to ask him because I fear the Guards won't be in action,' he added as though excusing himself.

'Very well, very well, we will talk it over presently,' said Prince Andrei. 'Only let me report on this gentleman's business and I am at your disposal.'

While Prince Andrei was away reporting the business of the purple-faced general, that gentleman, evidently not sharing Boris's conception of the advantages of the unwritten code of subordinancy, glared so fiercely at the presumptuous lieutenant who prevented him having his say to the adjutant that Boris began to feel uncomfortable. He moved away and waited impatiently for Prince Andrei's return from the commander-in-chief.

'Well, my dear fellow, as I said, I have been thinking about you,' resumed Prince Andrei, when they had gone into the large room with the clavichord. 'It's no use your going to the commander-in-chief. He would be extremely civil and polite, ask you to dine with him' ('That wouldn't be so bad as regards that unwritten code,' thought Boris), 'but nothing more would come of it: there will soon be enough of us aides-de-camp and staff-officers to form a battalion! But I tell you what we will do: I have a friend, an adjutant-general and an excellent fellow, Prince Dolgorukov; and though you may not know it, the fact is now that Kutuzov and his staff and the rest of us are of mighty little account. Everything at present is centred round the Emperor. So let us go to Dolgorukov. I have to call on him anyhow, and I have already spoken to him about you. We shall see whether he can't attach you on his own staff or find you a post somewhere nearer the sun.'

Prince Andrei always showed particular energy when the chance occurred of taking a young man under his wing and furthering his ambitions. Under cover of obtaining assistance of this kind for another, which his pride would never have let him accept for himself, he kept in touch with the circle which confers success and which attracted him. He most readily took up Boris's cause and went with him to Prince Dolgorukov.

It was already quite late in the evening when they made their way into the palace at Olmütz occupied by the Emperors and their retinues.

That same day there had been a council of war in which all the members of the Hofkriegsrath and both Emperors had been present. At the council it had been decided – against the advice of the elder generals, Kutuzov and Prince Schwartzenberg – to advance at once and give battle to Bonaparte. The sitting was only just over when Prince Andrei, accompanied by Boris, arrived at the palace to seek out Prince Dolgorukov. Everyone at headquarters was still under the spell of the day's council which had resulted in a triumph for the younger party. The voices of those who favoured delay and advised further postponement of the attack had been so unanimously drowned, and their arguments confuted by such conclusive evidence of the advantages of attacking, that the subject of their deliberations – the impending engagement and the victory certain to follow it – already seemed to be a thing of the past rather than of the future. All the advantages were on our side. Our immense forces, undoubtedly superior to those of Napoleon, were concentrated in one place; the armies were inspired by the presence of their Emperors and eager for action; the strategic position on which the battle must be fought was known in the minutest detail to the Austrian general, Weierother, who was in command of the troops (a lucky accident had ordained that the previous year the Austrian army had chosen for their manoeuvres the very field where they now had to fight the French); every feature of the locality was familiar and marked down on maps, while Bonaparte's present inaction argued a state of weakness.

Dolgorukov, one of the warmest advocates of an immediate offensive, had only just returned from the council, weary and exhausted but full of excitement and proud of the victory he had obtained. Prince Andrei introduced his *protégé* but Prince Dolgorukov, though he pressed his hand politely and firmly, said nothing to Boris, and evidently unable to suppress the thoughts which were uppermost in his mind addressed Prince Andrei in French.

'Ah, my dear fellow, what a battle we have won! God grant that the victory to follow may be equally brilliant. However, my dear fellow,' he said brusquely and eagerly, 'I must confess to having been unjust to the Austrians and particularly to Weierother. What accuracy and meticulousness! What knowledge of the locality! What foresight for every eventuality, every contingency down to the minutest detail! No, my dear boy, anything more propitious than present circumstances could not have been devised. The combination of Austrian precision with Russian valour – what more could one wish for?'

'So it has been definitely decided to attack?' said Bolkonsky.

'And do you know, I fancy Bonaparte has completely lost his head. You know that a letter came from him today addressed to the Emperor?' Dolgorukov smiled significantly.

'You don't say so! What does he write?' asked Bolkonsky.

'What can he write? Bubble and froth and so forth ... all simply to gain time. I tell you he's in our hands, that's certain! But the most amusing thing of all,' he continued with a sudden good-natured laugh, 'is that we couldn't for the life of us think how to address the reply! If not "Consul" – and of course not "Emperor" – it would have to be "General Bonaparte", it seemed to me.'

'But there is a considerable difference between not recognizing him as Emperor and calling him General Bonaparte,' remarked Bolkonsky.

'That's just the point,' interrupted Dolgorukov quickly, laughing. 'You know Bilibin – he's a very clever fellow. He suggested writing "To the Usurper and Enemy of the Human Race".' Dolgorukov broke into a hearty peal of laughter.

'And nothing more?' observed Bolkonsky.

'All the same, in the end it was Bilibin who found a suitable form of address. He's a shrewd clever fellow.'

'What was it?'

'"To the Head of the French Government ... *Au chef du gouvernement français*,"' said Dolgorukov with grave satisfaction. 'Good, don't you think?'

'Yes, but it won't please him at all,' observed Bolkonsky.

'Not one bit! My brother knows him, he's dined with him – with this self-styled Emperor – more than once in Paris, and tells me he's never met a subtler or more cunning diplomatist – French finesse plus Italian play-acting, you know! You've heard the anecdotes about him and Count Markov? Count Markov was the only person who could meet him on his own ground. The story of the handkerchief's a gem!'

And the loquacious Dolgorukov, turning now to Boris now to Prince Andrei, told them the story of how Bonaparte, to try out Markov, our ambassador, purposely dropped his pocket-handkerchief at Markov's feet and stood still to see if he would pick it up for him, and how Markov promptly dropped his own beside Bonaparte's and picked it up again, leaving Bonaparte's where it lay.

'Delicious!' said Bolkonsky. 'But prince, I have come to you as a supplicant on behalf of this young man. You see ...' But, before Prince Andrei could finish, an aide-de-camp came in to summon Dolgorukov to the Emperor.

'Oh, how annoying!' said Dolgorukov, hurriedly rising and shaking hands with Prince Andrei and Boris. 'You know I should be very glad to do all in my power either for you or for this charming young man.' He pressed Boris's hand again with a sincere good-natured expression of careless gaiety. 'But you see how it is ... another time!'

Boris was greatly excited by the thought of being so close to the higher powers as he felt himself to be at that moment. He was conscious that here he was in contact with the springs that set in motion all those vast movements of the mass, of which he in his regiment felt himself a tiny, humble and insignificant atom. They followed Prince Dolgorukov out into the corridor and met (emerging from the door of the Emperor's room at which Dolgorukov went in) a short man in civilian clothes with an intelligent face and sharply projecting jaw which, far from being a disfigurement, lent peculiar energy and mobility to his expression. This short man nodded to Dolgorukov as to an intimate friend, and fixed Prince Andrei with a cold stare, walking straight towards him and apparently expecting him to bow or step out of his way. Prince Andrei did neither: a look of animosity crossed his features and the short young man turned away and walked down the side of the corridor.

'Who was that?' asked Boris.

'That is one of the most remarkable but to me most unpleasant of men – the minister of foreign affairs, Prince Adam Czartoryski. It is such men as he who decide the fate of nations,' added Bolkonsky with a sigh he could not suppress as they left the palace.

Next day the armies took the field, and up to the time of the battle of Austerlitz Boris found no opportunity of seeing either Prince Andrei or Dolgorukov again, and remained for the time being with the Ismailov regiment.

10

AT dawn on the 16th Denisov's squadron, in which Nikolai Rostov was serving and which formed part of Prince Bagration's detachment, marched out from its bivouac into action, so it was said, and after proceeding for about three-quarters of a mile behind other columns was halted on the highway. Rostov saw the Cossacks and then the first and second squadrons of hussars, and infantry battalions and artillery pass by and go forward; and then Generals Bagration and Dolgorukov ride past with their adjutants. As before, all the panic he had felt at the prospect of battle, all the struggle he had had with himself to overcome that fear, all his dreams of distinguishing himself in true hussar style in this battle went for nothing. His squadron was held back in reserve, and Nikolai Rostov spent a tedious and wretched day. Soon after eight in the morning he heard firing ahead of him and shouts of *hurrah*, and saw wounded being carried back (there were not many of them), and finally beheld a whole detachment of French cavalry being brought in, conducted by a unit of a hundred Cossacks. Evidently it was all over and, though only a small affair, had been attended with success. The returning men and officers spoke of a brilliant victory, of the occupation of the town of Wischau and the capture of a whole French squadron. The morning was bright and sunny after a sharp night frost, and the cheerful glitter of the autumn day was in keeping with the news of victory, which was conveyed not only by the accounts of those who had taken part in it but by the happy faces of soldiers, officers, generals and adjutants passing this way and that before Rostov. And Nikolai felt all the more depressed that he should have suffered to no purpose all the dread that precedes a battle, and then been obliged to spend this glorious day in inactivity.

'Wostov, come here. Let's dwink to dwown our gwief!' shouted Denisov, who had settled by the roadside with a flask and some food.

The officers gathered in a ring round Denisov's canteen, eating and chatting.

'Here they come, bringing in another prisoner!' cried one of the officers, pointing to a captive French dragoon being escorted in on foot by two Cossacks.

One of them was leading by the bridle a fine large French horse taken from the prisoner.

'Sell us that horse!' Denisov called out to the Cossacks.

'If you like, your Honour.'

The officers sprang up and crowded round the Cossacks and their prisoner. The dragoon was a young Alsatian lad who spoke French with a German accent. He was breathless with agitation, his face was red, and when he heard French spoken he at once turned to the officers, addressing first one then another of them. He said he would not have been captured, and it was not his fault but the corporal's who had sent him to seize some horse cloths, though he had told him the Russians were there. And at every word he added: 'But don't let any harm come to my little horse!' and stroked the animal. It was plain that he did not quite grasp where he was. At one moment he was finding excuses for having been taken prisoner, at the next imagining himself before his own officers and insisting on his soldierly discipline and zeal for the service. He brought with him into our rearguard in all its freshness the very atmosphere of the French army, which was so alien to us.

The Cossacks sold the horse for two gold pieces, and Rostov, being the richest of the officers now that he had received his money, became its owner.

'But don't hurt my little horse,' said the Alsatian good-naturedly to Rostov, when the animal was handed over to the hussar.

Rostov reassured the dragoon with a smile and gave him some money.

'Alley! Alley!' said the Cossack, touching the prisoner's arm to make him go on.

'The Emperor! The Emperor!' was suddenly heard among the hussars.

All was stir and bustle, and down the road behind Rostov saw a number of horsemen with white plumes in their hats riding towards them. In a moment everyone was in his place, waiting.

Rostov did not remember and had no consciousness of how he ran to his place and mounted. Instantly his regret at not having taken part in the action and his humdrum mood among men he saw every day had gone – instantly every thought of himself had vanished. He was entirely absorbed by happiness at the nearness of the Emperor. This nearness by itself, he felt, made up to him for the morning's disappointment. He was happy as a lover is happy when the moment arrives for the longed-for rendezvous. Not daring to look down the line, and not glancing round, he was conscious by an ecstatic instinct of *his* approach. And he felt it not only from the sound of the tramping hooves of the approaching cavalcade, but because as *he* drew nearer everything around him grew brighter, more joyous and full of meaning, more festive. Nearer and nearer moved this sun, as he seemed to Rostov, shedding around him rays of blissful and majestic light, until Rostov felt himself enfolded in that radiance and heard *his* voice, caressing, serene, regal and yet so simple. A deathly silence ensued, just as Rostov felt ought to be the case, and in this silence the Sovereign's voice was heard.

'The Pavlograd Hussars?' he inquired.

'The reserves, sire!' replied some other voice, a very human voice compared with the one that had asked in French: 'The Pavlograd Hussars?'

The Emperor came level with Rostov and reined in his horse. Alexander's face was even more beautiful than it had been at the review three days before. It shone with such gaiety and youth – such innocent youthfulness that it suggested the high spirits of a boy of fourteen – and yet it was still the face of the majestic Emperor. Casually glancing up and down the squadron, the Sovereign's eyes met Rostov's and for upwards of two seconds rested on them. Whether or no the Tsar realized all that was going on in Rostov's soul (it seemed to Rostov that he saw everything), at any rate for the space of two seconds his blue eyes gazed into Rostov's face. A soft, mild light poured from them. Then all at once he raised his eyebrows, and with a sharp movement of his left foot touched his horse and galloped on.

At the sound of gunfire from the advance troops the young Emperor had not been able to restrain his desire to be present at the battle and, in spite of the expostulations of his courtiers, at noon had left the third column under whose escort he had been moving and had spurred off towards the vanguard. But before he could come up with the hussars several adjutants met him with news of the successful issue of the skirmish.

The action, which had consisted merely in the capture of a French squadron, was represented as a brilliant victory over the enemy. Consequently the Emperor and the whole army, especially while the smoke still hung over the battlefield, believed that the French had been defeated and forced to retreat. A few minutes after the Tsar had passed, the Pavlograd division was ordered to advance. In Wischau itself, a little German town, Rostov saw the Emperor once more. In the market-place, which just before the Sovereign's arrival had been the scene of a fairly lively interchange of shots, lay a number of dead and wounded whom there had not been time to move. The Emperor, surrounded by his suite of officers and courtiers, was mounted on a bob-tailed chestnut mare, a different horse from the one he had ridden at the review. Leaning over and gracefully holding a gold lorgnette to his eye, he was looking at a soldier lying on his face with blood on his bare head. The wounded soldier was so dirty, coarse and revolting that Rostov was shocked that he should be so close to the Sovereign. Rostov saw how the Tsar's stooping shoulders contracted as though a cold shiver had run across them, how his left foot began convulsively tapping the horse's side with the spur. The well-trained animal looked round indifferently and did not stir. Adjutants, dismounting, lifted the soldier under the arms to lay him on a stretcher that had been brought up. The soldier groaned.

'Gently, gently, can't you be more gentle?' exclaimed the Emperor, apparently suffering more than the dying soldier, and he rode away.

Rostov saw that his eyes were full of tears, and heard him say in French to Tchartorizhsky as they moved off:

'What a terrible thing war is, what a terrible thing! *Quelle terrible chose que la guerre!*'

The troops of the vanguard were posted before Wischau, in sight of the enemy's lines, which all day long had yielded ground to us at the first shot. The Emperor's gratitude was conveyed to the van-guard, rewards were promised and a double ration of vodka was served out to the men. Camp-fires crackled and soldiers' songs rang out even more merrily than on the previous night. Denisov was cele-brating his promotion to the rank of major, and Rostov, who had already drunk quite enough, at the end of the carousal proposed a toast to the health of the Emperor. 'Not "Our Sovereign the Em-peror", as they say at official dinners,' he explained, 'but to the health of our Sovereign, that good, enchanting, great man! Let us drink to his health, and to the certain defeat of the French! If we fought be-fore' said he, 'and gave no quarter to the French, as at Schön Graben, what shall we not do now when he himself is at our head. We will all die – die gladly for him. Is that not so, gentlemen? Perhaps I am not expressing myself very well, I have drunk a good deal – but that's how I feel, and so do all of you. To the health of Alexander the First! Hurrah!'

'Hurrah!' rang the hearty voices of the officers.

And the old cavalry captain Kirsten shouted no less heartily and sincerely than the twenty-year-old Rostov.

When the officers had drunk the toast and smashed their glasses, Kirsten filled others and in shirt-sleeves and riding breeches went glass in hand to the soldiers' camp-fires and with his long grey whis-kers, his white chest visible under his unbuttoned shirt, stood in a stately pose in the light of the camp-fire, waving his uplifted arm.

'Lads! here's to the health of our Sovereign Emperor, and to vic-tory over our enemies! Hurrah!' he roared in his dashing old hussar baritone.

The hussars crowded round and responded with a loud shout in unison.

Late that night, when they had all separated, Denisov with his stubby hand slapped his favourite, Rostov, on the shoulder.

'No one to fall in love with in the field, so he's fallen in love with the Tsar,' he said.

'Denisov, don't joke about that,' cried Rostov. 'It's such a lofty, such a sublime feeling, so ...'

'I agwee, I agwee, fwiend, and I share and appwove ...'

'No, you don't understand!'

And Rostov got up and took himself off to wander about among the camp-fires, dreaming of what happiness it would be to die, not saving the Emperor's life (of that he did not even dare dream), but simply to die before his eyes. He really was in love with the Tsar and the glory of the Russian arms and the hope of coming victory. And he was not the only one to experience this feeling during those memorable days that preceded the battle of Austerlitz: nine-tenths of the men in the Russian army were at that moment in love, though perhaps less ecstatically, with their Tsar and the glory of the Russian arms.

II

THE following day the Emperor remained in Wischau. His physician, Villier, was several times summoned to him. At headquarters and among the troops near by the news circulated that the Emperor was unwell. He was eating nothing and had slept badly that night, so those about him reported. The cause of this indisposition was said to be the painful impression produced upon his sensitive nature by the sight of the killed and wounded.

At daybreak on the 17th a French officer with a flag of truce was conducted from our outposts into Wischau. This officer was Savary. The Tsar had only just fallen asleep, and so Savary had to wait. At midday he was admitted to the Emperor and an hour later he rode off with Prince Dolgorukov to the advanced post of the French army.

It was rumoured that Savary had been sent to propose peace and a meeting between the Emperor Alexander and Napoleon. To the rejoicing and pride of the whole army a personal interview was refused and, instead of the Sovereign, Prince Dolgorukov, the victor at Wischau, was dispatched with Savary to negotiate with Napoleon, if, contrary to expectations, these negotiations were founded on a genuine desire for peace.

Towards evening, Dolgorukov returned, went straight to the Tsar and remained closeted with him for a long time.

On the 18th and 19th of November the army moved forward two days' march, and the enemy's outposts, after a brief interchange of shots, retired. In the highest army circles from noon on the 19th an intense, bustling excitement and activity began which lasted until the morning of the 20th, when the famous battle of Austerlitz was fought.

Up to midday of the 19th the activity, the eager talk, the running to and fro and the dispatching of adjutants was confined to the head-quarters of the Emperors. But on the afternoon of that day the excitement communicated itself to Kutuzov's headquarters and the staffs of the divisional commanders. By evening the adjutants had spread it in every direction and to every part of the army, and in the night of the 19th the eighty thousand men comprising the allied forces arose from their bivouacs with a hum of voices, and swayed forward in one enormous mass six miles long.

The concentrated activity, which had begun in the morning at the headquarters of the Emperors and had given the impetus to all the activity that followed, was like the first movement of the centre wheel of a great tower-clock. One wheel moved slowly, another was set in motion, then a third, and wheels began to revolve faster and faster, levers and cogwheels to work, chimes to play, figures to pop out and the hands to advance in measured time, as a result of that activity.

Just as in the mechanism of a clock, so in the mechanism of the military machine, an impetus once given leads on to the final result; and the parts of the mechanism which have not yet been started into action remain as indifferently stationary. Wheels creak on their axles as the cogs engage, the revolving pulleys whirr in rapid motion, while the next wheel stands as apathetic and still as though it would stay so for a hundred years; but the momentum reaches it – the lever catches and the wheel, obeying the impulse, creaks and joins in the common movement, the result and aim of which are beyond its ken.

Just as in the clock the result of the complex action of innumerable wheels and pulleys is merely the slow and regular movement of the hand marking the time, so the result of all the complex human activities of these 160,000 Russians and French – of all their passions, hopes, regrets, humiliations, sufferings, outbursts of pride, fear and enthusiasm – was only the loss of the battle of Austerlitz, the battle of the three Emperors, as it was called; that is to say, a slow movement of the hand on the dial of human history.

Prince Andrei was on duty that day, in constant attendance on the commander-in-chief.

At six in the evening Kutuzov visited the headquarters of the Emperors and after a brief audience with the Tsar went to call on the earl marshal, Count Tolstoy.

Bolkonsky took advantage of this interval to drop in on Dolgorukov to try and learn details of the coming action. He felt that Kutuzov was upset and disgruntled about something, and that they were displeased with him at headquarters; also that at imperial headquarters everyone adopted the tone with him of men who know something other people are not aware of; and for that reason he was anxious to have a talk with Dolgorukov.

'Well, how d'you do, *mon cher*,' said Dolgorukov, who was sitting at tea with Bilibin. 'The fête comes off tomorrow. How is your old fellow? Out of sorts?'

'I should not say he was out of sorts, but I fancy he would like to get a hearing.'

'But he did get a hearing at the council of war, and will again when he is willing to talk sense. But to delay and hang about now when Bonaparte fears nothing so much as a combined attack is impossible.'

'Yes, you've seen him, haven't you?' said Prince Andrei. 'Well, what did you think of Bonaparte? How did he impress you?'

'Yes, I saw him, and I'm convinced he fears nothing on earth so much as a general engagement,' repeated Dolgorukov, evidently setting great store by this all-round conclusion drawn from his interview with Napoleon. 'If he weren't afraid of battle, why did he ask for that interview? Why propose negotiations, and, above all, why retreat when retreat is so entirely contrary to his whole method of conducting warfare? Believe me, he is afraid, afraid of a large-scale offensive. His hour has come. Mark my words!'

'But tell me, what is he like, eh?' asked Prince Andrei again.

'He's a man in a grey overcoat, very anxious to be called "Your Majesty", but to his chagrin he got no title from me! That is the sort of man he is – and that's all I can say,' replied Dolgorukov, looking round at Bilibin with a smile.

'In spite of my profound respect for old Kutuzov,' he continued, 'we should be a pretty set of fools to wait about and give him the chance to escape, or trick us, just when he's right in our hands. No, we mustn't forget Suvorov and his maxim: "It is better to attack than be attacked". I assure you, the energy of young men is often a safer guide in warfare than all the experience of old slow-coaches.'

'But in what position are we going to attack him? I have been at the outposts today and there was no making out where his main forces are concentrated,' said Prince Andrei.

He was longing to explain to Dolgorukov a plan of attack of his own that he had devised.

'Oh, that's of no consequence whatever,' Dolgorukov said quickly, getting up and spreading a map out on the table. 'Every contingency has been provided for. If he is at Brünn ...'

And Prince Dolgorukov gave a rapid and vague account of Weierother's plan for a flanking movement.

Prince Andrei began to point out objections and to expound his own plan, which may have been as good as Weierother's but for the disadvantage that Weierother's had already been accepted. As soon as Prince Andrei began to demonstrate the defects of the latter and the merits of his own scheme, Prince Dolgorukov ceased to attend and gazed absent-mindedly not at the map but at Prince Andrei's face.

'In any case, there is to be a council of war at Kutuzov's tonight: you can say all this then,' remarked Dolgorukov.

'I intend to,' said Prince Andrei, moving away from the map.

'Whatever are you bothering about, gentlemen?' said Bilibin, who till then had been listening with an amused smile to their conversation and now was evidently ready with a joke. 'Whether tomorrow brings victory or defeat the glory of our Russian arms is assured. Except your Kutuzov there is not a single Russian in command of a column! The commanders are: *Herr General* Wimpfen, *le comte de* Langeron, *le prince de* Lichtenstein, *le prince de* Hohenlohe, and finally Prshprsh-plus-every-letter-in-the-alphabet-to-follow, like all those Polish names.'

'Be quiet, you slanderer!' said Dolgorukov. 'It's not true, there are a couple of Russians now, Miloradovich and Dokhturov, and there would have been a third, Count Arakcheyev, but for his weak nerves.'

'However, I think General Kutuzov has come out,' said Prince Andrei. 'I wish you good luck and success, gentlemen!' he added, and having shaken hands with Dolgorukov and Bilibin he left them.

On the way back Prince Andrei could not refrain from asking Kutuzov, who sat in moody silence beside him, what he thought of tomorrow's battle.

Kutuzov looked sternly at his adjutant and after a pause replied: 'I think the battle will be lost, and I said so to Count Tolstoy and

asked him to tell the Emperor. What do you think was his answer?
"My dear general, rice and cutlets are my affair, military matters
you must look after yourself." Yes ... that was the answer I got!'

12

SHORTLY after nine o'clock that evening Weierother with his plans
drove over to Kutuzov's quarters, where the council of war was to be
held. All the commanders of columns had been summoned to the
commander-in-chief and with the exception of Bagration, who declined to come, all appeared at the appointed hour.

Weierother, who had the arranging of the proposed engagement,
by his urgent eagerness presented a sharp contrast to the ill-pleased,
sleepy-looking Kutuzov who reluctantly played the part of chairman and president of the council of war. Weierother evidently felt
himself to be at the head of a movement that already there was no
stopping. He was like a horse in harness running downhill with a
heavy cart-load behind him. Whether he was pulling it or it was
pushing him, he did not know – but he was borne along, helter-
skelter, with no time to consider where this movement might land
him. Weierother had been twice that evening to the enemy's picket-
line to reconnoitre personally, had made two visits to the Emperors,
Russian and Austrian, to report and expound, and between whiles
had called at his own headquarters to dictate the dispositions for the
German troops. Now, exhausted, he arrived at Kutuzov's.

He was evidently so deeply engrossed that he even forgot to be
respectful to the commander-in-chief: he interrupted him, talked
rapidly and indistinctly, without looking at the person he was addressing, and failed to answer questions that were put to him. He was
bespattered with mud and had a woe-begone, haggard, distracted
air, and at the same time he was haughty and self-confident.

Kutuzov was occupying a nobleman's castle of modest dimensions
near Ostralitz. In the large drawing-room, which had become the
commander-in-chief's office, were gathered Kutuzov himself,
Weierother and the members of the council of war. They were
drinking tea, and only awaited Prince Bagration before opening the
council. Shortly after seven Bagration's orderly rode over with the
message that the prince was unable to attend. Prince Andrei came in to
inform the commander-in-chief of this and, availing himself of

permission previously granted by Kutuzov to be present at the meeting, remained in the room.

'Well, since Prince Bagration is not coming, we can begin,' said Weierother, hastily jumping up from his seat and going over to the table on which an enormous map of the environs of Brünn was spread out.

Kutuzov, with his uniform unbuttoned so that his fat neck bulged over his collar as if escaping from bondage, was sitting in a low chair with his podgy old hands laid symmetrically on the arms. He was almost asleep. At the sound of Weierother's voice he opened his solitary eye with an effort.

'Yes, yes, pray do, it's late as it is,' he exclaimed, and nodding his head he let it droop and again closed his eye.

If at first the members of the council believed Kutuzov was pretending to be asleep, the nasal sounds to which he gave vent during the subsequent reading were sufficient proof that the commander-in-chief was absorbed by a vastly more serious matter than the desire to show his contempt for the dispositions or anything else – he was engaged in satisfying the irresistible human need for sleep. He was, in point of fact, sleeping soundly. Weierother, with the gesture of a man too busy to lose a moment, glanced at Kutuzov and, persuaded that he was asleep, took up a paper and in a loud, monotonous voice began reading the dispositions for the impending battle, under a heading which he also read out:

'Dispositions for an attack on the enemy position behind Kobelnitz and Sokolnitz, 20th November, 1805.'

The disposals were very intricate and obscure. They began as follows (in German):

'Whereas the enemy's left wing rests on wooded hills and his right extends along Kobelnitz and Sokolnitz behind the ponds that are there, while we on the other hand with our left wing far outflank his right, it will be to our advantage to attack this last-named wing, especially if we occupy the villages of Sokolnitz and Kobelnitz, whereby we can fall on his flank and pursue him over the plain between Schlapanitz and the Thuerassa forest, avoiding the defiles of Schlapanitz and Bellowitz which cover the enemy's front. To this end it will be necessary ... The first column will proceed ... The second column will proceed ... The third column will proceed ...'

and so on, read Weierother.

302

The generals appeared to listen grudgingly to these complicated instructions. The tall fair-haired General Buxhöwden stood leaning his back against the wall and, staring at a burning candle, he seemed not to be listening, or even wishing it to be supposed that he was listening. Directly opposite Weierother, with his brilliant wide-open eyes fixed upon him, sat the ruddy Miloradovich in martial attitude, hands on knees with elbows bent outwards, moustache twisted upwards and shoulders raised. He preserved a stubborn silence, gazing at Weierother's face and only taking his eyes off him when the Austrian chief-of-staff finished speaking. Then Miloradovich looked round significantly at the other generals. But it was quite impossible to tell from this knowing glance whether he agreed or disagreed, was satisfied or not with the arrangements. Next to Weierother sat Count Langeron, who all through the reading, with a subtle smile that never left his typically southern French face, watched his own delicate fingers twirling by its corners a gold snuff-box adorned with a miniature portrait. In the middle of one of the longest sentences he stopped the rotatory motion of the snuff-box, lifted his head and with polite hostility lurking in the corners of his thin lips interrupted Weierother to make some remark. But the Austrian general, continuing to read, frowned angrily and jerked his elbows as much as to say: 'You can tell me your ideas later, but now be so good as to look at the map and listen.' Langeron threw up his eyes with an expression of perplexity, glanced at Miloradovich as though seeking enlightenment but, meeting the latter's impressive gaze that meant nothing, looked away gloomily and fell to revolving the snuff-box again.

'A geography lesson!' he muttered as if to himself but loud enough to be heard.

Przhebyzhewski, with respectful but dignified courtesy, held one hand to the ear nearest Weierother, with the air of one all attention. Dokhturov, a little man, sat opposite Weierother with an assiduous and modest mien, and bending over the outspread map conscientiously studied the dispositions and the unfamiliar locality. Several times he asked Weierother to repeat words he had not caught or the difficult names of villages. Weierother complied and Dokhturov noted them down.

When the reading, which lasted more than an hour, was ended, Langeron again brought his snuff-box to rest and, without looking at Weierother or at anyone in particular, began to discourse on the difficulties of carrying out a plan depending on hypothetical knowledge of the enemy's position, which might well be uncertain, seeing that he was in movement. Langeron's objections were valid but it was obvious that their principal aim was to show General Weierother – who had read out his dispositions with as much self-confidence as though he were addressing a pack of schoolboys – that he had to do not with fools but with men who could teach him a thing or two about the art of waging war.

When the monotonous sound of Weierother's voice ceased Kutuzov opened his eye, as a miller wakes up at any interruption in the soporific drone of the mill-wheel. He listened to Langeron, and then as though saying to himself: 'So you are still at the same silly nonsense!' quickly closed his eye again and let his head sink still lower.

Langeron, doing his utmost to sting Weierother's military vanity as author of the plan, argued that Bonaparte might easily attack instead of waiting to be attacked, and consequently render the whole plan completely futile. Weierother met all objections with a firm and contemptuous smile that was evidently prepared beforehand against any piece of criticism, whatever it might be.

'If he could attack us, he would have done so today,' said he.

'So you think he isn't strong enough?' said Langeron.

'I doubt if he has as many as forty thousand men,' replied Weierother with the smile of a doctor to whom an old wife tries to explain how to treat a patient.

'In that case he is courting destruction by waiting for us to attack him,' said Langeron with a subtly ironical smile, again looking round to his neighbour, Miloradovich, for support.

But Miloradovich was obviously miles from the discussion.

'*Ma foi!*' said he, 'tomorrow we shall see all that on the field of battle.'

Weierother again indulged in that smile which said that it was absurd and strange for *him* to meet with objections from Russian generals, and to have to prove to them what he had not only thoroughly convinced himself of but had convinced their majesties the Emperors of too.

'The enemy has extinguished his fires and a continual noise is heard from his camp,' said he. 'What does that mean? Either he is retreating, which is the only thing we need fear, or he is changing his position.' (He smiled sardonically.) 'But even if he should take up a position in the Thuerassa, it would only be saving us a great deal of trouble, and all our arrangements to the minutest detail remain the same.'

'How can that be? ...' began Prince Andrei, who had for some time been watching for an opportunity to express his doubts.

Kutuzov woke up at this point, cleared his throat huskily and looked round at the generals.

'Gentlemen, the dispositions for tomorrow – or rather for today, since it is past midnight – cannot be altered now,' said he. 'You have heard them, and we shall all do our duty. But before a battle there is nothing more important' – he paused – 'than a good night's rest.'

He made a show of rising from his chair. The generals bowed and retired. It was after midnight. Prince Andrei went out.

*

The council of war at which Prince Andrei was not given a chance to express his opinion, as he had hoped to do, left him doubtful and uneasy. He did not know who was right – Dolgorukov and Weierother, or Kutuzov and Langeron and the others who did not approve of the plan of attack. 'But had it really been impossible for Kutuzov to state his views directly to the Emperor? Could it really not have been managed differently? Must court and personal considerations be allowed to imperil tens of thousands of lives, and my life, *mine* too?' he wondered.

'Yes, I may very likely be killed tomorrow,' he reflected. And suddenly at this thought of death a whole chain of most remote, most intimate memories rose up in his imagination: he recalled his last parting from his father and his wife; he remembered the early days of his love for her; thought of her approaching motherhood, and began to feel sorry for her and for himself, and in a nervously overwrought and softened mood he went out of the hut in which he and Nesvitsky were billeted and walked up and down outside.

The night was foggy and the moonlight gleamed mysteriously through the mist. 'Yes, tomorrow, tomorrow!' he thought. 'Tomorrow, maybe, all will be over for me, all these memories will be no more – all these memories will have no more meaning for me.

305

Tomorrow perhaps – indeed, tomorrow for sure – I have a presentiment that for the first time I shall at last have to show what I can do.' And his fancy painted the battle, the loss of it, the concentration of the fighting at one point and the hesitation of all the commanders. And then the happy moment – the Toulon for which he had been waiting so long – presenting itself to him at last! Firmly and clearly he speaks his opinion to Kutuzov and Weierother, to the Emperors. All are struck by the truth of his arguments but no one offers to put them into execution, so he takes a regiment, a division – stipulates that no one is to interfere with his arrangements – leads his division to the critical spot and wins the victory alone. 'What about agony and death?' said another voice. Prince Andrei, however, does not answer this voice but continues to dream of his triumphs. The dispositions for the next battle are planned by him alone. Nominally he is only an adjutant on Kutuzov's staff, but he does everything alone. He wins the next battle by himself. Kutuzov is removed, he is appointed. ... 'Well, and then?' asks the other voice again. 'Supposing a dozen times you escape being wounded or killed or betrayed – well, what then?' 'Why, then ...' Prince Andrei answered himself, 'I don't know what will happen then. I can't know, and have no wish to; but if I want glory, want to be famous and beloved, it's not my fault that I want it, that it's the only thing I care for, the only thing I live for. Yes, the only thing! I shall never tell anyone, but, oh God, what am I to do if all I care for is fame and the affections of my fellow-men? Death, wounds, the loss of my family – nothing holds any terrors for me. And precious and dear as many people are to me – father, sister, wife – those I cherish most – yet dreadful and unnatural as it seems, I would exchange them all immediately for a moment of glory, of triumph over men, of love from men I don't know and never shall know, for the love of those men there,' he thought, as he listened to voices in Kutuzov's courtyard. They came from the orderlies who were packing up; one voice, probably a coachman's, was teasing Kutuzov's old cook, whom Prince Andrei knew and who was called Tit.

'Tit, I say, Tit?' he called.

'What?' answered the old man.

'Tit, go thresh a tit-bit,' said the wag.

'Pshaw! you go to the devil!' growled the old man, his voice smothered by the laughter of the orderlies and servants.

'All the same, the only thing I love and prize is triumph over all of them. I care for nothing but this mysterious power and glory which I seem to feel in the haze that hangs above my head!'

13

ROSTOV that same night was with a platoon on picket duty to the line of outposts in front of Bagration's detachment. His hussars were posted along the line in couples; he himself rode up and down, struggling to overcome an irresistible inclination to drowsiness. Behind him could be seen an immense expanse of ground with our army's camp-fires glowing dimly in the fog; in front of him was misty darkness. Peer as he would into this foggy distance, Rostov could see nothing: at one moment it seemed to lighten up a little, at the next it looked black; did tiny lights glimmer over there where the enemy ought to be, or had the glimmer been only in his own eyes? His eyes kept closing and the image now of the Emperor, now of Denisov or of memories of Moscow floated across his mind, until he hurriedly opened his eyes again and saw right in front of him the head and ears of the horse he was riding and sometimes, when he came within half a dozen paces of them, the black figures of hussars, but in the distance still the same misty darkness. 'Why not? ... It might easily happen,' mused Rostov. 'The Emperor might meet me and give me some order as he would to any other officer. "Go and find out what's over there," he will say. I have heard a lot of stories of his getting to know an officer quite by chance and attaching him to his person. What if he were to take me into his service? Oh, how I would watch over him, how I would tell him the whole truth and unmask those who deceive him!' And, in order to give greater colour to his picture of his love and devotion to the Sovereign, Rostov imagined some enemy or treacherous German whom he would delight not only in killing but in slapping in the face in the presence of the Emperor. Suddenly a shout in the distance roused him. He started and opened his eyes.

'Where am I? Oh yes, in the picket line ... the pass and watchword: *draught-bar*, *Olmütz*. What bad luck that our squadron will be in reserve tomorrow ...' he thought. 'I'll ask to go to the front. It may be my only chance of seeing the Emperor. It won't be long now before I'm relieved. I'll take another turn up and down and when I get back I'll go to the general and ask him.' He adjusted him-self in the saddle and touched up his horse to ride once more round his hussars. It seemed to him that it was getting lighter. To the left he could see the gleam of a slope and facing it a black knoll that looked as steep as a wall. On the top of this knoll, was a white patch which Rostov could not account for. Was it a clearing in the woods lit up by the moon, or the remains of snow, or white houses? He even thought something moved on the white patch. 'It must be snow, that patch ... a patch – *une tache*,' he thought, half in French, half in Russian. 'There now, it's no *tache*. ... Na-tash-a, my sister, black eyes. Na-tash-a ... (won't she be surprised when I tell her I've seen the Emperor!) Na-tash-a ... take my *sabretache*. ...' 'Keep to the right, your Honour, there are bushes here,' said the voice of a hussar past whom Rostov was riding, in the very act of falling asleep. Rostov hastily lifted his head, which had almost dropped on to his horse's mane, and pulled up beside the hussar. He could not shake off the youthful, childish drowsiness that overcame him, 'But, I say, what was I thinking? I mustn't forget. How I shall speak to the Emperor? No, that's not it – that's for tomorrow. Oh yes! Na-tash-a ... *sabretache* ... sabre them. ... Whom? The hussars ... Ah, the hussars with moustaches. Along the Tversky boulevard rode the hussar with the moustaches, and I was thinking about him just opposite Guryev's house. ... Old man Guryev. ... Oh, but Denisov's a fine fellow! No, but that's all nonsense. The great thing now is that the Emperor's here. How he looked at me and longed to say something but dared not. ... No, it was I who did not dare. But that's nonsense, the great thing is not to forget the important thing I was thinking of. Yes, Na-tash-a, *sabretache* ... oh yes, yes. That's it.' And again his head sank forward on to his horse's neck. All at once it seemed to him that he was being fired at. 'What? What? What? ... Cut them down! What? ...' said Rostov, waking up. At the instant that he opened his eyes he heard in front of him, in the direction of the enemy, the long-drawn shouts of thousands of voices. His horse and the horse of the hussar near him pricked up their ears at these shouts. Over where the shouting came from a light flared up and died again, followed by another and another, and all along the French line on the hillside lights flared, while the clamour grew louder and louder. Rostov heard that it was French but could not distinguish the words in the roar of voices. All he could hear was 'a ha ah!' and 'rrr!'

'What's that? What do you make of it?' said Rostov to the hussar beside him. 'It must be in the enemy's camp, surely?'

The hussar did not reply.

'Why, don't you hear it?' Rostov asked again, after waiting some time for a reply.

'Who can tell, your Honour?' the hussar answered reluctantly.

'From the direction it must be the enemy,' Rostov repeated.

'Maybe 'tis, and maybe 'tisn't,' muttered the hussar. 'It's dark. There now, steady!' he cried to his fidgeting horse.

Rostov's horse, too, was getting restive and pawed the frozen ground as it listened to the noise and looked at the lights. The shouting increased in volume and merged into a general roar that only an army of several thousand could produce. The lights spread farther and farther until no doubt they stretched all along the line of the French camp. Rostov was no longer sleepy. The gay, triumphant huzzas of the enemy army had a stimulating effect on him. '*Vive l'Empereur! l'Empereur!*' he now heard distinctly.

'They can't be far off – probably just beyond the brook, don't you think?' he said to the hussar beside him.

The man only sighed without replying, and cleared his throat angrily. The sound of horse's hooves was heard approaching at a trot along the line of hussars, and out of the foggy darkness the figure of a sergeant suddenly loomed huge as an elephant.

'Your Honour, the generals!' said the sergeant, riding up to Rostov.

Rostov, still looking round towards the fires and the shouts, joined the sergeant and rode to meet several horsemen who were moving along the line. One was mounted on a white horse. Prince Bagration and Prince Dolgorukov with their adjutants had come to investigate the curious phenomenon of lights and shouts in the enemy's camp. Rostov rode up to Bagration, made his report and fell in with the adjutants, who were listening to what the generals were saying.

'Take my word for it,' said Prince Dolgorukov, addressing Bagration, 'this is nothing but a trick! He has retreated and ordered the rearguard to light fires and make a noise to deceive us.'

'I hardly think so,' said Bagration. 'I saw them this evening on that knoll; if they had retreated they would have withdrawn from there too. ... Officer!' said Bagration to Rostov. 'Are the enemy's pickets still there?'

'They were there this evening, but I can't be sure now, your Excellency. Shall I take some hussars and find out?' replied Rostov.

Bagration hesitated and before answering tried to see Rostov's face in the mist.

'Well, go and see,' he said, after a brief pause.

'Yes, sir.'

Rostov put spurs to his horse, called to Sergeant Fedchenko and two other hussars to follow him, and trotted off down the slope in the direction of the shouting, which still continued. He felt a mixture of trepidation and excitement at riding alone with three hussars into that mysterious and dangerous, misty distance where no one had been before him. Bagration shouted to him from the hill not to go beyond the stream but Rostov pretended not to hear and rode on and on without stopping, continually mistaking bushes for trees and gullies for men, and continually discovering his mistakes. Descending the hill at a trot, he lost sight both of our own and the enemy's fires, but the shouts of the French were louder and more distinct. In the valley he saw ahead of him something that looked like a river but when he reached it he found it was a road. Having come out on to this road, he reined in his horse, hesitating whether to go along it or cut across and ride over the black field up the hillside. To keep to the highway which gleamed white in the mist would have been less dangerous because it would be easier to see people coming along it. 'Follow me!' he said, as he crossed the road and began galloping up the hill towards the point where the French pickets had been that evening.

'Your Honour, there he is!' cried one of the hussars behind him.

And before Rostov had time to make out what the black thing was that suddenly loomed up in the fog there was a flash followed by a report, and a bullet whizzed high in the mist, with a plaintive sound, and sped out of hearing. Another musket missed fire but flashed in the pan. Rostov turned his horse and rode back at a gallop. Four more shots followed at varying intervals, and the bullets whistled past each in a different pitch somewhere in the fog. Rostov pulled at his horse, exhilarated like himself by the firing, and brought him to a walk. 'More! Go on, fire again!' a light-hearted voice was saying inside himself. But no more shots came.

Only as he approached Bagration did Rostov put his horse to the gallop again, and with his hand at the salute rode up to the general.

Dolgorukov was still insisting that the French had retreated and the lighted fires were merely to deceive us. 'What does that prove?' he was saying as Rostov rode up. 'They might retreat and leave pickets.'

'It's plain they have not all gone yet, prince,' said Bagration. 'We must wait till morning. We'll find out about everything tomorrow.'

'The picket's still on the hill, your Excellency, just where it was in the evening,' reported Rostov, bending forward, his hand to his cap, and unable to repress the smile of delight induced by his expedition and especially by the whizz of the bullets.

'Very good, very good,' said Bagration. 'Thank you, officer.'

'Your Excellency,' said Rostov, 'may I ask a favour?'

'What is it?'

'Tomorrow our squadron is to be in reserve. May I beg to be attached to the first squadron?'

'What's your name?'

'Count Rostov.'

'Ah, very well! You may stay in attendance on me.'

'Count Ilya Rostov's son?' asked Dolgorukov.

But Rostov made him no reply.

'Then I may reckon on it, your Excellency?'

'I will give the order.'

'Tomorrow very likely I may be sent with some message to the Emperor,' thought Rostov. 'Hallelujah!'

*

The lights and shouting in the enemy's camp had been occasioned by the fact that while Napoleon's proclamation was being read to the troops the Emperor himself came on horseback to ride round the bivouacs. The soldiers on seeing him lighted wisps of straw and ran after him shouting, '*Vive l'Empereur!*' Napoleon's proclamation was as follows:

Soldiers! The Russian army is advancing against you to avenge the Austrian army of Ulm. They are the same battalions you broke up at Hollabrünn* and have been pursuing ever since, up to this place. The position we occupy is a strong one, and while they are marching to outflank me on the right they will be exposing their own flank. Soldiers! I myself will lead your battalions. I will keep out of fire, if you, with your habitual valour, carry disorder and confusion into the

* The battle which Tolstoy calls Schön Graben. (Tr.)

enemy's ranks, but should victory for one instant be in doubt you will see your Emperor exposing himself to the foremost fire of the enemy, for victory must not tremble in the balance, especially on a day when the honour of the French infantry, on which rests the honour of our nation, is at stake.

Do not, on the plea of removing the wounded, break your ranks! Let each man be animated by the thought that we must subdue these hirelings of England who are inspired with such hatred of our nation. This victory will conclude our campaign and we can return to winter quarters, where we shall be joined by fresh troops now mobilizing in France; and then the peace I shall conclude will be one worthy of my people, of you, and of myself.

NAPOLEON.

14

AT five in the morning it was still quite dark. The troops of the centre, of the reserves, and of Bagration's right flank had not yet moved; but on the left flank the columns of infantry, cavalry and artillery, destined to be the first to descend from the heights to attack the French right flank and drive it into the Bohemian mountains, according to plan, were already up and astir. The smoke from the camp-fires, into which they were throwing everything that was not wanted, made the eyes smart. It was cold and dark. The officers were hurriedly drinking tea and breakfasting; the soldiers, munching biscuit and beating a tattoo with their feet to warm themselves, were crowded round the fires, throwing into the flames the remains of huts, chairs, tables, wheels, tubs and everything else they did not want or could not carry away with them. Austrian column guides were moving in and out among the Russian troops, serving as heralds of the advance. As soon as an Austrian officer showed himself near the quarters of a regimental commander the regiment began to rouse itself: the soldiers ran from the fires, thrust their pipes into the tops of their boots, bags into the baggage-wagons, got their muskets ready and fell into line. The officers buttoned their jackets, buckled on their swords and pouches, and strode up and down the ranks shouting. The orderlies and men in charge of the baggage-train harnessed the horses and packed and tied up the wagons. The adjutants, battalion commanders and colonels mounted their chargers, crossed themselves, gave final orders, exhortations and commissions to men remaining behind with the baggage, and the monotonous tramp of thousands of feet began. The columns moved forward, not knowing where they were going and, because of the throngs around them, the smoke and the thickening fog, unable to see either the place they were leaving or the one to which they were advancing.

A soldier on the march is as much shut in and borne along by his regiment as a sailor is by his ship. However far he goes, however strange, unknown and dangerous the regions to which he penetrates, all about him – just as the sailor sees the same decks, masts and rigging – he has always and everywhere the same comrades and ranks, the same sergeant-major Ivan Mitrich, the same regimental dog Nigger, and the same officers. The soldier rarely cares to find out the latitude in which his ship is sailing; but on the day of battle – heaven knows why or how – a stern note, of which all are conscious, sounds in the moral atmosphere of an army, announcing the approach of something decisive and solemn, and rousing the men to a curiosity unusual in them. On the day of battle soldiers make excited efforts to get beyond the interests of their regiment, they become all ears and eyes and ask eager questions about what is going on around them.

The fog had become so dense that though it was growing light they could not see ten paces ahead of them. Bushes looked like gigantic trees, and level ground like cliffs and slopes. Anywhere, on any side, they might stumble upon the enemy who, ten paces away, would be invisible. But for a long while the columns advanced always in the same fog, marching downhill and up, skirting gardens and orchards, in new and unfamiliar country, and nowhere encountering the enemy. On the other hand, the soldiers became aware that in front and behind and on all sides of them other Russian columns were all moving in the same direction. Every soldier felt cheered to know that where he was going, to that unknown spot were also going many many more of our men.

'See there, the Kurskies have gone on too,' said various voices in the ranks.

'Stupendous lot of our troops here, chum! 'Ad a look at the camp-fires last night – no end to 'em. Good as Moscow!'

Though none of the column commanders rode up to the ranks or talked to the soldiers (the commanding officers, as we saw at the council of war, were out of humour and disapproving of the affair,

313

and so they merely carried out their orders without exerting themselves to encourage the men), yet the troops marched gaily, as troops always do when advancing into action, especially on the offensive. But, after they had been marching for about an hour, all the time in thick fog, the greater part of the army had to halt, and an unpleasant impression of confusion and mismanagement spread through the ranks. How such a feeling communicates itself is very difficult to explain; but there is no doubt that it is transmitted with extraordinary accuracy and rapidity and spreads, imperceptible and irresistible, like water along a mountain valley. Had the Russian army been acting alone, without allies, it might possibly still have taken a considerable time for this impression of mismanagement to become a general conviction; but as things were, there was a keen and natural satisfaction in ascribing the mix-up to the stupid Germans, and everyone was convinced that the German sausage-makers were responsible for a dangerous muddle.

'What are we stopping for? Is the way blocked? Or have we already run up against the French?'

'No, we should have heard from them. They'd have started firing.'

'They were in hurry enough to start us, and now here we stand without rhyme or reason in the middle of a field. It's those damned Germans making a muddle of everything! Silly devils!'

'Yes, I'd have sent them on in front. But no fear, they keep behind. And here we are stuck with nothing to eat.'

'I say, are we to be planted here all day? The cavalry's blocking the road, I'm told,' exclaimed an officer.

'Ach, those damned Germans! They don't know their own countryside!' said another.

'What division are you?' shouted an adjutant, riding up.

'Eighteenth.'

'Then what are you doing here? You ought to have been in front long ago. Now you won't get there before nightfall.'

'What fool arrangements, they don't know themselves what they're about,' said the officer, and rode off.

Next a general trotted by, shouting something angrily in a foreign tongue.

'Jabber-jabber! Can't make out a word of it,' said a soldier, mimicking the general who had ridden away. 'I'd like to shoot the lot of them, the blackguards!'

314

'We were ordered to be in position before nine, but we're not half-way yet. Fine orders!' was being repeated on different sides.

And the feeling of energy with which the army had started out began to curdle into vexation and anger at the stupid arrangements, and at the Germans.

The muddle originated when, with the Austrian cavalry moving towards the left flank, the higher command discovered that our centre was too far separated from our right flank, and ordered all the cavalry to switch to the right. Several thousand cavalry crossed in front of the infantry, and the infantry had to wait till they had passed.

Ahead of the troops an altercation had arisen between an Austrian guide and a Russian general. The general shouted a demand that the cavalry should be halted; the Austrian argued that not he but the higher command was responsible. Meanwhile the troops were at a standstill, growing listless and dispirited. After an hour's delay they moved on at last and found themselves going downhill. The fog that was dispersing on the heights lay as thick as ever on the low ground to which they were descending. In front in the fog a shot was heard and then another, at first erratic, at varying intervals – tratta ... tat, and then the firing became more frequent and regular, and the skirmish of the little stream, the Holdbach, began.

Not having expected to come on the enemy down by the stream, and suddenly stumbling on him in the fog, not hearing a word of encouragement from their commanders, with a general sense of being too late, and, worst of all, unable to see a thing before or about them in the thick mist, the Russians fired back slowly and languidly at the enemy, advancing and then halting again, never receiving a command in time from the officers and adjutants, who wandered about in the fog over unfamiliar ground, searching vainly for their own units. This was how the action began for the first, the second and the third columns, who had gone down into the valley. The fourth column, with which Kutuzov was, stayed on the Pratzen heights.

Below, where the engagement was beginning, the fog lay dense; higher up it was clearing but still nothing could be seen of what was going on in front. Whether all the enemy forces were, as we had assumed, six miles away, or whether they were close by in that sea of mist, no one knew till after eight o'clock.

Nine o'clock came. The fog stretched, an unbroken sea, over the plain below, but at the village of Schlapanitz on the high ground where Napoleon stood surrounded by his marshals it was quite light. Overhead was a clear blue sky and the sun's vast orb quivered like a huge, hollow, purple float on the surface of the milky sea of mist. Not only the whole French army but Napoleon himself with his staff were – not on the far side of the streams and hollows of the villages of Sokolnitz and Schlapanitz, beyond which we had intended to take up our position and begin the attack – but on this side, so close indeed that Napoleon could distinguish a cavalryman from a foot soldier in our army with the naked eye. Napoleon, in the blue cloak he had worn throughout the Italian campaign, sat on his small grey Arab horse a little in front of his marshals. He gazed in silence at the hills which seemed to rise out of the sea of mist, and the Russian troops moving across them in the distance, and he listened to the sounds of firing in the valley. Not a muscle of his face – still thin in those days – moved; his glittering eyes were fixed intently on one spot. His forecasts were proving correct. Part of the Russian force had already descended into the valley towards the ponds and lakes, part were abandoning the Pratzen heights which he had intended to attack and which he regarded as the key to the position. He saw through the fog, in a hollow between two hills near the village of Pratzen, Russian columns, their bayonets gleaming, moving continuously in one direction, towards the valleys, and disappearing one after another into the mist. From information he had received overnight, from the sounds of wheels and footsteps heard by the outposts during the dark hours, from the slack formation of the Russian columns, from all the evidence he thought it plain that the allies believed him to be a long way in front of them, that the columns moving in the vicinity of Pratzen constituted the centre of the Russian army, and that this centre was now sufficiently extenuated for him to attack with success. But still he did not begin the battle.

That day was a high-day and holiday for him – it was the anniversary of his coronation. He had slept for a few hours up to dawn, and waking refreshed, vigorous and in good spirits, he mounted his horse and rode out into the field in that happy mood in which everything seems possible and success certain. He sat motionless, looking at the heights rising out of the mist, and his cold face wore that peculiar look of confident, self-complacent happiness sometimes seen on the face of a young lad happily in love. His marshals were grouped behind him, not venturing to distract his attention. He looked now at the Pratzen heights, now at the sun floating up out of the mist.

When the sun had completely emerged from the fog, and fields and mist were a dazzling brilliance – as though he had only been waiting for this to begin the action – he drew the glove from his shapely white hand, made a sign with it to the marshals and gave the order for battle. The marshals, accompanied by their adjutants, galloped off in different directions, and a few minutes later the main body of the French army was making rapidly for those Pratzen heights which the Russian troops were fast abandoning as they filed down the valley to their left.

15

AT eight o'clock that morning Kutuzov rode up to Pratzen at the head of Miloradovich's fourth column, the one that was to take the place of Przhebyzhewski's and Langeron's columns, which were now on their way down into the valley. He greeted the men of the foremost regiment and gave them the order to march, thereby indicating that he intended to lead that column in person. When he reached the village of Pratzen, he halted. Prince Andrei stood just behind him, one of the immense number of his staff. Prince Andrei was in a state of excitement, of nervous irritability and at the same time of repressed calm, as a man often is at the approach of a long-awaited moment. He was firmly convinced that this day was to be his Toulon, or his bridge of Arcola. How it would come about he did not know, but he felt sure it would do so. He was as familiar with the locality and the position of our troops as anyone could be in our army. His own strategic plan, which obviously could not conceivably be carried out now, was forgotten. Now, entering into Weierother's plan, Prince Andrei was deliberating over possible contingencies and inventing new combinations in which his rapidity of resource and decision might be called for.

To the left, below in the mist, the musketry fire of unseen forces could be heard. There, it seemed to Prince Andrei, the fight would be concentrated. 'That is where we shall encounter difficulties,' he thought, 'and that is where I shall be sent with a brigade or a division, and there, standard in hand, I shall march forward and sweep everything before me.'

317

Prince Andrei could not look unmoved upon the standards of the passing battalions. Seeing them he kept thinking: 'Perhaps that is the very standard with which I shall lead the army.'

Towards morning nothing was left of the night mist on the heights but a hoar-frost now turning to dew; in the valleys however it still lay like a milk-white sea. Nothing was visible in the valley on the left into which our troops had descended and from whence came the sounds of firing. Above the heights stretched a dark clear sky, and to the right the vast orb of the sun. In the distance in front, on the farther shore of that sea of mist, some wooded hills were discernible, and it was there that the enemy should have been, and something could be descried there. On the right the Guards plunged into the region of mist with a tramp of hooves and rumble of wheels, and an occasional glint from a bayonet. To the left, beyond the village, similar masses of cavalry came up and disappeared into the sea of fog. In front and behind were the marching infantry. The commander-in-chief was standing at the end of the village, letting the troops pass by him. Kutuzov seemed worn and irritable that morning. The infantry filing past him came to a halt without any command being given, apparently obstructed by something in front.

'Do tell them to form into battalion columns and go round the village!' he said angrily to a general who had ridden up. 'How is it you don't understand, your Excellency, my dear sir, that it's out of the question to have them defile through narrow village streets when we are advancing to meet the enemy?'

'I intended to re-form them beyond the village, your Excellency,' replied the general.

Kutuzov laughed sourly.

'A fine thing that'll be, deploying in sight of the enemy! A fine thing!'

'The enemy is a long way off yet, your Excellency. According to the dispositions ...'

'The dispositions!' cried Kutuzov bitterly. 'Who told you that? ... Kindly do as you are commanded.'

'Yes, sir.'

'Mon cher,' Nesvitsky whispered to Prince Andrei, 'the old man's in a vile temper.'

An Austrian officer in a white uniform with green plumes in his hat galloped up to Kutuzov and asked him in the Emperor's name: Had the fourth column started?

Kutuzov turned away without answering, and his eye fell casually upon Prince Andrei, standing beside him. Seeing him, Kutuzov let his malevolent and caustic expression soften, as though acknowledging that his adjutant was not to blame for what was being done. And, still not answering the Austrian adjutant, he addressed Bolkonsky.

'Go and see, my dear fellow, whether the third division has passed the village. Tell them to stop and await my orders.'

No sooner had Prince Andrei set off than he called him back.

'And ask whether the sharpshooters have been posted,' he added. 'What are they about? What are they about?' he murmured to himself, still making no reply to the Austrian.

Prince Andrei galloped off to do his bidding.

Overtaking all the advancing battalions, he stopped the third division and satisfied himself that actually there were no sharpshooters in front of our columns. The colonel at the head of the foremost regiment was greatly amazed at the commander-in-chief's order to post sharpshooters forward. He had been resting in the full conviction that there were other troops in front of him and that the enemy could not be less than six miles away. There was really nothing to be seen ahead except a barren stretch of ground sloping downhill and shrouded in dense mist. Having given orders in the commander-in-chief's name to rectify this omission, Prince Andrei galloped back. Kutuzov, still in the same place, his bulky frame slumped in the saddle with the lassitude of age, sat yawning wearily with closed eyes. The troops were not moving now but stood with the butts of their muskets on the ground.

'Good, very good,' he said to Prince Andrei, and turned to a general who, watch in hand, was saying it must be time they started, since all the columns of the left flank had gone down already.

'Plenty of time, your Excellency,' muttered Kutuzov in the midst of a yawn. 'Plenty of time!' he repeated.

At that moment in the distance behind Kutuzov there were sounds of regiments cheering, and the cheers came rapidly nearer, as they swept along the whole extended line of the advancing Russian columns. Evidently the object of these greetings was riding quickly. When the soldiers of the regiment in front of which Kutuzov was standing began to shout, he rode off a little to one side and looked round with a frown. Along the road from Pratzen galloped what appeared to be a squadron of horsemen in different-coloured uniforms. Two of them rode side by side ahead of the others, at full gallop. One was in a black uniform with white plumes in his hat, on a bob-tailed chestnut horse, the other in a white uniform on a black charger. These were the two Emperors followed by their suites. Kutuzov, affecting the style of an old soldier in the line, gave the command 'Atten – tion!' and rode up to the Emperors, saluting. His whole appearance and manner were suddenly transformed. He put on the air of a subordinate who obeys without question. With a pretence of respectfulness, which unmistakably struck Alexander unpleasantly, he rode up and saluted.

This unpleasant impression merely flitted across the young and happy face of the Emperor, like traces of haze in a clear sky, and vanished. After his indisposition he looked a trifle thinner that day than on the field at Olmütz, where Bolkonsky had seen him for the first time abroad, but there was the same bewitching combination of majesty and gentleness in his fine grey eyes, and on his delicate lips the same capacity for varying expression and the same predominating look of noble-hearted, innocent youth.

At the Olmütz review he had been more majestic, here he was livelier and more energetic. He was a little flushed from the two-mile gallop, and reining in his horse he drew a long breath and looked round at the faces of his suite, all as young and eager as his own. Tchartorizhsky, Novosiltsov, Prince Volkonsky, Stroganov and the others, all richly attired, gay young men on splendid, well-groomed, fresh, only slightly heated horses, chatting and laughing together, had pulled up behind the Emperor. The Emperor Francis, a ruddy, long-faced young man, sat bolt upright on his handsome black horse, looking about him in a leisurely preoccupied way. He beckoned to one of his white-uniformed adjutants and asked him some question. 'Most likely at what o'clock they started,' thought Prince Andrei, observing his old acquaintance with a smile, which he could not repress, as he recalled his reception at Brünn. In the Emperors' suite were the pick of the young orderly-officers of the Guards and the regiments of the line, Russian and Austrian. Among them were grooms leading extra horses, beautiful beasts from the Tsar's stables, covered with embroidered saddle-cloths.

Like a fresh breeze from the fields blowing into a stuffy room through an open window so a breath of youthfulness, energy and confidence in victory reached Kutuzov's dispirited staff with the advent of this cavalcade of brilliant young people.

'Why don't you begin, Mihail Ilarionovich?' the Emperor Alexander impatiently addressed Kutuzov, while he glanced courteously towards the Emperor Francis.

'I was waiting, your Majesty,' Kutuzov answered, bowing deferentially.

The Emperor bent his ear forward, with a slight frown and an air of not having quite caught his words.

'I was waiting, your Majesty,' repeated Kutuzov (Prince Andrei noticed that Kutuzov's upper lip twitched unnaturally when he repeated the word 'waiting'). 'Not all the columns have formed up yet, sire.'

The Emperor heard him but it was obvious that the answer did not please him. He shrugged his rather sloping shoulders and glanced at Novosiltsov, who stood near, with a look that seemed to complain of Kutuzov.

'We are not on the Empress Field, you know, Mihail Ilarionovich, where the parade is not begun until all the regiments are present,' said the Tsar with another look at the Emperor Francis as though inviting him, if not to take part, at least to listen to what he was saying. But the Emperor Francis continued to gaze about him and paid no heed.

'That is the very reason I do not begin, sire,' said Kutuzov in a ringing voice, apparently to preclude the possibility of not being heard, and again something in his face twitched. 'That is the very reason I do not begin, sire, because we are not on parade and not on the Empress Field,' he articulated clearly and distinctly.

All those in the Tsar's suite exchanged swift looks and their faces expressed disapproval and reproach. 'However old he may be, he ought not – he certainly ought not – to speak like that,' said their glances.

The Tsar stared steadily and attentively into Kutuzov's eyes, waiting to hear what more he might have to say. But Kutuzov for his part, with respectfully bowed head, also seemed to be waiting. The silence lasted nearly a minute.

'However, if it be your Majesty's command,' said Kutuzov, lifting his head and again affecting to be the dull-witted, unreasoning general who obeys orders.

He touched his horse and calling Miloradovich, the commander of the column, gave him the command to advance.

The troops began to move again, and two battalions of the Novgorod and one of the Apsheron regiment filed forward past the Emperor.

While the Apsheron battalion was marching by, the florid Miloradovich, without his greatcoat, his uniform covered with orders, and wearing his cocked hat with its enormous tuft of plumes on one side and with the points front and back, galloped forward with a flourish and, saluting jauntily, reined up his horse in front of the Emperor.

'God be with you, general!' said the Tsar.

'Indeed, sire, we shall do everything it is possible to do, sire,' he answered gaily, arousing none the less ironic smiles among the gentlemen of the Tsar's suite by his execrable French.

Miloradovich wheeled his horse round sharply and stationed himself a little behind the Emperor. The Apsheron men, excited by the presence of the Tsar, marched past the Emperors and their suites at a vigorous pace, keeping perfect step.

'Lads!' shouted Miloradovich in a loud, self-confident and cheery voice, obviously so elated by the sound of firing, the prospect of battle and the sight of the intrepid Apsherons, who had been his comrades in the campaigns under Suvorov and were now swinging so gallantly past the Emperors, that he forgot his Majesty's presence. 'Lads, it's not the first village you've had to take!'

'We're ready!' roared the soldiers.

The Emperor's horse started at the sudden shout. This horse, who had carried the Sovereign at reviews in Russia, also bore her rider here on the field of Austerlitz, patiently enduring the careless thrusts of his left heel and pricking up her ears at the sound of musketry just as she had done on the Empress Field, not understanding the significance of the volleys nor of the nearness of the Emperor Francis's black cob, nor of all that was being said, thought and felt that day by the man upon her back.

The Tsar turned with a smile to one of his immediate suite and, pointing to the Apsheron lads, made some remark.

16

KUTUZOV, accompanied by his adjutants, rode behind the cara-
bineers at a walking pace.

After continuing for half a mile at the tail of the column he
stopped at a solitary, deserted house – it had probably once been an
inn – almost at the fork of two roads, both of which led downhill
and were crowded with marching troops.

The fog was beginning to clear and about a mile and a half away
on the opposite heights the enemy troops were dimly visible. Down
below, on the left, the firing was becoming more distinct. Kutuzov
had stopped and was in conversation with an Austrian general.
Prince Andrei, who was a little behind, watching them, turned to an
adjutant to ask him for a field-glass.

'Look! Look!' exclaimed this adjutant, pointing not at the troops
in the distance but down the hill before him. 'It's the French!'

The two generals and the adjutants reached for the field-glass,
trying to snatch it from one another. The expression on all their faces
suddenly changed to horror. The French were supposed to be a mile
and a half away, and all of a sudden here they were right in front of
us.

'The enemy? ... No, it can't be! ... Yes, look, it is! ... It certainly
is! ... But how can it be?' cried different voices.

With the naked eye Prince Andrei saw below them to the right,
not more than five hundred paces from where Kutuzov was standing,
a dense column of French soldiers moving up to meet the Apsherons.

'Here it is! The decisive moment is at hand! My moment has
come,' thought Prince Andrei, and striking his horse he rode up to
Kutuzov.

'The Apsherons must be halted, your Excellency,' he shouted.

But at that very instant a pall of smoke spread over everything,
firing was heard close by and barely a couple of steps from Prince
Andrei a voice in naïve terror cried: 'Hey, mates, it's all up with us!'
And at this voice, as if at a command, they all started to run.

Ever-increasing masses of men rushed back in confusion to where
five minutes before they had marched past the Emperors. Not only
would it have been difficult to check the mob; it was impossible not
to be carried back with it oneself. Bolkonsky only tried not to lose

touch with Kutuzov, and gazed round bewildered and unable to grasp what was taking place under his eyes. Nesvitsky with an angry crimson face, utterly unlike himself, was shouting to Kutuzov that if he didn't get away at once he would be taken prisoner for a certainty. Kutuzov remained in the same spot and without answering drew out a handkerchief. Blood was flowing from his cheek. Prince Andrei forced his way up to him.

'You are wounded?' he asked, with difficulty controlling the trembling of his lower jaw.

'The wound is not here, it is there!' said Kutuzov, pressing the handkerchief to his wounded cheek and pointing to the fleeing soldiers.

'Stop them now!' he shouted, and at the same time, realizing probably that there was no stopping them, he lashed at his horse and rode off to the right.

A fresh wave of fugitives caught him up and carried him away with them.

The troops were pouring back in such a dense mass that once surrounded by them it was difficult to extricate oneself. A soldier was shouting: 'Get on! What are you waiting for?' Another in the same spot turned round to fire in the air. A third struck the very horse on which Kutuzov was mounted. Having succeeded with the greatest effort in struggling through the torrent of men to the left, Kutuzov, his suite diminished by more than half, rode towards the sound of nearby artillery fire. Freeing himself from the racing multitude, Prince Andrei, trying to keep near Kutuzov, saw on the side of the hill amid the smoke a Russian battery still firing away while the French came running towards it. Higher up stood some Russian infantry, neither moving forward to protect the battery nor back in the same direction as the runaways. A general on horseback detached himself from this brigade of infantry and approached Kutuzov. Of Kutuzov's suite only four were left. They were all pale and looking at one another dumbly.

'Stop those wretches!' Kutuzov gasped to the regimental commander, pointing to the flying soldiers; but at that instant, as though in revenge for the words, a shower of bullets, like a flock of little birds, flew buzzing over the heads of the regiment and Kutuzov's suite.

The French were attacking the battery and, catching sight of

Kutuzov, were shooting at him. With this volley the regimental commander clapped his hand to his leg; several soldiers fell and a second lieutenant who was holding the flag let it drop from his hands. The flag tottered and caught on the muskets of the nearest soldiers. The soldiers started to load and fire without orders.

With a groan of despair Kutuzov looked round. 'Bolkonsky,' he whispered in a voice shaking with the consciousness of his age and helplessness. 'Bolkonsky,' he whispered, pointing to the demoralized battalion and the enemy, 'what's this?'

But before he had uttered the words, Prince Andrei, feeling tears of shame and rancour choking him, had already leaped from his horse and run to the standard.

'Forward, lads!' he shouted in a voice shrill as a child's.

'This is my hour!' thought Prince Andrei, seizing the staff of the standard and exulting as he heard the whistle of bullets unmistakably aimed at him. Several soldiers fell.

'Hurrah!' shouted Prince Andrei, and scarcely able to hold up the heavy standard he ran forward in the unhesitating conviction that the whole battalion would follow him.

And it was indeed only for a few steps that he ran alone. One soldier started after him, then another, until the whole battalion with a shout of 'Hurrah' had dashed forward and overtaken him. A sergeant of the battalion darted up and grasped the standard which was swaying from its weight in Prince Andrei's hands, but he was immediately shot down. Prince Andrei snatched up the standard again and dragging it along by the staff ran on with the battalion. In front he saw our artillerymen, some of whom were fighting, while others had deserted their guns and were running towards him. He also saw French infantry pouncing on the artillery horses and reversing the field-pieces. Prince Andrei and the battalion were now within twenty paces of the cannon. He heard the incessant whizz of bullets overhead, and to right and left of him soldiers continually groaned and dropped. But he did not look at them: he kept his eyes fixed on what was going on in front of him – on the battery. He could now see distinctly the figure of a red-haired gunner, with his shako knocked awry, pulling one end of a mop while a French soldier tugged at the other. He could see distinctly the distraught yet furious faces of these two men, who were obviously quite unconscious of what they were doing.

'What are they about?' wondered Prince Andrei as he looked at them. 'Why doesn't the red-haired gunner make off, since he is unarmed? Why doesn't the Frenchman finish him off? He wouldn't get far, though, before the Frenchman remembered his bayonet and ran him through.'

In point of fact another Frenchman, with his musket at the ready, hurried up to the struggling pair, and the fate of the red-haired gunner, who had no idea of what was coming to him and had just triumphantly secured the mop, was probably sealed. But Prince Andrei did not see how it ended. It seemed to him as though one of the nearby soldiers, brandishing a heavy cudgel, dealt him a violent blow on the head. It hurt a little but the worst of it was that the pain distracted his attention and prevented him from seeing what he was looking at.

'What's this? Am I falling? My legs are giving way,' he thought, and fell on his back. He opened his eyes, hoping to see how the struggle between the Frenchmen and the gunners ended, and anxious to know whether the red-haired artilleryman was killed or not, whether the cannon had been captured or saved. But he saw nothing. Above him there was now only the sky – the lofty sky, not clear yet still immeasurably lofty, with grey clouds creeping softly across it. 'How quiet, peaceful and solemn! Quite different from when I was running,' thought Prince Andrei. 'Quite different from us running and shouting and fighting. Not at all like the gunner and the Frenchman dragging the mop from one another with frightened, frantic faces. How differently do these clouds float across that lofty, limitless sky! How was it I did not see that sky before? And how happy I am to have found it at last! Yes, all is vanity, all is delusion except these infinite heavens. There is nothing, nothing but that. But even it does not exist, there is nothing but peace and stillness. Thanks be to God! ...'

17

ON our right flank, commanded by Bagration, at nine o'clock the battle had not yet begun. Not caring to assent to Dolgorukov's demand that he should advance into action, and anxious to be rid of all responsibility, Prince Bagration proposed to Dolgorukov to send to inquire of the commander-in-chief. Bagration knew that as the distance separating the two flanks was almost seven miles the messenger, even if he were not killed (which he very likely would be), and even if he found the commander-in-chief (which would be extremely difficult), he could hardly succeed in making his way back before evening.

Bagration cast his large, expressionless, sleepy eyes round his suite, and the boyish face of Rostov, breathless with excitement and hope, was the first to catch his eye. He sent him.

'And if I should meet his Majesty before I find the commander-in-chief, your Excellency?' asked Rostov, with his hand to his cap.

'You can give the message to his Majesty,' said Dolgorukov, anticipating Bagration.

After being relieved at the outposts Rostov had managed to get a few hours' sleep before daybreak, and felt cheerful, bold and resolute, brimming with elasticity of movement and confidence in his luck, and in that state of mind which makes everything seem possible, pleasant and easy.

All his hopes were being fulfilled that morning: there was to be a general engagement, and he was taking part in it; more than that, he was in attendance on the bravest of generals; and, still more, he was being sent with a message to Kutuzov, perhaps even to the Sovereign himself. It was a fine morning, he had a good mount under him. His heart was full of joy and happiness. Having received his instructions, he gave his horse the rein and galloped off along the line. At first he rode along the line of Bagration's troops, which had not yet advanced into action but were standing motionless; then he came out into the region occupied by Uvarov's cavalry, and here he noticed activity and signs of preparation for battle. Once past Uvarov's cavalry he could clearly hear the sound of musketry and gunfire ahead of him. The firing grew louder and louder.

The sound that now reached him in the fresh morning air was not of two or three musket shots at irregular intervals as before, followed by one or two cannon shots; down the slopes of the hills before Pratzen he could hear volleys of musketry, interspersed with such frequent thunder from the cannon that sometimes there was no distinguishing them apart and they merged into one general roar.

He could see puffs of musketry smoke chasing one another down the hillsides, while smoke from the cannon rolled up in clouds, spread and became one. He could see, from the glint of bayonets in the smoke, moving masses of infantry and narrow lines of artillery with green caissons.

Rostov stopped his horse on a hillock for a moment to try and make out what was going on, but strain his attention as he would he could not understand or interpret anything of what was happening: there were men of some sort moving about in the smoke, lines of troops were hurrying this way and that – but what they were doing, who they were, where they were going, it was impossible to tell. This spectacle and these sounds, so far from exciting any feeling of depression or fearfulness, only stimulated his energy and determination.

'Go on, give it them! Go on!' was his mental response to the sounds he heard, and he resumed his gallop along the line, penetrating farther and farther into the area where the army was already in action.

'How it is going to turn out there, I don't know, but it will all be all right!' thought Rostov.

After passing some Austrian troops he noticed that the next part of the line (the Guards) were already engaged.

'So much the better! I shall see it at close quarters,' he thought.

He was riding almost along the front line. A handful of horsemen came galloping towards him. They were our Uhlans returning in disorder from the attack. Rostov passed them, not without noticing that one of them was covered with blood, and galloped on.

'That's no affair of mine!' he thought.

He had not ridden many hundred yards after that before he saw to his left, across the whole width of the field, an immense body of cavalry in dazzling white uniforms and mounted on coal-black chargers, trotting straight towards him, across his path. Rostov urged his horse to its utmost to get out of their way, and would have succeeded had they continued at the same speed but they kept increasing their pace so that some of the horses broke into a gallop. Rostov heard the thud of hooves and the clatter of arms coming nearer and nearer; in a minute they were close enough for him to distinguish their horses, their figures and even their faces. They were our Horse Guards about to charge the French cavalry, who were advancing to meet them.

The Horse Guards were galloping, though still holding in their horses. Rostov could see their faces now, and heard the command 'Charge!' shouted by an officer as he pressed his thoroughbred forward. Fearing to be crushed or swept into the attack on the

French, Rostov spurred along the front as hard as his horse could go, but still was not in time to escape them.

The last rider in the line, a huge pock-marked fellow, scowled viciously on seeing Rostov just in front of him, where they must inevitably collide. This Guardsman would certainly have overturned Rostov and his Bedouin with him (Rostov felt how small and slight he was compared to these gigantic men and horses), had it not occurred to Rostov to flourish his whip in the eyes of the Guardsman's horse. The heavy, coal-black charger shied and laid back its ears; but the pock-marked Guardsman drove his great spurs in violently and the horse, lashing its tail and stretching its neck, flew on faster than ever. Hardly had the Horse Guards passed Rostov before he heard their shout of 'Hurrah!' and looking back saw their foremost ranks mixed up with some foreign cavalry, probably French, with red epaulets. After that it was impossible to see anything, for cannon began to belch forth smoke which enveloped everything.

At the moment that the Horse Guards dashed past him and disappeared in the smoke Rostov hesitated whether to gallop after them or continue on his errand. This was the brilliant charge of the Horse Guards which filled the French themselves with so much admiration. Rostov was appalled to hear later that of all that mass of fine enormous men, of all those splendid, wealthy young officers and cadets who had galloped past him on horses worth thousands of roubles, only eighteen survived the charge.

'I have no need to envy them. My turn will come, and maybe I shall see the Emperor any minute now!' thought Rostov, and he sped on.

When he came up to the Foot Guards he realized that cannon-balls were flying over and about them – not so much because he heard the sounds of the missiles as because of the uneasy looks of the men and the unnatural martial solemnity of the officers.

As he was passing behind one of the lines of a regiment of Foot Guards he heard a voice calling him by name.

'Rostov!'

'Eh?' he called back, not recognizing Boris.

'I say, we've been in the front line! Our regiment went in to attack!' said Boris with the happy smile seen on the faces of young men who have been under fire for the first time.

Rostov stopped.

'Have you indeed!' said he. 'Well, how was it?'

'We drove them back!' said Boris eagerly, and becoming talkative. 'Fancy ...'

And Boris began describing how the Guards having taken up their position and seeing troops in front of them thought they were Austrians, and all at once discovered from the cannon-balls aimed at them by those same troops that they themselves were in the front line and had quite unexpectedly to go into action. Rostov set his horse moving, without waiting to hear Boris to the end.

'Where are you off to?' asked Boris.

'To his Majesty with a message.'

'There he is!' said Boris, thinking Rostov had said 'his Highness' and pointing to the Grand Duke with his high shoulders and frowning brows standing a hundred paces from them, wearing a helmet and Horse Guards' jacket, and shouting something to a pale, white-uniformed Austrian officer.

'No, that's the Grand Duke, and my errand is to the commander-in-chief or the Emperor,' said Rostov, and was about to spur his horse again.

'Count! Count!' shouted Berg, running up on the other side, no less excited than Boris. 'Count! I was wounded in my right hand' (he pointed to his blood-stained wrist bound up with a pocket-handkerchief), 'and I kept my place at the front. Count, I had to hold my sword in my left hand. All our family – the von Bergs – have been true knights.'

He was still talking but Rostov did not wait to hear any more, and rode on.

Passing the Guards and across a vacant space, Rostov – to avoid getting into the front line again as he had when the Horse Guards charged – followed the line of reserves, making a wide circuit round the place from whence came the hottest musket-fire and cannonade. Suddenly, quite close in front of him and behind our troops, where he could never have expected the enemy to be, he heard musketry-firing.

'What can it be?' wondered Rostov. 'The enemy in the rear of our troops? Impossible!' And all at once he was overwhelmed by panic for himself and for the issue of the whole battle. 'But whatever it is,' he reflected, 'there's no riding round it now. I must look for the commander-in-chief here, and if all is lost it will be my duty to perish with the rest.'

The foreboding of evil that had suddenly come upon Rostov was more and more confirmed the farther he advanced into the region behind the village of Pratzen, which was full of troops of all kinds.

'What does it mean? What is it? Who are they firing at? Who's doing the firing?' Rostov kept asking as he met Russian and Austrian troops running in confused crowds across his path.

'The devil only knows! We're all massacred! Everything's lost!' he was told in Russian, in German, in Czech by the fleeing rabble, who understood what was happening as little as he did.

'Hang the Germans!' shouted one.

'To hell with them – the traitors!'

'Damn these Russians!' muttered a German.

A number of wounded were among the crowds on the road. Oaths, cries and groans mingled in a general hubbub. The firing subsided, and Rostov learned later that Russian and Austrian soldiers had been firing at one another.

'Great heavens!' thought Rostov, 'and the Emperor may be here at any moment and see this rout. ... But no, these can only be a handful of scoundrels. It will soon be over, it's not the real thing, it *can't* be! I must make haste and get past them as fast as I can.'

The idea of defeat and flight could not enter Rostov's head. Though he saw French cannon and French troops on the Pratzen heights, the very spot where he had been told to look for the commander-in-chief, he could not and would not believe *that*.

18

Rostov had been directed to seek out Kutuzov and the Emperor in the vicinity of the village of Pratzen. But neither they nor even a single commanding officer were there – only disordered mobs of the rank and file. He urged on his now weary horse to get quickly past these crowds but the farther he went the more demoralized they were. The high road on which he had come out swarmed with calèches, carriages and vehicles of all kinds, with Russian and Austrian soldiers of every corps, wounded and unwounded. The whole rabble droned and jostled in confusion under the sinister whizz of cannon-balls from the French batteries stationed on the Pratzen heights.

'Where is the Emperor? Where is Kutuzov?' Rostov kept asking of everyone he could stop, but nobody could vouchsafe him any answer.

At last, seizing a soldier by the collar, he forced him to reply.

'Aye, brother! They've all bolted long ago!' said the soldier, laughing for some reason and shaking himself free.

Releasing this soldier, who was evidently drunk, Rostov held up the horse of a batman or groom to some important personage, and began to question him. The man declared that the Tsar had been driven in a carriage at full speed about an hour before along that very road, and that he was dangerously wounded.

'It can't be!' exclaimed Rostov. 'It must have been someone else.'

'I saw him with my own eyes,' said the man with a self-satisfied smirk. 'I ought to know the Emperor by now, after the times I've seen him in Petersburg. He was leaning back in the carriage as white as anything. My goodness, the way those four black horses thundered past! It's time I knew the imperial horses and Ilya Ivanich – why, I don't believe Ilya ever drives anyone but the Tsar.'

Rostov let go of the horse and was about to ride on when a wounded officer passing by addressed him.

'Who is it you want?' asked the officer. 'The commander-in-chief? Oh, he was killed by a cannon-ball – it got him in the chest. He was in front of our regiment when it happened.'

'Not killed – wounded,' another officer corrected him.

'Who? Kutuzov?' asked Rostov.

'Not Kutuzov, but what's his name – oh well, it's all the same ... there are not many left alive. If you go that way, to the village over there, all the commanders are there together,' said the officer, pointing to the village of Gostieradeck, and he walked on.

Rostov rode on at a foot-pace, not knowing to whom he was going, or why. The Emperor was wounded, the battle lost. It was impossible to doubt it now. Rostov rode in the direction indicated to him, and where he saw turrets and a church in the distance. What need to hurry? What was he to say now to the Tsar or to Kutuzov, even supposing they were alive and unwounded?

'Take this road, your Honour, that way you'll be killed straight off!' a soldier shouted to him. 'That way you'll get killed!'

'What are you talking about?' said another. 'Where is he to go? That way's nearest.'

Rostov considered, and then went in the direction where they said he would be killed.

'Nothing matters now. If the Emperor's wounded, am I to try and save my skin?' he thought. He rode on into the sector where there had been the heaviest slaughter of men escaping from Pratzen. The French had not yet occupied this ground, and the Russians – those, that is, who were unhurt or only slightly wounded – had long before abandoned it. All about the field, like heaps of manure on well-kept plough-land, lay the dead and wounded, a dozen or fifteen bodies to each couple of acres. The wounded had crawled together in twos and threes, and their cries and groans were distressing to hear (though it seemed to Rostov that sometimes they were simulated). He put his horse to a trot, to avoid the sight of all this suffering, and he felt afraid – afraid not for his life but for the courage he needed and which would not stand the spectacle of these unfortunates.

The French had ceased firing at this field strewn with dead and wounded where there was no one left to kill, but seeing an adjutant riding across they trained a gun on him and fired several shots. The sensation caused by those terrible whistling sounds and the spectacle of the corpses around him merged in Rostov's mind into a single feeling of terror and self-commiseration. He recalled his mother's last letter. 'How would she feel,' he thought, 'if she could see me now here on this field, with the cannon aimed at me?'

At the village of Gostieradeck there were Russian troops retiring from the field of battle, who though in some confusion were less disordered. Here they were out of range of the French cannon, and the musketry-fire sounded far away. Here everyone clearly saw and openly said that the battle was lost. No one to whom Rostov applied could tell him where the Emperor was, or Kutuzov. Some said that the rumour was true that the Emperor had been wounded, others said not and explained the widely-spread false report by the fact that the Emperor's carriage had dashed from the field of battle with the pale and terrified Grand Marshal Count Tolstoy, who had ridden out to the battle-field with others of the Emperor's suite. One officer told Rostov that he had seen someone from headquarters behind the village to the left, and thither Rostov rode, with no hope now of finding anyone but simply to satisfy his conscience. After going a couple of miles and passing the last of the Russian troops, he saw, near a kitchen-garden with a ditch round it, two mounted men facing the ditch. One with a white plume in his hat somehow seemed a familiar figure to Rostov; the other, a stranger on a beautiful chestnut (which Rostov fancied he had seen before) rode up to the ditch, put spurs to his horse and giving it its head leaped lightly over and into the garden. Only a little earth from the bank crumbled off under the animal's hind hooves. Turning sharply, he jumped the ditch again and deferentially addressed the horseman with the white plume, apparently urging him to do the same. The rider, whose figure Rostov seemed to know, somehow riveted his attention, shook his head and made a gesture of refusal with his hand, and by that gesture Rostov immediately recognized his lamented, his idolized Sovereign.

'But it can't be he, alone in the middle of this empty field!' thought Rostov. At that moment Alexander turned his head and Rostov saw the beloved features that were so deeply engraved on his memory. The Emperor was pale, his cheeks looked sunken and his eyes hollow, but the charm, the gentleness of his face, was all the more striking. Rostov felt happy in the certainty that the rumours about the Emperor being wounded were false. He was happy to be seeing him. He knew that he might, that indeed he ought to go straight to him and deliver the message Dolgorukov had commanded him to deliver.

But as a youth in love trembles and turns faint and dares not utter what he has spent nights in dreaming of, and looks around in terror, seeking aid or a chance of delay and flight, when the longed-for moment arrives and he is alone with *her*, so Rostov, now that he had attained what he had longed for beyond everything in the world, did not know how to approach the Emperor, and a thousand reasons occurred to him why it would be untimely, improper and impossible to do so.

'Why, it's as though I were glad to take advantage of his being alone and despondent! It might be disagreeable or painful for him to see a strange face at this moment of sorrow. Besides, what could I say to him now, when my heart fails me and my mouth feels dry at the mere sight of him?' Not one of the innumerable speeches he had addressed to the Tsar in his imagination could he recall now. Those speeches were for the most part framed for quite different conditions: to be spoken pre-eminently at moments of victory and triumph, above all, on his death-bed, as he lay dying of wounds and the Sovereign thanked him for his heroic exploits, while he gave expression as he died to the love he had proved by his conduct.

'Besides, how am I to ask the Emperor for his instructions to the right flank when it's four o'clock in the afternoon and the battle is lost? No, I certainly ought not to ride up to him, I must not intrude on his melancholy. Better die a thousand deaths than meet with an angry look, or give him a bad opinion of me,' Rostov decided, and with grief and despair in his heart he rode away, continually looking back at the Tsar, who still stood in the same attitude of indecision.

While Rostov was thus arguing with himself and riding sadly away, Captain von Toll chanced to ride up to the same spot, and seeing the Emperor went straight up to him, offered his services and assisted him to cross the ditch on foot. The Emperor, feeling unwell and in need of rest, sat down under an apple-tree, and von Toll remained beside him. Rostov from a distance saw with envy and heart-burning how von Toll talked long and ardently to the Emperor and how the Emperor, apparently weeping, covered his eyes with one hand and with the other pressed von Toll's hand.

'And I might have been in his place,' thought Rostov, and with difficulty restraining his tears of pity for the Emperor he rode away in utter despair, not knowing where he should go or for what reason.

His despair was all the more bitter because he felt that his own weakness was the cause of his unhappiness.

He might ... not only might but ought to have gone up to the Sovereign. It was a unique chance of showing his devotion to the Emperor and he had not made use of it.... 'What have I done?' he thought. And he turned his horse about and galloped back to the spot where he had seen the Emperor; but there was no one on the other side of the ditch now. A train of baggage-wagons and carriages was winding along. From one of the drivers he learnt that Kutuzov's staff were not far off, in the village the vehicles were bound for. Rostov followed them.

In front of him walked Kutuzov's groom, leading horses in horse-cloths. Then came a cart, and behind that went an old bandy-legged domestic serf in a peaked cap and jacket.

'Tit! I say, Tit!' cried the groom.

'What?' responded the old man absent-mindedly.

'Go, Tit, thresh a tit-bit!'

'Ugh, fool you!' said the old man, spitting angrily. A short interval of silence followed, and then the same joke was repeated.

*

Before five o'clock that evening the battle had been lost at every point. More than a hundred cannon were already in the possession of the French.

Przhebyzhewski and his corps had laid down their arms. Other columns, after losing half their strength, were retreating in confused, disorderly masses.

All that were left of Langeron's and Dokhturov's forces were crowded together around the pools and sluices of the village of Augest.

By six o'clock the only firing still to be heard was a heavy cannonade directed at the dam of Augest by the French who had established numerous batteries on the slopes of the Pratzen and were trying to cut down our men as they retreated.

In the rearguard Dokhturov and others, rallying their battalions, kept up a musketry-fire at the French cavalry who were pursuing our troops. It was growing dark. On the narrow Augest dam where for so many years the old miller in his tasselled cap had sat peacefully angling, while his grandson, with shirt-sleeves rolled up, plunged his arms into the water-can among the wriggling silvery fish; on that dam where for so many years the Moravians in their shaggy caps and blue jackets had peacefully driven their two-horse teams, loaded with wheat, to the mill, and returned dusty with flour that whitened their carts – on that narrow dam amid army vans and field-pieces, under the horses' hooves and between the wagon-wheels, men with faces distorted with fear of death now crowded together, crushing one another, expiring, trampling on the dying and killing each other, only to move on a few steps and be killed themselves in the same way.

Every ten seconds a cannon-ball flew over, lashing the air, or a shell burst in the midst of that dense throng, slaying some and spurting their blood on those who were near.

Dolohov, wounded in the arm, with ten men of his company on foot (he was an officer again now), and the regimental commander on horseback, represented all that remained of an entire regiment. Carried along by the press, they had got wedged in the approach to the dam and stood, jammed in on all sides, because a horse in front had fallen under a cannon and the crowd were dragging it out. A cannon-ball killed someone behind them, another fell in front, and Dolohov was splashed with blood. The mob, pushing forward desperately, squeezed together, moved a few steps and stopped again.

'A hundred paces more and I shall be safe; but another couple of minutes here is certain death,' each man was thinking.

Dolohov, standing in the centre of the crowd, forced his way to the edge of the dam, knocking down two soldiers, and ran on to the slippery ice that covered the mill-pool.

'Turn this way!' he shouted, leaping over the ice, which creaked under him. 'Turn this way!' he cried to the men with the gun. 'It holds!'

The ice bore him but it swayed and cracked, and clearly, far from supporting a cannon or a number of people, it would very shortly give way under his weight alone. The others looked at him and crowded to the bank, unable to bring themselves to step on to the ice. The general on horseback at the entry to the dam raised his hand and opened his mouth to speak to Dolohov. Suddenly a cannon-ball hissed so low overhead that everyone ducked. There was a flop as though the ball had struck something soft, and the general fell from his horse in a pool of blood. No one gave him a look, let alone thought of picking him up.

'On to the ice! Go over the ice! Get on! Turn round! Don't you hear? Go on!' quickly shouted innumerable voices, after the ball had struck the general, though they knew not what nor why they were shouting.

One of the guns in the rear that was just moving on to the dam turned off on to the ice. A crowd of soldiers from the dam began running on to the frozen pond. The ice cracked under one of the first of them, and his leg slipped into the water. He tried to right himself and floundered in up to the waist. The soldiers nearest shrank back, the gun-driver pulled up his horse, but from behind still came the shouts: 'Take to the ice! What are you stopping for? Get on! Get on!' And screams of terror were heard in the crowd. The soldiers near the cannon waved their arms and lashed the horses to make them turn and move forward. The horses started off the bank. The ice that held under the foot-soldiers broke in a huge sheet and some forty men dashed, some forward, some back, pushing each other under water.

All the time the cannon-balls whizzed regularly by, smacking on to the ice, into the water and oftenest of all into the crowd that covered the dam, the ponds and the bank.

19

On the Pratzen heights, at the spot where he had fallen with the flagstaff in his hand, lay Prince Andrei Bolkonsky, losing blood and, without realizing it, moaning a soft, plaintive moan like a child.

Towards evening his complaining ceased and he became quite still. He did not know how long his unconsciousness lasted. Suddenly he felt again that he was alive and suffering from a burning, lacerating pain in his head.

'Where is it, that lofty sky I saw today and had never seen before?' was his first thought. 'And this agony I did not know either,' he thought. 'Yes, I knew nothing, nothing till now. But where am I?'

He listened, and heard the sound of approaching hooves and voices speaking French. He opened his eyes. Above him again was the same lofty sky with clouds floating higher than ever and between them stretches of blue infinity. He did not turn his head and did not see those who, judging from the voices and the clatter of hooves, had ridden up to him and stopped.

The horsemen were Napoleon escorted by two aides-de-camp. Bonaparte, making a tour of the field of battle, had been giving final orders to strengthen the batteries firing at the Augest dam, and was now inspecting the dead and wounded left on the field.

'Fine men!' remarked Napoleon, looking at a dead Russian grenadier who lay on his belly with his face half buried in the soil, his neck turned black and one arm flung out and stiffened in death.

'The field-guns have exhausted their ammunition, sire,' said an adjutant arriving that moment from the batteries that were firing at Augest.

'Have more brought from the reserve,' said Napoleon, and having gone on a few yards he stopped by Prince Andrei, who lay on his back with the flagstaff that he had dropped beside him. (The flag had been carried off by the French as a trophy.)

'That's a fine death!' said Napoleon, looking down at Bolkonsky.

Prince Andrei grasped that this was said of him, and that it was Napoleon saying it. He heard the speaker addressed as *Sire*. But he heard the words as he might have heard the buzzing of a fly. Not only did they not interest him – they made no impression upon him, and were immediately forgotten. There was a burning pain in his head;

he felt that his life-blood was ebbing away, and he saw far above him the remote, eternal heavens. He knew it was Napoleon – his hero – but at that moment Napoleon seemed to him such a small, insignificant creature compared with what was passing now between his own soul and that lofty, limitless firmament with the clouds flying over it. It meant nothing to him at that moment who might be standing over him, or what was said of him: he was only glad that people were standing near, and his only desire was that these people should help him and bring him back to life, which seemed to him so beautiful now that he had learned to see it differently. He made a supreme effort to stir and utter some sound. He moved his leg feebly and gave a weak, sickly groan which aroused his own pity.

'Ah, he is alive!' said Napoleon. 'Pick up this young man – *ce jeune homme* – and carry him to the dressing-station.'

Having said this, Napoleon passed on to meet Marshal Lannes, who, hat in hand, rode smiling up to the Emperor to congratulate him on the victory.

Prince Andrei remembered nothing more: he became insensible from the excruciating pain of being lifted on to the stretcher, the jolting while he was being moved, and the probing of his wound at the dressing-station. He did not regain consciousness till late in the day, when with the other wounded and captured Russian officers he was being taken to the hospital. During this transfer he felt a little stronger and was able to look about him, even to speak.

The first words he heard on coming to himself were those of a French convoy officer who was saying hurriedly:

'We must halt here: the Emperor will be coming this way directly. He will like to see these gentlemen-prisoners.'

'There are so many prisoners today – practically the whole Russian army – that I should think he's sick of them,' said another officer.

'All the same! They say this one was the commander of all the Emperor Alexander's Guards,' said the first speaker, pointing to a wounded Russian officer in the white uniform of the Horse Guards.

Bolkonsky recognized Prince Repnin whom he had met in Petersburg society. Next to him stood another officer of the Horse Guards, a lad of nineteen, also wounded.

Bonaparte rode up at a gallop and reined in his horse.

'Who is the senior officer here?' he asked, on seeing the prisoners.

They named the colonel, Prince Repnin.

'Were you the commander of the Emperor Alexander's regiment of Horse Guards?' asked Napoleon.

'I commanded a squadron,' replied Repnin.

'Your regiment did its duty honourably,' said Napoleon.

'Praise from a great general is the highest reward a soldier can have,' said Repnin.

'I bestow it upon you with pleasure,' said Napoleon. 'And who is that young man beside you?'

Prince Repnin named Lieutenant Suhtelen.

Napoleon looked at him and smiled. 'He is very young to try odds with us.'

'Youth is no bar to courage,' muttered Suhtelen in a choked voice.

'A fine answer!' said Napoleon. 'Young man, you will go far!'

Prince Andrei, who had also been thrust forward under the Emperor's eyes to complete the array of prisoners, could not fail to attract his attention. Napoleon apparently remembered seeing him on the battlefield, and addressing him he used the same epithet *'jeune homme'* with which his first sight of Bolkonsky was associated in his memory.

'Well, and you, young man,' said he. 'How do you feel, *mon brave?*'

Although five minutes previously Prince Andrei had been able to say a few words to the soldiers who were carrying him, now with his eyes fixed steadily on Napoleon he was silent.... So trivial seemed to him at that moment all the interests that engrossed Napoleon, so petty did his hero with his paltry vanity and delight in victory appear, compared to that lofty, righteous and kindly sky which he had seen and comprehended, that he could not answer him.

Everything did indeed seem so futile and insignificant in comparison with the stern and solemn train of thought induced in him by his lapsing consciousness, as his life-blood ebbed away, by his suffering and the nearness of death. Gazing into Napoleon's eyes, Prince Andrei mused on the unimportance of greatness, the unimportance of life which no one could understand, and the still greater unimportance of death, the meaning of which no one alive could understand or explain.

The Emperor, after pausing in vain for an answer, turned away and said to one of the officers as he moved on:

'See that these gentlemen are looked after and taken to my bivouac. Let my surgeon, Dr Larrey, attend to their wounds. *Au revoir*, Prince Repnin!' and he spurred his horse and galloped away.

His face was radiant with happiness and self-satisfaction.

The soldiers who had been carrying Prince Andrei had removed from him the little gold icon Princess Maria had placed round her brother's neck, but when they saw the friendly manner with which the Emperor treated the prisoners they hastened to restore the holy image.

Prince Andrei did not see how or by whom it was replaced but the little icon with its delicate gold chain suddenly appeared on his chest outside his uniform.

'How good it would be,' thought Prince Andrei, letting his eyes rest on the icon which his sister had hung round his neck with such emotion and reverence, 'how good it would be if everything were as clear and simple as it seems to Marie. How good it would be to know where to seek help in this life, and what to expect after it, beyond the grave! How happy and at peace I should be if I could say now: "Lord, have mercy on me! ..." But to whom am I to say that? Is it to the great Power, indefinable, incomprehensible, which I not only cannot turn to but which I cannot even express in words – the great All or Nothing,' said he to himself, 'or is it to that God who has been sewn into this amulet by Marie? Nothing, nothing is certain, except the unimportance of everything within my comprehension and the grandeur of something incomprehensible but all important.'

The stretchers started off. At every jolt he felt intolerable pain again; his fever increased and he sank into delirium. The visions of his father, his wife, his sister and his unborn son, and the tenderness he had felt on the night before the battle, the figure of the insignificant little Napoleon, and over all these the lofty sky, formed the chief substance of his delirious fancies.

The quiet home life and peaceful happiness of Bald Hills passed before his imagination. He was enjoying that happiness when that little Napoleon suddenly appeared with his indifferent, narrow look of satisfaction at the misery of others, and was followed by doubts and torments, and only the heavens promised peace. Towards morning all these dreams ran together and slid into the chaos and obscurity of unconsciousness and oblivion, the outcome of which in the opinion of Napoleon's surgeon, Dr Larrey, was far more likely to be death than recovery.

'A nervous, spleeny subject,' said Larrey, 'he won't recover.'

And Prince Andrei, together with the other hopeless cases, was handed over to the care of the inhabitants of the district.

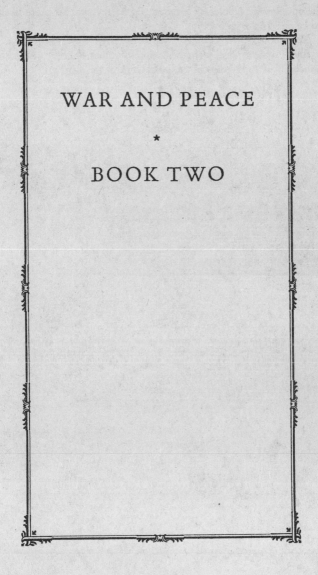

WAR AND PEACE

*

BOOK TWO

PART ONE

I

EARLY in the year 1806 Nikolai Rostov returned home on leave. Denisov, too, was going home to Voronezh and had been persuaded by Rostov to travel with him as far as Moscow and there pay the Rostovs a visit. Denisov met his comrade at the last posting-station but one, emptied three bottles of wine with him, and after that, in spite of the ruts on the road to Moscow, slept soundly, lying at the bottom of the sledge beside Rostov, who grew more and more impatient as they got nearer to Moscow.

'Is it much farther? Is it much farther? Oh, these insufferable streets, these shops and bakers' signs, street-lamps, and sledges!' thought Rostov, when they had presented their leave-permits at the city gates and were driving into Moscow.

'Denisov, we're here! Asleep!' he exclaimed, leaning forward with his whole body as if by that position he hoped to hasten the progress of the sledge.

Denisov made no response.

'There's the corner at the cross-roads, where Zahar the cabman has his stand – and there's Zahar himself, and still the same horse. And here's the little shop where we used to buy gingerbread! Oh, when shall we be there? Hurry!'

'Which house is it?' asked the driver.

'Why, that one over there at the end – the big one, don't you see? That's our house,' said Rostov. 'That's our house, of course! Denisov, Denisov, we shall be there in a minute!'

Denisov raised his head, cleared his throat, and said nothing.

'Dimitri,' said Rostov to his valet on the box, 'those lights are in our house, aren't they?'

'To be sure, sir; and there's a light in your father's study.'

'So they haven't gone to bed yet? What do you think? Mind now, don't forget to put out my new Hungarian tunic,' added Rostov, fingering his new moustache. 'Now then, get on,' he shouted to the driver. 'And do wake up, Vasska,' he continued, turning to Denisov, whose head was nodding again. 'Come on, get along – you shall have three roubles for vodka, but do get on!' Rostov shouted, when the sledge was only three doors away. It seemed to him that the horses were not moving. At last the sledge bore to the right and drew up at the steps. Rostov saw the familiar cornice with the bit of broken plaster overhead, the porch, the kerb-stone. He sprang out while the sledge was still moving, and ran into the vestibule. The house stood cold and silent, as though it were not concerned that he had come home. There was no one in the hall. 'Oh, God, is everything all right?' he thought, stopping for a moment with a sinking heart and then immediately starting to run through the vestibule and up the familiar crooked steps. There was the same old door-handle, which always annoyed the countess when it was not properly cleaned, as loose and as much askew as ever. A solitary tallow candle burned in the ante-room.

Old Mihail was asleep on his perch. Prokofy, the footman, who was so strong that he could lift the back of the carriage off the ground, sat plaiting bast shoes out of odd strips of cloth. He looked up as the door opened, and his expression of sleepy indifference was suddenly transformed into one of delighted amazement.

'Merciful heavens! The young count!' he cried, recognizing his young master. 'Is it possible? Me darlin'!' And Prokofy, trembling with excitement, rushed towards the drawing-room door, probably with the intention of announcing him; but apparently he changed his mind, for he came back and fell on his young master's neck.

'All well?' asked Rostov, drawing away his arm.

'Yes, yes, God be praised! They've just finished supper! Let us have a look at you, your Excellency!'

'Everything quite all right?'

'Yes, praise be!'

Rostov had entirely forgotten Denisov. Not wishing anyone to forestall him and announce his arrival, he pulled off his fur coat and ran on tiptoe into the great dark ballroom. Everything was the same: the same old card tables and the same chandelier with a cover over it; but someone had already seen the young master, and before he could reach the drawing-room something swooped out of a side door like a tornado and began hugging and kissing him. A second and a third figure sprang in from a second and a third door; more hugging, more kissing, more outcries and tears of joy. He could not distinguish which was Papa, which Natasha, which Petya. Everyone shouted and talked and kissed him at the same time. Only his mother was not there, he noticed that.

'And to think I never knew. ... My little Nikolai ... my own dear boy!'

'Here he is ... our Nikolai. ... How he's changed! ... Where are the candles? Let us have some tea!'

'And me, kiss me!'

'Darling Nikolai ... me too!'

Sonya, Natasha, Petya, Anna Mihalovna, Vera and the old count were all hugging him; and the men-servants and maids flocked into the room, exclaiming and oh-ing and ah-ing.

Petya, clinging to his legs, kept shouting, 'And me too!'

Natasha, after pulling him down to her and covering his face with kisses, skipped back and keeping hold of his jacket pranced up and down like a goat in the same spot, uttering shrill shrieks.

On all sides were loving eyes glistening with tears of joy, and on all sides were lips seeking a kiss.

Sonya too, as red as turkey twill, clung to his arm and radiant with bliss looked eagerly into the eyes she had been so longing to see. Sonya was turned sixteen now and very pretty, especially at this moment of happy, rapturous excitement. She gazed, unable to take her eyes off him, smiling and holding her breath. He gave her a grateful glance, but was still expectant and looking for someone else. The old countess had not yet made her appearance. But now footsteps were heard at the door, steps so rapid that they could hardly be his mother's.

Yet she it was, in a new gown which he did not know, made, probably, during his absence. The others all let him go, and he ran to her. When they came together she fell on his breast sobbing. She could not lift her face but only pressed it to the cold braiding of his hussar's jacket. Denisov, who had come into the room unnoticed by anyone, stood there looking at them and rubbing his eyes.

'Vasili Denisov, your son's fwiend,' he said, introducing himself to the count who looked at him inquiringly.

'Welcome! I know, I know,' said the count, kissing and embracing him. 'Nikolai wrote us. ... Natasha, Vera, look – here is Denisov!'

347

Denisov was surrounded, the same happy ecstatic faces turned to his shaggy countenance with its black moustaches.

'Darling Denisov!' squealed Natasha, and beside herself with delight she darted up, threw her arms round him and kissed him. Everyone was embarrassed at this. Denisov too blushed, but smiled and taking Natasha's hand kissed it.

Denisov was conducted to the room prepared for him, while the Rostovs all gathered round Nikolai in the sitting-room.

The old countess, not letting go of his hand, which she kept kissing every minute, sat beside him. The rest, crowding round, caught his every movement, word, look, and could not take their blissfully adoring eyes off him. His brother and sisters quarrelled and disputed with each other for the places nearest to him, and fought with one another as to who should bring him tea, a handkerchief or his pipe.

Rostov was very happy in the love they showed him; but the first moment of meeting had been so blissful that his happiness now seemed a little tame, and he kept expecting something more and more, and yet more.

Next morning, after their journey, the travellers slept on till ten o'clock.

The adjoining room was littered with sabres, bags, sabretaches, open portmanteaux and dirty boots. Two pairs of clean boots with spurs had just been placed by the wall. Servants were bringing in wash-basins, hot water for shaving and clothes well-brushed. There was a masculine odour and a smell of tobacco.

'Hey, Gwishka – my pipe!' shouted Vasska Denisov in his husky voice. 'Wostov, get up!'

Rostov, rubbing his eyes that seemed glued together, lifted his tousled head from the warm pillow.

'Why, is it late?'

'Late! It's getting on for ten o'clock,' answered Natasha's voice, and in the next room they heard the rustle of starched petticoats and girlish whispering and laughter. The door was opened a crack, to reveal a glimpse of something blue, of ribbons, black hair and merry faces. It was Natasha, with Sonya and Petya, come to see whether their brother was up.

'Nikolai! Do get up!' Natasha's voice was heard at the door again. 'Directly!'

Meanwhile Petya in the outer room had espied and seized upon the sabres with the rapture small boys feel at the sight of a military elder brother, and forgetting that it was hardly correct for his sisters to see the young men undressed pushed upon the bedroom door.

'Is this your sabre?' he shouted.

The girls skipped back. Denisov hid his hairy legs under the counterpane, looking with a scared face to his comrade for help. The door admitted Petya and closed after him. A giggle was heard from outside.

'Nikolai darling, come out in your dressing-gown,' cried Natasha's voice.

'Is this your sabre?' asked Petya. 'Or is it yours?' he said, addressing the black-moustached Denisov with slavish respect.

Rostov hurriedly put something on his feet, threw his dressing-gown over his shoulders and went out. Natasha had got one spurred boot on and was just slipping her foot into the other. Sonya when he came in was spinning round to make her skirts into a balloon and then duck down. They were dressed alike in new pale-blue frocks, and both were fresh, rosy and full of spirits. Sonya ran away, but Natasha, taking her brother's arm, led him into the sitting-room, where they began talking. They hardly gave one another time to ask and answer all the questions in regard to a thousand and one trifles which could only be of interest to themselves. Natasha laughed at every word he said and at every word she said herself, not because what they were saying was amusing but because she felt happy and was unable to contain her joy which brimmed over into laughter.

'Oh, how nice, how splendid!' she said to everything.

Rostov felt that, under the influence of the warm sunshine of Natasha's love, for the first time for eighteen months his soul and his face were expanding into the pure childlike smile which had not once appeared on his countenance since he left home.

'No, but listen,' she said, 'you're a grown-up man now, aren't you? I'm awfully glad you're my brother.' She touched his moustache. 'I want to know what men are really like. Are you like us? Yes? No?'

'But why did Sonya run away?' asked Rostov.

'Oh, that is a whole long story! How are you going to speak to Sonya – shall you call her "thou" or "you"?'

'I don't know – just as it happens,' said Rostov.

'Call her "you", please. I'll tell you why afterwards.'

349

'But why?'

'All right, I'll tell you now. You know Sonya's my dearest friend – so much my friend that I would burn my hand off for her. Here, look!'

She pulled up her muslin sleeve and showed him a red scar on her long, thin, soft arm, well above the elbow, near the shoulder (in a place where it would be covered even in a ball-gown).

'I did that to prove how much I loved her! I just heated a ruler in the fire and pressed it there.'

Sitting in his old schoolroom on the sofa with the little cushions on its arms, and looking into Natasha's wildly excited eyes, Rostov was carried back into that world of home and childhood which had no meaning for anyone else but gave him some of the sweetest joys of life. And burning one's arm with a ruler as a proof of love did not seem nonsense to him: he understood, and was not surprised.

'So that was what you did? No more?' he asked.

'We are such friends, such great friends! All that with the ruler is nothing, but we are friends for ever and ever. If she loves anyone, it's for ever. I don't understand that. I forget so quickly.'

'Well, what then?'

'Well, she loves me and you like that.' Natasha suddenly flushed. 'Well, you remember before you went away? ... Well, she says you are to forget all that. ... She said, "I shall always love him, but let him be free." Isn't that lovely, lovely and noble now? Yes, yes, very noble! It is, isn't it?' asked Natasha so seriously and with such feeling that evidently what she was saying now she had talked of before with tears.

Rostov was silent.

Then, 'I never go back on my word,' he said. 'And besides, Sonya is so charming that only a fool would refuse such happiness.'

'No, no!' cried Natasha. 'She and I have already talked it over. We knew you'd say that. But it won't do, because, don't you see, if you say that – if you consider yourself bound by your promise – it would look as if she had said it on purpose? It makes it as though you were marrying her because you were obliged to, and that wouldn't do at all.'

Rostov saw that they had considered the whole question thoroughly. He had already been struck the evening before by Sonya's beauty; in the glimpse he had caught of her today she seemed even lovelier. She was a charming girl of sixteen, obviously passionately in love with him (he did not doubt that for an instant). Why should he not love her now, and even marry her, mused Rostov; but not just at present. At present he had so many other pleasures and interests before him! 'Yes, they have come to a wise conclusion,' he thought. 'I must remain free.'

'Well, that's all right then,' said he. 'We'll talk it over later on. Oh, how glad I am to be back with you!' he added. 'Well, and are you still true to Boris?' he asked.

'Oh, that's all nonsense!' cried Natasha, laughing. 'I don't think about him or anyone else, and I don't want to.'

'Oh, you don't, don't you! Then what are you up to now?'

'I?' queried Natasha, and a happy smile lit up her face. 'Have you seen Duport?'

'No.'

'Never seen Duport, the famous dancer? Well, then, you won't understand. That's what I'm up to.'

Curving her arms, Natasha held out her skirt in the way dancers do, ran back a few steps, turned round, executed a pirouette, brought her little feet sharply together and walked a few steps on the very tips of her toes.

'See, I'm standing on my toes! Look!' she said, but could not keep up on her toes. 'That's what I'm going to do. I'll never marry anyone: I'm going to be a dancer. Only don't tell anybody.'

Rostov laughed so loudly and merrily that Denisov in his room felt envious, and Natasha could not help joining in.

'No, but don't you think it a nice idea?' she kept repeating.

'Oh, quite. So you don't want to marry Boris now?'

Natasha flared up.

'I don't want to marry anyone. I'll tell him so myself when I see him.'

'Dear me!' said Rostov.

'But this is all nonsense,' Natasha prattled on. 'Is Denisov nice?' she asked.

'Very.'

'Well, good-bye for now. You go and dress. Is he a frightening person, Denisov?'

'Why should he be frightening?' asked Nikolai. 'No, Vasska's a capital fellow.'

'You call him Vasska? How funny! So he's very nice, is he?'

'Very nice.'

'Well, make haste now. We'll all have breakfast together.'

And Natasha rose on her toes and glided out of the room like a ballet dancer, but smiling as only happy girls of fifteen can smile. When Rostov met Sonya in the drawing-room he reddened. He did not know how to behave with her. Yesterday they had kissed in the first joyful moment of meeting again, but today he felt that out of the question. He sensed that everybody, including his mother and sisters, was looking inquiringly at him and watching to see how he would behave with her. He kissed her hand and called her *you* and *Sonya*. But their eyes met and said *thou*, and exchanged tender kisses. Her eyes asked his forgiveness for having dared, through Natasha, to remind him of his promise, and thanked him for his love. His were thanking her for offering him his freedom, and telling her that one way or another he would never cease to love her, for it was impossible not to love her.

'But how funny it is,' said Vera, choosing a moment when all were silent, 'that Sonya and Nikolai meet as though they were strangers and call each other "you".'

Vera's remark was true enough, like all her observations, but like most of them it made everyone – not only Sonya, Nikolai and Natasha – feel uncomfortable, and the old countess, who feared lest her son's love for Sonya should stand in the way of his making a brilliant match, also coloured up like a girl.

To Rostov's surprise, Denisov, pomaded and perfumed and in his new uniform, cut quite as dashing a figure in the drawing-room as on the field of battle, and showed himself more amiable and courtly to the ladies than Rostov had ever expected.

2

ON his return to Moscow from the army, Nikolai Rostov was welcomed by his home circle as the best of sons, a hero, their beloved Nikolai; by his relations as a charming, attractive and polite young man; by his acquaintances as a handsome lieutenant of hussars, a graceful dancer and one of the best matches in town.

The Rostovs knew everybody in Moscow. The old count had money enough that year, as all his estates had been remortgaged, and so Nikolai, acquiring a swift trotter of his own, very stylish riding-breeches such as no one else in Moscow yet had, and boots of the latest fashion with extremely pointed toes and small silver spurs, was able to spend his time very agreeably. After a short period of adapting himself to the old conditions of life, Nikolai found it very pleasant to be at home again. He felt that he had grown up and become very much a man. His despair at failing in a Scripture examination, the days when he had borrowed money from Gavrila to pay a sledge-driver, the secret kisses he had given Sonya he now looked back on as childishness which he had left immeasurably behind. Now he was a lieutenant of hussars in a jacket laced with silver and wearing the cross of St George (awarded to soldiers for bravery in action), and in the company of well-known racing men, elderly and respected persons, was training a trotter of his own for a race. There was a lady of his acquaintance on the boulevard whom he visited of an evening. He led the mazurka at the Arharovs' ball, talked about the war with Field-Marshal Kamensky, frequented the English Club, and was on intimate terms with a colonel of forty to whom Denisov had introduced him.

His passion for the Emperor had cooled somewhat in Moscow, since he did not see him and had no opportunity of doing so all that time. But still he often talked about him and his love for him, letting it be understood that he could say more and that there was something in his feelings for the Emperor which not everyone could understand; and with his whole soul he shared the adoration, general in that period in Moscow, for the Emperor Alexander Pavlovich, who was spoken of as the 'angel incarnate'.

During this brief stay in Moscow, before rejoining the army, Rostov did not draw closer to Sonya but, on the contrary, drifted away from her. She was very pretty and sweet, and obviously deeply in love with him; but he was going through that phase of young manhood when there seems so much to do that there is *no time* for that sort of thing, and the young man dreads to bind himself, and prizes his freedom which he needs for so much else. When he thought of Sonya during this stay in Moscow he said to himself, 'Ah well, I shall find plenty more like her, plenty whom I have not yet seen! There will be time enough to think about love when I want to, but now I am too busy.' Besides, it seemed to him that feminine society was somehow beneath his manly dignity. He went to balls and into

353

ladies' society with an affectation of doing so against his will. The races, the English Club, junketing with Denisov and visits to a certain house were another matter and quite the thing for a dashing young hussar.

At the beginning of March old Count Rostov was much occupied with the arrangements for a dinner at the English Club in honour of Prince Bagration. Walking up and down the hall in his dressing-gown, he gave directions to the club steward and to Feoktist, the famous head chef, concerning asparagus, fresh cucumbers, straw-berries, veal and fish for the dinner to the prince. From the day of its foundation the count had been a member of the club, and on the committee. To him had they entrusted the preparations for this ban-quet for Bagration, since few men knew so well how to organize a dinner on an open-handed, hospitable scale, and still fewer who would be so well able and willing to advance money, if funds were needed for the success of the fête. The chef and club steward listened to the count's orders with cheerful faces, aware that with no one else could it be so easy to extract a handsome profit for themselves out of a dinner costing several thousands.

'Well, then, mind and have scallops in the turtle soup, you know.'

'So there'll be three cold *entrées*, will there?' asked the chef.

The count pondered.

'I don't see how we can do with less – yes, three ... the mayonnaise, that's one,' said he, bending down a finger.

'Then am I to order those large sterlets?' asked the steward.

'Yes, it can't be helped, we must take them if they won't knock the price down. Oh dear, I nearly forgot! Of course we must have another *entrée* on the table. Ah, goodness gracious!' he clutched at his head. 'Who's going to get me the flowers? Mitenka! Here, Mitenka! You sprint off to our country place' (this was just outside Moscow) 'and tell Maxim the gardener to set the serfs to work. Say that everything out of the hothouses is to come here, packed in felting. I must have a couple of hundred pots here by Friday,' he said to the factotum who appeared at his call.

Having given several further commands and directions, he was about to go to his 'little countess' to rest from his labours when he remembered something else of importance, turned back, summoned the chef and the club steward again, and began giving more orders. A light, masculine step and the jingling of spurs were heard at the door, and the young count came in, handsome and rosy, with his darkening moustache, visibly sleeker and in better trim for his easy life in Moscow.

'Ah, my dear boy, my head's in a whirl!' said the old man with a somewhat shamefaced smile at his son. 'You might come to my aid! There are still the singers to get. I shall have my own orchestra, but shouldn't we arrange for some gipsy singers as well? You military gentlemen like that sort of thing.'

'Upon my word, papa, I do believe Prince Bagration took less trouble preparing for the battle of Schön Graben than you are taking now,' said his son, smiling.

The old count pretended to be angry.

'Yes, you can talk, but just you try it yourself!'

And he turned to the chef, who with a shrewd and respectful expression looked observantly and sympathetically from father to son.

'What are the young people coming to, eh, Feoktist?' said the count. 'Laughing at us old fellows!'

'That's so, your Excellency, all they have to do is to eat a good dinner, but providing it and serving it all up – that's no affair of theirs!'

'True, true!' exclaimed the count, and gaily seizing his son by both hands he cried, 'Now I've got you, so take the sledge and pair at once, and go to Bezuhov's, and say your father has sent you to ask for strawberries and fresh pineapples. We can't get them from anyone else. If he's not at home himself, you'll have to go in and ask the princesses; and from there go on to the Gaiety – the coachman Ipatka knows the way – and look up Ilyushka, the gipsy who danced at Count Orlov's, you remember, in a white Cossack coat, and bring him along to me.'

'And am I to fetch some of the gipsy girls with him?' asked Nikolai, laughing.

'Now, now! ...'

At that moment Anna Mihalovna stepped noiselessly into the room with that air of meek Christianity mingled with practical and anxious preoccupation that never left her face. Though she came upon the count in his dressing-gown every day, he was invariably embarrassed and each time apologized for his costume. He did so again now.

'It does not matter at all, my dear count,' she said, modestly closing her eyes. 'But I'll go to Bezuhov's myself. Young Bezuhov has

355

arrived and now we shall get all we want from his hothouses. I have to see him in any case. He has forwarded me a letter from Boris. Thank God, Boris is now on the staff.'

The count was delighted to have Anna Mihalovna take upon herself one of his commissions, and ordered the small closed carriage to be brought round for her.

'Tell Bezuhov to come. I'll put his name down. Is his wife with him?' he asked.

Anna Mihalovna turned up her eyes, and an expression of profound sadness came over her face.

'Ah, my dear, he is very unfortunate,' she said. 'If all we hear is true, it is a dreadful business. Little did we dream of this when we were rejoicing so in his happiness! And such a lofty, angelic nature, that young Bezuhov! Yes, I pity him from the bottom of my heart, and shall try to give him what consolation I can.'

'Why, what has happened?' asked both Rostovs, old and young together.

Anna Mihalovna sighed deeply.

'Dolohov, Maria Ivanovna's son,' she said in a mysterious whisper, 'has, they say, compromised her completely. Pierre took him up, invited him to his house in Petersburg, and now ... she has come here and that scapegrace after her!' said Anna Mihalovna, meaning to show sympathy for Pierre but by the involuntary inflexions of her voice and the half-smile on her face betraying her sympathy for the 'scapegrace', as she called Dolohov. 'They say Pierre is quite broken up by the situation.'

'Well, anyway, tell him to come to the club. It'll all blow over. It will be a sumptuous banquet.'

On the next day, the 3rd of March, soon after one o'clock, the two hundred and fifty members of the English Club and their fifty guests were awaiting the guest of honour, the hero of the Austrian campaign, Prince Bagration. At first Moscow had been quite bewildered by the tidings of the battle of Austerlitz. The Russians at that period were so used to victories that news of a defeat made some people simply incredulous, while others looked for exceptional circumstances of some kind to explain so strange an event. At the English Club, where everyone of note and importance, everyone who had trustworthy sources of information foregathered, when the news began to arrive in December not a word was said about the war or the last battle, as though all were in a conspiracy of silence. The men who generally gave the lead in conversation – Count Rostopchin, Prince Yuri Vladimirovich Dolgoruky, Valuyev, Count Markov and Prince Vyazemsky – did not put in an appearance at the club but met privately together at each other's houses, and that section of Moscow society which took its opinions from others (to which, indeed, Count Rostov belonged) remained for a short time without leaders and without definite views in regard to the progress of the war. People in Moscow felt that something was wrong, and that it was difficult to know what to think of the bad news, and so better to be silent. But after a while, like jurymen emerging from the jury room, the bigwigs who guided opinion in the club reappeared, and a clear and definite formula was produced. Reasons were discovered to account for the incredible, unheard-of and impossible fact that the Russians had been beaten, all became plain and in every corner of Moscow one and the same story was current. The defeat was due, so people told each other, to the treachery of the Austrians, to a defective commissariat, to perfidy on the part of the Pole Przhebyzhewski and the Frenchman Langeron, to Kutuzov's inefficiency and (this in a whisper) to the youth and inexperience of the Sovereign, who had put faith in men of no character or ability. But the army, the Russian army, everyone declared, had been extraordinary and had performed miracles of valour. Soldiers, officers and generals were heroes to a man. But the hero of heroes was Prince Bagration, who had distinguished himself at the Schön Graben affair and in the retreat from Austerlitz, where he alone had withdrawn his column unbroken, and the livelong day had fought back an enemy of twice his strength. What also contributed to Bagration's selection for the rôle of popular hero in Moscow was the fact that he had no connexions in the city and was a stranger there. In his person, honour could be done to the ordinary Russian soldier who had won his way without influence or intrigue, and was still associated, through memories of the Italian campaign, with the name of Suvorov. And besides, paying such honour to Bagration was the best possible way of showing dislike and disapproval of Kutuzov.

'Had there been no Bagration somebody would have had to invent him,' said the wit Shinshin, parodying the words of Voltaire.

Kutuzov, no one spoke of, except those who whispered abuse, calling him the court weathercock and an old satyr.

All Moscow repeated Prince Dolgoruky's dictum: 'If you work with glue, sooner or later you're bound to get stuck,' which offered consolation for our defeat, in the reminder of former victories. Rostopchin, too, was quoted everywhere: 'The French soldier,' pronounced Rostopchin, 'has to be incited to battle by high-sounding phrases; the German must have it logically proved to him that it is more dangerous to run away than to advance; but the Russian soldier has to be held back and urged to go slowly!' Every day fresh stories were to be heard on all sides of individual feats of gallantry performed by our officers and the rank and file at Austerlitz. Here a man had saved a standard, another had killed half a dozen Frenchmen, a third had loaded five cannon single-handed. It was even related of Berg, by strangers, how when wounded in his right hand he had taken his sword in his left and gone forward. Nothing was said about Bolkonsky and only those who had known him intimately lamented that he had died so young, leaving a wife with child, and his eccentric old father.

3

On the 3rd of March all the rooms in the English Club buzzed with conversation, and, like bees swarming in spring, members and their guests wandered back and forth, sat, stood, met and separated, some in uniform, some in tailcoats and a few here and there with powdered hair and in Russian kaftans. Powdered and liveried footmen wearing buckled shoes and silk stockings stood at every door, anxiously trying to anticipate every movement of the guests and club members so as to proffer their services. The majority of those present were elderly and respected persons with broad, self-satisfied faces, plump fingers, and resolute gestures and voices. The guests and members of this class occupied certain habitual places and met together in certain habitual circles. A small proportion of those present were casual guests – chiefly young men, among them Denisov, Rostov, and Dolohov, now reinstated in the Semeonovsk regiment again. The faces of these younger men, especially the officers, bore that expression of condescending deference for their elders which seems to say to the older generation: 'We are ready to respect and honour you, but don't you forget that the future belongs to us.'

Nesvitsky was there too, as an old member of the club. Pierre, who at his wife's command had let his hair grow and abandoned his spectacles, walked about the rooms dressed in the height of fashion but looking sad and depressed. Here, as everywhere else, he was surrounded by an atmosphere of subservience to his wealth, and he treated the sycophants with the careless, contemptuous air of sovereignty that had become habitual with him.

In years, he belonged to the younger generation, but his fortune and connexions gave him a place among the senior and more influential set, and so he drifted from one group to another. Some of the most distinguished of the elder members formed the centres of circles which even strangers respectfully approached for the purpose of listening to the great. The largest groups were gathered round Count Rostopchin, Valuyev and Naryshkin. Rostopchin was describing how the Russians had been trampled underfoot by the fleeing Austrians, and had had to force their way through at the point of the bayonet.

Valuyev was confidentially informing his circle that Uvarov had been sent from Petersburg to ascertain what Moscow was thinking about Austerlitz.

In the third group Naryshkin was repeating the old story of the Austrian council of war at which Suvorov crowed like a cock in reply to the nonsense talked by the Austrian generals. Shinshin, who stood near, tried to make a joke, saying that Kutuzov had evidently not been able to learn from Suvorov even so simple a thing as the art of crowing like a cock, but the elder members looked sternly at the wag, giving him to understand that here and on this day it was out of place to speak so of Kutuzov.

Count Ilya Rostov, in his soft boots, hovered anxiously between dining-room and drawing-room, muttering hasty greetings to the important and unimportant alike, all of whom he knew, while every now and then his eyes sought out and feasted on the graceful, dashing figure of his young son, to whom he would send a wink of satisfaction. Young Rostov stood at the window with Dolohov, whose acquaintance he had recently made and greatly prized. The old count went up to them and shook hands with Dolohov.

'You will come and visit us, I hope. So you're a friend of my youngster's ... been playing the hero together out there. ... Ah, Vasili Ignatich ... How d'ye do, *mon vieux* ?' he said, turning to an old man who was passing them, but before he had finished his greeting there was a general stir and a footman came running in to announce with awe-struck countenance: 'He's arrived!'

Bells rang, the stewards rushed forward and the guests, who had been scattered about in the different rooms, congregated like rye shaken together in a shovel, and crowded at the door of the great drawing-room.

Bagration appeared in the doorway of the ante-room without hat or sword, which in accord with the club custom he had given up to the hall-porter. He had no astrakhan cap on his head, nor whip over his shoulder, as when Rostov had seen him on the eve of the battle of Austerlitz, but wore a tight new uniform with Russian and foreign orders, and the star of St George on his left breast. Evidently, with a view to the dinner, he had had his hair and whiskers trimmed, which did not change his appearance for the better. His face had a sort of naïvely festive expression which, in conjunction with his firm, virile features, gave him a rather comical look. Bekleshov and Fiodr Petrovich Uvarov, who had arrived with him, paused at the doorway to allow him, as guest of honour, to precede them. Bagration was embarrassed, and unwilling to avail himself of their courtesy: this caused some delay at the door, but finally Bagration did, after all, enter first. He walked shyly and awkwardly over the parquet floor of the reception-room, not knowing what to do with his hands: he would have been more at home and at his ease tramping over a ploughed field under fire, as he had at the head of the Kursk regiment at Schön Graben. The stewards met him at the first door and, expressing their delight at seeing such an illustrious guest, took possession of him, as it were, and, without waiting for his reply, surrounded and led him to the drawing-room. It was impossible to get into the room for the crowd of members and guests, jostling one another in their efforts to look over each other's shoulders at Bagration, as if he were some rare sort of wild animal. Count Ilya Rostov, laughing and repeating the words, 'Make way, *mon cher!* Make way, make way!' pushed through the throng more energetically than anyone, conducted the guests into the drawing-room and seated them on the sofa in the middle. The bigwigs, the most respected members of the club, beset the new arrivals. Count Ilya, again thrusting his way through the crowd, left the drawing-room and reappeared a minute later with another steward bearing a huge silver salver which he presented to Prince Bagration. On the salver lay some verses composed and printed in the hero's honour. At the sight of the salver

Bagration glanced about him in dismay, as though seeking help. But all eyes demanded that he should submit, and feeling himself in their power he resolutely took the salver in both hands and looked irately and reproachfully at the count who had brought it. Someone obligingly relieved Bagration of the tray (or he would, it seemed, have held it till nightfall and gone into dinner with it) and drew his attention to the ode. 'Well, I'll read it, then,' Bagration seemed to say, and fastening his weary eyes on the paper began to read with a concentrated and serious expression. But the author himself took the verses and started reading them aloud. Prince Bagration bowed his head and listened.

> Be thou the pride of Alexander's reign,
> Be of our Titus' throne the stern defender!
> Be thou our chieftain and our country's stay!
> At home a Rhipheus, a Caesar in the fray!
> Yea, e'en victorious Napoleon
> By sad experience has learned Bagration
> And dare not Herculean Russians trouble ...

But before he could finish, a stentorian major-domo announced that dinner was served. The door opened, and from the dining-room thundered the strains of the polonaise:

> Raise the shout of victory,
> Valiant Russia, now festive sing!

and Count Rostov, glancing angrily at the author who went on reading his verses, bowed Bagration in. All the company rose, feeling that dinner was of more importance than poetry, and Bagration, again preceding the rest, led the way into the dining-room. He was seated in the place of honour between two Alexanders – Bekleshov and Naryshkin (this was a delicate allusion to the name of the Sovereign). Three hundred persons took their places at the table, according to their rank and importance: those of greater consequence, nearer to the distinguished guest, as naturally as water flows to find its own level.

Just before dinner Count Ilya Rostov presented his son to Bagration, who recognized him and mumbled a few words, disjointed and awkward, as was everything else that he said that day. Count Ilya looked joyfully and proudly around at the assembled company while Bagration was speaking to his son.

Nikolai Rostov, with Denisov and his new acquaintance Dolohov, sat together almost at the middle of the table. Opposite them was Pierre, next to Prince Nesvitsky. Count Ilya Rostov and the other stewards sat facing Bagration and, as the very impersonation of Moscow hospitality, did the honours to the prince.

His labours had not been in vain. The fare – both for those who were keeping Lent and those who were not – was sumptuous, but still he could not feel perfectly at ease until the very end. He kept beckoning to the butler, whispered directions to the footmen and not without anxiety awaited each expected dish. Everything was excellent. With the second course, a gigantic sterlet (at the sight of which Ilya Rostov blushed with self-conscious pleasure), the footmen began popping corks and pouring out champagne. After the fish, which made a certain sensation, the count exchanged glances with the other stewards. 'There will be a great many toasts, it's time to begin,' he whispered, and glass in hand he got up. All were silent, waiting for what he would say.

'To the health of our Sovereign, the Emperor!' he cried, and at the same moment his kindly eyes grew moist with tears of joy and enthusiasm. The band immediately struck up 'Raise the shout of victory!' All rose from their seats and cheered 'Hurrah!' Bagration too shouted 'Hurrah', exactly as he had on the field at Schön Graben. Young Rostov's ecstatic voice could be heard above the three hundred others. He was on the point of tears. 'To the health of our Sovereign, the Emperor!' he roared, 'Hurrah!' and emptying his glass at a gulp he dashed it to the floor. Many followed his example, and the loud shouts continued for a long time. When the uproar subsided, the footmen cleared away the broken glass and everybody sat down again, smiling at the noise they had made and exchanging remarks. Then the old count rose again, glanced at a note that lay beside his place, and proposed a toast 'To the health of the hero of our last campaign, Prince Piotr Ivanovich Bagration!' and again his blue eyes were dimmed with tears. 'Hurrah!' cried the three hundred voices again, but this time instead of the band a choir began singing a cantata composed by a certain Pavel Ivanovich Kutuzov:

> No let can bar a Russian's way,
> Valour's the pledge of victory,
> For we have our Bagration
> And all our foes will be brought down ... etc.

As soon as the singers had finished, toast followed toast and Count Ilya Rostov became more and more moved, more glasses were smashed and the shouting grew louder. Healths were drunk to Bekleshov, Naryshkin, Uvarov, Dolgorukov, Apraksin, Valuyev, the stewards, the committee, all the club members and their guests, and finally and separately to the organizer of the banquet, Count Ilya Rostov. At this toast the count took out his handkerchief and hiding his face wept outright.

4

PIERRE was sitting opposite Dolohov and Nikolai Rostov. As usual he ate much and drank heavily. But those who knew him intimately noticed that a great change had come over him that day. He was silent all through dinner, and blinking and knitting his brows looked about him, or with fixed eyes and an air of complete absent-mindedness rubbed the bridge of his nose with his finger. His face was depressed and gloomy. He appeared to see and hear nothing of what was going on around him, and to be thinking of one thing only, that was painful and concerning which he had come to no conclusion.

This unresolved matter that tormented him arose out of hints from the princess in Moscow concerning Dolohov's close friendship with his wife, and an anonymous letter received that very morning, which in the vile facetious manner characteristic of anonymous letters told him that his spectacles were of little use to him and that his wife's intimacy with Dolohov was a secret to no one but himself. Pierre decidedly did not believe either the princess's hints or the letter but he flinched at the sight of Dolohov, who sat opposite him. Every time he chanced to meet Dolohov's handsome insolent eyes Pierre felt as though something hideous and awful was rising up in his soul, and he made haste to turn away. Involuntarily recalling his wife's past and her relations with Dolohov, Pierre saw clearly that what was said in the letter might well be true, or might at least appear to be the truth, if only it had nor referred to *his wife*. He could not help recalling how Dolohov, who had been completely reinstated after the campaign, had returned to Petersburg and come to him. Taking advantage of his friendship with Pierre as an old boon companion, Dolohov had made straight for Pierre's house and Pierre had put him up and lent him money. Pierre recalled how Hélène had smilingly expressed dissatisfaction at having Dolohov living under their roof; and how cynically Dolohov had praised his wife's beauty to him and from that day forth until they came to Moscow had never left their side.

'Yes, he is very handsome,' thought Pierre, 'and I know him. He would find it particularly alluring to besmirch my name and hold me up to ridicule after I had exerted myself on his behalf and befriended and helped him. I know, I understand what spice that would add to the pleasure of deceiving me, if it really were true. Yes, if it were true; but I don't believe it. I have no right to, and I can't believe it.' He remembered the expression on Dolohov's face in his moments of cruelty, as for instance when he had tied the policeman to the bear and dropped them into the water, or when without any provocation he challenged a man to a duel, or shot the post-boy's horse dead with a pistol. That expression often came over Dolohov's face when he was looking at him. 'Yes, he is a bully,' thought Pierre. 'It means nothing to him to kill a man. He must think that everyone is afraid of him, and find it pleasant. He must think that I am afraid of him too. And in fact I am afraid of him,' Pierre mused, and again felt something terrible and monstrous rising inside him. Dolohov, Denisov and Rostov were sitting opposite Pierre and seemed to be very lively. Rostov was chattering gaily to his two friends, one of whom was a dashing hussar and the other a notorious duellist and madcap, and every now and then he glanced ironically at Pierre, whose preoccupied, abstracted and solid appearance was very noticeable at this dinner. Rostov looked with disfavour upon Pierre, in the first place because Pierre in the eyes of the hussar was merely a millionaire civilian and husband of a beauty, and altogether an old woman, and secondly because Pierre in his preoccupation and absent-mindedness had not recognized Rostov or responded to his bow. When the Emperor's health was drunk, Pierre, lost in thought, did not rise or lift his glass.

'What's the matter with you?' shouted Rostov, looking at him in an ecstasy of exasperation. 'Don't you hear – it's a toast to the health of his Majesty the Emperor?'

Pierre sighed and got submissively to his feet, emptied his glass and waiting till all were seated again turned with his kindly smile to Rostov.

'Why, I didn't recognize you!' he said. But Rostov was otherwise engaged, shouting 'Hurrah!'

'Aren't you going to renew the acquaintance?' said Dolohov to Rostov.

'Oh, confound him, he's a fool!' said Rostov.

'One should always be civil to the husbands of pwetty women,' remarked Denisov.

Pierre did not catch what they were saying, but he knew they were talking about him. He reddened and turned away.

'Well, now to the health of beautiful women!' proposed Dolohov, and with a serious expression, though a smile lurked at the corners of his mouth, glass in hand, addressed Pierre.

'Here's to the health of all lovely women, Peterkin – and their lovers!' he added.

Pierre with downcast eyes drank out of his glass, not looking at Dolohov or answering him. A footman, who was distributing copies of Kutuzov's cantata, laid a copy before Pierre as one of the principal guests. Pierre was just going to take it when Dolohov leaned across, snatched the sheet from his hand and began reading it. Pierre looked at Dolohov and his eyes dropped: the awful and hideous something that had been tormenting him all through the dinner rose up and took possession of him. He bent the whole of his ungainly person across the table.

'How dare you?' he shouted.

Hearing this cry and seeing to whom it was addressed, Nesvitsky and his neighbour on the right turned in haste and alarm to Bezuhov.

'Hush! Hush! What are you about?' they whispered in panic-stricken voices.

Dolohov stared at Pierre with clear, mirthful, cruel eyes, and that smile of his which seemed to say, 'Ah! This is what I like!'

'I am not giving it up!' he said, measuring his words.

Pale, with quivering lips, Pierre snatched the sheet of paper.

'You ... you ... blackguard! I challenge you!' he ejaculated, and pushing back his chair rose from the table.

At the very instant he did this and uttered these words Pierre felt that the question of his wife's guilt, which had been torturing him for the past twenty-four hours, was finally and incontestably answered in the affirmative. He hated her and was severed from her for ever. In spite of Denisov's entreaties that he should not get mixed up in the affair Rostov consented to act as Dolohov's second, and after dinner he discussed with Nesvitsky, Bezuhov's second, the arrangements for the duel. Pierre went home but Rostov, together with Dolohov and Denisov, stayed on at the club, listening to the gipsies and the other singers until late in the evening.

'Well, good-bye till tomorrow at Sokolniky,' said Dolohov, taking leave of Rostov on the club steps.

'And you're not worried?' asked Rostov.

Dolohov paused.

'Look here, in a couple of words, I'll let you into the whole secret of duelling. If you are going to fight a duel and the day before you make a will and write loving letters to your parents, and if you think you may be killed – you're a fool and as good as done for. But go with the firm intention of killing your man as quickly and surely as possible, then everything will be all right. As our bear-huntsman from Kostroma used to say to me: "A bear," he'd say, "sure, everyone's afraid of a bear – but once you set eyes on him your only fear is that he'll get away!" Well, that's how it is with me. *A demain, mon cher!*'

Next day at eight o'clock in the morning Pierre and Nesvitsky drove to the Sokolniky woods and found Dolohov, Denisov and Rostov already there. Pierre had the air of a man preoccupied with reflections in no way connected with the matter in hand. His haggard face was yellow. He had evidently not slept that night. He looked about him vaguely and screwed up his eyes as though dazzled by glaring sunshine. Two considerations absorbed him exclusively: his wife's guilt, of which after a sleepless night he had not a vestige of doubt, and the guiltlessness of Dolohov, who was certainly not called upon to protect the honour of a man who meant nothing to him. 'Maybe I should have done the same thing in his place,' thought Pierre. 'Indeed, I am sure I should. Then why this duel, this man-slaughter? Either I shall kill him, or he will put a bullet through my head, my elbow or my knee. Can't I get away from here, run off and disappear somewhere?' was the thought that passed through his mind. But at the very moments when such ideas occurred to him, he would be asking with a peculiarly calm and unconcerned face, which inspired the respect of the onlookers, 'Will it be long? Aren't we ready?'

When they were all set, with swords stuck in the snow to mark the limits to which they were to advance, and the pistols loaded, Nesvitsky went up to Pierre.

'I should not be doing my duty, count,' he faltered, 'or be worthy of your confidence and the honour you have done me in choosing me for your second, if at this grave moment, this very grave moment, I did not speak the whole truth to you. I consider this affair has not sufficient grounds, and does not warrant the shedding of blood. ... You were in the wrong, you lost your temper ...'

'Oh yes, it is horribly foolish ...' said Pierre.

'Then allow me to express your regrets, and I am sure our opposite numbers will agree to accept your apology,' said Nesvitsky (who like the other participants, and like all men in similar cases, did not believe even now that the business had actually come to a duel). 'You know, count, it is far more honourable to admit one's mistake than to let matters proceed to the irrevocable. There was no insult on either side. Allow me to confer ...'

'No, what is there to talk about?' said Pierre. 'It doesn't matter. ... Is everything ready then?' he added. 'Only tell me where I am to go, and where to fire,' he said with an unnaturally gentle smile. He took up the pistol and began to inquire about the working of the trigger, as he had never held a pistol in his hands before – a fact he was unwilling to confess.

'Oh yes, like that, of course. I know, I had only forgotten,' said he.

'No apologies, none whatever,' Dolohov was saying to Denisov (who on his side had been making an attempt at reconciliation), and he too went up to the appointed spot.

The place selected for the duel was some eighty yards from the road where the sledges had been left, in a small clearing in the pine woods, covered with melting snow after the thaw of the last few days. The antagonists stood forty paces from one another at the farther edge of the clearing. The seconds, in marking off paces, left tracks in the deep wet snow from the spot where they had been standing to the swords of Nesvitsky and Dolohov, which were stuck into the ground ten paces apart to mark the barrier. It was thawing and misty; forty yards away nothing could be seen. For three minutes everything had been ready, but still they delayed. Everyone was silent.

5

'WELL, let us begin!' said Dolohov.

'To be sure,' said Pierre, still with the same smile.

A feeling of dread was in the air. It was obvious that the affair that had begun so lightly could not now be averted in any way but was bound to run its course to the very end, irrespective of the will of men. First Denisov moved forward to the barrier and announced:

'Since the adve'sawies wefuse a weconciliation, may we not pwoceed? Take your pistols, and at the word *thwee* both of you advance. O-ne! T-wo! Thwee!' he shouted wrathfully, and stepped aside.

The combatants advanced along the trodden tracks, coming closer and closer, beginning to discern one another through the mist. They had the right to fire when they liked as they approached the barrier. Dolohov walked slowly, not raising his pistol, and fastening his bright sparkling blue eyes on his opponent's face. His mouth wore its usual semblance of a smile.

At the word 'three' Pierre moved quickly forward, missing the beaten path and stepping into the deep snow. He held the pistol at arm's length in his right hand, apparently afraid of shooting himself with it. His left arm he carefully kept behind his back because he felt inclined to use it to support his right arm, which he knew he must not do. Having gone half a dozen paces and strayed off the track into the snow, Pierre looked down at his feet, then glanced rapidly at Dolohov and, bending his finger as he had been shown, fired. Not at all expecting so loud a report, Pierre jumped at the sound, then smiled at his own sensations and stood still. The smoke, rendered denser by the mist, prevented him from seeing anything for a moment, but there was no second report as he had expected. All he could hear was Dolohov's hurried footsteps, and his figure came into view through the smoke. One hand was pressed to his left side, while the other clutched his drooping pistol. His face was pale. Rostov ran towards him and said something.

'No-o-o!' muttered Dolohov through his teeth. 'No, it's not over.' And struggling on a few staggering steps up to the sword he sank on the snow beside it. His left hand was covered with blood; he wiped it on his coat and leaned on it. His face was pale and frowning, and it trembled.

'Plea ... ' began Dolohov, but could not at first get the word out. 'Please,' he uttered with an effort.

Pierre, hardly able to restrain his sobs, started to run to Dolohov and would have crossed the space between the barriers when Dolohov cried: 'To your barrier!' and Pierre, grasping what was wanted, stopped by his sabre. Only ten paces divided them. Dolohov lowered his head, greedily sucked up a mouthful of snow, lifted his head again, straightened himself, drew in his legs and sat up, trying to find a firm centre of gravity. He gulped and swallowed the cold snow; his lips quivered but still smiled; his eyes glittered with strain and exasperation as he struggled to muster his remaining strength. He raised his pistol and aimed.

'Stand sideways! Cover yourself with your pistol!' ejaculated Nesvitsky.

'Covah you'self!' Denisov even shouted, in spite of himself for he was Dolohov's second.

With his gentle smile of compassion and regret, Pierre stood with legs and arms straddling helplessly, and his broad chest directly exposed to Dolohov, while he looked at him mournfully. Denisov, Rostov and Nesvitsky blinked. At the same instant they heard a report and Dolohov's angry cry.

'Missed!' howled Dolohov, and lay impotently face downwards in the snow.

Pierre clutched his temples and, turning round, walked away into the woods, plunging into the deep snow and muttering incoherent words.

'Folly ... folly! Death ... Lies ...' he repeated, with knitted brows. Nesvitsky stopped him and took him home.

Rostov and Denisov drove away with the wounded Dolohov, who lay silent in the sledge with closed eyes, answering not a word in reply to questions addressed to him. But as they entered Moscow he suddenly came to and, lifting his head with an effort, took Rostov, who was sitting beside him, by the hand. Rostov was struck by the totally transformed and unexpectedly exalted, tender expression on Dolohov's face.

'Well? How do you feel now?' he asked.

'Bad! But that is no matter. My friend,' said Dolohov in a gasping voice, 'where are we? In Moscow, I know. I don't count, but I have killed her, killed her.... She won't get over this. She won't get over ...'

'Who won't?' asked Rostov.

'My mother. My mother, my angel, my adored angel of a mother,' and Dolohov pressed Rostov's hand and burst into tears.

When he had grown a little calmer he explained to Rostov that he was living with his mother and if she were to see him dying she would not get over the shock. He begged Rostov to go on and prepare her.

Rostov went on ahead to carry out his mission, and to his immense surprise he learned that Dolohov the brawler, Dolohov the bully, lived in Moscow with an old mother and a hunchback sister, and was the most affectionate of sons and brothers.

6

PIERRE had of late rarely seen his wife alone. Both in Petersburg and Moscow their house was always full of guests. The night following the duel, instead of going to his bedroom, he remained, as he often did, in his huge study, the very room where old Count Bezuhov had died. With his mind going round and round, he had not slept the previous night. Now he was to be even more restless.

He stretched himself on the sofa with the idea of falling asleep and forgetting all that had taken place, but this he could not do. Such a tornado of thoughts, feelings, recollections suddenly arose inside him that, far from being able to sleep, he could not even keep still in one place but was compelled to leap up from the couch and pace the room with rapid strides. Now he seemed to see her in the early days of their marriage, with her bare shoulders and languid, passionate eyes, and then by her side he immediately saw Dolohov's handsome, insolent, hard, mocking face as he had seen it at the banquet, and then that same face pale, quivering and in agony as it had been when he reeled and sank in the snow.

'What has happened?' he asked himself. 'I have killed *her lover* – yes, killed my wife's lover. Yes, that was it. And why? How did I come to this?'

Because you married her, answered an inner voice.

'But how was I to blame?' he asked.

Because you married her without loving her; because you deceived both yourself and her. And vividly he recalled that moment after supper at Prince Vasili's, when he spoke those words he had found so difficult to utter: '*Je vous aime* – I love you.' 'It all started from that! I felt at the time' – he reflected – 'I felt at the time that it was wrong, that I had no right to do it. And so it has turned out.' He remembered their honeymoon and flushed at the recollection. Particularly vivid, humiliating and shameful was the memory of how one day shortly after his marriage he had come out of the bedroom into his study a little before noon in his silk dressing-gown, and found his head-steward there, who, with an obsequious bow, looked into his face and at his dressing-gown, and smiled faintly, as though to express by that smile respectful understanding of his master's happiness.

'And yet how many times I have been proud of her – proud of her majestic beauty, her social tact,' he reflected; 'been proud of my house in which she received all Petersburg, proud of her unapproach-ability and beauty. So this was what I prided myself on! I used to think then that I did not understand her. How often, pondering over her character, I have told myself that I was to blame for not under-standing her, for not understanding that everlasting composure and complacency and the absence of all preferences and desires, and the key to the whole riddle lies in the terrible word depravity: she is a depraved woman. Now that I have uttered the terrible word to myself everything has become clear.

'Anatole used to come to borrow money from her and kiss her on her naked shoulders. She didn't give him the money but she let her-self be kissed. Her father in jest tried to rouse her jealousy: with a serene smile she would reply that she was not so stupid as to be jealous. "Let him do as he likes," she used to say about me. I asked once if she felt no symptoms of pregnancy. She laughed contemp-tuously and said she was not such a fool as to want children, and that *I* should never have a child by her.'

Then he recalled the coarseness and bluntness of her ideas, and the vulgarity of the expressions that were characteristic of her, though she had been brought up in the most aristocratic circles. 'Not quite such a fool,' 'Just you go and try it on,' 'Get out,' she would say. Often, watching her success with young and old, men and women, Pierre could not understand why it was he did not love her. 'Yes, I never loved her,' Pierre said to himself. 'I knew she was a dissolute woman,' he repeated, 'but I did not dare admit it to myself. And now Dolohov, sitting there in the snow and forcing himself to smile, dying maybe and meeting my remorse with some swaggering affectation!'

Pierre was one of those people who, in spite of an appearance of what is called weak character, do not seek a confidant in their troubles. He worked through his trouble alone.

'It is all, all her fault,' he said to himself; 'but what of that? Why did I bind myself to her? Why did I say "*Je vous aime*" to her, which was a lie, and worse than a lie? I am to blame and must endure ... But what? The besmirching of my name? Unhappiness for life? Oh, that's all rubbish,' he thought. 'The disgrace to my name, my honour – all that's relative and apart from myself.

'Louis XVI was executed because they said he was dishonourable and a criminal' (Pierre developed the idea that came into his mind), 'and from their point of view they were right, just as were those who canonized him as a saint and died a martyr's death for his sake. Then Robespierre was guillotined for being a tyrant. Who is right, who is wrong? No one! But while you are alive – live: tomorrow you die, as I might have died an hour ago. And is it worth worrying oneself when one has only a second left to live, in comparison with eternity?' But at that moment when he believed himself soothed by such reflections he suddenly had a vision of *her* as she was at those moments when he had most violently expressed his insincere love for her, and he felt the blood rush to his heart, and had to jump up again and move about and break and tear to pieces whatever his hands came across. 'Why did I say to her "I love you"?' he kept asking himself. And as he repeated the question for the tenth time a phrase of Molière's came into his head: '*Mais que diable allait-il faire dans cette galère*? – But what the deuce was he doing in that mess?' and he began to laugh to himself.

In the night he called his valet and told him to pack up to go to Petersburg. He could not stay under the same roof with her. He could not imagine himself having anything more to say to her. He resolved that next day he would go away, leaving her a letter in which he would tell her of his intention of parting from her for ever.

In the morning when the valet came into the study with his coffee Pierre was lying on the ottoman, asleep with an open book in his hand.

He woke up and looked about him for a long while with a startled expression, unable to realize where he was.

'The countess sent to inquire if your Excellency was at home,' said the valet.

But before Pierre could decide what answer to send, the countess herself, in a white satin dressing-gown embroidered with silver and with her hair simply dressed (two immense plaits coiled twice round her exquisite head like a coronet), walked into the room, calm and majestic, except for a frown of fury on her rather prominent marble brow. With her imperturbable self-control she said nothing in front of the servant. She knew of the duel and had come to talk about it. She waited until the valet had set down the coffee and left the room. Pierre looked timidly at her through his spectacles, and like a hare surrounded by hounds who lays back her ears and continues to crouch motionless before her enemies so he tried to go on reading; but he was conscious that this was a senseless and impossible thing to do, and again he glanced timidly at her. She did not sit down but stood looking at him with a contemptuous smile while she waited for the valet to go.

'Well, what is this I hear ? Now what have you been up to, I should like to know ?' she said sternly.

'I – what have I – ?' stammered Pierre.

'Setting up as a hero, are you ? Well, answer, what about this duel ? What was it meant to prove ? Eh ? I am asking you.'

Pierre turned heavily on the sofa and opened his mouth but could not make a sound.

'If you won't answer, I'll tell you …' continued Hélène. 'You believe everything you're told. You were told' – Hélène laughed, 'that Dolohov was my lover,' she said in French with her coarse plainness of speech, uttering the word *amant* as casually as any other word, 'and you believed it! Well, what have you proved ? What did this duel show ? Only that you're a fool, *que vous êtes un sot*, but everybody knew that before. What will be the outcome ? That I'm made the laughing-stock of all Moscow; that everyone will say you were drunk and didn't know what you were doing, and challenged a man you are jealous of for no reason.' Hélène raised her voice and grew more and more excited. 'A man who's superior to you in every sense of the word …'

'Er … er …' growled Pierre, frowning and neither looking at her nor stirring.

'And how came you to believe that he was my lover ? … Eh ?

Because I like his company? If you were more intelligent and agreeable I should have preferred yours.'

'Don't speak to me ... I beg of you,' muttered Pierre hoarsely.

'Why shouldn't I speak to you? I can speak as I like, and I tell you bluntly – there are not many wives with husbands like you who would not have taken lovers (des amants), although I have not done so,' said she.

Pierre tried to say something, looked at her with strange eyes, the expression of which she did not understand, and lay down again. He was suffering physical pain at that moment: there was a weight on his chest and he could not breathe. He knew that he must do something to put an end to this agony, but what he wanted to do was too horrible.

'We had better part,' he murmured in a broken voice.

'By all means, on condition you provide for me,' said Hélène. 'Part! There's a threat to frighten me with!'

Pierre sprang up from the sofa and rushed staggering towards her.

'I'll kill you!' he shouted, and seizing a slab of marble from the table with a strength he had not known in himself till then he took a step towards her, brandishing it.

Hélène's face was dreadful to see. She shrieked and jumped back. His father's nature showed itself in Pierre. He felt the transports and fascination of frenzy. He flung down the slab, smashing it into fragments, and with outstretched arms advanced on Hélène, shouting 'Go!' in a voice so terrible that the whole house heard it with horror. God knows what he would have done at that moment had Hélène not fled from the room.

Within a week Pierre had made over to his wife the revenue from all his estates in Greater Russia, which constituted the larger half of his property, and had gone away alone to Petersburg.

7

Two months had elapsed since tidings of the battle of Austerlitz and of the fact that Prince Andrei was missing had reached Bald Hills. And in spite of all the letters sent through the Embassy, and the searches made, his body had not been found nor was he on the list of prisoners. What made it worst of all for his relatives was that there was still the possibility that he might have been picked up on the

374

battlefield by the people of the country, and now be lying, recovering or dying, alone among strangers and incapable of sending word of himself. The newspapers from which the old prince first heard of the defeat at Austerlitz had, as usual, given the briefest and vaguest accounts of how the Russians had been obliged, after brilliant feats of arms, to retreat, and had made their withdrawal in perfect order. The old prince understood from this official report that our army had been defeated. A week after the newspapers had carried the news of Austerlitz a letter came from Kutuzov informing the prince of the fate that had befallen his son.

Your son [wrote Kutuzov] fell before my eyes, a standard in his hand and at the head of his regiment – like a hero worthy of his father and his Fatherland. To the regret of myself and of the whole army it has not been ascertained up to now whether he is alive or not. I comfort myself and you with the hope that your son is living, for otherwise he would have been mentioned among the officers found on the field of battle, a list of whom has been handed to me under flag of truce.

After receiving this letter, late in the evening when he was alone in his study, the old prince said nothing to anyone. He went for his regular walk next day, but he was silent with the bailiff, the gardener and the architect, and though he looked very grim no word escaped him.

When Princess Maria went to him at the customary hour he was standing at his lathe and, as usual, did not look round at her.

'Ah, Princess Maria!' he said suddenly in an unnatural voice, throwing down his chisel. (The wheel continued to revolve from its own impetus. Princess Maria was long to remember the dying whirr of the wheel, which associated itself in her memory with what followed.)

She approached him, caught sight of his face, and something suddenly seemed to give way within her. Her eyes grew dim. By the expression on her father's face – not sad nor crushed but angry and working unnaturally – she saw that some terrible misfortune was hanging over her, about to crush her, the worst in life, a calamity she had not yet experienced, irreparable and incomprehensible – the death of one beloved.

'Father! Andrei?' said the ungainly, awkward princess with such an indescribable enchantment of grief and self-forgetfulness that her father could not bear to meet her eyes and turned away with a sob.

375

'I have had news! He is not among the prisoners, not among the killed. Kutuzov writes ...' he screamed shrilly, as though he would drive his daughter away with that shriek, 'he is killed!'

The princess did not sink down nor swoon. She was already pale but when she heard these words her face altered and a radiance shone from her beautiful, luminous eyes. It was as if joy, a supernatural joy independent of the joys and sorrows of this world, overlaid the great grief within her. She forgot all fear of her father, went up to him, took his hand and, drawing him to her, put her arm round his thin scraggy neck.

'Father,' she said, 'do not turn away from me: let us weep together.'

'Scoundrels! Blackguards!' screamed the old man, averting his face from her. 'Destroying the army, destroying men! And what for? Go – go and tell Lisa.'

The princess dropped helplessly into an arm-chair beside her father and wept. She could see her brother now as he looked when he said good-bye to her and Lisa with his tender and at the same time haughty expression. She could see him gentle and amused as he slipped the little icon round his neck. 'Did he believe now? Had he repented of his unbelief? Was he there now – there in the realm of eternal peace and blessedness?' she wondered.

'Father, tell me how it happened?' she asked through her tears.

'Go away, go away – he was killed in an action in which the finest men of Russia and Russia's glory were led out to slaughter. Go, Princess Maria. Go and tell Lisa. I will follow.'

When Princess Maria returned from her father the little princess was sitting at her work, and she looked up at her sister-in-law with that expression of happy inner serenity peculiar to women in her condition. It was evident that her eyes did not see Princess Maria but were looking within, deep into herself, at some joyful mystery being accomplished there.

'Marie,' she said, moving away from her embroidery-frame and leaning back, 'give me your hand.' She took the princess's hand and laid it on her belly.

Her eyes smiled, expectant, her little downy lip lifted and stayed so in childlike rapture.

Princess Maria knelt down before her and hid her face in the folds of her sister-in-law's dress.

'There – there – can you feel? I feel so strange. And do you know,

Marie, I am going to love him very much,' said Lisa, looking with shining, happy eyes at her husband's sister.

Princess Maria could not raise her head: she was weeping.

'What is the matter, Masha?'

'Nothing … only I felt sad … sad about Andrei,' she said, wiping away her tears against Lisa's knee.

Several times in the course of the morning Princess Maria attempted to prepare her sister-in-law, and each time began to cry. Unobservant as was the little princess in general, these tears, which she could not account for, agitated her. She said nothing but looked about uneasily as if in search of something. Before dinner the old prince, of whom she was always afraid, came into her room with a particularly restless and malign expression, and went out again without saying a word. She looked at Princess Maria with that appearance of attention concentrated within herself that is only seen in women with child, and suddenly burst into tears.

'Is there any news from Andrei?' she asked.

'No, you know it's too soon to hear anything, but Father is worried and I feel frightened.'

'So there's nothing?'

'Nothing,' answered Princess Maria, letting her lustrous eyes rest resolutely on her sister-in-law.

She had made up her mind not to tell her, and had persuaded her father to conceal the terrible tidings from Lisa, until after her confinement, which was expected before many days. Princess Maria and the old prince each bore and hid their grief in their own way. The old prince refused to cherish any hope: he decided that Prince Andrei had been killed, and though he sent an official to Austria to seek for traces of his son he ordered a monument from Moscow which he intended to erect in the garden to his son's memory, and told everybody that his son was dead. He tried to keep to his old routine but his strength started to fail him: he walked less, ate less, slept less, and every day he grew weaker. Princess Maria went on hoping. She prayed for her brother as though he were alive and was always expecting news of his return.

8

'DEAREST,' said the little princess after breakfast on the morning of the 19th of March, and her downy little lip was lifted as of old;

but as in that house since the terrible news had come smiles, tones of voice and even footsteps bore the stamp of mourning, so now the smile of the little princess, who was influenced by the general temper without knowing its cause, was such as to remind one still more of the general sorrow.

'Dearest, I'm afraid this morning's *fruschtique* (as Foka the cook calls breakfast) has disagreed with me.'

'What's the matter, sweetheart? You look pale. Yes, you do look very pale,' said Princess Maria in alarm, running up to her sister-in-law with her soft, ponderous tread.

'Shouldn't we send for Maria Bogdanovna, your Excellency?' said one of the maids who was present. (Maria Bogdanovna was the midwife from the neighbouring town who had been at Bald Hills for the last fortnight.)

'Oh yes,' assented Princess Maria, 'perhaps that's it. I'll go. Courage, my angel.' She kissed Lisa and was about to leave the room.

'No, no!' And, besides her pallor, the face of the little princess expressed childish terror at the inevitable physical suffering before her.

'No, it's only indigestion. ... Say it's only indigestion, say so, Marie, say ...' And the little princess began to cry and wring her hands in a capricious and even rather exaggerated fashion, like a child. Princess Maria hurried out of the room to fetch Maria Bogdanovna.

'*Mon Dieu! Mon Dieu!* Oh!' she heard behind her.

The midwife was already on her way to meet her, rubbing her small plump white hands with an air of significant composure.

'Maria Bogdanovna, I think it's beginning!' said Princess Maria, looking at the midwife with wide-open frightened eyes.

'Well, the Lord be praised, princess,' said Maria Bogdanovna, not hastening her step. 'You young ladies should not know anything about it.'

'But how is it the doctor from Moscow is not here yet?' said the princess. (In accordance with the wishes of Lisa and Prince Andrei it had been arranged for a doctor to come in good time from Moscow, and he was expected at any moment.)

'No matter, princess, don't be alarmed,' said Maria Bogdanovna. 'We shall manage quite well without a doctor.'

Five minutes later Princess Maria from her room heard something heavy being carried by. She looked out. Footmen were for some reason moving the leather sofa from Prince Andrei's study into the

378

bedroom. On their faces was a solemn and subdued look.

Princess Maria sat alone in her room listening to the sounds in the house, every now and again opening her door when anyone went along, and watching what was happening in the passage. A number of women made their way to and fro treading softly. They glanced at the princess and turned away. She did not venture to ask any questions, and going back into her room shut the door again and sat in an arm-chair, or took up her prayer-book, or knelt down before the icons. To her distress and surprise she found that prayer did not quiet her agitation. Suddenly the door opened softly and her old nurse, Praskovya Savishna, who hardly ever came into her room as the old prince had forbidden it, appeared on the threshold with a kerchief over her head.

'I've come to sit with 'ee a bit, dearie,' said the old nurse, 'and see, I've brought the prince's wedding candles to light before his saint, my angel,' she said with a sigh.

'Oh nurse, I'm so glad!'

'God is merciful, birdie.'

The old nurse lit the gilded candles before the icons and sat down by the door with her knitting. Princess Maria took a book and began reading. Only when they heard steps or voices did they look at one another, the princess anxious and inquiring, the old nurse reassuring. In every corner of the house everyone was dominated by the same feelings which Princess Maria experienced as she sat in her room. In accordance with the old superstition that the fewer people who know of the sufferings of a woman in labour, the less she suffers, everyone pretended to be ignorant of what was going on; no one mentioned it, but over and above the habitual staid and respectful good manners that obtained in the prince's household there was apparent a common anxiety, a mellowing of the heart and a consciousness that some great, unfathomable mystery was being accomplished at that very moment.

There was no laughter in the maids' large hall. In the men-servants' hall the men all sat in silence, as it were on the alert. In the serfs' quarters torches and candles were burning, and no one slept. The old prince walked about his study, treading on his heels, and sent Tikhon to Maria Bogdanovna to ask what news. 'Simply say, "The prince sends to inquire," and come back and tell me what she says.'

'Inform the prince that labour has commenced,' said Maria Bogdanovna, giving the messenger a significant look.

Tikhon returned and told the prince.

'Very good,' said the prince closing the door behind him, and Tikhon heard not the slightest sound from the study after that. Waiting a while, he went into the study on the pretext of attending to the candles. Seeing the prince lying on the sofa, Tikhon looked at him, observed his worried face, shook his head and dumbly going up to him kissed him on the shoulder, then went out without snuffing the candles or saying why he had come. The most solemn mystery in the world was in process of consummation. Evening passed, night wore on. And the feeling of suspense and softening of heart in the presence of the unfathomable did not wane but was heightened. No one slept.

It was one of those March nights when winter seems determined to resume its sway and lets loose a last desperate onslaught of howling winds and squalls of snow. A relay of horses had been sent to the high road to meet the German doctor from Moscow, who was expected every moment, and men were despatched on horseback with lanterns to the cross-roads to guide him over the ruts and snow-covered watery hollows.

Princess Maria had long since abandoned her book; she sat silent, her lustrous eyes fixed on her old nurse's wrinkled face, every line of which she knew so well, on the lock of grey hair that escaped from under the kerchief, on the baggy folds of skin under her chin.

Nurse Savishna, knitting in hand, was telling in low tones, scarcely hearing or following her own words, the story she had told hundreds of times before of how the late princess had been brought to bed of Princess Maria in Kishinyov, with only a Moldavian peasant woman to help instead of a midwife.

'God is merciful, no doctors bain't needed,' she was saying.

Suddenly a gust of wind beat violently against one of the window-frames (by the prince's decree the double frames were always taken out of one window in each room as soon as the larks returned), and forcing open a carelessly fastened latch set the damask curtain flapping and blew out the candle with its chill snowy draught. Princess Maria shuddered; the old nurse laying down the stocking she was knitting went to the window and leaning out tried to catch the open casement. The cold wind fluttered the ends of her kerchief and the escaping locks of her grey hair.

'Princess, my dearie, there's someone driving up the avenue!' she said, holding the casement and not closing it. 'With lanterns – it must be the doctor ...'

'Thank God, thank God!' cried Princess Maria. 'I must go and meet him: he does not know Russian.'

Princess Maria threw a shawl over her shoulders and ran to meet the stranger. As she was crossing the ante-room she looked through the window and saw a carriage with lanterns standing at the entrance. She went out on to the stairs. On a banister-post stood a tallow candle guttering in the draught. On the landing below was Philip the footman with another candle, looking scared. Still lower down, beyond the turn of the staircase, advancing footsteps were heard in thick overshoes, and a voice which seemed familiar to Princess Maria was saying something.

'Thank God!' said the voice. 'And father?'

'He has gone to bed,' answered the voice of the butler, Demyan, who was below.

Then the voice said something else and Demyan replied, and the footsteps in the thick overshoes approached more rapidly up the unseen part of the staircase.

'It's Andrei!' thought Princess Maria. 'No, it can't be, that would be too extraordinary,' and at the very moment she was thinking this the face and figure of Prince Andrei, in a fur cloak with a deep collar which was covered with snow, appeared on the landing where the footman stood with the candle. Yes, it was he, but pale and thin, and with an altered, strangely softened, agitated expression on his face. He came up the stairs and clasped his sister in his arms.

'You did not get my letter?' he asked, and not waiting for a reply which indeed he would not have received, for the princess was unable to speak – he turned back, and with the doctor who was behind him (they had met at the last post-station) he flew swiftly up the stairs again, and again embraced his sister.

'What a strange coincidence!' he cried. 'Dear Masha!' And flinging off his cloak and felt overshoes he went to his wife's apartment.

9

THE little princess lay supported by pillows, with a white night-cap on her head. (The pains had just left her.) Strands of her black hair curled about her hot perspiring cheeks; her rosy delightful little mouth with its downy lip was open and she was smiling joyfully. Prince Andrei entered and paused, facing her, at the foot of the couch on which she was lying. Her glittering eyes, staring in childish terror and excitement, rested on him with no change in their expression. 'I love you all,' they seemed to say, 'I have done no one any harm: why must I suffer like this? Help me!' She saw her husband but did not take in the meaning of his appearance before her just at this time. Prince Andrei went round to the side of the sofa and kissed her on the forehead.

'My darling!' he said. He had never called her this before. 'God is merciful ...'

She looked at him inquiringly, full of childish reproach.

'I expected help from you and none comes, none, even from you!' said her eyes. She was not surprised at his arrival: she did not realize that he was there. His coming had nothing to do with her agony or with its relief. The pains began again and Maria Bogdanovna advised Prince Andrei to leave the room.

The doctor came in. Prince Andrei left the room and meeting Princess Maria joined her again. They talked in whispers but kept breaking off. They were waiting and listening.

'Go, dear,' said Princess Maria.

Prince Andrei went to his wife's apartment again and sat waiting in the room next to hers. A woman ran out of the bedroom with a frightened face and was disconcerted when she saw Prince Andrei. He hid his face in his hands and sat thus for some minutes. Piteous, helpless, animal moans were heard through the door. Prince Andrei got up, went to the door and tried to open it. Someone was holding it shut.

'You can't come in! No!' said a terrified voice on the other side.

He began walking about the room. The moaning ceased; several seconds went by. Then suddenly a fearful shriek – it could not be her, she could not shriek like that – came from the bedroom. Prince Andrei ran to the door; the scream died away and he heard another cry – the wail of an infant.

'What have they taken a baby in there for?' wondered Prince Andrei for a second. 'A baby? What baby? ... Why a baby there? Or is the baby born?'

When he suddenly took in all the glad significance of that wail tears choked him, and leaning both elbows on the window-sill he began to cry, sobbing like a child. The door opened. The doctor with his shirt-sleeves tucked up and no coat on, came out of the room, pale and lower jaw trembling. Prince Andrei turned to him but the doctor gave him a distracted look and passed by without a word. A woman rushed out and seeing Prince Andrei stopped, hesitating, in the door. He went into his wife's room. She was lying dead in the same position he had seen her in five minutes earlier, and despite the fixed eyes and the pallor of her cheeks there was the same expression as before on the charming childlike, timid little face with its upper lip shaded with fine dark hair.

'I love you all, and have done no one any harm; and what have you done to me, oh, what have you done to me?' said the lovely, piteous, lifeless face.

In a corner of the room something red and tiny grunted and squealed in Maria Bogdanovna's shaking white arms.

*

Two hours later Prince Andrei stepped softly into his father's study. The old man knew everything already. He was standing near the door and as soon as it opened his rough old arms closed like a vice round his son's neck, and without a word he burst into sobs like a child.

*

Three days later the little princess was buried, and Prince Andrei stepped up to the side of the bier to take his last farewell of her. Even in the coffin the face was the same, though the eyes were closed. 'Ah, what have you done to me?' it still seemed to say, and Prince Andrei felt that something had broken away in his soul and that he was guilty of a wrong he could never set right nor forget. He could not weep. The old man also came up and kissed one of the waxen little hands lying peacefully crossed on her breast, and to him, too, her face said: 'Ah, what have you done to me, and why?' And the old man turned angrily away when he caught sight of this face.

*

In another five days there followed the christening of the young Prince Nikolai Andreich. The wet-nurse held back the swaddling-clothes with her chin while the priest with a goose feather anointed the baby's red and wrinkled little palms and soles.

His grandfather, who was his godfather, trembling and afraid of dropping him, carried the infant round the battered tin font, and handed him over to the godmother, Princess Maria. Prince Andrei sat in another room, his heart in his mouth lest they should let the child drown in the font, waiting for the conclusion of the ceremony. He looked up joyfully at the baby when the nurse brought him in, and nodded with satisfaction when she told him of the good omen that the bit of wax with the baby's hairs in it had floated and not sunk when it was thrown into the font.

10

ROSTOV'S part in the duel between Dolohov and Bezuhov was hushed up by the efforts of the old count, and instead of being reduced to the ranks, as he expected, he was appointed an adjutant to the governor-general of Moscow. In consequence of this, he was unable to go to the country with the rest of the family but was kept in Moscow all the summer by his new duties. Dolohov recovered, and Rostov became very friendly with him during his convalescence. Dolohov lay in bed at his mother's house. Old Maria Ivanovna, who was tenderly and passionately devoted to her son, took a liking to Rostov on account of his friendship with her Fedya, and often talked to him about her son.

'Yes, count,' she would say, 'he is too noble and pure-souled for the corrupt society of our time. No one cares about virtue nowadays – virtue is a thorn in everybody's flesh. Come, tell me, count, was it right, was it honourable of Bezuhov? And Fedya, in his noble-hearted way, loved him and even now never says a word against him. Those pranks in Petersburg, when they played all those tricks on the policeman – they were in it together, weren't they? But there, Bezuhov got off scot-free while Fedya had to bear the whole brunt of it on his shoulders. What he has had to go through! True, he has been reinstated, but how could they help reinstating him? I don't suppose there were many other such gallant sons of the Fatherland out there! And now what? This duel! Have these people no feelings, no honour? Knowing he was an only son, to challenge him to a duel and then fire right at him! Fortunately God had mercy on us. And what was it all about? Who doesn't have love affairs nowadays? Why, if he was so jealous, as I see things he ought to have shown it sooner, but he lets it go on for twelve months. And then to call him out, reckoning on Fedya not fighting, because he owed him money! What baseness! What infamy! I know you understand Fedya, my dear count, and so, believe me, I feel deep affection for you. Few understand him. His is such a lofty, celestial nature!'

Dolohov himself during his convalescence often said things to Rostov which could never have been expected of him.

'People think me an ugly customer, I know,' he would say, 'and they're welcome to. I don't give a damn unless I'm fond of a person; but I'd sacrifice my life for those I *am* fond of; the rest I'd throttle if they stood in my way. I have an adored and precious mother and two or three friends, of whom you are one; but as for everyone else – I only pay attention to them in so far as they are useful to me or mischievous. And most of them are mischievous, especially the women. Yes, my dear fellow,' he went on, 'I have met men who were tender, noble and high-minded; but I have never yet come across a woman – be she countess or cook – who could not be bought. I have yet to meet with the angelic purity and devotion which I look for in woman. If I found such a one I'd give my life for her! But those others!...' He made a gesture of contempt. 'And you may not believe me but if I still set a value on life it is only because I still hope one day to meet such a heavenly creature who will regenerate me, purify me and elevate me. But you don't understand that.'

'On the contrary, I understand perfectly,' answered Rostov, who was very much under the influence of his new friend.

*

In the autumn the Rostovs returned to Moscow. Early in the winter Denisov, too, came back and stayed with them. The first half of this winter of 1806 which Nikolai Rostov spent in Moscow was one of the happiest, merriest periods for him and the whole family. Nikolai brought a lot of young men to his parents' house. Vera was a handsome girl in her twentieth year; Sonya, at sixteen, had all the charm of an opening flower; Natasha, half child, half grown-up, at one moment was droll and immature, at the next girlishly bewitching.

Love was in the air in the Rostov house at this time, as commonly happens in every household where there are very young and very charming girls. Every young man who came to the Rostovs and saw those impressionable, smiling young faces (smiling probably at their own happiness), and the eager bustle, and heard the young feminine chatter, so inconsequent but so friendly to everyone, so ready for anything, so full of hope, and the spontaneous bursts of singing and music, felt the same disposition to fall in love and live happily ever after which the young people of the Rostov household were feeling themselves.

Among the young men Rostov brought home one of the foremost was Dolohov, whom everyone in the house liked except Natasha. She almost had a quarrel with her brother over him. She insisted that he was a bad man, that in the duel with Bezuhov Pierre had been right and Dolohov wrong, and that he was disagreeable and affected.

'There's nothing for me to understand!' she would cry with self-willed obstinacy. 'He is spiteful and heartless. Now your Denisov I like, though he is a rake and all that, still I like him; so that shows I do understand things. I don't know how to put it ... everything *he* does is thought out beforehand, and I don't like that. But Denisov...'

'Oh, Denisov's another matter,' answered Rostov, implying that even Denisov was nothing compared to Dolohov. 'One must understand what a soul there is in Dolohov – you should see him with his mother. What a tender heart!'

'Well, I don't know anything about that, but he makes me uncomfortable. And he has fallen in love with Sonya – did you know that?'

'What nonsense ...'

'I'm certain of it, you'll see.'

Natasha proved to be right. Dolohov, who did not as a rule care for feminine society, began to be a frequent visitor, and the question for whose sake he came (though no one ventured to remark on it) was soon settled – he came because of Sonya. And Sonya, though she would never have dared to acknowledge it, knew, and she blushed scarlet every time Dolohov appeared.

Dolohov often dined at the Rostovs', never missed a play performance at which they were present, and attended Iogel's 'balls for young people', at which the Rostovs were always to be found. He paid marked attention to Sonya and looked at her in such a way that not only could she not bear his eyes on her without turning crimson but even the old countess and Natasha coloured when they saw that look of his.

It was evident that this powerful, strange man was falling under the spell of the dark, graceful girl, who was in love with another man.

Rostov noticed something new in Dolohov's relations with Sonya but he did not define to himself what these new relations were. 'Every one of them's in love with someone,' he said to himself, thinking of Sonya and Natasha. But he was not so much at ease with Sonya and Dolohov as before, and was less often at home.

In the autumn of 1806 everybody began to talk again about the war with Napoleon, and with even greater fervour than in the previous year. It was decreed that ten out of every thousand of the population should be recruited for the regular army, besides a further nine of the militia. Everywhere anathemas were heaped on Bonaparte, and the impending war was Moscow's only topic of conversation. For the Rostov family interest in these preparations for war entirely centred in the fact that Nikolai would not hear of remaining in Moscow, and was only waiting for the end of Denisov's furlough to rejoin their regiment with him after Christmas. His approaching departure, far from preventing him from enjoying himself, gave an added zest to his pleasures. He spent the greater part of his time away from home, at dinners, parties and balls.

II

On the third day of the Christmas holidays Nikolai dined at home, a thing he had rarely done of late. It was a grand farewell dinner, as he and Denisov were leaving to join their regiment after Epiphany. About twenty people sat down at the table, including Dolohov and Denisov.

Never had love been so much in the air, and never had the amorous atmosphere made itself so strongly felt in the Rostovs' house as during these days of Christmas. 'Seize the moments of happiness – love and be loved! This is the only reality in the world: all else is fiddlesticks. And this is the one thing we are interested in here,' was the prevailing mood.

After exhausting two pairs of horses, as he did every day without having visited all the places he should have gone to or to which he had been invited, Nikolai returned home just before dinner. As soon as he went in he noticed, and felt, the tension of love about the house, and was conscious too of a curious embarrassment existing between certain of the company. Sonya, Dolohov and the old countess seemed particularly disturbed and in a lesser degree Natasha. Nikolai perceived that something must have happened before dinner between Sonya and Dolohov, and with his instinctive tact was very sympathetic and wary with both of them during the meal. That evening there was to be one of the dances that Iogel (the dancing-master) gave for all his pupils during the holidays.

'Nikolai darling, will you come to Iogel's? Please do!' said Natasha. 'He asked you specially, and Vasili Dmitrich' (this was Denisov) 'is coming.'

'Where would I not go at the young countess's wequest!' exclaimed Denisov, who at the Rostovs' had jestingly taken up the role of Natasha's knight. 'I'm even weady to dance the *pas de châle*.'

'I will if I can get away in time,' answered Nikolai. 'I promised to go to the Arharovs' – they're giving a party.'

'What about you?' ... he turned to Dolohov, but as soon as he had asked the question he saw that he should not have done so.

'Yes, possibly ...' Dolohov replied coldly and angrily, glancing at Sonya, and then, scowling, gave Nikolai just such a look as he had given Pierre at the club dinner.

'Something's wrong,' thought Nikolai, and still further confirmed in his surmise when Dolohov left immediately after dinner, he called Natasha and asked her what had happened.

'I was just looking for you,' said Natasha running out to him. 'I told you so but you wouldn't believe me,' she said triumphantly. 'He proposed to Sonya!'

Little as Sonya had occupied Nikolai's thoughts of late, he felt a sort of pang when he heard this. Dolohov was a suitable and in some respects a brilliant match for the dowerless orphan girl. From the old countess's point of view, and that of society, it was out of the question for her to refuse him. And so Nikolai's first feeling on hearing the news was one of indignation with Sonya. He had it on the tip of his tongue to say, 'Fine; of course she must forget her childish promises and accept the offer,' but before he could get it out Natasha went on:

'And fancy – she refused him! Definitely refused him! She told him that she loved another,' added Natasha after a pause.

'Yes, my Sonya could not have done otherwise,' thought Nikolai.

'Mamma begged her ever so many times not to, but she refused, and I know she will never change her mind once she has said a thing ...'

'And Mamma begged her not to refuse!' said Nikolai reproachfully.

'Yes,' said Natasha. 'Do you know, dearest Nikolai – don't be angry – but I know you won't marry her. I am sure of it, heaven knows how, but I know for certain that you won't marry Sonya.'

'Now you don't know anything about it,' said Nikolai. 'But I must go and talk to her. What a darling Sonya is!' he added, smiling.

'Indeed she is! I'll send her to you.' And Natasha kissed her brother and ran off.

A minute later Sonya came in, looking frightened, troubled and guilty. Nikolai went up to her and kissed her hand. This was the first time since his return that they had been alone together and talked of their love.

'Sophie,' he began, timidly at first but growing bolder as he went on, 'in case you are thinking of refusing not only a brilliant, an advantageous match – but he's a splendid, noble fellow ... he's my friend ...'

Sonya interrupted him.

'I have already refused him,' she said hurriedly.

'If you are refusing him for my sake, I am afraid that I ...'

Sonya again cut him short, giving him a frightened, beseeching look.

'Nicolas, don't say that to me!' she implored.

'No, I must. Perhaps it is conceited of me, but still it's better to speak out. If you are refusing him on my account, I ought to tell you the whole truth. I love you, I believe, more than anyone else ...'

'That is enough for me,' said Sonya, flushing crimson.

'No, but I have been in love a thousand times and shall fall in love again, though I don't feel for anyone else the friendship, trust and love that I do for you. Then I am young. Mamma does not wish it. Well – in fact – I can't make any promises. And I beg you to consider Dolohov's offer,' he said, finding it hard to bring out his friend's name.

'Do not say such things to me. I ask for nothing. I love you as a brother, and I shall always love you, and that's all I want.'

'You are an angel! I am not worthy of you, but I am only afraid of misleading you.' Nikolai once more kissed her hand.

12

IOGEL's were the most enjoyable balls in Moscow. So the mammas said as they watched their daughters executing the steps they had lately learnt; so said the young people themselves as they danced till they were ready to drop; and so said the grown-up young men and women who came to these evenings in a spirit of condescension, and found them the greatest entertainment. That very year two matches had been made at the dances. The two pretty young princesses Gorchakov had found husbands there, which had further increased Iogel's fame. What distinguished these balls from others was the absence of host and hostess, and the presence of the kind-hearted Iogel, who fluttered about like a feather, scraping and bowing according to the rules of his art, as he collected their tickets from each of his pupils. Another feature was that only those came to these balls who really wanted to dance and enjoy themselves, in the way that girls of thirteen and fourteen do who are wearing long dresses for the first time. All with rare exceptions were pretty, or seemed to be, so rapturous were their smiles and so sparkling their eyes. Sometimes the best pupils, of whom Natasha, being exceptionally graceful, was the very best, even danced the *pas de châle*; but at this last ball only the *écossaise*, the *anglaise* and a mazurka which was just coming into fashion were danced. Iogel had taken a ballroom in Bezuhov's house, and the ball, as everyone said, was a great success. There were pretty faces by the dozen and the Rostov girls were among the prettiest. They were both particularly happy and gay that evening. Elated by Dolohov's proposal, her own refusal and the talk with Nikolai, Sonya had waltzed about her room at home so that the maid could hardly get her hair plaited, and now at the dance she was transparently radiant with impulsive happiness.

Natasha, no less elated by her first long skirt and at being at a real ball, was even happier. Both the girls wore white muslin dresses with pink ribbons.

Natasha fell in love the moment she walked into the ballroom. She was not enamoured of anyone in particular, but of everyone. She was in love with everyone on whom her eyes happened to fall for that moment.

'Oh, how lovely it is!' she kept saying, running up to Sonya.

Nikolai and Denisov strolled through the room, looking with kindly patronage at the dancers.

'How pwetty she is – she will be a waving beauty!' said Denisov.

'Who?'

'Countess Natasha,' answered Denisov.

'And how she dances! What gwace!' he said again after a pause.

'Who are you talking about?'

'Why, your sister,' cried Denisov testily.

Rostov smiled.

'My dear count, you were one of my best pupils – you must dance,' said little Iogel, coming up to Nikolai and speaking in French. 'Look at all these attractive young ladies.' He turned with the same request to Denisov, who was also a former pupil of his.

'*Non, mon cher*, I pwefer to be a wall-flower,' said Denisov. 'Don't you wecollect how ill I pwofited by your teaching?'

'Oh no!' said Iogel, hastening to reassure him. 'You were only somewhat inattentive, but you had talent – oh yes, you had talent.'

The band struck up the first notes of the newly-introduced mazurka. Nikolai could not refuse Iogel, and invited Sonya to dance. Denisov sat down by the elderly ladies and leaning on his sword and beating time with his foot he kept them in fits of laughter with his stories, while he watched the young ones dancing. Iogel with Natasha, his pride and his best pupil, were the first couple. Placing his little slippered feet lightly in position, Iogel flew across the room with Natasha – shy, but conscientiously executing her steps. Denisov did not take his eyes off her, and tapped his sword in time with the music with an air which made it plain that if he were not dancing it was because he did not care to and not because he could not. In the middle of a figure he beckoned to Rostov who was passing.

'This is not the weal thing at all,' he said. 'What sort of a Polish mazurka is this? But she does dance admiwably.'

Knowing that Denisov was celebrated even in Poland for his masterly dancing of the mazurka, Nikolai ran up to Natasha.

'Go and choose Denisov. There's a dancer for you – he's a miracle!' he said.

When it came to Natasha's turn to choose a partner, she got up and tripping across the hall in her dainty dancing-slippers trimmed with little knots of ribbon she timidly made her way alone to the corner where Denisov was sitting. She saw that everybody was looking at her and waiting. Nikolai noticed that Denisov and Nətasha were smilingly disputing, and that Denisov was refusing though he grinned with delight. He ran up to them.

'Please, Vasili Dmitrich,' Natasha was saying. 'Do come.'

'Oh no, countess, weally and twuly,' Denisov replied.

'Now then, Vasska,' said Nikolai.

'They twy to coax me as if I were Vasska the cat,' laughed Denisov.

'I'll sing for you a whole evening,' said Natasha.

'The little enchantwess can do what she likes with me!' said Denisov, and he unhooked his sabre. He came out from behind the chairs, clasped his partner's hand firmly, threw back his head and put one foot forward, waiting for the beat. Only on horseback and in the mazurka was Denisov's short stature not noticeable and he looked the dashing fellow he felt himself to be. At the right beat of the music he glanced sideways with a triumphant and amused air at his partner, suddenly stamped with one foot, bounded from the floor like a ball and spun round the room, whirling his partner with him. Noiselessly he flew half across the hall on one foot and apparently not seeing the chairs ranged in front of him was dashing straight at them, when suddenly, clinking his spurs and spreading his legs, he stopped short on his heels, stood so for a second, with a clanking of spurs stamped with both feet, twisted rapidly round and striking his left heel against his right flew round in a circle again. Natasha divined what he meant to do, and abandoning herself to him followed his lead hardly knowing how. First he spun her round, holding her now with his right hand now with his left, then falling on one knee he twirled her round him, and again jumping up dashed so impetuously forward that it seemed as if he intended to race through the whole suite of rooms without drawing breath. Then he stopped suddenly again and executed some new and unexpected steps. When at last, after dexterously spinning his partner round in front of her chair, he drew up with a click of his spurs and bowed to her, Natasha did not even make him a curtsey. She fixed her eyes on him in amazement, smiling as if she did not recognize him.

'Whatever dance was that?' she brought out.

Although Iogel would not acknowledge this to be the proper mazurka, everyone was enthralled with Denisov's skill and he was continually being chosen as partner, while the old men, smiling, began to talk about Poland and the good old days. Denisov, flushed after the mazurka and mopping his face with his handkerchief, sat down by Natasha and would not leave her side for the rest of the evening.

13

FOR two days after this Rostov did not see Dolohov at his own or at Dolohov's home; on the third day he received a note from him.

As I do not intend to visit your house again for reasons you are aware of, and am going to rejoin the regiment, I am giving a farewell supper to my friends tonight – come to the English Hotel.

About ten o'clock that evening Rostov went to the English Hotel straight from the theatre, where he had been with his family and Denisov. He was at once shown to the best room in the place, which Dolohov had taken for the occasion.

Some twenty men were gathered round a table at which Dolohov was sitting between two candles. On the table lay a pile of gold and paper money, and Dolohov was keeping the bank. Rostov had not seen him since his proposal and Sonya's refusal, and felt uncomfortable at the thought of how they would meet.

As soon as Rostov entered the door Dolohov looked up with a clear cold glance, as though he had long been expecting him.

'We have not met for some time,' he said. 'Thanks for coming. I'll just finish dealing here, and Ilyushka will make his appearance with his chorus.'

'I called at your house once or twice,' said Rostov, reddening.

Dolohov made no reply.

'You might put down a stake,' he said.

Rostov at that instant recalled a singular conversation he had once had with Dolohov. 'Only a fool believes in gambling,' Dolohov had said then.

'Or are you afraid to play with me?' Dolohov asked, as though divining Rostov's thought, and he smiled.

Behind the smile Rostov saw the mood that Dolohov had been in at the club dinner and at various other times when, weary as it were of the monotony of daily life, he had felt the need to escape from it by some odd and usually cruel action.

Rostov felt ill at ease. He racked his brain without success for some

393

repartee in reply to Dolohov's words. But before he could think of anything, Dolohov, looking straight into Rostov's face, said slowly and deliberately so that everyone could hear:

'Do you remember, you and I were talking about cards. ... He's a fool who trusts to luck: one should play a safe game, and I want to try.'

'Try what – your luck, or play a safe game?' wondered Rostov.

'You're right, you'd better not play,' Dolohov added, and springing a new pack of cards said: 'Bank, gentlemen!'

Moving the money forward, Dolohov began to deal. Rostov sat down by his side and at first did not play. Dolohov kept glancing at him.

'Why don't you play?' said Dolohov. And strangely enough, Rostov felt impelled to take a card, stake a trifling sum on it and begin to play.

'I have no money on me,' said Rostov.

'I'll trust you!'

Rostov staked five roubles on a card and lost, staked again, and lost. Dolohov 'killed' – in other words, took Rostov's stake ten times running.

'Gentlemen,' said Dolohov after he had been holding the bank for some time, 'pray place your money on the cards or else I may get muddled over the reckoning.'

One of the players said he hoped that they could trust him.

'Yes, but I am afraid of getting the accounts mixed; so I beg you to lay the money on your cards,' replied Dolohov. 'Don't worry yourself, we'll settle up afterwards,' he added, turning to Rostov.

The game continued; a waiter kept bringing round champagne.

All Rostov's cards were beaten, and the sum of eight hundred was scored up against him. He was just writing '800 roubles' on a card, but while the waiter filled his glass he changed his mind and altered it to his usual stake of twenty roubles.

'Leave it,' said Dolohov, though he did not seem to be looking at Rostov at all, 'you'll win it back all the sooner. I lose to the others but win from you. Is it that you are afraid of me?' he asked again.

Rostov submitted, let the stake of eight hundred remain and laid down a seven of hearts with a torn corner, which he had picked up from the floor. Well he remembered that card afterwards. He placed the seven of hearts, on which he had written '800 roubles' with a broken bit of chalk in bold round figures; he emptied the glass of warm champagne that had been handed to him, smiled at Dolohov's words, and with sinking heart as he waited for the seven to turn up watched Dolohov's hands which held the pack. A great deal depended on Rostov's winning or losing on that seven of hearts. The previous Sunday the old count had given his son two thousand roubles, and although he never liked speaking of money difficulties had told Nikolai that this was the last money he could let him have till May, and so he begged him to be a little more careful this time. Nikolai had replied that it was enough and to spare, and gave his word of honour not to come for more before the spring. Now out of that sum only twelve hundred roubles was left, so on this seven of hearts hung not only the loss of sixteen hundred roubles but the necessity of going back on his word. Feeling sick and frightened, he watched Dolohov's hands and thought, 'Now then, make haste and deal me that card and I'll take my cap and drive home to supper with Denisov, Natasha and Sonya, and I'm sure I'll never touch a card again.' At that moment his home life – the jokes with Petya, his talks with Sonya, duets with Natasha, the games of picquet with his father, even his comfortable bed in the house in Povarsky street – rose before him with such force and vividness and attraction that it seemed like some long past, lost and hitherto unappreciated happiness. He could not conceive that a stupid chance, letting the seven be dealt to the right rather than to the left, might deprive him of all this newly-perceived, newly-comprehended happiness, and plunge him into the depths of unknown and undefined misery. That could not be, yet it was with dread in his heart that he waited for the movement of Dolohov's hands. Those broad, reddish hands with hairy wrists visible from under the shirt-cuffs laid down the pack of cards and took up a glass and the pipe that were passed to him.

'So you're not afraid to play with me?' repeated Dolohov; and as though he were about to tell a good story he leaned back in his chair, and began deliberately with a smile:

'Yes, gentlemen, I've been told there's a rumour going about Moscow that I'm too sharp with cards, so I advise you to be somewhat on your guard with me.'

'Come on, deal now!' said Rostov.

'Ugh, these Moscow rabbits!' said Dolohov, and with a smile he took up the cards.

'Aaah!' Rostov almost screamed, lifting both hands to his head. The seven he needed was lying uppermost, the first card in the pack. He had lost more than he could pay.

'Still, don't go ruining yourself,' said Dolohov with a passing glance at Rostov as he continued to deal.

14

AN hour and a half later most of the players were no longer seriously interested in their own play.

The whole game centred on Rostov. Instead of the sixteen hundred roubles, he had a long column of figures scored against him, which he had reckoned up to ten thousand but which he now vaguely supposed must have risen to at least fifteen thousand. In reality the sum already exceeded twenty thousand roubles. Dolohov was no longer listening to stories or telling them; he followed every movement of Rostov's hands and occasionally ran his eyes over the score against him. He had decided to play until that score reached forty-three thousand. He had fixed on this figure because forty-three was the sum of his and Sonya's ages. Rostov, supporting his head in both hands, sat at the table which was scrawled over with figures, wet with spilt wine, and littered with cards. One torturing sensation never left him – that those broad-boned reddish hands with the hairs visible under the shirt-cuffs, those hands which he loved and hated, held him in their power.

'Six hundred roubles, ace, a corner, a nine ... winning it back's out of the question! ... And how happy I should be if only I were at home! ... The knave, double or quits ... it can't be! And why is he doing this to me?' Rostov pondered and thought. Sometimes he put a higher stake on a card, but Dolohov refused it and fixed the stake himself. Nikolai submitted to him, and at one moment he was praying to God as he had prayed under fire on the bridge over the Enns; at the next it would occur to him that perhaps the first card that came to hand from the crumpled heap under the table would save him; then he reckoned up the rows of braiding on his jacket and tried staking the total of his losses on a card of that number; then he looked round for help from the other players, or stared at the now stony face of Dolohov and tried to read what was passing in his mind.

'He knows, of course,' he said to himself, 'what this loss means to me. Surely he can't want to ruin me? Why, he was my friend. Why, I love him. ... But it isn't his fault; what's he to do if he has all the luck? And it's not my fault either,' he thought to himself. 'I have done nothing wrong. Have I ever murdered or hurt anyone, or wished harm to anyone? Why, then, this horrible misfortune? And when did it begin? Such a little while ago, when I came to this table with the idea of winning a hundred roubles to buy that little casket for Mamma's name-day and then going home, I was so happy, so free, so light-hearted! And I did not realize then how happy I was! When did that end and when did this new, awful state of things begin? What outward sign marked the change? I have sat all the time in this same place at this same table, picking out cards and putting them down in the same way, and looking at those deft, broad-boned hands. Whenever did it happen, and what has happened? I am well and strong and just the same as I was, and in the self-same place. No, it cannot be! Surely it will all end in nothing.'

He was flushed and bathed in perspiration, though the room was not hot. And his face was all the more painful and piteous to see because of its futile efforts to seem calm.

The score against him reached the fateful figure of forty-three thousand. Rostov had just prepared a card by bending the corner, with which he meant to double the three thousand he had just won, when Dolohov, slapping the pack of cards down on the table, pushed them aside and taking a piece of chalk began rapidly adding up the total of Rostov's losses in his clear, firm hand, breaking the chalk as he did so.

'Supper, it's time for supper! And there are the gipsies!'

And a number of dark-skinned men and women were in fact coming in from the cold outside, saying something in their gipsy accent. Nikolai realized that all was over; but he said in an indifferent voice:

'What, won't you go on? And I had such a nice little card all ready,' as though what really interested him was the fun of the game itself.

'It's all over, I'm done for!' he thought. 'Now a bullet through my brains – that's all that is left to me!' And at the same time he said in a cheerful voice:

'Come now, just this one card.'

'All right!' said Dolohov, having completed the addition. 'All right! Make it twenty-one roubles then,' he said, pointing to the figure twenty-one, which was over and above the round sum of forty-three thousand; and taking up a pack he prepared to deal. Rostov submissively unbent the corner of his card and instead of the 6,000 he had intended to write carefully put 21.

'It's all the same to me,' he said. 'I only wanted to see whether you would win on this ten or let me have it.'

Dolohov gravely began to deal. Oh, how Rostov at that moment detested those hands with their short reddish fingers and the hairy wrists emerging from the shirt-bands, which held him in their power! ... The ten fell to him.

'Well, you owe me forty-three thousand, count,' said Dolohov, stretching himself and getting up from the table. 'One gets tired, though, sitting still so long,' he added.

'Yes, I'm tired too,' said Rostov.

Dolohov cut him short, as if to remind him that it was not for him to take a light tone.

'When do you propose to let me have the money, count?'

Rostov, flushing, drew Dolohov into the next room.

'I cannot pay it all immediately. Will you take an I.O.U.?' he asked.

'I say, Rostov,' exclaimed Dolohov, smiling brightly and looking Nikolai straight in the eye, 'you know the saying, "Lucky in love, unlucky at cards!" Your cousin is in love with you, I know.'

'Oh, how horrible to feel myself in this man's power,' thought Rostov. He knew the shock the news of his losses would be to his father and mother; he felt what happiness it would be not to have to confess to all this; and he was aware that Dolohov knew that he could set him free from this shame and sorrow, and now wanted to play cat and mouse with him.

'Your cousin ...' Dolohov was saying, but Nikolai cut him short.

'My cousin has nothing to do with this, and there is no need to mention her!' he cried with fury.

'Then when will you pay me?' demanded Dolohov.

'Tomorrow,' said Rostov, and left the room.

15

To say 'tomorrow' and maintain a dignified tone was not difficult, but to go home alone, see his sisters, brother, his mother and father, confess and ask for money he had no right to after giving his word of honour, was terrible.

At home they had not yet gone to bed. The younger members of the family after returning from the theatre had had supper and were now grouped round the clavichord. As soon as Nikolai entered the room he felt himself enfolded in the romantic atmosphere of love which pervaded the Rostov household that winter and now, after Dolohov's proposal and Iogel's ball, seemed to hang breathlessly around Sonya and Natasha, like the air before a thunderstorm. Sonya and Natasha in the light-blue dresses they had worn to the theatre, looking pretty, and conscious of it, were standing by the clavichord, happy and smiling. Vera was playing chess with Shinshin in the drawing-room. The old countess, waiting for her husband and son to come in, sat playing patience with an old gentlewoman who lived in the house with them. Denisov, with shining eyes and ruffled hair, was sitting with one leg behind him at the clavichord, striking chords with his short little fingers and rolling his eyes as he sang in his small, husky but true voice a poem of his own composition called *The Enchantress*, to which he was trying to fit music:

> Enchantress, say what magic fire
> Draws me to my forsaken lyre ?
> What ardour sets my heart aglow ?
> What rapture thrills my fingers slow ?

he sang in passionate tones, his black agate eyes sparkling at the tremulous but happy Natasha.

'Splendid! Excellent!' cried Natasha. 'Now another verse,' she said, not noticing Nikolai.

'Everything's just the same with them,' thought Nikolai, peeping into the drawing-room, where he saw Vera and his mother and the old lady.

'Ah. and here's our Nikolai!' Natasha ran up to him.

'Is Papa home ?' he asked.

'I am so glad you've come,' said Natasha, not answering his

question. 'We're having such a lovely time. Vasili Dmitrich is staying on another day for me, did you know?'

'No, Papa is not back yet,' said Sonya

'Nikolai, my dearest, you in? Come here to me, dear boy,' called the old countess from the drawing-room.

Nikolai went to his mother, kissed her hand and without saying a word took a seat near her table and began to watch her hands as they laid out the cards. From the music-room he kept hearing the sound of laughter and merry voices trying to persuade Natasha to sing.

'All wight! All wight!' shouted Denisov. 'It's no good making excuses now! It's your turn to sing the ba'cawolle – I entweat you!'

The countess glanced at her silent son.

'What is the matter?' she asked.

'Oh, nothing,' said Nikolai, as if he were sick of continually being asked one and the same question. 'Will Papa be in soon?'

'I expect so.'

'Everything's the same for them. They know nothing about it. What am I to do with myself?' thought Nikolai, and he went back to the music-room where the clavichord was.

Sonya was sitting at the instrument playing the opening bars of Denisov's favourite barcarolle. Natasha was preparing to sing. Denisov was looking at her with enraptured eyes.

Nikolai began to pace up and down the room.

'Why do they want to make her sing? What can she sing? And there's nothing to be happy about,' thought Nikolai.

Sonya struck the first chord of the prelude.

'My God, I'm a dishonoured man – I'm ruined! A bullet through my brain is the only thing left for me – not singing!' his thoughts ran on. 'Could I go away? But where to? I don't care – let them sing!'

He continued to stride about the room looking gloomily at Denisov and the girls, avoiding their eyes.

'Darling Nikolai, what is the matter?' Sonya's eyes asked, looking intensely at him. She had seen at once that something had happened to him.

Nikolai turned away from her. Natasha too, with her quick instinct, had instantly noticed her brother's state of mind. She had observed it but felt in such high spirits at that moment, so far removed from sorrow, melancholy or self-reproach, that she purposely deceived herself (as young people often do). 'No, I am too happy

400

just now to spoil my happiness by having to sympathize with someone else's misery,' she felt; and she said to herself: 'Very likely it is
only my fancy, and he's really as happy as I am.'

'Now, Sonya,' she said, walking into the very middle of the room
where she considered the acoustics were best. Lifting her head and
letting her arms droop lifelessly as ballet-dancers do, Natasha, rising
energetically from her heels to her toes, took a turn about the centre
of the room and stood still.

'Behold me, here I am!' she seemed to say, in response to the rapt
gaze with which Denisov followed her.

'And what can she find to be so pleased about?' thought Nikolai,
looking at his sister. 'How is it she isn't bored to death, why has she
no conscience?'

Natasha took the first note, her throat swelled, her chest rose, her
eyes became serious. At that moment she was oblivious of everyone
and everything, and from her smiling lips flowed sounds which anyone may produce at the same intervals and hold for the same length
of time, yet a thousand times they leave one unmoved, and on the
thousand and first occasion set one thrilling and weeping.

Natasha that winter had for the first time begun to take her
singing seriously, mainly because Denisov had been so enthusiastic
over her voice. She no longer sang like a child, there was no longer
any of that comical, immature, painstaking effort which used to be
in her performance; but she did not yet sing well, pronounced the
musical connoisseurs who heard her. 'A beautiful voice. Not trained
though. It must be trained,' everyone said. Only they generally
said it some while after the sound of her voice had died away. While
they were actually listening to that untrained voice with its incorrect
breathing and labouring transitions even the connoisseurs said
nothing but only delighted in it and wanted to hear it again. Her
voice had a virginal purity, an unconsciousness of its own powers and
an unforced velvety tone, which so combined with its lack of
knowledge of the art of singing that it seemed as though nothing in
that voice could be altered without spoiling it.

'What is this?' thought Nikolai, listening to her and opening his
eyes wide. 'What has happened to her? How she is singing today!'
And suddenly the whole world centred for him on anticipation of
the next note, the next phrase, and everything in the world was
divided into three beats: *Oh mio crudele affetto* ... One, two, three ...

One, two, three ... One ... *Oh mio crudele affetto* ... One, two, three ... One. 'Ugh, this senseless life of ours!' mused Nikolai. 'All that misery, money, Dolohov, and anger, and honour – it's all trash ... but this is real. ... Now, Natasha, now darling! Now my girl! How will she take that top B? Yes, she's taken it, glory be to God!' And without being conscious that he was singing, to support her top B he sang seconds and gave her the third to her high note. 'Oh God, how fine! Did I really get that note? How glorious!' he thought.

Oh, how that chord vibrated, and how all that was best in Rostov's soul thrilled in harmony! And this best was something apart from everything else in the world, and above all else. What were gambling losses, Dolohovs and promises? ... All rubbish. One might murder and steal and yet be happy. ...

16

IT was a long time since Rostov had derived such enjoyment from music as he did that day. But no sooner had Natasha finished her barcarolle than reality again presented itself. Without a word he got up and went downstairs to his own room. A quarter of an hour later the old count came in from the club, cheerful and contented. Hearing him drive up, Nikolai went to meet him.

'Well, had a good time?' asked the old count, smiling gaily and proudly at his son.

Nikolai tried to say 'Yes', but found it impossible, and nearly burst into sobs. The count was lighting his pipe and did not notice his son's state.

'Well, I've got to do it!' thought Nikolai for the first and last time. And suddenly, in the most casual tone, which made him feel utterly ashamed of himself, he said to his father, as though he were asking for the carriage to drive into town:

'Papa, I have come on a matter of business. I was almost forgetting. I need some money.'

'What's that!' said his father who was in particularly good spirits. 'I told you it wouldn't be enough. Need much, do you?'

'Very much,' said Nikolai flushing and smiling a stupid careless smile for which he was long unable to forgive himself. 'I have lost a little at cards, I mean a good deal, a great deal – forty-three thousand.'

'What! To whom? ... You're not serious!' cried the count, flushing, as old people flush, an apoplectic red over his neck and the back of his head.

'I have promised to pay tomorrow,' said Nikolai.

'Well! ...' said the old count, spreading out his arms and sinking helplessly on the sofa.

'It can't be helped. It happens to everyone!' said the son in a free and easy tone, while in his heart he was feeling himself a worthless scoundrel whose whole life could not atone for his crime. He longed to kiss his father's hands, kneel and beg his forgiveness, while in a careless and even rude voice he was telling him that it happens to everyone!

The old count dropped his eyes when he heard these words from his son, and began to fidget about as though in search of something.

'Yes, yes,' he murmured, 'it will be difficult, I fear, difficult to raise ... happens to everybody! Yes, yes, it might happen to anyone ...' And with a furtive glance at his son's face the count went out of the room. Nikolai had been prepared for opposition, but had not at all expected this.

'Papa! Pa-pa!' he called after him, sobbing. 'Forgive me!' And clutching at his father's hand he pressed it to his lips and burst into tears.

★

While father and son were having this conversation, another and no less important one was taking place between mother and daughter. Natasha came running to her mother in great excitement.

'Mamma! ... Mamma! ... He has done it ...'

'Done what?'

'Made me – made me an offer. Mamma! Mamma!' she cried.

The countess could not believe her ears. Denisov had proposed. To whom? To this chit of a girl, Natasha, who not so long ago was playing with dolls, and who was still in the school-room?

'Don't, Natasha! What nonsense!' she said, hoping it was a joke.

'Nonsense indeed! I am telling you a fact,' said Natasha indignantly. 'I came to ask you what to do, and you call it "nonsense". ...'

The countess shrugged her shoulders.

'If it is true that *Monsieur* Denisov has proposed to you, though it's an absurd idea, then tell him he is a donkey, that's all.'

'No, he isn't a donkey,' replied Natasha seriously, affronted.

'Well then, what do you want? You are all in love nowadays, it seems. Well, if you are in love, better go and marry him,' said the countess with a laugh of annoyance. 'Good luck to you!'

'No, mamma, I'm not in love with him. I suppose I'm not in love with him.'

'That's all right then, go and tell him so.'

'Mamma, are you cross? Don't be cross, dearest. It's not my fault, is it?'

'No, my dear, but what is it you want? Would you like me to go and tell him?' said the countess, smiling.

'No, I will do it myself, only tell me what to say. Everything comes easily to you,' said Natasha, responding to her smile. 'And you should have seen how he said it! You know, I am sure he did not mean to speak: it came out by accident.'

'Well, all the same, you must refuse him.'

'No, I mustn't. I am so sorry for him! He's so nice.'

'Then accept his proposal. It's high time you were married!' exclaimed the countess sharply and sarcastically.

'No, mamma, but I feel so sorry for him. I don't know how to tell him.'

'There's no need for you to tell him anything. I'll speak to him myself,' said the countess, indignant that anyone should dare to look upon her little Natasha as grown up.

'No you won't! I'll say it myself, and you come and listen at the door,' and Natasha ran across the drawing-room to the music-room, where Denisov was still sitting on the same chair by the clavichord with his face in his hands. He jumped up at the sound of her light step.

'Natalie,' he said, moving towards her with rapid steps, 'decide my fate. It is in your hands!'

'Vasili Dmitrich, I'm so sorry for you! ... No, but you are so nice ... but it cannot be ... not that ... but I shall always, always love you as a friend.'

Denisov bent over her hand and she heard strange incomprehensible sounds. She kissed his rough curly black head. At that moment they heard the hurried rustle of the countess's skirts. She came up to them.

'Vasili Dmitrich, I thank you for the honour you do us,' she said in an embarrassed voice, which sounded severe to Denisov, 'but my daughter is so young, and I should have thought that as my son's friend you would have addressed yourself to me first. In that case you would not have forced me to make this refusal.'

'Countess ...' began Denisov with downcast eyes and a guilty face. He tried to say more, but faltered.

Natasha could not see him in such a piteous plight, and remain calm. She began to sob aloud.

'Countess, I have acted w'ongly,' Denisov went on in an unsteady voice, 'but pway believe me, I so adoah your daughter and all your family that I would gladly sacwifice my life twice over. ...' He looked at the countess, and seeing her stern face said: 'Well, good-bye, countess,' and kissing her hand he left the room with quick resolute steps, without a glance at Natasha.

*

Next day Rostov saw Denisov off, as he was unwilling to remain another day in Moscow. All his Moscow friends gave him a farewell entertainment at the Gipsies', with the result that he had no recollection of how they got him into the sledge, or of the first three stages of his journey.

After Denisov's departure Rostov spent another fortnight in Moscow, waiting for the money which the old count was unable to raise all at once. He did not leave the house, and passed most of his time in the girls' sitting-room.

Sonya was more affectionate and devoted to him than ever. It seemed as if she were anxious to show that his gambling loss was an exploit for which she loved him all the more; but Nikolai now considered himself unworthy of her.

He filled the girls' albums with verses and music, and after having finally sent Dolohov the whole forty-three thousand roubles, and received his receipt he went away at the end of November, without taking leave of any of his acquaintances, to rejoin his regiment which was already in Poland.

PART TWO

I

AFTER the scene with his wife Pierre left for Petersburg. At the Torzhok post-station either there were no horses or the post-master was unwilling to supply them. Pierre was obliged to wait. Without undressing, he stretched himself on the leather sofa in front of a round table on which he put up his heavy feet in their thick over-boots and sank into thought.

'Will you have the portmanteaux brought in ? And a bed got ready ? Would you care for tea ?' the valet kept asking.

Pierre did not answer, he heard and saw nothing. He had begun to reflect while at the last station and still pondered the same question – one so important that he took no notice of what went on around him. Far from being concerned whether he reached Petersburg earlier or later, or whether there would or would not be a place for him to rest in at this station, in comparison with the thoughts that engrossed him now it was a matter of indifference to him whether he spent a few hours or the rest of his life here.

The post-master, his wife, Pierre's valet, and a peasant woman selling Torzhok embroidery, came into the room offering their services. Without removing his feet from the table Pierre looked at them through his spectacles, unable to understand what they could want or how they managed to live without having decided the questions that so absorbed him. These same problems had occupied his mind ever since the day he had returned from the Sokolnik woods after the duel and had spent that first agonizing, sleepless night. But now in the solitude of the journey they seized on him with especial force. No matter what he began to think about, he always came back to these questions, which he could not answer, yet could not cease asking himself. It was as though the thread of the principal screw which held his life together had worn smooth. The screw would not go in or come out but went on twisting round in the same groove without catching, and it was impossible to stop turning it.

The post-master came in and began obsequiously begging his Excellency to wait just a little couple of hours, after which (come what might of it) he would let his Excellency have the horses reserved for the mail. It was plain that the man was lying and only wanted to get an extra tip out of the traveller. 'Was that good or bad?' Pierre wondered. 'For me good, for the next traveller bad, and for himself unavoidable because he needs the money for food. He tells me an officer once gave him a thrashing for letting a private traveller have the courier-horses. But the officer thrashed him because he was in a hurry. And I shot Dolohov because I considered myself injured. And Louis XVI was executed because they believed him to be a criminal, and a year later they executed those who had executed him – also for some reason. What is wrong? What is right? What should one love and what hate? What is life for, and what am I? What is life? What is death? What is the power that controls it all?' he asked himself. And there was no answer to any of these questions, except the one illogical reply that in no way answered them. This reply was: 'One dies and it's all over. One dies and either finds out about everything or ceases asking.' But dying, too, was dreadful.

The Torzhok pedlar-woman in a whining voice kept offering her wares, especially some goat-skin slippers. 'I have hundreds of roubles I don't know what to do with, and she stands there in her tattered cloak looking timidly at me,' thought Pierre. 'And what does she want the money for? As if it could add a hair's breadth to her happiness or peace of mind. Can anything in the world make her or me less enslaved to evil and death? Death which is the end of all things and must come today or tomorrow – at any rate in an instant of time as compared with eternity.' And again he twisted the screw with the stripped thread, and the screw still went on turning in the same place.

His servant handed him a half-cut novel in the form of letters by Madame de Souza. He began reading about the sufferings and virtuous struggles of a certain Amélie de Mansfeld. 'And why did she resist her seducer when she loved him?' he thought. 'God could not have put into her heart an impulse that was against His will. My wife – as she once was – didn't struggle, and perhaps she was right. Nothing has been discovered, nothing invented,' Pierre said to himself again. 'All we can know is that we know nothing. And that is the sum total of human wisdom.'

Everything within him and without seemed to him confused, meaningless and loathsome. But in this very repugnance to all his circumstances Pierre found a kind of tantalizing satisfaction.

'May I venture to ask your Excellency to make the least little bit of accommodation for this gentleman here,' said the post-master, coming into the room and introducing another traveller held up for lack of horses. The new-comer was a thick-set, large-boned, sallow, wrinkled old man with grey bushy eyebrows overhanging bright eyes of an indefinite grey colour.

Pierre took his feet off the table, stood up and went to lie down on the bed that had been made ready for him, occasionally glancing at the stranger, who with a tired, gloomy air, without paying any heed to Pierre, wearily allowed his servant to help remove his wraps, leaving him in a shabby nankeen-covered sheepskin coat with felt high-boots on his thin bony legs. The new-comer took a seat on the sofa, leant his large head with its broad temples and close-cropped hair against the back of it, and looked at Bezuhov. The stern, intelligent and penetrating expression of his gaze impressed Pierre. He felt a wish to speak to the new-comer, but by the time he had made up his mind to put a question about the state of the roads the traveller had closed his eyes and folded his shrivelled old hands, on one finger of which there was a heavy iron ring with a seal representing a skull. He sat without stirring, either resting or sunk, as it seemed to Pierre, in profound and calm meditation. The stranger's servant was also a sallow wrinkled old man without beard or moustache, evidently not because he was shaven but because they had never grown. The old servant was nimbly unpacking his master's canteen, preparing tea and bringing in a samovar of boiling water. When everything was ready the new-comer opened his eyes, moved up to the table, and after pouring out a tumbler of tea for himself filled another for the beardless old man and passed it to him. Pierre began to feel a sense of uneasiness, and the need, even the inevitability, of entering into conversation with this stranger.

The servant brought back his empty glass turned upside down with an unfinished bit of nibbled sugar beside it, and asked if anything more would be wanted.

'No. Give me my book,' said the stranger.

408

The servant handed him a book which Pierre took to be of a devotional character, and the traveller buried himself in his reading. Pierre looked at him. All at once the stranger laid down the book, put a marker in the page and closed it, and again, shutting his eyes and leaning back on the sofa, fell into his former attitude. Pierre looked at him, and had not time to turn away when the old man opened his eyes and fastened his severe, resolute gaze directly on Pierre's face.

Pierre felt confused, and tried to escape that searching look, but the brilliant old eyes drew him irresistibly.

2

'I HAVE the pleasure of addressing Count Bezuhov, if I am not mistaken,' said the stranger, in a loud deliberate voice.

Pierre looked silently and inquiringly at him through his spectacles.

'I have heard of you, my dear sir,' continued the stranger, 'and of the misfortune that has befallen you.' He seemed to lay special stress on the word *misfortune*, as much as to say: *Yes, misfortune! Call it what you please, I know that what happened to you in Moscow was a misfortune.* - 'I feel for you deeply, my dear sir.'

Pierre flushed, and hurriedly dropping his legs down from the bed leant forward towards the old man, with a forced and timid smile.

'I have not referred to this out of curiosity, my dear sir, but for graver reasons.'

He paused, still gazing at Pierre, and moved aside on the sofa by way of inviting Pierre to sit next to him. Pierre felt reluctant to enter into conversation with this old man, but involuntarily submitting he came over and sat by his side.

'You are unhappy, my dear sir,' the stranger continued. 'You are young, I am old. I should like, so far as lies in my power, to help you.'

'Oh yes,' said Pierre with an unnatural smile. 'Very much obliged to you. ... May I ask where you are travelling from?'

The stranger's face was not genial, it was even cold and severe, but in spite of this to Pierre both the speech and the face of his new acquaintance were irresistibly attractive.

'But if for any reason you feel averse from talking to me,' said the old man, 'say so, my dear sir.' And suddenly he smiled a quite unexpected, tender, fatherly smile.

'Oh no, not at all, on the contrary, I am very happy to make your acquaintance,' said Pierre, and glancing once more at the stranger's hand he examined the ring more closely. He perceived the skull on it – the symbol of Masonry.

'Allow me to inquire,' he said, 'are you a mason?'

'Yes, I belong to the Brotherhood of Freemasons,' said the stranger, looking more and more searchingly into Pierre's eyes. 'And in their name and my own I hold out a brotherly hand to you.'

'I am afraid,' said Pierre, smiling and hesitating between the confidence inspired in him by the personality of the freemason and his own habit of ridiculing the articles of the masonic creed – 'I am afraid I am very far from a comprehension – how shall I put it? – I am afraid my way of thinking in regard to the whole theory of the universe is so opposed to yours that we shall not understand one another.'

'I am familiar with your way of thinking,' said the freemason, 'and the outlook you mention, which seems to you the result of your own mental efforts, is the way of thinking of the majority of men, and is the invariable fruit of pride, indolence and ignorance. Forgive me, my dear sir, but if I had not been sure of it I should not have addressed you. Your way of thinking is a melancholy delusion.'

'In exactly the same manner I might take it for granted that you are in error,' said Pierre with a faint smile.

'I should never be so bold as to assert that I know the truth,' said the mason, impressing Pierre more and more with the precision and assurance of his speech. 'No one can attain truth by himself. Only by laying stone upon stone with the co-operation of all, through millions of generations from our forefather Adam to our own day, is the temple raised which is to be a worthy dwelling-place for the Most High God,' said the freemason, and closed his eyes.

'I ought to tell you that I don't believe ... I do not believe in God,' said Pierre regretfully and with an effort, feeling it essential to confess the whole truth.

The mason looked intently at Pierre and smiled, much as a rich man holding millions in his hands might smile upon a poor wretch who told him that he, the poor man, was without the five roubles that would secure his happiness.

'Yes, you do not know Him, my dear sir,' said the freemason. 'You cannot know Him. You do not know Him, that is just why you are unhappy.'

'Yes, yes, I am unhappy,' assented Pierre; 'but what am I to do?'

'You do not know Him, my dear sir, and so you are very unhappy. You do not know Him, but He is here, He is in me. He is in my words – He is within thee, and even in those impious words thou hast just uttered!' pronounced the mason in a stern, vibrating voice.

He paused and sighed, evidently trying to master his emotion.

'If He did not exist,' he said quietly, 'you and I would not be speaking of Him, my dear sir. Of what, of whom have we been speaking? Whom hast thou denied?' he suddenly asked with triumphant austerity and authority in his voice. 'Who invented Him, if He does not exist? Whence came your hypothesis of the existence of such an inconceivable Being? How came you and all the rest of the world to postulate the existence of such an incomprehensible Being, a Being all-powerful, eternal and infinite in all His attributes? ...'

He stopped and remained silent for some time.

Pierre could not and had no wish to break this silence.

'He exists, but to understand Him is hard,' the freemason began again, looking not at Pierre but straight before him, while his old hands, which the fullness of his heart made it impossible for him to keep still, turned over the pages of his book. 'If it were a man whose existence thou didst doubt I could bring him to thee, I could take him by the hand and show him to thee. But how can I, an insignificant mortal, show all His omnipotence, all His infinity, all His goodness and mercy to one who is blind, or to one who shuts his eyes that he may not see or comprehend Him, and may not see or understand his own vileness and depravity?' He paused again. 'Who art thou? What art thou? Thou dost imagine thyself a wise man because thou could'st utter those blasphemous words,' he went on with sombre irony, 'while thou art more foolish and artless than a little babe playing with the parts of a cunningly-fashioned watch and, because he does not understand its use, dares to say he does not believe in the master who made it. To know Him is difficult. For centuries, from our forefather Adam to our own day, we have toiled after this knowledge and we are an infinity from the attainment of our aim; but in our lack of understanding we see only our own weakness and His greatness. ...'

Pierre listened with swelling heart, gazing into the freemason's face with shining eyes; he did not interrupt, nor ask questions, but with all his soul believed what this stranger was telling him. Whether he was convinced by the rational arguments contained in the freemason's words, or was persuaded, as children are, by the tone of authority and sincerity, or the tremor in the speaker's voice, which sometimes almost failed him, or those brilliant aged eyes grown old in that conviction, or the calm firmness and security of purpose which radiated from his whole being and which particularly impressed Pierre by contrast with his own desolation and hopelessness – at any rate Pierre longed with all his soul to believe, and he did believe, and experienced a joyous sense of comfort, regeneration, and return to life.

'It is not the mind that comprehends Him; it is life that makes us understand,' said the mason.

'I don't understand,' said Pierre, feeling with dismay the reawakening of doubt. He dreaded to detect any obscurity, any weakness in the mason's argument; he dreaded not being able to believe. 'I don't understand,' he said, 'how it is that human reason cannot attain the knowledge of which you speak.'

The freemason smiled his gentle, fatherly smile.

'Supreme wisdom and truth may be compared to the purest dew which we should like to imbibe,' said he. 'Can I receive this pure dew into an impure vessel and judge of its purity? Only by the inner purification of myself can I bring that dew contained within me to some degree of purity.'

'Yes, yes, that is so,' said Pierre joyfully.

'Supreme wisdom is not founded on reason alone, not on those worldly sciences of physics, history, chemistry and the like, into which intellectual knowledge is divided. The highest wisdom is one. The highest wisdom has but one science – the science of the All, the science which explains all creation and man's place in it. In order to absorb this science it is absolutely essential to purify and regenerate one's inner self, and so, before one can know, it is necessary to have faith and be made perfect. And for this purpose we have the divine light called conscience, which God has implanted in our souls.'

'Yes, yes,' cried Pierre.

'Turn thy spiritual gaze into thine inmost being and ask of thyself if thou art satisfied with thyself. What hast thou attained with no guide but the intellect? What art thou? You are young, you are rich, intelligent, well educated – what have you made of all the blessings vouchsafed you? Are you satisfied with yourself and your life?'

'No, I hate my life,' muttered Pierre, frowning.

'If thou hatest it, then alter it. Purify thyself, and as thou art purified thou wilt gain wisdom. Examine your life, my dear sir. How have you spent it? In riotous orgies and debauchery, taking everything from society and giving nothing in return. You have become the possessor of great wealth. How have you been using it? What have you done for your fellow-men? Have you ever given a thought to your tens of thousands of serfs? Have you done anything to help them physically and morally? No! You have profited by their toil to lead a dissipated life. That is what you have done. Have you tried to employ yourself for the good of others? No! You have eaten the bread of idleness. Then you married, my dear sir – took upon yourself the responsibility of guiding a young woman through life, and how did you do it? You did not help her to find the path of truth, my dear sir, but flung her into an abyss of deceit and misery. A man offended you and you shot at and might have killed him, and you say you do not know God and detest your life. There is nothing surprising about that, my dear sir!'

After these words the freemason again leant back on the sofa and closed his eyes, as though wearied by his long discourse. Pierre studied the stern, impassive, almost lifeless face of the old man, and moved his lips without uttering a sound. He wanted to say, 'Yes, I've led a vile, idle, vicious life!' but dared not break the silence.

The freemason cleared his throat huskily, as old men do, and called his servant.

'How about horses?' he asked, without looking at Pierre.

'Some have just come in,' answered the servant. 'Will you not rest here a little?'

'No, tell them to harness.'

'Can he really be going away and leaving me alone, without telling me everything and promising help?' thought Pierre, getting up and beginning to walk about the room with bowed head, occasionally glancing up at the freemason. 'Yes, I never thought of it before: I have led a contemptible, dissolute life, though I did not like it and did not want to,' mused Pierre. 'And this man knows the truth and if he liked he could disclose it to me.' Pierre longed but had not the courage to say this to the mason.

The traveller, having packed his things with his practised old hands, began buttoning up his sheepskin. When he had finished he turned to Bezuhov, and said in a tone of indifferent politeness:

'Where are you going now, my dear sir?'

413

'I? ... I'm going to Petersburg,' answered Pierre in a childlike, hesitating voice. 'I am very grateful to you. I agree with every word you said. But do not think me altogether bad. With my whole soul I have wished that I were what you would have me be; but I have never met with any help from anyone. ... Though I am myself most to blame for everything. Help me, teach me, and some day perhaps ...'

Pierre could not go on. He gulped and turned away.

There was a long silence: the freemason was evidently considering.

'Help is given from God alone,' he said, 'but such measure of aid which it is within the power of our Craft to give you will be afforded you, my dear sir. You are going to Petersburg. Hand this to Count Willarski' (he took out his note-book and wrote a few lines on a large sheet of paper folded in four). 'Allow me to offer you one piece of advice. When you reach the capital, first of all devote some time to solitude and self-examination, and do not return to your old manner of life. And now I wish you a good journey, my dear sir,' he added, seeing that his servant had come in, 'and all success. ...'

The traveller was Osip Alexeyevich Bazdeyev, as Pierre discovered from the post-master's register. Bazdeyev had been one of the most well-known freemasons and Martinists even in Novikov's time. For a long while after he had gone Pierre did not go to bed, or ask for horses, but paced up and down the room reviewing his evil past, and with the enthusiasm of regeneration pictured to himself a blissful, irreproachably virtuous future, which now appeared to him so easy of attainment. It seemed to him that he had gone wrong only because he had somehow forgotten how nice it was to be virtuous. Not a trace of his former doubts remained in his soul. He firmly believed in the possibility of the brotherhood of men united in the aim of supporting one another in the path of virtue, and Freemasonry he saw as such a brotherhood.

3

ON reaching Petersburg Pierre informed no one of his arrival, went nowhere, and spent whole days in reading Thomas à Kempis which some unknown person had sent him. One thing and one thing only he realized as he read: the hitherto unknown bliss of believing in the possibility of attaining perfection, and in the possibility of active brotherly love between men, which Osip Alexeyevich had revealed to him. A week after his arrival the young Polish Count Willarski,

414

whom Pierre knew very slightly in Petersburg society, came into his room one evening with the same official and ceremonious air with which Dolohov's second had called on him. Closing the door behind him, and having satisfied himself that he was alone with Pierre, he addressed him:

'I have come to you with a suggestion and a message, count,' he said, not sitting down. 'A personage of very high standing in our Brotherhood has applied for you to be received into our Craft before the usual term, and has asked me to be your sponsor. I regard it as a sacred duty to fulfil this person's wishes. Do you desire to join the Fraternity of Freemasons under my sponsorship?'

Pierre was struck by the cold austere tone of this man, whom he had almost always seen before at balls, smiling amiably in the society of the most brilliant women.

'Yes, I do wish it,' said Pierre.

Willarski bowed his head.

'One more question, count,' he said, 'which I beg you to answer in all sincerity – not as a future mason but as an honest man (*galant homme*): have you renounced your former opinions? Do you believe in God?'

Pierre considered.

'Yes ... yes, I believe in God,' he said.

'In that case ...' began Willarski, but Pierre interrupted him.

'Yes, I do believe in God,' he repeated.

'In that case we can go,' said Willarski. 'My carriage is at your service.'

Throughout the drive Willarski sat silent. To Pierre's inquiries as to what he would have to do, and how he should answer, Willarski merely replied that brethen more worthy than he would prove him, and that Pierre had only to tell the truth.

They drove in at the gates of a large house where the lodge had its quarters, and passing up a dark staircase they entered a small lighted ante-room where they took off their overcoats without the assistance of a footman. From the ante-room they proceeded into another room. A man in strange attire appeared at the door. Willarski, stepping forward to meet him, said something to him in an undertone in French, and then went up to a small cupboard, where Pierre noticed various apparel unlike any he had ever seen. Taking a handkerchief from the cupboard, Willarski put it over Pierre's eyes and tied it in a knot behind, catching his hair painfully in the knot. Then he drew his face down, kissed him and with a hand on his arm led him forward. Pierre's head hurt where the hair was caught in the knot, and he frowned with the pain and gave a shamefaced smile. His burly figure, with arms hanging down at his sides and face puckered up though smiling, moved after Willarski with timid, uncertain steps.

After leading him by the hand for about ten paces Willarski stopped. 'Whatever happens to you,' he said, 'endure bravely if you are determined to become one of us.' (Pierre nodded affirmatively.) 'When you hear a knock at the door, you will uncover your eyes,' added Willarski. 'I wish you good courage and success,' and pressing Pierre's hand Willarski went away.

Left alone, Pierre still continued to smile. Once or twice he shrugged his shoulders and put his hand to the handkerchief, as though he would have liked to take it off, but let it drop again. The five minutes he had spent with his eyes bandaged seemed to him an hour. His arms felt numb, his legs almost gave way, as if he were tired out. He was aware of the most complex and conflicting sensations. He was afraid of what they were going to do to him, and still more afraid of showing his fear. He felt curious to know what was coming, what would be revealed to him; but above all he was filled with joy that the moment had come when he would at last set out upon that path of re-generation and the actively virtuous life of which he had been dreaming ever since his meeting with Osip Alexeyevich. Loud knocks were heard at the door. Pierre took the bandage from his eyes and looked about him. The room was pitch dark, except in one spot where a small lamp was burning inside something white. Pierre went nearer and saw that the lamp stood on a black table on which lay an open book. The book was the Gospel, and the white thing in which the lamp was burning was a human skull with its eye-sockets and teeth. After reading the first verse of the Gospel: 'In the beginning was the Word, and the Word was with God,' Pierre wandered round the table and caught sight of a large open box filled with something. It was a coffin full of bones. He was not in the least surprised at what he saw. Hoping to enter on an entirely new life absolutely removed from the old one, he expected to meet with strange things, even more extraordinary than what he had already seen. A skull, a coffin, the Gospel - it seemed to him that he had been looking for all this, and indeed for still more. Trying to stir up a devotional feeling in himself, he peered around. 'God, death, love, the brotherhood of man,' he kept saying to himself, associating with these words vague but joyful conceptions of some kind. The door opened and someone came in.

By the dim light to which Pierre however had already become accustomed he saw a not very tall man. Evidently coming from light into darkness, the man paused, then with cautious steps approached the table and placed on it his small leather-gloved hands.

This short man was wearing a white leather apron which covered his chest and part of his legs; round his neck he had a sort of necklace and above that there was a high white ruffle, framing his oblong face, lighted from below.

'For what are you come hither?' asked the new-comer, turning in Pierre's direction at a faint rustle made by the latter. 'Why have you, who do not believe in the truth of the light, who have not seen the light, come here? What do you seek from us? Is it wisdom, virtue, enlightenment?'

At the moment the door opened and the unknown man came in Pierre felt a sense of awe and reverence such as he had experienced in his boyhood at confession; he felt himself in the presence of one who, in the routine of daily life, was a complete stranger, and yet his kin by the tie of human brotherhood. With bated breath and beating heart he moved towards the tyler (the term in Freemasonry for the brother who prepares a candidate for initiation into the Fraternity). Drawing nearer, he recognized the tyler as a man he knew, one Smolyaninov, and it jarred on him to think of the new-comer as a familiar figure: he would rather he were simply a brother and in-structor in virtue. For a long time he could not utter a word, so that the tyler was obliged to repeat his question.

'Yes, I ... I ... seek regeneration,' Pierre got out with an effort.

'Very well,' said Smolyaninov, and went on at once. 'Have you any idea of the means by which our holy Order can help you to the attainment of your desire?' said the tyler quietly and rapidly.

'I ... hope ... for guidance ... help ... in regeneration,' said Pierre with a trembling voice and some difficulty in utterance, due to his excitement and to being unaccustomed to speak of abstract matters in Russian.

'What conception have you of Freemasonry?'

'I imagine that Freemasonry is the *fraternité* and equality of men with virtuous aims,' said Pierre, feeling ashamed, as he spoke, of the

417

incongruity of his words with the solemnity of the moment. 'I imagine ...'

'Good!' said the tyler quickly, apparently quite satisfied with this answer. 'Have you sought the means of attaining your aim in religion?'

'No, for I thought religion contrary to truth, and so did not pursue it,' said Pierre, so softly that the tyler did not hear and asked him what he was saying. 'I was an atheist,' answered Pierre.

'You seek after truth for the purpose of observing its laws in your life; therefore you seek wisdom and virtue, do you not?' said the tyler, after a moment's silence.

'Yes, yes,' confirmed Pierre.

The tyler cleared his throat, crossed his gloved hands on his breast, and began to speak.

'It is now my duty to unfold to you the chief aim of our Craft,' he said, 'and if this aim harmonizes with yours you may with profit enter our Brotherhood. The first and principal object of our Order, the foundation on which it rests and which no human power can destroy, is the preservation and handing on to posterity of a certain important mystery ... which has come down to us from the most ancient times, and even from the first man – a mystery upon which perhaps the fate of the human race depends. But since this mystery is of such a nature that nobody can know or profit by it unless he be prepared by long and diligent self-purification, not everyone can hope to discover it speedily. Hence we have a secondary aim, that of preparing our brethren as far as possible to reform their hearts, to purify and enlighten their minds by those means which have been revealed to us by tradition through men who have striven to attain this mystery, and thereby to render them capable of receiving it. By purifying and regenerating our brethren we endeavour, thirdly, to improve the whole human race also, presenting in our brethren of the Craft an example of piety and virtue, and in this way we exert ourselves with all our might to combat the evil that is paramount in the world. Reflect on what I have said, and I will come to you again,' he concluded and went out of the room.

'To combat the evil that is paramount in the world ...' Pierre repeated, and a mental image of his future activity in that direction rose before him. He imagined men such as he had himself been a fortnight ago, and he mentally addressed an edifying exhortation to them. He pictured to himself vicious and unfortunate people, whom he would assist by word and deed; he saw oppressors whose victims he would deliver. Of the three aims enumerated by the tyler this last – the reformation of mankind – appealed particularly to Pierre. The great mystery mentioned by the tyler, though it excited his curiosity, did not seem to be of material importance; while the second aim, self-purification and regeneration, interested him very little since at that moment he was full of a blissful sense of already being completely cured of all his former vices, and geared to nothing but goodness.

Half an hour later the tyler returned to instruct the candidate in the seven virtues, corresponding to the seven steps of Solomon's Temple, which every freemason should cultivate in himself. These virtues were: (1) *discretion*, the keeping of the secrets of the Order; (2) *obedience* to those of higher rank in the Craft; (3) *morality*; (4) *love for mankind*; (5) *courage*; (6) *generosity*; (7) *the love of death*.

'Concerning the *seventh* of these,' said the tyler, 'by frequent meditation on death bring yourself to regard death not as an enemy to be dreaded but as a friend who sets free the soul, grown weary in the labours of virtue, from this miserable life, and leads it into the place of recompense and peace.'

'Yes, that's as it should be,' thought Pierre, when the tyler, after delivering himself of these words, again retired, leaving him to solitary reflection. 'It must be so, but I am still so weak as to love this life, the meaning of which is only now gradually opening before me.' But the other five virtues, which Pierre recalled, counting them on his fingers, he felt already in his soul: *courage, generosity, morality, love of mankind*, and, above all, *obedience* – which last seemed less a virtue to him than a pleasure. (He felt so glad now to be escaping from self-will and surrendering to those who knew the indubitable truth.) The seventh virtue Pierre had forgotten and he could not recall it.

The third time the tyler came back sooner, and asked Pierre if he were still firm in his intention to submit to everything that would be demanded of him.

'I am ready for anything,' said Pierre.

'I must inform you further,' said the tyler, 'that our Craft promulgates its teaching not by word only but makes use of certain other means which may perhaps have a more potent effect on the earnest seeker after wisdom and virtue than merely verbal explanations. This chamber with the objects you see therein must already, if you are sincere at heart, have told you more than any words could do; and in the course of your initiation it may be that you will be met with a like method of enlightenment. Our Craft follows the usage of ancient societies which explained their teaching through hieroglyphics. A hieroglyphic,' said the tyler, 'is the image of an abstract idea, embodying in itself the properties of the thing it symbolizes.'

Pierre knew very well what a hieroglyphic was, but he did not venture to speak. He listened to the tyler in silence, feeling from all he said that his ordeal was about to begin.

'If you are fully resolved, I must proceed to your initiation,' said the tyler, coming closer to Pierre. 'In token of generosity I request you to give me all your valuables.'

'But I have nothing with me,' replied Pierre, supposing that he was being asked to give up all his possessions.

'What you have with you: watch, money, rings ...'

Pierre made haste to get out his purse and his watch, and struggled for some time to remove the wedding ring from his fat finger. When this had been accomplished the tyler said:

'In token of obedience I ask you to undress.'

Pierre took off his coat, waistcoat and left boot according to the tyler's instructions. The mason drew the shirt back from Pierre's left breast, and stooping down pulled up the left leg of his trousers to above the knee. Pierre hurriedly began taking off his right boot and was going to tuck up the other trouser-leg to save this stranger the trouble, but the mason told him this was not necessary and gave him a slipper for his left foot. With a childlike smile of embarrassment, doubt and self-mockery, which would appear on his face in spite of himself, Pierre stood up, with his arms hanging by his sides, and legs apart, before the tyler, awaiting his next commands.

'And finally, in token of sincerity, I ask you to reveal to me your chief temptation.'

'My chief temptation! I *had* so many,' replied Pierre.

'The temptation which did more than all the rest to make you stumble on the path of virtue,' said the freemason.

Pierre paused, trying to think.

'Wine? Gluttony? Idleness? Laziness? Hasty temper? Anger? Women?' He went over his vices, mentally balancing them and not knowing to which to give preference.

'Women,' he said in a voice so low that it was scarcely audible.

420

The mason did not stir or speak for a long time after this reply. At last he moved up to Pierre, took the handkerchief lying on the table, and again blindfolded his eyes.

'For the last time I say to you – examine yourself thoroughly, put a bridle on your senses, and seek felicity not in your passions but in your heart. The fountain-head of happiness is not without but within us. ...'

Pierre was already conscious of this refreshing fount of blessedness within him which now flooded his heart with joy and emotion.

4

SHORTLY after this there came into the dark chamber to fetch Pierre, not the tyler but Pierre's sponsor, Willarski, whom he recognized by his voice. To fresh inquiries as to the firmness of his resolve, Pierre answered:

'Yes, yes, I agree,' and with a beaming, childlike smile, his fat chest uncovered, stepping timidly and unevenly with one booted and one slippered foot, he advanced, while Willarski held a drawn sword against his bare breast. He was conducted out of the room along corridors that twisted backwards and forwards, and at last brought to the doors of the lodge. Willarski coughed, he was answered by a masonic rapping with hammers; the door opened before them. A bass voice (Pierre was still blindfolded) questioned him as to who he was, when and where he was born, and so on. Then he was again led away somewhere, the handkerchief still over his eyes, and as he went along they spoke to him in allegories of the toils of his pilgrimage, of sacred friendship, of the Eternal Architect of the Universe, and of the courage with which he must endure perils and labours. During these wanderings Pierre noticed that sometimes he was called the 'Seeker', sometimes the 'Sufferer' or the 'Candidate', and that at each new appellation they made various tapping sounds with gavels and swords. While he was being led up to some object he was aware of hesitation and uncertainty among his guides. He heard a whispered dispute, and one of the people round him insisting that he should be made to walk along a certain carpet. After that they took his right hand, laid it on something, while they bade him hold a pair of compasses to his left breast with his other hand, and repeat after someone who read the words aloud the oath of fidelity to the laws of the Order. Then the candles were extinguished and some spirit lighted, as Pierre guessed by the smell, and he was told that he would see the lesser light. The bandage was removed from his eyes and by the faint illumination of the spirit lamp Pierre saw as in a dream a number of men standing before him, all wearing aprons like the tyler's and holding swords pointed at his breast. Among them stood a man whose white shirt was stained with blood. On seeing this Pierre moved forward with his breast towards the swords, meaning them to pierce it. But the swords were drawn back and he was at once blindfolded again.

'Now thou hast seen the lesser light,' said a voice. Then the candles were relit and he was told that he had now to see the full light; and again the bandage was taken off, and ten or a dozen voices declaimed together: '*Sic transit gloria mundi.*'

Pierre gradually began to recover himself and look about the room and at the people in it. Round a long table covered with black sat some twelve brethren in garments like those he had already seen. Several of them Pierre had met in Petersburg society. At the head of the table sat a young man he did not know, with a peculiar cross hanging from his neck. On his right sat the Italian *abbé* whom Pierre had seen at Anna Pavlovna's two years before. There were also present a very important dignitary, and a Swiss tutor who used to be in the Kuragin family. All preserved a solemn silence, listening to the words of the Worshipful Master, who held a gavel in his hand. Let into the wall was a star-shaped light. On one side of the table was a small carpet with various figures worked upon it; on the other was something resembling an altar on which lay the New Testament and a skull. Round the table stood seven large candlesticks of ecclesiastical design. Two of the brethren led Pierre up to the altar, placed his feet at right angles and bade him lie down, saying that he must prostrate himself at the gates of the Temple.

'He ought to receive the trowel first,' whispered one of the brethren.

'Oh, quiet, please!' said another.

Perplexed, Pierre peered about him with his short-sighted eyes, without obeying, and suddenly doubts rose in his mind. 'Where am I? What am I doing? They are making fun of me, surely? Will not the time come when I shall be ashamed of all this?' But these doubts only lasted a moment. He looked at the serious faces of those around him, thought of all he had just been through and realized that there was no stopping half-way. He was aghast at his hesitation, and trying to summon back his former feeling of devotion cast himself down at the gates of the Temple. And the devotional feeling did in fact return to him, and more powerfully than before. After he had lain there some little time he was told to get up, and a white leather apron such as the others wore was put on him, and he was given a trowel and three pairs of gloves. The Grand Master then addressed him. He told him that he must try never to stain the whiteness of that apron, which symbolized strength and purity; next, of the mysterious trowel, he said that Pierre was to toil with it to eradicate vice from his own heart and with forbearing patience smooth the hearts of his fellow-men. He was not to know the significance of the first pair of men's gloves, but must cherish them. The second pair, also men's, he would wear at the meetings of the lodge, and finally of the third pair – they were women's gloves – he said:

'Dear brother, these women's gloves are intended for you too. Give them to the woman whom you shall honour above all others. By this gift you pledge the purity of your heart to her whom you select to be your worthy helpmeet in Masonry.' Then after a pause he added: 'But beware, dear brother, that these gloves never deck hands that are unclean.'

Pierre fancied that the Grand Master was embarrassed as he said these last words. Pierre himself was even more embarrassed; he blushed to the point of tears, as children blush, looking about him uneasily, and an awkward silence followed.

The silence was broken by one of the brethren who led Pierre to the carpet and began reading to him, out of a manuscript book, an interpretation of all the symbols delineated upon it: the sun, the moon, the gavel, the plumb-line, the trowel, the untrimmed and four-square foundation stone, the pillar, the three windows, and so on. After this a place was assigned to Pierre, he was shown the masonic signs, told the password, and at last permitted to sit down. Then the Grand Master began reading the charges and regulations. They were very long, and Pierre, from joy, agitation and embarrassment, was not in a condition to understand what was being read. He managed to follow only the last words of the statutes and these impressed themselves on his memory.

'In our Temples we recognize no other degrees,' read the Grand Master, 'but those between virtue and vice. Beware of making any distinctions that may transgress against equality. Fly to a brother's aid whoever he may be, exhort him that goeth astray, raise him that falleth, and never harbour anger or enmity against thy brother. Be kindly and courteous. Kindle in all hearts the fire of virtue. Share thy happiness with thy neighbour, and may envy never dim the purity of this bliss.

'Forgive thine enemy, and avenge not thyself upon him, except by returning good for evil. Fulfilling in this wise the highest law, thou shalt recover traces of the ancient dignity which thou hast lost,' he concluded, and getting up he embraced and kissed Pierre.

Pierre looked round him with tears of joy in his eyes, not knowing what reply to make to the greetings and congratulations of acquaint-ances on all sides. He acknowledged no acquaintances: in all these men he saw only brethren, and he burned with impatience to set to work with them.

The Grand Master rapped with his gavel. All sat down in their places, and one of the masons read an exhortation on the necessity of humility.

The Grand Master proposed that the last duty be performed, and the important dignitary who bore the title of 'Collector of Alms' went round to all the brethren. Pierre would have liked to subscribe all the money he had in the world but the fear of being thought ostentatious checked him and he wrote down the same amount as the others.

The meeting was over, and it seemed to Pierre on reaching home that he had come back after a long journey of dozens of years' dura-tion, completely changed and quite divorced from his former life and habits.

5

THE day following his initiation into the lodge Pierre was sitting at home reading a book and trying to fathom the significance of the Square, one side of which symbolized God, another the world of ethics, the third the physical world and the fourth a combination. Now and then his attention wandered from the book and the Square and in his imagination he began to formulate a new plan of life for himself. On the previous evening he had been told at the lodge that rumours of his duel had reached the Emperor's ears, and that it would be as well for him to leave Petersburg for a time. Pierre proposed to go to his estates in the south and there attend to the welfare of his peasants. He was dreaming joyfully of this new life when Prince Vasili suddenly walked into the room.

'My dear fellow, what have you been up to in Moscow? Why have you quarrelled with Hélène, *mon cher*? You are under a misapprehension,' said Prince Vasili, as he came in. 'I know all about it, and I can tell you positively that Hélène stands as innocent before you as Christ was before the Jews.'

Pierre was about to reply but Prince Vasili interrupted him.

'And why didn't you simply come straight to me as to a friend? I know how it was: I understand it all,' he said. 'You behaved as becomes a man who cares for his honour – a bit too hastily perhaps, but we won't go into that. But just consider the position you are placing her and me in, in the eyes of society and even of the court,' he added, lowering his voice. 'She is in Moscow, you are here. But enough, my dear boy,' and he drew Pierre down by the arm, 'this is simply a misunderstanding: I expect you feel it so yourself. Let us write her a letter together, now at once, and she'll come here, all will be explained and there'll be an end to all this gossip. Otherwise, let me tell you, my dear boy, I am afraid you will live to repent of it.'

Prince Vasili gave Pierre a significant look.

'I have it from the best source that the Dowager Empress is taking a keen interest in the whole affair. You know she is very graciously disposed to Hélène.'

Several times Pierre prepared himself to speak, but on the one hand Prince Vasili would not give him the chance, hastily interrupting the conversation, and on the other Pierre himself was loath to embark on the tone of determined refusal and dissent in which he was firmly resolved to answer his father-in-law. Moreover the words of the masonic precept, 'Be thou kindly and courteous,' recurred to his mind. He blinked, went red, got up and sank back again, struggling with himself to do what was for him the most difficult thing in life – to say something unpleasant to a man's face, to say the opposite of what the other, whoever he might be, expected. He was so much in the habit of submitting to Prince Vasili's accent of careless authority that he felt he would be unable to resist it even now; but he was also aware that on what he said now his whole future depended: what he said now would decide whether he continued along the same old road or advanced along the new path that had been so attractively

425

pointed out to him by the masons, and where he firmly believed he would find regeneration.

'Come, dear boy,' said Prince Vasili playfully, 'just say "Yes", and I will write to her myself, and we'll kill the fatted calf.' But before Prince Vasili had time to finish his pleasantry, Pierre, not looking at him and with a flash of fury reminiscent of his father, exclaimed in a quiet whisper:

'Prince, I did not invite you here. Go, please go!' He jumped up and opened the door for him. 'Go!' he repeated, amazed at himself and enjoying the expression of confusion and alarm that showed it-self on Prince Vasili's face.

'What's the matter with you? Are you ill?'

'Go!' the threatening voice repeated once more. And Prince Vasili was obliged to withdraw, without receiving a word of explanation.

A week later Pierre, after taking leave of his new friends, the free-masons, and placing large sums in their hands for charity, set out for his estates. His new brethren gave him letters to the masons of Kiev and Odessa, and promised to write to him and guide him in his new way of life.

6

THE duel between Pierre and Dolohov was hushed up and, in spite of the Emperor's severity at that time in regard to duelling, neither the principals nor their seconds suffered for it. But the scandal of the duel, confirmed by Pierre's rupture with his wife, was the talk of society. Pierre had been looked upon with patronizing condescension when he was an illegitimate son, had been made much of and ex-tolled for his virtues when he was the best match in Russia; but after his marriage – when marriageable daughters and their mothers had nothing to hope from him – he had fallen greatly in the esteem of society, especially as he had neither the wit nor the wish to court public favour. Now, all the blame for what had happened was thrown on him alone: he was said to be insanely jealous, and subject, like his father, to fits of bloodthirsty rage. And when, after Pierre's departure, Hélène returned to Petersburg she was received by all her acquaint-ances not only cordially but with a shade of deference that was a tribute to her misfortune. If the conversation turned on her husband Hélène, prompted by her characteristic *nous*, would assume a dignified expression, though she had no idea what impression it gave. This expression suggested that she had resolved to endure her troubles uncomplainingly, and that her husband was a cross laid upon her by God. Prince Vasili expressed his opinion more openly. He shrugged his shoulders when Pierre was mentioned, and pointing to his forehead remarked:

'A bit touched – I always said so.'

'I said from the first,' declared Anna Pavlovna, referring to Pierre, 'I said at once and before anyone else' (she always insisted on her priority) 'that he was a lunatic young man ruined by the dissolute notions of the age. I said so even at the time when everybody was in ecstasies over him, after he had just returned from abroad, and when, if you remember, he posed at one of my *soirées* as a sort of Marat. Well, and this is the result. I was against the marriage even then, and predicted what would come of it.'

On evenings when she was free Anna Pavlovna continued to give her *soirées* as before – *soirées* such as she alone had the gift of arranging – at which was to be found 'the cream of really good society, the flower of the intellectual essence of Petersburg,' to use her own words. Over and above this discriminating selection of society Anna Pavlovna's receptions were also distinguished by the fact that at each one she presented some new and interesting individual, and that nowhere else in Petersburg could the political thermometer reflecting the disposition of loyal court society be more accurately studied than in her drawing-room.

Towards the end of the year 1806, when all the melancholy details of Napoleon's destruction of the Prussian army at Jena and Auerstadt, and the surrender of the majority of the Prussian fortresses, had been received, when our troops had already entered Prussia and our second campaign against Napoleon was beginning, Anna Pavlovna gave one of her *soirées*. The 'cream of really good society' consisted of the fascinating and unhappy Hélène, deserted by her husband; of Mortemart; of the delightful Prince Hippolyte just home from Vienna; of two diplomats; of the old aunt; of a young man known simply as *un homme de beaucoup de mérite*; of a newly-appointed maid of honour and her mother, and several other less noteworthy persons.

The novelty of the evening on this occasion was Boris Drubetskoy, who had just arrived on a special mission from the Prussian army and was aide-de-camp to a very important personage.

What the political thermometer indicated at that *soirée* was something as follows:

'Whatever the rulers and commanders of Europe may do to countenance Bonaparte, with the object of causing *me* and *us* in general
these annoyances and mortifications, our opinion in regard to Bonaparte cannot alter. We shall not cease to express our views on the
subject in the plainest terms, and can only declare to the king of
Prussia and others: "So much the worse for you. You made your bed,
and now you must lie on it" – that is all we have to say!'

This was the reading of the political thermometer at Anna Pavlovna's that evening. When Boris, the choice morsel to be served up
to the company, entered the drawing-room, almost all those invited
had assembled, and the conversation, guided by Anna Pavlovna,
turned on our diplomatic relations with Austria and the hope of an
alliance with her.

Boris, elegantly dressed in the uniform of an aide-de-camp, looking
fresh and rosy and grown to man's estate, came into the drawing-
room with easy assurance, and was duly conducted to pay his respects
to the aunt and then brought back to the general circle.

Anna Pavlovna held out her shrivelled hand for him to kiss, and
introduced him to several persons whom he did not know, giving
him a whispered description of each.

'Prince Hippolyte Kuragin – *charmant jeune homme*. Monsieur
Krug, *chargé d'affaires* from Copenhagen – a man of great intellect';
and simply, of the young man always thus described, 'Monsieur
Shitov – *un homme de beaucoup de mérite*.'

Thanks to his mother's efforts, his own inclinations and the peculiarities of his canny nature, Boris had with time succeeded in making
a very snug place for himself in the service. He was aide-de-camp to
a very eminent personage, had been sent on a most important mission
to Prussia, and had only just returned from there as a special messenger. He had become thoroughly conversant with that unwritten code
which had so pleased him at Olmütz, in virtue of which an ensign
might rank incomparably higher than a general, and all that was
needed to ensure success in the service was not exertion, not work,
not courage or perseverance, but simply the art of knowing how
to get on with the dispensers of promotions and awards; and he
often marvelled at the rapidity of his own progress, and at the inability of others to grasp the secret. His whole manner of life, all his

relations to former friends and acquaintances, all his plans for the future were completely transformed in consequence of this discovery. He was not well off but he would spend his last farthing to be better dressed than others, and would rather deprive himself of many pleasures than allow himself to be seen in a shabby carriage or appear in the streets of Petersburg in an old uniform. He cultivated the friendship and sought the acquaintance only of those who were above and could therefore be of use to him. He liked Petersburg and despised Moscow. He found it distasteful to look back on the Rostovs' house and his boyish passion for Natasha, and since the day of his departure for the army had not once been to see the Rostovs. To be in Anna Pavlovna's drawing-room he considered an important step up in the service, and he at once understood his rôle, and allowed his hostess to make the most of whatever interest he had to offer, while himself carefully scanning every face and appraising the advantages and possibilities of establishing intimacy with each of those present. He took the seat indicated to him beside the fair Hélène, and listened to the general conversation being carried on in French.

' "Vienna considers the bases of the proposed treaty so unattainable that not even a succession of the most brilliant victories would put them within reach, and she doubts the means we have of gaining them." Those are the actual words of the Vienna cabinet,' said the Danish *chargé d'affaires*.

'The doubt is flattering,' said the *man of great intellect* with a subtle smile.

'One should distinguish between the Cabinet in Vienna and the Emperor of Austria,' said Mortemart. 'The Austrian Emperor could never have thought of such a thing: it can only be the Cabinet who says that.'

'Ah, my dear *vicomte*,' put in Anna Pavlovna, 'Urope' (for some reason she pronounced it *Urope* as if that were a special refinement of French which she could allow herself in conversing with a Frenchman), 'Urope will never be a sincere ally of ours.'

After that, Anna Pavlovna led the conversation round to the courage and firmness of the king of Prussia, with the object of bringing Boris into action.

Boris listened attentively to each of the speakers, awaiting his turn, but every now and then he managed to glance in the direction of his neighbour, the beautiful Hélène, whose eyes several times met those of the handsome young aide-de-camp with a smile.

Speaking of the position of Prussia, Anna Pavlovna very naturally appealed to Boris to tell them about his journey to Glogau, and the state in which he found the Prussian army. Boris, without undue haste, in pure and elegant French, related a number of interesting particulars about the armies and the court, studiously abstaining from any expression of personal opinion in regard to the facts which he communicated. For some time he engrossed the general attention, and Anna Pavlovna felt that her guests appreciated the treat she had set before them. Hélène above all listened with the greatest concentration to what Boris had to say, asking him various questions about his expedition, and apparently much interested in the position of the Prussian army. As soon as he had finished, she turned to him with her habitual smile.

'You absolutely must come and see me,' she said in a tone which implied that certain considerations of which he could have no knowledge made it indispensable that he should call on her. 'Tuesday, between eight and nine. It will give me great pleasure.'

Boris promised to do so and was about to engage her in further conversation when Anna Pavlovna called him away, on the pretext that her old aunt wished to hear his story.

'You know her husband, of course?' said Anna Pavlovna, closing her eyes and indicating Hélène with a melancholy gesture. 'Ah, she is such an unfortunate, such an exquisite woman! Never mention him in her presence, I beg you. It is too painful for her!'

7

WHEN Boris and Anna Pavlovna returned to the others Prince Hippolyte had the ear of the company. Bending forward in his low chair he was saying:

'Le roi de Prusse!' and having said this he laughed. Everyone turned towards him. 'The king of Prussia?' repeated Hippolyte with another laugh, and then calmly and seriously settled himself in the depths of his arm-chair. Anna Pavlovna waited for him to go on, but as Hippolyte seemed quite decided to say no more she began to speak of how the impious Bonaparte had at Potsdam carried off the sword of the Great Frederick.

'It is the sword of Frederick the Great which I ...' she began, but Hippolyte interrupted her with the words: '*Le roi de Prusse ...*' and again, as soon as they turned towards him, excused himself and fell silent. Anna Pavlovna frowned. Mortemart, Hippolyte's friend, addressed him peremptorily.

'Come now, what about your *roi de Prusse*?'

Hippolyte laughed as though he were ashamed of laughing.

'Oh, nothing. I only meant ...' (He had intended to repeat a quip he had heard in Vienna which he had been trying all the evening to get in.) 'I only wanted to say that we are wrong to make war *pour le roi de Prusse* – the French idiom for having one's trouble for one's pains!'

Boris smiled discreetly, a smile that could be taken as ironical or appreciative, according to the way the pleasantry was received. Everybody laughed.

'Your pun is too bad! Very clever, but quite unjust,' said Anna Pavlovna, shaking her little shrivelled finger at him. 'We are not fighting *pour le roi de Prusse* but for right principles. Oh, that wicked Prince Hippolyte!' she said.

The conversation did not flag at all throughout the evening, dwelling chiefly on the political news. Towards the end of the *soirée* it became particularly eager, when the rewards bestowed by the Emperor were mentioned.

'You know, last year what's-his-name received a snuff-box with the portrait,' said the *man of great intellect*. 'So why shouldn't X get the same distinction?'

'I beg your pardon – a snuff-box with the Emperor's portrait is a reward, no doubt, but not an official distinction,' said one of the diplomats. 'Or rather, it's a present.'

'There have been precedents. I would instance Schwarzenberg.'

'It's impossible,' retorted another.

'Will you wager? The ribbon of the order, of course, is a different matter. ...'

When everybody rose to go, Hélène, who had spoken very little all the evening, turned to Boris again, graciously bidding him in a tone of pressing significance not to forget Tuesday.

'It is of great importance to me,' she said with a smile, looking round at Anna Pavlovna, and Anna Pavlovna, with the same melancholy expression with which she accompanied any reference to her royal patroness, gave her support to Hélène's wish. It appeared that from some words Boris had uttered that evening about the Prussian army Hélène had suddenly found it necessary to see him. Her manner seemed to convey that she would explain that necessity to him when he came on Tuesday.

But on Tuesday evening, in Hélène's magnificent salon, Boris received no clear explanation of the urgent reasons for his visit. Other guests were present, the countess talked little to him, and only as he kissed her hand on taking leave said unexpectedly and in a whisper, without any smile, which was strange for her:

'Come to dinner tomorrow evening. ... You must come. ... Do!'

During that stay in Petersburg Boris was constantly at the house of the Countess Bezuhov on a footing of the greatest intimacy.

8

THE war was blazing up and nearing the Russian frontier. Everywhere one heard curses on Bonaparte, 'the enemy of the human race'. Militiamen and recruits were being called out in the villages, and from the theatre of war came news of a conflicting character, as usual false and hence variously interpreted.

The life of old Prince Bolkonsky, Prince Andrei and Princess Maria had changed in many respects since 1805.

In 1806 the old prince had been appointed one of the eight commanders-in-chief created at that time to supervise recruiting all over Russia. Despite the infirmity of age, which had become particularly noticeable during the period when he supposed his son to have been killed, he did not think it right to refuse a duty assigned to him by the Sovereign in person, and this fresh opportunity for action gave him new energy and strength. He spent his time continually travelling about the three provinces entrusted to him; was pedantic in the performance of his duties, severe to the point of cruelty with his subordinates, and looked into everything down to the minutest details himself. Princess Maria had no more lessons in mathematics, and on mornings when he was at home only went to her father's study accompanied by the wet-nurse and little Prince Nikolai (as his grandfather called him). The baby Prince Nikolai lived with his wet-nurse and Nanny Savishna in the late princess's rooms, and Princess Maria passed most of the day in the nursery, doing all she could to take the place of mother to her little nephew. Mademoiselle Bourienne, too, appeared to be passionately fond of the child, and Princess Maria would often sacrifice herself to give her friend the pleasure of dandling and playing with the little *angel* (as she called the infant).

Near the chancel of the church at Bald Hills a small shrine had been made over the resting place of the little princess, and in the shrine was a marble monument brought from Italy, representing an angel with outspread wings ready to fly up to heaven. The angel's upper lip curled into the hint of a smile, and one day as Prince Andrei and Princess Maria were leaving the shrine they admitted to one another that the angel's face reminded them strangely of the little princess. But what was still stranger – though this Prince Andrei did not confess to his sister – was that in the expression the sculptor had chanced to give the angel's face Prince Andrei read the same gentle reproach which he had read on the face of his dead wife: 'Ah, why have you done this to me? ...'

Soon after Prince Andrei's return the old prince made over a large estate to him, Bogucharovo, twenty-five miles or so from Bald Hills. Partly because of the painful memories associated with Bald Hills, partly because Prince Andrei did not always feel equal to bearing placidly with his father's idiosyncrasies, and partly because of a craving for solitude, Prince Andrei made use of Bogucharovo, began building, and spent most of his time there.

After the battle of Austerlitz Prince Andrei had firmly resolved to have done with the army, and, to escape active service when war broke out again and everybody had to serve, he placed himself under his father's orders and assisted in the levying of the militia. The old prince and his son seemed to have exchanged rôles since the campaign of 1805. The father, stimulated by activity, expected the best results from the new campaign, while Prince Andrei on the contrary, taking no part in the war and secretly regretting his inaction, saw only the dark side.

On the 26th of February 1807 the old prince set off on one of his circuits. Prince Andrei, as usual during his father's absences, was staying at Bald Hills. Little Nikolai had not been well for the last three or four days. The coachman who had driven the old prince to the next town returned bringing documents and letters for Prince Andrei.

Not finding the young prince in his study, the valet went with the

433

letters to Princess Maria's apartments, but he was not there either. He was told that the prince had gone to the nursery.

'If you please, your Excellency, Petrusha has brought some papers,' said one of the nursemaids to Prince Andrei, who was sitting in a child's small chair while, frowning and with trembling hands, he poured drops of medicine from a bottle into a wine-glass half full of water.

'What is it?' he said crossly, and his hand shaking he accidentally let too many drops fall into the glass. He tipped the contents on to the floor and asked for some more water. The maid handed it to him.

In the room were a child's cot, two chests, a couple of arm-chairs, a table, a child's table, and the little chair on which Prince Andrei was sitting. The curtains were drawn, and a single candle was burning on the table, screened by a bound volume of music, so that no light might fall on the cot.

'My dear,' said Princess Maria, turning to her brother from beside the cot where she was standing, 'better wait a bit ... later on ...'

'Oh, do stop, you don't know what you are talking about. You always want to put things off, and now see what comes of it!' said Prince Andrei in an exasperated whisper, with the manifest intention of wounding his sister.

'My dear, truly it would be better not to wake him – he's asleep,' implored the princess.

Prince Andrei got up and went on tiptoe to the little bed, wine-glass in hand.

'Perhaps we'd really better not, do you think?' he said, hesitating.

'Just as you please – really ... I think so ... but you must judge,' said Princess Maria, obviously intimidated and uneasy that her opinion should prevail. She drew her brother's attention to the maid, who was calling him in a whisper.

It was the second night that both of them had gone without sleep, watching over the baby who was feverish. These last days, lacking confidence in their own household doctor and expecting another who had been sent for from the town, they had spent trying a succession of remedies. Tired and overwrought, they vented their anxiety on each other, finding fault and quarrelling with one another.

'Petrusha is here with papers from your father,' whispered the maid. Prince Andrei went out.

'What is it now?' he muttered angrily, and after listening to the

434

verbal instructions his father had sent and taking the correspondence and his father's letter he returned to the nursery.

'How is he now?' queried Prince Andrei.

'Just the same. Wait, for heaven's sake. Karl Ivanich always declares that sleep is better than anything,' whispered Princess Maria with a sigh.

Prince Andrei went up to the baby and felt him. He was very hot.

'Confound you and your Karl Ivanich!' He fetched the glass with the medicine and came up to the cot again.

'André, you shouldn't!' said Princess Maria.

But he scowled at her spitefully, yet with a stricken look in his eyes, and bent over the child with the glass.

'But I wish it,' he said. 'Come, I beg you, give it to him.'

Princess Maria shrugged her shoulders but obediently took the glass and, calling the nurse, began giving the child the medicine. The baby screamed and choked. Prince Andrei winced and, clutching his head, went out and sat down on a sofa in the next room.

He was still holding the letters. Opening them mechanically, he began to read. The old prince in his large, oblong hand, now and then making use of abbreviations, wrote on blue paper as follows:

Have just this moment received by special messenger v. joyful news – unless it's a *canard*. Bennigsen seems to have obtained a complete victory over Bonaparte at Preussisch-Eylau. In Petersburg everyone's wild with delight, and innumerable awards have been sent to the army. Though he's a German – I congratulate him. I can't make out what that fellow in charge at Korchevo – one Handrikov – is up to: so far no reinforcements or stores have come from him. Gallop over at once and say I'll have his head off if everything's not here within the week. Have received a letter about the Preussisch-Eylau battle from Petenka too – he took part in it – it's all true. When people who have no business to don't meddle, even a German beats Bonaparte. They say he is retreating in great disorder. Mind you get off to Korchevo without delay and see to things!

Prince Andrei sighed and broke the seal of another envelope. This contained a closely-written letter covering two sheets from Bilibin. He folded it up without reading it, and re-read his father's letter, ending with the words: 'Get off to Korchevo without delay and see to things!'

'No, you must forgive me, I'm not leaving now till the child is better,' he thought, going to the door and looking into the nursery.

Princess Maria was still standing by the cot, gently rocking the baby.

'Yes, what in the name of goodness was the other disagreeable news he wrote about?' thought Prince Andrei, recalling his father's letter. 'Oh, I know: we have gained a victory over Bonaparte just when I'm not taking part. Yes, yes, he's always getting at me. ... Ah well, let him!' And he began reading the letter in French from Bilibin. He read without understanding half of it, read for the sake of diverting his mind, if only for a moment, from what it had been too long and too anxiously dwelling upon to the exclusion of everything else.

9

BILIBIN was now at the headquarters of the army, in a diplomatic capacity, and though he wrote in French with French jests and French turns of speech he described the whole campaign with fearless impartiality, in true Russian fashion, sparing his own side neither reproaches nor sarcasms. Bilibin wrote that the obligations of diplomatic *discrétion* were a torture to him, and that he was happy to have in Prince Andrei a trustworthy correspondent to whom he could pour out all the spleen that had been accumulating in him at the sight of what was going on in the army. The letter was dated some time back, before the battle of Preussisch-Eylau.

Since the day of our brilliant success at Austerlitz [wrote Bilibin] as you know, my dear prince, I have not left headquarters. I have acquired a decided taste for war, and it is just as well for me. What I have seen during the last three months is beyond belief.

I will begin *ab ovo* – at the very beginning. The 'enemy of the human race', as you are aware, attacks the Prussians. The Prussians are our faithful allies who have only betrayed us three times in three years. We take up their cause. But it turns out that the 'enemy of the human race' pays not the slightest heed to our fine speeches, and in his ill-mannered, savage way flings himself on the Prussians without giving them time to finish the parade they had begun, and hey presto! wipes the floor with them and installs himself in the palace at Potsdam.

'It is my most earnest desire,' writes the king of Prussia to Bonaparte, 'that your Majesty should be received and treated in my palace in a manner agreeable to your Majesty, and to this end I have hastened to take every step that circumstances allow. I hope I may have succeeded.'

436

The Prussian generals pride themselves on their politeness to the French, and lay down their arms at the first summons. The commander of the garrison at Glogau, with ten thousand men, asks the king of Prussia what he shall do if he is called upon to surrender.... Fact!

In short, hoping to settle matters by assuming a warlike attitude, lo and behold! we find ourselves at war in good earnest, and, what is worse, at war on our own frontiers with and for *le roi de Prusse*. Everything is all ready: we only lack one little item – a commander-in-chief. As it is now thought that our success at Austerlitz might have been more decisive had the commander-in-chief not been so young, all the octogenarians have been reviewed, and of Prozorovsky and Kamensky the choice is in favour of the latter, who arrives in a covered cart, *à la* Suvorov, and is received by us with acclamations of joy and triumph.

On the 4th *voilà*! – the first courier from Petersburg. The mails are taken to the field-marshal's room, for he likes to see to everything personally. I am called in to help sort the letters and take those meant for us. The field-marshal looks on and waits for the packages addressed to him. We hunt through – there isn't a single one. The field-marshal waxes impatient and sets to work himself, and finds letters from the Emperor to Count T., Prince V. and others. Then he flies into one of his wild furies. Blood and thunder right and left. He snatches the letters, tears them open and reads those from the Tsar addressed to others. 'Ah, so that's the way they treat me! No confidence in me! Ah, ordered to keep an eye on me! Very well then, get out, all of you!' And he writes the famous order of the day to General Bennigsen:

'I am wounded and cannot ride on horseback, and consequently cannot command the army. You have led your *corps d'armée* defeated to Pultusk: here it remains exposed, without fuel or forage, so something must be done, and, as you yourself reported to Count Buxhöwden yesterday, measures must be devised for retiring to our frontier. Proceed to do so this day.

'All my expeditions on horseback,' he writes to the Emperor, 'have given me a saddle-sore, which, coming on top of all my previous journeying, quite prevents me sitting a horse and commanding an army so widely scattered; and I have therefore handed over the said command to the general next in seniority, Count Buxhöwden, sending him my whole staff and appurtenances of the same, and advising him if he is short of bread to move farther into the interior of Prussia, seeing that only one day's ration of bread is left, and some regiments have none at all, as reported by division-commanders Ostermann and Sedmoretsky, and all that the local peasants had has been eaten up. I shall myself remain in hospital at Ostrolenka till I recover. In most humbly submitting my report I would add further that if the army continues another fortnight in its present bivouac, by spring there will not be a healthy man left.

'Permit an old man to retire to the country who is already sufficiently disgraced by his inability to perform the great and glorious task for which he was chosen. I shall await your Majesty's most gracious permission here in hospital, that I may not have to play the part of *office clerk* rather than *commander* at the head of the army. My removal will make no more difference than would that of a man gone blind. Russia has thousands more where I came from!'

The field-marshal is vexed with the Emperor and punishes all of us; isn't that logical!

Thus ends the first act. Those that follow are naturally increasingly interesting and entertaining. After the field-marshal's departure it appears that we are within sight of the enemy and must give battle. Buxhöwden is commander-in-chief by right of seniority but General Bennigsen does not see it like that; more particularly as it is he and his corps who face the enemy and he wants to seize the opportunity to fight a battle 'on his own hand', as the Germans say. He fights it. This is the battle of Pultusk, which is considered a great victory but to my mind was nothing of the sort. We civilians, as you are aware, have a very undesirable way of deciding whether a battle was won or lost. The side that retreats after a battle has lost is what we say; and going by that, we lost the battle of Pultusk. In short, we retreat after the battle but we send a courier to Petersburg with news of a victory, and the general does not relinquish the command to Buxhöwden, hoping as a reward for his success to receive from Petersburg the title of commander-in-chief. During this interregnum we embark on a remarkably interesting and original series of manoeuvres. Our aim is no longer, as it should be, to avoid or attack the enemy, but solely to avoid General Buxhöwden, who by right of seniority should be our chief. We pursue this aim with so much energy that when we cross an unfordable river we even burn our bridges to cut off the enemy, who for the nonce, is not Bonaparte but Buxhöwden. General Buxhöwden was within an ace of being attacked and captured by superior enemy forces as a result of one of the pretty little manoeuvres by which we escaped him. Buxhöwden comes after us – we scuttle. No sooner does he cross to our side of the river than we cross back again. At last our enemy – Buxhöwden – catches up on us and attacks. Both generals lose their tempers. There is even a challenge to a duel on Buxhöwden's part and an epileptic fit on Bennigsen's. But at the critical moment the courier

438

who carried the news of our Pultusk victory to Petersburg returns bringing our appointment as commander-in-chief, and our enemy number one – Buxhöwden – is done for: we can now turn our attention to number two – Bonaparte. But at this juncture what should happen but a third enemy rises against us – namely, the *Orthodox Russian* soldiery clamouring for bread, meat, biscuits, fodder and I don't know what else! The storehouses are empty, the roads impassable. The 'Orthodox' take to looting, and that after a fashion of which our last campaign can give you no idea. Half the regiments have formed themselves into free companies, scouring the countryside and putting everything to fire and sword. The inhabitants are ruined, root and branch; the hospitals overflow with sick, and famine is everywhere. Twice, bands of marauders have attacked headquarters, and the commander-in-chief has to ask for a battalion to drive them off. In one of these raids my empty trunk and my dressing-gown were carried away. The Emperor proposes to authorize all commanders of divisions to shoot marauders, but I very much fear this will oblige one half of the army to shoot the other.

At first Prince Andrei read with his eyes only but after a while, and in spite of himself, what he found (though he knew how much faith to put in Bilibin) began to interest him more and more. Having got thus far, he crumpled up the letter and threw it aside. It was not what he read that vexed him, but the fact that the life out there, in which he had no part, could still unsettle him. He shut his eyes, rubbed his forehead with his hand as though to rid himself of all interest in what he had been reading, and listened to the sounds in the nursery. Suddenly he fancied he heard a strange noise through the door. Panic seized him lest something should have happened to the child while he was reading the letter. He crossed on tiptoe to the nursery door and opened it.

Just as he went in he saw that the nurse was hiding something from him with a scared look, and Princess Maria was no longer beside the cot.

'My dear,' he heard what seemed to him his sister's despairing whisper behind him.

As often happens after sleepless nights and prolonged anxiety, he was overwhelmed by an unreasoning dread: the notion came into his head that the boy was dead. All that he saw and heard seemed a confirmation of his terror.

'It is all over,' he thought, and a cold sweat broke out on his fore-

439

head. He went to the cot, beside himself, convinced that he would find it empty, that the nurse had been hiding the dead baby. He opened the curtains and for a long while his frightened, wandering eyes could not find the baby. At last he saw him: the rosy-cheeked child had tossed about till he lay sprawled across the bed with his head lower than the pillow, in his sleep making a sucking noise with his lips and breathing evenly.

Prince Andrei was as rejoiced at seeing the child like that as if he had got him back from the dead. He bent down and as his sister had shown him tried with his lips whether the baby was still feverish. The soft forehead was moist. Prince Andrei passed his hand over the little head – even the hair was wet, so profusely had the child perspired. Not only was he not dead but, on the contrary, the crisis was over and he was on the mend. Prince Andrei longed to snatch up and hug and press this helpless little creature to his heart, but dared not do so. He stood over him, gazing at his head and at the little arms and legs that showed beneath the blanket. He heard a rustle at his elbow and a shadow appeared under the canopy of the cot. He did not look round, but still watching the infant's face listened to his regular breathing. The dark shadow was Princess Maria, who had come up to the cot with noiseless steps, lifted the cot-curtains and let them fall again behind her. Prince Andrei recognized her without looking round, and held out his hand to her. She pressed it.

'He is in a perspiration,' said Prince Andrei.

'I went to tell you so.'

The baby stirred faintly in his sleep, smiled and rubbed his forehead against the pillow.

Prince Andrei looked at his sister. In the dim shadow of the curtain her luminous eyes shone more than usually bright with the tears of happiness that stood in them. She leaned over to her brother and kissed him, slightly disturbing the curtains of the cot. Each made the other a warning gesture and stood quiet in the twilight under the canopy, as though unwilling to leave that seclusion where they three were alone, shut off from all the world. Prince Andrei was the first to move away, ruffling his hair against the muslin hangings.

'Yes, this is the one thing left me now,' he said with a sigh.

10

SHORTLY after his initiation into the Masonic Brotherhood Pierre set out for the province of Kiev, where most of his serfs were, taking with him the directions he had written for his own guidance in the management of his estates.

When he reached Kiev he summoned all his stewards and explained to them his intentions and wishes He told them that steps would be taken shortly to complete the liberation of his serfs, and that till then they were not to be overburdened with labour, that women with young children were not to be sent to work, that assistance was to be given to the peasants, and punishments were to be admonitory instead of corporal, and that hospitals, alms-houses and schools were to be established on all the estates. A section of the stewards (there were some semi-literate foremen among them) listened in dismay, supposing the upshot of the young count's remarks to mean that he was dissatisfied with their management and embezzlement of his money. Others, after their first fright, found amusement in Pierre's lisp and the new words they had not heard before. Others, again, derived a simple satisfaction in hearing the sound of their master's voice; while the fourth and most intelligent group, which included the chief steward, divined from this speech how best they could handle the master for their own ends.

The chief steward expressed great sympathy with Pierre's projects; but observed that, these innovations apart, matters needed thoroughly going into, as they were in a bad way.

In spite of Count Bezuhov's enormous wealth Pierre, ever since he had inherited it and stepped into an annual income which was said to amount to five hundred thousand roubles, had felt himself much poorer than in the days when his father was making him an allowance of ten thousand roubles a year. He reckoned his budget pretty much as follows:

About 80,000 went in payments to the Land Bank; upkeep of the estate near Moscow and the town house, together with the allowance he made to the three princesses, accounted for 30,000; pensions took some 15,000, as did subscriptions to charitable institutions; the countess received 150,000 for her maintenance; about 70,000 were paid away in interest on loans; the building of a new church, which he had begun a couple of years before, was costing him a round 10,000; and the 100,000 that were left went, he did not know how, but so effectually that almost every year he was obliged to borrow. Moreover, every twelve months the chief steward wrote to inform him of fires and bad harvests, or of the necessity of rebuilding factories and workshops. And so the first task which confronted Pierre was one for which he had very little aptitude or inclination – practical business.

Every day Pierre *went into* things with his chief steward. But he felt that what he was doing did not advance matters one inch. He felt that what he was doing was somehow detached from reality, and did not link up with what was happening or advance it. On the one hand there was the chief steward picturing the state of affairs to him in the very worst light, pointing out to Pierre the absolute necessity of paying off his debts and undertaking new activities with serf-labour, to which Pierre would not agree. On the other hand, there was Pierre demanding that they should proceed to the work of liberating the serfs, which the steward countered by showing the necessity of first paying off the loans from the Land Bank, and the consequent impossibility of any early emancipation.

The steward did not say that this could not be done; he proposed to make it possible through the sale of forests in the province of Kostroma, the sale of some land lower down the river and of the Crimean estate. But all these operations according to the head steward entailed such complicated measures – the lifting of restrictive covenants and statutory provisions, the obtaining of licences and permits, etc. – that Pierre was lost in the labyrinth and confined himself to saying:

'Yes, yes, do that, then.'

Pierre had none of the practical tenacity which would have enabled him to attend to the business himself, and so he disliked the whole thing and merely tried in the steward's presence to keep up a pretence of activity. The steward for his part did his best to pretend to the count that he considered their consultations of great use to his master and a great inconvenience to himself.

In Kiev Pierre found some people he knew; others hastened to make his acquaintance and offer a warm welcome to the young man of fortune, the largest landowner of the province. Temptations to Pierre's besetting weakness – the one to which he had confessed at his initiation into the Lodge – were so strong that he could not resist them. Again, as in Petersburg, whole days, weeks and months of his life were busily filled with parties, dinners, lunches and balls, allowing him no time for reflection. Instead of the new life Pierre had hoped to lead, he still lived the old one, only in different surroundings.

Of the three precepts of Freemasonry Pierre had to admit that he was not fulfilling the one which enjoined every mason to set an example of moral uprightness; and that of the seven virtues he was entirely devoid of two – clean living and the love of death. He consoled himself with the thought that, on the other hand, he was fulfilling another of the precepts – the improvement of the human race – and had other virtues – love for his neighbour and generosity.

In the spring of 1807 Pierre decided to return to Petersburg. On the way he intended to visit all his estates and see for himself how far his orders had been carried out, and discover how the serfs whom God had entrusted to his care, and on whom he was doing his best to lavish benefits, were now faring.

The chief steward, who considered the young count's projects almost insane – unprofitable to himself, to his master and to the peasants – had made some concessions. While continuing to represent the liberation of the serfs as impracticable, he had arranged for the erection on all the estates of large schools, hospitals and alms-houses against the master's arrival. Demonstrations of welcome were organized – not on a sumptuous or magnificent scale, which he knew Pierre would not care for, but pious thanksgivings with icons and the traditional bread and salt, which knowledge of his master's character suggested would be more likely to affect him and pull the wool over his eyes.

The southern spring, the comfortable, rapid journey in his Vienna carriage and the solitude of the road all had a gladdening effect on Pierre. The estates, which he had not visited before, were each more picturesque than the other; the peasantry everywhere appeared prosperous and touchingly grateful for the favours conferred on them. He was met with such a welcome everywhere that, though he was embarrassed, Pierre's heart was overcome with a joyous sensation. At one place the peasants presented him with bread and salt and an icon of St Peter and St Paul, begging him to allow them, as a token of their love and gratitude for all that had been done for them to add a new chantry to the church at their own expense, in honour of his patron saints, Peter and Paul. In another place he was greeted by women with infants in arms who thanked him for releasing them from the obligation of heavy work. On a third estate the priest, bearing a cross, came to meet him, surrounded by children whom, through the count's generosity, he was instructing in reading, writing and religion. On all his estates Pierre saw with his own eyes brick buildings erected or in the course of erection, all to the same plan, for hospitals, schools and alms-houses, which were shortly to be opened. Everywhere he was shown the stewards' accounts, according to which the serfs' manorial labour had been cut down, and listened to the touching thanks of deputations of serfs in their full-skirted blue coats.

Pierre did not know that the village which had presented him with bread and salt and wanted to build a chantry in honour of St Peter and St Paul was a market village where a fair was held on St Peter's day, that the chantry had been begun long before by some well-to-do *muzhiks* of the village (the ones who formed the deputation), while nine-tenths of the peasants of that village lived in the utmost destitution. He did not know that since by his orders nursing mothers were not sent to work on his land they did vastly heavier work on their own bit of ground. He did not know that the priest who met him with the cross oppressed the peasants by his exactions, and that the pupils gathered round him had been yielded up to him with tears and were often ransomed back to their parents at a high price. He did not know that the brick buildings being raised according to plan were being built by serfs whose manorial labour was thus increased, and only lessened on paper. He did not know that where the steward had pointed out to him in the account-books that the serfs' payments had been reduced by a third their obligatory manorial work had been put up by a half. And so Pierre was in raptures with his visit to his estates and quite recovered the philanthropic frame of mind in which he had left Petersburg, and wrote enthusiastic letters to his 'brother-preceptor' as he called the Grand Master.

'How easy it is, how little effort is needed, to do so much good,' thought Pierre, 'and how little we trouble ourselves to do it!'

He was pleased at the gratitude shown him but felt ashamed at being the recipient of it. This gratitude reminded him of how much more he might do for these simple, kindly people.

The head steward, a thoroughly stupid sly man, quickly had the measure of the intelligent but naïve count, and played with him like a toy; and, seeing the effect produced on Pierre by the carefully arranged receptions, pressed him still harder with arguments proving the impossibility and, above all, the uselessness of emancipating the serfs, who were perfectly happy as they were.

Pierre in his secret soul agreed with the steward that it would be difficult to imagine more contented people, and that heaven only knew what would happen to them when they had their freedom, but he insisted, though reluctantly, on what he thought right. The steward promised to do all in his power to carry out the count's wishes, perceiving clearly that not only would the count never be in a position to verify whether every measure had been taken for the sale of the land and the forests to redeem the mortgage at the Land Bank, but in all probability would never even inquire, and would never find out that the newly-erected buildings were standing empty, and that the serfs continued to give in labour and money just what other people's serfs gave – that is to say, all that could be got out of them.

II

RETURNING from his southern tour, in the happiest frame of mind, Pierre paid a long-intended visit to his friend Bolkonsky, whom he had not seen for two years.

At the last post-stage he had heard that Prince Andrei was not at Bald Hills but on his other, new estate, and he went to him there.

Bogucharovo lay in a flat, uninteresting part of the country among fields and forests of fir and birch, in parts cut down. The manor was at one end of the village, which stretched straight along the high road. In front was a pond recently dug and filled to overflowing, though the grass had not yet had a chance to grow over its banks. The house stood in the midst of a young copse having several large pines among the smaller trees.

The homestead consisted of a threshing-floor, out-buildings, stables, a bath-house, a lodge and a large stone house with a semicircular façade still in course of construction. Round the house was a garden recently laid out. The fences and gates were solid and new; two fire-pumps and a water-barrel painted green stood under a penthouse; the paths were straight, the bridges were strong and furnished with hand-rails. Everything gave the impression of having been done efficiently and with care. Some domestic serfs Pierre met, in answer to his inquiries as to where the prince lived, pointed to a small newly-built lodge at the very edge of the pond. Anton, an old servant who had looked after Prince Andrei in his boyhood, helped Pierre down from the carriage, said that the prince was at home and showed him into a neat little ante-room.

Pierre was struck by the unpretentiousness of this diminutive though scrupulously clean little house, after the brilliant surroundings in which he had last seen his friend in Petersburg. He quickly entered the tiny parlour, still unplastered and smelling of pine wood, and would have gone farther but Anton ran ahead on tiptoe and knocked at a door.

'Well, what is it?' came a sharp, forbidding voice.

'A visitor,' answered Anton.

'Ask him to wait,' and there was the sound of a chair being pushed back.

Pierre went with rapid steps to the door and suddenly found himself face to face with Prince Andrei, who came out frowning and looking older. Pierre threw his arms round him, and lifting his spectacles kissed his friend on the cheek and considered him intently.

'Well, this is a surprise! I *am* glad to see you,' exclaimed Prince Andrei.

Pierre said nothing; he could not take his eyes off his friend, so struck was he by the change in his appearance. His words were kindly, there was a smile on his lips and face, but his eyes were dull and lifeless in spite of the effort he made to give them a joyous, happy sparkle. It was not only that Prince Andrei had grown thinner, paler and more set: what disturbed and alienated Pierre till he got used to it was his friend's inertia, and the line on his brow which bore witness to continued preoccupation with some one thought.

As is usually the case when friends meet after a long separation the conversation took some time to settle down. They asked each other questions and gave brief replies about things they knew ought to be talked over at length. At last the conversation gradually came to rest on some of the topics previously touched upon only in passing, and the two discussed things that had happened in the past, their plans for the future, Pierre's travels and what he had been doing, the war, and so on. The preoccupied, crushed look which Pierre had remarked in Prince Andrei's eyes was still more noticeable now in the smile with which he listened to Pierre, especially when Pierre spoke with earnest delight of the past or the future. It was as though Prince Andrei wanted to interest himself in what his friend was saying, but was unable to, so that Pierre began to feel it was in bad taste to speak of his enthusiasms, dreams and hopes of happiness or goodness in Prince Andrei's presence. He felt shy of coming out with all his new masonic ideas, which the tour he had just made had in particular revived and strengthened. He restrained himself for fear of appearing naïve; at the same time he was bursting to show his friend that he was now an entirely different and much better Pierre than the one Prince Andrei had known in Petersburg.

'I can't tell you all I have gone through since then. I hardly recognize myself.'

'Yes, we have altered a great deal, a very great deal since those days,' said Prince Andrei.

'Well, and what of you?' asked Pierre. 'What are your plans?'

'Plans?' echoed Prince Andrei ironically. 'My plans?' he repeated, as if wondering at the word. 'Well, as you see, I'm building. I mean to move in here altogether next year. ...'

Pierre was silent, looking searchingly into Prince Andrei's face, which had grown so much older.

'No, I meant ...' Pierre began, but Prince Andrei interrupted him. 'But what is the use of talking about me. ... *You* must tell me – yes, tell me about your travels, and about all you have been doing on your estates.'

Pierre began describing what he had done on his estates, trying so far as he could to disguise his own share in the improvements that had been made. Prince Andrei several times finished Pierre's sentence for him, as though all that Pierre had done was an old familiar story, and listened not only without interest but even as if he blushed a little for what Pierre was telling him.

Pierre began to feel awkward and uncomfortable, and finally relapsed into silence.

'I know what, my dear fellow,' said Prince Andrei, who apparently also felt depressed and constrained with his visitor, 'I am only camping here – I just came over to have a look round. I am going back again to my sister today. I'll introduce you to her. But of course you know her already,' he added, evidently for the sake of saying something to a guest with whom he now found nothing in common. 'We'll set off after dinner. And now would you care to see my place?'

They went out and walked about till dinner-time, talking of the political news and mutual acquaintances, like people who are not very intimate. Only the new homestead and premises he was building

447

produced any show of animation and interest in Prince Andrei, but even here, while they were on the scaffolding and he was in the middle of describing the plan of the house, he suddenly interrupted himself:

'However, this is very dull. Let us go and have dinner, and then we'll start.'

At the dinner-table the subject of Pierre's marriage came up.

'I was very much surprised when I heard of it,' said Prince Andrei.

Pierre coloured as he always did at any reference to his marriage, and said hurriedly:

'I'll tell you one day how it all happened. But you know it's all over and finished with for ever.'

'For ever?' said Prince Andrei. 'Nothing's for ever.'

'But you know how it all ended, don't you? You heard about the duel?'

'Yes, you had to go through that too!'

'The one thing which I thank God for is that I didn't kill the man,' said Pierre.

'Why so?' asked Prince Andrei. 'To kill a vicious dog is a very good thing really.'

'No, to kill a man is bad, wrong ...'

'Why is it wrong?' pressed Prince Andrei. 'It is not given to man to judge of what is right or wrong. Men always did and always will err, and in nothing more than in what they regard as right or wrong.'

'What does harm to another is wrong,' said Pierre, pleased to see that for the first time since his arrival Prince Andrei was roused and had begun to talk, wanting to come out with what it was that had brought him to his present state.

'And who has told you what does harm to another man?' he asked.

'Harm? Harm?' exclaimed Pierre. 'We all know what harms ourselves.'

'Yes, we know that, but the harm I am conscious of in myself is something it would be impossible for me to inflict on others,' said Prince Andrei, growing more and more animated and evidently eager to express his new outlook to Pierre. He spoke in French. 'I know of only two real evils in life: remorse and illness. The only good is the absence of those evils. To live for myself so as to avoid those two evils: that's the sum of my wisdom now.'

'And how about love of one's neighbour, and self-sacrifice?' began

448

Pierre. 'No, I cannot agree with you. To live with the sole object of avoiding doing evil so as not to have to repent is not enough. I used to do that – I lived for myself and I spoilt my life. And only now, when I am living for others – or at least trying to –' (modesty impelled Pierre to correct himself) 'only now do I realize all the happiness life holds. No, I cannot agree with you, and indeed you don't believe what you are saying yourself.'

Prince Andrei looked at Pierre in silence, with an ironic smile.

'Well, you'll soon be seeing my sister, Princess Maria. You'll get on with her,' said he. 'Perhaps you are right for yourself,' he added after a brief pause, 'but everyone must live after his own fashion. You used to live for yourself, and you say that by doing so you nearly ruined your life and only found happiness when you began to live for others. But my experience has been exactly the opposite. I lived for honour and glory. (And, after all, what is honour and glory? The same love for others, the desire to do something for them, the desire for their praises.) In that way I lived for others, and not almost but quite spoilt my life. And only since I started living for myself have I found peace.'

'But what do you mean when you say you live only for yourself?' asked Pierre, growing excited. 'What about your son, your sister, your father?'

'Ah, but they are part of myself – they are not other people,' explained Prince Andrei. 'But other people, one's *neighbour – le prochain* – as you and Princess Maria call them, are the great source of error and evil. One's neighbours are those – your Kiev peasants – whom one wants to do good to.'

And he looked at Pierre with a mocking, challenging expression. He obviously wished to draw him on.

'You are not serious,' replied Pierre, getting more and more worked up. 'What error or evil can there be in my wishing to do good (though I accomplished very little, and that badly)? But still, I tried and even met with some small success. What possible harm can there be in giving instruction to unfortunate people, our serfs – people like ourselves – who were growing up and dying with no idea of God and truth beyond meaningless prayer and church ceremonies? How can it be wrong to teach them the consoling doctrines of a future life, where they will find recompense, reward and solace? Where is the evil and error in my providing people who were helplessly dying of disease, while material assistance could so easily be rendered, with a doctor, a hospital and asylum for the aged? And is it not palpably and unquestionably a good thing if a peasant, or a woman with a young baby, never knowing a moment's respite day or night, and I give them rest and leisure time?' said Pierre, talking fast and lisping. 'And that is what I have done, though badly and to a small extent, but I have made a start, and you cannot persuade me that it wasn't good, and, more than that, you can't make me believe that you do not think so yourself. And the great thing is,' he continued, 'I know – and know for certain – that the enjoyment of doing this good is the only sure happiness in life.'

'Oh, if you put the question like that it's quite a different matter,' said Prince Andrei. 'I build a house and lay out a garden, and you build hospitals. Either occupation may serve to pass the time. But as to what's right and what's good – you must leave that to Him Who knows all things: it is not for us to decide. Well, I see you want an argument,' he added, 'come on then.'

They got up from the table and sat out in the entrance-porch which served as a verandah.

'Come, let's argue the matter,' said Prince Andrei. 'You talk of schools,' he went on, crooking a finger, 'education, and so forth. In other words, you want to lift him' (he pointed to a peasant who passed by them taking off his cap) 'out of his animal existence and awaken in him spiritual needs, when in my opinion animal happiness is the only happiness possible, and you want to deprive him of it. I envy him, while you are trying to make him what I am, without providing him with a mind or feelings like mine, or with my means. Then you say, "We must lighten his toil". But as I see it, physical labour is as essential to him, as much a condition of his existence, as intellectual activity is for you or me. You can't help thinking. I go to bed after two in the morning, thoughts come into my mind and I can't sleep but toss about till dawn, because I think and cannot help thinking, just as he can't help ploughing and mowing; if he didn't he would go to the tavern, or fall ill. Just as I could not stand his terrible physical labour, a week of which would kill me, so my physical idleness would be too much for him: he would put on weight and that would be the end of him. Thirdly – what was it now?' and Prince Andrei crooked a third finger. 'Oh, yes. Hospitals, medicine. Our peasant has a stroke and is dying, but you have him bled and patched up. He will drag about, a cripple, for another ten years, a burden to everybody. It would be far easier and simpler for him to die. Plenty of others are being born to take his place. It would be different if you grudged losing a worker – which is how I look at him – but you want to cure him out of love for him. And he does not want that. And besides, what an illusion that medicine ever cured anyone! Killed them, yes!' said he, frowning sardonically and turning away from Pierre.

Prince Andrei gave such clear and precise utterance to his ideas that it was evident he had reflected on this subject more than once, and the words came out readily in quick succession, as happens when a man has not talked for a long time. His eyes became brighter, the more pessimistic the views he expressed.

'Oh, that is dreadful, dreadful!' said Pierre. 'What I don't understand is how you can live with such ideas. I had moments of thinking like that myself not long ago – it was in Moscow, and on a journey – but then I sink into such depths that I'm not really living at all. Everything seems hateful to me ... myself most of all. Then I don't eat, don't wash ... how is it with you? ...'

'Why not wash? That's not clean,' said Prince Andrei. 'On the contrary, one has to try to make one's life as pleasant as possible. I'm alive, and it's not my fault that I am, and so it behoves me to make the best of it, not interfering with anybody else until death carries me off.'

'But what point is there for you in life? With ideas like these one would just sit without stirring, not embarking on anything ...'

'Life won't leave one in peace even so. I should be glad to do nothing, but here on the one hand the local Nobility did me the honour of selecting me to be their Marshal: it was all I could do to get out of it. They could not understand that I have not the required qualifications – the kind of busy, good-natured vulgarity – necessary for the position. Then there's this house here, which had to be built in order that I might have a nook of my own where I could be quiet. And now it's the recruiting.'

'Why aren't you serving in the army?'

'After Austerlitz?' said Prince Andrei gloomily. 'No, thank you very much. I vowed to myself I would never go on active service in the Russian army again. And I won't – not even if Bonaparte were here at Smolensk, threatening Bald Hills: even then I wouldn't serve in the Russian army. Well, as I was saying,' he continued, recovering his composure, 'now there's this recruiting. My father is chief in command of the 3rd circuit, and my only way of avoiding active service is to work with him.'

'So you are in the service after all?'

'Yes.'

He paused a little.

'But why?'

'I'll tell you why. My father is one of the most remarkable men of his time. But he is growing old, and though he is not exactly cruel he has too energetic a character. He is so accustomed to unlimited power that he is terrible, and now the Emperor has given him further authority as commander-in-chief over the recruiting. If I had arrived a couple of hours later a fortnight ago, he would have had the register-clerk at Yukhnovo hanged,' said Prince Andrei with a smile. 'And so I am serving, because no one but myself has any influence over him, and now and then I am able to save him from an act which would be a source of regret to him afterwards.'

'Ah, there, you see!'

'Yes, but it is not as you imagine,' Prince Andrei continued. 'It was not that I felt, or feel, kindly to the scoundrelly register-clerk who had been stealing boots or something from the recruits. Indeed, I should have been very glad to see him hanged, but I was sorry for my father – which means for myself again.'

Prince Andrei grew more and more eager. His eyes glittered feverishly as he tried to prove to Pierre that in his actions there was never any desire to do good to his neighbour.

'Look here, you want to liberate your serfs,' he went on. 'That is a very good thing, but not for you – I don't suppose you ever had any-one flogged or sent to Siberia – and still less for your peasants. If they are beaten, flogged and sent to Siberia, I dare say they are none the worse for it. In Siberia they can lead the same brute existence: the stripes on their bodies heal, and they are as happy as before. The men who would really benefit are those serf-owners whose moral nature is depraved, who bring remorse upon themselves, stifle that remorse and grow callous, all because of their power to inflict punishment justly and unjustly. It is such as they who have my pity, and for their sakes I should like to see the serfs liberated. You may not have come across it, but I have seen how good men brought up in those traditions of unlimited power grow more irritable with the years, turn cruel

452

and harsh, and although aware of it cannot control themselves and daily add to the sum of their misery.'

Prince Andrei spoke so earnestly that Pierre could not help thinking that these ideas had been suggested to him by his father. He made no reply.

'So that is who I am sorry for, what I lament over: human dignity, peace of mind, purity, and not backs and heads, which remain the same backs and heads, beat and convict as you may.'

'No, no, a thousand times no! I shall never agree with you,' cried Pierre.

12

IN the evening Prince Andrei and Pierre got into an open carriage and drove to Bald Hills. Prince Andrei, glancing at Pierre, broke the silence now and then with remarks which showed that he was in good humour.

Pointing to the fields, he spoke of the improvements he was making in his husbandry.

Pierre preserved a gloomy silence, answering in monosyllables and apparently immersed in his own thoughts.

He was reflecting that Prince Andrei was unhappy, that he had gone astray and did not see the true light, and that it was his, Pierre's, duty to go to his aid, enlighten him and lift him up. But as soon as he began to deliberate on what he should say, and how he should say it, he foresaw that Prince Andrei by a single word, a single argument, would upset all his teaching, and he shrank from beginning, afraid of exposing everything he cherished and held sacred to the possibility of ridicule.

'No, but what makes you think so?' Pierre began all at once, lowering his head and looking like a bull about to charge; 'what makes you think so? You ought not to think so.'

'Think what?' asked Prince Andrei in surprise.

'About life, about man's destiny. It can't be so. I had the same ideas, and do you know what saved me? Freemasonry. No, don't smile. Freemasonry is not a religious sect, nor mere ceremonial rites, as I used to suppose. Freemasonry is something much better: it is the one expression of the highest, of the eternal in humanity.'

And he began to expound Freemasonry as he understood it to Prince Andrei.

He declared that Freemasonry was the teaching of Christianity freed from the fetters of State and Church: the doctrine of equality, fraternity and love.

'Our holy Brotherhood is the only thing that has real meaning in life; all the rest is a dream,' said Pierre. 'Understand, my dear fellow, that outside this fraternity all is falsehood and deceit, and I agree with you that an intelligent and good man has no alternative but, like you, to get through life trying only not to hurt others. But make our fundamental convictions your own, join our Brotherhood, give yourself heart and soul to us, let yourself be guided, and you will at once feel, as I did, that you are a link in a vast invisible chain, the beginning of which is hidden in the skies,' said Pierre.

Prince Andrei, looking straight before him, listened to Pierre's discourse in silence. More than once when he failed to catch a word owing to the rumble of the carriage wheels he asked Pierre to repeat it, and by the peculiar light that glowed in Prince Andrei's eyes, and by his silence, Pierre saw that he had not spoken without effect, and that Prince Andrei would not interrupt him nor laugh at what he said.

They reached a river that had overflowed its banks and which they had to cross by ferry. While the carriage and horses were being seen to, the two young men stepped on to the ferry-boat.

Leaning his elbows on the rail, Prince Andrei gazed silently at the flooding waters glittering in the setting sun.

'Well, what do you think of it?' Pierre asked. 'Why don't you speak?'

'What do I think? I was listening to you. It's all all right,' answered Prince Andrei. 'You say: join our Brotherhood and we will show you the purpose of life, the destiny of man, and the laws which govern the universe. But who are "we"? Men. How is it you know everything? Why am I the only one not to see what you see? You behold a reign of goodness and truth on earth, but I don't.'

Pierre interrupted him. 'Do you believe in a future life?' he asked.

'A future life?' Prince Andrei repeated, but Pierre gave him no time to reply, taking this echo of his words for a denial, the more readily as he knew Prince Andrei's atheistic views in the past.

'You say you can't see any reign of goodness and truth on earth. Nor could I, and it's impossible to, if we accept our life here as the end of all things. On *earth* – here on this earth' (Pierre pointed to the open country) 'there is no truth: it is all lies and wickedness. But in the universe, in the whole universe, there is a kingdom of truth, and we who are now the children of earth are – in the eternal sense – children of the whole universe. Don't I feel in my soul that I am a part of that vast, harmonious whole? Don't I feel that I constitute one link, that I mark a degree in the ascending scale from the lower orders of creation to the higher ones, in this immense innumerable multitude of beings in which the Godhead – the Supreme Force, if you prefer the term – is manifest? If I see, see clearly the ladder rising from plant to man, why should I suppose that this ladder, the foot of which I can't see, it is hidden in the plant world – why should I suppose that it breaks off with me and does not lead further and further, up to superior beings? I feel not only that I cannot vanish, since nothing in this world ever vanishes, but that I always shall exist and always have existed. I feel that besides myself, above me, there are spirits, and that in their world there is truth.'

'Yes, that is Herder's theory,' commented Prince Andrei, 'but that won't convince me, my dear boy – life and death are what convince. What convinces is when you see a being dear to you, whose existence is bound up with yours, to whom you have done wrong that you had hoped to put right' (Prince Andrei's voice shook and he turned away) 'and all at once that being is seized and racked with pain, and ceases to exist. … Why? There must be an answer. And I believe there is. … That is what can convince a man, that is what convinced me,' said Prince Andrei.

'Yes, yes, of course,' exclaimed Pierre. 'Isn't that the very thing I'm saying?'

'No. I only mean that one is not persuaded by argument that there must be a future life: it is when you are journeying through life hand in hand with someone, and suddenly your companion vanishes *there*, *into nowhere*, and you are left standing on the edge of the abyss, and you look down into it. As I have …'

'Well, that's it then! You know there is a *there*, and there is a *Someone*? The *there* is the future life. The *Someone* is God.'

Prince Andrei did not reply. The carriage and horses had long ago been taken across to the other bank and reharnessed, and the sun was already half hidden and an evening frost was starring the puddles near the ferry; but Pierre and Andrei, to the astonishment of the footmen, coachmen and ferryhands, still stood on the ferry and talked.

'If there is a God and a future life, then there is truth and goodness, and man's highest happiness consists in striving to attain them. We must live, we must love, we must believe that we have life not only

455

today on this scrap of earth but that we have lived and shall live for ever, there, in the Whole,' Pierre was saying, and he pointed to the sky.

Prince Andrei stood leaning with his elbows on the rail of the ferry, and as he listened to Pierre he kept his eyes fixed on the red reflection of the sun on the blue waters. Pierre fell silent, and all was still. The ferry had long reached the other bank, and only the ripples of the current eddied softly against the bottom of the boat. It seemed to Prince Andrei that the water was lapping a refrain to Pierre's words: 'It's the truth, believe it.'

He sighed, and glanced with a radiant, childlike, tender look at Pierre's face, flushed and jubilant though still timidly conscious of his friend's superior intelligence.

'Yes, if only it were so!' said Prince Andrei. 'However, let us be going,' he added, and stepping off the ferry he looked up at the sky to which Pierre had pointed, and for the first time since Austerlitz saw those lofty eternal heavens he had watched while lying on the battlefield; and something long dormant, something better that had been in him, suddenly awoke with new and joyful life in his soul. The feeling vanished as soon as Prince Andrei fell back again into the ordinary conditions of life, but he knew that this feeling, which he was ignorant how to develop, lived within him. Pierre's visit marked an epoch in Prince Andrei's life. Though outwardly he continued to live in the same way, inwardly he began a new existence.

13

IT was dark by the time Prince Andrei and Pierre drove up to the main entrance at Bald Hills. As they approached, Prince Andrei, with a smile, drew Pierre's attention to the hubbub going on behind the house. An old woman bent with age, with a wallet on her back, and a short, long-haired young man in a black garment had returned hastily to the gate on seeing the carriage. Two women ran out after them, and all four, looking round at the *calèche*, with scared faces, hurried up the steps of the back porch.

'Those are some of my sister's "God's folk",' said Prince Andrei. 'They mistook us for my father. This is the one matter in which she disobeys him. His orders are to drive away these pilgrims, but she welcomes them.'

'But what are "God's folk"?' asked Pierre.

Prince Andrei had no time to answer. The servants came out to meet them, and he inquired where the old prince was and whether they expected him home soon.

The old prince was still in town, and expected back at any minute.

Prince Andrei led Pierre to his own apartments, which were always kept in perfect order and readiness for him in his father's house, and himself went to the nursery.

'Let us go and find my sister,' he said, rejoining Pierre. 'I have not seen her yet: she is hidden away somewhere, sitting with her "God's folk". It is her own fault – she will be embarrassed, and you will meet her "God's folk". A strange sight, I can tell you.'

'But who are these "God's folk"?' asked Pierre.

'You shall see.'

Princess Maria certainly was greatly disconcerted, and she coloured in red patches when they went in. In her cosy room, with lamps burning before the icon-stand, a young lad with a long nose and long hair, wearing a monk's habit, sat on the sofa beside her, behind a samovar. Near them in a low chair was a thin, shrivelled old woman with a meek expression on her childlike face.

'André, why didn't you let me know?' said the princess with mild reproach, standing up in front of her pilgrims like a hen protecting her chicks.

'Delighted to see you. I am very glad to see you,' she said to Pierre as he kissed her hand. She had known him as a child, and now his friendship with Andrei, his unhappy marriage, and above all his kindly, simple face disposed her favourably towards him. She looked at him with her beautiful luminous eyes as if to say: 'I like you very much, only, please, don't laugh at my flock.' After the first exchange of greetings they sat down.

'Ah, Ivanushka here too!' said Prince Andrei, with a smile indicating the pilgrim-lad.

'André!' said Princess Maria imploringly.

'It's a girl, you know,' Prince Andrei told Pierre in French.

'André, for pity's sake!' repeated Princess Maria.

It was plain that Prince Andrei's ironical tone towards the pilgrims and Princess Maria's unavailing championship had become a habit between them.

'But, my dear girl,' said Prince Andrei, still in French, 'on the contrary, you ought to feel obliged to me for giving Pierre some explanation of your bosom friendship with this young man.'

'Indeed?' said Pierre, gazing through his spectacles with curiosity and seriousness (for which Princess Maria was especially grateful to him) into Ivanushka's face, who perceiving that he was the subject under discussion considered them all with crafty eyes.

Princess Maria's embarrassment on her flock's account was quite unnecessary. They were not in the least abashed. The old woman, lowering her eyes but stealing sidelong glances at the new-comers, had turned her cup upside down in the saucer, placing her nibbled bit of sugar beside it, and sat quietly in her arm-chair, waiting to be offered another cup of tea. Ivanushka, sipping out of the saucer, peeped from under his brows with sly, womanish eyes at the young men.

'Where have you been? In Kiev?' Prince Andrei asked the old woman.

'I have, good sir,' answered the old woman garrulously. 'On the very Feast of Christmas it was given to me to partake of the holy, heavenly sacrament at the shrine of the saints. But now I'm from Kolyazin, sir, where a great and wonderful blessing has been revealed.'

'And was Ivanushka with you?'

'I take the road by myself, benefactor.' said Ivanushka, trying to make his voice sound deep. 'It was only at Yukhnovo that I fell in with Pelageya ...'

Pelageya interrupted her companion, evidently anxious to tell of what she had seen.

'In Kolyazin, master, a wonderful blessing has been revealed.'

'What was it? Some new relics?' asked Prince Andrei.

'Come, Andrei, that's enough,' said Princess Maria. 'Don't you tell him, Pelageya.'

'And why not, my dear, why ever shouldn't I? I like him. He's a good gentleman, one of God's elect, he's a benefactor, he once gave me ten roubles, I remember. When I was in Kiev, Crazy Kirill says to me (one of God's own, he is, goes barefoot winter and summer) – "Why aren't you going to the right place?" he says. "Go you to Kolyazin, there's a wonder-working icon revealed there, of the Holy Mother of God." So I took farewell of the saints and went. ...'

All were silent, only the pilgrim woman talked on in measured tones, breathing evenly.

'So I come, master, and folks say to me: "A great blessing has been vouchsafed, drops of holy oil trickle from the cheeks of the Most Holy Mother of God" ...'

'That will do, that will do, you can tell us another time,' said Princess Maria, flushing.

'Let me ask her something,' said Pierre. 'Did you see it with your own eyes?' he inquired.

'Oh yes, master, I was found worthy. Such a brightness was on her face, like light from heaven, and from the blessed Mother's cheeks first one drop, and then another ...'

'Of course it's a trick,' said Pierre naïvely, after listening intently to the pilgrim.

'Oh, master, whatever are you saying?' exclaimed Pelageya aghast, turning to Princess Maria for support.

'That's the way they impose on the people,' he repeated.

'Lord Jesus Christ!' cried the old woman, crossing herself. 'Oh, don't speak so, sir. There was a general once who didn't believe, and said he, "The monks are cheats," yes, and as soon as he said it he was struck blind. Well, and then he dreamed a dream, the Holy Virgin Mother of the Catacombs at Kiev comes to him and says: "Believe in me and I will make you whole." And so he kept beseeching, "Take me to her, take me to her." It's Gospel truth I'm telling you, I saw it with my own eyes. So they led him, stone blind as he was, straight to her, and he goes up and falls on his knees and says, "Make me whole," says he, "and I will give thee all I had from the Tsar." And, sir, I seen the star on her myself, just as he gave it to her. Well, and what do you think – he got back his sight. It's a sin to speak so. God will punish you,' she said admonishingly to Pierre.

'How did the star get into the icon?' Pierre asked.

'And was the Holy Mother promoted to the rank of general?' said Prince Andrei, smiling.

Pelageya suddenly turned pale and clasped her hands.

'Oh, master, master, what a sin! And you with a son too!' she began, turning from white to a vivid red. 'For what you have said, God forgive you.' She crossed herself. 'Oh Lord, forgive him! Dearie, what does it mean? ...' she asked Princess Maria. She got to her feet and, almost crying, began gathering up her wallet. Plainly she was both frightened and sorry for Prince Andrei who had spoken like that, and ashamed at having accepted charity in a house where such things could be said, and at the same time sorry that she must henceforth deprive herself of the bounty to be found there.

'Now what did you want to do this for?' said Princess Maria. 'Why did you come to my room? ...'

'No, Pelageya, I am not in earnest,' said Pierre. 'Princess, I give you my word I didn't mean to upset her,' he said in French. 'Forget it, I was only joking,' he said smiling shyly, and trying to efface his crime.

Pelageya paused doubtfully, but Pierre's face showed such sincere penitence, and Prince Andrei looked so meekly and earnestly from her to Pierre and back again, that she was gradually reassured.

14

THE pilgrim-woman was appeased and, being encouraged to talk, told them a long story of Father Amphilochy, who led such a holy life that his dear hands smelt of incense, and of how on her last pilgrimage to Kiev some monks she knew let her have the keys to the catacombs, and of how, taking some dried bread with her, she had spent two days and two nights in the catacombs among the saints. 'I'd say a little prayer to one, read a passage from the Bible, and go on to another. Then I'd have a little nap, and once more go and kiss the holy relics; and such peace, dearie, such blessedness that a body has no wish to come out even into God's daylight again.'

Pierre listened to her gravely and attentively. Prince Andrei went out of the room. And leaving 'God's folk' to finish their tea, Princess Maria followed him with Pierre into the drawing-room.

'You are very kind,' she said to him.

'Ah, I truly did not mean to hurt her feelings. I understand them so well and have the greatest respect for them.'

Princess Maria looked at him without speaking, and a gentle smile played over her lips.

'I have known you a long time, you see, and am as fond of you as of a brother,' she said. 'What do you think of Andrei?' she asked hastily, not giving him time to respond to her expressions of affection. 'I feel very worried about him. His health in the winter was better, but last spring his wound reopened and the doctor said he ought to go away and have proper treatment. His state of mind makes me afraid too. His is not a nature that would let him weep away his suffering, in the way we women do. He carries it buried in him. Today he is cheerful and in good spirits, but that is thanks to your visit – he is not often like that. If you could only persuade him to go abroad! He needs activity, and this quiet regular life is very bad for him. Other people don't notice it, but I do.'

Soon after nine the footmen rushed to the front door, hearing the bells of the old prince's approaching carriage. Prince Andrei and Pierre also went out on to the steps.

'Who's that?' asked the old prince, alighting and catching sight of Pierre.

'Ah! Very glad! Kiss me,' he said, having learnt who the young stranger was.

Prince Bolkonsky was in high good humour and treated Pierre in the most cordial manner.

Before supper Prince Andrei, on returning to his father's study, found him disputing hotly with their visitor. Pierre was maintaining that a time would come when there would be no more war. The old prince chaffingly joined issue with him, but without getting angry.

'Drain the blood from men's veins and pour water in instead, and then there'll be no more war. Old women's nonsense, old women's nonsense,' he was saying, but still he patted Pierre affectionately on the shoulder as he went over to the table where Prince Andrei, evidently not caring to enter into the discussion, was glancing through the papers his father had brought from town. The old man began to talk of business.

'The marshal, a Count Rostov, hasn't sent half his contingent. Came to town and thought fit to invite me to dinner – I gave him dinner! ... And here, have a look at this. ... Well, my boy,' Prince Bolkonsky went on, addressing his son and clapping Pierre on the shoulder, 'your friend's a capital fellow – I like him! He wakes me up. Other people will talk sense but one has no wish to listen; whereas this fellow pours out rubbish and it does an old man good. Well, get along, get along! Perhaps I'll come and sit with ye at supper. We'll have another argument. Make friends with my little goose, Princess Maria,' he shouted after Pierre through the door.

It was only now on his visit to Bald Hills that Pierre appreciated fully the strength and charm of his friendship with Prince Andrei. This charm was not expressed so much in his relations with Prince Andrei himself as in his relations with all his family and household. With the stern old host and the gentle timid Princess Maria, though he scarcely knew them, Pierre at once felt like an old friend. They were all fond of him already. Not only Princess Maria, who had been won by his kindliness with the pilgrims, gave him her most radiant looks, but even the little yearling Prince Nikolai (as his grandfather called him) smiled at Pierre and let himself be taken in Pierre's arms, and Mihail Ivanich and Mademoiselle Bourienne watched him with happy smiles when he talked to Prince Bolkonsky.

The old prince came in to supper; this was evidently on Pierre's account. And during the two days the young man stayed at Bald Hills he was extremely genial with him, and told him to come and visit them again.

When Pierre had gone, and all the members of the household were together, they began to discuss him, as people always do after the departure of a new face, but, as rarely happens, no one had anything but good to say of him.

15

RETURNING from this furlough, Rostov for the first time felt and recognized how strong were the ties that bound him to Denisov and all the others in the regiment.

When he was approaching the Pavlograds he felt as he had on nearing his home in Moscow. At the first sight of a hussar, of his regiment, with uniform unbuttoned, at the sight of Dementyev's red head, and the picket-ropes of the roan horses, and when he heard Lavrushka gleefully shout to his master, 'The count has come!' and Denisov, who had been asleep on his bed, ran all dishevelled out of the mud hut to embrace him, and the officers gathered round to greet the new arrival, Rostov felt exactly as he had when his mother and father and sisters had hugged him, and tears of joy so choked him that he could not say a word. The regiment was home, too, and one as unalterably dear and precious as his parental home.

After reporting himself to his colonel and being reassigned to his former squadron, after taking his turn as officer for the day and going for forage, after getting back into the current of all the little interests of the regiment, after taking leave of his liberty and letting himself be nailed down within one narrow inflexible framework, Rostov experienced the same sense of peace, of moral support, and the same sense of being at home and in his right corner as he felt under the paternal roof. Here was none of that turmoil of the world at large in which he found himself out of his element and made mistakes in exercising his free will. There was no Sonya with whom he ought or ought not to reach a clear understanding. Here he did not have to make up his mind whether he would or would not go to this or that place. Here there were not twenty-four hours in the day which could be spent in such a variety of ways; here there was an end to that innumerable throng of individuals whose presence or absence was a matter of indifference to him; there was an end to those vague and undefined money-relations with his father, and nothing to remind him of that terrible loss to Dolohov. Here in the regiment everything was straightforward and simple. The whole world was divided into two unequal parts: one, our Pavlograd regiment; the other, all the remainder. And with that remainder one had no concern. In the regiment everything was definite: who was lieutenant, who captain, who was a good fellow, who was not, and, above all, who was a comrade. The canteen-keeper gave one credit, one's pay came every four months; there was nothing that had to be thought out and decided. One had only to behave honourably by the standards of the Pavlograd Hussars, and when given an order carry out what was clearly, distinctly, and unmistakably commanded – and all would be well.

Stepping back into these explicit conditions of regimental life, Rostov felt the delight and relief a tired man feels in lying down to rest. To Rostov army life was all the more agreeable during this campaign because after his gambling loss to Dolohov (for which, in spite of all his family's efforts to console him, he could not forgive himself) he had made up his mind to atone for his fault by serving not as he had done before but really well; by being a thoroughly admirable comrade and officer – in other words, a first-rate man, a thing which seemed so difficult out in the *world* but so possible in the regiment.

He had determined to repay his debt to his parents within five years. They were sending him ten thousand roubles a year, but now he resolved to take only two thousand and leave the rest towards repayment of the debt.

★

Our army, after various retreats, advances, and engagements fought at Pultusk and Preussisch-Eylau, was concentrated in the vicinity of Bartenstein, awaiting the Emperor's arrival and the beginning of a new offensive.

The Pavlograd regiment, belonging to that part of the army which had served in the hostilities of 1805, had been recruiting up to strength in Russia, and arrived too late for the first actions of the campaign. The Pavlograds had not been at Pultusk nor at Preussisch-Eylau, and when they reached the army in the field in the second half of the campaign were attached to Platov's division.

Platov's division was acting independently of the main army. Several times units of the Pavlograd regiment had exchanged shots with the enemy, had taken prisoners, and on one occasion had even captured Marshal Oudinot's carriages. In April the Pavlograd Hussars were stationed near a totally ruined and deserted German village, where they remained without stirring for several weeks.

A thaw had set in, it was muddy and cold, the ice on the river had broken, and the roads become impassable. For days neither provisions for the men nor fodder for the horses had been issued. As no transports could arrive, the men scattered about the abandoned and empty villages, searching for potatoes, but even these were few and far between.

Everything had been devoured and the inhabitants had all fled – if any remained they were poorer than beggars and there was nothing to be taken from them; even the soldiers, usually pitiless enough, instead of robbing them further often gave up the last of their rations to them.

The Pavlograd regiment had lost only two men wounded in action, but famine and sickness had reduced their numbers by almost half. In the hospitals death was so certain that soldiers suffering from fever, or the swelling caused by bad food, preferred to remain on duty, dragging their feeble legs to the front, rather than go to the hospitals. With the coming of spring the soldiers found a plant just showing above ground that looked like asparagus, which for some reason they called 'Molly's sweet-wort', and they wandered about the fields and meadows hunting for this 'Molly's sweet-wort' (which was very bitter), digging it up with their sabres and eating it, in spite of orders not to touch this noxious root. That spring a new disease broke out among the men, a swelling of the arms, legs and face, which the doctors attributed to this plant. But, orders notwithstanding, the soldiers of Denisov's squadron fed chiefly on 'Molly's sweet-wort' because, this was the second week of eking out the last of the biscuits – half-pound rations being doled out to each man – and the last consignment of potatoes were frozen and sprouting.

The horses, too, had subsisted for a fortnight on straw from the thatched roofs; they had become shockingly thin and their winter coats still hung about them in tufts.

Despite this terrible destitution officers and men continued with the usual routine. Despite their pale, swollen faces and tattered uniforms, the hussars formed up for roll-call, attended to their duties, groomed their horses, polished their arms, tore down thatch from the roofs in place of fodder, and gathered round the cauldrons for their meals, from which they rose unsatisfied, joking about their vile food and their hunger. And just as usual during the hours when they were off duty they lit bonfires, stripped, and stood steaming themselves, smoked, picked out and baked sprouting rotten potatoes, while they told and listened to stories of Potemkin's and Suvorov's campaigns, or popular legends about Alyosha-the-artful-one or Mikolka who worked for the priest.

The officers also lived as usual in twos and threes in roofless, tumble-down houses. The seniors did what they could to get straw and potatoes and means of sustenance for the soldiers generally. The younger ones spent their time as they always did, some playing cards (money was plentiful if provisions were not), others with more innocent games such as quoits and skittles. The progress of the campaign as a whole was rarely spoken of, partly because they had no positive information of any sort and partly because of a vague feeling that in the main the war was going badly.

Rostov lived as before with Denisov, and the bond of friendship between them had become still closer since their furlough. Denisov never mentioned Rostov's family, but by the warmth of the affection his commander showed him Rostov felt that the elder hussar's luckless passion for Natasha had something to do with the strengthening of their friendship. There was no doubt that Denisov tried to take care of Rostov and to expose him to danger as seldom as possible, and after an action greeted his safe return with undisguised joy. On one of his foraging expeditions in a deserted and ruined village where he had gone in search of provisions, Rostov found a Polish family consisting of an old man and his daughter with an infant at the breast. They were half-naked, starving, too weak to get away on foot, and had no means of obtaining transport. Rostov brought them to his quarters, installed them in his own lodgings, and kept them for several weeks while the old man was recovering. One of his comrades, talking of women, began chaffing Rostov, declaring that he was the slyest fellow of them all and that it would not be a bad thing if he introduced them to the pretty little Polish girl he had rescued. Rostov took the joke as an insult, flared up and was so disagreeable to the officer that it was all Denisov could do to prevent a duel. When the officer had gone away, and Denisov, who knew nothing himself of Rostov's relations with the Polish girl, began to upbraid him for his quick temper, Rostov said to him:

'But how could I help it? ... she was like a sister to me, and I can't tell you how it offended me ... because ... well, because ...'

Denisov patted him on the shoulder, and took to walking rapidly up and down the room without looking at Rostov, a habit of his at moments of emotional disturbance.

'What a cwazy bweed you Wostovs are!' he muttered, and Rostov noticed tears in his eyes.

16

In the month of April the troops were cheered by news of the Emperor's arrival, but Rostov had no chance of being present at the review the Tsar held at Bartenstein: the Pavlograds were at the advance posts, a long way beyond Bartenstein.

They were bivouacking. Denisov and Rostov were living in a mud hut, dug out for them by the soldiers and roofed with branches and turf. The hut was made after a pattern then in vogue. A trench was dug three and a half feet wide, four feet eight inches deep, and eight feet long. At one end of the trench steps were cut and these formed the entrance, the approach. The trench itself was the room, in which the lucky ones such as the squadron commander had a plank lying on four piles at the end opposite the entrance, to serve as a table. On each side of the trench the earth was hollowed out to a depth of about two and a half feet, and this did duty for bedsteads and couches. The roof was so constructed that one could stand upright in the middle of the trench, and even sit up on the beds if one lent over towards the table. Denisov, who fared luxuriously because he was popular with the soldiers of his squadron, had a board in the front part of the roof of his hut, with a piece of broken but mended glass in it for a window. When it was very cold embers from the soldiers' camp-fires were brought on a bent sheet of iron and put on the steps in the 'reception room' – as Denisov called that part of the hut – and this made it so warm that the officers, of whom there were always a number with Denisov and Rostov, could sit in their shirt-sleeves.

In April Rostov was on orderly duty. Returning between seven and eight one morning after a night without sleep, he sent for hot embers, changed his rain-soaked clothes, said his prayers, swallowed some tea, warmed himself, then tidied up the things on the table and in his own corner and, his face glowing from exposure to the wind, and with nothing on but his shirt, lay down on his back, his hands behind his head. He was pleasantly reflecting on the promotion which was likely to follow his last reconnoitring expedition, and was awaiting Denisov, who had gone out somewhere. He was anxious to have a talk with him.

Suddenly he heard Denisov shouting behind the hut in a voice vibrating with anger. Rostov moved to the window to learn whom he was speaking to, and saw the quartermaster Topcheyenko.

'I told you not to let them eat that Molly-woot stuff!' Denisov was roaring. 'And then with my own eyes I see Lazarchuk bwinging some fwom the field.'

'I did give the order, your Honour, over and over again, but they won't listen,' answered the quartermaster.

Rostov lay down again on his bed, and thought complacently: 'It's his turn now, let him look to things: I've done my day's work and now I'm having a lie-down – hurrah!' Through the wall he could hear Lavrushka, Denisov's smart rogue of a valet, talking as well as the quartermaster. Lavrushka was saying something about loaded wagons, biscuits and oxen he had seen when he had gone for provisions.

Then Denisov's voice from farther off was heard shouting: 'Second troop – to the saddle!'

'Where are they off to now?' wondered Rostov.

Five minutes later Denisov came into the hut, climbed with muddy boots on the bed, angrily lit his pipe, rummaged through his belongings, got out his riding-whip, buckled on his sabre and started out of the hut. To Rostov's 'Whither away?' he answered gruffly and vaguely that he had business to attend to.

'Let God be my judge afterwards, and our gweat monarch!' said Denisov as he went out, and next Rostov heard the hooves of several

467

horses splashing through the mud. He did not even trouble to find out where Denisov had gone. Warm and comfortable in his corner, he fell asleep and stayed in the hut until late in the afternoon. Denisov had not returned. The weather had cleared, and near the next hut two officers and a cadet were playing *svayka*, laughing as they threw their pegs, which buried themselves in the soft mud. Rostov joined them. In the middle of a game the officers saw some wagons approaching with some fifteen hussars on their scraggy horses riding behind. The escorted wagons drove up to the picket-ropes and were surrounded by a crowd of hussars.

'There now, Denisov never left off worrying,' said Rostov, 'and here are the provisions.'

'So they are!' said the officers. 'Won't the men be pleased!'

A little behind the hussars came Denisov, accompanied by two in-fantry officers with whom he was discussing something. Rostov went to meet them.

'I warn you, captain,' one of the officers, a short thin man, evidently very angry, was saying.

'And I have told you that I am not weturning them,' replied Denisov.

'You will answer for it, captain. It's mutiny – carrying off trans-ports from your own army! Our men have had no food for two days.'

'And mine have had nothing for two weeks,' retorted Denisov.

'It's highway robbery! You'll answer for this, sir!' repeated the infantry officer, raising his voice.

'Now what are you pestewing me for?' shouted Denisov, suddenly losing his temper. 'I am the one who is wesponsible, and not you, and you'd better not buzz about here till you get hurt. Be off!' he shouted at the officers.

'Very well then!' cried the little officer, undaunted and not budg-ing. 'If you are determined on robbery, I'll …'

'Take yourself to the devil! Quick ma'ch, while you're safe and sound!' and Denisov rode his horse at the officer.

'Very good, very good!' muttered the officer threateningly, and turning his horse he trotted away, bouncing in the saddle.

'A dog astwide a fence! Vewily a dog astwide a fence!' Denisov called after him – the most insulting remark a cavalryman can make to an infantryman on horseback – and riding up to Rostov he broke into a guffaw.

468

'I appwopwiated 'em from the infantwy – I've taken their twans-ports by main force!' he said. 'Why, I can't let my men pewish of starvation.'

The wagons that had reached the hussars had been consigned to an infantry regiment, but learning from Lavrushka that the transport was unescorted Denisov with his hussars had forcibly seized it. The soldiers got as many biscuits as they wanted: there were even enough to share with other squadrons.

Next day the regimental commander sent for Denisov, and holding his fingers spread out before his eyes said:

'This is the way I look at the business: I know nothing about it and shall take no action, but I advise you to ride over to H.Q. and make matters right with the commissariat, and if possible sign a receipt for such and such stores received. If you don't, and the stuff is debited against the infantry regiment, there will be trouble and it may end unpleasantly.'

Denisov went straight from the colonel to headquarters with a sincere desire to act on this advice. In the evening he came back to his dug-out in a state such as Rostov had never seen him in before. He could not speak and was gasping for breath. When Rostov asked him what was wrong, he could only splutter incoherent oaths and threats in a faint voice.

Alarmed at Denisov's condition, Rostov suggested he should un-dress, and drink some water, while he sent for the doctor.

'Me to be twied for wobbewy – oh, some more water. ... Let them twy me, but I shall always thwash wascals, and I'll tell the Empewo' ... Give me some ice,' he kept muttering.

The regimental surgeon said it was necessary to bleed Denisov. A soup-plateful of black blood was taken from his hairy arm and only then was he able to relate what had happened.

'I get there,' began Denisov. '"Well, where are your chief's quar-ters?" I ask. They show me. "Will you be kind enough to wait?" "I've widden twenty miles, I have duties to attend to and no time to wait. Announce me." Vewy well: out comes the wobber-in-chief – he, too, thinks fit to lecture me: "This is wobbewy!" says he. "A wobber," I tell him, "is not a man who takes pwovisions to feed his soldiers but one who fills his own pockets!" "Will you please be silent?" Wight. "Go and sign a weceipt in the commissioner's office," says he, "but your affair will be weported to headquarters." I pwo-

469

ceed to the commissioner's. I enter, and there at the table ... who do you suppose? No, think! ... Who is it that's starving us to death?' roared Denisov, banging the table so violently with the fist of his newly-bled arm that the board almost collapsed and the tumblers danced on it. 'Telyanin! "What," I shouted, "so it's you starving us to death, is it?" and I gave him one stwaight on the snout. ... "Ah, you unspeakable ... you ...!" and I started thwashing him. ... I enjoyed it, I can tell you,' cried Denisov with malignant glee, showing his white teeth under his black moustache. 'I'd have killed him if they hadn't pulled me away.'

'Here, here, what are you shouting for, keep quiet,' said Rostov. 'Now you've started your arm bleeding. Wait, we must tie it up again.'

Denisov was bandaged up once more and put to bed. Next morning when he woke he was in good spirits and unruffled.

But at noon the adjutant of the regiment appeared in Denisov's and Rostov's dug-out and with a grave and serious face regretfully showed them a formal communication addressed to Major Denisov from the regimental commander inquiring about the incidents of the previous day. The adjutant told them that the affair was likely to take a very ugly turn, that a court-martial had been convened, and that in view of the severity with which marauding and insubordination were now regarded he might think himself fortunate if he escaped with being reduced to the ranks.

The case as presented by the aggrieved parties was that Major Denisov, after seizing the transports, had appeared, unbidden and the worse for liquor, before the chief quartermaster, called him a thief, threatened to strike him and, when he was led away, had rushed into the office and given two officials a thrashing, dislocating the arm of one of them.

In reply to further inquiries from Rostov, Denisov laughed and said that it did certainly seem as though some other fellow had got mixed up in it, but that it was all stuff and nonsense, that he would not dream of being afraid of any court-martial, and that if those scoundrels dared to pick a quarrel with him he would give them an answer they would not easily forget.

Denisov spoke contemptuously of the whole matter, but Rostov knew him too well not to detect that at heart (though he hid it from the others) he feared a court-martial and was worried over the affair,

470

which was obviously certain to have disastrous consequences. Forms to be filled in, and notices from the court, began to arrive daily, and on the 1st of May Denisov was ordered to hand his squadron over to the next in seniority and appear before the divisional staff to give an account of his violence at the commissariat office. On the previous day Platov made a reconnaissance of the enemy with two Cossack regiments and two squadrons of hussars. Denisov, as was his wont, rode out in front of the outposts parading his courage. A bullet fired by a French sharpshooter hit him in the fleshy upper part of the leg. Possibly at any other time Denisov would not have left the regiment for so slight a wound, but now he took advantage of it to excuse himself from appearing at headquarters, and retired into hospital.

17

In June the battle of Friedland was fought, in which the Pavlograds did not take part, and after that an armistice was declared. Rostov, who felt his friend's absence very keenly, having had no news of him since he left and feeling anxious about his wound and the progress of his affairs, took advantage of the truce to get leave to visit Denisov in hospital.

The hospital was in a small Prussian town which had twice been sacked by Russian and French troops. For the very reason that it was summer, when everything is so lovely out in the fields, the little town presented a particularly dismal appearance with its broken roofs and fences, its foul streets and ragged inhabitants, and the sick and drunken soldiers wandering about.

The hospital, which stood in a courtyard surrounded by the remnants of a wooden fence, had been established in a brick building with many of the window-frames and panes broken. A number of bandaged soldiers, with pale swollen faces, were walking about or sitting in the sunshine in the yard.

Directly Rostov entered the door he was enveloped by a smell of putrefaction, disease and disinfectant. On the stairs he met a Russian army doctor with a cigar in his mouth. The doctor was followed by a Russian assistant.

'I can't be everywhere at once,' the doctor was saying. 'Come this evening to Makar Alexeyevich, I'll be there.' The assistant asked some further question. 'Oh, do as you think best! What difference will it make?' The doctor caught sight of Rostov coming upstairs.

'What are you doing here, sir?' said the doctor. 'What are you here for? Couldn't you meet with a bullet that you want to pick up typhus? This is a pest-house, my good sir.'

'What do you mean?' asked Rostov.

'Typhus, sir. It's death to come in these walls. Makeyev' (he pointed to the assistant) 'and I are the only two still hanging about. Half a dozen of our colleagues have been carried off. ... As soon as a new man comes it's all up with him within a week,' said the doctor with evident satisfaction. 'Prussian doctors have been invited here but our allies don't care for the idea at all.'

Rostov explained that he wanted to see Major Denisov of the Hussars, who was lying wounded there.

'I don't know, can't tell you, my good sir. You can imagine: I've got three hospitals on my hands – over four hundred patients! It's just as well the kind ladies of Prussia send us a couple of pounds of coffee and some lint each month or we should be lost!' He laughed. 'Four hundred, sir, and fresh cases arriving all the time. It *is* four hundred, isn't it? Eh?' he asked, turning to his assistant.

The assistant looked tired out. It was evident that he was in a hurry for the talkative doctor to be gone, and waited irritably.

'Major Denisov,' repeated Rostov. 'He was wounded at Moliten.'

'Dead, I fancy. Eh, Makeyev?' queried the doctor in a tone of indifference.

The assistant, however, did not confirm the doctor's words.

'Is he tall, with reddish hair?' asked the doctor.

Rostov described Denisov's appearance.

'Yes, there was someone like that,' exclaimed the doctor almost with glee. 'But I'm sure he's dead, but anyway I'll make inquiries. We had lists. Have you got them, Makeyev?'

'The lists are at Makar Alexeyevich's,' answered the assistant. 'But go to the officers' ward and you'll see for yourself,' he added, turning to Rostov.

'Ah, you'd better not, sir,' said the doctor, 'or you might find yourself having to stay here!'

But Rostov took leave of the doctor with a bow and asked the assistant to show him the way.

'Don't blame me, mind!' the doctor shouted up the stairs after him.

Rostov and the assistant entered a corridor. The hospital stench was so strong in this dark passage that Rostov held his nose and was obliged to pause and brace himself before he could go on. A door opened on the right, and an emaciated, sallow-looking man limped out on crutches, wearing his underlinen only and with nothing on his feet. Propping himself up against the doorpost, he gazed with glittering envious eyes at them as they passed. Glancing in at the door, Rostov saw that the sick and wounded were lying on the floor, some on straw, some on their greatcoats.

'May one go in and look?' asked Rostov.

'What is there to see?' said the assistant.

But just because the assistant was obviously disinclined to let him, Rostov went into the soldiers' ward. The foul air which he had already begun to get used to in the corridor was still stronger here. It was a little different, more pungent, and one felt that this was where it originated.

In the long room, brightly lit by the sun which poured in through the large windows, the sick and wounded lay in two rows with their heads to the walls, leaving a passage down the middle. Most of them were unconscious and paid no attention to the visitors. The others raised themselves or lifted their thin yellow faces, and all gazed intently at Rostov with the same expression of hope that help had come, and of reproach and envy of another's health. Rostov stepped into the middle of the ward, and looking through the open doors of the two adjoining rooms on both sides saw the same spectacle. He stood still silently looking round. He had never expected anything like this. Close to his feet, almost across the empty space down the middle, a sick man lay on the bare floor, a Cossack probably, to judge by the way his hair was cut. The man was lying on his back, with his huge arms and legs outstretched. His face was purplish-red, his eyes were rolled back so that only the whites were visible, and the veins in his bare legs and arms, which were still red, stood out like cords. He was beating the back of his head against the floor, hoarsely muttering some word which he repeated over and over again. Rostov tried to hear what he was saying and made out the word he kept repeating. It was 'drink – drink – a drink!' Rostov looked round in search of someone who would lay the sick man back in his place and give him water.

'Who is it looks after the sick here?' he asked the assistant.

473

Just at that moment an army service corps soldier, a hospital orderly, came in from the next room, marched up to Rostov and stood to attention.

'Good day, your Honour!' bawled this soldier, rolling his eyes at Rostov and evidently mistaking him for someone in authority.

'Get him to his place and give him some water,' said Rostov, pointing to the Cossack.

'Certainly, your Honour,' the soldier replied complacently, rolling his eyes more strenuously than ever and drawing himself up still straighter, but not stirring from the spot.

'No, there's nothing I can do here,' thought Rostov, lowering his eyes, and he was about to leave the room when he became aware of an intense look fixed on him from over on the right. Almost in the corner, sitting on a military overcoat, was an old soldier with a stern sallow face, thin as a skeleton's, and an unshaved grey beard. He was looking persistently at Rostov. The man next the old soldier was whispering something to him, pointing to Rostov. Rostov realized that the old man wanted to ask him some favour. He went closer and saw that the old man had only one leg bent under him, the other had been amputated above the knee. At some distance from him, his neighbour on the other side, lay the motionless figure of a young soldier with head thrown back. The pale waxen face with its snub nose was still freckled, the eyes were rolled up under the lids. Rostov looked at the snub-nosed soldier and a cold chill ran down his back.

'Why, that man seems to be ...' he began, turning to the assistant.

'We've begged and begged, your Honour,' said the old soldier with a quiver in his lower jaw. 'He's been dead since morning. After all, we're men, not dogs. ...'

'I'll send someone at once. He shall be taken away – taken away at once,' said the assistant hurriedly. 'Come, your Honour.'

'Yes, yes, let us go,' said Rostov hastily, and dropping his eyes and shrinking into himself, trying to pass unnoticed between the rows of reproachful, envious eyes fastened upon him, he went out of the ward.

18

PASSING along the corridor, the assistant led Rostov to the officers' wards, consisting of three rooms opening into each other. Here there were bedsteads on which sick and wounded officers sat or lay. Others were walking about in hospital dressing-gowns. The first person Rostov met in the officers' ward was a thin little man who had lost one arm. He was walking about the first room in a night-cap and hospital dressing-gown, with a stumpy pipe between his teeth. Rostov looked at him, trying to recall where he had seen him before.

'What a place for us to meet again!' said the little man. 'I'm Tushin, Tushin, don't you remember? – I gave you a lift at Schön Graben. They've lopped a bit off me, see ...' he went on with a smile and indicating the empty sleeve of his dressing-gown. 'Looking for Vasili Dmitrich Denisov, are you? A room-mate of mine!' he added when he heard who Rostov wanted. 'Here, this way,' and Tushin drew him into the second room, from which came the sound of loud laughter.

'How can they exist in this place, much less laugh?' thought Rostov, with the odour of the dead body which he had seen in the soldiers' ward still strong in his nostrils, and still seeing those envious glances fixed on him, following him out of the room, and the face of that young soldier with upturned eyes.

Denisov, with his head buried under the blanket, was sound asleep on his bed, though it was nearly noon.

'Ah, Wostov? How are you, how are you?' he called out, in exactly the same tone as in the regiment, but Rostov noticed sadly that for all his customary light-heartedness and swagger there was some new, sinister, smothered feeling which revealed itself in the expression of Denisov's face and the intonations of his voice.

His wound, though trifling, had still not healed even after a lapse of six weeks. His face had the same swollen pallor as all the other faces in the hospital. But it was not this that struck Rostov: what struck him was that Denisov did not seem pleased to see him, and his smile was forced. He did not ask about the regiment, nor about what was happening generally, and when Rostov spoke of the war he did not listen.

Rostov noticed that Denisov disliked even to be reminded of the regiment or of that other free life going on outside the hospital. He seemed to be trying to forget that old life, and was only interested in the affair with the commissariat officers. In reply to Rostov's inquiry as to how that matter stood, he at once produced from under his pillow a communication he had received from the commission and a rough draft of his answer to it. He brightened up as he began to read his own reply, and particularly drew Rostov's attention to the stinging rejoinders he made to his enemies. Denisov's fellow-patients, who had gathered round Rostov – a fresh arrival from the world outside – one by one drifted away as soon as Denisov began reading his answer. From their faces Rostov could tell that all these gentlemen had already heard the whole story more than once and were heartily sick of it. Only the man who had the next bed, a stout Uhlan, continued to sit on his bed, scowling gloomily and smoking a pipe, and little one-armed Tushin still listened, shaking his head disapprovingly. In the middle of the reading the Uhlan interrupted Denisov.

'But what I say is,' he broke in, turning to Rostov, 'he ought simply to petition the Emperor for pardon. They say that rewards and honours are to be rained on us now, so surely the mere matter of a pardon ...'

'Me petition the Empewo'!' exclaimed Denisov in a voice into which he tried hard to throw his old energy and fire but which sounded like an expression of impotent irritability. 'What for? If I were a highway wobber I might beg for mercy but I'm to be court-martialled for bwinging wobbers to book. Let them twy me, I'm not afwaid of anyone. I've served the Tsar and my countwy honouwably, and I am not a thief! And am I to be degwaded? ... Listen, I'm w'iting to them stwaight. This is what I say: "If I had wobbed the Tweasuwy ..."'

'It's neatly put, no question about that,' remarked Tushin, 'but that's not the point, Vasili Dmitrich,' and he too turned to Rostov. 'One has to submit, and that is what Vasili Dmitrich here won't hear of. You know, the auditor himself told you that it was a bad business?'

'Let it be a bad business, then,' said Denisov.

'The auditor wrote out a petition for you,' continued Tushin, 'and you ought to sign it and entrust it to this gentleman. No doubt he' (indicating Rostov) 'has connexions on the staff. You won't find a better opportunity.'

'Haven't I said I won't go cwinging and gwovelling?' Denisov interrupted him, and he went on reading his answer.

Rostov did not venture to try and persuade Denisov, though he felt instinctively that the course advised by Tushin and the other officers was the safest, and though he would have been glad to be of service to Denisov. He knew his friend's stubborn will and impetuous temper.

When Denisov had finished reading his venomous diatribe, which took over an hour, Rostov had nothing to say, and in the most dejected frame of mind spent the rest of the day in the society of Denisov's hospital companions who had gathered round again, telling them what he knew and listening to their stories. Denisov maintained a gloomy silence all the evening.

At length, when it was late and Rostov was about to leave, he asked Denisov whether there was anything he could do for him.

'Yes, wait a bit,' said Denisov glancing round at the officers, and taking his papers from under his pillow he went to the window where he had an inkpot, and sat down to write.

'It seems it's no use knocking one's head against a stone wall,' he said, coming from the window and handing Rostov a large envelope. It was the petition addressed to the Emperor which the auditor had drawn up for him, in which Denisov, making no reference to the shortcomings of the commissariat officials, simply asked for a pardon.

'Hand it in. It seems ...' He did not finish but forced his lips to a painfully unnatural smile.

19

HAVING returned to the regiment and reported to the commander the state of Denisov's affairs, Rostov rode to Tilsit with the letter to the Emperor.

On the 13th of June the French and Russian Emperors met at Tilsit. Boris Drubetskoy had asked the important personage on whom he was in attendance to include him in the suite appointed for the occasion.

'I should like to see the great man,' he said in French, alluding to Napoleon, whom hitherto he, like everyone else, had always called Bonaparte.

'You are speaking of Bonaparte?' the general said to him, smiling.

Boris looked at his general inquiringly, and immediately saw that he was being quizzed.

'I am speaking, *mon prince*, of the Emperor Napoleon,' he replied. The general patted him on the shoulder with a smile.

'You will go far,' he said, and took him to Tilsit with him.

Boris was among the few present at the Niemen on the day the two Emperors met. He saw the rafts with the royal monograms, saw Napoleon's progress past the French Guards on the opposite bank, saw the pensive face of the Emperor Alexander as he sat silent in the inn on the bank of the Niemen awaiting Napoleon's arrival. He saw both Emperors get into boats, and Napoleon, who was the first to reach the raft, go forward with swift steps to meet Alexander and hold out his hand to him; then they disappeared together into the pavilion. Ever since he had begun to move in the highest circles Boris had made a practice of watching attentively all that went on around him, and noting it down. At Tilsit he inquired the names of those who had come with Napoleon and about the uniforms they wore, and listened carefully to the utterances of persons of consequence. At the moment the Emperors went into the pavilion he looked at his watch, and did not forget to look at it again when Alexander came out. The interview had lasted one hour and fifty-three minutes, an item which he recorded that evening among other facts which he felt to be of historic importance. As the Emperor's suite was a very small one, to be at Tilsit on the occasion of this interview between the two Emperors was a matter of great moment for a man who prized success in the service, and Boris, having succeeded in this, felt that henceforth his position was perfectly secure. He was not only known by name but people had grown accustomed to his presence and expected to see him. Twice he had executed commissions to the Emperor himself, so that the Sovereign knew his face, and the court, far from cold-shouldering him as at first, when they considered him a new-comer, would now have been surprised had he been absent.

Boris was lodging with another adjutant, the Polish Count Zhilinksy. Zhilinsky, a Pole brought up in Paris, was wealthy and passionately fond of the French, and almost every day of their stay at Tilsit French officers of the Guard and from the French High Command came to lunch or dine with him and Boris.

On the evening of the 24th of June Count Zhilinsky was giving a supper to his French acquaintances. The guest of honour was an aide-de-camp of Napoleon's. Others present included several French officers of the Guard and a page of Napoleon's, a young lad belonging to an old aristocratic French family. That same day Rostov, profiting by the darkness to pass unrecognized, arrived in Tilsit in civilian dress and went straight to the lodging occupied by Zhilinsky and Boris.

Rostov, in common with the whole army from which he rode, was as yet far from having undergone the change of feeling which had taken place at headquarters and in Boris towards Napoleon and the French – who had suddenly been transformed from foes to friends. In the army Bonaparte and the French were still regarded

478

with mixed feelings of animosity, contempt and fear. Only a short time back, in talking with a Cossack officer of Platov's Rostov had argued that if Napoleon were taken prisoner he would be treated not as a sovereign but as a criminal. Quite lately, falling in on the road with a wounded French colonel, Rostov had maintained with heat that no peace could be concluded between a legitimate sovereign and a criminal like Bonaparte. He was therefore strangely startled by the presence of French officers in Boris's rooms, wearing the uniform he had been accustomed to see with very different eyes from the line of pickets. The moment he saw a French officer, who thrust his head out of the door, that warlike feeling of hostility which always took possession of him at the sight of the enemy suddenly seized him. He stood still on the threshold and asked in Russian whether Drubetskoy lived there. Boris, hearing a strange voice in the ante-room, came out to meet him. A shade of annoyance crossed his face when he recognized Rostov.

'Ah, it's you! Glad to see you, very glad,' he said, however, coming forward with a smile. But Rostov had noticed his first reaction.

'I have come at a bad time, it seems. I shouldn't have come but it's a matter of business,' he said coldly.

'No, I was only surprised at your managing to get away from the regiment. I'll be with you in a moment,' he added in French to some-one calling him from within.

'I see I'm intruding,' repeated Rostov.

By this time the look of annoyance had disappeared from Boris's face. Having evidently reflected and made up his mind how to act, with marked ease of manner he took Rostov by both hands and led him into the next room. His eyes, gazing serenely and unflinchingly at Rostov, seemed to be veiled by something – shielded as it were by the blue spectacles of conventional society. So it seemed to Rostov.

'Oh, please now! As if you could come at a wrong time!' said Boris, and he led him into the room where supper was laid and intro-duced him to his guests, mentioning his name and explaining that he was not a civilian but an officer of the hussars and his old friend.

'Count Zhilinsky – *le Comte* N.N. – *le Capitaine* S.S.,' said he, naming his guests. Rostov looked frowningly at the Frenchmen, bowed stiffly and said nothing.

Zhilinsky was obviously not pleased at the advent of this unknown Russian outsider into his circle, and did not speak to Rostov. Boris appeared not to notice the constraint produced by the new-comer and, with the same amiable composure and the same veiled look in his eyes with which he had welcomed Rostov, endeavoured to enliven the conversation. One of the Frenchmen, with characteristic Gallic courtesy, addressed the stubbornly-taciturn Rostov, remarking that the latter had probably come to Tilsit to see the Emperor.

'No, I came on business,' replied Rostov shortly.

Rostov's ill-humour had come on from the moment he detected the dissatisfaction on Boris's face, and as always happens with people who are in a bad temper he imagined they were all looking at him with hostile eyes, and that he was in everyone's way. And in fact he was in everyone's way, for he alone took no part in the conversation, which again became general. The glances the others cast on him seemed to say: 'And what is he sitting here for?' He rose and went up to Boris.

'I do really feel I'm embarrassing you,' he said in a low tone. 'Let me tell you my business, and I'll be off again.'

'Oh no, not at all,' said Boris. 'But if you are tired, come and lie down in my room and have a rest.'

'Yes, really ...'

They went into the little room where Boris slept. Rostov, without sitting down began at once, speaking irritably (as if Boris were in some way to blame), to tell him about Denisov's affair, asking him whether, through his general, he could and would intercede with the Emperor on Denisov's behalf, and get the petition for pardon to him. When they were alone together Rostov felt for the first time that he could not look Boris in the face without a sense of awkwardness. Boris, with one leg crossed over the other and stroking the slender fingers of his right hand with his left, listened to Rostov after the manner of a general listening to the report of a subordinate, now looking away now gazing straight at Rostov with the same veiled look. Each time he did so Rostov felt uncomfortable and cast down his eyes.

'I have heard of cases of this sort, and I know that his Majesty is very strict on such points. I think it would be best not to bring it to the Emperor's attention but to apply directly to the commander of the corps. ... But generally speaking, I believe ...'

'So you don't want to do anything? Well then, say so!' Rostov almost shouted, not looking at Boris.

Boris smiled.

'On the contrary, I will do what I can. Only I thought ...'

At that moment Zhilinsky's voice was heard at the door, calling Boris.

'Well, go along, go along,' said Rostov, and refusing supper and remaining alone in the little room he walked up and down for a long time, listening to the light-hearted French chatter from the next room.

20

THE day on which Rostov arrived in Tilsit could not have been less favourable for proceedings on behalf of Denisov. It was out of the question for him to go himself to the general in attendance, since he was not in uniform and had come to Tilsit without permission, while Boris, even had he wished to, could not have done so on the day following Rostov's appearance. On that day, the 27th of June, the preliminaries of peace were signed. The Emperors exchanged decorations: Alexander received the *Légion d'honneur*, and Napoleon the Russian Order of St Andrew of the first degree; and that was the day arranged for the dinner to be given by a battalion of the French Guards to the Preobrazhensky battalion. The Emperors were to be present at this banquet.

Rostov felt so ill at ease and uncomfortable with Boris that when the latter looked in at him after supper he pretended to be asleep, and next morning left early to avoid another meeting. In a frock-coat and round hat he strolled about the town, staring at the French and their uniforms, and examining the streets and the houses where the Russian and French Emperors were staying. In the main square he saw tables being set up and preparations made for the dinner; in the streets he saw the Russian and French colours draped across from one side to the other, with the letters A and N in huge monograms. In the windows of the houses, too, there were flags and monograms.

'Boris doesn't care to help me, and I don't want to apply to him. That's settled,' thought Nikolai. 'All is over between us, but I'm not going away from here without having done everything I can for Denisov, and certainly not without getting his letter to the Emperor. The Emperor? ... He is here!' thought Rostov, who had unconsciously wandered back to the house occupied by Alexander.

Horses ready saddled were standing before the door and the suite were assembling, evidently preparing for the Emperor to come out.

'At any moment I may see him,' thought Rostov. 'If only I could give him the letter direct, and tell him all. ... Could they really arrest me for my civilian clothes? Surely not. He would understand on whose side justice lies. He understands everything, knows everything. Who can be juster and more magnanimous than he? Besides, even if they did arrest me for being here, what would it matter?' thought he, looking at an officer who was entering the house the Emperor occupied. 'Why, people are going in, I see. Oh, it's all nonsense! I'll go in and hand the letter to the Emperor myself: so much the worse for Drubetskoy who has driven me to it!' And suddenly, with a determination he would never have expected of himself, Rostov, fingering the letter in his pocket, went straight up to the house where the Emperor was staying.

'No, this time I won't miss my opportunity as I did after Austerlitz,' he thought, prepared every moment to meet the Monarch, and conscious of the blood rushing to his heart at the idea. 'I will fall at his feet and beseech him. He will lift me up, hear me out and even thank me. "I am happy when I can do good, but to remedy injustice is my greatest happiness,"' Rostov fancied the Emperor saying. And passing people who looked after him with curiosity, he entered the porch of the Emperor's house.

A broad staircase led straight up from the porch. On the right was a closed door. Below, under the stairs, was a door leading to the rooms on the lower floor.

'Who is it you want?' someone inquired.

'I have a letter, a petition, to hand to his Majesty,' said Nikolai, with a tremor in his voice.

'A petition? This way, please, to the officer on duty' (he was shown the door below). 'Only it won't be accepted.'

On hearing this indifferent voice Rostov grew panic-stricken at what he was doing; the thought of finding himself face to face with the Emperor at any moment was so alluring and consequently so terrifying that he felt like running away, but the attendant who met him opened the door to the officer's room for him, and Rostov went in.

A short stout man of about thirty, in white breeches, high boots and a batiste shirt which he had evidently only just put on, was standing in this room, while his valet buttoned on to the back of his breeches a pair of handsome new braces embroidered in silk that for some reason attracted Rostov's notice. The stout man was speaking to someone in the adjoining room.

'Devilish good figure and in her first bloom,' he was saying, but seeing Rostov he broke off and frowned.

'What do you want? A petition? ...'

'What is it?' asked the person in the other room.

'Another petitioner,' answered the man in the braces.

'Tell him to come back. He'll be out directly, we must go.'

'Come back another time, another time, tomorrow. It's too late. ...'

Rostov turned and was about to go but the man in the braces stopped him.

'Who is the petitioner? What's your name?'

'I come from Major Denisov,' replied Rostov.

'Who are you – an officer?'

'Lieutenant Count Rostov.'

'What audacity! Send it in through the proper channel. And go along with you ... go'; and he began putting on the uniform the valet handed him.

Rostov went back into the hall and noticed that by this time there were a great many officers and generals in full dress standing in the porch, and that he would have to pass through their midst.

Cursing his temerity, his heart sinking at the thought that he might at any moment meet the Emperor and be put to shame before him and placed under arrest, fully alive now to the impropriety of his conduct and repenting of it, Rostov with downcast eyes was making his way out of the house through the brilliant suite when a familiar voice called to him and a hand detained him.

'What are you doing here, sir, in a frock-coat?' demanded a deep voice.

It was a cavalry-general who had won the signal favour of the Emperor during this campaign, and who had formerly commanded the division in which Rostov was serving.

Rostov in dismay began to try and justify himself but, seeing the kindly, jocular face of the general, he drew him aside and in an excited voice explained the whole affair, begging him to intercede for Denisov, whom the general knew.

Having heard Rostov to the end, the general shook his head gravely.

'I'm sorry, very sorry for the gallant fellow. Give me the letter.'

Rostov had scarcely time to hand him the letter and finish telling him about Denisov's case before there were quick steps and the jingling of spurs on the stairs, and the general left his side to move to the porch. The gentlemen of the Emperor's suite ran down the steps and went to their mounts. Hayne, the same groom who had been at Austerlitz, led up the Emperor's horse, and on the stairs was heard the faint creak of a footstep which Rostov knew at once. Forgetting the danger of being recognized, Rostov made his way to the porch together with some inquisitive bystanders, and again after an interval of two years saw the features he adored: the same face, the same glance, the same walk, the same combination of majesty and mildness. ... And the feeling of enthusiasm and love for his Sovereign rose up again in Rostov's heart with all its old force. In the uniform of the Preobrazhensky regiment – white elk-skin breeches and high boots – and wearing a star Rostov did not know (it was the star of the *Légion d'honneur*), the Monarch came out on the steps, carrying his hat under his arm and putting on his glove. He paused and looked about him, brightening everything around by his glance. To one of the generals he spoke a few words, and also recognized Rostov's former commander, gave him a smile and beckoned to him.

All the suite drew back, and Rostov watched the general talking at some length to the Emperor.

The Emperor spoke a word or two in reply and took a step towards his horse. Again the crowd of the suite and the spectators in the street, with Rostov among them, moved closer to the Emperor. Stopping beside his horse with his hand on the saddle, the Emperor turned to the cavalry-general and said in a loud voice, evidently intended to be heard by all:

'I cannot do it, general. I cannot, because the law is mightier than I,' and he put his foot in the stirrup.

The general respectfully inclined his head, and the Monarch got into the saddle and rode down the street at a gallop. Beside himself with enthusiasm, Rostov ran after him with the crowd.

21

IN the public square to which the Emperor rode a battalion of the Preobrazhensky regiment was drawn up facing a battalion of the

French Guards in their bearskin caps, the Russians on the right, the French on the left.

As the Tsar rode up to one flank of the battalions, who presented arms, another group of horsemen galloped up to the opposite flank, and at the head of them Rostov recognized Napoleon. It could be no one else. He came at a gallop, wearing a small hat, a blue uniform open over a white vest, and the ribbon of St Andrew across his breast. He was mounted on a very fine thoroughbred grey Arab horse with a crimson gold-embroidered saddle-cloth. Riding up to Alexander, he raised his hat and as he did so Rostov, with his cavalryman's eye, could not help noticing that Napoleon sat neither well nor firmly in the saddle. The battalions shouted 'Hurrah' and *Vive l'Empereur!* Napoleon said something to Alexander. Both Emperors dismounted and took each other by the hand. Napoleon's face wore a disagreeably artificial smile. Alexander was saying something to him with an affable expression.

In spite of the kicking of the French gendarmes' horses which were keeping the crowd back, Rostov watched every movement of the Emperor Alexander and Bonaparte, never taking his eyes off them. It struck him with surprise that Alexander treated Bonaparte as an equal and that Bonaparte was perfectly at ease with the Russian Tsar, as if this proximity to a monarch were a natural everyday matter to him

Alexander and Napoleon with the long train of their suites moved towards the right flank of the Preobrazhensky battalion, coming straight towards the crowd standing there. The crowd unexpectedly found itself so close to the Emperors that Rostov, in the front row, was afraid he might be recognized.

'Sire, I ask your permission to present the *Légion d'honneur* to the bravest of your soldiers,' said a harsh, precise voice speaking in French and articulating every letter.

It was the diminutive Bonaparte who spoke, looking up straight into Alexander's eyes. Alexander listened attentively to what was said to him and inclining his head smiled amiably.

'To the man who has conducted himself with the greatest courage in this last war,' added Napoleon, laying equal stress on each syllable and, with an assurance and composure revolting to Rostov, scanning the rows of Russian soldiers drawn up before him, all presenting arms and all gazing immovably at their own Emperor.

485

'Will your Majesty allow me to consult the colonel?' said Alexander, and he took a few hasty steps towards Prince Kozlovsky, the commander of the battalion.

Bonaparte meanwhile began to draw the glove from his small white hand, tore it in so doing and threw it away. An aide-de-camp behind him rushed forward and picked it up.

'To whom shall it be given?' the Emperor Alexander asked Kozlovsky in Russian, in a low voice.

'As your Majesty commands.'

The Emperor frowned with annoyance and glancing round said: 'But we must give him an answer.'

Kozlovsky ran his eyes over the ranks with a resolute air, including Rostov, too, in his scrutiny.

'Could he by any possibility choose me?' thought Rostov.

'Lazarev!' the colonel called with a scowl; and Lazarev, the first man in the front rank, stepped briskly forward.

'Where are you off to? Stand still!' various voices whispered to Lazarev, who did not know where he was to go. Lazarev stopped short, with a sidelong scared look at his colonel, and his face twitched, as often happens to soldiers called forward out of the ranks.

Napoleon slightly turned his head and stretched out his plump little hand behind him, as if to take something. The members of his suite, guessing at once what he wanted, whispered and stirred as they passed a small object from one to another, and a page – the same one Rostov had seen the previous evening at Boris's – sprang forward and, bowing respectfully over the outstretched hand and not keeping it waiting a single instant, laid in it an order on a red ribbon. Napoleon, without looking, pressed two fingers together and the badge was between them. Then he approached Lazarev, who stood rolling his eyes and still gazing obstinately at his own Monarch. Napoleon looked round at the Emperor Alexander to imply that what he was doing now he did out of consideration for his ally, and the small white hand holding the order touched one of Lazarev's buttons. It was as though Napoleon knew that it was enough for his hand to deign to touch the soldier's breast for that soldier to be for ever happy, rewarded and distinguished from everyone else in the world. Napoleon merely laid the cross on Lazarev's breast and, dropping his hand, turned towards Alexander as though sure that the cross must needs stay in position. The cross did, in fact, stick on because officious hands, both Russian

486

and French, instantly seized it and fastened it to the uniform. Lazarev glanced morosely at the little man with the white hands who had been doing something to him, and still standing rigidly, presenting arms, looked again into Alexander's eyes, as though he were asking whether he should continue to stand there, or was it his pleasure for him to go now, or perhaps do something else. But receiving no orders he remained for some time, motionless as a statue.

The Emperors remounted and rode away. The Preobrazhensky battalion, breaking ranks, began to mingle with the French Guards, and sat down at the tables prepared for them.

Lazarev was seated in the place of honour. Russian and French officers embraced him, congratulated him and pressed his hand. Crowds of officers and civilians flocked up simply to get a sight of him. A rumble of Russian and French voices and laughter filled the air round the tables in the square. Two officers with flushed faces, looking gay and happy, passed by him.

'What do you say to the banquet, my boy? All served on silver plate,' remarked one of them. 'Seen Lazarev?'

'Yes.'

'Tomorrow, I hear, the Preobrazhenskys are to give them a dinner.'

'I say, but what luck for Lazarev! Twelve hundred francs pension for life.'

'How's this for a head-piece, lads!' shouted a Preobrazhensky soldier, donning a shaggy French cap.

'First-class! Suits you down to the ground!'

'Have you heard the password?' asked one Guards officer of another. 'The day before yesterday it was "*Napoléon, France, bravoure*"; yesterday was "*Alexandre, Russie, grandeur*". Our Emperor gives it one day and Napoleon the next. Tomorrow the Emperor will present a St George's cross to the bravest man in the French Guards. He can't help it. Must return the compliment.'

Boris and his friend Zhilinsky also came along to see the banquet to the Preobrazhensky regiment. On his way back Boris noticed Rostov standing by the corner of a house.

'Rostov! How are you? We missed each other,' he said, and could not refrain from asking what was the matter, so strangely dismal and troubled was Rostov's face.

'Nothing, nothing,' replied Rostov.

'You'll call round ?'

'Yes, by and by.'

Rostov stood a long while at the corner, watching the feast from a distance. His brain was seething in an agonizing confusion which he could not work out to any conclusion. Horrible doubts were stirring in his soul. He thought of Denisov and the change that had come over him, and his surrender, and the whole hospital with those amputated legs and arms, and its dirt and disease. So vividly did he recall that hospital stench of putrefaction that he looked round to see where the smell was coming from. Then he thought of that self-satisfied Bonaparte with his little white hand, who was now an emperor, liked and respected by Alexander. For what, then, those severed arms and legs, why those dead men ? Then his mind went to Lazarev rewarded and Denisov punished and unpardoned. He caught himself harbouring such strange reflections that he was terrified at them.

Hunger and the savoury smell of the Preobrazhensky dinner roused him from his reverie: he must have something to eat before going away. He went to an hotel he had noticed that morning. There he found so many people, among them officers who like himself had come in civilian dress, that he had difficulty in getting dinner. Two officers of his own division joined him at table. The conversation naturally turned on the peace. The two officers, Rostov's comrades, like most of the army, were dissatisfied with the peace concluded after the battle of Friedland. They declared that if we had only held out a little longer Napoleon would have been done for, as his troops had neither provisions nor ammunition. Nikolai ate and drank (chiefly the latter) in silence. He finished a couple of bottles of wine by himself. The conflict working within him still fretted him, and found no solution. He was afraid to give way to his thoughts yet could not rid himself of them. Suddenly, when one of his companions remarked that it was humiliating to see the French, Rostov began to shout with uncalled-for violence, and therefore much to the officers' surprise:

'And how, pray, can you judge what would have been best ?' he cried, the blood rushing to his face. 'Why do you criticize the Emperor's actions ? What right have we to sit in judgement on him ? We cannot appreciate or understand the Emperor's aims or actions!'

'But I never said a word about the Emperor!' protested the officer, unable to find any other interpretation for Rostov's outburst than that he was drunk.

But Rostov did not heed him.

'We are not in the diplomatic service, we are soldiers and nothing more,' he went on. 'Command us to die – then we die. If we are punished, it means we're in the wrong; it's not for us to judge. If it's his Majesty the Emperor's pleasure to recognize Bonaparte as emperor and to conclude an alliance with him, it must be the right thing to do. If once we begin sitting in judgement and arguing about everything, there will be nothing sacred left. If we take that line we shall soon be saying there is no God, no nothing!' shouted Nikolai, banging the table with his fist. His outcry seemed utterly irrelevant to his listeners, but it was quite consistent with the train of his own thoughts.

'Our business is to do our duty, to fight, and not to think! And that's the sum of it!' he concluded.

'And to drink!' said one of the officers, who had no desire for a quarrel.

'Yes, and to drink!' agreed Nikolai. 'Hey, there!' he shouted. 'Another bottle!'

PART THREE

I

In the year 1808 the Emperor Alexander went to Erfurt for another interview with the Emperor Napoleon, and in the upper circles of Petersburg society there was much talk of the magnificence of this imperial occasion.

By 1809 the intimacy between 'the world's two arbiters', as Napoleon and Alexander were called, was such that when Napoleon declared war on Austria a Russian corps crossed the frontier in support of their former enemy, Bonaparte, against our former ally, the Austrian Emperor, and court circles speculated on a possible marriage between Napoleon and one of the Emperor Alexander's sisters. But besides considerations of foreign policy the attention of Russian society was at that time directed with keen interest on the internal changes taking place in every department of the administration.

Meanwhile life – actual everyday life with its essential concerns of health and sickness, work and recreation, and its intellectual preoccupations with philosophy, science, poetry, music, love, friendship, hatred, passion – ran its regular course, independent and heedless of political alliance or enmity with Napoleon Bonaparte and of all potential reforms.

*

Prince Andrei had spent two years uninterruptedly in the country. All the projects Pierre had attempted on his estates – and continually switching from one thing to another and never carried through – had been brought to fruition by Prince Andrei quietly and with no noticeable exertion. He possessed in the highest degree a quality Pierre lacked, that practical tenacity which without fuss or undue effort on his part gave impetus to any enterprise.

On one of his estates the three hundred serfs were transformed into free agricultural labourers (this was one of the first instances of the kind in Russia). On other estates the forced husbandry service was commuted for a quit-rent. At Bogucharovo a trained midwife was engaged at his expense to assist the peasant women in childbirth, and a priest paid to teach reading and writing to the children of the peasants and household servants.

Prince Andrei spent half his time at Bald Hills with his father and son, who was still in the nursery. The other half he passed at what his father called his 'Bogucharovo Hermitage'. Despite the indifference to the affairs of the world he had displayed to Pierre, he diligently followed all that went on, received many books, and was amazed to find that visitors arriving fresh from Petersburg, the very vortex of life, to see him or his father, lagged far behind himself – who never left the country – in knowledge of what was happening in home and foreign affairs.

In addition to looking after his estates and much general reading of the most varied kind, Prince Andrei was engaged at this time upon a critical survey of our last two unfortunate campaigns, and in working out a scheme of reform for our army rules and regulations.

In the spring of 1809 Prince Andrei set off to visit the Ryazan estates which his son, whose trustee he was, had inherited.

Warmed by the spring sunshine he sat in the *calèche*, looking at the new grass, the young leaves on the birch-trees and the first flecks of white spring clouds floating across the clear blue sky. He was not thinking of anything, but looked about him, carefree and absent-minded.

They crossed the ferry where he had talked with Pierre a year before. They drove through the muddy village, past threshing floors and green fields of winter rye, downhill by a drift of snow still lying near the bridge, uphill along a clay road hollowed into runnels by the rain, past strips of stubble land and a copse touched here and there with green, and into a birch forest extending along both sides of the road. In the forest it was almost hot; there was not a breath of wind. The birches, all studded with sticky green leaves, did not stir, and lilac-coloured flowers and the first blades of green grass lifted and pushed their way between last year's leaves. Dotted here and there among the birches, small fir-trees were an unpleasant reminder of winter with their coarse evergreen. The horses began to snort as they entered the forest and the sweat glistened on their coats.

The footman, Piotr, made some remark to the coachman; the coachman agreed. But apparently this was not enough for Piotr: he turned round on the box to his master.

'How mild it is, your Excellency!' he said with a respectful smile.

'What?'

'Mild, your Excellency.'

'What is he talking about?' wondered Prince Andrei. 'Oh, the spring, I suppose,' he thought, looking about him on either side. 'And indeed everything is green already. ... How early! And the birches and the wild cherry and alder too are all beginning to come out. ... But I don't see any sign of the oak yet. Oh yes, there's one, there's an oak!'

At the edge of the road stood an oak. Probably ten times the age of the birches that formed the bulk of the forest, it was ten times as thick and twice as tall as they. It was an enormous tree, double a man's span, with ancient scars where branches had long ago been lopped off and bark stripped away. With huge ungainly limbs sprawling unsymmetrically, with gnarled hands and fingers, it stood, an aged monster, angry and scornful, among the smiling birch-trees. This oak alone refused to yield to the season's spell, spurning both spring and sunshine.

'Spring, and love, and happiness!' this oak seemed to say. 'Are you not weary of the same stupid, meaningless tale? Always the same old delusion! There is no spring, no sun, no happiness! Look at those strangled, lifeless fir-trees, everlastingly the same; and look at me too, sticking out broken excoriated fingers, from my back and my sides, where they grew. Just as they grew; here I stand, and I have no faith in your hopes and illusions.'

Prince Andrei turned several times to look back at this oak, as they drove through the forest, as though expecting some message from it. There were flowers and grass under the oak, too, but it stood among them scowling, rigid, misshapen and grim as ever.

'Yes, the oak is right, a thousand times right,' mused Prince Andrei. 'Others – the young – may be caught anew by this delusion, but we know what life is – our life is finished!'

A whole sequence of new ideas, pessimistic but bitter-sweet, stirred up in Prince Andrei's soul in connexion with that oak-tree. During this journey he considered his life as it were afresh, and arrived at his old conclusion, restful in its hopelessness: that it was not for him to begin anything new, but that he must live out his life, content to do no harm, dreading nothing and aspiring after nothing.

2

PRINCE ANDREI was compelled by his obligations as trustee of the Ryazan property to call upon the local Marshal of the Nobility. This was Count Ilya Rostov, and in the middle of May Prince Andrei went to see him.

It was by now the hot period of spring. The woods were already in full leaf. It was dusty, and so hot that the sight of water made one long to bathe.

Depressed and preoccupied with the business about which he had to consult the Marshal, Prince Andrei drove along the avenue leading to the Rostovs' house at Otradnoe. Behind some trees on the right he heard merry girlish cries, and caught sight of a bevy of young girls running to cross the path of his *calèche*. In front of the rest, and nearer to him, ran a dark-haired, remarkably slight, black-eyed girl in a yellow print dress, with a white pocket-handkerchief on her head from under which strayed loose locks of hair. The girl was shouting something, but then, seeing a stranger, ran back laughing, without looking at him.

Prince Andrei for some reason felt a sudden pang. The day was so lovely, the sun so bright, everything around so gay; but that slim pretty girl did not know or care to know of his existence, and was content and happy in her own life – foolish no doubt – but light-hearted and carefree and remote from him. 'What is she so glad about? What are her thoughts? Not of army regulations or Ryazan serfs and their quit-rents. What is she thinking of? Why is she so happy?' Prince Andrei asked himself with instinctive curiosity.

In 1809 Count Rostov was living at Otradnoe just as he had done in previous years; that is, entertaining almost the whole province with hunts, theatricals, dinner-parties and music. He welcomed Prince Andrei, as he did any new visitor, and insisted on his staying the night.

Several times in the course of a tedious day during which he was monopolized by his elderly hosts and the more distinguished of the guests (the old count's house was crowded on account of an approaching name-day), Prince Andrei found himself glancing at Natasha, laughing and amusing herself among the young people of the party, and wondering each time, 'What is she thinking about? What makes her so happy?'

That night, alone in new surroundings, it was long before he could get to sleep. He read awhile, then put out his candle but afterwards relit it. It was hot in the room with the inside shutters closed. He was annoyed with the silly old man (as he called Rostov) who had detained him, declaring that the necessary documents had not yet arrived from town, and he was vexed with himself for having stayed.

He got up and went to the window to open it. As soon as he drew the shutters the moonlight flooded the room as though it had long been waiting at the window. He unfastened the casement. The still night was cool and beautiful. Just outside the window was a row of pollard-trees, looking black on one side and silvery bright on the other. Under the trees grew some sort of lush, wet, bushy vegetation with leaves and stems touched here and there with silver. Farther away, beyond the dark trees, a roof glittered with dew; to the right was a great, leafy tree with satiny white trunk and branches, and above it shone the moon, almost full, in a pale, practically starless, spring sky. Prince Andrei leaned his elbows on the window-ledge, and his eyes gazed at the heavens.

His room was on the first floor. Those above were also occupied, and by people who were not asleep either. He heard feminine voices overhead.

'Just once more,' said a girlish voice above him which Prince Andrei recognized at once.

'But when are you coming to bed?' replied a second voice.

'I shan't sleep – I can't, what's the use? Come, this will be the last time. ...'

Two girlish voices broke into a snatch of song, forming the final phrase of a duet.

'Oh, it's exquisite! Well, now let's say good-night and go to sleep.'

'You go to sleep, but I can't,' said the first voice, coming nearer to the window. She evidently thrust her head right out, for he could hear the rustle of her dress and even her breathing. Everything was hushed and turned to stone – the moon and her light, and the shadows. Prince Andrei, too, dared not stir, for fear of betraying his unintentional presence.

'Sonya! Sonya!' said the first voice again. 'Oh, how can you sleep? Just look how lovely it is! Oh, how glorious! Do wake up, Sonya!'

494

and there were almost tears in the voice. 'There never, never was such an exquisite night.'

Sonya made some reluctant reply.

'No, but do look what a moon! ... Oh, how lovely! Do come here. Darling, precious, come here! There, you see? I feel like squatting down on my heels, putting my arms round my knees like this, tight – as tight as can be – and flying away! Like this. ...'

'Take care, or you'll fall out.'

He heard the sound of a scuffle and Sonya's disapproving voice: 'Why, it's past one o'clock.'

'Oh, you only spoil things for me. All right, go to bed then, go along!'

Again all was silent, but Prince Andrei knew she was still sitting there. From time to time he heard a soft rustle or a sigh.

'O God, O God, what does it mean?' she exclaimed suddenly. 'To bed then, if I must!' and she slammed the casement.

'And for her I might as well not exist!' thought Prince Andrei while he listened to her voice, for some reason hoping yet dreading she might say something about him. 'And there she is again! As if it were on purpose,' thought he.

All at once such an unexpected turmoil of youthful thoughts and hopes, contrary to the whole tenor of his life, surged up in his heart that, feeling incapable of explaining his condition to himself, he made haste to lie down and fall asleep.

3

NEXT morning, having taken leave of no one but the count, and not waiting for the ladies to appear, Prince Andrei set off for home.

It was already the beginning of June when, on his return journey, he drove into the birch-forest where the gnarled old oak had made so strange and memorable an impression on him. In the forest the harness-bells sounded still more muffled than they had done four weeks earlier, for now all was thick, shady and dense, and the young fir-trees dotted about here and there did not jar on the general beauty but, yielding to the mood around, showed delicately green with their feathery young shoots.

The whole day had been hot. Somewhere a storm was gathering, but only a small rain-cloud had sprinkled the dust of the road and the

495

sappy leaves. The left side of the forest lay dark in the shade, the right side gleamed wet and shiny in the sunlight, faintly undulating in the breeze. Everything was in blossom, the nightingales trilled and carolled, now near, now far away.

'Yes, that old oak with which I saw eye to eye was here in this forest,' thought Prince Andrei. 'But whereabouts?' he wondered again, looking at the left side of the road and, without realizing, without recognizing it, admiring the very oak he sought. The old oak, quite transfigured, spread out a canopy of dark, sappy green, and seemed to swoon and sway in the rays of the evening sun. There was nothing to be seen now of knotted fingers and scars, of old doubts and sorrows. Through the rough, century-old bark, even where there were no twigs, leaves had sprouted, so juicy, so young that it was hard to believe that aged veteran had borne them.

'Yes, it is the same oak,' thought Prince Andrei, and all at once he was seized by an irrational, spring-like feeling of joy and renewal. All the best moments of his life of a sudden rose to his memory. Austerlitz, with that lofty sky, the reproachful look on his dead wife's face, Pierre at the ferry, that girl thrilled by the beauty of the night, and that night itself and the moon and ... everything suddenly crowded back into his mind.

'No, life is not over at thirty-one,' Prince Andrei decided all at once, finally and irrevocably. 'It is not enough for me to know what I have in me – everyone else must know it too: Pierre, and that young girl who wanted to fly away into the sky; all of them must learn to know me, in order that my life may not be lived for myself alone while others, like that young girl, live so apart from it, but may be reflected in them all, and they and I may live in harmony together.'

*

On reaching home Prince Andrei decided to go to Petersburg in the autumn, and invented all sorts of grounds for this decision. A whole series of sensible, logical reasons showing it to be essential for him to visit Petersburg, and even to re-enter the service, kept springing to his mind. Indeed, it now passed his comprehension how he could ever have doubted the necessity of taking an active share in life, just as a month before he could not have believed that the idea of leaving the country could ever enter his head. It seemed clear to him that all he had experienced would be wasted and pointless unless he applied it to work of some kind and again played an active part. He could not understand how formerly he could have let such wretched arguments convince him that he would be lowering himself if after the lessons he had received from life he were to believe in the possibility of being useful or look forward to happiness and love. Now reason suggested quite the opposite. After his journey to Ryazan Prince Andrei began to tire of the country; his old pursuits ceased to interest him, and often when sitting alone in his study he got up, went to the looking-glass and contemplated his own face for a long while. Then he would turn away to the portrait of his dead Lisa, who, with her curls pinned up *à la grecque*, looked down at him tenderly and gaily out of the gilt frame. She no longer said those terrible words to him, but watched him with a simple, merry, quizzical look. And Prince Andrei, clasping his hands behind his back, would spend much time walking up and down the room, now frowning, now smiling, as he brooded over those preposterous, inexpressible ideas, secret as a crime, which were connected with Pierre, with fame, with the girl at the window, the oak, with woman's beauty, and love, which had altered his whole life. And if anyone came into his room at such moments he would be particularly curt, forbidding, determined and, above all, disagreeably rational.

'*Mon cher*,' Princess Maria might happen to say, entering at such a moment, 'little Nikolai can't go out today, it is very cold.'

'If it were hot,' Prince Andrei would answer his sister with peculiar dryness, 'he could go out in nothing but a smock, but as it is cold you will have to dress him in the warm clothes which were designed for that purpose. That is what follows from the fact that it is cold; not keeping a child indoors when it needs the fresh air,' he would say with exaggerated logicality, as it were punishing someone else for all that secret illogical element working within him.

On such occasions Princess Maria would think to herself how much intellectual activity dries up a man.

4

PRINCE ANDREI arrived in Petersburg in the August of 1809. It was the period when the youthful Speransky was at the zenith of his fame and his reforms were being pushed forward with the utmost vigour. That same August the Emperor was thrown from his carriage, injured his leg and was laid up for three weeks at Peterhof, seeing Speransky every day and no one else. At this period were elaborated the two famous decrees that so alarmed society – abolishing court ranks and introducing examinations to qualify for the grades of Collegiate Assessor and State Councillor. A complete imperial constitution was also under discussion, destined to revolutionize the existing order of government in Russia, legal, administrative and financial, from the privy council down to the district tribunals. Now those vague liberal dreams with which the Emperor Alexander had ascended the throne, and which he had tried to put into effect with the aid of Tchartorizhsky, Novosiltsov, Kochubey and Stroganov – whom he himself in jest had called his *comité du salut public* – were taking shape and being realized.

Now all these men were replaced by Speransky on the civil side and Arakcheyev on the military. Soon after his arrival Prince Andrei, as a gentleman of the chamber, presented himself at court and at a levée. The Emperor, though he met him twice, did not favour him with a single word. It had always seemed to Prince Andrei that he was antipathetic to the Emperor and that the latter disliked his face and general personality, and the cold repellent glance the Emperor gave him further confirmed this surmise. Courtiers explained to Prince Andrei that the Tsar's neglect of him was due to his Majesty's displeasure at Bolkonsky's not having served since 1805.

'I know myself that one cannot help one's likes and dislikes,' thought Prince Andrei, 'so it would be no use to present my proposal for the reform of the military code in person to the Emperor, but the project will speak for itself.'

He mentioned his memorandum to an old field-marshal, a friend of his father's. The field-marshal made an appointment to see him, received him graciously and promised to put the matter before the Emperor. A few days later Prince Andrei was notified that he was to call upon the minister of war, Count Arakcheyev.

At nine o'clock on the morning of the day appointed Prince Andrei entered Count Arakcheyev's waiting-room.

He did not know Arakcheyev personally and had never seen him; but what he had heard about him inspired but little respect for the man.

'He is minister of war, a person the Emperor trusts; his personal qualities are no concern of anyone's; it is his business to examine my project, consequently he alone could get it adopted,' reflected Prince Andrei as he waited among a number of important and unimportant people in Count Arakcheyev's ante-room.

During the period of his service – for the most part as an adjutant – Prince Andrei had seen the ante-rooms of many high dignitaries, and he was quick to recognize the various types. Count Arakcheyev's ante-room had quite a special character. The faces of the unimportant people awaiting their turn for an audience showed embarrassment and servility; those of higher rank gave a general impression of awkwardness concealed behind a mask of ease and ironical derision of themselves, their position, and the person they were waiting to see. Some walked thoughtfully up and down, others whispered and laughed, and Prince Andrei caught the nickname 'Strong-man Andreich' and 'We shall get it hot from the governor', referring to Count Arakcheyev. One general (a person of consequence), unmistakably chagrined at being kept waiting so long, sat crossing and uncrossing his legs and smiling disdainfully to himself.

But the moment the door opened all faces expressed one and the same sentiment – terror. Prince Andrei for the second time asked the adjutant on duty to take in his name, but he received a sarcastic stare and was told that his turn would come in due course. After several others had been shown in and out of the minister's room by the adjutant on duty, an officer whose abject, terrified air struck Prince Andrei was admitted to the fearful audience. The officer's interview lasted a long time. Suddenly a harsh bellowing was heard on the other side of the door, and the officer, pale and trembling, came out and clutching his head passed through the ante-room.

Immediately after this, Prince Andrei was conducted to the door and the officer on duty said in a whisper: 'To the right, at the window.'

Prince Andrei entered a plain, tidy study, and saw at the table a man of forty with a long waist, a long closely-cropped head, deep wrinkles, scowling brows over dull greenish-hazel eyes and a red drooping nose. Arakcheyev turned his head towards him without looking at him.

'What is your petition?' asked Arakcheyev.

'I am not ... petitioning – for anything, your Excellency,' replied Prince Andrei quietly.

Arakcheyev's eyes turned to him.

'Sit down,' he said. 'Prince Bolkonsky?'

'I have no petition to make. His Majesty the Emperor has deigned to put into your Excellency's hands a project submitted by me ...'

'Allow me to inform you, my dear sir – I have read your project,' interrupted Arakcheyev, speaking the first words with a certain courtesy and then – without looking at Prince Andrei – gradually relapsing into a tone of querulous contempt. 'You are proposing new military laws? There are regulations in plenty and no one carries them out. Nowadays everyone's drawing up new regulations: it's easier to write 'em than to carry them out.'

'I have come at his Majesty the Emperor's wish to learn from your Excellency how you propose to deal with the memorandum I have presented,' said Prince Andrei politely.

'I have endorsed a resolution on your memorandum and forwarded it to the Committee. I do *not* approve of it,' said Arakcheyev, getting up and taking a paper from his writing-table. 'Here!' and he handed it to Prince Andrei.

Across the paper was scrawled in pencil, without capital letters or punctuation, and misspelt: 'unsound seeing its only an imitation of the french military coad and needlessly departing from our own articles of war.'

'To what Committee has the memorandum been referred?' inquired Prince Andrei.

'To the Committee on Army Regulations, and I have recommended your Honour being enrolled as a member. Only without salary.'

Prince Andrei smiled.

'I have no wish for one.'

'A member without salary,' repeated Arakcheyev. 'I wish you good day. Hey! Call the next one! Who else is there?' he shouted, bowing to Prince Andrei.

5

WHILE waiting for the formal notification of his appointment to the Committee, Prince Andrei looked up old acquaintances, especially those he knew to be in power and whose assistance he might need. He experienced now in Petersburg a sensation analogous to that which he had had on the eve of a battle, when he was fretted by restless curiosity and irresistibly attracted to those higher spheres where the future was being shaped, that future on which hung the fate of millions. From the angry irritability of the older generation, the inquisitiveness of the uninitiated, the reserve of the initiated, the hurry and preoccupation of everyone, and the innumerable committees and commissions – he heard of new ones every day – he felt that now, in the year 1809, here in Petersburg, some vast civil battle was in preparation, the commander-in-chief of which was a mysterious person whom he did not know but imagined to be a man of genius – Speransky. And this activity for reform, of which Prince Andrei had a confused idea, and Speransky its moving spirit, began to interest him so keenly that the matter of the army regulations very soon receded to a secondary place in his mind.

Prince Andrei found himself most favourably placed for securing a good reception in the highest and most diverse Petersburg circles of the day. The reforming party warmly welcomed and courted him, in the first place because he was said to be clever and very well read, and secondly because his emancipation of his serfs had gained him the reputation of being a liberal. The party of the dissatisfied older generation turned to him expecting his sympathy in their disapproval of the innovations, simply because he was the son of his father. The feminine world, *society*, received him gladly because he was rich, distinguished, a good match, and almost a new-comer, with a halo of romance on account of his supposed death in battle and the tragic loss of his wife. Moreover, the general opinion of all who had known him previously was that he had greatly improved during these last five years, having softened and grown more manly, lost his former affectation, pride and contemptuous irony, and had acquired the serenity that comes with years. People talked about him, were interested in him and eager to see him.

The day after his interview with Count Arakcheyev, Prince Andrei spent the evening at Count Kochubey's. He described to the count his interview with Strong-man Andreich (Kochubey spoke of Arakcheyev by that nickname with the same vaguely scoffing note in his voice which Prince Andrei had noticed in the minister of war's ante-room).

'Mon cher,' said Kochubey, 'even in this case you can't do without Mihail Mihailovich Speransky. He is the great factotum. I'll speak to him. He promised to come in this evening.'

'But what has Speransky to do with army regulations?' asked Prince Andrei.

Kochubey shook his head smilingly, as if wondering at Bolkonsky's simplicity.

'He and I were talking about you the other day,' Kochubey continued, 'about your free husbandmen ...'

'Oh, so it was you, prince, who freed your serfs?' said an old man of Catherine's time, looking disdainfully at Bolkonsky.

'It was a small estate which brought in a very meagre income,' replied Prince Andrei, trying to minimize what he had done so as not to irritate the old man needlessly.

'Afraid of being late,' said the old man, looking at Kochubey. 'There's one thing I don't understand,' he continued. 'Who is to till the land if they are emancipated? It is easy to write laws, but hard work to govern. In the same way now, I should like to ask you, count, who will be departmental heads when everybody has to pass examinations?'

'Those who pass the examinations, I suppose,' answered Kochubey, crossing his legs and looking about him.

'Take Pryanichnikov now, one of my subordinates, a capital fellow, a priceless man, but he's sixty - is he to go up for examination?'

'Yes, that is where the difficulty lies, since education is not at all general, but ...'

Count Kochubey did not finish. He got up, and taking Prince Andrei by the arm went to meet a tall, bald, fair-haired man of about forty with a large open forehead and a long face of strange and singular pallor. The new-comer wore a blue swallow-tail coat with a cross suspended from his neck and a star on his left breast. It was Speransky. Prince Andrei recognized him at once, and his heart thrilled, as happens at the great moments of one's life. Whether it was a thrill of respect, envy or anticipation, he did not know. Speransky's whole figure was of a peculiar type so that it was impossible to mistake him for a second. Never in any one of the circles in which Prince Andrei lived had he seen such calm, such self-possession allied to such awkward, ungainly movements; never had he seen so resolute yet gentle an expression as that in those half-closed, rather humid eyes, or such firmness as in that smile that meant nothing. Never had he heard a voice so delicate, smooth and soft; but what struck him most of all was the tender whiteness of face and hands - the hands, especially, which were rather broad yet extraordinarily plump, soft and white. Such whiteness and softness Prince Andrei had seen only in the faces of soldiers who had lain long in hospital. This was Speransky, Secretary of State, the Emperor's confidential adviser and his companion at Erfurt, where he had more than once met and talked with Napoleon.

Speransky did not shift his eyes from one face to another as people involuntarily do on entering a large company, and he was in no hurry to speak. He spoke slowly, sure of being listened to, and looked only at the person to whom he was talking.

Prince Andrei followed Speransky's every word and gesture with keen attention. As is often the case with men, particularly with those who judge their fellows severely, Prince Andrei, on meeting anyone new – especially anyone whom, like Speransky, he knew by reputation – always hoped to discover in him the perfection of human qualities.

Speransky told Kochubey he was sorry he had been unable to come sooner, as he had been detained at the palace. He did not say that the Emperor had kept him, and this affectation of modesty did not escape Prince Andrei. When Kochubey presented Prince Andrei, Speransky slowly transferred his eyes to Bolkonsky with the same smile on his face, and gazed at him in silence.

'I am very glad to make your acquaintance. I have heard of you, as everyone has,' he said.

Kochubey gave a brief account of Bolkonsky's reception by Arakcheyev. Speransky's smile broadened.

'The chairman of the Committee on Army Regulations is my good friend Monsieur Magnitsky,' he said, articulating every syllable and every word distinctly, 'and if you like I can put you in touch with him.' (He paused at the full stop.) 'I hope that you will find him sympathetic and willing to further anything that is reasonable.'

A little circle had immediately formed round Speransky, and the old man who had talked of his subordinate Pryanichnikov addressed a question to him.

Prince Andrei, taking no part in the conversation, watched Speransky's every gesture – Speransky, not long since an insignificant divinity student, who now held in his hands, those plump white hands, the fate of Russia, so Bolkonsky thought. He was struck by the extraordinarily scornful composure with which Speransky answered the old man. He appeared to drop him condescending words from an immeasurable height. When the old man began to speak too loudly

Speransky smiled and said that he could not judge of the advantage or disadvantage of what the Sovereign saw fit to approve.

Having talked for a little while in the general circle, Speransky rose and going over to Prince Andrei drew him away to the other end of the room. It was plain that he thought it necessary to interest himself in Bolkonsky.

'I have not had a chance to exchange two words with you, prince, thanks to the animated conversation in which that venerable gentleman involved me,' he said with a smile of bland contempt by which he seemed to imply that he and Prince Andrei were at one in recognizing the insignificance of the people with whom he had just been talking. This flattered Prince Andrei. 'I have known of you for a long time: to begin with from your action with regard to your serfs, the first instance of the kind among us, an example which it would be desirable to find generally followed; and secondly because you are one of those gentlemen of the chamber who have not considered themselves affronted by the new decree concerning the ranks allotted to courtiers, which is provoking so much discussion and cavil.'

'No,' said Prince Andrei, 'my father did not wish me to take advantage of the privilege. I began the service from the lower grades.'

'Your father, a man of the older generation, evidently stands far above our contemporaries who so condemn this measure, which merely re-establishes natural justice.'

'I think, however, that there is some ground for criticism,' said Prince Andrei, trying to resist Speransky's influence, of which he was beginning to feel conscious. It was distasteful for him to agree at every point: he felt a desire to contradict. Though he usually spoke easily and well, he now found some difficulty in expressing himself while talking with Speransky. He was too much absorbed in studying the personality of the famous man.

'The ground of personal ambition maybe,' Speransky put in quietly.

'And to some extent in the interests of the State too,' said Prince Andrei.

'How do you mean?' asked Speransky, mildly lowering his eyes.

'I am an admirer of Montesquieu,' replied Prince Andrei, 'and his idea that *le principe des monarchies est l'honneur* seems to me incontrovertible. Certain rights and privileges for the aristocracy appear to me to be the means of maintaining this sentiment.'

The smile vanished from Speransky's pallid face, which gained enormously from the change. Apparently Prince Andrei's thought interested him.

'If you regard the question from that point of view,' he began in French, which he pronounced with obvious difficulty, and speaking even more slowly than in Russian but with perfect composure. He went on to say that honour, *l'honneur*, cannot be upheld by privileges prejudicial to the working of the government service; that honour, *l'honneur*, is either a negative concept of not doing what is reprehensible, or it is a notorious source of the impulse which stimulates us to win commendation and rewards that bear witness to it.

His arguments were concise, simple and clear.

'An institution that upholds honour, that source of emulation, similar to the *Légion d'honneur* of the great Emperor Napoleon, is not prejudicial but helpful to the success of the service, but that is not true of class or court prerogatives.'

'I do not dispute that but it cannot be denied that court privileges have attained the same end,' returned Prince Andrei. 'Every courtier considers himself bound to fulfil his functions worthily.'

'Yet you do not care to avail yourself of your prerogatives, prince,' said Speransky, indicating by a smile that he wished to conclude amiably an argument embarrassing to his companion. 'If you will do me the honour of calling on me on Wednesday,' he added, 'I shall by that time have seen Magnitsky and have something to tell you that may interest you; and, moreover, I shall have the pleasure of a more circumstantial conversation with you.' Closing his eyes, he bowed and, trying to escape unnoticed, slipped from the room *à la française*, without saying good-bye.

6

DURING the first weeks of his stay in Petersburg Prince Andrei found all the habits of thought he had formed during his life of seclusion in the country entirely obscured by the petty preoccupations which engrossed him in that city.

Every evening on his return home he would jot down in his note-book four or five unavoidable visits or appointments for specified times. The mechanism of life, the arrangement of the day so as to be punctual everywhere, absorbed the greater part of his vital energy. He did nothing – he neither thought nor had time to think, and whatever he said in conversation, and he talked well, was merely the fruit of his meditations in the country.

He sometimes noticed with dissatisfaction that he repeated the same remark on the same day in different circles. But he was so busy for whole days together that he had no time to reflect that he was doing nothing.

As on their first meeting at Kochubey's, Speransky produced a strong impression on Prince Andrei on the Wednesday, when he received him *tête-à-tête* at his own house and talked to him long and confidentially.

To Bolkonsky so many people appeared contemptible and insignificant, and he had such a powerful longing to find in someone the living pattern of perfection towards which he was striving, that it was easy for him to believe he had discovered in Speransky his ideal of a perfectly rational and virtuous man. Had Speransky sprung from the same class in society to which Prince Andrei belonged, had he possessed the same breeding and moral traditions, Bolkonsky would soon have detected the weak and prosaically human side of his character; but as it was, Speransky's strange and logical turn of mind inspired him with respect the more because he did not altogether understand it. Besides this, Speransky, either because he appreciated Prince Andrei's abilities or because he considered it necessary to win him to his side, showed off his cool, easy wit before Prince Andrei and flattered him with that subtle flattery which goes hand in hand with conceit, and consists in a tacit assumption that one's companion is the only man besides oneself capable of understanding the folly of the rest of the world, and the sagacity and profundity of one's own ideas.

In the course of their long conversation on the Wednesday evening Speransky more than once remarked: '*We* regard everything that rises above the common level of rooted custom ...'; or, with a smile, 'But *our* idea is that the wolves should be fed and the sheep kept safe ...'; or '*They* cannot understand this ...'; and always with a tone and look that implied: '*We* – you and I – understand what *they* are and who *we* are.'

This preliminary long conversation with Speransky only served to strengthen the feeling produced in Prince Andrei at their first meeting. He saw in him a man of vast intellect and sober, accurate judgement who by his energy and persistence had attained power, which he was using solely for the welfare of Russia. In Prince Andrei's eyes Speransky was precisely the man he would have liked to be himself – able to find a rational explanation for all the phenomena of life, recognizing as important only what was logical, and capable of applying the standard of reason to everything. Everything seemed so simple, so lucid, in Speransky's exposition of it that Prince Andrei involuntarily agreed with him on every point. If he argued and raised objections it was for the express purpose of maintaining his independence and not submitting to Speransky's opinions entirely. Everything was right, everything was as it should be: only one thing disconcerted Prince Andrei. This was Speransky's cold, mirror-like eye which seemed to refuse all admittance to his soul, and his flabby white hands which Prince Andrei instinctively watched as one watches the hands of those who possess power. That mirror-like gaze and those delicate hands somehow irritated Prince Andrei. He was disagreeably struck too by the excessive contempt for others that he observed in Speransky, and the various shifts in the arguments he employed to buttress his opinion. He made use of every possible mental device, except analogy, and was too venturesome, it seemed to Prince Andrei, in passing from one to another. At one moment he would take his stand as a practical man and condemn visionaries; next as a satirist he was making ironical sport of his opponents; then he would become severely logical, or suddenly fly off into the domain of metaphysics. (This last resource was one he very frequently employed.) He would transfer a question to metaphysical heights, pass on to definitions of space, time and thought, and having deduced the refutation he needed descend again to the plane of the original discussion.

What impressed Prince Andrei as the leading trait of Speransky's mentality was his absolute and unshakable belief in the power and authority of reason. It was plain that it would never occur to him, as it did so naturally to Prince Andrei, that after all it is impossible to express the whole of one's thought; and that he had never known doubt, never asked himself, 'Might not everything I think and believe be nonsense?' And it was this very peculiarity of Speransky's mind that attracted Prince Andrei most.

During the first period of their acquaintance Bolkonsky conceived a passionate admiration for him akin to what he had once felt for

Bonaparte. The fact that Speransky was the son of a priest, which enabled many foolish persons to regard him with vulgar contempt as a member of a despised class, caused Prince Andrei to cherish his sentiment for him the more, and unconsciously to strengthen it.

On that first evening Bolkonsky spent with him, having mentioned the Commission for the Revision of the Legal Code, Speransky told Prince Andrei sardonically that the Commission had existed for fifty years, had cost millions and had done nothing except that Rosenkampf had stuck labels on the corresponding paragraphs of the various articles.

'And that's all the State has got for the millions it has spent!' said he. 'We want to give the Senate new juridical powers but we have no laws. That is why it is a sin for men like you, prince, not to be in the government.'

Prince Andrei remarked that such work required legal training which he did not possess.

'But there is no one who does, so what are you going to do? It is a *circulus viciosus* which we must break out of by main force.'

Within a week Prince Andrei was a member of the Committee on Army Regulations, and – a thing he had never expected – was chairman of a sub-committee of the Commission for the Revision of the Legal Code. At Speransky's request he took the first part of the Civil Code that was being drawn up, and with the help of the *Code Napoléon* and the *Institutes of Justinian* set to work at formulating the section on Personal Rights.

7

NEARLY two years before this, in 1808, Pierre, on his return to Petersburg after visiting his estates, found himself by no design of his own in a leading position among the Petersburg freemasons. He organized memorial and dining lodge meetings, initiated new members and took an active part in uniting various lodges and acquiring authentic charters. He gave money for the building of masonic temples and did what he could to supplement the collection of alms, in regard to which the majority of the members were niggardly and irregular. He was almost alone in defraying the expenses of the almshouse the Order had founded in Petersburg.

His life meanwhile continued as before, with the same infatuations and dissipations. He liked to dine and drink well, and, though he considered it immoral and degrading to yield to them, he was unable to resist the temptations of the bachelor circles in which he moved.

Amid the hurly-burly of his activities and distractions, however, Pierre began to feel before a year was over that the more firmly he tried to rest upon it the more the ground of Freemasonry on which he stood slipped away from under his feet. At the same time he was conscious that the deeper the ground gave under him the more inextricably he was committed to it. When he had first entered the Brotherhood he experienced the sensations of a man who confidently steps on to the smooth surface of a bog. He puts down one foot and it sinks in. To convince himself of the firmness of the ground he puts his other foot down and sinks in farther, becomes stuck and must now wade knee-deep in the bog.

Osip Alexeyevich Bazdeyev was not in Petersburg. (He had of late stood aside from the affairs of the Petersburg lodges and now never left Moscow.) All the brethren, the members of the lodges, were men Pierre came across in everyday life and it was difficult for him to regard them merely as brothers in Freemasonry and not as Prince B. or Ivan Vasilyevich D., whom he knew in society mostly as people of weak and commonplace character. Under their masonic aprons and insignia he saw the uniforms and decorations which were their aim in ordinary life. Often after collecting alms, and reckoning up twenty to thirty roubles received for the most part in promises from a dozen members of whom half were as well-off as Pierre himself, he thought of the masonic vow whereby each brother bound himself to devote all his belongings to his neighbour; and doubts on which he tried not to dwell stirred in his soul.

He divided the brothers he knew into four categories. In the first he put those who took no active part in the affairs either of their lodges or of humanity but were exclusively occupied with the mystical science of the Order: with questions relating to the threefold designation of God, or the three primordial elements – sulphur, mercury and salt – or the meaning of the Square and all the various figures of the Temple of Solomon. Pierre respected this class of freemason, to which the elder brethren chiefly belonged, together, Pierre thought, with Osip Alexeyevich himself, but he did not share their interests. His heart was not drawn to the mystical side of Freemasonry.

In the second category he reckoned himself and brothers like him, seeking and vacillating, who had not yet found in Freemasonry a straight and comprehensible path but hoped to do so.

In the third category he placed the brethren (and they formed the majority) who saw nothing in Freemasonry but an external form and ceremonial, and prized the strict performance of these ceremonies, caring nothing for their purport or significance. Such were Willarski and even the Grand Master of the Supreme Lodge.

Finally, to the fourth category also belonged a great many brethren, particularly those who had entered the Brotherhood of late. These, so far as Pierre could observe, were men who had no belief in anything, nor desire for anything, but joined the freemasons simply for the sake of associating with the wealthy young members who were influential through their connexions or rank, and who abounded in the lodge.

Pierre began to feel dissatisfied with what he was doing. Freemasonry, at any rate as he saw it here, sometimes seemed to him to rest on externals. He never dreamed of doubting Freemasonry itself, but suspected that Russian masonry had got on to a false track and had deviated from its original principles. And so towards the end of the year he went abroad to devote himself to the higher mysteries of the Order.

*

It was in the summer of 1809 that Pierre returned to Petersburg. From the correspondence that passed between our freemasons and those abroad, it was known in Russia that Bezuhov had obtained the confidence of many highly placed persons, that he had been initiated into many mysteries, had been raised to a higher grade and was bringing back with him much that would be of advantage to the masonic cause at home. The Petersburg freemasons all came to see him, tried to ingratiate themselves with him, and all fancied that he had something in reserve that he was preparing for them.

A solemn meeting was convened of the lodge of the second degree, at which Pierre promised to communicate to the Petersburg brethren the message with which he had been entrusted by the highest leaders of the Order. The assembly was crowded. After the usual ceremonies Pierre got up and started on his address.

'My dear brethren,' he began, blushing and stammering, with a written speech in his hand, 'it is not enough to observe our mysteries in the seclusion of the lodge – we must act ... act. We are slumbering while we should be active.' Pierre took his manuscript and began to read.

For the propagation of pure truth and to secure the triumph of virtue, [he read], we must purge men of prejudice, diffuse principles in harmony with the spirit of the times, undertake the education of the young, unite ourselves by indissoluble bonds with the most enlightened men, boldly yet prudently contend with superstition, infidelity and folly, and form of men devoted to us a body linked together by singleness of purpose and possessed of authority and power.

To attain this end the scale must be weighted against vice and on the side of virtue; we must strive that the honest man may obtain his eternal reward even in this world. But in these great endeavours we are gravely hampered by the existing political institutions. What then is to be done in these circumstances? Are we to welcome revolutions, to overthrow society, oppose force with force? ... No! We are very far from that. All violent reforms are to be deprecated, because they can never do away with evil so long as men remain what they are, and also because wisdom has no need of violence.

The whole plan of our Order should be based on the idea of preparing men of character and virtue, bound together by unity of conviction – a conviction that it is their duty everywhere and with all their might to suppress vice and folly, and encourage talent and virtue, raising worthy men from the dust and attaching them to our Brotherhood. Not till then will our Order have the power imperceptibly to bind the hands of the promoters of disorder and to control them without their being aware of it. In a word, we must found a form of government holding universal sway, which would spread over the whole world without encroaching on civil ties or hindering other administrations from continuing their customary course and abandoning nothing except what stands in the way of the great aim of our Order – the triumph of virtue over vice. This aim is that of Christianity itself. Christianity taught men to be wise and good, and for their own profit to follow the example and precepts of the best and wisest men.

At that time, when all was plunged in darkness, preaching alone was of course sufficient: the novelty of truth endowed it with peculiar strength, but today we are obliged to have recourse to far more powerful means. Nowadays a man governed by his senses needs to find in virtue a charm palpable to those senses. The passions cannot be eradicated: we must strive to direct them to noble ends, and so it is necessary that everyone should be able to satisfy his passions within the limits of virtue. Our Order should provide means to that end.

So soon as we have a certain number of worthy men in every land, each of them in his turn training two others and all working in close co-operation, then all things will be possible for our Fraternity, which has already in secret accomplished so much for the welfare of mankind.

This discourse not only made a marked impression but caused agitation in the lodge. The majority of the brethren, affecting to see in it the dangerous doctrines of the German Illuminati, received it with a coldness that surprised Pierre. The Grand Master began to raise objections, and Pierre with growing heat went on to develop his view. It was a long time since there had been such a stormy session. The lodge split into parties, some accusing Pierre of Illuminism, others supporting him. At this meeting Pierre was for the first time struck by the endless variety of the human mind, preventing any truth from ever presenting itself in the same way to any two persons. Even those brethren who seemed to be on his side interpreted him after their own fashion with provisos and modifications to which he could not agree, since his chief desire was to convey his thought to others exactly as he himself understood it.

At the conclusion of the sitting the Grand Master reproved Pierre with irony and ill-will for his vehemence, and observed that it was not love of virtue alone but a liking for strife that had been his guide in the discussion. Pierre made no reply, and inquired briefly whether his proposal would be accepted. He was told that it would not, and without waiting for the usual formalities he left the lodge and went home.

8

AGAIN Pierre was overtaken by the despondency he so dreaded. For three days after the delivery of his speech at the lodge he lay on a sofa at home, seeing no one and going nowhere.

It was during this time that he received a letter from his wife, who implored him to see her, describing her sorrow at what had happened and her desire to devote her whole life to him.

At the end of the letter she informed him that in a day or two she would be arriving in Petersburg from abroad.

On top of the letter one of the masonic brethren whom Pierre respected least burst in upon his solitude, and, leading the conversation to the subject of Pierre's matrimonial affairs, by way of fraternal advice expressed the opinion that his severity to his wife was wrong, and that he was departing from the first principles of Freemasonry in not forgiving the penitent.

At the same time his mother-in-law, Prince Vasili's wife, sent to him beseeching him to call upon her, if only for a few minutes, in regard to a matter of supreme importance. Pierre saw there was a conspiracy, that they meant to reconcile him with his wife, and in the mood in which he then was he did not even dislike the idea. It was all the same to him. Nothing in life seemed to him of much consequence, and under the influence of the depression that engulfed him he no longer cared about his own freedom nor his obstinate determination to punish his wife.

'No one is right, no one is wrong, and so she, too, is not to blame,' he thought.

If he did not at once give his consent to a reconciliation with his wife it was only because in the despondent state into which he had lapsed he had not the energy to take any step. Had his wife come to him he would not have turned her away. In comparison with what preoccupied him was it not a matter of complete indifference whether he lived with his wife or not?

Vouchsafing no reply either to his wife or his mother-in-law, Pierre late one evening set out and drove to Moscow to see Osip Alexeyevich Bazdeyev. This is what he wrote in his diary.

Moscow, November 17th

I have just returned from seeing my benefactor, and hasten to note down all that I felt with him. Osip Alexeyevich lives in poverty, and for three years past has been suffering with a painful affection of the bladder. No one has ever heard him utter a groan or a word of complaint. From morning till late at night, except for the short while he gives up to his very frugal meals, he devotes himself to his scientific studies. He received me graciously and made me sit beside him on the bed where he lay. I made him the sign of the Knights of the East and of Jerusalem, and he responded in the same manner, and with a gentle smile asked me what I had learned and gained in the Prussian and Scottish lodges. I told him everything as best I could, repeating to him the proposal I had laid before our Petersburg lodge and describing the unfriendly reception I had encountered, and the rupture which had occurred between myself and the brethren. After he had been silent and taken thought for some little time, Osip Alexeyevich put his view of the matter before me, so that all the past was immediately made plain to me, as well as the course that lies before me. He surprised me by asking whether I remembered the threefold aim of the Order: (1) the preservation and study of the Mystery; (2) the purification and reformation of oneself for its reception; and (3) the improvement of the human race through striving for such purification. Which, he asked, is the first and greatest of these three aims? Undoubtedly self-reformation and self-purification. It is only towards this aim that we can always strive, independently of whatever circumstances. But at the same time it is just this aim which requires of us the greatest effort, and so, led astray by pride, we let this aim drop, and occupy ourselves either with the Mystery which in our impurity we are unworthy to receive, or we seek the reformation of the human race while ourselves setting an example of depravity and abomination. Illuminism is not a pure doctrine precisely because it has been seduced by social activity and puffed up with pride. On this ground Osip Alexeyevich condemned my speech and all I had done. At the bottom of my heart I agreed with him. Talking of my domestic affairs, he said to me, 'The principal duty of a true mason, as I have told you, lies in perfecting himself. But we often think that by removing all the difficulties of our life we shall the more quickly attain our purpose; on the contrary, my dear sir,' he said to me, 'it is only in the midst of worldly cares that we can attain our three great aims: (1) self-knowledge – for man can only know himself by comparison with others; (2) greater perfection, which can only be obtained through struggle, and (3) the chief virtue – love of death. Only the vicissitudes of life can teach us the vanity of life and stimulate our innate love of death or rebirth into new life.' These words were all the more remarkable in that Osip Alexeyevich, in spite of grievous physical suffering, is never weary of life, though he loves death, for which – notwithstanding all his spiritual purity and loftiness – he does not yet feel himself sufficiently prepared. Next my benefactor explained to me the full significance of the Great Square of Creation and pointed out that the numbers three and seven are the basis of everything. He counselled me not to withdraw from the Petersburg brethren, and, while taking upon myself only the obligations of the second degree in the lodge, to endeavour to win the brethren from the seductions of pride, and try and turn them into the true path of self-knowledge and self-perfecting. Besides this, for myself personally, he advised me above all things to keep a watch over myself, and to that end he gave me a note-book, the one in which I am writing now, and in future I shall keep an account of all my actions.

Petersburg, November 23rd

I am living with my wife again. My mother-in-law came to me with tears in her eyes, and said that Hélène was back and implored me to hear her: she was innocent, and miserable that I had left her, and much besides. I knew that if I once let myself see her I should not have the strength to refuse her. In my perplexity I did not know where to turn for help and advice. Had my benefactor been here he would have told me what to do. I shut myself up in my room, read over Osip Alexey-evich's letters and recalled my conversations with him, and, taking all things together, I came to the conclusion that I ought not to refuse a suppliant and must hold out a helping hand to everyone – and especi-ally to the person so closely bound to me – and that I must bear my cross. But if I forgive her for the sake of doing right, then let my reunion with her have a spiritual aim only. That is what I decided, and what I wrote to Osip Alexeyevich. I told my wife that I begged her to forget the past, to forgive me whatever wrong I might have done her, and that I had nothing to forgive. It gave me joy to tell her this. May she never know how painful it was to me to see her again! I have installed myself on the upper floor of this great house, and am rejoicing in a pleasant sense of regeneration.

9

AT that time, as always indeed, the upper strata of society that met at court and at the grand balls was divided into a number of separate circles, each having its own particular tone. The largest of these was the French circle – supporting the Napoleonic alliance – the circle of Count Rumyantsev and Caulaincourt. In this group Hélène, as soon as she and her husband had resumed residence together in Petersburg, took a very prominent part. Members of the French Embassy fre-quented her drawing-room, and a great number of people distin-guished for their intellect and polished manners, and belonging to the same political persuasion.

Hélène had been at Erfurt during the famous meeting between the Emperors, and had there made the acquaintance of all the Napoleonic celebrities of Europe. At Erfurt she had enjoyed a most brilliant suc-cess. Napoleon himself had noticed her at the theatre, asked who she was and admired her beauty. Her triumphs as a beautiful and elegant woman did not surprise Pierre, for as time went on she had grown handsomer than ever. What did surprise him was that during these last two years his wife had succeeded in acquiring the reputation of being 'une femme charmante, aussi spirituelle que belle'. The distinguished Prince de Ligne wrote her eight-page letters. Bilibin saved up his epigrams to fire off for the first time in Countess Bezuhov's presence. To be received in Countess Bezuhov's *salon* was regarded as a certificate of intelligence. Young men read up books before one of Hélène's parties so as to have something to say in her drawing-room, and Embassy secretaries and even ambassadors confided diplomatic secrets to her, so that Hélène was a power in a certain way. Pierre, who knew she was very stupid, sometimes attended her receptions and dinner-parties, where politics, poetry and philosophy were discussed, and he listened with a strange feeling of perplexity and alarm. At these parties he felt as a conjurer must feel who is all the time afraid that at any moment his tricks will be seen through. But whether because only stupidity was just what was needed to run such a *salon*, or because those who were deceived found pleasure in the deception itself, at any rate the secret did not come out and Hélène Bezuhov's reputation as a lovely and intelligent woman became so firmly established that she could say the most commonplace and stupidest things and still everybody would go into raptures over her every word and discover a profound meaning in it of which she herself had no conception.

Pierre was the very husband for this brilliant society woman. He was that absent-minded, eccentric, *grand seigneur* of a husband who got in no one's way and, far from spoiling the general impression of lofty tone in the drawing-room, he provided, by his contrast to his wife's elegance and *savoir faire*, an advantageous background for her. Pierre's constant absorption in abstract interests during the last two years, and his genuine contempt for everything else, gave him in his wife's circle, which did not interest him, that air of unconcern and indifference combined with benevolence towards all alike, which cannot be acquired artificially, and, for that reason, inspires involuntary respect. He would enter his wife's drawing-room as though it were a theatre, was acquainted with everybody, equally pleased to see everyone and equally reserved with them all. Sometimes he joined in a conversation which appealed to him and, regardless of whether any 'gentlemen of the Embassy' were present or not, mumbled out his opinions, which were by no means always in accord with those current at the moment. But society had grown so used to the queer husband of the 'most distinguished woman in Petersburg' that no one took his idiosyncrasies seriously.

Among the many young men who were daily to be seen in Hélène's house Boris Drubetskoy, who had already achieved marked success in the service, was, since Hélène's return from Erfurt, the most intimate friend of the Bezuhov household. Hélène called him *'mon page'*, and treated him like a child. The smile she gave him was the same as she bestowed on everybody, but sometimes it gave Pierre an unpleasant feeling. Boris behaved towards Pierre with a peculiar grave deference that was perfectly proper. This shade of deference also disturbed Pierre. He had suffered so painfully three years before from the mortification to which his wife had subjected him that he now protected himself from the danger of similar mortification, firstly by not being a husband to his wife, and secondly, by not allowing himself to be suspicious.

'No, now that she has become a *bas bleu* she has renounced her old inclinations for ever,' he told himself. 'There has never been an instance of a blue-stocking being carried away by affairs of the heart' – an axiom he had picked up somewhere and believed implicitly. Yet, strange to say, the presence of Boris in his wife's drawing-room (and he was almost always there) had a physical effect upon Pierre: it seemed to paralyse his limbs, to awaken all his self-consciousness and take away his freedom of movement.

'Such a strange antipathy,' thought Pierre, 'and yet at one time I really liked him very much.'

In the eyes of the world Pierre was a fine gentleman, the rather blind and ridiculous husband of a distinguished wife, a clever eccentric who did nothing but was no trouble to anyone, a good-natured, capital fellow – while all the time in the depths of Pierre's soul a complex and arduous process of inner development was going on, revealing much to him and bringing him many spiritual doubts and joys.

10

HE kept up his diary, and this is what he was writing in it at this time:

November 24th

Got up at eight, read the Scriptures, then proceeded to my duties –

(Pierre, on his benefactor's advice, had entered the service of the State and was on one of the government committees.)

Returned home for dinner and dined alone (the countess has a lot of guests I do not care for), ate and drank with moderation, and after dinner copied out some passages for the brethren. In the evening I went down to the drawing-room and told a funny story about B., and only bethought myself that I ought not to have done so when everybody was laughing loudly at it.

I go to bed with a happy tranquil mind. Lord God, help me to walk in Thy paths: (1) to conquer anger by gentleness and deliberation, (2) to vanquish lust by self-restraint and a turning away, (3) to shun the vanities of this world but without shutting myself off from (a) the service of the State, (b) family cares, (c) relations with my friends and (d) the management of my affairs.

November 27th

Got up late and lay a long while in bed after I was awake, yielding to sloth. O God, help and strengthen me that I may walk in Thy ways. Read the Scriptures but without proper feeling. Brother Urusov came and we talked about the vanities of the world. He told me of the Emperor's new projects. I was on the point of criticizing them but remembered my principles and my benefactor's words – that a true mason should be a zealous worker for the State when his services are required and a quiet onlooker when not called upon to assist. My tongue is my enemy. Brothers G.V. and O. visited me and we had a preliminary talk about the initiation of a new brother. They charge me with the duty of tyler. Feel myself weak and unworthy. Then we turned to the interpretation of the seven pillars and steps of the Temple, the seven sciences, the seven virtues, the seven vices, the seven gifts of the Holy Spirit. Brother O. was very eloquent. The initiation took place in the evening. The new decoration of the lodge contributed much to the magnificence of the spectacle. It was Boris Drubetskoy who was admitted. I nominated him and was the tyler. A strange feeling agitated me all the time I was alone with him in the dark chamber. I caught myself harbouring a feeling of hatred towards him which I vainly strove to overcome. For this reason I really wanted to save him from evil and lead him into the path of truth, but evil thoughts about him never left me. It seemed to me that his object in entering the Brotherhood was merely to be intimate and in favour with members of our Lodge. Apart from the fact that he had asked me several times whether N. and S. were members of our lodge (a question to which I could not reply), and that, so far as my observation goes, he is incapable of genuine respect for our holy Order and is too much occupied and too well satisfied with the outer man to care much for spiritual improvement, I had no grounds for doubting him; but he seemed to me insincere, and all the time I stood alone with him in the dark chamber I kept fancying that he was smiling contemptuously at my words, and I could gladly have

518

stabbed his bare breast with the sword I held to it. I was unable to speak with any fluency, and I could not frankly communicate my misgivings to the brethren and the Grand Master. May the Great Architect of the Universe help me to find the true path out of the labyrinth of falsehood!

The next three pages in the diary were left blank, and then came the following:

Had a long and instructive private conversation with Brother V., who advised me to hold fast by Brother A. Much was revealed to me, though I am so unworthy. Adonai is the name of the creator of the world. Elohim is the name of the ruler of all. The third name, the name unutterable, means the *All*. Talks with Brother V. strengthen and refresh me, and confirm me in the path of virtue. In his presence there is no opportunity for doubt. I can see clearly the distinction between the poor doctrines of mundane science and our sacred, all-embracing teaching. Human sciences dissect in order to comprehend, and destroy in order to analyse. In the sacred science of our Order all is one, all is known, everything is known in its entirety and life. The trinity – the three elements of matter – are sulphur, mercury and salt. Sulphur is oil and fire; amalgamated with salt the fiery quality of sulphur arouses an appetite in salt by means of which mercury is attracted, seized, held and in combination produces other bodies. Mercury is the fluid, volatile, spiritual essence – Christ, the Holy Spirit, He.

December 3rd

Awoke late, read the Scriptures but was apathetic. Afterwards went down and walked to and fro in the large hall. Wanted to meditate but instead my imagination brought before me an incident which happened four years ago, when Dolohov, meeting me in Moscow after our duel, said he hoped I was enjoying complete peace of mind in spite of my wife's absence. At the time I made him no reply. Now, though, I recalled every detail of the encounter and in my mind answered him with the most vindictive and biting retorts. I recovered myself and banished the subject only when I found I was burning with anger; but I did not sufficiently repent. After this Boris Drubetskoy came and began describing various adventures. From the first moment I was annoyed at his visit and made some contrary remark. He retaliated. I flared up and said a great deal that was disagreeable and even rude. He was silent, and I recollected myself only when it was too late. O God, I cannot get on with him at all. The fault lies in my own self-esteem. I set myself above him and consequently become a thousand times worse than he, for he condones my rudeness while I, on the contrary, nourish contempt for him. O God grant that in his presence I may rather see my own vileness and behave in such fashion that it may profit him too. After dinner I had a nap and just as I was falling asleep I distinctly heard a voice saying in my left ear, 'Thine is the day'.

I dreamt that I was walking in the dark and was suddenly surrounded by dogs but I went on undismayed. Suddenly a smallish dog seized my left thigh with its teeth and would not let go. I began to strangle it with my hands. Scarcely had I succeeded in throwing it off when another, a bigger one, gripped me by the chest. I shook it off but a third, even bigger dog began biting me. I lifted it up but the higher I lifted it the bigger and heavier it grew. And suddenly Brother A. came along, and taking my arm led me to a building, to enter which we had to go along a narrow plank. I stepped on it but the plank bent and gave way, and I began clambering up a fence which I just managed to get hold of with my hands. After great efforts I dragged myself up so that my legs were hanging down on one side and my body on the other. I looked round and saw Brother A. standing on the fence and pointing me to a broad avenue and garden, and in the garden was a large and beautiful building. I woke up. O Lord, Great Architect of Nature, help me to tear from myself these dogs – my passions – especially the last, which unites in itself the violence of all the others, and aid me to enter that temple of virtue of which I was vouchsafed a vision in my dream.

December 7th

I dreamed that Osip Alexeyevich was sitting in my house, and I was very glad and eager to entertain him. But in my dream I kept chattering away to other people and all at once I bethought myself that this could not be to his liking, and I wanted to go up to him and embrace him. But as soon as I drew near I saw that his face had changed and grown younger, and in a low, low tone – so low that I could not hear – he was telling me something from the teachings of our Order. Then we all seemed to go out of the room and something strange happened. We were sitting or lying on the floor. He was telling me something. But in my dream I longed to let him see how moved I was, and not listening to what he was saying I began picturing to myself the condition of my inner man and the grace of God sanctifying me. And tears came into my eyes, and I was glad he noticed this. But he glanced at me with vexation and jumped up, breaking off his remarks. I was abashed and asked him whether what he had been saying did not concern me; he made no reply but gave me a kindly look, and then all of a sudden we found ourselves in my bedroom with a big double bed in it.

He lay down on the edge of it and I, on fire, as it were, with longing to caress him lay down too. And in my dream he asked me, 'Tell me honestly, what is your chief temptation? Have you found out? I believe you have.' Put out of countenance by this question, I replied that sloth was my besetting sin. He shook his head incredulously. Still more disconcerted, I told him that though I was living with my wife, as he had counselled me, I was not living with her as a husband. To this he replied that a wife ought not to be deprived of her husband's embraces, and gave me to understand that this was my duty. But I answered that I should feel ashamed, and with this everything was gone. I awoke and in my mind was the Scripture text: 'The life was the light of men. And the light shineth in darkness; and the darkness comprehended it not.' Osip Alexeyevich's face had looked young and radiant. That day I received a letter from my benefactor in which he wrote of the obligations of the married state.

December 9th

I had a dream from which I awoke with my heart throbbing. I dreamt I was in my house in Moscow, in the big sitting-room, and Osip Alexeyevich came in from the drawing-room. I knew instantly that the process of regeneration had already taken place in him, and I rushed towards him. I embraced him and kissed his hands, and he said, 'Hast thou noticed that my face is different now?' I looked at him, still holding him in my arms, and saw that his face was young but there was no hair on his head, and his features were greatly altered. And I said, 'I should have recognized you had we met by accident,' and at the same time I thought, 'Am I telling the truth?' And suddenly I saw him lying like a dead body; then he gradually came to himself again and went with me into the big study, carrying a folio book of cartridge paper. I said, 'I drew that,' and he answered me by an inclination of his head. I opened the book and on all the pages were drawings superbly done. And in my dream I knew that the drawings represented the adventures of the soul with her beloved. And among them I saw a beautiful picture of a maiden in diaphanous raiment and with a transparent body flying up to the clouds. And I seemed to know that this damsel was nothing else than a representation of the Song of Songs. And as I looked at the drawings in my dream I felt that I was doing wrong, yet could not tear myself away from them. O Lord, help me! O God if Thy forsaking me is Thy doing, then Thy will be done; but if I am myself the cause, teach me what I must do. I must perish from my corruption if Thou dost utterly abandon me.

The Rostovs' monetary affairs had not improved during the two years they had spent in the country.

Though Nikolai Rostov had kept firmly to his resolution and was still serving quietly in an obscure regiment, spending comparatively little, the scale of life at Otradnoe – and particularly Mitenka's management of affairs – was such that debts increased like a snowball with every year. The old count saw but one way out of the difficulty, and that was to apply for some government appointment, so he had come to Petersburg to look for one and also, as he said, to let the lassies enjoy themselves for the last time.

Soon after their arrival in Petersburg Berg proposed to Vera and was accepted.

In spite of the fact that in Moscow the Rostovs moved in the highest society (without giving a thought to it one way or the other), in Petersburg their acquaintance was rather mixed. In Petersburg they were provincials, and the very people they had entertained in Moscow without inquiring to what set they belonged here looked down on them.

The Rostovs kept open house in Petersburg as in Moscow, and the most heterogeneous collection met at their suppers: a country neighbour from Otradnoe, an impoverished old squire with his daughters, Madame Peronsky, who was a maid of honour, Pierre Bezuhov, and the son of their district postmaster, who was in an office in Petersburg. Among the men who very soon became frequent visitors at the Rostovs' house in Petersburg were Boris, Pierre whom the count had met in the street and dragged home with him, and Berg who spent whole days at the Rostov's and paid the elder daughter, Countess Vera, the attentions a young man pays when he intends to propose.

Not in vain had Berg shown everybody his right arm wounded at Austerlitz, and affected to hold his wholly unnecessary sword in his left hand. He related the episode so persistently and with so important an air that everyone had come to believe in the expediency and merit of his action, and he had received two decorations for Austerlitz.

In the Finnish campaign he had also succeeded in distinguishing himself. He had picked up a fragment of the grenade that had killed an aide-de-camp standing near the commander-in-chief, and had taken it to the commander. Again, as after Austerlitz, he talked to everyone about the incident at such length and so insistently that people ended up believing that it had been necessary to do this also, and the Finnish war brought him two more decorations. In 1809 he was a captain in the Guards, wore medals on his breast, and held some particular, lucrative posts in Petersburg.

Though there were some sceptics who smiled when Berg's merits were mentioned to them, it could not be denied that he was a painstaking and gallant officer, extremely well thought of at headquarters, and a modest, upright young man with a brilliant career before him and enjoying an assured position in society.

Four years before, meeting a German comrade in the *parterre* of a Moscow theatre, Berg had pointed out Vera Rostov to him and said in German, 'There is the girl who shall be my wife,' and there and then had determined that he would marry her. Now in Petersburg, after duly considering the Rostovs' position and his own, he decided that the time had come to propose.

Berg's proposal was received at first with a hesitation by no means flattering for him. It seemed a strange idea at first that the son of an obscure Livonian gentleman should ask for the hand of a Countess Rostov; but Berg's most characteristic *trait* was an egoism so naïve and good-natured that the Rostovs found themselves thinking that it must be a good thing since he himself was so firmly convinced that it would be – and indeed that it would be even more than a good thing. Moreover, the Rostovs' affairs were in an embarrassing state, a circumstance of which the suitor could not but be aware; and above all, the chief consideration, Vera, was now four-and-twenty, had been taken about everywhere, and, though she was undeniably good-looking and sensible, no one up to now had made her an offer. So consent was given.

'You see,' said Berg to his comrade, whom he called his friend only because he knew that everyone has friends. 'You see, I have weighed it all up carefully, and I shouldn't think of marrying if I had not considered it all round or if there were any difficulties. But now on the contrary, my papa and mamma are well provided for – I have made over to them the income from that land in the Baltic Provinces – and my wife and I can live in Petersburg on my pay, and with her little fortune and my careful habits we can get along nicely. I am not marrying for money – I call that sort of thing dishonourable – but a wife ought to bring her share and a husband his. I have my position in the service, she has her connexions and some small means. That's something in these days, isn't it? But best of all, she's a handsome, estimable girl, and she loves me ...'

Berg blushed and smiled.

'And I love her, because she has plenty of sense and a nice nature. The other sister now, though they are the same family, is quite different – a disagreeable character and not the same intelligence. She is so ... you know? ... I don't like. ... But my betrothed. ... Well, you will be coming' – he was going to say 'to dine' but thought better of it and said – 'to take tea with us.' and hastily curling his tongue he blew a little round ring of tobacco smoke, the emblem of the happiness of which he dreamed.

After the first rather doubtful reactions of Vera's parents to Berg's proposal the family settled down to the festivity and happiness usual at such times, but the rejoicing was on the surface and not genuine. A certain awkwardness and constraint were perceptible in the feelings of the relations. It was as if their consciences smote them for not having been very fond of Vera and for being so ready now to get her off their hands. The old count was the most disturbed over this. He would probably have been unable to say what made him uncomfortable but his financial difficulties were at the root of the trouble. He had no idea how he stood or how much he owed, or what dowry he could give Vera. When his daughters were born he had assigned to each of them as a marriage portion an estate with three hundred serfs; but one of these estates had already been sold, and the other was mortgaged and the interest so much in arrears that they were bound to foreclose, so Vera could not have this estate either. Nor was there any money.

Berg had already been the accepted bridegroom for over a month, and only a week remained before the wedding, yet still the count had not decided in his own mind the question of the dowry, nor broached the subject to his wife. At one moment he considered giving Vera the Ryazan estate, then he thought of selling a forest or raising money on a note of hand. A few days before the wedding Berg entered the count's study early one morning and with a pleasant smile respectfully invited his future father-in-law to let him know what Countess Vera's dowry would be. The count was so disconcerted by this long-anticipated inquiry that without thinking he said the first thing that came into his head.

'I like your being businesslike about it, I like it. You will be quite satisfied. ...'

And patting Berg on the shoulder he got up, hoping to cut short the conversation. But Berg, smiling blandly, explained that if he did not know for certain how much Vera would have, and did not receive at least part of the dowry in advance, he would be obliged to withdraw.

'Because, consider, count – if I were to allow myself to marry now without knowing what I had to depend on to maintain my wife I should be acting abominably ...'

The conversation ended by the count, in his anxiety to be generous and to avoid further importunity, saying that he would give him a note of hand for eighty thousand roubles. Berg smiled sweetly, kissed the count on the shoulder and declared that he was very grateful but that he could not make his arrangements for his new life without receiving thirty thousand in ready money. 'Or at least twenty thousand, count,' he added, 'and in that case a note of hand for only sixty thousand.'

'Yes, yes, to be sure,' said the count hurriedly. 'Only you must allow me, my dear fellow, to give you twenty thousand and the note of hand for eighty thousand as well. Yes, that's it! Kiss me.'

12

NATASHA was sixteen and it was the year 1809, the year to which she had counted on her fingers with Boris after they had kissed four years ago. Since then she had not once seen him. With Sonya, and with her mother, if Boris happened to be mentioned, she would quite unconcernedly treat all that had gone before as childish nonsense, not worth talking about and long forgotten. But in the secret depths of her heart the question whether her engagement to Boris was a jest or a solemn, binding promise tormented her.

Ever since Boris had left Moscow in 1805 to join the army he had not been back to the Rostovs. Several times he had been in Moscow, and in travelling had passed within a short distance of Otradnoe, but not once had he gone to see them.

It sometimes occurred to Natasha that he did not want to see her, and this conjecture was confirmed by the sorrowful tone in which her elders referred to him.

'Nowadays it is the fashion to forget old friends,' the countess would say immediately Boris was mentioned.

Anna Mihalovna's visits too had been less frequent of late. There was a marked dignity in her manner and she never failed to allude rapturously and gratefully to her son's merits and the brilliant career on which he was embarked. When the Rostovs arrived in Petersburg Boris came to call upon them.

It was not without emotion that he drove to their house. His memories of Natasha were the most poetic memories Boris had. But at the same time he was going with the firm intention of making both her and her parents clearly understand that the childish vows between himself and Natasha could not be considered binding on either of them. He had a brilliant position in society, thanks to his intimacy with Countess Bezuhov; a brilliant position in the service, thanks to the patronage of an important personage whose complete confidence he enjoyed; and he was now busy begetting plans for marrying one of the richest heiresses in Petersburg, plans which might very easily be realized. When Boris entered the Rostovs' drawing-room Natasha was in her own room. On being told of his arrival she almost ran into the drawing-room, flushed and radiant with a more than friendly smile.

Boris remembered Natasha in a short dress, with dark eyes flashing under her curls and a wild childish laugh, as he had known her four years before; and so he was taken aback when a quite different Natasha came in, and his face expressed surprise and admiration. This expression on his face delighted Natasha.

'Well, do you recognize your mischievous playmate of old?' asked the countess.

Boris kissed Natasha's hand, and said that he was astonished at the change in her. 'How pretty you have grown!'

'I should hope so!' replied Natasha's shining eyes. 'And does Papa look older?' she asked.

Natasha sat down and, taking no part in Boris's conversation with her mother, silently and minutely studied her childhood's suitor. He felt the weight of that resolute and affectionate scrutiny, and now and again stole a glance at her.

Boris's uniform, his spurs, his cravat and the way his hair was brushed were all in the latest fashion and *comme il faut*. This Natasha noted at once. He sat a little sideways in the arm-chair next to the countess, with his right hand smoothing the most immaculate of gloves that fitted his left hand like a skin, while he spoke with a peculiar, delicate compression of the lips about the gaieties of high life in Petersburg, and with mild irony recalled the old days in Moscow and their Moscow acquaintances. It was not without design, Natasha felt sure, that in speaking of the flower of the aristocracy he alluded to an ambassador's ball that he had attended and to invitations that he had received from So-and-so and Such-and-such.

All this time Natasha sat silent, watching him from under her brows. This gaze disconcerted Boris and made him more and more uneasy. He kept turning to her and breaking off what he was saying. He did not stay above ten minutes, then rose and bowed his leave. Still the same inquisitive, challenging and rather mocking eyes looked at him. After his first visit Boris confessed to himself that Natasha attracted him just as much as ever, but that he must not yield to his feelings because to marry her – a girl almost without a dowry – would ruin his career, while to renew their former friendship without intending to marry her would be dishonourable. Boris determined that he would avoid seeing Natasha, but notwithstanding this resolution he appeared again a few days later, and began calling often and spending whole days at the Rostovs'. He told himself more than once that he must come to an understanding with Natasha and tell her that they must forget the old times, that in spite of everything ... she could not be his wife, that he had no means and they would never let her marry him. But he always failed to do so, and felt awkward about approaching the subject. Every day he became more entangled. Natasha, it seemed to her mother and Sonya, was in love with Boris as she had been before. She sang him his favourite songs, showed him her album, made him write in it, would not let him refer to the past, making him feel how delightful was the present; and every day he went away in a whirl without having said what he meant to say, not knowing what he was doing or why he kept going there, or how it would all end. He left off visiting Hélène, received reproachful notes from her daily, and yet still spent whole days together at the Rostovs'.

ONE night when the old countess, in night-cap and dressing-jacket, with her false curls and with her one poor little knob of hair showing under her white calico nightcap, knelt sighing and groaning on a rug and bowing to the ground in prayer, her door creaked and Natasha, also in dressing-jacket with slippers on her bare feet and her hair in curl-papers, ran in. The countess looked round and frowned. She was repeating her last prayer 'And if this pallet should be my deathbed.' Her devotional mood was dispelled. Natasha, flushed and eager, checked her rush when she saw her mother was praying, made a little bob and unconsciously put out her tongue at herself. Seeing that her mother still went on with her devotions, she danced on tiptoe to the bed, kicked off her slippers by quickly rubbing one little foot against the other, and sprang into the bed which the countess feared might become her bier. It was a high feather-bed with five pillows, each one smaller than the one below. Natasha skipped on to the bedstead, sank into the feather mattress, rolled over to the wall and began snuggling down under the quilt, tucking herself up, bending her knees up to her chin and then kicking out, and giving faintly audible giggles as she alternately hid her face under the counterpane and peeped out at her mother. The countess finished her prayers and came over to the bed with a stern face, but seeing that Natasha's head was hidden under the bedclothes she smiled her good-natured, weak smile.

'Come, come, come!' said she.

'Mamma, can we have a talk – may we?' said Natasha. 'There now, just one on your throat, and one more and that's all.' And she threw her arms round her mother's neck and kissed her under the chin. Natasha's manner with her mother appeared rough, but she was so dexterous and careful that however she hugged her mother she always managed to do it without hurting or upsetting her and making her feel annoyed.

'Well, what is it tonight?' said her mother, arranging her pillows and waiting until Natasha, who rolled over a couple of times, should cuddle down close to her under the quilt, drop her hands and become serious.

These visits of Natasha to her mother at night before the count came home from the club were one of the greatest joys of both mother and daughter.

'What is it tonight? And I want to talk to you about –'

Natasha put her hand on her mother's lips.

'About Boris. ... I know,' she said gravely. 'That's what I have come about. Don't say it – I know. No, do!' and she took away her hand. 'Go on, mamma. He's nice, isn't he?'

'Natasha, you are sixteen. At your age I was already married. You say Boris is nice. He is very nice, and I love him like a son, but what is it you're after? ... What is in your mind? You have quite turned his head, I can see that. ...'

As she said this the countess looked round at her daughter. Natasha lay staring straight before her at one of the mahogany sphinxes carved on the corners of the bedstead, so that the countess could only see her daughter's face in profile. She was struck by its serious, intent expression.

Natasha was listening and considering.

'Well, what then?' said she.

'You have completely turned his head, and what for? What do you want of him? You know you can't marry him.'

'Why not?' said Natasha, without altering her position.

'Because he is very young, because he is poor, because he is a relation ... because you yourself don't love him.'

'How do you know?'

'I know. It is not right, darling!'

'But if I want to ...' began Natasha.

'Leave off talking nonsense,' said the countess.

'But if I choose ...'

'Natasha, I am in earnest ...'

Natasha did not let her finish. She drew the countess's large hand to her, kissed it on the back and then on the palm, turned it over again and began kissing first one knuckle, then the space between the knuckles, then the next knuckle, whispering: 'January, February, March, April, May. Speak, mamma, why don't you say something? Speak!' said she, looking up at her mother, who was gazing tenderly at her daughter and in her contemplation had apparently forgotten what she had meant to say.

'It won't do, my love! Not everyone will understand that this friendship dates from the time when you were both children, and to see him on such intimate terms with you may prejudice you in the eyes of other young men who come to the house, and above all it is making him wretched for nothing. He may very likely have found a match that would suit him, some rich girl, and now he's going half out of his mind.'

'Out of his mind?' repeated Natasha.

'I'll tell you something that happened to me. I once had a cousin ...'

'I know – Kirill Matveich, but he's old, isn't he?'

'He was not always old. But this is what I'll do, Natasha. I will have a talk with Boris. He must not come so often. ...'

'Why mustn't he, if he wants to?'

'Because I know it can't lead to anything.'

'How do you know? No, mamma, don't speak to him. Don't you dare speak to him. What foolishness!' said Natasha in the tone of one being robbed of her property. 'All right, I won't marry him, but let him come if he enjoys it and I enjoy it.' Natasha smiled and looked at her mother. 'Not get married, but go on *as we are*,' she added.

'What do you mean, my pet?'

'Why, as we are, of course. I quite see I shouldn't marry him, but ... as we are.'

'As we are, as we are!' repeated the countess, and, shaking all over, she went off into a good-humoured, unexpected, elderly laugh.

'Don't laugh, stop!' cried Natasha. 'You're shaking the whole bed. You're awfully like me, just another giggler. ... Wait. ...' She snatched both the countess's hands and kissed a knuckle of the little finger, saying 'June,' and continued kissing – 'July, August' – on the other hand. 'Mamma, is he very much in love? What do you think? Was anybody ever so much in love with you? And he's very nice, very, very nice. Only not quite to my taste – he's so narrow, like the dining-room clock. ... Don't you understand? ... You know, narrow, pale grey, light-coloured. ...'

'What nonsense you do talk!' exclaimed the countess.

Natasha continued:

'Don't you really understand? Nikolai would ... Bezuhov, now, he's blue – dark-blue and red, and all square. ...'

'You flirt with him too,' said the countess, laughing.

'No, I found out he's a freemason. He's a jolly person, dark-blue and red. ... How can I make you see?'

'Little countess!' the count's voice called the other side of the door.

'Aren't you asleep?' Natasha jumped up, seized her slippers in her hand and ran off barefoot to her own room.

She could not get to sleep for a long while. She kept thinking that no one could ever understand all the things she understood, and what there was in her.

'Sonya?' she thought, glancing at that curled-up sleeping little kitten with her enormous plait of hair. 'No, how could she? She is all virtue. She's in love with Nikolai, and that's all she cares about. Even mamma doesn't understand. It is wonderful how clever I am and how ... charming she is,' she went on, speaking of herself in the third person and imagining that some very intelligent, extraordinarily intelligent and most superior man was saying this about her. 'She possesses everything, everything,' continued this man. 'She is unusually intelligent, charming and pretty too – uncommonly pretty – and graceful. She can swim, she rides horseback splendidly, and what a voice! One might really say a marvellous voice!'

She hummed a few favourite bars from a Cherubini opera, flung herself into bed, laughed happily at the thought that she would be asleep in a trice, called to Dunyasha to snuff out the candle, and before the maid was out of the room had already crossed into that other still happier world of dreams, where everything was as buoyant and lovely as in real life, and even more so because it was different.

*

Next day the countess sent for Boris and had a talk with him, after which he gave up going to the Rostovs'.

14

ON the 31st of December, on the eve of the new year 1810, an old grandee of Catherine's day was giving a ball to see out the old year. The diplomatic corps and the Emperor were to be present.

The grandee's well-known mansion on the English Quay blazed with innumerable lights. Police were stationed at the brilliantly-lit, red-carpeted entrance – not only gendarmes but the chief of police himself and dozens of officers. Carriages drove away, and new ones kept arriving with red-liveried footmen and grooms in plumed hats. From the carriages emerged men wearing uniform, stars and ribbons, while ladies in satin and ermine cautiously descended the carriage steps, which were let down for them with a clatter, and swiftly and noiselessly passed along the red baize into the porch.

Almost every time a new carriage drove up a whisper ran through the crowd and caps were doffed.

'The Emperor ? ... No, a minister ... prince ... ambassador. Don't you see the plumes ? ...' said the crowd among themselves. One man, better dressed than the rest, seemed to know who everybody was, and announced the names of all the most celebrated personages of the day.

Already a third of the guests had arrived, but the Rostovs, who were to be present, were still hurrying to get dressed.

There had been much discussion and numerous preparations for this ball in the Rostov family. Would the invitation arrive ? Would their gowns be ready in time ? Would everything turn out as it should ?

Maria Ignatyevna Peronsky, an old friend and relative of the countess, was to accompany the Rostovs to the ball. She was a thin and sallow maid of honour at the Empress Dowager's court, who was acting as guide to her country cousins in their entry into Petersburg high society.

They were to call for her at ten o'clock at her house in the Tavrichesky gardens, but it was already five minutes to ten and the girls were not yet dressed.

Natasha was going to her first grand ball. She had got up at eight that morning and had been in a fever of excitement and energy all day. All her energies from the moment she woke had been directed to the one aim of ensuring that they all – herself, mamma and Sonya – should look their very best. Sonya and the countess put themselves entirely in her hands. The countess was to wear a dark red velvet gown; the two girls, white tulle dresses over pink silk slips, with roses on their bodices. Their hair was to be arranged à la grecque.

All the essentials had been done: feet, hands, neck and ears most carefully washed, perfumed and powdered, as befits a ball. The openwork silk stockings and white satin slippers with ribbons were already on; their hair was almost finished. Sonya was nearly ready, so was the countess; but Natasha, who had bustled about helping everyone, was less advanced. She was still sitting before the looking-glass with a *peignoir* thrown over her thin shoulders. Sonya, on the last stage, stood in the middle of the room fastening on a final bow and hurting her dainty finger as she pressed the pin that squeaked as it went through the ribbon.

'Not like that, Sonya, not like that!' cried Natasha, turning her head and clutching with both hands at her hair which the maid, who was dressing it, had not time to let go. 'That bow isn't right. Come here!'

Sonya sat down and Natasha pinned the ribbon differently.

'If you please, miss, I can't get on like this,' said the maid, still holding Natasha's hair.

'Oh, goodness gracious, wait then! There, that's better, Sonya.'

'Will you soon be ready?' came the countess's voice. 'It is nearly ten.'

'Coming, coming! What about you, mamma?'

'I have only my cap to pin on.'

'Don't do it without me!' cried Natasha. 'You won't do it right.'

'Yes, but it's ten o'clock.'

It had been agreed that they should arrive at the ball at half past ten, but Natasha had still to get her dress on before they called for Madame Peronsky.

When her hair was done, Natasha, in a short petticoat from under which her dancing-slippers showed, and her mother's dressing-jacket, ran up to Sonya, inspected her critically, and then flew on to her mother. Turning the countess's head this way and that, she fastened on the cap, gave the grey hair a hasty kiss and scurried back to the maids who were shortening her skirt.

The cause of the delay was Natasha's skirt, which was too long. Two maids were at work turning up the hem and hurriedly biting off the threads. A third, with her mouth full of pins, was running backwards and forwards between the countess and Sonya, while a fourth held the gossamer garment high on one uplifted hand.

'Hurry up, Mavra, darling!'

'Hand me that thimble, please, miss.'

'Aren't you ever going to be ready?' asked the count, coming to the door. 'Here are you still perfuming yourselves. Madame Peronsky must be tired of waiting.'

'Ready, miss,' said the maid, lifting up the shortened tulle skirt with two fingers, and giving it a puff and a shake to show her appreciation of the airiness and immaculate freshness of what she held in her hands.

Natasha began putting on the dress.

'In a minute, in a minute! Don't come in, papa!' she cried to her father at the door, her face eclipsed in a cloud of tulle. Sonya slammed the door to. But a moment later they let the count in. He was wearing a blue swallow-tail coat, stockings and buckled shoes, and was perfumed and pomaded.

'Oh, papa, how nice you look! Lovely!' exclaimed Natasha, as she stood in the middle of the room stroking out the folds of her tulle.

'If you please, miss, allow me,' said the maid, who was on her knees pulling the skirt straight, and shifting the pins from one side of her mouth to the other with her tongue.

'You can say what you like,' cried Sonya in despairing tones, as she surveyed Natasha's dress, 'you can say what you like, it is still too long!'

Natasha stepped back to see herself in the pier-glass. The dress *was* too long.

'Really, madam, it is not at all too long,' said Mavra, crawling on her knees after her young lady.

'Well, if it's too long we'll tack it up ... we can do it in a second,' said the determined Dunyasha, taking a needle from the kerchief she wore crossed over her bosom and, still on the floor, setting to work again.

At that moment the countess in her cap and velvet gown crept shyly into the room.

'Oo-oo, my beauty!' cried the count. 'She looks nicer than any of you!'

He would have embraced her but, blushing, she stepped back, for fear of getting her gown rumpled.

'Mamma, your cap wants to go more to one side,' said Natasha. 'I'll alter it for you,' and she darted forward so that the maids who were tacking up her skirt could not follow her fast enough and a piece of the tulle got torn off.

'Mercy, what was that? Really it was not my fault. ...'

'Never mind, I'll put a stitch in, it won't show,' said Dunyasha.

'My beauty – my little queen!' exclaimed the old nurse, coming in at the door. 'And little Sonya too! Ah, the beauties! ...'

At last at a quarter past ten they seated themselves in the carriage and were on their way. But they still had to call at the Tavrichesky gardens.

Madame Peronsky was all ready and waiting. In spite of her advanced age and absence of looks she had gone through the same process as the Rostovs, though with less flurry since to her it was a matter of routine. Her unprepossessing old body had been washed, perfumed and powdered in exactly the same way. She had washed just as carefully behind her ears, and when she had come down into the drawing-room in her yellow gown, wearing her badge as a maid of honour, her old maid had been just as enthusiastic in her admiration of her mistress's toilette as at the Rostovs'.

Madame Peronsky praised the Rostovs' dresses. They praised her taste and her attire, and at eleven o'clock, careful of their *coiffures* and their gowns, they settled themselves in the carriages and drove off.

15

NATASHA had not had a moment to herself since early morning, and not once had she had time to think of what was before her.

In the damp chill air, in the closeness and half dark of the swaying vehicle, she vividly pictured to herself for the first time what was in store for her there at the ball, in those brilliantly-lighted rooms – the music, the flowers, the dances, the Emperor, all the dazzling young people of Petersburg. The prospect was so splendid that she could hardly believe it would come true, so out of keeping was it with the cold outside and the stuffy darkness of the carriage. She only realized all that was in front of her when she walked along the red baize at the entrance into the vestibule, took off her fur cloak and, together with Sonya, preceded her mother between the flowers up the lighted stair-case. Only then did she remember how she should behave at a ball, and tried to assume the dignified air she considered to be the proper thing for a girl on such an occasion. But, fortunately for her, she felt her eyes growing misty: she could not see anything clearly, her pulse was beating a hundred to the minute and the blood throbbed at her heart. It was impossible for her to put on the manner that would have made her ridiculous, and she moved on almost swooning with ex-citement and trying with all her might to hide it. And this was the very behaviour that became her best. Before and behind them other guests were mounting the stairs, also talking in low tones and wearing ball-dresses. The looking-glasses along the staircase reflected ladies in white, pale blue and pink gowns, with diamonds and pearls on their bare arms and bosoms.

Natasha looked in the mirrors and could not distinguish her reflection from the others. Everything intertwined into one brilliant procession. At the entrance to the ballroom the continuous hum of voices, footsteps and greetings deafened Natasha; and the light and glitter dazzled her still more. The host and hostess, who had already been standing at the door for half an hour repeating the same words of welcome – '*Charmé de vous voir*' – to the various arrivals, greeted the Rostovs and Madame Peronsky in like manner.

The two young girls in their white dresses, each with a rose in her black hair, curtsied alike, but the hostess's eye involuntarily rested longer on the slender figure of Natasha. She looked at her and gave her a special smile for herself as well as her hostess smile. Looking at her, she was reminded perhaps of the golden days of her own girlhood, gone never to return, and of her own first ball. The host too followed Natasha with his eyes and asked the count which of the two was his daughter.

'*Charmante!*' said he, kissing the tips of his fingers.

In the ballroom guests stood crowding about the entry in expectation of the Emperor. The countess took up a position in one of the front rows of this crowd. Natasha heard and was conscious that several people were asking about her and looking at her. She realized that she was making a pleasant impression on those who noticed her, and this observation calmed her somewhat.

'There are some looking as nice as we do, and some not so nice,' she thought.

Madame Peronsky was pointing out to the countess the most interesting of the people in the ballroom.

'That is the Dutch ambassador, do you see? The grey-haired man,' she said, indicating an old man with a profusion of silver-grey curls, who was surrounded by ladies laughing at some story he was telling.

'Ah, and here comes the Queen of Petersburg, Countess Bezuhov,' she exclaimed, as Hélène made her appearance. 'How lovely she is! She quite holds her own beside Maria Antonovna –' (this was the Tsar's favourite) '– see how the men pay court to her, young and old alike. She's both beautiful and intelligent. They say a royal prince is head over heels in love with her. But look at those two – not a bit good-looking but even more run after.'

She pointed out a lady who was crossing the room followed by a very plain daughter.

'That girl's heiress to a million,' said Madame Peronsky. 'And look, here come her suitors. .... That's Countess Bezuhov's brother, Anatole Kuragin,' she said, indicating a handsome officer of the Horse Guards who passed by them, holding himself very erect and looking at something over the heads of the ladies. 'Handsome, isn't he? I'm told he is to marry the heiress. And your cousin, Drubetskoy, is very attentive to her too. They say she has millions. Oh yes, that is the French ambassador himself,' she replied in answer to the countess's inquiry as to the identity of Caulaincourt. 'He might be a king! All the same, the French are charming, very charming. No one more charming in society. Ah, here she is! Yes, after all, there is no one to compare with our Maria Antonovna! And how simply she is dressed! Exquisite! And that stout fellow in spectacles is the great freemason,' she went on, referring to Pierre. 'Set him beside his wife, and what a ridiculous creature!'

Swinging his portly figure, Pierre advanced through the throng, nodding to right and left as casually and good-naturedly as if he were making his way through crowds at a fair. He pushed forward, evidently looking for someone. Natasha was delighted to see the familiar face of Pierre, that 'ridiculous creature', as Madame Peronsky had called him, and knew it was they, and herself in particular, of whom he was in search. He had promised to be at the ball and find partners for her.

But before reaching them Pierre stopped beside a very handsome, dark man of medium height in a white uniform, who was standing by a window talking to a tall man wearing stars and a ribbon. Natasha at once recognized the shorter and younger man in the white uniform: it was Bolkonsky, who seemed to her to have grown much younger, happier and better looking.

'There's someone else we know – Bolkonsky, do you see, Mamma?' said Natasha, pointing out Prince Andrei. 'You remember, he stayed a night with us at Otradnoe.'

'Oh, do you know him?' said Madame Peronsky. 'I can't bear him. Everyone is crazy over him just now. And the conceit of him: it's beyond words! Takes after his father. And he's hand in glove with Speransky over some project or other. See how he treats the ladies! There's one talking to him, and he turns his back on her,' she said, pointing to him. 'I'd give him a piece of my mind if he behaved with me as he does with them.'

16

THERE was a sudden stir: a whisper ran through the assembly, which pressed forward and then back, separating into two rows down the middle of which walked the Emperor to the strains of the orchestra which struck up at once. Behind him came his host and hostess. He entered rapidly, bowing to right and left as if anxious to get through the first formalities as quickly as possible. The band played the polonaise in vogue at the moment on account of the words that had been set to it, beginning: 'Alexander, Elisaveta, our hearts ye ravish quite...' The Emperor passed on into the drawing-room; the crowd surged to the doors; several persons dashed backwards and forwards, their faces transformed. The wave receded from the doors of the drawing-room, where the Emperor appeared engaged in conversation with his hostess. A young man, looking distraught, bore down on the ladies, begging them to move away. Several ladies, with faces betraying complete disregard of all the rules of decorum, squeezed forward to the detriment of their toilettes. The men began to select partners and take their places for the polonaise.

Space was cleared, and the Emperor, smiling, came out of the drawing-room leading his hostess by the hand but not keeping time to the music. The host followed with Maria Antonovna Naryshkin; and after them ambassadors, ministers and various generals, whom Madame Peronsky diligently named. More than half the ladies had partners and were taking up or preparing to take up their positions for the polonaise. Natasha felt that she would be left with her mother and Sonya among the minority who lined the walls, not having been invited to dance. She stood with her slender arms hanging by her sides, her scarcely defined bosom rising and falling regularly, and with bated breath and glittering, frightened eyes gazed straight before her, evidently equally prepared for the height of joy or the depths of misery. She was not interested in the Emperor or any of the great personages whom Madame Peronsky was pointing out – she had but one thought: 'Can it be that no one will come up to me, that I shall not be among the first to dance? Is it possible that not one of all these men will notice me? They don't even seem to see me, or if they do they look as if they were saying, "No, she's not the one I'm after, it's no use looking at her!" No, it cannot be,' she thought. 'They must know how I am longing to dance, and how splendidly I dance, and how much they would enjoy dancing with me.'

The strains of the polonaise, which had now lasted some little time, began to have a melancholy cadence in Natasha's ears, like some sad reminiscence. She wanted to cry. Madame Peronsky had left them. The count was at the other end of the ballroom. She and the countess and Sonya were as much alone in this crowd of strangers as though they stood in the heart of a forest: no one took any interest in them or wanted them. Prince Andrei passed with a lady, obviously not recognizing them. The handsome Anatole was smilingly talking to a partner on his arm, and he glanced at Natasha's face as one glances at a wall. Twice Boris passed them, and each time turned his head away. Berg and his wife, who were not dancing, came up to them.

Natasha was mortified at this family gathering here in the ball-room – as though there were nowhere else for family talk but here at the ball. She did not listen or look at Vera, who was telling her something about her own green dress.

At last the Emperor stopped beside his last partner (he had danced with three) and the music ceased. An officious aide-de-camp bustled up to the Rostovs requesting them to stand farther back, though as it was they were already close to the wall, and from the gallery came the precise, regular, enticing strains of a waltz. The Emperor glanced down the room with a smile. A minute passed – no one had as yet begun dancing. An aide de camp, the master of ceremonies, went up to Countess Bezuhov and asked her to dance.

Smiling, she raised her hand and laid it on his shoulder, without looking at him. The aide-de-camp, a master of his art, grasped his partner firmly round the waist, and with confident deliberation glided smoothly first round the edge of the circle, then at the corner of the room he caught Hélène's left hand and turned her, the only sound audible, apart from the ever-quickening music, being the rhythmic clicking of the spurs on his swift and agile feet, while at every third beat his partner's velvet skirts seemed to flash as she whirled round. Natasha watched them and was ready to weep that it was not she who was dancing that first round of the waltz.

Prince Andrei, in the white uniform of a cavalry-colonel, wearing silk stockings and buckled dancing-slippers, stood looking animated and in the best of spirits in the front row of the circle not far from the Rostovs. Baron Firhoff was talking to him about the preliminary sitting of the Council of State to be held next day. Prince Andrei, as one closely connected with Speransky and participating in the work of the legislative commission, could give reliable information in regard to the approaching session, concerning which there were many conflicting rumours. But he was not listening to what Firhoff was saying, and looked now at the Sovereign, now at the various gentlemen who were all ready but had not yet gathered courage to take the floor.

Prince Andrei was observing these gentlemen abashed by the Emperor's presence, and the ladies who were dying to be asked to dance.

Pierre came up to Prince Andrei and caught him by the arm.

'You always dance. I have a *protégée* here, the little Rostov girl. Do invite her,' he said.

'Where is she?' asked Bolkonsky. 'Excuse me, baron,' he added, turning to the man he had been talking to, 'we will finish this conversation elsewhere – at a ball one must dance.' He stepped forward in the direction Pierre indicated. Natasha's dejected, despairing face caught his eye. He recognized her, guessed her feelings, saw that it was her *début*, remembered the conversation he had overheard between her and Sonya at the window, and with an eager expression went up to Countess Rostov.

'Allow me to introduce you to my daughter,' said the countess, with heightened colour.

'I have the pleasure of her acquaintance already, if the countess remembers me,' said Prince Andrei with a low and courteous bow, quite belying Madame Peronsky's remarks about his rudeness; and approaching Natasha he started to put his arm round her waist even before he had completed his invitation to her to dance. He suggested that they should take a turn of the waltz. Natasha's face with the tremulous expression prepared for despair or rapture suddenly lighted up with a happy, childlike smile of gratitude.

'I have been waiting an eternity for you,' this frightened, happy little girl seemed to be saying with a smile shining through the threatened tears, as she raised her hand to Prince Andrei's shoulder. They were the second couple to take the floor. Prince Andrei was one of the best dancers of his day. Natasha danced exquisitely. Her little feet in their satin dancing-shoes performed their rôle swiftly, lightly, as if they had wings, while her face was radiant and ecstatic with happiness. Her thin bare arms and neck were not beautiful compared to Hélène's. Her shoulders looked thin and her bosom undeveloped. But Hélène seemed, as it were, covered with the hard polish left by the thousands of eyes that had scanned her person, while Natasha was a girl appearing décolletée for the first time in her life, and who would certainly have felt very much ashamed had she not been assured by everyone that it was the proper thing.

Prince Andrei was fond of dancing, and wishing to lose no time in escaping from the political and intellectual conversations into which everyone tried to draw him, and anxious as quickly as possible to break through that burdensome barrier of constraint caused by the Emperor's presence, he danced, and had chosen Natasha for his partner because Pierre pointed her out to him and because she was the first pretty girl who caught his eye. But he had no sooner put his arm round that slender supple quivering figure, and felt her stirring so close to him and smiling up into his face, than her charm mounted to his head like wine, and he felt himself revived and rejuvenated when they stopped to get breath and he released her and stood watching the other couples.

17

AFTER Prince Andrei, Boris came up to ask Natasha for a dance, and he was followed by the aide-de-camp who had opened the ball, and several other young men, so that Natasha, flushed and happy, and passing on her superfluous partners to Sonya, did not miss a single dance throughout the rest of the evening. She noticed and saw nothing of what interested everyone else. Not only did she fail to remark that the Emperor had a long conversation with the French ambassador, that his manner was particularly gracious to a certain lady, or that Prince So-and-so and Monsieur So-and-so had done and said this and that, and that Hélène had a great success and was honoured by the special attentions of such-and-such a person, but she did not even see the Emperor, and was only aware that he had gone because the ball became livelier after his departure. For one of the jolliest cotillions before supper Prince Andrei was again her partner. He reminded her of their first encounter in the avenue at Otradnoe, and of how she had been unable to sleep that moonlight night, and told her how he had involuntarily overheard her. Natasha blushed at this reminiscence and tried to excuse herself, as if there had been something to be ashamed of in what Prince Andrei had accidentally listened to.

Like all men who have grown up in society, Prince Andrei enjoyed meeting someone not of the conventional society stamp. And such was Natasha, with her wonder, her delight, her shyness and even her mistakes in speaking French. His manner was particularly tender and careful. As he sat beside her talking of the simplest and most insignificant matters, he admired the radiance of her eyes and her smile which had to do with her own inner happiness and not with what they were saying. When Natasha was invited to dance, and got up with a smile and glided round the room, her shy grace particularly charmed him. In the middle of the cotillion, having completed one of the figures, Natasha, still out of breath, was returning to her seat when another cavalier importuned her. She was tired and panting, and evidently thought for a moment of declining, but immediately she put her hand on her partner's shoulder and was off again, with a smile to Prince Andrei.

'I would rather rest and stay with you, I'm tired,' said that smile; 'but you see how they keep asking me, and I'm glad of it, and happy, and I love everybody, and you and I understand all about it.' That and much more this smile of hers seemed to say. When her partner left her, Natasha flew across the room to choose two ladies for the figure.

'If she goes first to her cousin and then to another lady, she will be my wife,' Prince Andrei – greatly to his own surprise – caught himself thinking as he watched her. She did go first to her cousin.

'What nonsense enters one's head sometimes!' thought Prince Andrei. 'But one thing's certain – that girl is so sweet, so out of the ordinary, that she won't spend a month in the ballroom before she's married. ... Such as she are rare here,' he thought, as Natasha, re-adjusting a rose that was slipping on her bodice, settled herself beside him.

At the end of the cotillion the old count in his blue coat came up to the young people who had been dancing. He invited Prince Andrei to come and see them, and asked his daughter whether she was enjoying herself. Natasha did not answer at once: she only looked up with a smile that said reproachfully: 'How can you ask such a question?'

'It's the loveliest time I ever had in my life!' said she, and Prince Andrei noticed how her thin arms rose quickly as though to embrace her father, and instantly dropped again. Natasha had never been so happy. She was at that highest pitch of bliss when one becomes completely good and kind, and cannot believe in the existence or possibility of evil, unhappiness and sorrow.

*

Pierre at this ball for the first time felt humiliated by the position his wife occupied in court circles. He was morose and abstracted. A deep furrow ran across his forehead, and standing by a window he stared through his spectacles, seeing no one.

On her way to supper Natasha passed him.

Pierre's gloomy, unhappy face struck her. She stopped in front of him. She felt a desire to help him, to bestow on him the superabundance of her own happiness.

'How delightful it is, count,' she said, 'don't you think so?'

Pierre smiled absent-mindedly, obviously not taking in what she said.

'Yes, I am very glad,' he replied.

'How can people not be pleased with anything?' thought Natasha. 'Especially anyone as nice as Bezuhov.' In Natasha's eyes all who were at the ball were alike good, kind, splendid people, full of affection for one another, incapable of harm – and so they all ought to be happy.

18

NEXT day Prince Andrei recalled the ball but it did not occupy his mind for long. 'Yes, it was a most brilliant ball. And then – oh yes, the little Rostov girl is very charming. There's something fresh, original, un-Petersburg-like about her that distinguishes her.' That was the extent of the thought he gave to the ball of the night before, and after his morning tea he set to work.

But either from fatigue or want of sleep he was ill-disposed for effort and could not get on. He was dissatisfied with what he did do, as was often the case with him, and was glad when he heard a visitor arrive.

The visitor was Bitsky, a man who served on various committees and frequented all the different cliques of Petersburg. He was a passionate devotee of the new ideas and of Speransky, and the most diligent purveyor of news in Petersburg – one of those men who select their opinions like their clothes, according to the prevailing fashion, and in consequence come to be regarded as the most eager supporters of the latest trends. Scarcely giving himself time to remove his hat, he hurried busily into Prince Andrei's room and at once began talking. He had just heard all about that morning's sitting of the Council of State opened by the Emperor. He dilated with enthusiasm on the Sovereign's speech: it had been an extraordinary one – the sort of speech only constitutional monarchs deliver. 'The Sovereign said in so many words that the Council and the Senate are *estates* of the realm; he said that the government must rest not on arbitrary authority but on solid principles. The Emperor said that the fiscal system must be reorganized and the budgets made public,' recounted Bitsky, laying stress on certain words and opening his eyes significantly. 'Yes, today's events mark an epoch, the greatest epoch in our history,' he concluded.

Prince Andrei listened to the account of the opening of the State Council, to which he had so impatiently been looking forward and to which he attached so much importance, and was astonished that now that it was an accomplished fact he was not only unmoved but completely unimpressed. He listened with quiet irony to Bitsky's rhapsody. A very simple thought occurred to him: 'What is it to me and Bitsky – what is it to us what the Emperor is pleased to say in the Council? Can it make me any happier or better?'

And this simple reflection suddenly destroyed all the interest Prince Andrei had formerly taken in the impending reforms. That very day he was to dine at Speransky's – 'just a few of us', his host had said when inviting him. The idea of this dinner in the intimate home circle of the man he so admired had seemed very attractive to Prince Andrei, especially as he had not yet seen Speransky in his domestic surroundings, but now he had lost all desire to go.

At the appointed hour, however, he entered the modest residence in the Tavrichesky gardens. The little house, which was Speransky's own property, was remarkable for its extreme spotlessness (suggesting that of a monastery). In the parquet-floored dining-room Prince Andrei, who was rather late, found the friendly gathering of his host's intimate friends already assembled at five o'clock. There were no ladies present except Speransky's young daughter (who had a long face like her father's) and the child's governess. The other guests were Gervais, Magnitsky and Stolypin. From the vestibule Prince Andrei caught the sound of loud voices and a ringing, staccato laugh – a laugh such as one hears on the stage. Someone – it sounded like Speransky

– was giving vent to a distinct *ha-ha-ha*. Prince Andrei had never heard Speransky laugh before, and this shrill, ringing laugh from the great statesman made a strange impression on him.

He went into the dining-room. The whole party were standing between the two windows at a small table laid with hors-d'œuvre. Speransky, wearing a grey swallow-tail coat with a star on his breast, and evidently still the same white waistcoat and high white stock in which he had appeared at the famous meeting of the Council of State, stood at the table with a beaming countenance. His guests formed a ring round him. Magnitsky, addressing himself to Speransky, was relating an anecdote, and Speransky was laughing in advance at what Magnitsky was going to say. Just as Prince Andrei walked into the room Magnitsky's words were again drowned by laughter. Stolypin gave a deep bass guffaw as he munched a little square of bread and cheese. Gervais softly hissed a chuckle, and Speransky laughed his high-pitched staccato laugh.

Still laughing, Speransky held out his soft white hand to Prince Andrei.

'So glad to see you, prince,' he said. 'One moment ...' he went on, turning to Magnitsky and interrupting his story. 'We have agreed that this is a dinner for recreation, and not a word about business!' and giving his attention to the narrator again, he began to laugh afresh.

Prince Andrei looked at the hilarious Speransky with a sense of wondering and melancholy disillusion. This was not Speransky but some other man, it seemed to him. All that had formerly appeared mysterious and fascinating in Speransky suddenly became commonplace and unattractive.

At dinner the conversation never stopped for a moment, and seemed to consist of the contents of a book of funny stories. Before Magnitsky had finished his story someone else was anxious to tell them something even more amusing. Most of the anecdotes, if not confined to the world of officialdom, at least related to individuals in the service. It was as though in this company the nonentity of those people was so thoroughly taken for granted that the only possible attitude to them was one of good-humoured ridicule. Speransky described how at the Council that morning a deaf dignitary, on being asked his opinion, replied that he thought so too. Gervais gave a long account of an incident to do with the census, remarkable for the imbecility of everybody concerned. Stolypin, stuttering, broke in and began talking of the abuses that existed in the old order of things, with a warmth that threatened to give the conversation a serious turn. Magnitsky started making fun of Stolypin's vehemence. Gervais intervened with a pun, and the talk reverted to its former frivolous tone.

Evidently Speransky liked to rest after his labours and find amusement in a circle of friends, and his guests, knowing this, did their best to cheer him and divert themselves. But their gaiety seemed forced and mirthless to Prince Andrei. Speransky's shrill voice struck him unpleasantly, and his incessant laughter had a false ring that grated on him. Prince Andrei did not laugh and feared that the company would find him a kill-joy, but no one noticed that he was out of harmony with the general mood. They all appeared to be enjoying themselves greatly.

He made several attempts to join in the conversation, but each time his remarks were tossed aside like a cork flung back out of the water, and he could not bandy jokes with them.

There was nothing wrong or unseemly in what they said: it was witty, and might have been amusing but it lacked just that something which is the salt of mirth, and they were not even aware that such an element existed.

After dinner, Speransky's daughter and her governess rose. Speransky patted the little girl with his white hand and kissed her. And that gesture, too, seemed unnatural to Prince Andrei.

The men remained at table, sitting over their port after the English fashion. In the middle of a conversation that sprang up about Napoleon's Spanish affairs, which they all approved unanimously, Prince Andrei took it upon himself to disagree. Speransky smiled, and with the evident intention of changing the subject told a story which was totally irrelevant. For a few moments all were silent.

After they had sat for some time at table, Speransky corked up a bottle of wine, and remarking 'Good wine is expensive these days,' handed it to the servant and got up. All rose, and still talking noisily passed into the drawing-room. Two letters were brought in which had come by a courier, and Speransky took them to his study. As soon as he left the room the general merriment was abandoned and the guests began to talk sensibly together in low tones.

'Well, now for the recitation,' said Speransky, returning from his study. 'A wonderful talent!' he said to Prince Andrei. Magnitsky immediately threw himself into an attitude and began to recite some humorous verses he had written in French about certain well-known Petersburg people. Several times he was interrupted by applause. At the conclusion of the recitation Prince Andrei went up to Speransky and took his leave.

'Where are you off to so early?' inquired Speransky.

'I promised to be at a *soirée.* ...'

They said no more. Prince Andrei looked closely into those mirror-like, impenetrable eyes, and felt that it had been ludicrous of him to have expected anything from Speransky, or of any of his own activities connected with him, and marvelled how he could have attributed importance to what Speransky was doing. The measured mirthless laugh rang in Prince Andrei's ears long after he had left Speransky's.

When he reached home Prince Andrei began to live over his life in Petersburg during the last four months, as though it were something new. He recalled his exertions, the efforts he had made to see people, and the history of his project of army reform, which had been accepted for consideration and which they were trying to shelve for the sole reason that another scheme, a very inferior one, had already been prepared and submitted to the Emperor. He thought of the sittings of the committee of which Berg was a member. He remembered the conscientious and prolonged deliberations that took place at those meetings on every point relating to form and procedure, and how sedulously and promptly all that touched the substance of the business was evaded. He recalled his labours on the legislative reforms, and how painstakingly he had translated the articles of the Roman and French codes into Russian, and he felt ashamed for himself. Then he vividly pictured Bogucharovo, his pursuits in the country, his expedition to Ryazan; thought of his peasants and Dron the village elder, and mentally applying to them the section on Personal Rights, which he had classified into paragraphs, he was amazed that he could have spent so much time on such useless work.

19

THE next day Prince Andrei paid calls on various people whom he had not visited before, and among them on the Rostovs, with whom he had renewed his acquaintance at the ball. Apart from considerations of politeness which demanded the call, he also had a strong desire to see in her own home that original, eager girl who had left such a pleasant impression in his mind.

Natasha happened to be the first to receive him. She was wearing a dark blue everyday dress, in which Prince Andrei thought she looked even prettier than in her ball-gown. She and all the family welcomed him as an old friend, simply and cordially. The whole family, whom he had once criticized so severely, now seemed to him charming, simple, kindly folk. The old count's pressing hospitality and his good nature, particularly conspicuous and appealing here in Petersburg, were such that Prince Andrei could not refuse to stay to dinner. 'Yes,' he thought, 'they are excellent people, who of course have not the slightest idea what a treasure they possess in Natasha; but they are good people, who make the best possible background for this wonderfully poetical, delightful girl, so overflowing with life!'

In Natasha Prince Andrei was conscious of a strange world, completely remote from him and brimful of joys he had not known, that different world which even in the avenue at Otradnoe and on that moonlight night at the window had tantalized him. Now it mocked him no longer, and was no longer an alien world: he himself had stepped into it and was finding new satisfactions for himself.

After dinner Natasha, at Prince Andrei's request, went to the clavichord and began singing. Prince Andrei stood at the window talking to the ladies, and listened to her. Suddenly in the middle of a sentence he fell silent, feeling a lump in his throat from tears, a thing he would not have believed possible for him. He looked at Natasha as she sang, and something new and blissful stirred in his soul. He felt happy and at the same time sad. He had absolutely nothing to weep about, yet he was ready to weep. For what? For his past love? For the little princess? For his lost illusions? ... For his hopes for the future? ... Yes and no. The chief reason for his wanting to weep was a sudden acute sense of the terrible contrast between something infinitely great and illimitable existing within him and the narrow material something which he, and even she, was. The contrast made his heart ache, and rejoiced him while she sang.

As soon as Natasha finished her song she went up to him and asked him how he liked her voice. She asked the question and was then embarrassed, realizing that she ought not to have put it. He smiled, looking at her, and said he liked her singing just as he liked everything else she did.

It was late in the evening when Prince Andrei left the Rostovs. He went to bed from habit, but soon saw that he could not sleep. Having lit his candle he sat up in bed, then got up, then lay down again, not at all oppressed by his sleeplessness: his soul was so full of new and joyful sensations that it seemed to him as if he had just emerged from a stuffy room into God's fresh air. It did not enter his head that he was in love with the little Rostov girl, he was not thinking about her but only picturing her to himself, and in consequence all life appeared in a new light. 'Why do I struggle ? Why am I toiling and moiling in this narrow, petty environment, when life, all life with its every joy, lies open before me ?' he said to himself. And for the first time for a very long while he began making happy plans for the future. He decided that he must attend personally to his son's education, finding a tutor and putting the boy in his charge; then he ought to retire from the service and go abroad, see England, Switzerland, Italy. 'I must make the most of my freedom while I feel myself so overflowing with strength and energy,' he said to himself. 'Pierre was right when he said one must believe in the possibility of happiness in order to be happy, and now I do believe in it. Let the dead bury their dead; but while one has life one must live and be happy,' he thought.

20

One morning Colonel Adolf Berg, whom Pierre knew just as he knew everybody in Moscow and Petersburg, came to see him. Berg arrived in an immaculate brand-new uniform, with his hair pomaded and curled over his temples in imitation of the Emperor Alexander.

'I have just been calling on the countess, your wife. Unfortunately she could not grant my request, but I hope, count, I shall have better luck with you,' he said with a smile.

'What is it you wish, colonel ? I am at your service.'

'I am now quite settled in my new quarters, count,' Berg informed him, evidently convinced in his own mind that this piece of news could not fail to be agreeable, 'and consequently I was hoping to arrange a little reception for my friends and those of my spouse.' (He smiled still more effusively.) 'I wanted to ask the countess and yourself to do me the honour of coming to us for a cup of tea and ... to supper.'

Only the Countess Hélène, considering it beneath her dignity to associate with nobodies like the Bergs, could have been cruel enough to refuse such an invitation. Berg explained so clearly why he wanted to gather a small but select company at his new rooms, and why this would give him pleasure, and why though he grudged money spent on cards and other disreputable occupations he was prepared to run to some expense for the sake of good society, that Pierre could not refuse, and promised to come.

'Only not too late, count, if I may venture to beg of you. About ten minutes to eight, if I may make so bold. We shall make up a rubber. Our general is coming. He is very kind to me. We will have a little supper, count. So do me the favour.'

Contrary to his usual habit of being late, Pierre that evening arrived at the Bergs' house not at ten but at fifteen minutes to eight.

The Bergs, having made every provision for the party, were ready for their guests to appear.

In their new, clean, light study, embellished with little busts and pictures and new furniture, sat Berg and his wife. Berg, tightly buttoned into his new uniform, sat beside his wife, explaining to her that one always could and should be acquainted with people above one in station, that being the only real satisfaction in having friends.

'You can always find something to imitate or ask for. Look at me now, how my life has gone since my first promotion.' (Berg measured his life not by years but by promotions.) 'My comrades are still nobodies, while at the first vacancy I shall be a regimental commander. I have the happiness of being your husband.' (He rose and kissed Vera's hand, but on the way he straightened a corner of the carpet which was rucked up.) 'And how did I accomplish all this? Principally by knowing how to select my acquaintances. It goes without saying, of course, that one must be conscientious and methodical.'

Berg smiled with the consciousness of his superiority over a weak woman, and paused, reflecting that this dear wife of his was after all but a feeble woman unable to appreciate the dignity of being a man—what it meant *ein Mann zu sein*. Vera meanwhile was smiling too with a sense of her superiority over her good, worthy husband, who nevertheless, like the rest of his sex, according to Vera's ideas of men, took an utterly wrong-headed view of the meaning of life. Berg, judging by his wife, considered all women weak and foolish. Vera, judging only by her husband and generalizing from her observation of him, supposed that all men believed that no one but themselves had any sense, though they had no real understanding and were conceited and selfish.

Berg rose and embracing his wife carefully so as not to crush her lace fichu, for which he had paid a round sum, kissed her full on the lips.

'The only thing is, we mustn't have children too soon,' he said, by a correlation of ideas of which he himself was unaware.

'No,' answered Vera, 'I don't at all want that. We must live for society.'

'Princess Yusupov was wearing one exactly like this,' said Berg, laying a finger on the fichu with a contented, happy smile.

Just then Count Bezuhov was announced. Husband and wife exchanged self-satisfied glances, each mentally claiming the credit for this visit.

'See the result of knowing how to make acquaintances,' thought Berg. 'This is what comes of possessing *savoir faire*!'

'Now I do beg of you,' said Vera, 'don't interrupt me when I am entertaining the guests, because I know very well what is likely to interest each of them and what to say to different people.'

Berg, too, smiled.

'Oh, but sometimes men must have their masculine conversation,' said he.

Pierre was shown into the brand-new drawing-room, where it was impossible to sit down without disturbing its symmetrical neatness and order; so it was perfectly comprehensible and not to be wondered at that Berg should magnanimously offer to sacrifice the symmetry of an arm-chair or of the sofa for his esteemed guest, and then, finding himself in a painful state of indecision on the matter, leave the visitor to decide the problem of where to sit. Pierre upset the symmetry by moving forward a chair for himself, and Berg and Vera immediately began their *soirée*, interrupting each other in their efforts to entertain their guest.

Vera, having decided in her own mind that Pierre ought to be entertained with conversation about the French Embassy, promptly embarked upon that subject. Berg, deciding that masculine conversation was required, cut in on his wife with some remarks on the war with Austria, and from general discussion involuntarily leapt to a personal review of the proposals made to him to take part in the Austrian campaign, and the reasons which had led him to decline them. Although the conversation was extremely desultory and Vera was indignant at the intrusion of this masculine element, both husband and wife felt with satisfaction that, even if only one guest was present, their *soirée* had begun very well and was as like as two drops of water to every other *soirée*, with the same conversation, tea and lighted candles.

Before long Boris, Berg's old comrade, arrived. There was a certain shade of patronage and condescension in his treatment of Berg and Vera. After Boris came the colonel and his lady, then the general himself, then the Rostovs, and now the party without a shadow of doubt began to resemble all other evening parties. Berg and Vera could not repress blissful smiles at the sight of all this stir in their drawing-room, at the sound of the disconnected chatter, and the rustle of skirts and of curtsies and bows. Everything was identically the same as it was everywhere else; especially so was the general, who admired the apartment, patted Berg on the shoulder, and with paternal authority superintended the setting out of the table for boston. The general sat down by Count Ilya Rostov, as the guest ranking next in precedence to himself. The elderly gathered near the elderly, the young people sat with the young, the hostess at the tea-table on which there were exactly the same kind of cakes in a silver cake-basket as the Panins had at their party. Everything was just as it was everywhere else.

21

PIERRE, as one of the most honoured guests, had to sit down to boston with Count Rostov, the general and the colonel. At the card-table he happened to be directly facing Natasha, and he was struck by the curious change that had come over her since the night of the ball. She scarcely spoke a word, and not only was she less pretty than she had been at the ball but would have looked positively plain but for the expression of gentle indifference on her face.

'What is the matter with her?' Pierre wondered, glancing at Natasha. She was sitting by her sister at the tea-table, making reluctant answers, without looking at him, to Boris who sat down beside her. After playing out a whole suit and to his partner's satisfaction taking five tricks, Pierre, hearing greetings and the steps of someone who had entered the room while he was picking up his cards, glanced again at Natasha.

'What has happened to her?' he asked himself with even more wonder than before.

Prince Andrei was standing before her, saying something with a look of tender solicitude. She had raised her head and was gazing at him with flushed cheeks, visibly trying to control her rapid breathing. And the radiance of some inner fire that had been extinguished before was alight in her again. She was completely transformed: instead of looking plain she was the beautiful creature she had been at the ball.

Prince Andrei went up to Pierre, and Pierre noticed a new and youthful expression in his friend's face.

Pierre changed places several times during the game, sitting now with his back to Natasha, now facing her, but during the whole six rubbers he watched her and his friend.

'There is something very important happening between them,' thought Pierre, and a mixed feeling of joy and bitterness agitated him and made him forgetful of the game.

After six rubbers the general got up, saying that it was no use playing like that, and Pierre was released. Natasha on one side was talking with Sonya and Boris. Vera, with a subtle smile, was saying something to Prince Andrei. Pierre went up to his friend and, asking whether they were talking secrets, sat down beside them. Vera, having observed Prince Andrei's attentions to Natasha, decided that a *soirée*, a real *soirée*, demanded some delicate allusions to the tender passion, and seizing an opportunity when Prince Andrei was alone, began a conversation with him about the emotions generally and her sister in particular. With so intellectual a guest as she considered Prince Andrei, she felt she must bring to bear all her art of diplomacy.

When Pierre joined them he noticed that Vera was being carried away by her own eloquence, while Prince Andrei seemed embarrassed – a rare thing with him.

'What do you think?' Vera was saying with an arch smile. 'You are so discerning, prince, and so quick at understanding people's characters. What do you think of Natalie? Is she capable of being constant in her attachments? Could she, like other women' (Vera meant herself) 'love a man once for all and remain faithful to him for ever? That is what I call true love. What is your opinion, prince?'

'I do not know your sister well enough,' replied Prince Andrei, with a sardonic smile behind which he hoped to hide his embarrassment, 'to be able to solve so delicate a question; and besides I have noticed that the less attractive a woman is the more constant she is likely to be,' he added, and looked up at Pierre who had just joined them.

'Yes, that is true, prince. In these days,' pursued Vera – speaking of 'these days' as people of limited intelligence are fond of doing, imagining that they have discovered and appraised the peculiarities of 'these days' and that human nature changes with the times – 'in these days a girl has so much freedom that the pleasure of being courted often stifles real feeling in her. And Natasha, it must be confessed, is very susceptible.' This return to the subject of Natasha caused Prince Andrei to contract his brows disagreeably. He made to rise, but Vera persisted with a still more subtle smile:

'Nobody, I imagine, has been so much run after as she has,' she went on, 'but till quite lately no one has ever made a serious impression on her. Of course, you know, count,' she turned to Pierre, 'even our charming cousin, Boris, who, between ourselves, journeyed very deep into the region of tenderness ...' (she was alluding to a map of love much in vogue at that time).

Prince Andrei frowned and remained silent.

'You and Boris are friends, are you not ?' asked Vera.

'Yes, I know him. ...'

'I expect he has told you of his boyish love for Natasha ?'

'Oh, so there was a romance between them, was there ?' suddenly asked Prince Andrei, going unexpectedly red.

'Yes, you know close intimacy between cousins often leads to love. *Le cousinage est un dangereux voisinage.* Don't you agree ?'

'Oh, undoubtedly !' said Prince Andrei, and with a sudden and unnatural liveliness he began chaffing Pierre, warning him to be very careful with his fifty-year-old cousins in Moscow, and in the midst of these jesting remarks he got up, and taking Pierre's arm drew him aside.

'Well ?' asked Pierre, who had been watching in startled wonder his friend's strange excitement and had noticed the glance he turned upon Natasha as he rose.

'I must ... I must have a talk with you,' said Prince Andrei. 'You know that pair of women's gloves ?' (He was referring to the masonic gloves given to a newly-initiated brother to present to the woman he loved.) 'I ... no, I will talk to you by and by ...' and with a queer light in his eyes and a restlessness in his movements Prince Andrei crossed over to Natasha and sat down beside her. Pierre saw that Prince Andrei asked her something, and how she coloured as she replied.

But at that moment Berg came to Pierre and began insisting that he should take part in a discussion between the general and the colonel on affairs in Spain.

Berg was satisfied and happy. The blissful smile never left his face. The *soirée* was being a great success, exactly repeating every other *soirée* he had been to. Everything was similar: the ladies' refined conversation, the cards, the general raising his voice over the game, the samovar and the tea cakes; only one thing was lacking, which he had always seen at the evening parties he wished to imitate. There had not yet been a loud conversation among the men and argument over some grave intellectual concern. Now the general had started such a discussion and it was to this that Berg carried Pierre off.

22

NEXT day, having been invited by the count, Prince Andrei dined with the Rostovs and spent the rest of the day there.

Everyone in the house realized on whose account Prince Andrei came, and, making no secret of it, he tried to be with Natasha the whole time. Not only was Natasha, in her heart of hearts, frightened yet happy and enraptured, but all the household felt a sort of awe in the anticipation of a great and solemn event. With sad and sternly-serious eyes the countess gazed at Prince Andrei as he talked to Natasha, and timidly started some artificial conversation about trifles as soon as he looked her way. Sonya was afraid to leave Natasha and afraid of being in the way if she stayed with them. Natasha turned pale in a panic of expectation every time she was left for a moment alone with him. Prince Andrei surprised her by his bashfulness. She felt that he wanted to say something to her but could not bring himself to speak.

In the evening after Prince Andrei had gone the countess went up to Natasha and whispered:

'Well?'

'Mamma, for pity's sake, don't ask me any questions now! One mustn't talk about it,' said Natasha.

But that night Natasha, excited and scared by turns, lay a long time in her mother's bed, gazing straight before her. She told her how he had complimented her, how he had said he was going abroad, asked her where they were going to spend the summer, and then how he had asked her about Boris.

'But I never ... I never felt like this before,' she said. 'Only I feel afraid in his presence. I am always afraid when I'm with him. What does it mean? Does it mean that it's the real thing? Does it? Mamma, are you asleep?'

'No, my love; I am frightened myself,' answered her mother. 'Run along now.'

'I shouldn't sleep anyway. How silly to go to sleep! Mummy, mummy! Nothing like this has ever happened to me before!' she said, amazed and awed at the feeling she was aware of in herself. 'And could we ever have dreamed ...!'

It seemed to Natasha that she had fallen in love with Prince Andrei even when she first saw him at Otradnoe. It was as if she were terrified at the strange unexpected happiness of meeting again with the very man she had then chosen (she was firmly convinced that she had done so), and finding that he was apparently not indifferent to her.

'And it seemed as though it all had to happen – his coming to Petersburg while we are here. And our meeting at that ball. It was all fate. It's plain it was fate making everything lead up to this! Already *then*, directly I saw him, I felt something peculiar.'

'What else did he say to you? What are those verses? Read them to me ...' said her mother thoughtfully, referring to some verses Prince Andrei had written in Natasha's album.

'Mamma, it's nothing to be ashamed of that he's a widower?'

'Hush, Natasha. Pray to God – marriages are made in heaven,' said her mother, quoting the French proverb.

'Darling Mummy, how I love you! How happy I am!' cried Natasha, shedding tears of joy and excitement, and hugging her mother.

At that very same hour Prince Andrei was at Pierre's, telling him of his love for Natasha and his firm intention to make her his wife.

*

That evening Countess Hélène Bezuhov was holding an informal party. The French ambassador was there, and a prince of the blood, who of late had been a frequent visitor at the countess's, and a great number of brilliant ladies and gentlemen. Pierre had come down and wandered through the rooms, his preoccupied, absent-minded air of gloom attracting general attention.

Since the ball he had felt the approach of one of his attacks of nervous depression, and had been making desperate efforts to combat it. Since his wife's intimacy with the royal prince Pierre had unexpectedly been appointed a gentleman of the bedchamber, and from that time he had begun to feel a sense of weariness and shame in court society, and dark thoughts of the vanity of all things human came to him oftener than of old. At the same time the growing love he had noticed between his protégée Natasha and Prince Andrei aggravated his melancholy by the contrast between his own position and his friend's. He strove alike to avoid thinking of his wife and of Natasha and Prince Andrei. Once more everything seemed to him insignificant in comparison with eternity; again the question confronted him: 'What is the point of it all?' And days and nights together he forced himself to work at his masonic labours in the hope of warding off the evil spirit. Towards midnight he had withdrawn from the countess's apartments and was sitting in a shabby dressing-gown at a table in his own low-ceilinged room, which was cloudy with tobacco-smoke, and copying out the original transactions of the Scottish freemasons, when someone came in. It was Prince Andrei.

'Ah, it's you,' said Pierre vaguely, with a dissatisfied air. 'I'm hard at it, as you see.' He pointed to his manuscript-book in the way of unhappy people who regard their work as a means of salvation from the ills of life.

Prince Andrei, his face ecstatic with renewed life, came and stood in front of Pierre, and not perceiving his friend's wretched expression smiled down on him with the egoism of happiness.

'Well, my dear boy,' said he, 'I wanted to tell you about it yesterday, and now I have come to do so today. I have never experienced anything like it before. I am in love, my friend!'

Pierre heaved a sudden ponderous sigh and dumped his heavy person down on the sofa beside Prince Andrei.

'With Natasha Rostov, is it?' said he.

'Yes, yes, who else should it be? I would never have believed it, but the feeling is stronger than I. Yesterday I was in torment, in agony, but I would not exchange even that agony for anything in the world.

I have never lived till now. Only now am I alive, but I cannot live without her. But can she love me? ... I'm too old for her. ... Why don't you speak?'

'I? I? What did I tell you?' said Pierre suddenly, rising and beginning to walk about the room. 'I have always thought. ... That girl is such a treasure, such a ... She is a rare girl. ... My dear fellow, don't, I beseech you, stop to reason, do not have doubts – marry, marry, marry. ... And there will be no happier man on earth, of that I am sure.'

'But how about her?'

'She loves you.'

'Don't talk rubbish. ...' said Prince Andrei, smiling and looking into Pierre's eyes.

'She does, I know,' Pierre cried fiercely.

'No, do listen,' returned Prince Andrei, taking hold of him by the arm and stopping him. 'Do you know the state I am in? I must tell someone all about it!'

'Well, go on, talk away. I am very glad,' said Pierre, and indeed his face had changed; the frown had smoothed itself out, and he listened gladly to Prince Andrei. Prince Andrei seemed, and really was, an utterly different, new man. What had become of his *ennui*, his contempt for life, his disillusionment? Pierre was the only person to whom he could bring himself to speak frankly, and to him he revealed all that was in his heart, now gaily and boldly making plans reaching far into the future, saying he could not sacrifice his own happiness to the caprices of his father, declaring that he would either force his father to agree to the marriage, and like her, or dispense with his consent altogether; then marvelling at the feeling which had taken possession of him, as something strange and apart, independent of himself.

'I should never have believed it if anyone had told me I could love like this,' said Prince Andrei. 'It is not at all the same feeling that I had before. The whole world is split into two halves for me: she is one half, and there all is joy, hope and light: the other is where she is not, and there everything is gloom and darkness. ...'

'Darkness and gloom,' repeated Pierre; 'yes, yes, I understand that.'

'I can't help loving the light, it is not my fault. And I am very happy! You understand me? I know you are glad for my sake.'

'Yes, yes,' Pierre assented, looking at his friend with a touched and sad expression in his eyes. The brighter Prince Andrei's lot appeared to him, the more sombre seemed his own.

23

PRINCE ANDREI required his father's sanction for his marriage, and to obtain this he started for the country next day.

The old prince received his son's communication with outward composure but inward wrath. He could not comprehend how anyone could wish to alter his life, to introduce any new element into it, when his own was so near its close. 'Why can't they let me end my days as I want to, and then do as they please?' the old man said to himself. With his son, however, he employed the diplomacy he reserved for matters of serious import. Adopting a quiet tone, he went into the whole matter judicially.

To begin with, the match was not a brilliant one from the point of view of birth, fortune or rank. Secondly, Prince Andrei was not in his first youth and his health was poor (the old man laid special stress on this), while the girl was very young. Thirdly, he had a son whom it would be a pity to entrust to a chit of a girl. 'Fourthly, and finally,' the father said, looking ironically at his son, 'I beg of you to put it off for a year; go abroad, take a cure, have a look round, as you wanted to, for a German tutor for Prince Nikolai; and then if your love or passion or obstinacy – whatever you choose – is still as great, marry! And that's my last word on the subject. Make no mistake, the last!...' concluded the prince, in a tone which showed that nothing would get him to alter his verdict.

Prince Andrei saw clearly that the old man hoped that either his feelings or those of his prospective bride would not stand the test of a year, or else that he (the old prince himself) would die before then, and he decided to conform to his father's wish – to propose, and then postpone the wedding for a year.

Three weeks after his last visit to the Rostovs Prince Andrei returned to Petersburg.

*

On the morrow of her talk with her mother Natasha all day expected Bolkonsky, but he did not come. The next day, and the day after, it was the same. Pierre did not appear either and Natasha, unaware that Prince Andrei had gone away to see his father, did not know how to interpret his absence.

Three weeks passed in this way. Natasha had no desire to go anywhere, and wandered from room to room like a ghost, listless and forlorn, weeping in secret at night and not going to her mother in the evenings. She was continually flushing and was very irritable. It seemed to her that everybody knew about her blighted hope, and was laughing at her and pitying her. In spite of all the intensity of her inward grief this wound to her vanity aggravated her misery.

Once she went to her mother, tried to say something and suddenly burst into tears. Her tears were the tears of an offended child who does not know why it is being punished.

The countess tried to comfort Natasha. At first Natasha listened to her mother's words, but all at once interrupted her.

'Stop, mamma! I am not even thinking about it, and I don't want to. He just came and then left off, left off. ...'

Her voice quivered, and she almost cried again but recovered herself and went on quietly:

'And I don't want to be married at all. And I am afraid of him; I have quite, quite got over it now. ...'

The day after this conversation Natasha put on an old frock, which she knew always made her feel cheerful when she wore it in the mornings, and as soon as she was dressed began to resume her old occupations which she had dropped since the ball. After morning-tea she went to the ballroom, which she particularly liked for its loud resonance, and got to work on her sol-fa exercises. Having sung the first, she stood in the middle of the room and repeated a single musical phrase which pleased her specially. She listened with delight, as though it were new to her, to the charm of the notes ringing out, filling the empty ballroom and dying slowly away; and suddenly her heart felt lighter. 'What's the good of making so much of it? Things are nice as it is,' she said to herself; and she began walking up and down the room, not stepping naturally on the echoing parquet floor, but setting her little heels down first and then her toes (she had on a cherished pair of new slippers), and listening to the rhythmical tap of the heel and creak of the toe with as much pleasure as she had listened to the sounds of her own voice. Passing a looking-glass, she glanced into it. 'There, that's me!' the expression of her face seemed to say as she caught sight of her reflection. 'Well, and very nice too! I don't need anybody.'

A footman wanted to come in to clear away something in the room but she would not let him, and having closed the door behind him continued her promenade. That morning she had returned to her favourite mood of liking and being ecstatic over herself. 'What an enchanting creature that Natasha is!' she said, putting the words into the mouth of some third, generic male person. 'Pretty, a good voice, young, and in nobody's way if only they leave her in peace.' But however much they left her in peace she could not now be at peace, and was immediately aware of it.

In the vestibule the hall-door opened and someone asked: 'Are they at home?' and then footsteps were heard. Natasha was gazing in the looking-glass but she did not see herself. She was listening to the sounds in the hall. When she saw herself, her face was pale. It was *he*. She was sure of it, though she hardly caught his voice through the closed doors.

Pale and agitated, Natasha ran into the drawing-room.

'Mamma, Bolkonsky has come!' she cried. 'Mamma, it is awful, unbearable! I don't want ... to be tortured! What am I to do? ...'

But before the countess could answer, Prince Andrei entered the room with a grave and anxious face, which lit up as soon as he saw Natasha. He kissed the countess's hand and Natasha's, and sat down near the sofa.

'It is a long time since we had the pleasure ...' began the countess, but Prince Andrei interrupted her by answering her implied question, obviously in haste to say what he had on his mind to say.

'I have not been to see you all this time because I went to my father. I had to talk over an exceedingly important matter with him. I only got back last night,' he said, glancing at Natasha. 'I should be very glad if I might have a few words with you, countess,' he added after a moment's pause.

The countess lowered her eyes, sighing heavily.

'I am at your disposal,' she murmured.

Natasha knew that she ought to go away but was unable to do so: something gripped her throat and regardless of manners she stared straight at Prince Andrei with wide-open eyes.

'What at once? This minute? ... No, it can't be!' she was thinking.

He glanced again at her, and that glance convinced her that she was

561

not mistaken. Yes, at once, this very minute, her fate was to be decided.

'Go, Natasha, I will send for you,' said the countess in a whisper.

With frightened, imploring eyes Natasha looked at Prince Andrei and her mother, and went out.

'I have come, countess, to ask for your daughter's hand,' said Prince Andrei.

The countess's face flushed hotly but she said nothing.

'Your offer ...' she began at last, sedately. He waited in silence, looking into her eyes. 'Your offer ...' (she hesitated in confusion) 'is agreeable to us, and ... I accept your offer. I am happy. And my husband ... I hope ... but it must rest with herself. ...'

'I will speak to her as soon as I receive your permission. ... Do you give it me?' said Prince Andrei.

'Yes,' replied the countess. She held out her hand to him, and with mingled feelings of aloofness and tenderness pressed her lips to his forehead as he bent to kiss her hand. She wanted to love him as a son, but felt that he was a stranger who filled her with alarm.

'I am sure my husband will consent,' said the countess, 'but your father. ...'

'My father, whom I have apprised of my plans, has made an express stipulation that the wedding should not take place for a year. I wanted to tell you that too,' said Prince Andrei.

'True, Natasha is very young, but – that is a long time!'

'There is no alternative,' said Prince Andrei with a sigh.

'I will send her to you,' said the countess, and left the room.

'Lord have mercy upon us!' she murmured over and over again as she went in search of her daughter.

Sonya told her that Natasha was in her bedroom. She was sitting on her bed, pale and dry-eyed, gazing at the icons and whispering something as she rapidly crossed herself. When she saw her mother she jumped up and flew to her.

'Well, mamma? ... Well?'

'Go, go to him. He asks for your hand,' said the countess, coldly it seemed to Natasha. 'Go ... go,' murmured the mother mournfully and reproachfully with a deep sigh as her daughter ran off.

Natasha never remembered how she entered the drawing-room. As she opened the door and caught sight of him she stopped short. 'Can it be that this stranger has now become *everything* to me?' she asked herself, and the reply came in a flash, 'Yes, everything: he alone is now dearer to me than all else in the world.' Prince Andrei approached her with downcast eyes.

'I have loved you from the first moment I saw you. May I hope?'

He looked at her and was struck by the grave impassioned expression of her face. Her face seemed to say: 'Why ask? Why doubt what you cannot help knowing? Why use words when words cannot express what one feels?'

She drew nearer to him and stopped. He took her hand and kissed it.

'Do you love me?'

'Yes, yes!' exclaimed Natasha, with something that seemed almost like vexation, and catching her breath more and more quickly she began to sob.

'What is it? What is the matter?'

'Oh, I am so happy!' she replied, smiling through her tears and, bending over closer to him, she hesitated for an instant, as if asking herself whether she might, and then kissed him.

Prince Andrei held her hand in his, looked into her eyes and could find no trace in his heart of his former love for her. Some sudden transformation seemed to have taken place in him: the former poetic and mystic charm of desire had given way to pity for her feminine and childish weakness, fear at her devotion and trustfulness, and an oppressive yet sweet sense of duty binding him to her for ever. The present feeling, though not so bright and poetical as the former one, was stronger and more serious.

'Did your mother tell you that it cannot be for a year?' asked Prince Andrei, continuing to gaze into her eyes.

'Can this really be I – this "chit of a girl", as everybody calls me?' Natasha was thinking. 'Is it possible that from this time forth I am to be the *wife*, the equal, of this stranger – this dear, clever man whom even my father looks up to? Can it be true? Can it be true that there can be no more playing with life, that now I am grown up, that now a responsibility lies on me for my every word and action? Oh, what did he ask me?'

'No,' she replied, but she had not understood his question.

'Forgive me,' said Prince Andrei, 'but you are so young, and I have already had so much experience of life. I am afraid for you, you do not yet know yourself.'

Natasha listened with concentrated attention, doing her best but failing to take in the meaning of his words.

'Hard as this year will be for me, delaying my happiness,' continued Prince Andrei, 'it will give you time to be sure of your own heart. I ask you to make me happy at the end of a year, but you are free: our engagement shall remain a secret, and should you discover that you do not love me, or if you should come to love ...' said Prince Andrei with a forced smile.

'Why do you say that?' Natasha interrupted him. 'You know that from the very day you first came to Otradnoe I have loved you,' she cried, quite convinced that she was speaking the truth.

'In a year you will have learned to know yourself. ...'

'A who-ole year!' suddenly exclaimed Natasha, only now realizing that the wedding would have to wait a year. 'But why a year? Why a year? ...'

Prince Andrei began to explain to her the reasons for this delay. Natasha did not hear him.

'And can't it be helped?' she asked. Prince Andrei made no answer but his face expressed the impossibility of altering the decision.

'It's awful! Oh, it's awful, awful!' Natasha cried suddenly, and burst into sobs again. 'I shall die if I have to wait a year: it's impossible, it's awful!' She looked into her lover's face and saw that it was full of commiseration and perplexity.

'No, no! I'll do anything!' she said, immediately checking her tears. 'I am so happy.'

Her father and mother came into the room and gave the betrothed pair their blessing.

From that day Prince Andrei began to frequent the Rostovs' as Natasha's accepted suitor.

24

THERE was no betrothal ceremony and Natasha's engagement to Bolkonsky was not announced: Prince Andrei insisted upon that. He said that since he was responsible for the delay he ought to bear the whole burden of it. He declared that he considered himself irrevocably bound by his word but that he did not want to bind Natasha and would leave her perfectly free. If after six months she felt that she did not love him she would have every right to refuse him.

Naturally neither Natasha nor her parents would hear of this but Prince Andrei insisted. He was at the Rostovs' every day but did not behave with Natasha as though he were engaged to her: he addressed her with a certain formality and kissed only her hand. The day of the proposal saw the beginning of quite different, simple, friendly relations between Prince Andrei and Natasha. It seemed as though they had not known each other till then. Both liked to recall how they had regarded one another when they were *nothing* to each other; now they felt that they were entirely different beings: then they dissembled, now they were natural and sincere. At first the family felt awkward with Prince Andrei; he seemed like a man from another world and it took Natasha a long time to get them used to him, proudly assuring them all that he only appeared to be different but was really just like everybody else, and that she was not afraid of him and no one need be. After a few days they grew accustomed to him and fell back without constraint into their ordinary routine of life, in which he took his part. He could talk rural economy with the count, fashions with the countess and Natasha, and albums and embroidery with Sonya. Sometimes when they were by themselves, or even in his presence, the family would marvel at the way it had all happened, and how the prognostics of it all had been so apparent: Prince Andrei's coming to Otradnoe and their coming to Petersburg, and the resemblance between Natasha and Prince Andrei, which the old nurse had remarked on his first visit, and Nikolai's encounter with Andrei in 1805, and many other portents betokening that it was to be were observed by the family.

That atmosphere of romantic, silent melancholy which always accompanies a betrothed couple pervaded the house. Often they all sat in the same room without uttering a word. Sometimes the others would get up and go away, and the engaged pair, left alone, would remain as silent as before. They rarely spoke of their future life. Prince Andrei avoided it with dread, as well as from conscientious motives. Natasha shared this feeling as she did all his feelings, which she was always divining. Once she began to ask him about his son. Prince Andrei blushed, as he often did now – Natasha particularly liked it in him – and replied that his son would not live with them.

'Why not?' exclaimed Natasha, startled.

'I could not take him away from his grandfather, and besides. ...'

'How I should have loved him!' said Natasha, instantly guessing what was in his mind. 'But I know how it is, you are anxious that there should be no pretext for finding fault with us.'

The old count would sometimes come up, embrace Prince Andrei and ask his advice about Petya's education or Nikolai's advancement in the army. The old countess was apt to sigh as she looked at the lovers; Sonya was always afraid of being in their way, and constantly on the look out for excuses to leave them together, even when they had no desire to be alone. When Prince Andrei talked (he could tell a story very well) Natasha listened with pride; when she spoke, she noticed with fear and joy that he watched her with an intent and scrutinizing look. 'What does he hope to find in me?' she would ask herself in perplexity. 'What are his eyes probing for? Supposing I have not got what he is in search of?' Sometimes she fell into one of the mad, merry moods characteristic of her, and then it was an especial delight to see and hear him laugh. He seldom laughed but when he did he abandoned himself completely to his mirth, and after such laughter she always felt nearer to him. Natasha would have been utterly happy had not the thought of their parting, which was now near at hand, filled her with terror.

On the eve of his departure from Petersburg Prince Andrei brought Pierre with him. Pierre had not been to the Rostovs' once since the ball, and seemed bewildered and embarrassed. He devoted all his attention to the countess. Natasha sat down beside a little chess-table with Sonya, thereby inviting Prince Andrei to join them. He did so.

'You have known Bezuhov a long while, haven't you?' he asked. 'Do you like him?'

'Yes, he's a dear, but quite absurd.'

And she began, as people always did when speaking of Pierre, to tell anecdotes of his absent-mindedness, some of which were even pure invention.

'You know, I have confided our secret to him,' said Prince Andrei. 'I have known him since we were boys. He has a heart of gold. I beg you, Natalie,' Prince Andrei said with sudden seriousness, 'I am going away, and heaven knows what may happen. You may cease to ... all right, I know I am not to say that. Only this, then – whatever happens to you after I am gone. ...'

'What could happen?'

'If any trouble were to come,' pursued Prince Andrei, 'I implore you, Mademoiselle Sophie, if anything should happen, to go to him and no one else for advice and help! He may be the most absent-minded, ludicrous fellow, but he has a heart of gold.'

Neither her father nor her mother, nor Sonya, nor Prince Andrei himself, could have foreseen the effect of the parting on Natasha. Flushed and agitated, she wandered about the house that whole day, dry-eyed, busying herself with all sorts of trifling matters as though not understanding what was before her. She did not cry even when he kissed her hand for the last time. 'Don't go!' was all she said in a tone that made him wonder whether he really ought not to stay and which he remembered long afterwards. When he had gone, she still did not weep; but for several days sat in her room, not crying but taking no interest in anything and only saying from time to time: 'Oh, why did he go?'

But a fortnight after his departure, to the surprise of those around her, she just as suddenly recovered from her mental sickness and became her old self again, only with a change in her moral physiognomy, as a child's face changes after a long illness.

25

In the twelve months following his son's departure abroad Prince Nikolai Bolkonsky's health and temper became much worse. He grew still more irritable, and it was Princess Maria who generally bore the brunt of his unprovoked outbursts of anger. It seemed as though he did all he could to seek out the most vulnerable spots in her nature so as to inflict on her the cruellest wounds possible. Princess Maria had two passions and consequently two joys – her nephew, little Nikolai, and religion; and both were favourite themes for the old prince's attacks and jeers. Whatever was being talked about, he would bring the conversation round to the superstitiousness of old maids, or the petting and spoiling of children. 'You want to make him' (little Nikolai) 'into an old maid like yourself! A fine idea! Prince Andrei needs a son and not an old maid,' he would say. Or, turning to Mademoiselle Bourienne, he would ask her in Princess Maria's presence how she liked our village priests and icons, and make jokes about them.

He was constantly wounding Princess Maria's feelings, but it cost her no effort to forgive him. Could he be to blame where she was concerned? Could her father, who loved her, she knew in spite of it all, be unjust to her? Besides what is justice? Princess Maria never gave a thought to that proud word 'justice'. All the complex laws of mankind for her were summed up in the one clear and simple law of love and self-sacrifice laid down for us by Him, Who in His love had suffered for all humanity though He was Very God. What mattered to her the justice or injustice of men? All she had to do was to endure and love, and this she did.

In the course of the winter Prince Andrei had come to Bald Hills, had been gay, gentle and more affectionate than Princess Maria had known him for many years. She felt that something had happened to him, but he said nothing to his sister about his love. Before he left he had a long talk with his father, and Princess Maria noticed that they were ill-pleased with each other at parting.

Shortly after Prince Andrei had gone Princess Maria wrote from Bald Hills to her friend in Petersburg, Julie Karagin, whom she had dreamed – as all girls do dream – of marrying to her brother, and who was at that time in mourning for her own brother killed in Turkey.

Sorrow, it seems, is our common lot, my dear, sweet friend Julie. Your loss is so terrible that I can only explain it to myself as a special providence of God Who, in His love for you, would chasten you and your incomparable mother. Ah, my dear, religion, and religion alone, can – I don't say comfort us – but save us from despair. Religion alone can interpret to us what, without its help, man cannot comprehend: why, for what purpose, kind and noble beings, able to find happiness in life, who have not only never injured a living thing but are indeed necessary to the happiness of others, are called away to God, while the wicked, the useless, or those who are a burden to themselves and other people, are left living. The first death I saw, and which I shall never forget – that of my dear sister-in-law – made just such an impression on me. Just as you ask fate why your splendid brother had to die, so I asked why that angel Lisa should be taken, who not only never wronged any one but never had a thought in her heart that was not kind. And what do you think, dear friend? Five years have passed since then, and already I with my humble intelligence begin to see clearly why she had to die, and in what way her death was but an expression of the infinite goodness of the Creator, Whose every action, though for the most part beyond our comprehension, is but a manifestation of His boundless love for His creature. Perhaps, so I often think, she was too angelically innocent to have the strength to perform all a mother's duties. As a young wife she was irreproachable: possibly she would not have been equally so as a mother. As it is, not only has she left us, and particularly Prince Andrei, with the purest memories and regrets, but in all likelihood there on the other side she will receive a place such as I dare not hope for myself. But, not to speak of her alone, that premature and terrible death has had the most blessed influence on me and on my brother, in spite of all our grief. At the time, at the moment of our loss, I could not have entertained such thoughts: I should have repelled them with horror, but now they are quite clear and incontestable. I write all this to you, dear friend, simply to convince you of the Gospel truth, which has become a principle of life for me: not one hair of our head shall fall without His will. And the one guiding principle of His will is His infinite love for us, and so whatever happens to us is for our good.

You ask if we are going to spend next winter in Moscow. In spite of all my desire to see you, I do not expect and do not wish to do so. And you will be surprised to hear that the reason for this is Bonaparte! I will tell you why: my father's health is noticeably worse – he cannot endure contradiction and is easily irritated. This irritability is, as you are aware, most readily aroused by political affairs. He cannot tolerate the idea that Bonaparte is negotiating on equal terms with all the sovereigns of Europe, and especially with our own, the grandson of the great Catherine! As you know, I am quite indifferent to politics, but from my father and his conversations with Mihail Ivanovich I am not ignorant of all that goes on in the world, and have heard in particular of the honours conferred on Bonaparte. It seems that Bald Hills is now the only spot on the terrestrial globe where he is not accepted as a great man - still less as emperor of France, the idea of which my father cannot stand. It appears to me that it is chiefly on account of his political views that my father feels reluctant to talk of going to Moscow. He foresees the clashes which would result from his habit of expressing his views regardless of anybody. All the benefit he would gain from medical treatment in Moscow would be undone through the inevitable quarrels about Bonaparte. In any case the matter will be decided very shortly.

Our home life continues as usual, except for my brother Andrei's absence. As I wrote to you before, he has greatly changed of late. It is only now, in this last year, that he has quite recovered his spirits after his grief. He has again become the way I remember him as a child: kind, affectionate, with that heart of gold to which I know no equal. He has realized, it seems to me, that life is not over for him. But, on the other hand, his health has deteriorated as his mind has mended: he is thinner and more nervous, and I feel anxious about him.

I am glad he is taking this trip abroad which the doctors recommended long ago. I hope that it will restore his health. You write that he is spoken of in Petersburg as one of the most energetic, cultivated and intelligent young men of the day. Forgive a sister's pride, but I have never doubted it. The good he did here to everyone – from his peasants to the local gentry – is incalculable. When he went to Petersburg he received only his due. I always wonder at the way rumours fly from Petersburg to Moscow, especially such false ones as the report you wrote to me about of my brother's betrothal to the little Rostov girl. I do not believe Andrei will ever marry again, and certainly not her. And this is why: in the first place, I know that though he rarely mentions his late wife he was too deeply afflicted by her loss ever to think of letting another fill her place in his heart, or of giving our little angel a stepmother. Secondly, because, so far as I know, that girl is not at all the kind of girl who would be likely to attract my brother. I do not think Andrei has chosen her for his wife; and I will frankly confess, I should not wish for such a thing. But I have been running on too long and am at the end of my second sheet. Farewell, dearest friend: God have you in His holy and almighty keeping. My dear companion, Mademoiselle Bourienne, sends you her fond love.

MARIE

26

In the middle of the summer Princess Maria received an unexpected letter from Prince Andrei, from Switzerland, in which he gave her strange and surprising news. He informed her of his engagement to Natasha Rostov. The whole letter breathed ecstatic love for his betrothed, and tender and confiding affection for his sister. He wrote that he had never loved as he loved now, and that it was only now that he realized and understood the meaning of life. He begged his sister to forgive him for not having told her of his plans on his last visit to Bald Hills, though he had spoken of them to his father. He had not told her because Princess Maria might have tried to persuade their father to give his consent and, without attaining her object, would irritate him and draw all the weight of his displeasure upon herself. Besides, he wrote, the matter was not then so definitely settled as it was now.

At that time Father insisted on a delay of a year, and now *six months*, half of the period, have passed, and my resolution is firmer than ever. If it were not for the doctors keeping me here at the waters I should be back in Russia myself, but as it is I must put off my return for another three months. You know me and my relations with Father. I have need of nothing from him. I have been, and always shall be, independent; but to go against his will and incur his anger, when there may be so short a time left to him to be with us, would destroy half my happiness. I am writing a letter to him now about the same question, and beg you to choose a good moment to hand it to him, and then let me know how he receives it and whether there is any hope of his agreeing to reduce the term by three months.

After many hesitations, doubts and prayers Princess Maria gave the letter to her father. The next day the old prince said to her quietly:
'Write and tell your brother to wait till I am dead. ... It won't be long – I shall soon set him free.'

The princess tried to make some reply but her father would not let her speak, and raising his voice higher and higher went on:
'Marry, let the dear boy marry! ... Nice connexions! ... Clever people, eh? Rich, eh? Oh yes, a fine stepmother she'll make for little Nikolai! Write and tell him he may marry tomorrow if he likes. Nikolushka can have her for a stepmother, and I'll marry the little Bourienne! ... Ha, ha, ha! He mustn't be without a stepmother either! Only there's one thing, I won't have any more women-folk in my house: let him marry and go and live by himself. Perhaps you'd like to go and live with him too?' he added, turning to Princess Maria. 'You're welcome to, in heaven's name! Go – get out of my sight ... out of my sight ...!'

After this outburst the prince did not once refer to the subject again. But simmering chagrin at his son's poor-spirited behaviour found expression in his treatment of his daughter, and a fresh theme for irony was added to the old ones – allusions to stepmothers, and gallantries to Mademoiselle Bourienne.

'Why shouldn't I marry her?' he would say to his daughter. 'She'd make a splendid princess!'

And latterly, to her surprise and bewilderment, Princess Maria began to notice that her father was really associating more and more with the Frenchwoman. She wrote to her brother and told him how the old prince had taken the letter but comforted him with hopes of reconciling their father to the idea.

Little Nikolai and his education, Andrei, and her religion were Princess Maria's joys and consolations; but apart from these, since everyone must have some personal aspirations, Princess Maria cherished in the profoundest depths of her heart a hidden dream and hope that supplied the chief comfort in her life. This hope and consolation came to her through her 'God's folk' – the crazy prophets and pilgrims she continued to receive without her father's knowledge. The longer she lived, the more experience and observation she had of life, the more she wondered at the short-sightedness of men who seek enjoyment and happiness here on earth: toiling, aching, striving and doing evil to one another in their pursuit of that impossible, visionary, sinful happiness. Prince Andrei had loved his wife, she died, but that was not enough: he wanted to commit his happiness to another woman. Her father objected to this because he wanted a more distinguished and wealthier match for Andrei. And they all struggled and suffered and tormented one another, and injured their souls, their immortal souls, for the sake of winning some blessing that was gone in the twinkling of an eye. 'Not only do we know this ourselves, but Christ, the Son of God, came down upon earth and told us that this life is but a flash, a time of probation; yet we cling to it and think to find happiness in it. How is it no one realizes this ?' thought Princess Maria. 'No one except these despised "God's folk", who come to me with wallets over their shoulders, climbing the back stairs, afraid of the prince catching them – not because they fear ill-usage at his hands, but to spare him the temptation to sin. To leave family and home, give up all thought of material blessings and, clinging to nothing, wander in hempen rags from place to place under an assumed name, never doing any harm but praying for people – praying alike for those who persecute them and those who shelter – there is no truth and life higher than that truth and life !'

There was one pilgrim, a quiet pock-marked little woman of fifty called Theodosia, who for over thirty years had gone about barefoot and wearing heavy chains. Princess Maria was particularly fond of her. One day when they were sitting together, in the dark except for the dim light of the lamp burning before the icons, and Theodosia was talking of her life, the feeling that Theodosia had found the only true path suddenly came over Princess Maria with such force that she resolved to become a pilgrim herself. After Theodosia had retired to sleep, Princess Maria pondered this for a long while, and at last made up her mind that, strange as it might seem, she must go on a pilgrimage. She confided her intention to no one but the monk who was her confessor, and Father Akinfi approved of her project. Pretending that she was getting presents for pilgrim-women, Princess Maria prepared for herself the complete outfit of a pilgrim: a coarse smock, bast shoes, a rough coat and a black kerchief. Many a time going up to the chest of drawers containing these treasures, Princess Maria would pause irresolute, wondering whether the moment had not arrived to carry out her plan.

Often as she listened to the pilgrims' tales she was so fired by their simple speech, natural to them but to her ears full of the deepest significance, that more than once she was on the point of abandoning everything and running away from home. In imagination she already saw herself with Theodosia, in rags, trudging along the dusty road with her staff and her wallet, going on her pilgrimage, free from envy, from earthly loves or desires, journeying from one shrine to another, and at last reaching that bourne where there is neither sorrow nor sighing, but everlasting joy and bliss.

'I shall stop at a place and pray there, and before I have time to grow used to it, become attached to it, I shall go on – on and on until my legs give way under me and I lie down and die somewhere, and find at last that eternal haven of peace where there is neither sorrow nor sighing ...' thought Princess Maria.

But afterwards at the sight of her father, and still more of little Nikolai, she wavered in her resolve, wept secretly and accused herself of being a sinner who loved her father and her little nephew more than God.

PART FOUR

I

THE Bible legend says that the absence of toil – idleness – was a circumstance of the first man's blessed state before the Fall. Fallen man, too, has retained a love of idleness but the curse still lies heavy on the human race, and not only because we have to earn our bread by the sweat of our brow but because our moral nature is such that we are unable to be idle and at peace. A secret voice warns that for us idleness is a sin. If it were possible for a man to discover a mode of existence in which he could feel that, though idle, he was of use to the world and fulfilling his duty, he would have attained to one facet of primeval bliss. And such a state of obligatory and unimpeachable idleness is enjoyed by a whole section of society – the military class. It is just this compulsory and irreproachable idleness which has always constituted, and will constitute, the chief attraction of military service.

Nikolai Rostov was experiencing this blissful condition to the full as after the year 1807 he continued to serve in the Pavlograd regiment, in command of the squadron that had been Denisov's.

Rostov had grown into a bluff, good-natured fellow, whom his Moscow acquaintances would have considered rather bad form but who was liked and respected by his comrades, subordinates and superiors, and who was well satisfied with his lot. Of late – in the year 1809, that is – he noticed that in her letters his mother lamented more and more frequently that their affairs were going from bad to worse, suggesting it was high time for him to return home to gladden and comfort his old parents.

Reading these letters, Nikolai felt a pang of dread at their wanting to drag him away from surroundings in which, fenced off from all the entanglements of existence, he was living quietly and peacefully. He foresaw that sooner or later he would have to plunge back into that whirlpool of life, with its confusions and affairs to be straightened out, its steward's accounts, with its quarrels and intrigues, its ties, with society, with Sonya's love and his promise to her. It was all terribly difficult and complicated; and he replied to his mother in cold, formal letters in French, beginning, 'My dear Mamma' and ending 'Your dutiful son', which said nothing of any intention of coming home. In 1810 he received letters from his parents in which they told him of Natasha's engagement to Bolkonsky, and of the wedding having to wait for a year because the old prince did not approve. This letter vexed and mortified Nikolai. In the first place, he was sorry that Natasha, for whom he cared more than for all the rest of the family, should be lost to the home; and secondly, from his hussar point of view, he regretted not to have been there at the time to show that fellow Bolkonsky that it was by no means such an honour to be connected with him, and that if he loved Natasha he might dispense with his lunatic old father's consent. For a moment he wondered whether to apply for leave so as to see Natasha as an engaged girl, but then came the army manoeuvres, and he thought of Sonya and the difficulties at home, and once more he postponed it. But in the spring of that year he received a letter from his mother, written without his father's knowledge, and that letter decided him. She wrote that if Nikolai did not return and take matters in hand their whole estate would go under the hammer and they would be left destitute. The count was so weak, and trusted Mitenka so much, and was so good natured, that everybody took advantage of him and things were going from bad to worse. 'For God's sake, I beg of you, come at once, if you don't want to make me and all the family wretched,' wrote the countess.

This letter had its effect on Nikolai. He possessed the common sense of the mediocre man which showed him what he ought to do.

The right thing now was, if not to retire from the service, at any rate to go home on leave. Why he had to go, he could not have said; but following his after-dinner nap he gave orders to saddle Mars, an extremely vicious grey stallion that he had not ridden for a long time, and when he returned with the horse in a lather he informed Lavrushka (Denisov's old servant who had remained with him) and his comrades who dropped in that evening that he was applying for leave and was going home. Difficult and strange as it was for him to reflect that he would go away without having heard from the Staff whether he had been promoted to a captaincy or would receive the order of St Anne for the last manoeuvres (a matter of the greatest interest to him); strange as it was to think that he would go away without having sold his three roans to the Polish Count Goluchowski, who was bargaining for the horses Rostov had wagered he would get two thousand roubles for; inconceivable as it seemed that the ball the hussars were giving in honour of the Polish Mademoiselle Przazdecki (to turn the tables on the Uhlans, who had just entertained their Polish belle, Mademoiselle Borzowski) would take place without him – he knew he must abandon this bright, pleasant existence and go where everything was upside-down and silly. A week later his leave came. His comrades – not only the hussars of his own regiment but the whole brigade – gave him a subscription dinner at fifteen roubles a head, at which there were two bands and two choruses. Rostov danced the *trepak* with Major Basov; tipsy officers tossed him in the air, embraced him and dropped him on the ground; the soldiers of the third squadron tossed him again, and shouted 'Hurrah!' Then they carried him to his sledge and escorted him as far as the first post-station.

For the first half of the journey, from Kremenchug to Kiev, as is always the way, all Rostov's thoughts were behind him, with the squadron; but after he had passed the half-way he began to forget his three roans, his quartermaster and Mademoiselle Borzowski, and to wonder anxiously how things would be at Otradnoe and what he would find there. The nearer he got, the more intense – far more intense – were his thoughts of home (as though moral feelings, like gravity, were subject to the inverse square law). At the last post-station before Otradnoe he gave the driver a three-rouble tip, and ran breathlessly up the steps of his home, like a boy.

After the excitement of the first meeting and the odd feeling of disappointment at the reality falling short of expectation – the feeling that 'everything is just the same, so why was I in such a hurry?' – Nikolai began to settle down in the old world of home. His father and mother were just the same, only a little older. What was new in them was a certain uneasiness and occasional difference of opinion, which there used not to be, and which, as Nikolai soon found out, was due to the wretched state of their affairs. Sonya was now nearly twenty. She would grow no prettier: there was no promise in her of more to come; but she was pretty enough as she was. She exhaled happiness and love from the moment Nikolai returned, and this girl's faithful, steadfast devotion gladdened his heart. Petya and Natasha surprised Nikolai most. Petya was a big, handsome boy of thirteen, merry, mischievous and witty, with a voice that was already beginning to break. As for Natasha, it was a long while before Nikolai could get over his wonder, and he laughed whenever he looked at her.

'You're not the same at all,' he said.

'How? Am I uglier?'

'On the contrary, but what dignity – princess!' he whispered to her.

'Yes, yes, yes,' cried Natasha gleefully.

She told him all about her romance with Prince Andrei, and his visit to Otradnoe, and showed him his last letter.

'Well, are you glad?' Natasha asked. 'I am so at peace and happy now.'

'Very glad,' answered Nikolai. 'He is a splendid fellow. Are you very much in love then?'

'How shall I put it?' replied Natasha. 'I was in love with Boris, with our teacher, with Denisov; but this is quite different. I feel at peace and settled. I know there is not a better man in the world, and so I feel quite quiet and contented. It is not a bit like the other times …'

Nikolai expressed his dissatisfaction at the marriage being delayed for a year; but Natasha fell on her brother with exasperation, proving to him that no other course was possible, that it would be a horrid thing to enter a family against the father's will, and that she herself wished it so.

'You don't understand in the least,' she kept saying.

Nikolai gave way and said no more.

Her brother often wondered as he looked at her. She did not seem at all like a girl in love and parted from her betrothed. She was even-tempered and serene, and quite as light-hearted as ever. This amazed Nikolai and even made him regard Bolkonsky's courtship rather sceptically. He could not believe that her fate was now sealed, especially as he had not seen her with Prince Andrei. It always seemed to him that there was something not quite right about this proposed marriage.

'Why the delay? Why no betrothal?' he thought. Once, when he started to talk to his mother about his sister, he discovered to his surprise and somewhat to his satisfaction that in the depths of her heart she too had doubts about the marriage.

'Here, you see,' said she, showing her son a letter of Prince Andrei's with that latent feeling of resentment a mother always has towards her daughter's future married happiness, 'he writes that he won't be coming before December. What can be keeping him? Illness, I suppose. His health is very delicate. Don't say anything to Natasha. And don't be surprised that she is so gay: these are the last days of her girlhood, but I know how she is every time she gets a letter from him. However, God grant, all may be well yet!' she concluded, adding as usual, 'He is an excellent man.'

2

At first after his return home Nikolai was grave and even depressed. He was worried by the impending necessity of going into the stupid business matters for which his mother had sent for him. To be rid of this burden as quickly as possible, on the third day after his arrival he marched off, angry and scowling and making no reply to Natasha's inquiries as to where he was going, to Mitenka's lodge, and demanded an *account in full*. What he meant by an *account in full* Nikolai knew even less than the panic-stricken and bewildered Mitenka. The conversation and the examination of the accounts with Mitenka did not last long. The village elder, a spokesman from the peasants, and the village clerk, who were waiting in the passage, heard with awe and delight first the young count's voice roaring and snapping and getting louder and louder, and then terrible words of abuse following one upon another.

'You robber!... You ungrateful wretch! I'll thrash you like a dog! ... You're not dealing with my father this time! ... Stealing everything we've got! ... Scoundrel!'

Then, with no less awe and delight, they saw the young count, his face purple with rage, his eyes bloodshot, drag Mitenka out by the scruff of the neck and with great dexterity apply his foot and knee to his rear whenever the pauses between his words gave him a convenient chance, as he shouted: 'Get out of here! Never let me see your face again, you blackguard!'

Mitenka flew headlong down the six steps and ran away into the shrubbery. (This shrubbery was a well-known haven of refuge for delinquents at Otradnoe. Mitenka himself was wont to hide there when he returned tipsy from town, and many of the residents of Otradnoe, anxious to keep out of Mitenka's way, were aware of its protecting powers.)

Mitenka's wife and her sisters, looking terrified, peeped into the passage from the door of their room, where a polished samovar was boiling and the steward's high bedstead stood with its patchwork quilt.

The young count paid no heed to them but, breathing hard, strode by with determined step and went into the house.

The countess, who heard at once through the maids of what had happened at the lodge, was comforted by the reflection that now their affairs would certainly improve, though on the other hand she was uneasy as to the effect of the scene on her son. She tiptoed several times to his door and listened as he lighted one pipe after another.

Next day the old count drew Nikolai on one side and with a timid smile said to him:

'But you know, my dear boy, you got excited for nothing! Mitenka has told me all about it.'

'Of course,' thought Nikolai. 'I knew I should never make head or tail of anything in this idiotic place.'

'You were angry at his not having entered those seven hundred roubles. But they were carried forward, and you did not look on the other page.'

'Papa, he is a blackguard and a thief, I am sure of it. And what I have done, I have done. Still, if you don't wish it, I won't say any more to him.'

'No, my dear boy' (the count, too, felt embarrassed. He was conscious that he had mismanaged his wife's property and wronged his children, but he did not know how to remedy matters). 'No, I beg of you to take charge of things. I am old, I ...'

'No, papa. Forgive me if I have caused you unpleasantness. I understand less about it than you do.'

'Devil take them all – peasants and money matters, and carrying forward on the next page,' he thought. 'I used to know well enough how to score at cards, but this carrying over to the next page is quite beyond me,' said he to himself, and after that he did not meddle in the management of the family affairs. But once the countess called her son and told him that she had a promissory note from Anna

579

Mihalovna for two thousand roubles, and asked him what he thought should be done about it.

'This is what I think,' answered Nikolai. 'You say it rests with me. Well, I don't like Anna Mihalovna, and I don't like Boris, but they were our friends and are poor. This is what I should do!' and he tore the note in two, and by so doing caused the old countess to weep tears of joy. After that, the young Rostov took no further part in business of any sort, but devoted himself with passionate interest to what was to him a new pursuit – hunting – for which his father kept a large establishment.

3

WINTRY weather was already setting in; morning frosts hardened the earth saturated by the autumn rains. Already the grass was full of tufts and stood out bright green against the brownish strips of winter rye trodden down by the cattle, and against the pale yellow stubble of the spring sowing and the russet lines of buckwheat. The uplands and copses, which at the end of August had still been green islands amid black fields and stubble, had turned into golden and lurid crimson islands among the green winter corn. The hares had already half changed their summer coats, the fox-cubs were beginning to scatter, and the young wolves were bigger than dogs. It was the best time of the year for hunting. The hounds belonging to that eager young sportsman Rostov were not only in good condition but almost over-trained, so that at a common council of the huntsmen it was decided to give them three days' rest and then, on the 16th of September, to go off on a distant expedition, starting with the oak grove where there was a litter of young wolves.

Such was the position on September the 14th.

All that day the hounds were kept at home. It was frosty and the air was sharp, but towards evening the sky became overcast and it began to thaw. On the 15th, when young Rostov in his dressing-gown looked out of the window, he saw an unsurpassable morning for hunting: the sky seemed to be dissolving and sinking to the earth without a breath of wind. The only movement in the air was the soft downward drift of microscopic beads of drizzling mist. The bare twigs in the garden were hung with transparent drops which dripped down on to the freshly fallen leaves. The earth in the kitchen-garden gleamed wet and black like the heart of a poppy, and within a short distance melted into the damp grey shroud of fog. Nikolai stepped out into the wet and muddy porch. There was a smell of decaying leaves and dogs. Milka, a black-spotted bitch with broad hind-quarters and big prominent black eyes, got up when she saw her master, stretched her hind legs and lay down like a hare; then suddenly jumped up and licked him right on his nose and moustache. Another borzoi, a dog, catching sight of Nikolai from the garden path, arched his back and, rushing headlong to the steps with lifted tail, began rubbing himself against Nikolai's legs.

At the same moment a loud 'O-hoy!' rang through the air – the inimitable halloo of the huntsman, which unites the deepest bass with the shrillest tenor notes; and round the corner came Danilo, whipper-in and head huntsman, a grey, wrinkled old man with hair cut straight over his forehead, Ukrainian fashion, carrying a long bent whip in his hand. On his face was that expression of independence and scorn of everything which is only seen in huntsmen. He doffed his Circassian cap to his master and looked at him witheringly. This scorn was not offensive to Nikolai: he knew that, disdainful and superior as this Danilo seemed to be, he was, nevertheless, his devoted servant and huntsman.

'Oh, Danilo!' Nikolai said, shyly conscious at the sight of this per-fect hunting weather, the hounds and the huntsman that he was being carried away by that irresistible passion for the chase which makes a man forget all his previous intentions, as a lover forgets everything in the presence of his mistress.

'What orders, your Excellency?' asked the huntsman in a bass voice deep as an archdeacon's and hoarse from hallooing, and a pair of flashing black eyes gazed from under their brows at the silent young master. 'Surely you can't resist it?' those two eyes seemed to be asking.

'It's a good day, eh? For a hunt and a gallop, eh?' said Nikolai, scratching Milka behind the ears.

Danilo made no reply but winked instead.

'I sent Uvarka out at daybreak to listen,' his bass voice boomed after a minute's pause. 'He says *she's* moved them into the Otradnoe enclosure. They were howling there.' (*She* meant the she-wolf, whom they both knew about, who had moved with her cubs to the Otradnoe copse, a small plantation a mile and a half from the house.)

'We ought to go after them, don't you think?' said Nikolai. 'Come to me and bring Uvarka.'

'Very good, sir.'

'Then put off feeding them.'

'Yes, sir.'

Five minutes later Danilo and Uvarka were standing in Nikolai's big study. Though Danilo was not a tall man, to see him in a room was like seeing a horse or a bear on the floor among the furniture, in domestic surroundings. Danilo felt this himself, and as usual stood just inside the door, trying to speak softly and not move for fear of breaking something in the master's apartment, and saying what he had to say as quickly as possible so as to get out into the open again, under the sky instead of a ceiling.

Having finished his inquiries and extracted from Danilo an opinion that the hounds were fit (Danilo himself was longing to go hunting), Nikolai ordered the horses to be saddled. But just as Danilo was about to go Natasha came hurrying in with swift steps, not yet dressed but wrapped in a big shawl of her old nurse's, and her hair not done. Petya ran in with her.

'You are going?' asked Natasha. 'I knew you would! Sonya said you wouldn't go, but I knew that today is the sort of day when you'd have to.'

'Yes, we are going,' replied Nikolai reluctantly, for he intended to hunt wolves seriously that day and did not want to take Natasha and Petya. 'We are going, but only wolf-hunting: it wouldn't interest you.'

'You know I like that best of all,' said Natasha. 'How mean of him – going himself, and having the horses saddled, with never a word to us.'

' "No obstacles bar a Russian's path!" – we'll go!' shouted Petya.

'But you can't. Mamma said you mustn't,' Nikolai objected to Natasha.

'Yes, I'm coming. I shall certainly come,' said Natasha firmly. 'Danilo, have them saddle for us, and tell Mihail to come with my dogs,' she added, turning to the huntsman.

Danilo had found it irksome and unsuitable to be in a room at all, but to have anything to do with a young lady seemed to him quite impossible. He cast down his eyes and made haste to get away, as though it were no affair of his, and being careful as he went not to inflict any accidental injury on the young lady.

4

THE old count, who had always kept up an enormous hunting establishment but had now handed it all over to his son's care, being in excellent spirits on this 15th of September, prepared to join the expedition.

Within an hour the whole party was at the porch. Nikolai, with a stern and serious air betokening that he had no time to waste on trifles, walked past Natasha and Petya who were trying to tell him something. He saw to everything himself, sent a pack of hounds and huntsmen ahead to find the quarry, mounted his chestnut Don horse and, whistling to his own leash of borzois, set off across the threshing-floor to a field leading to the Otradnoe preserve. The old count's horse, a sorrel gelding called Viflyanka, was led by his groom, while the count himself was to drive in a light gig straight to a spot reserved for him.

Fifty-four hounds were led out under the charge of six hunt-attendants and whippers-in. Besides members of the family there were eight borzoi kennel-men and more than forty borzois, so that with the hounds in leashes belonging to the family there were about a hundred and thirty dogs and a score of riders on horseback.

Each dog knew its master and its call. Each man in the hunt knew his business, his place and what he had to do. As soon as they had passed the fence they all spread out evenly and quietly, without noise or talk, along the road and field leading to the Otradnoe covert.

The horses stepped over the field as over a thick carpet, now and then splashing into puddles as they crossed a road. The misty sky still seemed to be falling imperceptibly and steadily down to the earth; the air was still and warm, and there was no sound save for the occasional whistle of a huntsman, the snort of a horse, the crack of a whip, or the whine of a hound that had straggled out of place.

When they had gone about three-quarters of a mile, five more horsemen accompanied by dogs appeared out of the mist, approaching the Rostovs. In front rode a fresh-looking, handsome old man with a large grey moustache.

'Morning, Uncle!' said Nikolai as the old man drew near.

'That's the mark! Come on ... I was sure of it,' began 'Uncle'. (He was a distant relative of the Rostovs' and had a small property near them.) 'I knew you wouldn't be able to resist coming out, and it's a good thing you have. That's the mark! Come on!' (This was 'Uncle's' favourite expression.) 'Take the covert at once, for my Girchik says the Ilagins are out with their hounds at Korniky. That's the mark! Come on, or they'll snatch the litter from under your noses.'

'That's where I'm going. Shall we join forces?' asked Nikolai.

The hounds were united into one pack, and 'Uncle' and Nikolai rode on side by side. Natasha, muffled up in shawls which did not hide her eager face and shining eyes, galloped up to them, followed by Petya, who always kept close to her, and Mihail, a hunt-groom who had been told to look after her. Petya was laughing, and whipping and pulling at his horse. Natasha sat her black Arabchik with ease and confidence, and reined him in effortlessly with a firm hand.

'Uncle' looked round disapprovingly at Petya and Natasha. He did not like any frivolity mixed with the serious business of hunting.

'Good morning, Uncle. We are coming too!' shouted Petya.

'Good morning, good morning! but don't go overriding the hounds,' said 'Uncle' sternly.

'Nikolai darling, what a lovely dog Trunila is. He recognized me,' said Natasha of a favourite hound.

'In the first place Trunila is not a "dog" but a harrier,' thought Nikolai, and looked sternly at his sister, trying to make her feel the distance that ought to separate them at that moment. Natasha understood.

'You mustn't think we'll be in any one's way, Uncle,' she said. 'We'll stay in our places without budging.'

'And a good thing too, little countess,' said 'Uncle'. 'Only mind you don't fall off your horse,' he added, 'or you'll never get on again. That's the mark – come on! You've nothing to hold on to.'

The oasis of the Otradnoe covert came in sight a couple of hundred yards off, and the huntsmen were already nearing it. Rostov, having finally settled with 'Uncle' where they should set on the hounds, and shown Natasha her place – a spot where nothing could possibly run out – went round above the ravine.

'Well, nephew, you're after a big wolf,' said 'Uncle'. 'See she doesn't give you the slip now!'

'That depends,' answered Rostov. 'Karay, here!' he shouted, replying to 'Uncle's' remarks by this call to his borzoi. Karay was a shaggy, ugly, nondescript old dog famous for having tackled a big wolf un-aided. All took their places.

The elder Rostov, knowing his son's ardour in the hunt, hurried so as not to be late, and the huntsmen had hardly taken up their stand before the old count, cheerful, flushed and with quivering cheeks, drove up with his black horses over the winter rye to the position reserved for him where a wolf might come out. Having straightened his coat and fastened on his hunting-knives and horn, he mounted his glossy, well-fed Viflyanka, who was quiet and good-tempered, and as grey as himself. The horses with the trap were sent home. Count Ilya Rostov, though not a keen sportsman at heart, was well acquainted with the rules of the hunt, and rode to the fringe of bushes where he was to stand, arranged his reins, settled himself in the saddle and, feeling that he was ready, looked about him with a smile.

Beside him was his personal attendant, Semeon Tchekmar, a vet-eran horseman now somewhat stiff in the saddle. Tchekmar held in leash three formidable wolf-hounds, though they too had grown fat like their master and his horse. Two wise old dogs lay down un-leashed. Some hundred paces farther along the edge of the wood stood Mitka, the count's other groom, a reckless rider and passion-ate enthusiast. Before the hunt, in accordance with time-honoured custom, the count had drunk a silver goblet of mulled brandy, taken a snack and washed it down with half a bottle of his favourite Bordeaux.

Count Rostov was somewhat flushed with the wine and the drive. His eyes were inclined to be moist and they glittered more than usual. Sitting in the saddle wrapped up in his fur coat, he looked like a child taken out for a drive.

The lean, hollow-cheeked Tchekmar, having attended to every-thing, kept glancing at his master, with whom he had lived on the best of terms for thirty years, and perceiving that he was in good humour he anticipated a pleasant chat. A third person rode circum-spectly out of the wood – he had evidently learned by experience – and stopped behind the count. This individual was a grey-bearded old man in a woman's cloak with a tall peaked cap on his head. It was the buffoon, who went by a woman's name, Nastasya Ivanovna.

'Well, Nastasya Ivanovna,' whispered the count, winking at him, 'just you see what Danilo will do to you if you scare the beast away!'

'I wasn't born yesterday,' said Nastasya Ivanovna.

'Sssh!' hissed the count, and he turned to Tchekmar. 'Have you seen the young countess?' he asked. 'Where is she?'

'With young Count Piotr, behind the high grass yonder by Zharov,' answered Tchekmar, smiling. 'Though she be a lady she be very fond of hunting.'

'And you're surprised at the way she rides, Semeon, eh?' said the count. 'As good as any man!'

'Who wouldn't be? So bold she is, and sits so easy-like!'

'And Nikolai? By the Lyadov uplands, I suppose?' asked the count, still in a whisper.

'Yes, sir. He knows the best places. And there's naught he don't know about riding – times Danilo and me's struck of a heap,' said Tchekmar, knowing what would please his master.

'Rides well, eh? Fine fellow on a horse, eh?'

'A reg'lar picture! How he run that there fox out of the steppe Zavarzino way t'other day! Come flying out of them woods, 'twas a caution! Horse worth thousand roubles but nobody could set no price to the rider. Aye, a man'd need to go a long way to find the likes of him!'

'To find the likes of him ...' repeated the count, evidently sorry that Tchekmar had come to an end with his praises. 'To find the likes of him,' he said, turning back the skirt of his coat to get at his snuff-box.

'T'other day now, when he come out of church in his smart uniform, and Mihail Sidorych ...' Tchekmar broke off: in the still air he had distinctly caught the baying of a hound or two, signifying that the hunt was on. He bent his head and listened, shaking a warning finger at his master. 'They be on the scent of them cubs ...' he whispered, 'making straight to the Lyadov uplands.'

The count, forgetting to smooth out the smile on his face, looked into the distance, along the narrow open space, holding the snuff-box in his hand but not taking a pinch. After the cry of the hounds came the bass note of the hunting-call for a wolf, sounded on Danilo's horn; the pack joined the first three hounds and they could be heard in full cry with that peculiar howl which indicates that they are after a wolf. The whippers-in were no longer halloo-ing the hounds but had changed to the cry of 'Tally-ho!', and above all the others rose Danilo's voice, passing from a deep bass to piercing shrillness. His voice seemed to fill the whole wood, to ring out beyond it and echo far away in the open country.

After listening for a few seconds in silence the count and his groom felt convinced that the hounds had separated into two packs: one, the larger, was going off into the distance, in particularly hot cry; the other pack was flying along by the wood past the count, and it was with this pack that Danilo's voice was heard urging the dogs on. The sounds from both packs mingled and broke apart again, but both were becoming more distant. Tchekmar sighed and stooped down to straighten the leash in which a young borzoi had caught his leg. The count sighed too, and noticing the snuff-box in his hand opened it and took a pinch.

'Back!' cried Tchekmar to a borzoi that was pushing forward out of the wood. The count started and dropped the snuff-box. Nastasya Ivanovna dismounted to pick it up.

The count and Tchekmar were looking at him. Then in a flash, as so often happens, the sound of the hunt was suddenly close at hand, as though the baying hounds and Danilo's 'Tally-ho!' were right upon them.

The count glanced round and on the right saw Mitka staring at him with eyes starting out of his head. Lifting his cap, he pointed in front to the other side.

'Look out!' he shouted in a voice that showed the words had long been on the tip of his tongue, fretting for utterance, and, letting the borzois slip, he galloped towards the count.

The count and Tchekmar galloped out of the bushes, and on their left saw a wolf swinging easily along and with a quiet lope making for an opening a little to the left of the very thicket where they had been standing. The angry borzois whined and, tearing themselves free of the leash, rushed past the horses' hooves after the wolf.

The wolf paused in its course; awkwardly, like a man with a quinsy, it turned its heavy forehead towards the hounds, and still with the same soft, rolling gait gave a couple of bounds and disappeared with a swish of its tail into the bushes. At the same instant, with a cry like a wail, first one hound, then another, and another, sprang out helter-skelter from the wood opposite, and the whole pack flew across the open ground towards the very spot where the wolf had vanished. The hazel bushes parted behind the hounds, and Danilo's chestnut horse appeared, dark with sweat. On its long back sat Danilo, hunched forward, capless, his dishevelled grey hair hanging over his flushed, perspiring face.

'Tally-ho! Tally-ho! ...' he was shouting. When he caught sight of the count his eyes flashed lightning.

'You —!' he roared, threatening the count with his whip. 'You've let the wolf slip! ... Hunters indeed!' and as though scorning to waste more words on the startled, shamefaced count he lashed the heaving flanks of his sweating chestnut gelding with all the fury meant for the count and flew off after the hounds. The count, like a schoolboy that has been chastized, looked round with a smile of appeal to Tchekmar for sympathy in his plight. But Tchekmar was not there: he had galloped round to try to start the wolf again. The field too was coming up on both sides, but the wolf got into the wood before any of the party could head it off.

5

MEANWHILE Nikolai Rostov remained at his post, waiting for the wolf. By the way the hunt approached and receded, by the cries of the dogs whose notes were familiar to him, by the shouts of the whippers-in, advancing and retreating, he could form a good idea of what was happening at the copse. He knew that there were young and old wolves in the enclosure, that the hounds had separated into two packs, that in one place they were close on their quarry, and that something had gone wrong. He expected every second to see the animal come his way. He made a thousand different conjectures as to where and from what side the brute would appear, and how he should attack it. Hope alternated with despair. Several times he addressed a prayer to God that the wolf might come in his direction. He prayed with that sense of passionate anxiety with which men pray at moments of great excitement arising from trivial causes. 'Why not grant me this?' he said to God. 'I know Thou art great and that it's wrong to pray about this; but for God's sake make the old wolf come my way and let Karay spring at it – in front of "Uncle" who is watching from over there – and fix his teeth in its throat and finish it off!' A thousand times during that half-hour Rostov cast eager restless glances over the thickets at the edge of the wood, with the two scraggy oaks rising above the aspen undergrowth and the ravine with its waterworn side and 'Uncle's' cap just visible behind a bush on the right.

'No, no such luck for me,' thought Rostov. 'But wouldn't it be fine! No hope though. I'm always unlucky – at cards, in the war, everywhere.' Memories of Austerlitz and of Dolohov flashed vividly through his imagination, in rapid succession. 'Just once in my life to kill an old wolf: that's all I want!' he thought, straining eyes and ears and looking to left and right and listening to every tiny variation in the cries of the hounds. He looked to the right again and saw something running across the open ground towards him. 'No, it can't be!' thought Rostov, taking a deep breath as a man does at the coming of something long hoped for. The height of happiness was upon him – and so simply, without noise or flourish or display. Rostov could not believe his eyes and for over a second remained in doubt. The wolf ran forward and jumped heavily over a gully that lay across her path. It was an old wolf with a grey back and full reddish belly, running without haste, evidently feeling sure that no one saw her. Rostov held his breath and looked round at the borzois. They were standing and lying about, unaware of the wolf and not realizing the situation. Old Karay had turned his head and was angrily searching for a flea, baring his yellow teeth and snapping at his hind legs.

'Tally-ho!' whispered Rostov, pouting his lips. The borzois leaped up, jerking the iron rings of the leashes and pricking up their ears. Karay finished scratching his hind-quarters and got up, cocking his ears and faintly wagging his tail from which tufts of matted hair hung down.

'Shall I loose 'em or not?' Nikolai asked himself as the wolf moved away from the copse towards him. Suddenly the wolf's whole appearance changed: she shuddered, seeing what she had probably never seen before – human eyes fixed on her, and turning her head a little towards Rostov she paused, in doubt whether to go back or forward. 'Oh, no matter – forward ...' the wolf seemed to say to herself, and she continued on, not looking round, with a quiet, long, easy yet resolute lope.

'Tally-ho!' cried Nikolai in a voice not his own, and, unprompted, his good horse bore him at breakneck pace downhill, leaping over gullies to head off the wolf, and the hounds outstripped them, speeding faster still. Nikolai did not hear his own shout nor was he conscious of galloping. He did not see the borzois, nor the ground over which he was carried: he only saw the wolf who, quickening her pace, bounded on in the same direction along the hollow. The first to get close to her was Milka, the bitch with the black markings and powerful quarters. Nearer, nearer … now she was level. But the wolf turned a sidelong glance upon her, and Milka, instead of putting on a spurt as she usually did, suddenly raised her tail and stiffened her forelegs.

'Tally-ho! Tally-ho!' shouted Nikolai.

The red hound, Lyubim, darted forward from behind Milka, sprang impetuously at the wolf and seized her by the hind-quarters, but immediately jumped aside in terror. The wolf crouched, gnashed her teeth, rose again and bounded forward, followed at a distance of a couple of feet by all the borzois, who did not try to come any closer.

'She'll get away! No, it's impossible!' thought Nikolai, still shouting in a hoarse voice.

'Karay! Tally-ho!…' he screamed, looking round for the old borzoi who was his only hope now. Karay, straining his old muscles to the utmost and watching the wolf intently, was running heavily alongside the beast to cut her off. But the swift lope of the wolf and the borzoi's slower pace made it plain that Karay had miscalculated. Nikolai could already see the wood not far ahead where the wolf would certainly escape if once she reached it. But in front dogs and a huntsman came into sight bearing almost straight down on the wolf. There was still hope. A long yellowish young borzoi, one Nikolai did not know, from another leash, rushed impetuously at the wolf from in front and almost knocked her over. But the wolf jumped up surprisingly quickly and gnashing her teeth flew at the yellowish borzoi, which with a piercing yelp fell with its head on the ground, bleeding from a gash in its side.

'Karay, old fellow!…' wailed Nikolai.

Thanks to this delay to the progress of the wolf, the old dog with the tufts of matted hair hanging from its haunches had now got within five paces of her. As though aware of her danger the wolf looked out of the corner of her eyes at Karay, tucked her tail yet farther between her legs and increased her speed. But here Nikolai saw that – wonder of wonders! – the borzoi was suddenly on the wolf, and the two had rolled head over heels into a gully just in front of them.

That instant when Nikolai saw the wolf struggling in the gully with the dogs, saw the wolf's grey coat under them, her outstretched hind-leg, her panting, terrified head with ears laid back (Karay was pinning her by the throat), was the happiest moment of his life. He had his hand on the saddle-bow ready to dismount and stab the wolf, when she suddenly thrust her head up from among the mass of dogs, and then her fore-paws were on the edge of the gully. She clicked her teeth (Karay no longer had her by the throat), gave a leap of her hind-legs out of the gully, and, having disengaged herself from the dogs, with tail tucked in again went forward. Karay, with bristling hair, apparently either bruised or wounded, crawled painfully out of the gully.

'Oh my God! Why?' cried Nikolai in despair.

'Uncle's' huntsman was galloping from the other side across the wolf's path, and his borzois stopped the animal's advance again. Again she was hemmed in.

Nikolai, his groom, 'Uncle' and his huntsman were all circling round the wolf, crying 'Tally-ho!', shouting and preparing to dismount whenever the wolf crouched back, and starting forward again every time she shook herself free and moved towards the copse where safety lay.

Right at the beginning of this onset Danilo, hearing the hunters' cries, had darted out from the wood. He saw Karay seize the wolf, and checked his horse, supposing the affair to be over. But, seeing that the horsemen did not dismount and that the wolf had shaken herself free and was making off, Danilo set his chestnut galloping not at the wolf but in a straight line for the copse, in the way Karay had done, to intercept the animal. As a result of this manoeuvre he came up with the wolf just when she had been stopped a second time by 'Uncle's' borzois.

Danilo galloped up silently, holding a drawn dagger in his left hand and thrashing the heaving sides of his chestnut with his riding whip as though it were a flail.

Nikolai neither saw nor heard Danilo until the chestnut, breathing heavily, panted past him, and he did not hear the sound of a falling body or see Danilo lying on the wolf's back among the dogs, trying to seize her by the ears. It was obvious to the hounds, to the hunters and to the wolf herself that all was over now. The beast, her ears drawn back in terror, tried to rise but the borzois clung to her. Danilo half rose, stumbled and as though sinking down to rest rolled with his full weight on the wolf, snatching her by the ears. Nikolai was about to stab her but Danilo whispered: 'Don't, we'll string her up!' and shifting his position he put his foot on the wolf's neck. A stake was thrust between her jaws and she was fastened with a leash, as if bridled, her legs were bound together, and Danilo swung her over once or twice from side to side.

With happy, exhausted faces they laid the old wolf, alive, on a horse that shied and snorted in alarm, and, accompanied by the hounds yelping at her, took her to the place where they were all to meet. The hounds had killed two of the cubs and the borzois three. The huntsmen assembled with their booty and their stories, and everyone came to look at the wolf, who with her broad-browed head hanging down and the bitten stick between her jaws, gazed with great glassy eyes at the crowd of dogs and men surrounding her. When they touched her she jerked her bound legs and looked wildly yet simply at them all. Count Ilya Rostov also rode up and touched the wolf.

'Oh, what a formidable brute!' said he. 'An old one, eh?' he asked Danilo, who was standing near.

'That she be,' answered Danilo, hurriedly doffing his cap.

The count remembered the wolf he had let slip, and Danilo's outburst.

'Still, but you're a crusty fellow, my lad!' said the count.

Danilo said nothing but gave him a shy, sweet, childlike smile.

6

THE old count went home. Natasha and Petya stayed with the hunt, promising to follow immediately. The hunting party went farther as it was still early. At midday they put the hounds into a ravine thickly overgrown with young trees. Nikolai, standing on stubble land above, could see all his whippers-in.

Facing Nikolai lay a field of winter rye, and there stood his own huntsman, alone in a hollow behind a hazel bush. The hounds had scarcely been loosed before Nikolai heard one he knew, Voltorn, giving tongue at intervals; other hounds joined in, now pausing and now again giving tongue. A moment later he heard from the ravine the cry that they were on the scent of a fox, and the whole pack rushed off together along the ravine towards the rye-field and away from Nikolai.

He saw the whips in their red caps galloping along the edge of the overgrown ravine. He even saw the hounds, and was expecting a fox to show itself at any moment in the rye-field opposite.

The huntsman standing in the hollow moved and loosed his borzois, and Nikolai caught sight of an odd, short-legged red fox with a fine brush scurrying across the field. The borzois bore down on it. Now they drew close to the fox which began to dodge between the field in sharper and sharper curves, trailing its brush, when suddenly a strange white borzoi dashed in followed by a black one, and all was confusion. The borzois formed a star-shaped figure, their bodies scarcely swaying and their tails all pointing outwards from the centre of the group. A couple of huntsmen galloped to the dogs, one in a red cap, the other, a stranger, in a green coat.

'What is the meaning of that?' wondered Nikolai. 'Where did that huntsman spring from? He's not one of "Uncle's" men.'

The huntsmen despatched the fox and stood on for a long time without strapping it to the saddle. Near by, bridled and with high saddles, were their horses, and the dogs lying down. The huntsmen were waving their arms and doing something to the fox. Presently from the same spot a horn sounded – the signal agreed upon in case of a dispute.

'That's Ilagin's huntsman having a row with our Ivan,' said Nikolai's groom.

Nikolai sent the groom back to fetch his sister and Petya, and rode at a walking pace to where the whips were getting the hounds together. Several of the field galloped to the scene of the squabble.

Nikolai dismounted and, with Natasha and Petya who had ridden up, stood near the hounds, waiting to see how the affair would end. Out of the bushes came the huntsman who had been disputing, and rode towards his young master with the fox tied to his crupper. While still some way off he took off his cap and tried as he came up to speak respectfully, but he was pale and out of breath, and his face was distorted with rage. One of his eyes was black, but of this he did not seem to be aware.

'What was the matter over there?' asked Nikolai.

'Why, he was going to kill the fox our hounds had hunted! And my bitch it was – the mouse-coloured one – that nipped her. Go and have me up for it! Snatching hold of the fox! I gave him one with the fox. Here she is on my saddle. Is it a taste of this you want?' said the

593

huntsman, pointing to his hunting-knife and apparently imagining that he was still talking to his enemy.

Nikolai did not waste words on the man but, asking his sister and Petya to wait for him, rode over to where the rival hunt of the Ilagins was collected.

The victorious huntsman joined his fellows, and there, the centre of a sympathetic and inquisitive crowd, recounted his exploits.

The facts were that Ilagin, with whom the Rostovs had some quarrel and were at law, hunted over places that by custom belonged to the Rostovs, and on this occasion had, it would seem purposely, sent his party to the very 'island' the Rostovs were hunting, and had allowed his man to snatch a fox their hounds had put up.

Though he had never seen Ilagin, Nikolai, who knew no moderation in his opinions and feelings, accepted certain reports of violent and arbitrary behaviour on the part of this country squire, cordially detested him and considered him his bitterest foe. So now, excited and angry, he rode up to him, clenching his fist round his whip and fully prepared to take the most energetic and desperate measures to punish his enemy.

He had hardly passed an angle of the wood before his eyes fell on a stout gentleman in a beaver cap, riding towards him on a handsome raven-black horse, accompanied by two hunt-servants.

Instead of an opponent, Nikolai discovered in Ilagin a courteous gentleman of stately appearance, who was particularly anxious to make the young count's acquaintance. Ilagin raised his beaver cap as he approached Rostov, and said that he greatly regretted what had occurred and would have the man punished for daring to seize a fox hunted by someone else's borzois. He hoped to become better acquainted with the count and invited him to draw his covert.

Natasha, apprehensive that her brother might do something dreadful, had followed him in some excitement. Seeing the enemies exchanging friendly greetings, she rode up to them. Ilagin lifted his beaver cap still higher to Natasha, and with a pleasant smile declared that the countess was indeed a Diana both in her passion for the chase and her beauty, of which he had heard much.

To expiate his huntsman's crime Ilagin pressed Rostov to come to an upland of his about three-quarters of a mile away which he usually kept for himself and which, he said, was teeming with hares. Nikolai consented, and the hunt, its numbers now doubled, moved on.

The way to Ilagin's upland lay across country. The hunt-servants fell into line. The masters rode together. 'Uncle', Rostov and Ilagin kept stealing furtive glances at each other's hounds, trying not to be observed by their companions and searching anxiously for possible rivals to their own borzois. Rostov was particularly impressed by the beauty of a small thoroughbred, slender, black-and-tan bitch of Ilagin's, with muscles like steel, a delicate muzzle and prominent black eyes. He had heard of the sporting qualities of Ilagin's borzois, and in that beautiful bitch he saw a rival to his own Milka.

In the middle of a sedate conversation begun by Ilagin about the year's harvest Nikolai pointed to the black-and-tan bitch.

'A fine little bitch you have there!' he said in a careless tone. 'Full of go, is she?'

'That one? Yes, she's a good dog, gets what she's after,' answered Ilagin indifferently of his black-and-tan Yerza, for which the year before he had given a neighbour three families of house-serfs. 'So in your parts, too, count, the harvest is nothing to boast of?' he went on, continuing their previous conversation. And feeling it only polite to return the young count's compliment Ilagin scanned his borzois and picked out Milka, whose broad back caught his eye.

'Your black-spotted there's all right – a useful animal!' said he.

'Yes, she's fast enough,' replied Nikolai. ('Oh, if only a good big hare would cross the field now, I'd soon show you what sort of a borzoi she is!' he thought.) And turning to his groom he said he would give a rouble to any of the huntsmen who unearthed a hare.

'I don't understand,' Ilagin went on, 'how it is some sportsmen can be so jealous about each other's game and packs. For myself, I can tell you, count, I enjoy the whole thing – riding, pleasant company – such as I have lighted on today, for instance ... what could be more delightful?' (He doffed his beaver cap to Natasha again.) 'But as for reckoning up pelts – I'm not interested in that.'

'Oh, no!'

'Or being upset because someone else's borzoi and not mine gets on the scent first. All I care about is the chase itself, is it not so, count? Besides, I consider ...'

A prolonged halloo from one of the beaters interrupted him. The man was standing on a knoll in the stubble, holding his whip aloft, and now he repeated the long-drawn cry. (This call and the uplifted whip meant that he saw a sitting hare.)

'On the scent, I fancy,' said Ilagin carelessly. 'Well, let us course it, count!'

'Yes, we must ride up. ... Shall we go together?' answered Nikolai, looking intently at Yerza and 'Uncle's' red Rugay, the two rivals against which he had never as yet had a chance of pitting his own borzois. 'What if they outdo my Milka from the first!' he thought, as he rode with 'Uncle' and Ilagin towards the hare.

'A full-grown fellow, is it?' asked Ilagin, moving up to the beater who had sighted the hare – and not altogether indifferently he looked round and whistled to Yerza. 'What about you, Mihail Nikanorovich?' he said, addressing 'Uncle'.

The latter was riding with a sullen expression on his face.

'What's the use of my joining in? Why, you've given a village for each of your borzois. That's the mark – come on! They're worth thousands. No, I'll look on while you two compete against each other.'

'Rugay, hey, hey!' he shouted. 'Rugay, good dog!' he added, thus involuntarily expressing his affection and the hopes he placed on the red borzoi. Natasha could see and feel the anxious excitement which these two elderly men and her brother were trying to conceal, and was herself infected by it.

The huntsman on the hillock still stood with upraised whip and the gentry rode up to him at a walking pace. The hounds moving on the rim of the horizon turned away from the hare, and the whips, but not the gentlefolk, also moved off. Everything was done slowly and deliberately.

'Which way is it pointing?' asked Nikolai, after riding a hundred paces towards the whip who had sighted the hare.

But before the whip could reply the hare, scenting the frost coming next morning, could not stay still: he leapt up and was off. The pack on leash flew downhill in full cry after the quarry, and from all sides the borzois who were not tied rushed after the hounds and the hare. All the hunt, who had been advancing so unhurriedly, galloped across the field, getting the hounds together with cries of 'Stop!', while the whips directed their course with shouts of 'A-too!' The staid Ilagin, Nikolai, Natasha and 'Uncle' flew along, reckless of where or how they went, seeing nothing but the borzois and the hare, and fearing only lest they should for a single instant lose sight of the chase. The hare they had started turned out to be strong and swift. When he jumped up he did not immediately race off but pricked his ears, listening to the shouting and trampling that resounded from all sides at once. He made a dozen bounds, in no great haste, letting the borzois gain on him, and finally, having chosen his direction and realizing his danger, laid back his ears and was off like the wind. He had been lying in the stubble, but in front of him was the autumn-sowing where the ground was soft. The two hounds belonging to the huntsman who had sighted him, being the nearest, were the first to be on the scent and lay for him, but they had not gone far before Ilagin's black-and-tan Yerza passed them, got within a length, sprang upon the hare with frightful swiftness, aiming at his scut, and rolled over, thinking she had hold of him. The hare arched his back and bounded off more nimbly than ever. From behind Yerza rushed the broad-beamed, black-spotted Milka, and began rapidly gaining on the hare.

'Milka good dog, oh good dog!' rose Nikolai's triumphant cry. Milka looked as though she were just going to pounce on the hare, but her impetus carried her too far and she flew beyond, the hare having stopped short. Again the graceful Yerza came to the fore and paused close to the hare's scut as if measuring the distance so as not to make a mistake this time but seize him by the hind-leg.

'Yerza, my beauty!' urged Ilagin pathetically in a voice unlike his own. Yerza did not fulfil his hopes. At the very moment when she should have seized her prey, the hare swerved and darted along the ridge between the winter rye and the stubble. Again Yerza and Milka, running side by side like a pair of carriage horses, began to gain on their quarry, but it was easier for the hare to run on the ridge and the borzois did not overtake him so quickly.

'Rugay, come on, old man! That's the mark, come on!' another voice shouted this time, and 'Uncle's' thick-shouldered red borzoi, stretching out and curving his back, caught up with the two fore-most borzois, pushed ahead of them, put on speed with dreadful self-abandonment when close to the hare, knocked it off the ridge into the rye-field, again put on speed still more viciously, sinking half-way to his shoulders in the muddy field, until all that could be seen was the dog rolling over and over with the hare, the mud sticking to his back in large patches. The hounds formed a star-shaped figure round them. A moment later the whole party had drawn up round the crowding dogs. Only the radiantly happy 'Uncle' dismounted and cut off a pad, shaking the hare for the blood to drip off, and looking round excitedly with wandering eyes, unable to keep his feet and hands still. He kept speaking, not knowing what he said or whom he addressed. 'That's something like – come on! There's a dog for you. ... Outdid them all, whether they cost a thousand roubles or one! That's the mark, come on!' said he, panting and looking furiously about him as if he were berating someone, and as if they were all his enemies, who had insulted him, and he had only now at last succeeded in clearing himself. 'So much for your thousand-rouble animals – that's the mark, come on! Here, Rugay, here's a pad for you!' he cried, throwing down the hare's muddy pad, which he had just hacked off. 'You've earned it – that's the mark, come on!'

'She was all in – she ran it down three times all by herself,' Nikolai was saying, also not listening to anyone and regardless of whether he was heard or not.

'Cutting in sideways like that!' said Ilagin's groom.

'Once she had overshot and got it down any mongrel could catch it,' Ilagin was saying at the same moment, flushed and breathless from his gallop and the excitement. At the same time Natasha, without drawing breath, gave vent to her delight in a shriek so ecstatic and shrill that it set everyone's ears tingling. By that shriek she expressed what the others were expressing by all talking at once, and it was so strange that she must herself have been ashamed of so wild a cry, and the others would have been amazed at it at any other time. 'Uncle' himself twisted up the hare, hitched it neatly and smartly across his horse's back, as if by that gesture he would rebuke them all, and, with an air of not wishing to speak to anyone, mounted his bay and rode off. The others all followed, dispirited and outraged, and only much later were they able to recover their previous affectation of indifference. For a long time they continued to stare after the red dog, Rugay, who with his round back spattered with mud, rattling his chain, trotted along behind 'Uncle's' horse with the serene air of a conqueror. He looked to Nikolai as though he were saying:

'As you see, I'm like any other dog until it's a question of coursing a hare. But when there is work to be done, you had better look out!'

When, some while later, 'Uncle' rode up to Nikolai and addressed a remark to him, Nikolai felt flattered that, after what had happened, 'Uncle' was condescending enough to talk to him.

7

IT was towards evening when Ilagin took leave of Nikolai, who found himself so far from home that he was glad to accept 'Uncle's' offer that the hunting-party should spend the night in his little village of Mihailovko.

'And suppose you put up at my place – that's the mark, come on!' said 'Uncle'. 'That would be better still. You see, the weather's wet. You could get a rest, and the little countess could be driven back in a trap.'

'Uncle's' invitation was accepted. A huntsman was sent to Otradnoe for a trap, while Nikolai rode with Natasha and Petya to 'Uncle's' house.

Four or five men-servants, big and little, rushed out to the front porch to meet their master. A score of women serfs, of every age and size, popped their heads out from the back entrance to have a look at the cavalcade. The appearance of Natasha – a woman, a lady on horseback – aroused their curiosity to such a pitch of astonishment that many of them came up and, unabashed by her presence, stared her in the face, making remarks as though she were some prodigy on show and not a human being who could hear and understand what was said about her.

'Arinka, look now, she sits sideways! Sitting on one side, while her skirt dangles... And, see, she's got a little hunting-horn!'

'My goodness! And a knife too ...'

'A regular Tartar, isn't she!'

'How is it you don't tumble off head over heels?' asked the boldest of them, addressing Natasha directly.

'Uncle' dismounted at the porch of his little wooden house, which was buried in the middle of an overgrown garden, and after a glance at his retainers shouted peremptorily to those who were not wanted that they should take themselves off and that the others should see to the comfort and entertainment of the guests and the hunting-train.

The serfs ran off in different directions. 'Uncle' lifted Natasha from her horse and giving her his hand led her up the rickety wooden steps of the porch. Indoors, the house with its bare unplastered timber walls was not over-clean – there was nothing to show that the occupants were concerned to keep it spotless – but neither was it noticeably neglected. A smell of fresh apples pervaded the entrance, and the walls were hung with the skins of wolves and foxes.

'Uncle' conducted his guests through the vestibule into a small hall with a folding table and red chairs, then into the drawing-room with a round birch-wood table and a sofa, and finally into his study, where there was a tattered couch, a threadbare carpet, and portraits of Suvorov, of the host's father and mother, and of himself in military uniform. The study smelt strongly of tobacco and dogs.

'Uncle', after begging his visitors to be seated and make themselves at home, left them. Rugay, his back still covered with mud, came into the room and lay on the sofa, cleaning himself with his tongue and teeth. Leading from the study was a passage in which a partition with ragged curtains could be seen. From behind the screen came the sound of women laughing and whispering. Natasha, Nikolai and Petya took off their wraps and sat down on the sofa. Petya leaned on his elbow and was instantly asleep. Natasha and Nikolai sat without speaking. Their faces were burning, they were very hungry and in high good humour. They looked at one another – now that the hunt was over and they were indoors, Nikolai no longer considered it necessary to display his masculine superiority over his sister – Natasha winked at her brother, and neither of them could refrain for long from bursting into a ringing peal of laughter even before they had any pretext ready to account for it.

After a brief interval 'Uncle' came in wearing a Cossack coat, blue trousers and short top-boots. And Natasha felt that this very costume – which she had regarded with surprise and amusement when 'Uncle' wore it at Otradnoe – was just the right thing and in no respect inferior to a swallow-tail or frock-coat. 'Uncle' too was in the best of spirits and, far from taking offence at the brother's and sister's merriment (it could never enter his head that they might be laughing at his mode of life), he joined in their inconsequent mirth himself.

'Well, this young countess here – that's the mark, come on! – I never saw anyone like her!' said he, offering Nikolai a pipe with a long stem while with a practised motion of three fingers he filled another – a short broken one – for himself. 'She's been in the saddle the whole day, just like a man, and is still fresh as a daisy!'

Shortly after 'Uncle's' reappearance the door was opened – judging from the sound by a barefooted servant-girl – and a stout, rosy-cheeked, handsome woman of about forty, with a double chin and full red lips, entered carrying a huge loaded tray. She looked round at the visitors, her eyes and every movement expressing a dignified cordial welcome, and with a genial smile dropped them a respectful curtsey. In spite of her exceptional stoutness which obliged her to hold her head flung back while her bosom and stomach were thrust forward, this woman (who was 'Uncle's' housekeeper) stepped about with amazing agility. She went to the table, set down the tray and with her plump white hands deftly took and arranged the bottles and various hors-d'œuvre and other dishes. When she had finished, she moved back to the door and stood there with a smile on her face. 'Look at me! Now do you understand your little "Uncle"?' was what her bearing seemed to Rostov to imply. And how could one help understanding? Not only Nikolai but even Natasha realized the meaning of his furrowed brow, and the happy complacent smile which slightly curved his lips when Anisya Fiodorovna came into the room. On the tray were a bottle of herb-brandy, different kinds of vodka, pickled mushrooms, rye-cakes made with buttermilk, honey in the comb, still mead and sparkling mead, apples, plain nuts and roasted nuts, and nuts in honey. Later Anisya Fiodorovna brought in preserves made with honey and with sugar, a ham and a fowl that had just been roasted to a turn.

All this was the work of Anisya Fiodorovna's own hands, selected and prepared by her, and redolent of Anisya Fiodorovna herself, having a savour of juiciness, cleanliness, whiteness and pleasant smiles.

'Try a taste of this, my little lady-countess!' she kept saying, offering Natasha first one thing and then another.

Natasha ate of everything, and it seemed to her she had never seen or tasted such buttermilk-cakes, such delicious preserves, such nuts in honey, or such a chicken. Anisya Fiodorovna withdrew. After supper, over their cherry brandy, Rostov and 'Uncle' talked of hunts past and to come, of Rugay and Ilagin's dogs, while Natasha sat upright on the sofa, listening with sparkling eyes. She made several attempts to rouse Petya to eat something, but he only muttered incoherent words without waking. Natasha felt so gay and happy in these novel surroundings that her only fear was lest the trap should come for her too soon. After one of those fortuitous silences that are almost inevitable when one is entertaining acquaintances for the first time in one's own house, 'Uncle', responding to a thought that was in his visitors' minds, said:

'Yes, so you see how I am finishing my days. ... Death has to come.

Yes, that's the mark all right – you can't take anything with you. So where's the sense in being prudish?'

'Uncle' looked impressive and even handsome as he said this, and Rostov found himself remembering how highly his father and the neighbours always spoke of the old man. Throughout the whole province 'Uncle' had the reputation of being the most noble-hearted and unself-seeking of eccentrics. He was called in to arbitrate in family quarrels, he was chosen as executor. Secrets were confided to him; he was elected to be a justice and to fill other offices; but he always persistently refused all public appointments, spending the autumn and spring in the fields on his bay gelding, sitting at home in the winter, and lounging in his overgrown garden during the summer.

'Why don't you enter the service, Uncle?'

'I did once but gave it up. I'm not suited for it – that's the mark, come on! – I can't make head or tail of it. That's a matter for you – I haven't brains enough. But hunting is quite another thing – that's the mark, come on! Open that door there!' he shouted. 'What did you shut it for?'

The door at the end of the corridor (which word 'Uncle' always pronounced 'collidor') led to the huntsmen's room, as the sitting-room for the hunt-servants was called. There was a rapid patter of bare feet, and an invisible hand opened the door into the huntsmen's room. From the passage came the clear sounds of a balalaika being played by someone who was unmistakably a master. Natasha had been listening to the music for some time and now went out into the corridor to hear better.

'That's Mitka, my coachman. ... I bought him a good balalaika, I'm fond of it,' said 'Uncle'.

It was the custom for Mitka to play the balalaika in the men's room when 'Uncle' returned from the chase. 'Uncle' liked that kind of music.

'How well he plays! It's really very nice,' said Nikolai with a certain unconscious superciliousness in his tone, as though he were ashamed to admit that the sounds pleased him very much.

'Very nice?' Natasha said reproachfully, noticing her brother's tone. 'Nice isn't the word – why it's absolutely lovely!'

Just as 'Uncle's' pickled mushrooms, honey and cherry-brandy had seemed to her the best in the world, so also did this tune at this moment strike her as the very perfection of musical delight.

'Go on playing, please, go on,' cried Natasha at the door as soon as the balalaika ceased. Mitka tuned up and began twanging away again at *My Lady*, with trills and variations. 'Uncle' sat listening with his head on one side, a faint smile on his lips. The refrain repeated itself again and again. The instrument had to be retuned more than once, after which the player would thrum the same air again, yet the listeners never wearied and their only desire was for ever the same tune. Anisya Fiodorovna came in and leaned her portly person against the doorpost.

'Listen to him now, little countess' she said to Natasha, with a smile extraordinarily like 'Uncle's'. 'That's a good player of ours,' she added.

'He doesn't get that bit right,' exclaimed 'Uncle' suddenly, with a vigorous gesture. 'It ought to come spilling out – that's the mark, come on! – he ought to spill it out.'

'Can you play then?' asked Natasha.

'Uncle' smiled and did not answer.

'Anisya, go and see if the strings of my guitar are all right. It's a long while since I last touched it. That's the mark, come on! I'd quite given it up.'

Anisya Fiodorovna readily went off with her light step to do her master's bidding, and brought back the guitar.

Without looking at anyone 'Uncle' blew the dust off it, tapped the case with his bony fingers, tuned up and settled himself in his arm-chair. He grasped the guitar a little above the finger-board, with a somewhat theatrical gesture arching his left elbow, and, winking at Anisya Fiodorovna, struck a single chord, pure and sonorous. Then quietly, smoothly and confidently he began playing in very slow time not *My Lady* but the well-known air *Came a maiden down the street*. The hearts of Nikolai and Natasha thrilled in rhythm with the steady beat, thrilled with the sober gaiety of the song – the same sober gaiety which radiated from Anisya Fiodorovna's whole being. Anisya Fiodorovna flushed, and drawing her kerchief over her face went laughing out of the room. 'Uncle' continued to play correctly, carefully, energetically, while he gazed, transfigured and inspired, at the spot where Anisya Fiodorovna had stood. A faint smile lurked at one corner of his mouth, under the grey moustache, and grew broader as the song developed, as the rhythm quickened and a string almost snapped under the flourish of his fingers.

'Lovely, lovely! Go on, Uncle, go on!' cried Natasha as soon as he came to a stop. Jumping up from her place she hugged and kissed him. 'Oh, Nikolai, Nikolai!' she said, turning to her brother as though words failed her to describe the wonder of it all.

Nikolai too was greatly delighted with the performance, and 'Uncle' had to play the piece over again. Anisya Fiodorovna's smiling face reappeared in the doorway and behind her other faces. ...

> At the crystal-flowing fountain
> A maiden cries 'Oh stay!'

played 'Uncle' once more, running his fingers skilfully over the strings, and broke off with a shrug of his shoulders.

'Go on, Uncle *dear*,' wailed Natasha imploringly, as if her life depended on it.

'Uncle' rose, and it was as though there were two men in him, one of whom smiled a grave smile at the merry fellow, while the merry fellow struck a naïve, formal pose preparatory to a folk-dance.

'Now then, niece!' he exclaimed, waving to Natasha the hand that had just struck a chord.

Natasha flung off the shawl that had been wrapped round her, ran forward facing 'Uncle', and setting her arms akimbo made a motion with her shoulders and waited.

Where, how and when could this young countess, who had had a French *émigrée* for governess, have imbibed from the Russian air she breathed the spirit of that dance? Where had she picked up that manner which the *pas de châle*, one might have supposed, would have effaced long ago? But the spirit and the movements were the very ones – inimitable, unteachable, Russian – which 'Uncle' had expected of her. The moment she sprang to her feet and gaily smiled a confident, truimphant, knowing smile, the first tremor of fear which had seized Nikolai and the others – fear that she might not dance it well – passed, and they were already admiring her.

Her performance was so perfect, so absolutely perfect, that Anisya Fiodorovna, who had at once handed her the kerchief she needed for the dance, had tears in her eyes, though she laughed as she watched the slender, graceful countess, reared in silks and velvets, in another world than hers, who was yet able to understand all that was in Anisya and in Anisya's father and mother and aunt, and in every Russian man and woman.

'Well done, little countess – that's the mark, come on!' cried 'Uncle' with a gleeful laugh when the dance was over. 'Well done, niece! Now all we need is to pick you a handsome young husband – that's the mark, come on!'

'He's chosen already,' said Nikolai, smiling.

'Oho?' said 'Uncle' in surprise, looking inquiringly at Natasha, who nodded her head with a happy smile.

'And he's such a fine one,' she said. But as soon as the words were out a new train of thoughts and feelings arose in her. 'What did Nikolai's smile mean when he said "He's chosen already"? Is he glad or sorry? He seems to be thinking that my Andrei would not approve of or understand this jolly evening we're having. But he would understand it every bit. Where is he now, I wonder?' she thought, and her face suddenly grew serious. But this lasted only a second. 'Don't think about it – don't you dare think about it,' she told herself, and smilingly sat down again beside 'Uncle', begging him to play some more.

'Uncle' played another song and a valse; then after a pause he cleared his throat and struck up his favourite hunting song:

As the evening sun sank low
Fell the soft and lovely snow ...

'Uncle' sang as the peasant sings, with the full and naïve conviction that the whole meaning of a song lies in the words, and that the tune comes as a matter of course and exists only to emphasize the words. This gave the unconsidered tune a peculiar charm, like the song of a bird. Natasha was in raptures over 'Uncle's' singing. She determined to give up her harp lessons and play only the guitar. She asked 'Uncle' for his guitar and at once picked out the chords of the song.

Towards ten o'clock a carriage arrived to fetch Natasha and Petya, with a droshky and three men on horseback, who had been sent to look for them. The count and countess did not know what had become of them, and were in a great state of agitation, so one of the men said.

Petya was carried out like a log and deposited in the carriage, still sound asleep. Natasha and Nikolai got into the trap. 'Uncle' wrapped Natasha up warmly, and said good-bye to her with quite a new tenderness. He accompanied them on foot as far as the bridge – which they had to ride round, fording the river lower down – and sent huntsmen to ride in front with lanterns.

'Good-bye, my dear niece,' his voice called out of the darkness – not the voice Natasha had known hitherto but the one that had sung *As the evening sun sank low.*

There were red lights in the village through which they drove, and a cheerful smell of smoke.

'What a darling "Uncle" is!' said Natasha, when they had come out on to the high road.

'Yes,' agreed Nikolai. 'You're not cold?'

'No, I'm quite all right, quite. I feel so happy!' answered Natasha, puzzled even by her sense of well-being. They were silent for a long while.

The night was dark and damp. They could not see the horses: they could only hear them splashing through the unseen mud.

What was passing in that receptive childlike soul that so eagerly caught and assimilated all the diverse impressions of life? How did they all find place in her? But she was very happy. As they were nearing home she suddenly hummed the air of *As the evening sun sank low* – the tune of which she had been trying to recapture all the way and had at last succeeded in remembering.

'Got it?' said Nikolai.

'What were you thinking about just now, Nikolai?' inquired Natasha.

They were fond of asking one another that question.

'I?' said Nikolai, trying to recollect. 'Let me see – at first I was thinking that Rugay, the red hound, was like "Uncle", and that if he were a man he would keep "Uncle" about him all the time, if not for hunting then for his harmony. What a peaceful being "Uncle" is! Don't you think so? Well, and what about you?'

'I? Wait a minute now. Yes, first I thought that here we are driving along and imagining that we are going home, but that heaven knows where we are really going in the darkness, and that all of a sudden we shall arrive and find we are not at Otradnoe but in fairyland. And then I thought … no, that was all.'

'I know, I expect you thought about *him*,' said Nikolai, smiling, as Natasha could tell by his voice.

'No,' replied Natasha, though she certainly had been thinking about Prince Andrei at the same time, and how he would have liked 'Uncle'. 'And then I was saying to myself all the way, "How well Anisya carried herself – how beautifully she walked!"' And Nikolai

606

heard her spontaneous, ringing, happy laugh. 'And do you know,' she suddenly added, 'I am sure I shall never again be as happy and at peace as I am now.'

'What rubbish – what silly nonsense!' exclaimed Nikolai, and he thought: 'What a darling this Natasha of mine is! I shall never find another friend like her. Why should she marry? I could drive like this with her for ever!'

'What a darling my Nikolai is!' Natasha was thinking.

'Ah, there's a light in the drawing-room still,' she said, pointing to the windows of the house which gleamed invitingly in the wet, velvety darkness of the night.

8

COUNT ILYA ROSTOV had resigned the office of Marshal of the Nobility because the position involved him in too much expense, but still his affairs showed no improvement. Natasha and Nikolai often found their parents engaged in anxious consultation, talking in low tones of selling the sumptuous ancestral Rostov house and estate near Moscow. Now that the count was no longer Marshal of the Nobility it was not necessary for them to entertain so extensively, and life at Otradnoe was quieter than in former years; but still the enormous house and the 'wings' were full of people, and more than twenty sat down to table every day. These were all dependants who had domiciled themselves almost like members of the family, or persons who were obliged, it seemed, to live in the count's house. Such were Dimmler, the musician, and his wife; Iogel, the dancing-master, with his family; an elderly maiden lady, Mademoiselle Byelov, who had her home there; and many others besides – Petya's tutors, the girls' former governess, and various people who simply found it preferable or more to their advantage to live at the count's than at home. There were not quite so many visitors as before, but the scale of living remained unchanged, for the count and countess could not conceive of any other. The hunting establishment was still there – indeed, Nikolai had even added to it – with fifty horses and fifteen grooms in the stables. Costly presents were still given on name-days, with formal dinner-parties to which the whole neighbourhood was invited. The count still played whist and boston, holding his cards spread out fanwise so that everyone could see them and thus allowing

607

himself to be plundered of hundreds of roubles every day by neighbours, who looked upon the privilege of making up a rubber with
Count Rostov as a most profitable source of income.

The count moved about in his affairs as though walking in a huge
net, striving not to believe that he was entangled but becoming more
involved at every step, aware that he had neither the strength to tear
through the meshes that snared him, nor the patience and care required to set about unravelling them. The countess's loving heart
told her that her children were being ruined, but she felt the count
was not to blame, for he could not help being what he was, and that
he was distressed himself (though he tried to hide it) by his knowledge
of the disasters facing him and his family; and she tried to find means
of remedying the position. Her feminine mind could see only one
solution – for Nikolai to marry a rich heiress. She felt this to be their
last hope, and that if Nikolai were to refuse the match she had found
for him she would have to say good-bye to all idea of restoring their
fortunes. The match she envisaged was Julie Karagin, the daughter of
worthy, excellent parents, a girl the Rostovs had known from childhood, and who had lately come into a large fortune on the death of
her last surviving brother.

The countess had written direct to Julie's mother in Moscow, suggesting a marriage between their children, and had received a favourable answer from her. Madame Karagin had replied that for her part
she was agreeable, and everything would depend on her daughter's
inclinations. She invited Nikolai to come to Moscow.

Several times the countess, with tears in her eyes, told her son that
now that both her daughters were settled her only wish was to see
him married. She declared that she would go to her grave content if
this desire of hers were fulfilled. Then she would add that she happened to know of a splendid girl, and try to get from him his views
on matrimony.

On other occasions she praised Julie and advised Nikolai to go to
Moscow during the holidays to amuse himself. Nikolai guessed what
was behind his mother's remarks, and during one of these conversations induced her to come out into the open. She told him frankly
that their only hope of disentangling their affairs lay in his marrying
Julie Karagin.

'But, mamma, suppose I loved a girl who was poor, would you
really expect me to sacrifice my feelings and my honour for the sake

of money?' he asked his mother, not realizing the cruelty of his question and simply wishing to show his noble-mindedness.

'No, you have not understood me,' said his mother, not knowing how to justify herself. 'You misunderstand me, Nikolai. It is your happiness I want,' she added, feeling that she was not telling the truth and had got into difficulties. She began to cry.

'Mamma, don't cry. You have only to tell me you wish it, and you know I will give my life, everything, for your peace of mind,' said Nikolai. 'I would sacrifice anything for you – even my feelings.'

But the countess did not want the question put like that: she did not want a sacrifice from her son, she would sooner have sacrificed herself for him.

'No, you have not understood me; don't let us talk about it,' she replied, wiping away her tears.

'Yes, maybe I am in love with a penniless girl,' said Nikolai to himself. 'But am I to sacrifice my feelings and my honour for money? I wonder how mamma could suggest such a thing. Does she think that because Sonya is poor I must not love her?' he thought. 'Must not respond to her faithful, devoted love? Yet I should certainly be far happier with her than with any doll of a Julie. I can always sacrifice my feelings for my family's welfare,' he went on to himself, 'but I cannot coerce them. If I love Sonya, then that for me is far more powerful and higher than everything else.'

Nikolai did not go to Moscow, and the countess did not renew her conversations with him about matrimony. But she saw with sorrow, and sometimes with exasperation, symptoms of a growing attachment between her son and the dowerless Sonya. Though she reproached herself for it, she could not refrain from grumbling and nagging at Sonya, often pulling her up without reason, grumbling at her, and addressing her stiffly as 'my dear' and using the formal 'you' instead of the intimate 'thou' in speaking to her. What made the kind-hearted countess more irritated than anything with Sonya was that this poor, dark-eyed niece of hers was so meek, so good, so devotedly grateful to her benefactors, and so faithfully, unchangingly and unselfishly in love with Nikolai, that there were no grounds for finding fault with her.

Nikolai stayed on at home until the end of his leave. A fourth letter had come from Prince Andrei, from Rome, in which he wrote that he would long ago have been on his way back to Russia had not his wound unexpectedly reopened in the warm climate, which obliged him to defer his return till the beginning of the new year. Natasha was as much in love with her betrothed as ever, found the same comfort in her love, and was still as ready to throw herself into all the joys of life; but by the end of the fourth month of their separation she began to suffer from fits of depression against which she was unable to contend. She felt sorry for herself, sorry that she was being wasted all this time and of no use to anyone though she knew she had such capacity for loving and being loved.

Things were not cheerful at the Rostovs'.

9

CHRISTMAS came, and except for the solemn celebration of the Liturgy, the formal and wearisome compliments of the season from neighbours and servants, and the new gowns that everyone put on, there were no particular festivities to mark the holidays, though the perfectly still weather with the thermometer at thirteen degrees below zero, the dazzling sunshine by day and the wintry starlit sky at night seemed to call for some special celebration of Christmas-tide.

After midday dinner on the third day of Christmas week all the household dispersed to different rooms. It was the most tedious time of the day. Nikolai, who had been paying a round of visits in the neighbourhood that morning, was asleep on the sitting-room sofa. The old count was resting in his study. Sonya sat at the round table in the drawing-room, copying a design for embroidery. The countess was playing patience. Nastasya Ivanovna, the buffoon, with a woebegone countenance, was sitting at the window with two old ladies. Natasha came into the room, went up to Sonya and glanced at what she was doing, and then crossed over to her mother and stood without speaking.

'Why are you wandering about like a homeless spirit?' asked her mother. 'What do you want?'

'*Him* – I want him ... now, this minute! I want *him*,' said Natasha, with glittering eyes and no sign of a smile.

The countess raised her head and gave her daughter a searching look.

'Don't look at me, mamma. Don't look, or I shall cry.'

'Sit down – come and sit here by me,' said the countess.

'Mamma, I must have him. Why should I be wasted like this,

mamma? ...' Her voice broke, the tears started to her eyes and in order to hide them she quickly turned away and left the room.

She went into the sitting-room, stood there for a moment lost in thought, and then continued into the maids' room. There an elderly housemaid was scolding a young girl who had just run in from the serfs' quarters, breathless with the cold.

'Give over playing,' said the old woman. 'There's a time for everything.'

'Let her be, Kondratyevna,' said Natasha. 'Run along now, Mavrushka, run along.'

And, having rescued Mavrushka, Natasha crossed the ballroom and went to the vestibule, where an old footman and two young lackeys were playing cards. They broke off and stood up as she entered.

'What shall I have them do?' thought Natasha.

'Yes, Nikita, please go. ... (Where can I send him?) Oh yes, go to the yard and fetch me a fowl, please, a cock, and you, Misha, bring some oats.'*

'Is it a handful of oats you want?' said Misha with cheerful readiness.

'Go on, make haste,' the old man urged him.

'And you, Fiodr, get me a piece of chalk.'

On her way past the butler's pantry she ordered the samovar to be put on, though it was not anywhere near the time for it.

Foka, the butler, was the most surly-tempered person in the house. Natasha liked to test her power over him. He could not believe his ears and went off to ask whether the samovar was really wanted.

'Oh dear, what a young lady!' said Foka, pretending to frown at Natasha.

No one in the house set so many feet flying or gave the servants so much trouble as Natasha. She could not see people without wanting to send them on some errand. It seemed as though she wanted to try whether one or another would not get cross or sulky with her; but no one's orders were so readily obeyed by the servants as Natasha's.

'Now what shall I do? Where can I go?' Natasha wondered, as she went slowly along the passage.

'Nastasya Ivanovna, what sort of children shall I have?' she asked the buffoon, who was coming towards her in his woman's jacket.

'Why, fleas, dragon-flies and grasshoppers,' answered the buffoon.

* Natasha had in mind to tell fortunes by making a pattern of oats on the floor for the fowl to pick up. — *Tr.*

'O Lord, O Lord, it's always the same: where shall I go? Oh, what shall I do with myself?' And tapping with her heels she ran quickly upstairs to see Iogel and his wife who lived on the top floor. Two governesses were sitting with the Iogels at a table spread with plates of raisins, walnuts and almonds. The governesses were discussing whether it was cheaper to live in Moscow or Odessa. Natasha sat down, listened to the conversation with a grave and thoughtful air, and then got up again.

'The island of Madagascar,' she said. 'Ma-da-gas-car,' she repeated, articulating each syllable distinctly, and without replying to Madame Schloss, who asked her what she was saying, she hastened from the room. Petya, her brother, was upstairs too: with his tutor he was preparing fireworks to let off that night.

'Petya! Petya!' she called to him. 'Carry me downstairs.'

Petya ran up and bent his back for her. She sprang on, putting her arms round his neck, and he pranced along with her.

'No, that's enough ... the island of Madagascar!' she exclaimed, and jumping off his back she went downstairs.

Having as it were reviewed her kingdom, tested her power and made sure that everyone was submissive, but that all the same she was utterly bored, Natasha betook herself to the ballroom, caught up her guitar, sat down with it in a dark corner behind a bookcase and began to run her fingers over the strings in the bass, picking out a passage she recalled from an opera she had heard in Petersburg with Prince Andrei. For other listeners the sounds she drew from the guitar would have had no meaning, but in her imagination they called up a whole series of reminiscences. She sat behind the bookcase with her eyes fixed on a streak of light escaping from the pantry door, and listened to herself, turning over her memories. She was in a mood for brooding on the past.

Sonya passed to the pantry with a wine-glass in her hand. Natasha glanced at her, and at the crack in the pantry door, and it seemed to her that she remembered the light falling through that crack once before, and Sonya passing with a glass in her hand. 'Yes, and it was exactly the same in every detail,' thought Natasha.

'Sonya, what is this?' she cried, twanging a thick string.

'Oh, there you are!' said Sonya with a start, and she came closer to listen. 'I don't know. Is it a storm?' she ventured timidly, afraid of being wrong.

'There! That's just how she started, and came up with that same timid smile when all this happened before,' thought Natasha, 'and in just the same way I felt there was something lacking in her.'

'No, it's the chorus from the *Water-Carrier*, listen!' and Natasha hummed the air of the chorus so that Sonya might catch it. 'Where are you going?' she asked.

'To change the water in my glass. I am just finishing the design.'

'You always find something to do, but I can't,' said Natasha. 'And where's Nikolai?'

'Asleep, I think.'

'Sonya, go and wake him,' said Natasha. 'Tell him I want him to come and sing.'

She sat a little longer, wondering what the meaning of it all having happened before could be, and without solving the problem, or being in the least disturbed at not having done so, she drifted into reminiscence again, dreaming of the time when she was with *him* and he was looking at her with eyes of love.

'Oh, if only he would come quickly! I am so afraid it will never be. And worst of all, I am getting older, that's the trouble! Soon I shall no longer be what I am now. But perhaps he will come today – perhaps he is arriving this very moment. Perhaps he has come and is sitting in the drawing-room. Perhaps he arrived yesterday, and I have forgotten.' She rose, put down the guitar, and went to the drawing-room. All the domestic circle, tutors, governesses and guests, were already sitting at the tea-table. The servants stood behind – but Prince Andrei was not there and the same old life was going on as before.

'Ah, here she is!' said the old count when he saw Natasha come in. 'Come and sit by me.'

But Natasha stayed by her mother, looking round as though in search of something.

'Mamma,' she murmured. 'Get him for me, get him, mamma – quickly, quickly!' and again she had difficulty in repressing her sobs. She sat down at the table and listened to the conversation between the elders and Nikolai, who had also come in to tea. 'Oh Lord, always the same faces, the same talk, papa holding his cup and blowing on it just as he always does!' thought Natasha, to her horror feeling an aversion rising in her for the whole household because they were always the same.

After tea Nikolai, Sonya and Natasha went into the sitting-room, to their favourite corner, where their most intimate talks always began.

10

'Do you ever feel,' Natasha said to her brother when they were comfortably settled in the sitting-room – 'do you ever feel that there is nothing left to happen – nothing? As if everything nice is already in the past? And it's not so much that you are bored, as melancholy?'

'I should think so!' said he. 'Many a time when everything was all right and everybody in high spirits it has suddenly struck me that I'm sick of it all and that there's nothing left for us but to die. Once in the regiment, when I did not go to some jollification where there was music ... and all at once I felt so depressed. ...'

'Oh yes, I know, I know – I know that feeling,' Natasha interrupted him. 'It used to be like that with me when I was quite little. Do you remember that time when I was punished on account of those plums, and you were all dancing while I sat sobbing in the school room? I sobbed so hard, I shall never forget it. I felt sad and sorry for everyone – sorry for myself and everyone in the world. And I hadn't done anything, that was the point,' said Natasha. 'Do you remember?'

'Yes,' said Nikolai. 'And I remember coming to you afterwards and wanting to comfort you, but, do you know, I felt shy about it. We were terribly ridiculous. I had a funny wooden doll then, and I wanted to give it to you. Remember?'

'And do you remember,' Natasha asked with a pensive smile, 'how once, long, long ago, when we were quite little, Uncle called us into the study – that was in the old house – and it was dark. We went in and all at once there stood ...'

'A Negro,' Nikolai finished for her with a smile of delight. 'Of course I remember! To this day I don't know whether there really was a Negro, or if we only dreamt it, or were told about him.'

'He had grey hair, remember, and white teeth, and he stood and stared at us. ...'

'Sonya, do *you* remember?' asked Nikolai.

'Yes, yes, I do remember something too,' Sonya answered timidly.

'You know, I've often asked papa and mamma about that Negro,' said Natasha, 'and they declare there never was a Negro. But you see, *you* remember about it.'

'Of course I do. I can see his teeth now.'

'How strange it is! As though it were a dream! I like that.'

'And do you remember how we rolled hard-boiled eggs in the ballroom, and all of a sudden two little old women appeared and began spinning round on the carpet? Was that real or not? Do you remember what fun it was?'

'Yes, and do you remember how papa in his blue overcoat fired a gun off in the porch?'

So, smiling with happiness, they went through their memories: not the melancholy memories of old age but the romantic reminiscences of youth – impressions from the most distant past in which dreams fuse with reality – and they laughed with quiet enjoyment.

Sonya, as usual, did not quite keep up with the other two, though they had grown up together.

Sonya had forgotten much that the others recalled, and what did come back to her failed to arouse the same romantic feeling as they experienced. She simply rejoiced in their enjoyment and tried to fit in with it.

She only really took part when they began to speak of her arrival in their home. She told them how afraid she had been of Nikolai because he wore braid on his jacket, and her nurse had said that she too would be sewn up in braid.

'And I remember they told me that you had been born under a cabbage,' said Natasha, 'and I remember not daring to disbelieve it then, though I knew it wasn't true and I felt so uncomfortable.'

While they were talking a maid popped her head in at the door of the sitting-room.

'They have brought the cock, miss,' she said in a whisper.

'I don't want it now, Polya. Tell them to take it away,' replied Natasha.

In the middle of their talk in the sitting-room Dimmler came in and went up to the harp that stood in a corner. He took off the cover, and the harp gave out a jarring sound.

'Herr Dimmler, please play my favourite nocturne by Field,' cried the old countess from the drawing-room.

Dimmler struck a chord and, turning to Natasha, Nikolai and Sonya, remarked, 'How quiet you young people are!'

'Yes, we're philosophizing,' said Natasha, glancing round for a moment and then pursuing the conversation. They were now discussing dreams.

Dimmler began to play. Natasha tiptoed noiselessly to the table, took the candle, carried it away and returned, seating herself quietly in her former place. It was dark in the room, especially where they were sitting on the sofa, but through the lofty windows the silvery light of the full moon fell on the floor.

'Do you know,' said Natasha in a whisper, moving closer to Nikolai and Sonya (while Dimmler, who had finished the nocturne, sat softly running his fingers over the strings, apparently uncertain whether to stop or to play something else), '– do you know that when one goes on and on recalling memories, in the end one begins to remember what happened before one was in the world? ...'

'That's metempsychosis,' said Sonya, who had always been a good scholar and remembered what she learned. 'The Egyptians used to believe that our souls once inhabited the bodies of animals, and will return into animals again.'

'No, I don't believe we were ever in animals,' said Natasha, still in a whisper though the music had ceased. 'But I know for certain that we were angels once, in some other world, and we have been here, and that is why we remember. ...'

'May I join you?' said Dimmler, coming up quietly, and he sat down by them.

'If we have been angels, why should we have fallen lower?' said Nikolai. 'No, that can't be!'

'Not lower – whoever told you we were lower? ... Because I know what I used to be,' rejoined Natasha with conviction. 'You see, the soul is immortal ... therefore if I am to live for ever in the future I must have existed in the past, existed for a whole eternity.'

'Yes, but it is hard for us to imagine eternity,' remarked Dimmler, who had joined the young folk with a mildly condescending smile but now spoke as quietly and seriously as they.

'Why is it hard to imagine eternity?' demanded Natasha. 'After today comes tomorrow, and then the next day, and so on for ever; and there was yesterday, and the day before. ...'

'Natasha! Now it is your turn. Sing me something,' they heard the countess's voice. 'Why are you sitting there like conspirators?'

'Mamma, I don't feel a bit like it,' said Natasha, but she got up all the same.

None of them, not even the middle-aged Dimmler, wanted to break off their conversation and leave that corner of the sitting-room, but Natasha rose to her feet and Nikolai seated himself at the clavichord. Standing as usual in the middle of the room, and choosing the place where the acoustics were best, Natasha began to sing her mother's favourite song.

She had said she did not feel like singing, but it was long since she had sung, and long before she was to sing again, as she did that evening. The count, from his study where he was talking to Mitenka, heard her, and like a schoolboy in a hurry to run out and play, stumbled over his instructions to the steward, and at last stopped speaking, while Mitenka stood in front of him, also listening and smiling. Nikolai did not take his eyes off his sister, and drew breath in time with her. Sonya, as she listened, thought of the immense difference there was between herself and her friend, and how impossible it was for her to be anything like as bewitching as her cousin. The old countess sat with a blissful yet sad smile, and with tears in her eyes, ever and anon shaking her head. She was thinking of Natasha, and of her own youth, and of how there was something unnatural and dreadful in this impending marriage between Natasha and Prince Andrei.

Dimmler, who had seated himself beside the countess, listened with closed eyes.

'No, countess,' he said at last, 'this talent of hers is European: she has nothing to learn – what softness, what tenderness and strength. ...'

'Oh, how afraid I am for her, how afraid I am!' said the countess, not realizing to whom she was speaking. Her maternal instinct told her that Natasha had too much of something, and that because of this she would not be happy. Before Natasha had finished singing, fourteen-year-old Petya rushed into the room in great excitement to announce that some mummers had arrived.

Natasha stopped abruptly.

'Idiot!' she screamed at her brother, and running to a chair flung herself into it, sobbing so violently that it was a long while before she could stop.

'It's nothing, mamma, really it's nothing. Only Petya startled me,' she said, trying to smile; but the tears still flowed and the sobs still choked her.

The mummers (some of the house-serfs dressed up as bears, Turks, tavern-keepers and fine ladies – awe-inspiring or comic figures) at first huddled bashfully together in the vestibule, bringing in with them the cold and hilarity from outside. Then, hiding behind one

617

another, they pushed into the ballroom, where, at first shyly but afterwards with ever-increasing merriment and zeal, they started singing, dancing and playing Christmas games. The countess, after identifying them and laughing at their costumes, went away to the drawing-room. The count sat in the ballroom with a beaming smile, applauding the players. The young people had vanished.

Half an hour later there appeared among the mummers in the ball-room an old lady in a farthingale – this was Nikolai. A Turkish girl was Petya. Dimmler was a clown. A hussar was Natasha, and a Circassian youth Sonya with burnt-cork moustaches and eyebrows.

After being received with well-feigned surprise, non-recognition or praise from those who were not mumming, the young people decided that their costumes were so good that they ought to be dis-played somewhere else.

Nikolai, who had a strong desire to go out in his troika, the roads being in splendid condition, proposed that they should take with them a dozen of the house-serfs who were dressed up, and drive to 'Uncle's'.

'No, why disturb the old fellow ?' said the countess. 'Besides, you wouldn't have room to turn round there. If you must go anywhere, go to the Melyukovs'.'

Madame Melyukov was a widow who lived with a host of children of various ages, and their tutors and governesses, about three miles from the Rostovs'.

'That's right, *ma chère*, an excellent idea,' chimed in the old count. 'I'll dress up at once and go with them. I'll make Pashette open her eyes.'

But the countess would not agree to let the count accompany them: his leg had been bad for several days. It was decided that the count must not go but that if Louisa Ivanovna (Madame Schoss) would act as chaperone, then the young ladies might visit the Melyukovs. Sonya, generally so reserved and timid, was more urgent than all the others in her entreaties to Madame Schoss not to refuse.

Sonya's costume was the best of all. Her moustaches and eyebrows were extraordinarily becoming to her. Everyone said how pretty she looked, and she was keyed up to an unusual pitch of energy and ex-citement. Some inner voice told her that now or never her fate would be decided, and in her masculine attire she seemed quite another person. Madame Schoss consented to go, and half an hour later four troikas, all jingling bells, drove up to the porch, their runners crunching and creaking over the frozen snow.

Natasha was the first to sound the note of Christmas gaiety, and this gaiety, spreading from one to another, grew wilder and wilder, reaching its climax when they all came out into the frosty air and, talking and calling to one another, laughing and shouting, got into the sledges.

Two of the troikas were the ordinary household sledges, the third was the old count's with a trotter from the Orlov stud as shaft-horse, the fourth was Nikolai's own troika with a short shaggy black horse between the thills. Nikolai, in his farthingale, over which he had belted his hussar's cloak, stood up in the middle of the sledge, holding the reins.

It was so light that he could see the metal of the harness shining in the moonlight, and the horses' eyes as they looked round in alarm at the noisy party gathered under the shadow of the porch roof.

Natasha, Sonya, Madame Schoss and two maids got into Nikolai's sledge. Into the old count's sledge went Dimmler and his wife, and Petya; while the rest of the mummers seated themselves in the other two sledges.

'You lead the way, Zahar!' shouted Nikolai to his father's coachman, so as to have the chance of racing past him on the road.

The old count's troika with Dimmler and his party started forward, its runners creaking as though they were frozen to the snow, its deep-toned bell clanging. The trace-horses pressed close to the shafts and, sinking in the snow, kicked it up, hard and glittering like sugar.

Nikolai followed the first sledge; behind him he heard the noise and crunch of the other two. At first they drove at a slow trot along the narrow road. As they passed the garden the shadows cast by the bare trees fell across the road and hid the bright moonlight, but as soon as they got beyond the fence the snowy plain, motionless and bathed in moonlight, stretched out before them, glittering like diamonds and dappled with bluish shadows. *Bump, bump!* went the first sledge over a cradle-hole in the snow; in exactly the same way the one behind dipped down and up again, and the others that followed; and then, rudely breaking the iron stillness, the troikas began to speed along the road, one after the other.

'A hare's track, a lot of tracks!' Natasha's voice rang out in the frost-bound air.

'How light it is, Nicolas!' came Sonya's voice.

Nikolai glanced round at Sonya, and bent down to look more closely into her face. It was quite a new, sweet face with black eyebrows and moustaches that peeped up at him from her sable furs – so close yet so distant – in the moonlight.

'That used to be Sonya,' thought Nikolai. He gave her a closer look and smiled.

'What is it, Nicolas?'

'Nothing,' said he, and turned to the horses again.

When they came out on to the beaten high road – polished by sledge-runners and cut up by rough-shod hooves, the marks of which were visible in the moonlight – the horses began to tug at the reins of their own accord, and quickened their pace. The near-side horse, arching his head and breaking into a short canter, strained at the traces. The shaft-horse swayed from side to side, pricking up his ears as though asking: 'Shall we go, or is it too soon?' In front, already a considerable distance ahead, the deep bell of the sledge rang farther and farther off, and the black horses driven by Zahar made a dark patch against the white snow. The shouts and laughter of his party of mummers could be clearly heard.

'Now then, my darlings!' cried Nikolai, pulling the reins to one side and flourishing the whip. And it was only the wind meeting them more sharply, and the tugging of the side-horses galloping faster and faster, that gave them an idea of how fast the sledge was flying along. Nikolai glanced behind. With screams and squeals and brandishing of whips, that caused even the shaft-horses to gallop, the other sledges speeded after them. The shaft-horse swung steadily beneath the shaft-bow over its head, with no thought of slackening pace but ready to increase it if need be.

Nikolai overtook the first sledge. They glided down a little slope and came out upon a broad trodden track that crossed a meadow near a river.

'Where are we?' wondered Nikolai. 'It must be the Kosoy meadow, I suppose. But no – this is a place I never saw before. It isn't the Kosoy meadow, nor Dyomkin hill – heaven only knows where we are. This is some new enchanted place. Well, no matter!' And, shouting to his horses, he began to gain on the first troika.

Zahar held back his steeds and turned his face, white to the eyebrows with hoar-frost.

Nikolai gave his team the rein, and Zahar, stretching out his arms, clucked his tongue and let his horses go.

'Steady there, master!' he cried.

Swifter still flew the two troikas, side by side, and swifter interwove the legs of the horses as they sped onward. Nikolai began to draw ahead. Zahar, arms still outstretched, raised one hand with the reins.

'You won't do it, master!' he shouted.

Nikolai urged his three to a gallop and passed Zahar. The horses kicked up the fine dry snow into the faces of those in the sledge – beside them sounded the jingle of bells and they caught confused glimpses of swiftly moving legs and the shadows of the sledge they were passing. From different sides came the whistle of runners on the snow and the voices of girls shrieking.

Checking his horses again, Nikolai looked around him. All about him lay the same magic plain bathed in moonlight and spangled with stars.

'Zahar's shouting that I'm to turn to the left, but why to the left?' thought Nikolai. 'Aren't we going to the Melyukovs'? Is this the way to Melyukovka? Heaven only knows where we are going – the Lord knows what is happening to us, but whatever it is it is very peculiar and nice.' He looked round in the sledge.

'See, his moustache and eyelashes are all white!' said one of the strange, pretty, unfamiliar figures sitting by him – the one with the fine eyebrows and moustaches.

'I believe that was Natasha,' thought Nikolai. 'And that's Madame Schoss, but perhaps I'm wrong, and I don't know that Circassian with the moustache, but I love her.'

'Aren't you cold?' he asked.

They did not answer but began to laugh. Dimmler from the sledge behind shouted something – it was probably something funny – but they could not make out what he said.

'Yes, yes!' other voices laughed back.

'But here we are in a sort of magic forest with shifting black shadows, and a glitter of diamonds, a flight of marble steps and the silver roofs of fairy buildings, and the shrill yells of wild beasts. And if this really is the Melyukov place, then it's stranger than ever that after driving heaven knows where we should come to Melyukovka,' thought Nikolai.

It was, in fact, Melyukovka, and maids and footmen with beaming faces came running out to the porch, carrying candles.

'Who is it?' asked someone from the front door.

'Mummers from the count's. I know by the horses,' answered various voices.

II

PELAGEYA DANILOVNA MELYUKOV, a broadly-built, energetic woman wearing spectacles and a loose house-dress, was sitting in the drawing-room surrounded by her daughters whom she was doing her best to keep amused. They were quietly occupied in dropping melted wax into water and watching the shadows the wax shapes cast on the wall, when the steps and voices of the visitors began to echo through from the hall.

Hussars, fine ladies, witches, clowns and bears, clearing their throats in the vestibule and wiping the hoar-frost from their faces, came into the ballroom where candles were hurriedly lit. The clown – Dimmler – and the lady – Nikolai – opened the dance. Surrounded by shrieking children, the mummers hid their faces and, disguising their voices, bowed to their hostess and arranged themselves about the room.

'Dear me, there's no recognizing them! And Natasha there! Whoever is it she looks like? She really does remind me of someone. And there's Herr Dimmler – isn't he good! I didn't know him. And how he dances! And oh, my goodness, look at that Circassian! Why, how it suits dear little Sonya! And who is that? Well, you have cheered us up! Nikita, Vanya – clear away the tables. And we were sitting here so quietly. Ha, ha, ha! ... That hussar – that hussar over there! Just like a boy! And the legs! ... I can't look at him ...' various voices were exclaiming.

Natasha, who was a great favourite with the young Melyukovs, disappeared with them into rooms at the back of the house, where a burnt cork and sundry dressing-gowns and male garments were called for and received from the footmen by bare girlish arms from behind the door. Ten minutes later all the young Melyukovs were ready to join the mummers.

Madame Melyukov, having seen to it that space was cleared for the visitors, and arranged about refreshments for the gentry and the serfs, went about among the mummers with her spectacles on her nose, peering into their faces with a suppressed smile and failing to recognize any of them. It was not only Dimmler and the Rostovs that she failed to recognize: she did not even know her own daughters, or identify her late husband's dressing-gowns and uniforms which they had put on.

'And who can this one be?' she kept saying, addressing the governess and staring into the face of her own daughter disguised as a Kazan Tartar. 'I suppose it is one of the Rostovs. Well, Mr Hussar – what regiment do you belong to?' she asked Natasha. 'Here, give some fruit-jelly to that Turk,' she told the butler who was carrying round refreshments. 'Turkish law doesn't forbid jelly.'

Sometimes, as she looked at the strange and ludicrous capers cut by the dancers, who, having made up their minds once for all that no one would recognize them in their fancy dresses, were not at all shy, Madame Melyukov would hide her face in her handkerchief, and her fat body would shake from head to toe with irrepressible, good-natured, elderly laughter.

'My little Sasha! Look at my little Sasha!' she said.

After Russian country-dances and choruses Madame Melyukov made the serfs and gentry form into one large circle; a ring, a string and a silver rouble were fetched, and they all began playing games.

By the end of an hour every costume was crumpled and untidy. The burnt-cork moustaches and eyebrows were smudged over the perspiring, flushed and merry faces. Madame Melyukov began to recognize the mummers and compliment them on their clever dresses, telling them how very becoming they were, especially to the young ladies, and she thanked them all for having entertained her so well. The visitors were invited to supper in the drawing-room, while the serfs had something served to them in the ballroom.

'Now to tell one's fortune in the empty bath-house is a terrifying thing!' exclaimed an old maid who lived with the Melyukovs, during supper.

'Why?' asked the eldest Melyukov girl.

'You wouldn't go. It takes courage. ...'

'I'll go,' said Sonya.

'Tell us what happened to that girl?' said the second Melyukov daughter.

'Well, this was the way of it,' began the old maid. 'A young lady

623

went and took a cock, laid the table for two, all properly, and sat down. After a little while she suddenly hears someone coming ... a sledge drives up, harness bells jingling. She hears him coming! He walks in, precisely in the shape of a man, like an officer – and comes and sits down at the table with her.'

'Oh! Oh!' screamed Natasha, rolling her eyes in horror.

'Yes, and then? Did he speak?'

'He did, like a man. Everything was ordinary, and he began to try and win her over, and all she had to do was to keep him talking till the cock crowed; but she got frightened, just got frightened and hid her face in her hands. Then he clasped her in his arms. Luckily at that minute the maids ran in. ...'

'Come, what is the good of scaring them?' said Madame Melyukov.

'Why, mamma, you used to try your fortune that way yourself ...' said her daughter.

'And how does one tell one's fortune in a barn?' inquired Sonya.

'Well, say you went to the barn now, and listened. It depends on what you hear: if there's hammering and tapping, that's bad; but the sound of shifting grain is a good sign. And sometimes one hears ...'

'Mamma, tell us what happened to you in the barn.'

Madame Melyukov smiled.

'Oh, I've forgotten, it was so long ago ...' she replied. 'Besides, I'm sure none of you would go?'

'Yes, I will. Let me – I'll go,' said Sonya.

'Very well, then, if you're not afraid.'

'Madame Schoss, may I?' asked Sonya.

Whether they were playing the ring-and-string game, or the rouble game, or talking as now, Nikolai did not leave Sonya's side, and gazed at her with quite new eyes. It seemed to him that it was only now, thanks to those burnt-cork moustaches, that he really knew her. Indeed that evening Sonya was gayer, more animated and prettier than Nikolai had ever seen her before.

'So this is what she is like! And what a fool I have been!' he kept thinking, looking at her sparkling eyes and watching the happy, rapturous smile dimpling her cheeks under the moustache – a smile he had never seen before.

'I am not afraid of anything,' said Sonya. 'May I go at once?' She got up.

They told her where the barn was, and how she must stand silent and listen, and gave her a fur cloak, which she flung over her head with a glance at Nikolai.

'What an exquisite girl she is!' he said to himself. 'And what have I been thinking about all this time?'

Sonya went out into the passage to go to the barn. Saying that he felt too hot, Nikolai hurried to the front porch. It certainly was stuffy indoors from the crowd of people.

Outside there was the same still cold, and the same moon, except that it shone brighter than before. The light was so strong and the snow sparkled with so many stars that one's eye was not drawn to look up at the sky, and the real stars passed unnoticed. The sky was black and dreary; the earth was radiant.

'I'm a fool, an idiot! What have I been waiting for all this time?' thought Nikolai; and, running out from the porch, he turned the corner of the house and went along the path that led to the back door. He knew Sonya would come that way. Half-way to the barn lay some snow-covered stacks of firewood, and across and along them a network of shadows from the bare old lime trees fell on the snow and on the path leading to the barn. The log walls of the granary and its snow-covered roof, that looked as if they were hewn out of some precious stone, shone in the moonlight. A tree in the garden snapped with the frost, and all was silent and still again. Nikolai's lungs seemed to breathe in not air but an elixir of eternal youth and joy.

From the back porch came the sound of feet descending the steps. There was a ringing crunch on the last step which was thickly carpeted with snow, and the voice of an old maidservant was saying:

'Keep straight on along the path, miss. Only don't look round.'

'I am not afraid,' replied Sonya's voice; then along the path towards Nikolai came the sliding, squeaking sound of Sonya's little feet in her thin slippers.

Sonya came muffled up in her cloak. She was only a couple of paces away when she saw him, and to her too he was different from the Nikolai she had known and always slightly feared. He was in woman's dress, with tousled hair and a blissful smile new to Sonya. She ran quickly towards him.

'She's quite different and yet exactly the same,' thought Nikolai, looking at her face all lit up by the moonlight. He slipped his arms under the fur cloak that covered her head, embraced her, strained her to his heart, and kissed her on the lips which wore a moustache and smelt of burnt cork. Sonya kissed him full on the mouth, and disengaging her little hands pressed them to his cheeks.

'Sonya!' ... 'Nicolas!' ... was all they said. They ran to the barn and then back again to the house, which they re-entered, he by the front and she by the back porch.

12

WHEN they all drove back from Madame Melyukov's, Natasha, who always saw and noticed everything, arranged a change of seating, so that she and Madame Schoss should return in the sledge with Dimmler, while Sonya went with Nikolai and the maids.

On the way home Nikolai drove at a steady pace instead of racing, and kept gazing in the weird, all-transforming light into Sonya's face, trying to discover beneath the eyebrows and moustaches the Sonya of the past, and his present Sonya from whom he had resolved never to be parted again. He watched her intently, and when he recognized the old Sonya, and the new, and recalled the smell of burnt cork mingled with the sensation of her kiss, he drew in a deep breath of the frosty air and, looking at the ground gliding by and the sky shining above, felt himself in fairyland once more.

'Sonya, is it well with *thee* ?' he asked from time to time.

'Yes,' Sonya would reply. 'And *thee* ?'

When they were half-way home Nikolai handed the reins to the coachman and ran for a moment to Natasha's sledge and stood on the wing.

'Natasha,' he whispered in French, 'do you know, I have made up my mind about Sonya ?'

'Have you told her ?' asked Natasha, suddenly all radiant with joy.

'Oh, how strange you look with that moustache and those eyebrows, Natasha! Are you glad ?'

'I am so glad, so glad! I was beginning to be vexed with you. I did not tell you, but you have been treating her badly. Such a heart she has, Nicolas! I'm horrid sometimes, but I was ashamed to be happy while Sonya wasn't,' continued Natasha. 'Now I am so glad! Well, run back to her.'

'No, wait a moment. ... Oh, how funny you look!' cried Nikolai, peering into her face and finding in his sister, too, something new, unusual and bewitchingly lovely that he had never noticed in her before. 'Natasha, it's like fairyland, isn't it?'

'Yes,' she replied. 'You have done splendidly.'

'Had I seen her before as she is now,' thought Nikolai, 'I should have asked her long ago what to do, and have done whatever she told me, and all would have been well.'

'So you are glad, and I have done right?'

'Oh, quite right! I had a quarrel with mamma about it a little while ago. Mamma said she was angling for you. How could she say such a thing! I almost stormed at mamma. And I will never allow anyone to say or think anything bad of Sonya, for she is goodness itself.'

'Then it's all right?' said Nikolai, giving another searching look at the expression of his sister's face to see if she was in earnest. Then he jumped down and, his boots scrunching the snow, ran back to his own sledge. The same happy smiling Circassian, with moustaches and beaming eyes peeping up from under the sable hood, was still sitting there, and this Circassian was Sonya, and this Sonya was beyond a doubt to be his happy and loving wife in the days to come.

After they reached home, and told their mother how they had spent the evening at the Melyukovs', the girls went to their bedroom. They undressed, but without wiping off their burnt-cork moustaches sat a long time talking of their happiness. They talked of how they would live when they were married, how their husbands would be friends, and how happy they would be. On Natasha's table stood two looking-glasses which Dunyasha had put there earlier in the evening.

'Only when will it all happen? I fear me never. ... It would be too good!' said Natasha, rising and going over to the looking-glasses.

'Sit down, Natasha; perhaps you'll see him,' said Sonya.

Natasha lit the candles and sat down.

'I do see someone with a moustache,' said Natasha, seeing her own face.

'You shouldn't make fun, miss,' said Dunyasha.

With the help of Sonya and the maid Natasha got into the proper position before the glass. Her face assumed a serious expression, and she fell silent. She sat a long time looking at the receding line of candles reflected in the glasses and expecting (in accordance with the tales she had heard) to see a coffin, or else *him*, Prince Andrei, in that last dim indistinct square. But ready as she was to accept the slightest blur as the image of a man or a coffin, she saw nothing.

Her eyes began to blink and she moved away from the mirror.

'Why is it other people see things and I don't?' she said. 'Now you sit down, Sonya. Tonight you really must. Do it for me. ... I feel so full of dread today!'

Sonya sat down to the looking-glass, settled herself in the right position and began to look.

'Miss Sonya, now, is sure to see something,' whispered Dunyasha. 'You always make fun.'

Sonya heard this, and heard Natasha's whispered reply:

'Yes, I know she will: she did last year, you remember.'

For two or three minutes the three of them were silent. 'Of course she will!' murmured Natasha, and did not finish. ... Suddenly Sonya pushed away the glass she was holding, and covered her eyes with her hand.

'Oh, Natasha!' she cried.

'Did you see something? Did you? What was it?' exclaimed Natasha.

'I said so,' said Dunyasha, supporting the looking-glass.

Sonya had not seen anything. She was just wanting to blink her eyes and get up when she heard Natasha say 'Of course she will!' She did not wish to disappoint either Dunyasha or Natasha, but she was tired of sitting there. She did not know herself how or why the exclamation had escaped her when she covered her eyes.

'Did you see him?' demanded Natasha, clutching her hand.

'Yes. Wait ... I ... saw him,' Sonya found herself saying, and not sure yet whether by *him* Natasha meant Nikolai or Andrei. ('Why not say I saw something? Other people see things. Besides, who can tell whether I saw anything or not?' flashed through Sonya's mind.)

'Yes, I saw him,' she said.

'How was he? How? Standing up or lying down?'

'No, I saw ... At first there was nothing. Then suddenly I saw him lying down.'

'Andrei lying down? Is he ill?' Natasha asked, looking at her friend with terrified eyes.

'No, on the contrary – on the contrary, his face was cheerful, and he turned round to me ...' and as she was saying this she fancied she really had seen what she was describing.

'What next? Go on, Sonya.'

'I could not make out after that – there was something blue and red. ...'

'Sonya, when will he come back? When shall I see him? Oh God, how afraid I am for him and for myself, afraid for everything ...' Natasha began, and paying no heed to Sonya's attempts to comfort her she got into bed, and long after her candle was out lay open-eyed and motionless, gazing at the frosty moonlight through the frozen window-panes.

13

SOON after the Christmas holidays Nikolai told his mother of his love for Sonya and announced his firm intention to marry her. The countess, who had long ago noticed what was going on between Sonya and Nikolai, and was expecting this declaration, listened to him in silence, and then told her son that he might marry whom he pleased but that neither she nor his father would give their blessing to such a marriage. For the first time in his life Nikolai felt that his mother was displeased with him, and that, notwithstanding all her love for him, she would not give way. Coldly, without looking at Nikolai, she sent for her husband, and when he came in she tried, in a few chilling words to explain the situation to him, in Nikolai's presence, but she could not control herself, and bursting into tears of vexation left the room. The old count made a feeble appeal to Nikolai, begging him to give up his intention. Nikolai replied that he could not go back on his word, and his father, sighing and visibly embarrassed, very quickly cut short the conversation and went in to the countess. In all his encounters with his son the count was always aware of a sense of guilt for having squandered the family fortune, and so he could not feel angry with him for refusing to marry an heiress, and choosing the dowerless Sonya. On this occasion he was more vividly conscious than ever that if his affairs had not been in disorder no better wife than Sonya could have been wished for for Nikolai, and that no one but himself and his Mitenka and his incorrigible bad habits was to blame for the condition of the family finances.

The father and mother did not speak of the matter to their son again, but a few days later the countess sent for Sonya and, with a cruelty that surprised them both, upbraided her niece for enticing Nikolai, and accused her of ingratitude. Sonya listened in silence and with downcast eyes to the countess's bitter words, at a loss to understand what was required of her. She was ready to make any sacrifice for her benefactors. The idea of self-sacrifice was her favourite idea;

629

but in this case she could not see what she ought to sacrifice, or for whom. She could not help loving the countess and the whole Rostov family, but neither could she help loving Nikolai and knowing that his happiness depended on that love. She stood silent and dejected, and made no reply. Nikolai felt he could not endure the situation any longer, and went to have it out with his mother. He first implored her to forgive him and Sonya, and to consent to their marriage; then he threatened that if she persecuted Sonya he would instantly marry her in secret.

The countess, with an iciness her son had never seen in her before, replied that he was of age, that Prince Andrei was marrying without *his* father's consent, and he could do the same, but that she would never receive that *scheming creature* as her daughter.

Stung to fury by the words *scheming creature*, Nikolai, raising his voice, told his mother that he had never expected her to try and force him to sell his feelings, but that if this were so it was the last time he would ever ... but before he could speak the fatal word which the expression of his face caused his mother to await with terror, and which would perhaps have remained an agonizing memory to them both for ever, Natasha, who had been listening at the door, ran into the room with a pale, set face.

'Nikolai, my darling, you don't know what you are saying! Be quiet, be quiet, I tell you! Be quiet! ...' she almost screamed, so as to drown his voice.

'Mamma, dearest, he doesn't mean it at all ... my poor, sweet darling,' she said to her mother, who, conscious that they had been on the edge of a rupture, was gazing at her son in terror, yet because of her obstinacy and the heat of the quarrel could not and would not give way.

'Nikolai, I'll explain to you, you go away. And you, mamma darling, listen,' she entreated, turning to her mother.

Her words were incoherent but they achieved their purpose.

The countess, sobbing heavily, buried her face in her daughter's bosom, while Nikolai got up, clutching his head, and left the room.

Natasha set to work to effect a reconciliation, and so far succeeded that Nikolai received a promise from his mother that Sonya should not be ill-used, while he on his side pledged himself not to do anything without his parents' knowledge.

Firmly resolved to retire from the service as soon as he could wind up his military career, and return and marry Sonya, Nikolai, grave and melancholy and at variance with his parents but, as it seemed to him, passionately in love, left at the beginning of January to rejoin his regiment.

After Nikolai had gone the atmosphere in the Rostov household was more depressing than ever. The countess fell ill with the mental upset.

Sonya was unhappy at being parted from Nikolai, and still more so on account of the hostile tone the countess could not help adopting towards her. The count was more than ever taken up with the precarious state of his finances, which called for some decisive action. Their town house and estate near Moscow would have to be sold, and for this it was necessary to go to Moscow. But the countess's health obliged them to delay their departure from one day to the next.

Natasha, who had at first borne the separation from her betrothed lightly and even cheerfully, now grew more restless and impatient every day. The thought that the best time of her life, which might have been spent in loving him, was being wasted to no purpose fretted her continually. His letters for the most part irritated her. It hurt her to think that while she lived only in the thought of him he was living a real life, seeing new places and new people interesting to him. The more engaging his letters were the more they provoked her. Her letters to him, far from giving her any comfort, seemed to her a wearisome and artificial duty. She could not write, because she could not conceive of the possibility of expressing sincerely in a letter even a thousandth part of what she was accustomed to say by the tone of her voice, a smile and a look. The letters she wrote to him were dry and formal, all after one pattern. She attached no importance to these compositions, in the rough copies of which her mother corrected her spelling mistakes.

There was still no improvement in the countess's health, but the journey to Moscow could not be deferred any longer. Natasha's trousseau had to be ordered and the house sold. Moreover, Prince Andrei was expected in Moscow, where his father was spending the winter, and Natasha felt certain he had already arrived.

So the countess remained in the country, while the count, taking Sonya and Natasha with him, went to Moscow towards the end of January.

631

PART FIVE

I

After Prince Andrei's engagement to Natasha, Pierre, without any apparent reason, suddenly felt it impossible to go on living as before. Firmly convinced as he was of the truths revealed to him by his benefactor, and happy as he had been in his first period of enthusiasm for the task of improving his spiritual self, to which he had devoted so much ardour – all the zest of such a life vanished with the engagement of Andrei and Natasha, and the death of Bazdeyev, the news of which reached him almost at the same time. Nothing but the empty skeleton of life remained to him: his house, a brilliant wife who now enjoyed the favours of a very important personage, acquaintance with all Petersburg, and his duties at court with all their tedious formalities. And this life suddenly began to fill Pierre with unexpected loathing. He ceased keeping a diary, avoided the company of the brethren, took to visiting the club again, drank a great deal and renewed his association with the gay bachelor sets, leading such a life that the Countess Hélène found it necessary to bring him severely to task. Pierre felt that she was right, and to avoid embarrassing her went away to Moscow.

In Moscow, as soon as he set foot in his enormous house with the faded and fading princesses and the swarm of servants; as soon as, driving through the town, he saw the Iversky chapel with innumerable tapers burning before the golden settings of the icons, the Kremlin square with its snow undisturbed by vehicles, the sledge-drivers and the hovels of the slum district; saw the old Moscovites quietly living out their days, with never a desire or a quickening of the blood; saw the old Moscow ladies, the Moscow balls and the English Club – he felt himself at home in a haven of rest. Moscow gave him the sensation of peace and warmth that one has in an old and dirty dressing-gown.

Moscow society, from the old ladies to the children, welcomed Pierre like a long-expected guest whose place was always ready waiting for him. In the eyes of Moscow society Pierre was the nicest, kindest, most intelligent, merriest and most liberal-minded of eccentrics, a heedless, genial Russian nobleman of the old school. His purse was always empty because it was open to everyone.

Benefit performances, wretched pictures, statues, charitable societies, gipsy choirs, schools, subscription dinners, drinking parties, the freemasons, the churches, and books – no one and nothing ever met with a refusal from him, and had it not been for two friends who had borrowed large sums from him and now took him under their protection he would have parted with everything. At the club no dinner or *soirée* was complete without him. The moment he sank into his place on the sofa after a couple of bottles of Margaux he would be surrounded by a circle of friends, and the discussions, the arguments and the joking began. Where there were quarrels his kindly smile and apt jests were enough to reconcile the antagonists. The masonic dinners were dull and dreary when he was absent.

When he rose after a bachelor supper and with his amiable, kindly smile yielded to the entreaties of the festive party to drive off somewhere with them the young men would make the rafters ring with their shouts of delight and triumph. At balls he danced if a partner was needed. Young women, married and unmarried, liked him because he paid court to no one but was equally agreeable to all, especially after supper. '*Il est charmant, il n'a pas de sexe,*' they said of him.

Pierre was one of those retired gentlemen-in-waiting, of whom there were hundreds, good-humouredly ending their days in Moscow.

How horrified he would have been seven years before, when he first arrived back from abroad, if anyone had told him there was no need for him to look about and make plans, that his track had long ago been shaped for him and marked out before all eternity, and that, wriggle as he might, he would be what everyone in his position was doomed to be. He would not have believed it. Had he not at one time longed with all his heart to establish a republic in Russia? Then that he might be a Napoleon? Then a philosopher, then a great strategist and the conqueror of Napoleon? Had he not seen the possibility of and passionately desired the regeneration of the sinful human race, and his own progress to the highest degree of perfection? Had he not established schools and infirmaries and liberated his serfs?

But instead of all that, here he was, the wealthy husband of a faithless wife, a retired gentleman-in-waiting, fond of eating and drinking, fond, too, as he unbuttoned his waistcoat after dinner, of abusing the government a bit, a member of the Moscow English Club, and a universal favourite in Moscow society. For a long while he could not reconcile himself to the idea that he was one of those same retired Moscow gentlemen-in-waiting he had so profoundly despised seven years before.

Sometimes he tried to console himself with the reflection that he was only temporarily leading this kind of life; but presently he was shocked by another reflection – how many men, like himself, with the same idea of its being temporary, had entered that life and that club in possession of all their teeth and a thick head of hair, only to leave it when they were toothless and bald?

In moments of pride, when he was reviewing his position, it seemed to him that he was quite different and distinct from those other retired gentlemen-in-waiting whom he had scorned in the past: they were vulgar and stupid, content and at ease with their position, 'while I am still dissatisfied – I still want to do something for mankind,' he would assure himself in moments of pride. 'But possibly all these comrades of mine struggled just as I do, trying to find some new and original path through life, and like myself have been brought by force of circumstances, by conditions of society and birth – that elemental force against which man is powerless – to the same point as I have,' he would say to himself in moments of humility; and after living for some time in Moscow he ceased to despise his companions in destiny, but began to grow fond of them, to respect and feel sorry for them as he was sorry for himself.

Pierre no longer suffered moments of despair, hypochondria and disgust with life, but the same malady that had formerly manifested itself in acute attacks was driven inwards and now never left him for an instant. 'What for? What is the use? What is going on in the world?' he asked himself in perplexity several times a day, involuntarily beginning to inquire into the meaning of the phenomena of life; but knowing by experience that there were no answers to these questions he made haste to put them out of his mind, and took up a book or hurried off to the club or to Apollon Nikolayevich's, to exchange the gossip of the town.

'Hélène, who has never cared for anything but her own body, and is one of the stupidest women in the world,' thought Pierre, 'is regarded by people as the acme of intelligence and refinement, and they pay homage to her. Napoleon Bonaparte was scorned by everybody while he was great, but since he became a pitiful buffoon the Emperor Francis seeks to offer him his daughter in an illegal marriage. The Spaniards, through their Catholic clergy, return thanks to God for their victory over the French on the 14th of June, while the French, through the same Catholic Church, offer praise because on that same 14th of June they defeated the Spaniards. My masonic brethren swear in blood that they are ready to sacrifice everything for their neighbour, but they don't give so much as one rouble to the collections for the poor, and the Astraea lodge intrigues against the "Manna Seekers", and fuss about getting an authentic Scottish carpet and a charter which nobody needs, and the meaning of which not even the man who copied it understands. We all profess the Christian law of forgiveness of injuries and love for our neighbour, the law in honour of which we have raised forty times forty churches in Moscow – but yesterday a deserter was knouted to death and a minister of that same law of love and forgiveness, the priest, gave the soldier the cross to kiss before his execution.' Thus mused Pierre, and this whole universal hypocrisy which everyone accepts, accustomed as he was to it, astonished him each time as if it were something new. 'I see this hypocrisy and muddle,' he thought, 'but how am I to tell them all that I see it? I have tried, and have always found that they, too, in the depths of their hearts know it as well as I do but are wilfully blind. Then so it must be, I suppose. But I – what am I to do with myself?' Pierre ruminated. He had the unlucky capacity many men, especially Russians, have of seeing and believing in the possibility of goodness and truth, but of seeing the evil and falsehood of life too clearly to be able to take any serious part in life. Every sphere of activity was, in his eyes, linked with evil and deception. Whatever he tried to be, whatever he engaged in, he always found himself repulsed by this knavery and falsehood, which blocked every path of action. Yet he had to live and to find occupation. It was too awful to be under the burden of these insoluble problems, and so he abandoned himself to the first distraction that offered itself, in order to forget them. He frequented every kind of society, drank much, purchased pictures, built houses, and above all – read.

He read, and read everything that came to hand. Returning home at night, he would pick up a book and begin to read even while his valets were taking off his things. From reading he passed to sleeping, from sleeping to gossip in drawing-rooms or the club, from gossip to carousals and women; from dissipation back to gossip, reading and wine. Drinking became more and more a physical and moral necessity alike. Though the doctors warned him that with his corpulence wine was dangerous to him, he drank heavily. He only felt quite comfortable when, having mechanically poured several glasses of wine down his capacious throat, he experienced a pleasant warmth in his body, an amiable disposition towards all his fellows, and a readiness to respond superficially to every ideal without probing it too deeply. Only after emptying a bottle or two did he feel vaguely that the terribly tangled skein of life which had appalled him before was not so dreadful as he had fancied. He was always conscious of some aspect of that skein, as with a buzzing in his ears he chatted or listened to conversation, or read his books after dinner or supper. But it was only under the influence of wine that he could say to himself: 'Never mind. I'll disentangle it. I have a solution all ready. But there isn't time now – I'll think it all out presently!' But that *presently* never came.

In the morning, on an empty stomach, all the old questions looked as insoluble and fearful as ever, and Pierre hastily picked up a book, and was delighted if anyone called to see him.

Sometimes he remembered having heard how soldiers under fire in the trenches, and having nothing to do, try hard to find some occupation the more easily to bear the danger. And it seemed to Pierre that all men were like those soldiers, seeking refuge from life: some in ambition, some in cards, some in framing laws, some in women, some in playthings, some in horses, some in politics, some in sport, some in wine, and some in government service. 'Nothing is without consequence, and nothing is important: it's all the same in the end. The thing to do is to save myself from it all as best I can,' thought Pierre. 'Not to see *it*, that terrible *it*.'

2

AT the beginning of the winter old Prince Bolkonsky and his daughter moved to Moscow. The fame of his past career, his wit and his

eccentricity caused Moscovites to regard him with peculiar venera-
tion; and as popular enthusiasm for the Emperor Alexander I's
régime was then cooling off, and a nationalist, anti-French tendency
was all the vogue in Moscow, he became the centre of opposition to
the government.

The prince had aged very much during the past year. Signs of sen-
ility showed themselves unmistakably in sudden naps, forgetfulness
of quite recent events while his memory retained incidents of the
remote past, and the childish vanity with which he accepted the rôle
of leader of the Moscow opposition. In spite of this, when the old
man came into the drawing-room for tea of an evening, in his old-
fashioned coat and powdered wig, and incited by someone or other
started on his abrupt observations on days gone by, or delivered still
more abrupt and scathing criticisms of the present, he inspired in all
his visitors a unanimous feeling of respectful esteem. For them the
old-fashioned house with its huge pier-glasses, pre-Revolution furniture, powdered footmen, and the stern shrewd old man (himself a
relic of a past century) with his gentle daughter and the pretty
Frenchwoman, both so reverently devoted to him, presented a majestic and agreeable spectacle. But the visitors did not reflect that over
and above the couple of hours during which they saw their hosts
there were also twenty-two hours of the day and night during which
the private and intimate life of the household continued its accustomed way.

Of late this private life had become very trying for Princess Maria.
In Moscow she was deprived of her greatest joys – talks with the
pilgrims, and the solitude which refreshed her at Bald Hills – and she
had none of the advantages and pleasures of town life. She did not go
out into society: everyone knew that her father would not allow her
anywhere without him, and his failing health prevented his going out
himself, so that she was not invited to dinners and evening parties.
She had abandoned all hope of ever getting married. She saw the
coldness and malevolence with which the old prince received and
dismissed such young men as occasionally came to the house, and
who might have been her suitors. She had no friends: since her arrival
in Moscow she had been disappointed in the two who had been
nearest to her. Mademoiselle Bourienne, with whom she had never
been able altogether to open her heart, she now regarded with dislike,
and for various reasons kept at a distance. Julie, with whom she had

corresponded for the last five years, was in Moscow, but she seemed like a stranger when they met again. By the death of her brothers Julie had become one of the wealthiest heiresses in Moscow, and was at that time engrossed in a giddy whirl of fashionable amusements. She was surrounded by young men who, she believed, had suddenly learnt to appreciate her worth. Julie was at that stage in the life of a society woman past her first youth when she feels that her last chance of finding a husband has come, and that her fate must be decided now or never. With a mournful smile Princess Maria reflected every Thursday that she now had no one to send letters to, since Julie – Julie whose presence gave her no pleasure – was here in town and they met every week. Like the old French *émigré* who declined to marry the lady with whom he had spent all his evenings for years, because if he were married he would not know where to spend his evenings, she regretted that Julie was in Moscow and so there was no one to write to. In Moscow Princess Maria had no one to talk to, no one in whom to confide her sorrows, and many fresh sorrows fell to her lot just then. The time for Prince Andrei's return and his marriage was drawing near, but his mission to her to prepare his father was so far from having been successfully carried out that the whole thing seemed quite hopeless – any reference to the young Countess Rostov set the old prince beside himself (who in any case was almost always in a bad temper). Another trouble that weighed on Princess Maria of late arose out of the lessons she gave to her six-year-old nephew. In her relations with little Nikolai, to her consternation she detected in herself symptoms of her father's irritability. No matter how often she told herself that she must not lose her temper when teaching her nephew, almost every time that, pointer in hand, she sat down to show him the French alphabet, she so longed to hasten, to make easy the process of pouring her own knowledge into the child – who by now was always afraid that at any moment Auntie would get angry – that the slightest inattention on the part of the little boy would make her tremble, become flustered and heated, raise her voice, and sometimes even seize him by the arm and stand him in the corner. Having stood him in the corner, she would begin to shed tears over her spiteful, wicked nature, and little Nikolai, his sobs vying with hers, would come unbidden out of his corner to pull her tear-wet hands from her face, and try to comfort her. But the heaviest, far the heaviest of the princess's burdens was her father's irascibility, which was invariably directed against his daughter, and had of late reached the point of cruelty. Had he forced her to spend the night on her knees in prayer, had he beaten her or made her chop wood and carry water, it would never have entered her head that her lot was a hard one; but this loving despot – the more cruel from the very fact that he loved her, and for that very reason tortured both himself and her – knew not merely how to wound and humiliate her deliberately but how to make her feel that she was always and for ever in the wrong. Latterly he had exhibited a new trait, which caused Princess Maria more misery than anything. This was his ever-increasing intimacy with Mademoiselle Bourienne. The farcical notion, first suggested to his mind by the news of his son's intentions, that if Andrei got married he himself would marry the Bourienne evidently flattered his fancy, and of late he had persistently, and as it seemed to Princess Maria merely to give offence to her, lavished endearments on Mademoiselle Bourienne, and expressed his dissatisfaction with his daughter by demonstrations of affection for the Frenchwoman.

One day in Moscow, in Princess Maria's presence (she thought her father did it on purpose because she was there), the old prince kissed Mademoiselle Bourienne's hand and, drawing her to him, embraced and fondled her. Princess Maria flushed hotly and ran out of the room. A few minutes later Mademoiselle Bourienne came into Princess Maria's room smiling and making cheerful remarks in her agreeable voice. Princess Maria hastily wiped away her tears, went resolutely up to Mademoiselle Bourienne, and evidently unconscious of what she was doing began screaming at the Frenchwoman in furious haste, her voice breaking:

'It's loathsome, vile, inhuman to take advantage of weakness. ...' She did not finish. 'Leave my room!' she cried, and burst into sobs.

The following day the prince did not say a word to his daughter, but she noticed that at dinner he gave instructions that Mademoiselle Bourienne should be served first. At the end of the meal, when the footman brought round the coffee and from habit began with the princess, the old prince flew into a sudden frenzy, flung his cane at Filipp, and instantly ordered that he should be sent off to the army.

'You disobey me ... twice I've told you! ... You disobey me! She is the first person in this house, she's my best friend,' shouted the old prince. 'And if you,' he cried in fury, addressing Princess Maria for the first time, 'ever again dare, as you did yesterday, to forget yourself in her presence, I'll show you who is master in this house. Go! Get out of my sight! Beg her pardon!'

Princess Maria asked Mademoiselle Bourienne's pardon, and also her father's pardon for herself and Filipp the footman, who implored her to intercede for him.

At such moments a feeling akin to the pride of sacrifice gathered in her soul. And then all of a sudden the father whom she was criticizing would look for his spectacles, fumbling near them and not seeing them, or forget something that had just happened, or totter on his failing legs and turn to see if anyone had noticed his feebleness, or, worst of all, at dinner if there were no guests to keep him awake, would suddenly fall into a doze, letting his napkin drop and his shaking head sink over his plate. 'He is old and feeble, and I presume to criticize him!' she would think at such moments, revolted by herself.

3

IN the year 1811 there was living in Moscow a French doctor called Métivier, who had rapidly become the fashion. He was enormously tall, handsome, polite and amiable as Frenchmen are, and, as everyone said, an extraordinarily clever doctor. He was received in the very best houses, not merely as a doctor but as an equal.

Old Prince Bolkonsky had always ridiculed medicine, but latterly on Mademoiselle Bourienne's advice had allowed this doctor to visit him, and had grown accustomed to him. Métivier came to see the old prince a couple of times a week.

On St Nikolai's day, the name-day of the prince, all Moscow drove up to the prince's front door, but he gave orders to admit no one. Only a select few, of whom he handed a list to Princess Maria, were to be invited to dinner.

Métivier, who arrived in the morning with his felicitations, considered himself entitled, as the old prince's doctor, to *forcer le consigne*, as he told Princess Maria, and went in to see the old man. It so happened that on that morning of his name-day the prince was in one of his very worst moods. He had been wandering wearily about the house the whole morning, finding fault with everyone and pretending not to understand what was said to him, and not to be understood himself. Princess Maria only too well knew this mood of lowering querulousness, which generally culminated in an outburst of fury, and she went about all that morning as though facing a cocked and loaded gun, in expectation of the inevitable explosion. Until the doctor's arrival the morning had passed off safely. Having admitted the doctor, Princess Maria sat down with a book in the drawing-room near the door, through which she could hear all that passed in the study.

At first the only sound was Métivier's voice, then her father's, then both voices speaking at once. The door flew open, and on the threshold appeared the handsome figure of the terrified Métivier with his shock of black hair, followed by the prince in his skull-cap and dressing-gown, his face distorted with rage and the pupils of his eyes dilated.

'You don't see it?' shouted the prince. 'Well, I do! French spy, slave of Bonaparte, spy, get out of my house – get out, I tell you!' And he slammed the door.

Métivier, shrugging his shoulders, went up to Mademoiselle Bourienne, who had rushed in from the adjoining room on hearing the noise.

'The prince is not very well – bile and rush of blood to the head. Do not worry, I will look in again tomorrow,' said Métivier, and putting his fingers to his lips he hurried away.

Through the study door came the sound of slippered feet and the shouting of 'Spies, traitors, traitors everywhere! Never a minute's peace even in my own house!'

After Métivier's departure the old prince sent for his daughter, and the whole brunt of his fury fell on her. She was to blame that a spy had been admitted to see him. Had he not told her, told her to make a list, and not to let anyone in who was not on that list? Then why had that scoundrel been shown in? It was all her fault. With her, he said, he could not have sixty seconds' quiet to die in peace.

'No, ma'am! we must part, we must part, I tell you. Make up your mind to it! I cannot stand any more,' he said, and left the room. And then, as though afraid she might find some means of consolation, he returned and trying to appear calm added: 'And don't imagine I said that to you in the heat of the moment. No, I am perfectly calm, and I have weighed my words, and it shall be so – we must part. Find a home for yourself somewhere else! ...' But he could not restrain himself and, with the virulence which can only exist where there is love, obviously in anguish himself, he shook his fists at her and screamed:

'If only some fool would take her to wife!' After that he slammed the door, sent for Mademoiselle Bourienne and subsided in his study.

At two o'clock the six chosen guests assembled for dinner. These guests – the famous Count Rostopchin, Prince Lopuhin and his nephew, General Chatrov, an old comrade in arms of the prince's, and, of the younger generation, Pierre and Boris Drubetskoy – awaited their host in the drawing-room.

Boris, who had come to Moscow on leave a few days before, had been anxious to be presented to Prince Nikolai Bolkonsky, and he had so far succeeded in ingratiating himself that the old prince in his case made an exception to his rule of not receiving young bachelors.

The prince's house was not what was called 'fashionable', but it was the centre of a little circle into which, though not much talked about in town, it was more flattering to be admitted than anywhere else. Boris had realized this the week before, when he heard Rostopchin tell the commander-in-chief of Moscow, who had invited him to dine on St Nikolai's day, that he could not accept his invitation.

'On that day I always go and pay my devotions to the relics of Prince Nikolai Bolkonsky.'

'Oh yes, of course,' replied the commander-in-chief. 'How is he ? ...'

The little party that met together before dinner in the lofty, old-fashioned drawing-room with its ancient furniture resembled the solemn gathering of a court of justice. No one had much to say, and if they spoke it was in low tones. Prince Nikolai came in, grave and taciturn. Princess Maria seemed even quieter and more diffident than usual. The guests showed no inclination to address her, for they saw that she was not attending to what they said. Count Rostopchin alone kept the conversation going, now relating the latest news of the town, now the most recent political gossip.

Lopuhin and the old general occasionally put in a word. Prince Bolkonsky listened as a presiding judge listens to a report presented to him, only now and then, by a grunt or some curt monosyllable, showing that he was taking cognizance of the facts laid before him. The tone of the conversation was based on the assumption that no one approved of what was being done in the political world. Incidents were related obviously confirming the opinion that everything was going from bad to worse; but in all their anecdotes and criticisms it was noticeable how each speaker came to a stop, or was brought to a stop, every time the point was reached beyond which his unfavourable opinion might reflect on the person of his Majesty the Emperor.

At dinner the talk turned on the latest political news: Napoleon's seizure of the possessions of the Duke of Oldenburg, and the Russian note – hostile to Napoleon – which had been sent to all the European courts.

'Bonaparte treats Europe the way a pirate treats a captured vessel,' said Count Rostopchin, repeating an epigram he had got off a number of times before. 'One only marvels at the long-suffering, or the blindness, of the ruling Sovereigns. Now it is the Pope's turn, and Bonaparte doesn't scruple to try and depose the head of the Catholic Church, and no one says a word. Our Emperor is the only one to raise a voice against the seizure of the Duke of Oldenburg's territory, and even …' Count Rostopchin paused, feeling that he was on the very borderline beyond which criticism was impossible.

'Other domains have been offered him in exchange for the Duchy of Oldenburg,' said Prince Bolkonsky. 'He shifts the dukes about as I might move my serfs from Bald Hills to Bogucharovo or my Ryazan estates.'

'The Duke of Oldenburg bears his misfortunes with admirable fortitude and resignation,' remarked Boris in French, putting in his word respectfully. He said this because on his journey from Petersburg he had had the honour of being presented to the duke. Prince Bolkonsky glanced at the young man as though he had it in mind to make some reply but thought better of it, evidently considering him too young to bother about.

'I read our protest about the Oldenburg affair and was surprised how badly the note was worded,' remarked Count Rostopchin in the casual tone of a man who knows what he is saying.

Pierre looked at Rostopchin in naïve wonder, unable to understand why he should be disturbed by the wretched style of the note.

'What difference does it make, count, how the note is written,' he asked, 'so long as the subject-matter is forcible ?'

'*Mon cher*, with our army of five hundred thousand men it should be easy to have a good style,' returned Count Rostopchin.

Pierre perceived the point of Count Rostopchin's dissatisfaction with the wording of the note.

'I should have thought there were plenty of quill-drivers about,' said the old prince. 'In Petersburg they do nothing but write – not notes only, but even new laws. My Andrei there has written a whole volume of laws for Russia. Nowadays they're always at it!' and he laughed unnaturally.

The conversation languished for a moment. The old general cleared his throat to draw attention to himself.

'Did you hear what happened recently at the review in Petersburg? The way the new French ambassador behaved!'

'What was that? Yes, I did hear something. He made some awkward remark in his Majesty's presence, I believe.'

'His Majesty drew his attention to the Grenadier division and the march past,' pursued the general, 'and it seems the ambassador took no notice and had the impudence to remark, "We in France do not trouble our heads over such trifles." The Emperor did not condescend to reply. At the next review, they say, the Emperor simply ignored his presence.'

All were silent. It was out of the question to pass any comment on this occurrence, since it related to the Monarch personally.

'Insolent rogues!' exclaimed the old prince. 'You know Métivier? I turned him out of my house this morning. He was here – they let him in to see me in spite of my request that no one should be admitted,' he went on, glancing angrily at his daughter. And he repeated from beginning to end his conversation with the French doctor, and his reasons for believing Métivier to be a spy. Though these reasons were very insufficient and obscure, no one made any rejoinder.

After the roast, champagne was served. The guests rose from their places to wish the old prince many happy returns. Princess Maria, too, went up to him.

He gave her a cold, angry look, and offered her his wrinkled, clean-shaven cheek to kiss. The whole expression of his face told her that he had not forgotten their conversation of that morning, that his mind was just as fully made up and only the presence of his guests prevented him from telling her so now.

When they went into the drawing-room for coffee, the old men sat together.

Prince Bolkonsky grew more animated, and began to express his views on the impending war.

He declared that our wars with Bonaparte would be disastrous so long as we tried to make common cause with the Germans and went meddling in European affairs, into which we had been drawn by the Peace of Tilsit. 'We had no business to fight either for or against

Austria. Our political interests are all in the east, and so far as Bonaparte is concerned the only thing is to have an armed force on the
frontier and a firm policy, and he will never again dare to set foot in
Russia, as he did in 1807!'

'How can we possibly make war against the French, prince?' asked
Count Rostopchin. 'Can we arm ourselves against our teachers – our
idols? Look at our young men, look at our ladies! The French are our
gods, and Paris is our Kingdom of Heaven.'

He raised his voice, evidently so that all might hear him.

'Our fashions are French, our ideas are French, our sentiments are
French! You sent Métivier packing because he is a Frenchman and a
scoundrel, but our ladies crawl after him on their hands and knees.
Yesterday I was at a party, and out of five ladies present three were
Roman Catholics and had a dispensation from the Pope allowing
them to do wool-work on Sundays. And there they sat, practically
naked, like the sign-boards outside our public bath-houses, if you'll
excuse my saying so. Ah, prince, when one looks at our young people,
one would like to take Peter the Great's old cudgel out of the museum
and break a few ribs in the good old Russian style. That would soon
knock the nonsense out of them!'

All were silent. The old prince looked at Rostopchin with a smile
and nodded his head approvingly.

'Well, good-bye, your Excellency, keep well!' said Rostopchin,
getting up with his usual abruptness and holding out his hand to the
prince.

'Good-bye, my dear fellow. ... His words are like music, I never
tire of listening to him,' said the old prince, keeping hold of Rostopchin's hand and offering him his cheek. The others, too, rose when
Rostopchin did.

4

PRINCESS MARIA, sitting in the drawing-room and listening to the
old men's talk and fault-finding, understood not a word of what she
was hearing; her one preoccupation was whether their guests had all
observed her father's hostile attitude towards her. She did not even
notice the marked attentions and amiabilities showed her all through
dinner by Boris Drubetskoy, though this was his third visit to the
house.

Princess Maria turned with an abstracted, inquiring look to Pierre

645

who, hat in hand and with a smile on his face, was the last to come up to her after the old prince had retired and they were left alone in the drawing-room.

'May I stay a little longer?' he asked, letting his bulky person sink into a low chair beside Princess Maria.

'Oh yes,' she answered. 'You noticed nothing?' her eyes asked.

Pierre was in an agreeable, after-dinner mood. He looked straight before him and smiled softly.

'Have you known that young man long, princess?' he asked.

'What young man?'

'Drubetskoy.'

'No, not long ...'

'Do you like him?'

'Yes, he's a pleasant young fellow. ... Why do you ask me that?' said Princess Maria, her mind still on the morning's conversation with her father.

'Because I have remarked that when a young man comes on leave from Petersburg to Moscow it is usually with the object of marrying an heiress.'

'You have observed that?' said Princess Maria.

'Yes,' continued Pierre with a smile, 'and this young man now so manages it that where there are wealthy heiresses – there he, too, is to be found. I can read him like a book. At present he is undecided whether to lay siege to – you or Mademoiselle Julie Karagin. He is very attentive to her.'

'He goes there then?'

'Yes, very often. And do you know the new-fashioned method of courting?' said Pierre with an amused smile, evidently in that gay mood of light-hearted raillery for which he had so often reproved himself in his diary.

'No,' replied Princess Maria.

'To please the Moscow girls nowadays one has to be melancholy. He is very melancholy with Mademoiselle Karagin,' said Pierre.

'Really?' said Princess Maria, looking into Pierre's kindly face and thinking all the time of her own trouble. 'It would ease my heart,' she thought, 'if I could make up my mind to confide what I am feeling to someone. And it is just Pierre I should like to tell it all to. He is so kind and generous. It would be a relief. He would give me advice.'

'Would you marry him?' asked Pierre.

'Oh heavens, count, there are moments when I would marry any-body!' exclaimed Princess Maria, to her own surprise and with tears in her voice. 'Ah, how bitter it is to love someone near to you and to feel that ...' she went on in a trembling voice, 'that you can do nothing but be a trial to him, and to know that you cannot alter it. Then there is only one thing left – to go away, but where could I go?'

'What is wrong? What is the trouble, princess?'

But without explaining further Princess Maria burst into tears.

'I don't know what is the matter with me today. Don't take any notice – forget what I said.'

Pierre's gaiety vanished completely. He questioned the princess anxiously, begged her to speak out, to confide her grief to him; but her only reply was to beseech him to forget what she had said, repeating that she did not remember it and that she had no troubles except the one which he knew about already – her fear lest Prince Andrei's marriage should cause a breach between father and son.

'Have you any news of the Rostovs?' she asked, to change the sub-ject. 'I am told that they will be arriving soon. And I expect André too any day now. I should have liked them to meet here.'

'And how does he regard the matter now?' asked Pierre, by he meaning the old prince.

Princess Maria shook her head. 'But it can't be helped. A few more months and the year will be up. And that's inevitable. I only wish I could spare my brother the first moments. I wish the Rostovs were coming sooner. I hope to get to be friends with her. ... You have known them a long time, haven't you?' said Princess Maria. 'Tell me truly, with your hand on your heart, what sort of a girl is she, and what do you think of her? I want the whole truth, because, you see, André is risking so much in doing this against his father's will that I should like to know. ...'

A vague instinct told Pierre that these explanations and repeated requests to be told the *whole truth* betrayed some covert ill-will on Princess Maria's part towards her future sister-in-law, and a wish that he should not approve of Prince Andrei's choice; but in reply he said what he felt rather than what he thought.

'I don't know how to answer your question,' he said, blushing though he could not have told why. 'I really don't know what kind of girl she is. I can never analyse her. She is fascinating. But what makes her so, I can't tell you. That is all one can say about her.'

Princess Maria sighed, and the expression on her face said: 'Yes, that's what I expected and feared.'

'Is she clever?' she asked.

Pierre considered.

'I think not,' he said, 'and yet – yes. She does not think it worth while to be clever. ... Oh no, she is enchanting, and that's all about it.'

Princess Maria again shook her head disapprovingly.

'Ah, I do so want to like her! Tell her so, if you see her before I do.'

'I hear they are expected very soon,' said Pierre.

Princess Maria confided to Pierre her plan to become friends with her future sister-in-law as soon as the Rostovs arrived, and to try to get the old prince accustomed to her.

5

BORIS had not succeeded in making a wealthy match in Petersburg, so with the same object in view he came to Moscow. Here he found himself hesitating between two of the richest heiresses, Julie and Princess Maria. Though Princess Maria, in spite of her plainness, seemed to him more attractive than Julie, without knowing why he felt uncomfortable about paying court to her. In his last conversation with her, on the old prince's name-day, she had met all his attempts to talk sentimentally with irrelevant replies, evidently not listening to what he was saying.

Julie, on the contrary, received his attentions eagerly, though she showed her readiness in a peculiar fashion of her own.

Julie was twenty-seven. At the death of her brothers she had become very wealthy. She was now decidedly plain, but believed herself to be not merely as pretty as before but far more captivating now than she had ever been. She was sustained in this illusion firstly by the fact of having become an extremely wealthy heiress, and secondly because the older she grew the less dangerous she was to men, and the more freely could they gather round her and avail themselves of her suppers, her *soirées* and the lively company that frequented her house, without incurring any obligation. Men who, ten years ago, would have thought twice before going every day to a house where there was a young girl of seventeen, for fear of compromising her and entangling themselves, now appeared constantly and treated her not as a marriageable girl but as a sexless acquaintance.

That winter the Karagins' house was the most agreeable and hospitable in Moscow. In addition to the formal receptions and dinnerparties, every evening there was a numerous gathering, chiefly of men, who ate supper at midnight and stayed till three in the morning. Julie never missed a ball, a play or a promenade. Her gowns were always of the latest fashion. Nevertheless Julie pretended to be disenchanted with everything, and told everybody that she had no faith in friendship or in love, or any of the joys of life, and hoped for peace only 'beyond the grave'. She affected the air of one who has suffered a great disappointment, like a girl who has either lost her lover or been cruelly deceived by him. Though nothing of the kind had happened to her, it began to be thought that such was the case, and she herself came to believe that she had suffered a great deal in her life. This melancholy neither hindered her from enjoying herself nor prevented the young people who came to her house from passing their time very pleasantly. Each one of her visitors paid his tribute to the melancholy mood of his hostess, and then proceeded to enjoy himself with society gossip, dancing, intellectual games, and *bouts rimés* which were in vogue at the Karagins'. Only a few of the young men, among them Boris, entered more deeply into Julie's melancholy, and with these she had longer and more confidential conversations on the vanity of all worldly things, and to them she showed her albums, filled with gloomy sketches, maxims and verses.

Julie was particularly gracious to Boris. She mourned with him over his early disillusionment with life, offered him such consolations of friendship as she, who had suffered so much, could render, and opened her album to him. Boris sketched two trees in the album, and wrote under them in French: 'Rustic trees, your sombre branches shed darkness and melancholy upon me.'

On another page he drew a tomb and inscribed below it:

Death gives us peace – 'tis death that brings release.
'Tis then alone our earthly sorrows cease!

Julie said this was exquisite.

'There is something so ravishing in the smile of melancholy!' she said to Boris, repeating word for word a passage copied from a book. 'It is a ray of light in the darkness, a *nuance* between sorrow and despair, heralding the possibility of consolation.'

Whereupon Boris wrote these lines for her in French:

Poisonous nourishment of a soul too sensitive,
Thou, the only joy my grieving spirit knows,
Tender melancholy, come! Thy consolation bring!
O come with respite from my solitary woes,
Mingle thy secret, soothing balm
With my tears that never cease to spring.

For Boris Julie played her most doleful nocturnes on the harp. Boris read *Poor Liza* aloud to her, and more than once had to interrupt his reading because of the emotion that choked him. When they met in society, Julie and Boris gazed at one another as if they were the only two kindred souls in the world who understood each other.

Anna Mihalovna, who often visited the Karagins, while playing cards with the mother would make careful inquiries as to Julie's dowry – which was to consist of two estates in Penza and the Nizhni Novgorod forest lands. Anna Mihalovna looked on with emotion and humble devotion to the will of Providence at the refined sadness that united her son to the wealthy Julie.

'You are still as charming and melancholy as ever, my dear Julie,' she would remark to the daughter. 'Boris says that here in your house he finds repose for his soul. He has suffered so many disappointments, and is so sensitive,' said she to the mother. 'Ah, my dear, I can't tell you how fond I have grown of Julie latterly,' she would say to her son. 'But who could help loving her? She is such an angelic being! Ah, Boris, Boris!' She paused for a moment. 'And how I pity her mother,' she went on. 'Today she was showing me her accounts and letters from Penza (they have enormous estates there), and she, poor thing, with no one to help her. They do take such advantage of her!'

Boris's face wore an almost perceptible smile as he listened to his mother. He was quietly amused at her naïve diplomacy, but listened to what she had to say and sometimes questioned her carefully about the Penza and Nizhni Novgorod estates.

Julie had for some time been expecting a proposal from her melancholy adorer, and was fully prepared to accept it; but some secret distaste for her, for her passionate desire to get married, for her affectation, and a feeling of horror at thus renouncing the possibility of true love, still restrained Boris. The term of his leave was expiring. He spent every day and all day at the Karagins', and each day, as he thought the matter over, Boris told himself that he would propose tomorrow. But in Julie's presence, looking at her red face and her chin (nearly always dusted with powder), her moist eyes, and her expression which betokened an ever-readiness to fly at a moment's notice from melancholy to unnatural ecstasies of wedded bliss, Boris could not bring himself to utter the decisive words, although in imagination he had long regarded himself as the master of those Penza and Nizhni Novgorod estates, and had more than once arranged how he would spend the income from them. Julie noticed Boris's hesitation and sometimes the thought occurred to her that he had an aversion for her; but her feminine vanity quickly restored her confidence, and she would assure herself that it was merely love that made him bashful. Her melancholy, however, was beginning to develop into irritability, and not long before Boris's departure she formed a definite plan of action. Just as Boris's leave of absence was drawing to a close Anatole Kuragin made his appearance in Moscow, and – it need hardly be said – in the Karagins' drawing-room, and Julie, abruptly abandoning her melancholy, became exceedingly gay and very attentive to Kuragin.

'My dear,' said Anna Mihalovna to her son, 'I hear from a reliable source that Prince Vasili has sent his son to Moscow to make a match with Julie. I am so fond of Julie that I should be very sorry for her. What is your opinion, my dear?'

The idea of being left to look a fool, and of having wasted that whole month in the arduous, melancholy service of Julie, and of seeing all the revenue from those Penza estates, which he had already assigned and put to proper use, fall into the hands of another, especially into the hands of that fool Anatole, outraged Boris. He drove off to the Karagins' with the firm intention of proposing. Julie met him in a lively, careless manner, casually mentioned how much she had enjoyed the ball the previous evening, and asked when he was leaving. Though Boris had come fully intending to speak of his love and was therefore resolved to take a tender tone, he began complaining irritably of feminine inconstancy, of how easily women could pass from sadness to joy, and how their moods depended solely on whoever happened to be paying court to them. Julie took offence at this, and replied that he was right: a woman needed variety, and the same thing over and over again would bore anyone.

'Then I should advise you ...' Boris was about to retort, meaning to say something cutting; but at that instant the galling reflection occurred to him that he might have to leave Moscow without having attained his object and having wasted his efforts in vain (an experience he had never known yet). He stopped short in the middle of the sentence, lowered his eyes to avoid seeing the disagreeable look of annoyance and indecision on her face, and said:

'But it was not to quarrel with you that I came here. On the contrary. ...'

He glanced at her to make sure that he might go on. All her irritation had suddenly vanished, and her anxious, imploring eyes were fastened upon him in greedy expectation. 'I can always manage so as to see very little of her,' thought Boris. 'And the thing's been begun and must be finished!' He blushed hotly, raised his eyes to hers, and said:

'You know my feelings for you!'

There was no need to say more: Julie's face beamed with triumph and self-satisfaction; but she forced Boris to say all that is usually said on such occasions – to say that he loved her and had never loved any woman more. She knew that for her Penza estates and the Nizhni Novgorod forests she could demand that, and she received what she demanded.

The engaged couple, with no further allusions to trees that enfolded them in gloom and melancholy, laid plans for a brilliant establishment in Petersburg, paid calls, and made every preparation for a brilliant wedding.

6

COUNT ILYA ROSTOV, together with Natasha and Sonya, arrived in Moscow at the end of January. The countess was still unwell and unable to travel, but it was out of the question to wait for her recovery: Prince Andrei was expected in Moscow any day. Besides that, the trousseau had to be ordered, the estate near Moscow sold, and advantage taken of old Prince Bolkonsky's presence in Moscow to present his future daughter-in-law to him. The Rostovs' town house had not been heated that winter, and as, moreover, they had come only for a short time and the countess was not with them the count decided to stay with Maria Dmitrievna Ahrosimov, who had long been pressing her hospitality on the count.

Late one evening the Rostovs' four sledges drove into Maria Dmitrievna's courtyard in Old Konyusheny street. Maria Dmitrievna lived alone. She had already married off her daughter, and her sons were all in the service.

She still held herself as erect as ever, still gave everyone her opinion in the same loud, outspoken, blunt fashion, and her whole bearing seemed a reproach to other people for any weakness, passion or temptation – the possibility of which she did not admit. She was up early in the morning, wearing a loose jacket, to attend to her household affairs, after which she drove out – on saints' days to church, and thence to gaols and prisons; of what she did there she never spoke to anyone. On ordinary days, after she was dressed, she received everyone, whoever they were, who came to seek her aid. Then she had dinner, a substantial and appetizing meal at which there were always three or four guests. After dinner she played a game of boston, and at night had the newspapers or a new book read to her while she knitted. She rarely made any exception to her routine, and if she did it was only to visit the very important persons in the town.

She had not yet retired when the Rostovs arrived and the door in the hall creaked on its pulleys, admitting the travellers and their retinue of servants from the cold. Maria Dmitrievna, with her spectacles slipping down her nose and her head flung back, stood in the hall doorway looking at the newcomers with a stern, grim face. It might have been supposed she was really angry with them and ready to pack them off again at once, had she not at the same time been heard giving careful instructions to the servants for the accommodation of the visitors and their belongings.

'The count's things? Bring them this way,' she said, pointing to the portmanteaux and not stopping to greet anyone. 'The young ladies'? Take them over there, on the left. Well, what are you pottering about for?' she cried to the maids. 'Get the samovar ready! ... The girl's grown plumper and prettier,' she remarked, drawing Natasha towards her by her hood. (Natasha's cheeks were glowing from the cold.) 'Phoo! You *are* cold! Now take off your things, quick!' she cried to the count who was going to kiss her hand. 'You're frozen, I'll warrant. Bring some rum with the tea! ... Sonya, dear, *bonjour!*' she added, addressing Sonya and indicating by this French greeting her slightly contemptuous though affectionate attitude towards her.

When they came in to tea, having taken off their wraps and tidied themselves after their journey, Maria Dmitrievna kissed them all in turn.

'I'm heartily glad you have come and are staying with me. It was high time,' she said, giving Natasha a significant look. 'The old man is here, and his son is expected any day. You'll certainly have to make his acquaintance. Well, we'll talk about that later on,' she added, with a glance at Sonya as much as to say that she did not care to speak of that subject in her presence. 'Now, listen,' she said to the count. 'What are your plans for tomorrow? Whom will you send for? Shinshin?' She crooked one finger. 'That snivelling Anna Mihalovna – two. She's here with her son. That son of hers is getting married! Then Bezuhov, eh? He and his wife are here. He ran away from her, but she came galloping after him. He dined with me on Wednesday. As for them' – and she pointed to the girls – 'tomorrow I'll take them first to the Iversky chapel, and then to Suppert-Roguet's. I suppose you'll have everything new? Don't judge by me: sleeves nowadays are this size! Young Princess Irina Vasilyevna came to see me recently: she was an awful sight – looked as if she had put two barrels on her arms. Not a day passes now, you know, without some new fashion. And what business have you on hand?' she asked the count severely.

'Oh, a little of everything,' replied the count. 'The girl's rags to buy, and now a purchaser has turned up for the Moscow estate and the house. If you will be so kind, I'll fix a time and drive over to the estate for the day, leaving my lassies with you.'

'Very well. Very well. They'll be safe with me, as safe as in chancery! I'll take them where they must go, and scold them a bit and pet them too,' said Maria Dmitrievna, touching her god-daughter and favourite, Natasha, on the cheek with her ample hand.

Next morning Maria Dmitrievna bore the young ladies off to the Iversky chapel and then to Madame Suppert-Roguet, who was so afraid of Maria Dmitrievna that she always let her have gowns at a loss simply to get rid of her as quickly as possible. Maria Dmitrievna ordered almost the whole trousseau. When they got home she turned everybody out of the room except Natasha, and called her favourite to sit beside her arm-chair.

'Well, now we can have a talk. I congratulate you on your betrothed. You've hooked a fine fellow! I am glad for you: I've known him since he was so high.' (She put her hand a couple of feet from the floor.) Natasha coloured with pleasure. 'I like him and all his family. Now listen! You know, of course, that old Prince Nikolai is very much against his son's marrying. He's a crotchety old boy. Of course

Prince Andrei is not a child and can get on without him, but still it's not a very nice thing to enter a family against the father's will. One must act peaceably, with affection. You're a clever girl, you'll know how to manage. You must use your wits and your kind heart. Then all will be well.'

Natasha remained silent, not as Maria Dmitrievna supposed from shyness, but because she disliked anyone interfering where her love for Prince Andrei was concerned, which seemed to her so above and beyond all ordinary human matters that she did not believe anyone could enter into her feeling about it. She loved Prince Andrei, and only him, and knew only him; he loved her and was to arrive in a day or two and carry her off. She did not care about anything else.

'I have known him for a long time, don't you see, and I am very fond of Maria, your future sister-in-law. "With husbands' sisters – look out for blisters!" says the proverb, but this one wouldn't hurt a fly. She begs me to bring the pair of you together. Tomorrow you'll be going with your father to see her. Be very nice to her – you are younger than she is. When that young man of yours comes he'll find you already know his sister and father, and that they like you. Am I not right? Won't that be best?'

'Yes, I suppose so,' Natasha answered reluctantly.

7

NEXT day, on Maria Dmitrievna's advice, Count Rostov took Natasha to call on Prince Nikolai Bolkonsky. The count set out in anything but a happy frame of mind: at heart he felt alarmed, for he remembered only too vividly the last interview he had had with the old prince, at the time of the levying of the militia. He had invited the prince to dinner, and in reply had had to listen to an angry repri-mand for not having furnished his full quota of men. Natasha, on the other hand, having put on her best gown, was in the highest spirits. 'They can't help liking me,' she thought. 'Everybody always does. And I am so willing to do anything they could wish for them, so ready to be fond of him for being *his* father and of her for being *his* sister that there can be no reason for them not to like me. ...'

They drove up to the gloomy old house in Vozdvizhenka street and entered the vestibule.

'Well, the Lord have mercy on us!' exclaimed the count, half in jest, half in earnest; but Natasha noticed that her father was flurried as he went into the ante-room and inquired timidly and softly whether the prince and the princess were at home. After they had given their names, some confusion was obvious among the servants. The footman who had hurried off to announce them was stopped by another footman at the drawing-room door, and the two stood whispering together. Then a maid ran into the hall and hurriedly said something, mentioning the princess. At last an elderly, cross-looking footman came and informed the Rostovs that the prince was not receiving but the princess would be glad to see them. The first person to come out to meet the visitors was Mademoiselle Bourienne. She greeted the father and daughter with effusive politeness, and conducted them to the princess's apartment. The princess, agitated and nervous, her face all crimson patches, hastened forward to welcome the visitors, treading heavily and endeavouring unsuccessfully to appear cordial and at ease. From the first she did not like Natasha. She thought her too fashionably dressed, too frivolous, too flighty and vain. Princess Maria had no idea that before having seen her future sister-in-law she was prejudiced against her through unconscious envy of her beauty, youth and happiness, as well as jealousy of her brother's love for her. Apart from this insuperable feeling of antipathy to her, Princess Maria was in a state of agitation at that moment because at the announcement of the Rostovs' visit the old prince had shouted at the top of his voice that he did not wish to see them, that Princess Maria might do so if she chose but they were not to be admitted to him. She had decided to receive them, but feared lest the prince might at any moment indulge in some vagary, as he seemed so upset by the Rostovs' arrival.

'Well now, princess, I have brought you my little songstress,' said the count with a bow and a scrape, and looking round uneasily as if he were afraid the old prince might appear. 'I am so glad that you are to get to know one another. ... Sorry, very sorry the prince is still ailing.' And after making a few more commonplace remarks he got up. 'If you'll allow me, princess, I will leave my Natasha in your hands for a little quarter of an hour, while I slip round to see Anna Semeonovna – in Dog's square, only a few steps from here. Then I'll come back for her.'

The count bethought himself of this diplomatic stratagem (as he told his daughter afterwards) to give the future sisters-in-law an opportunity to talk to one another freely, but also to avoid the possibility of meeting the prince, of whom he was afraid. He did not mention this to his daughter, but Natasha perceived her father's nervousness and anxiety, and felt mortified by it. She blushed for him, grew still more annoyed with herself for having blushed, and flung the princess a bold, defiant look which said that she was not afraid of anybody. The princess told the count that she would be delighted, and only begged him not to hurry away from Anna Semeonovna's, and he departed.

Despite the restless glances thrown at her by Princess Maria – who wanted to have a tête-à-tête with Natasha – Mademoiselle Bourienne would not leave the room, and persisted in keeping up a steady stream of chatter about the delights of Moscow, and the theatres. Natasha felt offended by the hesitation she had noticed in the ante-room, by her father's nervousness and by the unnatural manner of the princess who, she thought, was making a favour of receiving her. Consequently she was displeased with everything. She did not like Princess Maria, who seemed to her very plain, affected and unsympathetic. Natasha suddenly shrank into herself, and involuntarily assumed an off-hand manner which alienated Princess Maria still more. After five minutes of laboured, artificial conversation they heard the sound of slippered feet approaching rapidly. A look of terror came over Princess Maria's face. The door opened, and the old prince appeared, wearing a white night-cap and dressing-gown.

'Ah, madam,' he began. 'Madam, countess ... Countess Rostov, if I am not mistaken. ... I beg your pardon, pray excuse me. ... I did not know, madam. God is my witness, I did not know that you were honouring us with a visit. I came to see my daughter – which accounts for this costume. I beg you to excuse me. ... God is my witness, I did not know,' he repeated, stressing the word 'God' so unnaturally and so unpleasantly that Princess Maria stood with downcast eyes, not daring to look either at her father or at Natasha. Natasha, too, having risen and curtsied, did not know what to do. Only Mademoiselle Bourienne smiled agreeably.

'I beg you to excuse me, I beg you to excuse me! God is my witness, I did not know,' muttered the old man, and after looking Natasha over from head to foot he went out.

Mademoiselle Bourienne was the first to recover herself after this apparition, and she began to talk about the prince's indisposition.

Natasha and Princess Maria looked at one another in silence, and the longer they did so, without saying what they wanted to say, the more they were confirmed in their mutual antipathy.

When the count returned, Natasha made an ill-mannered display of relief, and immediately prepared to take her departure: at that moment she almost hated the stiff, elderly princess, who could place her in such an embarrassing position and spend half an hour with her without once mentioning Prince Andrei. 'Of course I couldn't be the first to speak of him in the presence of that Frenchwoman,' thought Natasha. A similar compunction was meanwhile tormenting Princess Maria. She knew what she ought to have said to Natasha, but she had been unable to say it both because Mademoiselle Bourienne was in the way and because – though she did not know why – she found it very difficult to speak of the marriage. The count was already leaving the room when Princess Maria hurried towards Natasha, took her by the hand and said with a deep sigh:

'Wait, I must ...'

Natasha gave her a mocking glance, though she could not have told what made her do so.

'Dear Natalie,' said Princess Maria, 'I want you to know how glad I am that my brother has found happiness. ...'

She paused, feeling that she was not telling the truth. Natasha noticed the pause and guessed the reason for it.

'I think, princess, this is not the time for speaking of that,' said Natasha coldly and with outward dignity, though she felt the tears rising in her throat.

'What have I said, what have I done?' she thought, as soon as she was out of the room.

They had to wait a long while for Natasha to come to dinner that day. She sat in her room crying like a child, blowing her nose and sobbing. Sonya stood beside her, kissing her hair.

'Natasha, what is there to cry about?' she asked. 'Why do you mind about them? It will all pass over, Natasha.'

'But if only you knew how insulting it was ... as if I ...'

'Don't talk about it, Natasha. It wasn't your fault, so why let it upset you? Kiss me now,' said Sonya.

Natasha lifted her head and, kissing her friend on the lips, pressed her wet face against her.

'I can't tell you. I don't know. No one's to blame,' said Natasha.

'It's my fault. But it all hurts terribly. Oh, why doesn't he come?'

She went down to dinner with red eyes. Maria Dmitrievna, who had heard how the prince had received the Rostovs, pretended not to notice Natasha's troubled face, and at table loudly and resolutely bandied jests with the count and her other guests.

8

THAT evening the Rostovs went to the opera, for which Maria Dmitrievna had taken a box.

Natasha did not want to go but could not refuse after Maria Dmitrievna's kindness, especially as it had been arranged expressly for her. Dressed and waiting for her father in the big hall, she surveyed herself in the tall looking-glass and when she saw how pretty, how very pretty she was, she felt even more melancholy than before, but it was a sweet, tender melancholy.

'Oh God, if he were here now I should not have that silly sort of shy feeling I had before. I would throw my arms round his neck and cling close to him, and make him look at me with those searching, inquiring eyes of his with which he has so often looked at me, and then I would make him laugh as he used to laugh then. And his eyes – how plainly I can see his eyes this very moment!' thought Natasha. 'And what do his father and sister matter to me? I love only him, him alone, him, with that dear face and his eyes and his smile – a man's smile and at the same time childlike. ... No, better not think of him, not think but forget. Better forget him altogether for the present, or I shan't be able to bear this waiting. I shall cry in a minute!' and she turned away from the looking-glass, making an effort not to weep. 'And how can Sonya love Nikolai so calmly and quietly, and wait so long and so patiently?' she wondered, seeing Sonya come in, dressed and ready with a fan in her hand. 'No, she's quite different from me. I can't be like her!'

Natasha at that moment felt so full of emotion and tenderness that it was not enough for her to love and know that she was loved: what she wanted now at this instant was to embrace her beloved, speak to him and hear from him the words of love that filled her own heart. As she rode along in the carriage, sitting beside her father and pensively watching the lights of the street lamps flickering on the frozen window, she felt still sadder and more in love, and forgot where she was going and with whom. The Rostovs' carriage fell into the line of carriages and drove up to the theatre, its wheels slowly creaking over the snow. Natasha and Sonya skipped down quickly, holding up their skirts. The count got out supported by the footmen, and making their way through the stream of ladies and gentlemen going in, and the programme-sellers, the three of them walked along the corridor to their box in the stalls. The sounds of music were already audible through the closed doors.

'Natasha, your hair!' whispered Sonya in French.

An attendant hurried up and slipped deferentially sideways past the ladies to open the door of their box. The music sounded louder, and through the door they beheld the rows of brightly-lit boxes occupied by ladies with bare arms and shoulders, and the noisy stalls below, brilliant with uniforms. A woman entering the adjoining box shot a glance of feminine envy at Natasha. The curtain had not yet risen and the orchestra was playing the overture. Natasha, smoothing her gown, went forward with Sonya and sat down, gazing at the glittering tiers opposite. A sensation she had not experienced for a long time – that of having hundreds of eyes looking at her bare arms and neck – suddenly affected her with mixed pleasure and discomfort, and called up a whole swarm of memories, desires and emotions associated with that sensation.

The two remarkably pretty girls, Natasha and Sonya, with Count Rostov, who had not been seen in Moscow for some long while, attracted general attention. Moreover, everybody had heard vaguely of Natasha's engagement to Prince Andrei, and knew that the Rostovs had been living in the country ever since, and so gazed with curiosity at the girl who was to make one of the best matches in Russia.

Natasha's looks, as everyone told her, had improved in the country, and that evening, thanks to her agitation, she was particularly pretty. Her exuberance and beauty combined with her indifference to everything around her impressed all those who saw her. Her black eyes wandered over the crowd without seeking anyone, and her slender arm, bare to above the elbow, lay on the velvet edge of the box, while, evidently unconsciously, she opened and closed her hand in time to the music, crumpling her programme.

'Look, there's Alenina,' said Sonya, 'with her mother, isn't it?'

'Saints alive, Mihail Kirillich is fatter than ever!' exclaimed the old count.

'And do look at our Anna Mihalovna – what a head-dress she's got on!'

'The Karagins, Julie – and Boris with them. It's easy to see they're engaged.'

'Drubetskoy has proposed! Didn't you know? I heard today,' said Shinshin, coming into the Rostovs' box.

Following the direction of her father's eyes, Natasha saw Julie sitting beside her mother with a blissful look on her face and a string of pearls round her thick red neck – which Natasha knew was covered with powder. Behind them, wearing a smile and inclining his ear towards Julie's mouth, was Boris's handsome, smoothly-brushed head. He looked from under his brows at the Rostovs, and said something, smiling, to his betrothed.

'They are talking about us, about me and him!' thought Natasha. 'And she's jealous of me most likely, and he is trying to reassure her. They need not worry themselves! If only they knew how little they matter to me, any of them.'

Behind them sat Anna Mihalovna wearing a green head-dress, her face expressing resignation to the will of God but looking happy and festive. Their box was redolent of that atmosphere which hangs about an engaged couple and which Natasha knew and liked so much. She turned away and suddenly all the humiliation of that morning's visit came back to her.

'What right has he not to want to receive me into his family? Oh, better not think about it – not till *he* comes back,' she said to herself, and began looking about at the faces, some familiar, some unknown, in the stalls. In the front row, in the very middle, leaning back against the orchestra-rail, stood Dolohov in a Persian dress, his curly hair brushed up into an enormous shock. He was standing in full view of the audience, well aware that he was attracting the attention of the whole theatre, yet as much at ease as though he were in his own room. Around him thronged Moscow's most brilliant young men, whom it was obvious he dominated.

Count Rostov, laughing, nudged the blushing Sonya, pointing out to her her former admirer.

'Did you recognize him?' he asked. 'And where has he sprung from?' he inquired of Shinshin. 'I thought he had disappeared somewhere.'

'So he did,' replied Shinshin. 'He was in the Caucasus, and ran away from there. They say he has been acting as minister to some ruling prince in Persia, and there killed the Shah's brother. Now all the ladies of Moscow have gone wild over him! "Dolohov the Persian" – that's what does it! Nowadays you hear nothing but Dolohov: they swear by him and invite you to meet him as if they were offering you a dish of choice sterlet. Dolohov and Anatole Kuragin have turned the heads of all our ladies.'

A tall, beautiful woman with a tremendous plait of hair and a great display of plump white shoulders and neck, round which she wore a double string of large pearls, entered the adjoining box, rustling her heavy silk gown and taking a long time to settle into her place.

Natasha found herself examining that neck and the shoulders, the pearls and the coiffure of the lady, and admired the beauty of the shoulders and the pearls. Just as Natasha was taking a second look at her, the lady glanced round, and meeting the count's eyes she nodded and smiled to him. It was Countess Bezuhov, Pierre's wife. The count, who knew everyone in society, leaned over and spoke to her.

'Have you been here long, countess?' he inquired. 'I'll call, I'll call to kiss your hand. I am in town on business and, see, I have brought my girls with me. They say Semeonova's acting is superb,' the count went on. 'Count Pierre never used to forget us. Is he here?'

'Yes, he said he would drop in,' answered Hélène, looking intently at Natasha.

Count Rostov resumed his seat.

'Handsome, isn't she?' he whispered to Natasha.

'Wonderful!' agreed Natasha. 'It would be easy to fall in love with her!'

At that moment the last chords of the overture were heard, and the conductor tapped with his stick. Some late-comers hurried to their places in the stalls, and the curtain rose.

With the rising of the curtain a hush fell on boxes and stalls, and all the men, old and young, in their uniforms and dress-coats, and all the women with precious stones on their bare flesh, concentrated their attention with eager expectation on the stage.

Natasha too began to look.

9

SMOOTH boards formed the centre of the stage, at the sides stood painted canvases representing trees, and in the background was a cloth stretched over boards. In the middle of the stage sat some girls in red bodices and white petticoats. One extremely fat girl in a white silk dress was sitting apart on a low bench, to the back of which a piece of green cardboard was glued. They were all singing something. When they had finished their chorus the girl in white advanced towards the prompter's box, and a man with stout legs encased in silk tights, a plume in his cap and a dagger at his waist, went up to her and began to sing and wave his arms about.

First the man in tights sang alone, then she sang, then they both paused while the orchestra played and the man fingered the hand of the girl in white, obviously waiting for the beat when they should start singing again. They sang a duet and everyone in the theatre began clapping and shouting, while the man and woman on the stage, who were playing a pair of lovers, began smiling, spreading out their arms and bowing.

To Natasha, fresh from the country, and in her present serious mood, all this seemed grotesque and extraordinary. She could not follow the opera, could not even listen to the music: she saw only painted cardboard and oddly dressed men and women who moved, spoke and sang strangely in a patch of blazing light. She knew what it was all meant to represent, but it was so grotesquely artificial and unnatural that she felt alternately ashamed and amused at the actors. She looked about her at the faces of the audience, trying to see if they felt as derisive and bewildered as she did; but all the faces appeared absorbed in what was happening on the stage, the while they expressed what seemed to Natasha to be an affected rapture. 'I suppose it has to be like this!' she thought. She kept looking in turn at the rows of pomaded heads in the stalls and then at the half-naked women in the boxes, especially at Hélène in the next box, who, quite uncovered, sat with a quiet, serene smile, not taking her eyes off the stage and basking in the bright light that flooded the theatre and the warm air heated by the crowd. Natasha little by little began to pass into a state of intoxication she had not experienced for a long time. She lost all sense of who and where she was, and of what was going on before her. As she gazed and dreamed, the strangest fancies flashed unexpectedly and disconnectedly into her mind. At one moment the idea occurred to her to leap over the footlights and sing the aria the actress was singing. Next she had an impulse to give a tap of her fan to an old gentleman sitting not far from her, or lean over to Hélène and tickle her.

At one time when there was a lull on the stage before the beginning of an aria an outer door creaked, and the masculine steps of a belated arrival were heard advancing along the carpeted stalls on the side nearest the Rostovs' box. 'Here comes Kuragin!' whispered Shinshin. Countess Bezuhov turned, smiling, to the new-comer. Natasha, following the direction of the countess's eyes, saw an extraordinarily handsome adjutant approaching their box, with self-assured yet courteous bearing. This was Anatole Kuragin whom she had seen and noticed long ago at the ball in Petersburg. He was now in an adjutant's uniform with one epaulet and a shoulder knot. He moved with a discreet swagger, which would have been ridiculous if he had not been so good-looking and his comely features had not expressed such good-natured complacency and high spirits. Although the performance was in progress he sauntered down the sloping carpeted gangway, accompanied by a slight jingling of sword and spurs, his perfumed, handsome head held high. With a glance at Natasha he went up to his sister, laid his finely-gloved hand on the edge of her box, nodded to her, and leaning forward asked her a question, with a gesture towards Natasha.

'Charming, charming!' said he, evidently referring to Natasha, who did not exactly hear the words but divined them from the movement of his lips. Then he took his place in the front row of the stalls, sitting beside Dolohov and giving a friendly, careless nudge with his elbow to the man whom most people treated so obsequiously. Anatole threw him a merry wink and a smile, and rested his foot on the orchestra screen.

'How alike brother and sister are!' remarked the count. 'And how handsome they both are!'

Shinshin, lowering his voice, began to tell the count some story of an intrigue of Kuragin's in Moscow, to which Natasha purposely listened just because he had called her charming.

The first act was over. In the stalls everyone stood up and began moving about, coming and going.

Boris arrived in the Rostovs' box, received their congratulations very simply and, with a lift of his eyebrows and an absent-minded smile, conveyed to Natasha and Sonya his fiancée's invitation to her wedding, and went away. Natasha, with a gay coquettish smile, had talked to him and congratulated him on his approaching marriage, though this was the very Boris she had once been in love with. In her present intoxicated, excited state everything seemed simple and natural.

The half-naked Hélène was sitting near her, smiling on all alike, and it was just such a smile that Natasha bestowed on Boris.

Hélène's box was filled and surrounded on the side of the stalls by the cleverest and most distinguished men, who seemed to be vying with one another in their desire to let everyone see that they knew her.

Throughout the *entr'acte* Kuragin stood with Dolohov in front of the footlights, never taking his eyes off the Rostovs' box. Natasha knew he was talking about her, and this afforded her gratification. She even turned so that he should see her profile from what she believed to be the most becoming angle. Before the beginning of the second act Pierre appeared in the stalls. The Rostovs had not seen him since their arrival. His face looked sad, and he had grown stouter since Natasha had seen him last. He walked to the front rows, not noticing anyone. Anatole went up to him and began saying something, with a look and a gesture towards the Rostovs' box. When he caught sight of Natasha, Pierre's face lighted up and he hurried along the row of stalls towards their box, where, leaning on his elbows and smiling, he talked to her for a long time. In the midst of her conversation with Pierre, Natasha heard a man's voice in Countess Bezuhov's box, and something told her it was Kuragin. She looked round and met his gaze. Almost smiling, he stared straight into her eyes with a look of such warmth and admiration that it seemed strange to be so near him, to look at him like that, to be so sure that he admired her, and yet not to be acquainted with him.

In the second act the stage was a cemetery, and there was a round hole in the back-drop to represent the moon. Shades were put over the footlights, and the horns and contra-bass began to play deep bass notes, while a number of people emerged from right and left, wearing black cloaks. These people began waving their arms, and in their hands they held things which looked like daggers. Then some other men ran in and began dragging away the maiden who had been in white but was now in light blue. They did not drag her away at once but spent a long while singing with her, until at last they did drag her off, and behind the scenes some iron object was struck three times, and everyone knelt down and sang a prayer. All these actions were repeatedly interrupted by the enthusiastic plaudits of the audience.

During this act every time Natasha looked towards the stalls she saw Anatole Kuragin, with an arm flung across the back of a chair, staring at her. She was pleased to see that he was so captivated by her and it did not occur to her that there could be anything amiss in it.

When the second act was over Countess Bezuhov stood up, turned towards the Rostovs' box – her whole bosom completely exposed – beckoned the old count with a small gloved finger, and paying no heed to those who had entered her box began talking to him with an amiable smile.

'Oh, you must introduce me to your lovely daughters,' said she. 'The whole town is singing their praises and I don't even know them.'

Natasha rose and curtsied to the magnificent countess. She was so delighted by praise from this brilliant beauty that she blushed with pleasure.

'I am determined to become a Moscovite too, now,' said Hélène. 'And aren't you ashamed of yourself for burying such pearls in the country?'

Countess Bezuhov had some right to her reputation of being a fascinating woman. She could say what she did not think – flattery especially – with perfect simplicity and naturalness.

'Now, my dear count, you must let me help to entertain your daughters. Though I am not here for long this time – nor are you either. But I'll do my best to amuse them. I heard a great deal about you when I was in Petersburg, and wanted to get to know you,' said she, turning to Natasha with her uniform lovely smile. 'I have also heard about you from my page, Drubetskoy – he is getting married, you know. And from my husband's friend, Bolkonsky, Prince Andrei Bolkonsky,' she went on with special emphasis, implying that she knew of his relation to Natasha. She asked that one of the young ladies should move into her box for the rest of the performance so that they might become better acquainted, and Natasha went over and sat next to her.

The third act took place in a palace in which a great many candles were burning and pictures of bearded knights hung on the walls. At the front of the stage stood a man and woman – the king and queen, no doubt. The king was gesticulating with his right arm and, obviously nervous, sang something badly and sat down on a crimson throne. The damsel who had appeared first in white and then in pale blue now wore only a shift, and stood beside the throne with her hair hanging down. She sang something dolefully, addressing the queen, but the king peremptorily waved his hand, and men and women with bare legs emerged from the wings on both sides and began dancing together. Next the violins played very shrilly and merrily. One of the women, with thick bare legs and thin arms, separated from the others, retired behind the scenes to adjust her bodice, then walked into the middle of the stage and began skipping into the air and kicking one foot rapidly against the other. Everyone in the stalls clapped and roared 'Bravo!' Then one of the men was seen standing by himself at one corner of the stage. The cymbals and horns struck up in the orchestra, and this bare-legged man began leaping very high and making quick movements in the air with his feet. (This was Duport, who earned sixty thousand roubles in silver for this accomplishment.) Everybody in the stalls, boxes and from up among the gods started clapping and shouting with all their might, and the man stopped and began smiling and bowing in all directions. Then other men and women with bare legs danced. Then one of the royal personages declaimed something in recitative and all the chorus replied. But suddenly a storm sprang up, chromatic scales and diminished sevenths were heard in the orchestra, and they all ran off, again dragging one of their number behind the scenes, and the curtain dropped. Once more there was a terrible uproar and tumult among the spectators, and the whole audience with rapturous faces began screaming:

'Duport! Duport! Duport!'

Natasha no longer thought this strange. She looked about her with a sense of satisfaction, smiling joyfully.

'Isn't Duport ravishing?' Hélène asked her.

'Oh yes,' answered Natasha.

10

DURING the *entr'acte* a draught of cold air blew into Hélène's box, the door was opened and Anatole came in, stooping and trying not to brush against anyone.

'Allow me to introduce my brother,' said Hélène, her eyes shifting uneasily from Natasha to Anatole.

Natasha turned her pretty little head towards the elegant young officer, and smiled at him over her bare shoulder. Anatole, who was as handsome at close quarters as he was from a distance, sat down beside her and told her he had longed for this pleasure ever since the Naryshkins' ball where he had had the happiness, which he had never forgotten, of seeing her. Kuragin was far more sensible and straight-forward with women than he was in the society of men. He talked boldly and naturally, and Natasha was agreeably surprised at finding there was nothing formidable in this man, about whom so many stories were rife, but, on the contrary, the smile on his face could not have been more artlessly jolly and good-natured.

Anatole Kuragin asked her what she thought of the performance, and told her how on a previous occasion Semeonova had fallen down on the stage.

'And do you know, countess,' said he, suddenly addressing her as though she were an old friend, 'we are getting up a fancy-dress ball. You ought to take part in it: it will be great fun. We are all assembling at the Arharovs'. Please come! Do – will you?'

As he was saying this he never took his smiling eyes off her face, her neck and her bare arms. Natasha had no doubt that he was en-raptured by her. This pleased her, yet his presence somehow made her feel constrained, hot and ill at ease. When she was not looking at him she felt that he was gazing at her shoulders, and she could not help trying to catch his eye, to divert it to her face. But looking into his eyes she was frightened, realizing that between her and him there was not that barrier of decorum she had always been conscious of between herself and other men. She did not know how it was that within five minutes she had come to feel terribly close to this man. When she turned away she feared he might seize her from behind by her bare arm, or kiss her on the neck. They talked of the most ordin-ary things, yet she felt that they were more intimate than she had ever been with any man. Natasha kept looking round to Hélène and her father, as though asking them what it all meant, but Hélène was engaged in conversation with a general and did not respond to her glance, while her father's eyes said nothing but what they always said: 'Enjoying yourself? I am so glad.'

In one such moment of awkward silence, during which Anatole's prominent eyes stared calmly and persistently at her, Natasha, to break the silence, asked him how he liked Moscow. She asked the question and blushed. She was feeling all the time that she was doing something improper by talking to him. Anatole smiled as though to encourage her.

'At first I wasn't particularly charmed – because what is it makes one like a town? It's the pretty women, isn't it? Well, but now I like it very much indeed,' he said, giving her a significant look. 'You'll come to the fancy-dress ball, countess? Do come!' and putting out his hand to her bouquet and dropping his voice he added in French, 'You will be the prettiest there. Do come, dear countess, and give me this flower as a pledge!'

Natasha did not understand what he was saying, any more than he did himself, but she felt that his uncomprehended words held some unseemly design. She did not know what to say, and turned away as though she had not heard his remark. But as soon as she turned away the thought came to her that he was there behind her, so close to her.

'What is he feeling now? Is he ashamed of himself? Angry? Ought I to mend matters?' she asked herself. She could not refrain from looking round. She looked straight into his eyes, and his nearness and self-assurance, and the simple-hearted warmth of his smile, vanquished her. She gave him an answering smile, looking straight into his eyes. And again she felt with horror that no barrier lay between him and her.

The curtain rose again. Anatole left the box, serene and gay. Natasha went back to her father in the other box, now completely under the spell of the world in which she found herself. All that was happening now seemed perfectly natural; while on the other hand all her previous thoughts concerning her betrothed, or Princess Maria, or her life in the country, had dissolved from her mind, as though all that belonged to a past that was far remote.

In the fourth act there was some sort of devil who sang and gesticulated until the boards were withdrawn from under him and he disappeared down below. That was all Natasha saw of the fourth act: she felt agitated and upset, and the cause of this agitation was Kuragin, whom she could not help watching. As they were leaving the theatre Anatole came up to them, called their carriage and helped them in. When it was Natasha's turn to take her seat he squeezed her arm above the wrist. Startled and flushed and happy, she looked round at him. He was gazing at her with flashing eyes and a tender smile.

*

Not until she reached home was Natasha able to form any clear idea of what had happened, and suddenly, remembering Prince Andrei, she was horrified, and at tea, to which they all sat down after the theatre, she groaned aloud, flushed crimson and ran from the room.

'O God, I am lost!' she said to herself. 'How could I have let it go so far?' she wondered. For a long time she sat hiding her burning cheeks in her hands, trying to realize what had happened to her, but she could not grasp either what had happened or what she was feeling. Everything seemed dark, obscure and dreadful. There in that huge, brilliant auditorium, where Duport with his bare legs and his spangled jacket had capered about on the damp boards to the sounds of music, where young girls and old men, and the nearly naked Hélène, with her proud, serene smile, had cried 'Bravo!' till they were hoarse – there in the protecting shadow of that Hélène it had all seemed simple and natural; but now, alone by herself, it was past comprehension.

'What does it mean? What was that terror I felt of him? What is the meaning of these stings of conscience which I feel now?' she asked herself.

Only to the old countess could Natasha have talked, at night in bed, of all she was feeling. She knew that Sonya, with her strict and single-minded outlook, would either not understand at all or would be horrified at such a confession. So Natasha accordingly had to try, by her own unaided efforts, to solve the riddle that tormented her.

'Have I really forfeited Prince Andrei's love or not?' she asked herself, and laughed reassuringly. 'What a fool I am to wonder that! What did happen? Nothing. I have done nothing. I didn't lead him on at all. Nobody will know and I shall never see him again,' she told herself. 'So it's plain that nothing happened, that there is nothing to repent of, and that Andrei can love me still. But why "still"? O God, O God, why isn't he here?'

For a moment Natasha felt comforted, but again some instinct told her that though it was all true, and though nothing had happened, yet the former purity of her love for Prince Andrei was lost. And again in imagination she went over the whole conversation with Kuragin, and saw the face, the gesture and the tender smile of that handsome, impudent man as he squeezed her arm.

ANATOLE KURAGIN was living in Moscow because his father had
sent him away from Petersburg, where he had been spending over
twenty thousand roubles a year in ready money, besides running up
bills for as much more, for which his creditors were dunning his
father.

Prince Vasili informed his son that he would, for the last time, pay
one-half of his debts, but only on condition that he went to Moscow
as adjutant to the commander-in-chief – a post his father had managed to procure for him – and finally made up his mind to try to
contract a good match there. He suggested either Princess Maria or
Julie Karagin.

Anatole consented and went to Moscow, where he took up residence at Pierre's house. Pierre at first received him unwillingly, but
got used to him after a while, occasionally accompanied him on his
carousals and gave him money in the guise of loans.

Shinshin spoke truly when he said that Anatole had begun the
moment he arrived to turn the heads of all the ladies in Moscow,
mainly by the fact that he treated them with nonchalance, and openly
preferred gipsy-girls and French actresses with the most prominent
of whom, Mademoiselle Georges, he was said to be on terms of close
intimacy. He never missed a drinking-party given by Dolohov or
any other member of Moscow's fast set, drank whole nights through,
leaving all his companions under the table, and was at every *soirée*
and ball in the best society. Rumours were widespread of his intrigues
with married ladies, and at balls he flirted with a few of them. But he
fought shy of young girls, especially the wealthy heiresses, who were
most of them plain. He had good reason for this, having been married a couple of years before – a fact known only to his closest friends.
Two years previously, when his regiment had been stationed in
Poland, a Polish landowner of small means had forced Anatole to
marry his daughter. Anatole had lost no time in abandoning his wife,
and in consideration of a sum of money which he agreed to send
periodically to his father-in-law he was allowed by the latter to pass
himself off as a bachelor.

Anatole was always very well satisfied with his position, with himself and with the rest of the world. He was instinctively and thor-

oughly convinced that he could not possibly live otherwise than in the way he did live, and that he had never in his life done anything evil. He was incapable of considering how his behaviour might affect others, or what the consequences of this or that action of his might be. He believed that just as a duck is so created that it must live in water, so he was created by God for the purpose of spending thirty thousand roubles a year and occupying the highest pinnacle in society. He was so firmly grounded in this opinion that others, looking at him, were persuaded of it too, and refused him neither the exalted position in society nor the money, which he borrowed right and left with obviously no notion of ever repaying it.

He was not a gambler – at least he was never interested in winning money at cards, and even did not care if he lost. He was not vain. He did not mind what people thought of him. Still less could he be accused of ambition. More than once he provoked his father by injuring his own prospects, and he laughed at honours of all kinds. He was not tight-fisted, and never refused anyone who asked of him. All that he cared for was 'a good time' and women, and as according to his ideas there was nothing ignoble about these tastes, and as he was incapable of considering the effect on others of the gratification of his desires, he was sincere in his opinion of himself as a man of unimpeachable character and in his contempt for rogues and wrong-doers, and with a tranquil conscience carried his head high.

Rakes, those male Magdalens, cherish a secret belief in their own innocence similar to the feeling women Magdalens have, and which is based on the same hope of forgiveness. 'All will be forgiven her, for she loved much, and all will be forgiven him because he enjoyed himself much.'

Dolohov, back again in Moscow that year after his exile and his Persian adventures, and once more leading a dissipated life of luxury and gambling, renewed his friendship with his old Petersburg comrade Kuragin, and made use of him for his own ends.

Anatole was genuinely fond of Dolohov for his cleverness and audacity. Dolohov, who needed Anatole Kuragin's name, renown and connexions as a bait to ensnare rich young men into his gambling circle, made use of him and amused himself at his expense without letting him suspect it. Apart from these interested motives for which he required Anatole, the very process of dominating another man's will was in itself an enjoyment, a habit and a necessity for Dolohov.

Natasha had made a deep impression on Kuragin. At supper after the opera he described to Dolohov, in the manner of a connoisseur, the attractions of her arms, shoulders, feet and hair, and expressed his intention of paying court to her. The possible consequences of such a flirtation Anatole was incapable of considering, just as he never had any notion of what might be the outcome of any of his actions.

'Yes, she's pretty, my lad, but she's not for us,' Dolohov said to him.

'I'll tell my sister to ask her to dinner,' said Anatole. 'How would that be?'

'You'd do better to wait till she's married. …'

'You know I adore little girls,' pursued Anatole. 'They lose their heads at once.'

'You've already come to grief once over one "little girl",' replied Dolohov, who knew of Anatole's marriage. 'Take care!'

'Well, one can't get caught a second time! What?' said Anatole, with a good-humoured laugh.

12

THE day after the opera the Rostovs stayed at home, and nobody came to call. Maria Dmitrievna had a private conversation with the count to discuss something which they kept from Natasha. Natasha guessed they were talking about the old prince and concocting some scheme, and this made her feel uneasy and humiliated. Every minute she expected Prince Andrei, and twice that day sent a man-servant to Vozdvizhenka street to find out whether he had arrived. He had not. She was having a more difficult time now than during her first days in Moscow. To her impatience and pining for him were now added the unpleasant memory of her interview with Princess Maria and the old prince, and a fear and anxiety of which she did not understand the cause. She was continually fancying either that he would never come or that something would happen to her before he came. She could no longer day-dream about him by herself for hours on end. As soon as she turned her mind to him recollections of the old prince, of Princess Maria, of the theatre and of Kuragin began to intrude on her thoughts. Once more she asked herself whether she had not done something wrong, whether she had not already broken faith with Prince Andrei, and again she found herself going over in the minutest detail every word, every gesture, every shade in the play of expression on the face of the man who had been able to arouse in her such incomprehensible and terrifying feelings. To the eyes of those about her Natasha seemed livelier than usual, but she was far from being as serene and happy as before.

On Sunday morning Maria Dmitrievna invited her guests to come to the service at her parish church – the Church of the Assumption.

'I don't like those fashionable churches,' she said, evidently priding herself on her independent ideas. 'God is the same everywhere. Our parish priest is an excellent man: he conducts the service decently and with dignity, and the deacon is the same. Where is the holiness in giving concerts in the choir? I don't like it: it's mischievous nonsense!'

Maria Dmitrievna liked Sundays and knew how to celebrate them. On Saturday her house was scrubbed and polished from top to bottom, and on the Lord's Day neither she nor her servants did any work, but wore their best clothes and went to church. She had some extra dishes for dinner in the dining-room, and there was vodka and roast goose or a sucking-pig in the servants' hall. But nowhere in the whole house was the influence of the day more distinctly legible than on the broad, severe face of Maria Dmitrievna herself which on Sundays wore a fixed expression of solemn festivity.

After church, when they had finished their coffee in the dining-room, where the loose covers had been removed from the furniture, a servant announced that the carriage was ready, and Maria Dmitrievna rose with a stern air. She wore her best shawl in which she paid calls, and announced that she was going to see Prince Nikolai Bolkonsky to have it out with him concerning Natasha.

After she had gone, a dressmaker from Madame Suppert-Roguet's waited on the Rostovs, and Natasha, very glad of this diversion, having shut herself in a room adjoining the drawing-room, began trying on her new dresses. Just as she had put on a bodice basted together, with the sleeves not yet tacked in, and was turning her head to see in the looking-glass how the back fitted, she heard her father's voice in eager conversation with another voice, a woman's voice, which made her flush red. It was Hélène's voice. Before Natasha had time to take off the bodice she was trying on, the door opened and in walked Countess Bezuhov, dressed in a velvet gown of dark heliotrope with a high collar, her face alive with amiable, friendly smiles.

'Oh my enchantress!' she cried to the blushing Natasha. 'Charm-

674

ing! No, this is really beyond anything, my dear count,' she said to Count Rostov, who had followed her in. 'The idea of being in Moscow and not going anywhere! No, I shall not let you off! This evening Mademoiselle Georges is to recite for me at my house, and I am having a few friends in. If you don't bring your lovely girls – who are much prettier than Mademoiselle Georges – I shall positively have to quarrel with you. My husband is away in Tver or I would send him to fetch you. You must come. You positively must! Between eight and nine.'

She nodded to the dressmaker, who knew her and was curtseying respectfully, and seated herself in an arm-chair beside the looking-glass, draping the folds of her velvet gown picturesquely about her. She kept up a flow of good-humoured, light-hearted chatter, and repeatedly expressed her admiration of Natasha's beauty. She examined the new dresses and praised them, as well as one of her own, *en gaze métallique*, which had just arrived from Paris, and advised Natasha to have a copy of it.

'However, anything suits you, my charmer!' she remarked.

The smile of pleasure on Natasha's face never left it. She felt happy, as if she were blossoming out under the praises of this nice Countess Bezuhov, who before had seemed so grand and unapproachable and was now so kind to her. Natasha's spirits rose, and she felt almost in love with this woman, who was so beautiful and so gracious. Hélène for her part was sincere in her admiration of Natasha and in her wish that she should enjoy herself. Anatole had more than once begged her to bring him and Natasha together, and it was with this object that she had come to the Rostovs. The idea of throwing her brother and Natasha together amused her.

Though at one time, in Petersburg, Hélène had been annoyed with Natasha for drawing Boris away from her, she did not think of that now and in her own way wished Natasha nothing but good. As she was leaving the Rostovs she called her *protégée* aside.

'My brother was dining with me yesterday, and we nearly died of laughter – he eats nothing and can only sigh for you, my charmer! He is madly, quite madly in love with you, my dear.'

Natasha flushed crimson when she heard this.

'How she colours up, how she colours up, *ma délicieuse!*' pursued Hélène. 'You must be sure to come. Though you are in love, that is no reason for shutting yourself up like a nun. And even if you are

675

betrothed, I cannot think your fiancé would not wish you to go into society rather than be bored to death.'

'Then she knows I am engaged,' thought Natasha. 'So she and her husband Pierre – that good, upright Pierre – must have talked and laughed about this. So there can be no harm in it.' And again under Hélène's influence what had struck her before as terrible now seemed simple and natural. 'And she is such a *grande dame*, so kind, and has obviously taken a great fancy to me. And why shouldn't I enjoy myself?' thought Natasha, gazing at Hélène with wide-open, wondering eyes.

Maria Dmitrievna returned in time for dinner, silent and grave-faced, having evidently suffered a rebuff at the old prince's. She was still too agitated by the encounter to be able to describe the interview calmly. To the count's inquiries she replied that everything was all right and that she would tell him about it next day. On hearing of Countess Bezuhov's visit and the invitation for that evening Maria Dmitrievna remarked:

'I don't care to associate with Countess Bezuhov, and I should advise you not to. However, go, since you have promised. It will be a little amusement for you,' she added, addressing Natasha.

13

COUNT ROSTOV took the girls to Countess Bezuhov's. There were a fair number of people present, nearly all strangers to Natasha. Count Rostov was displeased to see that the company consisted almost entirely of men and women notorious for the freedom of their conduct. Mademoiselle Georges was standing in a corner of the drawing-room surrounded by young men. There were several Frenchmen there, among them Métivier, who had been a constant visitor at Countess Bezuhov's ever since her arrival in Moscow. The count decided not to sit down to cards or let his girls out of his sight, and to get away as soon as Mademoiselle Georges' performance was over.

Anatole was at the door, evidently on the look-out for the Rostovs. Having exchanged greetings with the count, he immediately went up to Natasha and followed her into the room. The moment Natasha saw him she was overcome by the same feeling she had had at the opera – a mixed feeling of gratified vanity at his admiration for her, and terror at the absence of any moral barrier between them.

Hélène welcomed Natasha with delight, and was loud in admiration of her loveliness and her dress. Soon after their arrival Mademoiselle Georges went out of the room to change her costume. In the meantime chairs were arranged in the drawing-room and the guests began to take their seats. Anatole found a chair for Natasha and was about to sit down next to her, but the count, keeping a sharp eye on his daughter, took the seat beside her himself. Anatole sat behind.

Mademoiselle Georges, with bare, plump, dimpled arms, and a red shawl flung across one shoulder, came into the empty space left for her between the chairs, and assumed an unnatural pose. A murmur of enthusiasm hailed her.

Mademoiselle Georges gazed round her audience with theatrical gloom, and began to declaim a long soliloquy in French describing her guilty passion for her son. In places she raised her voice, in others she dropped to a whisper, solemnly lifting her head; sometimes she broke off or spoke huskily, rolling her eyes.

'*Adorable!*' ... '*Divin!*' ... '*Délicieux!*' was heard on all sides.

Natasha's eyes were fastened on the fat actress, but she neither saw nor heard nor understood anything of what went on before her. She was only aware of being borne irrevocably away again into that strange and senseless world so remote from her old one, a world in which there was no knowing what was good and what was bad, what was sensible and what was folly. Behind her sat Anatole, and conscious of his proximity she experienced a frightened sense of expectancy.

After the first monologue the whole company rose and crowded round Mademoiselle Georges, rapturously expressing their admiration.

'How beautiful she is!' Natasha remarked to her father, who had got up with the rest and was moving through the throng towards the actress.

'I don't think so when I look at you,' said Anatole, following Natasha. He said this at a moment when only she could hear him. 'You are enchanting ... from the first moment I saw you I have never ceased. ...'

'Come along, Natasha, come along!' said the count, turning back for his daughter. 'How pretty she is!'

Making no reply, Natasha stepped up to her father with a dazed look in her eyes.

After several more recitations Mademoiselle Georges took her departure, and Countess Bezuhov invited her guests into the ballroom.

The count would have liked to go home, but Hélène besought him not to spoil her impromptu ball. The Rostovs stayed on. Anatole asked Natasha for a valse and as they danced together he pressed her waist and her hand, and told her she was bewitching and that he loved her. During the *écossaise*, which she also danced with him, Anatole said nothing when they happened to be by themselves but merely gazed at her. Natasha wondered whether she had not dreamed what he said to her during the valse. At the end of the first figure he pressed her hand again. Natasha lifted frightened eyes to him, but there was such confident tenderness in his fond expression and smile that she found it impossible to look at him and say what it was she had it on her tongue to say. She lowered her eyes.

'Do not say such things to me. I am betrothed and I love another,' she murmured rapidly. She glanced up at him. Anatole was neither disconcerted nor hurt by what she had said.

'Don't speak to me of that. What is that to do with me ?' said he. 'I tell you I am madly, madly in love with you. Is it my fault if you are irresistible ? ... It's our turn to lead.'

Natasha, excited and agitated, looked about her with wide, scared eyes, and seemed gayer than usual. Afterwards she remembered almost nothing of what took place that evening. They danced the *écossaise* and the *gross vater*. Her father suggested that they should go but she begged to remain. Wherever she was, whoever was talking to her, she felt *his* eyes upon her. Later she recalled how she had asked her father to let her go to the dressing-room to rearrange her dress, that Hélène had followed and spoken laughingly of her brother's passion for her, and that she again met Anatole in the little sitting-room. Hélène vanished somewhere, leaving them alone, and Anatole had taken her hand and said in a tender voice:

'I cannot come to call upon you, but is it possible that I am never to see you ? I love you to distraction. Can I never ... ?' and, barring her way, he brought his face close to hers.

His large, shining, masculine eyes were so close to hers that she saw nothing but them.

'Natalie ?' he whispered inquiringly, and she felt her hands being squeezed till they hurt. 'Natalie ?'

'I don't understand. I have nothing to say,' her eyes replied.

Burning lips were pressed to hers, and at the same instant she felt herself set free, and Hélène's footsteps and the rustle of her gown were heard in the room. Natasha looked round at her, and then, crimson and trembling, threw a frightened look of inquiry at Anatole and moved towards the door.

'One word, just one, for God's sake!' cried Anatole.

She paused. She so wanted a word from him that would explain to her what had happened, and to which she could find an answer.

'Natalie, just one word ... only one!' he kept repeating, evidently not knowing what to say, and he repeated it till Hélène came up to them.

Natasha returned with Hélène to the drawing-room. The Rostovs went away without staying for supper.

When they got home Natasha lay awake all night, tormented by the problem she could not solve: which did she love – Anatole or Prince Andrei? She loved Prince Andrei – she remembered distinctly how deeply she loved him. But she loved Anatole too: of that there was no doubt. 'Otherwise, how could all that have happened?' she said to herself. 'If, after that, I could return his smile when we said good-bye; if I could let things go so far, it means that I fell in love with him at first sight. So he must be kind, noble and splendid, and I could not help loving him. What am I to do if I love him and the other too?' she asked herself, and was unable to find an answer to those terrible questions.

14

MORNING came with its daily cares and bustle. Everyone got up and began to move about and talk, dressmakers came again, Maria Dmitrievna appeared and they were summoned to breakfast. Natasha kept looking uneasily at everybody with wide-open eyes, as though she wanted to intercept every glance directed towards her, and did her utmost to seem exactly as usual.

After breakfast (this was always her favourite time), Maria Dmitrievna settled herself in her easy chair and called Natasha and the count to her.

'Well now, my friends, I have thought the whole matter over and this is my advice,' she began. 'Yesterday, as you know, I went to see Prince Bolkonsky. Well, I had a talk with him. ... He thought fit to scream at me, but I am not one to be shouted down. I said what I had to say!'

'And he – what did he say?' asked the count.

'He? He's an old fool ... will not listen to anything. But what is the use of talking? As it is, we have worn this poor girl out,' said Maria Dmitrievna. 'My advice to you is, finish your business and go back home to Otradnoe ... and wait there.'

'Oh no!' exclaimed Natasha.

'Yes, go back,' said Maria Dmitrievna, 'and wait there. If your betrothed comes here now, there'll be no escaping a quarrel; but alone with the old man he will talk things over and then come to you.'

Count Rostov approved of this suggestion, seeing the sound sense of it at once. If the old man were to come round, it would be all the better to visit him in Moscow or at Bald Hills later on; and if not, then the wedding, against his wishes, could only take place at Otradnoe.

'That is perfectly true,' said the old count. 'I am only sorry I went to see him and took her.'

'No, why be sorry about that! Being here, you had to pay your respects. But if he won't have it ... that is his affair,' said Maria Dmitrievna, searching for something in her reticule. 'Besides, the trousseau is ready, so there is nothing to keep you; and what isn't ready yet I will send on. Though I don't like to lose you, it's the best way, and God bless you.' Finding what she was looking for in her reticule she handed it to Natasha. It was a letter from Princess Maria. 'She has written to you. What a state she is in, poor thing! She's afraid you might think she does not like you.'

'Well, and she doesn't like me,' said Natasha.

'Don't talk nonsense!' cried Maria Dmitrievna.

'I shall accept no one's word for that: I know she doesn't like me,' replied Natasha boldly as she took the letter, and an expression of such resolute, cold anger came over her face that Maria Dmitrievna looked at her more intently and frowned.

'Don't you contradict me like that, my good girl,' she said. 'What I say is true! You answer that.'

Natasha did not reply, and retired to her room to read Princess Maria's letter.

Princess Maria wrote that she was in despair at the misunderstanding that had arisen between them. Whatever her father's feelings might be, she begged Natasha to believe that she could not fail to love her, as the girl chosen by her brother, for whose happiness she was ready to make any sacrifice.

'Do not believe, however,' she wrote, 'that my father is ill-disposed towards you. He is ailing and old, and one must make excuses for him; but he is good-hearted and generous, and will come to love the woman who makes his son happy.' Princess Maria went on to ask Natasha to fix a time when she could see her again.

After reading the letter Natasha sat down at the writing-table to pen a reply.

'*Chère Princesse*,' she began, writing rapidly and mechanically, and then paused. What more could she write after all that had happened the evening before? 'Yes, yes! All that did happen, and now everything is different,' she thought as she sat before the letter she had started. 'Must I break off with him? Must I really? This is frightful!...' and to escape these dreadful thoughts she ran in to Sonya and began looking through embroidery designs with her.

After dinner Natasha went to her room and again took up Princess Maria's letter. 'Can it be that all is over?' she thought. 'Can all this have happened so quickly and have destroyed everything that went before?' She recalled in all its former strength her love for Prince Andrei, and at the same time felt that she loved Kuragin. She vividly pictured herself as Prince Andrei's wife, remembered the dreams of happiness with him which her imagination had so often painted, and at the same time, aglow with emotion, went over every detail of yesterday's meeting with Anatole.

'Oh why may I not love them both at once?' she kept asking herself in the depths of bewilderment. 'Only so could I be perfectly happy; but now I have to choose, and I can't be happy if I let either of them go. One thing is certain,' she thought, 'to tell Prince Andrei what has happened, or to hide it from him, is equally impossible. But with the *other* nothing is spoilt. But must I really part for ever from the happiness of loving Prince Andrei, whom I have been living for for so long?'

'Please, miss!' whispered a maid, entering the room with a mysterious air. 'A man told me to give you this –' and she handed Natasha a letter. 'Only, for mercy's sake, miss ...' the girl went on, as Natasha, without thinking, mechanically broke the seal and began reading a love-letter from Anatole, of which, without taking in a word, she understood only that it was a letter from him – from the man she loved. Yes, she loved him. Otherwise how could what had happened have happened? How could a love-letter from him be in her hand?

With trembling hands Natasha held that passionate love-letter, composed for Anatole by Dolohov, and as she read she found in it an echo of all that she imagined herself to be feeling.

'Since yesterday evening my fate is sealed: to be loved by you or to die. There is no other alternative for me,' the letter began. Then he went on to say that he knew her parents would never consent to her marriage to him, Anatole, for various secret reasons which he could reveal to her alone, but that if she loved him she need only say the word *Yes*, and no human power could hinder their bliss. Love would conquer all. He would spirit her away and carry her off to the ends of the earth.

'Yes, yes, I love him!' thought Natasha, reading the letter for the twentieth time and looking for some peculiarly deep meaning in every word.

That evening Maria Dmitrievna was going to the Arharovs' and proposed taking the girls with her. Natasha pleaded a headache and stayed at home.

15

On her return late in the evening Sonya went to Natasha's room, and to her surprise found her still dressed and asleep on the sofa. Open on the table beside her lay Anatole's letter. Sonya picked it up and read it.

As she read she glanced at the sleeping Natasha, trying to discover in her face some key to the mystery of what she was reading, but found none. Natasha's face was calm, gentle and happy. Clutching at her breast to keep herself from choking, Sonya, pale and trembling with fright and agitation, sat down in a low chair and burst into tears.

'How is it I noticed nothing? How can it have gone so far? Can she have left off loving Prince Andrei? And how could she have let Kuragin go to such lengths? He is a deceiver and a scoundrel, that's plain! What will Nicolas, dear noble Nicolas, do when he hears of it? So that was the meaning of her excited, determined, unnatural look the day before yesterday, and yesterday and today,' thought Sonya. 'But it's impossible that she can care for him! She probably opened the letter without knowing who it was from. Most likely she feels insulted by it. She could not do such a thing!'

Sonya wiped away her tears and went up to Natasha, scrutinizing her face again.

'Natasha!' she murmured, hardly audibly.

Natasha awoke and saw Sonya.

'Ah, you're back?'

And impulsively, as often happens at the moment of awakening, she gave her friend a tender hug. But noticing Sonya's look of embarrassment her own face became troubled and suspicious.

'Sonya, you read that letter?' she demanded.

'Yes,' answered Sonya softly.

Natasha smiled ecstatically.

'No, Sonya, I can't any longer—' she said, 'I can't hide it from you any longer! You know, we love one another! Sonya, darling, he writes ... Sonya ...'

Sonya stared wide-eyed at Natasha, unable to believe her ears.

'But Bolkonsky?' she asked.

'Ah, Sonya, if you only knew how happy I am!' cried Natasha. 'You don't know what love ...'

'But, Natasha, do you mean to say the *other* is all over?'

Natasha stared at Sonya with her large eyes, as though she could not grasp the question.

'What, are you breaking it off with Prince Andrei?' said Sonya.

'Oh, you don't understand a thing! Don't talk nonsense. Listen!' exclaimed Natasha with a flash of temper.

'No, I can't believe it,' insisted Sonya. 'I don't understand. How can you have loved one man for a whole year and suddenly.... Why, you have only seen him three times! Natasha, I don't believe you, you're joking. In three days to forget everything and be like this. ...'

'Three days?' interrupted Natasha. 'It seems to me as if I'd loved him a hundred years. It seems to me as if I had never never loved anyone before. Never loved anybody the way I love him. You can't understand, Sonya, wait – sit here.' Natasha threw her arms round her and kissed her. 'I have heard of this happening – and so have you too, surely? But it's only now that I feel such love. It's not what I felt before. As soon as I saw him I felt he was my master and I his slave, and that I could not help loving him. Yes, his slave! Whatever he bids me, I shall do. You don't understand that. What am I to do? What am I to do, Sonya?' cried Natasha with a blissful yet frightened face.

'But just think what you are doing,' said Sonya. 'I can't leave it like

683

this. This secret correspondence. . . . How could you let him go so far ?' she asked, with a horror and disgust she could with difficulty conceal.

'I told you, I have no will,' Natasha replied. 'Why can't you understand ? I love him !'

'Then I won't let it go on. ... I shall tell !' cried Sonya, bursting into tears.

'What do you mean ? For God's sake. ... If you tell, you are my enemy,' declared Natasha. 'You want me to be miserable, you want to see us separated. ...'

When she saw Natasha's alarm Sonya wept tears of shame and pity for her friend.

'But what has passed between you ?' she asked. 'What has he said to you ? Why doesn't he come to the house ?'

Natasha did not answer.

'For God's sake, Sonya, don't tell anyone; don't torture me,' implored Natasha. 'Remember, you oughtn't to interfere in such matters. I have confided in you. ...'

'But why this secrecy ? Why doesn't he come to the house ?' Sonya persisted. 'Why doesn't he ask for your hand straight out ? You know Prince Andrei left you perfectly free, if anything like this happened; but I don't believe it. Natasha, have you considered what these *secret reasons* can be ?'

Natasha fixed wondering eyes on Sonya. Evidently this question had not occurred to her before and she did not know how to answer it.

'I don't know what his reasons are. But there must be reasons !'

Sonya sighed and shook her head distrustfully.

'If there were reasons ...' she began.

But Natasha, divining her doubts, interrupted her in dismay.

'Sonya, one can't doubt him ! One can't, one can't ! Don't you understand ?' she cried.

'Does he love you ?'

'Does he love me ?' repeated Natasha with a smile of pity at her friend's stupidity. 'Why, you have read his letter, haven't you ? You've seen him.'

'But supposing he's not an honourable man ?'

'*He!* ... Not an honourable man ? If you only knew !' exclaimed Natasha.

'If he is an honourable man he should either declare his intentions or give up seeing you; and if you won't tell him, I will. I'll write to him. I'll tell papa!' said Sonya resolutely.

'But I can't live without him!' cried Natasha.

'Natasha, I don't understand you. And what are you saying? Think of your father, of Nicolas.'

'I don't want anyone, I love no one but him. How dare you say he's dishonourable? Don't you know that I love him?' screamed Natasha. 'Sonya, go away! I don't want to quarrel with you; go away, for God's sake, go! You see how wretched I am,' Natasha cried angrily, in a voice of repressed irritation and despair. Sonya burst into sobs and ran from the room.

Natasha went to the table and without a moment's reflection wrote the answer to Princess Maria which she had been unable to write all the morning. In her letter she briefly informed Princess Maria that all their misunderstandings were at an end; that availing herself of the magnanimity of Prince Andrei, who when he went abroad had given her her freedom, she begged Princess Maria to forget everything and forgive her if she had been at fault in any way; but that she could not be his wife. At that moment this all seemed so easy, simple and clear to Natasha.

*

The Rostovs were to return to the country on Friday, but on Wednesday the count departed with the prospective purchaser to his estate near Moscow.

On the day the count went out of town Sonya and Natasha were invited to a big dinner-party at the Karagins', whither they were chaperoned by Maria Dmitrievna. At that party Natasha again met Anatole, and Sonya noticed that she said something to him, trying not to be overheard, and that all through dinner she was more worked up than ever. When they got home Natasha was the first to embark on the subject Sonya was waiting for.

'There, Sonya, you said all sorts of silly things about him,' Natasha began in a meek voice – the voice in which children speak when they want to be praised for being good. 'I have had it all out with him today.'

'Well, what happened? What did he say, then? Natasha, how glad I am you're not angry with me. Tell me everything. What did he say?'

Natasha pondered.

'Oh, Sonya, if you knew him as I do! He said. ... He asked me what promise I had given Bolkonsky. He was so glad I was free to refuse him.'

Sonya sighed miserably.

'But you haven't refused Bolkonsky, have you?' she said.

'Perhaps I have! Maybe all is over between me and Bolkonsky! Why do you have such hard thoughts of me?'

'I don't think anything, only I don't understand this. ...'

'Wait a little while, Sonya, you'll understand everything. You'll see the sort of man he is! Don't think hard thoughts of me, or of him either.'

'I don't think hard thoughts of anyone: I love and am sorry for everybody. But what am I to do?'

Sonya would not let herself be won over by the affectionate tone Natasha used with her. The more tender and ingratiating grew Natasha's face, the more serious and stern was Sonya's expression.

'Natasha,' said she, 'you asked me not to speak to you of all this, and I haven't, but now you yourself have begun. Natasha, I don't trust him. Why this secrecy?'

'There you go again!' interrupted Natasha.

'Natasha, I am afraid for you!'

'Afraid of what?'

'I am afraid you are rushing to your ruin,' declared Sonya resolutely, herself horrified at what she had said.

A spiteful look showed on Natasha's face again.

'Then I'll go to my ruin, so I will, and the sooner the better! It's not your business! It won't be you, but I, who'll suffer. Leave me alone, leave me alone! I hate you!'

'Natasha!' moaned Sonya, aghast.

'I hate you, I hate you! You're my enemy for ever!' And Natasha ran out of the room.

Natasha did not speak to Sonya again, and avoided her. With the same agitated expression of astonishment and guilt she wandered about the house, trying one occupation after another and instantly abandoning them.

Hard as it was for Sonya, she kept watch on her friend and never let her out of her sight.

The day before the count was to return, Sonya noticed that Natasha sat by the drawing-room window all the morning, as if expecting something, and that she made a sign to an officer who drove past, whom Sonya took to be Anatole.

Sonya began watching her friend still more attentively, and observed that at dinner and throughout the evening Natasha was in a strange and unnatural state, quite unlike herself. She answered questions at random, began sentences and did not finish them, and laughed at everything.

After they had drunk tea Sonya noticed a housemaid at Natasha's door timidly waiting for her to pass. She let the girl go in, and then listening at the door learned that another letter had been delivered. And all at once it became clear to Sonya that Natasha had some dreadful plan on foot for that evening. Sonya knocked at the door. Natasha would not let her in.

'She is going to run away with him!' thought Sonya. 'She is capable of anything. There was something particularly piteous and determined in her face today. And she cried when she said good-bye to papa,' Sonya remembered. 'Yes, that's it, she means to elope with him – but what am I to do?' she wondered, recalling all the incidents that so clearly betokened some terrible intention on Natasha's part. 'The count is away. What am I to do? Write to Kuragin, demanding an explanation? But who is to make him answer me? Write to Pierre, as Prince Andrei asked me to in case of trouble? ... But perhaps she really has already refused Bolkonsky – she sent a letter to Princess Maria yesterday. And Uncle is not here!'

To tell Maria Dmitrievna, who had such trust in Natasha, seemed to Sonya a fearful step to take.

'But one way or another,' thought Sonya as she stood in the dark corridor, 'now or never the time has come for me to show that I am mindful of the family's goodness to me and that I love Nicolas. Yes, if I have to stay awake for three nights running I'll not leave this passage and will hold her back by force, and not let the family be disgraced,' she said to herself.

16

ANATOLE had lately moved to Dolohov's house. The plan for abducting Natasha had been suggested and arranged by Dolohov a few days before, and on the day that Sonya, after listening at Natasha's door, resolved to safeguard her, it was to have been put into execution. Natasha had promised to come out to Kuragin at the back porch at ten o'clock in the evening. Kuragin was to get her into a troika he would have waiting, and drive with her forty miles to the village of Kamenka, where an unfrocked priest was prepared to perform a marriage ceremony over them. At Kamenka a relay of horses was to be in readiness which would take them as far as the Warsaw high road, and from there they would hasten abroad by means of post-horses.

Anatole had a passport and an order for post-horses, ten thousand roubles borrowed from his sister and another ten thousand raised with Dolohov's assistance.

The two witnesses for the mock marriage – Hvostikov, a retired petty official whom Dolohov made use of in his gambling transactions, and Makarin, once a hussar, a weak, good-natured fellow who had an unbounded affection for Kuragin – were sitting in Dolohov's front room taking tea.

In his large study, the walls of which were hung to the ceiling with Persian rugs, bearskins and weapons, sat Dolohov in a travelling tunic and high boots in front of an open bureau on which lay an abacus and some bundles of paper money. Anatole, with uniform unbuttoned, was walking to and fro, from the room where the witnesses were sitting through the study into a room behind, where his French valet and other servants were packing the last of his things. Dolohov was counting the bank-notes and jotting down various amounts.

'Well,' he said, 'Hvostikov must have a couple of thousand.'

'Give it him then,' said Anatole.

'Makarka –' (their name for Makarin) 'now he would go through fire and water for you for nothing. So here are our accounts all settled,' said Dolohov, showing him the memorandum. 'Is that right?'

'Yes, of course,' answered Anatole, evidently not attending to Dolohov and looking into space with a smile that did not leave his face.

Dolohov banged down the lid of his desk, and turned to Kuragin, smiling sardonically.

'But see here, now – you'd really better drop the whole business. There's still time!'

'Fool!' retorted Anatole. 'Don't talk rubbish! If you only knew… the devil only knows what!'

'No, really, throw it all up,' urged Dolohov. 'I'm speaking in earnest. It's no joking matter, this plot of yours.'

'What, teasing again? Go to the devil with you! Eh? …' said

688

Anatole, frowning. 'Really, I'm in no humour for your stupid jokes.'
And he left the room.

Dolohov smiled a contemptuous, supercilious smile when Anatole had gone.

'Wait now,' he called after Anatole. 'I'm not jesting, I'm talking sense. Come here, come here!'

Anatole returned and looked at Dolohov, trying to concentrate his attention and evidently submitting to him against his will.

'Listen to me. I'm speaking for the last time. Why should I joke? Have I ever done anything to thwart you? Who is it made all the arrangements for you? Who found the priest and got the passport? Who raised the money? I did.'

'Well, and I am very much obliged to you. Do you suppose I am not grateful?' Anatole sighed and embraced Dolohov.

'I have been helping you, but all the same I must tell you the truth: this is a dangerous game and, if you think about it, a stupid one. You carry her off – well and good. But do you imagine they'll let it stop at that? It will come out that you are already married. Why, they'll have you up on a criminal charge. ...'

'Oh, rubbish, rubbish!' ejaculated Anatole again, scowling. 'Haven't I explained to you again and again?' And Anatole, with the peculiar infatuation of the dull-witted for any deduction they have arrived at by their own reasoning, repeated the argument he had put to Dolohov a hundred times already. 'I have told you time after time – I see it like this: if this marriage turns out to be invalid,' he went on, crooking one finger, 'then it follows I have nothing to answer for. But if it is valid, no matter! Abroad no one will ever know anything about it. Isn't that so? So don't, don't, don't talk to me!'

'Seriously, you'd better drop it! You'll only get yourself into a mess. ...'

'Go to the devil!' cried Anatole and, clutching at his hair, left the room, but returned at once and sank into an arm-chair facing Dolohov, with his legs doubled up under him. 'It's the very devil! What? Feel how it beats!' He took Dolohov's hand and placed it on his heart. 'Ah, what an ankle, my dear fellow! What eyes! She's a goddess! What?'

Dolohov, with a cold smile and a gleam in his handsome, insolent eyes, looked at him, obviously disposed to get some more amusement out of him.

'Well, and when your money's gone, what then?'

'What then? Eh?' repeated Anatole, with genuine perplexity at the thought of the future. 'What then? I don't know what then. ... But what is the use of talking nonsense!' He glanced at his watch. 'It's time!'

Anatole went into the back room.

'Hurry up there! Dawdling about!' he shouted to the servants.

Dolohov put away the money, called a footman and, telling him to bring them something to eat and drink before the journey, went into the room where Hvostikov and Makarin were sitting.

Anatole lay on the sofa in the study, leaning on his elbow and smiling dreamily as he murmured softly to himself.

'Come and eat something. Here, have a drink!' Dolohov called from the next room.

'I don't want anything!' replied Anatole, continuing to smile.

'Come, Balaga is here.'

Anatole rose to his feet and went into the dining-room. Balaga was a famous troika-driver who had known Dolohov and Anatole some six years and had given them good service with his troikas. More than once when Anatole's regiment was stationed at Tver he had started out with him from Tver in the evening, set him down in Moscow before daybreak and driven him back again the next night. More than once he had enabled Dolohov to escape when pursued. More than once he had driven them about the town with gipsies and 'ladykins' as he called the *cocottes*. More than once in their service he had run over pedestrians and upset vehicles in the streets of Moscow, and always 'his gentlemen' as he called them had protected him from the consequences. He had ruined more than one horse in their service. They thrashed him now and again, and many a time they had made him drunk on champagne and madeira, which he loved; and he knew of more than one exploit of each of them which would long ago have condemned any ordinary man to Siberia. They often called Balaga into their orgies and made him drink and dance at the gipsies', and many a time thousands of roubles of their money had passed through his hands. In their service he risked his skin and his life twenty times a year, and wore out more horses than the money they gave him would ever pay for. But he was fond of them, liked driving at the mad pace of twelve miles an hour, liked upsetting a driver or running down a pedestrian, and flying full gallop through the Moscow streets.

He liked to hear those wild, tipsy shouts behind him, urging him on when it was impossible to go any faster. He liked giving a painful lash round the neck to some peasant who was already hurrying out of his way more dead than alive. 'Real gentlemen,' he thought them.

Anatole and Dolohov were fond of Balaga too, for his spirited driving and because he liked the things they liked. With other people Balaga haggled and bargained, charging twenty-five roubles for a couple of hours' excursion, and rarely went himself, generally sending one of his young men. But 'his gentlemen' he always took personally, and never demanded payment for the job. Only when he happened to know through the valets that there was cash in the house he would turn up of a morning two or three times a year, quite sober, and with a deep bow would ask them to help him out. The gentlemen always made him sit down.

'Please give me a helping hand, Fiodr Ivanich, sir,' or 'your Excellency,' he would say. 'I am right out of horses. Spare me what you can to go to the fair.'

And Anatole and Dolohov, when they were in funds, would let him have a thousand or two.

Balaga was a flaxen-haired, squat, snub-nosed peasant of around seven-and-twenty, with a red face and a particularly red, thick neck, little twinkling eyes and a small beard. Now he wore a fine dark-blue, silk-lined coat over a sheepskin.

He turned to the corner where the icons hung and crossed himself before going up to Dolohov and holding out a small black hand.

'Fiodr Ivanich – my respects!' said he, bowing.

'Good-day to you, my good fellow. Well, here he comes!'

'Good-day, your Excellency!' he said, again holding out his hand, this time to Anatole who was just entering.

'I say, Balaga,' exclaimed Anatole, clapping his hands on the man's shoulders, 'have you a soft spot for me or not, eh? Now's the time to do me a service. What horses have you come with, eh?'

'The ones your man ordered – your favourites,' replied Balaga.

'Now see here, Balaga! Drive all three to death, but get me there in three hours, understand?'

'If we kill them, how shall we get there?' said Balaga with a wink.

'None of your jokes now, or I'll smash your snout for you!' cried Anatole suddenly, his eyes glaring.

'Who's joking?' laughed the driver. 'As if I'd grudge my gentlemen anything! We'll drive as fast as ever the horses can gallop.'

'Ah!' grunted Anatole. 'Well, sit down.'

'Yes, sit down!' said Dolohov.

'I'll stand, Fiodr Ivanich.'

'Nonsense! Sit down! Have a drink,' said Anatole, and poured him out a large glass of madeira.

The driver's eyes lit up at the sight of the wine. After refusing it at first for manners' sake, he tossed it off and wiped his mouth with a red silk handkerchief which he took out of his cap.

'And when are we to start, your Excellency?'

'Let me see. ...' Anatole looked at his watch. 'We must set off at once. Mind now, Balaga! You'll get us there in time, eh?'

'That depends on our luck at the outset. If we get off well, why shouldn't we do it in time?' said Balaga. 'Didn't we get to Tver in seven hours once? I'll warrant you remember that, your Excellency!'

'Do you know, one Christmas I drove from Tver,' said Anatole, smiling at the recollection and turning to Makarin, who was gazing at him adoringly. 'Would you believe it, Makarka, we went so fast we could hardly breathe. We ran into a train of loaded sledges and jumped right over two of them. How's that, eh?'

'What horses those were!' Balaga took up the tale. 'I'd put a couple of young horses in the traces with the bay in the shafts,' he went on, turning to Dolohov, 'and just fancy, Fiodr Ivanich, those beasts galloped forty miles! There was no holding 'em. My hands were numb with the frost, and I flung down the reins. "Hold on, your Excellency!" thinks I, and I rolls over backward into the sledge and lays there sprawling. No need of driving 'em. Why, we couldn't hold 'em in till we reached the place. Those devils got us there in three hours! Only the near one died of it.'

17

ANATOLE left the room and returned a few minutes later wearing a fur coat girdled with a silver belt, and a sable cap jauntily set on one side and very becoming to his handsome face. Having glanced in the looking-glass and then standing before Dolohov in the same attitude he had assumed for the mirror, he took up a glass of wine.

'Well, Fiodr, good-bye, and thanks for everything – farewell!' said Anatole. 'Now, companions and friends ...' – he considered for a moment – '... of my youth ... farewell!' he said, turning to Makarin and the others.

Although they were all going with him, Anatole evidently wished to make something touching and solemn out of this address to his comrades. He spoke in a loud, deliberate voice, squaring his shoulders and swinging one leg.

'All of you take your glasses. You, too, Balaga. Well, comrades, friends of my youth, we have had jolly good times together, we've lived and had our fling, what? And now when shall we meet again? I am going abroad. We have had a good time together – so farewell, lads! Here's to our health! Hurrah! ...' he cried, draining his glass and flinging it on the floor.

'Here's to your good health!' said Balaga, who wiped his mouth with his handkerchief when he too had emptied his glass.

Makarin embraced Anatole with tears in his eyes.

'Alas, prince, how it grieves my heart to part from you,' he said.

'Come, let us be off!' cried Anatole.

Balaga was about to leave the room.

'No, stop!' said Anatole. 'Shut the door. We must sit down for a moment first. That's the way.'

They closed the door and all sat down.*

'Now, quick march, lads!' said Anatole, rising.

Joseph, his valet, handed him his sabretache and sabre, and they all went out into the vestibule.

'But the fur cloak – where is it?' asked Dolohov. 'Hey, Ignashka! Run in to Matriona Matveyevna and ask her for the sable cloak. I've heard what happens at elopements,' continued Dolohov with a wink. 'She's sure to come skipping out more dead than alive, wearing indoor things. Delay for an instant and there'll be tears and "dear papa" and "dear mamma", and next minute she's frozen and for going back again – but you wrap her up in the fur cloak right away and carry her to the sledge.'

The valet brought a woman's fox-lined pelisse.

'Fool, I told you the sable. Hey, Matriona, the sable!' he shouted, so that his voice rang out through the room.

A handsome, slim, pale-faced gipsy-girl with brilliant black eyes

---

* For the sake of the traditional Russian custom of pausing to reflect before setting out on a journey. – Tr.

and purple-black curls, wearing a red shawl, ran out with a sable mantle on her arm.

'Here, I don't grudge it – take it!' she said, visibly afraid of her master and regretful of the cloak.

Dolohov, making her no answer, took the cloak, threw it over Matriona and wrapped her up in it.

'That's the way,' said Dolohov. 'And then like this!' and he turned the collar up round her head, leaving only a small opening for her face. 'That's how to do it, see?' and he moved Anatole's head forward to meet the opening left by the collar, from which Matriona's flashing smile peeped out.

'Well, good-bye, Matriona,' said Anatole, kissing her. 'Ah me, my follies here are over. Remember me to Stioshka. There, good-bye! Good-bye, Matriona, wish me luck!'

'The good God now grant you great happiness, prince!' said Matriona with her gipsy accent.

Outside before the porch two troikas were standing, with two stalwart young drivers holding the horses. Balaga took his seat in the foremost, and holding his elbows high slowly and carefully arranged the reins in his hands. Anatole and Dolohov got in with him. Makarin, Hvostikov and the valet seated themselves in the other sledge.

'All ready?' asked Balaga. 'Off!' he shouted, twisting the reins round his hands, and the troika flew at breakneck speed down the Nikitsky boulevard.

'Grrrh! … Look out there! Hi! … Grrh!' yelled Balaga and the sturdy young fellow seated on the box. In Arbatsky square the troika knocked against a carriage: there was a cracking sound, shouts were heard, and the troika flew off along Arbat street.

After driving the length of Podnovinsky boulevard a couple of times, Balaga began to rein in, and turning back drew up at the crossing by Old Konyusheny street.

The smart young fellow on the box jumped down to hold the horses by their bridles, while Anatole and Dolohov strode along the pavement. When they reached the gate, Dolohov whistled. The whistle was answered, and a maidservant ran out.

'Come into the courtyard, or you'll be seen. She'll be here directly,' she said.

Dolohov stayed by the gate. Anatole followed the maid into the courtyard, turned the corner, and ran up into the porch.

He was met by Gavrilo, Maria Dmitrievna's gigantic footman.

'Kindly walk this way to the mistress,' said the footman in his deep bass, blocking all retreat.

'What mistress? And who are you?' asked Anatole in a breathless whisper.

'Kindly step in. My orders are to bring you in.'

'Kuragin! Come back!' shouted Dolohov. 'Treachery! Come back!'

Dolohov, at the little wicket-gate where he had waited, was struggling with the yard-porter who was trying to lock it and keep Anatole in. With a last desperate effort Dolohov shoved the porter aside, and grabbing Anatole by the arm as he came running back pulled him through the gate and made off with him to the troika.

18

MARIA DMITRIEVNA, coming upon Sonya weeping in the corridor, had forced her to confess everything. Intercepting Natasha's note to Anatole and reading it, she marched into Natasha's room with the note in her hand.

'You shameless hussy!' she said to her. 'I won't hear a word!'

Pushing back Natasha, who looked at her with amazed but tearless eyes, she locked her in her room, and having given orders to the yard-porter to admit the persons who would be coming that evening but not to let them out again, and having instructed the footman to show these persons up to her, she seated herself in the drawing-room to await the abductors.

When Gavrilo came to inform her that the persons who had come had run away again, she rose frowning, and, with her hands clasped behind her back, for a long while paced to and fro through the rooms, pondering what she should do. Towards midnight she went to Natasha's room, fingering the key in her pocket. Sonya was sitting sobbing in the corridor.

'Maria Dmitrievna, for God's sake let me in to her!' she pleaded.

Making no reply, Maria Dmitrievna unlocked the door and went in.

'Disgusting! Abominable! ... In my house. ... Shameless wench! Only I'm sorry for her father!' thought she, trying to restrain her wrath. 'Hard as it may be, I'll tell them all to hold their tongues, and keep it from the count.'

Maria Dmitrievna walked into the room with resolute steps. Natasha was lying on the sofa, her head hidden in her hands, and she did not stir. She was lying in the same position in which Maria Dmitrievna had left her.

'Pretty conduct, pretty conduct, indeed!' exclaimed Maria Dmitrievna. 'Making assignations with lovers in my house! It's no use dissembling: you listen when I speak to you!' And Maria Dmitrievna shook her by the arm. 'Listen when I speak. You've disgraced yourself like any common hussy. I don't know what I wouldn't do to you, but I feel for your father, so I will keep it quiet.'

Natasha did not change her position, but her whole body began to heave with noiseless, convulsive sobs which choked her. Maria Dmitrievna glanced round at Sonya and sat down on the edge of the sofa beside Natasha.

'It's lucky for him he escaped; but I'll catch up with him!' she said in her rough voice. 'Do you hear what I say?'

She put her large hand under Natasha's face and turned it towards her. Both Maria Dmitrievna and Sonya were startled when they saw how Natasha looked. Her eyes were dry and glittering, her lips tightly compressed, her cheeks sunken.

'Let me be. ... What do I care? ... I shall die!' she muttered, wrenching herself free from Maria Dmitrievna's grasp and falling back into her former position.

'Natalie!' said Maria Dmitrievna. 'I wish for your good. Lie still, stay like that then, I won't touch you. But listen ... I shan't tell you how wrongly you have acted. You know that yourself. But when your father comes back tomorrow – what am I to say to him? Eh?'

Again Natasha's body shook with sobs.

'Suppose he hears of it, and your brother, and your betrothed?'

'I have no betrothed. I have refused him!' cried Natasha.

'That makes no difference,' pursued Maria Dmitrievna. 'If they hear of this, will they let it pass? There's your father, I know him ... if he challenges him to a duel, will that be all right? Eh?'

'Oh, leave me alone! Why did you have to spoil everything? Why? Why? Who asked you to interfere?' screamed Natasha, raising herself on the sofa and glaring spitefully at Maria Dmitrievna.

'But what was it you wanted?' cried Maria Dmitrievna, losing patience again. 'You weren't kept under lock and key, were you?

Who hindered him from coming to the house? Why carry you off like some gipsy singing-girl? ... And if he had carried you off – do you suppose they wouldn't have found him? Your father, or your brother, or your betrothed? He's a scoundrel, a knave – that's a fact!'

'He's better than any of you!' shrieked Natasha, sitting up. 'If you hadn't meddled. ... O my God, why has it come to this? What does it mean? Sonya, how could you? Go away!'

And she burst into a passion of tears, sobbing with the despairing vehemence of those who feel that they are the instruments of their own misery. Maria Dmitrievna was about to speak again, but Natasha cried out:

'Go away! Go away! You all hate and despise me!' And she flung herself back on the sofa.

Maria Dmitrievna continued for some time to admonish her, insisting that it must all be kept from the count and assuring her that nobody would know anything about it if only Natasha herself would undertake to forget it all and not let it be seen that anything had happened. Natasha did not answer. She ceased to sob, but grew cold and was seized with a fit of shivering. Maria Dmitrievna put a pillow under her head, covered her with two quilts, and herself fetched some lime-flower water, but Natasha had nothing to say to her.

'Well, let her sleep,' said Maria Dmitrievna, as she went out of the room, supposing Natasha to be asleep.

But Natasha was not asleep: her fixed, wide-open eyes stared straight before her out of her pale face. All that night she did not sleep or weep, and did not speak to Sonya who got up and went to her several times.

On the following day Count Rostov returned from his estate near Moscow, in time for lunch as he had promised. He was in capital spirits. The purchaser and he were coming to terms very nicely and there was nothing to keep him in Moscow any longer, away from the countess whom he missed. Maria Dmitrievna met him and told him that Natasha had been very unwell the day before and they had sent for the doctor, but that now she was better. Natasha did not leave her room that morning. With compressed, parched lips and dry, staring eyes she sat at the window, uneasily watching the people who drove past, and hurriedly glancing round at anyone who entered the room. She was obviously expecting news of him – expecting that he would either come himself or write to her.

697

When the count went in to see her she turned round nervously at the sound of a man's footstep, and then her face resumed its cold, almost vindictive expression. She did not even get up to greet him.

'What is it, my angel? Are you ill?' asked the count.

Natasha was silent for a moment.

'Yes, ill,' she answered.

To the count's anxious inquiries as to why she was so dejected and whether anything had happened with her betrothed she protested that it was all right and begged him not to worry. Maria Dmitrievna confirmed Natasha's assurances that nothing had befallen. From the pretended illness, from his daughter's distress and the troubled faces of Sonya and Maria Dmitrievna, the count saw clearly that something had gone wrong during his absence; but it was so terrible for him to imagine anything discreditable occurring in connexion with his beloved daughter, and he so prized his own cheerful tranquillity, that he avoided asking questions and did his best to persuade himself that there was nothing very much out of the way, and his only regret was that her indisposition would delay their return to the country.

19

FROM the day of his wife's arrival in Moscow Pierre had been intending to go away somewhere, so as not to be with her. Then, soon after the Rostovs came to the capital, the impression made upon him by Natasha hastened the carrying out of his intention. He went to Tver to see Bazdeyev's widow, who some time since had promised him her deceased husband's papers.

On his return to Moscow Pierre was handed a letter from Maria Dmitrievna asking him to come and see her on a matter of great importance concerning Andrei Bolkonsky and his betrothed. Pierre had been avoiding Natasha. It seemed to him that his feeling for her was stronger than a married man's should be for his friend's betrothed. And some fate was continually throwing them together.

'What can have happened? And what do they want with me?' he wondered as he dressed to go to Maria Dmitrievna's. 'If only Prince Andrei would hurry up and come home and marry her!' thought he on his way to the house.

On the Tverskoy boulevard someone hailed him.

'Pierre? Been back long?' called a familiar voice. Pierre raised his head. In a sledge drawn by a pair of grey trotting-horses that were bespattering the splashboard with snow Anatole and his constant companion Makarin dashed by. Anatole was sitting bolt upright in the classic pose of the stylish army officer, the lower part of his face muffled in a beaver collar and his head bent a little forward. His face was fresh and rosy, his white-plumed hat was set jauntily on one side, displaying his curled and pomaded hair besprinkled with powdery snow.

'Yes, there goes a true sage,' said Pierre to himself. 'He sees nothing beyond the enjoyment of the moment. Nothing worries him and so he is always cheerful, satisfied and serene. What wouldn't I give to be like him!' he thought enviously.

In Maria Dmitrievna's ante-room the footman who helped him off with his fur coat told him that the mistress asked him to come to her in her bedroom.

Opening the ballroom door Pierre caught sight of Natasha sitting at the window, looking pale, thin and bad-tempered. She glanced round at him, frowned and with an expression of frigid dignity walked out of the room.

'What has happened?' asked Pierre, going on to Maria Dmitrievna.

'Fine doings!' answered Maria Dmitrievna. 'Fifty-eight years have I lived in this world and never have I witnessed anything so disgraceful!'

And having exacted from Pierre his word of honour not to repeat a syllable of what he should hear from her, Maria Dmitrievna informed him that Natasha had broken her engagement with Prince Andrei without the knowledge of her parents; that the cause of her doing so was Anatole Kuragin into whose society Pierre's wife had thrown her, and with whom Natasha had attempted to elope during her father's absence, in order to be secretly married.

Pierre, with hunched shoulders, listened open-mouthed to what Maria Dmitrievna was saying, hardly able to believe his ears. That Prince Andrei's dearly-loved betrothed – that the hitherto charming Natasha Rostov should throw over Bolkonsky for that fool Anatole, who was already married (Pierre was in the secret of the marriage), and should be so enamoured of him as to agree to run away with him, was more than Pierre could comprehend or imagine.

He could not reconcile the agreeable impression he had of Natasha, whom he had known since her childhood, with this new picture of baseness, folly and cruelty. He thought of his wife. 'They are all alike,' he said to himself, reflecting that he was not the only man whose unhappy fate it was to be tied to a worthless woman. But at the same time he could have wept for Prince Andrei and his wounded pride. And the more he grieved for his friend, the deeper was the contempt and even disgust he felt for that Natasha who had just passed him with such icy dignity in the ballroom. He could not know that Natasha's soul was overflowing with despair, shame and humiliation, and that she was not to blame if her face happened to express cold dignity and severity.

'Married?' exclaimed Pierre, catching at Maria Dmitrievna's last words. 'He could not marry her: he already has a wife.'

'Worse and worse!' ejaculated Maria Dmitrievna. 'A nice youth! What a scoundrel! And there she sits waiting for him. These two days she's been expecting him. That at least must stop: we must tell her.'

When she had learned from Pierre the details of Anatole's marriage, and poured out the vials of her wrath against Anatole in abusive words, Maria Dmitrievna explained to Pierre why she had sent for him. She was afraid that the count or Bolkonsky, who might arrive at any moment, might hear of the affair (though she hoped to conceal it from them), and challenge Anatole to a duel. She therefore begged Pierre to tell his brother-in-law in her name to leave Moscow and never dare to let her set eyes on him again. Pierre – only now realizing the risk to the old count, Nikolai and Prince Andrei – promised to do as she desired. After briefly and precisely expounding to him her wishes, she let him go to the drawing-room.

'Mind, the count knows nothing. Behave as if you knew nothing either,' she said. 'And I will go and tell her it's no use expecting him! And do stay to dinner if you care to,' she called after Pierre.

Pierre met the old count, who seemed nervous and upset. That morning Natasha had told him that she had broken off her engagement to Bolkonsky.

'Trouble, trouble, *mon cher*!' he said to Pierre. 'Nothing but trouble with these girls away from their mother! I am only sorry I ever came. I'll be plain with you. Have you heard that she has broken off her engagement without consulting any of us? True, the engagement never was much to my liking. Of course he's a fine man and all that, but there you are – with his father against it they wouldn't have been happy, and Natasha will never want for suitors. Still, it has been going on for so long – and then to take such a step without a word to her father or mother! And now she's ill, and God knows what it is! Yes, it's a bad thing, count, a bad thing for girls to be away from their mother. ...'

Pierre saw that the count was deeply disturbed, and he tried to bring the conversation round to some other subject, but the count kept returning to his troubles.

Sonya entered the drawing-room, looking agitated.

'Natasha is not very well: she's in her room and would like to see you. Maria Dmitrievna is with her and she too asks you to come.'

'Yes, of course you are a great friend of Bolkonsky's, no doubt she wants to give you some message for him,' said the count. 'Oh dear, oh dear, how happy it all was before this!' And clutching the spare grey locks on his temples the count left the room.

Maria Dmitrievna had told Natasha that Anatole was married. Natasha had refused to believe her, and demanded confirmation from Pierre himself. Sonya told Pierre this as she led him along the corridor to Natasha's room.

Natasha, pale and unbending, was sitting beside Maria Dmitrievna, and the moment Pierre appeared at the door she met him with feverishly glittering, imploring eyes. She did not smile or nod. She simply looked hard at him, her look asking only one thing: was he a friend, or, like the others, an enemy in regard to Anatole? Pierre as himself obviously did not exist for her.

'He knows all about it,' said Maria Dmitrievna, indicating Pierre and addressing Natasha. 'Let him tell you whether I was speaking the truth.'

Natasha glanced from one to the other as a hunted and wounded animal watches the approaching dogs and sportsmen.

'Natalia Ilyinichna,' Pierre began, dropping his eyes with a feeling of pity for her and loathing for the thing he had to do, 'whether it is true or not should make no difference to you . ...'

'Then it is not true that he is married?'

'Yes, it is true.'

'Has he been married long?' she asked. 'On your word of honour?'
Pierre gave his word of honour.

'Is he still here?' she asked quickly.

'Yes, I have just seen him.'

She was obviously incapable of speaking, and made a sign with her hands that they should leave her alone.

20

PIERRE did not stay for dinner, but left the room and went away at once. He drove about the town in search of Anatole, the mere thought of whom now made his blood boil and his heart beat till he could hardly breathe. He was not on the ice-hills, nor at the gipsies', nor at Comoneno's. Pierre drove to the club. At the club everything was going on as usual: the members who had dropped in for dinner were sitting about in groups. They greeted Pierre, and talked of the news of the town. The footman, after welcoming Pierre, told him, knowing his friends and his habits, that there was a place left for him in the small dining-room, that Prince Mihail Zakarich was in the library, but Pavel Timofeich had not arrived yet. One of Pierre's acquaintances in the middle of a remark about the weather asked him if he had heard of Kuragin's abduction of the young Countess Rostov which was talked of in the town, and was it true? Pierre laughed and said it was nonsense, for he had just come from the Rostovs'. He asked everyone about Anatole. One man told him he had not come in yet, another that he would be there for dinner. It gave Pierre an odd sensation to see this calmly indifferent crowd of people who had not the slightest inkling of what was passing in his mind. He walked about the rooms, waiting till everyone had arrived, and then, as Anatole had not turned up, did not stay for dinner but drove home.

Anatole, for whom Pierre was looking, dined that day with Dolohov, consulting him as to ways and means of achieving the exploit that had miscarried. It seemed to him essential to see Natasha. In the evening he went to his sister's to discuss with her how to arrange a meeting. When Pierre returned home after vainly ransacking all Moscow his valet told him that Prince Anatole was with the countess. The countess's drawing-room was full of guests.

Pierre, without greeting his wife whom he had not seen since his return to Moscow – at that moment she seemed to him more utterly detestable than ever – entered the drawing-room and catching sight of Anatole walked straight up to him.

'Ah, Pierre,' said the countess, approaching her husband. 'You don't know what a plight our poor Anatole is in. ...'

She stopped short, seeing in the hanging head, in her husband's face, in his flashing eyes and resolute tread, the terrible indications of that fury and might which she knew and had herself experienced after his duel with Dolohov.

'Wherever you are, depravity and evil are to be found,' said Pierre to his wife. 'Anatole, come with me, I want a word with you,' he added in French.

Anatole glanced round at his sister and got up obediently, prepared to follow Pierre.

Pierre took him by the arm, pulled him to him and was leading him out of the room.

'If you dare in my drawing-room ...' muttered Hélène in a whisper, but Pierre walked out of the room without replying.

Anatole followed him with his usual jaunty swagger. But his face betrayed uneasiness.

Reaching his study, Pierre shut the door, and addressed Anatole without looking at him.

'You promised Countess Rostov to marry her? You were about to elope with her? Is that so?'

'*Mon cher*,' returned Anatole (the whole conversation proceeded in French), 'I consider myself under no obligation to answer questions put to me in that tone.'

Pierre's face, already pale, became distorted with fury. With his great hand he seized Anatole by the collar of his uniform, and shook him from side to side till Anatole's features registered a sufficient degree of terror.

'When I tell you that I *want a word with you* ...' insisted Pierre.

'Well, what? This is ridiculous, what?' said Anatole, fingering a button of his collar that had been wrenched off together with a bit of the cloth.

'You are a scoundrel and a blackguard, and I don't know what restrains me from the pleasure of cracking your skull with this,' said Pierre, expressing himself so artificially because he was speaking French. He took up a heavy paper-weight and lifted it threateningly, but at once hurriedly put it back in its place.

'Did you promise to marry her?'

'I – I – I didn't think ... in fact I never promised because ...'

Pierre interrupted him.

'Have you any letters of hers? Have you any letters?' he demanded, advancing upon Anatole.

Anatole cast him one look and immediately thrust a hand into his pocket and drew out his pocket-book.

Pierre took the letter Anatole handed him, and pushing aside a table that stood in his way plumped down on the sofa.

'I shan't do anything to you, don't be afraid,' said Pierre in response to Anatole's gesture of alarm. 'The letters – that's one,' he continued, as if repeating a lesson to himself. 'Two – ' he went on after a moment's silence, getting to his feet again and beginning to pace up and down the room, 'tomorrow you leave Moscow.'

'But how can I? ...'

'Three – ' pursued Pierre, not heeding him, 'you are never to breathe a word of what has passed between you and Countess Rostov. I know I can't prevent your doing so, but if you have a spark of conscience ...' Pierre took several turns about the room in silence. Anatole sat at the table, scowling and biting his lips.

'You must surely understand that besides your pleasure there is such a thing as other people's happiness, other people's peace of mind; that you are ruining a whole life for the sake of a little amusement for yourself. Amuse yourself with women like my wife – with such you are within your rights: they know what it is you want of them. They are armed against you by a similar experience of depravity; but to promise an innocent girl to marry her ... to deceive, to kidnap. ... Don't you see that it's as low-down as hitting an old man or a child! ...'

Pierre paused and glanced at Anatole, with a look of inquiry now in place of anger.

'I don't know about that, what?' said Anatole, growing bolder in proportion as Pierre mastered his wrath. 'I don't know about that, and don't want to,' he said, not looking at Pierre and with a slight tremor of his lower jaw, 'but you have used words to me – talked about being low-down, and so on – which as a man of honour I can't allow from anyone.'

Pierre stared at him in amazement, unable to understand what he was after.

'Though it was only tête-à-tête,' Anatole went on, 'still I can't. ...'

'Is it satisfaction you want?' said Pierre ironically.

'At least you can retract what you said, what? If you want me to do as you wish, what?'

'I will! I'll take it back!' exclaimed Pierre. 'And I beg you to forgive me.' Pierre involuntarily glanced at the torn button. 'And if you require money for your journey ...'

Anatole smiled. That base, cringing smile which Pierre knew so well in his wife revolted him.

'Oh you vile, heartless breed!' he exclaimed, and walked out of the room.

Next day Anatole left for Petersburg.

21

PIERRE drove to Maria Dmitrievna's to report to her that her wishes had been carried out and Kuragin banished from Moscow. The whole house was in a state of alarm and commotion. Natasha was very ill, having, as Maria Dmitrievna told him in confidence, poisoned herself the night she had heard that Anatole was married, with some ratsbane procured by stealth. After swallowing a little she had been so frightened that she woke Sonya and confessed what she had done. The necessary antidotes had been administered in time and she was now out of danger, though still so weak that there could be no question of moving her to the country, and the countess had been sent for. Pierre saw the distracted count and Sonya, red and swollen with weeping, but he was not allowed to see Natasha.

Pierre dined at the club that day and heard on every side gossip about the attempted abduction of the young Countess Rostov. He strenuously denied these rumours, assuring everyone that nothing had happened except that his brother-in-law had proposed to her and been refused. It seemed to Pierre that it was his bounden duty to conceal the whole affair and re-establish Natasha's reputation.

He was awaiting Prince Andrei's return with dread, and called daily on the old prince for news of him.

Prince Bolkonsky had heard all the stories flying about the town from Mademoiselle Bourienne, and had read the note to Princess Maria in which Natasha had broken off her engagement. He seemed in better spirits than usual and looked forward with impatience to his son's home-coming.

A few days after Anatole's departure Pierre received a note from

Prince Andrei announcing his arrival and asking him to come to see him.

Directly Prince Andrei reached Moscow his father had handed him Natasha's note to Princess Maria breaking off her engagement (Mademoiselle Bourienne had purloined it from Princess Maria and given it to the old prince), and from his father's lips Prince Andrei heard the story of Natasha's elopement, with various supplementary details.

Prince Andrei arrived in the evening and Pierre came to see him the following morning. Pierre expected to find Prince Andrei almost in the same state as Natasha, and was therefore surprised on entering the drawing-room to hear him in the study loudly and eagerly discussing some intrigue going on in Petersburg. The old prince's voice and another interrupted him from time to time. Princess Maria came out to meet Pierre. She sighed, turning her eyes towards the door of the room where her brother was, obviously wanting to make a show of sympathy with his sorrow; but Pierre saw by her face that she was both glad at what had happened and at the way her brother had taken the news of Natasha's faithlessness.

'He says he expected it,' she remarked. 'I know his pride will not let him express his feelings, but still he has borne up under it better, far better, than I expected. Evidently it had to be. ...'

'But is everything really all over between them?' asked Pierre.

Princess Maria looked at him in astonishment. She could not understand how anyone could even ask such a question. Pierre went into the study. Prince Andrei, greatly altered and apparently restored to health, but with a new and perpendicular line between his brows, was standing in civilian clothes facing his father and Prince Meshchersky, arguing hotly and making forceful gestures.

They were talking about Speransky, news of whose sudden banishment and alleged treachery had just reached Moscow.

'Now he is being criticized and accused by the very men who a month ago were lauding him to the skies,' Prince Andrei was saying, 'and were incapable of appreciating his aims. It is very easy to find fault with a man when he's out of favour, and throw upon him the blame for everybody else's mistakes; but I maintain that if anything good has been accomplished in the present reign it has been done by him – by him alone. ...' He caught sight of Pierre and paused. His face quivered and immediately assumed a malicious expression. 'And posterity will vindicate him,' he wound up, and at once turned to Pierre.

'Well, how are you? Still getting stouter?' he said in an animated tone, but the newly-formed furrow on his forehead deepened. 'Yes, I am very well,' he replied in answer to Pierre's inquiry, and smiled. It was clear to Pierre that his smile meant: 'Yes, I am well, but my health is of no use to anyone now.'

After a few words to Pierre about the awful roads from the Polish frontier, about people he had met in Switzerland who knew Pierre, and about Monsieur Dessalles, whom he had brought back from abroad to be his son's tutor, Prince Andrei warmly took part again in the conversation about Speransky which was still going on between the two elderly men.

'If there had been any treason, or if there were any proofs of secret relations with Napoleon, they would have been made public,' he said, speaking hurriedly and excitedly. 'I personally don't like and never have liked Speransky, but I do like justice!'

Pierre was now beginning to realize that his friend was labouring under that necessity, with which he himself was only too familiar, of getting thoroughly worked up and argumentative over some irrelevant topic for the purpose of stifling thoughts too painful and too near the heart to be endured.

When Prince Meshchersky had gone, Prince Andrei took Pierre's arm and invited him into the room that had been prepared for him. A bed had been made up there, and some open portmanteaux and trunks stood about. Prince Andrei went to one and took out a small casket, from which he drew a packet wrapped in paper. All this he did in silence and with speed. He stood up and cleared his throat. His face was gloomy and his lips set.

'Forgive me for troubling you. ...'

Pierre perceived that Prince Andrei was going to speak of Natasha, and his broad countenance expressed pity and sympathy. This expression on Pierre's face irritated Prince Andrei. He went on in a clear, resolute, disagreeable voice:

'I have received my dismissal from Countess Rostov, and reports have come to my ears that your brother-in-law has been seeking her hand, or something of the kind. Is that true?'

'Both true and untrue,' began Pierre; but Prince Andrei interrupted him.

'Here are her letters,' he said, 'and her portrait.' He took the packet from the table and handed it to Pierre.

'Give this to the countess ... if you happen to see her.'

'She is very ill,' said Pierre.

'Then she is here still?' inquired Prince Andrei. 'And Prince Kuragin?' he asked quickly.

'He left some time ago. She has been at death's door. ...'

'I am very sorry to hear of her illness,' said Prince Andrei with a disagreeable smile – a cold, spiteful smile like his father's.

'So Monsieur Kuragin has not honoured Countess Rostov with his hand?' said Andrei. He snorted several times.

'He could not have married her, for the reason that he is married already,' said Pierre.

Prince Andrei laughed unpleasantly, again reminding one of his father.

'And where is your brother-in-law now, if I may ask?' he said.

'He has gone to Peters. ... But I don't really know,' replied Pierre.

'Well, that's no matter,' said Prince Andrei. 'Tell Countess Rostov from me that she was and is perfectly free, and that I wish her all happiness.'

Pierre took the packet. Prince Andrei, who seemed to be considering whether he had said everything he wanted to say, or was waiting to see if Pierre would say anything, looked fixedly at him.

'Listen. You remember our discussion in Petersburg?' said Pierre. 'About ...'

'I remember,' returned Prince Andrei hastily. 'I said that a fallen woman should be forgiven, but I did not say I could forgive her. I can't.'

'But how can you compare ...?' said Pierre.

Prince Andrei cut him short. He cried harshly:

'Yes, ask her hand again, be magnanimous, and so on? ... Yes, that would be very noble, but I'm not equal to following where that gentleman has walked. If you wish to remain my friend never speak to me of that ... of all this business! Good-bye now. So you'll give her the packet?'

Pierre left the room, and went to the old prince and Princess Maria.

The old man seemed livelier than usual. Princess Maria was the same as always, but beneath her sympathy for her brother Pierre could see that she was delighted that the engagement had been broken off. Looking at them, Pierre realized what contempt and animosity they all felt for the Rostovs, and understood that it was hopeless in their presence even to mention the name of the girl who could give up Prince Andrei for anyone in the world.

At dinner the conversation turned on the war, of the imminence of which there could now be no doubt. Prince Andrei talked incessantly, arguing now with his father, now with the Swiss tutor Dessalles, and displaying an unnatural animation, the cause of which Pierre so well understood.

22

THAT same evening Pierre went to the Rostovs' to fulfil the commission entrusted to him. Natasha was in bed, the count at the club, and Pierre, after giving the letters to Sonya, went to Maria Dmitrievna, who was greatly interested to know how Prince Andrei had taken the news. Ten minutes later Sonya came to Maria Dmitrievna.

'Natasha insists on seeing Count Bezuhov,' said she.

'But how? Are we to take him up to her? Why, your room is all in a muddle,' protested Maria Dmitrievna.

'No, she is dressed and has come down to the drawing-room,' said Sonya.

Maria Dmitrievna could only shrug her shoulders.

'If only her mother would come! The girl has worried me to death! Now mind, don't go telling her everything,' she said to Pierre. 'One hasn't the heart to scold her, she is such a piteous object, poor thing!'

Natasha was standing in the middle of the drawing-room, looking much thinner, and with a pale set face (though not in the least overcome with shame as Pierre had expected). When he appeared in the doorway she hesitated, flustered and evidently undecided whether to go to meet him or wait for him to come to her.

Pierre hastened forward. He thought she would offer her hand as usual; but stepping near him she stopped, breathing hard, her arms hanging lifelessly, in exactly the same pose in which she used to stand in the middle of the ballroom to sing, but with an utterly different expression on her face.

'Count Bezuhov,' she began rapidly, 'Prince Bolkonsky was your friend – is your friend,' she corrected herself. (It seemed to her that everything was in the past, and now all was changed.) 'He once told me to turn to you if ...'

Pierre choked dumbly as he looked at her. Till then he had in his heart reproached her and tried to despise her, but now he felt so sorry for her that there was no room in him for reproach.

'He is here now: tell him ... to for ... forgive me!' She paused and her breath came still faster, but she shed no tears.

'Yes ... I will tell him,' murmured Pierre; 'but ...' He did not know what to say.

Natasha was evidently dismayed at the thought that might occur to Pierre.

'Of course I know all is over between us,' she said hurriedly. 'No, that can never be. I am only tortured by the wrong I have done him. Only tell him that I beg him to forgive, to forgive – forgive me for everything. ...' Her whole body trembled and she sat down on a chair.

A feeling of compassion such as he had never known before flooded Pierre's heart.

'I will tell him, I will tell him everything once more,' said Pierre. 'But ... I should like to know one thing. ...'

'Know what?' Natasha's eyes asked.

'I should like to know, did you love ...' Pierre did not know what to call Anatole, and flushed at the thought of him – 'did you love that vile man?'

'Don't call him vile!' said Natasha. 'But I – I don't know – I don't know at all. ...'

She began to cry again, and Pierre was more than ever overwhelmed with pity, tenderness and love. He felt the tears trickling under his spectacles and hoped they would not be noticed.

'We won't speak of it any more, my dear,' said Pierre, and it suddenly seemed so strange to Natasha to hear his affectionate, gentle, sympathetic tone.

'We won't speak of it, my dear – I'll tell him everything. But one thing I beg of you: look on me as your friend, and if you need help, advice, or simply to open your heart to someone – not now, but when your mind is clearer – think of me.' He took her hand and kissed it. 'I shall be happy if I am able. ...'

Pierre grew confused.

'Don't speak to me like that. I am not worthy of it!' cried Natasha, and she would have left the room but Pierre held her hand. He knew he had something more to say to her. But when he had spoken he was amazed at his own words.

'Hush, hush! You have your whole life before you,' he said to her.

'Before me? No! All is over for me,' she replied, in shame and self-abasement.

'All over?' he echoed. 'If I were not myself, but the handsomest, cleverest, best man in the world, and if I were free I would be on my knees this minute to beg for your hand and your love.'

For the first time for many days Natasha wept soft tears of gratitude, and giving Pierre one look she fled from the room.

Pierre, too, when she had gone almost ran into the ante-room, restraining the tears of tenderness and happiness that choked him, and without stopping to find the sleeves of his fur coat, flung it over his shoulders and got into his sledge.

'Where to now, your Excellency?' asked the coachman.

'Where to?' Pierre wondered. 'Where can I go now? Surely not to the club or to pay calls?' All men seemed to him so pitiful, such poor creatures in comparison with this feeling of tenderness and love in his heart – in comparison with that softened, grateful last look she had turned upon him through her tears.

'Home!' said Pierre, and despite the twenty-two degrees of frost he threw open the bearskin coat from his broad chest and joyously inhaled the air.

It was clear and frosty. Above the dirty ill-lit streets, above the black roofs, stretched the dark starry sky. Only as he gazed up at the heavens did Pierre cease to feel the humiliating pettiness of all earthly things compared with the heights to which his soul had just been raised. As he drove out on to Arbatsky square his eyes were met with a vast expanse of starry black sky. Almost in the centre of this sky, above the Prichistensky boulevard, surrounded and convoyed on every side by stars but distinguished from them all by its nearness to the earth, its white light and its long uplifted tail, shone the huge, brilliant comet of the year 1812 – the comet which was said to portend all manner of horrors and the end of the world. But that bright comet with its long luminous tail aroused no feeling of fear in Pierre's heart. On the contrary, with rapture and his eyes wet with tears, he contemplated the radiant star which, after travelling in its orbit with inconceivable velocity through infinite space, seemed suddenly – like an arrow piercing the earth – to remain fast in one chosen spot in the black firmament, vigorously tossing up its tail, shining and playing with its white light amid the countless other scintillating stars. It seemed to Pierre that this comet spoke in full harmony with all that filled his own softened and uplifted soul, now blossoming into a new life.

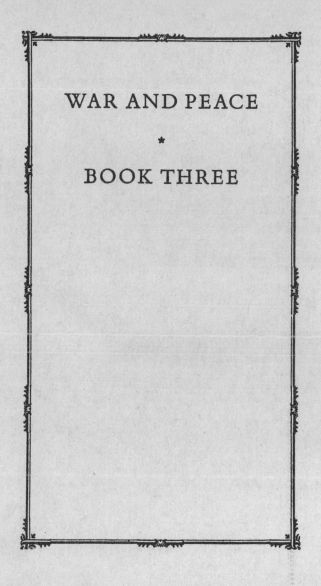

WAR AND PEACE

*

BOOK THREE

PART ONE

I

THE last months of the year 1811 saw the sovereigns of Western Europe beginning to reinforce their armies and concentrate their strength, and in 1812 these forces – millions of men, reckoning in those concerned in the transport and victualling of the army – moved eastwards towards the Russian frontiers, where the Russians, too, had been massing since 1811. On the 12th of June 1812 the forces of Western Europe crossed the frontiers of Russia, and war began: in other words, an event took place counter to all the laws of human reason and human nature. Millions of men perpetrated against one another such innumerable crimes, deceptions, treacheries, robberies, forgeries, issues of false monies, depredations, incendiarisms and murders as the annals of all the courts of justice in the world could not muster in the course of whole centuries, but which those who committed them did not at the time regard as crimes.

What brought about this extraordinary occurrence? What were its causes? The historians, with naïve assurance, tell us that behind this event lay the wrongs inflicted on the Duke of Oldenburg, the non-observance of the Continental System forbidding trade with England, the ambition of Napoleon, the firmness of Alexander, the mistakes of the diplomats, and so on.

Of course, if that were so it would only have been necessary for Metternich, Rumyantsev or Talleyrand, in the interval between a levée and an evening party, to have taken a little trouble and penned a more judicious diplomatic note; or Napoleon to have written to Alexander: '*Monsieur mon frère*, I consent to restore the duchy to the Duke of Oldenburg' – and there would have been no war.

We can understand that this was not the view taken at the time. We can understand how it naturally seemed to Napoleon that the war was caused by England's intrigues (as in fact he said on the island of St Helena). We can understand how to the English Parliament

Napoleon's ambition seemed to be the cause of the war; to the Duke of Oldenburg it was the outrage done to him; to the merchants the cause of the war was the Continental System which was ruining Europe. Generals and veterans of the army traced the cause of the war to the necessity of providing them with employment, while to the legitimists of the day it was the vital need for re-establishing *les bons principes*; and the diplomats set it down to the alliance between Russia and Austria in 1809 not having been concealed tactfully enough from Napoleon, and to the awkward wording of Memorandum No. 178. We can understand how these and an incalculable and endless number of other reasons – the number corresponding to the infinite variety of points of view – presented themselves to men of that day; but for us of posterity, contemplating the accomplished fact in all its magnitude, and seeking to fathom its simple and terrible meaning, these explanations must appear insufficient. To us it is incomprehensible that millions of Christian men killed and tortured each other either because Napoleon was ambitious or Alexander firm, or because England's policy was astute or the Duke of Oldenburg wronged. We cannot grasp the connexion between these circumstances and the actual fact of slaughter and violence: why because the Duke was wronged thousands of men from the other end of Europe slaughtered and pillaged the inhabitants of Smolensk and Moscow, and were slaughtered by them.

For us their descendants, who are not historians and are not carried away by the process of research, and so can look at the facts with common sense unobscured, a countless number of causes offer themselves. The deeper we delve in search of these causes the more of them do we discover; and each separate cause or whole series of causes appears to us equally valid in itself and equally unsound by its insignificance in comparison with the size of the event, and by its impuissance (without the co-operation of all the other coincident causes) to occasion the event. To us the willingness or unwillingness of this or that French corporal to serve a second term has as much weight as Napoleon's refusal to withdraw his troops beyond the Vistula and to restore the duchy of Oldenburg; for had the corporal refused to serve, and a second and a third and a thousand corporals and soldiers with him, Napoleon's army would have been so greatly reduced that the war could not have occurred.

If Napoleon had not taken offence at the demand that he should retire beyond the Vistula, and had not ordered his troops to advance, there would have been no war. But if all his sergeants had objected to serving in a second campaign, then also there could have been no war. Nor could there have been a war had there been no English intrigues and no Duke of Oldenburg, and had Alexander not felt insulted, and had there not been an autocratic government in Russia, or a Revolution in France and consequent dictatorship and Empire, or all the things that produced the French Revolution, and so on. Had any one of these causes been absent, nothing could have happened. And so all these causes – these myriads of causes – coincided to bring about what happened. And so there was no exclusive reason for that occurrence: the war came about because it was bound to come about. Millions of men, renouncing their human feelings and their common sense, had to march from west to east to slay their fellows, just as some centuries previously hordes of men had moved from east to west, slaying their fellows.

The deeds of Napoleon and Alexander, on whose fiat the whole question of war or no war apparently depended, were as little spontaneous and free as the actions of every common soldier drawn into the campaign by lot or by conscription. This could not be otherwise, for in order that the will of Napoleon and Alexander (the people on whom the whole decision appeared to rest) should be effected a combination of innumerable circumstances was essential, without any one of which the event could not have taken place. It was necessary that millions of men in whose hands the real power lay – the soldiers who fired the guns or transported provisions and cannon – should consent to carry out the will of those weak individuals, and should have been induced to do so by an infinite number of diverse and complex causes.

We are forced to fall back on fatalism to explain the irrational events of history (that is to say, events the intelligence of which we do not see). The more we strive to account for such events in history rationally, the more irrational and incomprehensible do they become to us.

Every man lives for himself, using his freedom to attain his personal aims, and feels with his whole being that he can at any moment perform or not perform this or that action; but, so soon as he has done it, that action accomplished at a certain moment in time becomes irrevocable and belongs to history, in which it has not a free but a predestined significance.

There are two sides to the life of every man: there is his individual existence which is free in proportion as his interests are abstract; and his elemental life as a unit in the human swarm, in which he must inevitably obey the laws laid down for him.

Man lives consciously for himself but unconsciously he serves as an instrument for the accomplishment of historical and social ends. A deed done is irrevocable, and that action of his coinciding in time with the actions of millions of other men assumes an historical significance. The higher a man stands in the social scale, the more connexions he has with others and the more power he has over them, the more conspicuous is the predestination and inevitability of every act he commits.

'The hearts of kings are in the hand of God.'

A king is the slave of history.

History, that is, the unconscious, universal, swarm-life of mankind, uses every moment of the life of kings for its own purposes.

*

Though Napoleon at that time, in 1812, was more convinced than ever that to shed or not to shed the blood of his peoples – *verser ou ne pas verser le sang de ses peuples,* as Alexander expressed it in his last letter to him – depended entirely on his will, he had never been more in the grip of those inevitable laws which compelled him, while to himself he seemed to be acting on his own volition, to perform for the world in general – for history – what was destined to be accomplished.

The people of the west moved eastwards to slay their fellow-men. And, by the law of coincidence of causes, thousands of minute causes fitted together and co-ordinated to produce that movement and that war; resentment at the non-observance of the Continental System, the Duke of Oldenburg's wrongs, the advance of troops into Prussia – a measure undertaken (as Napoleon thought) solely for the purpose of securing armed peace – and the French Emperor's passion for war, and the habit of fighting which had grown upon him, coinciding with the inclinations of his people, who were carried away by the grandiose scale of the preparations, and the expenditure on those preparations, and the necessity of recouping that expenditure. Then there was the intoxicating effect of the honours paid to the French Emperor at Dresden, the diplomatic negotiations which in the opinion of contemporaries were conducted with a genuine desire to achieve a peace, though they only inflamed the *amour propre* of both sides, and millions upon millions of other coincident causes that adapted themselves to the fated event.

Why does an apple fall when it is ripe? Is it brought down by the force of gravity? Is it because its stalk withers? Because it is dried by the sun, because it grows too heavy, or the wind shakes it, or because the boy standing under the tree wants to eat it?

None of these is the cause. They only make up the combination of conditions under which every living process of organic nature fulfils itself. And the botanist who finds that the apple falls because the cellular tissue decays, and so forth, is just as right and just as wrong as the child who stands under the tree and says the apple fell because he wanted to eat it and prayed for it to fall. In the same way the historian who declares that Napoleon went to Moscow because he wanted to, and perished because Alexander desired his destruction, will be just as right and wrong as the man who says that a mass weighing thousands of tons, tottering and undermined, fell in consequence of the last blow of the pickaxe wielded by the last navvy. In historical events great men – so-called – are but labels serving to give a name to the event, and like labels they have the least possible connexion with the event itself.

Every action of theirs, that seems to them an act of their own freewill, is in the historical sense not free at all but is bound up with the whole course of history and preordained from all eternity.

2

On the 29th of May Napoleon left Dresden, where he had spent three weeks surrounded by a Court that included princes, dukes, kings and even one emperor. Before his departure Napoleon lavished his favours on the princes, the kings and the emperor who had earned them, upbraided the kings and princes with whom he was not entirely satisfied, presented his own diamonds and pearls – those, that is, which he had taken from other kings – to the Empress of Austria, and having, as his historian tells us, tenderly embraced the Empress Marie Louise (who regarded herself as his consort though he had left another consort in Paris), he proceeded on his way, leaving her deeply distressed by the parting, which she seemed scarcely able to bear. Although the diplomats still firmly believed in the possibility of peace, and were zealously working to that end; although the Emperor Napoleon penned a letter to Alexander calling him *Monsieur mon frère* and sincerely assuring him that he had no wish for war and would always hold him in affection and esteem – yet he set off to join his army, and at every station gave fresh orders to accelerate the progress of his troops from west to east. He travelled in a closed coach drawn by six horses, accompanied by pages, aides-de-camp and a bodyguard, along the road through Posen, Thorn, Dantzig and Königsberg. At each of these towns thousands of people rushed to greet him with enthusiasm and trepidation.

The army was moving from west to east, and relays of six horses bore him in the same direction. On the 10th of June, coming up with the army, he spent the night in quarters prepared for him on the estate of a Polish count in the Wilkowiski forest.

The following day Napoleon drove on ahead of the army, reached the Niemen and, changing into Polish uniform, went to the river bank in order to select a place for the crossing.

When he saw the Cossacks posted on the opposite bank and the expanse of the steppes, in the midst of which lay the holy city of Moscow – *Moscou, la ville sainte* – capital of an empire, like the Scythian empire into which Alexander the Great had marched, Napoleon unexpectedly, and contrary alike to strategic as well as diplomatic considerations, ordered an immediate advance, and the next day his army began to cross the Niemen.

Early on the morning of the 12th of June he came out of his tent, which was pitched that day on the steep left bank of the Niemen, and looked through a field-glass at his troops pouring out of the Wilkowiski forest and flowing over the three bridges thrown across the river. The troops, knowing of the Emperor's presence, were on the lookout for him, and when they caught sight of a figure in a greatcoat and cocked hat standing apart from his suite in front of his tent on the hill they threw up their caps, shouting *'Vive l'Empereur!'* And rank after rank, never ending, they streamed out of the vast forest that had concealed them, and splitting up crossed the three bridges to the other side.

'Now we shall get on! Things warm up when he himself takes a hand! ... By Jove! ... There he is! ... *Vive l'Empereur!* So those are the steppes of Asia! Nasty country, all the same. Good-bye, Beauché!

720

I'll reserve the best palace in Moscow for you! Good-bye! Good luck! . . . Did you see the Emperor? *Vive l'Empereur!* . . . *pereur!* If they make me governor of the Indies, Gérard, I'll make you minister of Kashmir – that's a bargain. Hurrah for the Emperor! Hurrah! hurrah! hurrah! Those rascally Cossacks – see how they run! *Vive l'Empereur!* There he is! See him? I've seen him twice, plain as I'm seeing you now. *Le petit caporal.* . . . I saw him present the Cross to one of our old 'uns. . . . Hurrah for the Emperor!' came the voices of men, old and young, of the most diverse characters and stations in life. The faces of all alike wore one common expression of delight at the commencement of the long-expected campaign, and of enthusiasm and devotion for the man in the grey coat standing on the hill.

On the 13th of June a rather small, thoroughbred Arab horse was brought to Napoleon. He mounted and rode at a gallop to one of the bridges over the Niemen, deafened all the while by rapturous acclamations which he evidently endured only because it was impossible to forbid the men to express their love of him by such shouting; but this shouting, which accompanied him everywhere he went, fatigued him and distracted his attention from the military problems which beset him from the time he joined the army. He rode over one of the swaying pontoon bridges to the farther side, turned sharply to the left and galloped in the direction of Kovno, preceded by ecstatic horse guards who, wild with excitement, tore ahead to clear a passage for him through the troops. On reaching the broad river Viliya he pulled up beside a regiment of Polish Uhlans stationed on the bank.

'Long live the Emperor!' shouted the Poles no less enthusiastically, breaking their ranks and pushing against one another to get a sight of him. Napoleon looked up and down the river, got off his horse and sat down on a log that lay on the bank. At a mute sign from him he was handed a telescope which he rested on the back of a page, who ran up delighted. He gazed at the opposite bank and then, with absorbed attention, studied a map spread out between logs. Without lifting his head he said something, and two of his aides-de-camp galloped off to the Polish Uhlans.

'What? What did he say?' was heard in the ranks of the Polish Uhlans as one of the adjutants rode up to them.

The order was that they should look for a ford and cross the river. The colonel of the Polish Uhlans, a handsome old man, flushing and stammering in his excitement, asked the aide-de-camp whether he

721

might be permitted to swim the river with his men instead of seeking a ford. In obvious dread of a refusal, like a boy asking permission to get on a horse, he begged to be allowed to swim across the river before the Emperor's eyes. The aide-de-camp replied that in all probability the Emperor would not be displeased at this excess of zeal.

No sooner had the aide-de-camp said this than the old whiskered officer, with beaming face and sparkling eyes, brandished his sabre in the air, shouted '*Vivat!*' and, calling on his men to follow him, spurred his horse and dashed down to the river. He gave a vicious thrust to his charger which had grown restive under him, and plunged into the water, heading for the deepest part where the current was swift. Hundreds of Uhlans galloped in after him. It was cold and forbidding in the middle in the rapid current. The Uhlans clung to one another as they fell from their horses. Some of the animals were drowned, some, too, of the men; the rest struggled to swim on and reach the opposite bank; and though there was a ford only about a quarter of a mile away they were proud to be swimming and drowning in the river under the eyes of the man who sat on the log and was not even looking at what they were doing. When the adjutant returned and, choosing an opportune moment, ventured to draw the Emperor's attention to the devotion of the Poles to his person, the little man in the grey overcoat got up and, having summoned Berthier, began pacing up and down the bank with him, giving him instructions and occasionally casting a glance of displeasure at the drowning Uhlans who distracted his thoughts.

It was nothing new in his experience and he did not need any convincing that his presence in any part of the world, from Africa to the steppes of Muscovy alike, was enough to turn men's heads and drive them to senseless acts of self-sacrifice. He ordered his horse and rode to his bivouac.

Some forty Uhlans were drowned in the river though boats were sent to their assistance. The majority scrambled back to the bank from which they had started. The colonel with several of his men got across and with difficulty clambered out on the other bank. But so soon as they were out of the water, their clothes streaming wet and flapping against their bodies, they shouted '*Vivat!*' and looked ecstatically at the spot where Napoleon had stood, though he was there no longer, and at that moment considered themselves happy.

In the evening, between issuing two orders – one for hastening the arrival of the counterfeit paper money prepared for circulation in Russia, and the other that a Saxon who had been caught with a letter containing information concerning the dispositions of the French army should be shot – Napoleon also gave instructions for the Polish colonel who had quite unnecessarily flung himself into the river to be enrolled in the *Légion d'Honneur* of which Napoleon was the head.

Quos vult perdere – dementat.

3

THE Emperor of Russia had meanwhile been in Vilna for over a month, reviewing troops and holding manoeuvres. Nothing was ready for the war which everyone expected and to prepare for which the Emperor had come from Petersburg. There was no general plan of action. Hesitation between all the various schemes that were proposed was only even more marked after the Tsar had been at Headquarters for a month. Each of the three armies had its own commander-in-chief, but there was no supreme commander of all the forces, and the Emperor did not see fit to assume that responsibility himself.

The longer the Emperor remained at Vilna the less did everybody – tired of waiting – do to prepare for the war. Every effort of the men who surrounded the Sovereign seemed directed solely to making his stay as pleasant as possible and enabling him to forget the impending clash of arms.

In June, after a series of balls and fêtes given by the Polish magnates, by members of the Court and by the Emperor himself, it occurred to one of the Polish aides-de-camp in attendance that all the generals on the staff should give a banquet and a ball for the Emperor. The idea was eagerly received. The Emperor expressed his consent. The imperial adjutants collected the necessary funds by subscription. The lady who was thought to be most pleasing to the Emperor was invited to act as hostess. Count Bennigsen, being a landowner in the Vilna province, offered his villa for the festivity, and the 13th of June was fixed for a banquet, ball, regatta and fireworks at Zakreto, Count Bennigsen's country seat.

The very day that Napoleon gave the order to cross the Niemen, and his vanguard, driving back the Cossacks, crossed the Russian frontier, Alexander was spending the evening at the entertainment given by his aides-de-camp at Bennigsen's country house.

It was a gay and brilliant fête. Connoisseurs of such matters declared that rarely had so many beautiful women been assembled in one place. Countess Bezuhov, who together with other Russian ladies had followed the Sovereign from Petersburg to Vilna, was at this ball, by her massive beauty – the Russian type, as it is called – eclipsing the dainty little Polish ladies. The Emperor noticed her and honoured her with a dance.

Boris Drubetskoy, having left his wife in Moscow and being for the present *en garçon*, as he said, was also there, and though not an aide-de-camp had subscribed a large sum towards the expenses. Boris was now a rich man who had risen to high honours and no longer sought patronage but stood on an equal footing with the most distinguished representatives of his own generation.

At midnight dancing was still going on. Hélène, finding no other partner to her taste, had herself offered to dance the mazurka with Boris. They were the third couple. Boris, glancing with cool indifference at Hélène's dazzling bare shoulders which emerged from a bodice of dark, gold-embroidered gauze, talked to her of old acquaintances, at the same time, though neither he himself nor anyone else was aware of it, never for an instant ceasing to observe the Emperor who was in the same room. The Emperor was not dancing: he stood in the doorway, stopping now one pair, now another with the gracious words that he alone knew how to utter.

As the mazurka began Boris saw that Adjutant-General Balashev, one of those in closest attendance on the Emperor, went up to him and, contrary to Court etiquette, stood near him while he conversed with a Polish lady. After a few remarks to her the Emperor looked inquiringly at Balashev and, evidently perceiving that only weighty considerations would have caused him to act thus, he gave the lady a slight bow and turned to the adjutant. Hardly had Balashev begun to speak before a look of amazement appeared on the Emperor's face. He took Balashev by the arm and crossed the room with him, unconsciously clearing a space three yards wide on each side of him as people hastily drew back. Boris noticed Arakcheyev's agitation when the Sovereign went out with Balashev. Arakcheyev looked at the Emperor from under his brows and, sniffing with his red nose, stepped forward from the crowd as though expecting the Emperor to turn to him. (It was clear to Boris that Arakcheyev was jealous of Balashev and annoyed that apparently important news had reached the Emperor otherwise than through himself.)

But the Tsar and Balashev walked on through the door into the illuminated garden, without noticing Arakcheyev. Arakcheyev, holding his sword and glancing wrathfully about him, followed some twenty paces behind them.

Boris continued to perform the figures of the mazurka but he was wondering all the time what the news could be that Balashev had brought, and how he could get hold of it before other people.

In the figure in which he had to choose two ladies, he whispered to Hélène that he meant to ask Countess Potocka who had, he thought, gone out on to the balcony, and gliding over the parquet floor he slipped through the door opening into the garden, where, seeing Balashev and the Emperor returning to the verandah, he stood still. They were moving towards the door. Boris, pretending he had not time to get out of the way, respectfully pressed back against the door-post and bowed his head.

The Emperor in the tone of a man resenting a personal insult was saying:

'To enter Russia with no declaration of war! I will not make peace so long as a single armed enemy soldier remains in my country!'

Boris fancied that the Tsar felt some satisfaction in saying these words: he was pleased with the form in which he had expressed his thought, but displeased that Boris had overheard it.

'Let no one know of this!' the Emperor added with a frown.

Boris understood that this was meant for him, and closing his eyes he inclined his head a little. The Emperor re-entered the ball-room and stayed another half an hour or so.

Boris was thus the first to learn that French troops had crossed the Niemen – which enabled him to give certain important personages to understand that much which was concealed from others was commonly known to him, and thereby he succeeded in rising still higher in their estimation.

*

The astounding information of the French having crossed the Niemen seemed particularly unexpected, coming after a month of unfulfilled expectancy, and at a ball! At the first instant of receiving the news, under the influence of indignation and resentment, the Emperor hit on the declaration which has since become famous – a declaration which pleased him and exactly expressed his feelings. On returning home from the ball at two o'clock in the morning, he sent for his secretary, Shishkov, and told him to write a general order to the troops, and a rescript to Field-Marshal Prince Saltykov, in which he insisted on the words being inserted that he would never make peace so long as a single armed Frenchman remained on Russian soil.

Next day the following letter was sent to Napoleon.

Monsieur mon frère,

Yesterday I learnt that, despite the fidelity with which I have adhered to my engagements with your Majesty, your troops have crossed the frontiers of Russia, and I have at this moment received a note from Petersburg in which Count Lauriston informs me, in explanation of this aggression, that your Majesty has considered yourself to be in a state of war with me from the time that Prince Kurakin requested his passports. The grounds on which the *duc de* Bassano based his refusal to deliver these passports would never have led me to suppose that that incident would serve as a pretext for aggression. In point of fact, my ambassador, as he himself has declared, was never authorized to make that request, and so soon as I was informed of it I manifested the extent of my disapproval by ordering him to remain at his post. If your Majesty is not bent upon shedding the blood of our peoples for such a *malentendu*, and consents to withdraw your troops from Russian territory, I will ignore what has happened, and a settlement between us will be possible. In the contrary case, your Majesty, I shall be forced to repel an invasion that nothing on my part has provoked. It is still in your Majesty's power to preserve humanity from the disasters of another war.

I am, etc.

(Signed) ALEXANDER

4

AT two in the morning of the 14th of June the Emperor, having sent for Balashev and read him his letter to Napoleon, ordered him to take and hand it personally to the French Emperor. As he dismissed Balashev the Sovereign once more repeated to him his declaration that he would never make peace so long as a single armed enemy soldier remained on Russian soil, and told him to be sure to quote those words to Napoleon. Alexander had not incorporated them in his letter because, with his characteristic tact, he felt that it would be injudicious to use them just when last attempts towards reconciliation were being made, but he expressly charged Balashev to give that message verbally to Napoleon.

Having set off in the small hours of June the 14th, accompanied by a bugler and two Cossacks, Balashev reached the French outposts at the village of Rykonty on the Russian side of the Niemen, by dawn. There he was stopped by French cavalry sentinels.

A French subaltern officer of hussars, in a crimson uniform and a shaggy cap, shouted to the approaching envoy and ordered him to halt. Balashev did not obey at once but continued to advance along the road at walking pace.

The subaltern, with scowls and muttered abuse, blocked Balashev's way with his horse, put his hand to his sabre and shouted rudely at the Russian general, asking him whether he was deaf that he did not hear when he was spoken to. Balashev gave his name. The subaltern sent a soldier to his superior officer.

Paying no further attention to Balashev, the subaltern began talking with his comrades about regimental matters.

It was an exceedingly strange experience for Balashev, used to living close to the very fountain-head of power and might, having only three hours before been conversing with the Tsar, and in general being accustomed to the deference due to his rank in the Service, to be subjected in his own person and on his native soil to this hostile and, still more, this disrespectful display of brute force.

The sun was only just appearing from behind the clouds; the air was fresh and dewy. A herd of cattle was being driven along the road from the village. Over the fields, one after another, like bubbles floating to the surface of water, larks soared trilling into the sky.

Balashev looked about him as he awaited the arrival of an officer from the village. The Russian Cossacks and the bugler and the French hussars looked at one another from time to time but no one spoke.

A French colonel of hussars, evidently just out of bed, came riding up from the village on a handsome sleek grey horse, accompanied by two of his men. The officer, the soldiers and their horses all looked smart and content with life.

It was that first stage in a campaign when troops are still in full trim, almost like that of peace-time manoeuvres but enhanced by a touch of martial swagger in their apparel and the gay spirit of adventure which always accompany the beginning of an expedition.

The French colonel with difficulty repressed a yawn but was courteous and apparently appreciated Balashev's importance. He conducted him past his soldiers and behind the line of outposts, and informed him that his desire for an audience with the Emperor would in all probability be satisfied immediately, since the Imperial Headquarters, he believed, were not far distant.

They rode through the village of Rykonty, past French picket ropes, and sentinels and soldiers who saluted their colonel and stared with curiosity at a Russian uniform. They came out at the other end of the village, and the colonel told Balashev that they were only a mile and a quarter from the commander of the division, who would receive him and take him to his destination.

The sun had by now fully risen and was shining cheerfully on the vivid green of field and tree.

They had hardly ridden up a hill, past a tavern, before they saw a group of horsemen coming towards them, led by a tall figure in a scarlet cloak with plumes in his hat and black hair curling down to his shoulders. He was mounted on a raven-black horse whose trappings glittered in the sun, and his long legs were thrust forward in the fashion affected by French riders. This personage came towards Balashev at a gallop, plumes fluttering and gems and gold lace glittering in the bright June sunshine.

Balashev was already within ten yards of this rider with the bracelets, plumes, necklaces and gold lace, who was galloping towards him with a theatrically solemn countenance, when Julner, the French colonel, whispered with reverence: 'The King of Naples!' It was in fact Murat, now styled 'King of Naples'. Though it was wholly incomprehensible why he should be King of Naples, still he was called so, and was himself convinced that so it was, and therefore assumed an air of greater solemnity and dignity than before. So firmly did he believe that he really was the King of Naples that when on the eve of departure from that city, as he was strolling through the streets of Naples with his wife, some Italians acclaimed him with cries of '*Viva il re!*' he turned to her with a pensive smile and said: 'Poor souls, they little know that I am leaving them tomorrow!'

But, though he so implicitly believed himself to be King of Naples, and sympathized with his subjects' grief at losing him, after he had been ordered to return to military service, and especially after his last interview with Napoleon at Dantzig, when his august brother-in-law had told him, 'I make you king to rule in my way, not your own!' he had cheerfully resumed his familiar business; and, like a well-fed but not over-fat horse fit for service, feeling itself in harness and prancing between the shafts, he decked himself out in the most gorgeous and costly array possible, and went gaily and contentedly galloping along the roads of Poland, with no notion where or why.

On seeing the Russian general he threw back his head, with its long hair curling to his shoulders, in royal majestic fashion and looked inquiringly at the French colonel. The colonel respectfully informed his Majesty of Balashev's mission, whose name he could not pronounce.

'De Bal-macheve!' said the King (overcoming by his assurance the difficulty that had presented itself to the colonel). 'Charmed to make your acquaintance, general!' he added with a gesture of regal condescension.

As soon as the King began to speak loudly and rapidly all his royal dignity instantly deserted him and, without himself being aware of it, he slipped into his natural tone of good-natured familiarity. He laid his hand on the withers of Balashev's horse.

'Well, general,' he said, 'everything looks like war,' as though he regretted a state of things on which he was unable to offer an opinion.

'*Sire*,' replied Balashev, 'the Emperor, my master, does not desire war, and as your Majesty sees . . .' said Balashev, using the words *your Majesty* at every possible opportunity, with the affectation unavoidable when reiterating a title and addressing one to whom that title is still a novelty.

Murat's face beamed with foolish satisfaction as he listened to 'Monsieur de Balacheff'. But royalty has its obligations: he felt it incumbent on him, as a King and an ally, to confer on affairs of state with Alexander's envoy. He dismounted, took Balashev's arm and, moving a few steps away from his suite, who remained dutifully waiting, began walking up and down with him, trying to speak with grave significance. He referred to the fact that the Emperor Napoleon had resented the demand made upon him to withdraw his forces from Prussia, especially now when that demand had been made public and the dignity of France was thereby offended.

Balashev replied that there was nothing offensive in the demand, seeing that . . . but Murat interrupted him:

729

'Then you do not consider the Emperor Alexander the aggressor?' he asked suddenly, with a silly good-natured smile.

Balashev explained why he considered Napoleon to be the one responsible for the war.

'Ah, my dear general!' Murat interrupted him again, 'I hope with all my heart that the Emperors may settle the matter between themselves, and that the war begun by no desire of mine may finish as quickly as possible!' said he in the tone of a servant anxious to remain on friendly terms with another despite a quarrel between their masters. And he turned the conversation, inquiring after the health of the Grand Duke and recalling the agreeable and amusing time he had spent with him in Naples. Then suddenly, as if remembering his royal dignity, Murat solemnly drew himself up, struck the attitude in which he had stood at his coronation, and with a wave of his right arm, said:

'I will detain you no longer, general. I wish you success in your mission,' and with a flutter of his embroidered scarlet cloak and his plumes, and a flash of his jewels, he rejoined his suite who were respectfully awaiting him.

Balashev rode on, supposing from Murat's words that he would very shortly be brought before Napoleon himself. But, instead of any speedy meeting with Napoleon, at the next village he was stopped by the sentinels of Davoust's infantry corps, just as he had been at the outposts, and an adjutant of the corps commander was sent for to conduct him into the village to Marshal Davoust.

5

DAVOUST was to the Emperor Napoleon what Arakcheyev was to Alexander. Though not a coward like Arakcheyev he was as exacting and cruel, and as unable to express his devotion to his monarch otherwise than by cruelty.

In the mechanism of administration such men are as necessary as wolves are in the economy of nature, and they are always to be found, making their appearance and holding their own, however incongruous their presence and their proximity to the head of the administration may be. This indispensability alone can explain how a man so cruel as Arakcheyev, who tore out grenadiers' moustaches with his own hands yet whose weak nerves rendered him unable to face danger, who was ill-bred and boorish, could retain such influence with a sovereign of gentle chivalry and nobility of character like Alexander.

Balashev found Davoust seated on a barrel in the shed of a peasant's hut, writing – he was auditing accounts. An adjutant stood near him. Better quarters could have been found for him, but Marshal Davoust was one of those men who purposely make the conditions of life as uncomfortable for themselves as possible in order to have an excuse for being gloomy. For the same reason they are always hard at work and in a hurry. 'How can I think of the bright side of existence when, as you see, I sit perched on a barrel in a dirty shed, hard at work ?' the expression of his face seemed to say. The chief satisfaction and requirement of such people is to make a great parade of their own dreary, persistent activity, whenever they encounter anyone enjoying life. Davoust allowed himself that gratification when Balashev was brought in. He buried himself more deeply than ever in his work when the Russian general entered, and after a glance through his spectacles at Balashev's face, which was animated by the beauty of the morning and his talk with Murat, he did not rise, did not stir even, but scowled more blackly than before and smiled malignantly.

Perceiving the disagreeable impression produced on Balashev by this reception, Davoust raised his head and asked him frigidly what he wanted.

Thinking he could have been received in such a manner only because Davoust did not know that he was adjutant-general to the Emperor Alexander and, what was more, his envoy to Napoleon, Balashev hastened to inform him of his rank and mission. But, contrary to his expectations, Davoust, after listening to his communication, became still more surly and rude.

'Where is your despatch ?' he demanded. 'Give it to me. I will forward it to the Emperor.'

Balashev replied that he had been ordered to hand it personally to the Emperor.

'Your Emperor's orders are obeyed in your army, but here,' said Davoust, 'you must do as you're told.'

And, as though to make the Russian general still more sensible that he was at the mercy of brute force, the marshal sent an adjutant to call the officer on duty.

Balashev took out the packet containing the Tsar's letter and laid it on the table (which consisted of a door placed across two tubs with the hinges still hanging on it). Davoust picked up the envelope and read the inscription.

'You are perfectly at liberty to show me respect or not, as you please,' protested Balashev, 'but permit me to observe that I have the honour to be adjutant-general to his Majesty....'

Davoust glanced at him in silence, plainly deriving satisfaction from the signs of disturbance and agitation on Balashev's face.

'You will be shown what is fitting,' said he and, putting the packet in his pocket, left the shed.

A minute later an adjutant of the marshal's, Monsieur de Castre, came in and conducted Balashev to the lodgings assigned him.

Balashev dined that day with the marshal in the same shed, sitting down to the door laid across the tubs.

The following morning Davoust rode out early, but before starting he sent for Balashev and peremptorily requested him to remain where he was, to move on with the baggage-train should orders arrive for it to move, and to have no communication with anyone save Monsieur de Castre.

After four days of solitude, ennui and a continued sense of impotence and insignificance – all the more acutely felt by contrast with the atmosphere of power to which he had until so lately been accustomed – and after a number of marches with the marshal's baggage and the French troops, who occupied the whole district, Balashev was brought back to Vilna – now in possession of the French – re-entering the town through the very gate by which he had left it four days previously.

Next day the Emperor's gentleman-in-waiting, Comte de Turenne, came to Balashev to inform him of the Emperor Napoleon's wish to honour him with an audience.

Four days before, sentinels of the Preobrazhensky regiment had mounted guard in front of the house to which Balashev was conducted, but now two French grenadiers stood there, wearing fur caps and blue uniforms open over the breast, while an escort of hussars and Uhlans and a brilliant suite of aides-de-camp, pages and generals were waiting for Napoleon to come out, forming a group round his saddle-horse and his Mameluke, Rustan. Napoleon received Balashev in the actual house in Vilna from which Alexander had despatched him on his mission.

6

THOUGH Balashev was used to imperial pomp he was amazed at the luxury and magnificence of Emperor Napoleon's Court.

Comte de Turenne led him into the great reception-room, where a throng of generals, gentlemen-in-waiting and Polish magnates – several of whom Balashev had seen at the Court of the Emperor of Russia – were waiting. Duroc said that Napoleon would receive the Russian general before going for his ride.

After some minutes the gentleman-in-waiting who was on duty came into the great reception-room and, bowing politely, invited Balashev to follow him.

Balashev went into the small reception-room, one door of which led into a study, that same room from which the Russian Emperor had sent him forth. He stood alone for a couple of minutes waiting. Hasty steps were heard the other side of the door, both leaves of which were quickly thrown open by a chamberlain who then halted, waiting respectfully, and in the ensuing silence came the sound of other steps, firm and resolute – those of Napoleon. He had just finished dressing for his ride, and wore a blue uniform opening in front over a white waistcoat, so long that it covered his round stomach, white doeskin breeches fitting tightly over the fat thighs of his stumpy legs, and Hessian boots. His short hair had evidently just been brushed, but one lock hung down in the middle of his broad forehead. His plump white neck stood out sharply above the black collar of his uniform, and he smelt of eau-de-Cologne. His youthful-looking, full face, with its prominent chin, wore an expression of benevolent welcome compatible with his imperial majesty.

He entered briskly, with a jerk at every step and his head slightly thrown back. The whole of his short corpulent figure with the broad thick shoulders and with the abdomen and chest unconsciously thrust forward had the imposing air of dignity common in men of forty who enjoy a life of ease. Moreover, it was evident that on this particular day he was in extremely good humour.

He nodded in response to Balashev's low and deferential bow, and, going up to him, at once began speaking like a man who values every moment of his time and does not condescend to prepare what he has to say but is sure of always saying the right thing and saying it well.

'Good day, general!' he began. 'I have received the letter you brought from the Emperor Alexander and am very glad to see you.' He scrutinized Balashev's face with his large eyes and then immediately looked past him.

It was plain that Balashev's personality did not interest him in the least. Nothing outside *his* own self held any significance for him, because everything in the world, it seemed to him, depended on his will alone.

'I do not, and did not, desire war,' he continued, 'but it has been forced on me. Even *now*' (he emphasized the word) 'I am ready to accept any explanations you can give me.'

And he proceeded clearly and concisely to state the grounds for his dissatisfaction with the Russian government.

Judging by the studiously composed and amicable tone of the French Emperor, Balashev was firmly persuaded that he was anxious for peace and intended to enter into negotiations.

'*Sire*, the Emperor, my master,' began Balashev when Napoleon had finished speaking and looked inquiringly at the Russian envoy. But the sight of the Emperor's eyes fastened upon him disconcerted him and drove from his mind the speech he had prepared long before. 'You are flurried – steady yourself!' Napoleon's gaze seemed to say, as with a scarcely perceptible smile he glanced at Balashev's uniform and sword.

Balashev recovered himself and began to speak. He said that the Emperor Alexander did not consider Kurakin's demand for his passports a sufficient ground for war; that Kurakin had acted on his own initiative and without his Sovereign's sanction; that the Emperor Alexander did not desire war and that he had no relations with England.

'Not *yet!*' interposed Napoleon and, as though fearing to give vent to his feelings, he frowned and nodded slightly as a sign that Balashev might continue.

Having said all he had been instructed to say, Balashev added that the Emperor Alexander wished for peace but that he would not enter into negotiations except on condition that ... Here Balashev stopped short: he remembered the words the Emperor Alexander had not written in his letter but had insisted on inserting in the rescript to Saltykov, and had commanded Balashev to repeat to Napoleon. Balashev remembered those words, 'so long as a single armed enemy soldier remains on Russian soil', but some complex feeling held him back. He could not utter those words, much as he had meant to do so. He hesitated, and said: 'On condition that the French army retires beyond the Niemen.'

Napoleon observed Balashev's embarrassment over this last sentence, and his face twitched and the calf of his left leg started to tremble rhythmically. Without moving from where he stood he began speaking in a louder and more hurried tone than before. During the speech that followed, Balashev, who more than once lowered his eyes, could not help watching the quivering of Napoleon's left calf, which increased as Napoleon raised his voice.

'I am no less desirous of peace than the Emperor Alexander,' he began. 'Have I not for the past eighteen months been doing everything to obtain peace? I have waited eighteen months for explanations. But in order to open negotiations what is it that is required of me?' he said, frowning and making a vigorous gesture of inquiry with his plump little white hand.

'The withdrawal of your forces beyond the Niemen, sire,' said Balashev.

'Beyond the Niemen?' echoed Napoleon. 'So now you want me to retire beyond the Niemen – only beyond the Niemen?' repeated Napoleon, looking straight at Balashev.

Balashev respectfully bowed his head.

Four months previously the demand had been for his withdrawal from Pomerania; now all that was required was a retirement beyond the Niemen. Napoleon swung round and began walking up and down the room.

'You say that I must retire across the Niemen before negotiations can be opened; but in exactly the same way two months ago the demand was that I should withdraw beyond the Oder and the Vistula, and yet you are willing to negotiate!'

He strode in silence from one corner of the room to the other and again stopped in front of Balashev. Balashev noticed that his left calf was twitching faster than ever and his face seemed petrified in its stern expression. This twitching of his left leg was something Napoleon was conscious of. 'The vibration of my left calf is a great sign with me,' he remarked at a later date.

'Such demands as to retreat beyond the Oder and the Vistula may be made to a prince of Baden, but not to me!' Napoleon almost screamed, quite to his own surprise. 'If you were to offer me Peters-burg and Moscow, I would not accept such conditions. You say I began this war! But which of us was the first to join his army? The Emperor Alexander, not I! And you propose negotiations when I have expended millions, when you are in alliance with England, and when your position is weak – you propose negotiations with me! Yes, and what is the object of your alliance with England? What has she given you?' he continued hurriedly, obviously no longer thinking of enlarging on the benefits or possibility of peace but entirely bent on proving his own righteousness and his own power, and Alexander's improbity and blundering.

He had plainly entered on his speech with the intention of pointing out the advantages of his position and indicating that he was never-theless willing to negotiate. But he had begun talking, and the more he talked the less able was he to control the tenor of his words.

The whole purport of his remarks now was clearly to exalt himself and insult Alexander – precisely what he had least intended to do at the outset of the interview.

'I hear you have concluded a peace with the Turks?'

Balashev bowed his head affirmatively.

'Yes, peace has been . . .' he began.

But Napoleon did not let him speak. It was obvious that he wanted to do all the talking himself, and he went on with the vehemence and irritable impatience to which people spoilt by success are so prone.

'Yes, I know you have made peace with the Turks without obtain-ing Moldavia and Wallachia – while I would have given your Sover-eign those, just as I presented him with Finland. Yes,' he went on, 'I promised Moldavia and Wallachia to the Emperor Alexander, and I would have given them to him, but now he will not get those fair provinces. Yet he might have united them to his Empire and in a single reign would have extended Russia from the Gulf of Bothnia to the mouth of the Danube. Catherine the Great could not have done more,' declared Napoleon, growing more and more excited as he paced up and down the room repeating to Balashev almost the very words he had used to Alexander himself at Tilsit. 'All that, he would have owed to my friendship. Ah, what a glorious reign, what a glorious reign . . . !' he repeated several times, then paused, drew from his pocket a gold snuff-box, lifted it to his nose and greedily sniffed at it. 'What a glorious reign the Emperor Alexander's *might have been!*'

He turned a commiserating glance on Balashev, and as soon as the latter started to make some rejoinder hastily interrupted him again.

'What could he wish or look for that he would not have secured through my friendship? . . .' demanded Napoleon, shrugging his shoulders with an air of perplexity. 'But no, he has preferred to surround himself with my enemies – and with whom? With the Steins, the Armfeldts, the Wintzingerodes, the Bennigsens! Stein, a traitor expelled from his own country; Armfeldt, a rake and an intriguer; Wintzingerode, a renegade French subject; Bennigsen, rather more of a soldier than the rest but all the same an incompetent, who was helpless in 1807 and who, I should have thought, must arouse horrible memories in the Emperor Alexander's mind. . . . We will grant that were they efficient they might be made use of,' pursued Napoleon, hardly able to keep pace in speech with the rush of arguments proving to him his right or his might (which to his mind meant one and the same thing), 'but they are not even that! They are no good for war or peace! Barclay is said to be the most capable of the lot, but I shouldn't say so, judging by his first manoeuvres. And what are they doing? What are all these courtiers doing? Pfuhl formulates plans, Armfeldt argues, Bennigsen considers, while Barclay, called upon to act, does not know what to decide on, and time slips by. Bagration alone is a soldier. He's stupid but he has experience, a quick eye and determination. . . . And what part does your young Emperor play in this unseemly crowd? They compromise him and throw upon him the responsibility for all that happens. A Sovereign should not be with the army unless he is a general!' said Napoleon, evidently intending these words as a direct challenge to the Russian Emperor. Napoleon knew Alexander's ambition to pass for a military commander.

'Why, the campaign opened a week ago, and you haven't even succeeded in defending Vilna. You are cut in two and have been driven out of the Polish provinces. Your army is discontented. . . .'

'On the contrary, your Majesty,' began Balashev, hardly able to remember what had been said to him, and with difficulty following these verbal fireworks, 'the troops are wild with enthusiasm. . . .'

'I know all that,' Napoleon interrupted him. 'I know all that, and I know the number of your battalions as well as I know that of my own. You have not two hundred thousand men, while I have three times as many. I give you my word of honour,' said Napoleon, forgetting that his word of honour could carry no weight – 'I give you my *parole d'honneur* that I have five hundred and thirty thousand men this side of the Vistula. The Turks will be no help to you. They are never any good, and have proved it by making peace with you. As for the Swedes, it's their destiny to be ruled by mad kings. Their king was insane. They changed him for another – Bernadotte, who promptly went mad, for no Swede would ally himself with Russia unless he were mad.'

Napoleon sneered maliciously and again lifted the snuff-box to his nose.

To each of Napoleon's remarks Balashev had a reply ready and would have come out with it: he kept making the gestures of a man who has something to say, but Napoleon always cut him short. For instance the allegation that the Swedes were insane Balashev would have refuted with the argument that when Russia is on her side Sweden is practically an island; but Napoleon shouted an angry exclamation to drown his voice. Napoleon was in that state of irritation in which a man has to talk and talk and talk, simply to prove to himself that he is in the right. Balashev began to feel uncomfortable: as envoy he was anxious to keep up his dignity, and felt it incumbent upon himself to reply; but as a man he shrank before the assault of Napoleon's unreasonable fury. He was aware that nothing Napoleon might say now had any significance, and that Napoleon himself would be ashamed of his words when he came to his senses. Balashev stood with downcast eyes, watching Napoleon's fat legs as they moved to and fro, and trying to avoid his eyes.

'But what do I care about your allies?' said Napoleon. 'I have allies too – the Poles. There are eighty thousand of them and they fight like lions! And before long they will number two hundred thousand.'

And probably still further exasperated at having told this palpable falsehood, and at Balashev's continuing to stand mutely before him in that attitude of resignation to fate, Napoleon turned abruptly and going right up to Balashev and gesticulating rapidly and vigorously in his face with his white hands, he almost shouted:

'Let me tell you that if you stir up Prussia against me I'll wipe her off the map of Europe!' he declared, his face pale and distorted with anger, as he smote one little hand energetically against the other. 'And as for you, I'll throw you back beyond the Dvina, beyond the Dnieper, and I'll restore the frontier that Europe was criminal and blind to allow you to overrun. Yes, that's what is in store for you.

That is what you have gained by alienating me!' And he took several turns up and down the room in silence, his fat shoulders twitching.

He put his snuff-box into his waistcoat pocket, took it out again, held it several times to his nose, and halted in front of Balashev. He paused, looked sardonically straight into Balashev's eyes and said in a quiet voice:

'And yet what a glorious reign your master *might have had!*'

Balashev, feeling it imperative to make some rejoinder, declared that Russians did not take so gloomy a view of the position. Napoleon was silent, still looking derisively at him and evidently not listening. Balashev said that in Russia the best results were expected from the war. Napoleon nodded condescendingly, as much as to say: 'I know it is your duty to say so, but you don't believe it yourself. My arguments have convinced you.'

When Balashev was done, Napoleon again pulled out his snuff-box, took a pinch and stamped his foot twice on the floor as a signal. The door opened, a gentleman-in-waiting, bending respectfully, handed the Emperor his hat and gloves; another brought him a pocket-handkerchief. Napoleon, without bestowing a glance on them, turned to Balashev:

'Assure the Emperor Alexander from me,' said he, taking his hat, 'that I am devoted to him as before: I know him perfectly, and have the highest esteem for his lofty qualities. I will detain you no longer, general: you shall receive my letter to the Emperor.'

And Napoleon walked rapidly to the door. Everyone in the reception-room rushed forward and down the stairs.

7

AFTER all that Napoleon had said to him, after those outbursts of anger and the last dryly spoken words, 'I will detain you no longer, general: you shall receive my letter,' Balashev felt certain that Napoleon would not wish to see him again – indeed, that he would avoid another meeting with the envoy he had treated with contumely and, what was more, who had been the eye witness of his unbecoming vehemence. But to his astonishment Balashev received, through Duroc, an invitation to dine that day with the Emperor.

Bessières, Caulaincourt and Berthier were present at the dinner. Napoleon met Balashev with a cheerful, affable air. There was not

739

the slightest trace of constraint or self-reproach for his outburst of the morning: on the contrary, he did his best to put Balashev at his ease. It was plain that it had long been Napoleon's conviction that no possibility existed of his making a mistake, and that, according to his understanding of things, whatever he did was right, not because it harmonized with any preconceived notion of right or wrong but because it was *he* who did it.

The Emperor was in excellent spirits after his ride through Vilna, where he had been greeted and followed by the acclamations of crowds of the inhabitants. Every window in the streets through which he rode was hung with rugs, flags or draperies with his monogram, and the Polish ladies waved their handkerchiefs to him in welcome.

At dinner, having placed Balashev beside him, Napoleon not only addressed him amiably but behaved as though he regarded him as one of his own courtiers, one of those who sympathized with his plans and must surely rejoice at his successes. In the course of conversation he mentioned Moscow, and questioned Balashev about the Russian capital, not merely as an interested traveller asks about a new place which he has in mind to visit, but with the apparent conviction that Balashev, as a Russian, must be flattered by his curiosity.

'What is the population of Moscow? How many houses are there? Is it true that Moscow is called *Moscou la sainte*? How many churches are there in Moscow?' he asked.

And when he was told that Moscow had over two hundred churches, he said:

'What is the good of so many?'

'Russians are very devout,' replied Balashev.

'Incidentally, a large number of monasteries and churches is always a sign of the backwardness of a people,' remarked Napoleon, looking round to Caulaincourt for appreciation of this pronouncement.

Balashev ventured respectfully to disagree with the French Emperor.

'Every country has its own customs,' said he.

'But nowhere else in Europe is there anything like that,' declared Napoleon.

'I beg your Majesty's pardon,' returned Balashev, 'besides Russia there is Spain, which also has a vast number of churches and monasteries.'

This retort of Balashev's, which suggested a covert allusion to the recent discomfiture of the French in Spain, was subsequently highly appreciated when Balashev repeated it at Alexander's Court but was little esteemed at Napoleon's dinner and excited no attention.

From the indifferent and doubtful faces of the marshals it was obvious that they were puzzled as to what Balashev's tone suggested. 'If there is a point, we fail to see it', or 'It is not at all witty' their expressions seemed to say. So little was his rejoinder appreciated that Napoleon did not notice it at all, and naïvely asked Balashev through what towns the direct road from there (Vilna) to Moscow passed. Balashev, who was on his guard all through the dinner, replied that just as 'all roads lead to Rome' so all roads led to Moscow; that there were many roads and among them 'the road through *Poltava*, which Charles XII chose'. Balashev involuntarily flushed with pleasure at the aptness of this answer, but hardly had he uttered the word *Poltava* before Caulaincourt began talking of the badness of the road from Petersburg to Moscow and of his Petersburg reminiscences.

After dinner they adjourned to drink coffee in Napoleon's study, which four days previously had been the study of the Emperor Alexander. Napoleon sat down, toying with his Sèvres coffee-cup, and motioned Balashev to a chair beside him.

There is a well-known after-dinner mood which is more potent than any rational consideration in making a man contented with himself and disposed to regard everyone as his friend. Napoleon was in this comfortable humour, fancying himself surrounded by men who adored him, and persuaded that after his dinner Balashev, too, was his friend and worshipper. Napoleon turned to him with a pleasant though slightly ironic smile.

'They tell me this is the very room the Emperor Alexander occupied. Strange, isn't it, general?' he said, obviously without the least misgiving that this remark could be other than agreeable to the Russian since it went to show his, Napoleon's, superiority over Alexander.

Balashev could make no reply, and inclined his head in silence.

'Yes, in this room, four days ago, Wintzingerode and Stein were holding council,' pursued Napoleon with the same confident, satirical smile. 'What I cannot understand,' he went on, 'is that the Emperor Alexander has taken to himself all my personal enemies. That I do not ... understand. Has it never occurred to him that I might do the

741

same?' and he turned inquiringly to Balashev, and obviously the question revived the hardly smothered furies of the morning.

'Aye, and I will, too: let him know that!' said Napoleon, rising and pushing his cup away with his arm. 'I'll drive all his kith and kin out of Germany – the Württembergs and Badens and Weimars. ... Yes, I'll drive them out. Let him prepare an asylum for them in Russia!'

Balashev bowed his head with an air indicating that he would be glad to take his leave and retire, and was simply listening because he had no alternative but to listen to what was said to him. Napoleon did not notice this expression; he was treating Balashev not as an envoy from his enemy but as a man now wholly devoted to him and certain therefore to rejoice at his former master's humiliation.

'And why has the Emperor Alexander assumed command of his armies? What is the good of that? War is my profession, but his business is to reign and not to command armies. Why has he taken such a responsibility on himself?'

Again Napoleon brought out his snuff-box, strode several times up and down the room in silence, and then suddenly and unexpectedly went up to Balashev, and with a slight smile, and as confidently, quickly and without ceremony as though he were doing something not merely important but even agreeable to Balashev, he raised his hand to the forty-year-old Russian general's face and taking him by the ear pulled it gently, smiling with his lips only.

To have one's ear pulled by the Emperor was considered the greatest honour and mark of favour at the French Court.

'*Eh bien*, adorer and courtier of the Emperor Alexander, why don't you say something?' he said, as though it were comic, in his presence, to be the adorer and courtier of anyone but himself, Napoleon. 'Are the horses ready for the general?' he added, with a slight nod in acknowledgement of Balashev's bow. 'Let him have mine. He has *a long way to go.* ...'

The letter carried back by Balashev was the last Napoleon sent to Alexander. Every detail of the interview was communicated to the Russian monarch, and the war began.

8

AFTER his meeting with Pierre in Moscow Prince Andrei went to Petersburg, on business as he told his family but in reality to seek out

Anatole Kuragin, whom he felt it necessary to see. Kuragin, for whom he inquired as soon as he reached Petersburg, was no longer there. Pierre had warned his brother-in-law that Prince Andrei was on his track. Anatole Kuragin had promptly obtained a commission from the minister of war, and gone to join the army in Moldavia. During this visit to Petersburg Prince Andrei met Kutuzov, his former commander, who was always well disposed towards him, and Kutuzov suggested that he should accompany him to the Moldavian army, of which the old general had been appointed commander-in-chief. So Prince Andrei, having received an appointment on the headquarters staff, left for Turkey.

Prince Andrei did not think it proper to write to Kuragin and challenge him. He considered that if he challenged him without some fresh cause it might compromise the young Countess Rostov, and so he was seeking to encounter Kuragin in person in order to pick a quarrel with him that would serve as a pretext for a duel. But in the Turkish army, too, Prince Andrei failed to come across Kuragin, who returned to Russia shortly after Prince Andrei's arrival. In a new country, amid new conditions, Prince Andrei found life easier to bear. After the faithlessness of his betrothed, which he felt the more acutely the more he endeavoured to conceal its effect on him, the surroundings in which he had been happy he now found painful, and the freedom and independence he had once prized so highly still more so. He not only no longer thought the thoughts which had first come to him as he lay gazing up at the heavens on the field of Austerlitz and which he had afterwards loved to enlarge upon with Pierre – the thoughts which had been the companions of his solitude at Bogucharovo, and later on in Switzerland and Rome: he even dreaded to recall them and the boundless vistas of light they had opened up to him. He now concerned himself solely with the practical interests lying closest to hand and in no way related to his old ideals. The more the latter were closed to him the more avidly he clutched at these new interests. It was as if that lofty infinite canopy of heaven that had once arched high above him had suddenly been transformed into a low solid vault that weighed him down, in which all was clear but nothing was eternal or mysterious.

Of the activities that presented themselves to his choice, army service was the simplest and most familiar. Accepting the duties of a general on the staff, he applied himself to his work so doggedly and

perseveringly that Kutuzov was amazed at his zeal and conscientious-
ness. Having missed Kuragin in Turkey, Prince Andrei did not feel it
necessary to gallop back to Russia after him, but all the same he knew
that however long it might be before he met Kuragin, despite his
contempt for him and despite all the arguments he used to convince
himself that it was not worth stooping to a clash with him – he knew
that when he did come across him he would not be able to resist
calling him out, any more than a starving man could resist rushing at
food. And the consciousness that the insult was not yet avenged, that
his rancour had not been expended but was still stored up in his heart,
poisoned the artificial tranquillity which he managed to obtain in
Turkey in the form of strenuously preoccupied, and rather vain-
glorious and ambitious activity.

In the year 1812, when news of the war with Napoleon reached
Bucharest (where Kutuzov had been living for two months, spending
his days and nights with a Wallachian woman), Prince Andrei asked
to be transferred to the western army. Kutuzov, who was already
weary of Bolkonsky's energy, which he felt as a standing reproach to
his own idleness, very readily let him go, and gave him a mission to
Barclay de Tolly.

Before joining the army of the west, which was then, in May, encamped at Drissa, Prince Andrei visited Bald Hills, which was directly
on his route, being only a couple of miles off the Smolensk high road.
During the last three years there had been so many changes in his life,
he had thought, felt and seen so much (having travelled both in the
east and the west), that it surprised and struck him as strange when he
reached Bald Hills to find life there continuing exactly as it always
had, down to the smallest detail. He drove through the stone gateway
into the avenue leading up to the house, feeling as though he were
entering an enchanted castle where everything was fast asleep. The
same sedate air, the same spotlessness, the same silence reigned in the
house; there was the same furniture, the same walls, the same sounds
and smells, and the same timid faces, only grown a little older. Princess
Maria was still the same timid, plain girl, no longer in her first youth,
wasting the best years of her life with her fears and eternal moral
searchings, and getting no benefit or happiness out of her existence.
Mademoiselle Bourienne was the same coquettish, self-satisfied young
woman, enjoying every moment of the day and full of the blithest
hopes for the future. Only she had become more sure of herself,

Prince Andrei thought. Dessalles, the tutor he had brought back from Switzerland, was wearing a coat of Russian cut and talking broken Russian to the servants, but he was still the same cultured, virtuous, pedantic preceptor of somewhat limited intelligence. The only physical change apparent in the old prince was the gap left at the side of his mouth caused by the loss of a tooth: in temper he was the same as ever, only even more irritable and sceptical concerning the good faith of what was happening in the world. Little Nikolai alone had grown and changed: his cheeks were rosier, his hair was dark and curly, and when he was laughing and happy he unconsciously lifted the lip of his pretty little mouth just as his dead mother had done. He alone did not obey the law of immutability in this spellbound sleeping castle. But though on the surface everything remained as of old, the relations to each other of all these people had altered since Prince Andrei had last seen them. The household was divided into two hostile camps, who came together now simply because he was there, on his account modifying their usual pattern of existence. To one camp belonged the old prince, Mademoiselle Bourienne and the architect; to the other – Princess Maria, Dessalles, little Nikolai and all the old nurses and maids.

During his stay at Bald Hills all the family dined together, but they were ill at ease and Prince Andrei felt that he was being treated as a guest for whose sake an exception was being made, and that his presence was a constraint upon them. On the first day at dinner, instinctively aware of this, he sat mute, and the old prince, remarking his unnatural quietness, relapsed into a moody silence, and immediately after dinner retired to his apartments. In the evening, when Prince Andrei joined him and began to tell him of young Count Kamensky's campaign, in the hope of rousing his interest, the old prince to his surprise began talking about Princess Maria, criticizing her for her religious superstitions and her dislike of Mademoiselle Bourienne, who was, he said, the only person really attached to him.

The old prince declared it was all Princess Maria's doing if he was not well: that she set out to plague and annoy him, and that she was spoiling little Nikolai with her coddling and silly talk. The old prince knew perfectly well that he tormented his daughter and that she had a very hard life; but he knew, too, that he could not help tormenting her and that she deserved it. 'Why does Prince Andrei, who sees this, say nothing about his sister?' wondered the old prince. 'Does he think me a scoundrel, or an old fool who for no reason has estranged himself from his daughter and taken the Frenchwoman in her place? He doesn't understand, so I must explain and he must hear me out,' thought the old prince. And he began expounding why it was he could not put up with his daughter's stupid character.

'If you ask me,' said Prince Andrei, not looking at the old man (it was the first time in his life that he was finding fault with his father), 'I had no wish to speak of it – but, if you ask me, I will give you my frank opinion. If there is misunderstanding and discord between you and Marie, I cannot lay the blame for it at her door. I know how she loves and reveres you. Since you ask me,' continued Prince Andrei, his temper rising, as of late it was apt to, 'I can only say that if there are misunderstandings the cause of them is that worthless woman, who is not fit to be my sister's companion.'

The old man at first stared at his son with fixed eyes, and a forced smile disclosed the fresh gap between his teeth to which Prince Andrei could not get accustomed.

'What companion, my dear boy? Eh? So you've already been talking it over, have you?'

'Father, I had no wish to pass judgement,' said Prince Andrei in a hard, bitter tone, 'but you insisted, and I have said, and always shall say, that Marie is not to blame. It is the fault of those – it is the fault of that Frenchwoman.'

'Ah, he has pronounced judgement ... pronounced judgement!' said the old prince in a low voice and, as it seemed to Prince Andrei, with some embarrassment. But the next moment he jumped to his feet and screamed: 'Get out of my sight, get out of my sight. Never let me lay eyes on you again.'

Prince Andrei would have left at once but Princess Maria persuaded him to stay another day, during which he did not see his father, who kept to his room and admitted no one save Mademoiselle Bourienne and Tikhon, and asked several times whether his son had gone. On the following day, just before setting out, Prince Andrei went to the part of the house where his son was to be found. The sturdy little boy, curly-headed like his mother, sat on his knee. Prince Andrei began telling him the story of Bluebeard but fell into a reverie before he got to the end. He was thinking not of the pretty child, his son whom he held on his knee, but of himself. He sought, and was horrified not to find in himself, either remorse for having angered his father or regret at leaving home for the first time in his life on bad terms with him. What disturbed him still more was that he could detect no trace in himself of the tenderness he had once felt for the boy and had hoped to revive in his heart when he petted the child and sat him on his knee.

'Well, go on!' said his son.

Prince Andrei, without replying, put him down from his knee and went out of the room.

As soon as Prince Andrei suspended his daily occupations, and especially the moment he returned to the old surroundings in which he had been happy, the anguish of life seized him with all its former strength, and he made haste to escape from these memories and to find some work to do without delay.

'Are you really leaving, André?' his sister asked him.

'Thank God that I can,' replied Prince Andrei. 'I am very sorry you can't.'

'Why do you say that?' exclaimed Princess Maria. 'How can you say that when you are going to this awful war, and he is so old? Mademoiselle Bourienne says he keeps asking about you. ...'

As soon as she began on that subject, her lips quivered while large tears rolled down her cheeks. Prince Andrei turned away and began walking up and down the room.

'Good God! And to think that such – such trash can bring misery on people!' he cried with a malignity that alarmed Princess Maria.

She realized that by the word 'trash' he was referring not only to Mademoiselle Bourienne, the cause of her misery, but also to the man who had destroyed his own happiness.

'André, one thing I beg, I entreat of you!' she said, touching his elbow and looking at him with eyes that shone through her tears. 'I understand you' (she looked down). 'Don't imagine that sorrow is the work of men. Men are His instruments.' She glanced upwards a little above Prince Andrei's head with the confident, accustomed look with which one glances towards the place where a familiar portrait hangs. 'Sorrow is sent by Him, not by men. Men are His instruments – they are not to blame. If it seems to you that someone has wronged you, forget it and forgive. We have no right to punish. And then you will know the happiness of forgiveness.'

'If I were a woman, I would, Marie. That is a woman's virtue. But a man should not and cannot forgive and forget,' he replied, and, though up to that minute he had not been thinking of Kuragin, all his

747

unexpended anger suddenly surged up in his heart. 'If Marie is already hoping to persuade me to forgive, it is proof positive that I ought long ago to have punished him,' he thought. And making no further reply to her he began picturing to himself the glad vindictive moment when he would meet Kuragin, who he knew was now with the army.

Princess Maria besought her brother to stay one day more, telling him she knew how unhappy her father would be if Andrei left without being reconciled to him, but Prince Andrei answered that he would probably soon be back again from the army, and would write to his father, but that the longer he delayed now the more embittered would their difference become.

'Adieu, André! Remember that misfortunes come from God, and men are never to blame,' were the last words he heard from his sister as he said good-bye to her.

'Such is fate!' thought Prince Andrei as he drove out of the avenue of the Bald Hills mansion. 'She, poor innocent creature, is left to be victimized by an old man who has outlived his wits. The old man knows he is wrong but he can't help himself. My boy is growing up and smiling at life in which like everybody else he will deceive or be deceived. And I am off to the army – why? I have no idea. And I am anxious to meet with a man whom I despise, so as to give him a chance to kill me and sneer at me!'

Life had been made up of the same conditions before, but then these conditions had seemed to him all of a piece, whereas now they had all fallen apart. His mind flitted inconsequently from one thing to another, and there was no sense or meaning anywhere.

9

PRINCE ANDREI reached Army Headquarters at the end of June. The first army, with the Emperor, occupied a fortified camp at Drissa; the second army was retreating, in an effort to effect a junction with the first, from which it was said to be cut off by large French forces. Everyone was dissatisfied with the general course of military affairs in the Russian army, but no one even dreamed that the Russian provinces might be in danger of invasion or that the war would not be confined to the western, the Polish, provinces.

Prince Andrei found Barclay de Tolly, to whom he had been

748

assigned, on the bank of the Drissa. As there was not a single small town or sizeable village in the neighbourhood of the camp, the immense multitude of generals and court functionaries accompanying the army had taken possession of the best houses of the villages on both sides of the river, over a radius of about six miles. Barclay de Tolly was quartered nearly three miles from the Emperor. He received Bolkonsky stiffly, and frigidly informed him in his German accent that he would refer to the Emperor concerning his employment, and proposed that for the time being he should remain on his staff. Anatole Kuragin, whom Prince Andrei had hoped to find in the army, was not there: he was in Petersburg, and Bolkonsky was glad to hear it. He was absorbed by the interest of being at the heart of a mighty war that was just at its beginning, and was thankful for a short respite from the resentment which the thought of Kuragin provoked in him. Having no immediate duties, he spent the first four days in riding all round the camp's fortifications, endeavouring with the help of his own experience and talks with the well-informed to conceive a specific opinion about it. But the question whether the camp was an advantage or not remained an open one in his mind. He had already, from his own military experience, come to the conclusion that in war the most deeply deliberated plans mean nothing (he had seen that at Austerlitz), and that everything depends on the way unexpected movements on the part of the enemy – which cannot possibly be foreseen – are met with, and on how and by whom operations are directed. To get light on this last point Prince Andrei, availing himself of his position and acquaintances, took every opportunity of studying the character of the control of the army and of the persons and parties engaged in its organization, and deduced for himself the following idea of the position of affairs.

While the Emperor was at Vilna the forces had been divided into three armies. First, the army under Barclay de Tolly; secondly, the army under Bagration; and thirdly, the one commanded by Tormasov. The Emperor was with the first army but not in the capacity of commander-in-chief. In the order of the day it was not announced that the Emperor would take command, only that he would be with the army. Moreover, the Emperor had with him not a commander-in-chief's staff but the Imperial Headquarters staff. In attendance on him was the Chief of the Imperial Staff, Quartermaster-General Prince Volkonsky, as well as generals, Imperial aides-de-

749

camp, diplomatic officials and a considerable number of foreigners, but it was not a military staff. Also accompanying the Emperor, in no definite capacity, were Arakcheyev, ex-minister of war; Count Bennigsen, the most senior in rank of the generals; the Tsarevich, the Grand Duke Constantine Pavlovich; Count Rumyantsev, the chancellor; Stein, a former Prussian minister; Armfeldt, the Swedish general; Pfuhl, the chief author of the plan of campaign; General-adjutant Paulucci, a Sardinian *émigré*; Wolzogen – and many others. Though these personages had no military appointment in the army their position gave them influence, and often a corps-commander or even one of the commanders-in-chief did not know in what capacity Bennigsen or the Tsarevich, Arakcheyev or Prince Volkonsky asked questions or proffered their counsel, and could not tell whether such and such an order, couched in the form of a piece of advice, emanated from the man who gave it or from the Emperor, and whether it had to be executed or not. But all this simply formed the external aspect of the situation: the inner import of the presence of the Emperor and all these other individuals was, from a courtier's point of view (and in an emperor's vicinity all men become courtiers), plain to everyone. All realized that, though the Emperor was not formally assuming the title of commander-in-chief, the control of all the armies was in his hands, and the persons about him were his assistants. Arakcheyev was the faithful custodian of law and order, and the Sovereign's body-guard. Bennigsen was a landowner in the Vilna province who appeared to be doing the honours of the district but was in reality a good general, useful as an adviser and ready to hand to replace Barclay. The Tsarevich was there because it suited him. The former Prussian minister, Stein, was there because his advice was valuable and the Emperor Alexander had a high opinion of his personal qualities. Armfeldt had a violent hatred of Napoleon, and was a general possessed of great confidence in his own ability, a trait which never failed to have influence with Alexander. Paulucci was there because he was bold and decided in his utterances. The adjutants-general were there because they were always to be found where the Emperor was; and the last and principal figure, Pfuhl, was there because, having drawn up the plan of campaign against Napoleon and having induced Alexander to believe in the efficacy of this plan of his, he was directing the entire action of the war. With Pfuhl was Wolzogen, who put Pfuhl's ideas in a more comprehensible form than Pfuhl himself – who was a rigid cabinet theorist, self-confident to the point of despising everyone else – was able to do.

In addition to the above-mentioned Russians and foreigners (with foreigners in the ascendancy and every day propounding new and startling suggestions with the audacity characteristic of people engaged in activities in spheres not their own) – there were many more persons of secondary importance who were with the army because their principals were there.

In this vast, restless, brilliant and haughty world, among all these conflicting opinions and voices, Prince Andrei distinguished the following sharply outlined sub-divisions of tendencies and parties.

The first party consisted of Pfuhl and his adherents: military theorists who believed in a science of war having its immutable laws – laws for oblique movements, outflankings and so forth. Pfuhl and his adherents demanded a retirement into the interior of the country, a withdrawal in accordance with precise principles defined by a pseudo-theory of war, and in every deviation from this theory they saw only barbarism, ignorance or evil intention. To this party belonged the German princes, Wolzogen, Wintzingerode and others, but chiefly the Germans.

The second faction, diametrically opposed to the first, fell, as always happens, into the other extreme. The members of this party were those who had clamoured for an advance from Vilna into Poland, and freedom from all prearranged plans. Besides being advocates of bold action, this section also represented nationalism, which made them still more one-sided in the dispute. They were the Russians: Bagration, Yermolov (who was just beginning to make his mark) and others. It was at this time that Yermolov's famous joke was being circulated – that he had petitioned the Emperor to promote him to the rank of 'German'. The men of this party were never tired of quoting Suvorov and arguing that there was no need for cerebration and sticking pins into maps: the point was to fight, beat the enemy, keep him out of Russia, and not let the army lose heart.

To the third party – in which the Emperor had most confidence – belonged the courtiers, who tried to effect a compromise between the other two. The members of this group, chiefly civilians and including Arakcheyev among their number, thought and spoke in the way men who have no convictions but wish to pass for having some usually do speak. They said that war, especially against such a genius as Bonaparte (they called him Bonaparte again now) did undoubtedly call for the profoundest tactical considerations and scientific knowledge, and in that respect Pfuhl was a genius; but at the same time it had to be acknowledged that theorists were often one-sided, and so one should not place implicit faith in them but should also listen to what Pfuhl's opponents had to say, and to the views of practical men with experience in warfare, and then choose a middle course. They insisted that the camp at Drissa should be retained according to Pfuhl's plan, but advocated altering the disposition of the other two armies. Though by this course neither one aim nor the other could be attained, this seemed to the party of compromise the best line to adopt.

Of a fourth tendency of opinion the most conspicuous representative was the Grand Duke and heir-apparent, who could not get over his rude awakening at Austerlitz, where he had ridden out at the head of the Guards in casque and cuirass as to a review, expecting to rout the French with a flourish, but had suddenly found himself in the front line and had a narrow escape from the general *mêlée*. The men of this party had at once the merit and the defect of sincerity in their convictions. They feared Napoleon, recognized his strength and their own weakness, and had no hesitation in saying so. 'Nothing but misfortune, ignominy and defeat can come of all this,' they said. 'Here we have abandoned Vilna, abandoned Vitebsk, and we shall likewise abandon Drissa. The only rational thing left for us to do is to make peace, and as soon as possible, before we are driven out of Petersburg!'

This view was widely prevalent in the higher military circles, and found support in Petersburg too, and from the chancellor Rumyantsev, who for other reasons of state was in favour of peace.

Partisans of Barclay de Tolly, not so much as a man but as minister of war and commander-in-chief, formed the fifth faction. They said: 'Whatever else he is' (they always began like that), 'he is an honest, practical man, and we have nobody better. Give him real power, because war can never be prosecuted successfully under divided authority, and he will show what he can do, as he did in Finland. If our army is well-organized and strong, and has withdrawn to Drissa without suffering a single defeat, we owe it entirely to Barclay. If Barclay is now to be replaced by Bennigsen all will be lost, for Bennigsen proved his incapacity as far back as 1807.' Thus spoke the fifth party.

The sixth element – the Bennigsenites – argued, on the contrary, that after all there was no one more capable and experienced than Bennigsen, 'and however much you twist and turn you'll have to come to Bennigsen in the end'. Our whole retirement to Drissa, they maintained, was a shameful reverse and an uninterrupted series of blunders. 'The more mistakes that are made the better. At least it will teach them all the sooner that things cannot go on like this. And we want none of your Barclays, but a man like Bennigsen, who showed what he was made of in 1807, and to whom Napoleon himself had to do justice – a man whose authority would be willingly recognized. And the only man of that stamp is Bennigsen.'

The seventh party consisted of individuals such as are always to be found, especially in the entourage of young monarchs, and of whom there was a particularly plentiful supply around Alexander – generals and Imperial aides-de-camp passionately devoted to their Sovereign, not merely as a monarch but sincerely and whole-heartedly worshipping him as a man, just as Rostov had done in 1805, and who saw in him not only all the virtues but all the human talents as well. These men, though enchanted with the Sovereign for declining to assume command of the army, deplored such excess of modesty, and desired and urged one thing only – that their adored Tsar should overcome his diffidence and openly proclaim that he was placing himself at the head of the army, gather round him a staff appropriate to a commander-in-chief and, consulting experienced theoreticians and practical veterans where necessary, himself lead his forces, whose spirits would thereby be raised to the highest pitch of enthusiasm.

The eighth and largest group, numbering ninety-nine to every one of the others, consisted of men who were neither for peace nor for war, neither for offensive operations nor a defensive camp at Drissa or anywhere else; who did not take the side of Barclay or of the Emperor, of Pfuhl or of Bennigsen, but cared only for the one thing most essential – as much advantage and pleasure for themselves as they could lay hold of. In the troubled waters of those cross-currents of intrigue that eddied about the Emperor's headquarters it was possible to succeed in very many ways that would have been unthinkable at other times. One courtier simply interested in retaining his lucrative post would today agree with Pfuhl, tomorrow with Pfuhl's opponents, and the day after, merely to avoid responsibility or to please the Emperor, would declare that he had no opinion at all on the matter. Another, eager to curry favour, would attract the

Tsar's attention by loudly advocating something the Emperor had hinted at the day before, and would dispute and shout at the Council, beating his breast and challenging those who did not agree with him to a duel, thus displaying his readiness to sacrifice himself for the common weal. A third, while his enemies were out of the way, and in between two Councils, would simply solicit a special gratuity for his faithful services, well aware that it would be quicker at the moment to grant it than to refuse it. A fourth would contrive to be seen by the Tsar quite overwhelmed with work. A fifth, in order to achieve his long-cherished ambition to dine with the Emperor, would vehemently debate the rights or wrongs of some newly emerging opinion, producing more or less forcible and valid arguments in support of it.

All the members of this party were fishing after roubles, decorations and promotions, and in their chase simply kept their eye on the weathercock of Imperial favour: directly they noticed it shifting to one quarter the whole drone-population of the army began buzzing away in that direction, making it all the harder for the Emperor to change course elsewhere. Amid the uncertainties of the position, with the menace of serious danger which gave a peculiarly feverish intensity to everything, amid this vortex of intrigue, selfish ambition, conflicting views and feelings, and different nationalities, this eighth and largest party of men preoccupied with personal interests imparted great confusion and obscurity to the common task. Whatever question arose, a swarm of these drones, before they had done with their buzzing over the previous theme, would fly off to the new one, to smother and drown by their humming the voices of those who were prepared to examine it fully and honestly.

Out of all these groups, just at the time Prince Andrei reached the army, another and ninth party was coming into being and beginning to make its voice heard. This was the party of the elders, of sound men of experience in state affairs, sharing none of the conflicting opinions and able to take a detached view of what was going on at Staff Headquarters, and to consider means for escaping from the muddle, uncertainty, confusion and weakness.

The members of this party said and thought that the whole evil was primarily due to the Emperor's presence in the army with his military court, and the consequent introduction of that indefinite, conditional and fluctuating uncertainty of relations which may be convenient at Court but is mischievous in an army; that it was for a sovereign to reign but not command the army, and that the only solution of the difficulty would be for the Emperor and his Court to take their departure; that the mere presence of the Tsar paralysed fifty thousand troops required to secure his personal safety; and that the most incompetent commander-in-chief if he were independent would be better than the very best one hampered by the presence and authority of the Monarch.

Just at the time Prince Andrei was continuing at Drissa with nothing to do, Shishkov, secretary of state and one of the chief representatives of this last group, concocted a letter to the Emperor to which Balashev and Arakcheyev agreed to add their signatures. In this letter, availing himself of the Emperor's permission to discuss the general course of affairs, he respectfully suggested – on the plea of the vital necessity for the Sovereign to rouse the people of the capital to enthusiasm for the war – that the Emperor should leave the army.

The fanning of this flame by the Sovereign, and his appeal to them to rise in defence of their Fatherland – the very factors (in so far as they can be said to have resulted from the Tsar's personal presence in Moscow) which led to Russia's ultimate triumph – were suggested to the Emperor, and accepted by him, as a pretext for quitting the army.

10

THIS letter had not yet been presented to the Emperor when Barclay, at dinner one day, informed Bolkonsky that his Majesty wished to see him personally, to question him about Turkey, and that Prince Andrei was to appear at Bennigsen's quarters at six o'clock that evening.

That very day news had reached the Emperor's staff of a fresh movement on the part of Napoleon which might prove dangerous for the army – a report which subsequently turned out to be false. And that morning Colonel Michaud, accompanying the Tsar on a tour of inspection of the Drissa fortifications, had pointed out to him that this fortified camp, constructed under Pfuhl's direction and hitherto regarded as a *chef d'œuvre* of tactical science which would ensure Napoleon's destruction, was a piece of folly and the ruin of the Russian army.

Prince Andrei proceeded to Bennigsen's quarters, a small manorhouse on the very bank of the river. Neither Bennigsen nor the

Emperor was there but Tchernyshev, the Emperor's aide-de-camp, received Bolkonsky and informed him that the Tsar, with General Bennigsen and the Marchese Paulucci, had set off for the second time that day to inspect the fortifications of the Drissa camp, of the utility of which they were beginning to entertain grave doubts.

Tchernyshev was sitting at a window of the outer room with a French novel in his hand. This room had at one time probably been a music-room: there was still an organ in it on which some rugs were piled, and in one corner stood the folding bedstead of Bennigsen's adjutant. This adjutant was also there, and sat dozing on the rolled-up bedding, apparently exhausted by work or festivities. Two doors led from the room, one straight into what had been the drawing-room, and another, on the right, opening into the study. Through the first came the sound of voices conversing in German and occasionally in French. In the former drawing-room were gathered, by the Emperor's request, not a Council of War (the Emperor preferred to have things vague) but certain persons whose opinion of the impending difficulties he wished to know. It was not a Council of War but a sort of council to elucidate various questions for the benefit of the Tsar personally. To this semi-council had been invited the Swedish general, Armfeldt, Adjutant-General Wolzogen, Wintzingerode (whom Napoleon had referred to as a renegade French subject), Michaud, Toll, Count Stein – by no means a military man – and finally Pfuhl, who was, so Prince Andrei had heard, the mainspring of the whole affair. Prince Andrei had an opportunity of getting a good look at him, as Pfuhl arrived shortly after himself, and stopped for a minute to say a few words to Tchernyshev before passing on into the drawing-room.

At first glance Pfuhl, in his badly-cut uniform of a Russian general, which sat on him awkwardly like some fancy dress costume, seemed a familiar figure to Prince Andrei though he had never seen him before. He was of the same order as Weierother, Mack and Schmidt, and many other German theorist-generals whom Prince Andrei had come across in 1805, but he was more typical than any of them. Never in his life had Prince Andrei beheld a German theorist who so completely combined in himself all the characteristics of those other Germans.

Pfuhl was short and very thin but big-boned, of coarse, robust build, broad in the hips and with prominent shoulder-blades. His face

756

was much wrinkled, and his eyes deep-set. His hair had obviously been hastily brushed smooth in front by the temples but it stuck up behind in odd little tufts. He walked in looking nervously and irritably about him, as if afraid of everything in that great room to which he was bound. Awkwardly holding up his sword, he addressed Tchernyshev, asking him in German where the Emperor was. It was evident that he was anxious to get across the room as speedily as possible, have done with the bows and greetings, and sit down to business in front of a map, where he would feel at home. He nodded abruptly in response to Tchernyshev, and smiled ironically on hearing that the Sovereign was inspecting the fortifications that he, Pfuhl, had planned in accord with his theory. He growled to himself in his bass voice, muttering something that might have been 'Stupid blockhead!' or '... Damn the whole business!' or 'A pretty state of affairs that will lead to!', after the manner of all conceited Germans. Prince Andrei did not catch his remarks, and would have passed on, but Tchernyshev introduced him to Pfuhl, observing that Prince Andrei had just come from Turkey, where the war had terminated so fortunately. Pfuhl gave a fleeting glance not so much at Prince Andrei as through him, and commented with a laugh: 'That war must have been a model of tactics!' And, laughing scornfully, he went on into the room from which the sound of voices came.

It was plain that Pfuhl, always inclined to be irritable and sarcastic, was particularly provoked that day by the fact of their having dared to inspect and criticize his camp in his absence. From this brief interview with Pfuhl, Prince Andrei, thanks to his Austerlitz experiences, was able to form a clear conception of the man's character. Pfuhl was one of those hopelessly, immutably conceited men, obstinately sure of themselves as only Germans are, because only Germans could base their self-confidence on an abstract idea – on science, that is, the supposed possession of absolute truth. A Frenchman's conceit springs from his belief that mentally and physically he is irresistibly fascinating both to men and women. The Englishman's self-assurance comes from being a citizen of the best-organized kingdom in the world, and because as an Englishman he always knows what is the correct thing to do, and that everything he does as an Englishman is undoubtedly right. An Italian is conceited because he is excitable and easily forgets himself and other people. A Russian is conceited because he knows nothing and does not want to know anything, since he does not believe that it is possible to know anything completely. A conceited German is the worst of them all, the most stubborn and unattractive, because he imagines that he possesses the truth in science – a thing of his own invention but which for him is absolute truth. Pfuhl was evidently of this breed. He had his science – the theory of oblique movements deduced by him from the history of Frederick the Great's wars, and everything he came across in more recent military history seemed to him preposterous and barbarous – crude struggles in which so many blunders were committed on both sides that such wars could not be called wars: they did not fit in with the theory, and therefore could not serve as material for science.

In 1806 Pfuhl had been one of those responsible for the plan of campaign that culminated in Jena and Auerstadt; but in the outcome of that war he did not see the slightest evidence of the fallibility of his theory. On the contrary, to his mind the disaster was entirely due to the deviations that were made from his theory, and with character-istically gleeful sarcasm he would remark: 'Didn't I always say the whole affair would go to the devil!' Pfuhl was one of those theoreti-cians who are so fond of their theory that they lose sight of the object of that theory – its application in practice. His passion for theory made him hate all practical considerations, and he would not hear of them. He even rejoiced in failure, for failures resulting from depar-tures in practice from abstract theory only proved to him the accuracy of his theory.

He said a few words to Prince Andrei and Tchernyshev about the present war, with the air of a man who knows beforehand that every-thing will go wrong, and indeed is not displeased that it should do so. The little tufts of uncombed hair sticking up behind and the hastily smoothed locks on his temples expressed this most eloquently.

He crossed into the other room, from where the querulous notes of his bass voice were at once audible.

II

PRINCE ANDREI was still following Pfuhl with his eyes when Count Bennigsen came hurrying into the room and, nodding to Bolkonsky but not stopping, passed into the study, giving instructions to his ad-jutant as he went. The Emperor was behind him, and Bennigsen had hastened on ahead to make some preparations and to be there to receive him. Tchernyshev and Prince Andrei went out into the porch, where the Emperor, who looked tired, was dismounting from his horse. The Marchese Paulucci was addressing him with particular warmth and the Emperor, with his head inclined to the left, was listening with a look of displeasure. The Emperor moved forward, evidently wishing to cut short the conversation, but the flushed and excited Italian, oblivious of etiquette, followed him, still talking.

'As for the man who advised this camp at Drissa –' Paulucci was saying as the Emperor mounted the steps and, noticing Prince Andrei, scanned his unfamiliar face, 'as to that person, sire . . .' Paulucci persisted desperately, apparently unable to restrain himself, 'the man who advised the Drissa camp – I see no alternative but the madhouse or the gallows.'

Without waiting for the Italian to finish, and as though not hearing his remarks, the Emperor, recognizing Bolkonsky, turned to him graciously.

'I am very glad to see you. Go in to the others and wait for me.'

The Emperor went into the study. He was followed by Prince Piotr Mihalovich Volkonsky and Baron Stein, and the door closed behind them. Prince Andrei, taking advantage of the Tsar's permission, accompanied Paulucci, whom he had met before in Turkey, into the drawing-room where the Council was assembled.

Prince Piotr Mihalovich Volkonsky occupied the position, as it were, of chief of the Emperor's staff. He came out of the study into the drawing-room, bringing with him some maps which he spread on a table, and announced the points on which he wished to hear the opinion of the gentlemen present. What had happened was that news (which afterwards proved to be false) had been received during the night of a movement by the French to outflank the Drissa camp.

The first to speak was General Armfeldt, who, to counter the difficulty that presented itself, unexpectedly proposed that they should choose an entirely new position away from the Petersburg and Moscow roads, and, united there, await the enemy. No one could see any reason for his advocating such a scheme, unless it was a desire to show that he, too, could have ideas of his own. It was obviously a plan that Armfeldt had thought out long ago, and put forward now not so much with the object of meeting the problem – to which it offered no solution – as to avail himself of the opportunity of airing it. It was one of a myriad assumptions, each as good as the other, which might be made in ignorance of what character the war would take. Some of those present attacked his suggestion, others defended it. The young Colonel Toll criticized the Swedish general's views with more heat than anyone, and in the course of the argument drew from his side-pocket a well-filled manuscript-book which he asked permission to read to them. In a voluminous note Toll propounded still another plan of campaign, totally different from Armfeldt's or Pfuhl's. Paulucci, in raising objections to Toll's ideas, suggested an advance and attack, which, he urged, was the only way to extricate ourselves from the present uncertainty and from the trap (as he called the camp at Drissa) in which we were placed. During all these discussions Pfuhl and his interpreter Wolzogen (his mouthpiece in his dealings with the court) sat silent. Pfuhl merely snorted contemptuously and turned his back to indicate that he would never stoop to reply to the rubbish he was hearing. So when Prince Volkonsky, who was in the chair, appealed to him for his opinion he simply answered:

'Why ask me? General Armfeldt has proposed a first-rate position with our rear exposed to the enemy. Or why not this Italian gentleman's attack – a capital idea! Or a retreat? Excellent, too. Why ask me?' he repeated. 'You all know better than I do, it appears.'

But when Volkonsky frowned and said that he asked his opinion in the name of the Emperor, Pfuhl rose to his feet and, suddenly animated, began to speak:

'Everything has been spoilt and thrown into a muddle. Everybody thought they knew better than I, and now you come to me! "What shall we do to put things right?" you say. There is nothing to be put right. You have only to carry out to the letter the principles laid down by me,' said he, drumming on the table with his bony knuckles. 'What is the difficulty? It's nonsense! Child's play!'

He went up to the table and, speaking rapidly and thrusting with his wrinkled finger at the map, began demonstrating that no contingency could affect the advantages of the Drissa camp, that everything had been foreseen and that if the enemy were actually to outflank them, then the enemy would infallibly be wiped out.

Paulucci, who did not know German, began questioning him in French. Wolzogen came to the assistance of his chief, who spoke French badly, and began translating for him, hardly able to keep pace with Pfuhl, who was demonstrating at top speed that everything – not only all that had happened but all that could possibly happen –

had been provided for in his plan, and that if difficulties had arisen now the whole fault lay in the fact that his plan had not been carried out with exactitude. He kept laughing sarcastically as he argued, and at last, like a mathematician who will waste no more time verifying the various steps in the solution of a problem already proved, he contemptuously abandoned his demonstration. Wolzogen took his place, continuing to explain his views in French and every now and then turning to Pfuhl with a 'Is that not right, your Excellency?' But Pfuhl, as a man in the heat of the fray will belabour those of his own side, shouted angrily at his supporter:

'To be sure – it's as plain as daylight.'

Paulucci and Michaud fell simultaneously on Wolzogen in French. Armfeldt addressed Pfuhl in German. Toll explained to Prince Volkonsky in Russian. Prince Andrei listened and watched the proceedings in silence.

Of all these men the irate, peremptory and absurdly conceited Pfuhl was the one who most attracted Prince Andrei's sympathy. He alone of all those present was obviously not seeking anything for himself, harboured no personal grudge, and desired one thing only – the adoption of his plan based on a theory arrived at after years of toil. He was ridiculous, he was disagreeable with his sarcasm, yet he inspired an involuntary feeling of respect by his boundless devotion to an idea. Besides this, with the single exception of Pfuhl, the remarks of every person present possessed a common trait, of which there had been no symptom at the council of war in 1805. This was a panic fear of Napoleon's genius, a dread which, though cloaked, betrayed itself in every argument. They took it for granted that Napoleon could do anything, expected him to appear from every quarter at once, and invoked his terrible name to demolish each other's proposals. Pfuhl alone, it seemed, considered Napoleon as much a barbarian as everybody else who opposed his theory. But, as well as respect, Pfuhl evoked pity in Prince Andrei. From the tone in which the courtiers addressed him, and the way in which Paulucci had ventured to speak of him to the Emperor, but above all from a certain desperation in Pfuhl's own utterances, it was clear that the others knew, and Pfuhl himself was aware, that his fall was at hand. And for all his conceit and querulous German irony he was pathetic with his hair flattened on the temples and sticking up in tufts behind. Although he did his best to conceal the fact under a show of irritation and contempt, he was visibly in despair that his sole remaining chance of testing his theory on a tremendous scale and proving its soundness to the whole world was slipping from him.

The discussion continued a long while, and the longer it lasted the more heated grew the arguments, culminating in shouts and personalities, and the less possible it was to arrive at any general conclusions from all that had been said. Prince Andrei, listening to this polyglot talk, to the presuppositions, plans, cries and objections, could only wonder in amazement. A thought which had early and often occurred to him during the period of his military activities – that there was not, and could not be any such thing as a science of war, and consequently no such thing as military genius – now appeared to him a completely obvious truth. 'What theory and science is possible where the conditions and circumstances of a subject are unknown and cannot be defined – and especially when the strength of the active forces engaged cannot be ascertained? No one could know – no one can know – the relative positions of our army and the enemy twenty-four hours from now, and no one can gauge the potential of this or that detachment. Sometimes, when there is no coward in front to cry, "We are cut off!" and start to run, but a brave, spirited lad who leads the way with shouts of "Hurrah", a division of five thousand is as good as thirty thousand, as was the case at Schön Graben, while at other times fifty thousand will fly from eight thousand, as happened at Austerlitz. What science can there be where everything is vague and depends on an endless variety of circumstances, the significance of which becomes manifest all in a moment, and no one can foretell when that moment is coming? Armfeldt says that our army is cut off, while Paulucci maintains that we have caught the enemy between two fires. Michaud asserts that the weak point of the Drissa camp is having the river behind it, while Pfuhl declares that that is what constitutes its strength. Toll proposes one plan, Armfeldt another, and all are good and all are bad, and the advantages of each and every suggestion can only be seen at the moment of trial. And why do they all talk of "military genius"? Is a man a genius because he knows when to order army biscuits to be sent up, and when to march his troops to the right and when to the left? He is called a genius merely because of the glamour and power with which the military are invested, and the crowds of sycophants always ready to flatter power and to ascribe to it qualities of genius it does not possess. Indeed the best generals I have known were stupid or absent-minded men. The best was Bagration, Napoleon himself admitted that. And Bonaparte himself! I remember his self-satisfied, insular expression on the field of Austerlitz. A good general has no need of any special qualities: on the contrary, he is the better for the absence of the loftiest and finest human attributes – love, poetry, tenderness and philosophic and inquiring doubt. He should be limited, firmly convinced that what he is doing is of great importance (otherwise he will not have the patience to go through with it), and only then will he be a gallant general. God forbid that he should be humane, should feel love or compassion, should stop to think what is just and unjust. It is understandable that a theory of their "genius" was invented for them long ago because they are synonymous with power! The success of a military action depends not on them but on the man in the ranks who first shouts "We are lost!" or "Hurrah!" And only in the ranks can one serve with the assurance of being useful.'

Thus mused Prince Andrei as he listened to the arguments, and he only roused himself when Paulucci called him and the meeting was breaking up.

At the review next day the Emperor asked Prince Andrei where he desired to serve, and Prince Andrei lost his standing in court circles for ever by asking permission to serve with the army, instead of begging for a post in attendance on the Sovereign's person.

12

BEFORE the beginning of the campaign Rostov had received a letter from his parents in which they told him briefly of Natasha's illness and the breaking off of her engagement to Prince Andrei (which they explained as having come about simply because Natasha rejected him), and again begged him to retire from the army and return home. On receiving this letter Nikolai made no attempt to secure either leave of absence or permission to go upon the retired list, though he wrote to his parents that he was very sorry about Natasha's illness and the rupture with her betrothed, and that he would do all he could to fall in with their wishes. To Sonya he wrote separately.

Adored friend of my heart [he wrote]. Nothing save honour could keep me from returning to the country. But now, at the commencement of a campaign, I should count myself disgraced not only in my

763

comrades' eyes but in my own were I to put my personal happiness before my duty and my love for the Fatherland. But this shall be our last separation. Be sure that directly the war is over, if I am still alive and you still love me, I shall throw up everything and fly to you, to clasp you for ever to my ardent breast.

It was, in point of fact, only the inauguration of the campaign that held Rostov back and prevented him from returning home, as he had promised, and marrying Sonya. The autumn at Otradnoe with the hunting, and the winter with the Christmas holidays and Sonya's love, had opened out to him a vista of quiet country delights and contentment such as he had never known before and which now beckoned to him invitingly. 'A nice wife, children, a good pack of hounds, a dozen leashes of spirited borzois, the estate to look after, neighbours to entertain, perhaps an active share in the functions of the nobility,' he mused. But now the campaign was on them and he must remain with his regiment. And since it had to be so, Nikolai Rostov was characteristically able to be content too with the life he led in the regiment, and to make that life a pleasant one.

He had been hailed with joy by his comrades on returning from his furlough, and then sent to obtain remounts for the regiments. From the Ukraine he brought back some excellent horses which gave him great satisfaction and earned him commendation from his superior officers. During his absence he had been promoted to the rank of captain, and when the regiment was put on war-footing with an increased complement he was again allotted his old squadron.

The campaign began, the regiment was moved into Poland on double pay, new officers arrived, new men and horses, and, above all, everybody was infected with the excitement and enthusiasm which always accompany the beginning of a war; and Rostov, fully appreciating the advantages of his position in the regiment, devoted himself heart and soul to the pleasures and interests of military service, though he knew that sooner or later he would have to relinquish them.

The troops retired from Vilna for various complex considerations of state, of policy and of tactics. Every yard of the retreat stimulated a complicated interplay of interests, arguments and passions at Headquarters. For the Pavlograd Hussars, however, the whole of the withdrawal during the finest period of the summer and with ample supplies was a very simple and agreeable business. At Headquarters men might lose heart, grow nervous and intrigue but in the body of the army no one even thought of wondering where and why they were going. If they regretted having to retreat, it was only because it meant leaving billets they had become used to, or some pretty little Polish lady. If the idea did occur to anyone that things looked bad, he tried, as a good soldier should, to put a cheerful face on it, concentrating his attention on the task nearest to hand and forgetting the general trend of events. At first they pitched camp gaily before Vilna, making acquaintance with the Polish landowners of the neighbourhood, preparing for reviews and being reviewed by the Emperor and other high-ranking officers. Then came an order to retreat to Swienciany and destroy any stores that could not be carried away. Swienciany stuck in the hussars' memory simply as the *drunken camp*, the name given to the encampment there by the whole army, and as the scene of many complaints against the troops, who had taken advantage of orders to collect provisions and under this heading had included and taken horses, carriages and rugs from the Polish gentry. Rostov remembered Swienciany because on the first day of their arrival in that small town he had dismissed his quartermaster and been unable to do anything with the men of his squadron, all of whom were tipsy, having, without his knowledge, appropriated five barrels of old beer. From Swienciany they had retired farther, and then farther still, until they reached Drissa, and from Drissa the retreat had continued, till they were nearing the frontiers of Russia proper.

On the 13th of July the Pavlograds took part for the first time in a serious action.

On the 12th of July, on the eve of that engagement, there had been a heavy storm of rain with thunder. In general, the summer of 1812 was remarkable for its tempestuous weather.

The two Pavlograd squadrons were bivouacking in a field of rye which was already in ear but had been completely trodden down by cattle and horses. Rain was falling in torrents, and Rostov was sitting with a young officer named Ilyin, a *protégé* of his, in a shelter that had been hastily rigged up for them. An officer of their regiment, with long moustaches hanging down from his cheeks, riding back from Staff Headquarters and caught in the rain, joined Rostov.

'I'm on my way from Staff, count. Heard about Raevsky's exploit?'

And the officer proceeded to relate the details of the Saltanov battle which had been told him at Headquarters.

Rostov, hunching his shoulders as the water trickled down his neck, smoked his pipe and listened carelessly, with an occasional glance at young Ilyin who was squeezed in close to him. This officer, a lad of sixteen who had recently entered the regiment, looked up to Nikolai in the same way as Nikolai had looked up to Denisov seven years before. Ilyin tried to copy Rostov in everything, and adored him as a girl might have done.

The officer with the twin moustaches, Zdrzhinsky by name, grandiloquently described the dam at Saltanov as being a 'Russian Thermopylae', and declared the heroic deed of General Raevsky on that dam to be worthy of antiquity. He recounted how Raevsky had led his two sons forward on to the dam under terrific fire, and had charged with them beside him. Rostov heard the story and not only said nothing to encourage Zdrzhinsky's enthusiasm but, on the contrary, looked like a man ashamed of what was being told him, though he had no intention of gainsaying it. After Austerlitz and the campaigns of 1807 Rostov knew from his own experience that men always lie when reporting deeds of battle, as he himself had done. In the second place his experience had taught him that in war nothing really happens exactly as we imagine and describe it. And so he did not care for Zdrzhinsky's tale, nor did he like Zdrzhinsky himself, who had, besides his moustaches, a habit of bending right over into the face of the person he was speaking to; and he took up too much room in the cramped little shelter. Rostov looked at him without speaking. 'To begin with, there must have been such a crush and confusion on the dam they were attacking that if Raevsky had really rushed forward with his sons it could have had no effect except perhaps on the ten or twelve men nearest to him,' thought Rostov. 'The rest could not have seen how or with whom Raevsky advanced on to the dam. And then even those who did see could not have been particularly inspired, for what did Raevsky's tender paternal feelings matter to them when they had their own skins to think about? And, moreover, the fate of the Fatherland did not depend on whether the Saltanov dam was taken, as we are told was the case at Thermopylae. So what was the use of such a sacrifice? And why expose his own children in battle? I wouldn't have taken my brother Petya there, nor even Ilyin, who's not my own kith and kin but he's a nice lad: I would have tried to keep them out of danger,' Nikolai reflected as he listened to Zdrzhinsky. But he did not give voice to his thoughts: in that, too, experience had taught him wisdom. He knew that this tale redounded to the glory of our arms, and so one had to pretend to take it in. And he acted accordingly.

'I can't stand this any more,' exclaimed Ilyin, perceiving that Rostov did not care for Zdrzhinsky's chatter. 'Stockings and shirt and all – I'm soaked through. I'm off to look for another place. I fancy the rain's not so heavy.'

Ilyin went out and Zdrzhinsky rode away.

Five minutes later Ilyin came splashing back through the mud to the shanty.

'Hurrah, Rostov! Stir your stumps, I've found somewhere. There's a tavern a couple of hundred yards from here and a lot of our fellows are there already. We can at least get dry, and Maria Hendrihovna's there.'

Maria Hendrihovna was the wife of the regimental doctor, a pretty young German woman whom he had married in Poland. The doctor, either because he could not afford to set up house for her or because he did not want to be parted from his young wife in the early days of their marriage, took her with him wherever he went in his travels with the regiment, and his jealousy became a standing joke among the hussar officers.

Rostov flung his cloak over his shoulders, shouted to Lavrushka to follow with their things, and set off with Ilyin, now slipping in the mud, now splashing straight through it, in the lessening rain and the darkness which was rent at intervals by distant lightning.

'Rostov, where are you?'
'Here. What a flash!' they called to one another.

13

IN the deserted tavern, before which stood the doctor's shabby covered cart, there were already some half-dozen officers. Maria Hendrihovna, a plump, flaxen-headed little German in a dressing-jacket and night-cap, was sitting on a broad bench in the front corner. Her husband, the doctor, lay asleep behind her. Rostov and Ilyin were greeted with merry shouts and laughter as they entered the room.

'I say, how jolly we are!' said Rostov, laughing.

'And what are you gaping over?'

'Fine specimens they are! Why, the water's streaming from them! Don't swamp our parlour floor.'

'Mind you don't drip on Maria Hendrihovna's dress!' cried different voices.

Rostov and Ilyin made haste to look for a corner where they could change their wet clothes without offending Maria Hendrihovna's modesty. They started for a tiny recess the other side of a partition, but found it completely filled by three officers sitting on an empty chest playing cards by the light of a solitary candle, and nothing would induce them to budge. Maria Hendrihovna obliged with the loan of her petticoat which they hung up by way of a curtain, and behind this Rostov and Ilyin, assisted by Lavrushka, who had brought their kits, got out of their wet things and into dry ones.

They lit a fire in the dilapidated brick stove, discovered a board and propped it across two saddles and covered it with a horse-cloth. A small samovar was produced, together with a luncheon-basket and half a bottle of rum; and having asked Maria Hendrihovna to preside they all crowded round her. One offered her a clean handkerchief to wipe her charming hands; another spread his tunic under her little feet to keep them from the damp floor; a third hung a cape over the window to screen her from the draught; while a fourth waved the flies away from her husband's face he should wake up.

'Let him be,' said Maria Hendrihovna with a shy, happy smile. 'He will sleep sound anyhow after being up all night.'

'Oh no, Maria Hendrihovna,' replied the officer, 'one must look after the doctor. Anything may happen, and I dare say he'll take pity on me one day, when he has to cut off my leg or my arm.'

There were only three glasses, the water was so muddy that there was no telling whether the tea was strong or weak, and the samovar would only hold water enough for six; but this made it all the more fun to take turns in order of seniority to receive a glass from Maria Hendrihovna's plump little hands with their short and not over-clean nails. All the officers seemed to be genuinely in love with her for that evening. Even those who had been playing cards behind the partition soon left their game and came over to the samovar, catching the general mood of courting Maria Hendrihovna. She, seeing herself surrounded by all these brilliant and devoted young men, beamed with satisfaction, which she sought in vain to conceal, unmistakably alarmed as she was every time her husband moved in his sleep behind her.

There was only one spoon, sugar there was in plenty, but it took so long to melt that it was decided that Maria Hendrihovna should stir the sugar for each in turn. Rostov took his glass of tea, and adding some rum to it, begged Maria Hendrihovna to stir it for him.

'But you take it without sugar, don't you ?' she said, smiling all the while as though everything she said and everything the others said was as amusing as could be and held a double meaning.

'It's not the sugar I care about – all I want is for your little hand to stir my tea.'

Nothing loath, Maria Hendrihovna began looking for the spoon, which someone had pounced upon.

'Use your pretty little finger, Maria Hendrihovna,' said Rostov. 'I shall like that still better.'

'Too hot!' said Maria Hendrihovna, colouring with pleasure.

Ilyin put a few drops of rum into a bucket of water and brought it to Maria Hendrihovna, begging her to stir it with her finger.

'This is my cup,' he said. 'Only dip your finger in and I'll drink every drop.'

When they had emptied the samovar Rostov took a pack of cards and proposed a game of 'Kings' with Maria Hendrihovna. They drew lots to settle who should make up her set. At Rostov's suggestion it was agreed that whoever was 'king' should have the privilege of kissing Maria Hendrihovna's little hand, while the 'knave' should have to put the samovar on again for the doctor's tea when he awoke.

'Well, but supposing Maria Hendrihovna is "king" ?' asked Ilyin.

'She is our queen already, and her word is law!'

The game had scarcely begun before the doctor's dishevelled head suddenly popped up behind Maria Hendrihovna. He had been awake for some time, listening to the conversation, and apparently found nothing entertaining or amusing in what was going on. His face was glum and forlorn. He did not greet the officers but, scratching himself, asked them to move to let him get by. As soon as he had left the room all the officers burst into loud peals of laughter, while Maria Hendrihovna blushed till the tears came, which made her still more bewitching in the eyes of the young men. Returning from the yard, the doctor told his wife (who had lost her happy smile and was looking at him in dismay, in expectation of the sentence in store for her) that the rain had stopped and they must go and spend the night in their covered cart, or everything in it would be stolen.

'But I'll send an orderly ... I'll send a couple!' said Rostov. 'What an idea, doctor!'

'I will mount guard myself!' cried Ilyin.

'No, gentlemen, you have slept your fill but I've been up these two nights,' replied the doctor, and he sat gloomily down beside his wife to wait for the end of the game.

Seeing his sombre face lowering at his wife, the officers grew still more hilarious and many of them could not suppress their laughter, for which they hurriedly sought to invent plausible pretexts. When the doctor had gone, taking his wife with him, and had settled himself with her in their covered cart, the officers lay down in the tavern, covering themselves with their damp cloaks, but it was a long time before sleep came. They stayed awake talking, recalling the doctor's misgivings and his wife's glee, or running out on to the porch and coming back to report what was happening in the covered trap. Several times Rostov muffled up his head and tried to go to sleep, but some remark would rouse him again and the conversation would be resumed and again they would break out into nonsensical merry laughter, as though they were children.

14

IT was going on for three o'clock but no one was yet asleep when the quartermaster appeared with orders that they were to move on to the small town of Ostrovna.

Still laughing and talking, the officers began hurriedly getting ready; once more the samovar was filled with dirty water. But Rostov went off to his squadron without waiting for tea. It was already light, the rain had ceased and the clouds were dispersing. It felt damp and cold, especially in clothes that had not dried. As they came out of the tavern in the twilight of the dawn, Rostov and Ilyin both glanced under the wet and glistening leather hood of the doctor's cart; the doctor's feet were sticking out from under the apron, and in the interior they caught a glimpse of his wife's night-capped head resting on a pillow, and heard her sleepy breathing.

'She's a dear little creature, isn't she?' said Rostov to Ilyin, who was following him.

'Yes, what a charming woman!' responded Ilyin with all the gravity of a boy of sixteen.

Half an hour later the squadron was lined up on the road. The command was given 'Mount!', and crossing themselves the soldiers climbed into their saddles. Rostov, riding in front, gave the order 'Forward!' and the hussars, with clanking sabres and the subdued buzz of voices, their horses' hooves splashing in the mud, filed off four abreast and trotted along the broad road planted with birch-trees on either side, following the infantry and a battery which had gone on ahead.

Tattered violet-grey clouds, reddening in the sunrise, were scudding before the wind. It was getting lighter every moment. The feathery grass which always grows by the roadside in the country could be seen quite plainly, still glistening from the night's rain. The drooping branches of the birch-trees, wet too, swayed in the wind and tossed sparkling drops of water aslant across the highway. The soldiers' faces showed more distinctly with the passing of every minute. Rostov, with Ilyin who never left him, rode along the side of the road between two rows of birch-trees.

On active service Rostov allowed himself the indulgence of a Cossack horse instead of a regimental horse of the line. A connoisseur and lover of horses, he had lately acquired a fine spirited animal from the Don steppes, a chestnut with light mane and tail, on whom he could out-gallop anyone. To be on this mount was a pleasure to him, and so he rode on, thinking of his horse, of the morning, of the doctor's wife, and never once of the peril awaiting him.

Advancing into action in the early days, Rostov had felt afraid, but now there was not the slightest sensation of fear. He was fearless not because he had grown used to being under fire (one cannot grow used to danger), but because he had learned how to control his thoughts in face of danger. He had schooled himself when going into action to think about anything except what one would have supposed to be the most pressing interest of all – the hazards that lay before him. During the first period of his service, earnestly as he had tried and bitterly as he had reproached himself with cowardice, he had not been able to do this, but with time it had come of itself. So now he rode beside Ilyin under the birch-trees, occasionally plucking leaves from a branch that met his hand, sometimes touching his horse's flank with his foot, or without turning his head, handing the pipe he had finished to an hussar behind him, all with as calm and careless an air as though he were merely out for a ride. He felt a pang of pity when he looked at the excited face of Ilyin, who talked fast and nervously. He knew from experience the agonizing state of anticipation of terror and death in which the cornet was plunged, and knew that only time could help him.

As soon as the sun appeared in the clear strip of sky below the clouds the wind died down, as though it dared not mar the beauty of the summer morning after the storm; the trees still dripped but now the drops fell vertically, and all was hushed. The sun came up full and round, poised on the horizon and then disappeared behind a long, narrow cloud that hung above it. A few minutes later it burst forth brighter than ever on the upper rim of the cloud, cutting its edge. Everything shone and sparkled with light. And with that light, as though in response to it, the sound of guns was heard ahead of them.

Before Rostov had had time to collect his thoughts and determine how far distant the firing was, Count Ostermann-Tolstoy's adjutant came galloping from Vitebsk with orders to advance at a trot along the road.

The squadron overtook and passed the infantry and the battery – which had also quickened their pace – rode down a hill and through an empty, deserted village and started to climb again. The horses were beginning to lather and the men looked hot.

'Halt! Dress ranks!' the command of the divisional colonel rang out in front. 'Forward by the left. Walking pace – forward!'

And the hussars made their way along the line of troops to the left flank of our position, and halted behind our Uhlans, who formed the front line. To the right stood our infantry in a dense column: they were the reserves. Higher up the hill, on the very horizon, our cannons could be seen in the crystal-clear air, shining in the slanting rays of the morning sun. In front, beyond a hollow dale, the enemy's columns and guns were visible. Down below in the hollow our advanced line had already gone into action and was briskly exchanging shots with the enemy.

At these sounds, which he had not heard for many a day, Rostov's spirits rose, as though the firing was the liveliest of music. *Trap-ta-ta-tap!* cracked the shots, now together, now in rapid succession. Again all was silent, and then again it sounded as though someone were walking on squibs and exploding them.

The hussars waited for about an hour in the same place. A cannonade began. Count Ostermann with his suite rode up behind the squadron, stopped to say a word to the colonel of the regiment and continued up the hill to the guns.

After Ostermann had gone, a command rang out to the Uhlans. 'Fall in! Prepare to charge!'

The infantry in front parted into platoons to allow the cavalry to pass. The Uhlans started forward, the pennons on their lances fluttering, and trotted downhill towards the French cavalry, which had come into sight below to the left.

As soon as the Uhlans moved down the slope the hussars were ordered up the hill to support the battery. As they took the places vacated by the Uhlans bullets came flying from the outposts, hissing and whining but falling wide.

This sound, which he had not heard for so long, had an even more joyous and exhilarating effect on Rostov than the previous crack of musketry. Drawing himself up in the saddle, he surveyed the field of battle opening out before him from the hill, and with his whole soul followed the Uhlans into the charge. The Uhlans swooped down close upon the French dragoons, there was a scene of confusion in the smoke, and five minutes later the Uhlans were dashing back, not towards the spot where they had been posted but more to the left, and among the orange-coloured ranks of Uhlans on chestnut horses, and in a great mass behind them, could be seen blue French dragoons on grey horses.

15

ROSTOV, with the keen eye of the hunting man, was one of the first to descry these blue French dragoons pursuing our Uhlans. Nearer and nearer came the disordered throng of Uhlans with the French dragoons in pursuit. He could already see separate figures – who looked so small at the foot of the hill – jostling and overtaking one another, and waving their arms or their sabres in the air.

Rostov gazed at what was happening before him as he might have watched a hunt. His instinct told him that if he were to charge with his hussars on the French dragoons now, the latter could not stand their ground; but if they were to strike it must be done immediately, on the instant, or it would be too late. He looked round. A captain, standing beside him, also had his eyes fixed on the cavalry below.

'Andrei Sevastyanich,' said Rostov, 'you know, we could hack 'em to bits. ...'

'Yes, glorious,' said the captain, 'in fact we could. ...'

Without waiting for him to finish, Rostov touched his horse and galloped to the front of his men; and before he had time to give the word of command the whole squadron, sharing his impulse, dashed after him. Rostov himself could not have said how or why he acted. He did it all without reflecting or considering, as he would have done out hunting. He saw the dragoons near and galloping in disorder; he knew they could not withstand an attack – knew that there was only that one minute in which to take action and that it would not return if he let it slip. The bullets were whizzing and whistling around him so stimulatingly, and his mount was so eager to be off, that he could not resist it.

He spurred his horse, shouted the command and at the same instant rode at full trot downhill towards the dragoons, hearing the tramp of his deployed squadron behind him. No sooner had they reached the bottom of the slope than their gait involuntarily changed from trot to gallop, which grew swifter and swifter as they approached our Uhlans and the French dragoons who were pursuing them. The dragoons were close now. The foremost, seeing the hussars, began turning back, those behind paused. With the same feeling with which he would have dashed forward in the path of a wolf Rostov gave full rein to his Don horse and speeded to cut off the broken ranks of the French dragoons. One Uhlan stopped, another who was on foot flung himself to the ground to avoid being knocked over, a riderless horse fell in with the hussars. Nearly all the French dragoons were galloping back. Rostov, picking out one on a grey horse, flew after him. On the way he found himself bearing down on a bush, his gallant horse cleared it, and almost before he had righted himself in the saddle he saw that he was within a few seconds of overtaking his man. This Frenchman, an officer to judge by his uniform, was crouching over his grey horse and urging it on with his sabre. An instant later Rostov's charger dashed its shoulder against the hindquarters of the officer's horse, almost knocking it over, and at the same second Rostov, without knowing why, raised his sword and struck at the Frenchman.

The instant he had done this all Rostov's eagerness suddenly vanished. The officer fell, not so much from the blow – which had but slightly grazed his arm above the elbow – as from fright and the collision of the horses. Rostov reined in, and his eyes sought his foe to see what sort of man he had vanquished. The French officer was hopping with one foot on the ground and the other caught in the stirrup. With eyes screwed up with fear, as though expecting another blow at any moment, he glanced up at Rostov in shrinking terror. His pale mud-stained face – fair-haired, boyish, with a dimple in the chin and clear blue eyes – was not at all warlike or suited to the battlefield, but a most ordinary homely countenance. Before Rostov could decide what to do with him the officer cried, 'I surrender!' He made frantic unavailing efforts to get his foot out of the stirrup, and kept his frightened blue eyes fixed on Rostov. Some hussars who galloped up freed his foot and helped him into the saddle. On all sides Rostov's men were busily engaged with the French dragoons: one dragoon was wounded but though his face was streaming with blood he would not give up his horse; another sat perched up behind an hussar with his arms round him; a third was being assisted on to his horse by an hussar. In front the French infantry were firing as they ran. The hussars galloped back in haste with their prisoners. Rostov spurred back with the rest, conscious of a sort of ache in his heart. With the capture of that French officer and the blow he had dealt him he had been overcome by a vague, confused feeling, which he could not at all account for.

Count Ostermann-Tolstoy met the returning hussars, sent for Rostov, thanked him and said he would report his gallant action to the Emperor and would recommend him for the St George Cross. When he was summoned to Count Ostermann, Rostov, remembering that he had charged without orders, had no doubt that his commanding-officer was sending for him to reprimand him for breach of discipline. Ostermann's flattering words and promise of a reward should, therefore, have been all the more pleasant a surprise, but he was still oppressed by that obscure, disagreeable feeling of moral nausea. 'What on earth is it that's worrying me so?' he asked himself as he rode back from the general. 'Is it Ilyin? No, he's safe and sound. Have I disgraced myself in any way? No, that's not it either.' Something else was fretting him, like remorse. 'Yes, yes, that French officer with the dimple. And I remember how my arm hesitated when I raised it.'

Rostov caught sight of the prisoners being led away, and galloped after them to have a look at his Frenchman with the dimple in his chin. He was sitting in his strange foreign uniform on an hussar pack-horse, glancing uneasily about him. The sword-cut on his arm could scarcely be called a wound. He simulated a smile for Rostov and waved his hand in greeting. Rostov still felt uncomfortable, as if something were weighing on his conscience.

All that day and the next his friends and comrades noticed that Rostov, without being exactly depressed or irritable, was silent, thoughtful and preoccupied. He drank under protest as it were, tried to be alone and obviously had something on his mind.

He was going over that brilliant exploit of his, which to his amazement had gained him the St George Cross and even given him a reputation for bravery, and there was something he could not make out at all. 'So they are even more afraid than we are!' he thought. 'Is this, then, all that is meant by what is called heroism? And did I do it for my country's sake? And where was he to blame, with his dimple and his blue eyes? And how frightened he was! He thought I was going to kill him. Why should I kill him? My hand trembled. But they have given me the St George Cross. I can't make it out, I can't make it out at all!'

But while Nikolai brooded over these questions in his mind, and still failed to arrive at any clear solutions to what puzzled him so, the wheel of fortune, where the Service was concerned, as often happens, turned in his favour. After the affair at Ostrovna he received recognition and was given the command of a battalion of hussars, and whenever an intrepid officer was needed it was he who was picked for the job.

16

As soon as she received news of Natasha's illness the countess, though still ailing and far from strong, set out for Moscow with Petya and the rest of the household, and the whole family moved from Maria Dmitrievna's house to their own, and settled down in town.

Natasha's illness was so serious that, fortunately for her and for her parents, all thought of what had caused it, of her conduct and the breaking off of the engagement, receded into the background. She was so ill that they could not stop to consider how far she was to blame for all that had happened, while she could not eat or sleep, was growing visibly thinner, coughed and, as the doctors gave them to understand, was in danger. There was only one thing to be thought of now, and that was how to get her well again. Doctors came to see her, both singly and in consultation, talked endlessly in French, German and

Latin, criticized one another and prescribed every sort of remedy to cure every complaint they had ever heard of. But it never occurred to one of them to make the simple reflection that the disease Natasha was suffering from could not be known to them, just as no complaint afflicting a living being can ever be entirely familiar, for each living being has his own individual peculiarities and whatever his disease it must necessarily be peculiar to himself, a new and complex malady unknown to medicine – not a disease of the lungs, liver, skin, heart, nerves, and so on, as described in medical books, but a disease consisting of one out of the innumerable combinations of the ailments of those organs. This simple reflection could not occur to the doctors (any more than it could ever occur to a sorcerer that he is unable to produce magic) because medicine was their life-work, because it was for that that they were paid and on that that they had expended the best years of their lives. But the chief reason why this reflection could never enter their heads was because they saw that they unquestionably were useful; and they certainly were of use to the whole Rostov family. Their help did not depend on making the patient swallow substances, for the most part harmful (the harm was scarcely appreciable because they were administered in such small doses), but they were useful, necessary and indispensable because they satisfied a moral need of the sick girl and those who loved her – and that is why there are and always will be pseudo healers, wise women, homoeopaths and allopaths. They satisfied the eternal human need for hope of relief, for sympathetic action, which is felt in the presence of suffering, the need that is seen in its most elementary form in the child which must have the bruised place rubbed to make it better. A child hurts itself and at once runs to the arms of mother or nurse to have the bad place kissed and rubbed, and feels better as soon as this is done. The child cannot believe that these people who are so much stronger and cleverer have no remedy for its pain. And the hope of relief and the expression of its mother's sympathy while she rubs the bump comforts it. The doctors in Natasha's case were of service because they kissed and rubbed the bad place, assuring her that the trouble would soon be over if the coachman drove down to the chemist's in Arbatsky square and got a powder and some pills in a pretty box for a rouble and seventy kopeks, and if she took those powders in boiled water at intervals of precisely two hours, neither more nor less.

What would have become of Sonya and the count and countess if they had had nothing to do but look at Natasha, weak and fading away – if there had not been those pills to give by the clock, the warm drinks to prepare, the chicken cutlets, and all the other details ordered by the doctors, which supplied occupation and consolation to all of them? The stricter and more complicated the doctors' orders, the more comfort did those around her find in carrying them out. How could the count have borne his beloved daughter's illness had he not known that it was costing him a thousand roubles, and that he would not grudge thousands more, if that would do her any good; or had he not known that if her illness continued he would find still further thousands to take her abroad for consultations, and had he not been able to tell people how Métivier and Feller had not understood the symptoms, but Friez had diagnosed them, and Mudrov had succeeded even better? What would the countess have done had she not been able every now and then to scold the invalid for not obeying the doctor's instructions to the letter?

'You'll never get well like that,' she would say, vexation making her forget her distress, 'if you won't listen to the doctor and take your medicine properly! We can't play about, you know, or it may turn to *pneumonia*,' she would go on, finding great comfort in repeating this mysterious word, incomprehensible to others as well as to herself.

What would Sonya have done without the glad consciousness that at first she had not had her clothes off for three nights running, so as to be in readiness to carry out the doctor's injunctions promptly, and that she still kept awake at night so as not to miss the right time for giving Natasha the not very harmful pills from the little gilt box? Even Natasha herself, though she declared that no medicines could do her any good and that it was all nonsense, found it pleasant to see so many sacrifices being made for her, and to know that she had to take medicine at certain hours. And it was even pleasant to be able to show, by disregarding the doctor's prescriptions, that she did not believe in medical treatment and did not value her life.

The doctor came every day, felt her pulse, looked at her tongue and laughed and joked with her, paying no attention to her dejected face. But afterwards, when he had gone into the next room, where the countess hurriedly followed him, he would put on a grave expression and, thoughtfully shaking his head, say that, though the patient was in a critical state, still he placed high hopes on the efficacy of this last medicine, and that they must wait and see; that the illness was more psychological than . . .

And the countess, trying to conceal the action from herself and from him, would slip a gold piece into his hand, and always returned to the sick-room with a lighter heart.

The symptoms of Natasha's illness were loss of appetite, sleeplessness, a cough and continual depression. The doctors declared that she could not dispense with medical treatment, so they kept her in the stifling atmosphere of the city, and the Rostovs did not visit the country all that summer of 1812.

In spite of the vast number of little pills Natasha swallowed, and all the drops and powders out of the little bottles and boxes, of which Madame Schoss, who had a passion for such things, made a large collection, and in spite of being deprived of the country life to which she was accustomed, youth prevailed: Natasha's grief began to be overlaid by the impressions and incidents of everyday life, and ceased to press so painfully on her heart. The ache gradually faded into the past, and little by little her physical health improved.

17

NATASHA was calmer but she did not recover her spirits. She not merely avoided everything that might have amused and cheered her, such as balls, drives, concerts and theatres, but she never laughed without a note of tears in her laughter. She could not sing. As soon as she began to laugh or attempted to sing when she was by herself tears choked her: tears of remorse, tears of regret for that time of pure happiness which could never return, tears of vexation that she should so wantonly have ruined her young life which might have been so happy. Laughter and singing in particular seemed to her like a blasphemy in face of her sorrow. As to flirtation, there was no need for restraint – the idea never entered her head to desire admiration. She declared and felt at that time that all men were no more to her than Nastasya Ivanovna, the buffoon. Something stood sentinel within her and forbade her every joy. And indeed she seemed to have lost all the old interests of her girlish, carefree life that had been so full of hope. Those autumn months, the hunting, 'Uncle', and the Christmas holidays spent with Nikolai at Otradnoe were the memories over which she brooded most of all and with the sharpest pangs. What would she not have given to bring back even one single day of that time! But now it was gone for ever. Her presentiment at the time had not deceived her – the feeling that that state of freedom and readiness for every enjoyment would never come again. Yet she had to live on.

It comforted her to reflect that she was not better, as she had once fancied, but worse, far worse than anybody else in the world. But this was not enough. She knew that, and asked herself, 'What next?' But there was nothing to come. There was no gladness in life, yet life was passing. Natasha's sole idea was evidently not to be a burden or a hindrance to anyone, but for herself she wanted nothing at all. She held aloof from all the household, and only with her brother Petya did she feel at ease. She liked to be with him better than with the others, and when they were alone together she sometimes laughed. She rarely went out, and of those who came to call she was only glad to see one person – Pierre. No one could have been more tender, circumspect and at the same time serious than Count Bezuhov in his manner to her. Natasha unconsciously fell under the spell of this affectionate tenderness, and so took great solace in his society. But she was not even grateful to him for it – it seemed to her that Pierre did not have to make an effort to be good: it appeared to come so naturally to him that there was no merit in his kindness. Sometimes Natasha noticed embarrassment and awkwardness on his part in her presence, especially when he wanted to do something nice for her or when he was apprehensive lest something in the conversation should revive memories painful to her. She observed this and put it down to his general kindliness and shyness, which she supposed would be the same with everyone else. After those involuntary words – that if he were free he would have asked on his knees for her hand and her love – uttered in a moment of violent stress for her, Pierre never mentioned his feelings to Natasha; and it seemed to her plain that those words, which had so comforted her at the time, held no more meaning than any thoughtless, unconsidered absurdities spoken to console a weeping child. It was not because Pierre was a married man but because Natasha was conscious that between him and her the moral barrier – which she had felt to be absent with Kuragin – stood firm and rigid that it never entered her head that her relations with Pierre might develop into love on her side, and still less on his, or even into that tender, self-conscious, romantic friendship between a man and a woman of which she had known several instances.

Towards the end of the fast of St Peter, Agrafena Ivanovna Byelov, a country neighbour of the Rostovs, came to Moscow to pay her devotions at the shrines of the saints there. She suggested that Natasha should prepare for the Sacrament with her, and Natasha gladly welcomed the idea. Although the doctors forbade her going out early in the morning Natasha insisted on fasting and preparing for the Sacrament, not as was generally done in the Rostov family, by taking part in three services in their own house, but in the way Agrafena Ivanovna was doing, and going to church every day for a whole week and not missing a single vespers, matins or Liturgy.

The countess was pleased with Natasha's zeal. After the poor results of medical treatment, at the bottom of her heart she hoped that prayer might do more for her daughter than medicines, and, though she concealed it from the doctor and had some inward misgivings, she fell in with Natasha's wishes and entrusted her to Mademoiselle Byelov.

Mademoiselle Byelov would go in at three o'clock in the morning to call Natasha but generally found her already awake. Natasha was afraid of oversleeping and being late for matins. Making hasty ablutions and humbly dressing in her shabbiest gown and an old mantle, Natasha, shivering in the chill air, went out into the deserted streets lit by the pale light of early dawn. On Mademoiselle Byelov's advice Natasha prepared herself not in her own parish but at a church where, according to the devout Mademoiselle Byelov, the priest was a man who led an austere and lofty life. There were never many people in the church. Natasha always stood beside Mademoiselle Byelov in the same place, before the icon of the Mother of God let into the screen by the choir on the left, and a new feeling of humility before something sublime and incomprehensible came over Natasha when at that unprecedented early hour she gazed at the dark face of Our Lady, lit up by the candles burning before it and the morning light falling from the window, and listened to the words of the service which she tried to follow with understanding. When she understood them, all the shades of her personal feeling became interwoven with her prayer. When she did not understand, it was sweeter still to think that the desire to understand all was pride, that it was impossible to comprehend everything, that all she had to do was to have faith and commit herself to God, Who was, she felt, at those moments guiding her soul. She crossed herself, bowed to the ground, and when she did not follow, in horror at her own vileness simply asked God to forgive her everything, everything, and have mercy on her soul. The prayers to

which she surrendered herself most of all were the prayers of repent-
ance. On the way home in the early morning when the only people
about were bricklayers going to work or men sweeping the street,
and everybody indoors was still asleep, Natasha experienced a new
sense of the possibility of correcting her wickedness, and leading a
fresh life of purity and happiness.

During all that week which she spent in this way the feeling grew
with every day. And the happiness of communicating, or 'commun-
ing' as Mademoiselle Byelov liked to call taking Communion, seemed
to Natasha so great that she thought she would never live till that
blessed Sunday.

But the happy day did come, and on that memorable Sunday when
Natasha, wearing a white muslin dress, returned from the Sacrament,
for the first time for many months she felt at peace and not oppressed
by the thought of the life that lay before her.

The doctor, who came to see her that day, ordered the powders to
be continued, that he had begun prescribing a fortnight previously.

'She must certainly go on taking them morning and evening,' said
he, with visible and simple-hearted satisfaction at the success of his
treatment. 'Now please be careful and don't forget them. You may
set your mind at rest, countess,' he continued playfully, as he deftly
received the gold piece in the palm of his hand. 'She will soon be
singing and frolicking about. The last medicine has done wonders.
She is very much better.'

The countess looked at her finger-nails and spat a little for luck as
she returned to the drawing-room with a cheerful face.

18

At the beginning of July more and more disquieting reports about
the war began to spread in Moscow: there was talk of an appeal by
the Emperor to the people, and of his coming himself from the army
to Moscow. And as up to the 11th of July no manifesto or appeal had
been received the most exaggerated rumours became current about
them and concerning the position of Russia. It was said that the
Emperor was leaving because the army was in danger; it was said
that Smolensk had surrendered; that Napoleon had a million men
and that nothing short of a miracle could save the Fatherland.

On the 11th of July, a Saturday, the manifesto was received but was not yet in print, and Pierre, who happened to be at the Rostovs', promised to come next day, Sunday, to dinner, and bring a copy of the manifesto and appeal, which he would obtain from Count Rostopchin.

That Sunday the Rostovs attended divine service as usual in the private chapel of the Razumovskys. It was a hot July day. Even by ten o'clock, when the Rostovs got out of their carriage at the chapel, the sultry air, the shouts of the street-hawkers, the bright, gay clothes of the crowd, the dusty leaves of the trees along the boulevard, the martial music and white trousers of a battalion marching by to parade, the rattling of wheels on the cobble-stones, and the blazing sunshine were all full of that summer languor, that content and discontent with the present, which is felt with particular poignancy on a brilliant scorching day in town. All the rank and fashion of Moscow, all the Rostovs' acquaintances were in the Razumovskys' chapel. (This year, as if anticipating serious events, a great many of the wealthy families who usually spent the summer on their estates in the country were staying in the city.) As Natasha walked beside her mother, preceded by a footman in livery who cleared the way for them through the throng, she heard a young man make a remark about her in too loud a whisper.

'That's the young Countess Rostov, the one who ...'
'How thin she's got! But she's still pretty!'

She heard, or fancied she heard, the names of Kuragin and Bolkonsky. But that was always happening. She was always fancying that anyone who looked at her could only be thinking of what she had done. With a sinking heart, wretched as she always was now when she found herself in a crowd, Natasha, in her lilac silk dress trimmed with black lace, walked on, presenting an appearance – as women can – of ease and dignity all the greater for the pain and shame in her heart. She knew for a fact that she was pretty but the knowledge no longer gave her the pleasure it used to afford. On the contrary, it had been a source of more misery than anything of late, and especially so on this bright, hot summer day in town. 'Sunday again, and another week,' she said to herself, recalling how she had been here the previous Sunday, 'and for ever the same life which is no life, and the same circumstances in which it had been so easy to live before. I'm pretty, I'm young and I know that now I am good. Before I was wicked, but now I am good, I know,' she thought, 'but yet my best years, my very best years are slipping by and all for nothing.' She stood by her mother's side and exchanged nods with acquaintances who were standing near. From force of habit she scrutinized the dresses of the ladies, and criticized the *tenue* of a lady close to them, and the awkward cramped way in which she crossed herself; and then she thought again with vexation that she herself was being found fault with and was judging others, and suddenly, at the first sounds of the service, she was horrified at her sinfulness, horrified that her purity of heart should be lost to her again.

A venerable, gentle old man was conducting the service with that quiet solemnity which has so elevating and soothing an effect on the souls of the worshippers. The sanctuary doors were closed, the curtain was slowly drawn, and from behind it a soft mysterious voice pronounced some words. Tears that she could not have explained made Natasha's breast heave, and a feeling of joyful agitation came upon her.

'Teach me what to do, show me how to put my life right for ever and ever, how to live! . . .' she prayed.

The deacon came out on to the raised space before the altar-screen and, holding his thumb extended, drew his long hair from under his dalmatic, and making the sign of the cross on his breast began in a loud and solemn voice to recite the words of the litany:

'In peace let us pray unto the Lord.'

'As one community, without distinction of class, without enmity, united in brotherly love – let us pray!' thought Natasha.

'For the peace which is from above, and for the salvation of our souls.'

'For the world of angels and the souls of all spiritual beings who dwell above us,' prayed Natasha.

When they prayed for the armed forces she thought of her brother and Denisov. When they prayed for all who travel on sea and land she thought of Prince Andrei and prayed for him, and asked God to forgive her the wrong she had done him. When they prayed for all who love us she prayed for the members of her own family, her father, her mother, Sonya, realizing now for the first time how wrongly she had acted towards them and how strong and deep was her love for them. When they prayed for those who hate us she tried to conjure up enemies and people who hated her, in order to pray for them. Among her enemies she reckoned her father's creditors and all those who had business dealings with him, and always at the thought of enemies and people who hated her she remembered Anatole, who had done her so much harm, and though he had not hated her she prayed gladly for him as for an enemy. Only at prayer was she able to think clearly and calmly of Prince Andrei and Anatole, with a sense that her feelings for them were as nothing compared with her awe and devotion to God. When they prayed for the Imperial family and the Synod she bowed and crossed herself more devoutly than ever, telling herself that even if she did not understand, still she could not doubt and, anyway, loved the ruling Synod and prayed for it.

When the litany was over, the deacon crossed the stole over his breast and said:

'Let us commit ourselves and our whole lives to Christ the Lord!'

'Commit ourselves to God,' Natasha repeated in her heart. 'O God, I submit myself to Thy will!' she thought. 'I ask for nothing, desire nothing: teach me how to act, what to do with my will! Take me, take me to Thee!' prayed Natasha, her heart filled with yearning impatience. She did not cross herself but stood with her thin arms hanging down as if expecting some invisible power at any moment to take her and deliver her from herself, from her regrets and desires, her remorse, her hopes and her sins.

Several times during the service the countess looked round at her daughter's rapt face and shining eyes, and prayed God to help her.

To the general surprise, in the middle of the service and contrary to the usual order of the Liturgy, which Natasha knew so well, the deacon brought out the little footstool on which the priest kneels when he reads the prayers on Trinity Sunday, and set it before the holy gates leading into the sanctuary. The priest came out in his purple velvet calotte, adjusted his hair, and with an effort dropped on his knees. All the congregation knelt with him, looking at one another in perplexity. There followed the prayer just received from the Synod – the prayer for the deliverance of Russia from enemy invasion.

'Lord God of might, God of our salvation!' began the priest in the clear, mild, unemphatic tones peculiar to the Slav clergy, which act so irresistibly on a Russian heart.

Lord God of might, God of our salvation, in Thy mercy and bounty look this day on Thy humble people, and graciously hear us, and spare us, and have mercy upon us. Behold the enemy, which is confounding

Thy land and would fain lay waste the universe, has risen against us. Behold these lawless men are gathered together to overthrow Thy kingdom, to destroy Thy holy Jerusalem, Thy beloved Russia: to defile Thy temples, to overturn Thine altars and profane our sanctuaries. How long, O Lord, how long shall the wicked triumph? How long shall they wield their unlawful power?

Almighty God, hear us when we pray to Thee: strengthen with Thy might our most gracious Sovereign Lord the Emperor Alexander Pavlovich; forget not his virtue and meekness, reward him according to his righteousness and let it preserve us, Thy chosen Israel! Bless his counsels, his undertakings and his deeds; fortify his kingdom by Thine Almighty Hand, and vouchsafe him victory over his enemy, even as Thou didst give Moses victory over Amalek, Gideon over Midian, and David over Goliath. Preserve his armies, put weapons of brass in the hands of those who go forth in Thy name, and gird their loins with strength for the battle. Take up Thy sword and Thy buckler, and arise and help us: confound and put to shame them that devise evil against us, and let them be scattered before the face of Thy faithful armament as dust before the wind, and may Thy mighty Angel chastise and defeat them. May they be ensnared in the net that they know not of, and their designs which they have hatched in secret be turned against them. Let them go down under the feet of Thy servants, and be laid low by our hosts. Lord, Thou art able to save both great things and small. Thou art God, and man cannot prevail against Thee.

O God of our fathers, remember Thy bounteous mercy and lovingkindness that Thou hast shown of old! Cast us not from Thy presence, nor let Thy wrath be kindled against our iniquities, but have mercy upon us according to Thy lovingkindness, according unto the multitude of Thy tender mercies heed not our transgressions and iniquities. Create in us a clean heart, and renew a right spirit within us. Fortify us every one by faith in Thee, confirm us with hope, breathe into us true love one for another, arm us with unity of spirit in the righteous defence of the inheritance which Thou gavest to us and to our forefathers, and let not the sceptre of the unrighteous be exalted over the destinies of those whom Thou hast sanctified.

O Lord our God, in Whom we believe and in Whom we put our trust, let us not be confounded as we look for Thy mercy, and vouchsafe us a sign for our blessing that they that hate us and our holy Orthodox faith may see and be put to shame and perish; and may all the nations know that Thou art the Lord and we are Thy people. Show Thy mercy upon us this day, O Lord, and grant us Thy salvation; make the hearts of Thy servants to rejoice in Thy mercy; strike down our enemies and be swift to vanquish them beneath the feet of Thy faithful servants. For Thou art the defence, the succour and the victory of them that put their trust in Thee, and to Thee be all glory, to Father, Son and Holy Spirit, as it was in the beginning, is now and ever shall be, world without end. Amen.

In Natasha's receptive condition this prayer had a deep effect on her. She listened to every word about Moses' victory over Amalek, and Gideon's over Midian, and David's over Goliath, and about the destruction of Thy Jerusalem, and she prayed to God with all the feeling and fervour with which her heart was overflowing, though she was not really clear what she was asking of God in the prayer. With all her soul she joined in the petition for a right spirit, for the strengthening of her heart by faith and hope and the breathing into them of love. But she could not pray that her enemies might be trampled underfoot when but a few minutes before she had been wishing she had more of them to love and pray for. Yet neither could she doubt the propriety of the prayer that was being read by the priest on his knees. Her heart knew a thrill of awe and horror at the punishment that overtakes men for their sins, and especially for her own sins, and she prayed to God to forgive them all, and her too, and grant them all, and her too, peace and happiness. And it seemed to her that God heard her prayer.

19

EVER since the day when Pierre, on his way home from the Rostovs' with Natasha's grateful look fresh in his mind, had gazed at the comet in the sky and felt as though something new was opening before him – from that day the haunting problem of the vanity and folly of all earthly things had ceased to torment him. That terrible question 'Why ? Wherefore ?', which till then had appeared to trouble him in the midst of every occupation, was now replaced not by another question or by the answer to the former question, but by *her* image. Whether he listened to or himself took part in trivial conversations, whether he read or heard tell of some instance of human baseness or stupidity, he was not horrified as of old: he did not ask himself why people fussed, when all was so transient and uncertain, but he pictured her to himself as he had last seen her, and all his doubts vanished – not because she was the answer to the questions that met him at every turn but because his image of her instantly lifted him into another world, a serene realm of spiritual activity, where there could be neither right nor wrong – a realm of beauty and love which it was worth living for. Whatever worldly infamy came to his notice, he would say to himself:

'Well, what does it matter if So-and-so who has robbed the country and the Tsar has honours conferred on him by the State and the Tsar, since yesterday she smiled on me, and begged me to come, and I love her, and no one will ever know.'

Pierre still went into society, drank as much as before, and led the same idle and dissipated life, because besides the hours he spent at the Rostovs' he had to get through the rest of his time somehow, and the habits and the acquaintances he had made in Moscow formed a current that bore him along irresistibly. But of late, when the news from the theatre of war daily became more alarming, and Natasha's health had begun to improve and she had ceased to call for the same tender pity, he fell more and more prey to a restlessness which he could not explain. He felt that the position in which he found himself could not go on much longer, that a catastrophe was coming which would change the whole course of his life, and he sought impatiently and everywhere for signs of this approaching disaster. One of his brother freemasons had revealed to Pierre the following prophecy concerning Napoleon, drawn from the Revelation of St John the Divine.

Chapter xiii, verse 18 of Revelations says:

Here is wisdom. Let him that hath understanding count the number of the beast: for it is the number of a man; and his number is Six hundred threescore and six.

And the fifth verse of the same chapter:

And there was given unto him a mouth speaking great things and blasphemies; and power was given unto him to continue forty and two months.

If the French alphabet is written out and given the same numerical values as the Hebrew, in which the first nine letters denote units and the next the tens and so on, we get the following:

a	b	c	d	e	f	g	h	i	k	l	m	n	o	p	q	r	s
1	2	3	4	5	6	7	8	9	10	20	30	40	50	60	70	80	90

t	u	v	w	x	y	z
100	110	120	130	140	150	160

Turning the words *l'empereur Napoléon* into numbers on this system, it appears that the sum of them equals 666 (including a 5 for the letter *e* dropped by elision from the *le* before *empereur*), and Napoleon is seen to be the beast prophesied in the Apocalypse. Moreover, by applying the same system to the words *quarante-deux* (forty-two), that is, the term allowed to the beast that spoke 'great things and blasphemies', the same number 666 obtains; from which it follows that the limit fixed for Napoleon's power had come in the year 1812, when the French Emperor reached his forty-second year. This prophecy made a great impression on Pierre, and he frequently asked himself what would put an end to the power of the beast, that is, of Napoleon, and tried by the same system of turning letters into figures and reckoning them up to find an answer to the question that engrossed him. He wrote the words *l'empereur Alexandre, la nation russe* and added up their numbers, but the sums came to far more or far less than the 666. Once when he was engaged with these calculations he wrote down his own name in French – *Comte Pierre Besouhoff,* but again the total did not come out right. He changed the spelling, substituting *z* for *s* and adding *de* and the article *le,* and still he failed to obtain the desired result. Then it occurred to him that if the answer he sought were contained in his name, it would certainly include his nationality too. So he tried *Le russe Besuhof,* and reckoning up the numbers got 671. This was only five too much, and five corresponded to *e,* the very letter elided from the article before the word *empereur.* Dropping the *e,* though of course incorrectly, gave Pierre the answer he was after: *l'russe Besuhof* – exactly 666. This discovery excited him greatly. How, and by what means, he was connected with the great event foretold in the Apocalypse he did not know, but he did not for a moment doubt that connexion. His love for Natasha, Antichrist, Napoleon's invasion, the comet, 666, *l'empereur Napoléon* and *l'russe Besuhof* – all these taken together had to mature and burst forth, and lift him out of that bewitched, futile round of Moscow habits to which he felt himself held captive, and lead him to some mighty exploit and great happiness.

*

On the eve of the Sunday on which the special prayer was read, Pierre had promised the Rostovs to bring them, from Count Rostopchin whom he knew well, both the appeal to the nation and the latest military news. In the morning, when he went to call at Count Rostop-chin's, Pierre met there a courier fresh from the army. This courier was an acquaintance of Pierre's, a regular *habitué* of the Moscow ball-rooms.

'For heaven's sake, can't you relieve me of something?' said the courier. 'I have a whole sackful of letters to parents.'

Among these letters was one from Nikolai Rostov to his father. Pierre took charge of that letter, and Count Rostopchin also gave him a copy of the Sovereign's appeal to Moscow which had just come from the press, the latest army orders and his own most recent bulle-tin. Glancing through the army orders, Pierre found in one of them, in the lists of killed, wounded and decorated, the name of Nikolai Rostov, awarded a St George's Cross of the fourth class for bravery displayed in the Ostrovna affair, and in the same announcement the appointment of Prince Andrei Bolkonsky to the command of a regi-ment of Chasseurs. Though he did not want to remind the Rostovs of Bolkonsky, Pierre could not resist the inclination to rejoice their hearts with the news of their son's decoration, so, keeping the Tsar's appeal, the bulletin and the other announcements to take with him when he went to dinner, he sent the printed army order and Nikolai's letter to the Rostovs.

His conversation with Count Rostopchin and the latter's hurried, preoccupied air, the meeting with the courier who had casually alluded to the disastrous way things were going in the army, the rumours of the discovery of spies in Moscow and of a broadsheet circulating in the city stating that Napoleon had sworn to be in both Russian capitals by the autumn, and talk of the Tsar's expected arrival next day – all combined to revive in Pierre with fresh intensity that feeling of agitation and suspense which he had been conscious of ever since the appearance of the comet, and especially since the beginning of the war.

The idea of entering the army had, for some time, been much in his mind, and he would assuredly have done so had he not been de-terred, first, by his membership of the Order of Freemasonry, to which he was bound by oath and which preached eternal peace and the abolition of war, and, secondly, by the fact that when he saw the great mass of Moscovites who had donned uniform and sang the praises of patriotism, he felt somehow ashamed to take the same step. But the chief reason which kept him from carrying out his design to enter upon military service lay in the obscure conception that he, *l'russe Besuhof*, who had the number of the beast, 666, was predestined from eternity to take some part in setting a limit to the power of the beast 'speaking great things and blasphemies', and that therefore he ought not to undertake anything but wait for what was bound to come to pass.

20

A FEW intimate friends were, as usual on Sundays, dining with the Rostovs.

Pierre went early so as to find them alone.

He had grown so stout that year that he would have been grotesque had he not been so tall and had such powerful limbs, and been so strong that he carried his bulk with evident ease.

Puffing and muttering something to himself, he went up the stairs. His coachman did not even ask whether he should wait. He knew that when the count was at the Rostovs' he stayed till near midnight. The Rostovs' footmen rushed eagerly forward to help him off with his cloak and take his stick and hat. Pierre, from club habit, always left both stick and hat in the ante-room.

The first person he saw at the Rostovs' was Natasha. Even before he saw her, while taking off his cloak, he heard her. She was practising sol-fa exercises in the music-room. He knew that she had not sung since her illness, and so the sound of her voice surprised and delighted him. He opened the door softly and saw her in the lilac dress she had worn at church, walking about the room singing. She had her back to him when he opened the door, but when she turned quickly and saw his broad, surprised face, she blushed and came swiftly up to him.

'I want to try and sing again,' she said. 'At least it's something to do,' she added as if by way of excuse.

'Quite right too!'

'How glad I am you have come! I am so happy today,' she said with the old animation Pierre had not seen in her for a long time. 'You know, Nicolas has got the St George's Cross? I'm so proud of him.'

'Oh yes, I sent you the announcement. Well, I don't want to interrupt you,' he added, and would have gone on to the drawing-room.

Natasha stopped him.

'Count, is it wrong of me to sing?' she said, blushing, but still keeping her eyes fixed inquiringly on Pierre.

'No. ... Why should it be? On the contrary. ... But why do you ask me?'

'I don't know myself,' replied Natasha quickly, 'but I shouldn't like to do anything you disapproved of. I have such complete faith in you. You don't know how important you are to me, and how much you have done for me! ...' She spoke rapidly and did not notice how Pierre flushed at these words of hers. 'I saw in the same announcement, *he*, Bolkonsky' (she uttered the name in a hurried whisper), 'he is in Russia, and in the army again. What do you think,' she said hastily, evidently hurrying for fear her strength might fail her, 'will he ever forgive me? Will he not always bear me ill will? What do you think? What do you think?'

'I think ...' said Pierre. 'He has nothing to forgive. ... If I were in his place ...'

Association of ideas carried Pierre back in imagination to the time when he had tried to comfort her and said that if instead of being himself he were the best man in the world and free he would beg on his knees for her hand, and the same feeling of pity, tenderness and love took possession of him and the same words rose to his lips. But she did not give him time to utter them.

'Yes, you – you ...' she said, rapturously pronouncing the word *you* – 'that's a different matter. Anyone kinder, more generous or better than you I have never known, and nobody could be! If it had not been for you then, and now too, I don't know what would have become of me, because ...'

Her eyes suddenly filled with tears; she turned away, lifted her music before her face, and began singing and walking up and down the room again.

At that moment Petya ran in from the drawing-room.

Petya was now a handsome ruddy lad of fifteen, with full red lips, very like Natasha. He was preparing for the university, but lately he and his friend Obolensky had secretly made up their minds to join the hussars.

Petya came rushing up to talk to his namesake of this important matter. He had asked Pierre to find out whether he would be accepted in the hussars.

Pierre walked about the drawing-room not listening to what Petya was saying.

The boy pulled him by the arm to attract his attention.

'Well, what about my business – please tell me, for mercy's sake! You are my only hope!' said Petya.

'Oh yes, your affairs. You want to join the hussars? I'll speak about it. This very day I'll tell them all about it.'

'Well, *mon cher*, did you get the manifesto?' asked the old count. 'My little countess was at the service in the Razumovskys' chapel and heard the new prayer. Very fine it was, she tells me.'

'Yes, I've got it,' replied Pierre. 'The Emperor will be here to-morrow ... there's to be an extraordinary meeting of the nobility, and a levy, so they say, of ten men per thousand. Oh yes, let me congratulate you!'

'Yes, indeed, praise God! Well, and what news from the army?'

'We have retreated again. I'm told we're already back nearly to Smolensk,' answered Pierre.

'Mercy on us, mercy on us!' exclaimed the count. 'Where's the manifesto?'

'The Emperor's appeal? Ah, yes!'

Pierre began feeling in his pockets for the papers and could not find them. Still slapping his pockets, he kissed the countess's hand as she came in, and then looked round uneasily, evidently expecting Natasha, who had left off singing now but had not yet appeared in the drawing-room.

'Upon my word, I don't know what I've done with it,' he said.

'There he is, always losing everything,' remarked the countess.

Natasha entered with a softened and agitated expression, and sat down looking mutely at Pierre. As soon as she came into the room Pierre's face, which had been overcast, suddenly lighted up, and while still searching for the papers he glanced at her intently several times.

'By heaven, I'll drive home, I must have left them there. Most certainly. ...'

'But you'll be late for dinner.'

'Oh, and my coachman has gone.'

But Sonya, who had gone to look for the papers in the ante-room, had found them in Pierre's hat, where he had carefully tucked them under the lining. Pierre wanted to begin reading them immediately.

'No, after dinner,' said the old count, obviously anticipating much enjoyment from the reading.

At dinner they drank champagne to the health of the new chevalier of St George, and Shinshin told them the gossip of the town about the illness of the old Georgian princess, Métivier's disappearance from Moscow, and how some German fellow had been brought before Rostopchin and accused of being a *champignon* – a French spy – (so Count Rostopchin had told the story), and how Rostopchin let him go, assuring the people that he was not a *champignon* but simply an old German toadstool.

'Yes, they keep arresting people,' said the count. 'I tell the countess she should not speak French so much. This is not the time for it.'

'And have you heard ?' said Shinshin. 'Prince Golitsyn has engaged a tutor to teach him Russian. It is becoming dangerous to speak French in the streets.'

'And how about you, Count Piotr Kirillich ? If there's a general call-up, you too will have to mount a horse, eh ?' remarked the old count, addressing Pierre.

Pierre had been silent and preoccupied all through dinner. He looked at the count as though not understanding.

'Oh yes, the war,' he said. 'No! A fine soldier I should make! And yet the whole business is so strange – so extraordinary – I am quite at sea. I don't know, I am far from having military tastes, but in these days no one can answer for himself.'

After dinner the count settled himself comfortably in an easy-chair, and with a serious face asked Sonya, who enjoyed the reputation of being an excellent reader, to read the appeal.

To Moscow, our chief capital:
The enemy has entered the confines of Russia with immense forces. He comes to lay waste our beloved country,

Sonya carefully read aloud in her thin treble. The count listened with closed eyes, heaving abrupt sighs at certain passages.

Natasha sat bolt upright, gazing with searching looks, now at her father, now at Pierre.

Pierre felt her eyes on him and tried not to look round. The countess shook her head disapprovingly and wrathfully at every solemn expression in the manifesto. In all these words she saw only one thing: that the danger menacing her son would not soon be over. Shinshin, pursing lips into a sardonic smile, was clearly preparing to make fun at the first opportunity – of Sonya's reading, of the count's next remark, or even of the very manifesto should no better pretext present itself.

After reading about the perils threatening Russia, the hopes the Emperor placed on Moscow and especially on its illustrious Nobility, Sonya, with a quiver in her voice due principally to the attention with which they were listening to her, came to the last words:

We shall not be slow to appear among our people in the capital, and in other parts of our dominion, for consultation and for the guidance of all our militia levies, both those now barring the enemy's path and those newly formed to overthrow him wherever he may show himself. May the ruin and destruction which he would precipitate on us recoil on his own head, and may Europe, delivered from bondage, glorify the name of Russia!

'That's the way!' cried the count, opening his moist eyes and sniffing repeatedly as if a strong vinaigrette had been held to his nose. 'Let our Sovereign but say the word and we will sacrifice everything, begrudging nothing.'

Before Shinshin had time to utter the joke he was ready to make at the expense of the count's patriotism Natasha sprang up from her seat and ran to her father.

'What a darling our Papa is!' she cried, kissing him, and then she glanced at Pierre again with the unconscious coquetry which had come back to her with the return of better spirits.

'Bravo, what a patriot you are!' said Shinshin.

'Not at all, but simply ...' Natasha began, offended. 'You think everything funny, but this is no laughing matter. ...'

'Laughing matter indeed!' put in the count. 'Let him but say the word and we'll all go. ... We're not a set of Germans. ...'

'But did you notice,' said Pierre, 'that it spoke about "consultation"?'

'Well, whatever it's for. ...'

At that moment Petya, to whom nobody was paying any attention, came up to his father and, with a very red face, said in a voice which was now breaking and so was alternately deep and shrill:

'Well, Papa, now is the time to tell you – and Mamma, too, please – to say to you that you positively must let me enter the army, because I cannot ... well, that's all. ...'

The countess, in dismay, raised her eyes to heaven, clasped her hands and turned angrily to her husband.

'There, that's what comes of your talking!'

But the count had already recovered from his excitement.

'What next!' said he. 'A pretty soldier you'd make! No – nonsense! You have your studies to attend to.'

'It's not nonsense, Papa! Fedya Obolensky is younger than me, and he's going too. Besides, I couldn't study now anyhow, when ...' Petya stopped short, flushed till his face perspired, yet stoutly went on '... when our Fatherland is in danger.'

'That'll do, that'll do – enough of this nonsense. ...'

'But you said yourself that we would sacrifice everything.'

'Petya! Be quiet, I tell you!' cried the count with a glance at his wife, who had gone pale and was staring fixedly at her young son.

'And I say – Piotr Kirillich here will tell you too. ...'

'I tell you it's nonsense. The milk's hardly dry on his lips and he wants to go into the army! Really, I must say!' And the count, taking the papers, moved to go out of the room, probably to read them once more before having a nap.

'Piotr Kirillich, what about it? – let's go and have a smoke. ...'

Pierre felt embarrassed and hesitating. Natasha's unwontedly brilliant and eager eyes, continually turned upon him with a more than cordial look, had reduced him to this condition.

'No, I think I'll go home.'

'Go home? Why, you meant to spend the evening with us. ... You don't often come nowadays as it is. And this girl of mine,' said the count good-humouredly, pointing to Natasha, 'only brightens up when you are here.'

'Yes, I had forgotten. ... I really must go home. ... Business ...' said Pierre hurriedly.

'Well, then, *au revoir!*' said the count and went out of the room.

'Why are you going? What are you upset for? What is it?' Natasha asked Pierre, looking challengingly into his eyes.

'Because I love you!' was what he wanted to say, but he did not say it, and only crimsoned till the tears came, and lowered his eyes.

'Because it is better for me not to be here so much. ... Because ... No, simply I have business. ...'

'Why? No, tell me!' Natasha was beginning resolutely, and suddenly stopped.

The two looked at each other in dismay and confusion. He tried to smile but could not: his smile expressed suffering, and he silently kissed her hand and left.

Pierre made up his mind not to go to the Rostovs' any more.

21

AFTER the uncompromising refusal he had received, Petya went to his room and, locking himself in, wept bitterly. When he came in to tea, silent, morose and with tear-stained face, everybody pretended not to notice anything.

Next day the Emperor arrived in Moscow, and several of the Rostovs' house-servants begged permission to go and see the Tsar. That morning Petya was a long time dressing and doing his hair and arranging his collar to look like a grown-up man. He frowned before the looking-glass, gesticulated, shrugged his shoulders and finally, without a word to anyone, took his cap and went out of the house by the back door, trying not to be observed. Petya had decided to go straight to where the Emperor was and to explain frankly to some gentleman-in-waiting (Petya imagined that the Emperor was always surrounded by gentlemen-in-waiting) that he, Count Rostov, in spite of his youth, wished to serve his country, that youth could be no hindrance to devotion, and that he was ready to ... Petya, while dressing, had prepared a great many fine speeches to make to the gentleman-in-waiting.

Petya relied for success in reaching the Emperor on the very fact of being so young – he even thought how surprised everyone would be at his youth – and at the same time by the arrangement of his collar and his hair and by the sedate, deliberate way he would walk he meant to give the impression of being a grown-up man. But the farther he went and the more his attention was diverted by the ever-increasing crowds round the Kremlin, the less he remembered to keep up the sedateness and deliberation characteristic of grown-up people. As he approached the Kremlin he had to struggle to avoid being crushed, and with a resolute and threatening mien stuck his elbows out on each side of him. But at Trinity Gate, in spite of his determined air, the throng of people, probably unaware of the patriotic intentions bringing him to the Kremlin, so pressed him against the wall that he was obliged to give in and stop while carriages rumbled in beneath the archway. Near Petya stood a peasant woman, a footman, two tradesmen and a discharged soldier. After standing for some time in the gateway Petya tried to push forward in front of the others, without waiting for all the carriages to pass, and began vigorously working his way with his elbows, but the peasant woman standing beside him, who was the first to be poked, shouted at him angrily:

'Here, my young gentleman, what are you shoving for? Can't you see we're all standing still? What do you want to push for?'

'That's a game everyone can play,' said the footman, and he, too, set to work with his elbows and squeezed Petya into a very ill-smelling corner of the gateway.

Petya wiped his perspiring face with his hands, and pulled up the damp collar which at home he had arranged so carefully to look like a man's.

He felt that he no longer offered a presentable appearance, and feared that if he showed himself in this guise to the gentlemen-in-waiting they would not admit him to the Emperor. But the crush made it impossible to tidy himself up or move to another place. One of the generals who drove by was an acquaintance of the Rostovs', and Petya wanted to ask his help but came to the conclusion that this would not be a manly thing to do. When all the carriages had passed in, the crowd, carrying Petya with it, streamed forward into the square, which was already full of people. Not only in the square but on the slopes and the roofs – everywhere were people. As soon as Petya found himself in the square he heard the bells ringing and the joyous hum of the crowd flooding the whole Kremlin.

For a while the crush was less in the square, but all at once heads were bared and there was another surge forward. Petya was so squashed that he could hardly breathe, and everybody shouted 'Hurrah! hurrah! hurrah!'

Petya stood on tiptoe, and pushed and pinched, but he could see nothing except the people about him.

Every face wore the same expression of excitement and enthusiasm. A shopkeeper's wife standing next to Petya sobbed and the tears ran down her cheeks.

'Father! Angel! Little father!' she kept repeating, wiping away her tears with her fingers.

'Hurrah!' shouted the crowd on all sides.

For a moment the mass of people stood still; then they rushed forward again.

Beside himself with excitement, Petya, teeth clenched and eyes rolling ferociously, plunged forward, elbowing his way and shouting 'Hurrah!' as though he were ready and willing that moment to kill himself and everyone else, but on either side of him equally fierce faces pushed and shoved, and everybody yelled 'Hurrah!'

'So this is what the Emperor is!' thought Petya. 'No, I could never petition him myself – that would be too presumptuous!'

Nevertheless, he continued to force his way desperately forward, and just beyond the backs in front of him he caught glimpses of an open space spread with a strip of red carpet; but just at that instant the crowd swayed and receded – the police in front were driving back those who had pressed too close to the procession: the Emperor was passing from the palace to the cathedral of the Assumption – and Petya received such a sudden blow in the ribs, and was squeezed so hard, that all at once everything went dim before his eyes and he lost consciousness. When he came to himself a man of clerical appearance with the long grey hair hanging down at the back and wearing a shabby blue cassock – probably a church clerk and chanter – was supporting him under the arm with one hand, while warding off the pressure of the crowd with the other.

'A young gentleman's been crushed!' the deacon was saying. 'Mind there! ... Gently. ... You're crushing him, you're crushing him!'

The Emperor had entered the cathedral of the Assumption. The crowd fanned out again more evenly, and the clerk got Petya, pale and breathless, to the big cannon. Several people felt sorry for Petya, and suddenly a whole crowd turned and milled round him. Those who were standing near tended him, unbuttoned his coat, seated him on the raised platform of the cannon, and showered abuse on whoever it was had squashed him.

'Anyone could get crushed to death like that! What next! Killing people! Why, the poor dear's as white as a sheet!' various voices were heard saying.

Petya soon recovered, the colour returned to his cheeks, the pain passed off, and at the cost of that temporary discomfort he had obtained a place on the cannon, from which he hoped to see the Emperor who was to walk back that way. Petya no longer thought of preferring his request. If only he could just see the Emperor he would be happy!

While the service was proceeding in the cathedral of the Assumption – it was a combined service of prayer on the occasion of the Emperor's arrival and of thanksgiving for the conclusion of peace with the Turks – the crowd dispersed about the square outside, and hawkers appeared, selling kvass, gingerbread and poppy-seed sweets (of which Petya was particularly fond), and ordinary conversation was heard again. One tradesman's wife was showing her torn shawl, and saying how much she had paid for it; another observed that all silk goods were very dear nowadays. The deacon who had rescued Petya was talking to a functionary about the different priests who were officiating that day with the bishop. The clerk several times used the words 'and chapter', which Petya did not understand. Two young workmen were jesting with some servant-girls cracking nuts. All these exchanges, especially the jokes with the servant-girls, which at any other time would have fascinated Petya at his age, did not interest him now. He sat on his high perch on the cannon, as much agitated as before by the thought of the Emperor and his love for him. The combination of the feeling of pain and terror when he was being crushed and that of rapture still further intensified his sense of the solemnity of the occasion.

Suddenly the roar of cannon was heard from the embankment (the firing was in celebration of the signing of peace with the Turks), and the crowd made a dash for the embankment to watch. Petya would have run off there too, but the deacon who had taken the young gentleman under his protection would not let him. The guns were still firing when officers, generals and gentlemen-in-waiting came running out of the cathedral, followed by others in less haste. Caps were lifted again, and those who had run to look at the cannon ran back. At last four men wearing uniforms and decorations emerged from the portals of the cathedral. 'Hurrah! hurrah!' shouted the crowd again.

'Which one is he? Which one?' asked Petya in a tearful voice of those around him, but no one answered; everybody was too excited and Petya, picking out one of the four, and hardly able to see him for the tears of joy that started to his eyes, concentrated all his enthusiasm on him – though it happened not to be the Emperor – frantically yelled 'Hurrah!' and vowed that tomorrow, come what might, he would join the army.

The crowd rushed after the Emperor, accompanied him to the palace and began to disperse. By this time it was late, and Petya had had nothing to eat and was drenched with perspiration; however, he did not go home but stood with a smaller though still considerable crowd before the palace while the Emperor dined. He gazed up at the palace windows, expecting he knew not what, and envying alike the grand personages who drove up to the entrance to dine with the Emperor and the footmen waiting at table, glimpses of whom could be seen through the windows.

While the Emperor was dining Valuyev, looking out of the window, said:

'The people are still hoping for another sight of your Majesty.'

They had nearly finished dinner, and the Emperor, munching a biscuit, got up and went out on to the balcony. The crowd, with Petya in the middle, rushed towards the balcony.

'Angel! Father! Hurrah! Little father!' ... cried the crowd, and Petya with it, and again the women and some of the men of weaker stuff, including Petya, wept for joy.

A fair-sized piece of the biscuit the Emperor was holding in his hand broke off, fell on the balcony railing, and from the railing to the ground. A coachman in a jerkin, who stood nearest, pounced on the piece of biscuit and snatched it up. Several people rushed at the coachman. Seeing this, the Emperor had a plateful of biscuits brought, and began throwing them from the balcony. Petya's eyes almost started out of his head; more keyed up than ever by the danger of being crushed, he flung himself on the biscuits. He did not know why, but he had to have a biscuit from the Tsar's hand and felt that he must stand his ground. He made a dash and upset an old woman who was just about to seize a biscuit. But the old woman refused to consider herself defeated, though she was lying on the ground – she grabbed at some biscuits but her hand did not reach them. Petya pushed her hand away with his knee, seized a biscuit and, as though afraid of being late, shouted 'Hurrah!' again in a hoarse voice.

The Emperor went in, and after that the greater part of the crowd began to disperse.

'There, I said if only we waited – and so it was!' said one and another delightedly among the throng.

Happy as Petya was, he felt sad at having to go home knowing that all the enjoyment of that day was over. He did not go straight back from the Kremlin but called in on his friend Obolensky, who was fifteen and also entering the regiment. When he got home Petya announced resolutely and firmly that if they would not give their permission, then he would run away. And next day Count Ilya Rostov, though he had not yet quite yielded, went to inquire how he could arrange for Petya to serve somewhere where it would be as safe as possible.

22

Two days later, on the morning of July the 15th, an immense number of carriages were drawn up outside the Slobodskoy Palace.

The great halls were full. In the first were the Nobility and gentry in their uniforms; in the second bearded merchants in full-skirted coats of blue cloth and wearing medals. The room where the nobles were gathered was all bustle and movement. The chief magnates sat on high-backed chairs round a large table under the portrait of the Emperor, but the majority of the gentry were strolling about the room.

All the nobles, whom Pierre saw every day either at the club or in their own houses, were in uniform – some in the uniform of Catherine's day, others in that of the Emperor Paul, others again in the new uniforms of Alexander's time, or the ordinary uniform of the Nobility, and the general guise of being in uniform imparted a certain strange and fantastic character to these diverse and familiar personalities, both old and young. Particularly striking were the old men, dim-eyed, toothless, bald, sallow and bloated, or gaunt and wrinkled. For the most part they sat quietly in their places, or if they walked about and talked attached themselves to someone younger. Just like the faces of the crowd Petya had seen in the Kremlin square, all these faces in general expectation of some solemn event offered a conspicuous contrast to their usual everyday – yesterday's – expression when interest was centred on a game of boston, Petrushka the cook, Zinaida Dmitrievna's health.

Pierre was there too, uncomfortably buttoned up since early morning in a nobleman's uniform that had become too tight for him. He was in a high state of agitation: this extraordinary assembly not only of nobles but also of the merchant class – les États généraux (States-General) – revived in his mind a whole series of ideas he had long laid aside but which were deeply imprinted in his soul: thoughts of the *Contrat social* and the French Revolution. The words that had struck him in the Emperor's manifesto – that the Sovereign was coming to the capital for *consultation* with his people – confirmed him in this chain of thought. And supposing that something of importance in that direction was at hand, the something which he had long been looking for, he wandered about, watching and listening but nowhere finding any echo of the ideas that engrossed him.

The Emperor's manifesto was read, evoking enthusiasm, and then the assembly broke up into groups to discuss matters. Besides the ordinary topics of conversation Pierre heard men debating where the marshals of the Nobility were to stand when the Emperor came in, when the ball should be given in the Emperor's honour, whether they should group themselves according to districts or the whole province together ... and so on; but as soon as the war and the whole object of convening the Nobility was mentioned the talk became uncertain and hesitating. Everyone seemed to prefer listening to speaking.

One middle-aged man, handsome and virile, in the uniform of a retired naval officer, was speaking in one of the rooms, and a little knot of people pressed about him. Pierre went up to the circle that had formed round the speaker, and began to listen. Count Ilya Rostov, in his uniform of Catherine's reign, was sauntering about with a pleasant smile among the crowd, with all of whom he was acquainted. He too approached this group and paused to listen, smiling kindly, as he always did, and nodding his head in approbation of what the speaker was saying. The retired naval officer was speaking very boldly (this could be seen from the expression on the faces of the listeners and from the fact that some persons whom Pierre knew for the meekest and most timid of men walked away disapprovingly, or expressed their disagreement). Pierre pushed his way into the middle of the group, listened, and convinced himself that the speaker was indeed a liberal but with views quite different from his own. The naval officer spoke in the peculiarly mellow, sing-song baritone characteristic of the Russian Nobility, agreeably slurring his r's and clipping his consonants – the voice of a man who calls to his servants, 'Heah! Bwing me my pipe!' It was a voice that betrayed familiarity with the pleasures of the table, and a note of authority.

'What if the inhabitants of Smolensk have offahd to waise militia for the Empewah? Is Smolensk to lay down the law fo' us? If the noble awistocwacy of the pwovince of Moscow thinks fit, it can show its loyalty to our Sov'weign the Empewah in othah ways. Have we fo'gotten the waising of the militia in the yeah 'seven? All that did was to enwich the pwiests' sons, and thieves and wobbahs. ...'

Count Ilya Rostov smiled blandly, and nodded his head in approval.

'And was our militia of any use to the Empia? Not the slightest! They only wuined our farming intewests. Bettah have another con-scwiption ... o' owah men will wetum to us neithah soldier no' peasants but simply spoiled and good fo' nothing. The Nobility don't gwudge theah lives – evewy man jack of us will go and bwing wecwuits, and the Sov'weign need only say the word and we will all die fo' him!' added the orator, warming up.

Count Rostov's mouth watered with satisfaction and he nudged Pierre, but Pierre wanted to speak himself. He moved forward, feel-ing stirred though not yet sure why he was stirred or what he would say. He was just opening his mouth when one of the senators, a tooth-less old man with a shrewd, choleric face, standing near the first speaker, interrupted him. Evidently accustomed to managing debates and keeping up an argument, he began in low but distinct tones:

'I imagine, sir,' said he, mumbling with his toothless mouth, 'that we are summoned here not for the purpose of discussing whether at the present moment it would be in the best interests of the Empire to levy recruits or call out the militia. We have been summoned to reply to the appeal which our Sovereign the Emperor graciously deigns to make to us. We may leave it to the supreme authority to judge be-tween conscription or the militia. ...'

Pierre suddenly found the right outlet for his excitement. He felt exasperated with the senator who was introducing this conventional and narrow attitude towards the duties that lay before the Nobility. Pierre stepped forward and cut him short. He himself did not yet know what he was going to say, but he began eagerly, expressing himself in bookish Russian and occasionally lapsing into French.

'Excuse me, your Excellency,' he began. (Pierre was well acquainted with the senator but he thought it necessary on this occasion to address him formally.) 'Though I cannot agree with the gentleman ...' (he hesitated: he would have liked to say with *mon très honorable préopin-ant* – the honorable gentleman who has just spoken), 'with the gentle-man ... whom I have not the honour of knowing; still I imagine that the Nobility have been called together not merely to express their sympathy and enthusiasm but also to deliberate upon the measures by which we may assist our Fatherland! I imagine,' he went on, warming to his subject, 'that the Emperor himself would be ill-pleased to find in us merely owners of peasants whom we are willing to devote to his service, together with our own persons, as *chair à canon* – cannon fodder – instead of obtaining from us any co-co-counsel.'

Several of those listening withdrew from the circle, when they noticed the senator's sardonic smile and the freedom of Pierre's remarks. Count Rostov was the only person who approved of Pierre's speech, just as he had approved of what the naval officer had said, and the senator, and in general agreed with whatever he heard last.

'Before discussing these questions,' Pierre continued, 'I consider we should do well to ask the Emperor – most respectfully to ask his Majesty – to inform us of the exact number of the troops we have, and the position in which our armies and our forces now find themselves, and then. . . .'

But scarcely had Pierre uttered these words before he was attacked from three sides at once. The most violent onslaught came from an old acquaintance, a boston player who had always been very well disposed towards him, Stepan Stepanovich Apraksin. Apraksin was in uniform, and whether it was due to the uniform or to other causes, Pierre saw before him quite a different man. With an expression of senile wrath suddenly flushing his face, Apraksin screamed out at Pierre:

'In the first place, I tell you we have no right to put such questions to the Emperor; and secondly, if the Russian Nobility had any such right the Emperor could make us no answer. The movements of the troops depend on the movements of the enemy the numbers rise and fall. . . .'

Another voice, that of a nobleman of medium height, some forty years of age, whom Pierre had seen in days gone by at the gipsies' entertainments and knew as a wretched card-player, interrupted Apraksin. But he too was quite transformed by his uniform, as he moved up to Pierre.

'Yes, and this is not the time for deliberation,' said this nobleman. 'The time has come for action: the war is in Russia. The enemy is advancing to destroy Russia, to desecrate the tombs of our fathers, to carry off our wives and children.' The speaker smote his breast. 'We will arise, we will go to war as one man for our father the Tsar!' he cried, rolling his bloodshot eyes. Several approving voices were heard in the throng. 'We are Russians and will not grudge our blood for the defence of our faith, the throne and the Fatherland! We must leave off our idle dreaming if we are sons of our Fatherland! We will show Europe how Russia rises to the defence of Russia!'

Pierre tried to reply but could not get a word in. He was conscious that the sound of his words, apart from any meaning they conveyed, was less audible than the sound of his adversary's excited voice.

Count Rostov at the back of the little group was nodding approval. Several of the audience turned their shoulders briskly to the orator at the conclusion of a phrase and said:

'Hear, hear!'

Pierre was anxious to say that he was by no means averse to sacrificing his money, his peasants or himself, only one ought to know the state of affairs in order to be able to apply the remedy, but it was impossible. A number of voices were shouting and talking together, so that Count Rostov had not time to signify agreement with all of them, and the group grew in size, split up, re-formed again and moved off, all talking at once, into the largest hall, to the big table there. Not only was Pierre prevented from speaking but he was rudely interrupted, pushed aside, and backs were turned to him as though he were the common enemy. This happened not because they disliked the tenor of his speech, which was already forgotten after all the subsequent speeches; but to animate it the crowd needed some tangible object for its love and a similar object for its hate. Pierre furnished it with the latter. Many orators spoke after the excited nobleman, and all in the same tone, a number of them eloquently and with originality. Glinka, the editor of the *Russian Messenger*, who was recognized and greeted with cries of 'Author! Author!', said that hell must be repulsed by hell, that he had watched a child smiling at the flash of lightning and the clap of thunder, 'but we will not be like that child'.

'Hear, hear! Smiling at the clap of thunder!' was echoed approvingly at the back of the assembly.

The throng drifted up to the large table, where grey or baldheaded old noblemen of seventy were sitting, wearing uniforms and decorations. Almost all of them Pierre had seen in their own homes with their private jesters, and playing boston at the club. With an incessant hum of voices the crowd advanced to the table. The orators, pressed against the high chair-backs by the surging mass, spoke one after another and sometimes two at once. Those who stood further back noticed what the speaker omitted to say and hastened to supply the gap. Others were busy in the heat and crush ransacking their brains to find some idea and hurriedly utter it. The old grandees,

whom Pierre knew, sat looking first at one and then at another, and
their expressions for the most part betrayed nothing but the fact that
they found the room very hot. Pierre, however, felt painfully agitated, and the general desire to show that they were ready to go to all
lengths – which found expression in tones and looks rather than in
the tenor of the speeches – infected him too. He did not renounce his
opinions but somehow felt himself in the wrong and anxious to
justify himself.

'I only said that we could make sacrifices to better purpose when
we know what is needed!' he cried, trying to be heard above the
other voices.

One little old man close by him looked round but his attention
was immediately diverted by an exclamation at the opposite side of
the table.

'Yes, Moscow will be surrendered! She will be our expiation!' one
man was shouting.

'He is the enemy of mankind!' cried another.

'Allow me to speak. ...'

'Gentlemen, you are crushing me! ...'

23

AT that moment Count Rostopchin with his protruding chin and
alert eyes strode into the room, wearing the uniform of a general with
sash over his shoulder. The crowd parted before him.

'Our Sovereign the Emperor will be here immediately,' announced
Rostopchin. 'I am straight from the palace. I presume that in the
position we are in there is little need for discussion. The Emperor has
deigned to summon us and the merchants. They will pour out their
millions' (he pointed to the merchants' hall), 'while it is our business
to raise men and not spare ourselves. ... That is the least we can do!'

A consultation took place confined to the grandees sitting at the
table. Their whole conference was more than subdued, and the old
voices saying one after another, 'I agree,' or, for the sake of variety,
'I am of the same opinion,' and so on, even sounded mournful after
all the hubbub that had gone before.

The secretary was told to write down the resolution adopted by
the Moscow Nobility and Gentry, that they would furnish a levy of
ten men in every thousand of their serfs, fully equipped, as Smolensk

had done. Their chairs made a scraping noise as the gentlemen who had been conferring rose with an air of relief, and began walking about to stretch their legs, taking their friends' arms and chatting in couples.

'The Emperor! The Emperor!' was the cry that suddenly resounded through the various halls, and the whole throng hurried to the entrance.

The Emperor entered through a broad lane between two walls of noblemen. Every face expressed reverent and awe-struck curiosity. Pierre was standing rather far off, and could not quite catch all the Emperor said. From what he did hear he understood that his Majesty was speaking of the peril threatening the Empire, and of the hopes he placed on the Moscow Nobility. The Emperor was answered by a voice informing him of the resolution just arrived at by the Nobility.

'Gentlemen!' said the Tsar in a trembling voice.

A ripple of excitement ran through the crowd, which then fell quiet again, so that Pierre distinctly heard the pleasantly warm and human voice of the Emperor saying with emotion:

'I never doubted the devotion of the Russian nobles. But this day it has surpassed my expectations. I thank you in the name of the Fatherland. Gentlemen, let us act! Time is more precious than anything. ...'

The Emperor ceased speaking, the crowd began pressing round him, and rapturous exclamations were heard on all sides.

'Yes, more precious than anything ... spoken royally,' said the voice of Count Rostov with a sob. He had heard nothing but understood everything in his own way.

From the hall of the Nobility the Emperor went into the merchants' room, where he remained for about ten minutes. Pierre was among those who saw him come back with tears of emotion in his eyes. As became known later, the Emperor had scarcely begun to address the merchants before the tears gushed from his eyes and he continued in a trembling voice. When Pierre saw the Emperor he was coming out accompanied by two merchants, one of whom Pierre knew, a stout contractor. The other was the mayor, a man with a thin sallow face and narrow beard. Both were weeping. Tears filled the thin man's eyes but the stout contractor was sobbing outright like a child, while he kept repeating:

'Take life and property too, your Majesty!'

Pierre's one feeling at that moment was a desire to show that he was ready to go to all lengths and make any sacrifice. The constitutional tendency of his speech weighed on his conscience: he sought an opportunity of glossing it over. On learning that Count Mamonov was furnishing a regiment, Bezuhov at once informed Count Rostopchin that he would provide and maintain one thousand men.

Old Rostov could not tell his wife of what had passed without tears, and there and then granted Petya's request, and went himself to enter his name.

Next day the Emperor left Moscow. All the assembly of nobles took off their uniforms and settled down again in their homes and clubs, and not without some groans gave orders to their stewards about the levy, wondering at what they had done.

PART TWO

I

NAPOLEON began the war with Russia because he could not resist going to Dresden, could not help his head being turned by the homage he received, could not help donning Polish uniform and yielding to the stimulating influence of a June morning, and could not refrain from giving way to outbursts of fury in the presence of Kurakin and afterwards of Balashev.

Alexander refused all negotiations because he felt himself personally insulted. Barclay de Tolly did his utmost to command the army in the best way possible because he wished to fulfil his duty and win the renown of being a great general. Rostov charged the French because he could not restrain his longing for a gallop across the level plain. And in the same fashion all the innumerable individuals who took part in the war acted in accordance with their natural dispositions, habits, circumstances and aims. They were moved by fear or vanity, they rejoiced or were indignant, they argued and supposed that they knew what they were doing and did it of their own free will, whereas they were all the involuntary tools of history, working out a process concealed from them but intelligible to us. Such is the inevitable lot of men of action, and the higher they stand in the social hierarchy the less free they are.

Now those who took part in the events of the year 1812 have long ago passed from the scene, their personal interests have vanished, leaving no trace, and nothing remains of that time save its historical results.

Providence compelled all these men, striving for the attainment of their own private ends, to combine for the accomplishment of a single stupendous result, of which no one man (neither Napoleon, nor Alexander, still less any of those who did the actual fighting) had the slightest inkling.

It is plain to us now what caused the destruction of the French army in 1812. No one will dispute that the cause of the loss of Napoleon's French forces was, on the one hand, their advance into the heart of Russia late in the season without any preparation for a winter campaign; and, on the other, the character given to the war by the burning of Russian towns and the hatred aroused among the Russian people for the enemy. But no one at the time foresaw (what now seems so obvious) that this was the only way an army of eight hundred thousand men – the best army in the world led by the best general – could be defeated in conflict with a raw army of half its numerical strength, led by inexperienced commanders as the Russian army was. *Not only did no one see this* but *on the Russian side* every effort was systematically directed towards preventing the only thing that could save Russia, while *on the French side,* despite Napoleon's experience and so-called military genius, every exertion was made to push on to Moscow at the end of the summer, that is, to do the very thing that was bound to lead to destruction.

In historical works on the year 1812 French writers are very fond of saying that Napoleon was aware of the danger of extending his line, that he sought to give battle and that his marshals advised him to halt at Smolensk; and of making similar statements to show that, even at the time, the perils of the campaign were understood. Russian authors are still fonder of telling us that from the commencement of the campaign there existed a plan to lure Napoleon into the depths of Russia – after the manner of the Scythians – and this plan some of them attribute to Pfuhl, others to some Frenchman, others to Toll, and others again to Alexander, in support of which they cite memoirs, projects and letters containing hints of such a course of action. But all these suggestions of foresight concerning what happened, on the part of French and Russians alike, stand out now only because they fit in with what befell. Had the event not occurred these intimations would have been neglected, as hundreds of thousands of contrary intimations and surmises are forgotten which were current at the period but are now consigned to oblivion because the event falsified them. There are always so many conjectures as to the issue of any event that, however the matter may end, there will invariably be people to declare: 'I said so at the time', entirely forgetting that among their numerous hypotheses were some in favour of quite the opposite.

The notion that Napoleon was aware of the danger of extending his line, and that the Russians had a scheme for luring the enemy into the depths of Russia, obviously belong to this category; and only by much straining can historians ascribe such reflections to Napoleon and his marshals, or such plans to the Russian generals. All the facts are in flat contradiction to such suppositions. During the whole period of the war not only was there no desire on the part of the Russians to decoy the French into the heart of the country but from the moment they crossed the frontier everything was done to stop them. And far from dreading the extension of his line of communications, Napoleon welcomed every step forward as a triumph, and did not seek pitched battles at all as eagerly as he had done in his previous military operations.

At the very beginning of the campaign our armies were broken up, and our sole aim was to unite them, though uniting the armies presented no advantage if our object was to retire and draw the enemy into the depths of the country. Our Emperor was with the troops to inspire them to dispute every inch of Russian soil and on no account to retreat. An immense camp was fortified at Drissa in accordance with Pfuhl's plan, and there was no intention to withdraw further. The Emperor reproached the commanders-in-chief for every yard they retreated. The Emperor could never have imagined letting the enemy reach Smolensk, still less could he have contemplated the burning of Moscow, and when our armies did unite he was indignant that Smolensk had been taken and burnt without a general engagement having been fought before its walls.

Thus it was with the Emperor, and the Russian commanders and the people as a whole were even more incensed at the thought that our forces were retreating far inside our borders.

Napoleon, having divided our armies, advanced deep into the interior, letting slip several opportunities of forcing an engagement. In August he was in Smolensk and thinking only of how to advance further, though, as we see now, that advance meant inevitable ruin.

The facts show perfectly clearly that Napoleon did not foresee the danger of an advance on Moscow, and that Alexander and the Russian generals had no idea at that time of luring Napoleon on but were bent on stopping him. Napoleon was enticed into the heart of the country not as the result of any plan, the possibility of which no one believed in, but in consequence of a most complex interplay of the intrigues, desires and ambitions of those who took part in the war, who had no perception whatever of what was to come or of the sole means of saving Russia. Everything happens fortuitously. The army is split up early in the campaign. We try to effect a junction between the different sections with the apparent intention of giving battle and checking the enemy's advance, but by this effort to unite, while avoiding battle with a far stronger enemy, we are forced to retreat at an acute angle, and so lead the French on to Smolensk. But it is not enough to say that we withdrew at an acute angle because the French were advancing between our two armies: the angle became still more acute and we retired still further because Barclay de Tolly was an unpopular foreigner detested by Bagration (who would come under his command), and Bagration, as leader of the second army, did his utmost to delay joining forces and coming under Barclay's command as long as he could. Bagration was slow in effecting the junction (though this was the chief aim of all at Headquarters) because it seemed to him he would be exposing his army to danger on this march, and that it would be better for him to retire more to the left and south, harassing the enemy's flank and rear, and securing recruits for the army from the Ukraine. Whereas it looks as if he thought this up because he did not want to come under the command of the detested foreigner Barclay, who was his junior in the Service.

The Emperor was with the army to encourage it, but his presence, and his ignorance of what steps to take, and the enormous number of advisers and plans, paralysed the first army and it retired.

In the Drissa camp the intention was to make a stand; but Paulucci, with ambitions to become commander-in-chief, unexpectedly employed his energy to influence Alexander, and Pfuhl's whole scheme was abandoned and the matter entrusted to Barclay. But as Barclay did not inspire complete confidence his power was limited.

The armies were split up, there was no unity of command and Barclay was not liked; but this confusion and division and the unpopularity of the foreign commander-in-chief resulted on the one hand in vacillation and the avoidance of a battle (which would have been inevitable had the armies been united and someone other than Barclay been in command) and, on the other, growing indignation against the foreigners and an increase of patriotic fervour.

At last the Emperor left the army, on the pretext – the most convenient and indeed the only one that could be found for his departure – that it was necessary for him to fan the enthusiasm of the inhabitants of the capitals to wage war on a national scale, and this visit of the Emperor to Moscow did in fact treble Russian armed might.

The Emperor left the army in order not to obstruct the commander-in-chief's undivided control, and hoping that more decisive action would then be taken; but the commander's position became still more difficult and impaired. Bennigsen, the Tsarevich and a swarm of adjutants-general remained with the army to keep the commander-in-chief under observation and urge him to greater activity, and Barclay, feeling less free than ever under the surveillance of all these 'eyes of the Emperor', waxed still more chary of undertaking any decisive operation, and avoided giving battle.

Barclay stood for prudence. The Tsarevich hinted at treachery and demanded a general engagement. Lubomirsky, Bronnitsky, Wlocki, and others of the same mind swelled the clamour to such a point that Barclay, using the excuse of sending papers to the Emperor, despatched these Polish adjutants-general to Petersburg, and plunged into an open struggle with Bennigsen and the Tsarevich.

At Smolensk, in spite of Bagration's wishes to the contrary, the armies at last united.

Bagration drove up in a carriage to the house occupied by Barclay. Barclay donned his official sash and came out to greet and present his report to his senior officer, Bagration. Bagration, not to be outdone in this contest of magnanimity, places himself under Barclay's command, despite his own seniority in rank, but, having assumed a subordinate position, agreed with him less than ever. By the Emperor's express order Bagration made his reports direct to him, and wrote to Arakcheyev:

My Sovereign's will is law but I cannot work with the *minister* [so he called Barclay]. For mercy's sake send me somewhere else, if only in command of a regiment, for I cannot stand it here. Headquarters are so crammed full of Germans that a Russian cannot breathe and there is no making head or tail of anything. I thought I was serving my Sovereign and the Fatherland but it turns out that I am really serving Barclay, which I confess I have no mind for.

The swarm of Bronnitskys and Wintzingerodes and their like still further poisoned relations between the commanders-in-chief, and resulted in even less unity. Preparations were made to attack the French before Smolensk. A general was sent to inspect the position. This general, detesting Barclay, rode off to visit a friend of his own, a corps-commander, and having spent the day with him, returned to Barclay and roundly condemned a proposed battleground which he had never seen.

While all this intriguing and argument over the battlefield was going on, and while we were looking for the French – having lost touch with them – the French stumbled upon Nevyerovsky's division and reached the walls of Smolensk.

We were surprised into having to fight at Smolensk to save our lines of communication. The battle was fought, and thousands were slain on both sides.

Smolensk was abandoned contrary to the wishes of the Emperor and of the whole people. But Smolensk was set fire to by its own inhabitants, who had been betrayed by their governor. And these ruined inhabitants, offering an example to other Russians, fled to Moscow, full of their losses and kindling hatred of the foe. Napoleon advances further; we retreat; and so the very thing is attained that is destined to overthrow Napoleon.

2

THE day after his son's departure Prince Nikolai Bolkonsky summoned Princess Maria to his study.

'Well, now are you satisfied?' he demanded. 'You have made me quarrel with my son! Are you satisfied? That was all you wanted! Satisfied? ... This is painful to me, painful. I am old and infirm, and this was your wish. Well, gloat over it, gloat over it! ...'

And after that Princess Maria did not see her father again for a week. He was ill and did not leave his study.

Princess Maria noticed to her surprise that during this illness the old prince excluded Mademoiselle Bourienne too from his room. Tikhon alone attended him.

At the end of the week the prince reappeared and resumed his former way of life, devoting himself with special zeal to the laying out of his farm buildings and gardens, and completely breaking off all relations with Mademoiselle Bourienne. His frigid tone and air with Princess Maria seemed to say: 'There, you see? You plotted against me, told lies to Prince Andrei about my relations with that Frenchwoman and made me quarrel with him, but you see I can do without you, and without that Frenchwoman either!'

One half of the day Princess Maria spent with little Nikolai, supervising his lessons, teaching him Russian and music herself, and talking to Dessalles. The rest of the time she spent in her own suite over her books, or with her old nurse or the 'God's folk', who sometimes came up by the back stairs to visit her.

Princess Maria's attitude to the war was the general attitude of women when there is a war. She feared for her brother who was in it, was horrified and amazed at the strange cruelty that impels men to slaughter one another; but she had no notion of the significance of this war, which seemed to her exactly like all those of the past. She did not realize the import of the war, although Dessalles, with whom she was always talking, was passionately interested in its progress and tried to explain to her his views about it, and although her 'God's folk' who came to see her all with terror reported, in their own way, the popular rumours about the invasion by Antichrist, and although Julie (now Princess Drubetskoy), who had renewed her correspondence with her, sent patriotic letters from Moscow – written in her curious Frenchified Russian.

I write to you in Russian, my good friend [wrote Julie], because I have a detestation towards all the French, and their language equally, which I cannot support to hear spoken. ... We in Moscow are all elated with enthusiasm for our adored Emperor.

My poor husband is enduring pains and hunger in miserable Jewish taverns; but the news which I have inspires me yet more.

You have without doubt heard of the heroic exploit of Raevsky, embracing his two sons and saying: 'I will perish with them but we will not budge!' And indeed, though the enemy was twice stronger than we, we were unshakeable. We pass the time as best we can, but in war as in war! Princess Aline and Sophie spend whole days with me, and we, unhappy widows of live husbands, have beautiful conversations while we scrape cloth to make lint. Only you, my friend, are wanting ...

and so on.

The principal reason why Princess Maria failed to grasp the significance of the war was because the old prince never spoke of it, ignored its existence and laughed at Dessalles when he mentioned the war at dinner. The prince's tone was so calm and confident that Princess Maria accepted it without question.

All that July the old prince was exceedingly active and even lively. He planned another garden and began a new building for the domestic serfs. The only thing that made Princess Maria anxious about him was that he slept very little and instead of having his bed in his study changed his sleeping-place every day. One day he would order his camp-bedstead to be set up in the gallery, another time he would remain on the couch or in a tall-backed chair in the drawing-room and doze there without undressing, while Petrushka, the lad who had replaced Mademoiselle Bourienne, read to him. Then he would try spending a night in the dining-room.

On the 1st of August a second letter came from Prince Andrei. In his first, received shortly after he had left home, Prince Andrei had dutifully asked his father's forgiveness for what he had allowed himself to say, and begged to be restored to his favour. To this letter the old prince had replied affectionately, and from that time had kept the Frenchwoman at a distance. Prince Andrei's second letter, written near Vitebsk after the French had occupied that town, contained a brief account of the whole campaign, with a sketch-map to illustrate it, and his reflections as to the further progress of the war. In this letter Prince Andrei pointed out to his father the inadvisability of staying at Bald Hills, so close to the theatre of war and in the direct line of the enemy's advance, and counselled him to move to Moscow.

At dinner that day, on Dessalles's observing that the French were said to have already entered Vitebsk, the old prince remembered his son's letter.

'Had a letter from Prince Andrei today,' he said to Princess Maria. 'Haven't you read it?'

'No, father,' the princess replied timidly. She could not possibly have read the letter, of whose arrival she had not even heard.

'He writes about this war,' said the prince, with the ironic smile that had become habitual to him in speaking of the present war.

'That must be very interesting,' said Dessalles. 'Prince Andrei is in a position to know. ...'

'Oh, most interesting!' said Mademoiselle Bourienne.

'Go and fetch it for me,' said the old prince to Mademoiselle Bourienne. 'You know – under the paper-weight on the little table.'

Mademoiselle Bourienne jumped up with alacrity.

'No, don't!' he exclaimed with a frown. 'You go, Mihail Ivanich.'

Mihail Ivanich rose and went to the study. But he had hardly left the room before the old prince, looking about him nervously, threw down his dinner-napkin and went himself.

'No one can do anything ... they always make some muddle,' he muttered.

While he was away Princess Maria, Dessalles, Mademoiselle Bourienne and even little Nikolai looked at one another without speaking. The old prince came hurrying back, accompanied by Mihail Ivanich and bringing the letter and a plan, which he laid beside him, not letting anyone read them at dinner.

When they had moved into the drawing-room he handed the letter to Princess Maria and, spreading out before him the plan of his new building and fixing his eyes upon it, told her to read the letter aloud. After she had done so Princess Maria looked inquiringly at her father. He was studying the plan, apparently absorbed in his own thoughts.

'What do you think about it, prince?' Dessalles ventured to ask.

'I! I! ...' said the prince, seeming to rouse himself with a painful effort and not taking his eyes from the plan of the building.

'Very possibly the theatre of war will move so near to us that ...'

'Ha-ha-ha! The theatre of war!' said the prince. 'I have always said, and I say still, that the theatre of war is Poland and the enemy will never get beyond the Niemen.'

Dessalles looked in amazement at the prince, who was talking of the Niemen when the enemy were already at the Dnieper; but Princess Maria, forgetting the geographical position of the Niemen, supposed that what her father said was true.

'When the snow melts they'll be swallowed up in the Polish swamps. It's only they who can't see that,' the old prince continued, evidently thinking of the campaign of 1807 which seemed to him so recent. 'Bennigsen ought to have entered Prussia earlier, then things would have taken a different turn. ...'

'But, prince,' Dessalles began timidly, 'the letter speaks of Vitebsk ...'

'Ah, the letter, yes. Yes ...' replied the prince peevishly. 'Yes ... yes ...' His face suddenly took on a morose expression. He paused. 'Yes, he writes that the French were beaten at ... at ... what river was it?'

Dessalles dropped his eyes.

'The prince says nothing about that,' he remarked gently.

'Doesn't he? Well, I didn't invent it, that's quite certain.'

A long silence ensued.

'Yes ... yes ... Well, Mihail Ivanich,' he said suddenly, raising his head and pointing to the plan of the building, 'tell me how you pro-pose to make that alteration. ...'

Mihail Ivanich went up to the plan, and the prince, after talking to him about the new building, cast a wrathful glance at Princess Maria and Dessalles and departed to his room.

Princess Maria saw Dessalles's embarrassed, wondering look fixed on her father, noticed his silence and was struck by the fact that her father had forgotten his son's letter on the drawing-room table; but she was not only afraid to speak of it and ask Dessalles why he sat disconcerted and silent: she was afraid even to think about it.

In the evening Mihail Ivanich, sent by the prince, came to Princess Maria for Prince Andrei's letter which had been forgotten in the drawing-room. Princess Maria gave him the letter, and then, much as she disliked asking, ventured to inquire what her father was doing.

'Very busy as usual,' replied Mihail Ivanich with a politely ironic smile which caused Princess Maria to turn pale. 'He worries a good deal over the new building. He has been reading a little, but now' – Mihail Ivanich lowered his voice – 'now he's at his bureau, engaged on his will, I expect.' (Of late one of the prince's favourite occupations had been the preparation of some documents he meant to leave at his death and which he called his 'will'.)

'And is Alpatych being sent to Smolensk?' asked Princess Maria.

'Oh yes, to be sure. He has been waiting to start for some time.'

3

WHEN Mihail Ivanich returned to the study with the letter the old prince, spectacles on and a shade over his eyes, was sitting at his open bureau with a screened candle, holding a paper at arm's length, and in a somewhat dramatic attitude was reading over his manuscript – his 'Remarks' as he called it – which were to be delivered into the hands of the Emperor after his death.

When Mihail Ivanich went in there were tears in the prince's eyes evoked by the memory of the time when the paper he was now read-ing had been written. He took the letter from Mihail Ivanich, put it in his pocket, folded up his papers and called in Alpatych, who had long been waiting.

The prince had a list of things he wanted done in Smolensk, and walking up and down the room past Alpatych, who stood by the door, he gave his instructions.

'First, writing-paper – do you hear? Eight quires, like this sample, gilt-edged ... it must be exactly like the sample. Varnish, sealing-wax – according to Mihail Ivanich's list.'

He paced backwards and forwards for a while and glanced at his memorandum.

'Then deliver the letter about the deed to the governor in person.'

Next bolts for the doors of the new building were required and had to be of a special pattern the prince had himself designed. After that a box bound with iron must be ordered to keep his 'will' in.

The instructions to Alpatych took over two hours and still the prince did not let him go. He sat down, sank into thought and, closing his eyes, dropped into a doze. Alpatych made a slight movement.

'Get you gone, now, get you gone! If there is anything else I'll send after you.'

Alpatych went out. The prince returned to his bureau, glanced into it, fingered his papers, shut the bureau again and sat down to the table to write to the governor.

It was late when he got to his feet after sealing the letter. He was tired and wanted to sleep but he knew he would not be able to, and that the most melancholy thoughts came to him in bed. He called Tikhon and went through the rooms with him, to show him where to set up his bed for that night. He walked about, measuring every corner.

There was no place that seemed satisfactory, but worst of all was his customary couch in the study. That couch had become an object of dread to him, no doubt because of the oppressive thoughts he had had when lying on it. Nowhere was quite right, but the corner behind the piano in the sitting-room pleased him best of all: he had never slept there yet.

With the help of a footman Tikhon brought in the bedstead and began putting it up.

'Not like that, not like that!' cried the prince, and himself pushed the bed a few inches further from the corner and then closer to it again.

'Well, at last I have finished! Now I shall rest,' thought the prince, and he let Tikhon undress him.

Frowning with vexation at the exertion necessary to divest himself of his coat and trousers, the prince undressed, dropped heavily down on the bed and appeared to sink into thought, staring contemptuously at his withered yellow legs. He was not really thinking but only deferring the moment of making the effort to lift his legs and heave himself over on the bed. 'Ugh, what a trial! Oh, that these toils might end and *you* release me!' he mused. Pressing his lips together he made the effort for the twenty-thousandth time and lay down. But hardly had he done so before he felt the bed rocking evenly to and fro beneath him as though it were breathing heavily and jolting. He had this sensation almost every night. He opened his eyes just as they were closing.

'No peace, damn them!' he grumbled in fury at some unknown person. 'Ah yes, there was something else of importance – something of great importance that I was keeping to think of in bed. The bolts? No, I told him about them. No, it was something, something in the drawing-room. Princess Maria talked some nonsense. Dessalles – that fool – said something. Something in my pocket – can't remember.'

'Tikhon, what were we talking about at dinner?'

'About Prince Andrei, Mihail Ivanich ...'

'Quiet, be quiet!' The prince slapped his hand down on the table. 'Yes, I know, Prince Andrei's letter! Princess Maria read it. Dessalles said something about Vitebsk. Now I'll read it.'

He bade Tikhon fetch the letter from his pocket and move the little table with the lemonade and a spiral wax candle on it closer to the bed, and putting on his spectacles he began reading. Only now for the first time, as he read the letter in the stillness of the night, by the feeble light under the green shade, did he grasp its meaning for a moment.

'The French at Vitebsk! Four days' march and they could reach Smolensk – perhaps they are there already! Tikhon!' Tikhon started up. 'No, never mind, never mind!' he cried.

He slipped the letter under the candlestick and closed his eyes. And the Danube rose before his mind – a brilliant noonday, the reeds, the Russian camp and himself a young general without a wrinkle on his face, hale and hearty and ruddy, going into Potemkin's gaily-coloured tent, and the burning sensation of jealousy of the favourite agitates him as violently now as it had done then. And he recalls every word uttered at that first interview with Potemkin. And then he sees a rather short, stout woman with a sallow, greasy skin, the Dowager-Empress, with her smile and the words she spoke at her first gracious reception of him, and then that same face on the catafalque, and the brush with Zubov by the coffin over his right to kiss her hand.

'Oh, to make haste, to make haste back to that time and have done with all the present. Oh, if only they would leave me in peace!'

4

BALD HILLS, Prince Nikolai Bolkonsky's estate, lay forty miles east of Smolensk and a couple of miles from the main road to Moscow.

The same evening that the prince gave Alpatych his instructions, Dessalles asked to see Princess Maria and told her that, since the prince was not very well and was taking no steps to secure his safety, though from Prince Andrei's letter it was clear that to remain at Bald Hills might be dangerous, he respectfully advised her to send a letter by Alpatych to the provincial governor at Smolensk, asking him to let her know the state of affairs and the degree of risk to which Bald Hills was exposed. Dessalles wrote the letter to the governor for Princess Maria, and she signed it and gave it to Alpatych with instructions to hand it to the governor and in the case of danger to come back as quickly as possible.

Having received all his orders Alpatych, wearing a white beaver hat – a present from the prince – and carrying a walking-stick as the prince did, went out, escorted by his family, to get into the leather gig with its three sleek roan horses.

The large bell was muffled and the little harness bells were stuffed with paper. The prince allowed no one at Bald Hills to drive with ringing bells. But Alpatych loved to have bells ringing when he went on a long journey. His satellites – the head clerk, a counting-house clerk, the cook and the cook's assistant, two old women, a boy footman in Cossack dress, the coachman and various other servants – were seeing him off.

His daughter placed chintz-covered down cushions under him and behind his back. His old sister-in-law popped in a small bundle, and one of the coachmen helped him into the vehicle.

'There, there, women's fuss! Oh, females, females!' said Alpatych, puffing and speaking rapidly just as the prince did, and he climbed into the trap.

After giving the head clerk parting instructions about the work to be done, Alpatych, now certainly no longer imitating the prince, lifted his hat from his bald head and crossed himself three times.

'If anything should ... you come back, Yakov Alpatych. For Christ's sake think of us!' his wife called to him, alluding to the rumours of the war and the enemy.

'Ah, these women and their fuss!' Alpatych muttered to himself as he drove off, looking about him at the fields of rye turning yellow, at the thickly growing oats still green, and at other quite black fields where they were only just beginning the second ploughing. Alpatych continued his journey, admiring the crop of corn that was singularly fine that season, staring at the rye fields in which here and there reaping was already in progress, meditating like a true husbandman on the sowing and the harvest, and asking himself whether he had not forgotten any of the prince's instructions.

Having stopped twice on the way to feed his horses, he reached the city towards evening on the 4th of August.

On the road Alpatych kept meeting and overtaking baggage-trains and troops. As he approached Smolensk he heard the sounds of distant firing, but these did not impress him. What struck him most was the sight, on the outskirts of Smolensk, of a splendid field of oats in which a camp had been pitched and which was being mown down by some soldiers, evidently for fodder. This did make an impression on Alpatych but he soon forgot it in thinking over his own business.

All the interests of Alpatych's life for upwards of thirty years had been bounded by the will of the prince, and he never stepped outside that limit. Anything not connected with the execution of the prince's orders had no interest, had in fact no existence, for Alpatych.

On reaching Smolensk on the evening of the 4th of August Alpatych put up in the suburb of Gachen, across the Dnieper, at the inn kept by Ferapontov, where he had been in the habit of stopping for the last thirty years. Twelve years before, Ferapontov, through Alpatych's good offices, had bought a wood from the prince and begun to trade, and now he had a house, an inn and a corn-chandler's shop in the same province. Ferapontov was a stout, dark, red-faced peasant in the forties, with thick lips, a broad knob of a nose, similar knobs over his black, knitted brows, and a round belly.

Wearing a waistcoat over his calico shirt, Ferapontov was standing outside his shop which opened on to the street. Catching sight of Alpatych, he went up to him.

'You're right welcome, Yakov Alpatych. Folks be all leaving town, but here you are arriving,' said he.

'Leaving town – how's that?' asked Alpatych.

'To be sure, I always say folks is foolish! All scared now of a Frenchman!'

'Old wives' gossip, old wives' gossip!' said Alpatych.

'That's just what I think, Yakov Alpatych. I tell 'em there's orders not to let *him* in, so it's all right. And the peasants charging as much as three roubles for the use of a horse and cart – they've no conscience!'

Yakov Alpatych listened without hearing. He asked for a samovar, and hay for his horses, and after he had sipped his tea he went to bed.

All night long troops tramped past the inn. Next day Alpatych donned a jacket which he kept for wearing in town, and set forth to do his errands. It was a sunny morning, and by eight o'clock already hot. 'A good day for harvesting,' thought Alpatych.

Beyond the city the sounds of firing had been audible since daybreak. At eight o'clock the boom of cannon mingled with the rattle of musketry. The streets were thronged with hurrying people, and there were many soldiers, but drivers still plied for hire, the shopkeepers stood at their doors and morning service was going on as usual in the churches. Alpatych bought the things he had to buy, called in at the government offices, went to the post and to the governor's. In the offices and shops and at the post office everyone was talking of the troops, and of the enemy who was already attacking the town: everybody was asking everybody else what was to be done, and trying to calm each other's fears.

Outside the governor's house Alpatych found a large gathering, and saw Cossacks and a travelling carriage belonging to the governor. On the steps he met two of the landed gentry, one of whom he knew. This gentleman, an ex-captain of the police, was exclaiming vehemently:

'But I tell you this is no joke! It's all very well if you're single – "One man though undone is but one", as the proverb says, but with a family of thirteen, and all the goods and chattels. ... Things have come to such a pass that we shall all be ruined – what do the authorities amount to if they allow that? They ought to be hanged, the brigands! ...'

'Come, come, hush now,' said the other.

'What do I care? Let him hear! We're not dogs,' said the ex-captain of police, and looking round he noticed Alpatych.

'Ah, Yakov Alpatych, what brings you here?'

'I'm come to see the governor, by command of his Excellency,' answered Alpatych, lifting his head proudly and thrusting his hand into the bosom of his coat as he always did when he mentioned the prince. ... 'His Excellency bid me inquire into the position of affairs,' he added.

'Well, you may as well know, then,' cried the gentleman, 'they've brought things to such a pretty state that there are no carts or anything! ... There, hear that?' said he, pointing in the direction from which the sounds of firing came.

'They've led us all to ruin ... the brigands!' he repeated, and descended the porch steps.

Alpatych shook his head, and went upstairs. The waiting-room was full of tradesmen, women and functionaries, looking dumbly at one another. The door of the governor's room opened and they all stood up and moved forward. A clerk ran out, said something to a merchant, beckoned to a stout official with a cross hanging round his neck to follow him, and vanished again, obviously anxious to avoid the inquiring looks and queries directed to him. Alpatych moved forward and the next time the clerk emerged, placing his hand in the breast of his buttoned coat he addressed him and held out the two letters.

'For his Honour the Baron Asch, from General in chief Prince Bolkonsky,' he announced with such solemnity and so portentously that the clerk turned to him and took the letters.

A few minutes later the governor received Alpatych and hurriedly said to him:

'Inform the prince and princess that I knew nothing: I acted on the highest instructions – here ...' he held out a printed paper to Alpatych. 'Still, as the prince is not well, my advice to them is to go to Moscow. I am just setting off there myself. Tell them. ...'

But the governor did not finish: a begrimed and perspiring officer ran into the room and began to say something in French. A look of dismay came over the governor's face.

'You can go,' he said, nodding to Alpatych, and fell to interrogating the officer.

Searching, panic-stricken, helpless glances were turned on Alpatych when he came out of the governor's room. He hurried back to the inn, unable to help listening now to the firing, which was closer and getting hotter all the time.

The document the governor had given to Alpatych ran as follows:

I assure you that the city of Smolensk is not in the slightest danger as yet, and it is unlikely that it will be so threatened. I from the one side and Prince Bagration from the other are marching to unite our forces before Smolensk, which junction will be effected on the 22nd instant, and the combined armies will proceed with their joint forces to defend their compatriots of the province entrusted to your care until their efforts shall have beaten back the enemies of our Fatherland, or until the last warrior in our valiant ranks has perished. From this you will see that you have a perfect right to reassure the inhabitants of Smolensk, for those defended by two such brave armies may well be confident that victory will be theirs. (Order of the day from Barclay de Tolly to the Civil Governor of Smolensk, Baron Asch, 1812.)

People were roaming uneasily about the streets.

Carts piled high with household utensils, chairs and clothes-presses kept emerging from the gates of houses and proceeding through the town. Carts were standing at the house next to Ferapontov's, and women were wailing and lamenting as they exchanged good-byes. A small yard-dog was frisking about in front of the harnessed horses, barking.

Alpatych's step was more hurried than usual as he entered the inn yard and went straight to the shed where his horses and trap were. The coachman was asleep. He woke him up, told him to get ready, and crossed to the house. From the private room of the family came the sounds of a child crying, the heartrending sobs of a woman, and the furious, husky shouting of Ferapontov. The cook, fluttering about the passage like a frightened hen, cried as soon as she saw Alpatych:

'He's been thrashing the life out of her – beating the mistress to death. ... Beat and beat her, he did, and knocked her about!'

'What for?' asked Alpatych.

'She kept begging to go away. She's a woman! "Take me away," says she, "don't let me perish with my little children. Folks," says she, "are all gone, so why," says she, "don't we go?" And so he began to thrash her and drag her round the room!'

At these words Alpatych nodded his head as if in approval, and not caring to hear more he went towards the door of the room opposite the innkeeper's, where he had left his purchases.

'You brute, you murderer!' screamed a thin, pale woman, bursting out of the door at that moment with a baby in her arms and her kerchief torn from her head. She ran down the steps into the yard. Ferapontov came out after her, but seeing Alpatych he pulled down his waistcoat, smoothed his hair, yawned and followed Alpatych into the other room.

'Going already, be you?' he asked.

Without answering the question, or looking round at the innkeeper, Alpatych sorted his packages and asked how much he owed.

'We'll reckon up! Well, been at the governor's, eh?' inquired Ferapontov. 'What did you hear?'

Alpatych replied that the governor had told him nothing definite.

'How can the likes of us with our business pack up and go?' said Ferapontov. 'Why, it'd be seven roubles a cartload as far as Dorogobuzh, and I tell 'em it's not Christian to ask it. Selivanov, now, made a good thing Thursday – sold flour to the army at nine roubles a sack. What do you say to some tea?' he added.

While the horses were being harnessed Alpatych and Ferapontov over their tea discussed the price of corn, the crops and the splendid harvesting weather.

'Well, it seems to be getting quieter,' remarked Ferapontov, finishing his third cup and getting up, 'Our men must have got the best of it. They said they wouldn't let 'em in. I suppose we're in force all right. I heard tell Matvey Ivanych Platov pitched eighteen thousand of 'em into the Marina t'other day, and drowned the lot.'

Alpatych gathered together his parcels, handed them over to the coachman who had come in, and settled up with the innkeeper. The noise of wheels, hooves and bells was heard from the gateway as a little trap passed out.

It was by now long after midday. Half the street lay in shadow, while the other half was in brilliant sunshine. Alpatych glanced out of the window and went to the door. All of a sudden there came a strange sound of a far-away hiss and thump followed by the boom of cannon blending into a dull roar that set the windows rattling.

Alpatych went out into the street. Two men were running past towards the bridge. From different sides came the whistle and crashing of round-shot and the bursting of shells falling on the town. But these sounds attracted little attention among the inhabitants compared with the noise of firing beyond the walls. Napoleon had ordered a hundred and thirty guns to open up on the town after four o'clock. The people did not at first grasp the meaning of this bombardment, and the crash of falling grenades and cannon-balls only excited curiosity. Ferapontov's wife, who till then had kept up a steady whimpering in the barn, became quiet and, with the baby in her arms, went out to the gate and stood silently staring at the people and listening to the noise.

The cook and a shopkeeper came to the gate. With lively interest they all tried to get a glimpse of the projectiles as they flew over their heads. Several people came round the corner talking eagerly.

'What force!' remarked one. 'Smashed the roof and ceiling to splinters!'

'Rooted up the earth like a pig!' said another.

'Capital business, makes one look alive!' laughed the first. 'Lucky you skipped aside or you'd have been no more!'

The crowd stopped them, and they described how a cannon-ball had fallen on a house close to them. Meanwhile other missiles, now a cannon-ball with a swift sinister hiss, now a grenade with its agreeable intermittent whistle, flew incessantly over the people's heads; but not one fell near them, they all flew over. Alpatych took his seat in the trap. The innkeeper stood at the gate.

'Will you never have done gaping?' he shouted to a kitchen-woman, who in her red petticoat, with sleeves rolled up and her bare elbows swinging, had stepped to the corner to listen to what was being said.

'There's a marvel for you!' she was saying, but hearing her master's voice she turned back, pulling down her skirt which had been tucked up.

Once more, but very close this time, something whistled, swooping down like a small bird. There was a flash of fire in the middle of the street, the sound of an explosion, and the street was shrouded in smoke.

'Scoundrel, what did you do that for?' shouted the innkeeper, rushing to the kitchen-woman.

At the same instant the piteous wailing of women rose from all sides, the terrified baby began to scream, and in silence, with pale faces, the people crowded round the cook. Above all the clamour rose the groans and exclamations of the kitchen-woman.

'Oh-h-h, good kind souls! Dear friends, don't let me die! Good kind souls! ...'

Five minutes later no one was left in the street. The cook, with her thigh broken by a fragment of the grenade, had been carried into the kitchen. Alpatych, his coachman, Ferapontov's wife and children, and the yard-man were all sitting in the cellar listening. The thunder of cannon, the hiss of projectiles and the piteous moaning of the cook, which prevailed over all else, never ceased for a single instant. Ferapontov's wife alternately rocked and hushed her baby, and when anyone came into the cellar asked in a pathetic whisper what had become of her husband who had stayed in the street. A shopman told her the master had gone with the crowd to the cathedral to fetch the wonder-working icon of Smolensk.

Towards dusk the cannonade began to subside. Alpatych left the cellar and stood in the doorway. The evening sky that had been so clear was overcast with smoke, through which the sickle of the new moon shone strangely, high up in the sky. After the terrible roar of the guns a hush seemed to hang over the city, broken only by the rustle of footsteps far and wide, the sound of groans and distant shouts, and the crackle of fires. The cook's moaning had now ceased. In two directions clouds of black smoke curled up from fires and drifted away. Soldiers in various uniforms walked or ran confusedly about the streets, like ants from a demolished ant-hill. Several of them slipped into Ferapontov's yard before Alpatych's eyes. Alpatych went out to the gate. A retreating regiment, the men jostling each other in their hurry, blocked the street.

Noticing him, an officer said: 'The town is being abandoned, get away, get away!' and turning immediately to the soldiers, he shouted: 'I'll teach you to keep out of the yards!'

Alpatych went back to the house, called the coachman and bade him set off. Ferapontov's whole household followed Alpatych and the driver out. The women, who had been silent till then, broke into sudden lamentations when they saw the smoke – and there were flames too – now visible in the twilight. As though echoing them, similar wails rose up in other parts of the street. Under the penthouse Alpatych and the coachman arranged the tangled reins and traces of their horses with trembling fingers.

As Alpatych drove out of the gate he saw some ten soldiers in

Ferapontov's open shop, talking loudly and filling their bags and knapsacks with wheaten flour and sunflower seeds. Just then Ferapontov returned and went into the shop. On seeing the soldiers he was about to shout at them but suddenly stopped short and, clutching at his hair, burst into a sobbing laugh.

'Carry it all away, lads! Don't leave it for those devils!' he cried, himself snatching up some sacks of flour and pitching them into the street. Some of the soldiers were frightened and ran away, others went on stuffing their bags. Catching sight of Alpatych, Ferapontov turned to him.

'Russia is done for!' he shouted. 'Alpatych, it's all over! I'll set fire to the place myself. We're done for! ...' and Ferapontov ran into the yard.

An unbroken stream of soldiers was blocking up the whole street, so that Alpatych could not get out and was obliged to wait. Ferapontov's wife and children were also sitting in a cart, waiting till it was possible to drive away.

Night had fallen now. There were stars in the sky and from time to time the new moon shone through the veil of smoke. On the slope down towards the Dnieper, Alpatych's cart and that of the innkeeper's wife, which had been slowly moving forward amid the rows of soldiers and other vehicles, were brought to a halt. In a side street not far from the cross-roads where the traffic had come to a full stop a house and some shops were burning. The fire was already dying down. The flames now sank down and were lost in the black smoke, then suddenly flared up to illumine with strange distinctness the faces of the people crowding at the cross-roads. Black figures flitted to and fro before the fire, and cries and shouts were heard above the incessant crackling of the flames. Seeing that it would be some time before his gig could proceed, Alpatych got down and turned into the side street to look at the fire. Soldiers were scurrying backwards and forwards, and he saw a couple of them and a man in a frieze coat dragging burning beams into another yard across the street, while others carried armfuls of hay.

Alpatych joined a great crowd of people standing before a high barn which was blazing briskly. The walls were all in flames and the back wall had fallen in; the wooden roof was collapsing and the rafters were alight. The crowd was obviously waiting to see the roof fall in, and Alpatych watched too.

'Alpatych!' a familiar voice suddenly hailed the old man.

'Mercy on us, your Excellency!' answered Alpatych, immediately recognizing the voice of the young prince.

Prince Andrei in his riding-cloak and mounted on a black horse, was looking at Alpatych from the back of the crowd.

'What are you doing here?' he asked.

'Your ... your Excellency,' stammered Alpatych, and broke into sobs. 'Your ... your ... Is it really all over with us? Your father. ...'

'What are you doing here?' Prince Andrei repeated.

The flames blazed up again at that moment, and Alpatych saw his young master's pale, worn face. He described how he had been sent to the town and had difficulty in getting away.

'What do you say, your Excellency – is it all over with us?' he asked again.

Prince Andrei, making no reply, took out a note-book and, raising his knee, began scribbling in pencil on a page he tore out. He wrote to his sister:

Smolensk has surrendered. Bald Hills will be occupied by the enemy within a week. Leave at once for Moscow. Let me know as soon as you start – send by special messenger to Usvyazh.

Having written this and handed the sheet of paper to Alpatych, he gave him verbal instructions about the arrangements for the departure of the prince, the princess, his son and the boy's tutor, and told him how and where to communicate with him immediately. Before he had time to finish, a staff-officer accompanied by a suite, galloped up to him.

'You a colonel!' shouted the staff-officer with a German accent, in a voice Prince Andrei knew. 'Under your very eyes houses are being set on fire and you stand by! What do you mean by it? You will have to answer for this!' shouted Berg, who was now assistant to the chief-of-staff of the commander of the left flank of the infantry of the First Army, a very agreeable and prominent position, as Berg said.

Prince Andrei glanced at him and, without replying, went on with his instructions to Alpatych.

'So tell them that I shall wait till the 10th for an answer, and if by that time I do not get word that they have all got away I shall be obliged to throw up everything and go myself to Bald Hills'.

'Prince,' said Berg, recognizing Prince Andrei, 'I only spoke as I did because it is my duty to carry out my orders, and I am always most scrupulous in carrying out … You must excuse me, please,' Berg tried to apologize.

There was a crash in the burning building. The fire died down for a moment and wreaths of black smoke rolled from under the roof. There was another fearful crash, followed by the collapse of something huge.

'Oooo!' yelled the crowd, as the ceiling of the granary fell in and the burning grain wafted a smell as of cakes baking. The flames flared up again, lighting the animated, delighted, harassed faces of the spectators.

The man in the frieze coat brandished his arms in the air and shouted:

'Hurrah, lads! Now she's raging! Well done!'

'That's the owner himself,' several voices were heard saying.

'So then,' continued Prince Andrei to Alpatych, 'tell them just what I have said.' And without a word to Berg, who stood mute beside him, he put spurs to his horse and rode down the side street.

5

FROM Smolensk the troops continued to retreat, with the enemy close on their heels. On the 10th of August the regiment Prince Andrei commanded was marching along the high road past the avenue that led to Bald Hills. The heat and drought had gone on for more than three weeks. Every day fleecy clouds floated across the sky, occasionally shutting out the sun, but towards evening the sky would clear again and the sun set in a sombre red haze. Only the heavy night-dews refreshed the earth. The wheat left in the fields was burnt up and dropping out of the ear. The marshes dried up. The cattle lowed from hunger, finding nothing to graze on in the sun-baked meadows. Only at night and in the forests while the dew lasted was it ever cool. But on the road, the high road along which the troops marched, there was no coolness even at night or where the road passed through the forest: the dew made no impression on the sandy dust inches deep. As soon as it was daylight the soldiers began to move. The artillery and baggage-wagons ploughed along noiselessly, buried almost to their axles, and the infantry sank ankle-deep in the soft, choking, burning dust that never cooled even at night. Sandy dust clung to their legs and to the wheels, rose and hung like a cloud overhead, and got into eyes, ears, hair and nostrils, and, worst of all, settled in the lungs of the men and beasts that moved along the road. The higher the sun rose, the higher rose that cloud of dust, and through the screen of tiny fiery particles one could look with naked eye at the sun, which showed like a huge crimson ball in the cloudless sky. There was not a breath of wind, and the men suffocated in the stagnant atmosphere. They marched with handkerchiefs tied over their noses and mouths. When they reached a village there was a rush for the wells. They fought over the water, and drank it down to the mud.

Prince Andrei was in command of a regiment, and deeply concerned with its organization, the welfare of the men and the necessity of receiving and giving orders. The burning and evacuation of Smolensk marked an epoch in his life. A novel feeling of intense indignation with the enemy made him forget his personal sorrow. He was devoted heart and soul to the interests of his regiment, and was considerate and kind to his men and his officers. In the regiment they called him 'our Prince', were proud of him and loved him. But he was kind and gentle only with those of his own regiment, with Timohin and his like – people quite new to him, belonging to a different world, who could have no notion of his past. So soon as chance threw him in the way of any of his old acquaintances, or anyone from the Staff, he bristled up immediately, and was vindictive, ironical and scornful. Everything that was reminiscent of the past was repugnant to him, and so in his relations with that former world he confined himself to trying to do his *duty* and not to be unfair.

In truth, everything appeared to Prince Andrei in a dark and gloomy light, especially after Smolensk had been abandoned on the 6th of August (he considered that the town could and should have been defended), and after his ailing father had been forced, as he supposed, to flee to Moscow, leaving his beloved Bald Hills, which he had built and peopled, to be plundered. But despite this, thanks to his position, Prince Andrei had something to think about entirely apart from general matters – his regiment. On the 10th of August the column of which his unit formed part reached the turning leading off to Bald Hills. Two days previously he had received news that his father, his son and his sister had left for Moscow. Though there was nothing for Prince Andrei to do at Bald Hills, he decided, with a characteristic desire to aggravate his own sufferings, that he must ride over there.

He ordered his horse to be saddled and, leaving his regiment on the march, rode off to his father's estate, where he had been born and had spent his childhood. Riding past the pond, where there always used to be dozens of peasant women chattering away as they rinsed their linen or beat it with wooden beetles, Prince Andrei noticed that there was not a soul about, and that the little washing-platform had been torn away and was floating on its side in the middle of the pond, half under water. He rode to the keeper's lodge. There was no one to be seen at the stone gates of the drive and the door was unlocked. Grass had already begun to grow over the garden paths, and calves and horses were straying about in the English park. Prince Andrei went up to the hot-house: some of the glass panes were smashed, and of the trees in tubs several were overturned and others dried up. He shouted for Taras, the gardener. No one answered. Going round the hot-house to the ornamental garden, he saw that the carved wooden fence was broken and branches of the plum-trees had been torn off with the fruit. An old peasant, whom Prince Andrei could remember seeing as a boy at the gate, was sitting on a green garden-seat plaiting a bast shoe.

He was deaf and did not hear Prince Andrei's approach. He was sitting on the old prince's favourite bench, and beside him strips of bast were hanging on the broken and withered branches of a magnolia.

Prince Andrei rode up to the house. Several lime-trees in the old garden had been cut down and a piebald mare and her foal were wandering about among the rose bushes in front of the house. The shutters were all up, except at one window downstairs which was open. A little serf-boy, catching sight of Prince Andrei, ran into the house.

Alpatych, having got his family away, remained alone at Bald Hills: he was sitting indoors reading the *Lives of the Saints*. On learning that Prince Andrei was there, he came out, with his spectacles on his nose and buttoning his coat; he hurried up to the prince, and without a word began weeping and kissing his young master's knee.

Then, vexed at his own weakness, he turned away and began to give an account of the position of affairs. Everything precious and valuable had been moved to Bogucharovo. Up to eight hundred bushels of grain had also been carted away. The hay and the spring corn, which, according to Alpatych, had been wonderful that year, had been commandeered by the troops and cut while still green. The peasants were ruined; some of them, too, had gone to Bogucharovo; a small number remained.

Without waiting to hear him out, Prince Andrei asked when his father and sister had left – meaning when had they left for Moscow. Alpatych, supposing the question to refer to their departure for Bogucharovo, replied that they had set off on the 7th, and again went into details concerning arrangements for the estate, asking for instructions.

'Is it your Honour's orders that I let the oats go, on getting a receipt from the officers?' he inquired. 'We still have six hundred quarters left.'

'What am I to say to him?' Prince Andrei wondered, looking down on the old man's bald head shining in the sun, and seeing by the expression on his face that Alpatych himself realized the untimeliness of such questions, and only asked them to deaden his own grief.

'Yes, let it go,' he said.

'In case your Excellency noticed some disorder in the garden,' pursued Alpatych, 'it could not be prevented. Three regiments were here and camped for the night. The dragoons especially behaved ... I took down the name and rank of their commanding officer to lodge a complaint.'

'Well, and what are you going to do? Shall you stay, if the enemy occupies the place?' Prince Andrei asked him.

Alpatych turned his face to Prince Andrei and looked at him; then suddenly, with a solemn gesture, he lifted his arm upwards.

'He is my refuge, and His will be done!' he exclaimed.

A group of peasants and indoor servants were coming across the meadow, uncovering their heads as they drew near Prince Andrei.

'Well, good-bye!' said Prince Andrei, bending over to Alpatych. 'You must go away too. Take what you can; and tell the peasants to make their way to the Ryazan estate, or the property near Moscow.'

Alpatych clung to Prince Andrei's leg and broke into sobs. Gently disengaging himself, Prince Andrei spurred his horse and rode down the avenue at a gallop.

He passed the old man again, still sitting in the ornamental garden, as impassive as a fly on the face of a loved one who is dead, tapping on the last on which he was making the bast shoe. Two little girls came running out from the hot-house, their skirts full of plums picked from the trees there, and stopped short on meeting Prince Andrei.

When she saw the young master the elder girl, with a look of alarm on her face, clutched her younger companion by the hand and hid with her behind a birch-tree, not stopping to gather up the green plums they dropped.

Prince Andrei turned away with startled haste, unwilling to let them see that they had been observed. A feeling of pity welled up in him for the pretty, frightened child. He was afraid to look at her, yet at the same time had an overwhelming desire to do so. Looking at these children, he was seized by a new, comforting sense of relief as he became aware of the existence of other interests in life, quite remote from his own and just as legitimate. These little persons were evidently possessed by the one passionate idea – to carry off and devour those green plums without being caught – and Prince Andrei shared their hope for success in their enterprise. He could not resist another glance at them. Fancying that the danger was over, they had darted out of their hiding-place and, chirruping something in their shrill little voices and holding up their skirts, they were scampering merrily across the meadow as fast as their bare, sunburned little legs would carry them.

Prince Andrei was somewhat refreshed by his ride away from the dusty high road along which the troops were marching. But not far from Bald Hills he came out on the road again and overtook his regiment at its halting-place by the dam of a small lake. It was towards two o'clock in the afternoon. The sun, a red ball through the dust, baked and scorched his back intolerably through his black coat. The dust hung motionless as ever above the buzz of talk that came from the resting troops. There was not a breath of wind. As he rode along the embankment Prince Andrei smelt the fresh, muddy smell of the lake. He longed to take a dive into the water, however dirty it might be. He glanced round at the pool from which came shrieks and laughter. The small lake, thickly covered with green slime, looked half a yard higher and overflowed the dam, being full of white, naked human bodies with brick-red hands, faces and necks, splashing about in it. All this bare white human flesh, laughing and shrieking, was floundering about in that dirty pool like carp crammed into a water-pot. There was a ring of merriment in that splashing, and that was what made it especially pathetic.

One fair-haired young soldier of the third company, whom Prince Andrei knew and who had a strap round the calf of his leg, crossed himself, stepped back to get a good run, and plunged into the water. Another, a swarthy non-commissioned officer who always looked shaggy, stood up to his waist in the water wriggling his muscular form and snorting with satisfaction as he poured the water over his head with hands black to the wrists. There was a noise of slapping, yelling and puffing.

Everywhere, on the bank, on the dam and in the lake, there was white, healthy, muscular flesh. The officer, Timohin, with his little red nose, was rubbing himself down on the embankment. He felt rather abashed at seeing the prince but decided to address him nevertheless.

'It's really pretty good, your Excellency! Wouldn't you like to try?' he said.

'Too dirty,' replied Prince Andrei, making a grimace.

'We'll clear it out for you in a jiffy,' said Timohin, and, not stopping to put his clothes on, ran to get the men out of the lake.

'The prince wants to bathe.'

'What prince? Ours?' cried various voices, and the men were all in such haste to make way for him that Prince Andrei hardly had time to deter them. He thought that he would far rather souse himself with water in the barn.

'Flesh, bodies, *chair à canon!*' he reflected, looking at his own naked body and shuddering, not so much with cold as with aversion and horror, incomprehensible even to himself, aroused by the sight of that immense multitude of bodies splashing about in the dirty lake.

*

On the 7th of August Prince Bagration wrote as follows from his quarters at Mihalovka on the Smolensk road:

Dear Count Alexei Andreyevich [he was writing to Arakcheyev but knew that his letter would be read by the Emperor, and therefore weighed every word to the best of his ability].

I presume that the *minister* – [as he called Barclay de Tolly] – has already reported the abandonment to the enemy of Smolensk. It is painful, it is sad, and the whole army is in despair that this most important place should have been wantonly relinquished. I, for my part, personally entreated him most urgently, and finally even by letter; but nothing would persuade him. Upon my honour I swear to you that

837

Napoleon was in a greater fix than he has ever been, and might have lost half his army but he could not have taken Smolensk. Our troops fought and are fighting as never before. With fifteen thousand men I kept the enemy at bay for thirty-five hours and beat them; but *he* was not willing to hold out for a mere fourteen hours. It is a blot and a disgrace on our armies, and as for him – methinks he ought not to be alive.

If he reports that our losses were heavy, it is not true: perhaps around four thousand, not that. But even had it been ten thousand, that's war! The enemy, on the other hand, lost untold numbers. ...

What would it have cost him to hold out for a couple of days longer? In any case the French would have had to retire of their own accord, for they hadn't a drop of water for their men or their horses. He gave me his word he would not retreat, and then all of a sudden sends a message that he is withdrawing that very night. We cannot wage war in this way, or we may soon bring the enemy to Moscow. ...

There is a rumour that you are thinking of making peace. God forbid! To make peace after our sacrifices, after such insane retreats – you would be setting all Russia against you and everyone of us would feel ashamed of wearing the Russian uniform. If it has come to that, we must fight so long as Russia can and so long as there are men able to stand. ...

One man ought to be in command, not two. Your minister may be all right in the ministry but as a general he is not merely bad but execrable, yet the fate of the whole Fatherland has been entrusted to his hands! ... I am, I assure you, nearly beside myself with vexation: forgive me for writing so boldly. It is plain, anyone who can advocate the conclusion of a peace, and approves of confiding the command of the army to the minister, is no friend to the Sovereign and hopes for the ruin of us all. And so I write frankly: call out the militia. For the minister is leading our visitors after him to the capital in the most masterly fashion. Wolzogen, the Imperial aide-de-camp, is held in great suspicion by the whole army. He is said to be more Napoleon's man than ours, and he is the minister's prime counsellor. I am not merely civil to him but as obedient as a corporal, although I am his senior. This is painful, but, as I am devoted to my Sovereign and Benefactor, I submit. Only I grieve for the Emperor that he should entrust our valiant army to such as he. Consider – in the course of this retreat we have lost, through fatigue or left sick in hospital, over fifteen thousand men; whereas had we attacked this would not have happened. Tell me for God's sake what will Russia – our mother Russia – say to such cowardice, and why are we abandoning our good and gallant country to such rabble and implanting feelings of hate and shame in every Russian?

What is there to fear? Whom are we afraid of? It is no fault of mine if the minister shilly-shallies, is a coward, is dense and dilatory, and has all the worst defects. The whole army bewails it and calls down every sort of curse upon him. ...

6

ALL the innumerable sub-divisions into which it is possible to classify the phenomena of life may be assembled into two categories: the one, where matter predominates; the other, where form is the prevailing factor. In the latter group – by contrast with life in the village, in the country, in the provincial town, or even in Moscow – may be placed the life of Petersburg, and especially the life of its *salons*. The life of the fashionable drawing-room continues unvarying.

Since 1805 we had been quarrelling and being reconciled with Napoleon, making constitutions and unmaking them again; but the *salons* of Anna Pavlovna and Hélène were the same as they had been – the former seven, the latter five years – before. At Anna Pavlovna's everybody was as perplexed as ever by Napoleon's successes, and saw in them and in the subservience of the sovereigns of Europe a malicious conspiracy, intended solely to cause unpleasantness and anxiety to the Court circle of which Anna Pavlovna was the representative. In Hélène's house, which Rumyantsev himself honoured with his visits, regarding Hélène as a remarkably intelligent woman, the same enthusiasm prevailed in 1812 as in 1808 for the 'great nation' and the 'great man', together with regret for the breach with France, which, in the opinion of those who gathered at Hélène's, ought without delay to be terminated by peace.

Of late, since the Emperor's return from the army, there had been some excitement in these rival *salons*, accompanied by demonstrations of mutual hostility, but the bias of each circle remained unaffected. Except for the most unimpeachable legitimists, Anna Pavlovna's set refused to receive anyone who was French, and patriotic views were expressed that one ought not to go to the French theatre, and that to maintain the French troupe there was costing the government as much as the maintenance of a whole army corps. The progress of the war was eagerly followed, and the most flattering reports of our army were circulated. In the Hélène-Rumyantsev-French circle the rumours of the barbarities of the enemy and of the war were discredited and every conciliatory effort on the part of Napoleon was discussed in full. This set upbraided the premature counsels of those who advised speedy preparations for the removal to Kazan of the Court and the girls' educational establishments under the patronage of the Dowager-Empress. In general, the whole war was looked on in Hélène's drawing-room as a series of formal demonstrations which would very soon end in peace, and Bilibin's view prevailed – Bilibin was now in Petersburg and constantly at Hélène's (where it behoved every sensible man to be seen) – that gunpowder would not mend matters but only by those who invented it. Moscow's patriotic fervour, tidings of which reached Petersburg with the return of the Emperor, they derided ironically, with much wit though with equal circumspection.

In Anna Pavlovna's circle, on the contrary, these patriotic demonstrations roused the greatest enthusiasm, and were spoken of as Plutarch speaks of the deeds of the heroes of antiquity. Prince Vasili, who still occupied his former important posts, constituted the connecting link between the two sets. He visited 'my good friend Anna Pavlovna' and was likewise to be seen in 'my daughter's diplomatic *salon*', and often in his constant comings and goings between the two camps became confused and said at Anna Pavlovna's what he should have said at Hélène's, and vice versa.

Soon after the Emperor's return Prince Vasili, in a conversation about the progress of the war at Anna Pavlovna's, sharply criticized Barclay de Tolly, but was undecided as to who ought to be appointed commander-in-chief. One of the visitors, usually spoken of as '*un homme de beaucoup de mérite*', described how he had that day seen Kutuzov, the newly elected chief of the Petersburg militia, presiding over the enrolment of recruits at the Treasury, and cautiously ventured to suggest that Kutuzov would be the man to satisfy all requirements.

Anna Pavlovna remarked with a melancholy smile that Kutuzov had done nothing but cause the Emperor annoyance.

'I told them so over and over again at the Assembly of the Nobility,' interposed Prince Vasili, 'but they wouldn't listen to me. I told them his election as chief of the militia would not please the Emperor. They would not listen.

'It's all this mania for opposition,' he went on. 'And what public are they playing to, I should like to know? It's all because we want to ape the silly enthusiasm of those Moscovites,' Prince Vasili continued, forgetting for a moment that it was at Hélène's one had to jeer at Moscow's fervour, while at Anna Pavlovna's it was as well to admire it. But he retrieved his mistake at once. 'Now is it suitable for Kutuzov, the oldest general in Russia, to be presiding at that tribunal? And he'll get nothing by that move! How could they possibly appoint a man commander-in-chief who cannot sit a horse, who drops asleep at a council – a man, too, of the lowest morals! A pretty reputation he gained for himself in Bucharest! I don't speak of his capacity as a general, but at a time like this how could we nominate a decrepit, blind old man, yes, positively blind? A fine idea to have a blind general! He can't see a thing. To play at blindman's-buff? ... He doesn't see at all!'

No one made any rejoinder to this.

On the 24th of July this was a perfectly correct view. But on the 29th of July Kutuzov received the title of prince. This mark of favour might indicate a desire to shelve him, and therefore Prince Vasili's way of thinking continued to be correct though now he was not in any hurry to express it. But on the 8th of August a committee, consisting of Field-marshal Saltykov, Arakcheyev, Vyazmitinov, Lopuhin and Kochubey, met to consider the progress of the war. This committee came to the conclusion that our failures were due to a lack of unity in the command, and, though the members of the committee were aware of the Emperor's dislike of Kutuzov, after a brief deliberation they agreed to advise his appointment as commander-in-chief. And that same day Kutuzov was appointed commander in chief with full powers over the armies and over the whole region occupied by them.

On the 9th of August Prince Vasili once more met the man 'de beaucoup de mérite'. The man 'de beacoup de mérite' was very attentive to Anna Pavlovna, in the hope of getting himself appointed director of one of the Empress Maria Feodorovna's educational establishments for young ladies. Prince Vasili strode into the room with an air of happy triumph, like a man who has attained the object of his desires.

'Well, have you heard the great news? Prince Kutuzov is field-marshal! All differences are settled. I am so glad, so delighted! At last we have a man!' said he, glancing sternly and significantly round at the whole company.

L'homme de beaucoup de mérite, in spite of his anxiety to obtain the post he coveted, could not refrain from reminding Prince Vasili of his former opinion. (This was a breach of manners to Prince Vasili in

Anna Pavlovna's drawing-room, and also to Anna Pavlovna herself, who had likewise received the tidings with eager satisfaction, but he could not resist the temptation.)

'But, prince, they say he is blind!' he observed, quoting Prince Vasili's own words.

'What next! He sees well enough,' said Prince Vasili quickly, in a deep voice and with a slight cough – the voice and cough with which he was wont to dispose of all difficulties. 'He sees well enough,' he repeated. 'And what I am particularly pleased about,' he went on, 'is that the Emperor has given him full powers over all the armies and the whole region – powers no commander-in-chief has ever had before. He is a second autocrat,' he concluded with a victorious smile.

'God grant it, God grant it!' said Anna Pavlovna.

L'homme de beaucoup de mérite, who was still a novice in Court society, wishing to flatter Anna Pavlovna by upholding her first opinion on this subject, observed:

'They say the Emperor was reluctant to give Kutuzov such authority. I hear that Kutuzov coloured like a young girl having La Fontaine's *Contes* read to her, when he said: "Your Sovereign and the Fatherland award you this honour".'

'Perhaps his heart was not altogether in it,' said Anna Pavlovna.

'Oh no, no!' protested Prince Vasili warmly. 'He would not now put Kutuzov second to anyone.' In Prince Vasili's opinion, not only was Kutuzov the best of men but everybody worshipped him. 'No, that is impossible,' said he, 'for our Sovereign has always appreciated him highly.'

'Only God grant that Prince Kutuzov assumes real power and does not allow *anyone* to put a spoke in his wheel – *des batons dans les roues*,' remarked Anna Pavlovna.

Prince Vasili understood at once who was meant by that *anyone*, and he said in a whisper:

'I know for a fact that Kutuzov made it an express condition that the Tsarevich should not be with the army. Do you know what he said to the Emperor?'

And Prince Vasili repeated the words supposed to have been spoken by Kutuzov to the Emperor: '"I can neither punish him if he does wrong nor reward him if he does well." Oh, a very shrewd fellow is Prince Kutuzov, and what a character! I have known him this many a day.'

'They even say,' remarked *l'homme de beaucoup de mérite*, who did not yet possess a courtier's tact, 'that his Excellency made it an express condition that the Emperor himself should not be with the army.'

At these words Prince Vasili and Anna Pavlovna simultaneously turned their backs on him and looked mournfully at one another, with a sigh of pity for his *naïveté*.

7

WHILE all this was happening in Petersburg the French, having already left Smolensk behind them, were steadily approaching nearer and nearer to Moscow. Napoleon's historian, Thiers, like others of his historians, tries to justify his hero by saying that Napoleon was drawn on to the walls of Moscow against his will. He is as right as any of his kind who look for the explanation of historic events in the will of one man; he is as right as his Russian *confrères* who maintain that Napoleon was lured to Moscow by the skilful strategy of the Russian generals. Here, besides the law of 'retrospectiveness', which makes all the past appear a preparation for events that occur subsequently, reciprocity comes in, confusing the whole matter. A good chess player who has lost a game is genuinely convinced that his failure resulted from a false move on his part, and tries to see the mistake he made at the beginning of the game, forgetting that at each stage of play there were similar blunders, so that no single move was perfect. The mistake on which he concentrates attention attracts his notice simply because his opponent took advantage of it. How much more complex is the game of war, which must be played within certain limits of time and where it is a question not of one will manipulating inanimate objects but of something resulting from the innumerable *collisions* of diverse wills!

After Smolensk Napoleon sought a battle beyond Dorogobuzh, at Vyazma, and then at Tsarevo-Zaimishche; but it turned out that owing to a combination of circumstances without number the Russians could not give battle before they reached Borodino, seventy miles from Moscow. From Vyazma Napoleon issued the order to advance direct upon Moscow. *Moscow, the Asiatic capital of this great Empire, the sacred city of the peoples of Alexander; Moscow, with its countless churches looking like Chinese pagodas* – this Moscow allowed Napoleon's imagination no rest. On the march from Vyazma to Tsarevo-Zaimishche Napoleon rode his bob-tailed light bay ambling horse, accompanied by his Guards, his bodyguard, his pages and aides-de-camp. Berthier, his chief-of-staff, had dropped behind to interrogate a Russian prisoner taken by the cavalry. Followed by Lelorgne d'Ideville, an interpreter, he overtook Napoleon at a gallop and pulled up with an amused expression.

'Well?' asked Napoleon.

'One of Platov's Cossacks – says that Platov is joining up with the main army, and that Kutuzov has been appointed commander-in-chief. A very shrewd rascal, with a long tongue!'

Napoleon smiled and bade them give the Cossack a horse and bring the man to him. He wanted to have a talk with him himself. Several adjutants galloped off, and an hour later Lavrushka, the serf Denisov had turned over to Rostov, rode up to Napoleon, wearing an orderly's short jacket and sitting on a French cavalry saddle, looking sly, tipsy and mirthful. Napoleon told him to ride by his side, and began questioning him.

'You are a Cossack?'

'Yes, a Cossack, your Honour.'

The Cossack, says Thiers, relating this episode, *ignorant in whose company he found himself, for there was nothing in Napoleon's plain appearance to suggest to the Oriental mind the presence of a monarch, talked in the most free-and-easy manner of the incidents of the war.* In reality, Lavrushka, having got drunk the day before and left his master dinnerless, had been thrashed for it and sent to the village in quest of fowls, where he engaged in looting till the French caught and took him prisoner. Lavrushka was one of those coarse, impudent lackeys who have seen a good deal of life, who consider it imperative to employ trickery and cunning whatever they do, are ready to render any sort of service to their master and can always smell out his baser impulses, especially those prompted by vanity and pettiness.

Finding himself in the society of Napoleon, whose identity he easily and confidently recognized, Lavrushka was not in the least abashed but merely set to work to win the favour of his new master.

He knew very well that this was Napoleon, and Napoleon's presence intimidated him no more than Rostov's or the sergeant-major's with his knout, for the simple reason that there was nothing which either the sergeant-major or Napoleon could deprive him of.

So he rattled on, repeating all the gossip he had heard among the orderlies. Much of it was true. But when Napoleon asked him whether the Russians thought they would beat Bonaparte or not Lavrushka screwed up his eyes and considered.

He detected a sharp piece of cunning in the question, as men of his type see cunning in everything, so he frowned and did not answer immediately.

'This is the size of it,' he said thoughtfully, 'if there's a battle pretty soon, yours will win. That's a fact. But let three days go by, and it's likely to be a long job.'

Lelorgne d'Ideville smilingly interpreted this to Napoleon as follows: 'If a battle takes place within the next three days the French will win, but if it were postponed after that God knows what would be the outcome.' Napoleon did not smile, though he was obviously in high good humour, and ordered these words to be repeated.

Lavrushka noticed this and to entertain him further added (affecting ignorance of Napoleon's identity):

'We know, you've got your Bonaparte, aye, and he's beaten everybody in the world; but we're of different kidney ...' hardly aware how or why this boastful bit of patriotism slipped out at the end. The interpreter translated these words without the conclusion, and Bonaparte smiled.

The young Cossack brought a smile to the lips of his august interlocutor, says Thiers.

After riding a few paces in silence Napoleon turned to Berthier and said that he would like to see the effect on *this child of the Don* of learning that the man he was addressing was the Emperor himself, the very Emperor who had carved his immortally victorious name on the Pyramids.

The fact was accordingly communicated to Lavrushka.

Realizing that this was meant to disconcert him and that Napoleon expected him to be panic-stricken, Lavrushka for the gratification of his new masters promptly pretended to be astounded, aghast. He opened round eyes and made the sort of face he put on when he was being led off to be whipped. *As soon as Napoleon's interpreter had spoken,* says Thiers, *the Cossack was dumbfounded. He did not utter another word, and rode with his eyes fixed on the conqueror whose fame had reached him across the steppes of the East. All his loquacity was suddenly arrested and gave place to a naïve and silent awe. Napoleon, having re-warded him, ordered him to be set free like a bird one restores to its native fields.*

Napoleon continued on, dreaming of the Moscow that filled his imagination, while the 'bird one restores to its native fields' galloped back to our outposts, inventing on the way the tale he would tell his comrades. What had really taken place he had no mind to relate, simply because it seemed to him not worth the telling. He found the Cossacks, inquired for the regiment operating with Platov's detachment, and by evening located his master, Nikolai Rostov, quartered at Yankovo. Rostov was just mounting his horse to ride round the neighbouring villages with Ilyin. He let Lavrushka have another horse and took him along with him.

8

PRINCESS MARIA was not in Moscow and out of harm's way as Prince Andrei supposed.

After Alpatych's return from Smolensk the old prince suddenly seemed to awake as from a dream. He gave orders for the militiamen to be called up from the villages and armed, and wrote a letter to the commander-in-chief informing him of his intention to stay at Bald Hills and defend himself to the last, leaving it to the commander-in-chief's discretion whether or not to take measures for the defence of Bald Hills, where one of Russia's oldest generals was preparing to be captured or killed. At the same time he announced to his household that he would remain at Bald Hills.

But, while determined himself not to leave, he made arrangements for sending the princess with Dessalles and the little prince to Bogucharovo, and from there to Moscow. Princess Maria, alarmed by her father's feverish, sleepless activity following on his previous apathy, could not bring herself to desert him, and for the first time in her life ventured to disobey. She refused to go, and a fearful tempest of wrath broke over her. The prince repeated every injustice he had ever inflicted on his daughter. Trying to put her in the wrong, he told her she had worn him out, estranged him from his son, had harboured the vilest suspicions of him and made it the object of her life to poison his existence; and he drove her from his study, declaring that he did not care if she did not go away. He said that he did not wish to be reminded of her existence, and warned her not to let him set eyes on her again. The fact that he did not, as she had feared, order her to be removed from Bald Hills by main force, but only forbade her to show

846

herself to him, was a comfort to Princess Maria. She knew it meant that in the secret depths of his soul he was glad she was remaining at home and had not gone away.

The morning after little Nikolai had left, the old prince donned full uniform and prepared to visit the commander-in-chief. The calèche was ready at the door. Princess Maria saw him walk out of the house in uniform with all his orders, and go down the garden to inspect his armed peasants and domestic serfs. She sat by the window listening to his voice which reached her from the garden. Suddenly several men came running up the avenue with frightened faces.

Princess Maria ran out on to the steps, down the flower-bordered path and into the avenue. She was met by a crowd of militiamen and servants moving towards her, and in the centre of this throng several men were half supporting half dragging along a little old man in a uniform and decorations. She ran up to him and, in the play of the tiny rings of sunlight that filtered through the shade of the lime-tree avenue, could not be sure what change there was in his face. All she could see was that his former stern, determined expression had altered to one of timidity and submission. When he caught sight of his daughter he moved his helpless lips and uttered a hoarse sound. It was impossible to understand what he meant. He was lifted up, carried to his study and laid on the couch he had so dreaded of late.

The doctor, who was fetched that same night, bled him and announced that the prince had had a stroke, paralysing his right side.

To remain at Bald Hills was becoming more and more dangerous, and the next day they moved the prince to Bogucharovo, the doctor travelling with them.

By the time they reached Bogucharovo, Dessalles and the little prince had already left for Moscow.

For three weeks the old prince lay stricken with paralysis, getting neither better nor worse, in the new house Prince Andrei had built at Bogucharovo. His mind had gone; he lay like a twisted corpse. He muttered without cease, twitching his eyebrows and lips, and it was impossible to tell whether he was aware of his surroundings or not. Only one thing was certain – that he was suffering and wished to say something. But what it was, no one could divine: was it some whim of a sick and semi-delirious brain, did it relate to public affairs, or had it to do with family matters?

847

The doctor maintained that this restlessness meant nothing and was due to physical causes; but Princess Maria believed (and the fact that her presence always intensified his agitation confirmed her supposition) that he wanted to tell her something.

He was obviously suffering both physically and mentally. There was no hope of recovery. It was impossible to move him – what if he were to die on the road? 'Wouldn't it be better if the end did come, if it were all over?' Princess Maria thought sometimes. Night and day, hardly sleeping at all, she watched over him, and, terrible to say, often watched, not in the hope of finding signs of improvement but looking for symptoms of the approach of the end.

Strange as it was to her to acknowledge this feeling in herself, yet there it was. And what was still more horrible to Princess Maria was the fact that since her father's illness (if not even before, when she elected to stay with him, vaguely anticipating that something would happen) all the aspirations and hopes that had been forgotten or slumbering within her came to life again. Thoughts that had not entered her head for years – dreams of a life free from perpetual fear of her father, even of the possibility of love and a happy married life – haunted her imagination like temptations of the devil. No matter how strenuously she tried to set them aside she returned to them again and again, and often caught herself thinking how she would order her life now, after *this* was over. It was temptation of the devil and Princess Maria knew it. She knew that the sole weapon against *him* was prayer, and she tried to pray. She put herself into the attitude of prayer, gazed at the icons, repeated the words of a prayer, but she could not pray. She felt that a different world had now taken possession of her – the world of activity, arduous and free – completely the opposite of the spiritual world which had enclosed her till now and in which her greatest comfort had been prayer. She could not pray and could not weep, and practical cares absorbed her mind.

To remain at Bogucharovo was becoming unsafe. From all sides came news of the approach of the French, and in one village, a dozen miles from Bogucharovo, a homestead had been sacked by French marauders.

The doctor insisted on the necessity of moving the prince; the Marshal of the Province sent an official to Princess Maria to persuade her to get away as quickly as possible. The head of the rural police visited Bogucharovo and urged the same thing, saying that the French were only some twenty-five miles away, that French proclamations were circulating in the villages, and that if the princess did not take her father away before the 15th he could not answer for the consequences.

The princess decided to go on the 15th. The whole of the 14th she was busy making preparations and giving instructions, for which everyone applied to her. That night she spent as usual, without undressing, in the room next to the one where the old prince lay. Several times she woke to hear his groans and muttering, the creak of his bed, and the steps of Tikhon and the doctor when they turned him over. Several times she listened at the door, and it seemed to her that his mutterings were louder than usual and that he was more restless. She could not sleep, and several times went to the door and listened: she wanted to go in but hesitated. Though he could not speak, Princess Maria saw and knew how he disliked any sign of anxiety on his account. She had noticed how he always looked away in displeasure when he saw her anxious eyes involuntarily fixed on him. She knew that her intrusion in the middle of the night, at an unusual hour, would irritate him.

But never had she felt so grieved for him, never had she so dreaded to lose him. She went over their lives together, and in every word of his, every action, found a manifestation of his love for her. Occasionally these recollections were interrupted by those promptings of the devil, the thoughts of what would happen after his death, and how she would arrange her new life of freedom. But she drove away such imaginings with loathing. Towards morning he became quieter and she fell asleep.

She woke late. The clear-sightedness which often accompanies the moment of waking showed her unmistakably what it was that was of most interest to her in her father's illness. She woke, listened to what was going on behind the door and, hearing him groan, said to herself with a sigh that things were still the same.

'But what change could there be? What did I hope for? I hope for his death!' she cried, revolted with herself.

She washed, dressed, said her prayers and went out to the porch. In front of the steps the carriages into which their things were being packed were standing without horses.

It was a warm, grey morning. Princess Maria lingered in the porch, still horrified at her own spiritual infamy and trying to arrange her thoughts before going in to see her father.

The doctor came downstairs and out to her.

'He is a little better today,' said he. 'I was looking for you. One can make out something of what he says. His head is clearer. Come in – he is asking for you. ...'

Princess Maria's heart beat so violently at this news that she turned pale and leaned against the door to keep from falling. To see him, to talk to him – feel his eyes on her now that her whole soul was over-flowing with those dreadful, wicked thoughts – was a torment of joy and terror.

'Come along,' said the doctor.

Princess Maria entered her father's room and went up to the bed. He was lying on his back propped up high, and his small bony hands with their knotted purple veins rested on the quilt. His left eye gazed straight before him, his right eye was awry and his lips and eyebrows were motionless. He looked so thin, so small and pathetic. His face seemed to have shrivelled or fallen away, so that his features appeared smaller. Princess Maria went up and kissed his hand. His left hand pressed hers in a way that showed he had long been waiting for her to come. He twitched her hand, and his eyebrows and lips quivered angrily.

She looked at him in dismay, trying to fathom what he wanted of her. When she changed her position so that his left eye could see her face he was calmer at once, not taking his eyes off her for some seconds. Then his lips and tongue moved, sounds came and he tried to speak, gazing at her timidly and imploringly, evidently afraid that she might not understand him.

Straining all her faculties, Princess Maria looked at him. The gro-tesque effort it cost him to manage his tongue made her drop her eyes and with difficulty repress the sobs that rose in her throat. He said something, repeating the same words several times. She could not understand them but tried to guess what he was saying and in-quiringly repeated the syllables he uttered.

'S-s ... tr-d ... tr-d ...' he got out two or three times. It was im-possible to make any sense of the sounds. The doctor thought he had guessed their meaning, and suggested 'The princess is afraid?' The prince shook his head, and again repeated the same words.

'My soul is troubled?' asked Princess Maria.

850

He uttered a sort of bellow in confirmation of this, took her hand and began clasping it to different parts of his breast as if trying to find the right place for it.

'Always thinking ... about you ... thinking ...' he then articulated far more intelligibly than before, now that he was persuaded of being understood.

Princess Maria pressed her head against his hand to hide her sobs and tears.

He moved his hand over her hair.

'I have been calling for you all night ...' he brought out.

'If only I had known ...' she said through her tears. 'I was afraid to come in.'

He squeezed her hand.

'Weren't you asleep?'

'No, I could not sleep,' said Princess Maria, shaking her head.

Unconsciously imitating her father, she now spoke like him, using signs as much as possible, and almost had the same difficulty with her tongue.

'Dear heart ...' or was it 'Dearest ...'? – Princess Maria could not tell; but from the look in his eyes she knew that he had called her something tender and affectionate, which he had never done before. 'Why didn't you come in?'

'And I – I was wishing for his death!' thought Princess Maria.

He was silent for a space.

'Thank you ... daughter dear ... for all the, for all ... forgive ... thank you ... forgive ... thank you! ...' and the tears trickled from his eyes. 'Call my Andrei,' he said suddenly, and a shy, childlike look of uncertainty showed itself in his face. It was as if he himself were aware that there was something out of the way about his request. So at least it seemed to Princess Maria.

'I have had a letter from him,' she replied.

He glanced at her with timid surprise.

'Where is he?'

'He's with the army, *mon père*, at Smolensk.'

He lay silent for a long time, his eyes shut. Presently, as if in answer to his doubts and as much as to say that now he understood and remembered everything, he nodded his head and opened his eyes again.

'Yes,' he said, softly and distinctly. 'Russia is lost! They have destroyed her!'

And once more he began to sob, and the tears flowed from his eyes. Princess Maria could contain herself no longer, and wept too as she gazed at his face.

He closed his eyes again. His sobs ceased. He pointed to his eyes, and Tikhon, understanding what he meant, wiped away the tears.

Then he opened his eyes and said something which none of them could understand, until at last Tikhon made out what it was and repeated it. Princess Maria tried to connect the sense of his words with what he had just been speaking about. First she thought he was referring to Russia – or perhaps to Prince Andrei, or herself, or his grandson, or his own death – and so she could not divine what it was he was saying.

'Put on your white dress. I like it,' he had said.

When she understood, Princess Maria sobbed louder than ever, and the doctor, taking her arm, led her out to the verandah, trying to persuade her to calm herself and go on with the preparations for the journey. After she had left the room the prince again began speaking about his son, about the war, about the Emperor, angrily twitching his eyebrows and raising his hoarse voice, and then came the second and final stroke.

Princess Maria stayed on the verandah. The day had cleared, and it was hot and sunny. She could not realize anything, could think of nothing and feel nothing except passionate love for her father, love which it seemed to her she had never felt until that moment. She ran sobbing into the garden, towards the pond, along the avenues of young lime-trees Prince Andrei had planted.

'Yes ... I ... I ... I wished him dead. Yes, I wanted it to end quickly ... that I might be at peace. ... But what will become of me? What use will peace be to me when he is gone?' Princess Maria murmured, walking round the park with hurried steps and pressing her hands to her bosom, which heaved with convulsive sobs.

When she had completed the tour of the garden, which brought her back to the house again, she saw Mademoiselle Bourienne (who had remained at Bogucharovo, refusing to leave) coming towards her with a stranger. It was the District Marshal, who had called in person to impress upon the princess the need for a prompt departure. Princess Maria listened but his words held no meaning for her. She took him into the house, offered him lunch, and sat down with him. Then, excusing herself, she went to the old prince's door. The doctor came out with an agitated face and told her she could not enter.

'Go away, princess! Go away, go away!'

She returned to the garden and sat on the grass by the pond at the foot of the slope, where no one could see her. She did not know how long she stayed there. A woman's footsteps running along the path roused her. She got up and saw Dunyasha, her maid, who had evidently been sent to look for her, stop short, as though in alarm, at the sight of her mistress.

'Please, princess. ... The prince ...' said Dunyasha in a breaking voice.

'Coming, here I am, coming!' the princess cried quickly, not giving Dunyasha time to finish what she was saying; and, trying to avoid seeing the girl, she ran towards the house.

'Princess, it is God's will! You must be prepared for the worst,' said the Marshal, meeting her at the door into the house.

'Leave me alone! It's not true!' she cried angrily.

The doctor tried to stop her. She pushed him aside and ran to her father's door. 'Why do they all look so frightened and try to stop me? I don't need them. And what are they doing here?' she thought. She opened the door and the bright daylight in that previously darkened room startled her. Her old nurse and some other women were in the room. They all drew back from the bed, making way for her. He was still lying on the bed as before, but the stern expression on his calm face arrested Princess Maria on the threshold.

'No, he is not dead – it cannot be!' Princess Maria said to herself. She approached, and struggling with the terror that seized her pressed her lips to his cheek. But she instantly recoiled. In a flash all the deep tenderness she had been feeling for him vanished before the horror and dread of what lay there on the bed before her. 'No, he is no more! He is no more, but here, in the place where he was, is something unfamiliar and sinister, some fearful, terrifying and loathsome mystery!' And covering her face with her hands Princess Maria sank into the arms of the doctor, who held her up.

*

Watched by Tikhon and the doctor, the women washed what had been the prince, bound a kerchief round the head that the jaw should not stiffen with the mouth open, and with another kerchief tied his legs together. Then they dressed him in his uniform, with his decorations, and laid the shrivelled little body on a table. Heaven only knows under whose direction and when all this was accomplished, but it all got done as if of its own accord. By nightfall candles were burning round the coffin, a pall was spread over it, the floor was strewn with sprays of juniper, a printed prayer scroll was tucked in under the wrinkled head, and a deacon sat in the corner of the room reading aloud the Psalter.

A concourse of members of the household and people from outside crowded about the coffin in the drawing-room – for all the world like horses who jostle, shying and snorting, round a dead horse. The Marshal was there, and the village elder, and peasant women, all staring with round, awe-stricken eyes, crossing themselves and bowing before they kissed the cold, stiff hand of the old prince.

9

UNTIL Prince Andrei went to live at Bogucharovo the estate had always been owned by absentee landlords, and so the Bogucharovo peasants were of quite a different character from those of Bald Hills, from whom they differed in speech, dress and disposition. They were steppe-peasants. The old prince would commend their industry and endurance when they came to Bald Hills to help with the harvest or to dig ponds and ditches; but he had never liked them because of their dourness.

Prince Andrei's most recent stay at Bogucharovo, when he introduced hospitals and schools and reduced the quit-rent the peasants had to pay, instead of softening them, had, on the contrary, only intensified the traits which made up what the old prince called their churlishness. Strange, obscure rumours were always finding credence among them: now they were all going to be enrolled as Cossacks, or forcibly converted to some new religion; or there was talk about some supposed proclamation of the Tsar's; or they got the notion that their freedom had been granted them when they took the oath of allegiance to the Tsar Paul in 1797 – only the gentry had denied them afterwards; then they expected Piotr Fiodorovich's return to the throne in seven years' time, when there would be freedom for all and everything would be so simple and easy that there would be no laws at all. Rumours of the war and of Bonaparte and his invasion were connected in their minds with the same sort of obscure notions of Antichrist, the end of the world and perfect freedom.

In the vicinity of Bogucharovo were a number of large villages belonging to the Crown or to proprietors whose serfs paid quit-rent and could work where they pleased. There were very few resident landowners in the neighbourhood, and consequently very few domestic or literate serfs and the lives of the peasantry of those parts were more noticeably and powerfully affected than elsewhere by the mysterious undercurrents in the life-stream of the Russian people, the causes and significance of which are so baffling to contemporaries. One such phenomenon had occurred some twenty years before, when the peasants took it into their heads to emigrate to some unknown 'hot rivers'. Hundreds of families, among them the Bogucharovo folk, suddenly began selling their cattle and moving towards the south-east. Like birds flying somewhere beyond the sea, so these men with their wives and children poured south-eastwards, to parts where none of them had ever been before. They set off in caravans, bought their freedom one by one, ran and drove and walked towards the 'hot rivers'. Many were caught and punished, sent to Siberia; many perished of cold and starvation on the road; many returned of their own accord; and the movement died down of itself, just as it had sprung up, without apparent reason. But such undercurrents still flowed among the people, and were gathering impetus for some new outbreak, likely to prove just as perplexing, as unexpected and, at the same time, as simple, natural and violent. Now, in 1812, to anyone living in close contact with the peasants it was patent that these hidden currents were working with extraordinary energy, and that an outbreak of some kind was at hand.

Alpatych, who had arrived at Bogucharovo shortly before the old prince's demise, noticed that there was considerable excitement among the peasantry; and that, unlike the Bald Hills district, where over a radius of forty miles all the peasants were moving away, abandoning their villages to be devastated by the Cossacks, here in the steppe region round Bogucharovo the peasants, so the report ran, were in communication with the French, received certain leaflets from them which passed from hand to hand, and had no thought of leaving their homes. He learned through domestic serfs loyal to him that a muzhik named Karp, who possessed great influence in the village commune and had recently been away driving a government transport, had returned with the news that the Cossacks were destroying deserted villages, but the French did not touch them. Alpatych also knew that on the previous day another peasant had even brought from the village of Vislouhovo, which was occupied by the French, a proclamation from the French general that no harm would be done to the inhabitants, and that everything taken from them would be paid for, provided they remained where they were. As proof of this the peasant brought from Vislouhovo a hundred roubles in notes (he did not know that they were forgeries) paid him in advance for hay.

And last, and most important of all, Alpatych knew that on the morning of the very day he gave the village elder orders to collect carts to convey the princess's luggage from Boucharovo there had been a meeting in the village at which it had been decided not to move but to wait. Yet there was no time to lose. On the 15th, the day of the old prince's death, the Marshal had insisted that Princess Maria should leave at once, as it was becoming dangerous. He had told her that after the 16th he could not answer for what might happen. On the evening of the day the old prince died the Marshal departed, promising to return on the morrow for the funeral. But this he was unable to do, for he received tidings that the French had unexpectedly advanced, and he had barely time to get his own family and valuables away.

For thirty years or so Bogucharovo had been managed by the village elder, Dron, whom the old prince used to call by the affectionate diminutive 'Dronushka'.

Dron was one of those peasants – physically and mentally vigorous – who grow patriarchal beards as soon as they reach man's estate, and go on unchanged till they are sixty or seventy years old, without a grey hair or the loss of a tooth, as straight and strong at sixty as at thirty.

Soon after the exodus to the 'hot rivers', in which he had taken part with the rest, Dron was made village elder and overseer of Bogucharovo, and had now filled those positions irreproachably for three and twenty years. The peasants were more afraid of him than they were of their master. Both the old prince and the young prince and the steward respected and jestingly called him 'the minister'. During all this time Dron had never once been drunk or ill, or shown the slightest sign of fatigue after nights without sleep or the most exhausting labour, and though he could not read or write he had never forgotten a single item of money, or the number of quarters of flour in any of the endless cartloads he sold for the prince, or missed a single shock of wheat on an acre of the Bogucharovo fields.

It was this peasant Dron whom Alpatych summoned on the day of the prince's funeral, after his arrival from the plundered estate of Bald Hills. He told him to have·a dozen horses got ready for the princess's carriages, and eighteen carts for the luggage which she was to take with her from Bogucharovo. Though the peasants paid rent instead of working as serfs, Alpatych never dreamed there would be any difficulty in having this order carried out, since the village contained two hundred and thirty taxable households and the peasants were well-to-do. But on hearing the order Dron lowered his eyes and stood silent. Alpatych named certain peasants he knew, and told him to requisition carts from them.

Dron replied that the horses of these peasants were away on hire. Alpatych mentioned the names of others, but they too, according to Dron, had no horses available: some of their horses were with the government transport trains, others were out of condition, still others had died for lack of forage. In Dron's opinion there was no hope of collecting horses enough for the carriages, much less for the carting of baggage.

Alpatych looked sharply at Dron and frowned. In the same way as Dron was a pattern of what a village elder should be, so Alpatych had not managed the prince's estates for nothing all those twenty years, and was a model overseer, possessing in the highest degree the faculty of divining the needs and instincts of those with whom he had to deal, and this made him an excellent steward. One glance at Dron was enough to tell him that his answers were not the expression of his personal views but the general mood of the Bogucharovo commune, by which the elder had already been carried away. But at the same time he knew that Dron, who had saved money and was detested by the village, must be hesitating between the two camps – the masters' and the peasants'. This wavering he detected in his eyes, and so Alpatych frowned and moved closer to Dron.

'Now, Dron, my friend, you listen to me!' he said. 'Don't tell me any more of this nonsense. His Excellency Prince Andrei himself gave me orders to move all the folk away and not leave them behind with the enemy, and those are the Tsar's orders too. Anyone who stays is a traitor to the Tsar. Do you hear ?'

857

'I hear,' answered Dron without lifting his eyes.

Alpatych was not satisfied with this reply.

'Aye, Dron, there'll be trouble!' he said, shaking his head.

'It's for you to command,' said Dron dejectedly.

'Aye, Dron, have done!' Alpatych repeated, withdrawing his hand from his bosom and solemnly pointing to the floor at Dron's feet. 'I can see right through you, and not only that – I can see three yards into the ground under you,' he continued, gazing at the floor by Dron's feet.

Dron was disconcerted. He glanced furtively at Alpatych and lowered his eyes again.

'You drop this nonsense, and tell the people to pack up their chattels and go to Moscow, and to have the teams ready tomorrow morning for the princess's things. And don't you go attending the meeting, do your hear?'

Dron suddenly fell on his knees.

'Yakov Alpatych, discharge me! Take the keys from me and discharge me, for Christ's sake!'

'Stop that!' cried Alpatych sternly. 'I can see into the earth three yards under your feet,' he repeated, knowing that his skill in bee-keeping, his knowledge of the right time to sow the oats, and the fact that he had been able to retain the old prince's favour for a score of years had long ago gained him the reputation of being a sorcerer, and that the power of seeing three yards under a man is considered an attribute of wizards.

Dron got up and was about to say something but Alpatych interrupted him.

'What is it you've all got into your heads, eh? … What are you thinking of? Eh?'

'What am I to do with the people?' said Dron. 'They're all in a ferment. And I've already told them. …'

'"Told them," I dare say!' exclaimed Alpatych. 'Are they drinking?' he asked abruptly.

'In a ferment they are, Yakov Alpatych. They have got hold of another barrel.'

'Then you listen to me. I'll go to the captain of police, and you let them know, and tell them they must stop all this and see about getting the teams ready.'

'Very good,' answered Dron.

Alpatych did not insist further. He had managed peasants too long not to be aware that the best way to make them obey was not to show the slightest suspicion that they might disobey. Having wrung a submissive 'Very good' from Dron, Alpatych contented himself with that, though he not only suspected but was practically certain in his own mind that without the intervention of the military authorities the carts would not be forthcoming.

And so it turned out: the evening came but no carts. In the village, outside the tavern, another meeting had been held which voted to drive the horses out into the forest and not provide carts. Without saying a word of all this to the princess, Alpatych had his own belongings unloaded from the wagons which had come from Bald Hills and those horses put to the princess's carriages, while he went off to the governor.

10

AFTER her father's funeral Princess Maria shut herself up in her room and would admit no one. A maid came to the door to say that Alpatych was there asking for instructions about their departure. (This was before his talk with Dron.) Princess Maria sat up on the sofa where she had been lying, and replied through the closed door that she would never go away anywhere, and begged to be left in peace.

The windows of the room in which she was lying looked to the west. She lay on the sofa with her face to the wall, picking with her fingers at the buttons on the leather cushion and seeing nothing but that cushion, while her confused thoughts were concentrated on one subject – the irrevocability of death and her own spiritual baseness, of which she had had no idea till it showed itself during her father's illness. She wanted to pray but did not dare to – in her present state of mind she dared not address herself to God. For a long time she lay thus.

The sun had reached the other side of the house, and its slanting rays shone in through the open window, lighting up the room and part of the morocco cushion at which Princess Maria was looking. The current of her thoughts was suddenly arrested. Unconsciously she sat up, smoothed her hair, got to her feet and walked over to the window, instinctively drawing into her lungs the freshness of the clear but windy evening.

'Yes, now you can enjoy your fill of the evening! He is gone, and there is no one to hinder you,' she said to herself, and sinking into a chair she let her head fall on the window-sill.

Someone spoke her name in a gentle tender voice from the garden, and kissed her on the head. She looked up. It was Mademoiselle Bourienne in a black dress and weepers. She softly approached Princess Maria, kissed her with a sigh and promptly burst into tears. Princess Maria looked at her. All the times they had been at loggerheads and her jealousy of the Frenchwoman came back to her; but she remembered too how *he* had changed of late towards Mademoiselle Bourienne, and could not bear the sight of her, thereby showing how unjust had been the strictures Princess Maria had heaped on her in her heart. 'Besides, is it for me, for me who wished he would die, to pass judgement on anyone?' she thought.

A vivid picture presented itself to Princess Maria of Mademoiselle Bourienne's position, kept at a distance of late and at the same time dependent on her and living in her house. And she began to feel sorry for her. She gave her a mild inquiring look and held out her hand. Mademoiselle Bourienne at once started crying again and kissing her hand, speaking of the affliction that had descended on the princess and claiming to participate in it. She declared that her only consolation in her own grief was the fact that the princess permitted her to share it with her. All their old misunderstandings, she said, must sink into nothing before this great sorrow, and she felt that her conscience was clear in regard to everyone, and that *he* from above saw her affection and gratitude. The princess heard her without taking in what she was saying, but occasionally glancing at her and listening to the sound of her voice.

'Your position is doubly terrible, dear princess,' said Mademoiselle Bourienne after a pause. 'I understand that you could not – that you cannot – think of yourself, but with my love for you I am bound to do so. ... Has Alpatych been to you? Has he spoken to you about going away?' she asked.

Princess Maria made no reply. She did not understand who was to go, and where to. 'Is it possible to plan or think of anything now? What does it matter?' she thought, and did not reply.

'You know, *chère Marie*,' said Mademoiselle Bourienne, 'that we are not safe; we are surrounded by the French. It would be dangerous to move now. If we go, we are almost certain to be taken prisoner, and God knows ...'

860

Princess Maria looked blankly at her companion.

'Oh, if anyone knew how nothing makes any difference to me now, nothing,' she said. 'Of course I would not on any account move away from *him*. ... Alpatych did say something about going ... Speak to him. I will have nothing to say to it, and I don't want ...'

'I have been talking to him. He hopes to get us away tomorrow; but in my opinion it would be better now to remain here,' said Mademoiselle Bourienne. 'Because, you will agree, *chère Marie*, to fall into the hands of the soldiers or of rioting peasants on the road would be dreadful.'

Mademoiselle Bourienne drew forth from her reticule a proclamation (printed on strange un-Russian paper) issued by the French General Rameau, telling people not to leave their homes and that the French authorities would afford them proper protection. She handed the document to the princess.

'I think the best thing would be to appeal to this general,' she continued, 'and I am sure all due respect would be shown you.'

Princess Maria read the paper, and her face worked spasmodically with dry sobs.

'How did you get this?' she asked.

'They probably realized I was French by my name,' replied Mademoiselle Bourienne, flushing.

Holding the proclamation in her hand, Princess Maria got up from the window, and with a pale face walked out of the room into Prince Andrei's old study.

'Dunyasha – send Alpatych to me, or Dron. Anyone!' she said. 'And tell Mademoiselle Bourienne that I want to be alone,' she added, hearing Mademoiselle Bourienne's voice. 'We must get off at once! At once!' she said, appalled at the idea of being left in the hands of the French.

'What if Prince Andrei were to know that she was in the power of the French! That she, the daughter of Prince Nikolai Bolkonsky, had asked General Rameau for protection and accepted his good offices!' The mere suggestion of such a thing filled her with horror, made her shudder, turn crimson and experience such a rush of anger and pride as she had never felt before. All the bitterness, and still more the humiliation, of her position rose keenly to her imagination. 'They, the French, would take up their quarters in this house; *Monsieur le général* Rameau would occupy Prince Andrei's study and amuse himself by looking through and reading his letters and papers. Mademoiselle Bourienne would do the honours of Bogucharovo. I should be given some small room as a favour, the soldiers would violate my father's newly-dug grave to steal his crosses and decorations, they would tell me of their victories over the Russians, would pretend to sympathize with my grief ...' thought Princess Maria, not thinking her own thoughts but feeling bound to think as her father and brother would have done. For herself she did not care where she stayed or what happened to her, but at the same time she felt that she was the representative of her dead father and of Prince Andrei. Unconsciously she thought their thoughts and felt their feelings. Whatever they would have said, whatever they would have done, it was now incumbent on her to do. She went into Prince Andrei's study, and trying to identify herself with his ideas she reviewed her position.

The exigencies of life, which her father's death had seemed to sweep away, all at once rushed back upon her with a new and hitherto unknown force, and took possession of her.

Agitated and flushed, she walked about the room, summoning now Mihail Ivanich, now Tikhon or Dron. Dunyasha, the old nurse and the maids could none of them say how far Mademoiselle Bourienne's statement was correct. Alpatych was not at home: he had gone to the police authorities. Neither could the architect, Mihail Ivanich, who came in with sleepy eyes on being sent for, tell Princess Maria anything. With precisely the same smile of acquiescence with which he had been accustomed during the course of fifteen years to meet the old prince's remarks without committing himself, he now replied to Princess Maria, so that there was no getting anything definite out of him. The old valet, Tikhon, whose wan and sunken face bore the stamp of inconsolable grief, answered, 'Yes, princess' to all Princess Maria's questions, and could scarcely refrain from sobbing as he looked at her.

At length the village elder, Dron, came into the room and with a deep bow to the princess stood near the door.

Princess Maria walked up and down the room and stopped facing him.

'Dear Dron,' she said, seeing in him a staunch friend – the same kind Dron who every year had brought home a special kind of gingerbread from the fair at Vyazma which he presented to her with a smile. 'Dear Dron, since our sad loss ...' she began, and paused, unable to continue.

'We are all in God's hands,' he said, with a sigh.

They were silent for a moment.

'Dron, Alpatych has gone off somewhere. I have no one to turn to. Is it true, as they tell me, that I can't even get away?'

'Why shouldn't you get away, your Excellency? Of course you can,' said Dron.

'I was told it would be dangerous because of the enemy. Dear friend, I am helpless, I do not understand, I am entirely alone. I want to leave without fail tonight or early tomorrow morning.'

Dron did not speak. He looked up from under his brows at Princess Maria.

'There are no horses,' he said. 'I told Yakov Alpatych so.'

'How is that?' asked the princess.

'It's all the visitation of the Lord,' said Dron. 'What horses we had have been taken for the army, or else they died – that's the way it is this year. It's not a case of feeding horses – we may perish of hunger ourselves! As it is, some go three days without a bite. We've nothing; we're ruined.'

Princess Maria listened attentively to what he told her.

'The peasants are ruined? They have no bread?' she asked.

'They're dying of hunger,' said Dron. 'It's no use talking of horses and carts.'

'But why didn't you tell me, Dron? Isn't it possible to help them? I'll do all I can. ...'

It seemed strange to Princess Maria that at a time when her heart was overflowing with sorrow there could be rich people and poor people, and the rich do nothing to succour the poor. She had heard vaguely that there was such a thing as 'seignorial corn' and that it was sometimes given to the peasants. She knew, too, that neither her brother nor her father would refuse the peasants in their need; she was only afraid of making some mistake in the wording of the instructions she meant to give for this distribution. She was glad that she had an excuse for doing something in which she could, without scruple, forget her own grief. She proceeded to inquire from Dron about the peasants' needs, asking him whether there was a reserve store of corn at Bogucharovo.

'I suppose we have grain belonging to my brother?' she asked.

'The master's grain has not been touched,' replied Dron proudly. 'The prince gave no orders about selling it.'

'Give it to the peasants, let them have all they need. I authorize you to do so in my brother's name,' said Princess Maria.

Dron was silent, except for a deep sigh.

'You distribute that corn among them, if it will be enough. Distribute it all. This is an order in my brother's name; and tell them that what is ours is theirs. We grudge them nothing. Tell them so.'

Dron gazed intently at the princess while she was speaking.

'Discharge me, ma'am, for God's sake! Bid me give up the keys,' said he. 'Twenty-three years I've served and done no wrong. Discharge me, for God's sake!'

Princess Maria had no notion what he wanted of her, or why he was asking to be discharged. She replied that she had never doubted his devotion and that she was ready to do anything for him and for the peasants.

II

An hour later Dunyasha came in to tell the princess that Dron had returned, and all the peasants were assembled at the granary by the princess's orders and wished to speak with their mistress.

'But I did not send for them,' said Princess Maria. 'I only told Dron to let them have the grain.'

'For the love of God, princess dear, have them sent away, and don't you go out to them. It's all a plot,' said Dunyasha, 'and as soon as Yakov Alpatych is back we will start ... and please don't ...'

'What do you mean – a plot?' asked Princess Maria in amazement.

'I am sure of it – please listen to me, for God's sake! Ask old nurse too. They say they won't agree to move away at your orders.'

'You are making some mistake. Why, I never ordered them to leave,' said Princess Maria. 'Fetch Dron.'

Dron came and confirmed what Dunyasha had said: the peasants were there by the princess's instructions.

'But I never sent for them,' declared the princess. 'You must have given my message wrong. I only said that you were to give them the grain.'

Dron only sighed in reply.

'If you order it, they will go away,' he said.

'No, no. I'll go out to them,' said Princess Maria.

In spite of Dunyasha's and the old nurse's attempts to dissuade her, Princess Maria went out on to the steps. Dron, Dunyasha, the old nurse and Mihail Ivanich followed.

'They probably think I am offering them the grain to keep them here, while I go away myself, leaving them at the mercy of the French,' reflected Princess Maria. 'I will promise them monthly provisions and housing on the Moscow estate. I am sure André would do more still for them in my place,' she thought, as she went out in the twilight towards the crowd waiting on the pasture by the barn.

There was a stir in the gathering as the men moved closer together and rapidly took off their hats. Princess Maria, with downcast eyes and her feet tripping over her skirt, went up to them. So many different eyes, old and young, were fixed on her, and there were so many different faces that she could not distinguish any one of them, and, feeling that she must speak to them all at once, did not know how to set about it. But again the sense that she was the representative of her father and her brother gave her courage, and she boldly began her speech.

'I am very glad you have come,' she said, not raising her eyes and conscious of the hurried, violent beating of her heart. 'My good Dron tells me that the war has ruined you. That is our common misfortune and I shall grudge nothing to help you. I am myself going away because it is not safe here now ... and the enemy is near ... because ... I am giving you everything, my friends, and I beg you to take everything, all our grain, that you may not suffer want. But if you have been told that I am giving you the corn to keep you here – that is not true. On the contrary, I ask you to move with all your belongings to our Moscow estate, and there I promise you I will see to it that you shall not be in need. You shall be given housing and food.'

The princess paused. In the crowd sighs were heard, and that was all.

'I am not doing this on my own account,' she continued. 'I do it in the name of my dead father, who was a good master to you, and for my brother and his son.'

Again she stopped. No one broke the silence.

'This is our common misfortune and we will share it together. All that is mine is yours,' she concluded, scanning the faces before her.

All eyes were gazing at her with one and the same expression, the meaning of which she could not fathom. Whether it was curiosity, devotion, gratitude, or apprehension and distrust, the expression on all the faces was identical.

'We're very thankful for your bounty, but it won't do for us to take the master's grain,' said a voice from the back of the crowd.

'But why not?' asked the princess.

No one answered, and Princess Maria, looking round at the crowd, noticed that every eye dropped at once on meeting hers.

'But why won't you take it?' she asked again.

There was no reply.

The silence began to oppress the princess and she tried to catch somebody's eye.

'Why don't you speak?' she said, addressing a very old man who stood just in front of her, leaning on his stick. 'If you think something more is wanted, tell me! I will do anything,' she said, catching his eye.

But as if this angered him he hung his head and muttered:

'Why should we? We don't want the grain.'

'What – us abandon everything? We don't agree to it!... Don't agree. ... We are sorry for you, but we're not willing. Go away yourself, on your own ...' rang out from the mob on different sides.

And again all the faces in the crowd wore the same expression, and now it was certainly not an expression of curiosity or gratitude but of angry determination.

'But you can't have understood me,' said Princess Maria with a sad smile. 'Why don't you want to go? I promise to give you new homes and provide for you, while here the enemy would rob and plunder you. ...'

But her voice was drowned by the voices of the crowd.

'We're not willing! Let them plunder us! We won't take your grain. We won't agree to it!'

Again Princess Maria tried to catch someone's eye, but not a single one was turned to her: evidently they were all trying to avoid her look. She felt strange and ill at ease.

'Oh yes, an artful tale!' – 'Follow her into slavery!' – 'Pull down your houses and go into bondage! I dare say!' – '"I'll give you grain," says she!' – voices in the crowd were exclaiming.

With drooping head Princess Maria left the crowd and went back to the house. Reiterating her orders to Dron to have the horses ready against their departure the next morning, she went away to her room and remained alone with her thoughts.

12

For a long while that night Princess Maria sat by the open window of her room, hearing the sound of the peasants' voices floating across from the village, but she was not thinking of them. She felt that she could not understand them, however long she thought. Her mind was concentrated on one thing: her affliction, which now, after the interruption caused by anxieties to do with the present, seemed already to belong to the past. Now she could remember, could weep and pray.

With the setting of the sun the breeze had dropped. The night was still and cool. Towards midnight the voices began to die down, a cock crowed, the full moon began to rise from behind the lime-trees, a fresh, white, dewy mist rose from the ground and quiet reigned over the village and the house.

One after another, pictures of the recent past – of her father's illness and last moments – came into her mind. With melancholy pleasure she dwelt on these images, repelling with horror only the last one, the vision of his death, which she felt she had not the courage to contemplate even in imagination at this still and mystic hour of the night. And these pictures presented themselves to her so clearly and in such detail that they seemed now in the actual present, now from the past, and now in the future.

She had a vivid picture of the moment when he had his first stroke and was being dragged in, held under the armpits, from the garden at Bald Hills, muttering something with his helpless tongue, twitching his grey eyebrows and looking anxiously and timidly at her.

'Even then he wanted to tell me what he told me the day he died,' she thought. 'What he said to me then was all the time in his mind.'

And then she recalled in every detail the night at Bald Hills before the stroke, when with a foreboding of disaster she had remained at home with him against his will. She had not slept and in the small hours had stolen downstairs on tiptoe and gone to the door of the conservatory, where his bed had been put that night, and listened at the door. He was saying something to Tikhon in a weary, exhausted voice. Evidently he wanted to talk. 'And why didn't he call me? Why didn't he let me be there instead of Tikhon?' Princess Maria had asked herself then and wondered again now. 'Now he will never tell anyone all that was in his heart. Now the moment will never return for him or for me when he might have said all he longed to say, and I and not Tikhon might have heard and understood him. Why didn't I go in then?' she thought. 'Perhaps he would have said to me then what he said the day he died. Twice he asked about me while he was talking to Tikhon. He wanted to see me, and I was standing there outside the door. It was sad and not easy for him to talk to Tikhon, who did not understand him. I remember how he began speaking to him about Lise as if she were alive – he had forgotten she was dead – and Tikhon reminded him that she was no more, and he shouted "Fool!" He was heavy-hearted. As I stood outside I heard him groan and lie down on the bed and cry: "Oh God!" Why didn't I go in then? What could he have done to me? What could I have lost by it? Perhaps he would have been comforted and called me then – what he did.' And Princess Maria repeated aloud the caressing word he had used to her on the day of his death. 'Dear-est!' she repeated, and burst into tears which relieved her aching soul. She could see his face before her now. And not the face she had known ever since she could remember and had always seen at a distance, but the timid frail face she had seen that last day when she bent close to catch what he was saying, close enough for the first time to see all the lines and wrinkles on it.

'Dear-est!' she repeated again.

'What was he thinking when he uttered that word? What is he thinking now?' she wondered suddenly. And in answer she saw him with the expression she had seen on the face bound up with a white kerchief as he lay in his coffin. And the horror which had seized her then, when she had touched him and known that *that* was not *he* but something ghastly and mysterious, seized her again. She tried to think of something else, tried to pray, but could do neither. With staring eyes she gazed at the moonlight and the shadows, every instant expecting to see his dead face, and she felt that the silence that reigned without and within the house held her fast.

'Dunyasha!' she whispered. 'Dunyasha!' she screamed wildly, and tearing herself from the spell she rushed to the servants' room, running into the old nurse and the maids who came hurrying towards her.

13

On the 17th of August Rostov and Ilyin, accompanied only by Lavrushka, just back from his brief captivity, and an hussar on orderly duty, set forth from their quarters at Yankovo, ten miles or so from Bogucharovo, to try out a new horse Ilyin had bought and discover whether there was any hay to be had in the villages.

For the last three days Bogucharovo had been half-way between the two hostile armies, so that it was as easy for the Russian rearguard to get to it as for the French vanguard. Consequently Rostov, like the careful squadron-commander he was, wanted to be the first to lay hands on such provisions as might be left there.

Rostov and Ilyin were in the highest of spirits. On the way to Bogucharovo, an estate which belonged to some prince and had a manor-house and farm where they hoped to find a large domestic staff with some pretty servant-girls, they questioned Lavrushka about Napoleon and laughed at his stories, and raced one another to try Ilyin's new horse.

Rostov had no idea that the village they were going to was the property of that very Bolkonsky who had been betrothed to his sister.

Rostov and Ilyin gave rein to their horses for a last race along the incline before reaching Bogucharovo, and Rostov, outstripping Ilyin, was the first to gallop into the village street.

'You win,' cried Ilyin, flushed.

'Yes, I'm always first, not only on grass-land but here too,' answered Rostov, patting his foaming Don horse.

'And I'd have won on my Frenchy, your Excellency,' said Lavrushka from behind, alluding to the wretched cart-horse he was riding, 'only I didn't want to put you to shame.'

They rode at a foot-pace to the barn, where a large crowd of peasants was standing.

Some of the men bared their heads, others stared at the new-comers without doffing their caps. Two lank old peasants with wrinkled faces and scanty beards emerged from the tavern, reeling and singing a tuneless song, and approached the officers with smiles.

'Fine fellows!' said Rostov, laughing. 'Is there any hay here?'

'And like as two peas,' said Ilyin.

'A me-r-r-y me-r-r-y c-o-o-m-pan ...!' sang the two with blissful smiles.

A peasant came out of the crowd and went up to Rostov.

'Which side will you be from?' he asked.

'The French,' replied Ilyin jestingly, 'and this is Napoleon himself' – and he pointed to Lavrushka.

'So you're Russians, are you?' the peasant inquired again.

'And is there a large force of you here?' asked another, a short man, advancing to them.

'Very large,' answered Rostov. 'But what brings you all together here?' he added. 'Is it a holiday?'

'The old men are met about village business,' answered the peasant, moving away.

At that moment two women and a man in a white hat made their appearance, on the road leading from the big house, coming towards the officers.

'The one in pink is mine, so keep off!' said Ilyin, catching sight of Dunyasha running resolutely towards him.

'She'll be the girl for us!' said Lavrushka, winking.

'What is it you want, my pretty?' asked Ilyin with a smile.

'The princess sent me to find out your regiment and your names.'

'This is Count Rostov, squadron-commander, and I am your humble servant.'

'Co-o-om-pa-ny!' roared the tipsy peasant with a beatific smile as he looked at Ilyin talking to the girl. Alpatych followed Dunyasha, taking off his hat to Rostov as he approached.

'I make bold to trouble your Honour,' said he respectfully but with a shade of contempt for the youthfulness of the officer, and with a hand thrust in his bosom. 'My mistress, the daughter of General-in-chief Prince Nikolai Bolkonsky, who died on the 15th of this month, finding herself in difficulties on account of the outlandishness of these people here' – he pointed to the peasants – 'asks you to come up to the house. ... If your Honour will be so good as to ride a few yards further on,' said Alpatych with a melancholy smile, 'as it is not seemly in the presence of ...' He indicated the two peasants who were hovering about him like gadflies about a horse.

'Hey! ... Alpatych. ... Yakov Alpatych. ... Ser'ous shing! 'Schuse us, for mershy's shake, eh?' said the peasants, smiling gleefully at him.

Rostov looked at the tipsy old men and smiled.

'Or perhaps they amuse your Honour?' remarked Alpatych with a sedate look, as he pointed at the old men with his free hand.

'No, there's nothing very entertaining here,' said Rostov, and he rode on a little way. 'What is the matter?' he inquired.

'I make bold to inform your Honour that these coarse peasants here are unwilling to let the mistress leave the estate, and threaten to unharness her horses, so that though everything has been ready packed since morning her Excellency cannot get away.'

'Impossible!' cried Rostov.

'I have the honour to be reporting to you the actual truth,' said Alpatych.

Rostov dismounted, gave his horse to the orderly and walked with Alpatych to the house, questioning him further about the state of affairs. It appeared that the princess's offer of corn to the peasants the previous day, and her talk with Dron and with the peasants at the meeting, had made matters so much worse that Dron had finally given up the keys of office, joined the peasants, and refused to come when Alpatych sent for him; and that in the morning when the princess ordered the horses to be put in for her journey the peasants had flocked in a great crowd to the barn and despatched a messenger to say they would not let the princess leave the village: that there was an edict that people were not to move from their homes and that they would unharness the horses. Alpatych had gone out to reason with them but was told (it was Karp who did most of the talking, Dron kept in the background of the crowd) that the princess could not be allowed to go since it was contrary to orders, but that if she stayed they would serve and obey her in everything as they had always done.

At the moment when Rostov and Ilyin were galloping along the road Princess Maria, in spite of the arguments of Alpatych, her old nurse and the maids, had given orders to have the horses put in, and had made up her mind to start, but seeing the horsemen cantoring up the coachmen took them for the French and ran away, and the women of the household set up a wail.

'Kind sir! Our blessed protector! God has sent you!' cried deeply affected voices as Rostov crossed the vestibule.

Princess Maria was sitting, helpless and distraught, in the large sitting-room when Rostov was shown in. She had no idea who he was and why he was there, or what was going to become of her. When she saw his Russian face, and recognized by his manner and the first words he uttered that he was a man of her own walk in life, she looked up at him with her deep, starry eyes and began speaking in a voice that faltered and trembled with emotion. Rostov found something very romantic in this meeting. 'A defenceless girl, overcome with grief, alone, abandoned to the mercy of coarse, rebellious peasants! And what strange destiny has brought me here!' thought

Rostov as he watched her and listened to her story. 'And what sweetness and nobility there is in her features and expression!'

When she began to tell him that all this had happened the day after her father's funeral her voice shook. She turned away, and then, as though afraid Rostov might ascribe her words to a desire to work on his pity, she glanced at him with an apprehensive look of inquiry. There were tears in Rostov's eyes. Princess Maria noticed it, and looked gratefully at him with the luminous eyes which made one forget the plainness of her face.

'I cannot express how glad I am, princess, that I happened to come riding this way and now have the occasion to put myself entirely at your service,' said Rostov, rising. 'You can start immediately, and I pledge you my word of honour that no one shall dare to cause you the slightest unpleasantness if only you will allow me to act as your escort.' And bowing respectfully, as if to a lady of royal blood, he moved towards the door.

Rostov's deferential tone implied that though he would consider it a happiness to be acquainted with her he did not wish to take advantage of her misfortune to intrude.

Princess Maria understood and appreciated his delicacy.

'I am very, very grateful to you,' she said in French, 'but I hope it was all only a misunderstanding and that no one is to blame for it.' She suddenly began to cry.

'Excuse me!' she said.

Rostov, knitting his brows, made another low bow and left the room.

14

'WELL, is she pretty? Ah, my boy – my pink girl's delicious; her name's Dunyasha. ...'

But a glance at Rostov's face silenced Ilyin. He saw that his hero and captain had come back in quite a different frame of mind.

Rostov cast Ilyin a wrathful look and, without replying, strode off towards the village.

'I'll show them! I'll pay them, the ruffians!' he muttered to himself.

Alpatych followed Rostov at a quick trot just short of a run, catching up with him with difficulty.

'What decision has your Honour come to?' said he, overtaking him.

Rostov halted and, doubling his fists, suddenly made a threatening movement towards Alpatych.

'Decision? What decision? You old dotard! ...' he shouted. 'What have you been thinking about? Eh? The peasants are unruly and you stand gaping at them! You're a traitor yourself! I know you. I'll flay the skin off the lot of you!' ... And as if afraid of wasting his store of anger he left Alpatych and hastened on. Alpatych, swallowing his wounded pride, sailed after Rostov, keeping pace as best he could and continuing to impart his views. He said the peasants had got themselves into such a refractory state that at the present moment it would be imprudent to 'contrary' them without the support of an armed force, so that would it not be better first to send for the military?

'I'll give them armed force. ... I'll "contrary" them!' growled Rostov mechanically, choking with irrational animal fury and the need to vent it. With no definite plan of action, without considering, he strode impetuously towards the crowd. And the nearer he drew to it the more Alpatych felt that this rashness might lead to good results. The peasants in the crowd were similarly impressed when they saw Rostov's swift, unswerving steps and resolute, scowling face.

After the hussars had ridden into the village and Rostov had gone to see the princess a certain hesitation and difference of opinion had arisen among the gathering. Some of the peasants said that the horse-men were Russians and might take it amiss that the mistress was being detained. Dron was of this way of thinking, but as soon as he expressed his view Karp and others attacked their ex-elder.

'How many years have you been fattening on the village?' Karp shouted at him. 'It's all one to you! You'll dig up the pot of money you've buried and be off! ... What do you care whether they burn up our homes or not?'

'We've been told to keep order, and no one to leave their places or take away a single grain – and there she goes with all she's got!' cried another.

''Twas your son's turn to be conscripted, but no fear! Not your noodle of a son!' a little old man suddenly burst out, pouncing on Dron. 'So they took my Vanka and shaved him for a soldier! But we all have to die.'

'To be sure, we all have to die!'

'I'm not against the commune,' said Dron.

873

'Not you! You've filled your belly. ...'

The two lanky peasants had their say. As soon as Rostov, followed by Ilyin, Lavrushka and Alpatych, came up to the crowd Karp, thrusting his fingers into his belt and smiling slightly, walked to the front. Dron, on the contrary, retired to the rear, and the crowd huddled closer together.

'Hey! Who is your elder here?' shouted Rostov, striding up to the mob.

'The elder? What do you want with him?' ... asked Karp.

But before the words were well out of his mouth his cap flew off and a fierce blow jerked his head to one side.

'Caps off, traitors!' thundered Rostov. 'Where's the elder?' he cried furiously.

'The elder. ... He's asking for the elder! ... Mr Dron, he wants you!' said one and another in meek flustered tones, while one by one caps were removed.

'We should never think of mutiny, we're observing orders,' insisted Karp, and at that moment several voices began speaking together.

'It's as the elders settle – there's too many of you be giving orders....'

'Argue, would you? ... Mutiny! ... Scoundrels! Traitors!' roared Rostov recklessly, in a voice not his own, while he gripped Karp by the collar. 'Bind him, bind him!' he roared, though there was no one to bind him but Lavrushka and Alpatych.

Lavrushka, however, ran up to Karp and seized his arms from behind.

'Shall I call our fellows from below the hill, your Honour?' he shouted.

Alpatych turned to the peasants and called upon two of them by name to come and bind Karp. The peasants obediently stepped out of the crowd and began undoing their belts.

'Where's the village elder?' demanded Rostov in a loud voice.

With a pale and frowning face Dron moved to the front.

'Are you the elder! Bind him, Lavrushka!' shouted Rostov, as if that order, too, could not possibly meet with any opposition. And in fact two more peasants began binding Dron, who took off his own belt and handed it to them as though to assist in the operation.

'And now all of you listen to me!' Rostov turned to the peasants. 'Back to your homes this instant – and don't let me hear another word from you!'

'Why, we wasn't doin' no harm!' – 'We just acted silly, that's all!'
– 'Only made fools of ourselves!' ... 'Didn't I say it wasn't right?'
murmured several voices at once, bickering with one another.

'There, what did I tell you?' said Alpatych, coming into his own
again. ''Twas wrong of you, lads!'

'We bin foolish, Yakov Alpatych,' replied the men, and the crowd
began to break up and disperse through the village.

The two men with their arms bound were led off to the main yard.
The two drunken peasants followed them.

'Aye, now look at you!' said one of them to Karp.

'Fancy speaking to your betters like that! What on earth were you
thinking of? An idiot you are, a downright idiot!' added the other.

Inside a couple of hours the teams were standing in the courtyard
of the Bogucharovo house. The peasants were briskly carrying out
the Bolkonsky belongings and packing them on to the carts, superintended by Dron, who at Princess Maria's desire had been released
from the lumber-room where he had been locked up.

'Mind, be careful – not like that!' said one of the peasants, a tall
man with a round, smiling face, taking a casket out of a housemaid's
hands. 'That cost money, that did. Why, if you chuck it in like that,
or shove it under the rope, it'll get scratched. I don't like to see things
done like that. Do everything properly, in the right way, I say.
There, look – put it under the matting and cover it with hay – that's
the way of it, see!'

'Oh these books, these books!' said another peasant, bringing out
Prince Andrei's library cupboards. 'Mind you don't stumble! Mercy,
what a weight, boys – they're a healthy lot of books!'

'Yes, that man kept his pen busy and didn't hop about,' remarked
the tall, round-faced peasant gravely, pointing with a significant wink
to the big dictionaries lying on top.

*

Unwilling to obtrude himself on the princess, Rostov did not go
back to the house but remained in the village, waiting for her to drive
out. When the carriages started he mounted and escorted her as far
as the road occupied by our troops, eight miles from Bogucharovo.
At the inn at Yankovo he respectfully took his leave, for the first time
permitting himself to kiss her hand.

'But it was nothing – nothing!' he blushingly replied to Princess

Maria's expressions of gratitude for having saved her life (as she called it). 'Any police-officer would have done as much. If we had only peasants to fight, we should not have let the enemy advance so far,' said he, trying with a sort of bashfulness to change the subject. 'I am only happy to have had the opportunity of making your acquaintance. Good-bye, princess. I wish you good fortune and consolation, and hope I may meet you again in happier circumstances. If you want to spare my blushes, please do not thank me!'

But the princess, if she did not thank him further in words, thanked him with the whole expression of her face, which shone with gratitude and warmth. She could not believe that there was nothing to thank him for. On the contrary, she had no doubt that had it not been for him she must inevitably have fallen a victim to the rebellious peasants and the French; that to save her *he* had exposed himself to obvious and terrible danger; and even more certain was the fact that he was a man of lofty and noble soul, able to sympathize with her position and her grief. His kindly, honest eyes, which had filled with tears when she herself had wept as she spoke of her loss, haunted her imagination.

When she had said good-bye to him and was left alone Princess Maria suddenly felt tears starting to her eyes, and then, not for the first time, the strange question occurred to her: 'Had she fallen in love with him?'

During the rest of the journey to Moscow, though the princess's position was not a cheerful one Dunayasha, who was in the carriage with her, more than once observed that her mistress's face wore a pensive, half-happy smile as she leaned to look out of the window.

'Well, supposing I do love him?' thought Princess Maria.

Ashamed as she was of acknowledging to herself that she had fallen in love with a man who would perhaps never care for her, she comforted herself with the reflection that no one would ever know, and that it could not be reprehensible if, without ever speaking of it to anyone, she continued to the end of her days to love the first and last love of her life.

Sometimes when she recalled the way he had looked at her, his sympathy and what he had said, happiness did not appear impossible to her. And then it was that Dunyasha would notice her smiling as she looked out of the carriage window.

'And to think that he should come to Bogucharovo and at that very moment too!' mused Princess Maria. 'And that his sister should have refused Andrei!'* And in all this Princess Maria saw the hand of Providence.

The impression made on Rostov by Princess Maria was a very agreeable one. To think of her gave him pleasure, and when his comrades, hearing of his adventure at Bogucharovo, rallied him on having gone to look for hay and picked up one of the richest heiresses in Russia he lost his temper. He lost his temper precisely because the idea of marrying the gentle Princess Maria, who had impressed him so pleasantly and who possessed such enormous means, had more than once, against his will, occurred to him. So far as he personally was concerned, Nikolai could not wish to find a better wife: by marrying her he would make the countess, his mother, happy, and would repair his father's broken fortunes; and would even – Nikolai felt it – be for the happiness of Princess Maria.

But what of Sonya? And his plighted word? And that was why it made Rostov angry to be rallied about the Princess Bolkonsky.

15

On receiving the command of the armies Kutuzov remembered Prince Andrei and sent word to him to report at Headquarters.

Prince Andrei arrived at Tsarevo-Zaimishche on the very day and at the very hour when Kutuzov was making his first inspection of the troops. He stopped in the village at the priest's house, in front of which the commander-in-chief's carriage was standing, and sat down on the bench at the gate to await his 'Serene Highness', as everyone now called Kutuzov. From the field beyond the village came the strains of regimental music interrupted by the roar of a vast multitude shouting 'Hurrah!' to the new commander-in-chief. A couple of orderlies, a courier and a major-domo stood by the gate, some ten paces from Prince Andrei, taking advantage of their master's absence to enjoy the fine weather. A swarthy little lieutenant-colonel of hussars, with a portentous growth of moustache and side-whiskers, rode up to the gate and, glancing at Prince Andrei, inquired whether

* A woman might not marry with her brother's or sister's brother-in-law. Therefore, a marriage between Natasha and Prince Andrei would have brought Princess Maria and Nikolai Rostov within the proscribed degrees of affinity. – Tr.

his Serene Highness was lodging there and whether he would soon be back.

Prince Andrei replied that he was not on his Serene Highness's staff and had likewise only just arrived. The lieutenant-colonel turned to one of the spruce-looking orderlies, who answered him with the peculiar disdain with which a commander-in-chief's orderly speaks to an ordinary officer:

'What? His Serene Highness? I expect he will be here before long. What do you want?'

The lieutenant-colonel of hussars grinned beneath his moustache at the orderly's tone, dismounted, gave his horse to a despatch-runner and approached Bolkonsky with a slight bow. Bolkonsky made room for him on the bench, and the lieutenant-colonel sat down beside him.

'You waiting for the commander-in-chief, too?' he began. 'They say he weceives evewyone, thank God! It was a vewy diffewent matter with those pork-butchers! Yermolov was not far out when he asked to be pwomoted a German. Now p'waps Wussians will get a look in. As it was, devil only knows what they were up to. Always wetweating and wetweating. Did you take part in the campaign?' he asked.

'I had the pleasure,' said Prince Andrei, 'not only of taking part in the retreat but of losing everything I valued in that retreat – not to speak of the estates and the home of my birth ... my father, who died broken-hearted. I am a Smolensk man.'

'Ah? ... Are you Pwince Bolkonsky? Vewy glad to make your acquaintance! I am Lieutenant-Colonel Denisov, better known as Vasska,' said Denisov, pressing Prince Andrei's hand and looking into his face with a particularly kindly interest. 'Yes, I heard about it,' he went on sympathetically, and after a short pause added: 'Yes, this is Scythian warfare all wight. All vewy well – only not for those who get a dwubbing. So you are Pwince Andwei Bolkonsky?' He nodded his head. 'Vewy pleased, pwince, vewy pleased to make your acquaintance!' he repeated with a melancholy smile, and again pressed Prince Andrei's hand.

Prince Andrei knew about Denisov from Natasha's stories of her first suitor. This recollection, at once sweet and bitter, carried him back to those painful sensations over which he had not lingered lately but which still found place in his soul. Of recent times he had been visited by so many other very grave impressions – like the evacuation of Smolensk, his visit to Bald Hills, the news of his father's death – and had experienced so many emotions that for a long while now those memories had left him alone, and when they returned did not affect him nearly so violently. And for Denisov, too, the associations awakened by the name of Bolkonsky belonged to a far-away, romantic past when one evening after supper and Natasha's singing he had proposed to a little girl of fifteen without realizing what he was doing. He smiled at the remembrance of that time and of his love for Natasha, and immediately passed on to what now interested him passionately and to the exclusion of everything else. This was a plan of campaign which he had developed while serving at the outposts during the retreat. He had laid the plan before Barclay de Tolly, and was now bent on putting it to Kutuzov. The plan was based on the fact that the French line of operations was too extended, and his idea was that, instead of or concurrently with a frontal attack to bar the advance of the French, we should harass their communications. He began explaining his plan to Prince Andrei.

'They can't hold all that line. It's impossible. I will undertake to bweak thwough. Give me five hundwed men and I will cut their communications, that's certain! There's only one way – guewilla warfare!'

Denisov had got to his feet as he expounded his plan to Bolkonsky. In the middle of his commentary they heard the acclamations of the army, growing more incoherent and widespread, mingling with music and song, and coming from the parade-ground. There were sounds of horses' hooves and cheering at the end of the village street.

'He's coming! He's coming!' shouted a Cossack standing at the gate.

Bolkonsky and Denisov moved up to the gate, at which a knot of soldiers (a guard of honour) was standing, and they saw Kutuzov coming down the street, mounted on a rather small bay horse. An immense suite of generals followed. Barclay was riding almost beside him, and a crowd of officers ran after and around them shouting 'Hurrah!'

His adjutants galloped on ahead into the yard. Kutuzov impatiently kicked his heels into his horse, which ambled slowly along under his weight, and continually nodded his head and raised his hand to his white Horse Guard's cap with a red band and no peak. When he reached the guard of honour, a stalwart set of Grenadiers, most of them wearing decorations, who were saluting him, he considered them for a minute in silence, with the steady intent gaze of a commander, and then turned to the crowd of generals and officers surrounding him. His face suddenly assumed an ambiguous expression, and he shrugged his shoulders with an air of perplexity.

'And to think that with fine fellows like these we retreat and retreat!' he said. 'Well, good-bye, general,' he added, and rode into the yard past Prince Andrei and Denisov.

'Hurrah! hurrah! hurrah!' The shouts rent the air behind him.

Since Prince Andrei had last seen him Kutuzov had grown still more corpulent, flabby and bloated with fat. But the familiar bleached eyeball, the scar and the expression of weariness in his face were still the same. He was wearing the white Horse Guard's cap and a military greatcoat with a whip on a narrow strap hanging over his shoulder. He sat slumped and swaying on his sturdy little horse.

'Whew! ... whew! ... whew!' he whistled almost distinctly as he rode into the courtyard. His face expressed the relief of a man who looks forward to resting after a performance. He drew his left foot out of the stirrup and with a lurch of his whole body, frowning with the exertion, brought it up on to the saddle, leaned on his knee, and with a groan let himself drop into the arms of the Cossacks and adjutants who stood ready to support him.

He pulled himself together, looked round with half-shut eyes, glanced at Prince Andrei and, evidently not recognizing him, moved with his shambling gait towards the porch. 'Whew ... whew ... whew!' he whistled, and shot another look at Prince Andrei. As is often the case with old men, it was only after a few seconds that he connected Prince Andrei's face with the personality he remembered.

'Ah, how are you, prince? How are you, my dear boy? Come along ...' he said wearily, and, glancing round, stepped heavily on to the porch which creaked under his weight. He unbuttoned his coat and sat down on a bench in the porch.

'Well, how's your father?'

'I received news of his death yesterday,' said Prince Andrei abruptly.

Kutuzov looked at him with eyes wide with dismay, and then took off his cap and crossed himself. 'God rest his soul! May the Lord's will be done with all of us!' He sighed deeply and was silent. 'I loved and respected him, and I sympathize with you with all my heart.'

He embraced Prince Andrei, holding him to his fat breast and for some time did not let him go. When he released him Prince Andrei saw that Kutuzov's flabby lips were trembling and there were tears in his eyes. He sighed and pressed with both hands on the bench to raise himself.

'Come – come to my room and we'll have a chat,' said he.

But at that moment Denisov, no more intimidated by his superiors than by the enemy, walked confidently up, his spurs clanking on the steps, regardless of the indignant whispers of the adjutants who tried to prevent him. Kutuzov, his hands still pressed on the seat, looked at him with displeasure. Denisov, introducing himself, announced that he had to communicate to his Highness a matter of great importance for the welfare of the Fatherland. Kutuzov bent his weary eyes on Denisov, and lifting his hands with a gesture of annoyance folded them across his stomach and repeated: 'For the welfare of the Fatherland? Well, what is it? Speak up!' Denisov blushed like a girl (it was strange to see the colour rise on that whiskered, time-worn, hard-drinking face) and began boldly expounding his plan of cutting the enemy's lines of communication between Smolensk and Vyazma. Denisov's home was in those parts and he knew every inch of the country. His plan seemed unquestionably a good one, especially with the energy of conviction he threw into his words. Kutuzov sat staring at his own legs, occasionally looking over into the yard of the adjoining cottage, as though expecting something unpleasant to appear from there. From the cottage there did in fact emerge, while Denisov was speaking, a general with a portfolio under his arm.

'What?' exclaimed Kutuzov in the middle of Denisov's exposition. 'Ready so soon?'

'Ready, your Highness,' said the general.

Kutuzov shook his head, as much as to say: 'How is one man to get through it all?' and gave his attention again to Denisov.

'I give you my word of honour as a Wussian officer,' Denisov was saying, 'that I can bweak Napoleon's line of communication!'

'What relation are you to Intendant-General Kirill Andreyevich Denisov?' asked Kutuzov, interrupting him.

'He is my uncle, your Highness.'

'Ah, we were very good friends,' said Kutuzov cheerfully. 'Right, right, my dear boy. You stay here at Headquarters, and tomorrow we'll have a talk.'

With a nod to Denisov he turned away and stretched out his hand for the papers Konovnitsyn had brought him.

'Would not your Highness find it more comfortable indoors?' suggested the general on duty in a disgruntled voice. 'There are plans to be examined and several papers to sign.'

An adjutant appeared at the door and announced that everything was in readiness within. But apparently Kutuzov preferred to be rid of business before going into the house. He scowled. ...

'No, have a table brought here, my dear boy. I'll look through them here,' said he. 'Don't go away,' he added, turning to Prince Andrei. Prince Andrei remained in the porch and listened to the general on duty.

While the report was being read, Prince Andrei heard the murmur of a woman's voice and the rustle of a silk dress through the half-open door of the house. Several times as he glanced that way he caught sight behind the door of a plump, rosy-faced, handsome woman in a pink dress with a lilac silk kerchief on her head. She was holding a dish in her hand and evidently waiting for the commander-in-chief to come in. Kutuzov's adjutant whispered to Prince Andrei that this was the wife of the priest whose home it was, who intended to offer his Highness the bread and salt of hospitality. 'Her husband met his Serene Highness with the Cross at the church, and she means to welcome him to the house. ... She's a pretty little thing,' added the adjutant with a smile. Kutuzov looked round at these words. He was listening to the general's report (which consisted chiefly of an appraisal of the position at Tsarevo-Zaimishche), just as he had listened to Denisov and, seven years before that, to the discussion at the council of war on the eve of Austerlitz. He was evidently listening merely because he had ears, which, in spite of the bit of tarred hemp* in one of them, could not help hearing; but it was plain that nothing the general could say would surprise or even interest him, that he knew beforehand all that would be said, and listened only because he must, just as he might have sat through a service in church. All that Denisov had said was sensible and to the point. What the general was saying was even more sensible and to the point, but Kutuzov made it clear that he despised knowledge and wisdom and knew of something else that would decide the matter – something that had nothing to do with cleverness and knowledge. Prince Andrei watched the commander-in-chief's face attentively, and the only expression he could detect was a mixture of boredom, curiosity as to the meaning of the

* A popular remedy in Russia against earache. – Tr.

882

feminine whispering behind the door, and a desire to observe propriety. It was obvious that Kutuzov scorned intellect and learning, and even the patriotic feeling shown by Denisov, but scorned them not because of his own intellect or sentiment or knowledge (for he made no effort to display anything of the kind), but because of something else. He despised them because he was old and had seen too much of life. The only clause of his own that Kutuzov inserted in the report related to looting by the Russian troops. At the end of the report the general put before him a document for signature concerning the recovery of payment from army-commanders, upon receipt of an application by the landowner, for the loss of standing oats.

Kutuzov smacked his lips together and shook his head when he was told about this.

'Into the stove with it ... burn it! And I tell you once for all, my dear fellow,' said he, 'throw all such things into the fire. Let 'em cut the crops and burn wood to their hearts' content. I don't order it, and it's not with my permission, but I can't pursue the matter either. It can't be helped. One must take life as it comes.' He glanced once more at the paper. 'Oh, this German punctilio!' he muttered, shaking his head.

16

'WELL, that's all!' said Kutuzov as he signed the last of the documents; and, rising clumsily and straightening the folds in his fat white neck, he moved towards the door with a more cheerful expression.

The priest's wife, flushing rosy red, snatched up the dish which, though she had been so long preparing, she did not succeed in presenting at the right moment after all. With a low bow she offered it to Kutuzov.

Kutuzov screwed up his eyes, smiled, chucked her under the chin and said:

'Ah, what a pretty face! Thanks, sweetheart!'

He took some gold coins from his trouser pocket and put them on the dish for her. 'Well, and how are things here?' he asked, moving to the door of the room that had been made ready for him. The priest's wife, with every dimple in her rosy cheeks smiling, followed him into the room. The adjutant came out to Prince Andrei in the porch and invited him to lunch. Half an hour later Prince Andrei was again called to Kutuzov. He found him reclining in an arm-chair, still in the same unbuttoned military coat. He had a French novel in his hand, which he laid aside as Prince Andrei came in, marking the place with a paper-knife. It was *Les Chevaliers du Cygne* by Madame de Genlis, as Prince Andrei saw by the cover.

'Well, sit down, sit down here. Let's have a little talk,' said Kutuzov. 'It's sad, very sad. But remember, my dear fellow, that I am a father to you, a second father. ...'

Prince Andrei told Kutuzov all he knew about his father's death, and what he had seen at Bald Hills when he had ridden that way.

'What a pass they have brought us to!' Kutuzov exclaimed suddenly in an agitated voice, evidently seeing from Prince Andrei's story a clear picture of the state Russia was in. 'But give me time, give me time!' he added with a grim look, and apparently unwilling to dwell on a subject that stirred him too deeply he said: 'I sent for you to keep you with me.'

'I thank your Highness,' answered Prince Andrei, 'but I am afraid I am no longer any good for staff work,' he explained with a smile which Kutuzov noticed.

Kutuzov glanced at him inquiringly.

'But above all,' added Prince Andrei, 'I have grown used to my regiment. I am fond of the officers, and I fancy the men have come to like me. I should be sorry to leave the regiment. If I decline the honour of being in attendance on you, believe me ...'

A shrewd, kindly and at the same time subtly ironic twinkle lit up Kutuzov's podgy face. He cut Bolkonsky short.

'I am sorry, for you would have been useful to me. But you are right, you are right! It is not here that *men* are wanted. Advisers are always plentiful but men are scarce. The regiments would be very different if all the advice-givers would serve with them as you do. I remember you at Austerlitz. ... I remember – yes, I remember you with the standard!' said Kutuzov, and a flush of pleasure suffused Prince Andrei's face at this recollection.

Kutuzov held out his hand and drew him close, offering him his cheek to kiss, and again Prince Andrei saw tears in the old man's eyes. Though Prince Andrei knew that Kutuzov's tears came easily and that he was now being particularly affectionate and tender with him from a wish to show sympathy with his loss, still this reminder of Austerlitz pleased and gratified him.

'Go your own way, and God bless you. I know your path is the path of honour.' He paused. 'I missed you at Bucharest: I wanted someone to send ...' And changing the topic Kutuzov began talking of the Turkish war and the peace that had been concluded. 'Yes, I have been roundly abused,' he said, 'both for the war and the peace ... but it all chanced opportune. *Tout vient à point à celui qui sait attendre.* And there were as many counsellors there as here ...' he went on, returning to the subject he was evidently full of. 'Ugh, those advisers, those advisers!' said he. 'If we had listened to all of them we should be in Turkey now – peace would not have been signed, and the war would not be over yet. It's all hurry, hurry – but more haste less speed! Kamensky would have come to grief there if he hadn't died first. He went storming fortresses with thirty thousand men. It's easy enough to take fortresses but not so easy to win a campaign. To do that, it's not storming fortresses and attacking but *patience and time* that are needed. Kamensky sent his soldiers to take Rustchuk, but I trusted to these two alone – patience and time – and took more fortresses than Kamensky ever did, and made the Turks eat horse-flesh!' He nodded his head. 'And the French shall too, you mark my words,' he went on, growing more vehement and pounding his chest. 'It'll be horse-flesh for them with me!' And again there was a glisten of tears in his eyes.

'But we shall have to accept battle, shan't we?' remarked Prince Andrei.

'Of course, if everybody insists on it, there's no help for it. ... But believe me, my dear boy, the two most powerful warriors are *patience and time*: they will do everything. Only our wise counsellors don't see it that way, that's the trouble. Some are in favour, others aren't. What's one to do?' he asked, evidently expecting an answer. 'Well, what would you have me do?' he repeated, and his eyes shone with a deep, knowing look. 'I'll tell you what to do,' he pursued, since Prince Andrei still did not reply. 'I'll tell you what to do, and what I do. *Dans le doute, mon cher,*' he paused, '*abstiens-toi.*' He spoke the words with slow emphasis. 'When in doubt, my dear fellow, do nothing.

'Well, good-bye, my dear fellow. Remember, with all my heart I feel for you in your sorrow, and that for you I'm not his Serene Highness, or prince, or commander-in-chief, but a father. If ever you want anything, come straight to me. Good-bye, my dear boy.'

Again he embraced and kissed Prince Andrei. And then, before

Prince Andrei had time to close the door after him, Kutuzov gave a sigh of relief and settled down with the novel he was reading, *Les Chevaliers du Cygne*, by Madame de Genlis.

Prince Andrei could not have explained how or why it was, but after this interview with Kutuzov he went back to his regiment feeling reassured as to the course of affairs generally and as to the man to whom it had been entrusted. The more he realized the complete absence of self-interest in the old man – who had as it were outlived the fire of his passions, leaving only the habit of them, and whose intellect (which co-ordinates events and draws conclusions) had resolved itself into the single faculty for quietly contemplating the progress of events – the more confident he felt that everything would turn out as it should. 'He will not introduce anything of his own. He will not scheme or start anything,' thought Prince Andrei, 'but he will listen, bear in mind all that he hears, put everything in its rightful place. He will not stand in the way of anything expedient or permit what might be injurious. He knows that there is something stronger and more important than his own will – the inevitable march of events, and he has the brains to see them and grasp their significance, and seeing that significance can abstain from meddling, from following his personal desires and aiming at something else. And above all,' thought Prince Andrei, 'one believes in him because he's Russian, in spite of the novel by Genlis and his French proverbs, and because his voice shook when he exclaimed "What a pass they have brought us to!" and had a sob in it when he said he would "make 'em eat horse-flesh!"'

It was this feeling, more or less unconsciously shared by all, that was behind the unanimous approval which accompanied the appointment of Kutuzov to the chief command, harmonizing, as it did, with national sentiment, and overriding every intrigue at Court.

17

AFTER the Emperor's departure from Moscow life in the capital flowed on in its ordinary channels, resuming its normal course to such an extent that it was difficult to recall those few days of patriotic fervour and enthusiasm, hard to believe that Russia was really in danger and that the members of the English Club were at the same time sons of the Fatherland prepared for any sacrifice. The one thing that brought back the universal uprush of patriotism that had swept Moscow during the Emperor's stay was the call for contributions of men and money – promises, once offered, and quickly invested in legal, official form, had to be complied with.

Though the enemy was nearing Moscow, Moscovites were not inclined to regard their situation with any greater degree of serious-ness: on the contrary they became even more frivolous, as is always the case with people who see a great catastrophe approaching. At the advent of danger there are always two voices that speak with equal force in the human heart: one very reasonably invites a man to con-sider the nature of the peril and the means of escaping it; the other, with a still greater show of reason, argues that it is too depressing and painful to think of the danger since it is not in man's power to foresee everything and avert the general march of events, and it is better therefore to shut one's eyes to the disagreeable until it actually comes, and to think instead of what is pleasant. When a man is alone he generally listens to the first voice; in the company of his fellow-men, to the second. So it was now with the inhabitants of Moscow. It was a long time since Moscow had seen so much gaiety as there was that year.

Rostopchin's broadsheets, headed by woodcuts of a drinking-shop, a tapster and a Moscow burgher called Karpushka Tchigirin – *an old soldier having had a drop too much at the inn, who flies into a great rage and abuses the French in the most colourful language when he hears that Bona-parte means to march on Moscow, comes out of the drink-shop and harangues the crowd collected under the Imperial sign of the eagle* – were as much read and discussed as the latest *bouts-rimés* of Vasili Lvovich Pushkin.

In the corner room at the club, members gathered to peruse these broadsheets, and some approved of the way Karpushka was made to jeer at the French, saying that *Russian cabbages will blow them up like balloons, Russian porridge burst their bellies and cabbage-soup finish them off. They are all dwarfs, and one peasant-woman will toss three of them at a time with a hay-fork.* Others did not like the tone, declaring that it was stupid and vulgar. People said that Rostopchin had expelled all Frenchmen, and, indeed, all foreigners, from Moscow, and that there had been some spies and agents of Napoleon among them, but this story was told chiefly for the sake of being able to introduce Rostop-chin's witty remark *à propos* of the occasion. The foreigners were put on a boat bound for Nizhni, and Rostopchin had said to them in

887

French: 'Keep yourselves to yourselves. Get into the boat and take care not to turn it into Charon's ferry.' There was talk of all the government offices having already removed from Moscow, and here Shinshin's *bon mot* was brought in – to the effect that for this, at least, Moscow ought to be grateful to Napoleon. It was said that Mamonov's regiment would cost him eight hundred thousand roubles; that Bezuhov had spent even more on his, but that the best thing of all was that the count himself was going to don a uniform and ride at the head of his regiment without charging anything for the spectacle.

'You have no mercy on anyone,' said Julie Drubetskoy as she picked up and pressed together a bunch of ravelled lint with her slender, beringed fingers.

Julie was about to leave Moscow next day and was giving a farewell *soirée*.

'*Bezuhov est ridicule*, but he is so kind and good-natured. What pleasure is there to be so *caustique*?'

'A forfeit!' cried a young man in a militiaman's uniform, whom Julie called '*mon chevalier*', and who was going with her to Nizhni.

In Julie's set, as in many other circles in Moscow, it had been agreed to speak nothing but Russian, and those who forgot and spoke French paid a fine to the Committee for Voluntary Contributions.

'A double forfeit for a Gallicism,' said a Russian author who was present. '"What pleasure is there to be" is not Russian.'

'You show no mercy on anyone,' pursued Julie to the young man, paying no heed to the author's criticism. '*Caustique*, I admit,' she said, 'and I'll pay, and I am prepared to pay again for the pleasure of telling you the truth. For Gallicisms I refuse to be answerable,' she remarked, turning to the writer. 'I have neither the money nor the time to engage a tutor to teach me Russian, like Prince Golitsyn. Ah, here he is!' she added. '*Quand on* ... No, no,' she protested to the militiaman, 'you're not going to catch me. Talk of the sun and out it comes!' and she smiled amiably at Pierre. 'We were just speaking about you, and saying that your regiment was sure to be better than Mamonov's,' she told him, with the society woman's natural facility for making free with the truth.

'Oh, don't talk to me of my regiment,' replied Pierre, kissing his hostess's hand and taking a seat beside her. 'I am sick to death of it.'

'You will lead it in person, of course?' said Julie, exchanging a derisive, knowing look with the militiaman.

The militiaman in Pierre's presence was by no means so ready to be caustic, and his countenance betokened perplexity as to what Julie's smile could mean. In spite of his absent-mindedness and good nature, Pierre's personality never failed to cut short any attempt to ridicule him to his face.

'No,' laughed Pierre, glancing down at his huge, bulky figure. 'I should make too good a target for the French; besides, I doubt whether I could hoist myself on to a horse's back. ...'

Among those whom Julie's guests picked upon as a subject for their gossip were the Rostovs.

'I hear that their affairs are in a very bad way,' said Julie. 'And he is so unreasonable – the count, I mean. The Razumovskys wanted to buy the house and estate near Moscow, but it drags on and on. He will ask too much.'

'No, I fancy the sale will come off in a few days now,' said someone. 'Though it is madness to buy anything in Moscow in these times.'

'Why?' asked Julie. 'Surely you don't think Moscow is in danger?'

'Why are you leaving then?'

'I? What a question! I am going because ... well, because everybody else is; and besides – I am not a Joan of Arc or an Amazon.'

'Yes, yes, of course. Give me some more strips of linen.'

'If he manages the business properly he ought to be able to pay off all his debts,' said the militiaman, speaking of Rostov.

'He's a nice old man, but a very *pauvre sire*. And why are they staying on in town so long? They meant to leave for the country ages ago. Natalie is quite well again now, isn't she?' Julie asked Pierre with a sly smile.

'They are waiting for their younger son,' Pierre replied. 'He joined Obolensky's Cossacks and was sent off to Belaya Tserkov. The regiment is being formed there. But now they have had him transferred to my regiment and he is expected every day. The count would have gone long ago but nothing would induce the countess to leave Moscow before her son arrived.'

'I met them the day before yesterday at the Arharovs'. Natalie has quite recovered her looks and her spirits. She sang a song. How easily some people get over everything!'

'Get over what?' inquired Pierre, looking displeased.

Julie smiled. 'You know, count, such chivalrous knights as you are only to be found in Madame de Souza's novels!'

'Knights? What do you mean?' demanded Pierre, blushing.

'Oh come, my dear count. All Moscow knows. Really, I am surprised at you,' said Julie, speaking in French again.

'A fine, a fine!' cried the militiaman.

'Oh, all right. One can't open one's mouth nowadays – what a bore it is!'

'What does all Moscow know?' Pierre asked angrily, rising to his feet.

'Oh fie, count, you know!'

'I do not,' said Pierre.

'I know what great friends you have always been with Natalie, and so ... But I was always more friendly with Vera – that dear Vera!'

'*Non, madame,*' Pierre continued in a tone of annoyance. 'I have certainly not taken upon myself the role of Natalie Rostov's knight. Indeed, it is almost a month since I was at their house. But I cannot understand the cruelty. ...'

'*Qui s'excuse – s'accuse,*' said Julie, smiling and waving the lint triumphantly, and to have the last word she promptly changed the subject. 'By the way, I heard that poor Marie Bolkonsky arrived in Moscow yesterday. You know she lost her father?'

'Really? Where is she? I should very much like to see her,' said Pierre.

'I spent the evening with her yesterday. She is going on today or tomorrow morning to their estate near Moscow, taking her little nephew.'

'Tell me, and how is she?' asked Pierre.

'All right, but sad. But do you know who rescued her? It is quite a romance. Nikolai Rostov. She was surrounded, and they wanted to kill her and some of her servants were wounded. He rushed in and saved her. ...'

'Another romance,' said the militiaman. 'Really this general stampede has been got up expressly to marry off all our old maids. Katishe is one, Princess Bolkonsky another.'

'Do you know, I verily believe she is *un petit peu amoureuse du jeune homme?*'

'Forfeit, forfeit, forfeit!'

'But how could I say that in Russian?'

18

WHEN Pierre returned home he was handed two of Rostopchin's broadsheets that had been brought that day.

The first denied the report that Count Rostopchin had forbidden people to leave Moscow: on the contrary, he was glad that ladies and merchants' wives were leaving the city. 'There will be less panic and less gossip,' ran the broadsheet, 'but I will stake my life on it that the scoundrel will never set foot in Moscow.' These words showed Pierre clearly for the first time that the French would set foot in Moscow. In the second broadsheet it was announced that our Headquarters were at Vyazma, that Count Wittgenstein had defeated the French but that, as many of the inhabitants of the capital were desirous of arming themselves, weapons were ready for them at the arsenal; sabres, pistols and muskets could be had at low prices. The tone of this proclamation was not as jocose as those which had been attributed to the tapster Tchigirin. Pierre pondered over these broadsheets. Evidently the terrible storm-cloud which his soul longed for with all its might, though it excited an involuntary thrill of horror, was drawing near.

'Shall I join the army and enter the Service, or shall I wait?' he asked himself for the hundredth time. He took up a pack of cards that lay on the table and began to spread them out for a game of patience.

'If this game comes out,' he said to himself, shuffling the cards, holding them in his hand and lifting his head, 'if it comes out, it means ... what does it mean?'

Before he had time to decide what it would mean he heard the voice of the eldest princess at the door of his study, asking whether she might come in.

'Then it will mean that I must go to the army,' Pierre told himself. 'Come in, come in!' he called to the princess.

Only the eldest princess, the one with the long waist and the stony face, was still living in Pierre's house. The two younger sisters had both married.

'Forgive me, *mon cousin*, for disturbing you,' said she in an accusing and agitated voice. 'You know it is high time to come to a decision. What is going to happen? Everyone has left Moscow and the people are rioting. Why do we stay?'

'On the contrary, everything looks satisfactory, *ma cousine*,' said Pierre in the bantering tone he habitually adopted towards her, to carry off his embarrassment at being in the position of a benefactor to her.

'Satisfactory – oh yes! Very satisfactory! Only this morning Varvara Ivanovna was telling me how our troops are distinguishing themselves. It certainly does them credit! And the people, too, are in a complete state of revolt and will listen to no one – even my maid has begun to be insolent. At this rate they will soon be slaughtering us. It isn't safe to walk in the streets. But, above all, the French will be here any day now, so what are we waiting for? I ask just one favour of you, *mon cousin*,' pleaded the princess, 'arrange for me to be taken to Petersburg. Whatever I may be, I couldn't live under Bonaparte's rule.'

'Oh come, *ma cousine!* Where do you get your information from? On the contrary ...'

'I tell you I won't submit to your Napoleon! Others may if they please. ... If you won't do this for me ...'

'But I will, I'll give the order at once.'

The princess, obviously provoked at having no one to quarrel with, sat on the very edge of her chair, muttering to herself.

'But you have been misinformed,' said Pierre. 'Everything is quiet in the city and there is not the slightest danger. See, I've just been reading ...' He showed her the broadsheet. 'Count Rostopchin writes that he will stake his life on it that the enemy will not set foot in Moscow.'

'Oh, that count of yours!' the princess began spitefully. 'He's a hypocrite, a rascal, who has himself been exciting the people to sedition. Didn't he write in those idiotic broadsheets promising honour and glory to whoever should drag anyone – no matter whom – by the hair of his head to the lock-up? (How silly?) This is what his cajolery has brought us to. Varvara Ivanovna told me the mob nearly killed her because she started to say something in French.'

'Ah well, that is the way of things. ... You take matters too much to heart,' said Pierre, and he began laying out his cards for patience.

Although his game of patience came out, Pierre did not join the army but stayed on in Moscow, now much depopulated, in the same fever of uncertainty and alarm and yet eagerly looking forward to something awful.

Towards evening of the following day the princess took her departure, and Pierre's head steward came to inform him that the money needed for the equipment of his regiment could not possibly be raised except by selling one of the estates. The steward impressed on Pierre generally that such expensive caprices as fitting out a regiment would be his ruin. Pierre listened, scarcely able to repress a smile.

'Well, then, sell,' said he. 'There's no help for it, I can't draw back now!'

The worse the position of affairs, and in particular of his own affairs, the better pleased Pierre felt, and the more apparent was it that the catastrophe he expected was at hand. Hardly anyone he knew was left in town. Julie had gone, Princess Maria had gone. Of his intimate friends only the Rostovs were still there, but he did not go to see them.

To distract his thoughts he drove out that day to the village of Vorontsovo to see the great balloon Leppich was constructing to use against the enemy, and a trial balloon that was to go up next day. The balloon was not yet ready; but Pierre learnt that it was being constructed by the Emperor's desire. The Emperor had written to Count Rostopchin about it as follows:

As soon as Leppich is ready, get together a crew of reliable and intelligent men for his car, and send a courier to General Kutuzov to let him know. I have informed him of the matter.

Impress upon Leppich, please, to be very careful where he descends for the first time, that he may not make any mistake and fall into the hands of the enemy. It is essential that he should co-ordinate his movements with those of the commander-in-chief.

On his way home from Vorontsovo, as he was driving through Bolotny square Pierre saw a great crowd collected round the place of execution. He stopped and got out of his trap. A French cook, accused of being a spy, had just been flogged. The executioner was untying from the flogging-bench a stout man with red whiskers, in blue stockings and a green jacket, who was groaning piteously. Another offender, thin and pale, stood near. Both, to judge by their faces, were French. Looking as sick with dread as the lean Frenchman, Pierre elbowed his way through the crowd.

'What does this mean? Who are they? What have they done?' he kept asking.

But the attention of the throng – clerks, burghers, shopkeepers, peasants and women in mantles and cloaks – was so intently riveted on what was happening on the place of execution that no one answered him. The stout man got up, shrugged his shoulders with a scowl, and clearly anxious to show fortitude began to pull on his jacket without looking about him; but suddenly his lips trembled and to his own rage he started to cry, in the way grown men of sanguine temperament do cry. The crowd fell to passing loud remarks, to stifle their feelings of pity, as it seemed to Pierre.

'Cook to some prince ...'

'Eh, mounseer, Russian sauce would appear a bit strong for French taste ... sets the teeth on edge, eh?' said a wrinkled chancery clerk standing near Pierre, just as the Frenchman broke into tears. The clerk glanced round, obviously hoping for signs of appreciation for his joke. Several people laughed, others continued to gaze in dismay at the executioner who was undressing the second Frenchman.

Pierre choked, and knitting his brows turned hastily away, went back to his trap, muttering to himself, and took his seat. As they drove along he shuddered, and exclaimed several times so audibly that the coachman inquired:

'Yes, sir?'

'Where on earth are you going?' shouted Pierre as the coachman turned down Lubyanka street.

'You told me to drive to the Governor-general's,' answered the coachman.

'Idiot! Ass!' shouted Pierre, berating his coachman – a thing he rarely did. 'Home, I said! And make haste, blockhead!' And then:

'I must get away this very day,' he murmured to himself.

At the sight of the tortured Frenchman and the crowd round the place of execution Pierre had so definitely made up his mind that he could no longer remain in Moscow, and must leave that very day for the army, that it seemed to him either that he had told the coachman so or that the man ought to have known it of himself.

On reaching home Pierre instructed his omniscient and omnipotent head-coachman, who was known to all Moscow, that he would leave that night for the army at Mozhaisk, and to have his saddle-horses sent there. All this could not be arranged in one day, so on Yevstafievich's representations Pierre delayed his departure for another twenty-four hours to allow time for the relay horses to be sent on ahead.

On the 24th the weather cleared up after a spell of rain, and after dinner Pierre left Moscow. Stopping to change horses in the night at Perhushkovo, he learned that a great battle had been fought that evening. (This was the battle of Shevardino.) He was told that the firing had made the earth tremble there at Perhushkovo; but when he inquired who had been victorious, no one could give him any information. By dawn the following morning Pierre was approaching Mozhaisk.

Every house in Mozhaisk had soldiers quartered in it, and at the hostel where Pierre was met by his groom and coachman there was not a room to be had. The whole place was full of officers.

Everywhere, in the town and on the outskirts, troops were stationed or on the march. On all sides were Cossacks, foot- and horse-soldiers, wagons, caissons and cannon. Pierre pushed forward as fast as he could, and the farther he went from Moscow and the deeper he plunged into this sea of troops the more he was overcome by anxiety and a new, pleasurable sensation which he had never experienced before. It was somewhat akin to the feeling he had felt at the Slobodskoy Palace at the time of the Emperor's visit – a sense of the urgent necessity for taking some step and making some sacrifice. He was conscious at this moment of a glad conviction that everything which constitutes the happiness of men – the comforts of life, wealth, even life itself – was rubbish which it was a joy to fling away, when one thought of. ... Thought of what, Pierre could not say, and indeed he did not attempt to analyse for whom or for what he found such peculiar delight in sacrificing everything. He was not interested in knowing the object of the sacrifice: the mere fact of sacrificing in itself afforded him a new and joyous sensation.

19

On the 24th of August the battle of the Shevardino Redoubt was fought; on the 25th not a shot was fired by either side; on the 26th came the battle of Borodino.

How and with what object were the battles of Shevardino and Borodino given and accepted? Why was the battle of Borodino fought? There was not the least sense in it, either for the French or the Russians. Its immediate result for the Russians was, and was bound to be, that we were brought a step further towards the destruction of

Moscow (the very thing we dreaded above all else in the world); and for the French, that they were brought nearer to the destruction of their whole army (which they, too, dreaded above everything in the world). What the result must be was perfectly obvious, and yet Napoleon offered and Kutuzov accepted the battle.

If military leaders were guided by reason it would seem that it must have been clear to Napoleon that in advancing thirteen hundred miles and giving battle with a probability of losing a quarter of his men, he was marching to certain destruction; and that it must have been equally clear to Kutuzov that by accepting battle and risking the loss of a quarter of his army, he would certainly lose Moscow. For Kutuzov this was a mathematical certainty, just as in a game of draughts if I have one man less and go on exchanging I am bound to lose, and so I mustn't exchange. When my opponent has sixteen men and I have fourteen I am only one-eighth weaker than he, but when I have exchanged thirteen more men he will be three times as strong as I am.

Up to the battle of Borodino our forces were to the French in the approximate proportion of five to six, but after the battle, of one to two. In other words, before the battle we had a hundred thousand as against their one hundred and twenty thousand, and after the battle it was our fifty thousand to a hundred thousand of them. Yet the shrewd and experienced Kutuzov accepted battle, while Napoleon, an acknowledged military genius, offered battle, losing a quarter of his army and lengthening his lines of communication further than ever. If we are told that he expected the occupation of Moscow to complete the campaign, as the taking of Vienna had closed a previous campaign, we may say that there are many evidences to the contrary. Napoleon's historians themselves relate that from Smolensk onwards he was anxious to call a halt; that he was fully aware of the danger of his extended position, and knew that the capture of Moscow would not see the end of the campaign, for Smolensk had shown him the state in which Russian towns were left, and he had not received a single reply to the repeated expressions of his desire to open negotiations.

In giving and accepting battle at Borodino, Kutuzov and Napoleon acted contrary to their intentions and their good sense. But later on, to fit the accomplished facts, the historians provided cunningly devised proofs of the foresight and genius of the generals, who of all the blind instruments of history were the most enslaved and involuntary.

The ancients have passed down to us examples of epic poems in which the heroes furnish the whole interest of the story, and to this day we are unable to accustom our minds to the idea that history of that kind is meaningless for our epoch.

As to the other question: how the battle of Borodino and the preceding battle of Shevardino came to be fought, there exists an explanation just as positive and well known but absolutely fallacious. All the historians describe the affair thus:

The Russian army, they say, in its retreat from Smolensk sought for itself the most favourable position for a general engagement, and such a position they found at Borodino.

The Russians, they say, fortified this position in advance on the left of the high road (from Moscow to Smolensk) and almost at right angles to it, from Borodino to Utitsa, at the very place where the battle was fought.

In front of this position, they tell us, a fortified earthwork was thrown up on the Shevardino Redoubt as an outpost for observation of the enemy's movements. On the 24th, we are told, Napoleon attacked this advanced post and took it, and on the 26th he fell on the whole Russian army, which had taken up its position on the field of Borodino.

So the histories say, and it is all quite wrong, as anyone may see who cares to investigate the facts.

The Russians did not seek out the most favourable position but, on the contrary, during their retreat passed by several positions superior to Borodino. They did not halt at any one of these positions because Kutuzov would not occupy a position he had not himself selected, because the popular clamour for an engagement had not yet expressed itself forcefully enough, and because Miloradovich had not yet arrived with the militia, and for countless other reasons. The fact is that there were stronger positions on the road the Russian army had passed along, and that the position at Borodino (where the battle was fought), far from being strong was no more a *position* than any other spot one might find in the Russian Empire by haphazardly sticking a pin in the map.

The Russians not only did not fortify the position on the field of Borodino to the left of and at a right angle to the high road (that is, the spot on which the battle was fought) – until the 25th of August 1812 they never dreamed of the possibility of the battle taking place there. This is shown, first by the fact that before the 25th there were no entrenchments there, and that the earthworks begun on the 25th were not completed by the 26th; and secondly, the evidence of the Shevardino Redoubt itself: situated in front of the position where battle was accepted it had no meaning. Why was it more strongly fortified than any other post? And why were all efforts exhausted and six thousand men sacrificed to defend it till late at night on the 24th? A picket of Cossacks would have sufficed to keep watch on the enemy. And as a third proof that the position of the battlefield was not foreseen and that the Shevardino Redoubt was not an advanced post of that position, we have the fact that up to the 25th Barclay de Tolly and Bagration were under the impression that the Shevardino Redoubt was the *left flank* of the position, and that Kutuzov himself in his report written in hot haste after the battle speaks of the Shevardino Redoubt as the *left flank* of the position. It was only much later, when detailed accounts of the battle of Borodino were penned at leisure, that the inaccurate and extraordinary statement was invented (probably to cover up the blunders of the commander-in-chief who had to be represented as infallible) that the Shevardino Redoubt was an *advanced* post – when in reality it was simply the fortified point of the left flank – and that the battle of Borodino was fought by us on an entrenched position previously selected, whereas it was fought on a position quite unforeseen and almost unfortified.

The affair obviously took place in this way: a position was selected on the river Kolocha – which intersects the high road not at a right but at an acute angle – so that the left flank was at Shevardino, the right flank near the village of Novoe and the centre at Borodino, at the confluence of the rivers Kolocha and Voina. To anyone who looks at the field of Borodino without thinking of how the battle was actually fought, this position, protected by the Kolocha, presents itself as an obvious choice for an army whose object was to check the advance of an enemy marching along the Smolensk road to Moscow.

Napoleon, riding up to Valuevo on the 24th, did not (we are told in the history books) discover the Russians in their position between Utitsa and Borodino (he could not have seen that position because it did not exist), and did not see the advanced post of the Russian army. It was only when in pursuit of the Russian rearguard that he stumbled upon the left flank of the Russian position – at the Shevardino Redoubt – and, to the surprise of the Russians, moved his troops across the Kolocha. And the Russians, since it was too late for a general engagement, withdrew their left wing from the position they had intended to occupy, and took up a new position which had not been foreseen and was not fortified. By crossing to the other side of the Kolocha to the left of the high road, Napoleon shifted the whole forthcoming battle from right to left (looking from the Russian side) and transferred it to the plain between Utitsa, Semeonovsk and Borodino – a plain no more advantageous as a position than any other plain in Russia – and there the whole battle of the 26th of August took place.

Had Napoleon not ridden out on the evening of the 24th to Kolocha, and had he not then ordered an immediate attack on the redoubt but had begun the attack next morning, no one could have felt any uncertainty as to the Shevardino Redoubt being the left flank of our position; and the battle would have been fought where we expected it. In that case we should probably have defended the Shevardino Redoubt – our left flank – still more obstinately; we should have attacked Napoleon in the centre or on the right, and the general engagement would have taken place on the 25th, on the position prepared and fortified for it. But as the attack on our left flank was made in the evening after the retreat of our rearguard (that is, immediately after the action at Gridneva), and as the Russian commanders would not or could not begin a general engagement then on the evening of the 24th, the first and most important operation of the battle of Borodino was already lost on the 24th, and that loss clearly led to the loss of the one fought on the 26th.

After the loss of the Shevardino Redoubt we found ourselves, on the morning of the 25th, without a position for our left flank, and were forced to draw in this left wing and hastily entrench it where it chanced to be.

But not only was the Russian army on the 26th of August defended by weak, unfinished earthworks, but the disadvantage of that position was aggravated by the fact that the Russian generals, not having fully realized what had happened (i.e. the loss of our position on the left flank and the shifting of the whole field of the forthcoming battle from right to left), maintained their extended formation from the village of Novoe to Utitsa, and consequently had to transfer their forces from right to left during the engagement. So it happened that throughout the entire operation the Russians had to face the whole French army launched against our left flank with but half as many men. (Poniatowski's action against Utitsa and Uvarov's on the right

899

flank against the French were quite independent of the main course of the fighting.)

And so the battle of Borodino was not fought at all as the historians describe, in their efforts to gloss over the mistakes of our leaders even at the cost of diminishing the glory due to the Russian army and people. The battle of Borodino was not fought on a carefully picked and fortified position with forces only slightly weaker on the Russian side. As a result of the loss of the Shevardino Redoubt the Russians fought the battle of Borodino on an open and almost unentrenched position, with forces only half as numerous as the French; that is to say, under conditions in which it was not merely unthinkable to fight for ten hours and still leave the contest in doubt, but unthinkable to preserve an army for even three hours from complete disintegration and flight.

20

ON the morning of the 25th Pierre was driving out of Mozhaisk. On the winding slope of the monstrously steep hill leading out of the town, just beyond the cathedral that crowns the hill on the right, where a service was being held and the bells were pealing, Pierre got out of his carriage and proceeded on foot. A cavalry regiment followed him down the hill, the singers of the regiment in front. A train of carts came up the hill towards him filled with casualties from the previous day's engagement. The peasant drivers, shouting and lashing their horses, kept crossing from side to side. The carts, in each of which three or four wounded soldiers were lying or sitting, jolted over the stones that had been flung on the steep incline to make it something like a road. The wounded men, bandaged with rags, and with pale cheeks, compressed lips and knitted brows, clung to the sides of the carts as they were shaken and thrown against one another. Almost all of them stared with naïve, childlike curiosity at Pierre's white hat and green swallow-tail coat.

Pierre's coachman shouted angrily at the convoy of wounded to keep to one side of the road. The cavalry regiment, coming down the hill with its singers, overran Pierre's carriage and blocked the way. Pierre halted, finding himself squeezed to the edge of the road that had been hollowed out in the hill. The sun did not reach over the side of the hill into the cutting, and there it felt cold and damp, but overhead it was a bright August morning and the chimes rang out merrily. One team with its load of wounded drew up at the side of the road close to Pierre. The driver in his bast shoes ran panting up to his cart, shoved a stone under one of the back wheels, which had no tyres, and began arranging the breeching on his worn-out horse, which had stopped.

One of the wounded, an old soldier with his arm in a sling, walking behind the cart, caught hold of it with his sound arm and turned to look at Pierre.

'Well, fellow-countryman, are we to be put down here or will they take us on to Moscow?' he asked.

Pierre was so deep in thought that he did not hear the question. He was staring now at the cavalry regiment, which had met face to face with the convoy of wounded, now at the cart he stood by, in which two wounded men were sitting and one was lying, and it seemed to him that here with them lay the answer to the problem he was concerned with. One of the pair sitting up in the cart had apparently been wounded in the cheek. His whole head was bound up with rags and one side of his face was swollen as big as a child's head. His nose and mouth were twisted to one side. This soldier was looking at the cathedral and crossing himself. The other, a young lad, a fair-haired recruit as white as though there was not a drop of blood in his thin face, gazed at Pierre with a fixed, good-natured smile. The third soldier lay prone so that his face was not visible. The cavalry singers were now abreast of the cart.

> Ah, my head's all mazed
> In foreign parts ...

they sang the military dance tune.

As if in response, but with a different strain of merriment, the metallic notes of the bells reverberated from the heights above, while the hot rays of the sun bathed the top of the opposite slope with still another sort of gaiety. But where Pierre stood under the hillside, by the cart full of wounded soldiers and the panting little nag, it was damp, sombre and dismal.

The soldier with the swollen cheek looked angrily at the cavalry-singers.

'Ah, the swells!' he muttered reproachfully.

'It's not soldiers only but peasants too I've seen today! The peasants – even they have to go,' said the soldier who was leaning against the cart, addressing Pierre with a melancholy smile. 'They're not so particular nowadays. ... They mean to throw the whole nation against them – in a word, it's Moscow. They want to make an end of it.'

In spite of the incoherence of this statement Pierre understood what the soldier wanted to say and nodded agreement.

The road was clear again. Pierre walked down the hill and got into his carriage. As he drove on he looked, first to one side and then to the other, for someone he knew, but encountered everywhere only unfamiliar faces belonging to all sorts of regiments, and all staring with the same astonishment at his white hat and green tail-coat.

He had gone nearly three miles before he met his first acquaintance, and hailed him eagerly. This was a doctor, one of the heads of the army medical service. He was driving towards Pierre in a covered gig, sitting beside a young doctor, and on recognizing Pierre he called to the Cossack on the driver's seat to pull up.

'Count! Your Excellency – how do you come to be here?' asked the doctor.

'Oh, I wanted to have a look. ...'

'Yes, there'll be plenty to see. ...'

Pierre got out to talk to the doctor, confiding to him his intention of taking part in the battle.

The doctor advised Bezuhov to apply direct to Kutuzov.

'Why should you hang about God knows where during the battle, unable to see a thing?' said he, exchanging glances with his young colleague. 'And his Serene Highness knows you, anyway, and will receive you gladly. Yes, you do that, my friend.'

The doctor seemed tired and in a hurry.

'So you think ... Oh yes, I was going to ask you – where exactly is our position?' said Pierre.

'Our position?' repeated the doctor. 'Well, that is something that is not in my line. Take the route through Tatarinova; there's a lot of digging going on there. Climb up on to the barrow: you can get a good view from the top.'

'Can one see from there? ... If you would ...'

But the doctor interrupted him and moved towards the gig.

'I would go with you but so help me God I'm up to here' – and he indicated his throat. 'I am racing to the commander of the corps. How do matters stand? ... You know, count, there'll be a battle tomorrow. Out of an army of a hundred thousand we must expect at least twenty thousand casualties; and we haven't stretchers or pallets or dressers or surgeons enough for six thousand. To be sure, we've got ten thousand carts, but we need other things as well. We shall have to do the best we can.'

The strange thought that of those thousands of men, alive and well, young and old, who had stared with such light-hearted amusement at his hat (perhaps the very men he had noticed), twenty thousand were inevitably doomed to suffer wounds and death – made a deep impression on Pierre.

'They may be dead tomorrow. How is it then they can think of anything but death?' And suddenly, by some mysterious association of ideas, he saw a vivid picture of the steep descent from Mozhaisk – the carts with the wounded, the jangling chimes, the slanting rays of the sun and the chorus of the cavalrymen.

'The cavalry ride into battle and meet the wounded on the way, and never for a moment do they think of what is in store for them. They ride by winking at their wounded comrades. Yet of those men twenty thousand are doomed to die, and they can still find it in them to wonder at my hat! Strange!' thought Pierre, as he went on towards Tatarinova.

Outside a gentleman's house on the left of the road stood carriages, wagons, and a crowd of orderlies and sentinels. This was where the commander-in-chief was putting up, but when Pierre arrived he found that his Serene Highness and almost all the staff were out – they had gone to a service of intercession. Pierre pushed on in the direction of Gorky.

Driving up the hill into the little village street he saw for the first time the peasants of the militia in their white shirts, with the badge of the cross on their caps. Shouting and laughing together, eager and perspiring, they were at work on a huge knoll overgrown with grass, to the right of the road.

Some were digging, others wheeling barrow-loads of earth along planks, while a third lot stood about doing nothing.

Two officers were standing on the knoll directing the men. Seeing these peasants evidently still amused by the novelty of finding themselves soldiers reminded Pierre of the wounded men at Mozhaisk again, and he understood what the soldier had tried to express when he said: 'They mean to throw the whole nation at the enemy's head.' The sight of these bearded peasants toiling on the field of battle, with their queer, clumsy boots, their perspiring necks, and here and there with shirts unbuttoned obliquely across their chests, exposing their sunburnt collar-bones, impressed Pierre more strongly than anything he had yet seen or heard with the solemnity and gravity of the moment.

21

PIERRE got out of his carriage and walking past the toiling militia-men climbed on to the knoll from which the doctor had told him he could get a view of the field of battle. It was around eleven o'clock in the morning. The sun was a little to the left and behind him, and in the clear rarefied atmosphere the huge panorama that stretched like an amphitheatre before him lay bathed in brilliant light.

The Smolensk high road ran winding through this amphitheatre, intersecting it towards the left at the top, and passing through a vil-lage with a white church some five hundred yards in front of and below the knoll. This was Borodino. Below the village the road crossed the river by a bridge and winding up and down rose higher and higher to the hamlet of Valuevo, visible about four miles away, where Napoleon now was. Beyond Valuevo the road disappeared into a yellowing forest on the horizon. Far away in the distance in that birch and fir forest to the right of the road the cross and belfry of the Kolotsky monastery gleamed in the sun. Here and there over the whole of that blue expanse, to right and to left of the forest and the road, smoking camp-fires could be seen, and blurred masses of troops – ours and the enemy's. The country to the right – along the course of the two rivers Kolocha and Moskva – was broken and hilly. Through the gaps between the hills the villages of Bezzubovo and Zaharino showed in the distance. On the left the ground was more level; there were fields of grain and the smoking ruins of the village of Semeonovsk that had been set on fire were visible.

All that Pierre saw to right and left of him was so negative that no part of the scene before his eyes answered his expectations. Nowhere was there a field of battle such as his imagination had pictured: there were only fields, clearings, troops, woods, the smoke of camp-fires, villages, mounds and streams; and try as he would he could descry no military 'position' in this landscape teeming with life. He could not even distinguish our troops from the enemy's.

'I must ask someone who knows,' he thought, and addressed him-self to an officer who was looking with curiosity at his huge un-military figure.

'Would you have the goodness to tell me,' said Pierre, 'the name of the village opposite?'

'Burdino, isn't it called?' said the officer, turning inquiringly to his companion.

'Borodino,' corrected the other.

The officer, evidently glad of an opportunity for a talk, moved nearer to Pierre.

'Are those our men there?' asked Pierre.

'Yes, the others farther away are the French,' said the officer. 'There they are, there you can see them.'

'Where? Where?' asked Pierre.

'You can see them with the naked eye.... Look, look there!'

The officer pointed to the smoke rising on the left beyond the river, and the same stern and serious expression came into his face that Pierre had noticed on many of the faces he had met.

'Ah, so those are the French! And there? ...' Pierre indicated a mound on the left, near which some troops could be seen.

'Those are ours.'

'Ours, are they? And over there? ...' Pierre waved his hand in the direction of another knoll in the distance, with a big tree on it, not far from a village that lay in a hollow where more camp-fires were smoking and something black was visible.

'That's *his* too,' said the officer. (It was the Shevardino Redoubt.) 'It was ours yesterday, but now it's *his*.'

'Then how about our position?'

'Our position?' replied the officer with a smile of satisfaction. 'I can tell you all about that because I had to do with the construction of practically all our entrenchments. There, do you see – that's our centre, at Borodino, just over there,' and he pointed to the village with the white church directly in front of them. 'There's where we cross the Kolocha. You see down there where the rows of hay are lying in the hollow – that's the bridge. That is our centre. Our right flank is over yonder' – he pointed sharply to the right, far away in the broken ground. 'That's where the river Moskva is, and we have thrown up three redoubts there, very strong ones. Our left flank ...' here the officer paused. 'Well, this is a bit difficult to explain. ... Yesterday our left flank was there at Shevardino – look, where that oak is – but now we have withdrawn our left wing. Now it's over there – do you see that village and the smoke? That's Semeonovsk, yes, there,' he pointed to Raevsky's Redoubt. 'But the battle will hardly be there. *His* having moved his troops there is only a blind. *He* will probably pass round to the right of the Moskva. However, at all events there'll be a lot of us missing at roll-call tomorrow!' he ended.

An elderly sergeant who came up during the officer's speech had waited in silence for him to finish speaking, but at this point, evidently not liking the last remark, he interrupted him.

'We must fetch up some gabions,' he said severely.

The officer looked disconcerted, as though he realized that though one might think of how many men would be missing next day one ought not to talk about it.

'Very well, send No. 3 Company again,' he replied hurriedly. 'And who are you? Are you one of the doctors?'

'No, I was just having a look round on my own,' answered Pierre, and he descended the hill again, passing the peasant militiamen.

'Oh, those damned fellows!' muttered the officer, who followed him holding his nose as he hurried past the men at work.

'Here they come! … They've got her. … There they are. … They'll be here in a minute …' voices were suddenly heard saying; and officers, soldiers and militiamen began running forward along the road.

A church procession was coming up the hill from Borodino. First along the dusty road marched a company of infantry with their shakos off and trailing arms. From behind them came the sound of chanting.

Soldiers and militiamen ran bareheaded past Pierre to meet the procession.

'They are bringing her, our Holy Mother, our Protectress! … The Iberian icon of the Mother of God!'

'The Holy Mother of Smolensk! …' someone corrected.

The militiamen, both those who had been in the village and those who had been at work on the battery, threw down their spades and ran to meet the procession. Behind the battalion which came marching along the dusty road walked the priests in their vestments – one little old man in a hood – with attendant deacons and choristers. Behind them soldiers and officers bore a huge icon with a blackened face and silver mountings. This was the icon that had been brought away from Smolensk and had since accompanied the army. Behind, before

906

and all around walked or ran crowds of soldiers with bared heads, making obeisances to the very ground.

At the top of the hill the procession stopped. The men who had been holding the icon aloft by the linen bands attached to it were relieved by others, the chanters relit their censers and the service began. The scorching rays of the sun beat down vertically; a faint fresh breeze played with the hair on bared heads and fluttered the ribbons trimming the icon; the singing sounded subdued under the open sky. A huge bare-headed crowd of officers, soldiers and militiamen stood round the icon. In a space apart, behind the priest and a chanter, were gathered the personages of rank. A bald general with the order of St George hanging from his neck stood directly at the priest's back, and not crossing himself (he was evidently a German) patiently waited for the end of the service, which he thought it necessary to listen to, probably so as to arouse the patriotism of the Russian people. Another general stood in a martial pose, looking about him and making swift little signs of the cross in front of his chest. Standing among the crowd of peasants, Pierre recognized several persons he knew in the circle of officials, but he did not look at them – his whole attention was absorbed in watching the serious expression on the faces of the throng of soldiers and militiamen, who were all gazing raptly at the icon. As soon as the weary chanters, who were singing the service for the twentieth time that day, began languidly and mechanically to sing: 'O Mother of God, save thy servants from all adversities,' and the priest and deacon came in with: 'For to thee under God every man doth flee as to a steadfast bulwark and defence,' all those faces were fired with the same consciousness of the solemnity of the approaching moment which Pierre had seen on the faces at the foot of the hill at Mozhaisk, and by fits and starts on many faces he had met that morning. And heads were bowed more frequently and hair tossed back, and there was the sound of sighing and beating the breast as men crossed themselves.

The crowd round the icon suddenly parted and pressed against Pierre. Someone, a very important personage to judge by the haste with which they made way for him, was going up to the icon.

It was Kutuzov, who had been reconnoitring the position and on his way back to Tatarinova had stopped to join in the service. Pierre recognized him at once by his peculiar figure, which distinguished him from everybody else.

In a long overcoat over his enormously stout, round-shouldered body, with his white head uncovered and his puffy face showing the white ball of the eye he had lost, Kutuzov advanced with his lunging, staggering gait into the ring and stopped behind the priest. He crossed himself with an accustomed movement, bent till he touched the ground with his hand, and sighing heavily bowed his grey head. Behind Kutuzov was Bennigsen and the suite. Despite the presence of the commander-in-chief, which drew the attention of all the superior officers, the militiamen and soldiers continued their prayers without looking at him.

When the service was over Kutuzov stepped up to the icon, dropped ponderously on his knees, touched the earth with his forehead, and then for a long time struggled to rise to his feet but he was too heavy and feeble. His grey head twitched with the effort. At last he got himself up, and naïvely thrusting out his lips as children do kissed the icon and again bowed and touched the ground with his hand. The other generals followed his example; then the officers, and after them the soldiers and militiamen, came up with excited faces, pushing each other and shoving breathlessly forward.

22

CAUGHT in the thick of the crowd and staggering in the crush, Pierre looked about him.

'Count – Count Bezuhov! How did you get here?' said a voice.

Pierre looked round. Boris Drubetskoy, brushing his knees with his hand (he had probably made them dusty kneeling before the icon like the others), came up to him smiling. Boris was elegantly attired, with just a suggestion of the wear and tear appropriate on active service. He wore a long coat, and like Kutuzov had a riding-whip slung across his shoulder.

Kutuzov, meanwhile, reached the village, where he seated himself in the shade of the nearest house, on a bench which one Cossack ran to fetch and another hastily covered with a rug. An immense and magnificent retinue surrounded the commander-in-chief.

The icon had gone farther on its way, accompanied by the throng. Pierre stopped some thirty paces from Kutuzov, talking to Boris, explaining his desire to be present at the battle and inspect the position.

'I tell you what you had better do,' said Boris. 'I will offer you the hospitality of the camp. You will see everything best from where Count Bennigsen is to be. I am in attendance on him, you know. I'll mention it to him. But if you would like to ride round the position, come along with us. We are just going to the left flank. And then when we get back, do spend the night with me and we'll arrange a game of cards. Of course you know Dmitri Sergeich? He lodges there,' and he pointed to the third house in Gorky.

'But I should have liked to see the right flank. I'm told it is very strong,' said Pierre. 'I should have liked to start from the Moskva river and ride round the whole position.'

'Well, that you can do later, but the great thing is – the left flank. ...'

'Oh yes. And where is Prince Bolkonsky's regiment? Can you point it out to me?' asked Pierre.

'Prince Andrei's? We shall pass it and I'll take you to him.'

'What were you saying about the left flank?' asked Pierre.

'To tell you the truth, between ourselves, there's no making out how things stand with our left flank,' said Boris, confidentially lowering his voice. 'Count Bennigsen intended something quite different. He meant to fortify that knoll over there, and not ... but' – Boris shrugged his shoulders – 'his Serene Highness would not hear of it, or else he was talked round. You see ...' But Boris did not finish, for at that moment, Kaisarov, Kutuzov's adjutant, came up to Pierre. 'Ah, Kaisarov,' said Boris with a free and easy smile, 'I was just trying to explain our position to the count. It is amazing how his Serene Highness was able to foresee the enemy's intentions so accurately!'

'You mean about the left flank?' asked Kaisarov.

'Yes, exactly. That left flank of ours is now extremely strong.'

Although Kutuzov had dismissed all superfluous personnel from the staff, Boris had contrived to remain at Headquarters after the changes. He had established himself with Count Bennigsen, who, like everyone on whom Boris had been in attendance, considered young Prince Drubetskoy invaluable.

In the higher command there were two sharply defined parties: Kutuzov's party and that of Bennigsen, the chief of staff. Boris belonged to the latter faction, and no one else was quite so skilful at insinuating – while at the same time showing servile respect to Kutuzov – that the old fellow was not much good and that it was Bennigsen who managed everything. Now the resolutive moment of battle had come which would mean either the downfall of Kutuzov and the transfer of power to Bennigsen, or if Kutuzov won the battle it could be made to seem that the credit was Bennigsen's. In either case many important rewards were bound to be distributed after the morrow's engagement, and new men would be brought to the fore. And all that day the anticipation of this put Boris in a state of nervous stimulation.

After Kaisarov, others of his acquaintance came up to Pierre, and he had not time to reply to all the questions about Moscow that were showered upon him, or to listen to all they had to tell him. Exhilaration and anxiety were written on every face. But it seemed to Pierre that the cause of the excitement which some of the faces betrayed could be traced more to preoccupation with their own individual advancement, and he could not help remembering the expression he had seen on other faces, which spoke of concern not with personal matters but with the universal questions of life and death. Kutuzov caught sight of Pierre's figure and the group gathered round him.

'Call him to me,' said Kutuzov.

An adjutant communicated his Serene Highness's message, and Pierre went towards the bench. But a militiaman was there before him. It was Dolohov.

'How did that fellow get here?' asked Pierre.

'Oh, he's such a sly dog, he pokes himself in everywhere!' was the answer. 'He was degraded to the ranks, you know. Now he wants to bob up again. He's been proposing some scheme or other, and at night goes crawling up to the enemy's picket line. ... There's no denying he's plucky!'

Pierre took off his hat and bowed respectfully to Kutuzov.

'I decided that if I laid the matter before your Highness, you would either dismiss me, or say you already knew what I had to tell you, and in that case I shouldn't be any the worse off ...' Dolohov was saying.

'Very true, very true.'

'But if I were right, I should be rendering a service to my Fatherland, for which I am ready to die.'

'Very true ... very true. ...'

'And should your Highness require a man who is not particular whether he keeps his skin whole or not, I beg you will remember me. ... Perhaps I might be of use to your Highness.'

'Very true ... very true,' Kutuzov repeated, looking with a laughing, narrowing eye at Pierre.

Meanwhile Boris, with the finesse of the courtier, stepped up to Pierre's side near Kutuzov, and in the most natural manner, without raising his voice, said to Pierre as though continuing an interrupted conversation:

'The militiamen have got themselves into clean white shirts to be ready to die. There's heroism for you, count!'

Boris said this to Pierre with the evident intention of being overheard by his Serene Highness. He knew Kutuzov's attention would be caught by those words, and so it was.

'What are you saying about the militiamen?' he asked Boris.

'They're preparing for tomorrow, your Highness – they've put on clean shirts to be ready for death.'

'Ah! ... A wonderful, unique people!' said Kutuzov, and closing his eyes he nodded his head. 'A unique people!' he repeated with a sigh.

'So you want to smell gunpowder?' he said to Pierre. 'Yes, it's a pleasant smell. I have the honour to be one of your wife's admirers. Is she well? My quarters are at your service.'

And, as old people often do, Kutuzov began looking abstractedly about him, as though forgetting all he wanted to say or do.

Then, apparently recollecting the object of his search, he beckoned to Andrei Sergeich Kaisarov, the brother of his adjutant.

'Those verses ... those verses of Marin's ... how do they go, eh? The lines he wrote about Geraktov: "To the corps, Preceptor shalt thou be ..." Recite them, recite them!' said he, relaxing his features in readiness to laugh.

Kaisarov recited the lines. ... Kutuzov smilingly nodded his head to the rhythm of the verses.

When Pierre left Kutuzov, Dolohov approached and took his hand.

'I am very glad to meet you here, count,' he said in a loud tone, disregarding the presence of strangers, and speaking with marked determination and solemnity. 'On the eve of a day which God alone knows who of us is fated to survive, I am glad to have the opportunity of telling you how sorry I am for the misunderstandings which existed between us, and I should like you to have no ill-feelings against me. I beg you to forgive me.'

Pierre looked at Dolohov with a smile, not knowing what to say to him. With tears in his eyes Dolohov embraced Pierre and kissed him.

Boris had said something to his general, and Count Bennigsen turned to Pierre and proposed that he should join him in a ride along the lines.

'You will find it interesting,' said he.

'Yes, indeed,' replied Pierre.

Half an hour later Kutuzov had left for Tatarinova, and Bennigsen and his suite, with Pierre among them, set out on their tour of inspection.

23

FROM Gorky, Bennigsen descended the high road to the bridge which the officer on the knoll had pointed out to Pierre as the centre of our position, and where rows of fragrant new-mown hay lay by the riverside. They crossed the bridge into the village of Borodino, then switched to the left and, passing immense numbers of men and guns, came to a high knoll where militiamen were digging. This was the redoubt, as yet unnamed, which afterwards became known as the Raevsky Redoubt or the Knoll-battery.

Pierre paid no special attention to this mound. He did not know that it was to be the most memorable spot for him on the whole plain of Borodino. Then they rode through the ravine to Semeonovsk, where soldiers were dragging away the last beams and timbers left to the huts and barns. After that they continued downhill and uphill, across a field of rye (trampled and laid flat as though by hail), along a track newly made by the artillery over the furrows of the ploughed land, until they reached some flèches, at which men were still at work.

Bennigsen drew up at the earthworks and began looking at the Shevardino Redoubt opposite (which had been ours the day before), where several horsemen could be descried. The officers said that either Napoleon or Murat was there, and all gazed eagerly at the little group of horsemen. Pierre too stared at them, trying to guess which of the scarcely discernible figures was Napoleon. At last the little band rode away from the mound and disappeared from sight.

Bennigsen, addressing a general who approached him, began explaining the whole position of our troops. Pierre listened, straining every faculty to grasp the essential points of the impending battle, but to his mortification he felt that his mental capacity was not equal to the task. He could make nothing of it. Bennigsen stopped speaking, and noticing that Pierre was listening, suddenly said to him:

'This doesn't interest you, I'm afraid?'

'Oh, on the contrary, it is most interesting!' replied Pierre, not quite truthfully.

From the flèches they rode still farther to the left, along a road which wound through a thick, low-growing birch-wood. In the middle of the wood a brown hare with white paws sprang out and, scared by the trampling of so many horses, grew so confused that it leapt along the road in front of them for a long while, exciting general attention and amusement, and only when several voices shouted at it did it dart to one side and vanish in the thicket. After about a mile and a half of woodland they came out on a clearing where troops of Tuchkov's corps were stationed to defend the left flank.

Here, at the very extremity of the left flank, Bennigsen talked a great deal and with much heat, and made, as it seemed to Pierre, dispositions of great military importance. In front of Tuchkov's forces was some high ground not occupied by troops. Bennigsen was loud in his criticism of this oversight, declaring that it was madness to leave a height which commanded the surrounding country unoccupied, and to be satisfied with placing troops below it. Several of the generals expressed the same opinion, one in particular maintained with martial heat that they were put there to be slaughtered. Bennigsen, on his own responsibility, ordered the corps to be moved to the height.

This disposition on the left flank made Pierre more than ever doubtful of his capacity to understand military matters. As he listened to Bennigsen and the other generals criticizing the position of the troops at the foot of the hill, he grasped their opinion perfectly and agreed with them; but for that very reason he could not imagine how the man who had placed them there on the low ground could have made so gross and palpable a blunder.

Pierre did not know that these troops were not, as Bennigsen supposed, put there to defend the position, but had been stationed in that concealed spot to lie in ambush, unobserved, and strike an approaching enemy without warning. Bennigsen did not know this, and moved the troops forward according to his own ideas, without saying anything about the change to the commander-in-chief.

24

On this bright evening of August the 25th Prince Andrei lay leaning on his elbow in a tumble-down shed in the village of Knyazkovo, at the farther end of the encampment of his regiment. Through a gap in the broken wall he could see, beside the wooden fence, a row of thirty-year-old birches with their lower branches lopped off, a field with shocks of oats lying about it, and some bushes near which rose the smoke of camp-fires – the soldiers' kitchens.

Narrow and burdensome and of no use to anyone as his life now seemed to Prince Andrei, he felt disturbed and irritable on the eve of action, just as he had done seven years before at Austerlitz.

He had received and issued the orders for next day's battle, and had nothing more to do. But his thoughts – the most straightforward, clearest and therefore most terrible thoughts – would give him no peace. He was aware that tomorrow's engagement would be the most dreadful of all he had taken part in, and for the first time in his life the possibility of death presented itself to him – not in relation to his earthly life, or to any consideration of the effect his death might have on others, but simply in relation to himself, to his own soul – and rose before him plainly and awfully with a vividness that made it seem almost a concrete reality. And from the height of this vision all that had hitherto tormented and preoccupied him suddenly became illumined by a cold white light, having no shadows, without perspective, without distinction of outline. His whole life appeared to him like a series of magic-lantern pictures which he had been staring at by artificial light through a glass. Now he suddenly saw those badly-daubed pictures, without the glass, in the clear light of day. 'Yes, yes! There they are, those lying images that agitated, enthralled and tormented me,' he said to himself, passing in review the principal pictures of the magic-lantern of his life and looking at them now in the cold white daylight of his clear perception of death. 'There they are, those rudely painted figures that once seemed splendid and mysterious. Honour and glory, the good of society, love for a woman, the Fatherland itself – what grand pictures they used to seem to me, with what profound meaning they seemed to be filled! And it is all so simple, so colourless and crude in the cold white light of the morning which I feel is dawning for me.' The three great sorrows of his life held his attention especially; his love for a woman, his father's death, and the French invasion which had overrun half Russia. 'Love! ... that little girl who seemed to me brimming over with mystic forces. How I loved her! I dreamed romantic dreams of love, of happiness with her! Oh, how naïve and callow I was!' he groaned aloud. 'Why, I believed in some ideal love which was to keep her faithful to me for the whole twelve months of my absence! Like the tender dove of the fable she was to pine away, parted from me! But it was all vastly more simple ... it was all horribly simple and loathsome!

'My father, too, laid out Bald Hills, and thought the place was his – that it was his land, his air, his peasants. But Napoleon came along and swept him aside, unconscious of his existence, as he might brush a chip of wood from his path, and his Bald Hills and his whole life fell to pieces. Princess Maria says that it is a trial sent from above. What is the trial for, since he is no more and never will be? He will never come back again! He is no more! So for whom is the trial intended? The Fatherland, the destruction of Moscow! And tomorrow I shall be killed, perhaps not even by a Frenchman but by one of our own side, by a soldier discharging a musket close to my ear, as one of them did yesterday; and the French will come along and take me by my head and my heels and pitch me into a hole that I may not stink under their noses; and life generally will go on under new conditions, just as natural in their turn as the old ones, and I shall not know about them, for I shall be no more.'

He gazed at the row of birch-trees with their motionless green and yellow foliage and the white bark, shining in the sun. 'To die ... to be killed tomorrow ... to be no more. ... That all this should still be, but no me. ...'

He pictured the world without himself. And the birches with their light and shade, the curly clouds and the smoke of the camp-fires – everything around him suddenly underwent a transformation into something sinister and threatening. A cold shiver ran down his spine. He started to his feet, went out of the shed and began walking up and down.

Returning indoors, he heard voices outside the shed.

'Who's there?' he called.

The red-nosed Captain Timohin, Dolohov's old squadron-commander but now from lack of officers promoted to the command of a battalion, shyly entered the shed, followed by an adjutant and the paymaster of the regiment.

Prince Andrei got up hurriedly, listened to the business they had come about, gave a few further instructions and was about to dismiss them when he heard a familiar, lisping voice outside the shed.

'Devil take it!' exclaimed this voice as its owner stumbled over something.

Prince Andrei looked out of the shed and saw Pierre, who had tripped and almost fallen flat over a pole lying on the ground. As a rule Prince Andrei disliked seeing people of his own set, and especially Pierre, who reminded him of all the painful moments of his last visit to Moscow.

'You? What a surprise!' he cried. 'What brings you here? I didn't expect to see you!'

As he said this his eyes and face expressed more than coldness – they expressed hostility, which Pierre noticed at once. He had approached the shed with the greatest eagerness but when he saw Prince Andrei's face he felt constrained and ill at ease.

'I came – well – you know – I came ... it was interesting to me,' stammered Pierre, who had so often that day stupidly repeated the word 'interesting'. 'I wanted to see the battle.'

'Oh yes, and what do your freemason brethren say about war? How would they prevent it?' said Prince Andrei ironically. 'Well, and how's Moscow? How are my folks? Have they got to Moscow at last?' he asked more seriously.

'Yes, they have. Julie Drubetskoy told me so. I went to call, but missed them. They had gone on to your estate near Moscow.'

25

THE officers would have retired but Prince Andrei, apparently reluctant to be left alone with his friend, invited them to stay and have tea. Benches were brought in, and tea. With some amazement the officers gazed at Pierre's huge, bulky figure, and listened to his talk of Moscow and the position of our army, round which he had ridden. Prince Andrei sat silent, and his expression was so forbidding that Pierre addressed himself chiefly to Timohin, the kindly battalion-commander.

'So you understand the whole disposition of our troops?' Prince Andrei interrupted him.

'Yes – that is, how do you mean?' said Pierre. 'Not being a military man I can't say I do fully; but still I understand the general arrangement.'

'Well, then, you know more than anyone else,' said Prince Andrei in French.

'Oh!' said Pierre incredulously, looking through his spectacles at Prince Andrei. 'Well, and what do you think of the appointment of Kutuzov?' he asked.

'I welcomed it. That is all I can say,' replied Prince Andrei.

'And tell me your opinion of Barclay de Tolly? In Moscow they are saying heaven knows what about him. ... What do you think of him?'

'Ask these gentlemen,' said Prince Andrei, indicating the officers.

Pierre looked at Timohin with the condescendingly doubtful smile with which everybody involuntarily addressed that officer.

'It was a gleam of *serene* light in the dark, your Excellency, when his *Serene* Highness took over,' said Timohin, stealing shy glances continually at his colonel.

'Why so?' asked Pierre.

'Well, to mention only firewood and fodder – let me tell you. You see, when we were retreating from Swiencíany we dared not touch a stick or a wisp of hay or anything. We were going away so *he* would get it all – wasn't that the way of it, your Excellency?' he said, turning to his prince. 'And woe to us if we so much as laid a finger on anything! In our regiment two officers were court-martialled for that sort of offence. Well, since his *Serene* Highness took command everything became perfectly straightforward. We see the matter *serene* as daylight. ...'

'Then why did the other forbid it?'

Timohin looked about in confusion, at a loss to know how and what to reply to such a question. Pierre turned to Prince Andrei with the same inquiry.

'Why, so as not to lay waste the country we were abandoning to the enemy,' said Prince Andrei with angry sarcasm. 'It's a sound principle: never allow pillage, never let your men get accustomed to marauding. Well now, at Smolensk, too, Barclay de Tolly was quite right when he argued that the French might outflank us, since they

917

outnumbered us. But he could not understand this,' cried Prince Andrei in shrill tones, as though he had suddenly lost control of his voice: 'he could not understand that for the first time we were fighting on Russian soil, that there was a spirit in the men such as I had never seen before, that we had held the French for two days and that that success had multiplied our strength tenfold. He ordered us to retreat, and all our efforts and losses went for nothing. Of course he did not mean to betray us, he tried to do everything for the best, he thought everything out beforehand; and that is why he is no good. He is no good at the present juncture just because he plans it all out in advance, very judiciously and accurately, as every German has to. How can I explain? ... Well, say your father has a German valet, and he's an excellent valet and satisfies your father's requirements better than you could, and all's well and good. But if your father is mortally ill you'll send away the valet and attend to your father with your own unpractised, awkward hands, and be more comfort to him than a skilled man who is a stranger could. That's what happened with Barclay de Tolly. While Russia was well, a foreigner could serve her and be a splendid minister; but so soon as she is in danger she needs one of her own kin. But in your club they go and make him out to be a traitor! The sole result of traducing him as a traitor will be that later on, ashamed of their false accusations, they will suddenly turn him into a hero or a genius, which would be still more unfair to him. He's an honest and conscientious German. ...'

'They say he's an able general, though,' remarked Pierre.

'I don't know what is meant by "an able general",' replied Prince Andrei ironically.

'An able general,' said Pierre, 'well, it's one who leaves nothing to chance ... who foresees the adversary's intentions.'

'But that's impossible,' cried Prince Andrei, as if this were a point that had been settled long ago.

Pierre looked at him in surprise.

'And yet,' he observed, 'don't they say war is like a game of chess?'

'Yes,' replied Prince Andrei, 'but with this little difference, that in chess you may think over each move as long as you please, taking your time, and with this further difference that a knight is always stronger than a pawn and two pawns are always stronger than one, while in war a battalion is sometimes stronger than a division and sometimes weaker than a company. The relative strength of opposing

918

armies can never be predicted. You may be quite sure,' he went on, 'that if things depended on arrangements made by the staff, I should be there helping to make those arrangements, but instead of that I have the honour to serve here in the regiment with these gentlemen, and I consider that the issue of tomorrow's engagement will rest with us rather than with them. ... Success never has and never will depend on position, or equipment, or even on numbers – least of all on position.'

'What does it depend on, then?'

'On the feeling that is in me and in him' – he pointed to Timohin, 'and in every soldier.'

Prince Andrei glanced at Timohin, who was staring at his colonel in alarm and bewilderment. In contrast to his former silent reserve Prince Andrei seemed excited now. Apparently he could not refrain from expressing the thoughts that had suddenly occurred to him.

'A battle is won by the side that has firmly resolved to win. Why did we lose the battle of Austerlitz? The number of French casualties was almost equal to ours, but very early in the day we said to ourselves that we were losing the battle, and we did lose it. And we said so because we had nothing to fight for then: we wanted to get away from the battlefield as soon as we could. "We're defeated, so let us run!" And we ran. If we had not said that till the evening, heaven knows what might not have happened. But tomorrow we shan't say that. You talk about our position, of the left flank being weak and the right flank too extended,' he went on. 'All that's nonsense. It doesn't come into it at all. But what awaits us tomorrow? A hundred million incalculable contingencies, which will be determined on the instant by whether they run or we do, whether this man or that man is killed; but all that is being done at this moment is mere pastime. The fact is, the people with whom you rode round inspecting the position not only do not help matters but are a positive hindrance. They are concerned with their own petty interests, and nothing else.'

'At such a moment?' said Pierre reproachfully.

'At such a moment,' repeated Prince Andrei. 'For them it is simply a propitious moment to oust a rival and win an extra cross or ribbon. To my mind tomorrow means this: a hundred thousand Russian and a hundred thousand French soldiers have met to fight, and the thing is that these two hundred thousand men will fight and the side that fights the more savagely and spares itself least will win. And if you like I will tell you that whatever happens, and whatever mess those at the top may make, we shall win tomorrow's battle. Tomorrow, happen what may, the day will be ours!'

'You are right there, your Excellency! That's the whole truth of it!' cut in Timohin. 'Who would spare himself now? The soldiers in my battalion, would you believe it, wouldn't touch their vodka! "It's not a time for that", they say.'

All were silent.

The officers rose. Prince Andrei went out of the shed with them, giving final orders to the adjutant. After the officers had gone Pierre moved nearer to Prince Andrei, and was about to start a conversation when they heard the clatter of three horses on the road not far from the shed, and looking in that direction Prince Andrei recognized Wolzogen and Clausewitz, accompanied by a Cossack. Still talking, they passed so close that Pierre and Prince Andrei could not help overhearing the following, in German:

'The war must be extended over a wider area. That is a conviction which I cannot advocate too highly,' one of them was saying.

'Oh, undoubtedly,' replied the other, 'since the aim is to wear out the enemy, one cannot, of course, take into account damage and injury suffered by private persons.'

'Certainly not,' confirmed the first voice.

'Oh yes, spread the war!' said Prince Andrei with an angry snort, when they had ridden by. 'In that "wider area" I had a father and a son and a sister at Bald Hills. He doesn't care about that. That's what I was just saying to you – those German gentlemen won't win the battle tomorrow, they will only make a mess of it, so far as they are able, because they have nothing in their German heads but theories not worth an empty egg-shell, while their hearts are void of the one thing that's needed for tomorrow, which Timohin has. They have handed all Europe over to *him*, and now they come here to teach us. Fine teachers, I must say!' and again his voice grew shrill.

'So you think that we shall win a victory tomorrow?' asked Pierre.

'Yes, yes,' answered Prince Andrei absently. 'One thing I would do if I had the power,' he began again. 'I would not take prisoners. What sense is there in taking prisoners? It's playing knights of old. The French have destroyed my home and are on their way to destroy Moscow; and they have outraged and are outraging me every moment. They are my enemies. In my opinion they are all criminals and that expresses the feeling of Timohin and the whole army with him. They must be put to death. Since they are my enemies, they cannot be my friends, whatever was said at Tilsit.'

'Oh yes,' murmured Pierre, looking with shining eyes at Prince Andrei. 'I entirely agree with you!'

The question that had worried Pierre on the Mozhaisk hill and all that day now seemed to him quite clear and fully solved. He now realized all the import and all the gravity of this war and the impending battle. All he had seen that day, all the significant, stern expressions on the faces he had seen in passing, appeared to him in a new light now. The latent heat (as they say in physics) of patriotism which was present in all these men he had seen was now intelligible to him, and explained the composure and almost light-heartedness with which they were all preparing for death.

'Not to take prisoners,' Prince Andrei continued. 'That by itself would transform the whole aspect of war and make it less cruel. As it is we have been playing at war – that's what's vile! We play at being magnanimous and all the rest of it. Such magnanimity and sensibility are like the magnanimity and sensibility of the lady who faints at the sight of a calf being killed: she is so tender-hearted that she can't look at blood – but fricassée of veal she will eat with gusto. They prate about the rules of warfare, of chivalry, of flags of truce and humanity to the wounded, and so on. All fiddle sticks. I saw chivalry and flags of truce in 1805: they humbugged us and we humbugged them. They plunder people's homes, circulate false paper money, and worst of all they kill our children and our fathers, and then talk of the rules of warfare and generosity to a fallen foe. No quarter, I say, but kill and be killed! Anyone who has reached this conclusion through the same suffering as I have ...'

Prince Andrei, who had believed it was a matter of indifference to him whether they took Moscow as they had taken Smolensk, was unexpectedly pulled up in his argument by a sudden cramp in his throat. He walked to and fro a few times in silence, but his eyes glittered feverishly and his lips quivered as he began to speak again.

'If there were none of this magnanimity business in warfare, we should never go to war, except for something worth facing certain death for, as now. Then there would not be wars because Paul Ivanich had given offence to Mihail Ivanich. And when there was a war, like this present one, it would be war! And then the spirit and determination of the fighting men would be something quite different. All these Westphalians and Hessians that Napoleon has dragged at his heels would never have come to Russia, and we should not have gone fighting in Austria and Prussia without knowing why. War is not a polite recreation but the vilest thing in life, and we ought to understand that and not play at war. Our attitude towards the fearful necessity of war ought to be stern and serious. It boils down to this: we should have done with humbug, and let war be war and not a game. Otherwise, war is a favourite pastime of the idle and frivolous ... there is no profession held in higher esteem than the military. And what is war? What makes for success in warfare? What are the morals of the military world? The aim and end of war is murder; the weapons employed in war are espionage, treachery and the encouragement of treachery, the ruining of a country, the plundering and robbing of its inhabitants for the maintenance of the army, and trickery and lying which all appear under the heading of the art of war. The military world is characterized by the absence of freedom – in other words, a rigorous discipline – enforced inactivity, ignorance, cruelty, debauchery and drunkenness. And yet this is the highest caste in society, respected by all. Every monarch in the world, except the Emperor of China, wears a military uniform, and bestows the greatest rewards on the man who kills the greatest number of his fellow-creatures. Tens of thousands of men meet – as they will tomorrow – to massacre one another: to kill and maim, and then they will offer up thanksgiving services for having slain such vast numbers (they even exaggerate the number) and proclaim a victory, supposing that the more men they have slaughtered the more credit to them. Think of God looking down and listening to them!' cried Prince Andrei in a shrill, piercing voice. 'Ah, my friend, life has become a burden to me of late. I see that I have begun to understand too much. And it doesn't do for man to taste of the tree of the knowledge of good and evil. ... Ah well, it's not for long!' he added. 'However, you're sleepy, and it's time I turned in, too. Get back to Gorky,' said Prince Andrei suddenly.

'Oh no!' Pierre replied, looking at Prince Andrei with eyes full of scared sympathy.

'Yes, you ought to be off: before a battle one needs a good night's rest,' repeated Prince Andrei. He went quickly up to Pierre and embraced and kissed him. 'Good-bye, be off with you!' he cried.

'Whether we meet again – no ...' and hastily turning away he entered the shed.

It was already dark, and Pierre could not make out whether the expression of Prince Andrei's face was angry or tender.

For some time he stood in silence, deliberating whether to follow him or go away. 'No, he does not want me!' Pierre decided, 'and I know that this is our last meeting!' He heaved a deep sigh and rode back to Gorky.

In the shed Prince Andrei stretched himself on a rug but he could not sleep.

He closed his eyes. One set of images succeeded another in his imagination. There was one picture on which he dwelt long and joyfully. It was an evening in Petersburg, and with an eager, excited face Natasha was telling him how she had gone to look for mushrooms the previous summer and had lost her way in the big forest. Incoherently she described the still depths of the forest, and her sensations, and her talk with a bee-keeper she met, and every minute she broke off to say: 'No, I can't, I'm not telling it properly; no, you won't understand,' although Prince Andrei tried to reassure and persuade her that he did understand, and he really had understood all she wanted to express. But Natasha had been dissatisfied with her own words – she felt that they did not give an idea of the passionately poetic feeling she had known that day and which she wanted to convey. 'He was such a delightful old man, and it was so dark in the forest ... and he had such a kind... No, I can't describe it,' she had said, flushed and agitated. Prince Andrei smiled now the same happy smile he had smiled then as he looked into her eyes. 'I understood her,' he thought. 'Not only did I understand her but it was just that inner, spiritual force, that sincerity, that ingenuousness – the very soul of her which seemed to be pinioned by her body – it was that soul I loved in her ... loved so intensely, so happily. ...' And suddenly he recalled what it was that had put an end to his love. '*He* cared nothing for all that. *He* did not see or understand anything of that kind. All he saw was a pretty, *fresh* young creature, with whom he did not deign to link his destiny. And I? ... And he is still alive and enjoying life!'

Prince Andrei jumped up as though he had been scalded, and began pacing to and fro in front of the shed again.

26

On the 25th of August, the eve of the battle of Borodino, M. de Beausset, prefect of the French Emperor's palace, and Colonel Fabvier arrived, the former from Paris and the latter from Madrid, at Napoleon's quarters at Valuevo.

Changing into court uniform, M. de Beausset ordered a box he had brought for the Emperor to be carried before him, and walked into the outer compartment of Napoleon's tent, where he busied himself in unpacking the box while conversing with Napoleon's aides-de-camp who crowded round him.

Fabvier remained at the entrance of the tent, talking to some generals of his acquaintance.

The Emperor Napoleon had not yet left his bedroom and was finishing his toilet. Uttering little snorts and grunts, he presented now his stout back, now his plump hairy chest to the flesh-brush with which a valet was rubbing him down. Another valet, with his finger over the mouth of a bottle, was sprinkling eau-de-Cologne on the Emperor's pampered person with an expression which seemed to say that he alone knew where and how much eau-de-Cologne should be applied. Napoleon's short hair was wet and matted on the forehead, but his face, though puffy and yellow, expressed physical satisfaction. 'Go on, harder, go on! ...' he said, slightly tensing himself and giving a grunt, to the valet who was rubbing him. An aide-de-camp, who had come into the bedroom to report the number of prisoners taken in the previous day's engagement, was standing at the door, having accomplished his errand, awaiting permission to withdraw. Napoleon, scowling, glared at the aide-de-camp under his brows.

'No prisoners!' said he, repeating the aide-de-camp's words. 'They are compelling us to annihilate them. So much the worse for the Russian army. ... Go on ... harder – put more energy into it!' he muttered, hunching his fat shoulders before the valet. 'All right. Show in Monsieur de Beausset, and Fabvier too,' he said, nodding to the aide-de-camp.

'Very good, sire,' and the aide-de-camp disappeared through the door of the tent.

The two valets quickly got his Majesty into the blue uniform of the Guards and he entered the reception-room with firm, swift steps.

Beausset meanwhile had been busily engaged in arranging the present he had brought from the Empress, on two chairs directly in front of the door the Emperor must come in by. But Napoleon had dressed and emerged with such unexpected promptness that he had not time to finish setting up the surprise.

Napoleon at once noticed what they were about and guessed they were not ready. He did not want to deprive them of the pleasure of preparing a surprise for him, so he pretended not to see Monsieur de Beausset and beckoned Fabvier to him. With a deep frown, and without speaking, Napoleon listened to what Fabvier was saying about the heroism and devotion of his army fighting before Salamanca, at the other end of Europe, and who had but one thought—to be worthy of their Emperor – and but one fear – to fail to please him. The result of that battle had been deplorable. Napoleon made ironic remarks during Fabvier's account, making it understood that he had not expected matters could go otherwise in his absence.

'I must make up for that in Moscow,' said Napoleon. 'I will see you later,' he added, and summoned de Beausset, who had by this time succeeded in preparing his effect, having placed some object on the chairs and covered it with a piece of drapery.

De Beausset made a courtier's low bow, such as only the old retainers of the Bourbons knew how to make, and stepped forward, presenting an envelope.

Napoleon turned to him gaily and pulled his ear.

'You have been quick, I am very glad to see you. Well, what is Paris saying?' he asked, his look of severity suddenly changing to one of friendliness.

'Sire, all Paris regrets your absence,' replied de Beausset, as was proper.

But though Napoleon knew de Beausset had to say this, or something of the kind, and though in his lucid moments he knew it was untrue, it pleased him to hear de Beausset say it. He honoured him with another touch on the ear.

'I am sorry to have given you such a long journey,' said he.

'Sire, I expected nothing less than to find you at the gates of Moscow,' replied de Beausset.

Napoleon smiled, and lifting his head absently looked round to the right. An aide-de-camp glided forward with a gold snuff-box and offered it. Napoleon took it.

'Yes, it has turned out luckily for you,' he said, lifting the open snuff-box to his nose. 'You are fond of travel, and in three days you will see Moscow. I am sure you did not expect to see the Asiatic capital. You will have a pleasant excursion.'

De Beausset bowed in gratitude at this regard for his taste for travel (of which he had not till then been aware).

'Ha, what have we here?' asked Napoleon, observing that all the suite kept glancing at something concealed under a cloth.

With courtly agility, not turning his back on his Sovereign, de Beausset retired two steps, swung half round and whipped off the covering, saying as he did so:

'A present to your Majesty from the Empress.'

It was a portrait, painted in vivid colours by Gérard, of the son born to Napoleon and the Austrian Emperor's daughter – the child whom for some reason everyone called the 'King of Rome'.

An exceedingly pretty curly-headed little boy with eyes like those of the Infant Christ in the Sistine Madonna was depicted playing stick and ball. The ball represented the terrestrial globe and the stick in his other hand was the sceptre.

Though it was not altogether clear what the artist had intended to express by painting the so-called King of Rome impaling the earth on a stick, the allegory apparently seemed to Napoleon, as it had to everyone who had seen it in Paris, perfectly intelligible and enchanting.

'The King of Rome!' he exclaimed, pointing to the portrait with a graceful gesture. 'Admirable!'

With the natural facility of an Italian for altering the expression of his face at will he approached the portrait and assumed a look of pensive tenderness. He felt that what he said and did at that moment would be history, and it occurred to him that the best line he could take now, when his great glory enabled his son to play stick and ball with the terrestrial globe, would be to display, in contrast to that grandeur, the simplest paternal affection. His eyes dimmed with emotion, he moved forward, looked round for a chair (a chair sprang up under him) and sat down in front of the painting. At a single gesture from him everyone withdrew on tiptoe, leaving the great man to himself and his sentiments.

Having sat for a little while and passed his fingers – he could not have said why – over the rough texture of the high lights, he got up and recalled de Beausset and the officer on duty. He commanded the portrait to be carried out in front of his tent, so that the Old Guard, stationed round about, might not be deprived of the happiness of seeing the King of Rome, the son and heir of their adored Monarch.

And as he anticipated, at breakfast, to which he had honoured M. de Beausset with an invitation, they heard the rapturous cries of the officers and men of the Old Guard who had run up to see the picture.

'*Vive l'Empereur! Vive le roi de Rome! Vive l'Empereur!*' came the ecstatic shouts.

After breakfast Napoleon, in Beausset's presence, dictated his order of the day to the army.

'Short and to the point!' he remarked, when he had read over the proclamation he had dictated straight off without corrections. It ran as follows:

Soldiers! The battle you have so longed for is at hand. Victory depends on you. It is essential for us; it will give us everything we need – comfortable quarters and a speedy return to our own country. Acquit yourselves as you acquitted yourselves at Austerlitz, Friedland, Vitebsk and Smolensk. Let posterity far down the ages recall with pride your achievements this day. May it be said of each man among you: 'He was in the great battle before Moscow!'

'Before Moscow!' repeated Napoleon, and inviting M. de Beausset, who was so fond of travel, to accompany him on his ride he went out of the tent to where the horses stood saddled.

'Your Majesty is too kind!' said Beausset in response to the invitation to accompany the Emperor: he wanted to sleep, he did not ride well and was afraid of horses.

But Napoleon nodded to the traveller and de Beausset was obliged to mount. When Napoleon came out of the tent the acclamations of the Guards before his son's portrait redoubled. Napoleon frowned.

'Take him away,' he said, pointing with a gracefully majestic gesture to the portrait. 'It is too early yet for him to look upon a field of battle.'

De Beausset lowered his eyelids and bent his head with a deep sigh, testifying thereby how profoundly he appreciated and comprehended the Emperor's words.

27

THE whole of that day of the 25th of August, so his historians tell us, Napoleon spent on horseback inspecting the locality, considering the plans submitted to him by his marshals and giving commands in person to his generals.

The original line of the Russian disposition along the river Kolocha had been dislocated by the capture of the Shevardino Redoubt on the 24th, and part of the line – the left flank – had been drawn farther back. That portion of the line was not entrenched, nor was it protected any longer by the river, and the ground in front was more open and level than elsewhere. It was evident to anyone, whether soldier or civilian, that it was here the French should attack. One would have thought that no great deliberation would be necessary to reach this conclusion, nor any particular care or trouble on the part of the Emperor and his marshal; nor would there be any need of that high degree of talent called genius, which people are so fond of attributing to Napoleon. Yet the historians who described the battle afterwards and the men who surrounded Napoleon at the time, and Napoleon himself, thought otherwise.

Napoleon rode over the plain, surveying the countryside with a sagacious air, wagging his head approvingly or dubiously to himself, and without communicating to the generals around him the profound chain of reasoning which guided him in his decisions conveyed to them merely the final conclusions in the form of commands. When Davoust, now styled Duke of Eckmühl, suggested turning the Russian left wing Napoleon replied, without explaining, that it would not be necessary. On the other hand to a proposal made by General Campan (who was to attack the flèches) to lead his division through the woods Napoleon signified his assent, although the so-called Duke of Elchingen (Ney) ventured to remark that moving through woodland was risky and might break up the formation of the division.

After examining the ground over against the Shevardino Redoubt Napoleon pondered a little in silence and then indicated two points where he wished batteries to be set up by the morrow to bombard the Russian entrenchments, and the positions where, in line with them, the field-artillery should be placed.

Having given these and other commands, he returned to his tent, and the dispositions for the battle were written down from his dictation.

These dispositions, of which French historians speak with rapture and other historians with deep respect, were as follows:

At daybreak the two new batteries established during the night on the plateau occupied by the Prince of Eckmühl will open fire on the two opposing batteries of the enemy.

At the same time the commander of the artillery of the 1st Corps, General Pernetti, with thirty cannon of Campan's division and all the howitzers of Dessaix's and Friant's division will move forward, open fire and shower shells on the enemy's battery, which will thus have in action against it:

24 guns of the artillery of the Guards
30 guns of Campan's division
 8 guns of Friant's and Dessaix's division
—

a total of 62 guns.

The commander of the artillery of the 3rd Corps, General Fouché, will place the howitzers of the 3rd and 8th Corps, sixteen in all, on the flanks of the battery that is to shell the entrenchment on the left, thus giving this battery an effective of some 40 pieces.

General Sorbier is to be in readiness to advance, at the first word of command, with all the howitzers of the Guards' artillery against one or other of the entrenchments.

During the cannonade Prince Poniatowski is to advance through the wood on the village and turn the enemy's position.

General Campan will move through the wood to seize the first fortification.

With the action fairly started on these lines subsequent commands will be issued in accordance with the enemy's movements.

The cannonade on the left flank will begin as soon as the guns of the right wing are heard. The sharpshooters of Morand's division and of the Viceroy's division will open a heavy fire the moment they see that the attack on the right wing has begun.

The Viceroy will occupy the village* and debouch by its three bridges, keeping on a level with Morand's and Gérard's divisions, which under his leadership will march on the redoubt and come into line with the rest of the forces of the army.

* Borodino.

929

All this must be done in good order (*le tout se fera avec ordre et méthode*), taking care to keep troops in reserve so far as possible.

The Imperial Camp near Mozhaisk,
6th September, 1812.*

These dispositions – which are seen to be exceedingly obscure and confused if one ventures to discard superstitious awe for Napoleon's genius and analyse them – contain four points, four different orders, not one of which could be, or was, carried out.

In the dispositions it is said, first, *that the batteries placed on the spot selected by Napoleon, with the guns of Pernetti and Fouché which were to come in line with them, in all 102 cannons, were to open fire and shell the Russian flèches and redoubts.* This could not be done, since from the spots chosen by Napoleon the projectiles did not carry to the Russian works; and those 102 guns shot into the air until the nearest commander, contrary to Napoleon's instructions, moved them forward.

The second instruction given was that *Poniatowski, advancing to the village through the wood, should turn the Russian left flank.* This could not be done, and was not done, because Poniatowski, advancing on the village through the wood, met Tuchkov there barring his way, and could not and did not turn the Russian position.

The third order was: *General Campan will move through the wood to seize the first fortification.* Campan's division did not seize the first fortification, but was driven back, for on emerging from the wood it was obliged to re-form under a hail of Russian grapeshot, of which Napoleon knew nothing.

The fourth instruction was that *the Viceroy will occupy the village (Borodino) and debouch by its three bridges, keeping on a level with Morand's and Gérard's divisions* (for whose movements no directions are given), *which under his leadership will march on the redoubt and come into line with the rest of the forces.*

As far as one can make out – not so much from the unintelligible phraseology as from the Viceroy's attempts to execute the orders he received – it seemed he was to move through Borodino from the left to the redoubt, while the divisions of Morand and Gérard were to advance simultaneously from the front.

All this, like the other paragraphs of the disposition, was impossible to carry out. After getting through Borodino the Viceroy was driven

* The date of the French proclamation is new style, corresponding to August 25th, old style. – *Tr.*

back to the Kolocha and could advance no farther; while the divisions of Morand and Gérard did not take the redoubt but were beaten off, and the redoubt was only taken at the end of the battle by the cavalry (a thing probably unforeseen and not heard of by Napoleon). So not one of the orders in the disposition was, or could be, executed. But the disposition stated that *after the action has begun on these lines subsequent commands will be issued in accordance with the enemy's movements*, and therefore it might be inferred that Napoleon would take all necessary measures during the progress of the engagement. But this was not, and could not be, the case because during the whole battle Napoleon was so far from the scene of action that (as it appeared later) the course of the battle could not have been known to him, and not a single instruction given by him during the fight could be executed.

28

MANY historians contend that the French failed at Borodino because Napoleon had a cold in the head, and that if it had not been for this cold the orders he gave before and during the battle would have been still more full of genius, and Russia would have been annihilated and the face of the world would have been changed. To historians who believe that Russia was shaped by the will of one man – Peter the Great – and that France was transformed from a republic into an empire and French armies marched into Russia at the will of one man Napoleon – the argument that Russia remained a power because Napoleon had a bad cold on the 26th of August may seem logical and convincing.

If it had depended on Napoleon's will whether to fight or not to fight the battle of Borodino, or had it depended on his will whether he gave this order or that, it is evident that a cold affecting the functioning of his will might have saved Russia, and consequently the valet who forgot to bring Napoleon his waterproof boots on the 24th would be the saviour of Russia. On that method of reasoning such a corollary is irrefutable, as irrefutable as Voltaire's verdict pronounced in jest (he did not realize what he was jesting about) that the Massacre of St Bartholomew was due to Charles IX's dyspepsia. But for minds which cannot admit that Russia was fashioned by the will of one man, Peter I, or that the French Empire was created and the war with Russia begun by the will of one man, Napoleon, such reasoning will seem not merely unsound and preposterous but contrary to the whole nature of human reality. The question, What causes historic events? will suggest another answer, namely, that the course of earthly happenings is predetermined from on high, and depends on the combined volition of all who participate in those events, and that the influence of a Napoleon on the course of those events is purely superficial and imaginary.

Strange as the proposition may seem at first sight that the Night of St Bartholomew, for which Charles IX gave the order, was not the outcome of his will, and that he only thought he had decreed it; or that the slaughter of eighty thousand men at Borodino was not due to Napoleon's will (though he gave the orders for the opening stages and the general conduct of the battle), and that he only fancied it was his doing – strange as this proposition appears, yet human dignity, which tells me that each one of us is, if not more, at least not less a man than the great Napoleon, demands the acceptance of this interpretation of the question, and historical research abundantly confirms it.

At the battle of Borodino Napoleon did not fire a shot nor kill anyone. All that was done by the soldiers. Therefore he did not do any killing himself.

The soldiers of the French army went out to slay Russian soldiers on the field of Borodino not because of Napoleon's orders but in answer to their own impulse. The whole army – French, Italians, Germans, Poles – famished, ragged and weary of the campaign, felt at the sight of an army barring the road to Moscow that the wine was drawn and must be drunk. Had Napoleon then forbidden them to fight the Russians they would have killed him and fought with the Russians because they had to.

When they heard Napoleon's proclamation offering them as compensation for crippling wounds and death the thought that posterity would say that they too had been in the battle before Moscow they shouted 'Vive l'Empereur!' just as they had cried 'Vive l'Empereur!' at the portrait of the little boy piercing the terrestrial globe with a toy stick, and just as they would have cried 'Vive l'Empereur!' to any absurdity that might be told them. There was nothing left for them to do but shout 'Vive l'Empereur!' and go into battle to get food and rest as conquerors in Moscow. So it was not because of Napoleon's commands that they killed their fellow-men.

And it was not Napoleon who ordained the course of the battle, for no part of his plan was executed and during the engagement he did not know what was going on before him. Therefore the way in which these men slaughtered one another was not decided by Napoleon's will but occurred independently of him, in accord with the will of the hundreds of thousands of individuals who took part in the common action. It *only seemed* to Napoleon that it was all happening because he willed it so. Hence the question whether Napoleon had or had not a cold in the head is of no more interest to history than whether the least of the transport soldiers had a cold or not.

Napoleon's cold on the 26th of August becomes of still less account in that the assertions made by various writers – that because of this cold his dispositions before, and orders during, the battle were not as skilful as on previous occasions – are completely wrong.

The dispositions cited above are by no means inferior, are indeed superior, to previous dispositions which had won him victories in the past. His supposed orders during the battle were also no worse than the commands he had given in the course of other actions, but were much the same as usual. But these dispositions and commands seem less fortunate only because the battle of Borodino was the first battle in which Napoleon was not victorious. The profoundest and most splendid dispositions and orders look wretched, and every military expert can criticize them with a consequential air, when they have not resulted in victory, and the feeblest dispositions and orders seem excellent, and learned people devote entire volumes to demonstrating their merits, when they relate to a battle that has been won.

The dispositions drawn up by Weierother at Austerlitz were a model of perfection of their kind but still they have been condemned – condemned for their very perfection, for their excessive minuteness.

Napoleon played his part as representative of authority quite as well at Borodino as at his other battles – perhaps better. He did nothing harmful to the progress of the battle; he inclined to the more reasonable opinions; he made no confusion, did not contradict himself, did not lose his head or run away from the field of battle, but with his sound judgement and great military experience calmly and with dignity performed his role of appearing to be in supreme control.

29

ON returning from a second careful inspection of the lines, Napoleon remarked:

'The chess-board is set, tomorrow we begin the game.'

Calling for some punch and summoning de Beausset, he began to talk to him about Paris, discussing various changes he intended to make in the Empress's household, and surprising the prefect by his memory for the minutest details relating to the Court.

He showed interest in trifles, joked about de Beausset's love of travel, and chatted carelessly, as a famous surgeon confident that he knows his job will often chat while he tucks up his sleeves and puts on his apron, and the patient is being strapped to the operating-table. 'I have the whole business at my finger-tips, and it's all clear and definite in my head. When the time comes to set to work I shall do it as no one else could, but now I can jest, and the more I jest and the cooler I am the more hopeful and reassured you ought to feel, and the more you may wonder at my genius.'

Having finished his second glass of punch, Napoleon went to rest before the serious business which, as he imagined, lay before him next day.

He was too much interested in the task that awaited him to sleep, and in spite of his cold, which had got worse with the evening damp, he got up at three o'clock in the morning and went into the other and larger division of the tent, noisily blowing his nose. He asked whether the Russians had not withdrawn. He was told that the enemy's lines were still in the same places. He nodded approval.

The adjutant on duty came into the tent.

'Well, Rapp, do you think we shall do good business today?' Napoleon asked him.

'Without doubt, sire,' answered Rapp.

Napoleon looked at him.

'Do you remember, sire, the remark you were pleased to make to me at Smolensk?' continued Rapp. 'The wine is drawn and must be drunk.'

Napoleon frowned, and sat for a long while in silence, his head resting on his hand.

'This poor army,' he said suddenly, 'it has greatly diminished since

Smolensk. Fortune is a fickle jade, Rapp. I have always said so and I am beginning to know it by experience. But the Guards, Rapp, the Guards are intact, are they not?' he inquired.

'Yes, sire,' replied Rapp.

Napoleon took a lozenge, put it in his mouth and glanced at his watch. He was not sleepy and it was still not nearly morning. There were no further orders to give for the sake of killing time, for they had all been given and were even now being executed.

'Have the biscuits and rice been served out to the regiments of the Guards?' asked Napoleon sternly.

'Yes, sire.'

'The rice too?'

Rapp replied that he had issued the Emperor's orders in regard to the rice, but Napoleon shook his head with a dissatisfied air, as though he doubted whether his instructions had been carried out. An attendant came in with punch. Napoleon called for another glass for Rapp and took a few sips from his own in silence.

'I have no taste or smell,' he remarked, sniffing at the glass. 'This cold is a nuisance. They talk about medicine – what is the good of medicine when they can't cure a cold! Corvisart gave me these lozenges but they do no good. What do the doctors know? They can't cure anything. Our body is a machine for living. That is what it is made for, and that is its nature. Leave life to take care of itself, and don't interfere: it will fight its own battles a great deal better than if you paralyse its powers by encumbering it with remedies. Our body is like a perfect watch meant to go for a certain time; the watchmaker cannot open it – he can only adjust it by fumbling his way blindfold. Yes, our body is a machine for living, that is all.'

And having as it were started making definitions, which he had a weakness for doing, Napoleon suddenly hazarded one on a fresh subject. 'Do you know, Rapp, what military art is?' he asked. 'It is the art of being stronger than the enemy at a given moment. *Voilà tout.*'

Rapp made no reply.

'Tomorrow we shall have Kutuzov to deal with!' said Napoleon. 'We shall see! Do you remember, at Braunau he was in command of an army for three weeks and never once mounted a horse to inspect his entrenchments? We shall see!'

He looked at his watch. It was still only four o'clock. He still had no desire for sleep, the punch was finished and there was still nothing to do. He got up, walked to and fro, put on a warm overcoat and a hat and went out of the tent. The night was dark and damp: one could almost hear the moisture falling. Nearby, the camp-fires of the French Guards burned dimly, and in the distance those of the Russian line glimmered through the smoke. All was still, and the rustle and tramp of the French troops already moving to take up their positions sounded distinctly.

Napoleon walked up and down in front of his tent, stared at the fires and listened to the stamping, and, as he was passing a tall guardsman in a shaggy cap who was on sentry duty before his tent and who had drawn himself up like a black pillar at sight of the Emperor, Napoleon stood still facing him.

'What year did you enter the Service?' he asked with that affectation of military bluntness and geniality with which he always addressed the soldiers.

The man answered.

'Ah, one of the veterans. Has your regiment had its rice?'

'It has, your Majesty.'

Napoleon nodded and walked away.

*

At half past five Napoleon rode to the village of Shevardino.

It was growing light, the sky was clearing, a single cloud lay in the east. The deserted camp-fires were burning themselves out in the pale light of the morning.

A solitary deep cannon-shot boomed out on the right, echoed and then died away in the prevailing silence. Several minutes passed. A second and a third report shook the air; a fourth and fifth boomed solemnly near by on the right.

The first shots had not ceased to reverberate before others rang out, and still others, mingling and overtaking one another in a continuous roar.

Napoleon and his suite made their way to the Shevardino Redoubt and there dismounted. Play had begun.

30

WHEN Pierre returned to Gorky after seeing Prince Andrei he directed his groom to get the horses ready and to call him early in the morning, and then immediately fell fast asleep behind a screen in the corner which Boris had given up to him.

Before Pierre was properly awake next morning there was not a soul left in the hut. The panes were rattling in the little windows. His groom was standing at his side shaking him.

'Your Excellency! Your Excellency! Your Excellency! ...' the groom kept repeating persistently while he shook Pierre by the shoulder without looking at him, having apparently lost hope of ever rousing him.

'Eh? Has it begun? Is it time?' Pierre asked, opening his eyes.

'Hark at the firing, sir,' said the groom, an old soldier. 'All the gentlemen have gone already, and his Serene Highness himself rode past long ago.'

Pierre dressed in haste and ran out into the porch. Outside it was bright, fresh, dewy and cheerful. The sun, just bursting forth from behind a cloud that had obscured it, splashed its rays through the rifts in the clouds, over the roofs of the street opposite, on the dew-besprinkled dust of the road, on to the walls of the houses, through the gaps in the wooden palings and on Pierre's horses standing before the hut. The roar of guns sounded more distinct in the open air. An adjutant accompanied by his Cossack passed by at a sharp trot.

'It's time, count, it's time!' called the adjutant.

Telling his groom to follow with a horse, Pierre walked down the street to the knoll from which he had surveyed the field of battle the day before. A crowd of military was collected there, the staff-officers could be heard talking French, and Pierre saw Kutuzov's grey head in a white cap with the red band, the grey nape of his neck sunk between his shoulders. Kutuzov was looking through a field-glass along the high road before him.

As he mounted the steps to the knoll Pierre glanced at the scene spread beneath his eyes and was spell-bound at the beauty of it. It was the same panorama which he had admired from the mound the day before, but now the whole prospect swarmed with troops, smoke-clouds from the guns hung overhead and the slanting rays of the bright sun, rising slightly to the left behind Pierre, filled the clear morning air with rosy golden light and long dark shadows. The distant forest which bound the horizon might have been carved out of some greeny-yellow precious stone, its undulating outline being pierced beyond Valuevo by the Smolensk high road thick with troops.

In the foreground glittered golden cornfields and copses. Everywhere, to right, to left and in front were soldiers. The whole scene was animated, majestic and unexpected; but what struck Pierre most of all was the view of the battlefield itself, of Borodino and the hollows on both sides of the Kolocha.

Over the Kolocha, over Borodino and on both sides of it, especially to the left where the Volna flowing through marshy ground falls into the Kolocha, a mist had spread, melting, parting, shimmering with light in the brilliant sunshine, magically colouring and outlining everything. The smoke of the guns mingled with this mist, and over the whole landscape, through the mist and smoke, sparkled the morning sun, gleaming on the water, on the dew, on the bayonets of the infantry congregated along the river banks and in Borodino. Through this transparent veil could be seen the white church, and here and there a cottage roof in Borodino, or thick clumps of soldiers, green ammunition-chests or cannon. And the whole scene moved, or seemed to move, as the mist and smoke trailed over the wide plain. Just as the mist wreathed about the hollows of Borodino, so beyond and above, and in particular farther to the left, along the entire line, over the woods, over the fields, in the valleys, on the ridges of the high ground curling clouds of powder-smoke continually formed out of nothing, here a solitary puff, now a bevy together, at longer intervals or in quick succession, swelling, thickening, swirling round, merging and fading away.

These puffs of smoke and the reports that accompanied them were, strange to say, what gave the chief beauty to the spectacle.

'*Pooff!*' – suddenly a round compact ball of smoke flew up, turning from violet to grey to a milky-white, and '*boom!*' followed the report a second later.

'*Pooff-pooff!*' – and two clouds rose up, pushing one another and merging together; and '*boom-boom!*' came the sounds confirming what the eye had seen.

Pierre glanced over at the first puff of smoke which an instant before had been a round compact ball, and in its place he saw balloons of smoke drifting sideways, and *pooff* ... (a pause) *pooff-pooff* rose three others, then four more, each one answered at the same interval by a beautiful, firm, precise *boom* ... *boom-boom-boom*. Sometimes the smoke-clouds seemed to scud across the sky, sometimes they hung still while woods, fields and glittering bayonets ran past them. From the left, over fields and bushes, these great balls of smoke were constantly rising, followed by their solemn reports, while nearer still, over the lowlands and the woods, burst little cloudlets of musket-smoke which had no time to form into balls but had their little echoes in just the same way. '*Trak-ta-ta-tak!*' crackled the musketry, but it sounded thin and irregular in comparison with the roar of artillery.

Pierre longed to be there in the midst of the smoke, the glittering bayonets, the cannon, the movement and the noise. He looked round at Kutuzov and his suite, to compare his impressions with those of others. They were all gazing at the field of battle, as he had done, and, he fancied, with the same feelings. Every face now shone with that *latent heat* of excitement which Pierre had noticed the day before and understood perfectly after his talk with Prince Andrei.

'Go, my dear fellow, go ... and Christ be with you!' Kutuzov was saying to a general standing beside him, but he kept his eyes fixed on the battlefield.

Having got this order, the general went past Pierre on his way down the knoll.

'To the crossing!' replied the general coldly and sternly, in reply to one of the staff who asked where he was going.

'So will I, I'll go there too,' thought Pierre, and followed in the same direction.

The general mounted a horse which his Cossack led forward. Pierre went to his groom who was holding the horses. Asking which was the quietest, Pierre clambered up, clutched at the horse's mane, pressed his heels into the animal's belly and, feeling that his spectacles were slipping but unable to let go of the mane and the reins, he galloped after the general, causing the staff-officers to smile as they watched from the knoll.

31

AT the bottom of the hill the general after whom Pierre was galloping turned sharply to the left, and Pierre, losing sight of him, rode into the back of some ranks of infantry marching ahead of him. He tried to pass either to the right of them or to the left; but there were soldiers everywhere, all with the same preoccupied expression, intent on some mysterious but evidently important matter. They all cast the same annoyed look of inquiry at this stout man in the white hat who for some unknown reason was trampling them under his horse's hooves.

'What do you want to ride into the middle of a battalion for?' one man shouted at him.

Another gave the horse a prod with the butt-end of a musket and Pierre, leaning over his saddle-bow and scarcely able to control the plunging animal, galloped ahead of the soldiers to where it was more open.

In front of him he saw a bridge and other soldiers stood there firing. Pierre rode up to them. Though he was unaware of it, he had come to the bridge over the Kolocha between Gorky and Borodino, which the French (having occupied Borodino) were attacking in the first phase of the battle. Pierre saw there was a bridge in front of him and that soldiers were doing something in the smoke on both sides of it and in the meadow, among the rows of new-mown hay he had noticed the day before; but despite the incessant firing going on there it never occurred to him that this was the very heart of the battle. He did not hear the bullets whistling from every side, or the projectiles flying over his head, did not see the enemy on the other side of the river, and it was a long time before he saw the dead and wounded, though many fell not far from him. With a smile that did not leave his lips he gazed about him.

'What's that fellow doing in front of the line?' somebody shouted at him again.

'To the left!' ... 'Keep to the right!' the men called to him.

Pierre went to the right and unexpectedly encountered one of General Raevsky's adjutants whom he knew. The adjutant looked furiously at him, evidently also intending to shout at him, but recognizing him he nodded.

'How did you come here?' he said, and galloped on.

Feeling out of place and useless there, and afraid of getting in the way again, Pierre galloped after the adjutant.

'What's happening here? May I come with you?' he asked.

'Just a moment, just a moment!' replied the adjutant, and riding up to a stout colonel who was standing in the meadow he gave him some message, and then turned to Pierre.

'What brings you here, count?' he asked with a smile. 'Still curious, are you?'

'Yes, yes,' said Pierre.

But the adjutant wheeled his horse about and rode on.

'Here it's tolerable,' remarked the adjutant, 'but on the left flank where Bagration is they're getting it frightfully hot.'

'Really?' said Pierre. 'Where is that?'

'Come along with me to our knoll. We can get a view from there, and it's not too bad with our battery,' said the adjutant. 'Will you come?'

'After you,' replied Pierre, looking round for his groom.

It was only then for the first time that Pierre noticed the wounded, staggering along or being carried on stretchers. In the very meadow with the rows of fragrant hay through which he had ridden the day before the motionless form of a soldier was lying crosswise, his head thrown awkwardly back and his shako off.

'Why have they left that poor fellow?' Pierre was about to ask, but seeing the adjutant's stern face looking in the same direction he checked himself.

Pierre did not find his groom and rode along the hollow with the adjutant towards Raevsky's Redoubt. His horse lagged behind the adjutant's and jolted him at every step.

'You're not used to riding, count, I fancy?' remarked the adjutant.

'No, it's not that, but her action seems so jerky,' said Pierre in a perplexed tone.

'Why ... she's wounded!' cried the adjutant. 'The off foreleg above the knee. A bullet, no doubt. Congratulations, count, on your baptism of fire!'

Making their way in the smoke past the 6th Corps, behind the artillery which had been moved forward and was keeping up a deafening cannonade, they came to a small wood. There it was cool and quiet and smelt of autumn. Pierre and the adjutant got off their horses and walked up the hill on foot.

'Is the general here?' asked the adjutant, on reaching the redoubt.

'He was here a minute ago – he went that way,' someone answered, pointing to the right.

The adjutant looked round at Pierre as if puzzled to know what to do with him now.

'Don't trouble about me,' said Pierre. 'I'll go up on the mound if I may?'

'Yes, do. You'll see everything from there and it's not so dangerous. And I'll come back for you.'

Pierre went up to the battery and the adjutant rode on. They did not meet again, and only much later did Pierre learn that he lost an arm that day.

The mound – afterwards known to the Russians as the Knoll-battery or Raevsky's Redoubt, and to the French as *la grande redoute, la fatale redoute, la redoute du centre* – was the famous spot around which tens of thousands fell and which the French regarded as the key to the whole position.

This redoubt consisted of a knoll, on three sides of which trenches had been dug. Within the entrenchment stood ten guns which fired through the gaps left in the earthwork.

In line with the knoll cannon were stationed on either side, and these too kept up an incessant fire. A little to the rear of the guns stood the infantry. Climbing the knoll, Pierre had no suspicions that this little space, dug with some not very big trenches and from which a few guns were firing, was the most important point of the battle.

He fancied indeed (simply because he happened to be there) that it was one of the least significant places in the field.

Having reached the knoll, Pierre sat down at one end of a trench which enclosed the battery, and gazed at what was happening around him, with an unconscious smile of happiness. Occasionally he rose to his feet and walked about the battery, still with the same smile, trying not to get in the way of the soldiers who were loading and hauling the guns and continually running past him with bags and charges. The guns of this battery never stopped firing, one after another, with a deafening roar, enveloping the whole neighbourhood in powder-smoke.

In contrast to the painful anxiety felt by the infantry soldiers of the covering force, here in the battery, where a limited number of gunners busy at their work were separated from the rest by a trench, there was a general feeling of eager excitement, a sort of family feeling shared by all alike.

At first the intrusion of Pierre's unmilitary figure in a white hat made an unpleasant impression. The soldiers cast sidelong glances of surprise and even alarm at him as they ran by. The senior artillery-officer, a tall, long-legged, pock-marked man, on the pretence of examining the action of the cannon at the far end, moved over to Pierre and stared at him inquisitively.

A boyish, round-faced little officer, still a mere lad and evidently only just out of the Cadet College, who was very diligently commanding the two guns entrusted to him, addressed Pierre sternly.

'Permit me to ask you to stand aside, sir,' he said. 'You cannot stay here.'

The soldiers shook their heads disapprovingly as they looked at Pierre. But when they satisfied themselves that this man in the white hat was not only doing no harm as he sat quietly on the slope of the trench, or with a shy courteous smile made way for the soldiers, but walked about the battery as calmly as though he were strolling along a boulevard, their feeling of hostile ill-will was gradually transformed into a playful tenderness like the affection soldiers feel for the dogs, cocks, goats and animals in general which share the fortunes of the regiment. The men soon accepted Pierre in their own minds as one of their family, adopted him, gave him a nickname ('our gentleman') and made kindly fun of him among themselves.

A shell tore up the earth a couple of paces from Pierre. Brushing off the dirt which the missile had scattered over his clothes, he glanced around him with a smile.

'How is it you baint feared, sir?' a red-faced, broad-shouldered soldier asked Pierre with a grin that disclosed a set of sound, white teeth.

'Are you afraid, then?' said Pierre.

'What else d'ye expect?' answered the soldier. 'She don't have no mercy, you know. Down she crashes and out fly your guts. A man can't help being feared,' he said, laughing.

Several of the soldiers stopped beside Pierre with amused, friendly faces. They somehow had not expected him to talk like anybody else, and the discovery that he did so delighted them.

'It's our job – we're soldiers. But it's a wonderful thing in a gentleman. There's a gentleman for you!'

'To your places!' cried the young officer to the men gathered round Pierre.

The young officer was evidently for the first or perhaps the second time on duty of this kind, and accordingly treated his superiors and the men with extravagant punctilio and formality.

The thunder of cannon and the rattle of musketry was growing fiercer all over the field, particularly on the left where Bagration's flèches were, but from where Pierre was hardly anything could be distinguished for the smoke. Moreover, his whole attention was taken up with watching the little family circle of men shut off from the rest of the world on the battery. His first unconscious delight in the sights and sounds of the battlefield had now given place to another feeling, especially since he had seen that soldier lying alone in the hayfield. Seated on the slope of the earthwork he observed the faces of those around him.

By ten o'clock a score of men had been carried away; a couple of cannon had been disabled and shells fell thicker and faster on the battery, while bullets hummed and whistled from out of the distance. But the men serving the battery did not seem to pay any heed: merry voices and joking were heard on all sides.

'Here's a beauty!' shouted a soldier as a grenade came hissing towards them.

'Not this way, my pretty – try the infantry!' added another with a chuckle as the shell flew across and fell among the ranks of the covering forces.

'Hallo! Bowing to a friend of yours?' laughed a third to a peasant who ducked as a cannon-ball sped past.

A few soldiers collected by the wall of the trench, trying to make out what was happening in front.

'They've drawn the line back, look. They've given way,' said they, pointing across the earthwork.

'Mind your own business,' an old sergeant shouted at them. 'If they've retired it's because there's work for them to do farther back.'

And taking one of the men by the shoulder the sergeant gave him a shove with his knee. They all laughed.

'Serve No. 5! Forward!' rang the command from the other end.

'Now then, a good pull, all together,' chorused the cheerful voices of the men shifting the cannon.

'That one nearly had our gentleman's hat off!' cried the red-faced humorist, showing his teeth and chaffing Pierre. 'Oh, you hussy!' he added reproachfully to a ball which hit a cannon-wheel and carried off a man's leg.

'Now, you foxes there!' laughed another to the militiamen who were creeping in and out among the guns after the wounded man. 'Don't care much for this gruel, do you? Oh, you crows! that pulls you up!' they shouted at the militiamen who stood hesitating before the soldier whose leg had been torn off.

'Oo ... oo ... lad,' they cried, mocking the peasants. 'They don't like it at all, they don't.'

Pierre noticed that every ball that hit the redoubt, every man that fell, increased the general elation.

The gleams of a hidden burning fire flashed like lightning from an approaching thunder-cloud, brighter and brighter, more and more often in the faces of all these men (as though in defiance of what was taking place).

Pierre did not look out at the battlefield and was not concerned to know what was happening there. He was entirely absorbed in the contemplation of that fire which blazed more fiercely with every moment, and which (so he felt) was flaming in his own soul too.

At ten o'clock the infantry that had been in the thickets and along the Kamenka streamlet in front of the battery retreated. From the battery they could be seen running back past it, bearing their wounded on their muskets. A general with his suite came on to the redoubt and after speaking to the colonel and giving Pierre an angry look went away again, having ordered the infantry supports behind the battery to lie down, so as to be less exposed to fire. Immediately after this, from the ranks of the infantry more to the right of the battery came the sound of a drum and shouts of command, and the men with the battery saw the ranks of infantry move forward.

Pierre looked over the breastworks. One face particularly caught his eye, belonging to a pale young officer who was walking backwards, letting his sword hang down and looking uneasily around.

The ranks of the infantry disappeared in the smoke but prolonged cheering and rapid musketry fire could still be heard. A few minutes later multitudes of wounded men and stretcher-bearers came back from that direction. Faster and faster the shells rained down on the battery. A number of casualties lay about unattended. The men round the cannon bustled more busily than ever. No one paid any attention to Pierre now. Once or twice he was furiously shouted at for being in the way. The senior officer strode with long swift steps from gun to gun, a scowl on his face. The officer-lad, his cheeks still more flushed, gave the men their orders more punctiliously than ever. The soldiers handed up the charges, turned, loaded and performed their work with strained smartness, giving little jumps as they walked, as though they were on springs.

The storm-cloud was close overhead, and the fire which Pierre had watched kindling flashed in every face. He was standing beside the commanding officer. The young little lieutenant, his hand to his shako, ran up to his superior.

'I have the honour to report, sir, that only eight rounds are left. Are we to continue firing?' he asked.

'Grapeshot!' the senior officer cried, looking over the wall of the trench without answering.

Suddenly something happened: the young officer gave a gasp and bending double collapsed sitting on the ground, like a bird shot on the wing. Everything went strange, confused and overcast before Pierre's eyes.

Cannon-ball after cannon-ball whistled by, striking the earthwork, the soldiers or a gun. Pierre, who had scarcely heard these sounds before, could now hear nothing else. On the right of the battery soldiers shouting 'Hurrah!' were running, not forward, it seemed to Pierre, but back.

A cannon-ball struck the very edge of the breastwork by which he was standing, sending earth flying; a black ball flashed before his eyes and at the same instant smacked into something. Some militiamen who were entering the battery ran back.

'All with grapeshot!' shouted the officer.

The sergeant hurried up to the officer and in a frightened whisper (like a butler informing his master at a dinner-party that there is no more of the wine he asked for), said that the charges were finished.

'The scoundrels! What are they about?' fulminated the officer, turning to Pierre.

The officer was perspiring and red in the face and his eyes glittered beneath the frowning brow.

'Run to the reserves and bring up the ammunition-boxes!' he yelled, angrily avoiding Pierre with his eyes and addressing the soldier.

'I'll go,' said Pierre.

Making no reply, the officer strode across to the other side.

'Cease firing. ... Wait!' he bellowed.

The man who had been ordered to go for ammunition stumbled against Pierre.

'Ah, sir, it's no place for you here,' he said, and ran down the slope.

Pierre hastened after him, steering away from the spot where the young officer was sitting.

One cannon-ball, a second and a third flew over him, hitting the ground in front, beside and behind him. Pierre ran down the slope.

'Where am I going?' he suddenly wondered just as he came up to the green ammunition-boxes. He halted irresolutely, uncertain whether to return or go on. Suddenly a fearful concussion flung him backwards to the ground. At the same instant he was dazzled by a great flash of flame, and a deafening roar, a hiss and crash set his ears ringing.

When he came to himself he was sitting on the ground leaning on his hands; the ammunition-box which had been beside him was gone – only a few charred green boards and rags littered the scorched grass – and a horse, dragging fragments of its shafts, galloped past, while another horse was lying, like Pierre, on the ground and screaming long and piercingly.

32

BESIDE himself with terror, Pierre jumped up and ran back to the battery as to the one refuge from the horrors encompassing him.

As he entered the earthwork he noticed that there was no sound of firing from the battery but that men were doing something there. He had no time to make out who these men were. He saw the senior officer leaning over the breastwork with his back to him, as if he were examining something below, and that one of the soldiers he had remarked before was struggling to tear free from some men who had got him by the arm, and crying 'Help! Help!' He also saw something else that was strange.

But he had not time to realize that the colonel had been killed, that the soldier shouting 'Help!' was a prisoner, and that another man had been bayonetted in the back before his eyes, for hardly had he set foot in the redoubt when a lean, sallow-faced, perspiring man in a blue uniform rushed on him sword in hand, shouting something. Instinctively guarding against the shock – as they had been running full tilt against each other without seeing – Pierre put out his hands and clutched the man (it was a French officer) by the shoulder with one hand and by the throat with the other. The officer, dropping his sword, seized Pierre by the collar.

For several seconds they gazed with startled eyes at one another's unfamiliar-looking faces, and both were bewildered at what they had done and what they were to do next. 'Am I taken prisoner or am I taking him prisoner?' each of them was wondering. But evidently the French officer was more inclined to believe that he had been taken prisoner because Pierre's powerful hand, impelled by instinctive fear, was tightening its grip on his throat. The Frenchman was about to say something when just above their heads a cannon-ball whistled, terrible and low, and it seemed to Pierre that the Frenchman's head had been torn off, so swiftly had he ducked it.

Pierre also ducked his head and let go with his hands. Giving no further thought to the question who had taken whom prisoner, the Frenchman ran back to the battery, while Pierre dashed downhill, stumbling over the dead and wounded, who it seemed to him were catching at his feet. But before he reached the foot of the knoll he was met by a dense crowd of Russian soldiers who, floundering, tripping up and cheering, were rushing in wild merriment towards the battery. (This was the charge for which Yermolov claimed the credit, declaring that it was only his gallantry and good fortune that made such a feat possible – the attack in which he is supposed to have flung on to the redoubt some St George Crosses he had in his pocket, for the first soldiers who got there.)

The French, who had captured the battery, fled. Our men shouting 'Hurrah!' pursued them so far beyond the guns that they were with difficulty called back.

The prisoners were brought down from the battery, among them a wounded French general whom the officers surrounded. Crowds of wounded, both Russians and French (Pierre recognized some of the Russians), walked or crawled or were carried on stretchers from the battery, their faces distorted with agony. Pierre went up on the knoll again where he had spent over an hour, and of that little family circle which had, as it were, adopted him, he found not one. There were many dead whom he did not know but some he recognized. The young officer was still sitting huddled up in a pool of blood at the edge of the earth wall. The red-faced soldier was still twitching convulsively, but they did not carry him away.

Pierre ran down the slope.

'They must surely leave off now. Now they will be horrified at what they have done!' he thought, aimlessly following in the wake of a procession of stretcher-bearers moving from the battlefield.

But behind the veil of smoke the sun still stood high, and in front, and especially on the left around Semeonovsk, a turmoil still seethed in the smoke, and the thunder of cannon and musketry, far from slackening, grew louder and more desperate, like a man who puts all his remaining strength into one final cry.

33

THE principal action of the battle of Borodino was fought on a seven-thousand-foot space between Borodino and Bagration's flèches. (Outside this radius the Russians had made a brief diversion in the middle of the day with Uvarov's cavalry, on the one side, and on the other, beyond Utitsa, there had been the skirmish between Poniatowski and Tuchkov; but these were isolated and relatively trifling episodes in comparison with what took place in the centre of the battlefield.) It was on the open tract of ground visible from both sides, between Borodino and the flèches beside the wood, that the real engagement was fought in the simplest and most artless manner imaginable.

The battle began with a cannonade from both sides of several hundred guns.

Then, when the whole field was shrouded in smoke, two divisions, Dessaix's and Campan's, advanced from the French right, while Murat's troops moved on Borodino from the left. It was about two-thirds of a mile from Bagration's flèches to the Shevardino Redoubt where Napoleon was standing; and nearly a mile and a half, as the crow flies, from Napoleon's post to Borodino, and therefore Napoleon could not see what was happening there, especially as the smoke mingling with the mist entirely hid that part of the plain. The soldiers of Dessaix's division advancing upon the flèches were visible only until they began to descend the ravine which separated them from the earthworks. As soon as they dropped into the hollow the smoke of the guns and musketry on the flèches grew so dense that it curtained off the whole of the farther slope. Now and then it was possible to catch a glimpse through the fog of some black object – probably men – or the glint of bayonets. But whether they were moving or stationary, whether they were French or Russian, was impossible to distinguish from the Shevardino Redoubt.

The sun had risen bright and its slanting rays shone full on Napoleon's face as, shading his eyes with his hand, he looked at the flèches. The smoke hung low before the flèches and sometimes it looked as if the smoke were stirring, at others as if the troops moved. Occasionally shouts were heard through the firing but there was no knowing what was being done there.

Napoleon, standing on the knoll, gazed through a field-glass, and in the tiny circlet of glass saw smoke and men, sometimes his own, sometimes Russians, but when he looked again with the naked eye he could not find what he had been looking at.

He descended the knoll and began to pace up and down in front of it.

Occasionally he paused to listen to the firing and strain his eyes towards the battlefield.

But not only was it impossible to make out what was happening from where he stood down below, or from the knoll above on which some of his generals had taken their stand, but even from the flèches themselves, where Russian and French soldiers now found themselves together or alternately – dead, wounded and alive, frightened or panic-stricken – it was impossible to make out what was taking place. For several hours in succession, amid incessant cannon- and musketry-fire, now only Russians were seen there, now only French, now infantry, now cavalry: they showed themselves, fell, fired, struggled hand to hand, not knowing what to do with one another, shouted and ran back again.

From the battlefield adjutants he had sent out and orderlies from his marshals were continually galloping up to Napoleon with reports of the progress of the action; but all these reports were deceptive, both because in the heat of the fray it was impossible to say what was happening at any given moment, and because many of the adjutants did not go to the actual place of conflict but simply repeated what they had heard from others; and also because while an adjutant was riding the couple of miles to Napoleon circumstances changed and the news he brought was already ceasing to be accurate. Thus an adjutant came galloping up from Murat with tidings that Borodino had been occupied and the bridge over the Kalocha was in the hands of the French. The adjutant asked whether Napoleon wished the troops to cross the bridge. Napoleon gave orders for the troops to form up on the farther side and wait. But before that command was given – almost as soon in fact as the adjutant had left Borodino – the bridge had been retaken by the Russians and burnt, in the very skirmish with which Pierre had got mixed up at the beginning of the day.

Another adjutant rushed up from the flèches with a pale and frightened face and reported to Napoleon that their attack had been repulsed, Campan wounded and Davoust killed; while in fact the entrenchments had been recaptured by other French troops (at the very time when the adjutant was told that the French had been driven back), and Davoust was alive and well except for slight bruising. On the basis of such inevitably untrustworthy reports Napoleon gave his orders, which had either been executed before he gave them, or else could not be, and never were, executed.

The marshals and generals who were closer to the scene of action but, like Napoleon, not actually taking part in the fighting and only occasionally went within bullet range made their own dispositions without referring to Napoleon, and themselves directed from where and in what direction to fire, and decided where the cavalry should gallop and the infantry should run. But even their orders, like Napoleon's, were seldom carried out, and then only partially. For the most part the opposite happened to what they enjoined. Soldiers ordered to advance fell back on meeting grape-shot; soldiers ordered to remain where they were, suddenly seeing an unexpected body of the enemy before them, would either turn tail or rush forward, and the cavalry dashed unbidden in pursuit of the flying Russians. In this way two cavalry regiments galloped through the Semeonovsk hollow and as soon as they reached the top of the incline faced about and bolted headlong back again. The infantry likewise often went flying about in directions quite contrary to those they had been told to take. All decisions as to where and when to bring up the guns, when to send infantry to fire or horsemen to ride down the Russian infantry – all such decisions were made by the officers on the spot nearest to the units concerned, without consulting Ney, Davoust or Murat, much less Napoleon. They had no fear of getting into trouble for not fulfilling orders or for acting on their own initiative, for in battle the issue at stake is man's most precious possession – his own life – and it sometimes seems that safety lies in running back, sometimes in running forward, and these men who were right in the thick of the fray acted in accordance with the temper of the moment. In reality, however, all these movements back and forth did not improve or affect the position of the troops. All their onslaughts on one another did little harm: the harm, the death and disablement was the work of the cannon-balls and bullets that were flying all about the open space where these men were floundering to and fro. As soon as they got out of range of the shot and the shell their superior officers located in the background promptly restored order and discipline, and under the influence of that discipline led them back to the zone of fire, where order fell victim to terror of death and a blind stampede in all directions.

34

NAPOLEON's generals – Davoust, Ney and Murat, who were near that region of fire and sometimes even entered it – more than once led huge masses of orderly troops that way. But, contrary to what had invariably happened in all their former battles, instead of the news they expected of the enemy's flight, these disciplined masses returned as disorganized, panic-stricken mobs. The generals re-formed them but their number was steadily dwindling. In the middle of the day Murat sent his adjutant to Napoleon to request reinforcements.

Napoleon was sitting at the foot of the knoll, drinking punch, when Murat's adjutant galloped up with the assurance that the Russians would be routed if his Majesty would let them have another division.

'Reinforcements?' exclaimed Napoleon in grim amazement, staring, as though failing to comprehend his words, at the handsome boyish adjutant who wore his black hair in floating curls (like Murat). 'Reinforcements,' thought Napoleon to himself. 'How can they require reinforcements when they already have half the army concentrated against one weak, unentrenched Russian wing?'

'Tell the King of Naples,' said Napoleon sternly, 'that it is not noon yet, and I do not yet see my chess-board clearly. Go. …'

The handsome young adjutant with the long hair sighed deeply, without removing his hand from his hat, and galloped back to the slaughter.

Napoleon got up and, summoning Caulaincourt and Berthier, began talking to them about matters unconnected with the battle.

In the midst of this conversation, which was beginning to interest Napoleon, Berthier's eyes were attracted to a general who was galloping towards the knoll on a lathering horse, followed by his suite. It was Belliard. Dismounting, he strode rapidly up to the Emperor and boldly, in a loud voice, started to explain the absolute necessity of reinforcements. He swore on his honour that the Russians were lost if the Emperor would release one more division.

Napoleon shrugged his shoulders and continued to pace up and down without answering. Belliard began to talk noisily and vehemently to the generals of the suite gathered round him.

'You are very fiery, Belliard,' said Napoleon, turning to the general again. 'It is easy to make a mistake in the heat of the battle. Go and have another look and then come back to me.'

Belliard had hardly disappeared before a fresh messenger from another part of the field galloped up.

'Well, what is it now ?' asked Napoleon in the tone of a man irritated at being continually disturbed.

'*Sire, le Prince* ...' began the adjutant.

'Wants reinforcements ?' said Napoleon with an angry gesture.

The adjutant bowed his head affirmatively and began to deliver his report, but the Emperor turned from him, took a couple of steps, stopped, came back and beckoned to Berthier.

'We must give them the reserves,' he said, with a slight upward gesture of his hands. 'Who do you think should go ?' he asked of Berthier ('that gosling I hatched into an eagle,' as he called him afterwards).

'Sire, send Claparède's division,' replied Berthier, who knew all the divisions, regiments and battalions by heart.

Napoleon nodded assent.

The adjutant galloped off to Claparède's division, and a few minutes later the Young Guards, who were drawn up behind the knoll, moved forward. Napoleon watched in silence.

'No !' he cried suddenly to Berthier. 'I can't send Claparède. Send Friant's division.'

Though there was no advantage of any kind in dispatching Friant's division rather than Claparède's, and even obvious inconvenience and delay now in recalling Claparède and sending Friant, the order was carried out to the letter. Napoleon did not observe that in relation to his army he played the part of the doctor, whose action in hindering the course of nature with his nostrums he so truly gauged and condemned.

Friant's division vanished like the rest into the smoke of the battle-field. From every side adjutants continued to arrive at a gallop, all with the same story to tell, as if they had conspired beforehand. They all asked for reinforcements, declaring that the Russians were standing firm and maintaining a hellish fire under which the French troops were melting away.

Napoleon sat on a camp-stool deep in thought.

Monsieur de Beausset, who was so fond of travelling and had eaten nothing that morning, came up to the Emperor and respectfully ventured to suggest lunch to his Majesty.

'I hope I may already congratulate your Majesty on a victory?' he said.

Napoleon shook his head. Monsieur de Beausset, supposing the negative referred to the assumed victory and not to lunch, took the liberty of remarking, in a half-jesting tone, that there could be no mortal reason for not having lunch when lunch was available.

'Go away ...' Napoleon jerked out morosely, and turned his back on him.

An Olympian smile of pity, regret and unction beamed on Monsieur de Beausset's face, and he glided away to the other generals.

Napoleon was in the grip of the depression which descends on the gambler who, after a long run of luck during which he recklessly flung his money about and won every time, suddenly finds, just when he has carefully calculated all the chances of the game, that the more he considers his play the more surely he loses.

His troops were the same, his generals the same, there had been the same preparations, the same dispositions, the same proclamation *court et énergique*, he himself was the same – he knew that and knew that he was vastly more experienced and skilful even than he had been before. The enemy too was the same as at Austerlitz and Friedland – yet the crushing weight of his arm fell impotent as though spellbound.

All the old methods that had invariably been crowned with success had already been employed. Today as usual he had concentrated his batteries on a single point, had thrown forward his reserves to break the enemy's line, had ordered a cavalry attack by 'the men of iron'; yet not only was there no victory but from all sides poured in the same tidings of generals killed and wounded, of reinforcements needed, of the impossibility of beating back the Russians, and of the disarray of his own troops.

Hitherto, after he had given two or three orders and uttered a couple of sentences, marshals and adjutants had come galloping up with congratulations and happy faces, announcing trophies in the shape of the capture of whole corps of prisoners, of sheaves of enemy eagles and standards, of cannon and stores, and Murat had begged leave only to loose the cavalry to gather in the baggage-trains. Thus it had been at Lodi, Marengo, Arcola, Jena, Austerlitz, Wagram and so on, and so on. But now something strange was happening to his armies.

Notwithstanding news of the capture of the flèches, Napoleon saw that things were not going the same way – not at all the same way – as they had in his other battles. He saw too that what he was feeling all the men about him, with their military experience, were feeling too. There was gloom on every face: each man avoided his neighbour's eye. Only de Beausset failed to grasp the import of what was happening. Napoleon, of course, with his extensive knowledge of war, well knew what it meant for the attacking side still not to be in sight of victory after straining every effort for eight hours on end. He knew that this was equivalent to defeat and that the least accident might now – at the critical point the battle had reached – involve him and his army in ruin.

When he ran his mind from the beginning over this strange Russian campaign, in which not a single victory had been won, in which not a flag, nor a cannon, nor an army corps had been captured in two months; when he looked at the underlying dejection in the faces round him and listened to reports of the Russians still holding their ground – a terrible nightmare feeling seized him, and all the ill-starred eventualities occurred to him that might seal his doom. The Russians might fall on his left wing, might break through his centre; he himself might be killed by a stray cannon-ball. All this was possible. In former battles he had only considered the chances of success, but now an infinite number of possible disasters presented themselves and he expected them all. Yes, it was like a dream in which a man imagines a murderer advancing to attack him. He raises his arm to strike his assailant a terrible blow which he knows should demolish him, and then feels his arm drop powerless and limp as a rag, and the horror of inevitable annihilation seizes him in his helplessness.

The news that the Russians were attacking the left flank of the French army filled Napoleon with just such horror. He sat in silence on a camp-stool below the knoll, with bowed head and elbows on his knees. Berthier approached and suggested that they should ride along the line to ascertain the position of affairs.

'What? What did you say?' asked Napoleon. 'Yes, tell them to bring my horse.'

He mounted and rode towards Semeonovsk.

In the slowly dispersing powder-smoke, over the whole plain through which Napoleon rode, horses and men were lying in pools of blood, singly or in heaps. Neither Napoleon nor any of his generals had ever before seen such a frightful sight or so many slain in so small an area. The roar of guns, that had not ceased for ten hours, wearied the ear and gave a peculiar character to the spectacle (like music accompanying *tableaux vivants*). Napoleon rode up to the high ground at Semeonovsk and through the haze he saw ranks of soldiers in uniforms of unfamiliar hues. They were the Russians.

The Russians stood in serried ranks behind Semeonovsk village and its mound, and their guns thundered unremittingly all along the line, filling the air with smoke. It was no longer a battle: it was a prolonged massacre, equally fruitless to the French and the Russians. Napoleon reined in his horse, and again sank into that brown study from which Berthier had roused him. He could not stop what was going on before and around him, and which he was supposed to be directing and which was apparently dependent on him, and for the first time, because of its ill success, the thing struck him as unnecessary and horrible.

One of the generals riding up to Napoleon ventured to offer to lead the Old Guard into action. Ney and Berthier, standing near Napoleon, exchanged looks and smiled contemptuously at so preposterous a suggestion.

Napoleon let his head sink on his breast and was long silent.

'At eight hundred leagues from France I am not going to have my Guard destroyed!' he said, and turning his horse, rode back to Shevardino.

35

KUTUZOV, his grey head bent and his heavy body slumped, was sitting on the same rug-covered bench where Pierre had seen him that morning. He issued no orders but simply gave or withheld his assent to what was proposed to him.

'Yes, yes, do so,' he would answer to the various proposals. 'Yes, yes, my dear boy, go and have a look,' he would say to this one or that of those about him; or, 'No, better not – better wait a little.' He listened to the dispatches that were brought him, and gave directions when his subordinates demanded that of him; but when listening to the dispatches he did not seem to be interested in the import of the words spoken but rather in something else – in the expression of the face and the tone of voice of those who were reporting. Long experience in war had taught him, and the wisdom of age had made him realize, that it was impossible for one man to direct hundreds of thousands of others waging a struggle with death, and he knew that the outcome of a battle is determined not by the dispositions of the commander-in-chief, nor the place where the troops are stationed, nor the number of cannon or the multitude of the slain, but by that intangible force called the spirit of the army, and he kept an eye on that force and guided it as far as lay within his power.

Kutuzov's general expression was one of concentrated, quiet attention. His face wore a strained look as if he found it difficult to master the fatigue suffered by his old and feeble frame.

At eleven o'clock they brought him news that the flèches captured by the French had been retaken but that Prince Bagration was wounded. Kutuzov groaned and shook his head.

'Ride over to Prince Bagration and find out the details,' he said to one of the adjutants, and then turned to the Duke of Württemberg, who was standing behind him.

'Would your Highness please take command of the 2nd Army?'

Soon after the duke's departure – before he could possibly have reached Semeonovsk – his adjutant came back with a message from him asking Kutuzov for more troops.

Kutuzov frowned and sent an order to Dokhturov to take over command of the 2nd Army, and a request to the duke – whom he said he could not spare at such a moment – to return to him. When news was brought that Murat had been taken prisoner, and the staff-officers congratulated him, Kutuzov smiled.

'Wait a little, gentlemen,' said he. 'The battle is ours, and there is nothing extraordinary in the capture of Murat. Still, we must not crow too soon.'

Nevertheless, he sent an adjutant to make the fact known to the troops.

When Shcherbinin came spurring up from the left flank with the report that the French had got possession of the flèches and the village of Semeonovsk, Kutuzov, judging by the sounds on the battlefield and by the look on Shcherbinin's face that he brought bad news, got up as though to stretch his legs and, taking Shcherbinin by the arm, led him to one side.

'Go, my dear fellow,' he said to Yermolov, 'and see whether something can't be done.'

Kutuzov was in Gorky, the centre of the Russian position. The assault directed by Napoleon against our left flank had been several times repulsed. In the centre the French had not got beyond Borodino, and on their left flank Uvarov's cavalry had put the enemy to flight.

Towards three o'clock the French attacks ceased. On the faces of all who came from the field of battle, and of those who stood around him, Kutuzov read an expression of extreme tension. He was satisfied with the day's success – a success exceeding his expectation – but the old man's strength was failing him. Several times his head sank forward, as though falling, and he dozed off. They brought him some dinner.

Adjutant-General Wolzogen, the man whom Prince Andrei had overheard saying the war 'must be extended over a wider area' as he rode by, and whom Bagration so detested, rode up while Kutuzov was at dinner. Wolzogen had come from Barclay de Tolly to report on the progress of affairs on the left flank. The sagacious Barclay de Tolly, seeing crowds of wounded men running back, and the rear ranks of the army in disorder, weighed all the circumstances, concluded that the battle was lost and sent his favourite officer to the commander-in-chief with this news.

Kutuzov was laboriously chewing roast chicken and he looked up at Wolzogen with narrowed, twinkling eyes.

Wolzogen, nonchalantly stretching his legs, approached Kutuzov with a half-contemptuous smile on his lips, scarcely touching the peak of his cap.

He behaved to his Serene Highness with a certain affectation of indifference intended to show that as a highly trained military man he left it to the Russians to make an idol of this useless old dotard but that *he* knew whom he was dealing with. '*Der alte Herr*' (the Germans among themselves always spoke of Kutuzov as 'the old gentleman') 'is taking things very easy,' thought Wolzogen, and glancing severely at the dishes set in front of Kutuzov he proceeded to report to 'the old gentleman' the position of affairs on the left flank as Barclay had told him to and as he himself had seen and interpreted it.

'All the points of our position are in the enemy's hands and they cannot be driven back because there are not the troops to do it; the men are running away and it is impossible to stop them,' he submitted.

Kutuzov ceased chewing and stared at Wolzogen in amazement, as though not comprehending what was said to him. Wolzogen, observing the effect produced on *der alte Herr*, said with a smile:

'I do not consider I should be justified in concealing from your Highness what I have seen. ... The troops are completely routed. ...'

'You have seen? You have seen? ...' shouted Kutuzov with a fierce frown, and rising quickly to his feet he went up to Wolzogen.

'How ... how dare you! ...' he shouted, choking and making a threatening gesture with his trembling arms. 'How dare you, sir, say that to *me*? You know nothing about it. Tell General Barclay from me that his information is wrong and that the real course of the battle is better known to me, the commander-in-chief, than to him.'

Wolzogen was about to make a rejoinder but Kutuzov interrupted him.

'The enemy has been repulsed on the left and defeated on the right flank. If you have seen amiss, sir, do not allow yourself to speak of what you do not know. Be so good as to return to General Barclay and inform him of my fixed intention to attack the enemy tomorrow,' said Kutuzov sternly.

All were silent and the only sound was the heavy breathing of the panting old commander-in-chief.

'They are repulsed everywhere, for which I thank God and our brave army. The enemy is defeated and tomorrow we shall drive him from the sacred soil of Russia,' said Kutuzov, crossing himself, and he suddenly ended with a sob as his eyes filled with tears.

Wolzogen, shrugging his shoulders and curling his lips, walked away in silence, marvelling at 'the old gentleman's conceited stupidity'.

'Ah, here he is, my hero!' said Kutuzov to a portly, handsome, black-haired general who at this moment approached the knoll.

This was Raevsky, who had spent the whole day at the most critical part of the field of Borodino.

Raevsky reported that the troops were standing their ground firmly and that the French were not venturing a further attack.

After hearing him, Kutuzov said in French:

'Then you do not think *like some others* that we must retreat?'

'On the contrary, your Highness, where the issue is undecided it is always the most stubborn who come out victorious,' replied Raevsky, 'and in my opinion ...'

'Kaisarov!' Kutuzov called to his adjutant. 'Sit down and write out the order of the day for tomorrow. And you,' he turned to another, 'ride along the line and announce that tomorrow we attack.'

While Kutuzov was talking to Raevksy and dictating the order of the day, Wolzogen returned from Barclay and announced that General Barclay de Tolly would be glad to have written confirmation of the order the field-marshal had given.

Kutuzov, without looking at Wolzogen, gave directions for the order to be written out which the former commander-in-chief very prudently desired to have to relieve himself of all responsibility.

And through the mysterious indefinable bond which maintains throughout an army one and the same temper, known as 'the spirit of the troops', and which constitutes the chief sinew of war, Kutuzov's words, his order for renewing the battle on the following day, immediately became known from one end of the army to the other.

The words – the exact form of the order – were by no means the same when they reached the farthest links in the chain. In fact there was not a syllable in the accounts passing from mouth to mouth at different ends of the lines that resembled what Kutuzov had actually said; but the drift of his words spread everywhere because what he had said was not the result of shrewd calculations but the outflow of a feeling that lay deep in the heart of the commander-in-chief and deep in the heart of every Russian.

And when they were told that tomorrow they were to attack the enemy, and from the highest quarters heard confirmation of what they wanted to believe, the exhausted, wavering men took comfort and courage again.

36

PRINCE ANDREI'S regiment was among the reserves which until after one o'clock were stationed inactive behind Semeonovsk, under heavy artillery fire. Towards two o'clock the regiment, having already lost more than two hundred men, was moved forward into a trampled oat-field in the gap between Semeonovsk and the Knoll-battery where thousands of men perished that day and on which an intense, concentrated fire from several hundred enemy guns was directed between one and two o'clock.

Without stirring an inch or firing a shot the regiment here lost another third of its effectives. In front, and especially on the right, the guns boomed amid perpetual smoke, and out of that mysterious domain of smoke which shrouded the whole space in front swift hissing cannon-balls and slow whistling shells flew unceasingly. Now and then, as if to allow them a respite, a quarter of an hour would pass during which the cannon-balls and shells all flew overhead, but at other times several men would be torn from the regiment in the course of a single minute, and the slain were continually being dragged away and the wounded carried off.

Each new explosion diminished the chances of life for the survivors. The regiment was drawn up in battalion-columns three hundred paces apart but, in spite of that, one and the same mood prevailed everywhere. All alike were taciturn and morose. At rare intervals talk was heard in the ranks but it was hushed at each thud of a successful shot followed by the cry of 'Stretchers!' Most of the time, by their officers' orders, the men sat on the ground. One, taking off his shako, carefully loosened the gathers of the lining and drew them tight again; another, crumbling some dry clay in his hands, polished his bayonet; another fingered the strap and altered the buckle of his bandolier; while still another carefully smoothed and rewound his leg-bands and pulled his boots on again. Some built little houses of the clods of the ploughed field, or plaited straws of stubble. All seemed entirely absorbed in their occupations. When anyone was killed or wounded, when the stretchers trailed by, when our troops were forced back, when the smoke opened a little and disclosed great masses of the enemy, no one paid any attention to these circumstances. But when our artillery or cavalry advanced, or some of our infantry were seen to move forward, approving remarks were heard on all sides. But quite extraneous incidents that had nothing to do with the battle were what attracted most notice; as though the minds of these mortally exhausted men found relief in the ordinary trifles of everyday life. A battery of artillery passed in front of the regiment. One of the horses of an ammunition-cart put its leg over a trace. 'Hey, look at that trace-horse! ... Get her leg out! She'll be down. ... Hey, haven't they any eyes?' Such were the comments shouted all along the line. Another time general attention was attracted by a small brown dog, come from heaven knows where, which trotted busily in front of the ranks with tail stiffly erect, till suddenly a shell fell close by, when it squealed and dashed away with its tail between its legs. Yells and shrieks of laughter rang out from the whole regiment. But distractions of this kind did not last more than a moment, and for eight hours the men had been without food or occupation, in constant fear of death, and their pale and haggard faces grew paler and more haggard.

Prince Andrei, pale and haggard like everyone else in the regiment, paced to and fro in the meadow next to the oat-field from one boundary-line to the other, with his hands clasped behind his back and his eyes fixed on the ground. There was nothing for him to do and no orders to be given. Everything was done of itself. The slain were dragged behind the line, the wounded carried away and the ranks closed up. If any soldiers ran to the rear they made haste to return at once. At first Prince Andrei, thinking it his duty to keep up the spirits of his men and to set them an example, had walked about among the ranks, but he soon became convinced that this was unnecessary and that there was nothing they could learn from him. All his energies, like those of every soldier, were unconsciously bent on keeping his mind off the horrors of their situation. He wandered about the meadow, dragging his feet, making the grass rustle, and contemplating the dust which covered his boots. Then he strode along trying to step in the tracks left by the mowers when they had scythed the meadow; or, counting his steps, calculated how many times he would have to walk from one boundary to another to make a mile; or he would strip the flowers from the wormwood that grew along the edge of the field, rub them in his palms and sniff their bitter-sweet, pungent scent. Nothing remained of the fabric of thought which he had so painfully elaborated the day before. He thought of nothing at all. He listened with weary ears to the ever-repeating sounds, distinguishing the whistle of flying projectiles from the booming of cannon-shot, looked from time to time at the faces of the men of the first battalion which he had looked at over and over again, and waited. 'Here it comes ... this one's coming our way again!' he would say to himself as he listened to the approaching screech of something flying out of that smoke-hidden realm. 'One! Another! More still! That one's down. ...' He paused and looked along the ranks. 'No, it's gone over. But that one struck!' and once more he would take to pacing up and down, trying to reach the boundary strip in sixteen strides.

A whizz and a thud! Five paces from him a cannon-ball tore up the dry soil and disappeared into the earth. A chill ran down his back. Again he glanced at the ranks. Probably a number of men had been hit – a large crowd had collected near the second battalion.

'Adjutant!' he shouted. 'Tell those men not to stand so close together.'

The adjutant, having obeyed the instruction, approached Prince Andrei. From the other side a battalion commander rode up on horseback.

'Look out!' cried a soldier in a terrified voice, and like a bird dropping to the ground with a swift whirr of wings a shell plopped down with a dull thud within a couple of yards from Prince Andrei and close to the battalion-commander's horse. The horse, heedless of whether it were right or wrong to manifest fear, snorted, reared and, almost unseating the major, galloped off. The horse's terror infected the men.

'Lie down!' yelled the adjutant, throwing himself flat on the ground.

Prince Andrei hesitated. The smoking shell spun like a top between him and the prostrate adjutant, near a clump of wormwood between the ploughed land and the meadow.

'Can this be death?' Prince Andrei wondered, casting a fleeting glance of quite unwonted envy at the grass, the wormwood and the thread of smoke that curled upward from the whistling black ball. 'I can't die, I don't want to die. I love life – I love this grass, this earth, this air, ...' These were the thoughts in his mind, and at the same time he remembered that people were looking at him.

'For shame, sir!' he said to the adjutant. 'What sort of ...'

He did not finish. Simultaneously there was an explosion, a splintering sound like a window-frame being smashed, a suffocating smell of powder, and Prince Andrei was jerked to one side and, flinging up his arm, fell on his face.

Several officers ran up to him. Blood was welling out from the right side of his abdomen, making a great stain on the grass.

The militiamen were called with the stretchers and stood behind the officers. Prince Andrei lay on his chest with his face in the grass, gasping painfully.

'Well, what are you waiting for? Come along!'

The peasants came close and took him by the shoulders and legs but he groaned piteously and the men, exchanging looks, set him down again.

'Pick him up, up with him, it must be done!' cried someone.

They lifted him by the shoulders again and laid him on the stretcher.

'Ah, my God, my God! –'

'What is it?' – 'In the belly? That means it's all over with him then!' – voices among the officers were heard saying.

'It practically grazed my ear,' said the adjutant.

The peasants, adjusting the stretcher to their shoulders, hastily directed their steps along the path they had trodden to the dressing-station.

'Keep in step! ... Ah! ... these peasants!' cried an officer, putting a hand on their shoulders and checking them as they jogged unevenly along, jolting the stretcher.

'In step there, Fiodr, can't you! Hey, Fiodr!' said the foremost peasant.

'That's got it!' said the one behind cheerfully when he had fallen into step.

'Your Excellency! Prince – Prince!' said the trembling voice of Timohin, who had run up and was looking down on the stretcher.

Prince Andrei opened his eyes and looked up at the speaker from the depths of the stretcher where his head had sunk back, and closed his eyelids again.

The militiamen carried Prince Andrei to the dressing-station by the wood, where the vans waited. The ambulance-station consisted of three tents with flaps turned back, pitched at the edge of the birch-grove. In the wood stood the ambulance-vans and horses. The horses were munching their oats from portable troughs and the sparrows flew down and pecked the scattered grains. Some crows, scenting blood, flew about among the birch-trees, cawing impatiently. All round the tents, over an area of more than five acres, blood-stained men variously attired stood, sat or lay. Crowds of stretcher-bearers, staring with dejected faces, hung about the wounded: the officers in charge kept trying to drive them away but to no avail. Deaf to the commands of their officers, the soldiers stood leaning against their stretchers and gazed steadily, as though trying to grasp the meaning of the terrible spectacle before their eyes. From the tents came the sound of loud, angry wailing mingled with plaintive moans. At intervals dressers ran out for water or to point out those who were to be brought in next. The wounded waiting their turn outside the tents groaned, sighed, wept, screamed, swore or begged for vodka. Some were delirious. Prince Andrei's bearers, stepping over the crowd of wounded who had not yet been seen to, carried him, as a regimental commander, close to one of the tents, where they halted, awaiting instructions. Prince Andrei opened his eyes and for a long while could not make out what was going on around him. He remembered the meadow, the wormwood, the ploughed field, the black whirling ball and his sudden passionate upsurge of love of life. A couple of steps from him stood a tall, handsome, black-haired non-commissioned officer with a bandaged head, leaning against a branch. He had bullet-wounds in the head and leg, and was talking loudly, attracting general attention. A crowd of wounded men and stretcher-bearers had gathered round him in an eager audience.

'We gave him such a dose of it that he chucked everything and we grabbed the king himself!' cried this sergeant, looking about him with feverishly glittering black eyes. 'If only them reserves 'ad come up right, lads, there wouldn't 'ave been a smell of him left, for I can tell you. ....'

Like all the others near the speaker. Prince Andrei gazed at him with bright eyes and felt a sense of comfort. 'But isn't it all the same now?' he thought. 'And what will it be like there, and what has there been here? What made me so reluctant to part with life? There was something in this life I did not and don't understand.'

37

ONE of the doctors came out of the tent in a blood-soaked apron, holding a cigar between the thumb and little finger of one of his blood-stained hands, so as not to besmear it. He threw his head back and looked about him, but beyond the wounded men. He evidently wanted a short respite. After turning his head this way and that, he sighed and looked down.

'All right, come along,' he said in reply to a dresser who called his attention to Prince Andrei, and he told them to carry him into the tent.

Murmurs arose among the wounded who were waiting.

'The quality only, it seems, in the next world too,' remarked one.

Prince Andrei was carried in and laid on a table that had only just been cleared, and which a dresser was washing down. He could not make out distinctly what was in the tent. The pitiful groans on all sides and the agonizing pain in his thigh and stomach distracted him. Everything he saw about him merged into a single general impression of naked, bleeding human bodies which seemed to fill the whole of the low tent, just as a few weeks before, on that hot August day, bodies had filled the dirty pond beside the Smolensk road. Yes, it was the same flesh, the same *chair à canon*, the sight of which had excited in him then a sort of horror prophetic of what he felt now.

There were three operating-tables in the tent. Two were occupied, on the third they had placed Prince Andrei. For a little while he was left alone, an involuntary witness of what was being done at the other tables. On the nearest one sat a Tartar, probably a Cossack judging by the uniform thrown down beside him. Four soldiers were holding him while a doctor in spectacles was cutting into his muscular brown back.

'Ugh, ugh, ugh!' grunted the Tartar, and suddenly lifting his swarthy, snub-nosed face with its high cheek-bones, and baring his white teeth, he began to wriggle and twitch his body, and set up a long, shrill, piercing screech. The other table was surrounded with people. A big stout man was stretched upon it, his head thrown back, and there was something strangely familiar to Prince Andrei in the curly hair, its colour and the shape of the head. Several dressers were pressing on his chest to hold him down. One large white plump leg kept twitching with a regular spasmodic jerk. The man was sobbing and choking convulsively. Two surgeons – one of whom was pale and trembling – were silently doing something to the man's other gory leg. When he had finished with the Tartar, over whom a great-coat was thrown, the spectacled doctor came across to Prince Andrei, wiping his hands.

He glanced at Prince Andrei's face and quickly turned away.

'Get his clothes off! What are you waiting for?' he cried angrily to the dressers.

His earliest, most distant childhood came back to Prince Andrei when the dresser with sleeves rolled up began hastily unbuttoning and taking off his clothes. The doctor bent close over the wound, probed it and sighed deeply. Then he made a sign to someone, and the excruciating pain in his abdomen made Prince Andrei lose consciousness. When he came to himself the splintered portions of his thigh-bone had been extracted, the torn flesh cut away and the wound bandaged. Water was being sprinkled on his face. As soon as Prince Andrei opened his eyes the doctor bent down, kissed him on the lips without a word and hurried away.

After the agony he had borne Prince Andrei was conscious of a well-being such as he had not experienced for a long time. His imagination reverted to all the best and happiest moments of his life, especially his earliest childhood when he used to be undressed and put to bed, when his nurse had sung lullabies over him, and burying his head in the pillows he had felt happy in the mere feeling of being alive. All this rose to his mind, not like the past even, but as though it were the actual present.

The doctors were busily engaged with the wounded man, the shape of whose head had seemed familiar to Prince Andrei: they were lifting him up and trying to quiet him.

'Show it to me ... Oh, ooh ... ooooh!' his frightened moans could be heard, abject with suffering and broken by sobs.

Hearing those groans, Prince Andrei wanted to weep. Whether because he was dying a death without glory, or because he was sorry to part with life, or because of those memories of a childhood that could never return, or because he was in pain and others were in pain and that man near him was moaning so piteously – at any rate he felt like weeping childlike, good, almost happy tears.

The wounded man was shown his amputated leg stained with clotted blood and with the boot still on.

'Oh! O-oo-h!' he sobbed like a woman.

The doctor who had been standing beside him, in the way of his face being seen, moved aside.

'My God! What is this? Why is he here?' said Prince Andrei to himself.

In the miserable, sobbing, shattered creature whose leg had just been amputated he recognized Anatole Kuragin. It was Anatole they were supporting in their arms and offering a glass of water but his trembling, swollen lips could not grasp the rim. Anatole drew a sobbing, convulsive breath. 'Yes, it is he! Yes, that man is somehow closely and painfully connected with me,' thought Prince Andrei, not yet quite taking in what he was looking at. 'What is that man's connexion with my childhood, with my life?' he asked himself, and could not find the answer. And all at once a new unexpected recollection from that childlike world of purity and love presented itself to Prince Andrei. He remembered Natasha as he had seen her for the first time at the ball in 1810, with her slender neck and arms, with her timid, happy face prepared for ecstasy, and his soul awoke to a love and tenderness for her which were stronger and more pulsing with life than they had ever been. Now he remembered the link between himself and this man who was gazing vaguely at him through the tears that filled his swollen eyes. Prince Andrei remembered everything, and a passionate pity and love for this man welled up in his happy heart.

Prince Andrei could no longer restrain himself, and wept tender compassionate tears for his fellow-men, for himself and for their errors and his own.

'Sympathy, love of our brothers, for those who love us and for those who hate us – yes, the love that God preached on earth, that Princess Maria tried to teach me and I did not understand – that is what made me sorry to part with life, that is what remained for me had I lived. But now it is too late. I know it!'

38

THE fearful spectacle of the battlefield heaped with dead and wounded, in conjunction with the heaviness of his head and the news that some twenty generals he knew personally were among the killed or wounded, and the sense of the impotence of his once mighty arm, produced an unexpected impression on Napoleon, who usually liked to contemplate the killed and wounded, thereby (as he thought) testing his strength of mind. On this day the horrible appearance of the battlefield was too much for this dauntless spirit, which he regarded as the source of his worth and greatness. He hastened away from the scene of action and returned to the Shevardino knoll, where he sat on his camp-stool, his sallow face bloated and downcast, his eyes dim, his nose red and his voice hoarse, looking down and involuntarily listening to the sounds of the firing. In sickly dejection he awaited the end of the business in which he considered himself the prime mover but which he was powerless to arrest. A natural, human sentiment for a brief moment gained the ascendant over the mirage that he had served so long. He felt in his own person the sufferings and death he had seen on the battlefield. The heavy feeling in his head and chest brought home the possibility for him too of agony and death. At that moment he did not desire Moscow, or victory, or glory (what need had he of more glory?). The one thing he wished for was rest, tranquillity and release. But when he had been on the Semeonovsk heights the officer in command of the artillery had proposed to him to bring several batteries up on to that high ground to increase the fire on the Russian troops massed in front of Knyaz-kovo. Napoleon had assented, and given orders that he should be informed of the effect those batteries produced.

An adjutant came now to report that, in obedience to the Emperor's bidding, two hundred guns had been concentrated on the Russians but that they still held their ground.

'Our fire mows them down in rows but they hang on,' said the adjutant.

'They want more! ...' said Napoleon in a husky voice.

'Sire?' asked the adjutant, who had not caught the words.

'They want more!' Napoleon croaked hoarsely, frowning. 'Well, give it them!'

Already, without orders from him, the thing he wanted, and for which he only gave the order because he thought it was expected of him, was being done. And he fell back into his old artificial realm of fantasies of grandeur, and again (as a horse walking a treadmill may imagine it is doing something for itself) he meekly resumed the cruel, mournful, irksome and inhuman rôle which was his destiny.

And not for that day and hour alone were the mind and conscience of this man darkened, on whom the burden of all that was happening weighed more heavily than on all the others who took part in it. Never to the end of his life had he the least comprehension of good-ness, beauty or truth, or of the significance of his actions, which were too contrary to goodness and truth, too remote from everything human for him ever to be able to grasp their import. He could not disavow his deeds, lauded as they were by half the world, and so he was obliged to repudiate truth and beauty and all humanity.

Not on that day alone, as he rode over the battlefield strewn with men killed and maimed (the work, he supposed, of his will) did he reckon as he looked at them how many Russians lay there for each Frenchman and, beguiling himself, find reason for rejoicing in the calculation that there were five Russians for every Frenchman. This was not the only time he wrote to Paris that 'the field of battle was a superb sight' because of the fifty thousand corpses lying there: even on the island of St Helena, in the peaceful solitude where he said he intended to devote his leisure to an account of the mighty deeds he had accomplished, he wrote:

The Russian war should have been the most popular war of modern times: it was a war on the side of good sense and sound interests, to bring peace and security to all. It was purely pacific and conservative.

It was a war for a great cause, the end of uncertainties and the beginning of security. A new horizon, new labours would have opened out, full of well-being and prosperity for all. The European system was established: all that remained was to organize it.

Satisfied on these great points, and at peace with all the world, I too should have had my *Congress* and my *Holy Alliance*. These are ideas stolen from me. In that assembly of great sovereigns we could have discussed our interests like one family and have rendered account to the peoples as clerk to master.

In this way Europe would soon have become in reality but a single people and every man travelling anywhere would have found himself in the common fatherland. He would have insisted on all navigable rivers being free to all, required that the seas should be common to all and that the great standing armies be reduced henceforth to mere bodyguards for sovereigns.

On my return to France, to the bosom of the great, strong, magnificent, serene and glorious Fatherland, I would have proclaimed her frontiers immutable; all future wars purely *defensive*; all fresh aggrandizement *anti-national*. I would have made my son my partner in the Empire; my *dictatorship* would have been over, and his constitutional reign would have begun. . . .

Paris would have been the capital of the world, and the French the envy of the nations! . . .

My time then and my old age would have been devoted, in company with the Empress and during the royal apprenticeship of my son, to visiting in leisurely fashion, with our own horses like a genuine country couple, every corner of the Empire, receiving complaints, redressing wrongs and scattering public buildings and benefactions wherever we went.

Yes, he, foreordained by Providence to the sad, dependent role of executioner of the peoples, persuaded himself that the motive of his actions had been the welfare of the peoples, and that he could control the destinies of millions and confer benefits by the exercise of his power!

Of the four hundred thousand men who crossed the Vistula [he wrote further concerning the Russian war], half were Austrians, Prussians, Saxons, Poles, Bavarians,[Wurttembergers, Mecklenburgers, Spaniards, Italians, Neapolitans. A third of the Imperial army, strictly speaking, consisted of Dutch, Belgians, inhabitants of the Rhineland, Piedmontese, Swiss, Genevese, Tuscans, Romans, inhabitants of the Thirty-second Military Division, of Bremen, of Hamburg, and so on; it included scarcely a hundred and forty thousand who spoke French. The Russian expedition actually cost France less than fifty thousand men; the Russian army in the retreat from Vilna to Moscow lost in various battles four times as many men as the French army; the burning of Moscow cost the lives of a hundred thousand Russians who perished of cold and starvation in the forests; finally, in its march from Moscow to the Oder, the Russian army also suffered from the inclemency of the season; so that by the time it reached Vilna it numbered only fifty thousand, and less than eighteen thousand at Kalisch.

He imagined that the war with Russia came about by his volition, and the horror of what was done made no impression on his soul. He boldly assumed full responsibility for what happened, and his darkened mind found justification in the fact that among the hundreds of thousands who met their deaths there were fewer Frenchmen than Hessians and Bavarians.

39

SEVERAL tens of thousands of men lay dead in various attitudes and uniforms on the fields and meadows belonging to the Davydov family and certain Crown serfs – those fields and meadows where for centuries the peasants of Borodino, Gorky, Shevardino and Semconovsk had harvested their crops and grazed their cattle. For nearly three acres round the dressing-stations the grass and earth were soaked with blood. Soldiers of different arms, wounded and unwounded, with scared faces, dragged themselves back to Mozhaisk from the one army and Valuevo from the other. Other crowds, exhausted and hungry, went forward led by their officers. Still others held their ground and continued to fire.

Over all the plain, which had been so gay and beautiful with bayonets glittering and little puffs of smoke in the morning sun, there now hung a fog of damp and smoke, and the air was foul with a strange, sour smell of saltpetre and blood. Clouds had gathered and drops of rain began to fall on the dead and wounded, on the panic stricken and the weary, and on those who were filled with misgiving. 'Enough, enough!' the rain seemed to be saying. 'Stop!... Bethink yourselves! What are you doing?'

A flicker of doubt began to creep into the minds of the tired and hungry men on both sides – were they to go on slaughtering one another? Hesitation could be read on every face, and every heart was occupied with the question: 'Why – for whom – must I kill and be killed? ... Let the others get on with it and do what they like, but I've had enough!' By the evening this thought had ripened in every soul. Horror at what they were doing was near the surface and all these men were in a condition at any moment to throw everything up and run away anywhere.

But though towards the end of the struggle the men were conscious of the nightmare of their actions, though they would have been glad to leave off, some mysterious, inexplicable power continued to control them, and the surviving gunners – one out of every three – soaked with sweat, grimed with powder and blood, still brought up the charges, loaded, aimed and applied the match, though they stumbled and panted with fatigue. The cannon-balls flew just as swiftly and cruelly from each side, smashing human bodies, and still the fearful work went on, not by the will of individual men but at the will of Him who governs men and worlds.

Anyone looking at the disorder in the rear of the Russian army would have said that the French had only to make one further slight effort and the Russian army would have disappeared into nothing; and anyone seeing behind the French lines would have said that one last little effort on the part of the Russians would be the end of the French. But neither the French nor the Russians put forth that last effort, and the flame of battle burnt slowly out.

The Russians did not make that effort because they were not attacking the French. At the beginning of the battle they merely stood on the road to Moscow, barring it to the enemy, and at the conclusion of the engagement they still stood there exactly as they had at the beginning. But even had the aim of the Russians been to drive the French from their positions they could not have made this final effort, because all the Russian forces had been routed: there was not a single section of the army that had not suffered in the battle, and the Russians in merely holding their positions lost ONE HALF of their effectives.

The French, with the thought of their fifteen years of victories, with their confidence in Napoleon's invincibility, with the knowledge that they had got possession of part of the battlefield and had lost only a quarter of their men and still had their Guards intact – twenty thousand strong – might easily have made that effort. The French, who had attacked the Russian army with the object of driving it from its position, ought to have made that effort, for so long as the Russians continued to bar the way to Moscow, as before, the aim of the French had not been attained, and all their exertions and losses had been in vain. But the French did not make that effort. Some historians declare that if only Napoleon had used his Old Guards, who were intact, the battle would have been won. To speak of what would have happened had Napoleon sent forward his Guards is like talking of what would happen if spring came in autumn. It could not be. Napoleon did not sacrifice his Guards, not because he did not want to, but because it could not be done. All the generals, officers and soldiers of the French army knew that this was out of the question, because the flagging spirit of the troops did not allow of it.

It was not Napoleon alone who experienced that nightmare feeling of the mighty arm being stricken powerless: all the generals and soldiers of his army, whether they had taken part in the battle or not, after all their experience of previous battles – when a tenth of such pressure had started the enemy fleeing – knew a similar feeling of awe and dread before this foe who, after losing ONE HALF of his men, still stood as formidable at the end as at the beginning of the battle. The moral force of the French, the attacking army, was exhausted. The Russians at Borodino won – not the sort of victory which is specified by the capture of scraps of material on the end of sticks, called standards, or of the ground on which the troops had stood and were standing – but a moral victory, the kind of victory which compels the enemy to recognize the moral superiority of his opponent and his own impotence. The French invaders, like a maddened wild beast that in its onslaught receives a mortal wound, became conscious that it was doomed, but could not call a halt, any more than the Russian army, of half its strength, could help giving way. By the impetus it had been given the French army was still able to roll forward to Moscow; but there, without further effort on the part of the Russians, it was bound to perish, bleeding to death from the wound received at Borodino. The direct consequence of the battle of Borodino was Napoleon's causeless flight from Moscow, his return along the old Smolensk road by which he had come, the destruction of the invading army of five hundred thousand men and the downfall of Napoleonic France, on which at Borodino for the first time the hand of an adversary of stronger spirit had been laid.

PART THREE

I

I⊤ is impossible for the human intellect to grasp the idea of absolute continuity of motion. Laws of motion of any kind only become comprehensible to man when he can examine arbitrarily selected units of that motion. But at the same time it is this arbitrary division of continuous motion into discontinuous units which gives rise to a large proportion of human error.

Take, for instance, the well-known sophism of the ancients which set out to prove that Achilles would never catch up with a tortoise that had the start of him, even though Achilles travelled ten times as fast as the tortoise: by the time Achilles has covered the distance that separated him from the tortoise, the tortoise has advanced one-tenth of that distance ahead of him. While Achilles does this tenth the tortoise gains a hundredth, and so on *ad infinitum*. This problem appeared to the ancients insoluble. The absurdity of the finding (that Achilles could never overtake the tortoise) follows from arbitrarily dividing motion into separate units, whereas the movement both of Achilles and the tortoise was continuous.

By adopting smaller and smaller units of motion we only approach the solution of the problem but never reach it. It is only by admitting infinitesimal quantities and their progression up to a tenth, and taking the sum of that geometrical progression, that we can arrive at the solution of the problem. A new branch of mathematics, having attained the art of reckoning with infinitesimals, can now yield solutions in other more complex problems of motion which before seemed insoluble.

This new branch of mathematics, which was unknown to the ancients, by admitting the conception, when dealing with problems of motion, of the infinitely small and thus conforming to the chief condition of motion (absolute continuity), corrects the inevitable error which the human intellect cannot but make if it considers separate units of motion instead of continuous motion.

In the investigation of the laws of historical movement precisely the same principle operates.

The march of humanity, springing as it does from an infinite multitude of individual wills, is continuous.

The discovery of the laws of this continuous movement is the aim of history. But to arrive at these laws of continuous motion resulting from the sum of all those human volitions human reason postulates arbitrary, separated units. The first proceeding of the historian is to select at random a series of successive events and examine them apart from others, though there is and can be no *beginning* to any event, for one event flows without any break in continuity from another. The second method is to study the actions of some one man – a king or a commander – as though their actions represented the sum of many individual wills; whereas the sum of individual wills never finds expression in the activity of a single historical personage.

Historical science in its endeavour to approximate the truth is constantly isolating smaller and smaller units for examination. But, however small the units it takes, we feel that to postulate any disconnected unit, or to assume a *beginning* to any phenomenon, or to say that the volitions of all men are expressed in the actions of any one historical character, is false *per se*.

The critic has only to select some larger or smaller unit as the subject of observation – as criticism has every right to do, seeing that whatever unit history observes must always be arbitrarily selected – for any deduction drawn from history to disintegrate into small particles like dust, without the slightest exertion on his part.

Only by assuming an infinitesimally small unit for observation – a differential of history (that is, the common tendencies of men) – and arriving at the art of integration (finding the sum of the infinitesimals) can we hope to discover the laws of history.

*

The first fifteen years of the nineteenth century in Europe present an extraordinary movement of millions of people. Men leave their customary pursuits, tear from one end of Europe to the other, plunder and slaughter one another, triumph and despair, and for some years the whole flow of life is transformed into a powerful current which at first runs higher and higher and then subsides. What was the cause of this activity, by what laws was it governed ? – asks the human intellect.

The historians, replying to this question, lay before us the sayings and doings of a few dozen men in a building in the city of Paris, calling these sayings and doings 'the Revolution'. Then they give us an elaborate biography of Napoleon and of certain persons favourably or hostilely disposed to him; talk of the influence some of these people had upon others; and say: 'That is what was at the back of this movement and those are the laws it followed.'

But the human intellect not only refuses to believe in their explanation but flatly declares that this method of interpreting is not sound, because in it a smaller phenomenon is taken as the cause of a greater one. The sum of men's individual wills produced both the Revolution and Napoleon, and only the sum of those wills first tolerated and then destroyed them.

'But whenever there has been conquest there has been a conqueror, and every subversion of an empire brings forth great men,' says history. 'Yes indeed, in every case where conquerors appear there have been wars,' human reason replies, 'but this does not prove that the conquerors were the cause of the wars, or that it is possible to discover the factors leading to warfare in the personal activity of a single man.' Whenever I look at my watch and see the hand pointing to ten I hear the bells beginning to ring in the church close by; but I have no right to assume that because the bells start ringing when the watch hand reaches ten the movement of the bells is caused by the position of the hands of my watch.

When I see a steam-engine move I hear the whistle, I see the valves opening and the wheels turning; but I have no right to conclude that the whistle and the turning of wheels cause the movement of the engine.

Peasants say that a cold wind blows in late spring because the oaks are budding, and it is a fact that a cold wind does blow every spring when the oak is coming out. But though I do not know what causes the cold winds to blow when the oak-buds unfold, I cannot agree with the peasants that the unfolding of the oak-buds is the cause of the cold wind, for the force of the wind is altogether outside the influence of the buds. I see only a coincidence of occurrences such as happens with all the phenomena of life, and I see that however long and however carefully I study the hands of the watch, the valve and the wheels of the engine, and the oak-bud, I shall never find out what makes the bells ring, the locomotive move and the wind blow in spring. To do that I must completely change my point of observation and consider the laws regulating steam, bells and the wind. The historians must do likewise. And experiments in this direction have already been made.

To elicit the laws of history we must leave aside kings, ministers and generals, and select for study the homogeneous, infinitesimal elements which influence the masses. No one can say how far it is possible for man to advance in this way towards an understanding of the laws of history; but it is obvious that this is the only path to that end, and that the human intellect has not, so far, applied in this direction one-millionth of the energy which historians have devoted to describing the deeds of various kings, generals and ministers, and propounding reflections of their own concerning those deeds.

2

THE forces of a dozen different European nations burst into Russia. The Russian army and people fall back, avoiding a clash, to Smolensk, and again from Smolensk to Borodino. The French army flows on to Moscow, its goal, with gathering impetus. As it approaches the goal, momentum increases, just as the velocity of a falling body increases as it nears the earth. Behind it lie hundreds of miles of devastated, hostile country; ahead, only a dozen or so miles separate it from its goal. Every soldier in Napoleon's army is conscious of this, and the invasion is propelled onward by its own momentum.

The more the Russian army retreats the more fiercely burns the spirit of fury against the enemy: every step back adds fuel to the flames. At Borodino the collision takes place. Neither army is destroyed, but the Russian army, immediately after the collision, retreats as inevitably as a ball rebounds after colliding with another flying with greater impetus to meet it; and just as inevitably the ball of invasion that has advanced with such momentum rolls on for some distance (though the collision has deprived it of all vigour).

The Russians retire eighty miles – to the other side of Moscow; the French reach Moscow and there come to a halt. For five weeks after this there is not a single battle. The French do not stir. Like a mortally wounded beast, bleeding and licking its wounds, they remain inert in Moscow for five weeks, and then suddenly, without any new reason, they turn tail; they make a dash for the Kaluga road and (after a victory, too, since the field of Malo-Yaroslavets is still theirs after the engagement) flee back, without risking a single serious action, faster and faster, to Smolensk, beyond Smolensk, beyond Vilna, beyond the Berezina, on and on.

On the evening of the 26th of August Kutuzov and the whole Russian army were convinced that the battle of Borodino was a victory. Kutuzov reported to that effect to the Emperor. He gave orders to prepare for a fresh assault to finish off the enemy, not because he wanted to deceive anybody but because he knew, as everyone who had taken part in the battle knew, that the enemy was beaten.

But all that evening and next day reports kept coming in, one after another, of unprecedented losses – of the loss of half the army – and another battle proved physically impossible.

It was out of the question to give battle before information had been collected, the wounded gathered in, the supplies of ammunition replenished, the dead counted, new officers appointed to replace those who had been killed, and before the men had had food and sleep. And meanwhile, the very next morning after the battle, the French army advanced of itself upon the Russians, carried forward by the force of its own impetus, accelerated now in inverse ratio to the square of the distance from its goal. Kutuzov wanted to renew the attack on the following day, and the whole army was with him. But the desire to make an attack is not enough: there must also be the possibility of doing so, and that possibility did not exist. It was impossible not to fall back one day's march, and then in the same way it was impossible not to retreat a second and a third day's march, and finally, on the 1st of September when the army drew near Moscow – despite the strength of the feeling that had arisen in all ranks – the force of circumstances compelled it to retire beyond Moscow. And the troops retreated one more last day's march, and abandoned Moscow to the enemy.

To those who are wont to suppose that plans of campaigns and battles are made by generals in the same way as any of us sitting over a map in our study may imagine how we would have arranged things in this or that battle the questions present themselves: Why did Kutuzov, if he had to retreat, do this or that ? – Why did he not take up a position before reaching Fili ? – Why did he not fall back at once by the Kaluga road, leaving Moscow to itself ? – and so on. People accustomed to reason in this way forget, or do not know, the inevitable conditions which always limit the action of any commander-in-chief.

The conditions in which a commander-in-chief operates in the field have no sort of resemblance to the conditions we imagine to ourselves sitting at our ease in our studies and going over some campaign on the map, with a certain given number of soldiers on the one side and the other, in a certain known locality, and starting our plan from some given moment. A commander-in-chief never finds himself at the *beginning* of an event – the position from which we always contemplate it. The general is always in the midst of a series of shifting events and so he can never at any point deliberate on the whole import of what is going on. Imperceptibly, moment by moment, an event takes shape in all its bearings, and at every instant of this uninterrupted, consecutive shaping of events the commander-in-chief is at the heart of a most complex play of intrigues, cares, contingencies, authorities, projects, counsels, threats and deceits, and is continually obliged to reply to innumerable, always mutually contradictory questions.

Learned military critics assure us quite seriously that Kutuzov should have moved his army to the Kaluga road long before reaching Fili, and that somebody actually submitted such a proposal to him. But the commander of an army, especially at a critical moment, has not one but dozens of schemes proposed to him, each based on the rules of strategy and tactics and contradicting all the rest. A commander-in-chief's business, it would seem, is merely to select one of these projects. But even this he cannot do. Events and time will not wait. It is suggested to him, let us suppose, on the 28th to cross on to the Kaluga road, but just then an adjutant gallops up from Miloradovich asking whether he is to engage the French or retire. An order must be given him immediately, on the instant. And the order to retreat carries us past the turn to the Kaluga road. And after the adjutant comes the commissariat officer to inquire where the stores are to be taken; the chief medical officer wants to know where the wounded are to go; a courier from Petersburg brings a letter from the Sovereign, refusing to admit the possibility of abandoning Moscow; while the commander-in-chief's rival, who is trying to cut the ground from under his feet (and there are always not one but several such), presents a new project diametrically opposed to the plan of retreating along the Kaluga road. Added to all this, the commander-in-chief's own energies require sleep and refreshment; a worthy general who has been overlooked when decorations were bestowed arrives to complain; the inhabitants of the district implore protection; an officer sent to inspect the locality returns with a report flatly contradicting what the officer sent out before him has said; and a spy, a prisoner and a general who has been on reconnaissance all describe the position of the enemy's army quite differently. People who do not understand or who forget these inevitable conditions in which a commander-in-chief has to operate show us, for instance, the position of the troops at Fili and take for granted that the commander-in-chief could, on the 1st of September, with complete freedom decide whether to abandon Moscow or defend the city; whereas, with the Russian army less than four miles from Moscow, no such option existed. When, then, was this question decided? It was decided at Drissa, at Smolensk, and most palpably of all it was decided on the 24th of August at Shevardino, on the 26th at Borodino and each day and hour and minute of the retreat from Borodino to Fili.

3

THE Russian army, having retreated from Borodino, paused at Fili. Yermolov, who had been sent to reconnoitre the position, rode up to the field-marshal.

'There is no possibility of fighting in this position,' he said.

Kutuzov looked at him in wonder and made him repeat what he had said. When he had done so, Kutuzov reached towards him.

'Give me your hand,' said he, and turning it over so as to feel the pulse, remarked: 'You are not well, my dear fellow. Think what you are saying.'

On the Poklonny hill, four miles from Moscow's Dorogomilov gate, Kutuzov got out of his carriage and sat down on a bench by the roadside. A great cluster of generals gathered round him, and Count Rostopchin, who had come out from Moscow, joined them. This brilliant company separated into several groups and discussed among themselves the advantages and disadvantages of the position, the state of the army, the various plans proposed, the situation of Moscow and military matters generally. Though they had not been summoned for the purpose, and though it was not so called, they all felt that this was really a council of war. Conversation was confined to matters of public interest. If anyone did repeat or inquire any piece of personal news, it was done in a whisper, and such digressions were immediately followed by a return to topics of general concern. Not a jest, not a laugh, not even a smile was exchanged among all these men. They were all making an obvious effort to rise to the occasion. And all the groups, while talking among themselves, tried to keep near the commander-in-chief (whose bench formed the centre of the whole crowd) and to speak so that he might hear them. The commander-in-chief listened, occasionally asking for something to be repeated, but did not himself enter into conversation or express any opinion. For the most part, after listening to the talk of some group, he turned away with an air of disappointment, as though at not hearing anything of what he hoped to hear. Some were commenting on the position that had been chosen, criticizing not so much the position itself as the intellectual qualifications of those who had selected it. Others argued that a blunder had been made earlier and that a battle should have been fought two days before. Others again were discussing the battle of Salamanca, which a Frenchman named Crosart, who had just arrived in a Spanish uniform, was describing to them. (This Frenchman and one of the German princes serving with the Russian army were analysing the siege of Saragossa with a view to the possibility of defending Moscow in a similar manner.) Count Rostopchin was telling a fourth little coterie that he was prepared to die with the city militia under the walls of the capital but that he still could not help regretting having been left in ignorance of what was happening, and that had he known it sooner things would have been different. . . . A fifth group, parading the profundity of their strategic insight, discussed the direction the troops would now have to take. A sixth talked sheer nonsense. Kutuzov's expression grew more and more preoccupied and gloomy. From all these conversations he drew one conclusion: that to defend Moscow was a *physical impossibility* in the fullest sense of the words. It was so utterly impossible that even if some insane commander were to give orders to fight confusion would ensue but no battle would take place. No battle would take place because all the officers of the high command not merely recognized the position to be impossible but had got to the point of discussing what was to be done after the inevitable abandonment of that position. How could generals lead their men to a field of battle which they regarded as untenable? The junior officers and even the soldiers themselves (they, too, form their conclusions) likewise thought that the position could not be held, and therefore could not march out to fight when they were morally sure of defeat. That Bennigsen continued to urge the defence of this position, and others still deliberated it, no longer had significance in itself: the only significance was the excuse it offered for dissension and intrigue. This Kutuzov was well aware of.

Bennigsen, who had chosen the position, was making a passionate display of his Russian patriotism (Kutuzov could not listen to him without wincing) by insisting that Moscow must be defended. His purpose was as clear as daylight to Kutuzov: if the defence failed, to throw the blame on Kutuzov who had brought the army as far as the Sparrow Hills without giving battle; if it succeeded, to claim the credit for himself; or if battle were not given, to clear himself of the crime of abandoning Moscow. But this intriguing did not occupy the old man's mind now. One single, terrible question absorbed him. And to that question he heard no reply from anyone. The question for him now was: 'Can I really have allowed Napoleon to reach Moscow, and when did I do it? What decided it? Was it yesterday when I ordered Platov to retreat, or was it the evening before when I had a nap and left Bennigsen in charge? Or was it earlier still? ... When, when was this fearful business set in motion? Moscow must be abandoned. The army must retire, and I must give the order for it.' To give that dreadful order seemed to him tantamount to resigning the command of the army. And apart from the fact that he loved power to which he was accustomed (the honours awarded to Prince Prozorovsky, under whom he had served when he was in Turkey, galled him), he was convinced that he was destined to save Russia and that that was why, against the Emperor's wish and by the will of the people, he had been placed in supreme command. He was persuaded that in these critical circumstances he was the one man who could remain at the head of the army, that he was the only man in the world capable of facing the invincible Napoleon undismayed; and he was filled with consternation at the thought of the order he must issue. But it was essential to come to some decision, and these discussions around him, which were beginning to assume altogether too free a character, must be cut short.

He beckoned the senior generals to him.

'For good or for evil I must trust my own judgement,' he said in French, getting up from the bench, and he rode off to Fili, where his carriages were waiting.

4

A COUNCIL OF WAR assembled at two in the afternoon in the better, larger part of the cottage belonging to a man named Andrei Savostyanov. The men, women and children of the big peasant family crowded into the back room across the passage. Only Malasha, Andrei's six-year-old granddaughter, whom his Serene Highness had petted, giving her a lump of sugar while he drank his tea, stayed behind on top of the stove in the front room. Malasha peeped down from the stove with shy delight at the faces, the uniforms and the decorations of the generals, who one after another came into the room and sat down on the broad benches in the corner under the icons. 'Grandad' himself, as Malasha in her own mind called Kutuzov, was sitting apart from the rest in a dark corner behind the stove. He sat slumped in a folding armchair and continually cleared his throat and pulled at the collar of his coat, which, though it was unbuttoned, still seemed to rub his neck. The officers, as they came in one after another, walked up to the field-marshal: he shook hands with some, to others he merely nodded. His adjutant, Kaisarov, was about to draw back the curtain from the window facing Kutuzov but the latter waved his hand angrily and Kaisarov understood that his Serene Highness did not wish his face to be seen.

Round the peasant's deal table, on which lay maps, plans, pencils and papers, there was such a crowd that the orderlies brought in another bench and put it near the table. Yermolov, Kaisarov and Toll, who had all just arrived, seated themselves on this bench. Immediately under the icons, in the place of honour, sat Barclay de Tolly, his high forehead merging into his bald crown. He had a St George Cross round his neck and looked pale and ill. For two days now he had been suffering from an attack of ague, and at this very moment was shivering feverishly. Beside him sat Uvarov, telling him something in low tones (they all spoke quietly) accompanied by rapid gesticulation. Chubby little Dokhturov was listening attentively with eyebrows raised and hands clasped over his stomach. On the other side, resting his broad head with its bold features and brilliant eyes on his hand, sat Count Ostermann-Tolstoy, apparently immersed in his own thoughts. Raevsky, as usual twisting his black hair forward into curls on his temples, glanced now at Kutuzov, now at the door with a look of impatience. Konovnitsyn's firm, handsome, kindly face was lighted by a tender, shrewd smile. He caught Malasha's eye and winked at her in a way that set the little girl smiling.

They were all waiting for Bennigsen, who, on the pretext of examining the position afresh, was taking his time over a tasty dinner. They waited for him from four o'clock till six and all that time did not enter on their deliberations but talked of extraneous matters in subdued tones.

Only when Bennigsen came into the hut did Kutuzov leave his corner and approach the table but still so as to avoid placing himself in the light of the candles that had been put there.

Bennigsen opened the proceedings with the question: 'Shall we abandon the sacred and ancient capital of Russia without a struggle, or shall we defend it?' A prolonged silence followed. Every face was overcast and only Kutuzov's angry grunts and occasional cough broke the stillness. All eyes were fixed on him. Malasha too gazed at 'Grandad'. She was nearer to him than any of the others and saw that his face was working: he seemed to be going to cry. But this did not last long.

'*The sacred and ancient capital of Russia!*' he cried suddenly, repeating Bennigsen's words in an irate voice and thereby underlining the false note in them. 'Allow me to tell your Excellency that that phrase has no meaning for a Russian.' (He lurched his heavy body forward.) 'That is not the way to formulate the question which I have invited these gentlemen here to discuss. It is a military problem, to be stated as follows: Since the safety of Russia depends on the army, would it be more to our advantage to risk the loss of the army and of Moscow by accepting battle or to give up Moscow without a battle? That is the question on which I want your opinion,' and he sank back in his chair.

A debate began. Bennigsen did not yet consider his game lost. Agreeing with the view of Barclay and others that it was impossible to make a stand at Fili, he aired his Russian patriotism and devotion to Moscow by proposing to move troops from the right to the left flank during the night, and strike at the French right wing next day. Opinions were divided, and arguments were advanced for and against this project. Yermolov, Dokhturov and Raevsky sided with Bennigsen. Whether they were dominated by a sense that some sacrifice was called for before abandoning the capital, or were influenced by other, personal considerations, these generals seemed not to realize that their present deliberations could not alter the inevitable course of events and that Moscow was to all intents already abandoned. The other generals understood this and, setting aside the question of Moscow, turned their attention to the direction the army should take in its retreat. Malasha, looking on, wide-eyed, interpreted the proceedings of the council differently. To her it was a private tussle between 'Grandad' and 'Long-coat' as she christened Bennigsen. She saw that they were spiteful to each other, and secretly she took 'Grandad's' part. In the middle of the conversation she caught the quick, sly glance 'Grandad' cast Bennigsen, and then immediately after she noted with glee that 'Grandad' said something to 'Long-coat' which settled him. Bennigsen suddenly reddened, and strode angrily up and down the room. What had so gone home was Kutuzov's quiet, softly-uttered comment on the advisability or inadvisability of Bennigsen's proposal to move troops by night from the right to the left flank to attack the French right wing.

'Gentlemen,' said Kutuzov, 'I could not give my consent to the count's plan. Moving troops in close proximity to the enemy is always risky, and military history supports that conviction. For instance' – Kutuzov paused, as though to reflect, searching for an example, and then with a bright, naïve glance at Bennigsen – 'well, take the battle of Friedland, which, as the count no doubt well remembers, was not ... completely successful, only because our troops were rearranged while too near the enemy. ...'

A silence, lasting perhaps a minute but which felt never-ending, hung over the meeting.

The discussion was renewed but frequent lulls occurred and the feeling was general that nothing more could be said.

During one of those pauses Kutuzov heaved a deep sigh, as though preparing to speak. They all looked at him.

'*Eh bien, messieurs!* I see that it is I who will have to bear the brunt of it,' he said, and rising slowly he moved to the table. 'Gentlemen, I have heard your views. Some of you will not agree with me. But I' (he stopped), 'on the authority entrusted to me by my Sovereign and my country, give the order to retreat.'

After that the generals began to disperse with the solemnity and silent circumspection which people observe when they separate after a funeral.

Certain of the generals in low tones, in an entirely different key from that in which they had spoken during the council, made some communication to the commander-in-chief.

Malasha, who ought to have been at supper long ago, cautiously let herself down from her perch, clinging with her little bare feet to the projections of the stove, and, slipping between the legs of the generals, she darted out of the room.

After he had dismissed the assembly Kutuzov sat for a long while with his elbows on the table, pondering the terrible question: 'When, at what point had it become inevitable that Moscow must be abandoned? When was the thing done that made it inevitable? And who is to blame for it?'

'I did not expect this – not this,' he said to his adjutant, Schneider, when the latter came in late that night. 'I did not expect this! I did not think this would happen!'

'Your Highness must get some rest,' said Schneider.

'But it's not over yet! They shall devour horse-flesh yet, like the Turks!' cried Kutuzov, not heeding him and bringing his podgy fist down on the table. 'They too ... if only ...'

5

MEANWHILE, in circumstances of even greater importance than the retreat of the army without a battle – namely, the evacuation and burning of Moscow – Rostopchin, who is generally represented as dictating this step, was acting in a very different manner from Kutuzov.

This event – the abandonment and burning of Moscow – was as inevitable after the battle of Borodino as the retreat of the army beyond Moscow without fighting.

Every Russian might have predicted it, not by reasoning things out but by hearkening to the sentiment inherent in each of us and in our forefathers.

In every town and village on Russian soil, from Smolensk onwards, without the assistance of Count Rostopchin and his broadsheets, the same thing took place as happened in Moscow. The nation awaited the enemy with indifference: there was no rioting, no excitement, no one was torn to pieces. People calmly awaited their fate, feeling that when the time came they would know what they must do. And as soon as the enemy drew near, the well-to-do elements of the population departed, abandoning their possessions, while the poorer classes remained and burnt and destroyed what was left.

The conviction that this must and always will be the way of things was, and is, deeply implanted in every Russian heart. And this consciousness – nay, more, the presentiment that Moscow would be taken – pervaded Russian society in Moscow in that year 1812. Those who started quitting Moscow as early as July and the beginning of August showed that this was what they expected. Those who went away, taking what they could and abandoning their houses and half their property, did so in obedience to that latent patriotism which expresses itself not in phrases, not in sacrificing one's children to save the Fatherland, and such-like unnatural exploits, but unobtrusively, simply, organically and so in the way that always produces the most powerful results.

'It is disgraceful to run away from danger; only cowards are deserting Moscow,' they were told. In his broadsheets Rostopchin urged that it was ignominious to leave Moscow. They were ashamed at being branded as cowards, ashamed of going away, but still they left, knowing that it must be so. Why did they go? It is impossible to suppose that Rostopchin had scared them with his tales of atrocities perpetrated by Napoleon in the countries he conquered. The first to leave were the wealthy, educated people, who knew quite well that Vienna and Berlin had remained intact, and that during Napoleon's occupation the inhabitants of those cities had spent their time pleasantly in the company of the bewitching Frenchmen whom the Russians, and especially the Russian ladies, at that time liked so much.

They went because for Russians the question was not whether they would be comfortable or not under French rule in Moscow. To live under French administration was out of the question: it would be worse than anything. They were going away even before the battle of Borodino, and still more rapidly after Borodino, regardless of appeals to defend the capital, regardless of the proclamations of the governor of Moscow announcing his intention to take the wonder-working icon of the Iberian Mother of God and sally forth to combat, or the air-balloons that were to destroy the French, and regardless of all the nonsense Rostopchin wrote in his broadsheets. They knew that it was for the army to fight, and that if the army could not it would be no use for them to rush out with young ladies and house-serfs to do battle with Napoleon on the Three Hills, and so they must make haste and get away, sorry as they were to abandon their property to destruction. They drove away with never a thought of the sublime import of forsaking this immense, flourishing city and thereby consigning it to the flames (for a great city of wooden buildings abandoned by its inhabitants was certain to burn). They drove away, each on his own account, and yet it was only in consequence of their departure that the illustrious event was accomplished which will for ever remain the crowning glory of the Russian people. The lady who as early as June set off from Moscow with her Negroes and her buffoons for her Saratov estates, with a vague feeling that she was not going to be a subject of Bonaparte's, and in fear of being stopped by Count Rostopchin's orders, was simply and genuinely helping in the great work which saved Russia. And Count Rostopchin himself, who now cried shame on those who were leaving and now had the government offices transferred; now distributed quite useless weapons to the drunken rabble; ordered a procession of icons one day and the next forbade Father Augustin to bring out the icons and holy relics; now seized all the private conveyances in Moscow and on one hundred and thirty-six of them removed the air-balloon that was being constructed by Leppich; now hinted that he would burn Moscow and related how he had set fire to his own house, and now wrote a proclamation to the French solemnly upbraiding them for having razed the home of his childhood; now claimed the glory for Moscow in flames, now repudiated it; now commanded the people to capture all spies and bring them to him, then blamed them for doing so; now expelled all the French residents from Moscow and then allowed Madame Aubert-Chalmé (the centre of the whole French colony in Moscow) to remain, but ordered the respected old postmaster, Klucharov, to be arrested and banished for no particular offence; now assembled the people on the Three Hills to fight the French and then, to get rid of them, handed a man over to them to murder and himself drove away by a back gate; now vowed that he would not survive the fall of Moscow, and later on wrote French verses in albums concerning his share in the affair* – this man had no inkling of the mean-

*Je suis né Tartare.	(I was born a Tartar.
Je voulais être Romain.	I wanted to be a Roman.
Les Français m'appelèrent barbare.	The French called me a barbarian,
Les Russes – Georges Dandin.	The Russians – George Dandin.)

ing of what was happening. All he wanted was to do something himself, to startle people, to perform some heroic feat of patriotism; and like a child he frolicked in the face of the momentous and inescapable circumstance of the abandonment and burning of Moscow, and tried with his puny hand now to speed and now to stay the prodigious tide of popular feeling that was bearing him along with it.

6

HÉLÈNE, having returned with the Court from Vilna to Petersburg, found herself in a difficult situation.

In Petersburg she had enjoyed the special patronage of a grandee who occupied one of the highest positions in the Empire. In Vilna she had formed a liaison with a young foreign prince. When she returned to Petersburg both the prince and the magnate were there, both claiming their rights, and Hélène was confronted with a new problem in her career – how to preserve her intimacy with both without offending either.

What might have seemed difficult, if not impossible, to another woman caused never a thought to the Countess Bezuhov, who plainly deserved her reputation of a most intelligent woman. Had she attempted concealment, or tried subterfuge to extricate herself from her awkward position, she would have spoilt her case by acknowledging herself guilty. But Hélène, like a truly great man who can do anything he pleases, at once put herself in the right, as she really believed, and placed the blame on everyone else.

The first time the young foreign prince ventured to reproach her she lifted her beautiful head and, half turning to him, said firmly:

'That's just like a man – selfish and cruel! I might have expected it. Woman sacrifices herself for you; she suffers, and this is her reward! What right have you, *monseigneur*, to demand an account of my friendships, of my attachments? He is a man who has been more than a father to me!'

The prince was about to say something but Hélène interrupted him.

'*Eh bien, oui*,' said she, 'it may be that he has other sentiments for me than those of a father but that is no reason why I should shut my door on him. I am not a man that I should repay kindness with ingratitude! Know, *monseigneur*, that in all that relates to my private feelings I render account only to God and my conscience,' she concluded, laying her hand on her lovely fully expanded bosom as she glanced up to heaven.

'But for God's sake listen to me!'

'Marry me, and I will be your slave!'

'But that is impossible.'

'You would not stoop to marriage with me, you ...' said Hélène, bursting into tears.

The prince made to comfort her, but Hélène (as if quite distraught) said through her tears that there was nothing to prevent her marrying, that there were precedents (there were up to that time very few but she mentioned the cases of Napoleon and some other exalted personages), that she had never been a wife to her husband, that she had been dragged an unwilling victim to the altar.

'But the law, religion ...' murmured the prince, already yielding.

'Laws, religion. ... What were they invented for, if they can't arrange that?' said Hélène.

The foreign prince was astonished that so simple a reflection had never occurred to him, and he applied for advice to the holy brethren of the Society of Jesus, with whom he was in close relations.

A few days later, at one of those enchanting fêtes which Hélène was in the habit of giving at her summer villa on Stone Island, a certain charming Monsieur de Jobert was presented to her: a man no longer young, with snow-white hair and brilliant black eyes, *un Jésuite à robe courte* – a lay member of the Society – who in the garden by the light of the illuminations and to the strains of music conversed long with her of love for God, for Christ, for the Heart of the Mother of God, and of the consolations the one true Catholic faith afforded in this world and the next. Hélène was touched, and more than once tears rose to her eyes and to Monsieur de Jobert's, and her voice trembled. A dance, for which her partner came to fetch her, cut short this conversation with her future *directeur de conscience*; but the next evening Monsieur de Jobert came alone to see Hélène, and after that he was a frequent visitor.

One day he took the countess to a Roman Catholic church, where she fell on her knees before the altar to which she was conducted. The fascinating, middle-aged Frenchman laid his hands on her head and, as she herself afterwards described it, she felt something like the waft-ing of a fresh breeze into her soul. It was explained to her that this was *la grâce*.

Next, a long-frocked *abbé* – *un abbé à robe longue* – was brought to her. He heard her confession and absolved her from her sins. The following day she received a little casket containing the Sacred Host, which was left at her house for her to partake of. A few days later Hélène learned to her satisfaction that she had now been admitted into the true Catholic Church, and that very shortly the Pope himself would hear of her case and would send her a certain document.

All that was done around her and with her at this time, all the attention devoted to her by so many clever men and expressed in such agreeable, refined ways, and the state of dovelike purity she was now in (she wore only white dresses and white ribbons all these days) afforded her gratification; but her gratification never for a moment caused her to lose sight of her objective. And as it always happens in contests of cunning that a stupid person gets the better of cleverer ones, Hélène – realizing that the real end of all these fine words and manoeuvres was to obtain money from her, having converted her to Catholicism, for the benefit of Jesuit institutions (concerning which she received several hints) – before parting with her money demanded that the various formalities should be carried out which were neces-sary to free her from her husband. According to her understanding, the whole point of any religion was merely to provide recognized forms of propriety as a background for the satisfaction of human desires. And with this idea in mind she insisted, in one of her con-versations with her spiritual director, on getting an answer to the question how far her marriage was binding.

They were sitting in the twilight by a window in the drawing-room. Through the window came the scent of flowers. Hélène was wearing a white dress, transparent over shoulders and bosom. The sleek, well-fed *abbé*, with his plump, clean-shaven chin, his pleasant, firm mouth, and his white hands meekly folded on his knees, sat close to Hélène and with a subtle smile on his lips and a discreet glance of admiration for her beauty gazed from time to time at her face as he expounded his opinion on the subject. Hélène, with a restless smile, looked at his curly hair and his full, smooth-shaven, dark-shaded cheeks, and every moment expected the conversation to take a fresh turn. But the *abbé*, though unmistakably enjoying his companion's beauty and proximity, was carried away by his own skilful handling of the question.

The course of the father confessor's arguments ran as follows:

'In your ignorance of the import of what you were undertaking you made a vow of conjugal fidelity to a man who on his part, by entering into matrimony without recognizing the religious solemnity of marriage, was guilty of an act of sacrilege. This marriage lacked the dual significance it should have had. Yet in spite of this your vow was binding upon you. You have deviated from it. What sin did you commit by so doing? *Péché véniel ou péché mortel* – a venial sin or a mortal sin? A venial sin, for you acted without evil intention. If now, with the object of bearing children, you married again your sin might be forgiven. But the question again becomes a twofold one: firstly ...'

'But I imagine,' Hélène, who was getting bored, said suddenly with one of her bewitching smiles, 'that having espoused the true faith I cannot be bound by any obligations laid upon me by a false religion.'

Her spiritual adviser was astounded at having the problem presented to him with such simplicity like Columbus's egg. He was delighted at the unexpected rapidity of his pupil's progress but could not abandon the edifice of his argument which he had constructed with so much intellectual pain.

'Let us understand one another, countess,' he said with a smile, and proceeded to do what he could to refute his spiritual daughter's contention.

7

HÉLÈNE perceived that the matter was very simple and easy from the ecclesiastical point of view, and that her spiritual counsellors were raising difficulties only because they were apprehensive as to how the secular authorities might regard the matter.

So she made up her mind that society must be prepared to look at the matter in the right light. She provoked the jealousy of the elderly grandee, and said the same thing to him as she had to her other suitor – that is, gave him to understand that the sole means of obtaining exclusive rights over her was to marry her.

The elderly magnate was at first just as much taken aback by this suggestion that he should marry a woman whose husband was alive as the younger man had been; but Hélène's imperturbable conviction that it was as simple and natural as marrying a young girl had its effect on him too. Had Hélène herself betrayed the least trace of hesitation, shame or dissembling, her cause would undoubtedly have been lost; but not only did she show no sign of reserve or shame – on the contrary, with frank and simple-hearted naïveté she told her intimate friends (and this meant all Petersburg) that both the prince and the magnate had proposed to her, and that she loved both and was afraid of grieving either.

The rumour instantly spread about Petersburg, not that Hélène desired a divorce from her husband (had this been the report very many persons would have protested strongly against so illegal an intention), but that the unhappy and interesting Hélène was in doubt which of her two suitors to marry. The question now was not how far any marriage was possible but which party would be the better match, and how the Court would look on it. There were, it is true, some rigid individuals unable to rise to the heights of the occasion who saw in the project a desecration of the sacrament of marriage; but such people were few and far between, and they held their peace, while the majority were interested in Hélène's happiness and which would be the better match for her. As to whether it were right or wrong for a woman to marry whose husband was alive, nothing was said – that question had evidently already been settled by persons 'wiser than you and I', and to express any doubts as to the regularity of the solution arrived at would be to risk exposing one's stupidity and lack of *savoir faire*.

Only Maria Dmitrievna Ahrosimov, who had come to Petersburg that summer to see one of her sons, allowed herself to express an opinion flatly contrary to the general point of view. Meeting Hélène at a ball, she stopped her in the middle of the room and amid widespread silence said in her gruff voice:

'So wives have now started marrying while their husbands are alive! I dare say you think you've discovered something new. But you have been forestalled, madam. That was thought of a long time ago. They do the same in all the broth ...', and with these words Maria Dmitrievna turned back her wide sleeves with her characteristic threatening gesture, glanced round sternly and walked across the ball-room.

Though people were afraid of Maria Dmitrievna, she was looked upon in Petersburg as an eccentric, and so of what she said they seized on only the one coarse word at the end, repeating it in a whisper and supposing the whole point of her remark to lie there.

Prince Vasili, whose memory of late was failing so that he often repeated himself a hundred times, said to his daughter whenever he chanced to see her:

'Hélène, I have a word to say to you,' and he would lead her aside, drawing her hand downwards. 'Rumours have come to my ears of certain projects concerning ... you know what. Well, my dear child, you know that my paternal heart would rejoice to feel. ... You have had so much to bear. ... But, *chère enfant* ... you must consult only your own heart. That is all I have to say,' and concealing an emotion identical on each occasion, he would press his cheek against his daughter's and move away.

Bilibin, who had in no wise lost his reputation for possessing a ready wit and was a friend of Hélène's – one of those disinterested allies such as a brilliant woman always manages to attach to herself, men who may be relied upon never to change from friend to lover – one day at a 'small and intimate gathering' gave her his view on the whole subject.

'Listen, Bilibin,' said Hélène (she always called friends of the category to which Bilibin belonged by their surnames), and she touched his coat-sleeve with her white, beringed fingers. 'Tell me, as you would a sister, what ought I to do? Which of the two?'

Bilibin wrinkled up the skin over his eyebrows and pondered, a smile on his lips.

'You do not take me aback, you know,' said he. 'As a true friend I have thought and thought about this business. You see, if you marry the prince' (the younger suitor) and he crooked a finger, 'you lose for ever the chance of marrying the other, and you displease the Court into the bargain. (There is some sort of blood-relationship there, as you are aware.) But if you take the old count you will make his *last* days happy, and afterwards as the widow of the great lord ... the prince would no longer be making a *mésalliance* in contracting a marriage with you.' And Bilibin unwrinkled his forehead.

'You are a true friend!' cried Hélène radiantly, and again touching Bilibin's sleeve. 'But the fact is I love them both, and I don't want to hurt either of them. I would give my life for the happiness of both,' she declared.

Bilibin shrugged his shoulders, as much as to say that not even he could help in that quandary.

'*Une maîtresse-femme!*' thought Bilibin. 'That is what is called putting things squarely. She would like to be married to all three at once.'

'But tell me, how is your husband going to look upon this matter?' he asked, the security of his reputation preserving him from all fear of discrediting himself by so naïve a question. 'Will he agree?'

'Oh, he is so fond of me!' said Hélène, who for some reason fancied that Pierre too adored her. 'He will do anything for me.'

Bilibin puckered his forehead to give intimation of the coming *mot*.

'Even divorce you?' he said.

Hélène laughed.

Among those who ventured to doubt the equity of the proposed marriage was Hélène's mother, Princess Kuragin. She was constantly gnawed by envy of her daughter, and now that the ground for her jealousy was the one nearest to her own heart she could not reconcile herself to the idea. She consulted a Russian priest as to the feasibility of divorce and re-marriage during the husband's lifetime. The priest assured her that this was impossible and, to her delight, referred her to a text in the Gospel which (so it seemed to him) plainly forbids re-marriage while the husband is alive.

Armed with these arguments, which appeared to her irrefutable, the princess drove round to her daughter's early one morning to be sure of finding her alone.

Hélène listened to her mother's objections and then smiled with gentle irony.

'Here, it says in so many words that whoso marrieth her which is divorced ...' said the old princess.

'*Ah, maman*, don't talk nonsense. You don't understand. In my position I have obligations,' began Hélène, speaking in French, which she felt suited her case better – Russian made it sound somehow dubious.

'But my dear ...'

'*Ah, maman*, how is it you don't understand that the Holy Father, who has the power to grant dispensations ...'

At this point the lady companion who lived with Hélène came in to announce that his Highness was in the drawing-room and wished to see her.

'No, tell him I don't wish to see him, that I am furious with him for not keeping his word.'

'*Comtesse*, there is mercy for every sin,' said a fair-haired young man with a long face and long nose, entering the room.

The old princess rose respectfully and curtsied. The young man took no notice of her. Princess Kuragin nodded to her daughter and sailed to the door.

'Yes, she is right,' mused the old princess, all her convictions dissipated by the appearance of his Highness. 'She is right; but how was it in our youth – gone now for ever – we knew nothing of this? Yet it is so simple,' she thought as she got into her carriage.

*

By the beginning of August Hélène's affairs were settled and she wrote to her husband (who, so she imagined, was deeply attached to her), making known to him her intention of marrying N.N. and telling him that she had embraced the one true faith. She requested him to execute all the formalities necessary for a divorce, in regard to which the bearer of her letter would give him due particulars.

'Whereupon, my dear, I pray God to have you in His holy and powerful keeping – Your friend Hélène.'

This letter was brought to Pierre's house in Moscow while he was away on the field of Borodino.

8

TOWARDS the end of the battle of Borodino Pierre fled for a second time from Raevsky's battery and joined a throng of soldiers hastening along the ravine to Knyazkovo, reached the dressing-station and, seeing blood and hearing cries and groans, hurried on, caught up in the mob of soldiers.

The one thing Pierre desired now with his whole soul was to get away quickly from the terrible scenes through which he had lived that day and return to ordinary conditions of life, and go to sleep quietly in his own room in his own bed. He felt that only in the ordinary conditions of life would he be able to understand himself and all that he had seen and experienced. But such ordinary conditions of life were nowhere to be found.

Though shells and bullets did not whistle over the road along which he travelled, still he saw here on all sides the same sights he had seen on the field of battle. There were the same suffering, exhausted and sometimes strangely indifferent faces; everywhere the same blood, the same military greatcoats, the same sound of firing, which though distant now still aroused horror. And in addition there was the suffocating heat and dust.

Having walked a couple of miles along the Mozhaisk highway, Pierre sat down by the roadside.

Dusk had fallen and the roar of guns had died away. Pierre lay leaning on his elbow for a long time, watching the shadowy figures that filed past him in the dark. He was continually fancying that a cannon-ball was sweeping down on him with a terrible screech, and then he started and half rose. He had no idea how long he had been there. In the middle of the night three soldiers, dragging some brushwood after them, settled themselves near him and began making a fire.

Casting sidelong glances at Pierre, the soldiers got the fire to burn and placed an iron pot on it into which they broke some biscuits and added a little fat. The appetizing odour of frying food mingled with the smell of smoke. Pierre sat up and sighed. The soldiers (there were three of them) were eating and talking among themselves, paying no heed to Pierre.

'And who are you?' one of them suddenly asked Pierre, evidently meaning by that, and Pierre understood it so, that they would give him a share of their food if he were hungry and could prove he were an honest man.

'I? ...' said Pierre, feeling it necessary to minimize his social position as far as possible, so as to be closer to the soldiers and more within their comprehension. 'Actually I am a militia officer but my men are not here. I went into the battle and got separated from them.'

'That so?' said one of the soldiers.

Another shook his head.

'Well, you can have some of our mash if you like!' said the first, and licking clean a wooden spoon he handed it to Pierre.

Pierre squatted by the fire and fell to eating the mixture in the pot which he thought more delicious than any food he had ever tasted. As he sat bending over the pot, helping himself to large spoonfuls and greedily swallowing them down one after another, his face was lit up by the fire, and the soldiers studied him in silence.

'Where've you to go to, tell us that?' asked one of them.

'To Mozhaisk.'

'You're gentry then?'

'Yes.'

'And what's yer name?'

'Piotr Kirillovich.'

'Well, Piotr Kirillovich, you come along of us, we'll take you there.'

In the pitch dark the soldiers walked with Pierre to Mozhaisk.

By the time they got as far as Mozhaisk and were climbing the steep hill into the town the cocks were already crowing. Pierre continued on with the trio, quite forgetting that his inn was at the bottom of the hill and he had passed it. He might not have remembered it at all (so generally bewildered was he), had he not chanced halfway up the hill to stumble on his groom, who had been to look for him in the town and was now returning to the inn. The groom recognized Pierre in the darkness by his white hat.

'Your Excellency!' he cried. 'Why, we had quite given you up! How is it you are on foot? And, mercy on us, where are you going?'

'Oh yes!' said Pierre.

The soldiers stood still.

'Found your own folks then?' said one of them. 'Well, good-bye – Piotr Kirillovich, wasn't it?'

'Good-bye, Piotr Kirillovich!' repeated the other voices.

'Good-bye!' said Pierre, and he started back with his groom towards the inn.

'I ought to give them something!' he thought, feeling in his pocket. 'No, better not,' some inner voice prompted him.

There was not a room to be had at the hostelry, they were all occupied. Pierre went out into the yard, and muffling himself up from head to foot lay down in his carriage.

9

PIERRE had scarcely laid his head on the cushion before he felt himself dropping asleep; but all of a sudden, with a vividness that was almost real, he heard the *boom-boom-boom* of the cannon, the slapping sound of falling shells, the groans and cries, smelt the blood and powder, and a feeling of horror and the dread of death took possession of him. He opened his eyes in panic and put his head out from the cloak. All was tranquil in the yard. There was only someone's orderly talking at the gate and splashing through the mud. Above Pierre's head some pigeons, disturbed by the movement he had made in sitting up, fluttered under the dark eaves of the penthouse. The peaceful strong smell of stables, which at that instant delighted Pierre's heart, pervaded the whole courtyard – a smell of hay, of manure and of birchwood tar. Between the dark roofs of two penthouses he could see the clear, starry sky.

'Thank God, that is all over!' he thought, covering his head up again. 'Oh, what an awful thing fear is, and how disgracefully I gave way to it! Whereas they – *they* were steady and cool all the time, to the very end ...' thought he. *They* in Pierre's mind were the soldiers, those who had been on the battery, those who had given him food and those who had prayed before the icon. *They* – those strange people of whom he had known nothing hitherto – *they* stood out clearly and sharply from everyone else.

'To be a soldier, an ordinary soldier!' thought Pierre as he dropped off to sleep. 'To throw oneself heart and soul into that common life, to learn the secret of what makes them what they are. But how cast off all the superfluous, devilish burden of the outer man? There was a time when I could have done it. I could have run away from my father, as I wanted to. I might even after the duel with Dolohov have been sent to serve as a soldier.' And his thoughts flashed back to the dinner at the English Club when he had challenged Dolohov, and his meeting with his benefactor at Torzhok. And here a picture of a solemn assembly of the Lodge at the English Club arose before his mind, with someone he knew, someone near and dear to him sitting at the end of the table. 'Why, it is he! It is my benefactor. But surely he died?' mused Pierre. 'Yes, he died; and I did not know he was alive. How sorry I am that he died, and how glad I am that he is alive again!' On one side of the table sat Anatole, Dolohov, Nesvitsky, Denisov and others like them (in Pierre's dream the category to which these men belonged was as defined as the category of those he termed *they*), and those people, Anatole and Dolohov, were shouting and singing at the tops of their voices; but through their clamour the voice of his benefactor was heard speaking all the while, and the sound of his words was as weighty and uninterrupted as the din of the battlefield, but pleasant and comforting. Pierre did not understand what his benefactor was saying, but he knew (species of thought were also quite distinct in his dream) that he was talking of goodness and the possibility of being like *them*. And *they* with their simple, kind, steadfast faces surrounded his benefactor on all sides. But though they were kindly they did not look at Pierre, did not know him. Pierre wanted to attract their attention and speak to them. He sat up but in that second became aware that his legs were bare and chill.

He felt ashamed and put an arm over his legs, from which the cloak had in fact slipped off. For a moment, as he rearranged his cloak, Pierre opened his eyes and saw the same penthouse roofs, posts and yard, but now everything was enveloped in a bluish light and sparkling with dew or frost.

'Dawn already!' thought Pierre. 'But that's not the point. I want to hear and understand my benefactor's words.' He muffled himself in the cloak again, but now neither the masonic dinner nor his benefactor was there. All that remained were ideas clearly expressed in words, ideas that someone was uttering or that he himself was formulating.

Afterwards when he recalled those thoughts Pierre was convinced that someone outside himself had spoken them, though they had been evoked by the impressions of that day. He had never, it seemed to him, been capable of thinking such thoughts and expressing them like that when awake.

'War,' the voice had said, 'is the most painful act of subjection to the laws of God that can be required of the human will. Single-heartedness consists in submission to the will of God; there is no escaping Him. And *they* are single-hearted. *They* do not talk, they act. Speech is silver but silence is golden. Man can be master of nothing while he is afraid of death. But he who does not fear death is lord of all. If it were not for suffering, man would not know his limitations, would not know himself. The hardest thing' (Pierre went on to think or hear in his dream) 'is to know how to unite in your soul the significance of the whole. To unite the whole?' he asked himself. 'No, not to unite. Thoughts cannot be united, but to *harness* all these ideas together – that's what's needed! Yes, we *must harness* them, *must harness* them!' Pierre repeated to himself with a thrill of ecstasy, feeling that these words and they alone expressed what he wanted to say and solved the problem that tormented him.

'Yes, we must harness together, it is time to harness.'

'Time to harness, time to harness, your Excellency! Your Excellency!' some voice was echoing. 'We must harness, it is time to harness. ...'

It was the groom waking Pierre. The sun was shining full in Pierre's face. He glanced at the dirty inn-yard in the middle of which soldiers were watering their lean horses at the well, while carts were moving out of the gate. Pierre turned away with repugnance and, closing his eyes, made haste to roll over again on the carriage-seat. 'No, I don't want any part of that – I don't want to see and understand that. I want to follow out the things revealed to me in my dream. Another second and I should have understood it all. But what am I to do? Harness it all, but how can I harness everything?' And Pierre found to his dismay that the meaning of all he had seen and thought in his dream had slipped away.

The groom, the coachman and the innkeeper told Pierre that an officer had come with information that the French were nearing Mozhaisk and that our troops were moving on.

Pierre got up and, having given orders for them to harness his horses and catch him up, he went through the town on foot.

The troops were marching out, leaving nearly ten thousand wounded behind them, who could be seen in the yards, at the windows of the houses and in the streets, where they crowded round the carts that were to take some of them away, shouting, cursing and exchanging blows. Pierre offered a seat in his carriage, which had overtaken him, to a wounded general he knew, and drove with him to Moscow. On the road he was told of the death of his brother-in-law, Anatole, and of Prince Andrei.

10

On the 30th of August Pierre reached Moscow. Almost at the city gates he was met by Count Rostopchin's adjutant.

'Well we have been searching for you everywhere,' said the adjutant. 'The count wants to see you urgently. He begs that you will come to him immediately on a very important matter.'

Without going home, Pierre hailed a conveyance and drove to the governor-general's.

Count Rostopchin had only that morning returned from his summer villa at Sokolniky. The ante-room and reception-room of the count's residence were full of officials who had been summoned or had come for instructions. Vasilchikov and Platov had already seen the count and explained to him that the defence of Moscow was out of the question, and the city would have to be surrendered. Though this news was being concealed from the inhabitants, the officials – the heads of the various government departments – knew that Moscow would soon be in the hands of the enemy, just as Count Rostopchin himself knew it; and to escape personal responsibility they had all come to the governor to inquire how they were to act with their respective departments.

As Pierre entered the waiting-room a courier from the army emerged from an interview with the count.

The courier made a despairing gesture in answer to the questions directed to him, and passed through the room.

While he waited, Pierre watched with weary eyes the different functionaries, old and young, military and civilian, important and unimportant, who were gathered there. They all had long faces and seemed agitated. Pierre went up to one group among whom he recognized an acquaintance. After greeting Pierre, they continued with their conversation.

'If they're evacuated and brought back again later on it will do no harm, but as things are now one can't answer for anything.'

'But look here, what he writes,' said another, pointing to a printed sheet he held in his hand.

'That's another matter. That's necessary for the populace.'

'What is it?' asked Pierre.

'Oh, a new broadsheet.'

Pierre took it and began to read.

His Serene Highness Prince Kutuzov, in order to effect an early junction with the troops moving towards him, has passed through Mozhaisk and occupied a strong position where the enemy will not find it easy to attack him. Forty-eight cannon with ammunition have been sent him from here, and his Serene Highness declares that he will defend Moscow to the last drop of his blood and is ready to fight even in the streets of the city. My friends, do not let the closing of the Courts of Law occasion any alarm: it was necessary to remove them but we will give the evil-doer a taste of our law, you may be sure! When the time comes I shall want some gallant lads from the town and the country too. I shall utter my call a day or two beforehand but it is not necessary yet, so I hold my peace. An axe is a good weapon, a hunting-spear is not bad, but best of all would be a three-pronged fork: a Frenchman is no heavier than a sheaf of rye. Tomorrow after dinner I shall take the Iberian icon of the Mother of God to the wounded in St Catherine's hospital. There we will have some water blessed: that will help them to get well quicker. I am all right now. I had a bad eye but now I can see out of both.

'Why, military authorities have assured me that there could be no fighting in the city itself,' said Pierre, 'and that the position ...'

'To be sure, that's just what we were saying,' replied the first speaker.

'And what does he mean by "I had a bad eye but now I can see out of both"?' asked Pierre.

'The count had a sty,' explained the adjutant, smiling, 'and was very much put out when I told him people had called to ask what was the matter with him. By the way, count,' he added suddenly, addressing Pierre with a smile, 'we heard that you are having domestic difficulties and that the countess, that your wife ...'

'I don't know anything,' said Pierre indifferently. 'What is it you have heard?'

'Oh well, you know how people so often invent things. I only say what I heard.'

'But what did you hear?'

'Oh, they say,' observed the adjutant with the same smile, 'that the countess, your wife, is preparing to go abroad. I expect it's nonsense. ...'

'It may be,' said Pierre, looking about him absentmindedly. 'And who is that?' he asked, indicating a short old man in a clean blue peasant-overcoat, with a big snow-white beard and eyebrows and a ruddy face.

'That? Oh, he's a certain tradesman – I mean, he's the eating-house-keeper, Vereshchagin. You have heard the story of the proclamation, I dare say?'

'Oh, so that's Vereshchagin!' said Pierre, scrutinizing the calm, self-reliant face of the old man and seeking for signs in it to denote a traitor.

'That's not the man himself – that's the father of the fellow who wrote the proclamation,' said the adjutant. 'The son is in custody, and I fancy it will go hardly with him.'

A little old gentleman wearing a star, and another official, a German with a cross round his neck, joined the group.

'You see,' proceeded the adjutant, 'it is a puzzling business. The proclamation appeared a couple of months back. The count was informed of it. He ordered an inquiry to be made. Gavrilo Ivanich here started to investigate and found that the proclamation had passed through exactly sixty-three hands. He goes to one man and asks: "How did you come by it?" – "Had it from So-and-so." He tried the next. "Where did you get it?" and so on until he reaches Vereshchagin, an ignorant merchant – you know, one of those self-made men,' said the adjutant, smiling. 'He is asked: "Who gave you this?" And the point is, we knew perfectly well where he got it. He could only have had it from the Postmaster. But evidently they had some secret understanding. "No one," says he. "I made it up myself." He was threatened and coaxed but he stuck to it that he wrote it himself. And so it was reported to the count, who sent for the man. "From whom did you get this proclamation?" – "I wrote it myself." Well, you know the count,' said the adjutant cheerfully, with a smile of pride. 'He flared up like anything – and just think of the fellow's audacity, his stubborn lying! ...'

'And the count wanted him to implicate Klucharov? I understand,' said Pierre.

'Not at all,' rejoined the adjutant in dismay. 'Klucharov had sins enough to answer for without that, and that is why he was banished. But this is the point: the count was furious. "How could you have written it yourself?" says he, and he picked up the *Hamburg Gazette* that was lying on the table. "Here it is! You did not write it yourself but translated it, and translated it atrociously too, because even in French you are an idiot!" And what do you think? "No," says he, "I didn't read any gazettes, I made it up myself." – "Well, if that's so, you're a traitor, and I'll have you tried and hanged! Confess now, who did you get it from?" – "I never seen any newspapers, I made it up myself." And there the matter stuck. The count summoned the father too but the fellow held out. He was sent for trial and sentenced to penal servitude, I believe. Now the father is here to intercede for him. But he's a worthless young scamp! You know the kind – tradesman's son, dandy, lady-killer. Picked up a bit of learning somewhere and now thinks himself a cut above everybody else. That's the sort he is. His father keeps a cookshop here on the Kamenny bridge – and you remember in the parlour there was a large icon of God the Father painted with a sceptre in one hand and an orb in the other? Well, he takes it home with him for a few days, and what do you suppose he does? Found some scoundrel of a painter. ...'

II

In the middle of this new anecdote Pierre was called in to the governor-general.

When he entered the private room Count Rostopchin, scowling, was rubbing his forehead and eyes with his hand. A short man was saying something but as soon as Pierre appeared he stopped and left the room.

'Ah, good-day, doughty warrior!' said Rostopchin immediately the other man had gone. 'We have been hearing about your *prouesses*! But that's not what I want to talk about just now. Between ourselves, *mon cher*, are you a freemason?' he asked in a severe tone, as though that were a crime but one which he intended to pardon. Pierre remained silent. 'I am well informed, my friend, but I know that there are masons and masons, and I hope that you are not one of those who, by way of regenerating the human race, are doing their best to ruin Russia.'

'Yes, I am a mason,' Pierre replied.

'There you are, you see, my dear fellow! I don't expect you are ignorant of the fact that Messrs Speransky and Magnitsky have been put in their proper places, as also has Klucharov. Others likewise, who under the guise of building up the temple of Solomon have been trying to destroy the temple of their Fatherland. You may take it for granted there are good reasons for what has been done, and that I could not have banished the Postmaster had he not been a dangerous person. It has now come to my knowledge that you lent him your carriage to take him from the city, and that you have even accepted papers from him for safe custody. I like you, and wish you no harm, and as you are half my age I advise you, as a father would, to break with men of that stamp and take yourself off from here as fast as you possibly can.'

'But what was Klucharov's crime?' asked Pierre.

'That is my business, and it's not yours to question me,' cried Rostopchin.

'If he is accused of having circulated Napoleon's proclamation it is not proved that he did so,' said Pierre (not looking at Rostopchin), 'and Vereshchagin ...'

'Now we have it!' Rostopchin shouted at Pierre louder than before, frowning suddenly. 'Vereshchagin is a renegade and a traitor who will be punished as he deserves,' he said with the vindictiveness with which people speak at the recollection of an insult. 'But I did not send for you to discuss my actions but to give you advice – or an order if you prefer that term. I request you to break off all connexion with Klucharov and his like, and to leave town. And I will knock the nonsense out of any and everybody' – but, probably realizing that he was railing at Bezuhov, who so far was guilty of no offence, he added in French, cordially seizing Pierre's hand: 'We are on the eve of a public disaster and I haven't time to say civil things to everyone who has business with me. My brain's often in a perfect whirl. Well, *mon cher*, what are you personally going to do?'

'Why, nothing,' answered Pierre, without raising his eyes and with no change in the thoughtful expression on his face.

The count frowned.

'A friendly word of advice, *mon cher*. Be off as soon as you can: that's all I have to say to you. Happy he who has ears to hear. Good-bye, my dear boy. Oh yes!' he called through the door after Pierre, 'is it true the countess has fallen into the clutches of the holy fathers of the Society of Jesus?'

Pierre did not answer, and walked out of Rostopchin's more angry and out of humour than he had ever been known to look before.

*

By the time he reached home it was already growing dark. About eight different people came to see him that evening: the secretary of some committee, the colonel of his battalion of militia, his steward, his major-domo, and various other persons with petitions. They all had business with Pierre and wanted decisions from him. Pierre did not understand and was not interested in any of the questions, and only answered in order to get rid of these people. When at last he was left alone he opened and read his wife's letter.

'*They* – the soldiers in the battery; Prince Andrei killed ... the old man. ... Single-heartedness is submission to God. Suffering is neces-sary ... the significance of everything ... one must harness ... my

wife is going to be married. ... One must forget and understand. ...'
And, without undressing, he threw himself on his bed and fell asleep
immediately.

When he awoke next morning the major-domo came in to inform
him that a special messenger, a police officer, had come from Count
Rostopchin to find out whether Count Bezuhov had left or was
leaving town.

A dozen people were waiting in the drawing-room to see Pierre on
business. He dressed hurriedly and, instead of going down to see
them, went to the back porch and out through the gate.

From that moment until after the devastation of Moscow, in spite
of every effort to trace him, no one of Bezuhov's household saw
Pierre again, or could discover his whereabouts.

12

THE Rostovs remained in Moscow till the 1st of September, the day
before the enemy entered the city.

After Petya had joined Obolensky's regiment of Cossacks and had
gone away to Byelaya Tserkov, where the regiment was being enrolled, the countess was seized with panic. The thought that both her
sons were at the war, that they had both gone from under her wing,
that today or tomorrow either or both of them might be killed, like
the three sons of a lady of her acquaintance, struck her that summer
for the first time with cruel explicitness. She tried to get Nikolai back,
wanted to go after Petya herself, place him somewhere in Petersburg,
but none of these ideas proved practicable. Petya could not return
unless his regiment did so, or unless he was transferred to another
regiment on active service. Nikolai was somewhere with the army
and nothing had been heard from him since his last letter in which he
had given a detailed account of his meeting with Princess Maria. The
countess could not sleep at nights, and when she did drop off dreamed
that both her sons had been killed. After many consultations and discussions the count at last hit on a plan to relieve the countess's anxiety.
He got Petya transferred from Obolensky's regiment to Bezuhov's,
which was in training outside Moscow. Though Petya would still
remain in the Service the transfer would give the countess the consolation of seeing at least one of her sons under her wing, and she hoped
to arrange matters for her Petya so as not to let him go again but

always get him appointed to places where there was no risk of his finding himself in a battle. While Nikolai had been the only one in danger the countess had fancied (and had suffered pangs of remorse over it) that she loved her first-born better than all her other children; but when her younger boy, the scapegrace who had been bad at his lessons, was always breaking things in the house and making himself a nuisance to everybody, that snub-nosed Petya with his merry black eyes and fresh rosy cheeks where soft down was just beginning to show, slipped away into the company of those big, dreadful, cruel men who were fighting somewhere about something and apparently finding pleasure in it – then his mother thought she loved him more, far more, than all her other children. The nearer the time came for the return of her longed-for Petya, the more restless grew the countess. She began to think she would never live to see such happiness. Not only Sonya's presence but her beloved Natasha's too, and even her husband's, irritated her. 'What do I want with them? I want no one but Petya,' she thought.

One day towards the end of August the Rostovs received another letter from Nikolai. He wrote from the province of Voronezh where he had been sent to procure remounts, but this letter did not soothe the countess's apprehensions. Knowing that one son was out of danger made her the more anxious about Petya.

Although by the 20th of August almost all the Rostovs' acquaintances had left Moscow, and although everybody tried to persuade the countess to get away as quickly as possible, she would not hear of leaving until her treasure, her adored Petya, had come back. On the 28th of August Petya arrived. The morbidly-passionate affection with which his mother received him did not please the sixteen-year-old officer. Though she concealed her intention of keeping him under her wing, Petya guessed her designs and, instinctively fearing that he might melt when he was with her and 'go soft' (as he expressed it in his own mind), he treated her coldly, avoided her and during his stay in Moscow attached himself exclusively to Natasha, for whom he had always cherished a peculiarly tender, brotherly affection, almost amounting to adoration.

Thanks to the count's characteristic carelessness, nothing was ready for their departure by the 28th of August, and the wagons that were to come from their Ryazan and Moscow estates to remove their household belongings only appeared on the 30th.

From the 28th to the 31st, Moscow was all bustle and commotion. Every day thousands of casualties wounded at Borodino were brought in by the Dorogomilov gate and deposited in various parts of Moscow, and thousands of carts conveyed the inhabitants and their possessions out by the other gates. In spite of Rostopchin's broadsheets, or because of them or independently of them, the strangest and most contradictory rumours circulated about the town. Some said that no one was to be allowed to depart; others, on the contrary, declared that all the icons had been taken out of the churches and everybody was to be forced to go. Some said there had been another battle after Borodino, at which the French had been routed, while others reported that the whole Russian army had been annihilated. Some asserted that the Moscow militia, with the clergy at their head, were going to the Three Hills; others whispered that Archbishop Augustin had been forbidden to leave, that traitors had been seized, that the peasants were rioting and plundering people on their way from Moscow, and so on. But all this was only talk, while in reality (though the council at Fili at which it was decided to abandon Moscow had not yet been held) both those who left and those who remained all felt that Moscow would assuredly be surrendered, though they did not say so freely, and that they must make all haste to get away and save their belongings. There was a feeling that everything was about to collapse, and that a sudden change was imminent, but up to the 1st of September things still continued the same. Like a criminal being led to the gallows, who knows that in a minute he must die but yet stares about him and straightens the cap sitting awry on his head, so Moscow automatically carried on with the routine of daily life, though aware that the hour of destruction was at hand when all the conventional conditions of existence would be torn asunder.

During the three days preceding the occupation of Moscow the whole Rostov family was absorbed in various activities. The head of the family, Count Rostov, continually drove about the city collecting all the rumours that were in circulation, and when at home gave superficial and hasty directions concerning the preparations for their departure.

The countess superintended the packing, was out of humour with everything, and kept in continual pursuit of Petya, who was always running away from her and exciting her jealousy by spending all his time with Natasha. Sonya was the only person who really saw to the practical business of getting things packed. But Sonya had been particularly silent and melancholy of late. Nicolas' letter in which he mentioned Princess Maria had occasioned, in her presence, the most joyful auguries from the countess, who saw in Nicolas' encounter with Princess Maria a direct dispensation of Providence.

'I never really felt happy about Bolkonsky's engagement to Natasha,' said the countess, 'but I always longed for Nikolai to marry the princess, and I have a presentiment that he will. And what a good thing it would be!'

Sonya felt this was true; that the only possibility of retrieving the fortunes of the Rostovs was for Nicolas to marry an heiress, and that the princess would be an excellent match. But this was a very bitter reflection for her. In spite, or perhaps in consequence, of her grief she took on herself all the difficult work of seeing after the storing and packing of the household goods, and was busy for whole days together. The count and countess referred to her when they had any orders to give. Petya and Natasha, on the contrary, far from helping their parents got in everybody's way and were a general nuisance. Almost from morning till night the house resounded with their flying footsteps, their cries and spontaneous laughter. They laughed and were gay, not because there was any reason for laughter but because gaiety and mirth were in their hearts and so everything that happened seemed to them a cause for rejoicing and laughter. Petya was in high spirits because he had left home a boy and returned (so everyone told him) a fine young man, because he was at home, because he had left Byelaya Tserkov, where there was no prospect of taking part in an early battle, and come to Moscow where any day there might be fighting, and above all because Natasha, whose lead he always followed, was in high spirits. Natasha was gay because for too long she had been sad and now nothing reminded her of the cause of her sadness, and she was feeling well again. She was happy too because she had someone to adore her – the adoration of others was the lubricant necessary if the wheels of her mechanism were to run quite smoothly – and Petya adored her. But above all they were gay because there was war at the very gates of Moscow, because there would be fighting at the barriers, arms were being distributed, everybody was rushing here and there, and altogether something extraordinary was happening, and that is always exciting, especially for the young.

On Saturday the 31st of August everything in the Rostovs' house seemed at sixes and sevens. All the doors stood wide open, all the furniture had been carried out or put somewhere else, looking-glasses and pictures had been taken down. The rooms were littered with trunks, bits of straw, wrapping-paper and cord. Peasants and house-serfs trod heavily over the parquet floors carrying out baggage. The courtyard was crowded with carts, some loaded high and already roped up, others still empty.

The voices and steps of the army of servants and peasants who had come with their carts rang through the courtyard and the house. The count had been out since morning. The countess had a headache, brought on by all the noise and turmoil, and was lying down in the new sitting-room with a vinegar compress on her head. Petya was not at home: he had gone to see a friend with whom he was planning to obtain a transfer from the militia to a regiment on active service. Sonya was in the ball-room superintending the packing of the glass and china. Natasha was sitting on the floor of her dismantled room with dresses, ribbons and scarves strewn about her, staring at the floor and holding in her hands an old ball-dress, the very one (quite out of date now) which she had worn at her first Petersburg ball.

Natasha's conscience had pricked her for being idle when everyone else was so busy, and several times in the course of the morning she had tried to do something to help, but her heart was not in it and she had always been incapable of doing any kind of work that did not captivate her completely. For a time she had stood beside Sonya while the china was being packed, with the idea of lending a hand, but she soon gave that up and went to her room to pack her own things. At first she had found it amusing to give away dresses and ribbons to the maids, but when it came to packing what was left she found it a wearisome task.

'Dunyasha, you pack! You will, won't you, dear?'

And when Dunyasha willingly agreed to do it all for her Natasha sat down on the floor with the old ball-dress in her hands and fell to dreaming of things far removed from what should then have been occupying her mind. She was roused from her reverie by the chatter of the maids in the next room (which was theirs) and the sound of their hurried footsteps going to the back porch. Natasha got up and looked out of the window. An enormous train of wounded men had come to a halt outside in the street.

The maids, the footmen, the housekeeper, the old nurse, the cooks, coachmen, post-boys and scullions were all at the gate, staring at the wounded.

Natasha flung a white pocket-handkerchief over her hair and holding the ends in both hands went out into the street.

The old housekeeper, Mavra Kuzminishna, had stepped out of the crowd by the gate and gone up to a cart with a hood constructed of bast mats, and was talking to a pale young officer who lay inside. Natasha moved a few steps forward and stopped shyly, still holding her handkerchief on, and listened to what the housekeeper was saying.

'So haven't you any kith or kin in Moscow, then?' she was asking. 'You'd be more comfortable in a house somewhere ... in ours for instance ... the family are leaving.'

'I don't know if they'd let me,' replied the officer in a weak voice. 'There's our commanding officer ... ask him,' and he pointed to a stout major who was walking back along the street past the row of carts.

Natasha glanced with frightened eyes into the face of the wounded man, and at once went to meet the major.

'Can some of the wounded stay in our house?' she asked.

The major raised his hand to his cap with a smile.

'Which one do you want, mam'selle?' he said, screwing up his eyes and smiling.

Natasha quietly repeated her question, and her face and her whole manner were so serious, though she was still holding on to the ends of her handkerchief, that the major ceased smiling and after some reflection – as if considering how far it were possible – replied in the affirmative.

'Oh yes, why not? Certainly they can,' he said.

Giving him a slight bow, Natasha stepped back quickly to Mavra Kuzminishna, who was still talking to the wounded officer, full of pity and sympathy.

'They may. He says they may!' whispered Natasha.

The cart in which the officer lay turned into the Rostovs' courtyard, and dozens of carts with wounded men began at the invitation of the townsfolk to draw up at the steps of the houses in Povarsky street.

Natasha was evidently pleased at having to do with strange people and circumstances. She and Mavra Kuzminishna tried to get as many of the wounded as possible into their yard.

'We must tell your papa, though,' said Mavra Kuzminishna.

'Never mind, never mind, what does it matter? For one day we can move into the drawing-room. They can have all our part of the house.'

'What an idea, young lady! Even if we give them the wing, the men's room and old nurse's room, we must still ask permission.'

'All right, I'll go and ask.'

Natasha ran into the house and tip-toed through the half-open door into the sitting-room where there was a strong smell of vinegar and Hoffman's drops.

'Are you asleep, mamma?'

'How can I sleep?' said the countess, waking up just as she was dropping into a doze.

'Mamma, darling!' said Natasha, kneeling by her mother and laying her cheek against hers. 'I am sorry, forgive me, I'll never do it again: I woke you up! Mavra Kuzminishna sent me: they have brought some wounded here - officers. Will you have them? They've nowhere to go. I knew you would ...' she said quickly all in one breath.

'What officers? Who has been brought here? I don't understand at all?' said the countess.

Natasha laughed, the countess too smiled faintly.

'I knew you'd give permission ... so I'll tell them,' and kissing her mother Natasha jumped up and darted to the door.

In the hall she met her father, who had come home with bad news.

'We have lingered on too long!' said the count with involuntary vexation. 'The club's closed and the police are leaving too.'

'Papa, you don't mind, I've invited some of the wounded into the house?' said Natasha.

'Of course not,' answered the count absently. 'That's not the point. I beg of you now to have done with trifling, and help to pack and get off - tomorrow we must go. ...'

And the count proceeded to give similar instructions to the major-domo and the servants.

Petya came back at dinner-time and told them the news he had heard. He said the people were fetching weapons from the Kremlin,

1013

and though Rostopchin had said in his broadsheet that he would sound the alarm a couple of days beforehand it was known in the town that tomorrow everyone was to go armed to the Three Hills, where a great battle would be fought.

The countess looked with nervous horror at her son's eager, excited face while he was saying this. She realized that if she uttered a word to dissuade him from going to this battle (she knew how delighted he was with the prospect) he would say something about *men* and *honour* and the *Fatherland* – some extravagant masculine absurdity which there would be no denying and that would be fatal to her plans; and so, hoping to arrange to leave before then and take Petya with them as their defender and protector, she said nothing to her son, but after dinner called the count aside and implored him with tears in her eyes to take her away quickly, that very night if possible. With the instinctive cunning of a woman where her affections are concerned she, who till then had not shown the slightest trace of alarm, declared that she would die of fright if they did not leave that very night. There was no pretence about it: she was now afraid of everything.

14

MADAME SCHOSS, who had been out to visit her daughter, increased the countess's terrors still further by describing the scenes she had witnessed outside a spirit-store in Myasnitsky street. She had taken that street on her way home but had been held up by a drunken mob rioting in front of the shop. She had hailed a cab and returned by a roundabout route and the driver had told her that the crowd had been breaking open the casks of spirit, having received orders to that effect.

After dinner the entire Rostov household set to work with eager haste to pack their belongings and prepare for departure. The old count, suddenly rousing himself to the task, kept trotting to and fro between the courtyard and the house, shouting confused instructions to the scurrying servants and urging them to still greater haste. Petya directed operations in the courtyard. Sonya was completely bewildered by the count's contradictory orders and did not know what to be at. The servants raced about the house and yard, shouting, quarrelling and making a din. Natasha too, with the ardour characteristic of her in all she did, suddenly threw herself into the fray. At first her intervention in the business of packing was received sceptically. No one expected anything but pranks from her, and they ignored her instructions; but her demands to be obeyed were so passionately earnest, and she grew angry and came so near weeping because they would not pay attention, that she at last succeeded in making them believe in her. Her first achievement, which cost her immense effort and established her authority, was the packing of the carpets. The count had a number of valuable Gobelin tapestries and Persian rugs in the house. When Natasha fell to work two large chests stood open in the ball-room, one almost full of china, the other of carpets. There was a great deal more china left waiting on the tables, and still more was coming from the pantry. There was nothing for it but to start on a third chest and the men had gone to fetch one.

'Sonya, wait, we can pack everything into these two,' said Natasha.

'Impossible, miss, we've already tried,' said the butler.

'No, wait a moment, please.'

And Natasha began taking out of the packing-case the plates and dishes wrapped in paper.

'We must put the dishes in here with the rugs,' said she.

'Why, it'll be a mercy if we get the carpets alone into three chests,' said the butler.

'Oh wait, please!' And Natasha rapidly and deftly began sorting out the things. 'These we won't want,' she said of some plates of Kiev ware. 'These, yes – these must go in among the rugs,' she decided, fishing out the Saxony dishes.

'Do stop, Natasha. Leave it alone, we can manage it all without you,' pleaded Sonya disparagingly.

'What a young lady!' exclaimed the major-domo.

But Natasha would not give in. She pulled everything out and quickly proceeded to repack, deciding that there was no need at all to take the ordinary cheaper carpets or the everyday crockery. When everything was out of the chests, they started again. And in fact, by rejecting almost everything which was not worth taking, all that was of value really did go into the two chests. Only the lid of the case containing the rugs would not shut. They could have taken out one or two things but Natasha was determined not to be beaten. She arranged and rearranged the contents, squeezed them down, made the butler and Petya – whose help she had enlisted – press on the lid, and added her own desperate efforts.

'There, that's enough, Natasha,' said Sonya. 'I see you were right, but now just take out the top one.'

'I won't!' cried Natasha, with one hand holding back the hair that hung over her perspiring face while with the other she pushed at the rugs. 'Now press, Petya! Press, Vasilich! Hard!' she cried.

The rugs yielded and the lid closed. Natasha, clapping her hands, squealed with delight, and tears gushed from her eyes. But this only lasted a second. She immediately applied herself to a new job, and now the servants put complete faith in her. The count did not take it amiss when they told him that Natasha had countermanded some order of his, or the servants went to her to ask whether a cart was sufficiently loaded and could it be roped up! Thanks to Natasha's supervision progress was swift now: everything of little account was left out and the most valuable things were packed as compactly as possible.

Still, in spite of their united efforts far into the night, they could not get everything done. The countess fell asleep and the count, deferring their departure till morning, went to bed.

Sonya and Natasha slept in the sitting-room without undressing.

That night another wounded man was driven along Povarsky street, and Mavra Kuzminishna, who was standing at the gate, had him brought into the Rostovs' courtyard. She supposed, she said, that he must be a very important personage. He was in a calèche with the hood raised, and was quite covered by the apron. On the box beside the driver sat a venerable-looking old valet. A doctor and two soldiers followed in a cart.

'Come into our house, come in. The family are all going, the whole house will be empty,' said the old woman, addressing the aged valet.

'Well, perhaps,' said he with a sigh. 'We don't expect to get him home alive! We've a house of our own in Moscow, but it's a long way from here, and there's no one living in it either.'

'This way, please, you are very welcome. There's plenty of everything in the master's house. Come in,' said Mavra Kuzminishna. 'Is the gentleman very bad, then?' she asked.

The valet made a hopeless gesture.

'There's no hope! We must ask the doctor.'

And the old servant got down from the box and went up to the cart behind.

'Very good,' said the doctor.

The valet returned to the calèche, peeped in, shook his head, bade the coachman turn into the yard, and stopped beside Mavra Kuzminishna.

'Merciful Saviour!' she murmured.

She invited them to take the wounded man into the house.

'The family won't object ...' she said.

But it was necessary to avoid carrying the wounded man upstairs, and so they took him into the wing and put him in the room that had been Madame Schoss's.

The wounded man was Prince Andrei Bolkonsky.

15

MOSCOW's last day had dawned. It was a clear, bright autumn morning, a Sunday. Just as on ordinary Sundays the church bells everywhere were ringing for service. It seemed that no one yet was able to realize what awaited the city.

Only two indications marked the crisis in which Moscow found herself: the rabble – that is, the unusual number of the poorer classes wandering the streets – and the price of commodities. Factory hands, house-serfs and peasants flocked out early that morning to the Three Hills in immense crowds, which were swelled by clerks, divinity students and gentry. After waiting there for Rostopchin, who did not turn up, and convinced now that Moscow would be surrendered, they dispersed about the town to the public-houses and cookshops. Prices, too, on that day indicated the state of affairs. Weapons, gold coin, carts and horses rose steadily, while the value of paper money and luxury goods for town use kept falling, so that by midday there were instances of carters, in lieu of payment, keeping for themselves half of any expensive goods, such as cloth, which they were delivering, and of peasant horses fetching five hundred roubles each, while furniture, mirrors and bronzes went begging.

In the Rostovs' staid old-fashioned house the collapse of all the usual conditions of life was scarcely noticeable. True, three out of their immense retinue of servants vanished during the night, but nothing was stolen; and as to the value of their possessions – the thirty peasant carts brought in from their estates in the country were in themselves worth a fortune and were the envy of many, people offering enormous sums of money for them. Not only were the

Rostovs offered huge sums for the horses and carts but all the previous evening and from early morning on the 1st of September orderlies and servants sent by wounded officers came to their courtyard, and wounded men dragged themselves out from the house and from neighbouring houses where they were accommodated, imploring the servants to try to get them a lift out of Moscow. The major-domo, to whom these entreaties were addressed, though he was sorry for the wounded, resolutely refused, saying that he would never even dare to hint at such a thing to the count. However hard it was to leave the wounded behind, it was self-evident that if one gave up one cart to them, why not another, and so on, until it came to putting one's own carriage too at their service? Thirty teams would not save all the wounded, and in the general catastrophe it was impossible not to think of oneself and one's own family first. So reasoned the major-domo on his master's behalf.

On waking up that morning Count Ilya Rostov slipped quietly from his bedroom, so as not to wake the countess who had only fallen asleep towards morning, and came out to the porch in his lilac silk dressing-gown. The loaded wagons were standing in the courtyard. The carriages were drawn up at the steps. The major-domo stood at the street-door talking to an elderly orderly and a pale young officer with his arm in a sling. Seeing his master, the major-domo made a significant and peremptory sign to them both that they should go.

'Well, Vasilich, is everything ready?' asked the count, rubbing his bald head; and looking benignly at the officer and the orderly he nodded to them. (The count liked new faces.)

'We can harness at once, your Excellency.'

'Well, that's capital. As soon as the countess wakes we'll be off, God willing! What is it, gentlemen?' he added, turning to the officer. 'Are you staying in my house?'

The officer came nearer. His pale face suddenly flushed crimson.

'Count ... for God's sake ... let me find a corner in one of your carts! I have nothing here with me. ... I could quite well travel with the luggage. ...'

Before the officer had finished speaking the orderly made the same request on behalf of his master.

'Of course, of course, only too glad!' said the count hastily. 'Vasilich, you see to it. Have a wagon or two cleared, that one there, say ... or ... well, whatever's needed ...' he added, muttering some vague order. But the glowing look of gratitude on the officer's face instantly set the seal on the order. The count glanced about him: everywhere – in the yard, at the gates, at the windows of the 'wing' – he saw wounded men and orderlies. They were all gazing at him and moving towards the porch.

'Please step into the gallery, your Excellency,' said the major-domo. 'What are your Excellency's instructions about the pictures?'

The count went into the house with him, repeating his injunctions not to refuse any of the wounded who asked for a lift.

'After all, we can always take some of the things out, you know,' he added in a low, confidential whisper, as though afraid of being overheard.

At nine o'clock the countess woke, and Matriona Timofyevna, who had been her lady's maid before her marriage and now performed the duties of a sort of chief gendarme for her, came to say that Madame Schoss was greatly incensed, and that the young ladies' summer dresses could not possibly be left behind. On the countess inquiring the cause of Madame Schoss's resentment, it appeared that her trunk had been taken off its cart, and that all the loads were being uncorded and the luggage removed to make room for wounded men, whom the count in the simplicity of his heart had said were to come with them. The countess sent for her husband.

'What's this, my dear? I hear the luggage is being unloaded.'

'You know, love, I wanted to tell you. ... Little countess, my dear ... an officer came up to me – they begged me to let them have a few carts for the wounded. After all, those things of ours are only things but think what it would mean for them to be left behind! ... Here they are in our very yard – we invited them ourselves, some of them are officers. ... You know, I really think, *ma chère* ... let them come with us ... what is the hurry anyway?'

The count said this timidly, in the way he spoke whenever the subject was in any way connected with money. The countess well knew this tone, which always ushered in some project prejudicial to her children's interests, such as the building of a new gallery or conservatory, the inauguration of a private theatre or orchestra, and she made it a habit and regarded it as a duty to oppose anything that was announced in that timid manner.

She assumed her air of tearful resignation and said to her husband: 'Listen to me, count, you have mismanaged things so that we are

1019

getting nothing for the house, and now you want to throw away all our – all *the children's* – property! Why, you told me yourself that we have a hundred thousand roubles' worth of valuables in the house. I don't agree, my dear, I don't agree. You must do as you please! It's the government's business to look after the wounded. They know that. Look at the Lopuhins opposite – every stick of theirs they cleared out two days ago. That's what other people do. It's only we who are such fools. If you have no consideration for me, do at least think of the children.'

Flourishing his arms in despair, the count left the room without a word.

'Papa, what is the matter?' asked Natasha, who had followed him to her mother's room.

'Nothing! Nothing that concerns you!' muttered the count testily.

'But I heard,' said Natasha. 'Why does mamma object?'

'What business is it of yours?' cried her father.

Natasha walked away to the window and pondered.

'Papa, here's Berg come to see us!' she said, looking out of the window.

16

BERG, the Rostovs' son-in-law, was by now a colonel wearing the orders of Vladimir and Anna, and he still filled the same pleasant, comfortable post of assistant to the chief of staff of the lieutenant-general of the 1st division of the Second Corps.

On the 1st of September he had come to Moscow from the army.

He had nothing to do in Moscow, but he had noticed that everyone in the army was asking for leave to go to Moscow and had some business there. So he considered it necessary to request leave of absence for family and domestic reasons.

Berg drove up to his father-in-law's house in his spruce little trap drawn by a pair of sleek roans, exactly like those of a certain prince. He looked closely at the carts in the yard and as he went up the steps took out a clean pocket-handkerchief and tied a knot in it.

From the ante-room Berg ran with smooth though impatient steps into the drawing-room, where he embraced the count, kissed Natasha's hand and Sonya's, and hastened to inquire after 'Mamma's' health.

'Health, at a time like this?' said the count. 'Come, tell us the news.

How about the army? Are they retreating, or will there be another battle?'

'Only the Eternal One can tell what will be the fate of our Fatherland, papa,' said Berg. 'The army is afire with the spirit of heroism, and even now its chieftains, so to speak, are assembled in council. No one knows what is coming. But in general I can tell you, papa, that no words can do justice to the heroic spirit, the truly "antique" valour of the Russian army, which they – which it' (he corrected himself) 'showed, or rather, displayed in the battle of the 26th. I can assure you, papa' (he smote himself on the chest as he had seen a general do who had made much the same speech, but Berg was a trifle late – he should have struck his breast at the words 'Russian army'), 'I can assure you that we officers, far from having to urge the men on, or anything of that sort, had much ado to restrain those ... those ... yes, those exploits recalling the valour of antiquity,' he rattled off. 'General Barclay de Tolly risked his life everywhere at the head of the troops, I can assure you. Our corps was posted on a hill-side. You can imagine!' And Berg proceeded to relate all that he had picked up from hearsay since the engagement. Natasha watched Berg with a persistent stare that disconcerted him, as if she were trying to find in his face the answer to some problem.

'Altogether such heroism as was displayed by our Russian fighting men is beyond description and beyond praise!' said Berg, glancing round at Natasha and, as though anxious to conciliate her, replying to her intent look with a smile. '"Russia is not in Moscow, she lives in the hearts of her sons!" Isn't that so, Papa?' said he.

At this point the countess came in from the sitting-room, looking tired and cross. Berg jumped to his feet, kissed her hand, inquired after her health and remained standing by her, shaking his head from side to side to express his sympathy.

'Yes, mamma, to tell the truth these are hard and sorrowful times for every Russian. But why are you so worried? You have still time to get away. ...'

'I can't make out what the servants are up to,' said the countess, turning to her husband. 'They've just told me nothing is ready yet. You see how necessary it is for someone to take charge. This is where we miss Mitenka. There won't be any end to it.'

The count was about to say something but with a visible effort restrained himself. He got up from his chair and went to the door.

Berg, meanwhile, had taken out his handkerchief as though to blow his nose, and, seeing the knot in it, pondered, shaking his head sadly and meaningly.

'Do you know, I have a great favour to ask of you, papa,' said he.

'H'm?' said the count, and stopped.

'I was driving past Yusupov's house just now,' said Berg with a laugh, 'when the steward, a man I know, ran out and asked me whether I wouldn't care to buy any of their things. I went in out of curiosity, you know, and there is a little chiffonier and a dressing-table. You remember how dear Vera wanted one and we quarrelled about it.' (At the mention of the chiffonier Berg unconsciously slipped into a tone expressive of his pleasure in his admirable domestic establishment.) 'And it's such a charming piece! The drawers pull out and there's one with a secret English lock, you know! Dear Vera's been wanting one for a long time. I should so like to make her a surprise. I saw what a number of peasant carts you have in the yard. Spare me one of them; I will pay the man well, and ...'

The count frowned and cleared his throat.

'Ask the countess; I don't give the orders.'

'If it's troublesome, pray don't,' said Berg. 'Only I should so have liked it on dear Vera's account.'

'Oh, to the devil with all of you! To the devil, the devil, the devil! ...' roared the old count. 'My head's in a whirl!'

And he left the room.

The countess began to cry.

'Yes, indeed, mamma, these are very trying times!' said Berg.

Natasha went out of the room with her father and, as though unable to make up her mind on some difficult point, at first followed him and then turned and ran downstairs.

Petya was in the porch, engaged in distributing weapons to the servants who were to leave Moscow. The loaded carts were still standing in the courtyard. Two of them had been uncorded, and a wounded officer was climbing into one, helped by an orderly.

'Do you know what it's about?' Petya asked Natasha.

Natasha knew that he meant what their father and mother had been quarrelling about. She did not answer.

'It's because papa wanted to give up all the carts to the wounded,' said Petya. 'Vasilich told me. In my opinion ...'

'In my opinion,' Natasha suddenly almost shrieked, turning a

1022

furious face on Petya, 'in my opinion, this is so horrid, so abominable, so. .... I don't know what. Are we a lot of wretched Germans?'

Her throat quivered with convulsive sobs and, afraid of weakening and letting the force of her anger run to waste, she turned and dashed headlong up the stairs.

Berg was sitting beside the countess, trying with filial duty to console her. The count, pipe in hand, was striding about the room, when Natasha, her face distorted with indignation, burst in like a hurricane and walked quickly up to her mother.

'It's horrible, disgraceful!' she screamed. 'It can't be true that it's by your orders!'

Berg and the countess gazed at her in alarm and bewilderment. The count stood still in the window, listening.

'Mamma, it's impossible: look what's happening in the courtyard!' she cried. 'They are being left! ...'

'What's the matter with you? Who are "they"? What do you want?'

'Why, the wounded! You can't do it, mamma! It's all wrong. ... No, mamma darling, it's not right. Forgive me, dearest. ... Mamma, what do we want with all those things? You only look at what's going on in the courtyard. ... Mamma! We can't ...!'

The count stood in the window and listened to Natasha without turning his head. Suddenly he gave a sort of gulp and put his face closer to the casement.

The countess glanced at her daughter, saw her face full of shame for her mother, saw her agitation, and understood why her husband kept his eyes averted, and she looked about her with a distracted air.

'Oh, do as you please! Am I interfering with anyone?' she said, not giving way all at once.

'Mamma, darling, forgive me.'

But the countess pushed her daughter away and went up to the count.

'Mon cher, you arrange what is right. ... You know I don't understand about it,' she said, with downcast eyes.

'Out of the mouth of babes ...' murmured the count through tears of joy, and he embraced his wife, who was glad to hide her ashamed face against his breast.

'Papa! Mamma! May I see to it? May I? ...' asked Natasha. 'And we'll take all that we really need.'

The count nodded, and Natasha was gone, darting through the ball-room to the ante-room and downstairs into the courtyard, her foot as light as when she used to play tag as a child.

The servants gathered round Natasha but could not believe the strange order she brought them until the count himself, in his wife's name, confirmed the instructions to give up all the carts to the wounded and take the trunks back to the store-rooms. When they understood, the servants set to work with a will at this new task. It no longer seemed strange to them but, on the contrary, no other course seemed possible, just as a quarter of an hour before not only had no one thought it strange that the wounded should be left behind while the furniture was taken: it was the natural thing.

The entire household, as if to atone for not having done it sooner, eagerly lent a hand with getting the wounded into the wagons. The wounded men crawled out of their rooms and crowded round the carts with pale, happy faces. The news spread that places were to be had in the Rostovs' carts, and wounded men began coming into the courtyard from other neighbouring houses. Many of the wounded begged them not to take out the chests but simply to let them sit on top of the luggage. But once the work of unloading had begun there was no stopping it. It seemed not to matter whether all or only half the things were left behind. Cases full of china, bronzes, pictures and mirrors that had been so carefully packed the night before now lay about the yard, and still they sought and found possibilities of taking out this or that and letting the wounded have another and yet another cart.

'There's room for four more here,' said the steward. 'They can have my trap, otherwise what is to become of them?'

'Give them my wardrobe cart,' said the countess. 'Dunyasha can come with me in the carriage.'

They cleared the wardrobe cart and sent it to fetch wounded men from two doors off. The whole household, servants included, were full of happy excitement. Natasha was worked up to a pitch of enthusiasm such as she had not known for a long time.

'What can we tie this to?' asked the servants, trying to fix a trunk on the narrow footboard at the back of the carriage. 'We must keep at least one cart.'

'What's in it?' asked Natasha.

'The master's books.'

1024

'Leave it. Vasilich will take care of it. It's not wanted.'

The phaeton was full of passengers, and there was a doubt as to where Count Petya was to sit.

'On the box. You'll go on the box, won't you, Petya?' cried Natasha.

Sonya, too, was busy all this time; but the object of her efforts was quite different from Natasha's. She was putting away the things that had to be left behind and making a list of them by the countess's desire, and doing her best to get as much taken with them as possible.

17

WELL before two o'clock in the afternoon the Rostovs' four carriages, packed full and ready to start, stood at the front door. One by one the wagons with the wounded filed out of the courtyard.

The calèche in which Prince Andrei was lying attracted Sonya's attention as it drove past the porch just as she and a maid were arranging a comfortable seat for the countess in the huge, lofty coach standing at the steps.

'Whose calèche is that?' she inquired, leaning out of the carriage window.

'Why, haven't you heard, miss?' replied the maid. 'It's the wounded prince: he spent the night in our house and is going on with us.'

'But who is it? What is his name?'

'It's our intended that was – Prince Bolkonsky!' sighed the maid. 'They say he is dying.'

Sonya jumped out of the coach and ran to the countess. The countess, ready dressed for the journey in shawl and bonnet, was wearily wandering up and down the drawing-room waiting for the rest of the party to assemble and sit for a moment with closed doors for the usual silent prayer before starting out. Natasha was not in the room.

'*Maman*,' said Sonya. 'Prince Andrei is here, wounded and dying. He is going with us.'

The countess opened her eyes in dismay and, clutching Sonya's arm, glanced about her.

'Natasha?' she whispered.

At that first moment this news had but one significance for both of them. They knew their Natasha, and alarm as to what might be the effect on her outweighed all sympathy for the man whom they both liked.

'Natasha does not know yet, but he is going with us,' said Sonya.

'You say he is dying?'

Sonya nodded.

The countess threw her arms around Sonya and burst into tears.

'The ways of the Lord are past finding out!' she thought, feeling that the omnipotent hand of Providence, hitherto unseen, was becoming manifest in all that was now taking place.

'Well, mamma, we're all ready. What's the matter? ...' asked Natasha with animated face, running into the room.

'Nothing,' answered the countess. 'If we're ready, then let us be off.'

And the countess bent over her reticule to hide her agitated face. Sonya hugged Natasha and kissed her.

Natasha looked inquisitively at her.

'What is it? What has happened?'

'Nothing – noth ...'

'Something very bad, concerning me? ... What is it?' persisted the intuitive Natasha.

Sonya sighed and made no reply. The count, Petya, Madame Schoss, Mavra Kuzminishna and Vasilich came into the drawing-room, and having closed the doors they all sat down and remained for several moments silently seated without looking at one another.

The count was the first to rise, and with a loud sigh crossed himself before the icon. All the others did the same. Then the count proceeded to embrace Mavra Kuzminishna and Vasilich, who were to stay behind in Moscow, and while they caught at his hand and kissed his shoulder he patted their backs, muttering some vaguely affectionate and reassuring words. The countess went off to the little prayer-room where Sonya found her on her knees before the icons that had been left here and there hanging on the wall. (The most precious ones, which were counted as family heirlooms, they were taking with them.)

In the porch and in the yard the servants who were going – all of whom had been armed with swords and daggers by Petya – with their trousers tucked inside their high boots, and belts and girdles tightened, were exchanging farewells with those who were to be left behind.

As is invariably the case at a departure, several things had been forgotten or packed in the wrong place, and two grooms were kept a long time standing one each side of the open carriage-door, waiting to help the countess up the carriage-steps, while maids bringing cushions and bundles flew backwards and forwards between the house, the carriages, the calèche and the phaeton.

'They always will forget everything as long as they live!' said the countess. 'You know that I can't sit like that.'

And Dunyasha, clenching her teeth to keep silent, but with an aggrieved look on her face, hastily got into the coach to rearrange the cushions.

'Ah, servants, servants!' muttered the count, shaking his head.

Yefim, the old coachman, who was the only one the countess trusted to drive her, sat perched up on the box and never so much as glanced round at what was going on behind him. His thirty years' experience had taught him that it would be some time yet before they would say, 'Off now, and God be with us!'; and that even after that he would be stopped at least twice while they sent back for some forgotten article; and then once more for the countess herself to lean out of the window and beg him in heaven's name to be careful driving downhill. He knew all this and therefore awaited what was to come with more patience than his horses, especially the near one, the chestnut Falcon, who was pawing the ground and champing the bit. At last all were seated, the carriage-steps pulled up, the door was shut with a bang, a forgotten travelling-case sent for, and the countess had popped her head out and said what was expected of her. Then Yefim slowly doffed his hat and began crossing himself. The postilion and all the other servants did the same.

'God be with us!' cried Yefim, putting on his hat. 'Off now!'

The postilion cracked his whip. The right shaft-horse tugged at his collar, the high springs creaked and the body of the coach swayed. The footman sprang on to the box as the coach jolted out of the courtyard and over the uneven pavement; the other vehicles bumped along behind, and the procession started up the street. The occupants of the carriages, the calèche and the phaeton all crossed themselves as they passed the church opposite. The servants who were remaining in Moscow walked on either side of the vehicles to see the travellers off.

Natasha had rarely experienced such keen delight as she felt at that moment sitting in the carriage beside the countess and gazing at the slowly receding walls of forsaken, agitated Moscow. Now and then she put her head out of the carriage-window and looked back, and then in front at the long train of wounded preceding them. Almost at the head of the line she could see the raised hood of Prince Andrei's calèche. She did not know who was in it but each time she took stock of the procession her eyes sought that calèche. She knew it would be right in front.

In Kudrino, from Nikitsky street, Presny and Podnovinskoy street emerged several other trains of vehicles similar to the Rostovs' and by the time they reached Sadovoy street the carriages and carts were two abreast all along the road.

As they were going round the Suharev water-tower Natasha, who was inquisitively and alertly scrutinizing the people driving or walking by, exclaimed with joyful surprise:

'My goodness! Mamma, Sonya, look, it's he!'

'Who? Who?'

'Look, do look! It *is* Bezuhov!' cried Natasha, putting her head out of the carriage-window and staring at a tall, stout man in a coachman's long coat, whose gait and the way he held himself made it obvious that he was a gentleman in disguise. He was passing under the arch of the Suharev tower accompanied by a sallow-faced, beardless little old man in a frieze coat.

'Yes, it really is Bezuhov in a coachman's coat, with a queer-looking old boy,' said Natasha. 'Do look, do look!'

'Of course it isn't. How can you talk such nonsense!'

'Mamma,' screamed Natasha, 'I'll stake my head it's he. I assure you! Stop, stop!' she cried to the coachman.

But the coachman could not stop, because more carts and carriages were filing out of Meshchansky street and the Rostovs were being shouted at to move on and not hold up the traffic.

However, though now at a much greater distance, all the Rostovs did indeed see Pierre - or someone extraordinarily like him - wearing a coachman's coat and going along the street with bent head and a serious face beside a small, beardless old man who looked like a footman. This old man noticed a face thrust out of the carriage-window staring at them, and respectfully touching Pierre's elbow said something to him, pointing to the carriage. Pierre appeared to be sunk in thought and it was some time before he understood what was being said to him. At length, when he realized, he looked in the direction indicated and, recognizing Natasha, immediately yielded to his first impulse and took a quick step towards the coach. But having gone a dozen paces he seemed to remember something and stopped short.

Natasha's face, leaning out of the window, beamed with mischievous affection.

'Piotr Kirillich, come here! You see, we recognized you! This is wonderful!' she cried, stretching out a hand to him. 'What are you doing? Why are you dressed like that?'

Pierre took the outstretched hand and kissed it awkwardly as he walked beside the carriage (which continued moving).

'What has happened, count?' asked the countess in an astonished, commiserating tone.

'I – I – Why? Don't ask me,' said Pierre, and he looked round at Natasha whose radiant, happy expression – which he felt without looking at her – flooded him with enchantment.

'What are you doing – or are you going to stay in Moscow?'

Pierre hesitated.

'In Moscow?' he said doubtfully. 'Yes, in Moscow. Good-bye.'

'Oh, how I wish I were a man, I'd stay with you! How splendid!' said Natasha. 'Mamma, do let me.'

Pierre glanced absently at Natasha and was about to say something but the countess interrupted him.

'We heard you were at the battle?'

'Yes, I was,' answered Pierre. 'Tomorrow there will be another battle ...,' he was beginning, but Natasha broke in.

'But what is the matter, count? You are not like yourself. ...'

'Oh, don't ask me, don't ask me! I don't know. Tomorrow. ... But no! Good-bye, good-bye!' he muttered. 'Terrible times!' and dropping behind the carriage he stepped on to the pavement.

Natasha for a long while still kept her head out of the window, beaming at him with her fond, slightly quizzical, joyous smile.

18

FROM the time he had disappeared from home, two days before, Pierre had been living in the empty abode of his deceased benefactor, Osip Bazdeyev. This is how it happened.

When he woke on the morning after his return to Moscow and his interview with Count Rostopchin, he could not at first make out where he was and what was required of him. When his major-domo mentioned among the names of those who were waiting to see him that of the Frenchman who had brought the letter from his wife, the Countess Hélène, one of the fits of bewilderment and despair to which he was so liable suddenly came over him. He felt all at once that everything was now at an end, everything was in confusion and crumbling to pieces, that no one was right or wrong, the future held nothing and there was no escape from this coil of troubles. With an unnatural smile on his lips and muttering to himself, he now sat down on the sofa in an attitude of helplessness, now rose, went to the door and peeped through the crack into the ante-room, then turned back with a fierce gesture and took up a book. His major-domo came in for the second time to say that the Frenchman who had brought the letter from the countess was very anxious to see him if only for a minute, and that someone from Bazdeyev's widow had called to ask Pierre to take charge of her husband's books, as she herself was leaving for the country.

'Oh yes, at once – wait. ... No, no, go and say I will be along directly,' Pierre replied to the major-domo.

But as soon as the man had left the room Pierre snatched up his hat which was lying on the table and left his study by the other door. There was no one in the passage. Pierre walked the whole length of the corridor to the stairs and, frowning and rubbing his forehead with both hands, went down as far as the first landing. The hall-porter was standing at the front door. From the landing where Pierre stood there was a second staircase leading to the back entrance. He ran down this staircase and out into the yard. No one had seen him. But as soon as he turned out of the gates into the street the coachmen waiting by their carriages, and the gate-porter, caught sight of him and took off their caps. Aware of their eyes fixed on him, Pierre behaved like an ostrich which hides its head in the shrub to avoid being seen: he hung his head and, quickening his pace, hurried down the street.

Of all the business awaiting Pierre that morning the task of sorting Bazdeyev's books and papers appeared to him the most urgent.

He hailed the first conveyance he met and told the driver to go to Patriarch's Ponds, where the widow Bazdeyev's house was.

He kept turning to look about him at the long lines of loaded carts that were making their way out of Moscow from all sides, and, balancing his bulky person so as not to be tipped out of the rickety old chaise, Pierre knew the light-hearted sensation of a runaway school-boy, as he chatted with the driver.

The man told him that arms were being distributed that day in the Kremlin and that next day everyone would be sent out beyond the Three Hills gate, where a great battle was to be fought.

When they reached Patriarch's Ponds Pierre had some difficulty in recognizing the house, where he had not been for some time. He went up to the garden-gate. Gerasim, the sallow, beardless old man Pierre had seen with Bazdeyev five years before at Torzhok, came out in answer to his knock.

'Anyone at home?' asked Pierre.

'Owing to present circumstances my mistress and the children have gone to their house in the country at Torzhok, your Excellency.'

'I'll come in all the same: I want to look through the books,' said Pierre.

'Be so good as to step this way. Makar Alexeyevich, the brother of my late master – God rest his soul! – has stayed behind; but as your Honour is aware he is in feeble health.'

Pierre knew that Makar Alexeyevich was Bazdeyev's half-witted brother, who was given to tippling.

'Yes, yes. Let us go in …' said Pierre, and he walked into the house.

A tall, bald-headed, red-nosed old man wearing a dressing-gown and with goloshes on his bare feet was standing in the vestibule. When he saw Pierre he muttered something angrily and shuffled off along the passage.

'He was a very clever man once but now, as your Honour can see, he has quite declined,' said Gerasim. 'Will you come this way into the study?' Pierre nodded. 'It has not been disturbed since it was sealed up. The mistress gave orders that if anyone should come from you they were to have the books.'

Pierre went into the gloomy study which he had entered with such trepidation in his benefactor's lifetime. Now thick with dust and un-touched since Bazdeyev's death, the room was gloomier than ever.

Gerasim opened one of the shutters and crept away on tiptoe. Pierre walked round the room, went up to the bookcase in which the manuscripts were kept and took out what had once been one of the most important and sacred documents of the Order. This consisted of some of the original acts of the Scottish Lodges, with Bazdeyev's notes and commentaries. He sat down at the dusty writing-table and, spreading the manuscripts before him, opened them out, then closed them and finally pushed them away, and resting his head on his hand fell to musing.

Gerasim peeped in cautiously several times and saw Pierre always sitting in the same atittude.

More than two hours passed. Gerasim ventured to make a slight noise at the door to attract Pierre's attention. Pierre did not hear him.

'Is the driver to be discharged, your Honour?'

'Oh, yes!' said Pierre, rousing himself and hastily getting to his feet. 'Listen,' he added, taking Gerasim by the button of his coat and looking down at the old man with moist, shining eyes full of exalta-tion. 'I say, you know that tomorrow there is to be a battle ... ?'

'So they've been saying,' replied Gerasim.

'I beg you not to tell anyone who I am, and to do what I ask you. ...'

'Certainly, sir,' said Gerasim. 'Would your Honour like something to eat?'

'No, but I want something else. I want peasant clothes and a pistol,' said Pierre, unexpectedly blushing.

'Certainly, your Excellency,' said Gerasim, after thinking for a moment.

All the rest of that day Pierre spent alone in his benefactor's study, and Gerasim heard him pacing restlessly from one corner of the room to the other and talking to himself, and he spent the night on a bed made up for him there.

Gerasim, with the equanimity of a servant who has seen many things in his time, accepted Pierre's installation in the house without surprise, and he seemed, indeed, pleased to have someone to wait on. That same evening – without even permitting himself to wonder what they were wanted for – he procured a coachman's coat and cap for Pierre, and promised to get him the pistol next day. Twice that evening Makar Alexeyevich shuffled along to the door in his goloshes, and stood there gazing ingratiatingly at Pierre. But as soon as Pierre turned to him he wrapped his dressing-gown round him with a shamefaced, irate look and hurried away. It was when Pierre, wearing the coachman's coat obtained and fumigated for him by Gerasim, was on his way with the old man to buy a pistol at the Suharev market that he met the Rostovs.

19

KUTUZOV'S order to fall back across Moscow to the Ryazan road was issued on the night of the 1st of September.

The vanguard started at once, marched slowly by night, without haste and in good order; but at daybreak the retiring troops nearing the city at the Dorogomilov bridge saw ahead of them masses of soldiers crowding and pushing across the bridge, toiling up the opposite side and blocking the streets and alleys, while endless multitudes of fighting-men were bearing down on them from behind; and they were seized with unreasoning hurry and alarm. There was a general surge forward on to the bridge, to the fords and to the boats. Kutuzov had himself driven round by the back streets to the other side of Moscow.

By ten o'clock on the morning of the 2nd of September the only troops left in the Dorogomilov suburbs were the regiments of the rearguard, and the crush was over. The main army was already on the far side of Moscow or beyond.

At this same time – ten in the morning of the 2nd of September – Napoleon was standing in the midst of his troops on the Poklonny hill gazing at the panorama spread out before him. From the 26th of August to the 2nd of September, that is from the battle of Borodino to the entry of the French into Moscow, all that agitating, memorable week, there had been that extraordinary autumn weather which always comes as a surprise, when the sun hangs low and shines more warmly than in spring; when everything sparkles so brightly in the pure, limpid atmosphere that the eyes are dazzled while the lungs are braced and refreshed by breathing in fragrant autumn air; when even the nights are warm and when in those dark mild nights golden stars slip from the skies, startling and delighting us.

At ten in the morning of the 2nd of September this weather still held. The early light was magical. Moscow, seen from the Poklonny hill, stretched far and wide with her river, her gardens and her churches, and seemed to be living a life of her own, her cupolas twinkling like stars in the sunlight.

The sight of the strange city with its peculiar architecture such as he had never seen before filled Napoleon with the rather envious and uneasy curiosity men feel when they contemplate an alien form of life which ignores their presence. This city appeared to be instinct with life. By those indefinable tokens by which one can infallibly distinguish, even at a distance, a living body from a dead one, Napoleon from the Poklonny hill could detect the throb of life in the town and felt, as it were, the breathing of that great and beautiful being.

'That Asiatic city of the innumerable churches, holy Moscow! Here it is at last – here is the famous city! It was high time,' said Napoleon, and dismounting from his horse, he bade them open the plan of Moscow before him, and he summoned his interpreter, Lelorgne d'Ideville.

'A town occupied by the enemy is like a maid who has lost her honour,' he thought (a remark he had already made to Tuchkov at Smolensk). And from that point of view he gazed at the oriental beauty before his eyes for the first time. Even to himself it seemed strange that the desire he had so long cherished, and thought so attainable, had at last been realized. In the clear morning light he gazed from the city to the map, from the map to the city, verifying details, and the certainty of possessing it agitated and awed him.

'But how could it be otherwise?' he thought. 'Here is this capital at my feet, awaiting her fate. Where is Alexander now, and what must he be feeling? Strange, beautiful, majestic city! And a strange and majestic moment! In what light do I appear to them now?' he mused, thinking of his soldiers. 'Here is this city – the reward for all those faint-hearted men,' he reflected, glancing at those near him and at the troops coming up and forming into line. 'One word from me, one wave of my arm, and the ancient capital of the Tsars would be no more. But my clemency is ever prompt to descend upon the vanquished. I must be magnanimous and truly great. ... But no,' he thought suddenly, 'it can't be true that I am in Moscow. Yet here she is lying at my feet, her golden domes and crosses flashing and scintillating in the sun. But I will spare her. On the ancient monuments of barbarism and despotism I will inscribe great words of justice and mercy. ... Alexander will feel that most painfully of all: I know him.' (It seemed to Napoleon that the principal significance of what was taking place lay in the personal contest between himself and Alexander.) 'From the heights of the Kremlin – yes, there is the Kremlin, yes – I will give them the laws of justice, I will teach them the meaning of true civilization, I will make generations of boyars remember with affection the name of their conqueror. I will tell the deputation that I did not and do not seek war, that I have waged war only against the false policy of their Court, that I love and respect Alexander and that in Moscow I will accept terms of peace worthy of myself and of my peoples. I have no wish to take advantage of the fortunes of war to humiliate an esteemed monarch. "Boyars," I will say to them, "I do not desire war. I desire peace and prosperity for all my subjects." In any case, I know their presence will inspire me, and I shall speak to them as I always do: clearly, impressively and magnanimously. But can it be true that I am in Moscow? Yes, there she lies!'

'Let the boyars be brought to me,' he said, addressing his suite.

A general with a brilliant following of adjutants galloped off at once to fetch the boyars.

Two hours passed. Napoleon had lunched and was again standing on the same spot on the Poklonny hill awaiting the deputation. His speech to the boyars had now taken definite shape in his mind. It was a speech full of dignity and majesty as Napoleon understood it.

Napoleon himself was carried away by the tone of great-hearted chivalry he intended to adopt towards Moscow. In imagination he appointed days for *une réunion dans le palais des Czars*, at which Russian grandees would mingle with the courtiers of the French Emperor. He mentally named a governor, one who would win over the population. Having heard that there were many charitable institutions in Moscow, he decided in his mind that he would shower his bounty on all of them. He thought that just as in Africa he had had to put on a burnous and sit in a mosque, so in Moscow he must be open-handed after the manner of the tsars. And in order conclusively to touch the hearts of the Russians – and being like all Frenchman unable to imagine anything affecting without a reference to '*ma chère, ma tendre, ma pauvre mère*' – he resolved to have an inscription on all these charitable foundations in large letters: THIS ESTABLISHMENT IS DEDICATED TO MY DEAR MOTHER. Or no, it should be simply: MAISON DE MA MÈRE. 'But am I really in Moscow? Yes, there she is before me, but why is the deputation from the city so long in appearing?' he wondered.

Meanwhile an agitated consultation was being carried on in whispers among his generals and marshals in the rear of the suite. The adjutants sent to fetch the deputation had returned with the news that Moscow was empty, that everyone had left the city, many on foot. The faces of those conferring together were pale and perturbed. It was not the fact that Moscow had been abandoned by its inhabitants (grave as that might seem) that alarmed them: the problem that dismayed them was how to tell the Emperor – without putting his Majesty in the terrible position of appearing what the French call *ridicule* – that he had been waiting for the boyars all this time in vain, that there were drunken mobs in Moscow but no one else. Some said that a deputation of some sort must be scraped together somehow; others opposed this idea, insisting that the Emperor, after being carefully and skilfully prepared for it, ought to hear the truth.

'He will have to be told, all the same,' said some gentlemen of the suite. '*Mais messieurs ...*'

The position was the more awkward because the Emperor, pondering on his magnanimous plans, was walking patiently up and down before the outspread map, shading his eyes to look from time to time along the road to Moscow, with a proud and happy smile.

'But it's impossible ...' the gentlemen-in-waiting kept repeating, shrugging their shoulders and unable to bring themselves to pronounce the terrible word which was in all their minds: *le ridicule. ...*

Meanwhile the Emperor, weary of his futile wait, his actor's instinct suggesting to him that the sublime moment by being too drawn out was losing its grandeur, made a sign with his hand. A single report of a signalling-gun followed, and the troops, already assembled outside the city, moved into Moscow through the Tver, Kaluga and Dorogomilov gates. Faster and faster, vying with one another, they advanced at the double or at a trot, concealed in the clouds of dust they raised and making the air ring with their deafening shouts.

Caught up in their enthusiasm, Napoleon rode with his army as far as the Dorogomilov gate, but there he halted again and, dismounting from his horse, for some considerable time strode about the Kamer-Kollezhsky rampart, waiting for the deputation.

20

MOSCOW meanwhile was empty. There were still people in the city – perhaps a fiftieth part of its former inhabitants still remained – but it was empty. It was empty in the sense that a dying, queenless hive is empty.

In a queenless hive no life is left, though to a superficial glance it seems as much alive as other hives.

The bees circle about a queenless hive in the heat of the midday sun as gaily as about other living hives; from a distance it smells of honey like the others, and the bees fly in and out just the same. But one has only to give a careful look to realize that there is no longer any life in the hive. The bees do not fly in and out in the same way, the smell and sound that meet the bee-keeper are different. A tap on the wall of the sick hive and, instead of the instant, unanimous response, the buzzing of tens of thousands of bees threateningly lifting their stings and by the swift fanning of wings producing that whirring, living hum, the bee-keeper is greeted by an incoherent buzzing from odd corners of the deserted hive. From the alighting-board, instead of the former winy fragrance of honey and venom, and the breath of warmth from the multitudes within, comes an odour of emptiness and decay mingling with the scent of honey. No sentinels watch there, curling up their stings and trumpeting the alarm, ready to die in defence of the community. Gone is the low, even hum, the throb of activity, like the singing of boiling water, and in its place is the fitful, discordant uproar of disorder. Black oblong robber-bees smeared with honey fly timidly, furtively, in and out of the hive: they do not sting but crawl away at the sign of danger. Before, only bees laden with honey flew into the hive, and flew out empty; now they fly out laden. The bee-keeper opens the lower chamber and peers into the bottom of the hive. Instead of black, glossy bees tamed by toil, that used to hang down, clinging to each other's legs, in long clusters to the floor of the hive, drawing out the wax with a ceaseless murmur of labour now drowsy shrivelled bees wander listlessly about the floor and walls of the hive. Instead of a neatly glued floor, swept by winnowing wings, the bee-keeper sees a floor littered with bits of wax, excrement, dying bees feebly kicking their legs and dead bees that have not been cleared away.

The bee-keeper opens the upper compartment and examines the top super of the hive. Instead of serried rows of insects sealing up every gap in the combs and keeping the hive warm, he sees the skil-ful, complex edifice of combs, but even here the virginal purity of old is gone. All is neglected and befouled. Black robber-bees prowl swiftly and stealthily about the combs in search of plunder; while the short-bodied, dried up home-bees, looking withered and old, lan-guidly creep about, doing nothing to hinder the robbers, having lost all desire and all sense of life. Drones, hornets, wasps and butterflies flutter about, knocking awkwardly against the walls of the hive. From here and there among the cells containing dead brood and honey comes an occasional angry buzz; here and there a couple of workers, faithful to old habits, are cleaning out the brood-cells, a task beyond their strength, laboriously dragging away dead bees or drones, without knowing why they do it. In another corner two old bees indolently fight, or clean themselves, or feed one another, themselves unaware whether with friendly or hostile intent. Elsewhere a crowd of bees, squashing one another, fall on some victim, attack and smother it. And the debilitated or dead bee drops slowly, light as a feather, among the heap of corpses. The keeper parts the two centre frames to look at the brood-cells. In place of the close dark circles of bees in their thousands sitting back to back and guarding the lofty mysteries of the work of generation he sees dejected, half-dead and drowsy shells of bees in hundreds only. They have almost all of them died unawares, sitting in the sanctuary they had guarded and which is now no more. They reek of decay and corruption. Only a few of them stir, rise up and idly fly to settle on the enemy's hand, lacking the spirit to die stinging him: the rest are dead and spill down as light as fish-scales. The bee-keeper closes the hive, chalks a mark on it and presently, when he has time, breaks it open and burns it clean.

So in the same way was Moscow empty when Napoleon, weary, uneasy and morose, paced up and down by the Kamer-Kollezhsky rampart, awaiting what to his mind was an essential if but formal observance of the proprieties – a deputation.

In various odd corners of Moscow a few people still remained aimlessly moving about, following their old habits, with no understanding of what they were doing.

When with due circumlocution Napoleon was apprised that Moscow was deserted he scowled furiously at his informant and, turning away, continued his silent promenade.

'My carriage!' he said.

He took his seat beside the aide-de-camp on duty and drove into the suburbs.

'Moscow deserted!' he said to himself. 'What an incredible climax!'

He did not drive into the town, but put up at an inn in the Dorogomilov suburb.

The *coup de théâtre* had not come off.

21

THE Russian troops poured through Moscow from two in the morning till two in the afternoon, bearing away with them the last departing inhabitants and the wounded.

The greatest crush during the movement of the troops took place at the Kamenny, Moskva and Yauza bridges.

While the troops, dividing into two streams to pass round the Kremlin were thronging the Moskva and Kamenny bridges a great mob of soldiers, taking advantage of the delay and congestion, turned back from the bridges and slipped stealthily and noiselessly past the church of Vasili Blazhenny and through the Borovitsky gate, back up the hill to Red Square, where some instinct told them that without much difficulty they could lay their hands on what did not belong to them. Crowds of the kind seen at cheap sales filled all the passages and alleys of the Bazaar. But there were no wheedling, honeyed voices inviting customers to enter, no hawkers, no brightly coloured press of women purchasers – only soldiers in uniforms and overcoats who had laid down their arms and were going into the rows of shops empty-handed to emerge silently, loaded with spoil. Tradesmen and their assistants (of whom there were but few) moved about among the soldiers quite bewildered. They unlocked their shops and locked them up again, and themselves helped the gallant soldier-lads to carry away their wares. On the square in front of the Bazaar drums were beating the roll-call. But the drums, instead of bringing the looting ranks rushing back, on the contrary set them running farther and farther from its signal. Among the soldiers in the shops and passages were men in grey coats, with the shaven heads of convicts. Two officers, one with a scarf over his uniform and mounted on a lean, iron-grey horse, the other in a cloak and on foot, stood talking at the corner of Ilyinka street. A third officer galloped up to them.

'The general's orders are that they are all to be driven out at once, without fail. Why, this is outrageous! Half the men have scattered. You, where are you off to? ... And you there?' he shouted to three infantrymen without muskets who were slipping past him into the Bazaar, holding up the skirts of their greatcoats. 'Stop, scoundrels!'

'Yes, you try collecting them together!' replied another officer.

'It can't be done! The only hope is to push on quickly before the rest bolt. There's nothing else for it.'

'But how? They are stuck there, wedged on the bridge, without moving. Shouldn't we put a cordon round to prevent the remaining few from breaking ranks?'

'Forward and drive them out!' shouted the senior officer.

The officer wearing the scarf dismounted, called up a drummer and went with him into the arcade. A number of soldiers started to make off together. A shopkeeper with red pimples on his cheeks about his nose, and a quietly persistent, calculating expression on his bloated face, hurried ostentatiously up to the officer, gesticulating.

'Your Honour!' said he. 'Be so good as to grant us protection. We are not close-fisted – any trifle now ... you are welcome. Wait now, I'll fetch out a piece of cloth – a couple of pieces now for a gentleman like yourself, 'twould be a pleasure. For we know how things are – but this is sheer robbery! Pray, your Honour, guards should be posted, if only to give us a chance to put up the shutters. ...'

Several shopkeepers gathered round the officer.

'Eh, it's no use whining!' said one of them, a thin man with a stern face. When one's head is gone one doesn't weep over one's hair! Let 'em take what they like!' And with a vigorous sweep of his arm he turned sideways, away from the officer.

'It's all very well for you to talk, Ivan Sidorich!' said the first tradesman angrily. 'Please step inside, your Honour!'

'Talk indeed!' shouted the thin man. 'In my three shops here I have a hundred thousand roubles' worth of goods. Can they be saved when the army has gone? Ah, my brethren, God's will is not in men's hands!'

'If you please, your Honour!' repeated the first shopkeeper, bowing.

The officer hesitated, and his face betrayed uncertainty.

'Why, what business is it of mine!' he exclaimed suddenly, and strode on rapidly down the arcade. From one open shop came the sound of blows and vituperation, and just as the officer was going up to it a man in a grey coat, with a shaven head, was flung violently out of the door.

The man doubled himself up and bounded past the tradesmen and the officer. The officer pounced on the soldiers who were in the shop. But at this point fearful screams reached them from the huge crowd

on the Moskva bridge, and the officer ran out into the square.
'What is it? What is it?' he asked, but his comrade was already
galloping off past Vasili Blazhenny in the direction of the outcry.
The officer mounted his horse and followed. As he neared the bridge
he saw two cannon unlimbered, the infantry marching across the
bridge, several overturned carts, a few frightened faces and the soldiers laughing. Next to the cannon stood a wagon with a pair of
horses harnessed to it. Behind, close to the wheels, huddled four grey-
hounds in collars. The wagon was piled high with a mountain of
goods, and on the very top, beside a child's chair with its legs in the
air, sat a peasant woman uttering shrill, despairing shrieks. He was
told by his fellow-officers that the screams of the crowd and the
woman's squeals arose from the fact that General Yermolov, riding
up to the mob and learning that soldiers were straying away to the
shops while civilians blocked the bridge, had ordered two guns to be
unlimbered and a show made of firing at the bridge. The crowd,
squashing together, upsetting carts, trampling one another and yelling desperately, had cleared off the bridge, and the troops had moved
forward.

22

MEANWHILE the city proper was deserted. There was scarcely a soul
in the streets. Gates and shops were all locked; only here and there a
solitary shout or drunken song echoed near the taverns. Nobody ventured abroad in a carriage and the sound of footsteps was rare. Povarsky street was silent and deserted. The immense courtyard of the
Rostovs' house was littered with wisps of straw and dung from the
horses, and no one was about. In the great drawing-room of the
house – abandoned with all its contents – were two human beings:
the yard-porter Ignat and the page-boy Mishka, Vasilich's grandson,
who had stayed in Moscow with his grandfather. Mishka had opened
the clavichord and was drumming on it with one finger. The yard-
porter, his arms akimbo, stood smiling with satisfaction before the
large looking-glass.

'Isn't this fine, eh, Uncle Ignat?' said the boy, beginning to bang
on the keyboard with both hands at once.

'Ay, ay!' answered Ignat, wondering at the broadening grin on his
face in the mirror.

'Oh, you shameless creatures! Right down shameless!' exclaimed the voice of Mavra Kuzminishna, who had come noiselessly in behind them. 'Look at you grinning at yourself, you fat mug! Is that what you're here for? There's nothing put away downstairs and Vasilich is fair worn out. Just you wait!'

Ignat left off smiling and, hitching up his belt, went out of the room with meekly downcast eyes.

'Auntie, I was only just touching ...' said the boy.

'I'll give you "just touching", you young scamp you!' cried Mavra Kuzminishna, shaking her fist at him. 'Go and get the samovar to boil for your grandad.'

Mavra Kuzminishna flicked the dust off the clavichord and closed it, and with a deep sigh left the drawing-room and locked the door.

Going out into the yard, she paused to consider where she should take herself next – to drink tea in the servants' hall with Vasilich, or into the store-room to put away the things that still lay about.

Quick footsteps sounded in the quiet street. Someone stopped at the gate and a hand rattled the latch, trying to open it.

Mavra Kuzminishna went to the gate.

'Who is it you want?'

'The count – Count Ilya Rostov.'

'And who are you?'

'An officer. I should very much like to see him,' came the reply in a pleasant, well-bred Russian voice.

Mavra Kuzminishna unlocked the gate and a round-faced lad of eighteen with a strong family resemblance to the Rostovs walked into the courtyard.

'They have gone away, sir. Set off yesterday evening at vesper-time,' said Mavra Kuzminishna cordially.

The young officer standing by the gateway as though hesitating whether to enter or not clicked his tongue.

'Ah, how annoying!' he muttered. 'I ought to have come yesterday. ... Oh, what a pity! ...'

Mavra Kuzminishna meanwhile was intently and sympathetically scrutinizing the familiar Rostov features of the young man's face, his tattered cloak and downtrodden boots.

'What did you want to see the count for?' she asked.

'Oh, well ... it can't be helped!' exclaimed the lad in a tone of vexation, and he placed his hand on the gate as if intending to go away. He paused again, undecided.

'It's like this,' he said all at once, 'I am a kinsman of the count's, and he has always been very kind to me. And as you can see' (he glanced down at his cloak and boots with a frank, merry smile), 'I am in rags and haven't a farthing, so I was going to ask the count ...'

Mavra Kuzminishna did not let him finish.

'Just you wait a wee minute, sir. Only a minute now,' said she.

And as soon as the officer let go of the latch she turned about and hurrying away on her old legs went through the back-yard to the servants' quarters.

While Mavra Kuzminishna was trotting to her room the officer walked up and down the courtyard, gazing at his tattered boots with lowered head and a faint smile on his lips. 'What a pity I have missed uncle! What a nice old body! Where has she run off to ? I must ask her the shortest way to pick up my regiment: they must have got to the Rogozhsky gate by this time,' he reflected. Just then Mavra Kuzminishna appeared round the corner of the house, looking scared and at the same time determined. She carried a check kerchief in her hand, tied in a knot. A few steps from the officer she undid the kerchief and took out of it a white twenty-five rouble note and thrust it at him.

'If his Excellency had been at home ... of course he would ... for a kinsman, but with times what they are ... perhaps ...'

Mavra Kuzminishna faltered in confusion. But the officer did not refuse, and showed no haste, but took the note and thanked her.

'If the count had been home ...' Mavra Kuzminishna murmured apologetically. 'Christ be with you, sir! God keep you safe!' she said, bowing and showing him out.

The officer, smiling and shaking his head as if amused at himself, ran almost at a trot through the deserted streets towards the Yauza bridge to overtake his regiment.

But Mavra Kuzminishna stayed on at the closed gate for some time with moist eyes, pensively nodding her head and feeling a sudden rush of motherly tenderness and pity for the young unknown soldier.

23

FROM an unfinished house in Varvarka, the ground floor of which was a dram-shop, came the sounds of drunken brawling and singing.

Some ten factory hands were sitting on benches at tables in a dirty little room. Tipsy, sweating, bleary-eyed, with wide gaping mouths, they were singing some sort of song. They sang discordantly, laboriously, with effort – not, plainly, because they felt like singing but simply to show they were drunk and out to enjoy themselves. One, a tall, fair-haired fellow in a clean blue coat, was standing over the others. His face with its fine, straight nose would have been handsome but for the thin, compressed, twitching lips and lustreless, frowning, fixed eyes. He stood over the singers and, apparently possessed by some notion, solemnly beat time above their heads with stiff jerks of his white arm, its sleeve rolled back to the elbow, while he tried to spread his dirty fingers out unnaturally wide. The sleeve of his coat kept slipping down and he always carefully tucked it up again with his left hand, as if it were of particular importance that the sinewy white arm he was flourishing should be bare. In the middle of the song scuffling and blows were heard in the passage and the porch. The tall lad waved his arm.

'That'll do!' he cried peremptorily. 'There's a fight outside, boys!' And still tucking up his sleeve he went out to the porch.

The factory hands followed him. They had been drinking under the leadership of the tall young man, having brought the tavern-keeper some skins from the factory that morning and been treated to drinks for their trouble. Some blacksmiths working in a smithy near by, hearing sounds of revelry in the tavern and supposing it to have been broken into, thought that they also would like to take a hand, and a fight had ensued in the porch.

The publican was exchanging blows with a blacksmith in the doorway and just as the factory hands arrived on the scene the smith, wrenching himself free from the tavern-keeper, fell flat on his face on the pavement.

Another smith plunged in at the door, shoving with his chest against the publican.

The young fellow with the sleeve rolled up dealt the intruding blacksmith a blow in the face and uttered a wild yell:

'Up, lads! We're being attacked!'

At that moment the first smith got to his feet and scratching his bruised face to make it bleed lifted up his voice and wailed:

'Police! Murder! ... Man killed! Help! ...'

'Lord have mercy, killed dead, a man killed dead!' screamed a woman running out of the gates next door. A crowd gathered round the blood-stained smith.

'Haven't you ruined folks enough, stripping the shirts off their backs?' said a voice, addressing the publican. 'And now you've killed a man, have you? Cut-throat!'

The tall lad, standing on the steps, turned his bleared eyes from the publican to the smiths and back again, as if considering which of them he ought to fight.

'Murderer!' he shouted suddenly to the publican. 'Tie him up, lads!'

'Tie me up, would you? You tie me up?' roared the publican, shaking off the men advancing on him, and snatching his cap from his head he flung it on the ground. As though this action had some mysterious, ominous significance, the factory hands who had surrounded the publican paused irresolute.

'I know the law, me boy, like the back of me hand. I'll take the matter to the captain of police. You think I won't get to him? No one can't commit robbery and violence these days!' shouted the publican, picking up his cap.

'Let's step along then! ...' 'Let's step along then!' the publican and the tall young fellow repeated one after the other, and they moved up the street together. The blood-stained blacksmith fell in beside them. The factory hands and others followed behind, talking and shouting.

At the corner of Murodavka, opposite a large house with closed shutters and bootmaker's sign-board, stood a group of some twenty bootmakers, thin, spent, dismal-faced men wearing overalls and tattered coats.

'Why don't he give us our wages we're entitled to?' a lean boot hand with a scanty beard and knitted brows was saying. 'He sucks our life-blood out of us, and then he thinks he's quit of us! Fooled us the whole week, and now he's brought us to this pass he's skipped it.'

Seeing the mob and the blood-bespattered smith, the man paused and all the bootmakers with eager curiosity joined the moving crowd.

'Where you folks be going to?'

'Why, to the police, to be sure!'

'Say, is it true our side's beaten?'

'What do you think? Look at what folks is saying!'

Questions and answers were exchanged. The publican, taking advantage of the increased numbers of the rabble, dropped behind and returned to his tavern.

The tall youth, not noticing the disappearance of his enemy, and waving his bare arm, went on talking vociferously, attracting general attention to himself. The people pressed round him in the main, expecting to get from him some explanation of the problems that filled their minds.

'"Show me order," he says. "Show me the law." "That's what the government's for!" Isn't it the truth I'm telling you, good Christians?' said the tall young man, almost perceptibly smiling. 'Does he think there's no government? How could we do without a government? Otherwise there'd be plenty willing to rob us!'

'Stuff and nonsense!' said a voice from the crowd. 'Do you suppose they'd give up Moscow like that? Someone's been codding you and you swallowed it hook, line and sinker! Aren't there troops in plenty about? Let *him* in, indeed! That's what the authorities are for. You'd better listen to what people are saying,' said some of the mob, pointing to the tall fellow.

Near the wall of China-town a little knot of people were gathered round a man in a frieze coat who held a paper in his hand.

'An edict – they're reading an edict!' cried various voices, and the crowd rushed towards the reader.

The man in the frieze coat was reading the broadsheet of August the 31st. When the mob pressed round he seemed disconcerted but, at the demand of the tall lad who had pushed his way up to him, in a rather tremulous voice he began to read the notice from the beginning.

'I am going early tomorrow morning to see his Serene Highness the Prince,' he read – ('Serin Highness,' repeated the tall fellow solemnly, with a smile on his lips and a frown on his forehead) – 'to consult with him, to act and to aid the army to exterminate the scoundrels. We, too, will take a hand ...' the reader went on and then paused – ('See,' shouted the youth triumphantly, 'he's going to put everything straight for you ...') – 'in rooting up and sending these visitors to the devil. I shall be back by dinner-time and we'll put our shoulders to the wheel, make a job of it and have done with the miscreants.'

The last words were received in complete silence. The tall lad hung his head gloomily. It was evident that no one had understood the end part. The words 'I shall be back by dinner-time' in particular plainly offended both reader and audience. The mood of the people was tuned to a high pitch and this was too simple and unnecessarily commonplace: it was exactly what anyone of them might have said, and therefore what an announcement emanating from the supreme authority had no business to say.

They all stood in despondent silence. The tall youth moved his lips and swayed slightly.

'Why don't we ask him? ... That's him himself! ... How'd it be to ask him? ... Why not? He'll explain ...' voices in the back rows of the crowd were suddenly heard saying, and the general attention turned to the police-superintendent's trap which drove into the square, escorted by two mounted dragoons.

The chief of police, who had driven out that morning by Count Rostopchin's orders to set fire to the barks in the river and had in connexion with that errand acquired a large sum of money which was at that moment in his pocket, on seeing a crowd bearing down upon him, told his coachman to stop.

'Who are these people?' he shouted to the men who were moving separately and timidly in the direction of his trap. 'Who are these people I should like to know?' he repeated, receiving no reply.

'Your Honour, they ...' said the clerk in the frieze coat, 'your Honour, in accordance with the proclamation of his most illustrious Excellency, the Count, they desire to serve, not sparing their lives, and it is not any kind of riot but as his most illustrious Excellency, the Count, said ...'

'The count has not gone. He is here and arrangements will be made for you,' said the chief of police. 'Drive on!' he cried to his coachman.

The crowd stood still, pressing round those who had heard what the representative of power had said, and staring after the departing trap.

Just then the superintendent of police looked back in alarm, said something to his coachman, and his horses trotted faster.

'We've been cheated, mates! Let us go to the count himself!' shouted the tall youth. 'Don't let him escape, lads! Let him answer us! Hold him!' cried different voices, and the mob dashed in pursuit of the trap.

Shouting noisily, the crowd set off after the chief of police, in the direction of Lubyanka street.

'Look at that – the gentry and the tradespeople have all gone away and left us to perish. Do they think we're dogs?' voices in the crowd caught up one after another.

24

On the evening of the 1st of September, after his interview with Kutuzov, Count Rostopchin had returned to Moscow mortified and offended at not having been invited to attend the Council of War, and because Kutuzov had paid no attention to his offer to take part in the defence of the city, amazed also at the novel discovery he had made at the camp, which treated the tranquillity of the capital and its patriotic fervour not only as matters of quite secondary importance but as altogether irrelevant and trivial. Chagrined, affronted and amazed by all this, Count Rostopchin had returned to Moscow. After supper he lay down on a sofa without undressing, and between midnight and one in the morning was awakened by a courier with a letter from Kutuzov. The letter requested the count to be good enough to dispatch police officers to conduct the troops across the city, as the army was to retire beyond Moscow on to the Ryazan highway. This was no news to Rostopchin. He had known that Moscow would be abandoned not merely since his interview the previous day with Kutuzov on the Poklonny hill but ever since the battle of Borodino, for all the generals who had come to Moscow after that battle had with one voice declared that another pitched battle was out of the question, and with Rostopchin's sanction government property had been removed by night, and half the inhabitants had left. Nevertheless this information, conveyed in the form of a simple note with a command from Kutuzov and received at night, rousing him out of his first sleep, astonished and irritated the count.

Afterwards, in his memoirs explaining his actions at this time, Count Rostopchin reiterates that his two great aims were: to maintain good order in Moscow and to expedite the departure of the public. If one accepts this twofold aim, everything Rostopchin did appears irreproachable. But if so, why were the holy relics, the arms, ammunition, gunpowder and stores of grain not removed? Why were thousands of the inhabitants deceived into a belief that Moscow would not be given up – and thereby ruined? 'To preserve the tranquillity of the city,' explains Count Rostopchin. Then why were masses of worthless documents from government offices, and Leppich's balloon, and other articles sent out? 'To leave the town empty,' says Count Rostopchin's explanation. One need only admit the premise that public peace of mind is in danger and any action finds justification.

All the horrors of the Reign of Terror in France were based entirely on solicitude for public tranquillity.

What foundation was there for Count Rostopchin's dread of popular disturbance in Moscow in 1812? What reason was there for assuming any probability of an uprising in the city? The inhabitants were leaving Moscow, their place being filled by the retreating troops. Why should that cause the masses to riot?

Neither in Moscow nor anywhere in Russia did anything resembling an insurrection ever occur at the approach of the enemy. On the 1st and 2nd of September more than ten thousand people were still in Moscow and, except for a mob which collected in the governor's courtyard – and that at his own instigation – there was no trouble. It is obvious there would have been still less reason to anticipate a disturbance among the people if after the battle of Borodino, when the surrender of Moscow became a certainty, or at least a probability, Rostopchin, instead of exciting the public by distributing arms and posting up broadsheets, had taken steps for the removal of the holy relics, the gunpowder, munitions and money, and had told the population plainly that the town would be abandoned.

Rostopchin, an impulsive, sanguine man who had always moved in the highest spheres of the administration, though he had patriotic sentiments had no understanding whatsoever of the people he supposed himself to be controlling. Ever since the enemy's entry into Smolensk, in imagination he had been seeing himself playing the part of directing national feeling – guiding the heart of Russia. He did not merely fancy – as every governing official always does fancy – that he was managing the external behaviour of the citizens of Moscow, but he also thought he was shaping their mental attitude by means of his broadsheets and placards composed in the vulgar, slangy jargon which the people despise in their own class and do not understand from those in authority. The picturesque rôle of leader of popular feeling was so much to Rostopchin's taste, he had grown so used to it, that the necessity of relinquishing it and surrendering Moscow with no heroic display of any kind took him unawares: the ground was suddenly cut from under his feet and he was utterly at a loss what to do. Though he knew it was coming, he could not really bring himself to believe till the last minute that Moscow must be sacrificed, and did nothing to prepare for it. The inhabitants left against his wishes. If the government offices were removed, it was only due to the insistence of the officials, to whom the count reluctantly yielded. He was entirely absorbed in the rôle he had created for himself. As is often the case with those endowed with a spirited imagination, though he had long known that Moscow would be abandoned he had known it only with his intellect: he was not convinced of it in his heart and did not mentally adapt himself to the new situation.

All his painstaking and energetic activity – how far it was useful or had any effect on the people is another question – had been directed simply towards arousing in the masses his own feeling of patriotic hatred of the French and confidence in himself.

But when the catastrophe began to assume its true historic proportions; when expressing hatred for the French in words was plainly insufficient; when it was not even possible to give expression to that hatred by fighting a battle; when self-confidence was of no avail in relation to the one question before Moscow; when the whole population streamed out of Moscow as one man, abandoning their belongings and proving by this negative gesture the strength of their patriotic fervour – then the part Rostopchin had chosen suddenly became meaningless. All at once he found himself alone, weak and ridiculous, with no ground to stand on.

Wakened from his sleep to receive that cold, peremptory note from Kutuzov, Rostopchin felt the more irritated the more he felt himself to be guilty. Everything that had been expressly entrusted to him, the state property which he should have removed, was still in Moscow. There was no possibility of getting it all away.

'Who is to blame for this? Who has let things come to such a pass?' he ruminated. 'Not I, of course. I had everything in readiness. I had Moscow firmly in hand. And now see what a pretty plight they have led us to! Villains! Traitors!' he thought, not exactly identifying the villains and traitors but feeling it necessary to pour hatred on those, whoever they might be, who were to blame for the false and ludicrous position in which he found himself.

All that night Count Rostopchin issued orders, for which people were continually coming to him from all parts of Moscow. His intimates had never seen the count so gloomy and irritable.

'Your Excellency, there's a messenger from the director of the Registrar's Department asking for instructions. ... From the Consistory, from the Senate, from the University, from the Foundling Hospital. ... The suffragan has sent to. ... So-and-so wants to know. ... What are your orders about the Fire Brigade? The governor of the prison asks ... The superintendent of the lunatic asylum is here. ...' And so it went on all night long.

To all these inquiries the count's replies were short and severe, their drift being that instructions from him were not needed now, that somebody had spoilt all his careful preparations, and that that somebody would have to shoulder full responsibility for anything that might happen from now on.

'Oh, tell the idiot,' he said in answer to the inquiry from the Registrar's Department, 'to stay and look after his archives. What is this nonsense about the Fire Brigade? Let 'em get on their horses and be off to Vladimir, and not leave them to the French.'

'Your Excellency, the superintendent of the lunatic asylum has come: what does your Excellency wish him to do?'

'Wish him to do? Leave, that's all. And turn the lunatics loose in the town. When we have madmen in command of our armies God evidently means these others to be at large too.'

When asked what was to be done about the convicts in the gaol the count shouted furiously at the governor:

'Do you expect me to provide you with a couple of battalions – which we have not got for a convoy? Release 'em, and that settles it!'

'Your Excellency, some of them are political prisoners – Meshkov, Vereshchagin. ...'

'Vereshchagin! Hasn't he been hanged yet?' roared Rostopchin. 'Bring him to me!'

25

By about nine o'clock in the morning, with the troops already moving through Moscow, the count had ceased to be importuned for instructions. Those who were able to get away were going of their own accord; those who had stayed behind were deciding for themselves what they had better do.

The count ordered his carriage round to take him to Sokolniky, and sat waiting in his study with folded hands, morose, sallow and taciturn.

In quiet, untroubled times every administrator believes that it is only by his efforts that the whole population under his charge is kept going; and in this consciousness of being indispensable lies the chief reward of his pains and exertions. So long as the calm lasts, the administrator-pilot holding on to the ship of the people with a boat-hook from his frail bark, and himself gliding along, naturally imagines that his efforts move the ship he is clinging to. But let a storm spring up, let the sea begin to heave and the great vessel toss about of itself, and any such illusion becomes impossible. The ship rides on in mighty independence, the boat-hook no longer reaches to the moving vessel and the pilot, from being the arbiter, the source of power, finds himself an insignificant, feeble, useless person.

Rostopchin felt this, and it riled him.

The chief of police, who had been stopped by the crowd, arrived to see him at the same time as an adjutant to say that the horses were ready. Both were pale, and the superintendent of police, after reporting the accomplishment of his mission, informed the count that a vast assembly had collected in the courtyard wanting to see him.

Without a word Rostopchin got up and walked with rapid steps to his light, luxuriously furnished drawing-room, crossed to the balcony door, laid his hand on the latch, let go of it and went to the window from which he could get a better view of the crowd. The tall young lad was standing in front, waving his arm and saying something with a dour look. The blood-stained smith stood beside him with a sombre air.

'Is my carriage ready?' asked Rostopchin, stepping back from the window.

'It is, your Excellency,' replied the adjutant.

Rostopchin went to the balcony door again.

'But what is it they want?' he asked the superintendent of police.

'Your Excellency, they say they have rallied, in accordance with your orders, to go against the French, and they were shouting something about treachery. But it is a turbulent mob, your Excellency. I had much ado to get away. Your Excellency, if I may venture to suggest ...'

'Have the goodness to retire! I know what to do without your assistance,' cried Rostopchin angrily. He stood by the balcony door looking at the crowd. 'This is what they have done with Russia! This is what they have done with me!' he brooded, irrepressible fury welling up within him against the someone to whom what was happening might be attributed. As is often the case with hot-tempered people he was overcome with rage, but had still to find a scapegoat on which to vent it. 'There they are – the mob, the dregs of the populace,' he said to himself in French as he gazed at the crowd. 'The rabble they have stirred up by their folly! They want a victim,' he thought as he watched the waving arm of the tall fellow in front. And this idea came into his head precisely because he, too, wanted a scapegoat, an object for his wrath.

'Is the carriage ready?' he asked again.

'Yes, your Excellency. What orders do you wish to give concerning Vereshchagin? He is waiting at the porch,' said the adjutant.

'Ah!' exclaimed Rostopchin, as though struck by some sudden recollection.

And quickly throwing open the door he strode resolutely out on to the balcony. The buzz of talk was instantly hushed, caps and hats were doffed and all eyes raised to the count.

'Good-day, lads!' said the count briskly and loudly. 'Thanks for coming. I'll be out with you in a moment but first we have to settle accounts with a miscreant. We must punish the blackguard who has been the undoing of Moscow. Wait for me!'

And the count stepped as briskly back into the room, slamming the door behind him.

An approving murmur of satisfaction ran through the crowd. 'He'll deal with all the villains, you'll see! And you said the French. ... He'll show us the rights and wrongs of it all!' the mob were saying, as if reproving one another for their lack of faith.

A few minutes later an officer hurried out of the front door, gave an order, and the dragoons formed up in line. The crowd pressed eagerly from the balcony towards the porch. Rostopchin, coming out with swift, irate, steps, looked quickly about him as if seeking someone.

'Where is he?' he demanded, and as he spoke he saw a young man with a long thin neck, and half of his head that had been shaven covered with short hair, appearing round the corner of the house between two dragoons. He was dressed in a threadbare blue cloth coat lined with fox fur, that had once been stylish, and filthy convict trousers of fustian, thrust into thin, dirty, down-at-heel boots. Heavy iron shackles dragged on his weak, thin legs, hampering his uncertain gait.

'Ah!' said Rostopchin, hastily averting his eyes from the young man in the fur-lined coat and pointing to the bottom step of the porch. 'Stand him there!'

With a clank of fetters the young man lurched clumsily to the spot indicated, putting a finger in the tight collar of his coat which rubbed his skin, twisted his long neck twice this way and that, and, sighing submissively, folded before him a pair of hands which were too delicate to belong to a workman.

For several seconds, while the young fellow was taking up his position on the step, there was complete silence. Only from the rear of the crowd, where the people were all trying to push forward to the one spot, came grunts and groans, jostling and the shuffling of feet.

Rostopchin stood frowning and passing his hand over his face while he waited for the young man to get to the step.

'My friends!' he said, with a metallic ring in his voice. 'This man, Vereshchagin, is the scoundrel who has lost us Moscow.'

The young man in the fur-lined coat, stooping a little, stood in a resigned attitude, his wrists crossed over his stomach. His emaciated young face, with its expression of hopelessness and the hideous disfigurement of the half-shaven head, hung down. At the count's first words he raised it slowly and stared up at him as though he wanted to say something, or at least catch his eye. But Rostopchin did not look at him. Like a cord, a vein behind the young man's ear swelled livid on his long thin neck, and suddenly his face flushed.

All eyes were fixed on him. He returned the gaze of the crowd and, as though made hopeful by the expression he read on their faces, he gave a timid, pitiful smile, and lowering his head again shifted his feet on the step.

'He has betrayed his Tsar and his country, he has sold himself to Bonaparte. He is the only man of us all to have disgraced the name of Russia. It is because of him that Moscow is meeting her end,' said Rostopchin in a harsh, monotonous voice, but all at once he glanced down at Vereshchagin, who continued to stand in the same meek attitude. As though what he saw drove him to frenzy, he raised his arm and almost yelled to the people:

'Take the law into your own hands! I pass him over to you!'

The crowd made no answer and merely packed closer and closer. The press was intolerable; to breathe in that stifling, infected atmosphere, to be unable to stir and to be expecting something unknown, uncomprehended and terrible was becoming an agony. Those standing in front, who saw and heard what was taking place before them, all stood, with wide, startled eyes and gaping mouths, straining all their strength to resist the forward thrust on their backs from behind.

'Slay him! ... Let the traitor perish and not bring shame on the name of Russia!' screamed Rostopchin. 'Cut him down! It is my command!'

Hearing not so much Rostopchin's actual words as their venomous tone, the mob groaned and heaved forward, but stopped again.

'Count! ...' the timid yet theatrical voice of Vereshchagin broke in upon the momentary lull that followed. 'Count! There is one God judges us. ...' He lifted his head and again the thick vein in his thin neck filled with blood and the colour rapidly came and went in his face. He did not finish what he was trying to say.

'Cut him down! It is my command! ...' shouted Rostopchin, suddenly growing as white as Vereshchagin.

'Draw sabres!' cried the officer to the dragoons, unsheathing his own sword.

Another still more violent wave surged through the crowd, and reaching the front ranks carried them forward and threw them staggering against the very steps of the porch. The tall young fellow, with petrified face and his hand arrested in mid-air, stood beside Vereshchagin.

'Cut at him!' the officer almost whispered to the dragoons, and one of the soldiers, his face suddenly convulsed with fury, struck Vereshchagin on the head with the flat of his sword.

Vereshchagin, uttering a sharp cry of surprise, looked round in alarm, as though not knowing why this was done to him. A like moan of surprise and horror ran through the crowd.

'Merciful Lord!' exclaimed someone compassionately.

But after the exclamation of surprise that had escaped from Vereshchagin he uttered a piteous cry of pain, and that cry was his undoing. The barrier of human feeling that had held the mob in check, strained to its utmost limit, suddenly snapped. The crime was begun, its consummation now inevitable. The plaintive groan of reproach was swallowed up in the fierce and maddened roar of the crowd. Like the seventh and last roller which wrecks a ship, that final irresistible wave lifted at the back of the concourse, surged through to the front ranks, sweeping them off their feet and engulfing everything. The dragoon prepared to strike again. Vereshchagin with a scream of terror, covering his head with his hands, flung himself into the crowd. The tall youth, against whom he stumbled, gripped him by the throat and with a wild cry fell with him under the feet of the shoving, frenzied mass.

Some hit and tore at Vereshchagin, others at the tall youth. The shrieks of those who were being trampled on and of those who were trying to rescue the tall lad only increased the virulence of the mob. It was long before the dragoons could extricate the bleeding, half-murdered factory hand. And in spite of the feverish haste with which the mob strove to finish off the work that had been begun, it was a long time before those who were hitting, throttling and mangling Vereschchagin were able to beat the life out of him: the crowd pushed on them from all sides, heaving to and fro like one man with them in the middle and making it impossible for them either to kill or release him.

'Hit him with an axe, eh ? ... They've trampled him to death.... Traitor, he sold Christ! ... Still alive, is he ? ... He's a tough one... serve him right! What about a hatchet ? ... Isn't he dead yet ?'

Only when the victim ceased to struggle and his shrieks had given way to a long-drawn, rhythmic death-rattle did the mob around the prostrate, bleeding corpse hurriedly begin to change places. Every-one came up, glanced at what had been done, and pushed back again, aghast, remorseful and astonished.

'O Lord, the people are like wild beasts! It's a wonder anyone was spared!' exclaimed some voice in the crowd. 'Quite a young fellow, too ... must have been a merchant's son, to be sure the people ... They do say he's not the right one. ... What d'you mean – not the right one ? ... Merciful Lord! ... And there's another got butchered too – they say he's nearly done for. ... Oh, what a people! There's no sin they're afraid of ...' said the same mob now as they stared with rueful pity at the dead body with its long, thin neck half-severed and the livid face fouled with blood and dust.

A punctilious police official, considering the presence of a corpse in his Excellency's courtyard unseemly, bade the dragoons drag it away into the street. Two dragoons took hold of the mangled legs and hauled the body along the ground. The dead, shaven head, gory and grimed, was trailed along, rolling from side to side on the long neck. The crowd shrank away from the corpse.

When Vereshchagin fell and the crowd burst forward with savage yells and heaved about him, Rostopchin suddenly turned pale and, instead of making for the back where his horses were waiting, strode rapidly along the passage leading to the rooms on the ground floor, looking down and not knowing where he was going or why. The count's face was white and he could not control the feverish twitching of his lower jaw.

'Your Excellency, this way. ... Where would your Excellency be going? ... This way, please ...' said a trembling, frightened voice behind him.

Count Rostopchin was incapable of making any reply. Turning obediently he went in the direction indicated. At the back entrance stood his calèche. The distant roar of the howling mob was audible even there. He hastily took his seat and told the coachman to drive to his country house at Sokolniky. When they reached Myasnitsky street and could no longer hear the shouting the count began to repent. He recalled with dissatisfaction the excitement and fear he had betrayed before his subordinates. 'The hoi polloi is dreadful – hideous,' he said to himself in French. 'They are like wolves, only to be appeased with flesh. "Count, there is one God judges us!"' – Vereshchagin's words suddenly recurred to him, and a disagreeable chill ran down his spine. But this was only a momentary feeling and Count Rostopchin smiled disdainfully at himself. 'I had other duties,' thought he. 'The people had to be mollified. Many another victim has perished and is perishing for the public good' – and he began reflecting on the social obligations he had towards his family and towards the city entrusted to his care, and on himself – not himself as Fiodr Vasilyevich Rostopchin (he fancied that Fiodr Vasilyevich Rostopchin was sacrificing himself for le bien public), but himself as governor of Moscow, as the representative of authority invested with full powers by the Tsar. 'Had I been simply Fiodr Vasilyevich my course of action would have been quite different; but it was my duty to safeguard my life and dignity as governor.'

Lightly swayed on the easy springs of the carriage and no longer hearing the terrible sounds of the crowd, Rostopchin grew calmer physically and, as always happens, simultaneously with physical relief his reason suggested arguments to salve his conscience. The thought which reassured Rostopchin was not a new one. Ever since the world was created and men began killing one another no man has ever committed a crime of this character against his fellow without comforting himself with this same idea – *le bien public*, the hypothetical welfare of other people.

The man not actuated by passion never knows what this good is; but the man who has committed a crime is always very sure where that welfare lies. And Rostopchin now knew it.

Not only did he not reproach himself in his deliberations for what he had done but he even found grounds for self-complacency in having so successfully made use of a convenient opportunity at once to punish a criminal and satisfy the rabble.

'Vereshchagin had been tried and condemned to death,' Rostopchin argued to himself (though the Senate had only sentenced Vereshchagin to hard labour). 'He was a traitor and a spy. I could not let him go unpunished, and thus I slew two birds with one stone: I appeased the mob by presenting them with a victim and I punished a miscreant.'

By the time he had reached his country house and begun to busy himself with private affairs the count had completely regained his composure.

Half an hour later he was driving behind swift horses across the Sokolniki plain, his mind no longer dwelling on past events but turned to the future and what was to come. He was off to the Yauza bridge where he had been told Kutuzov was. Count Rostopchin was rehearsing to himself the angry, biting reproaches he meant to address to Kutuzov for his deception. He would make that foxy old courtier feel that the responsibility for all the calamities bound to follow the surrender of the capital and the annihilation (as Rostopchin regarded it) of Russia would redound entirely on his doting old grey head. Thinking over beforehand what he would say to Kutuzov, Rostopchin twisted about on the seat of the calèche and angrily surveyed the landscape on either side.

The Sokolniki plain was deserted. Only at one end, in front of the alms-house and the lunatic asylum, little knots of people in white could be seen, and a few others like them were wandering separately about the field, shouting and gesticulating.

One of these was running across the path of Count Rostopchin's carriage, and the count himself, his coachman and escort of dragoons watched with a vague mixture of consternation and curiosity these mad creatures who had just been turned loose, and especially the one running towards them. His long thin legs catching in his dressing-gown, he reeled along at breakneck speed, his eyes fixed on Rostopchin, shouting something in a hoarse voice and signalling for the carriage to stop. The lunatic's sombre, impassioned face, overgrown with uneven tufts of beard, was haggard and yellow. His dark agate eyes with their saffron whites rolled frenziedly.

'Wait! Stop, I tell you!' he cried piercingly, and again fell to shouting breathlessly with emphatic gestures and intonations.

He reached the calèche and ran beside it.

'Thrice have they slain me, thrice have I risen from the dead. They stoned me, crucified me. ... I shall rise again ... shall rise again ... shall rise again. They tore my body to pieces. The Kingdom of God will be overthrown. ... Thrice will I overthrow it and thrice set it up again,' he shrieked, his voice growing shriller and shriller.

Count Rostopchin suddenly paled as he had done when the crowd closed in on Vereshchagin. He turned away. 'Dri-drive faster!' he called to the coachman in a quaking voice.

The calèche flew over the ground as fast as the horses could go, but for a long time Count Rostopchin still heard the insane, despairing scream echoing away in the distance, while his eyes saw nothing but the wondering, frightened, bleeding face of the 'traitor' in the fur-lined coat.

Recent as that image was, Rostopchin felt that it had already cut deep into his heart, etching its imprint there. He knew now that time would never dim the bloody trace of that recollection: on the contrary, the longer he lived the more cruelly, the more vindictively would that fearful memory lacerate his heart. It seemed to him that he could hear now the ring of his own words: 'Cut him down! If you don't, you shall answer for it with your heads!'

'Why did I utter those words? They came out somehow by accident. ... I need not have said them,' he thought. 'Then nothing would have happened.' He saw the frightened face of the dragoon who had struck the first blow – his expression had suddenly changed to one of ferocity – and the look of silent, timid reproach that boy in the fur-lined coat had cast on him. ... 'But I did not do it on my own account. I had no choice. ... The mob, the traitor ... public welfare,' he mused.

Troops were still crowding the bridge over the Yauza. It was hot.

Kutuzov, beetle-browed and dejected, was sitting on a bench by the bridge tracing patterns with his whip in the sand, when a calèche dashed up noisily. A man in the uniform of a general, with plumes in his hat, approached Kutuzov and addressed him in French, half hesitatingly, half wrathfully, his eyes shifting uneasily. It was Count Rostopchin. He told Kutuzov that he had come because Moscow, the capital, was no more and there was nothing left but the army.

'Things might have been very different if your Highness had not assured me you would not abandon Moscow without a battle: none of this would have happened,' he said.

Kutuzov stared at Rostopchin as though, not grasping the significance of what was said, he was exerting all his energies to read the special meaning at that moment written on the face of the man addressing him. Rostopchin, disconcerted, fell silent. Kutuzov quietly nodded and, still keeping his searching eyes on Rostopchin's face, murmured softly:

'No, I shall not give up Moscow without a battle!'

Whether Kutuzov was thinking of something else entirely when he pronounced those words, or spoke them purposely, knowing them to be meaningless, at all events Rostopchin made no reply and hastily withdrew. And – wonder of wonders! – the governor-general of Moscow, the haughty Count Rostopchin, taking a Cossack whip in his hand, went to the bridge, and began to shout and hurry along the carts that were blocked together there.

26

TOWARDS four o'clock in the afternoon Murat's troops were entering Moscow. In front rode a detachment of Württemberg hussars, and behind them the King of Naples in person, accompanied by a numerous suite.

Near the centre of Arbat, not far from the church of St Nikolai of the Miraculous Apparition, Murat halted to await information from the advanced detachment as to the condition of the 'citadel,' le Kremlin.

A little group of the inhabitants left in Moscow gathered round Murat. They all stared with shy perplexity at this strange, long-haired commander decked in feathers and gold.

'I say, is that their tsar? He's not bad,' queried low voices.

An interpreter approached the knot of onlookers.

'Caps ... caps off!' they muttered to each other. The interpreter picked out an old porter and asked if it were far to the Kremlin. Puzzled by the unfamiliar Polish accent and not realizing that the interpreter was speaking Russian, the porter had no notion what was being said to him and took refuge behind the others.

Murat approached the interpreter and told him to ask where the Russian army was. One of the Russians understood this question and several voices began answering the interpreter simultaneously. A French officer from the advance detachment rode up to Murat and reported that the gates into the citadel had been barricaded and that probably there was an ambush there.

'Right,' said Murat, and turning to one of the gentlemen of his suite he commanded four light cannon to be moved forward and the gates to be shelled.

The artillery emerged at a trot from the column following Murat and advanced up Arbat. When they reached the end of Vozdvizhenky street they halted and drew up in the square. Several French officers superintended the placing of the guns and examined the Kremlin through field-glasses.

The bells in the Kremlin were ringing for vespers, and this sound troubled the French. They imagined it to be a call to arms. A few infantrymen ran to the Kutafyev gate. Beams and barriers made of planks lay across the gateway. Two musket shots rang out as soon as an officer with some men began running towards it. A general standing by the guns shouted words of command to the officer, and the latter and his men ran back again.

Three more shots came from the direction of the gate.

One shot grazed the leg of a French soldier and from behind the barricade a few voices were heard uttering a strange cry. Immediately, as though at a word of command, the expression of quiet good humour on the faces of the French general, officers and men was replaced by a look of stubborn, concentrated preparedness for action and suffering. To all of them, from the marshal to the humblest private, this was not a particular street in Moscow, not the Troitsa gate, but a new battlefield likely to be the scene of a bloody conflict. And all were ready for that conflict. The cries from behind the gates ceased. The guns were brought forward. The artillery men blew the ash off their linstocks. An officer shouted 'Fire!' and two whistling sounds of canister-shot rent the air one after another. The shot rattled against the stone of the gateway, on the wooden beams and barriers, and two wavering clouds of smoke fluttered up over the square.

A second or two after the echoes of the shots had died away over the stone Kremlin the French heard a curious sound above their heads. Thousands of jackdaws flew up from the walls and circled in the air, cawing and noisily flapping their wings. At the same instant a solitary human cry rose from the gateway, and amid the smoke appeared the figure of a man, bare-headed and wearing a long peasant coat. Grasping his musket, he took aim at the French. 'Fire!' repeated the artillery officer, the crack of a rifle rang out simultaneously with the roar of two cannon. The gate was again hidden in smoke.

Nothing more stirred behind the barricade, and the French infantry with their officers advanced to the gate. In the gateway lay three wounded and four dead. Two men in peasant coats were in full flight along the foot of the walls towards Znamenka street.

'Clear this lot away!' said the officer, pointing to the beams and the corpses, and the French soldiers, after dispatching the wounded, threw the bodies over the parapet.

Who those men were nobody knew. 'Clear this lot away!' was all that was said of them, and they were flung aside and later on removed that they might not stink. Thiers alone dedicates a few eloquent lines to their memory: 'These wretches had invaded the sacred citadel, supplied themselves with fire-arms from the arsenal and fired (the wretches) on the French. Some of them were hacked down with the sword, and the Kremlin was purged of their presence.'

Murat was informed that the way was clear. The French entered the gates and began pitching their camp in the Senate square. The soldiers hurled chairs out of the windows of the Senate House into the square to use as fuel for the fires they lit there.

Other detachments marched through the Kremlin and encamped along Moroseyka, Lubyanka and Pokrovka streets. Others bivouacked in Vozdvizhenka, Nikolsky and Tverskoy streets. Not finding citizens to entertain them, the French instead of billeting themselves on the inhabitants, as was the usual practice in a town, lived in the city as if it were a camp.

Their uniforms were tattered, they were famished, worn-out and reduced to a third of their original strength, but the French troops nevertheless entered Moscow in good order. It was a harassed and exhausted yet still active and menacing army. But it was an army only up to the moment when the soldiers of that army scattered to their different quarters. As soon as the units of the various regiments started to disperse among the wealthy and deserted mansions the army *qua* army ceased to exist and something nondescript came into being that was neither citizen nor soldier but what is known as marauder. Five weeks later, when these same men left Moscow, they no longer formed an army. They were a mob of marauders, each dragging away with him a quantity of articles which seemed to him valuable or useful. The aim of each of these men when he left Moscow was not, as it had been, to conquer but simply to keep the booty he had acquired. Like the monkey which slips its paw into the narrow neck of a pitcher to grasp a handful of nuts and will not open its fist for fear of losing its plunder, and is thereby the undoing of itself, so the French when they left Moscow were doomed to perish because they lugged their loot with them, yet to relinquish what they had stolen was as impossible for them as for the monkey to let go of its handful of nuts. Ten minutes after each regiment had made its entry into any given quarter of Moscow not a soldier, not an officer was to be found. Through the windows of the houses men could be seen in military uniforms and Hessian boots, laughing and strolling through the rooms. In cellars and store-rooms other men were busy among the provisions; in the yards they were unlocking or breaking open coach house and stable doors; they kindled fires in kitchens, rolled up their sleeves and kneaded, baked and cooked while frightening, amusing or wheedling women and children. Men such as these there were in plenty everywhere, in all the shops and houses; but the army was no more.

The very first day order after order was issued by the French command forbidding the troops to disperse about the town, severely prohibiting violence to the inhabitants, or looting, and announcing a general roll-call for that same evening. But in spite of all such measures the men, who only yesterday had still constituted an army, poured over the opulent, deserted city with its comforts and copious supplies. Like a hungry herd of cattle that keeps together over a barren plain but which there is no holding as soon as it reaches rich pastures, so did the army stray far and wide about the wealthy city.

Moscow was without its inhabitants, and the soldiers were sucked into her like water into sand, radiating out in all directions from the

Kremlin which they had entered first. Cavalrymen would go into a merchant's house which had been abandoned, find stabling and to spare for their horses – yet move on, all the same, and take possession of the house next door which looked better to them. Many appropriated several houses, chalking their names on them, and quarrelled and even came to blows with other companies for them. Soldiers had no sooner settled into their quarters than they ran out into the streets to see the city, and hearing that everything had been abandoned hurried off to where objects of value were to be had for the taking. The officers followed to try and control the soldiers, and were involuntarily lured into behaving in the same fashion. In Carriage Row shops had been left full of vehicles, and generals flocked there to select calèches and coaches for themselves. The few remaining citizens invited senior officers into their houses, hoping thereby to secure themselves against being plundered. Wealth there was in abundance: there seemed no end to it. The parts occupied by the French were surrounded by other regions still unexplored and unoccupied where, they thought, still greater treasure was to be found. And Moscow engulfed the army deeper and deeper into herself. Just as when water is spilt on dry ground both water and dry ground disappear into mud, so when the famished army marched into the luxurious deserted city, it was the destruction of army and wealthy city alike, and filth, conflagrations and marauding bands sprang up in their place.

*

The French attributed the burning of Moscow *au patriotisme féroce de Rostopchine*; the Russians to the barbarity of the French. In reality, however, responsibility for the burning of Moscow was not due and cannot be ascribed to any one person or number of persons. Moscow burned, as any city must have burned which was built of wood – quite apart from the question whether there were or were not one hundred and thirty inefficient fire-engines in the town. Deserted Moscow had to burn, as inevitably as a heap of shavings is sure to burn if sparks are scattered on it for several days in succession. A wooden city, which has its conflagrations almost every day in spite of the presence of householders careful of their property, and a watchful police, could not fail to burn when its inhabitants were gone and their places taken by soldiers who smoked their pipes, made campfires of the Senate chairs in the Senate square, and cooked themselves meals twice a day. In peace-time it is only necessary to billet troops in the villages of any district for the number of fires in that district to increase immediately. How much then must the probability of fire increase in an abandoned timber-constructed town occupied by a foreign army! *Le patriotisme féroce de Rostopchine* and the barbarity of the French do not enter in. Moscow was set on fire through soldiers smoking pipes, through cook-stoves and camp-fires, through the carelessness of enemy soldiers living in houses that were not their own. Even if there was any arson (which is very doubtful, for no one had any reason for starting fires – in any case a troublesome and dangerous proceeding), arson cannot be regarded as responsible, for the same thing would have happened without any incendiarism.

However tempting it might be for the French to blame Rostopchin's savage patriotism and for the Russians to throw the blame on the scoundrel Bonaparte, or, in after years, to place the heroic torch in the hands of their own people, it is impossible not to see that there could be no such direct cause of the fire, since Moscow was as certain to be burned as any village, factory or house forsaken by its owners for strangers to take possession of and cook their porridge in. Moscow was burned by its inhabitants – that is true; but by those who had left her and gone away, not by those who stayed behind. Moscow under enemy occupation was not treated with respect like Berlin, Vienna and other towns simply because her citizens, instead of welcoming the French with the bread and salt of hospitality and the keys of the gates, preferred to abandon her.

27

It was not till the evening of the 2nd of September that the tide of invasion, spreading out starwise as it did, reached the quarter where Pierre was staying.

After the last two days spent in solitude and in such unusual circumstances, Pierre was in a state bordering on insanity. One insistent train of thought wholly obsessed him. He could not have told how or when it had first come but now it had such complete possession of him that he remembered nothing of the past, realized nothing of the present; and all he saw and heard about him seemed like a dream.

Pierre had left home solely to escape from the intricate tangle of life's daily demands which held him fast, and which in his present condition he was incapable of unravelling. On the pretext of sorting the deceased's books and papers he had gone to Bazdeyev's house in search of relief from the turmoil of life, for in his mind Bazdeyev was connected with a world of eternal, quiet, solemn thoughts, the very opposite of the restless confusion into which he felt himself being dragged. He sought a peaceful refuge, and in Bazdeyev's study did indeed find it. As he sat leaning his elbows on the dust-covered writing-table in the deathlike stillness of the library impressions and recollections of the last few days began to rise before him in calm and significant succession, among them memories of the battle of Borodino in particular and of that overwhelming sense of his own unimportance and spuriousness compared with the truth, simplicity and strength of character of those whose image was stamped on his soul and whom he thought of as *they*. When he was roused from his reverie by Gerasim the idea occurred to him of taking part in the popular defence of Moscow which he knew was projected. And with this end in view he had asked Gerasim to procure him a peasant coat and a pistol, confiding to him his intention of keeping his identity secret and remaining in Bazdeyev's house. Then during the first day of solitude and idleness (Pierre tried several times to fix his attention on the masonic manuscripts but in vain), his mind more than once reverted vaguely to something that had struck him before – the cabalistic significance of his name in connexion with Bonaparte's. But the notion that he, *L'russe Besuhov*, was destined to set a term to the power of *the Beast* came to him as yet only as one of those fancies which flit idly through the brain, leaving no trace behind.

When, following the purchase of the peasant coat simply with the object of taking part in the defence of Moscow by the people, Pierre had met the Rostovs and Natasha had said to him: 'Are you going to stay in Moscow? Oh, how splendid!' the thought flashed into his mind that it really might be splendid, even if Moscow were taken, to remain and do what he was predestined to do.

Next day, full of the idea of not sparing himself and not lagging in any way behind *them*, Pierre went with the crowd to the Three Hills gate. But back in the house again, convinced that Moscow would not be defended, he suddenly felt that what before had only occurred to him as a possibility had now become absolutely necessary and inevitable. He must remain in Moscow, *incognito*, must meet Napoleon and kill him – and either perish or deliver all Europe from her misery, which it seemed to him was entirely due to Napoleon.

Pierre knew all the details of the attempt on Bonaparte's life by a German student in Vienna in 1809, and knew that the student had been shot. And the risk to which he would be exposing his life in carrying out his design excited him still more.

Two sentiments of equal intensity attracted Pierre irresistibly to this purpose. The first was the feeling that sacrifice and suffering were demanded from him in view of his consciousness of the common calamity, the feeling that had impelled him to go to Mozhaisk on the 25th and to place himself in the very thick of the battle, and had now caused him to run away from his own house, to give up the luxury and comfort to which he was accustomed, and sleep in his clothes on a hard sofa and eat the same food as Gerasim. The other was that vague and typically Russian contempt for everything conventional, artificial and accepted – for everything the majority of mankind regards as the highest good in the world. Pierre had first experienced this strange and fascinating feeling in the Slobodskoy Palace, when he had suddenly seen that wealth and power and life – all that men so painstakingly acquire and cherish – if they are worth anything at all are only worth the measure of joy afforded by renouncing them.

It was the same impulse that induces a volunteer-recruit to spend his last farthing on drink, the drunken man to smash looking-glasses and windows for no apparent reason, although he knows he will have to empty his purse to pay for the damage; the urge which impels a man to commit actions which from an ordinary point of view are insane, to essay, as it were, his personal power and strength and testify to the existence of a higher criterion of life outside mere human limitations.

Ever since the day Pierre experienced this sensation for the first time in the Slobodskoy Palace he had been continuously under its influence but only now found full satisfaction for it. Moreover at this present moment Pierre was supported in his design and prevented from abandoning it by the steps he had already taken in that direction. If he were now to leave Moscow like everyone else, his flight from home, the peasant coat, the pistol and his announcement to the Rostovs that he would be staying in Moscow would lose all meaning and appear laughable and ridiculous (a point on which Pierre was very sensitive).

Pierre's physical condition, as is always the case, corresponded to his mental state. The coarse fare to which he was unused, the vodka he drank during those days, the absence of wine and cigars, his dirty unchanged linen, two almost sleepless nights spent on a short couch without bedding – all this helped to keep him in a state of nervous excitement bordering on madness.

*

It was two o'clock in the afternoon. The French had already entered Moscow. Pierre knew this but instead of acting he only brooded on his scheme, going over it in the minutest detail. Pierre in his imaginings never clearly pictured to himself the striking of the blow or the death of Napoleon, but with extraordinary vividness and melancholy enjoyment dwelt on his own destruction and heroic fortitude.

'Yes, alone, for the sake of all, I must accomplish this deed or perish!' he mused. 'Yes, I will go up to him … and then suddenly … Shall it be with a pistol or a dagger? But no matter. "Not I but the hand of Providence punishes thee," I shall tell him,' thought Pierre, pondering the words he would say as he killed Napoleon. 'Well, then, take me and execute me!' he went on, murmuring to himself and bowing his head with a sad but firm expression on his face.

While Pierre was standing in the middle of the room reflecting in this fashion the study door opened and the figure of Makar Alexeyevich appeared on the threshold, his usual timid self transformed out of all recognition. His dressing-gown hung open. His face was red and distorted. He was unmistakably drunk. At first he was disconcerted at seeing Pierre, but observing embarrassment on Pierre's countenance too he was at once emboldened and, staggering on his thin legs, advanced into the middle of the room.

'They're scared,' he exclaimed in a husky, confidential voice. 'I say, I won't surrender, I say … Am I not right, sir?'

He deliberated for a moment; then, suddenly catching sight of the pistol on the table, seized it with surprising rapidity and ran out into the corridor.

Gerasim and the porter, who had followed at Makar Alexeyevich's heels, stopped him in the vestibule and tried to take the pistol from him. Pierre, coming out into the corridor, looked with pity and repugnance at the half-crazy old man. Makar Alexeyevich, scowling

with exertion, clung to the pistol and screamed in his hoarse voice
something that he evidently considered very exalted.

'To arms! Board them! No, you shan't have it!' he yelled.

'There now, that'll do, thank'ee. Pray let go, sir. Come along, sir,
please! ...' pleaded Gerasim, cautiously trying to steer Makar Alexeyevich by his elbows towards the door.

'Who are you? Bonaparte! ...' shouted Makar Alexeyevich.

'It ain't right of you, sir. You come along to your room now, and
have a lie down. Let me have the pistol please.'

'Off with you, scurvy knave! Touch me not! Do you see this?'
shrieked Makar Alexeyevich, brandishing the pistol. 'Board 'em!'

'Catch hold!' whispered Gerasim to the porter.

They seized Makar Alexeyevich by the arms and dragged him to
the door.

The vestibule was filled with an unseemly noise of scuffling and
drunken, husky gasping.

Suddenly a new sound, a shrill, feminine scream, reverberated from
the porch, and the cook came running into the vestibule.

'It's them! Oh heavens above! ... O Lord, they're here! Four on
'em, on horseback!' she cried.

Gerasim and the porter let go of Makar Alexeyevich and in the
hush that followed in the passage several hands were heard banging
at the front door.

28

Pierre, having decided that until the time came for him to carry out
his project it would be best not to disclose his identity or his knowledge of French, stood at the half-open door into the passage, intending to conceal himself as soon as the French entered. But the French
entered and still Pierre did not retire – an irresistible curiosity kept
him riveted there.

There were two of them. One, an officer – a tall, handsome, soldierly figure; the other evidently a private or an orderly, a squat,
thin, sunburnt man with sunken cheeks and a dull expression. The
officer walked in front, leaning on a stick and limping a little. When
he had advanced a few steps he stopped, having apparently made up
his mind that these were good quarters, turned round and shouted in
a loud, peremptory voice to the soldiers standing in the doorway to
put up the horses. Having done this, the officer with a jaunty gesture,

crooking his elbow high in the air, stroked his moustaches and lightly touched his hat.

'Good-day, everybody!' said he gaily, smiling and looking about him.

No one made any reply.

'Are you the master here?' the officer asked Gerasim.

Gerasim gazed at the officer with anxious inquiry.

'Quarters, quarters, lodgings!' exclaimed the officer, looking down at the little man with a condescending and good-natured smile. 'The French are good fellows. What the devil! Don't let us get touchy, *mon vieux*!' he went on, clapping the scared and silent Gerasim on the shoulder. 'Well, does no one speak French in this establishment?' he asked (still speaking in French), glancing round and meeting Pierre's eyes. Pierre moved away from the door.

The officer addressed himself to Gerasim again, asking to see the rooms in the house.

'Master not here – me no understand ... my – your ...' said Gerasim, striving to render his words more comprehensible by speaking in broken Russian.

Still smiling, the French officer spread his hands out before Gerasim's nose, intimating that he did not understand him either, and limped towards the door where Pierre was standing. Pierre was about to retreat in order to go and hide but at that very second he caught sight of Makar Alexeyevich appearing at the open kitchen door with the pistol in his hand. With a madman's cunning Makar Alexeyevich eyed the Frenchman, raised the pistol and took aim.

'Board 'em!' yelled the tipsy man, pressing his finger on the trigger.

The Frenchman, hearing the shout, turned round and at that instant Pierre flung himself on the drunkard. Just as Pierre snatched at the pistol and jerked it up Makar Alexeyevich at last succeeded in pressing the trigger. There was a deafening report and all were enveloped in a cloud of smoke. The Frenchman went pale and rushed to the door.

Forgetting his intention of concealing his knowledge of French, Pierre, snatching away the pistol and throwing it on the floor, ran to the officer and addressed him in French.

'You are not wounded?' he asked.

'I think not,' answered the officer, examining himself, 'but I had a narrow escape that time,' he added, pointing to the damaged plaster on the wall. 'Who is that man?' he demanded, looking sternly at Pierre.

'Oh, I am really in despair at what has happened,' said Pierre quickly, quite forgetting the part he had intended to play. 'He is mad, an unfortunate wretch who did not know what he was doing.'

The officer went up to Makar Alexeyevich and took him by the collar.

Makar Alexeyevich, pouting his lips, stood swaying and leaning against the wall as though dropping asleep.

'Brigand! You shall pay for this,' said the Frenchman, letting go of him. 'We French are merciful after victory but we do not pardon traitors,' he continued, with a look of morose dignity and a graceful, vigorous gesture.

Pierre in French pleaded further with the officer not to be too hard on the drunken imbecile. The Frenchman listened in silence, with the same gloomy air, and then suddenly turned to Pierre with a smile. For a second or two he scrutinized him without speaking. His handsome face assumed a melodramatically sentimental expression, and he held out his hand.

'You saved my life. You must be French,' said he.

For a Frenchman the deduction was axiomatic. Only a Frenchman could perform an heroic action, and to save the life of Monsieur Ramballe, a captain of the 13th Light Brigade, was undoubtedly a most heroic action.

But however impeccable this logic, however well-grounded the conviction the officer based upon it, Pierre felt it necessary to disillusion him.

'I am Russian,' he said shortly.

'Tut-tut-tut! Tell that to others,' said the Frenchman, waving his finger before his nose and smiling. 'You shall let me hear all about that presently. I am delighted to meet a compatriot. Well, what are we to do with this man?' he added, applying to Pierre now as to a brother. Even if Pierre were not a Frenchman, having once received that loftiest of appellations the officer's tone and look suggested that he did not care to disavow it. In reply to his last question Pierre again explained who Makar Alexeyevich was, and how just before his arrival the drunken imbecile had carried off the loaded pistol which they had not had time to recover from him, and begged the officer not to punish him.

'You saved my life. You are French. You ask me to pardon him? I grant your request. Take this man away!' he exclaimed with rapidity and energy, and linking his arm in Pierre's, whom he had promoted Frenchman for saving his life, he went with him into the house.

The soldiers in the yard, hearing the shot, came into the passage asking what had happened and proclaiming their readiness to punish the offenders but the officer stopped them sternly.

'You will be called when you are wanted,' he said.

The men withdrew. The orderly, who had meanwhile explored the kitchen, came up to his officer.

'Captain, there is soup and a leg of mutton in the kitchen,' said he. 'Shall I serve them up?'

'Yes, and bring some wine,' answered the captain.

29

WHEN the Frenchman went into the house with Pierre the latter thought it his duty to assure him once more that he was not French and wished to retire, but the officer would not hear of it. He was so extremely courteous, amiable, good-natured and genuinely grateful to Pierre for saving his life that Pierre had not the heart to refuse, and sat down with him in the parlour – the first room they entered. To Pierre's asseverations that he was not French the captain, plainly at a loss to understand how anyone could refuse so flattering a title, shrugged his shoulders and said that if Pierre absolutely insisted on passing for a Russian, so be it, but for all that he would be bound in eternal gratitude to Pierre for saving his life.

Had this man been endowed with even the slightest capacity for perceiving the feelings of others, and had he had the faintest inkling of Pierre's feelings, the latter would probably have left him; but his lively insensibility to everything other than himself disarmed Pierre.

'Frenchman or Russian prince *incognito*,' said the French officer, eyeing Pierre's fine though soiled linen and the ring on his finger, 'I owe my life to you, and offer you my friendship. A Frenchman never forgets an insult or a service. I offer you my friendship. That is all I can say.'

There was so much good nature and nobility (in the French sense of the word) in the officer's voice, in the expression of his face and in his gestures that Pierre unconsciously responded with a smile to his smile and pressed the hand held out to him.

'Captain Ramballe, of the 13th Light Brigade, Chevalier of the *Légion d'Honneur* for the affair of the 7th' (this was Borodino), he introduced himself, an irrepressible smile of complacency curling the lips under his moustache. 'Will you be so good as to tell me now with whom I have the honour of conversing so agreeably instead of lying in an ambulance with that maniac's bullet in my body?'

Pierre replied that he could not give his name, and coloured up while he tried to invent a name and some plausible excuse for not revealing it, but the Frenchman hastily interrupted him.

'I beg of you!' said he. 'I appreciate your reasons. You are an officer ... a staff-officer, perhaps. You have borne arms against us. It is no concern of mine. I owe you my life. That is enough for me. I am wholly at your service. You are a nobleman?' he concluded with a shade of inquiry in his voice. Pierre bent his head. 'Your Christian name? I ask nothing more. Monsieur Pierre, you say? ... Excellent. That is all I want to know.'

When the mutton and an omelette, a samovar, vodka and some wine which the French had taken from a Russian cellar were brought in Ramballe invited Pierre to share his dinner, and himself immediately fell to, greedily and without delay attacking the viands like a healthy, hungry man, munching vigorously with his strong teeth, constantly smacking his lips and exclaiming, 'Excellent! Delicious!' His face flushed and perspired. Pierre was hungry and glad to share the repast. Morel, the orderly, appeared with some hot water in a saucepan and placed a bottle of claret in it. He also fetched a bottle of kvass from the kitchen for them to try. The French called it *limonade de cochon*, and Morel spoke well of the 'pig's lemonade' he had found in the kitchen. But as the captain had the wine they had looted on their way across Moscow he left the kvass to Morel and devoted himself to a bottle of Bordeaux. He wrapped a table-napkin round the neck of the bottle and poured out wine for himself and Pierre. Hunger appeased and the wine made the captain even more lively and he chatted non-stop all through dinner.

'Yes, my dear Monsieur Pierre, I must offer up a fine votive candle for you for having saved me from that – that madman. ... You see, I have bullets enough in my body already. Here is one I got at Wagram' (he touched his side) 'and this was Smolensk' – he indicated the scar on his cheek. 'And there's this leg, which, as you have noticed, is reluctant to walk: that happened at the great battle of *la Moskowa*' (which was the French name for the battle of Borodino) 'on the 7th. Ye gods, that was something tremendous! You should have seen it – a deluge of fire. A tough job you set us there, upon my word! That is something you can be proud of all right. And, *ma parole*, in spite of the nasty smack I received there I should be ready to begin all over again. I pity those who missed it.'

'I was there,' said Pierre.

'No, really? So much the better!' said the Frenchman. 'You certainly are brave enemies, though. The big redoubt held out well, *nom d'une pipe*. And you made us pay dear for it. I was at it three times – sure as I sit here. Three times we were right on the cannon and three times we were knocked back like cardboard soldiers. Beautiful it was, Monsieur Pierre! Your grenadiers were superb, by Jove! Half a dozen times in succession I saw them close up their ranks and march as though on parade. Fine fellows! Our King of Naples, who knows what's what, cried "Bravo!" Well, well, so you're one of us soldiers!' he smiled after a momentary pause. 'So much the better, so much the better, Monsieur Pierre! Terrible in battle ... gallant ... with the fair' (he winked and smiled), 'that's your Frenchman for you, eh, Monsieur Pierre?'

The captain was so naïvely and good-naturedly gay, so obtuse and self-satisfied that Pierre almost winked back as he looked at him cheerfully. Probably the word 'gallant' led the captain to reflect on the state of things in Moscow.

'*À propos*, tell me, is it true all the women have left Moscow? What a queer idea! What had they to be afraid of?'

'Would not the French ladies leave Paris if the Russians were to enter?' asked Pierre.

'Ha, ha, ha!' The Frenchman gave vent to a merry, hearty chuckle, and slapped Pierre on the shoulder. 'That's a good one, that is!' he exclaimed. 'Paris? ... Why Paris – Paris is ...'

'Paris is the capital of the world ...' Pierre finished for him.

The captain looked at Pierre. He had a habit of stopping short in the middle of a sentence and staring intently with his laughing, genial eyes.

'Well, if you hadn't told me you were Russian, I would have wagered you were a Parisian. You have that ... I don't know what, that ...' and having pronounced this compliment he again gazed at him mutely.

'I have been in Paris. I spent some years there,' said Pierre.

'Oh yes, one can see that quite plainly. Paris! ... The man who doesn't know Paris is a barbarian. You can tell a Parisian two leagues off. Paris is Talma, la Duschénois, Potier, the Sorbonne, the boulevards,' and, perceiving that this conclusion was somewhat of an anti-climax, he added quickly: 'There is only one Paris in the world. You have been in Paris and you remain Russian. Well, I don't esteem you the less for that.'

Under the influence of the wine, and after the days spent in solitude with his sombre thoughts, Pierre could not help taking pleasure in talking to this jolly and good-tempered person.

'To return to your ladies – I hear they are lovely. What a wretched idea to go and bury themselves in the steppes when the French army is in Moscow. What a chance those girls have missed. Your peasants now – that's another thing; but you are civilized beings, you ought to know us better than that. We have occupied Vienna, Berlin, Madrid, Naples, Rome, Warsaw – all the capitals of the world. We are feared, but we are loved. We are worth knowing. And then the Emperor ...' he began, but Pierre interrupted him.

'The Emperor?' echoed Pierre, and his face suddenly wore a mournful and embarrassed look. 'Is the Emperor ...?'

'The Emperor? He is generosity, clemency, justice, order, genius themselves – that's what the Emperor is! It is I, Ramballe, who tell you so ... I, the Ramballe you see before you, was his enemy eight years ago. My father was an émigré count. ... But that man was too much for me. He has taken hold of me. I could not resist the spectacle of the grandeur and glory with which he was covering France. When I realized what he was aiming at, when I saw that he was preparing a bed of laurels for us, you know, I said to myself: "This is something like a monarch!" and I gave myself up to him. Oh yes, *mon cher*, he is the greatest man of the ages, past or future.'

'Is he in Moscow?' Pierre stammered with a guilty look.

The Frenchman glanced at Pierre's guilty face and smiled.

'No, he will make his entry tomorrow,' he replied, and went on with his talk.

Their conversation was interrupted by several voices shouting at the gate and Morel coming in to inform the captain that some

Württemberg hussars had appeared and wanted to put up their horses in the yard where the captain's horses were. This difficulty had arisen chiefly because the hussars did not understand what was said to them in French.

Ramballe had their senior N.C.O. called in, and in a stern voice asked to what regiment he belonged, who was his commanding officer and by what right he allowed himself to claim quarters that were already occupied. The German, who knew very little French, answered the first two questions and gave the names of his regiment and of his commanding officer, but in reply to the third, which he did not understand, he began to explain in German interlarded with a few words of broken French that he was the quartermaster of his regiment and his colonel had ordered him to occupy all the houses in the row. Pierre, who knew German, interpreted for the captain what the quartermaster said and translated the captain's reply into German for the Württemberg hussar. When he grasped what was being said to him the German gave in, and took his men elsewhere. The captain went out into the porch and shouted some orders.

When he returned to the room Pierre was sitting in the same place as before, with his hands clasped on his head. His face expressed suffering. He really was suffering at that moment. As soon as the captain had gone out and he was left alone he suddenly came to himself and realized the position he was in. It was not that Moscow had been taken, not that these happy conquerors were making themselves at home there and patronizing him. Painful as that was, it was not that which tortured Pierre at that moment. He was tortured by the consciousness of his own weakness. A few glasses of wine and a chat with this good-natured fellow had been enough to dissipate the black and determined mood in which he had spent the last few days and which was essential for the execution of his design. Pistol and dagger and peasant coat were ready. Napoleon was to make his entrée to-morrow. Pierre was still just as convinced that it would be a praise-worthy and public-spirited act to slay the malefactor; but he felt now that he would not do it. Why ? – he did not know but he had a sort of presentiment that he would not carry out his intention. He struggled against this recognition of his own weakness but was dimly aware that he could not overcome it, that his former dark thoughts of vengeance, assassination and self-sacrifice had been blown away like dust by contact with the first human being.

The captain came into the room, limping slightly and whistling a tune.

The Frenchman's chatter, which had previously amused Pierre, now repelled him. The tune he was whistling, his gait and the gesture with which he twirled his moustache, now all seemed offensive. 'I will go away at once. I won't say another word to him,' thought Pierre. He thought this but still sat on in the same place. Some strange feeling of impotence tied him to the spot; he longed to get up and go but could not.

The captain, on the contrary, appeared to be in high spirits. He walked a couple of times up and down the room. His eyes sparkled and his moustaches twitched as if he were smiling to himself at some amusing fancy.

'Charming fellow, the colonel of those Württembergers,' he said suddenly. 'He's a German but a good chap if ever there was one. But – a German.' He sat down facing Pierre. 'By the way, you know German, then?'

Pierre looked at him in silence.

'What is the German for "shelter"?'

'Shelter?' repeated Pierre. 'Shelter in German is Unterkunft.'

'How do you pronounce it?' the captain asked quickly, with a shade of distrust in his voice.

'Unterkunft,' Pierre repeated.

'Onterkoff,' said the captain, and looked at Pierre for several seconds with mischievous eyes. 'Awful fools these Germans, don't you think so, Monsieur Pierre?' he concluded.

'Well, another bottle of this Moscow claret, eh? Morel will warm us up another little bottle – Morel!' he called out gaily.

Morel brought candles and a bottle of wine. The captain studied Pierre in the candlelight and was obviously struck by his companion's troubled expression. With genuine concern and sympathy in his face, Ramballe went up to Pierre and bent over him.

'Down in the mouth, are we, eh?' he said, touching Pierre's hand. 'Have I upset you? No, tell me the truth, have you anything against me?' he asked Pierre. 'Perhaps it's the state of affairs?'

Pierre did not answer but looked cordially into the Frenchman's eyes. He found the sympathy he read in them pleasing.

'Parole d'honneur, to say nothing of what I owe you, I feel real liking for you. Can I do anything for you? You have only to command me.

For life and death. I say it with my hand on my heart!' he declared, slapping himself on the chest.

'Thank you,' said Pierre.

The captain gazed at Pierre as he had done when he learnt the German word for 'shelter,' and his face suddenly brightened.

'Well, in that case, I drink to our friendship!' he cried gaily, filling two glasses with wine.

Pierre took one of the glasses and emptied it. Ramballe drained his too, pressed Pierre's hand again and leaned his elbow on the table in a pose of pensive melancholy.

'Yes, my dear friend,' he began, 'such are the caprices of fortune. Who would have thought I should be a soldier and captain of the dragoons in the service of Bonaparte, as we used to call him? And yet here I am in Moscow with him. I must tell you, *mon cher*,' he continued in the sad, measured tones of a man about to embark on a long story, 'our name is one of the most ancient in France.'

And with the easy-going, naïve frankness of a Frenchman the captain told Pierre the history of his forefathers, his childhood, boyhood and youth, and all about his relations, and his financial and family affairs, *ma pauvre mère* playing, of course, a prominent part in the recital.

'But all that is only the stage-setting of life; the real thing is love – love! Am I not right, Monsieur Pierre?' said he, warming up. 'Another glass?'

Pierre again emptied his glass and poured himself out a third.

'*Oh! les femmes, les femmes!*' and the captain, gazing at Pierre with liquid eyes, began talking of love and his adventures with the fair sex, which were very numerous, as might readily be believed, seeing the officer's handsome, self-satisfied face and the eager enthusiasm with which he spoke of women. Although all Ramballe's accounts of his love-affairs had that sensual character in which the French find the unique charm and poetry of love, yet he told his story with such honest conviction that he was the only man who had ever tasted and known all the sweets of love, and he gave such alluring descriptions of women, that Pierre listened to him with curiosity.

It was evident that *l'amour* which the Frenchman was so fond of was not that low and simple sensual passion Pierre had at one time felt for his wife, nor was it the romantic sentiment which he had kindled in himself for Natasha. (Ramballe held both these kinds of love in equal contempt – the one was all very well for clodhoppers,

the other for nincompoops.) *L'amour* which the Frenchman worshipped consisted pre-eminently in an unnatural relation to the woman
and in a combination of monstrous circumstances which lent the chief
charm to the emotion.

Thus the captain related the touching story of his love for a fascinating marquise of five-and-thirty and at the same time for a delightful, innocent child of seventeen, the daughter of the bewitching marquise. Mother and daughter had vied with each other in generosity,
and the rivalry which ended in the mother sacrificing herself and
offering her daughter in marriage to her lover even now, though it
was a memory of a distant past, moved the captain deeply. Then he
narrated an episode in which the husband played the part of the lover,
while he – the lover – assumed the rôle of husband, as well as several
comic incidents from his reminiscences of Germany, where *Unterkunft* means *shelter* and husbands eat sauerkraut and the young girls
are 'too blonde'.

Finally he came to his latest adventure, in Poland, still fresh in the
captain's memory and described by him with rapid gestures and
glowing face: the story of how he had saved the life of a Pole (on the
whole saving life featured strongly in the captain's recitals) and the
Pole had entrusted to him his enchanting wife (*parisienne de cœur*)
while he himself entered the French service. The captain was fortunate, the enchanting Polish lady had wanted to elope with him, but
prompted by a magnanimous impulse the captain had restored the
wife to the husband, remarking as he did so: 'I saved your life, and
now I save your honour!' As he repeated these words the captain
wiped his eyes and gave himself a shake as though to shake off the
weakness which assailed him at this touching memory.

As men often do at a late hour, and under the influence of wine,
Pierre listened to the captain's tales, and while he followed and took
in all that was told him he was also following a train of personal
recollections which for some reason suddenly flooded his imagination.
Hearing these stories of love, his own love for Natasha suddenly rose
before him in a succession of pictures which he mentally compared
with Ramballe's descriptions. When the captain enlarged on the
struggle between love and duty Pierre was reminded in every detail
of his last meeting with the object of his love at the Suharev water-
tower. At the time, that meeting had not made much impression on
him – he had not once thought of it since. But now it seemed to him

that there was something very significant and poetic in the encounter.

'Piotr Kirillich, come here! You see, we recognized you!' He could hear her words now, could see her smile, her travelling hood and the curl straying out from beneath it ... and there seemed to him something pathetic and touching in it all.

Having finished his account of the bewitching Polish lady, the captain turned to Pierre with the inquiry whether he had experienced a similar impulse to sacrifice himself for love, or known a feeling of envy of the legitimate husband.

Pierre, thus challenged, raised his head and felt an urgent craving to give vent to the thoughts that filled his mind. He began to explain that he looked upon love for women somewhat differently. He said that in all his life he had loved and still loved only one woman, and that she could never be his.

'*Tiens!*' exclaimed the captain.

Pierre then confided that he had loved this woman from his earliest youth but had not dared to think of her because she was too young, and because he had been an illegitimate son without a name. Afterwards, when he had received a name and a fortune he had not dared think of her because he loved her too well, setting her high above all the world and especially, therefore, above himself.

When he reached this point Pierre asked the captain whether he could understand that.

The captain made a gesture signifying that even if he did not understand it he begged Pierre to proceed.

'Platonic love. Moonshine! ...' he muttered to himself.

Whether it was the wine he had drunk, or a necessity to pour out his heart, or the certainty that this man did not know and would never know any of the persons concerned in his tale, or whether it was all these things together, something loosened Pierre's tongue. Speaking thickly, and with a far-away look in his shining eyes, he told the whole story of his life: his marriage, Natasha's love for his best friend, her perfidy, and all his own simple relations with her. Impelled on by Ramballe's questions, he told him too what he had at first kept secret—his position in society and even his name.

What impressed the captain more than anything else in Pierre's account was the fact that Pierre was very wealthy, owned two palatial mansions in Moscow and had abandoned everything and not left the capital but was staying on, concealing his name and rank.

It was a very late hour when they went out into the street together. The night was mild and light. To the left of the house, in Petrovsky street, was the glow of the first fire to break out in Moscow. On the right a young crescent moon hung high in the sky, and in the opposite quarter of the heavens blazed the comet which was connected in Pierre's heart with his love. Gerasim, the cook and two Frenchmen stood laughing and talking by the gate, in two mutually incomprehensible languages. They were looking at the glow of the fire burning in the town.

There was nothing alarming in a small remote fire in the immense city.

Gazing at the high starry sky, at the moon, at the comet and at the glare from the fire, Pierre felt a thrill of joyous and tender emotion. 'How lovely it all is – what more could one want ?' he thought. And suddenly remembering his intention he grew dizzy and faint, and must have fallen had he not leaned against the fence to save himself.

Without taking leave of his new friend Pierre moved away from the gate with unsteady steps and returning to his room lay down on the sofa and instantly fell asleep.

30

THE glow of the first fire that broke out on the 2nd of September was watched from various roads and with various feelings by the fugitive Muscovites and the retreating troops.

The Rostovs spent that night at Mytishchy, fourteen miles from Moscow. They had started so late on the 1st of September, the road had been so encumbered by vehicles and troops, so many things had been forgotten and servants sent back for them, that they had decided to halt for the first night at a place three miles out of Moscow. The next morning they set off late and there were again so many delays that they got no farther than Great Mytishchy. At ten o'clock that evening the Rostov family and the wounded travelling with them were all distributed in the yards and huts of that large village. After settling their masters for the night the Rostovs' servants and coachmen and the orderlies of the wounded officers had supper, fed their horses and came out into the porches.

In a hut nearby lay Raevsky's adjutant with a fractured wrist, and the dreadful pain he was in made him groan piteously and incessantly, and his moaning had a gruesome sound in the darkness of the autumn night. He had spent the previous night in the same yard as the Rostovs. The countess declared she had been unable to close her eyes on account of his groaning, and at Mytishchy she moved into a less comfortable hut simply to be farther away from the wounded man.

One of the servants suddenly noticed against the dark sky beyond the high body of the coach standing before the porch the small glow of another fire. One such glow had long been visible and everybody knew it was the village of Little Mytishchy burning – set on fire by Mamonov's Cossacks.

'Look over there, boys! Another fire!' remarked the orderly.

They all looked round.

'Yes, they said as how them Cossacks of Mamonov's had fired Little Mytishchy.'

'Nay, that's not Mytishchy! 'Tis too far off.'

'It must be Moscow!'

Two of the men went round to the other side of the coach and squatted on the step.

'That there fire's too far to the left – why, Mytishchy lies yonder and this be way round on t'other side.'

Several more men joined the first.

'I say, it's flaring up right enough,' said one. 'That's a fire in Moscow, my friends – in Sushchevsky or mebbe Rogozhsky.'

No one made any comment and for some time they all stared in silence at the flames of this new conflagration spreading in the distance.

Old Danilo Terentyich, the count's valet (as he was called) came up to the group and shouted at Mishka.

'What are you standing there gaping at, fat-head? ... The count will be callin' and no one about. Go and tidy up the master's clothes.'

'I only just run out for some water,' said Mishka.

'What's your opinion, Danilo Terentyich? Isn't that there fire in Moscow?' asked one of the footmen.

Danilo Terentyich made no reply, and again for a long while they all watched dumbly. The glow spread, rising and falling, wider and wider.

'God have mercy! The wind and this dry weather ...' said another voice.

'Look'ee! See how far it's gone! O Lord above! Why, you can

even see the crows flying. Lord have mercy on us poor sinners!'

'They'll put it out, never fear!'

'Who's to put it out?' cried Danilo Terentyich, who had hitherto been silent. His voice was quiet and deliberate. ''Tis Moscow sure enough, lads,' said he. 'Our white-walled Mother Mosc ...' His voice faltered and broke into an old man's sob.

And it seemed as though they had all only been waiting for this to make them realize the meaning of the red glare they were watching. There were sighs, the murmur of prayer and the sobbing of the count's old valet.

31

THE valet returned to the count and told his master that Moscow was burning. The count put on his dressing-gown and went out to look. Sonya and Madame Schoss, who had not yet undressed, went with him. Natasha and the countess were left alone indoors. (Petya was no longer with the family, having gone on ahead with his regiment, which was making for Troitsa.)

The countess burst into tears when she heard the news that Moscow was in flames. Natasha, pale, with staring eyes, was sitting on the bench under the icons (in the same spot she had dropped into when they arrived), and had paid no attention to her father's words. She was listening to the ceaseless moaning of the adjutant, three houses off.

'Oh, how awful!' exclaimed Sonya, returning from the yard, chilled and frightened. 'I do believe all Moscow will burn, there's a dreadful glow! Natasha, do look! You can see it now from the window,' she said to her cousin, obviously trying to distract her mind. But Natasha gazed at her as though not understanding what was asked of her, and again fixed her eyes on the corner of the stove. She had been in this condition of stupor since early that morning, when Sonya, to the surprise and annoyance of the countess, had for some unaccountable reason found it necessary to tell Natasha that Prince Andrei was among the wounded travelling with them. The countess had seldom been so angry with anyone as she was with Sonya. Sonya had cried and begged to be forgiven, and now, as though striving to atone for her fault, continued doubly attentive to her cousin.

'Look, Natasha, what a frightful fire it is!' said she.

'What is?' asked Natasha. 'Oh yes, Moscow.'

And as though not to offend Sonya, and to get rid of her, she

1083

turned her head to the window and looked out in such a way that it was evident she could see nothing, and then resumed her former attitude.

'But you didn't see?'

'Yes, really I did,' Natasha declared in a voice that pleaded to be left in peace.

And it was plain both to the countess and Sonya that in the nature of things neither Moscow nor the burning of Moscow nor anything else could be of any interest to Natasha.

The count returned and lay down behind the partition. The countess went up to her daughter and rested the back of her hand on her head as she was wont to do when Natasha was ill, then pressed her lips to her forehead to feel whether she was feverish, and finally kissed her.

'Are you cold? You are trembling all over. You'd better lie down,' said the countess.

'Lie down? All right, I will. I'll lie down at once,' answered Natasha.

When Natasha had been told that morning that Prince Andrei was seriously wounded and was travelling with them she had at first asked endless questions: Where was he going? How had he been wounded? Was it serious? And could she see him? But after she had been told that she could not see him, that he was gravely wounded but his life was not in danger, she gave up asking questions or speaking at all, obviously having no faith in what they said and convinced that whatever she tried she would get the same answers. All the way she had sat motionless in a corner of the coach with those wide eyes, the expression in which the countess knew so well and dreaded so much, and now she was sitting in just the same way on the bench in the hut. She was planning something, was either coming or had come to some decision – this the countess knew but what the decision might be she did not know, and that alarmed and worried her.

'Natasha, undress, darling. Come and lie on my bed.'

(The countess was the only one for whom a bed had been made up on a bedstead. Madame Schoss and the two girls were to sleep on some hay on the floor.)

'No, mamma, I'll lie here on the floor,' Natasha replied irritably, and she went to the window and opened it. Through the opened window the moans of the adjutant came more distinctly. She leaned her head out into the damp night air, and the countess saw her slender shoulders shaking with sobs and throbbing against the window-frame. Natasha knew it was not Prince Andrei moaning. She knew Prince Andrei was in the same courtyard as themselves, that he was in the next hut across the passage; but these terrible incessant groans made her sob. The countess exchanged a look with Sonya.

'Come to bed, darling; come to bed, my pet,' said the countess, gently touching Natasha's shoulder. 'Come along now and lie down.'

'Yes, yes, all right. … I'll lie down at once,' said Natasha, hurriedly undressing and tugging at the strings of her petticoat.

When she had thrown off her dress and put on a dressing-jacket she sat down with her feet tucked under her, on the bed that had been made up on the floor, jerked her short braid of fine hair to the front and began re-plaiting it. Her long, thin, practised fingers rapidly and deftly parted, plaited and tied up the braid. Natasha's head moved from side to side from habit but her eyes, feverishly wide, stared straight before her with the same fixed intensity. When her toilet for the night was finished she sank quietly on to the sheet spread over the hay on the side nearest the door.

'Natasha, you lie in the middle,' said Sonya.

'No, I shall stay here,' muttered Natasha. 'And do go to bed,' she added crossly, and buried her face in the pillow.

The countess, Madame Schoss and Sonya hurriedly undressed and went to bed. The small lamp in front of the icons was the only light left in the room. But out in the yard there was the glare from the fire at Little Mytishchy a mile and a half away, and the tipsy clamour of peasants shouting in the tavern across the street, which Mamonov's Cossacks had broken into, and the adjutant's uninterrupted moaning.

For a long time Natasha lay listening to the sounds that reached her from within and without, and did not stir. First she heard her mother praying and sighing, and the creaking of her bed under her, Madame Schoss's familiar whistling snore and Sonya's soft breathing. Then the countess called to Natasha. Natasha did not answer.

'I think she's asleep, mamma,' whispered Sonya.

After a brief silence the countess spoke once more but this time no one answered her.

Soon after that Natasha heard her mother's even breathing. Natasha did not move, though her little bare foot poking out from under the quilt felt frozen against the uncovered floor.

A cricket chirped in a crack in the wall, as though celebrating a victory over all the world. Far away a cock crowed, and others responded near by. The shouts had died down in the tavern; only the moaning of the adjutant was heard. Natasha sat up.

'Sonya, are you asleep? Mamma?' she whispered.

No one answered. Slowly and carefully Natasha got up, crossed herself and stepped cautiously on to the cold, dirty floor with her slim, supple bare feet. A board creaked. Tripping lightly from one foot to the other she ran like a kitten the few steps to the door and took hold of the cold door-handle.

It seemed to her that something was banging on the walls of the hut with heavy, rhythmical strokes: it was the beating of her own heart, torn with dread, with love and terror.

She opened the door, stepped across the threshold and on to the chill damp earth of the passage outside. The cold all about her refreshed her. Her bare foot touched a sleeping man; she stepped over him and opened the door of the hut in which Prince Andrei was lying. It was dark in the hut. In the far corner, on a bench beside the bed where something lay, stood a tallow candle with a great smouldering wick.

From the moment she had been told that morning of Prince Andrei's wound and his presence there, Natasha had resolved that she must see him. She did not know why she had to: she knew the meeting would be painful and felt the more certain that it was essential.

All day long she had lived in the hope of seeing him that night. But now when the moment had come she was filled with dread of what she might see. How was he disfigured? What was left of him? Was he like that unceasing moan of the adjutant's? Yes, he was like that. In her imagination he was that terrible moaning personified. When she caught sight of an indistinct shape in the corner and mistook his knees raised under the counterpane for his shoulders she pictured some fearful body there, and stood still in terror. But an irresistible force drew her forward. She made one cautious step, then another, and found herself in the middle of a small room cumbered with baggage. Another man – Timohin – was lying in a corner on the benches beneath the icons, and two others – the doctor and a valet – lay on the floor.

The valet sat up and whispered something. Timohin, in pain from a wound in his leg, was not asleep and gazed wide-eyed at this strange apparition of a girl in a white chemise, dressing-jacket and night-cap. The valet's sleepy, frightened exclamation, 'What is it ? What do you want ?' only made Natasha hasten to the figure lying in the corner. Horribly unlike a human being as that body looked, she must see him. She slipped past the valet, the snuff fell from the candle-wick and she saw Prince Andrei quite clearly with his arms stretched out on the quilt, looking just as she had always seen him.

He was the same as ever; but the feverish flush on his face, his glittering eyes directed rapturously towards her, and especially his neck, soft as a child's, showing above the turn-down collar of his nightshirt, gave him a peculiarly innocent, boyish look which was quite new to her in Prince Andrei. She went up to him and with a swift, supple, youthful movement dropped on her knees.

He smiled and held out his hand to her.

32

SEVEN days had passed since Prince Andrei had come to himself in the ambulance-station on the field of Borodino. All that time he had been in a state of almost continuous unconsciousness. His feverish condition and the inflammation of his intestines, which were injured, were in the doctor's opinion certain to carry him off. But on the seventh day he ate with relish a slice of bread and drank some tea, and the doctor noticed that his temperature was lower. Prince Andrei had regained consciousness in the morning. The first night after they left Moscow had been fairly warm and he had remained in the calèche, but at Mytishchy the wounded man had himself asked to be carried indoors and given some tea. The pain caused by moving him into the hut had made him groan aloud and lose consciousness again. When he had been stretched on his camp bedstead he lay for a long while motionless with closed eyes. Then he opened them and murmured softly: 'How about the tea ?' The doctor was amazed by this ability to remember such a small everyday thing. He felt Prince Andrei's pulse, and to his surprise and regret found that it had improved. He was regretful because he knew by experience that his patient could not live and that if he did not die now he would do so a little later with greater suffering. With Prince Andrei was the red-nosed major of his regiment, Timohin, who had joined him in Moscow with a wound in the leg received at the same battle of Borodino.

They were accompanied by the surgeon, Prince Andrei's valet, his coachman and two orderlies.

They gave Prince Andrei some tea. He drank it eagerly, looking with feverish eyes at the door in front of him, as though trying to understand and remember something.

'I don't want any more. Is Timohin here?' he asked.

Timohin edged along the bench towards him.

'I'm here, your Excellency.'

'How's the wound?'

'Mine? All right, sir. But how are you?'

Prince Andrei pondered again, apparently in an effort to recollect.

'Couldn't they get me the book?' he asked.

'What book?'

'A New Testament. I haven't one.'

The doctor promised to procure it for him, and began to inquire of the prince how he was feeling. Prince Andrei answered all his questions reluctantly, though rationally, and then said he would like a bolster placed under him as he was uncomfortable and in great pain. The doctor and the valet lifted the cloak with which he was covered, and making wry faces at the noisome smell of putrefying flesh that came from the wound began to examine the fearful place. The doctor was deeply troubled over something, made some slight change in the dressings and turned the wounded man over so that he groaned and lost consciousness again and grew delirious with the pain. He kept asking them to be quick and get him the book and put it 'just here'.

'What trouble would it be to you?' he said. 'I haven't one – please get one for me. Put it under me just for a minute,' he pleaded in a piteous voice.

The doctor went into the passage to wash his hands.

'You fellows have no conscience,' said he to the valet who was pouring water over his hands. 'I take my eyes off you for half a second, and you go and lie him right on his wound. He's in such agony, I wonder how he lives through it.'

'I thought we had put something under him, as Christ is my witness I did!' said the valet.

The first time Prince Andrei realized where he was and what was the matter with him, and remembered being wounded and how, was when the calèche stopped at Mytishchy and he asked to be carried into the hut. Pain clouded his senses again until he came to himself inside the hut, and while he was drinking tea he went over in his mind all that had happened to him, remembering most vividly the moment in the ambulance station when at the sight of the sufferings of a man he disliked those new thoughts had come to him with such promise of happiness. And those thoughts – though vague now and cloudy – again possessed his soul. He remembered that he had a new source of happiness now, and that this happiness was somehow connected with the New Testament. That was why he had asked for the New Testament. But the uncomfortable position in which they had laid him, without support for his wound, and being turned over, confused his mind and it was only in the complete stillness of the night that he came to himself for the third time. Everybody around him was asleep. A cricket chirped across the passage; someone was shouting and singing in the street; cockroaches rustled over the table and the icons, and a big autumn fly flopped on his pillow and fluttered about the tallow candle beside him, the wick of which was charred into a shape like a mushroom.

His mind was not in a normal state. A man in good health usually thinks of, feels and remembers an immense number of different things simultaneously but has the power and resolution to select one series of ideas or phenomena on which to concentrate his whole attention. A man who is not ill can break away from the profoundest of meditations to say a civil word to anyone who comes in, and then return again to his own thoughts. But Prince Andrei's mind was not in a normal condition in this respect. All the powers of his mind were more active and clearer than ever but they acted apart from his will. The most heterogeneous notions and visions occupied him at one and the same moment. Sometimes his brain suddenly began to work with a vigour, clarity and depth it had never attained when he was in health. And then, just as suddenly, in the midst of its work it would switch to some unexpected obsession, and he lacked the strength to turn it back again.

'Yes, a new happiness was revealed to me – a happiness which is man's imprescriptible right,' he said to himself as he lay in the semi-darkness of the quiet hut gazing fixedly before him with feverish, wide-open eyes. 'A happiness beyond the reach of material forces, unaffected by the external material influences which touch man – a happiness of the soul alone, the happiness of loving! To feel it is in every man's power but only God can conceive and enjoin it. But how did God ordain this law? Why was the Son ... ?' The thread of these ideas was suddenly broken, and Prince Andrei heard (though he could not tell whether it was delirium or reality) a low, lisping voice repeating over and over in measured rhythm: '*I piti-piti-piti*' and then again '*i ti-ti*' and '*i piti-piti-piti*' and '*i ti-ti*' once more. At the same time he felt as though a strange, ethereal edifice of delicate needles or splinters was rising over his face, from the very centre of it, to the sound of this whispered music. He felt that he must balance carefully (though it was difficult) so that the airy structure should not collapse; but nevertheless it kept collapsing and then slowly rising again to the rhythmic murmur of the music. 'It is stretching out, stretching out, spreading and growing!' said Prince Andrei to himself. And while he listened to the whispering beat, and felt the edifice of needles drawing out and lifting, the red halo of light round the candle caught his eye by fits and starts, and he heard the rustle of cockroaches and the buzzing of the fly that flopped against his pillow and his face. Each time the fly brushed his cheek it burnt him like a hot iron; and yet to his surprise, though it struck the very spot where the strange fabric of needles was rising from his face, it did not demolish it. But apart from all this there was one other thing of importance. That something white by the door – the statue of a sphinx – which weighed on him too.

'But perhaps it's my shirt on the table,' thought Prince Andrei, 'and those are my legs, and that is the door, but why is it always stretching and expanding – and that *piti-piti-piti* and *ti-ti* and *piti-piti-piti*. ... That's enough, please leave off – stop!' Prince Andrei besought someone wearily. And all at once his mind cleared again, and thought and feeling floated to the surface, having extraordinary clarity and force.

'Yes – love' (he reflected again, quite lucidly). 'But not that love which loves for something, to gain something or because of something, but the love I knew for the first time when, dying, I saw my enemy and yet loved him. I experienced the love which is the very essence of the soul, the love which requires no object. And I feel that blessed feeling now too. To love one's neighbours, to love one's enemies, to love everything – to love God in all His manifestations. Human love serves to love those dear to us but to love one's enemies we need divine love. And that is why I knew such joy when I felt I loved that man. What became of him? Is he alive? ... Human love may turn to hatred but divine love cannot change. Nothing, not even death, can destroy it. It is the very nature of the soul. Yet how many people have I hated in my life? And of them all none did I love and hate as much as her.' And he vividly pictured Natasha to himself, not as he had pictured her in the past with her charms only, which gave him such delight, but for the first time imagining her soul. And he understood her feelings, her suffering, her shame and remorse. Now, for the first time, he realized all the cruelty of his rejection of her, the cruelty of breaking with her. 'If only I might see her once more. Just once to look into those eyes and say …'

Piti-piti-piti and *ti-ti*, and *piti-piti – boom!* flopped the fly. … And his attention was suddenly transported into the other mixed world of reality and hallucination in which something peculiar was taking place. The edifice was still rising, unbroken, something was still stretching out and the candle with its red halo was still burning, and the same shirt which looked like a sphinx lying by the door; but in addition to all this there was a creaking sound and a whiff of fresh air, and a new white sphinx appeared, standing in the doorway. And that sphinx had the white face and shining eyes of the very Natasha of whom he had just been thinking.

'Oh, how wearisome this everlasting delirium is!' thought Prince Andrei, trying to expel that face from his imagination. But the vision stayed before his eyes with all the strength of reality, was coming nearer. … Prince Andrei tried to return to the world of pure thought but he could not, and delirium drew him back into its domain. The soft murmuring voice kept up its rhythmic whisper, something was squeezing, stretching out, and the strange face was before him. Prince Andrei summoned all his might in an effort to recover his senses, he moved slightly, and suddenly there was a humming in his ears, a dimness in his eyes, and like a man sinking under water he lost consciousness. When he came to himself Natasha, the veritable living Natasha, whom of all people he most longed to love with the new, pure, divine love that had been revealed to him, was on her knees before him. He recognized that it was the real living Natasha, and did not wonder but was quietly happy. Natasha knelt rooted to the ground (she could not have stirred), gazing at him with frightened eyes and restraining her sobs. Her face was pale and rigid. Only her lips and chin quivered a little.

Prince Andrei fetched a sigh of relief, smiled and held out his hand.

'You ?' he said. 'What happiness!'

With a swift but circumspect movement Natasha came nearer, still on her knees, and cautiously taking his hand she bent her face over it and began kissing it, just touching it lightly with her lips.

'Forgive me!' she said in a whisper, lifting her head and glancing at him. 'Forgive me!'

'I love you,' said Prince Andrei.

'Forgive ...'

'Forgive what ?' he asked.

'Forgive me for what I di – d!' faltered Natasha in a scarcely audible, broken whisper, and again began quickly covering his hand with kisses, softly brushing her lips against it.

'I love you more, better than before,' said Prince Andrei, raising her face with his hand so as to look into her eyes.

Those eyes, swimming with happy tears, gazed at him with timid commiseration and joyous love. Natasha's thin, white face with its swollen lips was more than plain - it looked ghastly. But Prince Andrei did not see her face, he saw the shining eyes which were beautiful. They heard the sound of voices behind them.

Piotr, the valet, wide awake by now, had roused the doctor. Timohin, who had not slept at all for the pain in his leg, had long been watching all that was going on, carefully covering his bare body with the sheet as he huddled up on his bench.

'What does this mean ?' said the doctor, getting up from his bed on the floor. 'Please to be gone, madam!'

At that moment a maid sent by the countess, who had noticed her daughter's absence, knocked at the door.

Like a somnambulist awakened in the middle of a trance Natasha walked out of the room, and returning to her hut sank sobbing on her bed.

*

From that day, during all the remainder of the Rostovs' journey, at every halting-place and wherever they spent a night, Natasha never left the wounded Bolkonsky's side, and the doctor was obliged to admit that he had never expected to see in a young girl such constancy or such skill in nursing a wounded man.

Terrible as it seemed to the countess to think that Prince Andrei might (and very probably would, too, from what the doctor said) die on the road in her daughter's arms, she had not the heart to oppose

Natasha. Although the idea did occur that, with the renewal of affectionate relations between the wounded Prince Andrei and Natasha, should he recover, their engagement might be renewed, no one – least of all Natasha and Prince Andrei – spoke of this. The open question concerning life or death which hung not only over Bolkonsky but over the whole of Russia shut out all other considerations.

33

On the 3rd of September Pierre awoke late. His head ached, the clothes in which he had slept without undressing chafed his body and he was oppressed by a vague sense of having done something shameful the day before. That something shameful was his talk the previous evening with Captain Ramballe.

It was eleven o'clock by his watch but it seemed peculiarly dark out of doors. Pierre got up, rubbed his eyes and, seeing the pistol with an engraved stock which Gerasim had put back on the writing-table, remembered where he was and what lay before him that day.

'But am I not too late already?' he wondered. 'No, *he* will surely not make his entry into Moscow before noon.'

Pierre did not allow himself to reflect on what lay ahead of him but made haste to act.

Straightening his clothes, Pierre took up the pistol and was about to set out. But then for the first time it occurred to him that he certainly could not carry the weapon in his hand through the streets. It would be difficult to conceal such a big pistol even under his full coat. He could not put it in his belt or carry it under his arm without its being noticeable. Moreover, the pistol had been discharged and he had not had time to reload it. 'No matter, the dagger will do,' he said to himself, though when planning the execution of his purpose he had more than once come to the conclusion that the great mistake made by the student in 1809 was that he had tried to kill Napoleon with a dagger. But as Pierre's chief aim seemed to be not so much to succeed in his project as to prove to himself that he was not renouncing his intention but was doing all he could to achieve it, he hurriedly took the blunt jagged dagger in a green sheath which he had bought together with the pistol at the Suharev market, and hid it under his waistcoat.

Tying the sash round his peasant's coat and pulling his cap forward,

Pierre walked along the corridor, trying not to make a noise and to avoid meeting the captain, and stepped out into the street.

The conflagration he had looked at so indifferently the evening before had grown sensibly bigger during the night. Moscow was on fire at various points. The buildings in Carriage Row, across the river, in the Bazaar and Povarsky street, as well as the barges on the Moskva river and the timber yards by the Dorogomilov bridge were all ablaze.

Pierre's route took him through side streets to Povarsky street, and from there along Arbat to the church of St Nikolai: this was the spot which he had long since fixed upon for the deed he was meditating. The gates of most of the houses were locked and the shutters up. The streets and alleys were deserted. The air was full of smoke and the smell of burning. From time to time he met a few scared and anxious Russians, and Frenchmen with a look not of the city but of the camp about them, walking in the middle of the road. Both Russians and French looked inquisitively at Pierre. Apart from his height and breadth, and the queer suggestion of morose and concentrated suffering in his face and whole figure, the Russians stared at him because they could not make out to what class he could belong. The French looked back at him with puzzled eyes mainly because Pierre, unlike other Russians who all gazed at the French in trepidation or curiosity, paid no attention to them. At the gates of one house three Frenchmen, who were trying to explain something to some Russians who did not understand them, stopped Pierre and asked him if he knew French.

Pierre shook his head and walked on. In another side street a sentinel on guard beside a green caisson shouted at him but it was only when the shout was threateningly repeated and he heard the click of the musket which the sentinel took up that he realized he ought to have taken the opposite pavement. He heard and saw nothing around him. With a sense of nervous haste and horror he carried his resolution within him like something terrible and alien, fearful – after his experience of the previous night – of losing it. But he was not destined to arrive with his mood intact at the place to which he was bending his steps. Moreover, even if nothing had happened to hinder him *en route*, his design could not now have been carried out, for the reason that Napoleon had passed Arbat more than four hours earlier on his way from the Dorogomilov suburb to the Kremlin, and was at that moment seated in the Imperial study in the Palace, in the worst of humours, giving precise and detailed orders in regard to the urgent measures to be taken for extinguishing the fire, preventing looting and reassuring the inhabitants. But Pierre did not know this; entirely absorbed in what lay before him, he was suffering the anguish men go through when they persist in undertaking a task impossible for them – not because of its inherent difficulties but because of its incompatibility with their own nature. He was tortured by the dread of weakening at the decisive moment and so forfeiting his self-respect.

Though he saw and heard nothing around him he found his way by instinct and did not go wrong in the lanes that led to Povarsky street.

The nearer he approached Povarsky street, the thicker was the smoke everywhere, and the atmosphere was positively warm from the heat of the conflagration. Tongues of flame curled up here and there behind the house-tops. He met more people in the streets, and these people were more agitated. But Pierre, though he was conscious that something unusual was happening around him, did not grasp the fact that he was getting near the fire. As he followed a foot-path across the large open space skirting Povarsky street on one side and the gardens of Prince Gruzinsky's house on the other, Pierre suddenly heard the desperate weeping of a woman close to him. He stopped as if awakening from a dream, and lifted his head.

On the parched dusty grass on one side of the path all sorts of household goods lay in a heap: feather-beds, a samovar, icons and boxes. On the ground, near the trunks, sat a thin woman no longer young, with long, projecting upper teeth, wearing a black cloak and cap. This woman, swaying to and fro and muttering something, was crying convulsively. Two little girls between ten and twelve years old, dressed in dirty short frocks and cloaks, were staring at their mother with a look of stupefaction on their pale, frightened faces. The youngest child, a boy of about seven, who wore an overcoat and a huge cap evidently not his own, was sobbing in the arms of an old nurse. A dirty, bare-legged servant-girl was sitting on a trunk, and having let down her flaxen tresses was tidying her plait and sniffing at the singed hair. The husband, a short, stooping man in a uniform, with sausage-shaped whiskers, and smooth locks of hair showing under his square-set cap, with expressionless face was sorting the trunks piled one on top of the other, and dragging some garments from under them.

As soon as she saw Pierre the woman almost flung herself at his feet.

'Merciful heavens – good Christian folk – save us, help me, kind sir! Help us, somebody,' she articulated through her sobs. 'My baby. ... My little daughter. ... My youngest girl left behind! ... Burnt to death! ... Oh-oh-oh, why did I give suck. ... Oh-oh-oh!'

'There, that'll do, Maria Nikolayevna,' expostulated her husband in a mild voice, evidently only to exonerate himself before the stranger. 'Sister must have taken care of her. Otherwise where else can she be?' he added.

'Monster! Villain!' screeched the woman furiously, her tears suddenly ceasing. 'There's no heart in you, you don't feel for your own child! Any other man would have rescued her from the fire. But he is a monster, not a man, not a father. You, honoured sir, are a well-born person,' she continued, addressing Pierre rapidly between her sobs. 'The place caught fire next door. It blew our way. The girl screamed "Fire!" and we rushed to get our things out, and escaped with what we laid our hands on. ... This is all we could snatch up ... the holy icons, and my dowry bed. All the rest is gone. We caught up the children. But not little Katya. O Lord! Ooh! ...' and again she fell to sobbing. 'My baby, my little one, burnt to death, burnt to death!'

'But where – where was she left?' asked Pierre.

The sympathetic, interested expression on his face told the woman that this man might help her.

'Good, kind sir!' she cried, clutching at his legs. 'Benefactor! Put me out of my misery. ... Aniska, go, you hussy, show him the way!' she screamed to the servant-girl, angrily opening her mouth and exposing her long teeth still more.

'Show me the way, show me, I ... I'll go,' Pierre gasped out quickly.

The dirty servant-girl stepped from behind the trunk, put up her plait and, sighing, walked in front along the path on her stumpy bare legs. Pierre felt as if he had suddenly come back to life after a heavy swoon. He held his head higher, his eyes shone with the light of life, and with swift strides he followed and overtook the girl, and came out on Povarsky street. The whole street was shrouded in black smoke. Here and there tongues of flame broke through the screen. A huge crowd had gathered in front of the conflagration. In the middle of the street stood a French general, saying something to those about him. Pierre, accompanied by the servant-girl, was advancing to the spot where the French general was standing, but the French soldiers stopped him.

'Not this way!' a voice shouted to him.

'Here, master,' said the girl. 'We'll cut across the Nikulins and go by the alley.'

Pierre turned back, giving a spring now and then to keep up with her. The girl ran across the street, scurried down a side alley on the left and, passing three houses, dived into a yard on the right.

'It's just here,' she said, and running across the yard opened a gate in a wooden fence and, stopping short, pointed out to Pierre a small timber-built 'wing', which was blazing away fiercely. One wall had fallen in, the other was on fire, and bright flames issued from the openings of the windows and under the roof.

As Pierre went in at the little gate he was met by a rush of hot air and instinctively drew back.

'Which is it? Which is your house?' he asked.

'Ooh!' wailed the girl, pointing to the annexe. 'That's it. That's where we lived. Sure, you're burnt to death, my treasure, my little Katya, my precious little missy! Ooooh!' lamented Aniska, feeling at the sight of the fire that she too must give expression to her emotions.

Pierre darted up to the 'wing' but the heat was so great that he found himself obliged to skirt round it, and came upon a large house, which so far was only burning at one end, just below the roof. A mob of Frenchmen swarmed round it. At first Pierre did not understand what these men, who were dragging something out of the house, were about; but seeing a French soldier in front of him hit at a peasant with the flat of his sabre, in an effort to get from him a coat lined with fox-fur, he became vaguely aware that looting was in progress here – but he had no time to dwell on the thought.

The crackling and rumble of falling walls and ceilings, the hiss and sizzle of the flames, and the excited shouts of the crowd; the sight of the swaying smoke, now belching out thick and black, now shooting upwards, glittering with sparks, with here and there dense red sheaves of flame (or little golden fish-scales licking the walls); the heat and smoke, the sense of urgent movement everywhere, produced in Pierre the exalted feeling of excitement which fires commonly cause. The effect on Pierre was particularly strong because all at once, at the sight of the fire, he felt himself suddenly liberated from the ideas weighing upon him. He felt young, gay, ready and resolute. He ran round to the other side of the annexe and was about to dash into the part which was still standing when he heard several voices shouting just above his head, followed by a cracking sound and the crash of something heavy falling close beside him.

Pierre looked up and saw at the windows of the house some Frenchmen who had just dropped the drawer of a chest filled with metal articles. Other French soldiers standing below went up to the drawer.

'What does that fellow there want?' shouted one of them, referring to Pierre.

'There's a child in that house,' cried Pierre in French. 'Haven't you seen a child?'

'What's he talking about? Get out!' several voices replied, and one of the soldiers, evidently afraid that Pierre might want to rob them of the silver and bronzes that were in the drawer, moved menacingly towards him.

'A child?' shouted a Frenchman from above. 'I did hear something squealing in the garden. Perhaps it's the brat the fellow's looking for. Got to help one another, you know. ...'

'Where is it? Where is it?' asked Pierre.

'Over there, that way!' called the Frenchman from the window, pointing to the garden at the back of the house. 'Wait, I'll come down.'

And in a minute the Frenchman, a black-eyed fellow with a patch on his cheek, in his shirt-sleeves, did in fact jump out of a window on the ground floor, and slapping Pierre on the shoulder ran with him into the garden. 'Look sharp, you there!' he cried to his comrades. 'It's warming up.'

Running behind the house to a gravel path, the Frenchman pulled Pierre by the arm and pointed to a circular space where a little girl of three in a pink frock was lying under a garden seat.

'There's your bratling for you. Oh, it's a girl, so much the better!' said the Frenchman. 'G'bye, old man. Got to help one another, we're all brothers, you know,' and the Frenchman with the patch on his cheek ran back to his comrades.

Pierre, breathless with joy, started up to the little girl and would have taken her in his arms. But seeing a stranger the sickly, scrofulous-looking child, unattractively like her mother, screamed and began to run away. Pierre grabbed her, however, and lifted her in his arms. She screeched in desperate fury, and struggled with her thin little fists to pull Pierre's hands away and to bite them with her slobbering

mouth. Pierre was seized with horror and revulsion such as he might
have had at contact with some small animal, and he had to make an
effort not to throw the child down. He ran back with her to the big
house. By now, however, it was impossible to return by the way he
had come: the maid, Aniska, was nowhere to be seen, and Pierre with
a feeling of pity and disgust pressed the 'wet, pitifully howling baby
to himself as tenderly as he could and hurried across the garden in
search of some other exit.

34

WHEN Pierre, after running across courtyards and down by-lanes,
got back with his little burden to the Gruzinsky garden at the corner
of Povarsky street he did not at first recognize the place from which
he had set out to look for the child, so packed was it with people and
goods that had been dragged out of the houses. Besides the Russian
families with their belongings saved from the fire, there were a good
many French soldiers about in a variety of clothing. Pierre took no
notice of them. He was in a hurry to find that civil servant's family,
in order to restore the daughter to her mother and go back and rescue
someone else. Pierre felt that he had a great deal more to do, and to
do quickly. Hot from the heat, and from running, the sense of youth,
energy and determination which had come upon him when he ran
off to save the baby glowed within him more strongly than ever.
The child was quiet now and, clinging to Pierre's coat with her little
hands, sat on his arm gazing about her like some small wild animal.
He glanced down at her occasionally, with a half smile. He fancied he
saw something pathetically innocent and angelic in the frightened,
sickly little face.

Neither the civil servant nor his wife was in the place where he
had left them. Pierre walked among the crowd with rapid steps,
scanning the various faces he met. Unconsciously he noticed a Georgian or Armenian family consisting of a very old man with beautiful
Oriental features, wearing a new, cloth-faced sheepskin and new boots,
an old woman of similar type and a young woman. The latter – a
very young woman – struck Pierre as the perfection of Oriental beauty
with her sharply-outlined, arched, black eyebrows, her extraordinarily soft bright colour and lovely, impassive oval face. Amid the chattels scattered about in the crowd on the open space, with her rich
satin mantle and the bright lilac kerchief on her head, she suggested a

delicate, exotic plant thrown down in the snow. She was sitting on some bundles a little behind the old woman, her big black almond eyes under the long lashes fixed on the ground before her. Evidently she was aware of her beauty and it made her fearful. Her face impressed Pierre and he looked round at her several times as he scurried along by the fence. When he had reached the end, still without finding the people he was seeking, he stopped and surveyed the scene about him.

Pierre's figure with the baby in his arms was now more conspicuous than before, and a group of Russians, both men and women, gathered round him.

'Have you lost someone, good sir?' – 'You're gentry, aren't you?' – 'Whose child is it?' they asked him.

Pierre explained that the baby belonged to a woman in a black cloak who had been sitting at this spot with her other children, and asked whether anyone knew her and where she had gone.

'Why, that must be the Anferovs,' said an old deacon, addressing a pock-marked peasant woman. 'Lord have mercy, Lord have mercy!' he added in his professional bass.

'The Anferovs! No,' said the woman. 'Why, the Anferovs went early this morning. It'll either be Maria Nikolayevna's child, or the Ivanovs'.'

'He says a woman, and Maria Nikolayevna's a lady,' remarked a house-serf.

'Surely you know her – a thin woman with long teeth,' said Pierre.

'That's Maria Nikolayevna all right. They moved off into the garden when these wolves swooped down,' said the woman, pointing to the French soldiers.

'O Lord, have mercy on us!' ejaculated the deacon again.

'Go over that way, they're yonder. That's where she is. Beside herself and crying her eyes out,' continued the woman. 'She's there. You'll find her all right.'

But Pierre was not listening to the women. For some seconds he had been intent on what was happening a few yards away. He was watching the Armenian family and two French soldiers who had approached them. One of these, a nimble little man, was wearing a blue coat with a piece of rope tied round his waist for a belt. He had a night-cap on his head and his feet were bare. The other, whose appearance struck Pierre particularly, was a long, lank, round-shouldered, fair-haired man with slow movements and an idiotic expression. He was clad in a frieze tunic, blue trousers and big torn Hessian boots. The little barefooted Frenchman in the blue coat went up to the Armenians, said something and grabbed at the old man's legs, and the old man at once began pulling off his boots as fast as he could. The other soldier, in the tunic, stopped in front of the beautiful Armenian girl and with his hands in his pockets stood staring at her, without speaking or moving.

'Here, take the child!' exclaimed Pierre peremptorily, handing the little girl to the peasant woman. 'You give her back to them – give her back!' he almost shouted, putting the child, who had started to scream, on the ground and turning to look at the Frenchmen and the Armenian family again. The old man was by now sitting barefoot. The little Frenchman had appropriated his second boot and was slapping one boot against the other. The old man was saying something in a voice broken by sobs, but all this Pierre only saw in a passing glimpse: his whole attention was directed to the Frenchman in the frieze tunic who had meanwhile swaggered leisurely up to the young woman and, taking his hands out of his pocket, caught hold of her neck.

The beautiful Armenian continued to sit motionless, in the same attitude, with her long lashes drooping, as if she did not see or feel what the soldier was doing to her.

By the time Pierre had run the few steps that separated him from the Frenchmen the tall marauder in the tunic was already tearing the necklace from the Armenian beauty's neck, and the young woman, clutching at her throat, uttered a piercing shriek.

'Let that woman alone!' cried Pierre in a husky, furious voice, seizing the lank soldier by his round shoulders and hurling him aside.

The soldier fell, scrambled to his feet and made off. But his comrade, throwing down the boots and drawing his sword, moved threateningly towards Pierre.

'Look here, no monkey tricks!' he shouted.

Pierre was in such a transport of rage that he was oblivious of everything and his strength increased tenfold. He rushed at the barefooted Frenchman and, before the latter could draw his sabre, knocked him off his feet and was hammering him with his fists. The crowd roared its approval, and at the same moment a patrol of French Uhlans came round the corner. The Uhlans rode up at a trot and surrounded Pierre and the Frenchman. Pierre remembered nothing of what happened after that. He only knew that he was hitting someone and being hit, until in the end he found that his hands were bound and that a group of French soldiers were standing round and searching him.

'Lieutenant, he has a dagger,' were the first words that meant anything to Pierre.

'Aha, a weapon,' said the officer, and he turned to the barefooted soldier who had been arrested with Pierre. 'All right, you can tell your story at the court-martial.' And then he addressed Pierre: 'Do you speak French?'

Pierre glared about him with bloodshot eyes and did not reply. Evidently his face must have looked frightful, for the officer said something in a whisper and four more Uhlans left the rest and stationed themselves on either side of Pierre.

'Do you speak French?' the officer asked again, keeping at a distance from Pierre. 'Call the interpreter.'

A little man in Russian civilian dress rode out from the ranks. By his clothes and speech Pierre immediately recognized him for a French salesman from one of the Moscow shops.

'He doesn't look like a man of the people,' pronounced the interpreter, eyeing Pierre narrowly.

'Oho! He looks very much like an incendiary to me,' remarked the officer. 'Ask him who he is,' he added.

'Who are yeou?' demanded the interpreter. 'Yeou must answer the officer.'

'I shall not tell you who I am. I am your prisoner. Take me away,' Pierre suddenly replied in French.

'Ah-ha!' muttered the officer with a frown. 'Right then, quick march!'

A crowd had collected round the Uhlans. Nearest to Pierre stood the pock-marked peasant woman with the child. When the patrol set off she stepped forward.

'Where be they taking 'ee, you poor dear you?' said she. 'And the little lass, the little lass – what am I to do wi' 'er if she ain't theirs?' she cried.

'What does that woman want?' asked the officer.

Pierre was like one intoxicated. His elation increased at the sight of the little girl he had rescued.

'What does she want?' he exclaimed. 'She has got my daughter there, whom I just saved from the flames,' he declared. '*Adieu!*' And without in the least knowing what had possessed him to tell this aimless lie he strode triumphantly off between the French soldiers.

The patrol of Uhlans was one of those sent out on Durosnel's orders into the various streets of Moscow to put a stop to pillage and, still more, to capture the incendiaries who, according to the general impression prevalent that day among the French High Command, were the cause of the conflagrations. After riding up and down a number of streets the patrol arrested five more Russian suspects: a small shopkeeper, two divinity students, a peasant and a house-serf – and a few marauders. But of all these suspicious characters Pierre seemed the most suspect of all. When they had all been brought for the night to a big house on the Zubov rampart, which was being used as a guardhouse, Pierre was separated from the others and placed under strict surveillance.

WAR AND PEACE

*

BOOK FOUR

PART ONE

I

In Petersburg all this time an intricate battle was raging in the highest circles, with greater violence than ever, between the parties of Rumyantsev, the French, Maria Feodorovna, the Tsarevich and others, overlaid as usual by the buzzing of the Court drones. But Petersburg's daily round – tranquil, luxurious, concerned only with phantoms and reflections of life – continued as before, so that it was not easy, and needed a determined effort, to form any true idea of the peril and the difficulty in which the Russian nation was placed. There were the same levées and balls, the same French theatre, the same activities at Court, the same interests and intrigues in the government service. It was only in the very highest circles that attempts were made to keep in mind the critical nature of the actual situation. The different behaviour of the two Empresses in these trying circumstances was commented upon in whispers. While the Dowager-Empress Maria Feodorovna, anxious for the welfare of the charitable and educational institutions under her patronage, had all the necessary steps taken for their transfer to Kazan (and the effects belonging to these institutions were already packed), the Empress Elizaveta Alexeyevna, when asked what instructions she was graciously pleased to give, with her wonted Russian patriotism had vouchsafed that she could issue no commands about State institutions, since that was the province of the Sovereign, but in so far as she personally was affected she declared that she would be the last to quit Petersburg.

At Anna Pavlovna's on the 26th of August, the very day of the battle of Borodino, there was a *soirée*, the crowning attraction of which was to be the reading of a letter from His Eminence the Metropolitan of Moscow to accompany a present to the Emperor of an icon of St Sergii. This letter was regarded as a model of ecclesi-astical, patriotic eloquence. Prince Vasili himself, famed for his elo-cution, was to read it aloud. (He had even read more than once at the Empress's.) His 'art' consisted in pouring out the words, quite independently of their meaning, in a loud, resonant voice alternating between a despairing wail and a tender murmur, so that it was wholly a matter of chance whether the wail or the murmur fell on one word or another. This reading, as was always the case with Anna Pavlovna's entertainments, had a political significance. On this particular evening she was expecting several important personages who were to be made to feel ashamed of frequenting the French theatre, and roused to a patriotic frame of mind. Already a considerable number of her guests had arrived but Anna Pavlovna, not yet seeing in her drawing-room all whose presence she deemed necessary, delayed the reading and kept the conversation on general topics.

The news of the day in Petersburg was the serious indisposition of Countess Bezuhov. She had fallen ill unexpectedly a few days previously, had missed several gatherings of which she would have been the ornament, and was said to be receiving no one and, instead of the celebrated Petersburg physicians who usually attended her, had put herself in the hands of some Italian medico who was treating her by some new and extraordinary method.

Everyone was very well aware that the lovely countess's illness arose from the complications of marrying two husbands at the same time, and that the Italian doctor's cure lay in the removal of this difficulty; but at Anna Pavlovna's no one ventured to think of this or even, as it were, to know what they did know.

'The poor countess is very ill, I hear. The doctor talks of angina pectoris.'

'Angina? Oh, that's a dreadful malady!'

'They say the rivals are reconciled, thanks to this angina. ...' The word *angina* was repeated with much relish.

'I hear the old count is very pathetic. He cried like a child when the doctor told him how serious it was.'

'Oh, it would be a terrible loss. She's such a bewitching creature.'

'Are you speaking of the poor countess?' said Anna Pavlovna, joining the group. 'I sent to ask how she was, and am informed that she is a little better. Oh, there's no doubt of it, she's the most delightful woman on earth,' she went on, with a smile at her own enthusiasm. 'We belong to different camps but that does not prevent me from appreciating her as she deserves. And she is so unhappy!' added Anna Pavlovna.

Supposing that by this last remark Anna Pavlovna was slightly lifting the veil of mystery that hung over the countess's illness, one unwary young man went so far as to express surprise that no well-known doctor had been called in and that the countess should be treated by a quack who might administer dangerous remedies to his patient.

'Your information may be better than mine,' retorted Anna Pavlovna suddenly, letting fly very venomously at the inexperienced young man, 'but I have it on good authority that this doctor is a most learned, able man. He is private physician to the Queen of Spain.'

And having thus annihilated the young man Anna Pavlovna turned to another little group where Bilibin was discoursing on the Austrians: he had wrinkled up the skin on his forehead and was evidently on the point of letting it smooth out again with the utterance of one of his *mots*.

'I find it quite charming,' he was saying, referring to a diplomatic note that had been sent to Vienna with some Austrian banners captured from the French by Wittgenstein, 'the hero of Petropol,' as he was called in Petersburg.

'What is that?' inquired Anna Pavlovna, securing silence for the witticism which she had heard before.

And Bilibin repeated the precise words of the diplomatic dispatch concocted by him.

'The Emperor returns these Austrian banners,' quoted Bilibin, 'friendly banners gone astray and found off their right way,' letting the wrinkles run off his brow.

'Charming, charming!' observed Prince Vasili.

'The road to Warsaw, perhaps,' Prince Hippolyte suddenly remarked in a loud voice. Everybody looked at him, at a loss to understand what he wanted to convey by this. Prince Hippolyte himself glanced about him in amused wonder. He knew no more than the others what his words meant. In the course of his diplomatic career he had more than once noticed that a few words thus unexpectedly thrown in passed for being very witty, and at every opportunity he thus uttered the first words that entered his head. 'They may turn out lucky,' he would think, 'but if not, someone is sure to arrange matters.' And the awkward silence that ensued was in fact broken by the appearance of the insufficiently patriotic individual whom Anna Pavlovna was waiting for and hoping to convert, and, smiling and shaking a finger at Hippolyte, she invited Prince Vasili to the table and setting two candles and the manuscript before him begged him to begin. There was a general hush.

'Most gracious Sovereign the Emperor!' declaimed Prince Vasili severely, looking round at his audience as much as to inquire whether anyone had anything to say to the contrary. But nobody breathed a word. 'Moscow, our ancient capital, the New Jerusalem, receives *her* Messiah' – he hurled a sudden emphasis on the '*her*' – 'even as a mother embraces in her arms her zealous sons, and through the gathering mists, foreseeing the dazzling glory of thy dominion, sings aloud in exultation, "Hosanna! Blessed is he that cometh!"'

Prince Vasili pronounced these last words in a tearful voice.

Bilibin attentively examined his nails, and many of the audience appeared abashed, as though wondering what they had done wrong. Anna Pavlovna whispered the next words in advance, like an old woman muttering the prayer to come at communion: 'Let the insolent and brazen Goliath ...' she murmured.

Prince Vasili continued:

'Let the insolent and brazen Goliath from the borders of France encompass the realm of Russia with the murderous terrors of death; lowly faith, the sling of the Russian David, shall be swift to smite at the head of his pride that thirsteth for blood. This icon of St Sergii, the ancient zealot of our country's weal, comes to your Imperial Majesty. I grieve that my failing strength prevents my rejoicing in the sight of your most gracious countenance. I send up fervent prayers to Heaven that the Almighty may exalt the generation of the righteous and in His mercy fulfil the hopes of your Majesty.'

'*Quelle force! Quel style!*' cried one and another, in praise of reader and author alike.

Animated by this oration, Anna Pavlovna's guests discussed for a long time the state of the Fatherland, and made various conjectures as to the issue of the battle to be fought in the next few days.

'You will see,' said Anna Pavlovna, 'tomorrow, on the Emperor's birthday, we shall get news. I have a happy presentiment.'

2

ANNA PAVLOVNA's presentiment was in fact realized. Next day, during a Te Deum at the Palace chapel on the occasion of the Emperor's birthday, Prince Volkonsky was called out of church to receive a dispatch from Prince Kutuzov. This was Kutuzov's report penned from Tatarinova on the day of the battle. Kutuzov wrote that the Russians had not fallen back a single step, that the French losses were much heavier than ours, and that he was writing in haste from the field of battle before he had had time to collect the latest intelligence. So apparently there must have been a victory. And immediately, without leaving the church, thanks were offered up to the Creator for His succour, and for the victory.

Anna Pavlovna's presentiment was realized, and all that morning a joyous high-day and holiday mood reigned in the city. Everyone believed our success to have been complete, and some people even went so far as to talk of Napoleon having been taken prisoner, of his deposition and of the selection of a new ruler for France.

It is very difficult for events to be reflected in their true force and perspective so far from the scene of action and amid the conditions of Court life. Public events inevitably group themselves round some personal circumstance. So now in the present instance the joy of the Court sprang as much from the fact that the news had arrived on the Emperor's birthday as from the victory itself. It was like a success-fully arranged surprise. Kutuzov's report also made mention of the Russian losses, naming among the killed Tuchkov, Bagration and Kutaissov. Here again the world of Petersburg centred its grief on one happening – the death of Kutaissov. Everybody knew him, the Emperor liked him, he was young and interesting. That day every-one met with the words:

'What a wonderful coincidence! To come just during the Te Deum! But Kutaissov – what a loss! Ah, what a pity!'

'What did I tell you about Kutuzov?' Prince Vasili kept repeating now with a prophet's pride. 'I always said he was the only man cap-able of beating Napoleon.'

But on the following day no news arrived from the army and the public voice began to waver. The courtiers suffered agonies over the agonies of suspense which the Emperor was suffering.

'Just think of the Emperor's position!' said those at Court, and instead of singing Kutuzov's praises as they had the day before they began to pass judgement on him as the cause of the Emperor's anxiety. Prince Vasili no longer boasted of his protégé Kutuzov, but remained silent when the commander-in-chief was spoken of. Moreover, towards the evening of that day, as if everything were conspiring to alarm and disquiet Petersburg society, a terrible piece of news was announced. Countess Hélène Bezuhov had suddenly died of that fearful malady, the name of which it had been so agreeable to pronounce. At large gatherings the official story was accepted that Countess Bezuhov had died of a terrible attack of angina pectoris, but in select circles details were forthcoming of how the private physician of the Queen of Spain had prescribed small doses of a certain drug to bring about a certain effect; but that Hélène, worried by the old count's suspicions of her and by the fact that her husband to whom she had written (that wretched, profligate Pierre) had not replied, had suddenly swallowed an enormous dose of the drug and died in agony before assistance could be given. It was said that Prince Vasili and the old count had at first turned on the Italian; but the latter had produced notes from the unfortunate deceased of such a character that they quickly let the matter drop.

Conversation in general centred round three melancholy circumstances: the Emperor's lack of news, the loss of Kutaissov and the death of Hélène.

On the third day after Kutuzov's dispatch a country gentleman arrived from Moscow, and the news of the surrender of that capital to the French was all over the town. This was awful! What a position for the Emperor to be in! Kutuzov was a traitor, and Prince Vasili assured those who came to condole with him on his daughter's death that nothing else was to be expected of a blind and depraved old man (whose praises he had once sung so loudly – but it was pardonable that in his grief he should forget what he had said before).

'I am only amazed that the fate of Russia could have been entrusted to such a man.'

So long as the news was not official it was still possible to doubt it, but twenty-four hours later the following communication came from Count Rostopchin.

Prince Kutuzov's adjutant has brought me a letter in which he demands that I should furnish police officers to escort the army to the Ryazan road. He writes that he is regretfully abandoning Moscow. Sire, Kutuzov's action decides the fate of the capital and of your Empire! The nation will shudder to learn that the city which represents the greatness of Russia, and in which lie the ashes of your ancestors, is in the hands of the enemy. I am following the army. I have had everything removed, and it only remains for me to weep over the lot of my Fatherland.

On receiving this dispatch the Emperor sent Prince Volkonsky to Kutuzov with the following rescript:

Prince Mihail Ilarionovich! No communication has come to hand from you since the 29th of August. Meanwhile I have received, by way of Yaroslavl, under date of September 1st, from the Governor-general of Moscow, the sad tidings that you, with the army, have decided to abandon Moscow. You may imagine the effect this news has had upon me, and your silence adds to my amazement. I send Adjutant-general Prince Volkonsky with this, to ascertain from you the situation of the army and the reasons which have impelled you to so melancholy a decision.

3

NINE days after the abandonment of Moscow a courier from Kutuzov reached Petersburg with the official announcement of the surrender of the city. This courier was a Frenchman, Michaud, who did not know Russian. But, though a foreigner, he was, as he himself was wont to declare, 'Russian in heart and soul'.

The Emperor at once received the messenger in his study in the Palace on Kamenny Island. Michaud, who had never seen Moscow before the campaign, and who did not speak a word of Russian, yet felt deeply moved (as he wrote) when he appeared before 'notre très gracieux souverain' with the news of the burning of Moscow, the flames of which had lighted up his route.

Though the source of Monsieur Michaud's chagrin must indeed have been different from that to which the grief of the Russian people was due, he had such a melancholy face when he was shown into the Emperor's study that the Tsar at once asked:

'Do you bring me sad news, colonel?'

'Very sad, sire,' replied Michaud, casting his eyes down with a sigh. 'L'abandon de Moscou.'

'Can they have surrendered my ancient capital without a battle?' exclaimed the Emperor quickly, the angry colour mounting to his cheek.

Michaud respectfully delivered the message Kutuzov had entrusted to him, to the effect that it had been impossible to fight before Moscow, and, seeing that the choice lay between losing the army as well

1113

as Moscow or losing Moscow alone, the field-marshal had been obliged to choose the latter.

The Emperor listened in silence, not looking at Michaud.

'Has the enemy entered the city?' he asked.

'Yes, sire, and by now Moscow is in ashes. I left it a blaze of flames,' replied Michaud in a decided tone, but glancing at the Emperor he was appalled at what he had said. The Tsar was breathing heavily and rapidly, his lower lip twitched and the tears gushed to his fine blue eyes.

But this lasted only a moment. The Emperor suddenly frowned, as though vexed with himself for his own weakness, and raising his head addressed Michaud in a firm voice:

'I see, colonel, from all that is happening to us, that Providence requires great sacrifices of us. ... I am ready to submit myself in all things to His will; but tell me, Michaud, how was my army when you left – when it saw my ancient capital abandoned without a blow struck. Did you perceive signs of discouragement?'

Observing that his *très gracieux souverain* had regained his composure, Michaud too recovered himself but was not immediately ready to reply to the Emperor's direct and relevant question, which called for a direct answer.

'Sire, have I your Majesty's permission to speak frankly as befits a plain, honest soldier?' he asked, to gain time.

'Colonel, that is what I always demand,' said the Tsar. 'Conceal nothing from me; I want to know exactly how matters stand.'

'Sire!' said Michaud with the faintest suggestion of a smile on his lips, having now managed to think of an answer in the form of a light and respectful quibble – 'Sire, I left the whole army, from the commanders to the lowest soldier, in a state of extreme and desperate terror. ...'

'How so?' the Emperor interrupted him, frowning severely. 'Are my Russians cast down by misfortune? ... Never!'

This was just what Michaud was waiting for to get in his *jeu de mots*.

'Sire,' he said with a respectful playfulness of expression, 'their only fear is lest your Majesty, out of goodness of heart, should be persuaded to make peace. They are burning for the combat,' declared this representative of the Russian people, 'and to prove to your Majesty by the sacrifice of their lives how devoted they are. ...'

'Ah!' said the Emperor, reassured, and with a friendly light in his

eyes he patted Michaud on the shoulder. 'You set me at ease, colonel.'
He bent his head and was silent for some time.

'Well, then, go back to the army,' he said, drawing himself up to
his full height and addressing Michaud with a genial and majestic
gesture, 'and tell our brave fellows – tell all my loyal subjects wherever you may go – that when I have not a soldier left I shall put myself at the head of my beloved Nobility, of my worthy peasants, and
so use the last resources of my Empire. I have more at my command
than my enemies suspect,' he added, growing more and more
animated. 'But if it should be written in the decrees of Divine Providence,' he continued, raising to heaven his beautiful, mild eyes, shining with emotion, 'that my dynasty should cease to reign on the
throne of my ancestors, then, after exhausting every means in my
power, I shall let my beard grow to here' (the Emperor put his hand
halfway down his chest) 'and go and eat potatoes with the meanest
of my peasants rather than sign the shame of my country and of my
dearly loved people, whose sacrifices I know how to appreciate.'

Uttering these words in a voice full of feeling, the Emperor suddenly turned away, as if to hide from Michaud the tears that rose to
his eyes, and walked to the farther end of his study. After standing
there a few moments he strode back to Michaud and gave his arm a
powerful squeeze below the elbow. His gentle, handsome face was
flushed and his eyes gleamed with determination and anger.

'Colonel Michaud, do not forget what I say to you here; perhaps
one day we may recall it with satisfaction. Napoleon or I,' said the
Emperor, touching his breast. 'We can no longer both reign. I have
learned to know him, he will not deceive me again. ...'

And the Emperor paused, with a frown.

Hearing these words and seeing the steadfast look of resolve in the
Emperor's eyes, Michaud – 'a foreigner but Russian in heart and soul'
– at that solemn moment felt himself *enthousiasmé* by all that he had
heard (as he used to recount later), and gave expression to his own
feelings and those of the Russian people, whose representative he
considered himself to be, in the following exclamation:

'Sire!' said he, 'your Majesty is at this moment signing the glory
of the nation and the salvation of Europe!'

With an inclination of his head the Emperor dismissed Michaud.

4

WITH half of Russia in enemy hands, and the inhabitants of Moscow fleeing to distant provinces, with one levy after another being raised for the defence of the Fatherland, we, who were not living in those times, cannot help imagining that all Russians, great and small, were solely engaged in immolating themselves, in trying to save their country or in weeping over its downfall. All the stories and descriptions of those years, without exception, tell of nothing but the self-sacrifice, the patriotic devotion, the despair, the anguish and the heroism of the Russian people. Actually, it was not at all like that. It appears so to us because we see only the general historic interest of the period, and not all the minor personal interests that men of that day had. Yet, in reality, private interests of the immediate present are always so much more important than the wider issues that they prevent the wider issues which concern the public as a whole from ever being felt – from being noticed at all, indeed. The majority of the people of that time paid no attention to the broad trend of the nation's affairs, and were only influenced by their private concerns. And it was these very people who played the most useful part in the history of their day.

Those who were striving to understand the general course of events, and trying by self-sacrifice and heroism to take a hand in it, were the most useless members of society; they saw everything upside down, and all they did for the common good proved to be futile and absurd – like Pierre's regiment, and Mamonov's, which looted Russian villages, and the lint scraped by the ladies, that never reached the wounded, and so on. Even the amateur dialecticians, who in their fondness for subtilties and the expression of their feelings endlessly discussed Russia's situation, unconsciously introduced into their speeches an impress of hypocrisy or falsity, or else of profitless fault-finding and animosity directed against persons who were blamed for what no one could help. The interdiction anent tasting the fruit of the tree of knowledge comes out more conspicuously in historical events than anywhere. It is only subconscious activity that bears fruit, and a man who plays a part in an historic event never understands its import. As soon as he tries to realize its significance his actions become sterile.

The more closely a man was engaged in the events then taking place in Russia the less did he perceive their meaning. In Petersburg and in the provincial towns remote from Moscow, ladies, and gentlemen in militia uniforms, mourned over the fate of Russia and her ancient capital, and talked of self-sacrifice and so forth; but in the army, which was withdrawing beyond Moscow, almost nothing was said or thought about Moscow, and looking back at the scene of the fire, no one swore to be avenged on the French: their minds were on the coming pay-day, the next halt, Matrioshka the *vivandière*, and the like. . . .

Nikolai Rostov, without any idea of self-sacrifice but casually, because the war had caught him in the Service, took a real and continuous part in the defence of his country, and consequently he looked upon what was happening in Russia without despair or sombre syllogizing. Had he been asked what he thought of the state of affairs in Russia he would have replied that it wasn't for him to think about it, that Kutuzov and others were there for that purpose, but that he had heard that the regiments were to be made up to their full strength, that fighting would probably go on for a good while yet, and that things being so, it was quite likely he might be in command of a regiment in a couple of years' time.

Since he regarded the matter in this light he took the announcement that he was being sent to Voronezh to buy remounts for his division not only without regret at being deprived of participation in the coming engagement but with the greatest satisfaction – which he did not conceal and which his comrades fully sympathized with.

A few days before the battle of Borodino Nikolai received the necessary money and official warrants, and sending some hussars on in advance he set out with post-horses for Voronezh.

Only those who know what it is to spend several months on end in the atmosphere of an army on active service can appreciate how blissfully happy Nikolai felt when he got beyond the region overrun with troops and their foraging parties, provision-trains and field hospitals – when, instead of soldiers, army wagons and the filth which betrays the presence of a military camp, he found himself among villages of peasant men and women, gentlemen's country houses, fields with grazing cattle, and post-houses with their sleepy masters. He was so happy that he might have been seeing everything for the first time. The sight of wholesome young women without a dozen officers hanging round each of them was a particular wonder and delight – women, too, who were pleased and flattered that a passing officer should joke with them.

Enchanted alike with himself and his fate, Nikolai arrived at night at an hotel in Voronezh, ordered all the things he had over so long a period missed in camp, and next day, after an extra careful shave, in full-dress uniform which he had not worn for some time past, went to present himself to the authorities.

The commander of the local militia was a civilian general, an old man who was evidently enjoying his military status and rank. He gave Nikolai a brusque reception (imagining this to be the proper military manner) and interrogated him importantly, as though he had a right to do so, approving and disapproving and apparently deliberating on the course of events generally. Nikolai was in such good spirits that this only amused him.

From the commander of the militia he drove to the governor. The governor was a brisk little man, very affable and unpretentious. He told Nikolai of the stud-farms where he might find horses, recommended him to a horse-dealer in the town and a landed proprietor fourteen miles out of town who had the best horses, and promised him every assistance.

'You are Count Ilya Rostov's son? My wife was a great friend of your dear mother's. We are at home on Thursdays – today is Thursday, so please come and see us, without ceremony,' said the governor as Nikolai took his leave.

Nikolai hired post-horses and making his quartermaster get in beside him set off at a gallop straight from the governor's to the gentleman with the stud fourteen miles away. Everything seemed pleasant and easy to Nikolai during that first part of his stay in Voronezh, and, as happens when a man is in a happy frame of mind, everything went well and without difficulty.

The country gentleman turned out to be an old cavalry officer, a bachelor, a great horse-fancier, a sportsman, the possessor of some century-old brandy, besides some old Hungarian wine, who had a den where he smoked, and some superb horses.

In a very few words Nikolai came to terms with him, acquiring seventeen picked stallions for six thousand roubles – to serve (as he explained) as show specimens of his remounts. After dining and doing rather more than ample justice to the Hungarian wine, Nikolai –

having exchanged embraces with the country gentleman with whom he was already on the friendliest of footings – drove back in the gayest of moods at a furious pace over the most abominable road, continually urging the driver on, so as to be in time for the governor's *soirée*.

When he had changed, sluiced cold water over his head and scented himself, Nikolai appeared at the governor's, a little late but with the adage 'Better late than never' ready on the tip of his tongue.

It was not a ball, and nothing had been said about dancing, but everyone knew that Katerina Petrovna would play walses and *écossaises* on the clavier and that there would be dancing, and so everyone had come dressed as for a ball.

Provincial life in 1812 went on very much as usual, the only difference being that there was more stir in the towns, owing to the advent of numerous wealthy families from Moscow, and in the air a marked devil-may-care, in for a penny, in for a pound spirit noticeable in everything all over Russia at that time, while the inevitable small talk, instead of being concerned with the weather and mutual acquaintances, now turned on Moscow, the army and Napoleon.

The gathering at the governor's consisted of the cream of Voronezh society.

There were any number of ladies, there were several of Nikolai's Moscow acquaintances; but of the men there was not one who could even begin to rival the chevalier of St George, the hussar remount-officer, the good-natured, well-bred Count Rostov. Among the men was an Italian prisoner, an officer of the French army, and Nikolai felt that the presence of this prisoner – a living trophy, as it were – enhanced his own importance as a Russian hero. It seemed to him that everyone shared this sentiment, and he treated the Italian cordially but with a certain dignity and reserve.

The moment Nikolai entered the room in his hussar uniform, diffusing about him a fragrance of perfume and wine, and had uttered and heard others repeat his 'Better late than never', people clustered round him. All eyes were turned on him, and he felt at once that he had stepped into his proper position in the province – that of universal favourite – always a pleasant position to be in, and intoxicatingly so after long deprivation. Not only at the posting-stations, at inns and in the country landowner's smoking-room had servant-girls been flattered by his notice, but here too at the governor's party it seemed to Nikolai there was an inexhaustible array of young married ladies and pretty girls impatient for a share of his attention. The ladies and the young girls flirted with him, the elderly ladies concerned themselves from the first day to get this gallant young rake of a hussar married and settled down. Among these was the governor's wife herself, who welcomed Rostov as a near relative and called him 'Nicolas'.

Katerina Petrovna did in fact proceed to play waltzes and *écossaises*, and dancing began, in which Nikolai still further captivated provincial society by his mastery. He even surprised them all by his exaggeratedly free-and-easy style. Nikolai wondered a little himself at the way he danced that evening. He had never danced like that in Moscow and would indeed have considered such an extremely lax manner indecorous and bad form; but here he felt it incumbent on him to astonish them all by something extraordinary, something they would be compelled to accept as the regular thing in the capitals though new to them in the provinces.

All the evening Nikolai devoted most of his attentions to a blue-eyed, plump and pleasing little blonde, the wife of a local official. With the naïve conviction of young men who are enjoying themselves that other men's wives were created for their especial benefit Rostov never left this lady's side, and treated her husband with a friendly air, almost as though there was a private understanding between them and they knew without putting it into words how excellently they, that is, Nikolai and the other man's wife, would get on together. The husband, however, appeared to think otherwise, and tried to take a lowering tone with Rostov. But the latter's frank good humour was so boundless that more than once the husband was obliged, in spite of himself, to yield before Nikolai's good cheer. But towards the end of the evening, as the wife's face grew more flushed and animated the husband's became paler and more melancholy, as though they had only a modicum of vivacity between them and when it rose in the wife it declined in the husband.

5

WITH a smile that never left his lips Nikolai sat leaning slightly forward in an arm-chair, bending closely over the pretty blonde and paying her mythological compliments.

Jauntily shifting the position of his legs in their tight riding-breeches, diffusing a smell of perfume, and admiring his fair companion, himself and the handsome shape of his legs in their well-fitting Hessian boots, Nikolai was telling the little blonde that he meant to carry off a certain lady here in Voronezh.

'What is she like?'

'Charming, divine. Her eyes' (Nikolai gazed at his companion) 'are blue, her mouth is coral and ivory; her figure' (he glanced at her shoulders) 'like Diana's. ...'

The husband came up and asked his wife darkly what she was talking about.

'Ah, Nikita Ivanych!' cried Nikolai, rising courteously. And as though anxious for Nikita Ivanych to share in the fun he began to tell him, too, of his intention of running off with a blonde lady.

The husband smiled grimly, the wife gaily. The governor's kindly wife came up with a disapproving look on her face.

'Anna Ignatyevna wants to see you, Nicolas,' said she, pronouncing the name in such a way that Rostov was at once aware that Anna Ignatyevna was a very important person. 'Come with me, Nicolas. You said I could call you that, didn't you?'

'Oh yes, *ma tante*. But who is she?'

'Anna Ignatyevna Malvintsev. She has heard about you from her niece whom you rescued. ... Can you guess?'

'I rescued such a lot of people!' said Nikolai.

'Her niece, Princess Bolkonsky. She is here in Voronezh with her aunt. Oho! He blushes! Why, are ...?'

'Not a bit of it – I assure you, *ma tante*.'

'Very well, very well! Oh, what a boy it is!'

The governor's wife led him up to a tall and very stout old lady in a sky-blue toque, who had just finished a game of cards with the most eminent personages of the town. This was Madame Malvintsev, Princess Maria's aunt on her mother's side, a wealthy, childless widow who had always lived in Voronezh. When Rostov approached she was standing and paying her debts after the game. Sternly and importantly screwing up her eyes, she glanced at him and went on berating the general who had won from her.

'Very glad to see you, my dear,' she then said, holding out her hand to Nikolai. 'Pray come and see me.'

After a few words about Princess Maria and her late father, whom

Madame Malvintsev had evidently not cared for, and inquiring what news Nikolai had of Prince Andrei, who was apparently no favourite of hers either, the dignified old lady dismissed him with a renewal of her invitation to come and see her.

Nikolai promised to do so and blushed again as he bowed. At the mention of Princess Maria he experienced a sensation of shyness, even of fear, which he himself could not understand.

Having left Madame Malvintsev, Nikolai started back to the dancing but the governor's little wife laid a plump hand on his sleeve and, saying that she wanted to have a talk with him, led him to her sitting-room, from which those who were there immediately withdrew so as not to be in her way.

'Do you know, *mon cher*,' began the governor's wife with a serious expression on her kind little face, 'that really would be the match for you: would you like me to arrange it?'

'Whom do you mean, *ma tante*?' asked Nikolai.

'I will make a match for you with the princess. Katerina Petrovna suggests Lili but I say, no – the princess. I am sure your mother will be grateful to me. Really, she's a charming girl! And by no means so plain as all that.'

'Indeed, she isn't!' exclaimed Nikolai, as though offended at the idea. 'For my part, *ma tante*, as befits a soldier I never force myself on anyone, nor do I refuse anything that turns up,' he said, without stopping to consider what he was saying.

'But you must remember: this is no light matter.'

'Of course not!'

'Yes, yes,' said the governor's wife, as though talking to herself. 'But listen, *mon cher*, just one thing, you are too attentive by far to that other lady – *la blonde*. The husband cuts a sorry figure, true ...'

'Oh no, he and I are good friends,' exclaimed Nikolai in the simplicity of his heart: it had never occurred to him that a pastime which he found so agreeable could be other than agreeable to anyone else.

'What a lot of nonsense I said to the governor's wife, though!' thought Nikolai suddenly at supper. 'Now she really will start arranging a match for me, and what about Sonya? ...' And when he was bidding the governor's wife good-night, and she said to him with a smile, 'Well, remember then,' he drew her aside.

'*Ma tante*, listen, to tell you the truth ...'

'What is it, my dear? Come and sit down here.'

Nikolai suddenly felt a desire, an irresistible impulse to confide his most private thoughts (which he would never have told his mother, his sister or an intimate friend) to this woman who was almost a stranger. Afterwards, when he recalled this unsolicited, inexplicable fit of candour, which nevertheless had very important consequences for him, it seemed – as it always does seem in such instances – that he had merely been seized by some silly whim; yet that burst of frankness, together with other trivial events, had immense consequences for him and for the whole family.

'It's like this, *ma tante*. For a long time *Maman* has been bent on marrying me to an heiress, but the very idea of marrying for money is repugnant to me.'

'Oh yes, I can quite understand that,' said the governor's wife.

'But Princess Bolkonsky – that's a different matter. I will tell you the truth: in the first place, I like her very much, I feel drawn to her; and then, after I met her in such circumstances – so strangely – it has often struck me that it was fate. Especially if you remember that *Maman* has had it in mind for a long time, only I never happened to meet her before – it always happened somehow that we did not meet. And then as long as Natasha was betrothed to her brother of course it was out of the question for me to think of marrying her. And just when Natasha's engagement had been broken off it must needs happen that I meet her ... well, and then everything, ... You see, it's like this. ... I have never spoken to anyone about this, and I never will. Only to you. ...'

The governor's wife pressed his elbow gratefully.

'You know Sonya, my cousin? I love her, and I promised to marry her, and I mean to marry her. ... So you see there can be no question ever about –' concluded Nikolai incoherently, flushing crimson.

'My dear boy, my dear boy, what a way to look at things! Why, Sonya hasn't a farthing, and you said yourself that your papa's affairs are in a very bad way. And what about your mamma? It would kill her, for one thing. Then Sonya, if she's a girl with a heart – what sort of life would it be for her? Your mother in despair, you all ruined. ... No, *mon cher*, you and Sonya must realize that.'

Nikolai did not speak. It was a comfort for him to hear these arguments.

'All the same, *ma tante*, it cannot be,' he said with a sigh, after a brief silence. 'And besides, would the princess have me? And another thing, she is in mourning. Why, it's not to be thought of!'

'But you don't suppose I'm going to take you by the throat and get you married out of hand, do you? There are ways of doing everything,' said the governor's wife.

'What a match-maker you are, *ma tante* ...' said Nikolai, kissing her plump little hand.

6

ON reaching Moscow after her meeting with Rostov, Princess Maria had found her nephew there with his tutor, and a letter from Prince Andrei telling her how to get to her aunt, Madame Malvintsev, at Voronezh. The arrangements for the journey, anxiety about her brother, the organization of her life in a new home, fresh faces, the education of her nephew – all this deadened the voice as it were of temptation which had tormented her during her father's illness and after his death, and especially since her encounter with Rostov. She was sad. Now, after a month passed in quiet surroundings, she felt more and more deeply the loss of her father, which was associated in her heart with the downfall of Russia. She was restless and agitated: the thought of the perils to which her brother, the only near relation left to her, was exposed was a continual torture. She worried too about the upbringing of her nephew, for which she constantly felt herself unfitted; but in the depths of her soul she was at peace with herself because she was conscious of having suppressed the dreams and hopes of happiness that had been on the point of springing up within her in connexion with Rostov's appearance on the scene.

When the governor's wife called on Madame Malvintsev the day after the party and, after discussing her plans with the aunt (and remarking that, though in present circumstances a formal courtship was of course not to be thought of, still the young people might be brought together and allowed to get to know one another), and Madame Malvintsev having expressed approval, began to speak of Rostov in Princess Maria's presence, singing his praises and describing how he had blushed on hearing Princess Maria's name mentioned, her emotion was not one of joy but of pain: her inner harmony was destroyed, and desires, doubts, self-reproach and hope rose up again.

During the two days that elapsed before Rostov called, Princess Maria never stopped pondering what her behaviour to him should be. First she decided not to go down to the drawing-room when he called to see her aunt – that it would not be proper, in her deep mourning, to receive visitors; then she thought this would be rude after what he had done for her; then it occurred to her that her aunt and the governor's wife had intentions concerning herself and Rostov (the glances they gave and some of the words they let fall seemed to confirm this surmise); then she told herself that only she with her inborn depravity could think such things of them: they could not fail to realize that in her position, while she was still wearing the heaviest mourning, such match-making would be an insult both to her and to her father's memory. Assuming for a moment that she did go down to see him, Princess Maria would start imagining the words he would say to her and what she would say to him, and at one moment they seemed to her unwarrantably frigid, at the next they struck her as carrying too much meaning. Above all, she dreaded the embarrassment which she felt sure would overwhelm and betray her as soon as she saw him.

But when on Sunday morning after church the footman came to the drawing-room to announce that Count Rostov had called, only a faint flush suffused her cheeks and her eyes lit up with a new and radiant light.

'You have met him, Aunt?' said Princess Maria in a composed voice, not knowing herself how she could be outwardly so calm and natural.

When Rostov entered the room the princess looked down for an instant, as though to give the visitor time to greet her aunt, and then just as Nikolai turned to her she raised her head and met his gaze with shining eyes. With a movement full of dignity and grace she half rose with a smile of delight, held out her slender, delicate hand to him, and began to speak in a voice in which for the first time new deep, womanly notes vibrated. Mademoiselle Bourienne, who was in the drawing-room, stared at Princess Maria in bewildered surprise. A most accomplished coquette, she could not have manoeuvred better on meeting a man whom she wanted to attract.

'Either black suits her wonderfully, or she really has grown better-looking without my noticing it. And, above all, what *savoir faire* and grace!' thought Mademoiselle Bourienne.

Had Princess Maria been capable of reflection at that moment she would have been even more astonished than Mademoiselle Bourienne at the change that had taken place in herself. From the moment she set eyes on that dear, loved face, some new vital force took possession of her and compelled her to speak and act irrespective of her own volition. From the time Rostov entered the room her face was transformed. Just as when a light is lit inside a carved and painted lantern, suddenly revealing in unexpected, breath-taking beauty of detail the fine, intricate tracery of its panels, which till then had seemed coarse, dark and meaningless, so was Princess Maria's face suddenly transfigured. For the first time all the pure, spiritual, inward travail in which she had lived till then came out into the open. All her inner searchings of spirit, her sufferings, her striving after goodness, her resignation, her love and self-sacrifice – all this now shone forth in those radiant eyes, in her sweet smile, in every feature of her tender face.

Rostov saw all this as clearly as though he had known her whole life. He felt that the being before him was utterly different from and better than anyone he had met before, and, above all, better than himself.

Their conversation was very simple and ordinary. They talked of the war, like everyone else unconsciously exaggerating their sorrow over it; they spoke of their last meeting – Nikolai trying to change the subject; they talked of the governor's kindly wife, of Nikolai's relatives and of Princess Maria's.

Princess Maria did not allude to her brother, diverting the conversation as soon as her aunt mentioned Andrei. It was evident that while there might be some pretence about her grief over the misfortunes of Russia her brother was too near her heart and she neither could nor would speak superficially of him. Nikolai noticed this, as he noticed every shade of Princess Maria's character, with a keenness of insight not at all typical of him, and everything confirmed his conviction that she was an altogether rare and unusual being. Nikolai, exactly like Princess Maria in her turn, blushed and was embarrassed when people spoke to him about the princess, and even when he thought of her, but in her presence he felt perfectly at ease, and by no means confined himself to the set speeches which he had prepared in advance but said what, always quite appropriately, came into his head at the moment.

When a pause occurred during his short visit Nikolai, as people always do where there are children, turned to Prince Andrei's little son, caressing him and asking him whether he would like to be a hussar. He took the child on his knee, played with him and looked round at Princess Maria. With a softened, happy, shy look she was watching the little lad she loved in the arms of the man she loved. Nikolai caught that look, and as though he divined its significance flushed with pleasure and fell to kissing the child with simple-hearted gaiety.

On account of her mourning Princess Maria was not going into society at all, and Nikolai did not think it the proper thing to visit her again; but the governor's wife still persisted in her match-making, passing on to Nikolai the flattering things Princess Maria said of him, and *vice versa*, and pressing him to declare himself to Princess Maria. For this purpose she arranged a meeting between the young people at the bishop's house before morning service.

Though Rostov told the governor's wife that he was not going to make any declaration to Princess Maria, he promised to be there.

Just as at Tilsit Rostov had not allowed himself to doubt that what everybody accepted as right was right, so now, after a brief but genuine struggle between his efforts to order his life as he felt it should be ordered and a humble submission to circumstances, he chose the latter alternative and surrendered to the power which, he felt, was irresistibly carrying him away. He was aware that to declare his feelings to Princess Maria after his promise to Sonya would be what he would call dastardly. And he knew that he would never behave in a dastardly fashion. But he also knew (or rather felt at the bottom of his heart) that in resigning himself now to the force of circumstances and of the people guiding him he was not only doing nothing wrong but was doing something very, very important – more important than anything he had ever done in his life.

After his visit to Princess Maria, though his manner of life remained externally the same, all his former amusements lost their charm for him and he often found himself thinking of her. But he never thought about her as he had thought of all the young girls, without exception, whom he had met in society, nor as he had over a long period, and sometimes rapturously, thought about Sonya. Like almost every up-right, honest young man he had pictured each of these young ladies as a possible future wife, setting her in his imagination against a back-ground of married life – the white morning wrapper, his wife behind the samovar, his wife's carriage, the little ones, *maman* and papa, their attitude to his wife, and so on and so forth; and these pictures of the future he found enjoyable. But when he thought of Princess Maria, to whom they were trying to get him betrothed, he could never see the two of them together as man and wife. If he tried to do so, everything seemed incongruous and false, and only filled him with dread.

7

THE dreadful news of the battle of Borodino, of our casualties in killed and wounded, and the even more terrible tidings of the loss of Moscow reached Voronezh in the middle of September. Princess Maria, having learnt of her brother's wound only from the newspapers and having no definite information, prepared to go in search of him (so Nikolai was told, though he had not seen her again himself).

When he heard the news of the battle of Borodino and the abandonment of Moscow Rostov was not seized with despair, rage, a desire for vengeance, or the like, but everything in Voronezh suddenly seemed to him dreary and irksome: his conscience almost reproached him, and he was ill at ease. All the talk that he listened to rang false in his ear; he did not know what to think of events and felt that only back in the regiment would everything become clear to him again. He made haste to conclude his purchase of horses, and was often without cause ill-tempered with his servant and quartermaster.

A few days before his departure a solemn Te Deum, at which Nikolai was present, was held in the cathedral in thanksgiving for the victory gained by the Russian armies. He stood a little behind the governor, and held himself with befitting decorum throughout the service, meditating the while on a great variety of subjects. When the ceremony was over, the governor's wife beckoned him to her.

'Did you see the princess?' she asked, with a motion of her head towards a lady in black standing behind the choir.

Nikolai immediately recognized Princess Maria, not so much by the profile he saw under her hat as by the feeling of shyness, awe and pity which instantly came over him. Princess Maria, evidently absorbed in her thoughts, was crossing herself for the last time before leaving the church.

Nikolai gazed at her in wonder. It was the same face he had seen before; there was the same general look of refined, inner, spiritual travail, but now there was an utterly different light in it. It had a pathetic expression of sorrow, prayer and hope. As he had done before when she was present, Nikolai went up to her without waiting to be prompted by the governor's wife, or asking himself whether or not it were right and proper to address her here in church, and told her that he had heard of her trouble and sympathized with all his heart. She no sooner heard his voice than a vivid glow suffused her face, lighting up at once her sorrow and her joy.

'One thing I wanted to tell you, princess,' said Rostov. 'If Prince Andrei were not alive, it would have been announced in the gazettes, since he is a colonel.'

The princess looked at him, not grasping what he was saying but comforted by the expression of sympathetic concern on his face.

'And I know so many cases of a splinter-wound (the papers said it was a shell) either proving fatal at once or else very slight,' continued Nikolai. 'We must hope for the best, and I am sure ...'

Princess Maria interrupted him.

'Oh, it would be so aw ...' she exclaimed, and agitation preventing her from finishing, she bent her head with a graceful movement (all her gestures were graceful in his presence) and glancing gratefully up at him she followed after her aunt.

That evening Nikolai did not go out anywhere but stayed in his lodgings in order to square up certain accounts with the horse-dealers. By the time he was through with the business it was too late for paying visits but still too early to go to bed, and for a long while he paced up and down the room reflecting on his life, a thing he rarely did.

Princess Maria had made an agreeable impression on him when he met her near Smolensk. The fact of having encountered her in such unusual circumstances, and of his mother having at one time pointed her out to him as a good match, had caused him to regard her with especial interest. When he came on her again in Voronezh the impression she made on him was not merely pleasing but powerful. Nikolai was struck by the peculiar moral beauty he remarked in her at this time. He had, however, been preparing to go away and it had not entered his head to regret that in leaving Voronezh he was depriving himself of the chance of seeing her. But that morning's encounter with her in church had, he felt, gone more deeply into his heart than was desirable for his general peace. That pale, delicate, sad face, those luminous eyes, the gentle, graceful gestures, and especially the profound and tender melancholy pervading all her features, troubled him and exacted his sympathy. In men Rostov could not endure to see the expression of a lofty spiritual life (that was why he did not like Prince Andrei) – he referred to it scornfully as philosophy and moonshine; but in Princess Maria that very sorrowfulness which revealed the depth of a whole spiritual world foreign to him was an irresistible attraction.

'She must be a marvellous girl! A real angel!' he said to himself. 'Why am I not free? Why was I in such a hurry with Sonya?' And involuntarily he compared the two: the poverty in the one and the abundance in the other of those spiritual gifts which he himself lacked and therefore prized so highly. He tried to picture what would have been were he free. How he would have wooed her and made her his wife. No, he could not imagine that. A chill came over him and nothing clear would present itself to his imagination. He had long ago pictured to himself the future with Sonya, and it was all simple and clear just because it had been thought out and he knew all about Sonya; but it was impossible to picture a future with Princess Maria, because he did not understand her but only loved her.

Reveries to do with Sonya had something gay and playful about them. But to dream of Princess Maria was always difficult and rather frightening.

'How she prayed!' he thought. 'One could see that her whole soul was in her prayer. Yes, that was the prayer that moves mountains, and I am convinced her prayers will be answered. Why don't I pray for what I want?' he bethought himself. 'What do I want? Freedom, release from Sonya. She was right,' he mused, remembering what the governor's wife had said, 'nothing but misery can come of my marrying Sonya. Entanglement, grief for Mamma ... our position ... business difficulties, fearful difficulties! Besides, I don't love her – not as I should. O God, get me out of this dreadful, hopeless situation!' he suddenly began to pray. 'Yes, prayer can move mountains but one must have faith and not just pray as Natasha and I used to as children, for the snow to turn to sugar, and then run out into the yard to see whether it had done so. No, but I am not praying for trifles now,' he said, putting his pipe down in a corner and standing with clasped hands before the icon. And, his heart melted by thoughts of Princess Maria, he started to pray as he had not prayed for a long time. He had tears in his eyes and a lump in his throat when Lavrushka came in at the door with some papers.

'Stupid fool! Bursting in when you're not wanted!' cried Nikolai, quickly changing his attitude.

'From the governor,' said Lavrushka in a sleepy voice. 'A courier has arrived and there's a letter for you.'

'Oh, very well, thanks, you can go!'

Nikolai took the two letters. One was from his mother, the other from Sonya. He recognized them by the handwriting and opened Sonya's first. He had only read a few lines when he turned pale and his eyes opened wide with dismay and joy.

'No, it's not possible!' he exclaimed aloud.

Unable to sit still, he strode up and down the room, holding the letter in both hands as he read. He skimmed through it, read it once, read it a second time, then with shoulders raised and arms stretched out, stood still in the middle of the room, mouth wide open and eyes staring. What he had just been praying for with confidence that God would hear him had come to pass; but Nikolai was as much astonished as if it were something extraordinary and unexpected, and as though the very fact of its happening so quickly proved that it had not come from God, to whom he had been praying, but was some ordinary coincidence.

The knot fastening his freedom, that had seemed so impossible to undo, had been cut by this unexpected (and to Nikolai quite chance) letter from Sonya. She wrote that recent unfortunate events – the loss of almost the whole of the Rostovs' property in Moscow – and the countess's frequently expressed wish that Nikolai should marry Princess Bolkonsky, together with his silence and coldness of late, had all combined to decide her to release him from his promise and set him completely free.

It would be too painful to me to think that I could be a cause of sorrow or discord in the family that has been so good to me [she wrote], and the one aim of my affections is the happiness of those I love; and so, Nicolas, I beg you to consider yourself free, and to know that, in spite of everything, no one can love you more truly than

Your Sonya

Both letters were written from Troitsa. The other, from the countess, described their last days in Moscow, their departure, the fire and the destruction of all their property. In her letter the countess also mentioned that Prince Andrei was among the wounded travelling with them. His condition was critical but the doctor said there was now more hope. Sonya and Natasha were nursing him.

With this letter Nikolai went next day to call on Princess Maria. Neither he nor she spoke a word as to the possible implications of Natasha attending Prince Andrei, but thanks to this letter Nikolai suddenly became almost as intimate with the princess as if they were relations.

The following morning he saw Princess Maria off on her journey to Yaroslavl, and a few days later left to rejoin his regiment.

8

SONYA's letter to Nikolai, which had come as an answer to his prayer, had been written from Troitsa. This was how it had come about. The idea of getting Nikolai married to a wealthy bride obsessed the old countess's mind more and more. She knew that Sonya was the chief obstacle in the way of this. And Sonya's life had of late, and especially after the letter in which Nikolai described his meeting with Princess Maria at Bogucharovo, become more and more difficult in the countess's house. The countess never missed an opportunity of making humiliating or cruel allusions to Sonya.

But a few days before they left Moscow, distressed and overwrought by all that was happening, the countess had sent for Sonya and, instead of upbraiding and demanding, had implored her with tears to sacrifice herself, and repay all that the family had done for her, by breaking off her engagement to Nikolai.

'I shall never know a moment's peace till you make me this promise,' she said.

Sonya sobbed hysterically, replied through her sobs that she would do anything, was ready for anything, but she did not promise in so many words and in her heart she could not bring herself to do what was demanded of her. She must deny herself for the happiness of the family which had brought her up and provided for her. To deny herself for the happiness of others was second nature to Sonya. Her position in the house was such that only thus could she show her quality, and she was used to sacrificing herself and liked to do so. But hitherto in all her acts of self-immolation she had been happily conscious that they raised her in her own esteem and in that of others, and so made her more worthy of Nikolai, whom she loved more than all the world; but now they wanted her to renounce what constituted for her the whole reward of renunciation and the entire meaning of life. And for the first time in her existence she felt bitterness against the people who had befriended her only to torture her the more agonizingly: she envied Natasha who had never experienced anything of this sort, had never been required to sacrifice herself but made others sacrifice themselves for her and yet was beloved by everybody. And for the first time Sonya felt that out of her pure, quiet love for Nikolai a passionate feeling was beginning to grow up which was stronger than principle, virtue or religion; and under the influence of this feeling Sonya, whose life of dependence had taught her instinctively to be secretive, having answered the countess in vague general terms, avoided further conversation with her and resolved to wait until she saw Nikolai, not with the idea of giving him his freedom but, on the contrary, of binding him to her for ever.

The bustle and horror of the Rostovs' last days in Moscow had stifled the gloomy thoughts that weighed on Sonya. She was glad to find escape from them in practical activity. But when she heard of Prince Andrei's presence in their house, in spite of all her very genuine compassion for him and for Natasha, a blithe and superstitious feeling that God did not mean her to be parted from Nikolai enveloped her. She knew Natasha loved no one but Prince Andrei, and had never ceased to love him. She knew that brought together now, in such terrible circumstances, they would fall in love with one another again, and that then Nikolai would not be able to marry Princess Maria as they would be within the prohibited degrees of affinity as stipulated by the Orthodox Church. Notwithstanding all the horror of what had happened during those last days and during the early part of their journey, this feeling, this consciousness that Providence was intervening in her personal affairs, cheered Sonya.

At the Troitsa monastery the Rostovs made the first break in their journey.

Three large rooms were assigned to them in the monastery hostel, one of which Prince Andrei occupied. The wounded man was much better that day. Natasha was sitting with him. In the next room the count and countess were respectfully conversing with the father superior, who was paying a visit to his old acquaintances and patrons.

Sonya was there, too, tormented by curiosity as to what Prince Andrei and Natasha were talking about. She could hear the sound of their voices through the door. The door of Prince Andrei's room opened. Natasha came out, looking agitated, and, not noticing the monk, who had risen to greet her and was drawing back the wide sleeve over his right hand, she went up to Sonya and took her hand.

'Natasha, what are you thinking of? Come here,' said the countess.

Natasha went up to receive the monk's blessing, and he counselled her to turn to God for help, and to the patron saint of the monastery, the blessed St Sergii.

As soon as the father superior withdrew, Natasha took her friend by the hand and went with her into the empty third room.

'Sonya, say yes! Say he will live?' she urged. 'Sonya, I am so happy and so wretched! Sonya, dearest, everything is as it was before. If only he lives! He cannot ... because ... because of ...' and Natasha burst into tears.

'Yes! I knew it! Thank God!' murmured Sonya. 'He will live.'

Sonya was no less overcome than her cousin by the latter's fears and distress, and by her own private thoughts, which she shared with no one. Sobbing, she kissed and comforted Natasha. 'If only he lives!' she said to herself. Having wept and talked together, and wiped away their tears, the two friends stole to Prince Andrei's door. Natasha opened it cautiously and glanced into the room. Sonya stood beside her at the half-open door.

Prince Andrei was lying raised high on three pillows. His pale face looked peaceful, his eyes were closed, and they could see his regular breathing.

'Oh, Natasha!' Sonya suddenly almost shrieked, grabbing her cousin's arm and stepping back from the door.

'What? What is it?' asked Natasha.

'It's the same, it's that ...' said Sonya, with a white face and trembling lips.

Natasha softly closed the door and walked away with Sonya to the window, not yet understanding what the latter was trying to tell her.

'Do you remember' – said Sonya, with a scared and solemn face – 'do you remember when I looked into the mirror for you ... at Otradnoe, at Christmas-time? ... You remember what I saw?'

'Yes, yes!' cried Natasha, opening her eyes wide, and vaguely recalling that Sonya had said something then about seeing Prince Andrei lying down.

'Do you remember?' Sonya went on. 'I saw him then and told everybody, you and Dunyasha too. I saw him lying on a bed,' said she, at each item making a gesture with her hand and a lifted finger, 'and that he had his eyes shut and was covered with a pink quilt, and had his hands folded,' she concluded, convincing herself that the details she had seen were exactly what she had seen in the mirror.

At the time she had seen nothing but had described the first thing that came into her head; but what she had invented then seemed to her now as real as any other recollection. She not only remembered what she had said at the time – that he looked round at her and smiled and was covered with something red – but was firmly convinced that she had seen and said then that he was covered with a pink quilt – yes, pink – and that his eyes were closed.

'Yes, yes, pink it was,' cried Natasha, who now fancied that she too remembered the word *pink*, and saw in this the most extraordinary and mysterious part of the vision.

'But what does it mean?' she added meditatively.

'Oh, I don't know, it's all so queer,' replied Sonya, clutching her head.

A few minutes later Prince Andrei rang and Natasha went to him; but Sonya, in a rare state of excitement and emotion, remained at the window, pondering over the strangeness of what had occurred.

*

That day there was an opportunity of sending letters to the army, and the countess was writing to her son.

'Sonya!' said the countess, raising her eyes from her letter as her niece passed. 'Sonya, won't you write to dear Nikolai?' She spoke in a soft, tremulous voice, and in the weary eyes that looked through her spectacles Sonya read all that the countess meant by those words. Those eyes expressed entreaty, dread of a refusal, shame at having to beg, and readiness for relentless hostility in case of such refusal.

Sonya went up to the countess and, kneeling down, kissed her hand.

'Yes, *maman*, I will write,' said she.

Sonya was softened, excited and moved by all that had happened that day, especially by the mysterious fulfilment she had just seen of

1135

her vision. Now that she knew that the renewal of Natasha's relations with Prince Andrei would prevent Nikolai from marrying Princess Maria she was joyfully conscious of a return of that self-sacrificing spirit in which she was accustomed and loved to live. So with a glad sense of performing a magnanimous action – held up several times by the tears that dimmed her velvety black eyes – she wrote the touching letter, the reception of which had so amazed Nikolai.

9

In the guard-room to which Pierre had been taken the officer and soldiers who had arrested him treated him with hostility but at the same time with respect. Their attitude towards him betrayed both their uncertainty as to who he might be – perhaps someone of great importance – and animosity in consequence of the struggle they had just had with him.

But when the guard was relieved the following morning Pierre felt that for the new guard – officers and men alike – he was not as interesting as he had been to his captors. And indeed those on duty the second day saw nothing in this big, stout man in a peasant coat of the vigorous person who had fought so desperately with the pillaging soldier and the convoy, and had uttered those exalted words about saving a child: they saw in him only No. 17 of the Russian prisoners, arrested and detained for some reason by order of the higher authorities. If they noticed anything remarkable about Pierre, it was only his undaunted air of concentrated thought, and the way he spoke French, which struck them as surprisingly good. Nevertheless that very day Pierre was put in with the other suspicious characters, as the separate room he occupied was wanted for an officer.

All the Russians detained with Pierre were men of the lowest class. And all of them, recognizing Pierre as a gentleman, held aloof from him, the more so as he spoke French. Pierre listened sadly to their jeers at his expense.

That evening Pierre learned that all the prisoners (with himself, probably, in their number) were to be tried for incendiarism. The day after, he was taken with the rest to a house where a French general with a white moustache sat with two colonels and other Frenchmen with scarves sewn on their sleeves. With a sharp precision customary in the examination of prisoners, and which is supposed to preclude human frailty, Pierre, like the others, was interrogated as to who he was, where he had been, with what object, and so on.

These questions, like those generally put at trials, left the essence of the living fact aside, shut out the possibility of that essence being discovered, and were designed only at supplying a channel along which the examining officials desired the accused's answers to flow so as to lead to the goal of the inquiry, namely, a conviction. The moment Pierre began to say anything that did not contribute to this end the channel was removed and the water allowed to flow to waste. Pierre felt, moreover, what the accused always do feel at all trials – a puzzled wonder as to why these questions were put to him. He had a feeling that it was only out of condescension or a kind of courtesy that this device of a directing channel was employed. He knew he was in the power of these men, that only by force had they brought him here, that force alone gave them the right to exact answers to their questions, that the sole object of the proceedings was to prove him guilty. And so, since they had the power and the wish to incriminate him, there was no need for this expedient of an inquiry and trial. It was obvious that any answer was bound to lead to his conviction. When asked what he was doing when he was arrested, Pierre replied in a rather tragic manner that he was restoring to its parents a child he had saved from the flames. Why had he fought the marauder? Pierre answered that he was 'protecting a woman', and that 'to protect a woman who was being insulted was the duty of every man; that ...' They pulled him up: this was not to the point. With what object had he been in the courtyard of a burning house, where he had been seen by witnesses? He replied that he had gone out to see what was happening in Moscow. They stopped him again: he had not been asked where he was going, but why he was found near the fire. Who was he? they inquired, repeating their first question, to which he had declined to answer. Again he replied that he could not answer that.

'Make a note of that, that's bad ... very bad,' sternly remarked the general with the white whiskers and the florid red face.

On the fourth day fires broke out on the Zubovsky rampart.

Pierre and thirteen others were moved to a coach-house belonging to a merchant's mansion near the Crimean ford. As they marched through the streets Pierre could hardly breathe for the smoke which seemed to hang over the whole city. Fires were visible on all sides.

Pierre did not at that time grasp the significance of the burning of Moscow, and gazed with horror at the fires.

He passed another four days in a coach-house near the Crimean ford, and in the course of those four days he learned, from the conversation of the French soldiers, that all those in detention there were awaiting a decision which might come at any moment from the marshal. What marshal this was, Pierre could not find out from the soldiers. Evidently for them 'the marshal' represented the highest and somewhat mysterious symbol of power.

These first days, up to the 8th of September when the prisoners were brought up for a second examination, were the hardest of all for Pierre.

10

ON the 8th of September an officer – of very great consequence, judging by the respect the guards showed him – entered the coach-house where the prisoners were. This officer, probably someone from the Staff, held a memorandum in his hand, and called over all the Russians there, naming Pierre as 'the man who will not give his name'. Glancing indifferently and indolently at all the prisoners, he ordered the officer in charge to have them decently dressed and tidied up before bringing them before the marshal. An hour later a squad of soldiers arrived and Pierre with the thirteen others was taken to the Dyevichy meadow. It was a fine day, sunny after rain, and the air was exceptionally clear. The smoke did not hang low, as it had on the day Pierre had been removed from the guard-room on the Zubovsky rampart, but rose in columns into the pure atmosphere. Flames were nowhere to be seen but columns of smoke were rising on all sides, and all Moscow, so far as Pierre could make out, was one vast, charred ruin. On every side were devastated spaces with only stoves and chimney-pieces still standing, and here and there the blackened walls of a stone house. Pierre stared at the ruins and did not recognize districts he had known well. Here and there he found churches that had not been touched by the fire. The Kremlin, undamaged, gleamed white in the distance, with its towers and the belfry of Ivan the Great. Close at hand the dome of the Novo-Dyevichy convent glittered brightly and its bells pealed out particularly sonorously. These chimes reminded Pierre that it was Sunday, and the feast of the Nativity of the Virgin. But there seemed to be no one to celebrate the festival;

everywhere were blackened ruins, and the few Russians they met were ragged, panic-stricken folk who tried to hide themselves at sight of the French.

It was plain that the Russian nest was wrecked and destroyed; but Pierre felt dimly that behind the overthrow of the Russian order of life, in place of this ruined nest, an entirely different, stable French order had been established. He was conscious of this when he looked at the soldiers, briskly and gaily marching along in a steady file escorting him and the other delinquents; he was aware of it when his eyes fell on an important French official in a carriage and pair driven by a soldier, whom they met on the way. He felt it at the cheerful sounds of regimental music which floated across from the left of the open space, and especially he felt it and realized it from the list of prisoners the French officer had read off when he came that morning. Pierre had been taken by one set of soldiers and led first to one place and then to another, with dozens of other men; it seemed to him they might easily have forgotten him, have got him mixed up with the others. But no: the answers he had given at his interrogation had come back to him in his designation as 'the man who will not give his name'. And under that appellation, which was dreadful to Pierre, they were now conducting him somewhere with unhesitating assurance on their faces that he and all the other prisoners were the right ones and were being taken to the proper place. Pierre felt himself an insignificant chip fallen among the wheels of a machine whose mechanism he did not understand but which worked without a hitch.

He and his fellow-prisoners were brought to the right side of the Dyevichy meadow, to a big white house with an immense garden, not far from the convent. This was Prince Shcherbatov's house, where Pierre had often visited in other days and which, as he gathered from the talk of the soldiers, was at present occupied by the marshal, the Duke of Eckmühl (Davoust).

They were taken to the entrance, and led into the house one at a time. Pierre was the sixth to go in. Through a glass gallery, an anteroom and a hall, all familiar to him, he was escorted to a long low study at the door of which stood an adjutant.

Davoust, spectacles on nose, was sitting bent over a table at the far end of the room. Pierre went close up to him. Davoust, apparently engaged in consulting some document that lay before him, did not look up. Without raising his eyes he asked in a quiet voice:

'Who are you?'

Pierre was silent because he was incapable of uttering a word. To him Davoust was not merely a French general but a man notorious for his cruelty. Looking at the cold face – Davoust sat like a stern schoolmaster who was willing to be patient for a time and wait for an answer – Pierre felt that every instant's delay might cost him his life; but he did not know what to say. He could not make up his mind to repeat what he had said at his first examination, yet to disclose his rank and position would be both dangerous and humiliating. He stood silent. But before he had time to arrive at a decision Davoust raised his head, pushed his spectacles up on his forehead, screwed up his eyes and looked intently at him.

'I know this man,' he said in an icy, measured tone, obviously calculated to frighten Pierre.

The chill that had been running down Pierre's back seemed to clutch his head in a vice.

'You cannot know me, General, I have never seen you. ...'

'He is a Russian spy,' Davoust interrupted him, addressing another general in the room, whom Pierre had not noticed.

And Davoust turned away. With an unexpected vibration in his voice Pierre suddenly began rapidly:

'*Non, Monseigneur,*' he said, all at once remembering that Davoust was a duke. '*Non, Monseigneur,* you cannot possibly know me. I am a militia-officer and have not been out of Moscow.'

'Your name?' repeated Davoust.

'Bezuhov.'

'What proof have I that you are not lying?'

'*Monseigneur!*' exclaimed Pierre in a tone that betrayed not offence but entreaty.

Davoust lifted his eyes and gazed searchingly at him. For some seconds they looked at one another, and that look saved Pierre. It went beyond the circumstances of war and the court-room, and established human relations between the two men. Both of them in that one instant were dimly aware of an infinite number of things, and they realized that they were both children of humanity, that they were brothers.

When Davoust had first half raised his head from his memorandum, where men's lives and doings were indicated by numbers, Pierre had been only a case, and Davoust could have had him shot without burdening his conscience with an evil deed; but now he saw in him a human being. He reflected for a moment.

'How can you prove to me that you are telling the truth?' said Davoust coldly.

Pierre thought of Ramballe, and mentioned his name and regiment and the street and house where he could be found.

'You are not what you say you are,' returned Davoust.

In a trembling, faltering voice Pierre began adducing proofs of the truth of his statements.

But at this point an adjutant entered and reported something to Davoust.

Davoust immediately beamed at the news the adjutant brought, and began buttoning up his uniform. Apparently he quite forgot about Pierre.

When the adjutant reminded him of the prisoner he jerked his head in Pierre's direction with a frown and ordered him to be taken away. But where they were to take him Pierre did not know: back to the coach-house or to the place of execution his companions had pointed out to him as they crossed the Dyevichy meadow.

He turned his head and saw that the adjutant was repeating some question.

'Yes, of course!' said Davoust, but what that 'Yes' referred to Pierre did not know.

Pierre had no idea afterwards how or where he went, or whether it was a long way. In a state of complete stupefaction and bewilderment, seeing nothing around him, he moved his legs in company with the others till they all stopped and he stopped too.

His brain was racked with a single thought. Who – who was it really that had sentenced him to death? Not the men on the commission who had first examined him – not one of them had wished to, or in all probability could have done so. It was not Davoust, who had looked at him in such a human fashion. Another moment and Davoust would have realized that he was making a bad mistake, but just then the adjutant had come in and interrupted. And the adjutant had obviously had no evil intent, though he might have refrained from coming in. Then who was it who was executing him, killing him, taking his life – his, Pierre's, with all his memories, yearnings, hopes and ideas? Who was doing it? And Pierre felt that it was no one's doing.

It was the system, the concatenation of circumstances.

A system of some sort was killing him – Pierre – robbing him of life, of everything, annihilating him.

11

FROM Prince Shcherbatov's house the prisoners were conducted straight down the Dyevichy meadow to the left of the nunnery as far as a kitchen-garden where a post had been set up. Beyond the post a big pit had been freshly dug in the ground, and a great crowd formed a semicircle about the post and the pit. The crowd consisted of a few Russians and a large proportion of soldiers from Napoleon's army not on duty – there were Germans, Italians and Frenchmen in a variety of uniforms. To right and left of the post stood rows of French soldiers in blue uniforms with red epaulets and high boots and shakos.

The prisoners were placed in a certain order, in accordance with a written list (Pierre was sixth), and led up to the post. A number of drums suddenly began beating on both sides of them, and Pierre felt that with the roll of the drums part of his soul had been torn away. He lost all capacity to think and understand. He could only look and listen. And he had only one desire – the desire that the dreadful thing which had to be done should be done as quickly as possible. Pierre looked round at his companions and studied their faces.

The first two were convicts with shaven heads. One was tall and thin; the other a dark, shaggy, muscular fellow with a flat nose. No. 3 was a house-serf, a man of five-and-forty, with grizzled hair and a plump, well-nourished body. The fourth was a peasant, a very handsome fellow with a full flaxen beard and black eyes. The fifth was a factory hand, a thin, sallow-faced lad of eighteen in a loose coat.

Pierre heard the French deliberating whether to shoot them singly or two at a time. 'In couples,' the officer in command replied in a voice of cold indifference. There was a stir in the ranks of the soldiers and it was observable that they were all in a hurry – not as men hurry to execute an order they understand but as people make haste to have done with an essential but unpleasant and incomprehensible task.

A French official wearing a scarf came up to the right of the file of prisoners, and read out the sentence in Russian and in French.

Then two pairs of French soldiers advanced to the criminals, and at the officer's command took the two convicts who stood first in the row. The convicts stopped when they reached the post and, while the sacks were being brought, looked dumbly about them, as a wounded animal watches the approaching huntsman. One of them kept crossing himself, the other scratched his back and worked his lips into the semblance of a smile. With hasty fingers the soldiers blindfolded them, drawing the sacks over their heads, and pinioned them to the post.

A dozen sharpshooters with muskets stepped out of the ranks with a firm, regular tread, and halted eight paces from the post. Pierre turned away so as not to see what was about to happen. There was a sudden rattle and crash which seemed to him louder than the most terrific thunderclap, and he looked round. There was some smoke, and the French soldiers, with pale faces and trembling hands, were doing something near the pit. Two more prisoners were led up. They, too, with the same silent appeal for protection in their eyes, gazed vainly round at the onlookers, evidently unable to comprehend or believe what was coming. They were incredulous because they alone knew what their life meant to them, and so they could not understand, could not believe that it could be taken from them.

Pierre wanted not to look, and again turned away; but again his ears were assailed by the sound as of a frightful explosion, and with the report he saw smoke, blood, and the white, scared faces of the Frenchmen who were again doing something by the post, their shaking hands knocking against each other. Breathing heavily, Pierre stared about him as though asking, 'What does it mean?' The same question was repeated in all the eyes that met his.

On the faces of all the Russians, on the faces of the French soldiers and officers, without exception, he read the same dismay, horror and conflict that he felt in his own heart. 'But who, after all, is doing this? They are all as much sickened as I am. Whose doing is it, then? Whose?' flashed for a second through his mind.

'Sharpshooters of the 86th, forward!' shouted someone. The fifth prisoner, the one next to Pierre, was led forward – alone. Pierre did not realize that he had been spared, that he and the rest had been brought there simply to witness the executions. With mounting horror, and no sense of joy or relief, he gazed at what was taking place. No. 5 was the factory hand in the loose coat. The moment they laid their hands on him he sprang back in terror and clung to Pierre. (Pierre shuddered and shook him off.) The lad was unable to walk. They dragged him along, holding him under the arms, while he shrieked something. When they got him to the post he was suddenly quiet, as if he had all at once understood something. Whether he understood that screaming was useless, or felt that it was impossible these men should kill him, at any rate he took his stand at the post, waiting to be blindfolded like the others, and like a wounded wild beast looked around him with glittering eyes.

Pierre could no longer bring himself to turn away and close his eyes. His curiosity and agitation, which was shared by the crowd, reached their highest pitch at this fifth murder. Like the other four this new victim seemed composed: he wrapped his loose coat closer round him and rubbed one bare foot against the other.

When they proceeded to bind his eyes he himself adjusted the knot which hurt the back of his head; then when they propped him against the blood-stained post he leaned back and, not being comfortable in that position, straightened himself, carefully placed his feet and settled at his ease. Pierre never took his eyes off him and did not miss the slightest movement he made.

The word of command must have been given, the reports of eight muskets must have followed; but try as he would to recollect it afterwards Pierre could never remember having heard the smallest whisper of a shot. He only saw the factory lad suddenly sag in the ropes that held him, blood oozing in two places, saw the ropes give under the weight of the hanging body and the factory lad, his head drooping unnaturally and one leg bent under him, sink down into a sitting position. Pierre ran up to the post. No one stopped him. Pale, frightened people were doing something round the factory hand. The lower jaw of one whiskered old Frenchman trembled as he untied the ropes. The body collapsed. The soldiers dragged it awkwardly from the post and hurriedly began shoving it into the pit.

They all plainly and beyond a doubt knew that they were criminals who must hide the traces of their crime as quickly as possible.

Pierre glanced into the pit and saw the factory lad lying with his knees close to his head and one shoulder higher than the other. And that shoulder was convulsively, rhythmically rising and falling. But earth in spadeful was already being shovelled over the whole body. One of the soldiers, in a tortured voice of angry impatience, shouted to Pierre to go back. But Pierre did not understand him, and remained near the post, and no one drove him away.

When the pit was quite filled up a command was given. Pierre was taken back to his place, and the French troops faced about on both sides of the post, made a half incline and marched past the stake with measured tread. The twenty-four sharpshooters, their muskets discharged, standing in the middle of the ring, ran back to their places as their companies passed by.

Pierre stared now with dazed eyes at these sharpshooters, who were running together in couples out of the circle. All but one had rejoined their companies. This one, a young soldier, face deadly pale, shako pushed to the back of his head, musket resting on the ground, still stood facing the pit on the spot from which he had fired. He swayed like a drunken man, taking a few steps forward and then back to save himself from falling. An old non-commissioned officer ran out of the ranks and, seizing the youngster by the elbow, hauled him back to his company. The crowd of Russians and Frenchmen began to disperse. They all walked off in silence, with lowered heads.

'That will teach them to start fires,' said one of the French.

Pierre glanced round at the speaker and saw that it was a soldier trying to reconcile himself somehow with what had been done, but without success. Without finishing what he had been going to say, he made a hopeless movement with his arm and went on his way.

12

AFTER the execution Pierre was separated from the other prisoners and put by himself in a small, ravaged and befouled church.

Towards evening a patrol-sergeant entered with two soldiers and informed him that he had been pardoned and would now proceed to the barracks for prisoners-of-war. Without understanding what was said to him, Pierre got up and went with the soldiers. They took him to the upper end of the open space, where some sheds had been rigged up out of charred planks, beams and battens, and led him into one of them. In the darkness some twenty various individuals surrounded Pierre. He stared at them, with no idea who they were, why they were there or what they wanted of him. He heard what they said but did not grasp the meaning of the words: his mind made no kind of deduction or interpretation of them. He replied to the questions put to him but had no notion who was listening, or how they would understand his answers. He looked at faces and figures, and they all seemed equally meaningless.

From the moment Pierre had witnessed that hideous massacre committed by men who had no desire to do it, it was as if the spring in his soul, by which everything was held together and given the semblance of life, had been suddenly wrenched out, and all had collapsed into a heap of senseless refuse. Though he did not realize it, his faith in the right ordering of the universe, in humanity, in his own self and in God had been destroyed. He had experienced this state of mind before but never with such intensity. When similar doubts had assailed him in the past they had had their origin in his own wrongdoing, and at the bottom of his heart he had felt that salvation from his despair and those doubts was to be found within himself. But this time he could not blame himself that the world had crumbled before his eyes, leaving only meaningless ruins. He felt that to get back to faith in life was not in his power.

Around him in the darkness stood a number of men: evidently something about him interested them greatly. They were telling him something, asking him about something, then leading him somewhere, and at last he found himself in a corner of the shed among men who were talking on all sides, and laughing.

'And so, friends ... the prince himself *who* ...' a voice was saying in the opposite corner of the shed, with special stress on the word *who*.

Sitting mute and motionless on a heap of straw against the wall, Pierre now opened, now closed his eyes. But as soon as he shut them he saw again the dreadful face of that factory lad – dreadful from its very simplicity – and the faces of the unwilling executioners, still more dreadful in their uneasiness. And he would open his eyes again and stare vacantly about him in the darkness.

Beside him, in a stooping position, squatted a little man of whose presence Pierre was first made aware by a powerful odour of perspiration which emanated from him every time he moved. This man was engaged in doing something to his legs in the darkness, and though Pierre could not see his face he was conscious that the man kept glancing at him. When his eyes were more accustomed to the dark Pierre made out that the man was taking off his leg-bands, and the way he did it aroused Pierre's attention.

Having unwound the string that tied the band round one leg, he carefully coiled it up and at once set to work on the other leg, glancing at Pierre. While with one hand he hung up the length of string, with the other he was already unwinding the band round the second leg.

In this fashion, with precise, rounded, rapid movements which lost no time in following one another, the man removed his leg-bands and hung them on pegs knocked in the wall just above his head, took out a knife, cut off something, shut the knife, put it under his bolster and, settling himself more comfortably, clasped both arms round his knees, which were drawn up, and stared straight at Pierre. Pierre was conscious of something pleasant, soothing and satisfying in those deft movements, in the man's well-ordered establishment of his belong-ings in his corner, even in the very smell of the man, and he returned his gaze, without dropping his eyes.

'Seen a lot o' trouble, sir, eh?' said the little man suddenly.

And there was so much kindliness and simplicity in the sing-song voice that Pierre felt his jaw tremble and the tears rise to his eyes as he tried to reply. At the same second, giving Pierre no time to betray his confusion, the little fellow continued in the same pleasant tones:

'Eh, lad, don't fret now,' said he in the tender, sing-song, caressing voice in which old Russian peasant-women talk. 'Don't fret, my friend: suffering lasts an hour but life goes on for ever! That's the way it is, lad. And we get on here fine, thank God, there's no offence. They're men too, with good ones among 'em as well as bad,' he said, and, while still speaking, twisted agilely on to his knees, got up, cleared his throat and walked off to another part of the shed.

'Hi, you've come back again, have you?' Pierre heard the same soft voice from the far end of the hut. 'So you remember me, do you? There, there, that'll do!' And pushing away a little dog that was jumping up at him the soldier returned to his place and sat down. In his hands he held something wrapped in a bit of cloth.

'Here, you have a taste of this, sir,' said he, resuming the respectful tone he had used at first, and unwrapping and passing Pierre some baked potatoes. 'We had soup for dinner. But these potatoes are a treat!'

Pierre had not eaten all day and the smell of the potatoes struck him as extraordinarily good. He thanked the soldier and began to eat.

'What do you eat 'em like that for?' inquired the soldier with a smile. 'You should try 'em like this.'

He took a potato, got out his clasp-knife, cut the potato in the palm of his hand into two equal halves, sprinkled them with salt from the rag and offered them to Pierre.

'The potatoes are a treat,' he reiterated. 'You try 'em like that!'

Pierre thought he had never tasted anything more delicious.

'Oh, I'm right enough,' said he, 'but why did they shoot those poor fellows? ... The last was a lad of barely twenty.'

'Tst, tst ...' said the little man. 'What a sin, what a sin ...' he added quickly, and just as though the words were always waiting ready in his mouth and flew out by chance he went on: 'And how was it, sir, you stayed in Moscow?'

'I didn't think they would come so soon. I stayed by accident,' replied Pierre.

'And how came they to arrest you, friend? Was it in your own house?'

'No, I went out to look at the fire, and it was then they took me up and tried me for being an incendiary.'

'Where there's law there's injustice,' put in the little man.

'And have you been here long?' asked Pierre, chewing the last of the potato.

'Me? It was last Sunday they fetched me out of hospital in Moscow.'

'Why, are you a soldier then?'

'Yes, we were all from the Apsheron regiment. Dying of fever, I was. We were never told nothing. There were twenty or more of us lying sick. And we had no idea – we never guessed nothing.'

'And are you cut up at being here?' asked Pierre.

'To be sure, friend. My name's Platon – Platon Karatayev,' he added, evidently to make it easier for Pierre to address him. 'In the regiment they called me the little falcon. How can a man help feeling cut up? Moscow – she's the mother of cities. How can us look on at all this and not feel sick at 'eart? But the worm that gnaws the cabbage is the first to die: that's what the old folk used to tell us,' he added quickly.

'What? What did you say?' asked Pierre.

'Who? Me?' said Karatayev. 'Man proposes, God disposes, I say,' he replied, supposing that he was repeating what he had said at first, and immediately went on: 'And you, you must have a family estate? And a house of your own? Your cup must be full. And a wife may-be? And your old parents living?' he asked.

And though it was too dark for Pierre to see, he felt that the soldier's lips were twisted into a restrained smile of kindliness as he put these questions. He seemed grieved to learn that Pierre had no parents, especially no mother.

'A wife for good sense, a mother-in-law for kind welcome, but there's none so dear as a man's own mother!' said he. 'Well, and have you little ones?' he went on to ask.

Again Pierre's negative answer seemed to distress him, and he hastened to add:

'Never mind, you're young, and please God there'll be bairns yet. The great thing is to live on good terms. ...'

'But it makes no difference now,' Pierre could not help saying.

'Ah, my good man,' rejoined Platon, 'you can't be sure a beggar's sack or the prison-house will never fall to your lot!'

He settled himself more comfortably and cleared his throat, evidently preparatory to a long story. 'For instance, my dear friend, I was still living at home,' he began. 'We had a nice place with no end of land. Peasants we were, and we lived well, our house was one to thank God for. When father and we went out mowing there were seven of us. Lived well, we did, like proper Christians. But one day ...'

And Platon Karatayev told a long story of how he had gone into someone else's copse after wood, how he had been caught by the keeper, had been tried, flogged and sent to serve in the army.

'Well, lad,' and a smile changed the tone of his voice, 'we thought it was a misfortune but it turned out to be a blessing. If I 'adn't done wrong it would have been my brother for the army, and him – my younger brother, with five little ones, but me, you see, I only left a wife behind. We had a little girl once but the good Lord took her before I went for a soldier. I comes home on leave, and what do you think – I finds 'em all better off than they was before. Yard full of live-stock, the women-folk at home, two brothers out earning wages. Only Mihailo, the youngest, at home. My old dad says to me, "A bairn's a bairn to me," he says. "No matter which finger gets nipped, it hurts just the same. And if they hadn't shaved Platon for a soldier, then Mihailo would've had to go." He gathered us all together and – if you'll believe me, he stands us all up in front of the holy icons. "Mihailo," he says, "come you here and kneel down before him; and you, woman, kneel; and all you grandchillun, kneel at his feet. Understand?" he says. And that's the way it is, my good sir. There's no escaping fate. But we are always findin' fault and complainin': this ain't right, and the other don't suit us. Happiness, friend, is like water in a drag-net – pull it along and it bulges: take it out and it's empty! Yes, that's the way of it.'

And Platon shifted his seat on the straw.

After a short pause he got up.

'Well, I dare say you're sleepy?' said he, and began rapidly crossing himself and repeating:

'Lord Jesus Christ, holy St Nikola, Frola and Lavra! Lord Jesus Christ, holy St Nikola, Frola and Lavra! Lord Jesus Christ, have mercy on us and save us!' he concluded, then touched the ground with his forehead, got up, straightened himself with a sigh and sat down again on the straw. 'That's the way of it. Lay me down like a stone, O God, and raise me up like new bread,' he muttered as he lay down, pulling his coat over him.

'What prayer was that you were saying?' asked Pierre.

'Eh?' murmured Platon, who was already half asleep. 'What was I saying? I was saying me prayers. Don't you say your prayers?'

'To be sure I do,' said Pierre. 'But what was that about Frola and Lavra?'

'Why,' replied Platon quickly, 'they're the horses' saints. We mustn't forget the poor dumb creatures. See the little rascal – she's curled up and warm all right,' he said, stroking the dog that lay at his feet; and turning over again he fell asleep at once.

Sounds of crying and screaming came from somewhere in the distance outside and the glare of fire was visible through the cracks in the walls, but inside the shed it was quiet and dark. It was a long time before Pierre got to sleep: he lay in the darkness with wide open eyes, listening to the rhythmical snoring of Platon at his side, and he felt that the world that had been shattered was once more stirring to life in his soul, in new beauty and on new and steadfast foundations.

13

IN the shed, where Pierre spent four weeks, there were twenty-three soldiers, three officers and two civilian functionaries, all prisoners like himself.

Pierre remembered them afterwards as misty figures, except Platon Karatayev, who for ever remained in his mind as a most vivid and precious memory, and the very personification of all that was Russian, warm-hearted and – 'round'. When Pierre beheld his neighbour next morning at dawn the first impression of him as something rotund was fully confirmed: Platon's whole figure – in a French military coat belted round the waist with rope, a soldier's cap and bast shoes – was round. His head was as round as a ball; his back, his chest, his shoulders, even his arms, which he always held as though he were about to embrace something, were round; his pleasant smile and his large gentle brown eyes were round, too.

Platon Karatayev must have been on the far side of fifty to judge by his stories of the campaigns he had taken part in as an old soldier. He himself had no idea, and could never have determined with any accuracy, how old he was. But his shining white, strong teeth, which projected in two unbroken semicircles whenever he laughed – which was often – were all sound and good; there was not a grey hair in his beard or on his head, and his whole physique gave an impression of suppleness and of unusual hardiness and endurance.

His face, in spite of a multitude of curving wrinkles, held an expression of innocence and youth; his voice had an agreeable sing-song note. But the chief peculiarity of his speech was its spontaneity and shrewdness. It was evident that he never considered what he had said or was going to say, and this lent an especial and irresistible persuasiveness to the quick, true modulations of his voice.

His physical strength and agility during the first period of his imprisonment were such that he seemed not to know what fatigue or sickness meant. Every night before going to bed he repeated: 'O Lord, lay me down like a stone and raise me up like new bread;' and when he got up in the morning he would give his shoulders a certain shake and say: 'Lie down and curl up, get up and shake up.' And indeed he had only to lie down to fall asleep like a stone, or give himself a shake and be ready without a second's delay for any sort of work, just as children are ready for their toys directly they open their eyes. He knew how to do everything, not particularly well but not badly either. He could bake, cook, sew, carpenter and cobble boots. He was always busy, and only at night allowed himself to indulge in conversation, which he loved, and singing. He sang not as a trained singer does who knows he is being listened to, but like the birds, obviously because he was as much obliged to give vent to those sounds as one sometimes is to stretch oneself or move about; and his singing was always light, sweet, plaintive, almost feminine, and his face the while was very serious.

Being in prison, and having let his beard grow, he had apparently cast off everything alien and military that had been forced upon him, and unconsciously relapsed into his old peasant habits.

'A soldier away from the army is the shirt worn outside the breeches again,' he would say.

He did not like talking about his soldiering days, though he had no complaints to make and was proud of repeating that he had never once been flogged in all his years of service. When he had stories to tell they were generally of some old and evidently precious memory of the time when he lived the life of a *Kristianin* – a Christian – as he called it, instead of *krestianin*.* The proverbs of which he made so much use were not the mainly coarse and indecent expressions common among soldiers but the popular saws which taken without a context seem to have so little meaning, but which suddenly acquire a profoundly wise significance when applied appropriately.

He would often say the exact opposite of what he had said on a previous occasion, yet both would be right. He liked to talk and he talked well, adorning his speech with terms of endearment and proverbial sayings, which Pierre fancied he often invented himself; but the great charm of his stories lay in the fact that he clothed the simplest incidents – incidents which Pierre might easily have witnessed without taking any particular notice – in a grave seemliness to befit their nature. He liked listening to the folk-tales which one of the soldiers used to tell of an evening (they were always the same ones), but most of all he liked to hear stories of real life. He would listen with a happy smile, now and then putting in a word or asking a question for the purpose of elucidating for himself the moral excellence of what was related to him. Karatayev had no attachments, friendships or loves, as Pierre understood them; but he felt affection for and lived on sympathetic terms with every creature with whom life brought him in contact, and especially with man – not any particular man but those with whom he happened to be. He loved his dog, loved his comrades and the French, loved Pierre who was his neighbour; but Pierre felt that for all Karatayev's warm-heartedness towards him (thus involuntarily paying tribute to Pierre's spiritual life) he would not suffer a pang if they were parted. And Pierre began to feel the same way about Karatayev.

In the eyes of the other prisoners Platon Karatayev was just an

* The Russian word for *peasant*. – [Tr.]

ordinary soldier like the rest of his kind. They called him 'Little falcon' or 'Platosha', chaffed him good-naturedly and sent him on errands. But to Pierre he always remained what he had seemed that first night – an unfathomable, rounded-off, eternal personification of the spirit of simplicity and truth.

Platon Karatayev knew nothing by rote except his prayers. When he opened his mouth to speak he appeared to have no idea how, having once begun, he would finish up.

Sometimes Pierre, struck by the force of his remarks, would ask him to repeat them, but Platon could never recall what he had said a moment before, just as he could never tell Pierre the words of his favourite song. *Mother, little birch-tree* and *my heart is sick* came in but they made no coherent sense. He did not understand and could not grasp the meaning of words apart from their context. Every utterance and action of his was the manifestation of a force uncomprehended by him, which was his life. But his life, as he looked at it, held no meaning as a separate entity. It had meaning only as part of a whole of which he was at all times conscious. His words and actions flowed from him as smoothly, as inevitably and spontaneously as fragrance exhales from a flower. He could not understand the value or significance of any word or deed taken separately.

14

WHEN Princess Maria heard from Nikolai that her brother was with the Rostovs at Yaroslavl she immediately prepared, in spite of her aunt's efforts to dissuade her, to go to him – and to go not alone but to take her nephew with her. She did not ask, and was not interested to find out, whether this would be difficult or not difficult, possible or impossible: it was her duty not only to be with her brother, who might be dying, but to do everything in her power to bring his son to him, and so she set to and made her arrangements. If Prince Andrei had not communicated with her himself no doubt it was because he was too weak to write, or because he considered the long journey too hard and perilous for her and little Nikolai.

In a few days Princess Maria was ready to start. She used the huge family coach in which she had travelled to Voronezh, a semi-open trap and a baggage-wagon, and was accompanied by Mademoiselle

Bourienne, little Nikolai and his tutor, her old nurse, three maids, Tikhon, a young footman and a courier whom her aunt was sending with her.

It was out of the question even to think of going by the usual route, through Moscow, and the roundabout way which Princess Maria was obliged to follow, via Lipetsk, Ryazan, Vladimir and Shuya, was very long and, owing to the dearth of post-horses, extremely arduous; and in the neighbourhood of Ryazan, where the French were said to have shown themselves, positively dangerous.

During this trying journey Mademoiselle Bourienne, Dessalles and Princess Maria's servants were astonished at her tenacity of spirit and energy. She was the last to bed and the first up in the morning, and no obstacle could daunt her. Thanks to her assiduity and verve, which infected her fellow-travellers, by the end of the second week they found themselves approaching Yaroslavl.

The last few days of her stay in Voronezh had been the happiest period of her life. Her love for Rostov no longer tormented or agitated her. It filled her whole soul, had become an integral part of herself, and she no longer struggled against it. Latterly she had become convinced – though she never plainly, in so many words, admitted it to herself – that she loved and was loved. Her last meeting with Nikolai, when he had come to tell her that her brother was with the Rostovs, had persuaded her of this. Not by a single syllable had Nikolai alluded to the possibility of Prince Andrei's engagement to Natasha being renewed (should he recover), but Princess Maria saw by his face that he was aware of this and that it was constantly in his mind. And yet his manner to her – so considerate, gentle and affectionate – not only underwent no change but it sometimes seemed to Princess Maria that he was even glad of the family connexion between them because it allowed him greater liberty to express his loving friendship. She knew that she loved for the first and only time in her life, and felt that she was loved in her turn, and she was happy and at peace with this state of things.

But this happiness did not prevent her feeling the keenest concern for her brother – on the contrary, this spiritual tranquillity, in one sense, left her mind the freer to surrender to her anxiety about Prince Andrei. Her anguish was so intense at the moment of setting out from Voronezh that those who saw her off felt sure as they looked at her care-worn despairing face that she would fall ill on the journey. But its very difficulties and trials, which she tackled so forthrightly, saved her for the time being from her grief, and lent her strength.

As is always the case when one is travelling, Princess Maria was entirely preoccupied with the journey's progress, ignoring its object. But as they approached Yaroslavl the thought presented itself of what might await her there – not now at some future date, at the end of many days, but that very evening – and her agitation increased to its utmost.

The courier, whom she had sent on ahead to find out where the Rostovs were staying in Yaroslavl, and the condition of Prince Andrei, was appalled, when he met the great travelling coach just entering the town gates, by the ghastly pallor of the princess's face that looked out at him from the window.

'I have ascertained everything, your Excellency: the Rostovs are staying in the square, at the merchant Bronnikov's house. It's not far from here, on the banks of the Volga,' said the courier.

Princess Maria gazed at him with frightened inquiry, not understanding what he was saying to her, why he did not answer what she chiefly wanted to know: How was her brother? Mademoiselle Bourienne put the question for her.

'How is the prince?' she asked.

'His Excellency is staying in the same house with them.'

'Then he is alive,' thought Princess Maria, and asked in a low voice 'How is he?'

'The servants say there is no change in his condition.'

What 'no change' might mean Princess Maria did not inquire, and with a swift, scarcely noticeable glance at the little seven-year-old Nikolai, who was sitting in front of her, delighted at the town, she bowed her head and did not look up again till the heavy coach, rumbling, jolting and swaying, came to a stop. The steps were let down with a clatter.

The carriage-door was opened. On the left there was water – a broad river; on the right a porch. There were people at the entrance: servants, and a rosy-faced girl with a thick coil of black hair, smiling as it seemed to Princess Maria in an unpleasantly affected manner. (This was Sonya.) Princess Maria ran up the steps. 'Come in, come in!' said the girl, with the same artificial smile, and the princess found herself in the hall facing an elderly woman with Oriental features, who advanced rapidly to meet her, looking moved. This was the countess.

She put her arms round Princess Maria and proceeded to kiss her.

'My child!' she said in French. 'I love you dearly and have known you a long while.'

In spite of her agitation Princess Maria realized that this was the countess and that she must say something to her. Hardly knowing how she did it, she contrived to utter a few polite phrases in French in the tone in which she had been addressed, and asked: 'How is he?'

'The doctor says there is no danger,' said the countess, but as she spoke she raised her eyes to heaven with a sigh that contradicted her words.

'Where is he? Can I see him, can I?' asked the princess.

'Directly, princess, directly, my dear. Is this his son?' said the countess, turning to little Nikolai who came in with Dessalles. 'We shall find room for everybody, this is a big house. Oh, what a sweet little boy!'

The countess led Princess Maria into the drawing-room, where Sonya was talking to Mademoiselle Bourienne. The countess fondled the child and the old count appeared to welcome the princess. He was extraordinarily changed since Princess Maria had seen him last. Then he had been an alert, cheerful, self-confident little old man: now he seemed a pitiful, bewildered creature. All the time he talked to Princess Maria he kept looking about him, as though he were asking everyone whether he was doing the right thing. After the destruction of Moscow and the loss of his property, thrown out of his accustomed groove, he seemed to have lost his bearings and to feel that there was no longer a place for him in life.

Despite her anxiety, despite her one desire to see her brother as speedily as possible, and her vexation that at the moment when all she wanted was to see him they should be trying to entertain her conventionally with praises of her nephew, the princess took note of all that was going on around her, and felt it incumbent upon her to conform for the time being to the new order of things into which she had stepped. She knew that all this was inevitable, and it was hard for her, yet she bore no grudge against them for it.

'This is my niece,' said the count, introducing Sonya. 'I do not think you have met her, have you, princess?'

Princess Maria turned to Sonya and, trying to smother the rising hostility she felt towards the girl, kissed her. But she was growing painfully aware of the wide gap between the mood of everyone around her and the emotions filling her own breast.

'Where is he?' she asked again, addressing them all.

'He is downstairs. Natasha is with him,' answered Sonya, colouring. 'We have sent to find out if it will be all right. You are tired, I expect, princess?'

Tears of vexation showed in Princess Maria's eyes. She turned away and was about to ask the countess again where to go to him when light, impetuous footsteps that sounded almost gay were heard at the door. The princess looked round and saw Natasha nearly running in – the Natasha whom she had so disliked at their meeting long ago in Moscow.

But Princess Maria had hardly looked at Natasha's face before she realized that here was a true comrade in her grief, and hence a friend. She flew to meet her, hugged her and burst into tears on her shoulder.

As soon as Natasha, sitting by Prince Andrei's bedside, learned of Princess Maria's arrival, she had softly left the room and hastened to her with those swift steps that had sounded so light-hearted to Princess Maria.

There was only one expression on her agitated face when she ran into the drawing-room – an expression of love, of boundless love for him, for her, for all that was near to the man she loved; an expression of pity, of suffering for others, of passionate desire to give herself completely to the task of helping them. It was plain that Natasha's heart at that moment held no thought of self, or of her own relations with Prince Andrei.

Princess Maria with her sensitive intuition saw all this at the first glance, and with sorrowful relief wept on her shoulder.

'Come, let us go to him, Marie,' said Natasha, drawing her away into the next room.

Princess Maria lifted her head, dried her eyes and turned to Natasha. She felt that from her she would be able to know and find out everything

'How ...' she was beginning but stopped short. She felt that no question or answer could be put into words. Natasha's face and eyes would have to tell her all more clearly and with profounder meaning.

Natasha was gazing at her but she seemed to be in dread and in doubt: ought she, or ought she not, to say all she knew? She seemed to feel that before those luminous eyes, piercing to the very depths of her heart, it would be impossible not to tell the truth, the whole truth as she saw it. Natasha's lip suddenly twitched, ugly wrinkles creased her mouth and she broke into sobs, hiding her face in her hands.

Princess Maria understood.

But still she hoped, and asked, though she had no faith in words: 'But how is his wound? What is his general condition?'

'You – you ... will see,' was all Natasha could say.

They sat for a little while downstairs near his room till they had left off crying and were able to go in to him with calm faces.

'What has been the course of his illness? Did the change for the worse occur recently? When did *this* happen?' asked Princess Maria.

Natasha told her that at first his high temperature and the great pain he was in had made his condition dangerous, but when they were at Troitsa this had passed off and the doctor had been afraid of one thing only – gangrene. But the risk of that too was almost over. On their arrival at Yaroslavl the wound had begun to fester (Natasha knew all about such things as festering), and the doctor had said that the festering might take a normal course. Fever had set in. The doctor said this fever was not particularly serious.

'But two days ago *this* suddenly happened,' said Natasha, struggling with her sobs. 'I don't know what it means, but you will see how he is.'

'Has he grown weaker? Is he thinner? ...' queried the princess.

'No, it's not that, but worse. You will see. Oh, Marie, Marie, he is too good, he cannot, cannot live because ...'

15

WHEN Natasha with a practised movement opened Prince Andrei's door for Princess Maria to go in first, the princess felt the sobs rising in her throat. In spite of every effort she made to prepare and control herself she knew that she would be unable to see him without tears.

She understood what Natasha had meant when she said: 'Two days ago *this* suddenly happened.' She understood it to signify that he had suddenly become gentle and resigned, and that this sweet humility could only be the precursor of death. As she approached the door she already saw in her imagination Andrei's face as she remembered it in childhood – tender, diffident, full of feeling. In later life he had rarely looked like that, and so when he did it always affected her deeply.

She was sure he would speak soft, loving words to her such as her father had uttered before his death, and that she would not be able to bear it and would break into sobs in his presence. Yet sooner or later it had to be, and she went into the room. The sobs rose higher and higher in her throat the clearer her short-sighted eyes distinguished his form and tried to make out his features, and then she saw his face and met his gaze.

He was lying on a couch, propped up with pillows, in a squirrel-lined dressing-gown. He was thin and pale. One thin, transparently white hand held a handkerchief; with the other he stroked the delicate moustache that had grown long, moving his fingers slowly. His eyes were turned towards them as they came in.

When she saw his face, and their eyes met, Princess Maria's step suddenly slackened; she felt her tears dry up and her sobs cease. As she caught the expression of his face and eyes she all at once felt shy and guilty.

'But how am I in fault?' she asked herself. 'Because you are alive and your thoughts are on living, while I ...' his cold, stern look replied.

In the deep gaze that seemed to look not outwards from within but inwards upon himself there was something that was almost hostility as he slowly scanned his sister and Natasha.

He kissed his sister, holding her hand in his as was their wont.

'How are you, Marie? How did you manage to get here?' he said in a voice as steady and aloof as his look. Had he uttered a shriek of despair the cry would have struck less horror into Princess Maria's heart than the tone of his voice.

'And have you brought little Nikolai?' he asked in the same slow, quiet manner and with an obvious effort to remember.

'How are you now?' said Princess Maria, wondering herself at what she was saying.

'That, my dear, you must ask the doctor,' he replied, and, evidently making another effort to be affectionate, he said with his lips only (his mind was clearly not on what he was saying):

'Thank you for coming, my dear.'

Princess Maria pressed his hand. The pressure made him wince just perceptibly. He was silent, and she did not know what to say. She understood the change that had come over him two days ago. His speech, his voice, and especially that calm, almost antagonistic look betrayed the detachment from all earthly things which is so terrible for a living man to witness. He plainly found it difficult now to understand the concerns of this world; yet at the same time one felt that he failed to understand, not because he had lost the power of understanding but because he understood something else – something the living did not and could not understand, and that entirely absorbed him.

'Yes, see how strangely fate has brought us together again,' he said, breaking the silence and pointing to Natasha. 'She looks after me all the time.'

Princess Maria listened and could not believe her ears. How could he, the sensitive, tender-hearted Prince Andrei, say such a thing before the girl he loved and who loved him ? If he had any thought of living he could not have said that in that cold, hurtful tone. If he had not known he was dying how could he have failed to feel for her, how could he have spoken like that in her presence ? There could only be one explanation – that he was indifferent to everything, and indifferent because of a revelation of something of far greater importance.

The conversation was unimpassioned, desultory and continually stopping short.

'Marie came by Ryazan,' remarked Natasha.

Prince Andrei did not notice that she called his sister *Marie*. And Natasha only noticed it then for the first time herself.

'Really ?' he said.

'They told her Moscow has been burnt down, right to the ground, as if ...'

Natasha broke off; it was impossible to talk. He was plainly making an effort to listen but yet could not manage to.

'Yes, so they say,' he murmured. 'It is very sad,' and he stared straight before him, his fingers straying absently about his moustache.

'And so you have met Count Nikolai, Marie ?' said Prince Andrei suddenly, apparently trying to say something to please them. 'He wrote home here that he had taken a great liking to you,' he went on, simply and calmly, obviously unable to realize all the complex significance his remark had for living people. 'If you liked him too, it would be a very good thing ... if you were to marry,' he added rather more quickly, as if pleased at having at last found words for which he had long been seeking. Princess Maria heard what he said but it had no significance for her, except inasmuch as it showed how terribly far he was now from all earthly interests.

'Why talk of me?' she said quietly, and glanced at Natasha. Natasha, conscious of this glance, did not look at her. Again the three of them were silent.

'André, would you like ...' Princess Maria said suddenly in a shaky voice. 'Would you like to see little Nikolai? He is always talking of you!'

For the first time Prince Andrei almost smiled, but Princess Maria, who knew his face so well, saw with horror that it was not a smile of pleasure, or of affection for his son, but of quiet, gentle irony at his sister's trying what she believed to be the last means of rousing him.

'Yes, I should like to see little Nikolai very much. Is he all right?'

*

When the little boy was brought into Prince Andrei's room he stared with dismay at his father but did not cry, because nobody else was crying. Prince Andrei kissed him and apparently did not know what to say to him.

After the child had been taken away Princess Maria went up to her brother again, kissed him and, unable to restrain her tears any longer, began to weep.

He looked at her attentively.

'Is it about little Nikolai?' he asked.

Princess Maria nodded her head, sobbing.

'Marie, you know the New Tes –' but he broke off.

'What did you say?'

'Nothing. You mustn't cry here,' he said, looking at her with the same cold expression.

*

When Princess Maria burst into tears he understood that she was crying at the thought of little Nikolai being left without a father. With a great effort he tried to return to life and see things from their point of view.

'Yes, it must seem sad to them,' he thought. 'But how simple it is!

'The fowls of the air sow not, neither do they reap, yet your Father feedeth them,' he said to himself and wanted to say to Princess Maria; 'but no, they would interpret it their own way and not understand! They can't understand that all these feelings of theirs which they set such store by – all the ideas which seem so important to us –

do not matter. We cannot understand one another.' And he fell silent.

*

Prince Andrei's little son was seven years old. He could scarcely read, he knew almost nothing. He was to go through much after that day, gaining knowledge, observation, experience; but had he enjoyed the mastery at that time of all he acquired later he could not have had a truer or more profound comprehension of the meaning of the scene he had witnessed between his father, Princess Maria and Natasha than he had then. He understood it from beginning to end and, without shedding a tear, left the room, crept up to Natasha who followed him out and looked shyly at her with his beautiful, dreamy eyes. His uplifted, rosy upper lip quivered, he leaned his head against her and wept.

From that day he avoided Dessalles and the countess, who would have petted him, and either stayed by himself or timidly joined Princess Maria or Natasha, of whom he seemed even fonder than of his aunt, and clung to them quietly and shyly.

Princess Maria left Prince Andrei's side, realizing to the full what Natasha's face had told her. She spoke no more to Natasha about any hope of saving his life. She took turns with her in sitting beside his couch, and shed no more tears but prayed without ceasing, addressing her spirit to the Eternal and Unfathomable Whose presence about the dying man was now so palpable.

16

PRINCE ANDREI not only knew he was going to die but felt that he was dying, that he was already half dead. He felt remote from everything earthly and was conscious of a strange and joyous lightness in his being. Neither impatient nor anxious, he awaited what lay before him. That sinister, eternal, unknown and distant something which he had sensed throughout his life was now close upon him and – as he knew by the strange lightness of being that he experienced – almost comprehensible and tangible. ...

In the past he had dreaded the end. Twice he had experienced the frightful agony which is the fear of death, of the end, but now that fear meant nothing to him.

The first time was when the shell was spinning like a top before him, and he had looked at the stubble-field, at the bushes, at the sky, and known that he was face to face with death. When he had recovered consciousness after his wound, and instantly, as though set free from the cramping bondage of life, the flower of eternal unfettered love had opened out in his soul, he had had no more fear and no more thought of death.

During the hours of solitude, suffering and half-delirium that he spent after he was wounded, the more deeply he penetrated this new principle of eternal love which had been revealed to him, the more he unconsciously detached himself from earthly life. To love everything and everybody, always to sacrifice self for love, meant to love no one in particular, meant not to live this mundane life. And the more imbued he became with this principle of love, the more he let go of life and the more completely he annihilated that fearful barrier which – in the absence of such love – stands between life and death. Whenever, during that first period, he remembered that he had to die, he said to himself: 'Well, what of it? So much the better!'

But after the night at Mytishchy when, half delirious, he had seen her for whom he longed appear before him, and pressing her hand to his lips had wept soft, happy tears, love for one particular woman had stolen unobserved into his heart and bound him again to life. And glad and agitating thoughts began to occupy his mind. Recalling the moment at the ambulance-station when he had seen Kuragin, he could not now regain the feeling he had then. He was tormented by the question: 'Is he alive?' And he dared not inquire.

His illness pursued its normal physical course, but what Natasha referred to when she said 'This suddenly happened' had occurred two days before Princess Maria's arrival. It was the last spiritual struggle between life and death, in which death gained the victory. It was the unexpected realization that life, in the shape of his love for Natasha, was still precious to him, and a last, though ultimately vanquished, onslaught of terror before the unknown.

It happened in the evening. As usual after dinner he was slightly feverish, and his thoughts were preternaturally clear. Sonya was sitting at the table. He fell into a doze. Suddenly he was conscious of a glow of happiness.

'Ah, she has come!' he thought.

And so it was: in Sonya's place sat Natasha who had just crept noiselessly in.

Ever since she had begun looking after him he had always had this instinctive awareness of her presence. She was sitting in a low chair placed sideways so as to screen the light of the candle from him, and was knitting a stocking. (She had learned to knit after Prince Andrei had casually remarked that no one made such a good sick-nurse as an old nanny who knitted stockings, and that there was something soothing about knitting.) The needles clicked in her swiftly moving fingers, and then he could see quite clearly the pensive profile of her bent head. She shifted a little, and the ball of wool rolled from her lap. She started, glanced round at him, and shading the candle with her hand stooped carefully with a supple, precise movement, picked up the ball and sat back as before.

He watched her without stirring and saw that she wanted to draw a deep breath after picking up the wool, but refrained from doing so and breathed cautiously.

At the Troitsa monastery they had spoken of the past, and he had told her that if he lived he would always thank God for his wound, which had brought them together again; but since then they had never mentioned the future.

'Could it be, or could it not?' he was wondering now as he looked at her and listened to the light click of the steel needles. 'Can fate have brought us together so strangely only for me to die? ... Can the truth of life have been revealed to me only to give my whole life the lie? I love her more than anything in the world! But what am I to do if I love her?' he said to himself, and he involuntarily groaned, from a habit he had fallen into in the course of his sufferings.

Hearing the sound, Natasha laid down her stocking, leaned nearer to him and suddenly, noticing his shining eyes, went up to him with a light step and bent over him.

'You are not asleep?'

'No, I have been looking at you a long time. I felt you come in. No one else gives me that sweet sense of tranquillity ... that radiance. I could weep for joy.'

Natasha moved closer to him. Her face shone blissful with happiness.

'Natasha, I love you too much. More than anything in the world.'

'And I?' She turned away for a second. 'But why too much?' she asked.

'Why too much? ... Well, what do you think, what do you feel in your heart – in your heart of hearts: am I going to live? What do you think about it?'

'I am sure of it, sure of it!' Natasha almost shouted, seizing both his hands in hers with a passionate gesture.

He was silent awhile.

'How good that would be!' – and taking her hand he kissed it.

Natasha felt happy and deeply stirred; but at once remembered that this would not do and that he must be kept quiet.

'But you have not slept,' she said, subduing her joy. 'Try and sleep ... please!'

He pressed her hand and let it go, and she moved back to the candle and sat down again in the same position as before. Twice she glanced round at him and met his shining eyes fixed on her. She set herself a stint on the stocking and resolved not to look round till she had finished it.

He did, in fact, soon shut his eyes and fall asleep. He did not sleep long, and woke with a start and in a cold perspiration.

As he fell asleep he was still thinking of the subject which now occupied his mind all the time – of life and death. And of death more than life. He felt nearer to death.

'Love? What is love?' he mused.

'Love hinders death. Love is life. Anything at all that I understand, I understand only because I love. Everything is – everything exists – only because I love. All is bound up in love alone. Love is God, and to die means that I, a tiny particle of love, shall return to the universal and eternal source.' These thoughts seemed comforting to him. But they were only thoughts. There was something lacking in them, they were confused and too one-sidedly personal, too intellectual. And he was a prey to the same restlessness and uncertainty. He fell asleep.

He dreamed that he was lying in the room in which he actually was lying, but that he had not been wounded and was quite well. Many various people, indifferent, insignificant people, appear before him. He is talking to them, arguing about some trifle. They are preparing to set off somewhere. Prince Andrei dimly realizes that all this is trivial and that he has other far more serious matters to attend to, but still he continues to speak, surprising them by empty witticisms. Gradually, imperceptibly, all these persons begin to disappear, to be replaced by a single question, that of the closed door. He gets up and goes towards the door in order to shoot the bolt and lock it. Everything depends on whether he can lock it quickly enough. He starts, tries to hurry but his legs refuse to move and he knows he will not be in time to lock the door, yet he still frenziedly strains every effort to get there. Agonizing fear seizes him. And this fear is the fear of death: *It* stands behind the door. But while he is helplessly and clumsily stumbling towards the door that dreadful something is already pushing against it on the other side and forcing its way in. Something not human – death – is breaking in through the door and he must hold the door to. He grapples with the door, straining every ounce of his strength – to lock it is no longer possible – but his efforts are feeble and awkward, and the door, under the pressure of that awful thing, opens and shuts again.

Once more *It* pushes on the door from without. His last superhuman struggles are vain and both leaves of the door are noiselessly opened. *It* comes in, and it is *death*. And Prince Andrei died.

But at the very instant when in his dream he died Prince Andrei remembered that he was asleep, and at the very instant when he died he exerted himself and was awake.

'Yes, that was death. I died – and woke up. Yes, death is an awakening!' His soul was suddenly flooded with light, and the veil which till then had concealed the unknown was lifted from his spiritual vision. He felt as if powers hitherto confined within him had been set free, and was aware of that strange lightness of being which had not left him since.

When, waking in a cold perspiration, he stirred on the couch, Natasha went up and asked him what was the matter. He did not answer and looked at her oddly, not understanding.

This was what had taken place two days before Princess Maria's arrival. From that hour the wasting fever assumed a malignant character, as the doctor expressed it, but Natasha was not interested in what the doctor said: she saw the terrible psychological symptoms which to her were far more convincing.

With his awakening from sleep that day there began for Prince Andrei an awakening from life. And in relation to the duration of life it did not seem to him more prolonged than the awakening from sleep compared to the duration of his dream.

There was nothing terrible or violent in this relatively slow awakening.

His last days and hours passed in an ordinary and simple way.

Both Princess Maria and Natasha, who never left his side, felt this. They did not weep or shudder, and towards the end felt that they were attending not on him (he was no longer there, he had gone from them) but on their most immediate remembrance of him – his body. Both were so deeply conscious of this that the external, horrible side of death did not affect them, and they did not find it necessary to foment their grief. Neither in his presence nor away from him did they weep, nor did they ever talk of him to one another. They felt that they could not express in words what was real to their understanding.

The two of them saw that he was slowly and quietly slipping farther and farther away from them, and both knew that this had to be so and that it was well.

He was confessed and given the sacrament; everyone came to bid him farewell. When they brought his son to him he pressed his lips to the boy's and turned away, not because his heart ached or was sorrowful (Princess Maria and Natasha saw that) but simply because he supposed he had done all that was required of him; but when they told him to give the child his blessing he did what was demanded, and looked round as though to ask whether there was anything else he must do.

When the last convulsions of the body occurred, which the spirit was leaving, Princess Maria and Natasha were in the room.

'Is it over?' said Princess Maria after the body had lain for some moments motionless and growing cold before them. Natasha went up, looked into the dead eyes and made haste to close them. She closed them and did not kiss them but clung to that which was the most actual reminder of him – his body.

'Where has he gone? Where is he now? ...'

When the body, washed and clothed, lay in the coffin on the table everyone went up to take leave of him, and everyone wept.

Little Nikolai cried because his heart was torn with perplexity. The countess and Sonya cried from pity for Natasha and because he was no more. The old count cried because he felt that before long he too must step over the same terrible threshold.

Natasha and Princess Maria wept too now, but they wept not because of their own personal grief: they wept from the emotion and awe which took possession of their souls before the simple and solemn mystery of death that had been accomplished before their eyes.

PART TWO

I

It is beyond the power of the human intellect to encompass *all* the causes of any phenomenon. But the impulse to search into causes is inherent in man's very nature. And so the human intellect, without investigating the multiplicity and complexity of circumstances conditioning an event, any one of which taken separately may seem to be the reason for it, snatches at the first most comprehensible approximation to a cause and says: 'There is the cause!' In historical events (where the actions of men form the subject of observation) the primeval conception of a cause was the will of the gods, succeeded later on by the will of those who stand in the historical foreground – the heroes of history. But we have only to look below the surface of any historical event, to inquire, that is, into the activity of the whole mass of people who took part in the event, to become convinced that the will of our historical hero, so far from ruling the actions of the multitude, is itself continuously controlled. It might be thought that it is a matter of indifference whether historical events are interpreted this way or that. But between the man who says that the nations of the West marched into the East because Napoleon wished it and the man who believes that it happened because it had to happen, the difference is as wide as between those who maintained that the earth is stationary and the planets revolve round it, and those who admitted that they did not know what holds the earth in place but knew there were laws directing its movement and that of the other planets. There is, and can be, no cause of an historical event save the one cause of all causes. But there are laws governing events: some we are ignorant of, others we are groping our way to. The discovery of these laws becomes possible only when we finally give up looking for such causes in the will of any one man, just as the discovery of the laws of the motion of the planets was possible only when men renounced the conception of the earth as stationary.

After the battle of Borodino and the enemy occupation of Moscow and its destruction by fire, the most important episode of the war of 1812, in the opinion of historians, was the movement of the Russian army from the Ryazan to the Kaluga road and to the Tarutino camp – the so-called flank march across the Krasnaya Pakhra river. Historians ascribe the glory of this achievement of genius to various commanders, and dispute as to whom the honour is due. Even foreign – even French – historians admit the genius of the Russian generals when speaking of that flank march. But why military writers, and others following their lead, should assume this oblique movement to be the perspicacious design of some one individual who thereby saved Russia and destroyed Napoleon – it is extremely difficult to see. In the first place it is difficult to see where the acumen and genius of this march lies; for no great mental effort is needed to perceive that the best position for an army (when it is not being attacked) is where supplies are most plentiful. And anyone, even a not very bright boy of thirteen, might have supposed that the most advantageous position for the army after its retreat from Moscow in 1812 would be on the Kaluga road. And so it is impossible to understand, in the first place, what conclusions lead the historians to see some profound wisdom in this manoeuvre. Secondly, it is even more difficult to understand just why they should attribute the salvation of Russia and the downfall of the French to this manoeuvre; for this flank march, had it been preceded, accompanied or followed by other circumstances, might have meant the ruin of the Russians and the saving of the French. If the position of the Russian army did, in fact, begin to improve from the time of that march, it does not at all ensue that the improvement was consequent on the march.

That flank march might not only have brought no advantage to the Russian army: it might have been fatal but for the conjunction of other circumstances. What would have happened had Moscow not been burned? If Murat had not lost track of the Russians? If Napoleon had not remained inactive? If, as Bennigsen and Barclay advised, the Russian army had given battle at Krasnaya Pakhra? What would have happened had the French attacked the Russians when they were on the march the other side of the Pakhra? What would have happened if later on Napoleon, on reaching Tarutino, had attacked the Russians with one-tenth of the energy he had displayed at Smolensk? What would have happened had the French moved on Petersburg?

... On any one of these hypotheses the oblique march that brought salvation might have proved disastrous.

The third point, and the most difficult of all to understand, is that students of history deliberately shut their eyes to the fact that this flank march cannot be ascribed to any one man, that no one ever anticipated it, that, like the retreat to Fili, the manoeuvre was, in reality, never conceived of as a whole but came about step by step, incident by incident, moment by moment, as the result of an infinite number of most diverse conditions, and was only seen in its entirety when it was a *fait accompli* and belonged to the past.

At the council at Fili the prevailing thought in the minds of the Russian command was retreat by the most direct and obvious route – the Nizhni Novgorod road. Evidence of this is that the majority of votes at the council were for adopting this course, and, above all, the commander-in-chief's famous conversation after the council with Lansky, who was in charge of the commissariat. Lansky reported to the commander-in-chief that the army supplies were for the most part stored along the Oka, in the Tula and Kaluga provinces, and that if they retreated along the Nizhni Novgorod road the army would be separated from its supplies by the broad river Oka, across which transport in early winter was impossible. This was the first indication of the necessity for revising the plan of a direct retreat on Nizhni, which had previously seemed so natural. The army kept more to the south, along the Ryazan road, closer to its supplies. Subsequently the inactivity of the French, who actually lost sight of the Russian army, concern for the defence of the arsenal at Tula and, in the main, the advantages of getting nearer to its provisions, made the army incline still further south, to the Tula road. Having crossed over, by a forced march, to the Tula road beyond the Pakhra, the Russian commanders intended to halt at Podolsk and had no thought of taking up a position at Tarutino; but innumerable circumstances, as well as the reappearance on the scene of the French troops, who for a time had lost touch with the Russians, and plans for giving battle and, above all, the abundance of supplies in Kaluga constrained our army to turn still more south and switch from the Tula to the Kaluga road and on to Tarutino, through the country where those supplies lay. Just as it is impossible to say at what date the decision was taken to abandon Moscow, so it is impossible to say precisely when and by whom it was decided to move to Tarutino. It was only after the army had got there, as the result of an infinite number of diverse factors, that people began to assure themselves that they had long desired and foreseen this move.

2

THE famous flank movement consisted simply in this: the Russian army, which had been retreating directly back as the invaders pushed forward, as soon as the French attack ceased digressed from the straight course they had embarked on at first and, finding they were not pursued, naturally inclined towards the locality where supplies were abundant.

If we imagine, instead of generals of genius at the head of the Russian army, an army acting alone, without leadership of any kind, such an army could not have done anything else but retire towards Moscow, describing a semicircle through country where provisions were the most plentiful and which was richest.

So natural was this transfer from the Nizhni to the Ryazan, Tula and Kaluga roads that even the stragglers from the Russian army fled in that direction, and Petersburg ordered Kutuzov to take that route. At Tarutino Kutuzov received what was almost a reprimand from the Emperor for moving the army to the Ryazan road, and he was enjoined to occupy the very position facing Kaluga in which he was encamped at the time the Tsar's letter reached him.

Having rolled like a ball in the direction of the impetus given by the campaign as a whole and by the battle of Borodino, the Russian army, as the force of the blow spent itself and no new blows came, assumed the position natural to it.

Kutuzov's merit did not lie in any strategic manoeuvre of genius, as it is called, but in the fact that he alone appreciated the significance of what had happened. He was the only one at the time to understand the meaning of the French army's inactivity; he alone persisted in maintaining that the battle of Borodino was a victory; he alone who as commander-in-chief might have been expected to favour aggressive measures – did everything in his power to hold the Russian army back from useless fighting.

The wild beast wounded at Borodino lay where the fleeing huntsman had left him; but whether he was still alive, whether he still had his strength and was only lying low, the huntsman did not know. Suddenly the animal was heard to moan. The moan of the wounded creature (the French army) which betrayed its hopeless plight was the dispatch of Lauriston to Kutuzov's camp with overtures for peace.

Napoleon, with his usual assurance, not that right was right but that whatever occurred to his mind was right, wrote to Kutuzov the first words to come into his head, words that were quite meaningless. He wrote:

Monsieur le prince Koutouzov [he wrote],

I am sending you one of my adjutants-general to discuss with you various matters of interest. I beg your Highness to credit what he says to you, *especially when he expresses the sentiments of esteem and particular regard that I have long entertained for your person.* ... This letter having no other object, I pray God, *Monsieur le prince Koutouzov*, to have you in His holy and gracious keeping.

(Signed) NAPOLÉON

Moscow, 3rd October, 1812.

Kutuzov replied:

I should be cursed by posterity were I regarded as the first to take any steps towards a settlement of any sort. *Such is the spirit of my nation.*

And he continued to put forth all his energies to restrain his troops from attacking.

During the month spent by the French in pillaging Moscow and by the Russian army quietly encamped at Tarutino a change had taken place in the relative strength of the two belligerent forces – a change both in spirit and in numbers – which was all to the advantage of the Russian side. Although the condition of the French army and its numerical strength were unknown to the Russians, as soon as that change occurred signs in plenty appeared urgently calling attention to the indispensability of attacking. These signs were: Lauriston's mission; the abundance of provisions at Tarutino; the reports coming in from all sides of the inactivity and disorder of the French; the flow of recruits to our regiments; the fine weather; the long spell of rest the Russian soldiers had enjoyed, and their impatience (usual in troops that have been resting) to do the work for which they had been brought together; curiosity as to what was going on in the French army, of which nothing had been seen for so long; the audacity with which our outposts now scouted around the French encamped at Tarutino; the news of easy successes gained by peasants and guerilla bands over the French, and the envy thus aroused; the desire for vengeance that lay in the heart of every Russian so long as the French were in Moscow; and – paramount factor – the vague consciousness in every soldier's mind that the relative strength of the armies was reversed, and now that we had the superiority. A substantial change had occurred in the relative strength of the opposing forces, and advance had become inevitable. And at once, as surely as a clock begins to strike and chime when the minute hand has completed a full circle, this change was reflected in an increased activity, whirring and chiming in the higher spheres.

3

THE Russian army was commanded by Kutuzov and his Staff, and by the Emperor from Petersburg. Even before the news of the abandonment of Moscow had reached Petersburg a detailed plan for the whole campaign had been drawn up and sent to Kutuzov for his guidance. Although this plan had been conceived on the supposition that Moscow was still in our hands, it was approved by the Staff and accepted as the basis for action. Kutuzov replied only that movements arranged from a distance were always difficult to execute. So fresh instructions were dispatched for the solution of problems that might be encountered, as well as fresh people whose duty it would be to watch Kutuzov's actions and report upon them.

Besides this, the entire high command of the Russian army was now reorganized. The posts left vacant by Bagration, who had been killed, and Barclay, who had gone away in dudgeon, had to be filled. Very serious consideration was given to the question whether it would be better to put A in B's place and B in D's, or on the contrary to put D in A's place, and so on – as though anything more than A's or B's satisfaction depended on this.

In consequence of the hostility between Kutuzov and his chief of staff, Bennigsen, of the presence of confidential representatives of the Emperor, and of these transfers, the play of party intrigue at headquarters was more than usually complicated: A was trying to undermine B, B was undermining C, and so on in all possible combinations and permutations. In all these plottings the subject of intrigue was for the most part the conduct of the war, which all these people believed they were controlling; but this affair of the war continued independently of them, following the course it had to – that is, a course that never corresponded to the schemes of these men but was the outcome of the intrinsic reaction of the masses. Only in the higher spheres did all these schemes, thwarting and conflicting with one another, appear as a true index of what must inevitably come to pass.

Prince Mihail Ilarionovich [wrote the Emperor on the 2nd of October in a letter that reached Kutuzov after the battle of Tarutino]

Since the 2nd of September Moscow has been in the hands of the enemy. Your last reports were dated the 20th, and in all this time not only has no action been attempted against the enemy or for the relief of the ancient capital but according to your last reports you have even made a further retreat. Serpuhov is already occupied by an enemy detachment, and Tula with its famous arsenal, so indispensable to the army, is in danger. From General Wintzingerode's reports I see that an enemy corps ten thousand strong is moving on the Petersburg road. Another, numbering several thousand men, is marching upon Dmitrov. A third has advanced along the Vladimir road. A fourth, of considerable size, is concentrated between Ruza and Mozhaisk. Napoleon himself was in Moscow as late as the 25th. In view of all this information, with the enemy having split up his effectives in these large detachments, with Napoleon himself and his Guards in Moscow, is it possible that the enemy force confronting you is so considerable as not to allow of your taking the offensive? One must, with far more probability, assume that you are being pursued by detachments, or at most an army corps far inferior to the army under your command. It would seem that, availing yourself of these circumstances, you might with advantage have attacked an enemy weaker than yourself, and annihilated him, or at least have obliged him to retreat, and have kept in our hands a goodly part of the provinces now occupied by the enemy, and thereby have averted danger from Tula and the other towns of the interior. You will be responsible if the enemy is able to direct a considerable body of men against Petersburg, to menace that capital in which it has not been possible to retain any great number of troops; for with the army entrusted to you, and acting with energy and decision, you have ample means at your disposal for averting this fresh calamity. Remember that you have still to answer to your injured country for the loss of Moscow. You have had experience of my readiness to reward you. That readiness will not grow less, but I and Russia have a right to expect from you all the zeal, firmness and success which your intellect, your military talents and the valour of the troops under your command presage.

But while this letter – which showed that the change in the relative strength of the opposing forces was by now making itself felt in

Petersburg too – was on the road Kutuzov had found himself unable to hold his army back, and a battle had already been fought.

On the 2nd of October a Cossack, Shapovalov, out scouting, shot a hare and wounded a second. In pursuit of the wounded hare, he made his way deep into the forest and stumbled upon the left flank of Murat's army encamped there and quite off its guard. The Cossack laughingly told his comrades how he had all but fallen into the hands of the French. An ensign who heard the story informed his commander.

The Cossack was sent for and questioned. The officers of the Cossacks wanted to take advantage of this chance to capture some horses from the French, but one of the superior officers, who was intimate with the higher authorities, reported the incident to a general on the Staff. Latterly, relations on the Staff had been strained to the limit. A few days back Yermolov had gone to Bennigsen and besought him to use his influence with the commander-in-chief to induce him to take the offensive.

'If I did not know you I should think you did not want what you are asking for. I have only to advise one course for his Serene Highness without fail to do exactly the opposite,' replied Bennigsen.

The news brought by the Cossacks, confirmed by scouts riding out on horseback, proved conclusively that the time was ripe. The tight coil sprang, the clock-wheels whirred and the chimes began to play. Despite all his supposed power, his intellect, his experience and his knowledge of men, Kutuzov – in view of a note from Bennigsen (who sent personal reports to the Emperor), the desire expressed by all the generals alike, the wishes the Emperor was presumed to hold, and the information brought by the Cossacks – could no longer restrain the inescapable move forward, and gave the order for what he regarded as useless and mischievous – gave his assent, that is, to the accomplished fact.

4

BENNIGSEN's note pressing for aggressive action and the report received from the Cossacks that the French left flank was uncovered were merely the final indications that the signal for an offensive could no longer be delayed, and the attack was fixed for the 5th of October.

On the morning of the 4th of October Kutuzov signed the dispositions. Toll read them to Yermolov, asking him to attend to the further arrangements.

'Very good, very good, but I can't possibly see about it now,' replied Yermolov, and left the hut.

The dispositions as drawn up by Toll were perfectly satisfactory. Just as for the battle of Austerlitz it was stated – though not in German this time – that 'the first column will proceed this way and that way, the second column will proceed to this place and that place', and so on. And on paper all these columns arrived in their places at the appointed moment and routed the enemy. Everything had been admirably thought out, as dispositions always are, and as is always the case not a single column reached its objective at the appointed time.

When the necessary number of copies of the dispositions were ready an officer was summoned and sent to deliver them to Yermolov to deal with. A young officer of the Horse Guards, Kutuzov's orderly, pleased with the importance of the mission entrusted to him, set off for Yermolov's quarters.

'The general has ridden out,' Yermolov's orderly told him.

The officer of the Horse Guards went to the lodgings of a general in whose company Yermolov was often to be found.

'Not here, nor the general either.'

The officer, mounting his horse again, rode off to someone else.

'No, he's gone out,'

'Hope I shan't be held accountable for this delay! Deuce take it!' thought the officer.

He rode all over the camp. One man declared he had seen Yermolov ride past with some other generals; others, that he must have returned home by now. Without stopping to eat, the officer searched till six o'clock in the evening. Yermolov was nowhere to be found, and no one knew where he was. The officer snatched a hasty meal at a comrade's and started off again to the vanguard to see Miloradovich. Miloradovich too was away, but here he was told that he had gone to a ball at General Kikin's and that Yermolov was probably there as well.

'But where is that?'

'Over yonder at Yechkino,' said a Cossack officer, pointing to a country house in the far distance.

'What, beyond our lines?'

'Two regiments of our fellows have been sent out to the outposts.

1176

The devil of a spree they're having! A couple of bands, three sets of singers!'

The officer rode out beyond our lines to Yechkino. When he was still a long way from the house he heard the cheerful strains of a soldier's dance boisterously sung in chorus.

'In the mea-dows ... in the mea-dows!' he heard, accompanied by whistling and the sound of an instrument like a balalaika, drowned every now and then in a roar of voices. The officer's spirits rose as he listened, but at the same time he was afraid that he would be blamed for having been so long in delivering the weighty message entrusted to him. It was by now past eight o'clock. He dismounted and walked up to the porch and into the hall of a large country house which had remained intact, half-way between the Russians and the French. In an ante-room and in the hall footmen were bustling about with wines and refreshments. Groups of singers stood under the windows. The officer was admitted and immediately saw all the top generals of the army together, among them the big, imposing figure of Yermolov. They all had their coats unbuttoned and were standing in a semicircle with flushed and animated faces. In the middle of the room a short, handsome general with a red face was performing the steps of the *trepak* with much skill and spirit.

'Ha, ha, ha! Bravo, Nikolai Ivanovich! Ha, ha, ha! ...'

The officer felt doubly guilty at breaking in with important business at such a moment, and he would have waited; but one of the generals caught sight of him, and on hearing what he had come about, informed Yermolov. Yermolov came forward with a frown, listened to what the officer had to say and took the papers from him without a word.

'Do you suppose it was mere chance that he had gone off?' said a comrade of the Horse Guards officer, who was on the Staff, speaking of Yermolov that evening. 'Not a bit of it! It was done on purpose, to get Konovnitsyn into trouble. You see, there'll be a pretty kettle of fish tomorrow!'

5

NEXT day the decrepit old Kutuzov rose early, said his prayers, dressed and, with an unpleasant consciousness that he must now direct a battle he did not approve of, got into his carriage and drove to Letashovka (a village three and a half miles from Tarutino) to the place where the attacking columns were to meet. As he was driven along in the calèche he kept dozing and waking again, and listening for any sound of firing on the right which might indicate that the action had begun. But all was still quiet. A damp, overcast autumn morning was just dawning. As they approached Tarutino Kutuzov noticed cavalrymen leading their horses to water across the road along which he was driving. Kutuzov looked at them searchingly, stopped his carriage and inquired what regiment they belonged to. They were part of a column which should have been far to the front and in ambush long ago. 'It may be a mistake,' thought the old commander-in-chief. But a little farther on he saw infantry with their arms stacked, and the men in their drawers busy cooking rye-porridge and fetching wood. He sent for their officer. The officer reported that no order to advance had been received.

'No or – ' Kutuzov began, but checked himself immediately and summoned a senior officer. He climbed out of his calèche and paced silently up and down as he waited, with drooping head and breathing heavily. When Eykhen, the officer of the General Staff whom he had sent for, appeared Kutuzov turned purple with rage, not because that officer was to blame for the blunder but because he was an officer of sufficient status for him to vent his wrath on. Shaking and spluttering, the old man fell into one of those paroxysms of fury in which he would sometimes roll on the ground in frenzy, and flew at Eykhen, shaking his fists at him and shouting abuse in the language of the gutter. Another officer, Captain Brozin, who happened to appear and who was in no way to blame, came in for the same fate.

'And – what *canaille* are you? I'll have you shot, you scoundrels!' yelled Kutuzov in a hoarse voice, waving his arms and reeling.

He was in a state of actual physical suffering. He, the commander-in-chief, his Serene Highness who, everybody kept saying, had more power than any man had ever possessed in Russia, to be placed in such a position – made the laughing-stock of the whole army! 'Worrying and praying about today, staying awake the whole night going over and over everything – all sheer waste!' he thought to himself. 'Why, when I was a mere junior officer no one would have dared make a fool of me like this ... but now!' He felt real physical pain as though he had suffered corporal punishment, and could not help giving expression to it by cries of anger and distress. But soon his strength was exhausted, and looking about him, conscious of having said a great deal that was amiss, he got into his carriage and drove back in silence.

His fury once spent did not return, and, feebly blinking his eyes, Kutuzov listened to excuses and self-justifications (Yermolov kept out of sight till next day), and to the urgent representations of Bennigsen, Konovnitsyn and Toll that the movement that had miscarried should be executed on the morrow. And once more Kutuzov had to consent.

6

NEXT day the troops assembled at their appointed places in the evening and advanced during the night. It was an autumn night with dark purple clouds but no rain. The ground was damp but not muddy, and the troops proceeded noiselessly, except for an occasional faint clanking of the artillery. The men had been forbidden to talk above a whisper, to smoke their pipes or strike a light, and they tried to keep the horses from neighing. The secrecy of the enterprise heightened its attraction. The men tramped on blithely. Several columns halted, stacked their arms and lay down on the chilly ground, supposing they had reached their destination; others (the majority) marched all night and arrived at places that were obviously not intended.

Count Orlov-Denisov with his Cossacks (the least important detachment of all) was the only one to get to the right place at the right time. This detachment halted at the outskirts of a forest, on the path leading from the village of Stromilovo to Dmitrovsk.

Towards dawn Count Orlov-Denisov, who had dozed off, was awakened. A deserter from the French camp had been brought in. It was a Polish sergeant of Poniatowski's corps. He explained in Polish that he had come over because he had been slighted in the Service: he ought long ago to have been made an officer, he was braver than any of them, and so he had left and wanted to pay them out. He said that Murat was spending the night less than three-quarters of a mile away, and if they would let him have a convoy of a hundred men he would capture him alive. Count Orlov-Denisov consulted with his fellow-officers. The offer was too tempting to be refused. Everyone clamoured to go, everyone was in favour of the attempt. After much disputing and arguing Major-General Grekov, with two regiments of Cossacks, decided to go with the Polish sergeant.

'Well mark my words,' said Count Orlov-Denisov to the Polish deserter, as he dismissed him, 'if you have been lying I'll have you hanged like a dog; but if your story's true there'll be a hundred gold pieces for you.'

The sergeant made no reply, and with a resolute air sprang into the saddle and rode away with Grekov, who had quickly mustered his men. The party disappeared into the forest. Count Orlov, having seen Grekov off, returned, shivering from the freshness of the early dawn and strung up by the step he had undertaken on his own responsibility, and began scanning the enemy camp, now just discernible in the deceptive light of approaching daybreak and the dying camp-fires. Our columns ought by now to be showing themselves on an open declivity to his right. He looked in that direction, but though they would have been visible a long way off there were no columns to be seen. In the French camp the count fancied – and his keen-sighted adjutant confirmed the impression – that things were beginning to stir.

'Oh, of course it's too late,' said Count Orlov, staring at the camp.

As often happens when someone we have trusted is no longer before our eyes, it suddenly seemed perfectly clear and obvious that the deserter was an impostor, that he had told them a pack of lies, and that the whole attack would now be ruined because of the absence of those two regiments, which the man would lead away heaven only knew where. How could they possibly seize and capture a commander-in-chief from among such a mass of troops?

'Of course the wretch was lying,' said the count.

'We could recall Grekov,' said one of his suite, who like Count Orlov felt doubtful of the adventure when he looked at the enemy's camp.

'Ha? You really think so? What would you do – let them go on, or not?'

'Are your orders to fetch them back?'

'Yes, fetch them back!' said Count Orlov with sudden determination, glancing at his watch. 'It would be too late. It's quite light.'

And the adjutant galloped into the woods after Grekov. When Grekov came back Count Orlov-Denisov, keyed up by the abandoned venture and the vain wait for the infantry column which still did not appear, as well as by the proximity of the enemy, decided to advance. (All his men were feeling the same way.)

'To horse!' he commanded in a whisper. Every man fell into his place and crossed himself. ...

'In God's name, forward!'

'Hurrah-ah-ah!' reverberated through the forest, and the Cossacks, trailing their lances, one company after another as though poured out of a sack, flew gaily across the brook towards the enemy camp.

One desperate frightened yell from the first French soldier to catch sight of the Cossacks, and all in the camp, half-dressed, half-asleep, fled blindly, abandoning artillery, muskets and horses.

Had the Cossacks chased the French, instead of turning their attention to what they left behind and around them, they could have taken both Murat and everything else that was there. This was what the officers tried to make them do. But it was impossible to budge the Cossacks once they got to capturing booty and prisoners. No one heeded the word of command. Fifteen hundred prisoners and thirty-eight guns were taken on the spot, besides standards and, what was of most consequence in the eyes of the Cossacks, horses, saddles, blankets and the like. All this they wanted to see after, to secure prisoners and guns, to divide the spoils – not without some shouting and even a certain amount of fighting – and it was on this that the Cossacks busied themselves.

The French, finding that they were no longer pursued, gradually began to rally: they formed up into detachments and began firing. Orlov-Denisov was still waiting for the other columns to arrive, and did not advance further.

Meanwhile, in accordance with the dispositions – *the first column will proceed,* and so on – the infantry of the belated columns, under the command of Bennigsen and the direction of Toll, had started off in due order and had, in the usual way, arrived somewhere, only not at the place that was intended. As always happens, men who had started out cheerfully began to falter; murmurs were heard, it was felt that a muddle had occurred, and they were marched back to some point. Adjutants and generals galloped to and fro, shouted, lost their tempers, quarrelled, told each other that they had come quite wrong and were late, gave vent to a little abuse, etc., and finally all washed their hands of the whole business and went forward simply in order to get somewhere. 'We must arrive at some place or other!' And so they did indeed, though not where they should have got – the few who did eventually reach their proper destination reached it too late to be of any use and only in time to be fired on. Toll, who in this battle played the part that Weierother had filled at Austerlitz, galloped assiduously from place to place, always finding everything at sixes and sevens. Thus he stumbled on Bagovut's corps in a wood when it was already broad daylight, though the corps ought long ago to have joined Orlov-Denisov. Exasperated at the miscarriage, and supposing that someone was to blame, Toll galloped up to the commander of the corps and began upbraiding him severely, saying that he deserved to be shot. Bagovut, a sturdy old general of placid temperament, also being upset by all the delay, confusion and contradictory orders, to everybody's amazement fell into a rage, quite out of keeping with his usual character, and answered Toll somewhat offensively.

'I am not going to be lectured by anyone. I know as well as the next man how to face death with my soldiers,' and he moved forward with a single division.

Coming out on to a field under the enemy's fire, the valiant general, without stopping to consider in his agitation whether (now and with only one division) his advance into action was likely to be of use or not, marched his men straight ahead into the enemy's fire. Danger, shell and shot were just what he needed in his angry mood. One of the first bullets killed him, others killed many of his men. And his division remained under fire for some time and to no avail.

7

MEANWHILE another column was to have attacked the French from the front, but Kutuzov was with this column. He knew only too well that nothing but muddle would come of this battle, undertaken against his judgement, and so far as was in his power he held his forces back. He did not advance.

He rode mutely about on his small grey horse, giving languid replies to the suggestions that were made to him to attack.

'The word *attack* is for ever on your lips, but you don't see that we are unable to execute these complicated manoeuvres,' he said to Miloradovich, who asked permission to advance.

'You weren't smart enough to take Murat prisoner this morning, or to be in your place on time: now there's nothing to be done!' he answered another.

When Kutuzov was informed that there were now two battalions of Poles in the rear of the French, where according to the earlier reports from the Cossacks there had been none, he gave a sidelong glance at Yermolov who was behind him and to whom he had not spoken since the previous day.

'That is the way! They come begging to attack, proposing all sorts of plans, but as soon as it comes to action nothing is ready, and the enemy, forewarned, takes his measures accordingly.'

Yermolov screwed up his eyes and smiled faintly as he heard these words. He realized that so far as he was concerned the storm had blown over, and that Kutuzov would content himself with this innuendo.

'That's his little joke at my expense,' said Yermolov softly, nudging Raevsky with his knee, who was at his side.

Shortly after this Yermolov approached Kutuzov and respectfully submitted:

'It is not too late yet, your Highness – the enemy has not gone away. If you were to give the word to attack. Otherwise the Guards won't see so much as a puff of smoke.'

Kutuzov said nothing, but when it was reported to him that Murat's troops were in retreat he ordered an advance, although at every hundred yards he halted for three-quarters of an hour.

The whole battle amounted to no more than what had been done by Orlov-Denisov's Cossacks: the rest of the army simply lost several hundred men for nothing.

The consequence to Kutuzov was a diamond decoration; Bennigsen, too, was rewarded with diamonds and a hundred thousand roubles; and the other generals received agreeable recognition corresponding to their rank; and following the engagement more changes were made on the Staff.

'That's how things always are with us – the cart before the horse!' said the Russian officers and generals after the Tarutino affair, just as people do to this day, implying that some fool is handling matters all wrong, which we ourselves would have arranged quite otherwise. But people who talk like that either do not know what they are talking about, or purposely deceive themselves. No battle – be it Tarutino, Borodino, Austerlitz – ever comes off as those who planned it anticipated. That is the *sine qua non*.

An infinite number of freely acting forces (and nowhere is a man freer than during a life and death struggle) influence the course taken by a battle, and that course can never be known beforehand and never coincides with the direction it would take under the impulsion of any single force.

If many simultaneously and variously directed forces act on a given body, the direction which that body will take cannot be the course of any one of the forces individually – it will always follow an intermediate, as it were, shortest path, or what is represented in mechanics by the diagonal of a parallelogram of forces.

If in the accounts given us by historians, especially French historians, we find their wars and battles conforming to previously prescribed plans, the only conclusion to be drawn is that their accounts are not true.

The battle of Tarutino obviously did not attain the aim which Toll had in view – to lead the troops into action in the order laid down by the dispositions; nor that which Count Orlov-Denisov may have had – to take Murat prisoner; nor the aim of destroying at one blow the whole corps, which Bennigsen and others may have entertained; nor the aim of the officer who wished to go into action to distinguish himself; nor that of the Cossack who wanted more booty than he got, and so on. But if the aim of the battle was what actually resulted and what was the universal desire of the country – the expulsion of the French from Russia and the destruction of their army – it is quite clear that the battle of Tarutino, just because of its incongruities, was exactly what was wanted at that stage of the campaign. It would be difficult and even impossible to imagine any issue of that battle more opportune than its actual outcome. With a minimum of effort and at the cost of trifling losses, despite almost unexampled muddle the most important results of the whole campaign were obtained: the transition from retreat to advance, exposure of the weakness of the French, and the administration of the shock which was all that was needed to start Napoleon's army on its flight.

8

NAPOLEON enters Moscow after the brilliant victory *de la Moskowa*; there can be no doubt about the victory, since the French are left in possession of the field of battle. The Russians retire, abandoning their ancient capital. Moscow, crammed with provisions, arms, munitions and incalculable wealth, is in Napoleon's hands. The Russian army, only half the strength of the French, during the course of a whole month makes not a single attempt to assume the offensive. Napoleon's position could hardly be more brilliant. He can either, with doubly superior forces, fall upon the remains of the Russian army and exterminate it; negotiate an advantageous peace; or, in the case of his offer being rejected, make a threatening move on Petersburg, or – should that somehow not be successful – return to Smolensk or Vilna, or stay on in Moscow: in short, no extraordinary genius would seem to be required in order to retain the brilliant position the French held at that time. To do so it was only necessary to take the simplest and easiest measures: to keep the troops from looting; to prepare winter clothing – there was enough in Moscow for the whole army; and to organize systematic collection of provisions, of which (on the showing of the French historians) Moscow had sufficient to supply the entire army for six months. Napoleon, that greatest of all military geniuses, with absolute power, so the historians assert, took none of these steps.

He not only did nothing of all this but, on the contrary, used his power to select out of all the various courses open to him the one that was the most foolish and the most disastrous. Of all the different things Napoleon might have done – such as wintering in Moscow, going on to Petersburg, on to Nizhni Novgorod, or back a little more to the north or south (say, by the route Kutuzov afterwards took) – nothing more stupid or ruinous can be thought of than what he actually did. He remained in Moscow till October, letting his troops plunder the city, then – after hesitating whether or not to leave a garrison behind him – he quitted Moscow, marched within reach of Kutuzov without giving battle, turned to the right and went as far as Malo-Yaroslavets, again without attempting to break through, and finally retired not by the route Kutuzov had taken but along the devastated Smolensk road to Mozhaisk. Nothing could have been more stupid or more pernicious to the army than this, as the sequel proved. Assuming that Napoleon's object was to destroy his army, the most expert strategist could hardly conceive of any other series of actions which would so completely and infallibly have accomplished that purpose, independently of anything the Russian army might do.

Napoleon, the man of genius, did just this! But to say that Napoleon sacrificed his army because he wished to, or because he was very stupid, would be as inaccurate as to say that he brought his troops to

Moscow because he wanted to, and because he was very clever and a genius.

In both cases his personal activity, which was of no more consequence than the personal action of the meanest private, merely coincided with the laws that guided the event.

Quite falsely (and simply because consequent happenings did not vindicate his action) the historians represent Napoleon's faculties as having failed in Moscow. He employed all his ability and powers to do the best thing possible for himself and his army, just as he had always done before and as he did afterwards in 1813. His activity at this time was no less astounding than in Egypt, in Italy, in Austria and in Prussia. We cannot know with any certainty how much actual genius there was about Napoleon's operations in Egypt, where forty centuries looked down upon his glory, for the reason that all his great exploits there are described to us exclusively by Frenchmen. We cannot fairly assess his genius in Austria or Prussia, for we have to draw our information from French or German sources, and the incomprehensible surrender of whole corps without a blow struck, and of fortresses without a siege, must incline Germans to postulate his genius as the unique explanation of the war as it was waged in Germany. But we, thank God, have no need to plead his genius to cloak our shame. We have paid for the right to look facts simply and squarely in the face, and we shall not relinquish that right.

His genius operated as fully and amazingly in Moscow as elsewhere. Order after order and plan after plan were issued by him from the time he entered Moscow till the time he left it. The absence of the inhabitants and of a deputation, and even the burning of Moscow, did not daunt him. He did not lose sight of the welfare of his army or of the doings of the enemy, or of the well-being of the people of Russia, or of the conduct of affairs in Paris, or of diplomatic considerations concerning the terms of the anticipated peace.

9

ON the military side Napoleon, immediately on his entry into Moscow, gives General Sebastiani strict orders to keep a watch on the movements of the Russian army, sends army corps out along the different roads, and charges Murat to find Kutuzov. Then he gives careful instructions about the fortification of the Kremlin; then draws up a brilliant plan for a future campaign over the whole map of Russia. On the diplomatic side Napoleon summons Captain Yakovlev, who had been robbed and was in rags and did not know how to get out of Moscow, expounds to him at full length his whole policy and his magnanimity, and, after writing a letter to the Emperor Alexander in which he deems it his duty to inform his friend and brother that Rostopchin has managed affairs very badly in Moscow, he dispatches Yakovlev with it to Petersburg.

Having similarly expatiated on his view and his chivalry to Tutolmin, he dispatches that old man too to Petersburg to open negotiations.

On the judicial side orders were issued, immediately after the fires broke out, for the guilty persons to be found and executed. And the miscreant Rostopchin was punished by having his own houses burnt down.

On the administrative side Moscow was presented with a constitution. A municipal council was founded, and the following proclamation posted about the town:

CITIZENS OF MOSCOW!

Your miseries are cruel, but his Majesty the Emperor and King desires to arrest their course. Terrible examples have shown you how he punishes disobedience and crime. Stern measures have been taken to put an end to disorder and to restore public security. A paternal administration, composed of men chosen from among yourselves, will form your municipality or city government. It will care for your welfare, your needs and your interests. Its members will be distinguished by a red ribbon worn across the shoulder, and the mayor of the city will, in addition, wear a white belt. But except when discharging their duties they will only wear a red ribbon round the left arm.

The city police is established on its former footing, and thanks to its vigilance better order already prevails. The government has appointed two commissioners-general, or chiefs of police, and twenty commissioners, or inspectors, for the different wards of the city. You will recognize them by the white band they will wear around the left arm. A number of churches of various denominations are open, and divine service continues in them unhindered. Your fellow-citizens are daily returning to their homes, and instructions have been given that they should find in them the help and protection to which misfortune entitles. These are the measures the government has adopted for the restoration of order and easement of your position. But to attain this end it is necessary that you should second these efforts by your own and should, so far as is possible, forget your past sufferings; should cherish the hope of a less cruel destiny; should be fully persuaded that inevitable and ignominious death awaits those who make any attempt on your persons or on what remains of your property, and, finally, that you should not doubt that these will be safeguarded, since such is the will of the greatest and most just of monarchs. Soldiers and citizens, of whatever nation you may be – re-establish public confidence, the source of the prosperity of a state. Live like brothers. Render mutual aid and protection one to another. Combine to frustrate the designs of the evil-minded. Obey the military and civil authorities, and soon your tears will cease to flow.

On the commissariat side Napoleon decreed that all the troops should take turns in plundering Moscow for supplies, which would suffice to victual the army for a certain time.

In the matter of religious worship Napoleon ordered the priests to be brought back and services resumed in the churches.

Concerning trade and the provisioning of the army the following manifesto was placarded everywhere:

PROCLAMATION

Peaceable inhabitants of Moscow, artisans and working men whom misfortune has driven from the city, scattered tillers of the soil who are still kept in the fields by causeless terror – listen! Tranquillity is return-ing to this capital, and order is being restored in it. Finding that they are respected, your fellow-countrymen are boldly emerging from their hiding-places. Any violence to them or to their property brings prompt punishment. His Majesty the Emperor and King protects them, and considers none among you his enemy but such as disobey his commands. His desire is to put an end to your sufferings and restore you to your homes and families. Co-operate, therefore, with his beneficent pur-poses and come to us without fear. Citizens, return with confidence to your dwellings! You will soon find means of satisfying your needs. Craftsmen and industrious artisans, return to your work! Your houses, your shops, and guards to protect them, await you. For your labour you shall receive the wage which is your due. And lastly you too, peasants, come out from the woods where you are lurking in terror. Return without fear to your huts, and be assured that you will find protection. Markets have been organized in the city where peasants can bring their surplus produce and the fruits of the earth. The govern-ment has taken the following measures to ensure the free sale of this produce: (1) From this day peasants, husbandmen and those living in the environs of Moscow may, without any danger, bring their goods of whatever nature to two appointed markets – Moss street and the Poultry market. (2) Such goods will be bought from them at prices agreed upon between seller and buyer; but if a seller is unable to obtain a fair price he will be at liberty to take his goods back to his village, and no one may hinder his doing so on any pretext whatsoever. (3) Sunday and Wednesday of each week are appointed as chief market days; on this score a sufficient number of troops will be stationed along the high roads on Tuesdays and Saturdays at such distances from the town as to protect carts coming in. (4) Similar measures will be taken that peasants and their carts and horses may meet with no hindrance on their return journey. (5) Steps will immediately be taken to re-establish ordinary trading.

Inhabitants of town and country, and you, working men and artisans, whatever your nationality – you are called upon to carry into effect the paternal designs of his Majesty the Emperor and King, and to co-operate with him for the public welfare. Lay your respect and trust at his feet, and do not delay in uniting with us!

To raise the spirits of troops and civilians reviews were constantly held and decorations distributed. The Emperor rode through the streets on horseback to console the people, and despite his preoccupation with state affairs himself visited the theatres set up by his orders.

In the matter of philanthropy – the fairest jewel in a monarch's crown – Napoleon also did all that lay in his power. He caused the words *Maison de ma Mère* to be inscribed on the charitable institutions – thereby combining tender filial piety with beneficent majesty. He visited the Foundling Hospital and, allowing the orphans saved by him to kiss his white hands, conversed graciously with Tutolmin. Then, as Thiers eloquently recounts, gave instructions for his troops to be paid in forged Russian money which he had prepared.

To enhance the employment of these methods by an act worthy of himself and of the French army, he saw to it that relief was distributed to those who had suffered loss from the fire. But as food was too precious to be given away to foreigners, who were for the most part hostile to him, Napoleon preferred to bestow money with which to procure provisions from outside, and had this money paid in paper roubles.

With reference to army discipline orders were continually being issued providing for severe punishment for non-fulfilment of military duties and for the suppression of pillaging.

10

BUT, strange to say, all these arrangements, these efforts and plans, which were no whit inferior to others made in similar circumstances, never touched the root of the matter. Like the hands of a clock disconnected from the mechanism behind the dial, they swung about in an arbitrary, aimless fashion without engaging the cogwheels.

On the military side the plan of campaign – that prodigious work à propos of which Thiers remarks that 'his genius never devised anything more profound, more skilful, or more admirable', and enters into a polemical discussion with Monsieur Fain to prove that this composition of genius must be referred not to the 4th but to the 15th of October – that plan never was and never could have been put into execution, because it was quite out of touch with the actual facts of the position. The fortifying of the Kremlin, for which la Mosquée (as Napoleon called the church of Vasili Blazhenny) was to have been razed to the ground, turned out to be perfectly useless. The mining of the Kremlin only helped towards the fulfilment of Napoleon's wish to see the Kremlin blown up – in other words, that the floor on which the child has hurt himself might be beaten. The pursuit of the Russian army, on which Napoleon laid so much stress, produced an unheard-of phenomenon. The French generals lost track of the sixty thousand men of the Russian army, and, according to Thiers, it was only thanks to the skill, and also apparently the genius, of Murat that they eventually succeeded in discovering, like a needle in a haystack, the whereabouts of this Russian army sixty thousand strong.

On the diplomatic side all Napoleon's arguments to prove his magnanimity and justice, both to Tutolmin and to Yakovlev (who was principally interested to obtain a greatcoat and a conveyance for travelling) were thrown away; Alexander would not receive these envoys and returned no answer to the message they brought.

As to his judicial administration: after the execution of the supposed incendiaries the other half of Moscow was burnt down.

Administratively, the establishment of a municipality did not check pillage, and was of no benefit to anyone but the few persons who were members of it and so able – on the pretext of preserving order – to loot Moscow or to save their own property from being looted.

In matters of religion, though the Imperial visit to a mosque had been a great success in Egypt, a similar visit had no effect in Moscow. Two or three priests, picked up in the city, did attempt to carry out Napoleon's wishes but one of them got slapped in the face by a French soldier during the service, while of another a French official reported that 'the priest whom I found and invited to say mass cleaned and locked up the church. That night the doors were forced open again, the padlocks smashed, the books torn and other disorders perpetrated.'

As for commerce, the proclamation to 'industrious artisans and peasants' met with no response. There were no industrious artisans, and the peasants set upon the commissioners who ventured too far from the town with their proclamation and killed them.

The attempts to entertain the people and the troops with theatres were equally unsuccessful. The theatres set up in the Kremlin and in Poznyakov's house had to be closed again at once because the actors and actresses were robbed of their belongings.

Even philanthropy did not have the desired results. The genuine as well as the counterfeit paper money which flooded Moscow lost its value. The French, accumulating booty, cared for nothing but gold. Not only were the counterfeit notes worthless which Napoleon so graciously bestowed on the unfortunate – even silver fell below its standard value in relation to gold.

But the most striking example of the ineffectiveness of the orders issued by the authorities at that time was Napoleon's endeavour to check looting and restore discipline.

Here are some of the reports which the army authorities were sending in:

'Looting continues in the city, in spite of injunctions to the contrary. Order is not yet restored, and there is not a single merchant engaging in legitimate trade. Only the sutlers venture to sell anything, and the articles they have for sale are stolen goods.'

'My district continues to be pillaged by soldiers of the 3rd Corps, who, not content with stripping the poor creatures hiding in under-ground cellars of what little they have left, are brutal enough to wound them with sword-cuts, as I have repeatedly witnessed.'

'Nothing new to report, except that the soldiers are given up to theft and pillage – 9th October.'

'Robbery and pillaging continue. There is a band of thieves in our district who ought to be put down by forceful measures – 11th October.'

'The Emperor is exceedingly displeased that, despite strict orders to stop pillage, parties of marauding Guards are continually seen returning to the Kremlin. In the Old Guards the disorder and pillage have been more violent than ever last night and today. The Emperor finds with regret that the picked soldiers appointed to guard his person, who should be setting an example of good discipline, carry insubordination to such a point that they break into the cellars and stores containing army supplies. Others have fallen so low that they defy sentinels and officers of the watch, abusing and even striking them.'

'The Grand Marshal of the Palace [wrote the governor] complains bitterly that, notwithstanding repeated prohibitions, the soldiers continue to perform the offices of nature in all the courtyards, and even under the Emperor's very windows.'

The army, like a herd of cattle run wild and trampling underfoot the fodder which might have saved it from starvation, was disintegrating and perishing with every day it remained in Moscow.

But it did not stir.

It started in flight only when suddenly seized by panic at the capture of transport trains on the Smolensk road, and the battle of Tarutino. The news of that battle of Tarutino, which reached Napoleon unexpectedly in the middle of a review, fired him with a desire to punish the Russians (so Thiers tells us), and he issued the order for departure which the whole army was clamouring for.

In their flight from Moscow the soldiers carried away with them all the booty they had stolen. Napoleon, too, had his own personal *trésor* to take with him. Seeing the baggage-trains that encumbered the army, Napoleon (Thiers says) was horror-struck. And yet, for all his experience of war, he did not order the collection of superfluous vehicles to be burnt, as he had done with those of a certain marshal on the way to Moscow; he gazed at the calèches and carriages in which the soldiers were riding and remarked that it was a very good thing – all those conveyances would come in useful for carrying provisions, the sick and the wounded.

The plight of the whole army was like the plight of a wounded animal which feels its death is at hand and does not know what it is doing. To study the ingenious manoeuvres and objectives of Napoleon and his army from the time of entering Moscow up to the hour of the final catastrophe is like watching the convulsions and death throes of a mortally wounded animal. Very often the wounded creature, hearing a rustle, rushes straight at the sportsman's gun, runs forward and back again, and itself hastens its end. Napoleon, under the pressure of his entire army, did likewise. The rustle of the battle of Tarutino alarmed the beast and it made a rush towards the shot, reached the hunter and turned back again; moved forward, backed again, and at last, like any wild creature, fled along the most inexpedient, the most perilous but the best known track – its former trail.

Napoleon, who is presented to us as the leader of all this movement backwards and forwards (just as the figure-head over the prow of a ship seems to the savage to be the power directing the vessel in its course) – Napoleon in whatever he did throughout this period was like a child holding on to the straps inside a carriage and imagining that he is driving it.

II

EARLY in the morning of the 6th of October Pierre stepped outside the prison-shed, and then, turning back, stood in the doorway to play with the little bluish-grey mongrel with the long body and short bandy legs, who was gambolling around him. This little dog had made her home in the shed, sleeping beside Karatayev at night, though occasionally she went off on excursions into the town from which she would always return again. Probably she had never had an owner, and still belonged to nobody and had no name. The French called her Azor; the story-teller christened her Jenny Daw, while Karatayev and the others called her Grey, or sometimes Floppy. The fact that she belonged to no one, and had no name or breed or definite colour, did not seem to trouble the blue-grey bitch in the least. Her fluffy tail stood up firm and round like a plume, her bandy legs served her so well that often, as though disdaining to use all four, she would gracefully raise one hind leg and run very easily and quickly on three. Everything was a source of satisfaction to her. At one moment she would be rolling on her back squealing with delight, or basking in the sun looking thoughtful and solemn. Now she would frolic about playing with a chip of wood or a straw.

Pierre's attire by now consisted of a dirty town shirt (the sole relic from the clothes he was originally wearing), a pair of soldier's drawers which by Karatayev's advice he tied with string round the ankles, for the sake of warmth, and a peasant coat and cap. Physically he had altered a great deal during this time. He no longer seemed stout, though he still retained the appearance of solidity and strength that was hereditary in his family. A beard and moustache covered the lower part of his face, and a tangle of hair, infested with lice, curled round his head like a cap. His eyes had a steady, quiet look of alert readiness they had never held before. The old laxity, which had shown even in his eyes, had given place to an energetic preparedness for action and resistance. His feet were bare.

Pierre gazed alternately below at the plain across which wagons and men on horseback were passing that morning, across the river into the distance, at the dog pretending she was going to bite him, and at his own bare feet which he shifted about with pleasure from one position to another, moving his dirty thick big toes. And every time he looked at his bare feet a smile of lively self-satisfaction flitted across his face. The sight of those bare feet reminded him of all he had experienced and learned during these weeks, and the recollection pleased him.

For some days the weather had been mild and clear, with light frosts in the mornings – what is called an 'old wives' summer'.

It was warm out of doors in the sun, and this warmth was particularly agreeable with the invigorating freshness of the morning frost still in the air.

Over everything, far and near, lay the magic crystal glitter only seen at this time in the autumn. The Sparrow hills were visible in the distance, with the village, the church and a large white house. And the leafless trees, the sand, the bricks and roofs of the houses, the green steeple of the church and the angles of the white house in the distance all stood out in the limpid air, in most delicate outline and with unnatural distinctness. Close by could be seen the familiar ruins of a half-burnt mansion, occupied by the French, with lilac bushes still showing dark green beside the fence. And even this charred and begrimed house – which in dull weather was repulsively ugly – now in the clear, still brilliance seemed soothingly beautiful.

A French corporal in a night-cap, with his coat carelessly unbuttoned, came round the corner of the shed, a short pipe between his teeth, and approached Pierre with a friendly wink.

'What sunshine, eh, Monsieur Kirill?' (This was the name the French had given Pierre.) 'Just like spring.'

And the corporal leaned against the door and offered Pierre his pipe, though he was always offering it and Pierre always declined. 'This is the weather to be on the march ...' he began.

Pierre asked what news there was of the departure of the French, and the corporal told him that nearly all the troops were starting to leave and that instructions about prisoners were expected that day. In Pierre's shed one of the Russian soldiers – Sokolov – was dangerously ill, and Pierre reminded the corporal that something ought to be done about this soldier. The corporal replied that Pierre need not worry – they had mobile as well as permanent hospitals, and arrangements would be made for the sick, and in fact every possible contingency was provided for by the authorities.

'Besides, Monsieur Kirill, you have only to say a word to the captain, you know. Oh, he's a ... he's a man who never forgets anything. Speak to the captain when he makes his round: he will do anything for you. ...'

(The captain in question often had long chats with Pierre and showed him all sorts of favours.)

'"You see, St Thomas," he says to me t'other day, "That Kirill's got education, he talks French; he is a Russian lord who has been unfortunate but he's a proper man. He knows what's what. ... If he wants anything, let him tell me – I won't refuse him. When a person's a scholar himself, he likes a bit of education, you see, and genuine, real refined people." It is for your sake I mention it, Monsieur Kirill. That job the other day now – if it hadn't been for you things would have ended bad.'

And after chatting a little while longer the corporal went away. (The affair he had alluded to was a fight a few days before between the prisoners and the French soldiers, in which Pierre had succeeded in restraining his comrades.) Some of the prisoners had seen Pierre talking to the corporal, and they immediately came up to ask what the Frenchman had said. While Pierre was repeating what he had been told about the army leaving Moscow a thin, sallow, ragged French soldier sidled up to the door of the shed. With a quick, timid gesture he raised his fingers to his forehead by way of a salute and addressed himself to Pierre, inquiring of him whether the soldier 'Platoche', who was making a shirt for him, was in that shed.

Seven or eight days before, the French had been issued with boot-leather and linen, which they had given out to the prisoners to make up into boots and shirts for them.

'Ready, ready, me duck!' cried Karatayev, coming out with a neatly folded shirt.

On account of the warm weather and for convenience at work, Karatayev was wearing nothing but a pair of drawers and a tattered shirt as black as soot. He had tied a wisp of bast round his hair, workman-fashion, and his round face looked rounder and more good-natured than ever.

'Make a bargain and stick to it!' said he. 'I promised it for Friday, and here it is all finished,' and Platon smilingly unfolded the shirt he had made.

The Frenchman glanced round uneasily and then, as if overcoming some hesitation, quickly stripped off his uniform and put on the shirt. Under his uniform he had no shirt but a long greasy flowered-silk waistcoat next to his thin yellow body. He was evidently afraid that the prisoners looking on would laugh at him, and lost no time in thrusting his head into the shirt. None of the prisoners said a word.

'There's a good fit now!' Platon kept saying, pulling the shirt down.

The Frenchman, having pushed his head and hands through without looking up, inspected the shirt and examined the seams.

'You see, me duck, this 'ere place ain't exactly a tailor's bench, and I 'adn't no proper sewing gear; and as the saying is, without the right 'strument you can't even kill a louse,' said Platon, with one of his round smiles and obviously pleased with his own work.

'C'est bien, c'est bien, merci,' said the Frenchman. 'But there must be some of the stuff left over.'

'It'll fit better still when it sets to your body,' Platon went on, still admiring his handiwork. 'Nice and comfortable you'll be. ...'

'Merci, merci, mon vieux. ... And the pieces?' insisted the French-man, smiling. And taking out a note, he gave it to Karatayev. 'But let me have the pieces.'

Pierre saw that Platon did not want to understand what the French-man was saying, and he looked on without interfering. Karatayev thanked the Frenchmen for the money and went on admiring his own work. The Frenchman persisted in his demands for the pieces that were left and asked Pierre to tralate what he said.

'What does he want with them bits?' said Karatayev. 'Fine leg-bands they'd make us. Oh well, never mind.'

And, his face suddenly crestfallen and melancholy, Karatayev took a small bundle of scraps from inside his shirt and gave it to the Frenchman without looking at him. 'Alas! Alack!' muttered Karatayev, and turned on his heel. The Frenchman looked at the linen, deliberated for a moment, then glanced inquiringly at Pierre, and, as though Pierre's eyes had told him something, blushed all at once and called in a squeaky voice:

'Here, Platoche – Platoche! You can keep them!' And handing back the odd bits he swung round and hurried away.

'There, look at that,' said Karatayev, nodding his head. 'They say they're heathens, but that one has a soul. The old folk were right: "A sweaty hand's an open hand, a dry fist's a close fist." 'Adn't a rag to 'is back, and 'e goes an' gives me this.'

Karatayev smiled thoughtfully, gazing at the bits of stuff in silence for a moment.

'But they'll come in fine for leg-bands, me boy,' he said, and went back into the shed.

12

Four weeks had passed since Pierre had been taken prisoner. Although the French had offered to transfer him to the officer's shed, he had stayed on in the shed where he had been put from the first, with the ordinary soldiers.

In burnt and devastated Moscow Pierre experienced almost the extreme limits of privation a man can endure; but thanks to his physical strength and good health, of which he had hardly been aware till then, and still more to the fact that these privations came upon him so gradually that it was impossible to say when they began, he bore his position not only lightly but cheerfully. And it was just at this time that he attained to the peace and content with himself for which before he had always striven in vain. He had spent long years in the search for that tranquillity of mind, that inner harmony, which had so impressed him in the men at the battle of Borodino. He had sought it in philanthropy, in Freemasonry, in the dissipations of society life, in wine, in heroic feats of self-sacrifice, in romantic love for Natasha; he had sought it by the path of intellectual reasoning –

and all these efforts and experiments had failed him. And now, without any thought on his part, he had found that peace and that inner harmony simply through the horrors of death, through privation, and through what he had seen in Karatayev. Those dreadful moments of anguish he had gone through at the executions had, as it were, washed for ever from his imagination and his memory the restless ideas and feelings that had formerly seemed so important. It did not now occur to him to cogitate about Russia, or the war, or politics, or Napoleon. He realized that all that was no business of his, that he was not called upon to pronounce on such matters and therefore could not judge. 'Russia and summer don't mix together,' he would think, repeating words of Karatayev's which he found strangely comforting. His intention of assassinating Napoleon and his calculations round the cabalistic number of the beast of the Apocalypse struck him now as incomprehensible and positively ludicrous. His indignation against his wife, and his anxiety that his name should not be smirched, now seemed not merely trivial but even amusing. What concern was it of his that somewhere or other the woman was leading the life she preferred? What did it matter to anybody – least of all to him – whether or not they found out that their prisoner was Count Bezuhov?

He often recalled now his conversation with Prince Andrei, and fully agreed with his friend, except that he interpreted Prince Andrei's idea rather differently. Prince Andrei had been wont to reflect that happiness was purely negative – but he had said so with a shade of bitterness and irony, as though he were really saying that all our cravings for positive happiness were implanted in us merely for our torment, since they could never be satisfied. But Pierre acknowledged the truth of this without any qualification. The absence of suffering, the satisfaction of elementary needs and consequent freedom in the choice of one's occupation – that is, of one's mode of living – now seemed to Pierre the sure height of human happiness. Here and now for the first time in his life Pierre fully appreciated the enjoyment of eating because he was hungry, of drinking because he was thirsty, of sleep because he was sleepy, of warmth because he was cold, of talking to a fellow creature because he felt like talking and wanted to hear a human voice. The satisfaction of one's needs – good food, cleanliness, freedom – now that he was deprived of these seemed to Pierre to constitute perfect happiness; and the choice of occupation, that is, of his manner of life, now that that choice was so restricted, seemed to him such an easy matter that he forgot that a superfluity of the comforts of life destroys all joy in gratifying one's needs, while too much liberty in choosing our occupations – liberty which in his case arose from his education, his wealth and his social position – is just what makes the choice of occupation hopelessly difficult, and destroys the very desire and possibility of having an occupation.

All Pierre's dreams were now centred on the time when he would be free; though afterwards, and to the end of his days, he thought and spoke with enthusiasm of that month of captivity, of those irrecoverable, intense, joyful sensations, and above all, of the perfect spiritual peace, the complete inner freedom, which he experienced only during that period of his life.

On the first morning of his imprisonment, when he got up early and went out of the shed at dawn, and saw the cupolas and crosses of the Novo-Dyevichy convent, dim and dark at first, saw the hoar-frost on the dusty grass, saw the Sparrow hills and the wooded banks above the winding river disappearing into the purple distance, when he felt the contact of the fresh air and heard the cawing of the jackdaws flying from Moscow across the field, and when a little later flashes of light suddenly gleamed from the east and the sun's rim floated triumphantly up from behind a cloud, and cupolas and crosses and hoar-frost and distant horizon and river began to sparkle in the glad light, Pierre knew an unaccustomed feeling of vigour and *joie de vivre* such as he had never known before.

And this feeling not only stayed with him during the whole of his imprisonment but even grew in strength as the hardships of his position increased.

This feeling of being ready for anything, of moral alertness, was still further reinforced by the high opinion his fellow-prisoners formed of him soon after his arrival in the shed. His knowledge of languages, the respect shown him by the French, the frank simplicity with which he gave away anything he was asked for (he received the allowance of three roubles a week made to officers), his physical strength, which the soldiers saw when he pushed nails into the walls of the hut with his fingers, his gentleness to his companions and his capacity – which they could not understand – for sitting stock-still, doing nothing, and thinking, made him appear to the soldiers a somewhat mysterious and superior being. The very qualities that had been a source of embarrassment if not actually prejudicial to him in the world he had previously lived in – his strength, his disdain for the amenities of life, his absent-mindedness and simplicity – here among these people gave him almost the status of a hero. And Pierre felt that their opinion placed responsibilities upon him.

13

THE French evacuation began on the night of the 6th of October: kitchens and sheds were dismantled, carts loaded up, and troops and baggage-trains moved off.

At seven in the morning a French convoy in marching trim, wearing shakos and carrying muskets, knapsacks and enormous sacks, stood in front of the sheds, and a running fire of eager French talk, interlarded with oaths, was kept up all along the line.

Inside the shed everyone was ready dressed, belted and shod, only awaiting the order to start. The sick soldier Sokolov, pale and thin, with dark shadows round his eyes, alone lay in his corner, barefoot and not dressed. His eyes – the emaciation of his face made him seem all eyes – gazed inquiringly at his comrades, who were paying no heed to him, and at regular intervals he moaned quietly. It was evidently not so much his sufferings that caused him to moan (he was ill with dysentery) as his fear and grief at being abandoned.

Pierre, with a length of rope tied round his waist for a belt, and shod in shoes Karatayev had made for him out of some strips of raw leather which a French soldier had brought to have his boots mended with, went up to the sick man and squatted on his heels beside him.

'You know, Sokolov, they are not going away altogether! They have a hospital here. Very likely you'll be better off than the rest of us,' said Pierre.

'O Lord! Oh, it'll be the death of me! O Lord!' groaned the soldier more loudly.

'I'll go and ask them straight away,' said Pierre, and getting up, he went to the door of the shed.

Just as Pierre reached the door the corporal who had offered him a pipe the day before came up with two soldiers. Both the corporal and the soldiers were in marching kit with knapsacks and shakos with chin-straps buttoned, which altered their familiar faces.

The corporal approached the door for the purpose of locking it in accordance with his orders. The prisoners had to be counted before being let out.

'Corporal, what is to become of the sick man? ...' Pierre was beginning; but even as he spoke doubts arose in his mind whether this was the corporal he knew, or some stranger, so unlike himself did the corporal look at that moment. Moreover, just as Pierre was speaking a sharp rattle of drums was suddenly heard from both sides. The corporal frowned at Pierre's words, and uttering a meaningless oath slammed the door to. It was half-dark now in the shed; the drums beat a crisp tattoo on two sides, drowning the sick man's moans.

'Here it is! ... Here's *that* again! ...' said Pierre to himself, and an involuntary shudder ran down his spine. In the changed face of the corporal, in the sound of his voice, in the agitating, deafening din of the drums, Pierre recognized that mysterious, callous force which drove men against their will to murder their kind – that force the workings of which he had witnessed during the executions. To be afraid or to try to escape that force, to address entreaties or exhortations to those who were serving as its tools, was useless. Pierre knew this now. One could but wait and endure. He did not go near the sick man again, nor look round at him. He stood scowling in silence at the door of the shed.

When the door was opened and the prisoners, crowding against one another like a flock of sheep, squeezed into the exit, Pierre elbowed his way in front of them and went up to the very captain who was, so the corporal had assured him, ready to do anything for him. The captain was also in marching dress, and on his cold face appeared that same *it* which Pierre had recognized in the corporal's words and the roll of the drums.

'Get on, get on!' the captain was saying, frowning sternly and looking at the prisoners as they pushed past.

Pierre knew that his venture would be in vain, but still he went up to him.

'Well, what is it?' asked the officer, scanning him coldly as though he did not recognize him.

Pierre told him about the sick man.

'He can walk, damn him!' said the captain. 'Get on, get on!' he continued, without looking at Pierre.

'No, he is dying ...' Pierre was beginning.

'Be so good ...' shouted the captain, frowning angrily.

Drrram-da-da-dam, dam-dam rattled the drums. And Pierre realized that this mysterious force had already complete possession of these men and that to say anything more now was useless.

The officers among the prisoners were separated from the soldiers and ordered to march in front. There were about thirty officers, with Pierre in their number, and some three hundred men.

These officers, who had come from other sheds, were all strangers to Pierre and much better dressed than he. They looked at him and his queer foot-gear with aloof, mistrustful eyes. Not far from Pierre walked a stout major with a bloated, sallow, irascible countenance. He was wearing a Kazan dressing-gown, belted with a towel, and evidently enjoyed the general respect of his fellow-prisoners. He kept one hand, in which he clasped a tobacco-pouch, inside the bosom of his dressing-gown, and clutched the stem of his pipe firmly with the other. Panting and puffing, this major grumbled and growled at everybody because he thought he was being pushed and that they were all hurrying when they had nowhere to hurry to, and were all wondering when there was nothing to wonder at. Another, a thin little officer, addressed remarks to everyone, speculating as to where they were being taken now, and how far they would get that day. An official in felt high boots and a commissariat uniform ran from one side to another to spy out the ruins of Moscow, making loud observations as to what had been burnt down, and what this or that part of the city was that they could see. A third officer, of Polish extraction by his accent, disputed with the commissariat official, arguing that he was mistaken in his identification of the various quarters of Moscow.

'What are you quarrelling about?' said the major angrily. 'What does it matter whether it's St Nicolai or St Vlas, it's all one. You can see 'tis all burnt down, and there's an end of it. ... What are you shoving for? Isn't the road wide enough?' he demanded angrily of a man behind him who was not pushing him at all.

'Oh, I say! Look what they have done!' was heard on all sides as the prisoners gazed at the charred ruins. 'All beyond the river there, and Zubovo, and in the Kremlin ... see, half of it's gone! I told you the whole quarter beyond the river went, and so it has.'

'Well, you know it's burnt down, so what's the point of talking about it?' said the major.

As they passed near a church in the Khamovniky area (one of the few unscathed quarters of Moscow) the whole mass of prisoners suddenly swerved to one side, and exclamations of horror and aversion were heard.

'Oh, the swine!'

'What heathens!'

'Yes, it's a dead man, a dead man all right. ... And they've smeared his face with something!'

Pierre, too, drew near the church where the object that had called forth these exclamations was, and he vaguely discerned a figure leaning against the palings round the church. From the words of his comrades, who saw better than he did, he learned that this was the dead body of a man, propped on its feet against the fence, with its face dirtied with lamp-black.

'Move on there! What the devil. ... Get on! Thirty thousand devils! ...' they heard the escort swearing, and the French soldiers, with renewed vindictiveness, used the flat of their swords to drive on the prisoners who had crowded to stare at the dead man.

14

THROUGH the by-ways and alleys of the Khamovniky quarter the prisoners marched alone with their guards, followed by the carts and baggage-wagons belonging to the escort; but as they emerged near the provision stores they found themselves in the midst of a huge and closely packed train of artillery mixed up with a number of private vehicles.

At the bridge they all halted, waiting for those in front to cross. From the bridge the prisoners had a view of endless lines of moving baggage-trains before and behind. To the right, where the Kaluga road twisted round by the Neskuchny Gardens, troops and carts dragged never-ending into the distance. These were the troops of Beauharnais's corps which had set off before any of the others. Behind, along the quays and across Kamenny bridge, stretched the troops and transport commanded by Ney.

Davoust's troops, in whose charge were the prisoners, were crossing the Crimean ford and some were already debouching on to the Kaluga road. But the baggage-trains were so long that the vanguard of Ney's army was already emerging from Great Ordynka before the last of Beauharnais's wagons had got on to the Kaluga road out of Moscow.

After crossing the Crimean ford the prisoners moved a few steps at a time and halted, then moved forward again, and from all sides vehicles and men pressed up closer and closer. When they had advanced the few hundred paces that separated the bridge from the Kaluga road, taking over an hour to do so, and got as far as the square where the streets of the Transmoskva ward and the Kaluga road converge, the prisoners stopped, jammed together, and were kept standing for some hours at the cross-roads. From all sides, like the roar of the sea, came an unceasing sound of the rumble of wheels, the tramp of feet, and continuous angry shouting and abuse. Pierre stood flattened up against the wall of a charred house, listening to the din, which in his imagination was one with the roll of drums.

To have a better view several of the officer-prisoners climbed on to the wall of the burned house against which Pierre was leaning.

'What a jam! Just look at the crowds! ... They've even loaded goods on to the cannon! And see over there – those are furs! ...' they exclaimed. 'Oh look what the vermin have been looting! Look what that one has got behind there, in the cart. ... It's – yes, it's the mount from an icon, by heaven! ... Those must be Germans! ... And there's a peasant of ours, by Jove! ... Oh, the scum! See how that fellow's loaded himself up – he can hardly walk! Good Lord, they've even grabbed those chaises! ... See that man there perched on the trunks. Saints alive! they've started fighting! ...

'That's right, fetch him one on the nose – right on the nose! At this rate we shan't get by before nightfall. Look – I say, look! Those must be Napoleon's own! See what horses – and the monograms with a crown! It's like a portable house. ... That fellow's dropped his sack and hasn't noticed. Fighting again. ... A woman with a baby, and not bad-looking either. Yes, I dare say, that's the way they'll let you through, my lass! ... Look, there's no end to it. Russian wenches, I do declare, so they are! In carriages – see how comfortably they've settled themselves!'

Again, as at the church in Khamovniky, a wave of general curiosity bore all the prisoners forward on to the road, and Pierre, thanks to his height, saw over the heads of the others what it was that so attracted the prisoners' interest. In three carriages caught among the ammunition-caissons rode a party of women with rouged faces and decked out in glaring colours. They were squeezed closely together, shouting something in shrill voices.

From the moment when Pierre had recognized the manifestation of that mysterious force nothing had seemed to him strange or terrible; neither the corpse with its face smeared for a jest with lampblack, nor these women hurrying away, nor the burnt ruins of Moscow. All that he, Pierre, now saw hardly made any impression on him – as though his soul, preparing itself for a hard struggle, was refusing to receive any impressions that might weaken it.

The carriages with the women drove by. Behind them followed more carts, soldiers, baggage-wagons, soldiers, carriages, soldiers, caissons, more soldiers, and here and there women.

Pierre could not make out individuals separately: he saw only their general movement.

All these people and horses seemed as if they were impelled forward by some invisible power. During the hour Pierre spent watching them they all came pouring from the different streets with one and the same desire, to get along as quickly as possible; all alike, they jostled one another, became angry and started fighting. White teeth flashed, brows scowled, the same oaths were bandied to and fro, and every face bore the same look of reckless determination and cold inhumanity that had struck Pierre that morning in the corporal's expression when the drums were beating.

It was not until towards nightfall that the officer commanding the escort rallied his men and with shouting and angry argument forced his way in among the baggage-trains; and the prisoners, hemmed in on all sides, emerged on to the Kaluga road.

They proceeded very rapidly, not stopping to rest, and halted only when the sun began to set. The baggage-carts drew up close to one another, and the men began preparing for the night. Everyone seemed sulky and bad-tempered. Cursing, rancorous shouts and blows continued until late into the night. A private carriage following the prisoners' guard drove into one of the carts and ran a shaft through it. Several soldiers rushed across, some to flog the carriage-horses about the head as they pushed them aside, others to fight among themselves, and Pierre saw a German receive a severe scalp wound from a short sabre.

It seemed that all these men, now that they had halted amid fields in the chill dusk of the autumn evening, were experiencing one and the same disagreeable feeling of reaction from the hurry and eagerness to push on that had possessed them at the start. It was as if they realized, now that they had come to a stop, that they did not yet know where they were going, and that much misery and hardship lay in store for them on the journey.

During this halt the soldiers in charge of the prisoners treated them more brutally even than at the outset. It was here that the prisoners for the first time received horse-flesh for their meat ration.

From the officers down to the lowest ranks all displayed a sort of personal spite against every one of the prisoners, in surprising contrast to their former friendliness.

This spite increased still more when the roll was called and it was found that in the bustle of leaving Moscow one Russian soldier, pretending to be ill with colic, had managed to get away. Pierre saw a Frenchman beat a Russian soldier unmercifully for straying too far from the road, and heard his friend the captain reprimand and threaten to court-martial a non-commissioned officer for the escape of the Russian. To the non-commissioned officer's excuse that the prisoner was ill and could not walk the officer replied that their orders were to shoot those who lagged behind. Pierre felt that that blind force which had trampled over him during the executions, and which he had not been conscious of during his imprisonment, again had him in its clutches. He was filled with dread; but he felt too that the harder that fatal force strove to crush him the more did his own individual vitality assert itself in his soul.

Pierre ate his supper of rye-flour soup with horse-flesh, and chatted with his comrades.

Neither Pierre nor any of his companions spoke of what they had seen in Moscow, or of the roughness of their treatment at the hands of the French, or of the order to shoot stragglers which had been announced to them. As though to counteract the worsening of their position they were all particularly lively and gay. They reminisced, they talked of comical incidents they had seen during the march, and avoided any reference to their present plight.

The sun had set long since. Here and there a star flashed bright in the sky. The rising full moon spread a red glow along the horizon like the glare from a fire, and soon the vast red ball hung swaying strangely in the grey haze. The sky was growing lighter. The evening was over but night had not yet begun. Pierre got up and leaving his new companions walked between the camp-fires to the other side of the road, where he had been told the common prisoners were camping. He wanted to talk to them. On the way he was stopped by a French sentinel, who ordered him back.

Pierre returned, not to his companions by the camp-fire but to an unharnessed wagon where there was nobody. Tucking his legs under him and dropping his head, he sat down on the cold ground against a wheel of the wagon, and sat there a long while without moving, deep in thought. Over an hour went by. No one disturbed Pierre. Suddenly he burst into a burly peal of jovial laughter, so loud that men looked round on every side in astonishment at this odd and plainly solitary hilarity.

'Ha-ha-ha!' laughed Pierre. And he said aloud to himself: 'The soldier did not let me pass. They took me and shut me up They keep me prisoner. What "me"? Me? Me – my immortal soul! Ha-ha-ha! Ha-ha-ha! ...' he laughed with the tears starting to his eyes.

Someone got up and came to see what this queer big fellow was laughing at all by himself. Pierre stopped laughing, scrambled to his feet, walked away from the inquisitive intruder and looked about him.

The immense, endless bivouac which shortly before had hummed with the crackling of camp-fires and the voices of many men was now quiet; the red camp-fires paled and died down. High overhead in the luminous sky hung the full moon. Forests and fields beyond the confines of the camp, unseen before, now stretched visible in the distance. And still farther beyond those forests and fields the bright, quivering, limitless distance lured the eye into its depths. Pierre glanced up at the sky and the stars twinkling remote and far-away. 'And all that is mine, all that is in me, and all that is *me*,' thought Pierre. 'And they took all that and shut it up in a shed barricaded with planks!' He smiled and went to lie down and sleep beside his companions.

15

EARLY in October Napoleon sent another envoy to Kutuzov with overtures for peace and a letter falsely professing to come from Moscow, though in fact Napoleon was not far from Kutuzov on the old Kaluga road. Kutuzov replied to this letter as he had done to the previous one brought by Lauriston: he said that there could be no question of peace.

Soon after this a report was received from Dorohov's guerrilla squad operating to the left of Tarutino that French troops had been seen at Fominsk, that these troops belonged to Broussier's division, and that that division being separated from the rest of the French army might easily be destroyed. Soldiers and officers again clamoured for action. Generals on the Staff, elated by the easy victory at Tarutino, urged Kutuzov to act upon Dorohov's suggestion. Kutuzov did not consider any move necessary. The result, inevitably, was a compromise: a small detachment was sent to Fominsk to attack Broussier.

By a strange coincidence this operation – which turned out to be a most difficult and important one – was entrusted to Dokhturov, that same modest little Dokhturov whom no one has ever described to us as elaborating plans of campaign, rushing about at the head of regiments, showering crosses on batteries, and so on; who was thought to be and was spoken of as lacking decision and discernment – but nevertheless that same Dokhturov whom we always find in command, all through the Russo-French wars, from Austerlitz to the year 1813, wherever the position was most difficult. At Austerlitz he was the last to leave the Augest dam, rallying the regiments, saving what he could when all was rout and ruin and not a single general left in the rearguard. Ill with fever, he marches with twenty thousand men to Smolensk to defend the town against the whole of Napoleon's army. At Smolensk no sooner had he dozed off by the Molohov gate in a paroxysm of fever than he was roused by the roar of cannon bombarding the city – and Smolensk held out all day long. At Borodino when Bagration was killed and nine-tenths of the men of our left flank had fallen and the full force of the French artillery was directed against it, no other than the hesitating, undiscerning Dokhturov is dispatched there when Kutuzov hastens to repair his blunder in first sending someone else. And off goes the quiet little Dokhturov, and Borodino became the greatest glory of the Russian arms. Many are the heroes whose praises have been sung to us in verse and prose, but of Dokhturov hardly a word.

It is Dokhturov again who is sent to Fominsk, and from there to Malo-Yaroslavets, the scene of the last battle fought with the French and where the disintegration of the French army obviously began. And, again, accounts of this period of the campaign tell of many a genius and hero, but of Dokhturov nothing, or very little – and that half-heartedly – is said. This very silence about Dokhturov is the clearest testimony to his merit.

It is natural for a man who does not understand the workings of a machine to imagine that the most important part of the mechanism is the shaving which has fallen in by accident and is seen tossing about and interfering with its action. Anyone who does not understand the construction of the machine cannot conceive that it is not the shaving, which merely gets in the way and does damage, but the small connecting cogwheel, noiselessly revolving, that is one of the most essential parts of the mechanism.

On the 10th of October, the same day on which Dokhturov had gone half-way to Fominsk and stopped at the village of Aristovo, in readiness faithfully to carry out the orders given him, the entire French army, its convulsive jerking having brought it as far as Murat's position, apparently for the purpose of giving battle, abruptly, without any reason, swerved off to the left on to the new Kaluga highway and began marching into Fominsk, where until then only Broussier had been. Dokhturov at this time had under his command, besides Dorohov's guerillas, the two small detachments of Figner and Seslavin.

On the evening of October the 11th Seslavin came to the Aristovo headquarters with a captured French guardsman. The prisoner said that the troops which had that day entered Fominsk were the vanguard of the whole army, that Napoleon was with them and the whole army had marched out of Moscow four days previously. That same evening a house-serf, who had come from Borovsk, brought word that he had seen an immense mass of soldiery entering the town. Some Cossacks of Dokhturov's detachment reported having sighted the French Guards marching along the road to Borovsk. From all these reports it was evident that where they had expected to meet a single division there was now the entire French force marching from Moscow in an unexpected direction – along the old Kaluga highway. Dokhturov was unwilling to take any action as it was not clear to him now where his duty lay. His orders had been to attack Fominsk. But then only Broussier had been there, and now there was the whole French army. Yermolov wanted to act on his own judgement, but Dokhturov insisted that he must have instructions from his Serene Highness, Kutuzov. It was decided to send a dispatch to the Staff.

For this mission a capable officer, Bolhovitinov, was chosen, who, in addition to delivering a written report, was to explain the whole affair by word of mouth. Towards midnight Bolhovitinov, having received the dispatch and his verbal instructions, galloped off to Headquarters, accompanied by a Cossack with spare horses.

THE autumn night was warm and dark. Rain had been falling for the last four days. Changing horses twice and galloping twenty miles in an hour and a half over a sticky muddy road, Bolhovitinov reached Letashovka between one and two in the morning. Dismounting at a cottage, on the wattle fence of which hung a sign-board 'General Staff', and throwing down the reins, he entered the dark passage.

'The general on duty, instantly! It's very important!' he cried to someone who started up, wheezing in the darkness of the passage.

'His Honour has been very unwell since last evening, he hasn't slept for two nights,' pleaded the orderly in a whisper. 'Better wake the captain first.'

'This is most urgent, I tell you, from General Dokhturov,' said Bolhovitinov, groping his way through an open door behind the orderly who had gone in and was waking someone.

'Your Honour, your Honour! A courier.'

'What? What's that? From whom?' asked a sleepy voice.

'From Dokhturov and from Alexei Petrovich. Napoleon is at Fominsk,' said Bolhovitinov, unable to see the speaker in the dark but surmising by the sound of the voice that it was not Konovnitsyn.

The man who had been roused yawned and stretched.

'I don't like waking him,' he said, fumbling for something. 'He's a very sick man. And this may be only a rumour.'

'Here is the dispatch,' said Bolhovitinov. 'My orders are to deliver it at once to the general on duty.'

'Wait till I strike a light. You damned rascal, where is it you always hide things?' said the voice of the officer who was stretching himself, to the orderly. (The speaker was Shcherbinin, Konovnitsyn's adjutant.) 'I've found it, I've found it!' he added.

The orderly was striking a light. Shcherbinin was feeling round the candlestick.

'Oh, the swine!' said he with disgust.

By the light of the sparks Bolhovitinov caught a glimpse of Shcherbinin's youthful face as he held the candle, and, in the front corner of the room, of another man still asleep. This was Konovnitsyn.

When the flame of the sulphur splinters kindled by the tinder flared up, first blue and then red, Shcherbinin lighted a tallow candle – the cockroaches that had been gnawing it scurried from the candle-stick – and looked at the messenger. Bolhovitinov was bespattered all over with mud and in wiping his face with his sleeve had daubed it also.

'Where did the report come from?' inquired Shcherbinin, taking the envelope.

'The news is trustworthy enough,' said Bolhovitinov. 'Prisoners and Cossacks and spies all tell the same story.'

'Well, there's no help for it, we shall have to wake him,' said Shcherbinin, getting up and going to the sleeping man who wore a nightcap and was wrapped in a military greatcoat. 'Piotr Petrovich!' he said. Konovnitsyn did not stir. 'Wanted at Headquarters!' he said with a smile, knowing those words would be sure to rouse him.

And the head in the night-cap was, in fact, lifted immediately. On Konovnitsyn's handsome, resolute face, with cheeks flushed by fever, there still lingered for an instant a far-away, dreamy expression remote from reality, but he gave a sudden start and his face assumed its usual quiet firm look.

'Well, what is it? From whom?' he asked at once but with no haste, blinking at the light.

As he listened to what the officer had to tell him, Konovnitsyn broke the seal and read the dispatch. Hardly had he done so before he lowered his legs in their worsted stockings to the earth floor and began putting on his boots. Then he pulled off the night-cap and, running the comb through the locks on his temples, donned his forage-cap.

'Did you get here quickly? Let us go to his Serene Highness.'

Konovnitsyn had realized directly that the news brought was of great importance and there was no time to lose. As to whether it was good news or bad, he had no opinion and did not even put the question to himself. That did not interest him. He regarded the whole business of the war not with his intellect nor with his reason but with something else. In his heart he had a deep, unexpressed conviction that all would be well; but that one must not trust to this, and still less speak about it, but must simply do one's duty. And this he did, giving all his energies to it.

Piotr Petrovich Konovnitsyn, like Dokhturov, seems to have been included merely as a matter of form in the list of so-called heroes of 1812 – the Barclays, Raevskys, Yermolovs, Platovs and Miloradoviches. Like Dokhturov he had the reputation of being a man of very limited ability and knowledge; and again, like Dokhturov, Konovnitsyn never drew up plans of campaign but was always to be found where the situation was most critical. Ever since he had been appointed general on duty he had slept with his door open, insisting that he should be roused whenever any courier arrived. In battle he was always under fire, so that Kutuzov even chided him about it and was afraid to send him to the front; and like Dokhturov, Konovnitsyn was one of those inconspicuous cogwheels which, without chatter or noise, constitute the most essential part of the machine.

Emerging from the hut into the damp dark night, Konovnitsyn frowned – partly because the pain in his head was worse and partly from the disagreeable thought that occurred to him of the stir this news would make in the nest of all the bigwigs on the Staff, especially Bennigsen, who ever since Tarutino had been at daggers drawn with Kutuzov. The suggestions they would make, the quarrelling there would be, the orders and counter-orders! And the presentiment was not a pleasant one, though he knew there was no getting round the fact.

And, indeed, Toll, to whom he went to communicate the news, immediately began to expound his ideas to the general who shared his quarters, until Konovnitsyn, after listening in weary silence, reminded him that they must go to his Serene Highness.

17

Kutuzov, like all old people, did not sleep much at night. In the daytime he would often drop off unexpectedly into a doze; but at night he lay on his bed without undressing, and generally remained awake thinking.

He was lying on his bed like that now, leaning his large, heavy, disfigured head on his plump hand and meditating, his one eye wide open staring into the darkness.

Since Bennigsen, who was in correspondence with the Emperor and had more influence than all the rest of the Staff, had taken to avoiding him, Kutuzov was more at ease on the score of not finding himself obliged to lead his men into useless aggressive actions. The lesson of Tarutino and the day before the battle, a memory that rankled in Kutuzov's mind, must, he thought, have some effect on others too.

'They must see,' he thought, 'that we can only lose by taking the offensive. Patience and time are my two valiant allies!' He knew the apple was better not picked while it was still green. It would fall of itself when ripe, but if you pick it green you spoil the apple, and the tree, and set your teeth on edge. Like an experienced huntsman he knew the beast was wounded – wounded as only the whole might of Russia could wound it. But was the hurt mortal? That was a point not yet decided. The fact that Lauriston and Barthélemy had been sent to him, and the reports of the guerrillas, made Kutuzov almost sure that the wound was a deadly one. But further proofs were wanted: it was necessary to wait.

'They would like to run and look at the damage they have done. Wait a bit, and you'll see. This everlasting talk of manoeuvres, of attacks!' thought he. 'What for? Only to gain distinction for themselves! As if fighting were some sort of jolly exercise! They are like children from whom there's no getting a sensible account of what has happened because they all want to show how well they can fight. But that's not the point now.

'And what ingenious manoeuvres all these fellows propose to me! They think that when they have thought of one or two contingencies' (he had in mind the general plan sent him from Petersburg) 'they have exhausted the list. But there's no end to them.'

The unanswered question whether the wound inflicted at Borodino was mortal or not had been hanging about over Kutuzov's head for a whole month. On the one hand the French had occupied Moscow. On the other, Kutuzov felt convinced in every fibre of his being that the terrible blow into which he and the whole Russian people had put the last ounce of their strength must have been mortal. But in any case proofs were needed, and he had been waiting for them a month now, and the longer he waited the more impatient he became. Lying on his bed through those sleepless nights of his, he did the very thing the younger generals did – the very thing he found fault with them for doing. Just like the younger men he imagined all sorts of possible contingencies embracing Napoleon's downfall, surely already effected. He imagined these contingencies, only with this difference, that he based nothing on them and saw them, not in twos or threes but in thousands. The more he conjectured, the more numerous the hypotheses that presented themselves. He worked out every kind of diversion the Napoleonic army might make, acting as a whole or in sections – against Petersburg, against himself, or to outflank him. He thought too of the possibility (which he feared most of all) that Napoleon might fight him with his own weapon – might settle down in Moscow and wait for him to move. Kutuzov even pictured Napoleon's army turning back via Medyn and Yukhnov; but the one thing he could not foresee was the very thing that happened – the insane, convulsive doubling to and fro of Napoleon's army during the first eleven days of its march from Moscow: the stampede which rendered possible what Kutuzov had not till then dared even to think of – namely, the complete annihilation of the French. Dorohov's report about Broussier's division, the guerrillas' accounts of the miseries of Napoleon's army, rumours of preparations for evacuating Moscow – all confirmed the presumption that the French army was worsted and about to take to its heels. But all this was only supposition, which appealed to the younger men but not to Kutuzov. With his sixty years' experience he knew how much dependence to put upon hearsay, knew how apt people are when they want anything to arrange all the evidence so that it appears to confirm what they desire, and how ready they are in such circumstances to overlook anything that makes for the contrary. And the more Kutuzov hoped, the less he allowed himself to believe that it might be so. This question engaged all the energies of his mind. All else was for him merely the ordinary routine of life. To such customary routine belonged his conversations with the Staff, the letters he wrote from Tarutino to Madame de Staël, the novels he read, the distribution of awards, his correspondence with Petersburg, and so on. But the destruction of the French, which he alone foresaw, was his heart's one desire.

On the night of the 11th of October he lay leaning on his arm and thinking of that.

There was a stir in the next room and he heard the steps of Toll, Konovnitsyn and Bolhovitinov.

'Eh, who's there? Come in, come in! Anything new?' the field-marshal called to them.

While a footman was lighting a candle Toll related the gist of the news.

'Who brought it?' asked Kutuzov with a face that impressed Toll when the candle was lighted by its cold severity.

'There can be no doubt about it, your Highness.'

'Call him in, call him here!'

Kutuzov sat up with one leg hanging down from the bed and his big paunch resting against the other leg which was bent under him. He screwed up his sound eye the better to scan the messenger, as though he hoped to read in his features the answer to what was occupying him.

'Speak up, tell me, my friend,' he said to Bolhovitinov in his low, aged voice, pulling the shirt together that gaped open over his chest. 'Come here, come closer. What is this news you have brought me? Eh? That Napoleon has left Moscow? Are you sure? Eh?'

Bolhovitinov gave him a detailed account from the beginning of all that had been committed to him.

'Out with it, make haste! Don't keep me in suspense,' Kutuzov interrupted him.

Bolhovitinov told the whole story and was then silent, awaiting instructions. Toll was about to speak but Kutuzov checked him. He tried to say something but all at once his face began to work and pucker up; waving his arm at Toll, he turned to the opposite corner of the hut which was dark with the icons hanging there.

'O Lord, my Creator, Thou hast heard our prayer ...' he said in a trembling voice, clasping his hands. 'Russia is saved! I thank Thee, O Lord!' And he wept.

18

FROM the time he received the news of the French leaving Moscow, to the end of the campaign, all Kutuzov's activity was directed exclusively towards restraining his troops, by the exercise of authority, by guile, by entreaty, from useless attacks, manoeuvres or encounters with the doomed enemy. Dokhturov goes to Malo-Yaroslavets, but Kutuzov lingers with the main army and gives orders for the evacuation of Kaluga – a retreat beyond that town seeming to him quite possible.

Kutuzov falls back on all sides, but the enemy, without waiting for him to retire, flees in the opposite direction.

Napoleon's historians describe to us his skilful manoeuvres at Tarutino and Malo-Yaroslavets, and make conjectures as to what would have happened had Napoleon managed to penetrate into the rich provinces of the south.

But not to speak of the fact that nothing hindered Napoleon from marching into these southern provinces (since the Russian army left the road open) the historians forget that nothing could have saved Napoleon's army, for it already carried within itself the germs of inevitable ruin. How could that army – which had found abundant supplies in Moscow and had trampled them underfoot instead of conserving them, and on arriving at Smolensk had looted instead of storing provisions – how could that army have recovered in the province of Kaluga, where the inhabitants were of the same stock as the Russians of Moscow, and where fire had the same property of consuming whatever they set fire to?

That army could not have retrieved itself anywhere. After Borodino and the sacking of Moscow it was to bear within itself, as it were, the chemical elements of dissolution.

The men of what had once been an army fled with their leaders, not knowing whither they went, Napoleon and every soldier with him concerned only to extricate themselves as quickly as might be from the hopeless position of which they were all, if but dimly, aware.

So it came about that at the council at Malo-Yaroslavets when the French generals, affecting to be conferring together, expressed their various views, the last opinion of all, uttered by General Mouton, a blunt soldier, who said what everyone was thinking – that the only course was to get away as quickly as possible – closed all mouths; and no one, not even Napoleon, could say anything against a truth which all recognized.

But though everybody knew it was necessary to get away, there still remained the shame of confessing that they must take to flight. Some external shock was needed to overcome that shame, and that shock came in due time. It was 'le Hourra de l'Empereur', as the French called it.

On the day after the council Napoleon rode out early in the morning amid the lines of his army, with a suite of marshals and an escort, on the pretext of inspecting the troops and the scene of battle, past and to come. A party of Cossacks on the prowl for booty fell in with the Emperor and very nearly captured him. What saved Napoleon from the Cossacks on this occasion was the very thing that was proving the downfall of the French: the booty, which here as at Tarutino, tempted the Cossacks to go after plunder and let the enemy

1216

slip. Disregarding Napoleon, they flung themselves on the spoils, and Napoleon succeeded in getting away.

With matters at such a pass that the 'children of the Don' might actually have snatched the Emperor himself in the midst of his army, it was clear that there was nothing else for it but to fly with all possible haste by the nearest familiar road. Napoleon, forty and paunchy, and not so nimble and daring as of old, accepted the intimation; and under the influence of the fright the Cossacks had given him he at once agreed with Mouton and issued the order – as the historians tell us – to retreat along the Smolensk road.

The fact that Napoleon agreed with Mouton and that the army retreated does not prove that Napoleon instigated the retreat but that the forces influencing the whole army to take to the Mozhaisk (the Smolensk) road were simultaneously exerting their influence on Napoleon too.

19

WHEN a man finds himself in motion he always devises some purpose for his bodily exertion. To be able to walk hundreds of miles a man must believe that something good awaits him at the end of those hundreds of miles. He needs the prospect of a promised land to give him the strength to keep on.

When the French invaded Russia their promised land was Moscow; when they were retreating it was their mother country. But their mother country was too far off, and a man who has six or seven hundred miles to walk before reaching his destination must be able to put his final goal out of his mind and say to himself that he will 'do thirty miles today and then spend the night somewhere'; and during this first stage of the journey that resting-place for the night eclipses the image of his ultimate goal and absorbs all his hopes and desires. And the instinctive impulses manifest in the individual are always magnified in a crowd.

For the French, marching back along the old Smolensk road the final goal – their native land – was too remote, and their immediate objective on which all their desires and hopes, enormously intensified in the mass, were concentrated, was Smolensk. It was not that they expected plentiful supplies and reinforcements awaiting them in Smolensk, nor that they were told any such thing (on the contrary, the higher ranks of the army and Napoleon himself knew that provisions were scant there), but because this alone could give them the strength to keep on and endure their present hardships. So both those who knew better, and those who did not, alike deceived themselves and struggled on to Smolensk as to a promised land.

Once out on the high road the French fled with surprising energy and unheard-of rapidity towards the goal they had fixed on. Besides the common impulse which united the French hosts into one whole and imparted a certain momentum there was something else which held them together – their great numbers. As with the law of gravity in physics, the enormous mass of the retreating army attracted the individual human atoms to itself. In their hundreds of thousands they moved like a solid empire.

Every man among them had but one longing – to give himself up and be taken prisoner, to escape from all this horror and misery. But on the one hand the driving force of the common impulse towards their goal, Smolensk, carried each one in the same direction; on the other hand, an army corps could not surrender to a company, and though the French availed themselves of every convenient opportunity to stray off and surrender on the smallest decent pretext such pretexts did not always occur. Their very numbers and the compact swiftness with which they moved ruled out that possibility and made it not only difficult but out of the question for the Russians to arrest the progress on which the entire energies of the French mass were bent. Beyond a certain limit no mechanical disruption of the body could accelerate the process of decomposition.

A lump of snow cannot be melted instantaneously. There is a certain measure of time in less than which no amount of heat can thaw the snow. On the contrary, the greater the heat the harder the remaining snow becomes.

Of the Russian generals Kutuzov was the only one to understand this. When the retreat of the French army took the definite shape of flight along the Smolensk road, what Konovnitsyn had foreseen on the night of the 11th of October began to come to pass. The entire high command of the Russian army were fired with a desire to distinguish themselves, to cut off, to seize, to capture, to overthrow the French, and all clamoured for action.

Kutuzov alone employed all his powers (and the powers of any commander-in-chief are very inconsiderable) to prevent an attack.

He could not tell them what we can say now: 'Why fight, why

block the road, losing our own men and inhumanly slaughtering poor unfortunate wretches? What is the point of that when from Moscow to Viazma, without battle, a third of their army melted away of itself?' Instead, drawing from his aged wisdom what they could understand, he reminded them of the golden bridge (of self-destruction), and they mocked him and slandered him, and swooped cock-a-hoop and hacked at the dying beast.

In the neighbourhood of Viazma, Yermolov, Miloradovich, Platov and others, finding themselves near the French, could not resist their desire to cut off and break up two French corps. In sending to inform Kutuzov of their intention, they enclosed a blank sheet of paper in the envelope instead of the dispatch.

And in spite of all Kutuzov's efforts to restrain the troops our men assailed the French and tried to bar the road. Infantry regiments, we are told, advanced to the attack with music and beating of drums, and slew and were slain in thousands.

But as for cutting off retreat – no one was cut off and no one was turned aside. And the French army, closing its ranks tighter at the danger, continued its fatal path to Smolensk, steadily melting away as it went.

PART THREE

I

THE battle of Borodino with the occupation of Moscow that followed and the flight of the French, without any more engagements, is one of the most instructive phenomena in history.

All historians are agreed that the external activity of states and peoples in their clashes with one another finds expression in wars; that the political power of states and peoples increases or diminishes in proportion to success or defeat in war.

Strange as we may find historical accounts of how some king or emperor, having quarrelled with some other emperor or king, levies an army, fights his enemy's army, gains a victory, killing three, five or ten thousand men, and consequently subjugates a whole dominion of several million souls; and unintelligible as it may be why the defeat of an army – a hundredth part of a nation's strength – should oblige that whole nation to submit, yet all the facts of history (so far as we know history) confirm the truth of the statement that the greater or lesser success of one army against another is the cause, or at least a material indication, of an increase or decrease in the power of that nation. An army gains a victory, and at once the rights of the conquering nation are increased to the detriment of the defeated. An army suffers defeat, and at once a people loses its rights in proportion to the severity of the reverse, and if its army is completely routed the nation is reduced to complete subjection.

So (according to history) it has been from the most ancient times, and up to our own day. All Napoleon's wars serve to confirm this rule. In proportion to the defeat of the Austrian army Austria is shorn of her rights, and the rights and might of France increase. The victories of the French at Jena and Auerstädt destroy the independent existence of Prussia.

But suddenly, in 1812, the French gain a victory near Moscow. Moscow is taken, and after that, with no more battles, it is not Russia that ceases to exist but the French army of six hundred thousand, and then Napoleonic France itself. To stretch the facts to fit the rules of history – to say that the Russians remained in possession of the field of Borodino, or that after Napoleon's army left Moscow it was cut up in a series of pitched battles – is impossible.

After the French victory at Borodino there was no general engagement, nor even a skirmish of any great importance, yet the French army ceased to exist. What does this signify? If such a thing had occurred in the history of China, we might say that it was not an historical reality (the favourite loophole of historians when facts do not fit theories); if it were a question of some brief conflict in which only a small number of troops took part, we might treat it as an exception to the general rule; but all this took place before the eyes of our fathers, for whom it was a matter of the life or death of their country, and the war was the most momentous of all known wars. ...

That period of the campaign of 1812, from Borodino to the final expulsion of the French, proved that the winning of a battle does not necessarily lead to conquest and may not even be a sure promise of conquest; it proved that the force which decides the fate of peoples lies not in the conquerors, nor even in armies and battles, but in something else.

French historians, describing the condition of the French forces before they marched out of Moscow, assert that everything was in good order in the *Grande Armée*, except the cavalry, the artillery and the transport – there being no forage for the horses and cattle. That was a misfortune no one could remedy, for the peasants of the surrounding country burnt their hay rather than let the French have it.

Victory did not bring forth its usual results because Tom, Dick and Harry, who were by no means burdened with heroic sentiment – after the French had evacuated Moscow they drove in in their carts to pillage the city – and the whole vast multitude of others like them refused to bring their hay to Moscow, in spite of the high prices offered them, but burnt it instead.

Let us imagine two men who have come out to fight a duel with swords in accordance with all the rules of the art of fencing. The parrying has continued for some time. Suddenly one of the combatants, aware that he has been wounded and realizing that the affair is no joke but that his life is at stake, throws down his sword and seizing the first cudgel that comes handy begins to brandish it. Then let us imagine that the combatant who thus so sensibly employed the best and simplest means for his purpose was at the same time influenced by traditions of chivalry and, wanting to conceal the facts of the case, insisted afterwards that he won his victory with the sword according to all the rules of the art of fencing. How confusing and unintelligible we should find the story of such a duel!

The fencer who demanded a contest in accordance with the rules of fencing is the French army; his opponent who threw away his sword and snatched up a club did like the Russian people; those who try to give an account of the issue consistent with the rules of fencing are the historians who have described the event.

After the burning of Smolensk a war began which did not fit any of the old traditions of warfare. The burning of towns and villages, the withdrawal after every battle, the blow dealt at Borodino, followed by another retreat, the abandoning and burning of Moscow, the hunting down of marauders, the seizing of provision-trains, guerrilla fighting – all this was a departure from the rules.

Napoleon was conscious of it, and from the time he took up the correct attitude of the fencer in Moscow and instead of his opponent's rapier saw a cudgel raised against him he never ceased complaining to Kutuzov and to the Emperor Alexander that the war was being conducted contrary to all the rules – as if there were any rules for killing people. In spite of the complaints of the French that the rules were not being kept to, in spite of the fact that to some highly placed Russians it seemed rather disgraceful to fight with a club – they would have liked to take up the correct position *en quarte* or *en tierce* and make an adroit thrust *en prime*, and so on – the cudgel of the people's war was lifted with all its menacing and majestic might, and, caring nothing for good taste and procedure, with dull-witted simplicity but sound judgement it rose and fell, making no distinctions, and belaboured the French until the whole army of invaders had perished.

And it is well for the people who, unlike the French in 1813, will not salute their magnanimous conqueror according to all the rules of the art, gracefully and ceremoniously presenting him with the hilt of their swords. Happy the people who in the moment of trial, without stopping to ask what rules others have observed in similar cases, simply and nimbly pick up the first cudgel to hand and deal blow after blow until the resentment and revenge in their souls give way to contempt and compassion.

2

ONE of the most tangible and advantageous departures from the so-called rules of warfare is the action of scattered groups against a body of men obliged to operate in a dense mass. This sort of independent action is always seen in wars which assume a national character. In fighting of this kind, instead of combining into a crowd to attack a crowd, men divide, attack separately and at once run away when threatened by superior forces, only to resume the offensive at the first favourable opportunity. Such were the methods of the guerrillas in Spain, of the mountain tribes in the Caucasus and of the Russians in 1812.

People have called this kind of war 'guerrilla warfare' and assumed that by giving it this label they have explained its meaning. Incidentally, this sort of warfare not only fails to come under any rules but is in direct contradiction to a well-known law of tactics which is accepted as infallible. This law lays down that the attacking party shall concentrate his forces in order to be stronger than his adversary at the moment battle is joined.

Guerrilla warfare (always successful, as history testifies) operates in flat contradiction to this rule.

The paradox arises from the fact that military science assumes the strength of an army to be identical with its numerical proportions. Military science says, the greater the numbers the greater the strength. *Les gros bataillons ont toujours raison* – God is on the side of the big battalions.

For military science to make this assertion is like defining energy in mechanics by reference to the mass only. It is like saying that the momenta of moving bodies will be equal or unequal according to the equality or inequality of their masses. But momentum (or 'quantity of motion') is the product of mass and velocity.

So too in warfare the strength of an army is the product of its mass and of something else, some unknown factor x.

Military science, finding in history innumerable instances of the size of an army not coinciding with its strength, and of small detachments defeating larger ones, vaguely admits the existence of this 'unknown' and tries to discover it – now in some geometrical disposition of the troops, now in superiority of weapons, or (more frequently) in the genius of the commanders. But none of these hypo-thetical identifications of the unknown factor yields results which accord with the historical facts.

Yet it is only necessary to renounce the false notion (flattering though it may be to the 'heroes') of the efficacy of dispositions issued in war-time by the higher authorities in order to arrive at our un-known x.

This x is the spirit of the army – in other words, the greater or lesser readiness to fight and face danger on the part of all the men composing an army, quite independently of whether they are, or are not, fighting under leaders of genius, of whether they fight in two- or three-line formation, with cudgels or with rifles that repeat thirty times a minute. Men who are eager to fight will always put them-selves in the most advantageous conditions for fighting.

The spirit of an army is the factor which multiplied by the mass gives the resulting force. To define and formulate the significance of this unknown factor, the spirit of the army, constitutes the scientific problem.

The problem is only solvable if we stop arbitrarily substituting for the unknown x the conditions under which it is seen to operate – such as the dispositions of the general, the military equipment, and so on – mistaking these for the significant factor. We must accept the un-known and see it for what it is: the more or less active desire to fight and to face danger. Only then, expressing the known historical facts by means of equations, shall we be able to compare the relative values of the unknown factor; only then may we hope to arrive at the un-known itself.

If ten men, battalions or divisions, fighting fifteen men, battalions or divisions, beat the fifteen – that is, kill or capture them all while losing four themselves, the loss will have been four on one side and fifteen on the other. Therefore the four were equal to the fifteen, and we may write $4x = 15y$. In other words, x is to y as 15 is to 4. Though this equation does not yet give us the absolute value of the unknown factor, it does give us a ratio between two unknowns. And by putting a whole variety of historical data (battles, campaigns, periods of warfare and so on) into the form of such equations, a series of figures will be obtained which must involve the laws inherent in equations and will in time reveal them.

The principle of tactics, that armies should act in masses when on the offensive and should break up into smaller groups for retreat, unconsciously confirms the truth that the strength of an army depends on its spirit. To lead men forward under fire requires more discipline (obtainable only by movement in compact formation) than is needed for self-defence when attacked. But as the rule leaves out of account the spirit of the army, it continually proves fallacious. Above all it is in flagrant contrast to the facts when some strong rise or fall in the spirit of the troops occurs, as in all national wars.

The French during their retreat in 1812, instead of separating – according to tactics – into small detachments to defend themselves, clung together in a horde because the spirit of the troops had fallen so low that it was only their number that kept them going. The Russians on the contrary ought, according to tactics, to have attacked in a body, whereas in actual fact they split up into small units, because the spirit of the men ran so high that individual men struck at the French without waiting for orders and needed no compelling to expose themselves to hardships and dangers.

3

THE so-called partisan war began with the entry of the French into Smolensk.

Before guerrilla warfare had been officially recognized by the government many thousands of enemy soldiers – marauding stragglers, foraging parties – had been exterminated by Cossacks and peasants, who killed them off as instinctively as dogs set upon a mad stray. Denis Davydov was the first to appreciate with his Russian instinct the value of this terrible cudgel which, regardless of the rules of military science, was annihilating the French, and to him belongs the credit of taking the first step towards regularizing this method of warfare.

On August the 24th Davydov's first partisan detachment was formed, and others soon followed. As the campaign proceeded so more and more of these detachments were organized.

The partisans destroyed the *Grande Armée* piecemeal. They swept up the fallen leaves that were dropping of themselves from that withered tree – the French army – and sometimes shook the tree itself. By October, when the French were fleeing back to Smolensk, there were hundreds of these bands, of various sizes and characters.

There were some that kept up the appearance of regular troops, had infantry, artillery and army staffs, and the comforts and decencies of life. Others consisted solely of Cossack cavalry. There were small haphazard collections of mixed infantry and cavalry, and little knots of peasants and landed proprietors who remained anonymous. A sacristan commanded one such party which captured several hundred prisoners in the course of a month. There was the village elder's wife, Vasilisa, who killed hundreds of the French.

The latter days of October saw this guerrilla warfare at its height. The first period of this kind of war – with the partisans themselves amazed at their own audacity, in continual fear of being surrounded and captured by the French, and never unsaddling, hardly daring to dismount, hiding in the woods and expecting to be pursued at any moment – was past. By the end of October this kind of warfare had taken definite shape: it had become clear to everybody what could be ventured against the French and what could not. By now it was only the commanders of detachments marching with staff-officers who kept at a respectful distance from the French, according to the rules, and still regarded many things as impossible. The small bands that had started their activities long before and had already had the French under close observation considered feasible what the leaders of the big detachments would not even dare contemplate. The Cossacks and the peasants, who crept in and out among the French, reckoned everything possible now.

On the 22nd of October Denisov (who was one of the irregulars) was with his group at the height of the guerrilla enthusiasm. Since early morning he and his party had been on the move. All day long, keeping under cover of the forest that skirted the high road, he had been stalking a large French convoy of cavalry baggage and Russian prisoners, which, separated from the rest of the army and moving under a powerful escort – as was learned from scouts and prisoners – was making its way to Smolensk. Not only Denisov and Dolohov (who also was a leader of a small band operating in Denisov's vicinity) but the generals in charge of some big detachments with proper staffs were aware of the presence of this convoy and, as Denisov expressed it, 'were sharpening their teeth for it'. Two of these generals, one a Pole and the other a German, sent almost simultaneously to Denisov, inviting him to join forces with them to attack the convoy.

'No, thank you, bwother, I wasn't born yesterday!' said Denisov on reading these missives, and he wrote to the German that, despite his heartfelt desire to serve under so valiant and renowned a general, he must forgo that pleasure because he was already under the command of the Polish general. To the Pole he replied in the same strain, informing him that he was already under the command of the German.

Having arranged matters thus, Denisov, without referring to the higher authorities, intended with Dolohov to attack and seize the convoy with their own small forces. On October the 22nd the transport was proceeding from the village of Mikulino to that of Shamshevo. On the left of the road between the two villages were great forests, in some places extending to the very edge of the road, in others receding up to three-quarters of a mile or more. It was through these forests that Denisov and his party rode all day, sometimes keeping well back and sometimes emerging to the fringe but never losing sight of the moving French. That morning, not far from Mikulino, where the forest ran close to the road, Cossacks of Denisov's party had pounced on two French baggage-wagons loaded with cavalry-saddles which had stuck in the mud, and made off with them into the forest. From that time right on to evening they had been watching the movements of the French without attacking. Denisov's idea was to let the French continue quietly on to Shamshevo, without alarming them, and then, joining Dolohov (who was to come that evening to a watchman's hut in the wood, three-quarters of a mile from Shamshevo, to concert measures with him), surprise the French at dawn, falling like an avalanche of snow on their heads, and rout and capture the whole lot at one blow. Six Cossacks had been left behind a mile and a half from Mikulino where the forest bordered the road, to bring word at once should any fresh columns of French show themselves.

Beyond Shamshevo Dolohov was to observe the road in the same way, to find out at what distance there were other French troops. They reckoned that the convoy had fifteen hundred men. Denisov had a couple of hundred, Dolohov about the same number. But numerical disparity did not deter Denisov. All that he now needed to know was what troops these were, and for this purpose he had to capture a 'tongue' – that is, a man from the enemy column. The morning's attack on the wagons had been accomplished in such haste that the French soldiers in charge of the two wagons had all been killed, and only a little drummer-boy had been taken alive, who had strayed away and could tell them nothing definite about the troops forming the column.

To make a second raid Denisov considered would be too dangerous – it might put the whole contingent on the alert – so he sent Tikhon Shcherbaty, a peasant who was with them, on ahead to Shamshevo to see if he could capture at least one of the French quartermasters from the vanguard.

4

It was a mild, rainy autumn day. Sky and horizon were both the colour of muddy water. At times a sort of mist descended, and then suddenly there would be a heavy downpour of slanting rain.

Denisov, in a felt cloak and an astrakhan cap from which the water streamed down, was riding a lean, pinched-looking thoroughbred. Like his horse, which had its head down and its ears laid back, he shrank from the driving rain and peered anxiously before him. His face was somewhat thinner than of old, and with its short growth of thick black beard had an irate look.

Beside Denisov, also in felt cloak and astrakhan cap, and mounted on a sleek, sturdy Don horse, rode the hetman of the Cossacks – Denisov's collaborator.

This hetman – Esaul Lovaisky the Third – was a tall creature, flat as a board, pale-faced, fair-haired, and with narrow, light eyes. His face and bearing were expressive of quiet self-confidence. Though it would have been very difficult to say what it was gave horse and rider their particular character, a glance at the hetman and at Denisov was enough to tell one that the latter was wet and uncomfortable and a man who merely rode his horse, while looking at the hetman it was plain that he was as comfortable and as much at ease as always – not a man who merely rode his horse but a man who was one with his steed, and thus possessed of twofold strength.

A little ahead of them walked a peasant guide, soaked to the skin through his grey kaftan and white woollen cap.

A little behind, on a thin, scraggy Kirghiz pony with a huge tail and mane and its mouth bloody and torn, rode a young officer in a blue French military coat.

Beside him rode a hussar, with a boy in a tattered French uniform and blue cap perched behind him on his horse's crupper. The lad clung to the hussar, his hands red with cold, and, wriggling his bare feet in an effort to warm them, gazed about him with bewildered eyes and uplifted brows. This was the French drummer-boy captured that morning.

Behind them along the narrow, sodden, churned-up forest track came hussars in threes and fours, and then Cossacks, some in felt cloaks, some in French greatcoats, and some with horse-cloths over their heads. The horses, whether chestnut or bay, all looked black from the drenching rain. Their necks seemed curiously narrow with their wet clinging manes. Steam rose from the horses in clouds. Everything – clothes, saddles, bridles – was wet, slippery and dank, like the ground and the fallen leaves that strewed the path. The men sat huddled up, their arms pressed close to their sides so as to keep the chill off the water that had already trickled through to their skins, and not to admit the fresh cold rain that leaked in under their seats, behind their knees and at the back of their necks. In the middle of the file of Cossacks two wagons drawn by French horses, and Cossack saddle-horses hitched on in front, rumbled over tree-stumps and branches, and splashed through ruts full of water.

Denisov's horse swerved to avoid a puddle in the track and bumped his rider's knee against a tree.

'Oh, the devil!' exclaimed Denisov angrily, and showing his teeth he struck the horse three times with his whip, splashing himself and his comrades with mud.

Denisov was in a bad temper, because of the rain and also from hunger (none of them had eaten anything since morning), but most of all because he still had no news from Dolohov, and the man sent to capture a 'tongue' had not returned.

'We aren't likely to get another chance to fall on a twansport twain like today. To attack them alone is too much of a wisk, and if we put it off till another day one of the big guewwilla detachments will snatch the pwey from under our vewy noses,' thought Denisov, continually peering ahead in the hope of discerning a messenger from Dolohov.

Emerging into a clearing in the forest from which he could see a long way to the right, Denisov reined in.

'There's someone coming,' said he.

The hetman looked in the direction Denisov was pointing.

'There are two of them – an officer and a Cossack. Only I wouldn't be *prepositive* that it is the lieutenant-colonel himself,' said the hetman, who was fond of using words the Cossacks did not know.

The two horsemen, riding down a hill, were lost to sight but they reappeared again a few minutes later. In front, at a weary gallop and using his leather whip, rode the officer, dishevelled and soaked through. His trousers had worked up to above his knees. Behind him, standing in the stirrups, trotted a Cossack. The officer, a very young lad with a broad, rosy face and keen, merry eyes, galloped up to Denisov and handed him a sopping envelope.

'From the general,' he said, 'I must apologize for its not being quite dry.'

Denisov, frowning, took the envelope and opened it.

'There now, they kept telling us it was so dangerous,' said the officer, addressing the hetman while Denisov was reading the letter. 'But Komarov here' – he indicated his Cossack – 'Komarov and I made our preparations. We each of us have two pisto ... But what's this?' he asked, noticing the French drummer-boy. 'A prisoner? You've already been in action? May I speak to him?'

'Wostov! Petya!' exclaimed Denisov, having skimmed through the dispatch. 'Why didn't you say who you were?' – and turning with a smile he held out his hand to the lad.

The officer was Petya Rostov.

All the way Petya had been rehearsing in his mind how he should behave with Denisov as befitted a grown man and an officer, making no reference to their previous acquaintance. But as soon as Denisov smiled at him Petya beamed at once, blushed with pleasure, forgot the official demeanour he had been intending to preserve, and began telling him how he had ridden past the French, and how glad he was to have been given this commission, and how he had already been in a battle near Vyazma, and how a certain hussar had distinguished himself there.

'Well, I'm wight glad to see you,' Denisov interrupted him, and his face again assumed its anxious expression.

'Mihail Feoklitych,' he said to the hetman, 'this is fwom the German again, you know. He' (he meant Petya) 'is serving under him.'

And Denisov told the hetman that the letter just delivered reiterated the German general's request that they should join forces with him for an attack on the transports.

'If we don't gwab their twansport tomowwow they'll snatch it fwom under our noses,' he ended up.

While Denisov was talking to the hetman, Petya, mortified by

Denisov's cold tone and supposing that it might be due to the state of his trousers, did his best to work them down again under his cloak without attracting attention, at the same time maintaining as martial an air as possible.

'Has your Honour any orders for me ?' he asked of Denisov, putting his hand to the peak of his cap in a salute and resuming the comedy of adjutant and general for which he had rehearsed himself, 'or am I to remain with your Honour ?'

'Orders ? ...' Denisov repeated thoughtfully. 'What about we-maining till tomowwow ?'

'Oh yes, please ... May I stay with you ?' cried Petya.

'But just what did your genewal tell you ? To weturn at once ?' asked Denisov.

Petya blushed.

'He didn't give me any instructions. I think I could, couldn't I ?' he replied inquiringly.

'All wight, then,' said Denisov.

And turning to his men he directed a party of them to go on to the watchman's hut in the forest, the halting-place arranged on, and told the officer on the Kirghiz pony (this officer performed the duties of adjutant) to go and look for Dolohov, find out where he was and whether he would be coming that evening. Denisov himself intended riding with the hetman and Petya to the edge of the forest where it reached out to Shamshevo, to reconnoitre the position of the French and determine the best spot for the attack next day.

'Now, old gweybeard,' said he to the peasant who was acting as their guide, 'take us to Shamshevo.'

Denisov, Petya and the hetman, accompanied by a few Cossacks and the hussar who had charge of the prisoner, rode off to the left across a ravine to the edge of the forest.

5

THE rain had stopped; only a mist was falling, and drops from the trees. Denisov, the hetman and Petya rode in silence, following the peasant in the woollen cap who, stepping lightly, toes turned out, and moving noiselessly in his bast shoes over roots and wet leaves, led them to the fringe of the forest.

At the top of a slope he paused, looked about him and advanced to where the screen of foliage was less dense. He stood still under a big oak which had not yet shed its leaves, and mysteriously beckoned with his hand.

Denisov and Petya rode up to him. From the place where the peasant was standing they could see the French. Immediately beyond the forest a field of spring corn ran sharply downhill. To the right, the other side of a steep ravine, was a small village and a manor-house with a dilapidated roof. In this hamlet, in the house, over the whole little hump, in the garden, by the wells, by the pond and all along the road leading up from the bridge to the village, not more than five hundred yards distant, masses of men could be seen in the rolling mist. Their shouts in a foreign tongue at the horses straining uphill with the carts, and their calls to one another, rang out clearly.

'Bwing the pwisoner here,' said Denisov in a low voice, not taking his eyes off the French.

A Cossack dismounted, lifted the boy down and took him to Denisov. Pointing to the French, Denisov asked the lad what troops those were – and those? The drummer-boy, stuffing his benumbed hands into his pockets and lifting his eyebrows, looked at Denisov in dismay and, in spite of his obvious anxiety to tell all he knew, got confused in his answers and merely said Yes to everything Denisov asked him. Denisov turned away from him, frowning, and addressed the hetman, conveying his own conjectures to him.

Petya, moving his head round quickly, looked from the drummer-boy to Denisov, and from him to the hetman and then at the French in the village and along the road, trying not to miss anything of importance.

'Whether Dolohov comes or not, we must make the attempt ... eh?' said Denisov with a merry sparkle in his eye.

'It is a very convenient spot,' said the hetman.

'We'll send the infantwy down below, by the swamps,' Denisov went on. 'They can cweep up to the garden. You wide up from there with the Cossacks' – he pointed to the woods beyond the village – 'while I swoop from here with my hussars. And at the signal shot ...'

'It won't do to go by the hollow – it's all bog,' said the hetman. 'The horses would sink. You must skirt round more to the left.'

While they were talking in undertones there was the crack of a shot from the low ground by the pond, then another. Two puffs of white smoke appeared, and the voices of hundreds of Frenchmen half-way up the slope rose as it were in merry chorus. Denisov and the hetman involuntarily started back. They were so close that they thought they were the cause of the firing and shouting. But the shots and cries had nothing to do with them. Down below, a man wearing something red was running through the marsh. The French were evidently firing and shouting at him.

'Why, that's our Tikhon!' said the hetman.

'So it is! So it is!'

'Oh, the wascal!' exclaimed Denisov.

'He'll get away!' said the hetman, screwing up his eyes.

The man whom they called Tikhon, having run down to the stream, plunged in so that the water splashed in the air and, disappearing for an instant, scrambled out on all fours, looking black with the wet, and dashed on. The French in pursuit stopped.

'Smart fellow!' said the hetman.

'What a knave!' snarled Denisov with the same look of vexation. 'And what has he been up to all this time?'

'Who is he?' asked Petya.

'It's our scout. I sent him to capture a "tongue" for us.'

'Ah, to be sure,' said Petya, nodding immediately, as though he knew all about it, though he really did not understand a word.

*

Tikhon Shcherbaty was one of the most useful members of the party He was a peasant from the village of Pokrovsk, near the river Gzhat. When Denisov had come to Pokrovsk at the beginning of his operations as a guerrilla leader and had as usual summoned the village elder to ask him what he knew about the French, the elder replied, as all village elders did, in self-defence as it were, that he knew nothing whatever about them and had never set eyes on them. But when Denisov explained that his object was to kill Frenchmen and inquired whether no French had strayed that way, the elder replied that there had been some 'miroderers' certainly but that Tikhon Shcherbaty was the only person in their village to busy himself with such matters. Denisov had Tikhon fetched, and after praising him for his activity continued with a few words, said in the elder's presence, on the subject of loyalty to Tsar and country, and the hatred of the French that all sons of the Fatherland should cherish in their hearts.

'We don't do the French no harm,' said Tikhon, evidently intimidated by Denisov's speech. 'We only just amused ourselves a bit, as you might say. Them *miroderers* now – we done in a score or so o' they fellows but we didn't do no other 'arm. ...'

Next day after Denisov, who had forgotten all about the peasant, had left Pokrovsk, it was reported to him that Tikhon had attached himself to their party and wanted to stay with them. Denisov instructed that he should be allowed to remain.

Tikhon who at first undertook the rough work of laying campfires, fetching water, skinning dead horses, and so on, soon showed a great liking and aptitude for partisan warfare. He would go out after booty at night and always returned with some French clothing and weapons, and when told to he would also bring back a French prisoner or two. Denisov then relieved him from the rough jobs and began taking him with him on expeditions and had him enrolled among the Cossacks.

Tikhon did not like riding and always went on foot, never lagging behind the cavalry. His weapons were a carbine (which he carried rather as a joke), a pike and an axe, which latter he wielded as skilfully as a wolf uses its teeth – to crunch either a bone or a flea. Tikhon with equal accuracy could swing his axe to split a log, or hold it by the head and cut thin skewers or carve spoons. Among Denisov's followers Tikhon was on a special footing of his own. When anything particularly difficult or obnoxious had to be done – such as heaving a cart out of the mud with one's shoulder, dragging a horse by its tail out of a swamp and flaying it, slinking into the very midst of the French, or walking thirty miles in a day – everybody pointed laughingly to Tikhon.

'It won't hurt that devil – he's as strong as an ox!' they would say of him.

Once a Frenchman Tikhon was trying to capture fired a pistol at him and shot him in the buttock. The wound (which Tikhon treated exclusively with applications of vodka – internal and external) was the subject of the liveliest jesting by the whole detachment – jesting to which Tikhon willingly lent himself.

'Hullo, me boy, had enough, eh? That put a kink in you, didn't it?' the Cossacks would banter him. And Tikhon, purposely making a long face, pretended to be angry and abuse the French with the most comical oaths. The only effect of the incident on Tikhon was to make him chary of bringing in prisoners, after his wound.

Tikhon was the bravest and most useful man in the guerrilla band. No one was so quick to find opportunities for attack, no one captured or killed so many Frenchmen, and consequently he was the butt of all the Cossacks and hussars, and willingly accommodated himself to the rôle. Now he had been sent by Denisov overnight to Shamshevo to capture a 'tongue'. But either because he was not satisfied to get only one French prisoner, or because he had slept through the night, he had crept by day among some bushes right in the very middle of the French, and, as Denisov had witnessed from the hill, had been discovered by them.

6

AFTER talking a little while longer with the hetman about the next day's attack, which now, seeing how near they were to the French, he seemed finally to have decided upon, Denisov turned his horse and rode back.

'Now, my lad, we'll go and get dwy,' he said to Petya.

As they approached the forester's hut Denisov stopped, peering into the trees. A man in a short jacket, bast shoes and a Kazan hat, with a gun over his shoulder and an axe stuck in his belt, was striding lightly through the forest on his long legs, his long arms swinging at his side. Catching sight of Denisov, he hastily threw something into the bushes, removed his sodden cap, the brim of which drooped limply, and walked up to his commander. It was Tikhon. His wrinkled, pock-marked face and narrow little eyes beamed with self-satisfied mirth. He lifted his head high and gazed at Denizov as though he could hardly refrain from laughing.

'Well, where have you been?' inquired Denisov.

'Where have I been? I went after the French,' answered Tikhon boldly and hurriedly, in a husky but melodious bass.

'What was the idea of crawling in among them in daylight? Ass! Well, why didn't you get one?'

'Oh, I got one all right.'

'Where is he, then?'

'Yes, I got one at daybreak, to go on with, as you might say,' pursued Tikhon, straddling his flat feet with their turned-out toes, in bast shoes. 'I takes 'im into forest. I sees 'e's no good, so I says to meself, I says, "Better go and fetch a likelier one".'

'You see? ... What a wogue – just as I thought,' said Denisov to the hetman. 'Why didn't you bwing that one?'

'Why, what use to bring him?' Tikhon, angry, interrupted quickly. 'That one wouldn't have done for you. Don't I know what sort you want?'

'What a wascal! ... Well?'

'Off I goes to get another,' Tikhon continued, 'and I creeps this-ways into forest and lays flat.' And abruptly he dropped down on his stomach to show them how he had crawled along. 'One shows up and I grabs 'im, like this.' Tikhon leaped lightly to his feet. '"Come along to the colonel," says I. He starts yelling and all on a sudden there were four of 'em. 'Urled themselves at me with they little swords. So I goes for 'em with me axe – this fashion. "What a to-do!" I says to 'em. "Taking on like that!"' cried Tikhon, waving his arms and squaring his chest with a menacing scowl.

'Oh yes, we saw from the hill how you took to your heels through the puddles and pools!' said the hetman, screwing up his glittering eyes.

Petya badly wanted to laugh but he noticed that all the others refrained from laughing. He turned his eyes rapidly from Tikhon's face to the hetman's and Denisov's, not knowing what to make of it all.

'Don't play the fool!' said Denisov, coughing angrily. 'Why didn't you bwing the first man?'

Tikhon began scratching his back with one hand and his head with the other, and suddenly his whole face expanded into a beaming, foolish grin, disclosing the gap where he had lost a tooth – the gap that had earned him his name Shcherbaty – the gap-toothed. Denisov smiled, and Petya went off into a peal of laughter in which Tikhon himself joined.

'Oh, but that was a reg'lar good-for-nothing,' said Tikhon. 'The clothes on 'im – poor stuff! How could I bring 'im? And such a coarse fellow, your Honour! "Why," says 'e, "me, I be a gineral's son. I'm not coming," he says.'

'Ugh, you wogue!' said Denisov. 'I wanted to question him. ...'

'Oh, I questioned him all right,' said Tikhon. ''E said 'e didn't rightly know much. "A powerful lot of us, there be," 'e said, "but not up to much. Not real soldiers at all at all. Shout at 'em loud enough," says 'e, "and you'll capture the whole lot of 'em",' Tikhon concluded, with a cheerful and determined look at Denisov.

'I'll have you thwashed a hot hundwed – that'll teach you to play the fool!' said Denisov severely.

'What's there to fly into a rage about?' protested Tikhon. 'Don't I know the sort of Frenchmen you want? Wait till it be dark and I'll fetch in any kind you like – three on 'em, so I will.'

'Well, let's go,' said Denisov, and all the way to the forester's hut he rode in silence, frowning angrily.

Tikhon fell in behind and Petya heard the Cossacks laughing and teasing him about a pair of boots he had thrown into the bushes.

When he had recovered from the fit of laughter that had overcome him at Tikhon's words and his grin, and understood in a flash that this Tikhon had killed the man, Petya had an uneasy feeling. He looked round at the captive drummer-boy and felt a pang in his heart. But this uneasiness lasted only a moment. He felt it necessary to hold his head higher, to brace himself and question the hetman with an air of importance about tomorrow's expedition, that he might not be unworthy of the company in which he found himself.

The officer who had been sent to find out about Dolohov met Denisov on the way with news that Dolohov would be there soon and that all was well with him.

Denisov at once recovered his spirits, and beckoning Petya to him, said: 'Well now, tell me about yourself.'

7

LEAVING his people after their departure from Moscow, Petya had joined his regiment and was soon taken on as orderly by the general of a large guerrilla detachment. From the time he received his commission, and especially after his transfer into the army in the field, and his introduction to active service at Vyazma, Petya had been in a constant state of blissful excitement at being grown-up, and chronically eager not to miss the slightest chance of covering himself with glory. He was highly delighted with what he saw and experienced in the army but at the same time it seemed to him that the really heroic exploits were always being performed just where he did not happen to be. And he was always in a hurry to get where he was not.

When on the 21st of October his general expressed a wish to send somebody to Denisov's detachment, Petya had begged so piteously to go that the general could not refuse. But as he was seeing him off he recalled Petya's foolhardy behaviour at the battle of Vyazma, where instead of keeping to the road Petya had galloped across the front line of sharpshooters under the fire of the French, and had there discharged a couple of pistol-shots. So in letting him go the general explicitly forbade Petya to take part in any enterprise whatever that Denisov might be planning. This was why Petya had blushed and been disconcerted when Denisov asked him if he could stay. Until he reached the outskirts of the forest Petya had fully intended to carry out his instructions to the letter and return at once. But when he saw the French and met Tikhon, and learned that there would certainly be an attack that night, he decided, with the swiftness with which young people change their opinions, that the general for whom up to that moment he had had the greatest respect was a rubbishy German, that Denisov was a hero, the hetman a hero, and Tikhon a hero too, and that it would be shameful of him to desert them at a critical moment.

It was growing dark when Denisov, Petya and the hetman rode up to the forester's hut. In the twilight they could see saddled horses, and Cossacks and hussars rigging up rough shelters in the clearing and kindling a glowing fire in a hollow where the smoke would not be seen by the French. In the entrance of the little watch-house a Cossack with sleeves rolled up was cutting up a sheep. In the hut itself three officers of Denisov's were converting a door into a table-top. Petya pulled off his wet clothes, gave them to be dried, and at once set to work helping the officers to fix up the dinner-table.

In ten minutes the table was ready, covered with a napkin, and spread with vodka, a flask of rum, white bread, roast mutton and salt.

Sitting at the table with the officers and tearing the fat, savoury mutton with greasy fingers, Petya was in an ecstatic childlike state of melting love for all men and a consequent belief that in the same way they loved him.

'So what do you think, Vasili Fiodorovich?' he said to Denisov. 'It won't matter my staying just one day with you, will it?' And not waiting for Denisov to reply he supplied an answer for himself: 'You see, I was told to find out – well, I am finding out. ... Only do let me into the very ... into the real ... I don't care about rewards and decorations. ... I just want ...'

Petya clenched his teeth and looked about him, tossing his head and waving his arm.

'The real thing …' Denisov said with a smile.

'Only please give me a command, just the smallest command to command myself,' Petya went on. 'What difference could it make to you? Oh, is it a knife you want?' he said to an officer who was trying to sever himself a piece of mutton. And he handed him his clasp-knife.

The officer admired the blade.

'Please keep it! I have several others like it …' said Petya, blushing. 'Heavens! I was quite forgetting,' he cried suddenly. 'I have some wonderful raisins with me – you know, those seedless ones. Our new sutler has such first-rate things. I bought ten pounds. I always like sweet things. Will you have some? …' And Petya ran out to his Cossack in the passage and returned with baskets containing about five pounds of raisins. 'Help yourselves, gentlemen, help yourselves.

'Don't you need a coffee-pot?' he said to the hetman. 'I got a marvellous one from our sutler. His things are first-rate. And he's very honest. That's the great thing. I'll be sure and send it to you. Or perhaps your flints are giving out, or you are out of them – that does happen sometimes. I've got some here' – he pointed to the baskets – 'a hundred flints. I bought them dirt cheap. Do take them – have as many as you want, all of them if you like. …'

Then suddenly, dismayed at the thought that he had let his tongue run away with him, Petya stopped short and blushed.

He tried to remember whether he had been guilty of any other folly. And passing the events of the day in review he remembered the French drummer-boy. 'We are very snug here, but what of him? Where have they put him? Have they given him anything to eat? I hope they aren't being nasty to him?' he wondered. But, having caught himself saying too much about the flints, he was afraid to speak now.

'I have a great mind to ask,' he thought. 'But won't they say: "He's a boy himself, so of course he feels for the other boy"? I'll show them tomorrow whether I'm a boy! Would I be embarrassed to ask?' Petya wondered. 'Oh well, I don't care,' and on the spur of the moment, colouring and looking anxiously at the officers to see if they would laugh at him, he said:

'May I call in that boy who was taken prisoner? Give him something to eat, perhaps? …'

'Yes, poor little chap,' said Denisov, who evidently saw nothing

1239

to be ashamed of in this thought. 'Fetch him in. His name is Vincent Bosse. Fetch him in.'

'I'll go,' said Petya.

'Yes, yes, do. Poor little chap,' said Denisov again.

Petya was standing at the door when Denisov said this. He slipped in between the officers and went up to Denisov.

'I must embrace you for that, my dear fellow!' he exclaimed. 'Oh, how good of you, how kind!'

And having embraced Denisov he ran out of the hut.

'Bosse! Vincent!' called Petya, stopping outside the door.

'Who is it you want, sir?' asked a voice from the darkness.

Petya explained that he wanted the French lad who had been taken prisoner that day.

'Oh, Vesenny?' said a Cossack.

The boy's name, Vincent, had already been transformed by the Cossacks into Vesenny, and by the peasants and the soldiers into Vesenya, and both these words which have to do in Russian with the spring-time seemed appropriate to the young lad who was little more than a child.

'He's warming himself by the fire there. Hey, Vesenya! Vesenya! – Vesenny!' laughing voices called, catching up the cry one after another.

'He's a sharp little fellow,' remarked an hussar standing near Petya. 'We gave him a meal not long ago. He was frightfully hungry!'

There was the sound of footsteps in the darkness, and the drummer-boy came towards the door, bare feet splashing through the mud.

'Ah, there you are!' said Petya in French. 'Would you like some food? Don't be afraid, no one will hurt you,' he added, shyly laying a friendly hand on his arm. 'Come along, come in.'

'Merci, monsieur,' said the drummer-boy in a trembling, almost childish voice, and he began wiping his muddy feet against the threshold. Petya had a great many things he longed to say to the drummer-boy but he did not dare. He stood irresolutely beside him in the passage. Then he took the boy's hand in the darkness and pressed it.

'Come along, come in!' he repeated in an encouraging whisper.

'Oh, I wonder what I could do for him?' he thought, and opening the door he ushered the boy in before him.

When the drummer-boy was in the hut Petya sat down at some distance from him, feeling that it would be lowering his dignity to take much notice of him. But he was fingering the money in his pocket and asking himself whether it would seem ridiculous if he gave some to the little prisoner.

8

THE arrival of Dolohov diverted Petya's attention from the drummer-boy, who on Denisov's orders had been given some mutton and a drink of vodka, and clad in Russian garments so that he might be kept with their band and not sent away with the other prisoners. Petya had heard a great many stories in the army about Dolohov's extraordinary courage and of his barbarity to the French, and so from the moment Dolohov entered the hut Petya could not take his eyes off him but put on more and more of a swagger, and held his head high, that he might not be unworthy even of such company as Dolohov.

Dolohov's appearance amazed Petya by its simplicity.

Denisov, dressed in a Cossack coat, wore a beard and had an icon of St Nikolai the Miracle-worker on his breast, and his way of speaking and his whole manner indicated his unusual position. But Dolohov, who in Moscow had affected Persian dress, now looked like the most meticulous of Guards officers. He was clean-shaven; he wore the padded coat of the Guards with a St George ribbon in his button-hole, and an ordinary forage-cap set straight on his head. He took his wet cloak off in the corner of the room, and without greeting anyone went straight up to Denisov and immediately began asking questions about the matter in hand. Denisov told him of the designs the large detachments had on the transport, of the message Petya had brought, and his own replies to both generals. Then he related all he knew about the position of the French convoy.

'That is all very well, but we must know what troops they are and their numbers,' said Dolohov. 'We must go and have a look. We can't rush into the business without knowing for certain how many there are of them. I like to do things properly. Here, I wonder, wouldn't one of you gentlemen like to ride over to the French camp with me? I have an extra uniform with me.'

'I, I ... I'll go with you!' cried Petya.

'You are pwecisely the one not to go,' said Denisov, addressing Dolohov, 'and as for him, I wouldn't let him go on any account.'

'I like that!' cried Petya. 'Why shouldn't I go?'

'Why, because there's no point.'

'Well, you must excuse me because ... because ... I'm going and that's all about it. You will take me, won't you?' he said, turning to Dolohov.

'Why not? ...' Dolohov answered absently, staring at the French drummer-boy. 'That youngster been with you long?' he asked Denisov.

'They took him today but he knows nothing. I'm keeping him with me.'

'Oh, and what do you do with the others?' inquired Dolohov.

'What do I do with them? Send 'em in and get a weceipt,' cried Denisov, suddenly flushing. 'And I may tell you fwankly, I haven't one single man's life on my conscience. What's the twouble of sending thirty, or for that matter thwee hundwed under escort to the city as against staining – I speak bluntly – one's honour as a soldier?'

'Such squeamishness would be all very well from this sixteen-year-old little countlet here,' said Dolohov with a cold sneer, 'but it's high time you dropped all that.'

'Well, I don't say anything! I only say I'm certainly coming with you,' put in Petya shyly.

'But you and I, my friend, are too old for such fads,' Dolohov went on, apparently deriving particular satisfaction from insisting on a subject which irritated Denisov. 'Now, why have you kept this lad?' he said, shaking his head. 'Because you are sorry for him, eh? Don't we know those "receipts" of yours! You send off a hundred prisoners and hardly more than a couple of dozen arrive. The rest either die of starvation or get killed. So isn't it just as well to make short work of them?'

The hetman, screwing up his light-coloured eyes, nodded approvingly.

'That's not the point. There's nothing to weason about here. I don't care to have their lives on my conscience. You say they die on the woad. All wight. Only it's not my doing.'

Dolohov laughed.

'Do you suppose they haven't been told to grab me twenty times over? And if they should catch me – or you either, for all your chivalry – they'd string us up from the nearest aspen-tree.' He paused. 'However, we must be getting to work. Have my Cossack bring in my pack. There are a couple of French uniforms in it. Well, are you coming with me?' he asked Petya.

'Me? Yes, yes, certainly!' cried Petya, blushing almost to tears and glancing at Denisov.

While Dolohov had been arguing with Denisov what should be done with prisoners, Petya had again had that uncomfortable, restless feeling; but once more he had no time to form a clear idea of what they were talking about. 'If famous grown-up men think like that, then that's the way to think and it must be all right, I suppose,' he reflected. 'And the great thing is, that Denisov shouldn't imagine I'll listen to him – that he can order me about. Most certainly I shall go with Dolohov to the French camp. If *he* can, so can I!'

And to all Denisov's efforts to dissuade him Petya replied that he too liked doing things properly and not just anyhow, and that he never thought about danger to himself.

'For – as you'll admit – if we don't know for sure how many of them there are, it might cost the lives of hundreds, as against the two of us, and besides, I badly want to go, and I certainly shall, so don't you try to stop me,' said he. 'It would only make it worse. ...'

9

HAVING put on French greatcoats and shakos, Petya and Dolohov rode to the clearing from which Denisov had reconnoitred the French camp, and emerging from the forest in pitch darkness descended into the hollow. When they reached the bottom of the hill Dolohov told the Cossacks accompanying them to wait there, and started off at a quick trot along the road towards the bridge. Petya, his heart in his mouth with excitement, rode by his side.

'If we're caught, I won't be taken alive. I have a pistol,' he whispered.

'Don't speak Russian,' said Dolohov in a hurried whisper, and at that moment they heard through the darkness the challenge 'Who goes there?' and the click of a musket.

The blood rushed into Petya's face and he clutched at his pistol.

'Lancers of the 6th Regiment,' replied Dolohov, neither hastening nor slackening his horse's pace.

The black figure of a sentinel stood on the bridge.

'Password ?'

Dolohov reined in his horse and advanced at a foot-pace.

'Tell me, is Colonel Gérard here ?' he asked.

'Password ?' repeated the sentinel, barring his way and not replying.

'When an officer is making his round sentinels don't ask him for the password .,.' cried Dolohov, suddenly losing his temper and riding straight at the sentinel. 'I ask you, is the colonel here ?'

And not waiting for an answer from the sentinel, who had stepped aside, Dolohov rode up the incline at a walk.

Noticing the black outline of a man crossing the road, Dolohov hailed him and inquired where the commander and officers were. The man, a soldier with a sack over his shoulder, stopped, came close up to Dolohov's horse, patted it and explained in a simple, friendly way that the colonel and the officers were higher up the hill, on the right, in the courtyard of the farm, as he called the little manor-house.

Having ridden farther along the road, on both sides of which French talk could be heard round the camp-fires, Dolohov turned into the courtyard of the manor-house. Riding in at the gateway, he dismounted and walked towards a big blazing camp-fire, around which sat a number of men engaged in loud conversation. Something was boiling in a small cauldron on one side of the fire and a soldier in a peaked cap and blue coat was kneeling in the bright glow, stirring the contents with a ramrod.

'Oh, he's a tough nut to crack,' said one of the officers, sitting in the shadow on the opposite side of the fire.

'He'll make those fellows get a move on !' said another, laughing.

Both fell silent, peering into the darkness at the sound of Dolohov's and Petya's steps as they advanced to the fire, leading their horses.

'*Bonjour, messieurs!*' called Dolohov loudly and distinctly.

There was a stir in the shadow beyond the fire, and one tall officer with a long neck skirted the fire and came up to Dolohov.

'That you, Clément ?' he asked. 'Where the devil ...' but perceiving his mistake he broke off and with a slight frown greeted Dolohov as a stranger, inquiring what he could do for him. Dolohov said that he and his companion were trying to overtake their regiment, and addressing the company in general asked whether they knew anything of the 6th Regiment. None of them could tell him anything and Petya fancied the officers were beginning to look at him and Dolohov with hostility and suspicion. For several seconds no one spoke.

'If you're reckoning on some supper, you have come too late,' said a voice from behind the fire, with a smothered laugh.

Dolohov replied that they were not hungry and must push on farther that night.

He handed the horses over to the soldier who was stirring the pot, and squatted down on his heels by the fire beside the officer with the long neck. The latter never took his eyes off Dolohov and asked him a second time what regiment he belonged to. Dolohov appeared not to hear the question. Making no answer, he lighted a short French pipe which he took from his pocket, and began asking the officers how far the road ahead of them was safe from Cossacks.

'The brigands are everywhere,' replied an officer from behind the fire.

Dolohov remarked that the Cossacks were only a danger to stragglers like himself and his companion but he supposed they would not venture to attack large detachments. 'Would they?' he added inquiringly. No one replied.

'Now surely he'll come away,' Petya was thinking every moment as he stood by the fire, listening to the talk.

But Dolohov re-started the conversation which had dropped, and proceeded to ask point-blank how many men they had in their battalion, how many battalions there were, and how many prisoners. Asking about their Russian prisoners, Dolohov said:

'Nasty business dragging these carcasses about with one! Far better shoot the vermin dead!' and burst into such a strange loud laugh that Petya thought the French must immediately see through their disguise, and he involuntarily took a step back from the fire.

Dolohov's remark and laughter elicited no response, and a French officer whom they had not seen (he lay wrapped in a greatcoat) sat up and whispered something to his neighbour. Dolohov got to his feet and called to the soldier who was holding their horses.

'Will they let us have the horses or not?' wondered Petya, instinctively drawing nearer to Dolohov.

The horses were brought.

'Good evening, gentlemen,' said Dolohov.

Petya wanted to say 'Bonsoir' too, but he could not utter a sound. The officers were whispering together. Dolohov was a long time getting into the saddle, for his horse was restive; then he rode out of the yard at a foot-pace. Petya rode beside him, longing to look round to see whether the Frenchmen were running after them, but not daring to.

When they came out on to the road Dolohov did not turn back towards the open country but continued along through the village. At one spot he reined in and listened. 'Hear that?' he asked. Petya recognized the sound of Russian voices and saw the dark outlines of Russian prisoners round their camp-fires. Reaching the bridge again, Petya and Dolohov rode past the sentinel, who, without saying a word, paced morosely up and down the bridge, and descended into the hollow where the Cossacks were waiting for them.

'Well, now, good-bye. Tell Denisov, at sunrise, at the first shot,' said Dolohov and was about to ride away but Petya seized him by the arm.

'Oh!' he cried, 'you are such a hero! Oh, how splendid! How glorious! How I like you!'

'That's all right,' said Dolohov, but Petya did not let go of him and in the dark Dolohov perceived that he was bending towards him and wanted to embrace him. Dolohov embraced him laughingly, turned his horse and vanished into the night.

10

REACHING the hut in the forest, Petya found Denisov in the passage. He was waiting for Petya's return in a great state of agitation, anxiety and vexation with himself for having let him go.

'Thank God!' he exclaimed. 'Thank God now!' he repeated, listening to Petya's ecstatic account. 'But, damn you, I haven't had a wink of sleep because of you! Well, thank God! Now go and lie down. We can still get a nap before morning.'

'Yes ... no,' said Petya. 'I don't feel sleepy yet. Besides I know what I am – if I once fall asleep there'll be no waking me. And then I'm used to not sleeping before a battle.'

Petya sat for a little while in the hut gleefully going over the details of his adventure and vividly picturing to himself what would happen next day. Then, observing that Denisov was asleep, he got up and went out of doors.

Outside it was still quite dark. The rain was over but the trees were still dripping. Close by could be seen the black shapes of the Cossacks' shanties and the horses tethered together. Behind the hut there was a dark blur where two wagons stood with their horses beside them, and in the hollow the dying camp-fire glowed red. Not all the Cossacks and hussars were asleep: here and there, mingling with the sounds of the falling rain-drops and the munching of the horses near by, low voices seemed to be whispering.

Petya came out, peered about him in the darkness, and went up to the wagons. Someone was snoring underneath one of the carts, and around them stood saddled horses munching their oats. In the dark Petya recognized his own horse, which he called Karabach (though it was a Ukrainian horse and not from Karabach in the Caucasus, famous for its breed of horses), and went up to it.

'Well, Karabach! We have work before us tomorrow,' he said, sniffing its nostrils and kissing it.

'What, sir, aren't you asleep?' said a Cossack who was sitting beneath a wagon.

'No, I ... your name's Lihachov, isn't it? You see, I've only just come back. We've been calling on the French.'

And Petya gave the Cossack a detailed account not only of his expedition but also of his reasons for going, and why he thought it better to risk his life than to do things in a haphazard way.

'Well, you should get some sleep now,' said the Cossack.

'No, I am used to this,' said Petya. 'I say, aren't the flints in your pistols worn out? I brought some with me. Could you do with any? You can have some.'

The Cossack popped out from under the wagon to take a closer look at Petya.

'Because I'm accustomed to seeing to things properly,' said Petya. 'Some men, you know, leave things to chance. They don't think of preparing beforehand, and then afterwards they regret it. I don't like that.'

'That's a fact,' said the Cossack.

'Oh yes, and another thing – please, my dear fellow, sharpen my sabre for me, will you? It got blunted ...' (but Petya could not bring out the lie). 'It has never been sharpened. Can you do it for me?'

'To be sure.'

Lihachov got up, rummaged in his pack, and soon Petya heard the warlike sound of steel on whetstone. He climbed on to the wagon and perched on the edge of it. The Cossack sharpened the sabre below.

'I say! Are the lads asleep?' asked Petya.

'Some are, and some aren't – like us.'

'And what about that boy ?'

'Vesenny, you mean ? Oh, he stowed himself away in the hay over there. Fast asleep after his fright. He was that pleased.'

For a long time after this Petya remained silent, listening to the noises. He heard footsteps in the darkness and a black figure loomed up.

'What are you sharpening ?' asked a man, coming up to the wagon.

'A sabre for the gentleman here.'

'That's right,' said the man, whom Petya took to be an hussar. 'Was the cup left over here with you ?'

'There it is by the wheel.'

The hussar took the cup.

'It must be getting on for daylight,' said he, yawning, as he walked off.

Petya ought to have needed no second thoughts to know that he was in a forest with Denisov's guerrilla band, three-quarters of a mile from the road, perched on a wagon captured from the French, with horses tethered round it, and the Cossack Lihachov sitting underneath sharpening his sabre for him; that the big dark blur to the right was the forester's hut and the bright red patch below on the left – the dying embers of a camp-fire; that the man who had come for the cup was an hussar who was thirsty. But he knew nothing of all this, and did not want to. He was in a fairy kingdom where nothing resembled reality. The big dark blur might be a hut certainly, but it might be a cavern leading down into the very depths of the earth. The red patch could be the camp-fire but perhaps it was the eye of a huge monster. Perhaps he, Petya, was in fact perched on a wagon but it might very well be that he was not sitting on a wagon but on a fearfully high tower, and if he fell off it would take him a whole day, a whole month, to reach the earth – he might fall for ever and never reach it ! Perhaps it was merely the Cossack Lihachov sitting under the wagon, but it might be the kindest, bravest, most wonderful, marvellous man in the world, whom no one knew of. Perhaps it really was an hussar who came after water and went back into the hollow, or perhaps he had simply vanished – disappeared altogether and dissolved into nothingness.

Whatever Petya had seen now, it would not have surprised him. He was in a magic kingdom where everything was possible.

He looked up at the sky. And the sky was a fairy realm like the earth. It had begun to clear and the clouds were scudding over the tree-tops as though unveiling the stars. Sometimes it looked as if the clouds were passing, and a stretch of black sky appeared. At other times these black patches seemed to be storm-clouds. At still others it was as if the sky were lifting high, high above his head, and then it seemed to sink so low that he could have touched it with his hand.

Petya's eyes began to close and he swayed a little.

Rain-drops dripped from the trees. There was a low hum of talk. The horses neighed and jostled one another. Someone snored.

Ozhik-zhik, ozhik-zhik ... hissed the sabre on the whetstone. And all at once Petya heard a melodious orchestra playing some unknown, sweet, solemn hymn. Petya was as musical as Natasha, and more so than Nikolai, but he had never learnt music or thought about it and so the harmonies that suddenly filled his ears were to him absolutely new and intoxicating. The music swelled louder and louder. The air was developed and passed from one instrument to another. And what was played was a fugue – though Petya had not the slightest idea what a fugue was. Each instrument – now the violin, now the horn, but better and purer than violin and horn – played its own part, and before it had played to the end of the *motif* melted in with another, beginning almost the same air, and then with a third and a fourth; and then they all blended into one, and again became separate and again blended, now into solemn church music, now into some brilliant and triumphant song of victory.

'Oh yes, of course, I must be dreaming,' Petya said to himself as he lurched forward. 'It's only in my ears. Perhaps, though, it's music of my own. Well, go on, my music! Now! ...'

He closed his eyes. And from different directions, as though from a distance, the notes fluttered, swelled into harmonies, parted, came together and again merged into the same sweet and solemn hymn. 'Oh, this is lovely! As much as I like, and as I want it!' said Petya to himself. He tried to conduct this tremendous orchestra.

'Hush, now, softly die away!' and the sounds obeyed him. 'Now fuller, still livelier. More and more joyful now!' And from unknown depths rose the swelling triumphal chords. 'Now the voices!' commanded Petya. And, at first from afar, he heard men's voices, then women's, steadily mounting in a slow *crescendo*. Awed and rejoicing, Petya drank in their wondrous beauty.

The singing fused into a march of victory, and the rain dripped, and *ozhik-zhik, ozhik-zhik* ... hissed the sabre, and the horses jostled one another again, and neighed, not disturbing the chorus but forming part of it.

Petya did not know how long this lasted: he revelled in it, all the while wondering at his enjoyment and regretting that there was no one to share it. He was awakened by Lihachov's friendly voice.

'Here it is, your Honour – all ready to split a Frenchie in half.'

Petya opened his eyes.

'Why, it's getting light – really getting light!' he exclaimed.

The horses, invisible before, could now be seen to their very tails, and a watery light showed through the leafless boughs. Petya shook himself, jumped down, took a rouble from his pocket and gave it to Lihachov, brandished his sabre to try it and slipped it into the sheath. The Cossacks were busy untying their horses and tightening the saddle-girths.

'And here's the commander,' said Lihachov.

Denisov came out of the hut and, calling to Petya, bade him get ready.

II

In the half-light of dawn the men speedily picked out their horses, tightened up their saddle-girths and fell into line. Denisov stood by the hut, giving final instructions. The infantry of the detachment, hundreds of feet splashing through the mud, passed along the road and quickly vanished among the trees in the early morning mist. The hetman gave some orders to the Cossacks. Petya held his horse by the bridle, impatiently awaiting the signal to mount. His face, and especially his eyes, burned after the cold water he had splashed over them; cold shivers ran down his spine and his whole body shook with a rapid, rhythmic trembling.

'Well, is ev'wything weady?' asked Denisov. 'Bwing the horses.'

The horses were led up. Denisov flew at the Cossack because the saddle-girths were slack, and swore at him as he mounted. Petya put his foot in the stirrup. His horse made to nip his leg (its general practice) but Petya leaped into the saddle, unconscious of having any weight, and, turning to look round at the hussars moving up from behind in the darkness, rode up to Denisov.

1250

'Vasili Fiodorovich, you will give me some assignment or other, won't you? Please ... for God's sake ...' said he.

Denisov seemed to have forgotten Petya's very existence. He glanced round at him.

'One thing I beg of you,' he said sternly, 'and that is to obey me and not shove yourself fo'ward anywhere.'

He did not say another word to Petya but rode in silence all the way. By the time they reached the edge of the forest it had grown quite light in the open country. Denisov held a whispered consultation with the hetman, and the Cossacks rode past Petya and Denisov. When they had all passed Denisov touched his horse and started off down the slope. Slipping and sinking back on their haunches, the horses slid down into the hollow with their riders. Petya kept beside Denisov. The trembling of his whole body kept increasing. It was getting lighter and lighter, only distant objects were still concealed in the mist. Having reached the valley, Denisov looked back and nodded to a Cossack standing near him.

'The signal!' he said.

The Cossack raised his arm and a shot rang out, followed immediately by the tramp of horses galloping in front, and shouts from different directions, and more shots.

At the first sound of trampling hooves and yelling Petya lashed his horse and, loosening his rein, galloped forward, heedless of Denisov who shouted at him. It seemed to Petya that it suddenly became broad daylight, as though it were midday, at the moment the shot was fired. He galloped to the bridge. The Cossacks were dashing along the road in front of him. On the bridge he collided with a Cossack who had fallen behind, but he tore on. In front Petya saw men of some sort – the French, he supposed – running from right to left across the road. One of them slipped in the mud under his horse's legs.

Cossacks were crowding round one peasant's cottage, doing something. A fearful shriek rose from the middle of the crowd. Petya galloped up, and the first thing he saw was the white face and trembling jaw of a Frenchman clutching the staff of a lance directed at his breast.

'Hurrah! ... Our lads! ...' shouted Petya, and giving rein to his excited horse he galloped on down the village street.

He could hear shooting ahead of him. Cossacks, hussars and tattered Russian prisoners, who had come running up from both sides of the road, were all shouting unintelligibly at the tops of their voices. A gallant-looking Frenchman in a blue coat, capless, and with a frowning red face, had been defending himself against the hussars. When Petya dashed up the Frenchman had already fallen. 'Too late again!' flashed through Petya's mind and he flew on to the spot where there was brisk firing. The shots came from the courtyard of the manor-house he had visited the night before with Dolohov. The French were making a stand behind a wattle fence in a garden thickly overgrown with bushes, and shooting at the Cossacks clustering at the gateway. Through the smoke as he rode up to the gates Petya caught a glimpse of Dolohov's pale, greenish face, as he shouted something to his men. 'Go round. Wait for the infantry!' he was yelling, just as Petya appeared.

'Wait? ... Hurra-a-h! ...' roared Petya, and without pausing a second threw himself into the fray where the firing and smoke were thickest. A volley rang out, bullets whistled past and landed with a thud. The Cossacks and Dolohov galloped in at the gates of the yard after Petya. In the dense billowing smoke some of the French flung down their arms and ran out of the bushes to meet the Cossacks, while others fled downhill towards the pond. Petya was tearing round the courtyard, but instead of holding the reins he was waving both arms about in a strange, wild manner, and slipping farther and farther to one side in the saddle. His horse stepped on the ashes of the camp-fire that was smouldering in the morning light, stopped short, and Petya fell heavily on to the wet ground. The Cossacks saw his arms and legs jerk rapidly, though his head was quite still. A bullet had pierced his skull.

After parleying with the senior French officer, who came out of the house with a handkerchief tied to his sword to announce that they surrendered, Dolohov got off his horse and went up to Petya, who lay motionless with outstretched arms.

'Done for!' he said with a frown, and walked to the gate to meet Denisov who was riding towards him.

'Dead?' cried Denisov, recognizing from a distance the unmistakably lifeless attitude – only too familiar to him – in which Petya's body was lying.

'Done for!' repeated Dolohov, as though the utterance of the words afforded him satisfaction, and he hastened over to the prisoners, who were surrounded by Cossacks who had hurried up. 'We're giving no quarter!' he called out to Denisov.

Denisov did not reply. He rode up to Petya, dismounted, and with trembling hands turned Petya's blood-stained, mud-bespattered face – which had already gone white – towards himself.

'I always like sweet things. Wonderful raisins, take them all,' he recalled Petya's words. And the Cossacks looked round in amazement at the sound, like the howl of a dog, which broke from Denisov as he quickly turned away, walked to the wattle fence and held on to it.

Among the Russian prisoners rescued by Denisov and Dolohov was Pierre Bezuhov.

12

DURING the whole of their march from Moscow no new orders had been issued by the French authorities concerning the party of prisoners with whom Pierre was. On the 22nd of October that party was no longer with the troops and transport in whose company they had left Moscow. Half the wagons laden with hard-biscuit ration that had travelled the first stages with them had been carried off by Cossacks, the other half had gone on ahead. Of the cavalrymen on foot who had marched in front of the prisoners, not one was left: all had disappeared. The artillery the prisoners had seen in front of them during the early days was now replaced by Marshal Junot's enormous baggage-train, convoyed by Westphalians. Behind the prisoners came a transport of cavalry accoutrements.

From Vyazma onwards the French army, which had till then moved in three columns, now pushed on in one mass. The signs of disorder which Pierre had observed at the first halt outside Moscow had by now reached their climax.

The road along which they moved was strewn on both sides with the carcasses of dead horses. Ragged soldiers, stragglers from various regiments, constantly shifted about, now tacked on to the marching column, now dropped behind again.

Several times during the progress there had been false alarms and the soldiers of the escort had raised their muskets, fired and run headlong, trampling one another underfoot, but had afterwards rallied again and abused each other for their needless panic.

These three bodies travelling together – the cavalry stores, the convoy of prisoners, and Junot's baggage-train – still made up a complete and separate whole, though each of its constituent parts was rapidly melting away.

Of the cavalry transport, which had at first consisted of a hundred and twenty wagons, not more than sixty were left, the others having been captured or abandoned. Several wagon-loads of Junot's baggage had likewise been discarded or seized. Three wagons had been attacked and rifled by stragglers from Davoust's corps. Pierre overheard the Germans saying that this baggage-train was more strongly guarded than the prisoners, and that one of their comrades, a German soldier, had been shot by the marshal's own order, because a silver spoon belonging to the marshal had been found in his possession.

The group of prisoners had dwindled even more than the other two convoys. Of the three hundred and thirty men who had set out from Moscow less than a hundred still survived. The prisoners were even more of a burden to the escort than the cavalry-stores or Junot's baggage. The cavalry-saddles and Junot's spoons they could understand might be of some use, but that cold and starving soldiers should have to stand and guard equally cold and starving Russians who froze and lagged behind on the road (in which case the order was to shoot them) was not merely incomprehensible but an offence. And the escort, as though afraid, in the miserable plight they themselves were in, of giving way to the pity they felt for the prisoners, and so making their own lot harder, treated them with marked sullenness and severity.

At Dorogobuzh while the soldiers of the convoy, leaving the prisoners locked up in a stable, went off to plunder their own stores several of the prisoners had tunnelled under the wall and run away, but they were caught by the French and shot.

The arrangement adopted on the departure from Moscow, by which the officers among the prisoners were kept apart from the common run, had been dropped long since: all who could walk went together, and after the third stage Pierre had rejoined Karatayev and the bluey-grey, bow-legged dog who had chosen Karatayev for her master.

On the third day out from Moscow Karatayev fell ill with another bout of the fever which had kept him in hospital in Moscow, and as he grew worse Pierre held more aloof from him. Pierre could not have said why it was but from the time Karatayev's strength began to fail it had needed an effort to go near him. And when he did so and heard the subdued moaning with which Karatayev generally lay down at the halting-places, and smelt the increasing odour emanating from the sick man, Pierre moved farther away and would not think about him.

While imprisoned in the shed Pierre had learned, not through his intellect but through his whole being, through life itself, that man is created for happiness, that happiness lies in himself, in the satisfaction of simple human needs; and that all unhappiness is due, not to privation but to superfluity. But now, during these last three weeks of the march, he had learned still another new and comforting truth – that there is nothing in the world to be dreaded. He had learned that just as there is no condition in which man can be happy and absolutely free, so there is no condition in which he need be unhappy and not free. He had learned that there is a limit to suffering and a limit to freedom, and that these limits are not far away; that the person in a bed of roses with one crumpled petal suffered as keenly as he suffered now, sleeping on the bare damp earth with one side of him freezing as the other got warm; that in the old days when he had put on his tight dancing-shoes he had been just as uncomfortable as he was now, walking on bare feet that were covered with sores – his footwear having long since fallen to pieces. He discovered that when he had married his wife – of his own free will as it had seemed to him – he had been no more free than now when they locked him up for the night in a stable. Of all that he himself subsequently termed his sufferings, but which at the time he scarcely felt, the worst was the state of his bare, rubbed, scabbed feet. (Horse-flesh was palatable and nourishing, the saltpetre flavour of the gunpowder they used instead of salt was positively pleasant, the weather was not very cold – it was always warm on the march in the daytime, and at night there were the camp-fires – and the lice that devoured his body helped to keep it agreeably warm.) The one thing that gave him a bad time of it at the beginning was – his feet.

Examining his sores by the camp-fire on the second day, Pierre thought he could not possibly go another step; but when everybody got up he hobbled along, and presently, when he had warmed to it, he walked without feeling the pain, though at night his feet were a still more shocking sight than before. But he did not look at them and thought of other things.

Now for the first time Pierre realized the full strength of the vitality in man, and the saving power innate in him of being able to transfer his attention, like the safety-valve in a boiler that lets off the surplus steam as soon as the pressure exceeds a certain point.

He did not see and did not hear the prisoners being shot who lagged behind, though more than a hundred had perished in that way. He did not think of Karatayev, who was growing weaker every day and would soon no doubt have to meet the same fate. Still less did Pierre think about himself. The harder his lot and the more appalling the future, the more independent of his present plight were the glad and consoling thoughts, memories and imaginings that came to him.

13

At midday on the 22nd Pierre was walking uphill along the muddy, slippery road, looking at his feet and at the unevenness of the road surface. Occasionally he glanced at the familiar crowd around him, and then again at his feet. The crowd was as familiar to and as much part of him as his own feet. The bluey-grey, bow-legged dog was scampering merrily along by the side of the road, every now and then, in token of her agility and contentment, picking up a hind leg and skipping along on three legs before again darting off on all four to bark at the crows that perched on the carrion. 'Floppy' was more frolicksome and sleeker than she had been in Moscow. All around lay the flesh of different animals – from men to horses – in various stages of decomposition, and as the wolves were kept off by the continual procession of marching men, 'Floppy' was able to eat her fill.

Rain had been falling since early morning, and although it continually seemed as if at any moment it would cease, and the skies would clear, after a short break the downpour would be heavier than ever. The road, saturated with rain, could not soak up any more, and the water ran along the ruts in streams.

Pierre plodded on, looking from side to side, counting his steps and reckoning them off in threes on his fingers. Mentally addressing the rain, he repeated over and over: 'Rain, rain, come again!'

It seemed to him that he was not thinking of anything at all; but somewhere deep down within him his soul was pondering grave and comfortable thoughts of a most subtle spiritual nature to do with a conversation the night before with Karatayev.

Half-frozen at a fire that had gone out, on the previous night's halt Pierre had got up and moved to the next fire, which was burning better. There Platon Karatayev was sitting, with his greatcoat over his head, like a priest's vestment, telling the soldiers in his flowing, pleasant voice, though feeble now and ailing, a story Pierre knew. It was past midnight, the time when Karatayev was usually free of his fever and particularly lively. As Pierre drew near the fire and heard Platon's weak, sickly voice, and saw his pathetic face in the bright firelight, he felt a painful prick at his heart. He was alarmed at his own pity for the man and would have gone away but there was no other fire, so, trying not to look at Platon, he sat down.

'Well, how are you?' he asked.

'How am I? Grumble at sickness, and God won't grant you death,' said Karatayev, and at once went back to the story he had begun.

'And so, brother,' he continued, with a smile on his thin, white face and a peculiar, happy light in his eyes. 'And so, brother ...'

Pierre had heard the story long before. Karatayev had told it to him quite half a dozen times, always taking particular pleasure in it. But, well as Pierre knew the story, he listened to it now as to something new, and the quiet rapture Karatayev evidently felt in telling it communicated itself to Pierre too. It was the tale of an old merchant who lived a good and God-fearing life with his family, and who set out one day to go to the annual fair at Makary with a friend of his, a rich merchant.

They put up for the night at an inn and both retired to bed, and next morning his friend was found robbed and with his throat cut. A blood-stained knife was discovered under the old merchant's pillow. The old man was tried, knouted, and after having the end of his nose slit off – all in due order, as Karatayev put it – he was sent to hard labour in Siberia.

'And so, brother' (it was at this point in the story that Pierre came up), 'ten years or more pass. The good old man is living as a convict, in proper submission and never doing no harm. Only he prays to God to let him die. Well, and one night the convicts was gathered together, just like it might be us here, and the old 'un with 'em. And they starts telling what each is being punished for, and what they was guilty of in the sight of God. This one had taken his brother's life, that one was sentenced for a couple of murders, a third had set a house on fire, while another had simply been a vagrant and 'adn't done nought. "What about you, grandad?" they asks the old man. "What are you here for?" they ask. "Me," says the old 'un. "Me, I'm here to suffer for my own sins, yes and for the sins of others. I have never taken life, nor another man's goods, and I used to give to any needy fellow-creature. A merchant I was, my friends, and great wealth was mine." And so on and so on, he tells the whole story, chapter and verse how it all came about. "For myself," says he, "I don't complain. 'Twas the Lord's doing to try me, no doubt. Only," says he, "'tis the old woman and the bairns I be sorry for." And the old man falls a-weeping. Now it so happened the very man who had murdered the other merchant, you know, was there in the company. "Where was it all, grandad?" he inquires. "What season of the year, and what was the month of it?" He asks this question and that, and his heart grows full, and 'e goes up to the old 'un and falls – plump! – at the feet of him. "Good old man," he says, "'tis me that has brought you here. Gospel truth it is, lads – the old 'un 'ere's innocent as a baby. I done it," says he, "I done the thing: I puts the knife under your pillow whilst you was asleep. Forgive me, grandad," he says, "forgive me, for Christ's sake!"'

Karatayev paused, smiling blissfully as he gazed into the fire and then drew the logs together.

'And the old man said, "God will forgive you," he says, "we are all sinners in His sight. I am suffering for my own sins," and he wept with bitter tears. Well, and what do you think, my friends?' exclaimed Karatayev, his face brightening more and more with a beatific smile, as though the great charm and whole point of his tale lay in what he was about to tell now, 'what do you think, my dear fellow – that murderer himself went and confessed to the authorities. "Six souls are on me conscience," he says (for he was a great evil-doer), "but it's the old 'un that worries me most. Don't let 'im suffer no more 'cause of what I done." So he showed up, and it was wrote down and the paper sent in the proper way. The place was a long way off, and the time goes by while they was judging and all the papers to be made out in right order, the authorities, I mean. The matter gets to the Tsar. Whiles, a decree comes from the Tsar: to set the merchant free and give him compensation like it had been awarded. The paper comes, and they begin looking for the old man. "Where is the old man who has been suffering innocently and in vain? A paper has come from the Tsar." And they fell to searching for him.'

Karatayev's lower jaw trembled. 'But God had pardoned him already – dead, he was! That was the way of it, my dears,' Karatayev concluded, and for a long time he sat staring before him with a smile on his lips.

It was not the story itself but its mysterious import and the solemn happiness which irradiated Karatayev's face as he told it, and the mystic significance of that happiness, which filled Pierre's soul with a vague sense of joy.

14

'FALL in!' a voice shouted suddenly.

There was a cheerful commotion among the prisoners and soldiers of the convoy – an air of expecting something festive and solemn. On every side commands were shouted and a party of smartly dressed cavalry on good horses came trotting up from the left, making a circuit round the prisoners. Every face wore the look of tension seen at the approach of important personages. The prisoners huddled together and were pushed off the road. The convoy formed up.

'L'Empereur! L'Empereur! Le maréchal! Le duc!' – and hardly had the sleek cavalry passed before a carriage drawn by six greys rattled by. Pierre caught a glimpse of a man in a three-cornered hat with a tranquil look on his handsome, fat white face. It was one of the marshals. His eye fell on Pierre's large and imposing figure, and in the expression with which he frowned and looked away Pierre fancied he detected sympathy and a desire to conceal it.

The general in charge of the transport galloped after the carriage with a red, panic-stricken face, whipping up his skinny horse. Several officers grouped together; the soldiers pressed round them. Everybody looked excited and uneasy.

'What did he say? What did he say? ...' Pierre heard them ask.

While the marshal was driving by, the prisoners had crowded in a bunch, and Pierre noticed Karatayev, whom he had not yet seen that morning. He was sitting in his little military coat leaning against a birch tree. His face still bore the look of joyful emotion with which he had told the story the night before of the merchant who had suffered innocently, but now it had an added quiet solemnity.

Karatayev turned on Pierre his kindly round eyes which at this moment were filled with tears, and there was unmistakable appeal in them – he wanted Pierre to come up so that he could say something to him. But Pierre was afraid for himself. He pretended not to see, and hastily moved away.

When the prisoners set off again Pierre looked back. Karatayev was sitting at the side of the road under the birch-tree, and two French-men were bending over him talking. Pierre did not look round again. He limped on up the hill.

From behind, from the spot where Karatayev had been sitting, came the sound of a shot. Pierre heard the report distinctly but at the moment he heard it he remembered that he had not yet finished reckoning up how many stages were left to Smolensk – a calculation he had begun before the marshal drove by. And he began to count. Two French soldiers, one of them carrying his smoking musket in his hand, ran past Pierre. They both looked pale and in their ex-pressions – one of them glanced timidly at Pierre – there was some-thing resembling what he had seen on the face of the young soldier at the execution. Pierre looked at the soldier and remembered that this man, two days before, had scorched his shirt in drying it at the camp-fire, and how they had all laughed at him.

The dog began to howl behind at the spot where Karatayev had been sitting. 'Silly creature! What is she howling for?' thought Pierre.

The prisoners, his companions marching at his side, like him re-frained from looking back to the place where the shot had been fired and the dog was howling; but there was a set look on all their faces.

15

THE cavalry-transport, and the prisoners and the marshal's baggage-train, halted at the village of Shamshevo. They all piled up together round the camp-fires. Pierre made his way to a fire, ate his roast horse-flesh, lay down with his back to the blaze and immediately fell asleep. He fell into the same sort of sleep that he had slept at Mo-zhaisk, after the battle of Borodino.

Once more real events mingled with his dreams, and once more someone, either himself or another person, was uttering thoughts in his ear, the same thoughts even as had been spoken to him at Mo-zhaisk.

'Life is everything. Life is God. Everything changes and moves to and fro, and that movement is God. And while there is life there is joy in consciousness of the Godhead. To love life is to love God. More difficult and more blessed than all else is to love this life in one's sufferings, in undeserved sufferings.

'Karatayev!' flashed into Pierre's mind.

And suddenly there rose before him, as vivid as though alive, the image of a long-forgotten, gentle old man who had given him geography lessons in Switzerland. 'Wait,' said the little old man, and he showed Pierre a globe. This globe was a living thing – a quivering ball of no fixed dimensions. Its whole surface consisted of drops closely squeezed together. And all these drops were shifting about, changing places, sometimes several coalescing into one, or one dividing into many. Each drop tried to expand and occupy as much space as possible, but others, striving to do the same, crushed it, sometimes absorbed it, at others melted into it.

'That is life,' said the old teacher.

'How simple and clear,' thought Pierre. 'How is it I never knew that before?'

'In the centre is God, and each drop does its best to expand so as to reflect Him to the greatest extent possible. And it grows, and is absorbed and crowded out, disappears from the surface, sinks back into the depths and emerges again. That was the case with Karatayev: he overflowed and vanished. Do you understand, my child?' said the teacher.

'Do you understand, damn you?' shouted a voice, and Pierre woke up.

He raised his head and sat up. A Frenchman who had just shoved a Russian soldier aside was squatting by the fire roasting a lump of meat on the end of a ramrod. His sleeves were rolled up and his sinewy, hairy red hands with their stubby fingers were deftly twirling the ramrod. The glow of the charcoal lighted up his tanned, melancholy face with its sullen brows.

'Much he cares,' he muttered, quickly addressing a soldier standing behind him. 'Brigand! Clear off!'

And twisting the ramrod he glanced gloomily at Pierre, who turned away and gazed into the darkness. A prisoner, the Russian soldier the Frenchman had pushed away, was crouched near the fire patting something with his hand. Looking more closely, Pierre recognized the bluey-grey dog, sitting beside the soldier wagging her tail.

'Followed us, has she?' said Pierre. 'But Plat –' he began, but did not finish. Suddenly several pictures sprang into his mind all at the same time and all sliding into each other – he saw the look Platon had fixed on him, as he sat under the tree; heard the shot from that same place, and the dog's howl; remembered the guilty faces of the two Frenchmen as they ran past him, and the lowered, smoking gun; was aware of Karatayev's absence at this halt – and he was on the point of letting the realization sink in that Platon had been killed but at that very instant a sudden recollection flashed into his memory, suggested by Heaven knew what, of a summer evening he had spent with a beautiful Polish lady on the veranda of his house in Kiev. And still without linking up the impressions of the day, or drawing any conclusion from them, Pierre closed his eyes and the vision of the country in summer-time mingled with memories of bathing and of that liquid, quivering globe, and he sank deep down into water, until the waters closed over his head.

*

Before sunrise he was awakened by loud and rapid firing and yells. French soldiers were flying past him.

'The Cossacks!' one of them shouted, and a moment later Pierre was surrounded by a throng of Russians.

For a long time he could not take in what was happening to him. All about him he heard his comrades sobbing with joy.

'Brothers! Our own folk! Friends!' Old soldiers were weeping as they embraced Cossacks and hussars.

The hussars and Cossacks crowded round the prisoners, one offering them clothing, another boots and a third bread. Pierre sat choked with tears in their midst, unable to utter a word; he hugged the first soldier who came up, and kissed him, weeping.

*

Dolohov was standing at the gate of the dilapidated manor-house letting the collection of disarmed Frenchmen file past him. The French, excited by all that had happened, were talking loudly among themselves; but as they passed before Dolohov, who stood lightly flicking his boots with his riding-whip and watching them with cold, glassy eyes that boded no good, they became silent. On the other side stood a Cossack of Dolohov's, counting the prisoners and marking off each hundred with a chalk stroke on the gate.

'How many?' Dolohov asked.

'Into the second hundred,' replied the Cossack.

'Get on, get on! – *filez, filez!*' Dolohov kept urging (having picked up the word from the French), and when his eyes met those of the passing prisoners they flashed with a cruel gleam.

Denisov, bare-headed and with a sombre face, walked behind some Cossacks who were carrying the body of Petya Rostov to a hole that had been dug in the garden.

16

AFTER the 28th of October, when the frosts began, the flight of the French assumed a still more tragic character, with men freezing, or roasting themselves to death by the camp-fires, while the Emperor, kings and dukes pursued their homeward way wrapped in furs and riding in carriages, with the treasures they had stolen; but in its essentials the process of the flight and disintegration of the French army continued unchanged.

From Moscow to Vyazma the French forces numbering seventy-three thousand – not counting the Guards (who did nothing all through the war except pillage) – was reduced to thirty-six thousand, though not more than five thousand had perished in battle. Such was the first term in the progression, from which the succeeding ones might be deduced with mathematical precision.

The French army went on melting away and being destroyed in the same proportions from Moscow to Vyazma, from Vyazma to Smolensk, from Smolensk to the Berezina, from the Berezina to Vilna, irrespective of the greater or lesser degree of cold, of pursuit by the Russians, of the barring of their way, or of any other particular conditions, operating separately. Beyond Vyazma the French army, instead of moving in three columns, huddled together into one mass, and went on thus to the end. Berthier wrote to his Emperor (and we know commanding officers feel it permissible to depart rather widely from the truth in describing the condition of their armies), and this is what he said:

I deem it my duty to acquaint your Majesty with the condition of the various corps which have come under my observation on the march the last two or three days. They are almost disbanded. Scarcely a quarter of the men remain with the standards of their regiments; the rest wander off on their own in different directions, with the idea of finding food and escaping discipline. In general they look to Smolensk as the place where they hope to pick up again. During the last few days many of the men have been seen to throw away their cartridges and muskets. In such a state of affairs, whatever your Majesty's ultimate plans may be, the interests of your Majesty's service demand that the army should be rallied at Smolensk and rid, first and foremost, of ineffectives, such as cavalrymen without horses, unnecessary baggage, and artillery-material that is no longer in proportion to our present numbers. As well as a few days' rest the soldiers, who are exhausted by hunger and fatigue, need supplies. Many in these last days have died by the roadside or at the bivouacs. This state of things continually worsens and makes one fear that unless swift measures are taken to avert the evil we shall be exposed to the risk of being unable to control the troops in the event of an engagement.

9th November: 20 miles from Smolensk.

After staggering into Smolensk, the promised land of their dreams, the French fell to fighting one another over the food there, sacking their own stores, until everything had been plundered, when they fled farther.

All hastened on, not knowing whither or why. Still less did that genius Napoleon know why they did so, for there was no one to issue any orders to him. But still he and those about him clung to their old habits: wrote commands, letters, reports, orders of the day; addressed one another as *sire, mon cousin, Prince d'Eckmühl, roi de Naples*, and so on. But the orders and reports were only on paper, no attempt was made to carry them out, because they could not be carried out, and though they called each other Majesty, Highness or Cousin, they all felt that they were miserable wretches who had done much evil, for which they now had to pay the penalty. And though they pretended to be concerned for the army each was thinking selfishly of how to get away quickly and save himself.

17

THE movements of the Russian and French armies during the retreat from Moscow back to the Niemen resemble a game of Russian blindman's-buff, in which two players are blindfolded and one of them rings a bell at intervals to let the other know of his whereabouts. At first he rings the bell with no fear of his opponent, but when he finds himself in a tight corner he tries to steal away noiselessly, and often, thinking to escape, runs straight into his adversary's arms.

At first Napoleon's army made its whereabouts known – that was in the early period of the retreat along the Kaluga highway – but afterwards, when they had taken to the Smolensk road, they ran holding the clapper of the bell, and often, supposing that they were getting away, blundered right into the Russians.

Owing to the rapidity of the French flight and the Russian pursuit, and the consequent exhaustion of the horses, the chief method of ascertaining roughly the enemy's position – reconnaissance by cavalry – was not available. Moreover, in consequence of frequent and rapid changes of position by both armies, what news did come always came too late. If word was received one day that the enemy had been in a certain position on the day before, by the day after when the information could be acted upon the army in question was already a couple of days' march farther on and occupying an entirely different position.

One army fled, the other pursued. Beyond Smolensk the French had a choice of routes and one would have thought that during their four-day stay there they might have found out where the enemy was, have contrived some profitable plan, and tried something new. But after a four-day halt the mob took to the road again, without plan or purpose, running not to the right or to the left but along their old beaten tracks – the worst route they could have chosen – through Krasnoe and Orsha.

Believing that the enemy lay in their rear and not in front, the French hastened on, spreading out and scattering twenty-four hours' march from one another. In front of them all fled the Emperor, then the kings, then the dukes. The Russian army, expecting Napoleon to take the road to the right beyond the Dnieper – the only sensible course – themselves turned to the right and came out on the high road at Krasnoe. And here, just as in the game of blindman's-buff, the French ran into our vanguard. Seeing their enemy thus unexpectedly, the French were thrown into confusion and stopped short in sudden panic but then resumed their flight, abandoning their comrades in the rear. Then for three days separate portions of the French army – first Murat's (the viceroy's), then Davoust's, then Ney's – ran the gauntlet, as it were, of the Russian army. They all abandoned one another, shed their heavy baggage, their artillery, half their men, working their way past the Russians by moving in semicircles only by night.

Ney, who came last because he had lingered to blow up the unoffending walls of Smolensk (in spite of their wretched plight or, rather, in consequence of it, they wanted to beat the floor against which they had hurt themselves) – Ney, coming last, reached Napoleon at Orsha with only a thousand men left of his corps of ten thousand, having forsaken all the rest and all his cannon and got across the Dnieper by stealth at night, at a wooded spot.

From Orsha they fled along the road to Vilna, still playing at blindman's-buff with the pursuing army. At the Berezina there was confusion again, numbers were drowned and many surrendered, but those who managed to ford the river dashed on. Their chief commander donned a fur coat and, seating himself in a sledge, was off, deserting his companions. Those who could escaped the same way; those who could not surrendered or perished.

18

ONE might have supposed that the historians, who ascribe the actions of the masses to the will of one man, would have found it impossible to fit the flight of Napoleon's armies into their theory, considering that during this period of the campaign the French did all they could to bring about their own ruin, and that not one single movement of that rabble of men, from the time they turned on to the Kaluga road up to the day their leader fled from his army, betrayed a hint of rhyme or reason. But no! Mountains of volumes have been written by historians about this campaign and in all of them we find accounts of Napoleon's masterly arrangements and deeply considered plans; of the manoeuvres executed by the troops, of the strategy with which they were led and the military genius shown by the marshals.

The withdrawal from Malo-Yaroslavets, when nothing hindered Napoleon from taking to country amply stocked with supplies, and the parallel road was open to him along which Kutuzov afterwards pursued him – this wholly unnecessary return via a devastated road is explained to us as being the outcome of profound considerations. We are offered similar profound considerations to account for his retreat from Smolensk to Orsha. Then we have a description of his heroism at Krasnoe, where he is reported to have been prepared to put himself at the head of his troops and give battle, and to have marched about with a birch-stick, saying:

'I have played the Emperor long enough: it is now time to be the general.'

And yet in spite of this, and immediately after, he takes to flight again, leaving to their fate the scattered fragments of his army struggling after him.

Then we are told of the nobility of some of the marshals, especially Ney – nobility which consisted in his sneaking by a roundabout way through the forest by night, and across the Dnieper and escaping into Orsha without his standards and his artillery, and with nine-tenths of his men gone.

And lastly, the final departure of the great Emperor from his heroic army is presented to us by the historians as something sublime – a stroke of genius. Even that final act of running away, which in ordinary language would be characterized as the lowest depth of baseness, such as every child is taught to be ashamed of – even that act finds justification in the historian's language.

When it is impossible to stretch the very elastic thread of historical ratiocination any farther, when an action flagrantly contradicts all that humanity calls good and even right, the historians fetch out the saving idea of 'greatness'. 'Greatness' would appear to exclude all possibility of applying standards of right and wrong. For the 'great' man nothing is wrong; there is no atrocity for which a 'great' man can be blamed.

'*C'est grand!*' cry the historians, and that is enough. Goodness and evil have ceased to be: there is only '*grand*' and not '*grand*'. *Grand* is good, not-*grand* is bad. To be *grand* is according to them the necessary attribute of certain exceptional animals called by them 'heroes'. And Napoleon, taking himself off home wrapped in a warm fur cloak and abandoning to their fate not only his comrades but men who (in his belief) were there because he had brought them there, feels *que c'est grand*, and his soul is at ease.

'From the sublime' (he saw something sublime in himself) 'to the ridiculous there is only one step,' said he. And for fifty years the whole world has gone on repeating, '*Sublime! Grand! Napoléon le grand!*'

Du sublime au ridicule il n'y a qu'un pas!

And it never enters anyone's head that to admit a greatness not commensurable with the standard of right and wrong is merely to admit one's own nothingness and immeasurable littleness.

For us who have the standard of good and evil given us by Christ, nothing can claim to be outside the law. And there is no greatness where simplicity, goodness and truth are absent.

19

WHAT Russian, reading the accounts of the latter period of the campaign of 1812, has not known an irksome feeling of vexation, dissatisfaction and perplexity. Who has not asked himself: How was it the French were not all captured or wiped out when all three of our armies surrounded them in superior numbers, when the French were a disorderly, starving, freezing rabble, surrendering in droves, and when (as history relates) the aim of the Russians was precisely to stop, cut off and take them all prisoner?

How was it that the Russian army, which when numerically weaker than the French had given battle at Borodino, did not achieve its purpose when it had surrounded the French on three sides and its intention was to capture them? Can the French be so immensely superior to us that we, with stronger and more numerous forces, after surrounding them are not equal to beating them?

History (or what is called by that name) in reply to these questions declares that we must look for an explanation in the failure of Kutuzov and Tormasov and Tchichagov, and this general and that general, to execute such and such manoeuvres.

But why did they not execute these manoeuvres? And why if they were guilty of not carrying out a prearranged plan were they not tried and punished? But even if we admit that Kutuzov and Tchichagov and the rest were responsible for the Russian non-success it is still incomprehensible why, the position of the Russian army being what it was at Krasnoe and the Berezina (in both cases our forces were numerically superior), the French army with its marshals, kings and emperors, was not captured if that was the Russian intention.

This strange phenomenon cannot be explained – as Russian military historians explain it – by saying that it was because Kutuzov prevented offensive operations, for we know that he was unable to restrain the troops from attacking at Vyazma and Tarutino.

Why was it that the Russian army, which with inferior forces had withstood the enemy in full strength at Borodino, was defeated at Krasnoe and the Berezina when fighting in superior numbers against the demoralized mob of the French?

If the aim of the Russians really was to cut off and take prisoner Napoleon and his marshals – and that aim was not only frustrated but every attempt in its direction failed most disgracefully – then this last period of the campaign is quite rightly considered by the French to be a series of victories, and quite wrongly represented by the Russians as redounding to our glory.

Russian military historians, in so far as they have any regard for logic, must come to this conclusion and, for all their lyrical rhapsodies about valour and devotion and so forth, are reluctantly obliged to admit that the French retreat from Moscow was a series of victories for Napoleon and of defeats for Kutuzov.

But, putting national vanity entirely aside, one cannot help feeling that such a conclusion involves a contradiction, seeing that the series of French victories brought them to complete annihilation, while the series of Russian defeats culminated in the absolute overthrow of their enemy and the liberation of their own country.

The source of this contradiction lies in the fact that historians, studying events in the light of the letters of kings and generals, of memoirs, reports, projects and so on, have attributed to this last period of the war of 1812 an aim that never existed – that of cutting off and capturing Napoleon with his marshals and his army.

Such a plan never was, and never could have been: there was no reason for it, and it would have been quite impossible to execute.

There was no object in such a plan, firstly because Napoleon's demoralized army was flying from Russia with all possible speed – that is to say, was doing just what every Russian desired. Where would have been the point in performing various military operations against the French who were running away as fast as they could go?

Secondly, it would have been senseless to try and block the passage of men whose whole energies were bent on flight.

Thirdly, it would have been absurd to sacrifice troops in order to destroy the French army which without external interference was destroying itself at such a rate that, although every road lay open and undisputed, they could carry across the frontier only the small number that remained to them in the month of December, namely, one-hundredth part of the original army.

Fourthly, it would have been senseless to wish to seize the Emperor, kings and dukes – whose capture would have been in the highest degree embarrassing for the Russians, as the ablest diplomatists of the time (Joseph de Maistre and others) recognized. Still more nonsensical would have been any desire to capture the French army, when our own forces had dwindled to half before reaching Krasnoe and a whole division would have been needed to convoy every corps of prisoners, and when our own soldiers were not always getting full rations and the prisoners already taken were dying of hunger.

All the deep-laid schemes to cut off and capture Napoleon and his army would have been like a market-gardener who, with the idea of driving out a herd of cattle trampling his beds, rushes to the gate to belabour them about the head as they come out. The only thing that could be said in the gardener's justification would be that he was very angry. But not even this excuse could be made for those who devised this project, for they were not the ones who had suffered from the trampled vegetable-beds.

But, besides being absurd, it would have been impossible to cut off Napoleon and his army.

Impossible, first, because, since experience shows that the movement of columns of soldiers about a battle area of two or three miles never quite coincides with the plans, the probability that Tchichagov, Kutuzov and Wittgenstein effecting a junction at a designated place on time was so remote as to be tantamount to impossibility, which, in fact, was what Kutuzov was thinking when he received the plan from Petersburg and remarked that diversions conceived over great distances never produce the desired results.

Secondly, it was impossible because to paralyse the force of inertia with which Napoleon's army was retiring back along its track would have required incomparably larger forces than the Russians possessed.

Thirdly, it was impossible because the military term 'to cut off' has no meaning. One can cut off a slice of bread, but not an army. To cut off an army – to bar its road – is quite impossible: there is always some way of making a *détour*, and there is the night, when nothing can be seen. The military strategist has only to look at Krasnoe and the Berezina to be convinced of this. Again, it is only possible to capture prisoners if they agree to be captured, just as it is only possible to catch a swallow if it perches on your hand. Men can be taken prisoner if they surrender, like the Germans, in due form by all the rules of strategy and tactics. But the French troops quite rightly did not see that there was anything to be gained by this, since death by hunger and cold awaited them alike in flight or captivity.

The fourth and chief reason why it was impossible is that never since the world began has a war been fought under such terrible conditions as those which obtained in 1812, and the Russian army strained every nerve to the utmost in its pursuit of the French, and could not have done more without perishing itself.

In its march from Tarutino to Krasnoe the Russian army lost fifty thousand sick or stragglers, that is, a number equal to the population of a large provincial town. Half of them fell out without a battle.

And it is in regard to this period of the campaign – when the troops lacked boots and sheepskin coats, were short of provisions and without vodka, and camping out at night for months in the snow with fifteen degrees of frost; when there were only seven or eight hours of daylight and the rest of the twenty-four was night during which discipline cannot exert the same influence; when men were put in peril of death (and death knows no discipline), not for a few hours only, as in a battle, but for months on end, every minute seeing a mortal struggle against hunger and cold; when half the army gave up the ghost in a single month – it is in regard to this period of the campaign that the historians tell us how Miloradovich ought to have executed a flank movement on one side, while Tormasov did the same on the other, and Tchichagov should have crossed over somewhere else (with the snow more than knee-deep), and how this one 'routed' and that one 'cut off' the French, and so forth, and so on.

The Russians, half of whom died, did all that could and should have been done to attain an end worthy of the nation, and they are not to blame because other Russians, comfortably ensconced in warm studies, proposed that they should do the impossible.

All the strange discrepancies, which we find incomprehensible to-day, between the events as they happened and the official records arise solely because the historians writing their histories have described the noble sentiments and fine speeches of various generals, instead of giving us a history of the facts.

They attach great consequence to what Miloradovich said, to the honours bestowed on this general or that, and their conjectures; but the question of those fifty thousand men who were left in hospitals or their graves holds not the slightest interest for them, for it does not come within the scope of their investigations.

And yet we have only to discard our researches among the reports and plans of the generals and consider the movements of those hundreds of thousands of men who took a direct part in the events, and all the questions that seemed insoluble before will at once be satisfactorily answered with extraordinary ease and simplicity.

The aim of cutting off Napoleon and his army never existed save in the imagination of some dozen individuals. It could not have existed because it was absurd and impracticable.

The people had but one object: to rid their land of invaders. That aim was effected primarily of itself, when the French ran away and all that was necessary was not to check their flight. In the second place it was promoted by the guerrilla warfare which exterminated the French piecemeal; and thirdly, by the fact of a large Russian army following in the rear of the French, ready to use its strength in case of any pause in their retreat.

The Russian army had to act like a whip urging on a springing animal. And the experienced driver knew that it was far more effective to threaten with whip upraised rather than lash the running animal about the head.

PART FOUR

I

WHEN a man sees an animal dying, horror seizes him: substance similar to his own is perishing before his eyes, is ceasing to be. But when the dying creature is a human being, and a beloved one, over and above horror at the extinction of life there is a severance, a spiritual wound, which like a physical wound is sometimes fatal, sometimes heals, but always aches and shrinks from any external chafing touch.

After Prince Andrei's death Natasha and Princess Maria both felt this alike. Crushed in spirit, they closed their eyes under the menacing cloud of death that hovered about them, and dared not look life in the face. Carefully they guarded their open wounds from every rough and painful contact. Everything – a carriage driving swiftly along the street, the announcement that dinner was ready, the maid asking which dress to put out; worse still, any word of insincere, perfunctory sympathy – set the wound throbbing, seemed an affront, and violated the urgent silence in which they were both striving to listen to the stern and terrible choir still echoing in their ears, and hindered their contemplation of the mysterious, limitless vistas which for an instant had opened out before them.

Only when they were alone together were they free from such outrage and hurt. They spoke little to one another. When they did speak it was of the most insignificant matters. And both of them alike avoided any allusion to the future.

To admit the possibility of a future seemed to them an insult to his memory. Still more sedulously did they shun in their talk everything that had reference to the departed. It seemed to them that what they had lived through and felt could not be expressed in words, and that any allusion to the details of his life profaned the majesty and sacredness of the mystery that had been accomplished before their eyes.

Continual restraint in what they said, their constant and studious avoidance of everything that might lead to mention of him – this halting on all sides at the barriers fencing off what might not be spoken about – brought before their minds with still greater purity and clearness what they were both feeling.

But pure, unmitigated grief is as impossible as pure, unmitigated joy. Princess Maria in her position as absolute and independent arbiter of her own fate and guardian and instructor of her nephew was the first to be called back by the exigencies of life from that world of sorrow in which she dwelt for the first fortnight. She received letters from her relatives which had to be answered; the room in which little Nikolai had been put was damp and he began to cough; Alpatych came to Yaroslavl with reports on the state of their affairs, and advice and suggestions that they should return to Moscow to the house in Vozdvizhenka street, which had not been damaged and only needed some trifling repairs. Life would not stand still, and it was necessary to live. Hard as it was for Princess Maria to emerge from the secluded realm of contemplation in which she had been living till then, and sorry and almost ashamed as she felt at leaving Natasha alone, the cares of everyday life demanded her participation, and against her will she had to give herself up to them. She went through the accounts with Alpatych, conferred with Dessalles about her nephew, and began her arrangements and preparations for the journey to Moscow.

Natasha was left to herself, and from the time Princess Maria started to be taken up with preparations for departure she held aloof from her too.

Princess Maria asked the countess to let Natasha come with her to Moscow, and both parents eagerly agreed to this suggestion, for they could see their daughter's physical strength declining more every day and hoped that a change of scene and the advice of Moscow doctors might do her good.

'I am not going anywhere,' Natasha replied, when the idea was put to her. 'All I ask is to be left in peace!' And she ran out of the room, scarcely able to restrain her tears – tears of vexation and irritation rather than of sorrow.

Since she had felt herself deserted by Princess Maria and alone in her grief, Natasha spent most of the time in her room by herself, sitting with her feet curled up in a corner of the sofa and, while her slender nervous fingers kept tearing or crumpling something or other, staring with fixed eyes at whatever fell under her gaze. This solitude exhausted her, tortured her, but it was exactly what she needed. As soon as anyone went in to her she would get up quickly, change her position and expression, and pick up a book or some needlework, obviously waiting impatiently for the intruder to leave.

She felt all the time as if she were on the verge of understanding, of penetrating the mystery on which her spiritual vision was fastened with a terrible questioning too terrible for her to bear.

One day towards the end of December Natasha, thin and pale, dressed in a black woollen gown, with her plait of hair coiled up into a careless knot, was sitting with her feet tucked under her at one end of the sofa, nervously crumpling and smoothing the ends of her sash while she looked at a corner of the door.

She was gazing as it were towards the place where he had vanished, to that farther shore on the other side of life. And that shore, of which she had never thought in the old days and which had seemed to her so far away, so improbable, was now nearer and more familiar and comprehensible to her than this side of life where everything was emptiness and desolation, or suffering and indignity.

She was gazing into the world where she knew him to be; but she could not picture him otherwise than as he had looked here on earth. She saw him again as he had been at Mytishchy, at Troitsa, at Yaroslavl.

She saw his face, heard his voice, repeated his words and words which she had said to him, and sometimes imagined other words they might have spoken.

She remembered seeing him lying back in a low chair in his velvet, fur-lined cloak, leaning his head on his thin pale hand. His chest looked dreadfully hollow, his shoulders hunched. His lips were firmly set, his eyes glittered and a wrinkle was coming and going on his pale forehead. One of his legs was just perceptibly twitching with a rapid tremor. Natasha knew that he was struggling with agonising pain. 'What is that pain like? Why did he have it? What does he feel? What pain he is in!' thought Natasha. He had noticed her watching him, had raised his eyes and begun to speak gravely:

'One thing would be awful,' he said, 'to bind oneself for ever to a suffering invalid. It would be continual torture.' And – Natasha could see his expression now – he had looked searchingly at her. Natasha, as usual, had answered without giving herself time to think. She had said: 'It can't go on like this – it won't. You will get well – quite well.'

She was seeing him now as she had then, and living over in her memory all that she had felt at the time. She recalled the long, sad, stern look he had given her at those words, and she understood all the reproach and despair in that protracted gaze.

'I agreed,' Natasha said to herself now, 'that it would be dreadful if he always continued to suffer. I said so only meaning that it would be awful for him, but he meant that it would be awful *for me*. He still wanted to live then, and was afraid of dying. And I said it so crudely and stupidly. I wasn't meaning it that way. I was thinking of something quite different. If I had said what I meant, I should have said: even if he had to go on dying – dying all the time before my eyes – I should have been happy compared with what I am now. Now … there is nothing, nobody. Did he know that? No. He didn't know and never will know. And now it can never, never be put right.' And again he was saying the same words but this time Natasha in her imagination made him a different answer. She stopped him and said: 'Horrible for you, but not for me. You know that for me life without you would be nothing, and to suffer with you is the greatest happiness for me,' and he took her hand and pressed it, just as he had pressed it on that terrible evening four days before his death. And in her imagination she said other words of tenderness and love which she might have uttered then but only spoke now: 'I love you … you … I love you, I love you …' she said, wringing her hands convulsively and clenching her teeth in her extremity.

And the bitter sweetness of grief was taking possession of her, and her eyes were filling with tears, but all at once she asked herself to whom she was saying this. 'Where is he and *what* is he now?'

And again everything was shrouded in a dull aching perplexity, and again with a strained frown she tried to peer into the world where he was. And – yes – yes – surely she was just penetrating the mystery … But at the very instant when the incomprehensible seemed about to reveal itself a loud rattling of the door handle struck painfully on her ears. With a frightened look on her face, and not thinking of Natasha, Dunyasha the maid burst abruptly into the room.

'Come, miss, come quickly to your papa,' said Dunyasha with a strange, excited expression. 'A misfortune … Count Petya … a letter,' she gasped out, sobbing.

NATASHA at this time was feeling generally remote from everybody, and most of all from her own family. All of them – her father, mother and Sonya – were so near to her, so familiar, so *everyday*, that every word they uttered, every sentiment they expressed, seemed to her to desecrate the world in which she had been living of late, and she looked upon them with eyes not only indifferent but positively hostile. She heard Dunyasha's cry about Count Petya, and a misfortune, but did not take them in.

'What misfortune could they have ? What misfortune could happen to them ? They just continue on in their old, humdrum, quiet way,' she thought to herself.

As she went into the drawing-room her father was hastily coming out of her mother's room. His face was puckered up and wet with tears. He had evidently run out of the room to give vent to the sobs that were choking him. Seeing Natasha, he waved his arms despairingly and broke into convulsive, painful sobs that distorted his soft round face.

'Pe ... Petya. ... Go to her ... go ... she ... she ... is calling ...' and weeping like a child he tottered on feeble legs to a chair and almost fell into it, covering his face with his hands.

Suddenly as it were an electric shock ran through Natasha's whole being. Terrible anguish stabbed her heart. She felt a dreadful agony as if something were being rent within her and she were dying. But the pain were immediately followed by a feeling of release from the impression of being suspended from life. At the sight of her father and the sound of a fearful harsh cry from her mother through the door she instantly forgot herself and her own grief.

She ran to her father but with a feeble gesture he pointed towards her mother's door. Princess Maria, pale and with trembling lower jaw, came out from the countess's room and took Natasha by the hand, saying something to her. Natasha neither saw nor heard her. With swift steps she went to the door, paused for a moment as if struggling with herself, and then ran to her mother.

The countess was lying back in a low chair in a strange awkward position, stiffening herself and beating her head against the wall. Sonya and some of the maids were holding her by the arms.

'Natasha! Natasha! ...' the countess was screaming. 'It's not true ... it's not true. ... He's lying. ... Natasha!' she shrieked, pushing Sonya and the maids away. 'Go away, all of you, it's not true! Killed! ... ha, ha, ha! ... It's not true!'

Natasha leaned a knee on the low chair, stooped over her mother, put her arms round her and with unexpected strength lifted her up, turned her face towards herself and pressed her close.

'Mamma! ... darling! ... I'm here, dearest mamma!' she murmured again and again, without a second's intermission.

She did not let go of her mother but struggled gently with her, demanded a pillow and water, and unfastened and tore open her mother's dress.

'Dearest, my darling ... mamma ... my precious,' she kept whispering while she kissed her hair, her hands, her face, and feeling the streaming, irrepressible tears tickling her nose and cheeks.

The countess squeezed her daughter's hand, closed her eyes and was quieter for a moment. All at once she sat up, unnaturally quickly, looked vacantly about her and, seeing Natasha, began hugging her head to her with all her might. Then she turned her daughter's face, wincing with pain, towards her and gazed long and searchingly into it.

'Natasha, you love me?' she said in a soft, trusting whisper. 'Natasha, you would not deceive me? You will tell me the whole truth?'

Natasha looked at her with eyes brimming with tears, her whole face a single entreaty for forgiveness and love.

'Mamma ... dearest!' she repeated over and over, putting forth all the strength of her love to try and find some way of taking on herself a little of the load of grief crushing her mother.

And again in the impotent struggle against reality her mother, refusing to believe that she could still exist when her beloved boy was killed in the bloom of life, took refuge from fact in the world of delirium.

Natasha could never afterwards remember how that day passed, nor that night, nor the following day and night. She did not sleep and did not leave her mother's side. Natasha's love, patient and persistent, seemed to enfold the countess every second, not with consolation, not with explanation, but simply beckoning her back to life. On the third night the countess was very quiet for a few minutes, and

Natasha rested her head on the arm of her chair and closed her eyes. The bedstead creaked; Natasha opened her eyes. The countess was sitting up in bed and speaking softly.

'How glad I am my boy has come. You are tired. Would you like some tea?' Natasha went up to her. 'You have grown so handsome and manly,' continued the countess, taking her daughter's hand.

'Mamma, what are you saying! ...'

'Natasha, he is dead, he is no more!'

And, embracing her daughter, the countess for the first time began to weep.

3

PRINCESS MARIA postponed her departure. Sonya and the count tried to take turns with Natasha but could not. They saw that she was the only one able to keep the mother from wild despair. For three weeks she stayed in her mother's room, sleeping on a lounge chair, feeding her and talking to her without pause because her tender caressing voice was the only thing that calmed the countess.

There was no healing the wound in the mother's heart. Petya's death had torn half her life away. When the news had come she had been a fresh and vigorous woman of fifty; a month later she emerged from her room a listless old woman with no interest in the world. But the same blow which almost killed the countess – this new blow brought Natasha back to life.

A spiritual wound caused by laceration of the spirit is like a physical wound and, strange as it may seem, slowly closes over. And after the deep wound – spiritual or physical – has cicatrized, and the torn edges have come together, it only heals completely as the result of a vital force thrusting up from within.

So healed Natasha's wound. She had believed that her life was over. But suddenly her love for her mother showed her that the essence of life – love – was still active within her. Love awoke, and life awoke.

Prince Andrei's last days had bound Princess Maria and Natasha together. This fresh trouble united them still more closely. Princess Maria put off her departure and for three weeks tended Natasha as though she were a sick child. Those weeks spent by Natasha in her mother's room had been a severe drain on her strength.

One afternoon, noticing Natasha shivering feverishly, Princess

Maria brought her to her own room and made her lie down on the bed. Natasha submitted, but when Princess Maria had drawn the blinds and was going away she called her back.

'I'm not sleepy, Marie, stay with me.'

'You are tired – try and have a sleep.'

'No, no. Why did you bring me away? She will be asking for me.'

'She is much better. She was talking so naturally today,' said Princess Maria.

Natasha lay on the bed and in the semi-darkness of the room studied Princess Maria's face.

'Is she like him?' Natasha wondered. 'Yes, and no. But there is something original, peculiar to herself about her – she's a quite new, unknown person. And she loves me. What is she like underneath? Entirely good. But what is it – what does she think? What is her opinion of me? Yes, she's a beautiful person.'

'Marie, dearest,' she said timidly, drawing Princess Maria's hand towards her. 'Marie, don't think that I'm wicked. You don't, do you? Marie, precious, I do so love you! Let us be real, bosom friends.'

And Natasha, throwing her arms round Princess Maria, began kissing her face and hands. Princess Maria felt both shy and happy at this demonstration of feeling.

From that day one of those tender and passionate friendships such as exist only between women was established between Princess Maria and Natasha. They were constantly kissing and saying tender things to one another, and spent most of their time together. If one went out the other became restless and hastened to join her. They felt more at peace together than when alone. A tie stronger than friendship sprang up between them: a singular feeling of life being possible only in each other's company.

Sometimes they were silent for hours on end; sometimes, in their beds at night they would begin talking and talk on till morning. They talked for the most part of the remote past. Princess Maria would speak of her childhood, of her mother, her father, her hopes and dreams; and Natasha, who with a carefree lack of understanding would have been repelled in the old days by this life of devotion and resignation, this poetry of Christian self-sacrifice, now with the sympathy born of the affection that bound her to Princess Maria, learnt to love her past too and to understand a side of life of which she had had no conception before. She had no thought of applying that humility and abnegation to her own life, because she was accustomed to look for other joys, but she understood and loved in another those previously incomprehensible virtues. Princess Maria, too, as she listened to Natasha's stories of her childhood and early girlhood, had a glimpse of horizons she knew nothing of – of a belief in life and the joys of life.

They still refrained from mentioning *him*, for fear of profaning (as it seemed to them) the exalted feeling in their hearts by words, but this reticence led them, though they would not have believed it, into gradually forgetting him.

Natasha had grown thin and pale, and physically so run down that everyone was always talking about her health, and she was glad it was so. But sometimes she was suddenly overcome by a dread not simply of death but of sickness, of ill-health, of losing her looks, and she would find herself examining her bare arm, surprised at its thinness, or gazing at her drawn, pitiful face in the looking-glass in the morning. It seemed to her that this was as it should be, and yet it was awfully sad.

One day after hurrying upstairs she noticed she was out of breath. Immediately, in spite of herself, she invented some excuse to go down, and then ran upstairs again, to try her strength and see what she could do.

Another time when she called Dunyasha her voice cracked, so she called again – though she could hear Dunyasha coming – called her in the deep chest tones in which she used to sing, and listened attentively.

She did not suspect it and would not have thought it possible, but underneath what seemed to her the impenetrable layer of mould which covered her soul tender, delicate young shoots of grass were already sprouting, destined to take root and with their living verdure so shroud the grief that weighed her down that soon it would no longer be seen or noticed. The wound had begun to heal from within.

At the end of January Princess Maria left for Moscow, and the count insisted on Natasha's going with her to consult the doctors.

4

AFTER the encounter at Vyazma, where Kutuzov had been unable to restrain the eagerness of his troops to overrun and cut off the enemy, and so on, the further flight of the French and pursuit by the Russians continued as far as Krasnoe without any pitched battle. The flight was so rapid that the Russian army racing after the French could not keep up with them: cavalry- and artillery-horses dropped on the road, and information as to the movements of the French was never reliable.

The Russian soldiers were so spent by this unbroken march at the rate of some twenty-seven miles a day that they could not move a step faster.

To appreciate the degree of exhaustion of the Russians it is only necessary to realize the significance of the fact that the army – a hundred thousand strong on leaving Tarutino, and losing no more than five thousand killed and wounded, and not a hundred prisoners – numbered only fifty thousand on reaching Krasnoe.

The rapidity of the Russian pursuit was as disintegrating to our army as the flight of the French was to theirs. The only difference was that the Russian army moved at will, free from the threat of annihilation that hung over the French, and that French sick and stragglers fell into enemy hands while Russian stragglers were among their own people. The principal cause of the reduction of Napoleon's army was the swiftness of its flight, and indubitable proof of this is furnished by the corresponding dwindling of the Russian army.

Just as at Tarutino and Vyazma, all Kutuzov's energies were directed not to arresting – so far as lay in his power – the fatal movement of the French (which was what Petersburg and the Russian army generals wanted) but to promoting it, and slackening the speed of his own troops.

But, in addition to the exhaustion of the men and the tremendous losses due to the swiftness of their advance, another reason for easing the pace and not being in a hurry presented itself to Kutuzov. The object of the Russian army was the pursuit of the French. The route the French would take was uncertain, and therefore the more closely our soldiers followed on their heels the greater the distance they had to traverse. Only by keeping some way in the rear could they take short cuts across the zigzags made by the enemy. All the artful manoeuvres proposed by our generals would have meant forced marches over longer distances, whereas the only reasonable course was to reduce these marches. And this was the aim to which Kutuzov devoted himself throughout the whole campaign from Moscow to

Vilna – not casually or intermittently, but so consistently that he never once deviated from it.

Kutuzov knew, not by reasoning or science but with every fibre of his Russian being – knew and felt, as did every Russian soldier, that the French were beaten, that the enemy was on the run and must be seen off the premises; but together with his soldiers he was aware of all the hardships of a campaign unprecedented for the speed of its marches and the time of year.

But to the generals (especially the foreign ones), burning to distinguish themselves, to dazzle the world, for some reason or other to take some duke or king prisoner, it seemed that now – just when any battle must be horrible and senseless – was the very time for fighting battles and conquering somebody. Kutuzov simply shrugged his shoulders when one after another they came to him with plans for manoeuvres to be executed by the ill-shod, insufficiently-clad and half-starved soldiers whose numbers in one month, and without a battle, had fallen to half, and who would even in the most favourable circumstances have a longer distance to traverse before they reached the frontier than they had come already.

This desire on the part of the generals to distinguish themselves, to perform manoeuvres, to overthrow and cut off, was particularly conspicuous whenever the Russian army came up against the French.

Such was the case at Krasnoe, where they had expected to find one of the three French columns and stumbled instead on Napoleon himself with a force of sixteen thousand. Despite all Kutuzov's efforts to avoid this disastrous engagement and to preserve his troops, the massacre of the shattered concourse of Frenchmen was kept up by the weary, worn-out Russians for three days at Krasnoe.

Toll wrote a disposition: 'First column to advance to this spot,' etc. And as usual everything took place otherwise than as laid down. Prince Eugène of Württemberg fired away from the hill-top at the mob of French as they raced by, and asked for reinforcements which did not arrive. By night the French dispersed to get round the Russians, hid themselves in the forest, and all who could struggled on again.

Miloradovich, who used to say that he cared nothing whatever about the commissariat arrangements of his detachment, and who could never be found when he was wanted – that self-styled *chevalier sans peur et sans reproche* – always eager for parleys with the French, sent envoys demanding their surrender, wasted time and did not carry out the orders he had received.

'I make you a present of that column, lads,' he said, riding up to his men and pointing out the French to his cavalry.

And the cavalry, with spur and sabre urging on their thin, worn out horses that could scarcely move, trotted with great effort to the column he had bestowed on them – that is to say, a rabble of frozen, benumbed and famished Frenchmen – and the column that had been presented to them threw down their weapons and surrendered, which was what they had been longing to do for weeks past.

At Krasnoe they took twenty-six thousand prisoners, several hundred cannon, a stick of some sort which was promptly dubbed a 'marshal's baton', and disputed as to who had distinguished himself, and were well content with their achievement, though they much regretted not having captured Napoleon, or at least some hero, a marshal, say, and blamed one another, and especially Kutuzov, for having failed to do so.

These men, carried away by their passions, were but the blind instruments of the most melancholy law of necessity; but they believed themselves heroes and imagined that they were doing most noble and honourable work. They criticized Kutuzov, and declared that from the very beginning of the campaign he had prevented them from vanquishing Napoleon, that he thought of nothing but the comforts of the flesh and was unwilling to leave the neighbourhood of the Linen Mills because he was comfortable there, that at Krasnoe he had checked the advance only because, having heard of Napoleon's presence, he had completely lost his head, and that it was quite probable that he had a secret understanding with Napoleon, that he had been bought over by him,* and so on and so forth.

Not only did his contemporaries, misled by the violence of their feeling, speak thus: posterity and history have acclaimed Napoleon as *grand*, while Kutuzov is qualified by foreigners as a sly, dissolute, feeble old intriguer, and by Russians as a nondescript creature – a sort of puppet, useful only because he had a Russian name. ...

★ Wilson's *Diary*. L.T.

5

IN 1812 and 1813 Kutuzov was openly accused of blundering. The Emperor was dissatisfied with him. And in a recent history inspired by promptings from the highest quarters Kutuzov is spoken of as a cunning Court liar, quaking at the name of Napoleon, and guilty through his mismanagement at Krasnoe and the Berezina of robbing the Russian army of the glory of complete victory over the French.*

Such is the lot, not of great men – *grands hommes* – whom the Russian mind does not acknowledge – but of those rare and always solitary individuals who, divining the will of Providence, subordinate their personal will to it. The hatred and contempt of the multitude is their punishment for discerning the higher laws.

For Russian historians (strange and terrible to say!) Napoleon, that most insignificant tool of history who never anywhere, even in exile, showed human dignity – Napoleon is the object of adulation and enthusiasm: he is *grand*. But Kutuzov, the man who from first to last in the year 1812, from Borodino to Vilna, was never once, by word or deed, false to himself, who presents an example, exceptional in history, of self-denial and present insight into the future significance of what was happening – Kutuzov appears to them as some colourless, pitiable being, and whenever they speak of him in connexion with the year 1812 they always seem a little ashamed of the whole episode.

And yet it is difficult to recall an historical character whose activity was so unswervingly and constantly directed to a single aim; and it would be difficult to imagine an aim more worthy or more consonant with the will of a whole people. Still more difficult would it be to find an instance in history where the aim of any historical personage has been so completely accomplished as that towards which all Kutuzov's efforts were devoted in 1812.

Kutuzov never talked of 'forty centuries looking down from the Pyramids,' of the sacrifices he was making for the Fatherland, of what he meant to do or had done. He did not as a rule talk about himself, adopted no pose, always appeared to be the plainest and most ordin-

* *History of the Year 1812: The character of Kutuzov and reflections on the unsatisfactory results of the battles at Krasnoe,* by Bogdanovich. L.T.

ary man, and said the plainest and most ordinary things. He wrote letters to his daughters and to Madame de Staël, read novels, liked the company of pretty women, joked with generals, officers and the soldiers, and never contradicted anybody who tried to argue with him. When Count Rostopchin galloped up to Kutuzov on the Yauza bridge and charged him personally with having lost Moscow, and said: 'Didn't you promise not to abandon Moscow without a battle?' Kutuzov replied: 'And I shall not abandon Moscow without a battle,' although Moscow was in fact already abandoned. When Arakcheyev arrived from the Emperor to say that Yermolov should be appointed to the command of the artillery Kutuzov answered: 'Yes, I was just saying so myself,' though a moment before he had said just the opposite. What did it matter to him – the one man amid a foolish crowd to grasp the whole mighty significance of what was happening – what did it matter to him whether Count Rostopchin attributed the disasters of the capital to him or to himself? Still less could it concern him who was appointed chief of artillery.

Not merely in these instances but on all occasions this old man, whose experience of life had taught him that ideas and the words which serve to express them are not what move men to action, frequently said things which were quite meaningless – uttering the first words which came into his head.

And yet this same man, so heedless of his words, never in the whole period of his command let fall a syllable which would have been inconsistent with the single aim towards the attainment of which he was working all through the war. With obvious reluctance, with bitter conviction that he would not be understood, he more than once, in very diverse circumstances, gave expression to his real thoughts. The battle of Borodino saw his first difference of opinion with those about him: he alone persisted in declaring that *the battle of Borodino was a victory*, and this view he continued to assert both verbally and in his dispatches and reports and right to his dying day. He alone said that *the loss of Moscow is not the loss of Russia*. His reply to Lauriston with his overtures for peace was: *There can be no peace, for such is the people's will*. He alone during the retreat of the French said that *all our manoeuvres are unnecessary, everything is being accomplished of itself better than we could desire*; that *what we have to do is to give the enemy a 'golden bridge'* (*and let them destroy themselves*); that *the battles of Tarutino, Vyazma and Krasnoe were none of them necessary*; that *as many men as possible must be saved to reach the frontier*; and that *he would not sacrifice one Russian for ten Frenchmen.*

And he alone, this intriguing courtier, as he is described to us, who lies to Arakcheyev to propitiate the Emperor – in Vilna he is the only one to say (thereby incurring the Emperor's displeasure) that *to carry the war beyond the frontier would be mischievous and useless.*

But words alone would be no proof that he grasped the significance of events at the time. His actions – without the smallest deviation – were all directed to one and the same threefold aim: (1) to brace all his forces to meet the French; (2) to defeat them; and (3) to drive them out of Russia, mitigating as far as possible the sufferings of the population and the army.

This procrastinator Kutuzov, whose motto was always 'Patience and Time', the sworn opponent of precipitate action, gives battle at Borodino, investing the preparations for it with unparalleled solemnity. This Kutuzov who at Austerlitz, before the battle began, declares that it will be lost, at Borodino, in the face of the conviction of the generals that the battle ended in defeat and the unprecedented instance of an army having to retire after winning a victory – he alone, in opposition to everyone else, persists to his dying day that Borodino was a victory. He was alone during the whole of the retreat in insisting that battles which now had no point should not be fought, that a new war should not be begun nor the frontiers of Russia crossed.

It is easy enough now that all the events with their consequences lie before us to understand their significance, provided we abstain from attributing to the masses the aims that existed in the brains of only a dozen individuals.

But how came that old man, alone, in opposition to universal opinion, so accurately to appreciate the import of events for the nation that never once throughout his career was he untrue to it?

This extraordinary power of insight into the significance of contemporary events sprang from the purity and fervour of his identification with the people.

It was their recognition of this feeling of his of oneness with them that led the people by such strange paths to choose him, an old man out of favour, to be their representative in the national war, against the wish of the Tsar. And it was this feeling alone which lifted him to the lofty pinnacle from which he, the commander-in-chief, exerted all his efforts, not to maim and exterminate men but to spare and have pity on them.

This simple, modest, and therefore truly great figure could not be cast in the lying mould invented by history for the European hero and so-called leader of men.

No great man is great to the flunkey, for the flunkey has menial ideas about what constitutes greatness.

6

THE 5th of November was the first day of what is called the battle of Krasnoe. Towards evening – after endless discussions and delays caused by generals not reaching their proper places; after much galloping to and fro of adjutants with counter-orders – when it was already self-evident that the enemy was everywhere in flight and that there could and would be no battle, Kutuzov left Krasnoe for Dobroe, to which place his Headquarters had that day been transferred.

It had been a clear, frosty day. Kutuzov, mounted on his plump little white horse, followed by an enormous suite of disgruntled generals whispering their discontent behind his back, rode towards Dobroe. All along the road knots of French prisoners taken that day (they numbered seven thousand) huddled round camp-fires warming themselves. Not far from Dobroe a huge buzzing crowd of tattered prisoners, bandaged and muffled up in anything they had been able to lay hands on, were standing beside a long row of unlimbered French cannon. At the approach of the commander-in-chief the hum died down and all eyes were fixed on Kutuzov, who moved slowly along the highway, wearing a white cap with a red band and a padded overcoat that bulged over his round shoulders. One of the generals started informing Kutuzov where the guns and prisoners had been captured.

Kutuzov seemed preoccupied and did not listen to what the general was saying. He screwed up his eyes with displeasure as he gazed attentively and fixedly at the prisoners who made a particularly wretched spectacle. Most of them were disfigured by frost-bitten noses and cheeks, and nearly all of them had red, swollen and festering eyes.

One group of Frenchmen was standing close by the road, and two soldiers – the face of one covered with sores – were tearing at a piece of raw meat with their hands. There was something horrible and bestial in the fleeting look they cast at the riders, and the malevolent scowl with which the soldier with the sores, after a glance at Kutuzov, turned away and went on with what he was doing.

Kutuzov stared long and intently at these two soldiers. Puckering his face still more, he half-closed his eyelids and shook his head thoughtfully. Farther on he noticed a Russian soldier laughingly clapping a Frenchman on the shoulder and making some friendly remark to him. Kutuzov shook his head again, with the same expression on his face.

'What were you saying? What was that?' he asked the general, who had continued with his report and was calling the commander-in-chief's attention to the captured French colours set up in front of the Preobrazhensky regiment.

'Ah, the standards!' said Kutuzov, rousing himself with an effort from the subject absorbing his thoughts.

He looked about him absently. Thousands of eyes were directed on him from all sides, waiting for him to speak.

He stopped in front of the Preobrazhensky regiment, sighed heavily and closed his eyes. One of his suite beckoned to the soldiers holding the standards to come forward and set up the flagstaffs round the commander-in-chief. Kutuzov was silent for a few seconds, and then with obvious reluctance, yielding to the obligations of his position, raised his head and began to speak. Crowds of officers gathered round him. He ran an attentive glance over the circle of officers, recognizing some of them.

'I thank you all!' he said, addressing the soldiers and then turning to the officers again. In the silence which reigned about him his slowly-spoken words were audible and distinct. 'I thank you all for your hard and faithful service. The victory is complete and Russia will not forget you. Honour and glory to you without end!'

He paused and looked round.

'Lower, lower with its head!' he said to a soldier holding the French eagle who had accidentally inclined it before the Preobrazhensky colours. 'Down with it, lower still, that's it! Hurrah, lads!' he cried, with a quick movement of his chin to the soldiers.

'Hur-rah-ah-ah!' roared thousands of voices.

While the soldiers were cheering, Kutuzov, leaning forward in his saddle, bowed his head, and his eye glinted with a mild and as it were ironic light.

'Yes, my men ...' he said when the shouts had ceased.

And all at once his voice and the expression of his face changed. It was not the commander-in-chief speaking now but an ordinary old man who wanted to tel' his comrades something very important.

There was a stir among the throng of officers and in the ranks of soldiers, as they pressed forward to catch what he was going to say.

'Yes, men, I know you're having a bad time but it can't be helped. Have patience – it won't last much longer. We'll see our visitors off and then we'll rest. The Tsar won't forget your services. It is hard for you but at any rate you are at home, whereas they – you see what they are reduced to,' he said, pointing to the prisoners. 'Worse off than the poorest of beggars. While they were strong we did not spare ourselves but now we can afford to spare them. They are human beings too. Isn't that so, lads?'

He looked about him and in the unflinching, respectfully wondering eyes staring at him read sympathy with what he had said. His face grew brighter and brighter with the gentle smile of old age which brought clusters of wrinkles to the corners of his mouth and eyes. He paused and bowed his head, as though uncertain.

'But with all said and done, who invited them here? It serves them right, the b — b — s!' he cried suddenly, lifting his head.

And flourishing his whip he rode off at a gallop for the first time during the whole campaign, leaving the soldiers guffawing gleefully and shouting 'Hurrah!' as they broke ranks.

Kutuzov's words were barely understood by the rank and file. No one could have repeated the field-marshal's address, solemn to begin with and ending up with the homely simplicity of an old man; but the sincerity behind his words was not only understood but the exalted feeling itself of triumph combined with pity for the enemy and consciousness of the justice of their cause – so exactly expressed by the old man's good-natured expletives – found an echo in every man's breast and inspired their delighted long-sustained cheering. After this, when one of the generals went up and asked the commander-in-chief whether he wished his calèche to be sent for, Kutuzov, evidently deeply moved, could only answer with a sob.

7

WHEN the troops reached their halting-place for the night on the 8th of November, the last day of the Krasnoe battles, it was already growing dusk. All day it had been still and frosty with a steady fall of light snow. Towards evening the snow-clouds began to clear, and a purplish starry sky appeared through the last of the falling flakes, and it got much colder.

A regiment of musketeers, which had left Tarutino three thousand strong but now numbered nine hundred, was one of the first to arrive at the halting-place – a village on the high road. The quarter-masters who met the regiment announced that all the cottages were full of sick and dead Frenchmen, cavalrymen and staff-officers. There was only one hut left for the colonel.

The colonel rode up to his hut. The regiment went on through the village and stacked their arms near the last cottages on the road.

Like a huge, many-limbed monster the regiment set to work to prepare a lair and food. One party of men trudged off, knee-deep in the snow, to the right of the village, into a birch-forest which a few minutes later reverberated with the ring of axes and short sabres, the crash of falling branches and the sound of merry voices. Another party bustled round the regimental baggage wagons and horses, which were drawn up together, getting out cauldrons and rye biscuit and feeding the horses. A third section dispersed about the village arranging quarters for the staff-officers, carrying out the dead bodies of the French that lay in the huts, and dragging away planks, dry wood and thatch from the roofs for the camp-fires, or wattle fencing to throw up some form of shelter.

Behind the cottages at the end of the village a dozen soldiers shouting boisterously were trying to shake down the high wattle wall of a barn from which they had already removed the roof.

'Now then, all together, heave!' cried the voices; and in the dark the fabric of the great snow-sprinkled wall began to give with a frosty creak. The lower stakes cracked more and more until at last the wattle wall collapsed, dragging down in its fall the men who had been pushing it. There was a loud exclamation, and then roars of coarse laughter.

'Come on, in pairs now! Give us a lever here! That's it. What the hell d'you think you're doing?'

'Now – heave. ... But wait a minute, boys. ... What about a song?'

They all stood silent, and a soft, pleasant, velvety voice began to sing. At the end of the third verse, as the last note died away, twenty voices roared out in chorus: 'Oo-oo-oo-oo! It's coming! All together! Heave, lads! ...' but in spite of their united efforts the wattle hardly moved, and in the silence that followed the men could be heard breathing heavily.

'Hi, you there of the 6th Company! You devils, you! Lend us a hand ... we'll do the same for you one day.'

Some twenty men of the 6th Company, who were on their way into the village, joined forces with them, and the wattle wall, about thirty-five feet long and seven wide, curving under its own weight, moved slowly along the village street, crushing and bruising the shoulders of the panting soldiers.

'Keep step there, can't you! ... Look out, you clumsy fathead. ... What are you stopping for? There now. ...'

The cheerful rough exchange of abuse never ceased.

'What are you up to?' cried a peremptory voice, as a sergeant came upon the party hauling their burden. 'There are staff here – the gen'ral 'imself's in that there 'ut and you foul-mouthed devils, you curs – I'll learn you!' shouted the sergeant, hitting the nearest soldier a swinging blow on the back.

The soldiers were quiet. The man who had been struck grunted and wiped his face, which was scratched and bleeding: he had been knocked forward against the wattle.

'The b — knows how to hit! My face's all bloody,' he muttered under his breath when the sergeant had walked away.

'And you don't like it? Fancy that!' mocked someone, and lowering their voices the soldiers continued on their way. Out of the village, they began again as loudly as before, punctuating their talk with the same aimless expletives.

In the hut which the men had passed were assembled officers of the higher command eagerly discussing over their tea the events of the day and the manoeuvres suggested for the morrow. It was proposed to execute a flank march to the left, to cut off and capture the viceroy (Murat).

By the time the soldiers had dragged the wattle fence to its place camp-fires ready for cooking were blazing on all sides. Wood crackled, the snow was melting and black shadowy figures flitted to and fro over the space where the snow had been trodden down.

Axes and choppers plied all around. Everything was done without any orders being given. Supplies of wood were piled high for the night, shanties rigged up for the officers, cauldrons put to boil and arms and accoutrements seen to.

The wattle wall brought in by the men of the 8th Company was curved in a semicircle and propped up by musket-rests to give shelter from the north, and a camp-fire built in front of it. The drums beat the tattoo, the roll was called, and the men had supper and settled themselves for the night round the fires – some repairing their foot-gear, some smoking pipes, others stripped naked and trying to steam the lice out of their clothes.

8

ONE might have supposed that under the almost inconceivably wretched conditions of the Russian soldiery at that time – lacking thick boots and sheepskin coats, without a roof over their heads in the snow with the temperature eight degrees below zero, and often with-out full rations (the commissariat did not always keep up with the troops) – they would have presented a most melancholy and de-pressing spectacle.

On the contrary, never, even in the happiest material circumstances, had the army worn a livelier and more cheerful aspect. This was because day by day it was able to shake off the weak or dejected. All the physically or morally frail had long since been left behind and only the flower of the army – physically and mentally – remained.

More men collected behind the wattle fence of the 8th Company than anywhere else. A couple of sergeant-majors were sitting by their camp-fire which blazed brighter than the others. A contribution of fuel was demanded in exchange for the right to shelter under the wattle screen.

'Hi, Makeyev – you lost? Or did the wolves get you? Fetch us some wood,' shouted a red-faced, red-haired man, screwing up his eyes and blinking from the smoke but not stirring from the fire. 'You, Jackdaw, you run and get us something to burn,' he cried to another soldier.

The red-headed man was neither a sergeant nor a corporal but being tough and strong he ordered the weaker ones about. The soldier they called 'Jackdaw', a thin little fellow with a sharp nose, got up submissively and was about to obey but at that moment there stepped into the light of the fire the slender, handsome figure of a young soldier carrying a load of wood.

'Give it here – that's fine!'

They broke up the wood and heaped it on the fire, blew at it with their mouths and fanned it with the skirts of their greatcoats, making the flames hiss and crackle. The men drew nearer and lit their pipes. The handsome young soldier who had brought the wood stuck his arms akimbo and began a brisk and nimble shuffle with his frozen feet on the spot where he stood.

'Ah me mother dear, the dew's cold an' clear, for a musketeer ...' he sang, with a sort of hiccough at each syllable.

'Look out, your soles will fly off!' shouted the red-haired man, noticing that one of the dancer's soles was loose. 'He's a rare devil for dancing!'

The dancer stopped, tore off the loose piece of leather and flung it on the fire.

'You're right there, old man,' said he, and sitting down he took out of his knapsack a strip of French blue cloth and proceeded to wrap it round his foot. 'It's the steam what spoils 'em,' he added, stretching his feet towards the fire.

'They'll soon be issuing us new ones. They say once we've finished *them* off we're all to get a double lot of stuff.'

'I say, that son of a bitch Petrov seems to have stayed behind after all,' remarked one of the sergeants.

'I've had an eye on him this long while,' said the other.

'Oh well, he's a rotten soldier. ...'

'The 3rd Company now – it appears they 'ad nine men missing at roll-call yesterday.'

'Yes, but when a man's feet are frozen off how's he to walk?'

'Oh b — s!' said one of the sergeants.

'Why – you thinking of doing the same maybe?' said an old soldier reproachfully to the man who had spoken of feet frozen off.

'Well, what do you take us for?' the sharp-nosed soldier they called Jackdaw exclaimed in a squeaky, unsteady voice, suddenly getting up from the other side of the fire. 'The fat grows lean, and

1294

the lean dies. Look at me now – I got no strength left in me. Tell 'em to cart me off to 'ospital,' he said with sudden resolution, turning to the sergeant. 'I aches all over with t'rheumatiz. It's me'll be the next to drop on the road.'

'That'll do – that's enough of that,' replied the sergeant calmly.

The soldier said no more and the talk went on.

'A rare lot of Frenchies been taken today, and not a decent pair of boots among the lot – nothing you could properly call a boot,' observed one of the soldiers, starting a new topic.

'The Cossacks took care of that. We was clearing out a hut for the colonel when they carried 'em out. A pitiful sight an' all it was, lads,' put in the dancer. 'They rolled 'em over, and one was alive, would you believe it, jabbering something in that lingo of theirs.'

'And they're clean in themselves,' the first man went on. 'White – why, 'e was white as birch-bark, and there're some brave-looking fellows among 'em, I must say – gentry too.'

'Well, what do you expect? They takes 'em from all stations for their army.'

'But they don't understand nothing,' said the dancer with a puzzled smile. 'I says to 'im: "Which king do you belong to?" and 'e gives me a string of gibberish. A queer lot!'

'It's a funny thing, mates,' continued the man who had wondered at the white skins of the French. 'The peasants round Mozhaisk way were saying as how when they went to take away the dead where the battle was, you understand – well, them dead 'ad been lyin' there nigh on a month, and, the peasant says – "they was lying there clean and white as paper, and not a whiff of smell of powder-smoke about 'em".'

'Was it the cold, perhaps?' asked someone.

'That's good, that is! Cold! Why, 'twas hot. If it'd 'ad bin cold, our chaps wouldn't 'ave rotted neither. "But no, go up to ours," 'e says, "and they'd be all maggoty rotten. We 'ad to tie 'ankerchiefs round our faces an' turn our 'eads away whiles we was shifting 'em. Almost more'n we could stomach. But them," 'e says, "they was white as paper, not a smell about 'em".'

All were silent.

'Most likely 'tis the food,' said the sergeant. 'They bin livin' like princes.'

No one contradicted him.

'That peasant at Mozhaisk, where the battle was, was tellin' us they was fetched out from a dozen villages round and was three weeks carting the dead away, and still there was more of 'em. And as for the wolves, he says. ...'

'That was something like a battle,' said an old trooper. 'The only one worth remembering. But since then ... it's been nothing but just goin' through with it.'

'Well, grandpa, we did 'ave a go at 'em day afore yesterday. But you can't get at 'em, they're that quick laying down their arms an' flopping on their knees. "*Pardong!*" they say. Take an example. I heard tell Platov twice took 'Poleon hisself. But 'e don't know t'right charm, see. Catches 'old on 'im and phttt! 'e turns into a bird in 'is 'ands and flies off. And no chance of killing 'im neither.'

'You be a prime liar, Kiselov, by the looks er you.'

'What d'ye mean – liar? 'Tis the honest-to-God truth.'

'Well, if you ask me, I'd bury 'im in the earth, if I caught 'un. With an aspen-stake to fix 'un down. The number of folk 'e's bin the death of!'

'Anyhows, we're soon going to make an end of 'im. 'E won't come 'ere again,' remarked the old soldier, yawning.

The conversation flagged and the soldiers began settling themselves for the night.

'Look at all them stars! Shining wonderful! Anyone'd say the women 'ad been spreading their washing out over the sky,' said one of the men, marvelling at the Milky Way.

'That's a sign of a good harvest for next year.'

'We shall want some more wood.'

'Warm your back and your belly freezes. That's funny!'

'O Lord!'

'What you shoving for? Think the fire's only for you, eh? Look at the way 'e's sprawled out!'

In the ensuing silence the snoring could be heard of those who had fallen asleep. The others kept turning over to warm themselves, now and again exchanging a few words. From a camp-fire a hundred paces off came a chorus of merry laughter.

'Hark at 5th Company guffawing over there,' said a soldier. 'And what a terrific lot of them there are!'

One of the men got up and walked across to the 5th Company.

"Aving a high old time, they are,' he said, coming back. 'A couple of Frenchies have turned up. One's pretty frozen but t'other's lively enough. Singing songs 'e is.'

'Oh? Let's go and have a squint. ...'

And several of the soldiers strolled over to the 5th Company.

9

THE 5th Company was bivouacking at the very edge of the forest. An immense camp-fire was blazing brightly in the midst of the snow, lighting up the branches of the trees heavy with hoar-frost.

About midnight the soldiers had heard footsteps in the snow of the forest and the cracking of dry boughs.

'A bear, lads,' said one of the men.

They all raised their heads to listen, and out of the forest into the bright firelight stepped two strangely garbed human figures clinging to one another.

They were two Frenchmen who had been hiding in the forest. They came up to the fire, hoarsely uttering something in a tongue our soldiers did not understand. One was taller than the other and wore an officer's hat; he seemed utterly spent. Approaching the fire, he tried to sit but fell to the ground. The other, a stumpy little soldier with his head tied round with a scarf, was stronger. He lifted his companion and said something, pointing to his mouth. The soldiers surrounded the Frenchmen, spread a greatcoat under the sick man, and brought both of them porridge and vodka.

The exhausted French officer was Ramballe and the man with a scarf tied round his head was his orderly, Morel.

When Morel had drunk some vodka and finished his bowl of porridge he suddenly became painfully hilarious and chattered incessantly to the soldiers, who could not understand him. Ramballe refused food and lay silently leaning on his elbow by the fire, staring at the Russians with red, vacant eyes. At intervals he emitted a long-drawn groan, and then relapsed into silence again. Morel, pointing to his shoulders, tried to make the soldiers understand that Ramballe was an officer and that what he needed was warmth. A Russian officer who had come up to the fire sent to ask his colonel whether he would take a French officer into his hut to warm him, and when the messenger returned and said that the colonel bade them bring the officer Ramballe was invited to go. He got up and tried to walk but staggered and would have fallen had not a soldier standing by caught hold of him.

'A drop too much, eh?' said a soldier with a humorous wink to Ramballe.

'Silly clown! Can't you talk sense? What an oaf the man is!' voices exclaimed on all sides, rebuking the jesting soldier.

They gathered round Ramballe, lifted him on to the crossed arms of two soldiers and carried him to the hut. Ramballe put his arms around their necks and as they carried him along he kept repeating plaintively:

'Oh you good fellows! Oh my kind, kind friends! Real decent fellows! Oh my brave, kind friends!' and he leaned his head against the shoulder of one of the men like a child.

Morel meanwhile was sitting in the best place by the fire, surrounded by soldiers.

Morel, a short, thickset Frenchman with inflamed, streaming eyes, was wearing a woman's shabby sheepskin jacket and had a kerchief tied over his forage-cap after the fashion of a peasant woman. He was unmistakably tipsy, and with one arm thrown round the soldier sitting next to him was singing a French song in a husky, broken voice. The soldiers held their sides as they looked at him.

'Now then, come on, teach us how it goes! I'll soon get the hang of it! How does it go? ...' said the soldier Morel was clasping – he was a singer and a wag.

Vive Henri quatre,
Vive ce roi vaillant!★

sang Morel, winking.

Ce diable à quatre ... †

'Vivarika! Vif-seruvaru! Sedyablyaka! ...' repeated the soldier, beating time with a flourish and really catching the tune.

'Bravo! Ha, ha, ha!' rose a rough cheerful guffaw from the audience. Morel, wrinkling up his face, laughed with them.

'Come on, what next, what next?'

★ *Long live Henry the Fourth,*
Long live that valiant king! etc. (French song).
† *That devil incarnate.*

Qui eut le triple talent,
De boire, de battre,
*Et d'être un vert galant …**

'That sounds all right too! Now, Zaletayev! …'

'Kiu …' Zaletayev articulated with a struggle. 'Kiu-iu-iu …' he drawled, laboriously pursing his lips, 'le-trip-ta-la-de-bu-de-bat-eh-de-tra-va-ga-la!' he sang.

'Fine! Just like the Frenchie! Ha-ha-ha! Like some more to eat, would you?'

'Give him some porridge. It takes a long time to fill up when you've been starving.'

They gave him some more porridge, and Morel with a laugh set to work on a third bowlful. Jovial smiles broadened the faces of all the young soldiers as they watched him. The older men, regarding such puerilities as beneath them, remained stretched out on the opposite side of the fire, raising themselves on an elbow now and then to glance at Morel with a smile.

'They are men like ourselves, after all,' said one, rolling himself up in his coat. 'Even wormwood has its roots and grows.'

'O Lord, just look at all those stars! No end to 'em! A sure sign of frost. …'

And silence descended.

The stars, as though they knew no one would see them now, began to disport themselves in the dark sky, flashing bright, disappearing again, shimmering and signalling some glad mystery to one another.

10

THE French army melted away with the regularity of some mathematical progression. And the passage of the Berezina, about which so much has been written, was only one of the intermediate stages in its destruction, and not at all the decisive episode of the campaign. If so much has been and still is written about the Berezina it is, so far as the French are concerned, only because at the broken bridge across the river the calamities their army had met with one by one were suddenly concentrated at a single moment into a tragic catastrophe

* *With the threefold talent,*
  For drinking, for fighting,
  For being a gallant.

no one ever forgot. On the Russian side the reason so much has been made of the Berezina was simply that in Petersburg – far from the theatre of war – a plan (again one of Pfuhl's) had been devised for drawing Napoleon into a strategic trap on the banks of the Berezina. Everyone was persuaded that the plan would work out exactly as arranged, and so they insisted that it was just the crossing of the Berezina that proved fatal to the French army. In reality the results of the Berezina crossing were far less disastrous to the French – in loss of guns and men – than Krasnoe had been, as the statistics show.

The sole significance of the passage of the Berezina lies in the fact that it proved beyond a doubt the fallacy of all plans for cutting off the enemy's retreat, and the soundness of the only possible line of action (the one demanded by Kutuzov and the army as a mass) – the idea of merely following on the enemy's heels. The mob of French fled at a continually increasing speed, with all their energies directed to reaching their goal. It fled like a wounded animal and it was impossible to stop its headlong flight. This was shown not so much by the ar- rangements made for the passage as by what occurred at the bridges. When the bridges broke, unarmed soldiers, people from Moscow and women and children who were with the French transport, all, carried forward by *vis inertiae*, instead of surrendering made a rush for the boats or threw themselves into the ice-covered water.

The impulse was a reasonable one. The state of fugitives and pur- suers was equally wretched. So long as they remained with those of their own side each might hope for help from his fellows and from the fact of belonging with them. But those who surrendered to the Russians found themselves in the same miserable plight, and worse off when it came to getting a share of the necessities of life. The French had no need to be told that half the prisoners – whom the Russians did not know what to do with – perished of cold and hunger however much their captors might want to save them: they felt that it could not be otherwise. The most compassionate and pro-French Russian generals, Frenchmen in the Russian service, could do nothing for the prisoners. The French perished of the miseries which attended the Russian troops. It was not possible to take bread and clothing from our hungry soldiers, whom we needed, to give to Frenchmen – who might not be objectionable, were not hated, were not to blame but who were simply not needed. A few Russians even did this but they were exceptions.

Behind the French lay certain destruction: in front there was hope. They had burned their boats, massed flight was their only salvation, and to this the French devoted all their strength.

The farther they fled, the more pitiable the condition of the French remnant, especially after the Berezina, on which (in consequence of the Petersburg plan) great hopes had been placed by the Russians, the more violent waxed the passions of the Russian generals who railed at each other and most of all at Kutuzov. Taking for granted that the failure of the Petersburg Berezina plan would be laid at his door, they expressed their dissatisfaction with him, their contempt and ridicule, more and more openly. Their ridicule and contempt were, of course, couched in a respectful form – in such a form that Kutuzov could not even ask what he was accused of. They did not treat him seriously: they submitted their reports and asked for his sanction with the air of performing a melancholy ritual, while behind his back they winked and tried to mislead him at every turn.

Because they could not understand him it was accepted as the recognized thing by all these people that it was useless to talk to the old man, that he could never grasp the profundity of their plans and would only reply with one of his phrases (it seemed to them they were nothing but phrases) about a 'golden bridge' or that crossing the frontier with a troop of vagabonds was not to be thought of, and so forth. They had heard all that before. And everything he said – that it was necessary to wait for provisions, for instance, or that the men had no boots – was so simple, whereas what they proposed was so complicated and clever, that it was obvious to them that he was an old dotard, while they were commanders of genius, without authority to take the lead.

This mood and this gossip of the Staff rose to a climax with the arrival in the army of Wittgenstein, the brilliant admiral and favourite hero of Petersburg. Kutuzov saw it and simply sighed and shrugged his shoulders. Only once, after the affair of the Berezina, did he lose his temper and wrote the following note to Bennigsen (who made separate reports to the Emperor):

On account of your Excellency's bouts of ill-health your Excellency will retire to Kaluga, on receipt of this present, there to await further commands and appointments from his Imperial Majesty.

But this dismissal of Bennigsen was followed by the arrival on the

1301

scene of the Grand Duke Konstantin Pavlovich, who had taken part in the beginning of the campaign but had subsequently been removed by Kutuzov. Now the Grand Duke, on rejoining the army, informed Kutuzov of the Emperor's displeasure at the poor success of our forces and the slowness of their advance. The Emperor himself intended to be with his troops in a few days.

The old man, as experienced in Court methods as in warfare – this same Kutuzov who in the August of that year had been chosen commander-in-chief against the Sovereign's will, who had removed the Grand Duke and heir-apparent from the army, and acting on his own authority and contrary to the Emperor's wishes had decreed the abandonment of Moscow – realized at once that his day was over, that his part was played, and that the semblance of power he had been allowed to wield was no more. And it was not only the attitude of the Court which told him this. He saw on the one hand that the military business in which he had played his part was at an end, and felt that his work was accomplished. And at the same time he began to be conscious of the physical weariness of his aged body and of the necessity of physical rest.

On the 29th of November Kutuzov entered Vilna – his dear Vilna, as he called it. Twice during his career Kutuzov had been governor of Vilna. In that wealthy town, which had escaped damage, he found old friends and associations, as well as the amenities of life of which he had so long been deprived. And at once turning his back on military and political cares and, so far as the passions raging all around him would permit, he immersed himself in the quiet routine of ordinary life, as if all that was taking place and all that had still to be done in the realm of history did not concern him in the slightest.

Tchichagov, one of the most zealous of the 'cutters-off' and 'over-throwers', who had at first advocated effecting a diversion in Greece and then in Warsaw but was never willing to go where he was sent – Tchichagov, who was famous for the boldness of his remarks to the Emperor – Tchichagov, who considered Kutuzov to be under an obligation to him because when he had been sent in 1811 to make peace with Turkey over Kutuzov's head and found on arriving that peace had already been concluded, he had frankly admitted to the Emperor that the credit for having secured that peace really belonged to Kutuzov – this same Tchichagov was the first to meet Kutuzov at the castle at Vilna where the latter was to stay. In undress naval uniform, with a dirk, and holding his cap under his arm, he handed the commander-in-chief a garrison report and the keys of the town. The contemptuously respectful attitude of youth to old age in its dotage was expressed in the most marked manner by the behaviour of Tchichagov, who was aware of the charges being levelled against Kutuzov.

In conversation with Tchichagov Kutuzov happened to mention that the vehicles packed with china that had been captured from him at Borisov had been recovered and would be restored to him.

'You mean to imply that I have nothing to eat from. ... On the contrary, I can supply you with everything you are likely to require, even if you should wish to give dinner-parties,' replied Tchichagov hotly in French. The motive behind Tchichagov's every word was always to demonstrate his own correctness and therefore he imagined Kutuzov to be animated by the same desire.

Shrugging his shoulders, Kutuzov replied, also in French, with his subtle, shrewd smile:

'I mean only what I say.'

In opposition to the Emperor's wishes Kutuzov detained the greater part of the army in Vilna. Those about him said that he went down-hill to an extraordinary extent and grew very feeble physically during his stay in that town. He attended to army matters with a bad grace, left everything to his generals and while waiting for the Emperor to arrive gave himself up to a life of dissipation.

The Emperor with his suite – Count Tolstoy, Prince Volkonsky, Arakcheyev and others – left Petersburg on the 7th of December and reached Vilna on the 11th, and drove straight to the castle in his travelling sledge. In spite of the severe frost some hundred generals and staff-officers in full parade uniform stood outside the castle, as well as a guard of honour of the Semeonovsk regiment.

A courier, dashing up to the castle ahead of the Tsar in a troika drawn by three foam-flecked horses, shouted: 'He's here!' and Konovnitsyn rushed into the vestibule to inform Kutuzov, who was waiting in the porter's little lodge.

A minute later the old man's big, heavy figure in full dress uniform, his breast covered with orders and a scarf pulled tight about his stomach, waddled out into the porch. He put on his *bicorne*, one peak over each ear, and, carrying his gloves, with an effort lowered himself sideways down the steps to the bottom, and took in his hand the report he had prepared for the Emperor.

There was much running to and fro and whispering, another troika flew furiously up, and all eyes were turned on an approaching sledge in which the figures of the Tsar and Volkonsky could already be descried.

From the habit of half a century all this had a physically agitating effect on the old general. He ran a nervous hand over his paunch, readjusted his hat and pulling himself together straightened his back and at the very moment the Emperor alighted from the sledge lifted his eyes to him, presented the report and began to speak in his measured, ingratiating voice.

The Emperor scanned Kutuzov from head to foot with a rapid glance, frowned for an instant but immediately mastering himself stepped forward and, stretching out his arms, embraced the old general. Once more, owing to old and long-standing habit of impression, this embrace, stirring some deep personal association, had its usual effect on Kutuzov and he gave a sob.

The Emperor greeted the officers and the Semeonovsk guard, and pressing the old man's hand again went with him into the castle.

When he was alone with the field-marshal the Emperor did not attempt to hide his dissatisfaction at the slowness of the pursuit and with the blunders made at Krasnoe and the Berezina, and informed him of his intentions for a future campaign abroad. Kutuzov offered no rejoinder or observation. The same submissive, vacant look with which he had listened to the Emperor's commands on the field of Austerlitz seven years before settled on his face now.

When Kutuzov came out of the study and with downcast head was crossing the ball-room with his heavy lurching gait he was arrested by a voice saying:

'Your Serene Highness!'

He raised his head and looked long into the eyes of Count Tolstoy, who stood before him holding a silver salver on which lay a small object. Kutuzov seemed not to grasp what was expected of him.

Suddenly he rallied as it were: a faint smile flashed across his puffy face, and with a low, respectful bow he picked up the object lying on the salver. It was the order of St George of the first class.

11

THE next day the field-marshal gave a dinner and ball which the Emperor honoured with his presence. Kutuzov had received the order of St George of the first class; the Emperor had conferred on him the highest marks of respect; but everyone was aware that the Tsar was displeased with the commander-in-chief. The proprieties were observed, and the Emperor was the first to set the example in doing so; but everybody knew that the old man was at fault and had shown his incapacity. When Kutuzov, conforming to a custom of Catherine's day, ordered the captured standards to be lowered at the Emperor's feet as he entered the ball-room the Emperor frowned and muttered something in which those nearest caught the words, 'the old comedian'.

The Emperor's displeasure was increased at Vilna in particular by the fact that Kutuzov evidently could not or would not see the importance of the coming campaign.

On the following morning when the Emperor said to the officers gathered about him: 'You have not only saved Russia, you have saved Europe!' they all understood that the war was not ended.

Kutuzov alone refused to see this and openly expressed his opinion that no fresh war could improve the position or add to the glory of Russia but could only spoil matters and detract from the lofty pinnacle of glory on which, to his mind, Russia was now standing. He tried to point out to the Emperor the impossibility of levying fresh troops, spoke of the hardships the people were suffering, of the possibility of failure, and so on.

This being the field-marshal's attitude, he was naturally regarded merely as a hindrance and an obstacle in the path of the impending war.

To avoid friction with the old man the obvious resource was to do as had been done at Austerlitz and with Barclay at the beginning of the Russian campaign – shift the ground from under the commander-in-chief's feet without upsetting the old man by informing him of the change, and transfer authority to the Emperor himself.

With this object his staff was gradually reconstructed and its real strength removed and passed to the Emperor. Toll, Konovnitsyn and Yermolov received new appointments. Everyone spoke loudly of how infirm the field-marshal had grown, and of his failing health.

It was necessary for him to be in poor health in order that his place could be given to his successor. And his health was, in fact, failing.

So just as naturally and simply and gradually as Kutuzov had come from Turkey to the Treasury in Petersburg to recruit the militia, and then to the army when he was needed there, now, his part being played, the new actor that was required took Kutuzov's place.

The war of 1812, besides its national significance dear to every Russian heart, was to assume another – a European – character.

The movement of peoples from west to east was to be followed by a movement from east to west, and for this fresh war another leader was needed, having other qualities and views and prompted by other impulses than Kutuzov's.

Alexander I was as necessary for the movement from east to west and for the re-establishment of national frontiers as Kutuzov had been for the salvation and glory of Russia.

Kutuzov had no notion of what was meant by the balance of power, or Napoleon. He could not understand all that. For the representative of the Russian people, after the enemy had been annihilated and Russia liberated and raised to the summit of her glory, there was nothing left for a Russian as a Russian to do. Nothing remained for the representative of the national war but to die. And Kutuzov died.

12

A s is generally the case, Pierre only felt the full effects of the physical privations and strain he had suffered as a prisoner when they were over. After his rescue he arrived at Orel and on the third day there, as he was preparing to start for Kiev, he fell ill and was laid up for three months. He had what the doctors termed 'bilious fever'. But in spite of the fact that they treated him, bled him and made him swallow drugs – he recovered.

All that had happened to him from the time of his rescue till his illness had left hardly any impression on his mind. He only remembered dull grey weather, now rainy, now snowy, internal physical aches, pains in his feet and side. He had a hazy memory of unhappy, suffering people, of the plaguing curiosity of officers and generals who persisted with their questions, of his difficulty in obtaining a conveyance and horses; and above all he remembered his incapacity all that time to think and feel. On the day that he was rescued he had seen the body of Petya Rostov. That same day he had learned that Prince Andrei, after surviving for upwards of a month after the battle of Borodino, had only a short time before died in the Rostovs' house at Yaroslavl. And on that day, too, Denisov, who told him this piece of news, in the course of conversation happened to mention Hélène's death, supposing that Pierre had heard of it long before. All this had at the time seemed merely strange to Pierre. He felt that he could not take in these tidings in all their bearings. Just then his one idea was to get away as fast as possible from the places where men were slaughtering each other to some quiet refuge where he could recover, rest and think over all the strange new things he had learned during this period. But as soon as he reached Orel he fell ill. When he came to himself after his illness he found in attendance on him two of his servants, Terenty and Vasska, who had come from Moscow, and the eldest of his cousins, who had been living on his estate at Elets, and hearing of his rescue and illness had come to nurse him.

It was only gradually during his convalescence that Pierre got rid of the impressions of the last few months and accustomed himself to the idea that no one would drive him forth tomorrow, that no one would dispossess him of his warm bed, and that he was quite sure of having dinner and tea and supper. But for a long time in his dreams he continued to see himself in the conditions of captivity. In the same way, little by little, he came to realize the significance of the news he had been told after his rescue: the news of the death of Prince Andrei, the death of his wife and the annihilation of the French.

A joyous feeling of freedom – that complete, inalienable freedom inherent in man of which he had first had a consciousness at the first halt outside Moscow – filled Pierre's soul during his convalescence. He was surprised to find that this inner freedom, independent as it was of external circumstances, now had as it were an additional setting of external liberty. He was alone in a strange town, without acquaintances. No one made any demands on him; no one forced him to go anywhere against his will. He had everything that he wanted; the thought of his wife which had been a continual torment to him in the old days was no longer there, since she herself was no more.

'Oh, how good! How nice!' he said to himself when a cleanly laid table was moved up to him with savoury beef-tea, or when he settled down for the night in his soft clean bed, or when he remembered that his wife and the French no longer existed. 'Oh, how good, how nice!' And from old habit he would ask himself the question: 'Well, what next? What am I going to do now?' And immediately he would answer himself: 'Nothing. I am going to live. Oh, how splendid!'

The very thing that had haunted him in the old days and that he had constantly sought in vain – an object in life – did not exist for him now. That search for an object in life was over not merely temporarily, for the time being – he felt that it no longer existed for him and could not present itself again. And it was precisely this absence of an aim which gave him the complete and joyful sense of freedom that constituted his present happiness.

He could have no object, because now he had faith – not faith in any rules or creed or dogma, but faith in a living, ever-manifest God. In the old days he had sought Him in the aims he set himself. That search for an aim had simply been a search for God, and suddenly during his captivity he had learnt, not through words or arguments but by direct feeling, what his old nurse had told him long ago: that God is here and everywhere. In his captivity he had come to see that God in Karatayev was grander, more infinite and unfathomable than in the Architect of the Universe recognized by the masons. He felt like a man who finds what he has been looking for at his very feet, when he has been straining his eyes to seek it in the far distance. All his life he had been seeking over the heads of those around him, while he had only to look straight in front without straining his eyes.

In the past he had been unable to see the great, the inscrutable, the infinite in anything. He had only felt that it must exist somewhere and had looked for it. In all that was near and comprehensible he had seen only what was limited, narrow, commonplace, meaningless. He had armed himself with a mental telescope and gazed into space, where what was petty and everyday, hidden in the misty distance, had seemed to him great and infinite merely because it was not clearly seen. This was the way European life, politics, freemasonry, philosophy and philanthropy had appeared to him. But even then, at moments of weakness as he had accounted them, his mind had penetrated that distance too and he had remarked the same triviality, worldliness and emptiness. But now he had learnt to see the great, the eternal, the infinite in everything; and therefore – to see it and revel in its contemplation – he naturally threw away the telescope through which he had hitherto been gazing over men's heads, and joyfully feasted his eyes on the ever-changing, eternally great, un-fathomable and infinite life around him. And the closer he looked, the more tranquil and happier he was. The awful question that had shattered all his mental edifices in the past – the question *Why?* – no longer existed for him. To that question *Why?* he now had always ready in his soul the simple answer: *Because God is* – the God without whose will not one hair falls from a man's head.

13

In external ways Pierre had hardly changed at all. In appearance he was just the same as before. As he always had been, he was absent-minded and seemingly absorbed not in what was before his eyes but in something special of his own. The difference between his former and his present self was that in the old days when he was oblivious of what was before him, or of what was being said to him, he had wrinkled his brows painfully as though striving, without success, to distinguish something far away. Now he still forgot what was said to him and still did not see what confronted him, but now he looked with a faint, apparently ironical smile at what was before him and listened to what was said, though it was evident that his eyes and his mind were concerned with something quite different. Hitherto he had seemed to be a kind-hearted person but unhappy, and so people had been inclined to hold a little aloof from him. Now a smile of *joie de vivre* constantly played round his lips and his eyes radiated sympa-thetic interest in others – in the question 'Were they as happy as he was?' – and people liked to be with him.

In the past he had talked a great deal, had got excited when he talked and had listened very little; now he was seldom carried away in conversation and knew how to listen, so that people were eager to tell him their most intimate secrets.

The princess, who had never had any affection for Pierre and had cherished a particular feeling of animosity towards him since she had felt herself under obligation to him following the old count's death, after a short stay at Orel, whither she had come with the intention of showing Pierre that in spite of his 'thanklessness' she considered it her duty to nurse him – the princess, to her surprise and annoyance, quickly felt that she was fond of him. Pierre did nothing to ingratiate himself with his cousin: he merely studied her with interest. In the old days she had always suspected him of mockery and indifference, and so had shrunk into herself as she did with other people, and had shown him only the combative side of her nature; now, on the contrary, she felt that he seemed to be trying to read and understand the most sacred recesses of her heart, and, mistrustfully at first and then with gratitude, she let him see the hidden, kindly sides of her character.

The craftiest of men could not have stolen into the princess's confidence more dexterously, tempting forth her memories of the best times of her youth, and entering into them. Yet the extent of Pierre's artfulness consisted in seeking his own pleasure in drawing out the human qualities in the embittered, hard and, after her own fashion, proud princess.

'Yes, he's a most excellent creature when he is not under bad influence but under the influence of people like myself,' thought the princess.

The change that had taken place in Pierre was noticed, in their own way, by his servants Terenty and Vasska too. They found that he had grown vastly more natural and human. Often after he had helped his master to undress and wished him good-night, Terenty would linger with boots and clothes in his hand in the hope that he would start a talk. And Pierre, seeing that Terenty was longing for a chat, generally kept him.

'Well, tell me … now how did you manage to get food?' he would ask.

And Terenty would begin about the destruction of Moscow or speak of the late count, and would stand for a long time with the clothes over his arm, telling stories or sometimes listening to Pierre's yarns, and then with a pleasant sense of intimacy with his master and affection for him finally withdrew.

The doctor who was attending Pierre and visited him every day, though he felt it incumbent on him, after the manner of doctors, to pose as a man whose every moment was precious for suffering humanity, sat for hours with Pierre, repeating his favourite anecdotes and observations on the *mœurs* of his patients in general, and of the ladies in particular.

'Yes, it's a pleasure to talk to a man like that – very different from what we are used to in the provinces,' he would say of Pierre.

There were several prisoners from the French army in Orel, and the doctor brought one of them, a young Italian, to see Pierre.

This officer became a frequent visitor, and the princess used to make fun of the sentimental affection which the Italian expressed for her cousin.

The Italian was apparently only happy when he could come to see Pierre and talk with him and tell about his past, his life at home, and his love, and pour out his indignation against the French and especially against Napoleon.

'If all Russians are in the least like you,' he would say to Pierre, 'it is sacrilege to wage war on such a people. You, who have suffered so much at the hands of the French, do not even bear a grudge against them.'

And this passionate devotion Pierre earned merely by bringing out what was best in the soul of the Italian and delighting in it.

During the latter part of Pierre's stay in Orel he received a visit from his old masonic acquaintance, Count Willarski, who had introduced him to the Lodge in 1807. Willarski was married to a Russian heiress who had large estates in the province of Orel, and he was filling a temporary post in the commissariat department in the town.

Hearing that Bezuhov was in Orel, Willarski, though they had never been in very close touch, called upon him with the professions of friendship and intimacy that men commonly display on meeting one another in the desert. Willarski was bored in Orel and rejoiced to meet a man of his own circle with, as he supposed, similar interests.

But to his surprise Willarski soon noticed that Pierre had quite dropped behind the times and was sunk, as he expressed it to himself, in apathy and egoism.

'You are turning into a fossil, my dear fellow,' he said.

But for all that Willarski felt much more at home with Pierre now than he had done in the past, and came to see him every day. To Pierre, as he looked at and listened to Willarski, it seemed strange and incredible to think that he had been the same sort of person himself until quite lately.

Willarski was a married man with a family, whose time was taken up in managing his wife's property, in performing his official duties and in looking after family affairs. He regarded all these occupations as hindrances to life, and considered them all despicable because their purpose was the welfare of himself and his family. Military, administrative, political and masonic questions constantly engrossed his attention. And Pierre, without criticizing or trying to change the other's views, watched this strange yet only too familiar phenomenon with the smile of quiet, amused irony now habitual with him.

There was a new feature in Pierre's relations with Willarski, with the princess, the doctor and all the people he met now, which gained for him universal goodwill. This was his acknowledgement of the freedom of everybody to think, feel and see things in his own way – his recognition of the impossibility of altering a man's convictions by words. This legitimate individuality of every man's views, which in the old days used to trouble and irritate Pierre, now formed the basis of the sympathy he felt for and the interest he took in other people. The diversity, sometimes the complete contradiction between men's opinions and their lives, and between one man and another, pleased Pierre and drew from him a gentle, satirical smile.

In practical affairs Pierre now suddenly felt within himself a centre of gravity he had previously lacked. Hitherto, every question concerning money, especially requests for money to which, as a wealthy man, he was very frequently exposed, had reduced him to a helpless state of worry and perplexity. 'To give or not to give?' he was always asking himself. 'I have the money and he needs it. But there's another who needs it more. Who needs it most? And perhaps both of them are impostors?' And in the days gone by he had been unable to discover any solution to all these conjectures, and had given to all and sundry so long as he had anything to give. He used to find himself in precisely the same quandary with regard to his property, when one person would advise him to adopt one course and another would recommend something else.

Now he found to his amazement that he was no longer troubled with misgivings and hesitation. Now there was a judge within him, settling, by some laws of which he himself was unaware, what should or should not be done.

He was just as unconcerned about money matters as before, but now he knew infallibly what he ought and what he ought not to do. The first time he had recourse to this new judgement was when a prisoner, a French colonel, came to him and after boasting for some time of his exploits ended by making what almost amounted to a demand that Pierre should give him four thousand francs to send to his wife and children. Without the least difficulty or effort Pierre refused, amazed afterwards to find how simple and easy it was to do what before had always seemed so insurmountably difficult. At the same time as he refused the French colonel he made up his mind that he must certainly resort to some stratagem when he left Orel to induce the Italian officer to accept assistance of which he was evidently in need. A further proof to Pierre of his own more stable outlook on practical matters was furnished by decisions he took in regard to his wife's debts and the rebuilding of his houses in and near Moscow.

His head steward came to Orel and with him Pierre went into the question of his diminished income. He had lost, according to the steward's calculations, about two million roubles by the burning of Moscow.

With the idea of compensating this loss the head steward pointed out that Pierre's income, far from being reduced, would be positively increased if he refused to honour his wife's debts, which he was under no obligation to meet, and did not rebuild his Moscow house or the country villa on his Moscow estate, which cost him eighty thousand a year to keep up and brought in nothing.

'Yes, yes, of course,' said Pierre with a beaming smile. 'I don't need any of all that. By being ruined I have become much richer!'

But in January Savelich arrived from Moscow and gave him an account of the state of things there, and the estimate the architect had made for restoring the house and the villa in the suburbs, speaking of this as though it were a matter already confirmed. At the same time he received from Prince Vasili and other acquaintances in Petersburg letters in which his wife's debts were mentioned. And Pierre decided that the steward's proposals which had so pleased him at first were wrong, and that he must go to Petersburg to wind up his wife's affairs and must rebuild in Moscow. Why he ought to do so he did not know, but he was convinced that he ought. His income would be reduced by three-quarters. But it had to be so; he felt that.

Willarski was going to Moscow and they agreed to travel together.

During the whole period of his convalescence in Orel Pierre had experienced a feeling of delight, of freedom, of life; but when he came out into the wide world and saw hundreds of new faces that feeling intensified. Throughout the journey he felt like a schoolboy on holiday. Everyone – the stage-coach driver, the overseers at the posting-stations, the peasants on the road and in the villages – all had a new significance for him. The presence and the observations of

Willarski, who was continually deploring the poverty and ignorance of Russia and her backwardness compared with Europe, only heightened Pierre's appreciation. Where Willarski saw lethargy Pierre saw an extraordinary strength of vitality, the strength which in the snow over a vast latitude sustained the life of that homogeneous, peculiar and unique people. He did not contradict Willarski, and even seemed to agree with him – apparent agreement being the simplest way of avoiding arguments which could lead to nothing – and smiled cheerfully as he listened.

14

JUST as it is difficult to explain why and whither ants speed about a scattered ant-hill, some dragging bits of rubbish, eggs and corpses away from it, others hurrying back to the wreck; or their object in jostling, overtaking and fighting one another – so it would be hard to give the reasons that induced the Russians, after the departure of the French, to flock to the place which had been known as Moscow. But just as when one watches the scurrying ants round their ruined ant-heap it is evident from the tenacity, the energy and the immense number of the delving insects that, though the ant-hill is totally destroyed, something indestructible, intangible – something that is the real strength of the colony – remains; so Moscow in the month of October, without a government, without church services or sacred icons, without its wealth and its houses – was still the Moscow it had been in August. Everything was shattered except something intangible yet mighty and indestructible.

The motives of those who rushed from all sides to Moscow after it had been cleared of the enemy were most diverse and personal, and at first mainly savage and animal. One impulse only they all had in common: attraction to the place which had been called Moscow, in order to set their energies to work there.

Within a week Moscow had fifteen thousand inhabitants; in a fortnight twenty-five thousand, and so it went on, the figures increasing until by the autumn of 1813 the population exceeded what it had been in 1812.

The first Russians to enter Moscow were the Cossacks of Wintzingerode's detachment, peasants from the adjacent villages and residents who had fled the capital to hide in the outskirts. The returning

Russians, finding Moscow plundered, plundered in their turn. They continued what the French had begun. Trains of peasant carts drove into Moscow to carry away to the villages all that had been abandoned in the ruined houses and streets. The Cossacks carried off what they could to their camps, and house-owners snatched everything possible from other houses, on the pretence that they were recovering their own property.

But the first pillaging parties were followed by a second and a third contingent, and as the numbers swelled plundering became more and more difficult and assumed more definite forms.

The French had found Moscow deserted but with all the machinery of an organically normal town life still existent – with diverse branches of commerce and craftsmanship, of luxury, of local government and religion. The machinery was inert but it still existed. There were markets, stalls, shops, corn-exchanges, bazaars – for the most part still stocked with goods; there were factories and workshops; there were palaces and stately houses filled with luxuries; there were hospitals, prisons, government offices, churches and cathedrals. The longer the French stayed the more these forms of town life fell away, until towards the end everything disintegrated into one confused, lifeless scene of pillage.

The longer the rapine by the French continued the more the wealth of Moscow and the strength of the pillagers was demolished. But the plundering which marked the return of the Russians to their capital – the longer that lasted, and the greater the number of people taking part in it, the more rapidly was the wealth of Moscow and the regular life of the city restored.

Besides the plunderers, people of all sorts, drawn some by curiosity, some by the duties of office, some by self-interest – householders, clergy, officials of high and low degree, tradesmen, artisans and peasants – streamed into Moscow from all directions, as blood flows to the heart.

Within a week the peasants who came with empty carts to carry off plunder were stopped by the authorities and made to cart away dead bodies from the town. Other peasants, hearing of their comrades' discomfiture, drove into the capital with corn, oats and hay, by competition with one another knocking prices down to lower than they had been in former days. Gangs of carpenters, hoping for fat jobs, arrived in Moscow daily, and on all sides new houses began to go up and burnt-out skeletons were repaired. Tradesmen carried on their business from booths. Cook-shops and taverns were set up in houses that had been through the flames. The clergy resumed services of divine worship in many of the churches that had escaped the fire. The faithful contributed ecclesiastical furnishings which had been stolen. Government clerks planted their baize-covered tables and pigeon-holes of documents in small rooms. The higher authorities and the police organized the distribution of goods left by the French. The owners of houses in which much property was found that had come from other houses complained of the injustice of the order to bring everything to the Granovitaya palace in the Kremlin; others insisted that as the French had collected things from different places into this or that house it would be unfair to allow the master of the house to keep the contents. The police were abused and they were bribed. Estimates were made out at ten times its value for Crown property destroyed in the conflagration. Demands for relief poured in. Count Rostopchin wrote his proclamations.

15

AT the end of January Pierre arrived in Moscow and settled into the wing of his house which had not been damaged. He called on Count Rostopchin and various acquaintances who were back in Moscow, and made plans to leave for Petersburg after a couple of days. Everybody was celebrating the victory; there was a ferment of life in the shattered but reviving city. Everyone was glad to see Pierre; everyone was eager to meet him and they all plied him with questions about what he had seen. Pierre felt particularly friendlily disposed to everyone he encountered; but now he was instinctively on his guard not to entangle himself in any way. To all the inquiries put to him, important or trivial – such as, Where did he mean to live? Was he going to rebuild? When was he leaving for Petersburg and would he mind taking a small parcel for someone? – he would answer vaguely 'Yes, very possibly,' 'I dare say I may,' and so on.

He heard that the Rostovs were in Kostroma but he seldom thought of Natasha. If she did come into his mind it was only as a pleasant memory of time long past. He felt himself set free, not only from social obligations but also from that feeling which, it seemed to him, he had wittingly let loose on himself.

On the third day after his arrival he learned from the Drubetskoys that Princess Maria was in Moscow. The death, the sufferings and the last days of Prince Andrei had often engaged his thoughts and now recurred to him with fresh vividness. Having heard at dinner that Princess Maria was in Moscow and living in her own house – which had escaped the fire – in Vozdvizhenka street, he drove that same evening to call upon her.

On his way to Princess Maria's Pierre's mind was full of Prince Andrei, of their friendship, of the different occasions when they had met, and especially of the last time at Borodino.

'Can he have died in the bitter mood he was in then? Is it possible that the meaning of life was not revealed to him before he died?' mused Pierre. He thought of Karatayev and his death and involuntarily began to compare the two men, so different and yet so alike in the love he had felt for them both and in that both had lived and both were dead.

In the most serious of humours Pierre drove up to the house of the old prince. The house had been spared: traces of damage were to be seen but its general aspect was unchanged. The old footman met Pierre with a stern face, as if wishing to impress on the visitor that the absence of the prince made no difference to the order of the establishment, and said that the princess had retired to her own apartments, and received on Sundays.

'Tell her I am here. Perhaps she will see me,' said Pierre.

'Yes, sir,' answered the man. 'Please step into the portrait-gallery.'

A few minutes later the footman returned accompanied by Des-salles with a message from the princess that she would be very glad to see Pierre if he would excuse her want of ceremony and come upstairs to her apartment.

In a low room lighted by a single candle he found the princess and someone with her dressed in black. Pierre recalled that the princess always had lady companions. Who they were and what they were like he never knew or remembered. 'This must be one of her companions,' he thought, glancing at the lady in the black dress.

The princess rose quickly to meet him and held out her hand.

'Yes,' she said, studying his altered face after he had kissed her hand, 'so this is how we meet again. He often talked of you even towards the end,' she went on, turning her eyes from Pierre to her companion with a hesitancy that surprised him for an instant.

'I was so glad to hear of your safety. It was the only piece of good news we had for a long time.'

Again the princess glanced round still more uneasily at her companion and was about to add something but Pierre interrupted her.

'Just imagine – I knew nothing about him!' he said. 'I thought he had been killed. All my news I have had second-hand from others. I only know that he fell in with the Rostovs. ... What a strange coincidence!'

Pierre spoke rapidly, with animation. He glanced once at the companion's face, saw her friendly, interested eyes fixed attentively on him, and, as often happens in the course of conversation, he gathered a general impression that this companion in the black dress was a good, kind, nice creature, who need be no hindrance to his conversing freely with Princess Maria.

But when he mentioned the Rostovs the embarrassment in Princess Maria's face became even more marked. She shot another quick look from Pierre to the lady in black, and said:

'Don't you recognize her?'

Pierre looked again at the companion's pale, delicate face with its black eyes and strange mouth. Something near and dear, something long forgotten and more than sweet, gazed at him from those intent eyes.

'But no, it can't be!' he thought. 'This austere, thin, pale face that looks so much older? It cannot be she. It merely reminds me of her.' But at that moment Princess Maria said 'Natasha!' And the face with the attentive eyes painfully, with effort, like a rusty door opening, smiled, and through that opened door there floated to Pierre a breath of fragrance suffusing him with a happiness he had long forgotten and which, certainly of late, had had no place in his thoughts. It breathed about him, penetrated his being and enveloped him entirely. When she smiled doubt was no longer possible: it was Natasha, and he loved her.

In that first moment Pierre involuntarily betrayed to her and to Princess Maria, and most of all to himself, a secret of which he himself had been unaware. He flushed joyfully and with agonizing distress. He tried to mask his emotion. But the more he tried to hide it the more clearly – more clearly than any words could have done – did he disclose to himself and to her, and to Princess Maria, that he loved her.

1318

'No, it's only the unexpectedness of it,' thought Pierre. But as soon as he tried to go on with the conversation he had begun with Princess Maria he glanced again at Natasha, and a still deeper flush spread over his face and a still more violent agitation of rapture and terror flooded his soul. He tripped over his words and stopped short in the middle of a sentence.

Pierre had not noticed Natasha because he had never expected to see her there; but he had not recognized her because of the immense change in her since they had last met. She had grown thin and pale. But it was not that which made her unrecognizable: she was un-recognizable when he first entered the room and glanced at her because there was no trace of a smile in the eyes that in the old days had always shone with suppressed *joie de vivre*; he saw only intent, kindly eyes full of mournful inquiry.

Pierre's confusion roused no answering confusion on Natasha's part, but only a look of pleasure that faintly lighted up her whole face.

16

'SHE has come to stay with me,' said Princess Maria. 'The count and countess will be here in a few days. The countess is in a dreadful state. But it was necessary for Natasha herself to see a doctor. They insisted on her coming away with me.'

'Yes, is there a family free of sorrow these days?' said Pierre, turning to Natasha. 'You know it happened the very day we were rescued. I saw him. What a charming boy he was!'

Natasha looked at him, and in response to his words her eyes only widened and grew brighter.

'What can one say or think of by way of comfort?' exclaimed Pierre. 'Nothing! Why should such a glorious young fellow, so full of life, have to die?'

'Yes, in our times it would be hard to live if one had not faith ...' remarked Princess Maria.

'Yes, yes, that is true, indeed!' Pierre put in hastily.

'Why is it true?' Natasha asked, looking closely into Pierre's eyes.

'How can you ask that?' said Princess Maria. 'Why, only the thought of what awaits ...'

Natasha, without waiting for Princess Maria to finish, looked again inquiringly at Pierre.

'And because,' Pierre continued, 'only one who believes that there is a God guiding us can bear such a loss as hers and ... yours.'

Natasha had already opened her mouth to speak but suddenly she stopped.

Pierre hurriedly turned away from her and again addressed Princess Maria, to ask about his friend's last days.

Pierre's agitation had now almost subsided but at the same time he felt that his freedom had vanished too. He felt that there was now a judge criticizing his every word and action, a judge whose verdict was of greater consequence to him than that of all the rest of the world. As he talked now he was considering what impression his words were making on Natasha. He did not purposely say things to please her but whatever he said he looked at from her point of view.

Princess Maria – reluctantly, as is usual – began telling Pierre of the condition in which she had found Prince Andrei. But Pierre's questions, the eager, restless look in his eyes, his face quivering with emotion, gradually induced her to go into details which she shrank for her own sake to recall.

'Yes, yes, and so ... ?' Pierre kept saying as he lent towards her with his whole body, listening earnestly. 'Yes; so he found peace ? He grew gentler ? With his whole soul he was always striving for one thing only – to be completely good – so he could not have been afraid of death. The faults he had – if he had any – were not of his making. So he did soften ? ... What a happy thing that he saw you again,' he added, suddenly turning to Natasha and looking at her with eyes full of tears.

Natasha's face twitched. She frowned and for an instant looked down. For a moment she hesitated: should she speak or not ?

'Yes, that was a great happiness,' she said in her quiet voice with its deep chest notes. 'For me it was happiness indeed.' She paused 'And he ... he ... he said he was wishing for just that at the very moment I entered the room. ...'

Natasha's voice broke. She flushed, pressed her clasped hands on her knees, and then, controlling herself with an evident effort, lifted her head and began to speak rapidly.

'We knew nothing about it when we started from Moscow. I had not dared to ask about him. Then suddenly Sonya told me he was travelling with us. I had no idea – I could not imagine what state he was in, all I wanted was to see him, to be with him,' she said, trembling and choking.

And, not letting them interrupt her, she went on to tell of what she had never yet mentioned to anyone – all she had gone through during those three weeks of their journey and their stay in Yaroslavl.

Pierre listened with parted lips and eyes full of tears fastened upon her. As he listened he was not thinking of Prince Andrei, nor of death, nor of what she was saying. He listened to her, conscious only of pity for the pain she was suffering as she told her story.

The princess, frowning in her effort to hold back her tears, sat by Natasha's side and heard for the first time the history of those last days of her brother's and Natasha's love.

It was evidently a pressing necessity for Natasha to speak of that agonizing yet joyful time.

She talked on, mingling the most trivial details with her most sacred feelings, and it seemed as though she would never come to an end. Several times she repeated the same thing twice.

Dessalles' voice was heard at the door asking whether little Nikolai might come in to say good-night.

'Well, that's all – everything ...' said Natasha.

She got up quickly just as little Nikolai was coming in and almost running to the door, which was hidden by a curtain, knocked her head against it and with a moan of mingled pain and grief rushed from the room.

Pierre gazed at the door through which she had disappeared, and wondered why he suddenly felt alone in the wide world.

Princess Maria roused him from his abstraction, calling his attention to her nephew who had come in.

Little Nikolai's face, so like his father, affected Pierre so deeply at this moment of emotional tension that after kissing the child he got up quickly, took out his handkerchief and walked over to the window. He would have taken leave of Princess Maria but she would not let him go.

'No, Natasha and I often sit up until past two, so please don't go. We will have some supper. Go downstairs, we will follow directly.'

Before Pierre went down the princess said to him:

'This is the first time she has talked of him like that.'

17

PIERRE was shown into the large brightly-lit dining-room. In a few minutes he heard footsteps and the princess entered with Natasha. Natasha was calm, though the severe, unsmiling expression had settled on her face again. Princess Maria, Natasha and Pierre were all three suffering under that sense of awkwardness which usually follows after a serious and intimate conversation. To continue on the same subject is impossible; to discuss trifles does not seem right; and silence is disagreeable because the desire to talk is there and silence feels like affectation. They sat down to table without a word. The footmen drew the chairs back and pushed them up again. Pierre unfolded his cold table-napkin, and making up his mind to break the silence glanced at Natasha and Princess Maria. They had evidently both reached the same decision at the same moment: in the eyes of both shone a satisfaction with life and an admission that there was gladness in it as well as sorrow.

'Do you drink vodka, count?' asked Princess Maria, and these words suddenly banished the shadows of the past. 'Now tell us about yourself,' said she. 'One hears such incredible stories about you.'

'Yes,' replied Pierre with the gentle smile of irony now habitual to him. 'I am even told of wonders I myself never dreamed of! Maria Abramovna invited me to her house and kept telling me what had happened to me, or was supposed to have happened. Stepan Stepanych also gave me a lesson in the way I should relate my experiences. Altogether I have noticed that it is a very comfortable matter to be an interesting person (I am now an interesting person); people invite me out and tell me all about myself.'

Natasha smiled and started to say something.

'We heard,' said Princess Maria, forestalling her, 'that you lost two millions in Moscow. Is that true?'

'Oh, I am three times as rich as before,' said Pierre.

Though his circumstances were altered by his decision to pay his wife's debts and the necessity of rebuilding, Pierre still said that he was three times as rich as before.

'What I have undoubtedly gained is freedom ...' he began seriously, but on second thoughts did not continue, feeling that this was too egotistic a theme.

'And are you building?'

'Yes, Savelich says I must!'

'So you did not know of the countess's death when you stayed on in Moscow?' asked Princess Maria, and at once flushed crimson, having seen that in putting this question to him immediately after his reference to 'freedom' she was ascribing a significance to his words which was perhaps not intended.

'No,' answered Pierre, obviously not finding anything awkward in the interpretation Princess Maria had given to his remark about his freedom. 'I heard of it in Orel and you cannot imagine how it affected me. We were not a model couple,' he added quickly, glancing at Natasha and observing in her face curiosity as to how he would speak of his wife, 'but her death was a terrible shock. When two people cannot agree, the fault always lies on both sides. And one's own guilt suddenly becomes horribly serious when the other is no longer alive. And then to die like that ... alone, away from friends, without consolation! I felt very, very sorry for her,' he concluded, and was pleased to see a glad look of approval on Natasha's face.

'And so you are single and an eligible *parti* again,' remarked Princess Maria.

Pierre blushed crimson and for a long time tried not to look at Natasha. When he ventured a glance her way her face was cold and severe – even, he fancied, disdainful.

'But did you really see and speak to Napoleon, as we have been told?' asked Princess Maria.

Pierre laughed.

'No, not once, ever! To hear people, one might imagine that to be a prisoner is synonymous with being on a visit to Napoleon. Not only did I never see him – I never even heard him mentioned. I was in much lower company!'

Supper was over and Pierre, who had at first declined to talk about his captivity, was gradually led on to do so.

'But it's true, isn't it, that you stayed behind in Moscow to kill Napoleon?' Natasha asked him with a slight smile. 'I guessed as much when we met you at the Suharev tower – remember?'

Pierre acknowledged that this was true and, thus started, allowed himself to be drawn by Princess Maria's questions, and still more by Natasha's, into giving them a detailed account of his adventures.

At first he spoke with the light irony with which he now always used towards others and especially towards himself; but when he came to describe the horrors and sufferings he had witnessed he was unconsciously carried away and began speaking with the suppressed emotion of a man re-living in imagination experiences which made an acute impression on him.

Princess Maria looked from Pierre to Natasha with a gentle smile. In the whole narrative from beginning to end she saw only Pierre and his goodness. Natasha, leaning on her elbow, the expression on her face continually changing with the story, watched Pierre without taking her eyes off him, evidently living with him through all that he was telling them. Not only her look but her exclamations and the brief questions she put showed Pierre that she understood just what he wanted to convey. It was plain that she understood not only what he said but also what he would have liked to say and could not express in words. The episode with the child and the woman whom he had tried to defend and so got himself arrested Pierre related in the following manner:

'It was an awful sight – children abandoned, some of them in the flames. ... I saw one child dragged out. ... There were women who had their things pulled off, their ear-rings snatched. ...'

Pierre coloured and hesitated.

'Then a patrol arrived on the scene and all those who were not looting – all the men, I mean – were arrested. And me with them.'

'I am sure you're not telling us everything – I am sure there was something you did ...' said Natasha, and after a pause added: 'something fine.'

Pierre continued. When he came to the execution he would have passed over the horrible details but Natasha insisted on his leaving nothing out.

Pierre was going on to Karatayev but stopped. (By this time he had risen from the table and was walking up and down the room, Natasha following him with her eyes.)

'No, you just can't understand what I learned from that illiterate man – that simple creature.'

'Go on, go on,' urged Natasha. 'What became of him?'

'They killed him, almost before my eyes.'

And Pierre went on to tell them about the last part of the retreat, and about Karatayev falling ill (his voice shook continually) and then his death.

Pierre recounted adventures of which he had never told anyone, which he had never thought of before. He now saw as it were a new significance in all he had been through. Now that he was telling it all to Natasha he experienced the rare happiness men know when women listen to them – not *clever* women who when they listen are either trying to assimilate what they hear for the sake of enriching their minds and, when opportunity offers, repeating it, or to apply what is told them to their own ideas and promptly bring out the clever comments elaborated in their own little mental workshop; but the happiness true women give who are endowed with the capacity to select and absorb all that is best in what a man shows of himself. Natasha, without knowing it, was all attention: she did not miss one word, one inflection of his voice, no twitch of a muscle in his face nor a single gesture. She caught the still unspoken word on the wing and took it straight into her open heart, divining the secret import of all Pierre's spiritual travail.

Princess Maria understood his story and sympathized with him but she was seeing something else that absorbed her entire interest. She saw the possibility of love and happiness between Natasha and Pierre. And this idea, which struck her now for the first time, filled her heart with gladness.

It was three o'clock in the morning. The footmen appeared with sad, forbidding faces, bringing fresh candles, but no one noticed them.

Pierre finished his story. Natasha still gazed intently and persistently at him with shining, eager eyes, as if wishing to read the portions of his story that he had perhaps not told. In shamefaced and happy confusion Pierre occasionally glanced at her and cudgelled his brains what to say next to change the subject. Princess Maria was silent. It did not occur to any of them that it was three o'clock in the morning and time to go to bed.

'People talk about adversity bringing suffering,' remarked Pierre, 'but if I were asked at this moment whether I would rather be what I was before I was taken prisoner, or go through all that again, my answer would be: "For heaven's sake give me captivity and horse-flesh!" We imagine that as soon as we are thrown out of our customary ruts all is over, but it is only then that the new and the good begins. While there is life there is happiness. There is a great deal, a great deal before us. I say that for you,' he added, turning to Natasha.

'Yes, yes,' she murmured, answering something quite different.

'I too would ask for nothing better than to go through it all again from the beginning.'

Pierre looked at her keenly.

'No, I could ask for nothing more,' Natasha repeated.

'No, no!' cried Pierre. 'I am not to blame for being alive and wanting to live – nor you either.'

Suddenly Natasha let her head drop into her hands, and burst into tears.

'What is it, Natasha?' said Princess Maria.

'Nothing, nothing.' She smiled at Pierre through her tears. 'Goodnight, it's bedtime.'

Pierre got up and took his leave.

*

Natasha, as she always did, went with Princess Maria into her bedroom. They talked of what Pierre had told them. Princess Maria did not express her opinion of Pierre. Nor did Natasha speak of him.

'Well, good-night, Marie,' said Natasha. 'Do you know, I am often afraid that by not speaking of him' (she meant Prince Andrei) 'for fear of desecrating our feelings, we forget him.'

Princess Maria sighed deeply and by this sigh acknowledged the justice of Natasha's remark, but she did not agree with her in words.

'Is it possible to forget?' said she.

'It did me so much good to tell all about it today. It was hard and painful, yet I was glad to … very glad,' said Natasha. 'I am sure he really loved him. That was why I told him … it didn't matter my telling him?' she asked suddenly, blushing.

'Telling Pierre? Oh, no! What a fine man he is!' said Princess Maria.

'Do you know, Marie,' said Natasha all of a sudden, with a mischievous smile such as Princess Maria had not seen on her face for a long time, 'he has somehow grown so fair and smooth and fresh-looking – as though he had just come out of a bath: do you understand? Out of a moral bath, I mean. Don't you agree?'

'Yes,' replied Princess Maria. 'He has improved very much.'

'And his short jacket and his cropped hair; exactly as though … well, exactly as though he had come straight out of the bath. … Papa used sometimes …'

'I can understand how it was *he*' [Prince Andrei] 'cared for him more than anyone else,' said Princess Maria.

'Yes, and they were quite different. They say men are better friends when they are not alike. That must be true. He is not a bit like him in anything, is he?'

'No, and he's a marvellous person.'

'Well, good-night,' said Natasha.

And the same mischievous smile lingered for a long time on her face as though it had been forgotten there.

18

IT was a long while before Pierre could go to sleep that night. He strode up and down his room, at one moment frowning, deep in some difficult train of thought, or shrugging his shoulders and giving a start, at the next smiling blissfully.

He was thinking of Prince Andrei, of Natasha, and of their love, now jealous of her past, now reproaching now forgiving himself for the feeling. It was six o'clock in the morning and still he paced the room.

'Well, what's to be done if it cannot be otherwise? What's to be done? It must be so then,' he said to himself; and hurriedly undressing he got into bed, happy and agitated but free from doubt and hesitation.

'Yes, strange and impossible as such happiness may seem, I must do everything to make her my wife,' he told himself.

Several days previously Pierre had appointed to go to Petersburg on the Friday. When he woke next morning – Thursday – Savelich came to ask about packing for the journey.

'Petersburg? What about Petersburg? Who is there in Petersburg?' he asked involuntarily, though only to himself. 'Oh yes, long, long ago, before this happened, I had some such thought – I was going to Petersburg for some reason or other,' he remembered. 'Why was it? And perhaps I shall go. How good and attentive he is, and how he remembers everything!' he thought, looking at Savelich's old face. 'And what a nice smile he has!'

'Well, Savelich, do you still not want your freedom?' Pierre asked him.

'What would be the good of freedom to me, your Excellency? We lived well while the old count was alive – God rest his soul! – and now with you we're comfortable-like and have nothing to complain of.'

'Yes, but what about your children?'

'The children too will do very well, your Excellency. With a master like you there is nothing to fear.'

'Well, but my heirs?' suggested Pierre. 'Supposing I suddenly marry ... that might happen, you know,' he added with an involuntary smile.

'If I may take the liberty – it would be a very good thing, your Excellency.'

'How lightly he thinks of it,' thought Pierre. 'He doesn't know how terrible it is, how perilous. Whether too soon or too late ... it is terrible!'

'What orders, your Excellency? Will you be going tomorrow?' asked Savelich.

'No, I am deferring it for a bit. I'll let you know later. I am sorry for the trouble I have put you to,' said Pierre, and watching Savelich smile he thought how odd it was, though, he should not know that now there is no Petersburg for me, that *that* must be settled before anything else. 'But of course he must know and is only pretending. Shall I have a talk with him and see what he thinks?' Pierre wondered. 'No, some other time.'

At breakfast Pierre told his cousin that he had been to call on Princess Maria the previous evening and had there met – 'Whom do you think? Natalie Rostov!'

The princess looked as though she saw nothing more extraordinary in that fact than if Pierre had seen Anna Semeonovna.

'Do you know her?' asked Pierre.

'I met the princess once,' she replied. 'I did hear they were arranging a match for her with young Rostov. It would be a fine thing for the Rostovs – they are said to be utterly ruined.'

'No, I meant, do you know Natasha Rostov?'

'I heard about that affair of hers at the time. A great pity.'

'No, either she doesn't understand or is pretending,' thought Pierre. 'Better not say anything to her either.'

The princess, too, had prepared provisions for Pierre's journey.

'How kind they all are,' thought Pierre, 'to take so much trouble about all this now, when it certainly can be of no interest to them. And all for my sake – that is what's so marvellous.'

That same morning the chief of police came to Pierre with the suggestion that he send someone to the Granovitaya palace to recover the things that were to be restored to their owners that day.

'And this man too,' thought Pierre, looking into the face of the chief of police. 'What a fine, good-looking officer, and how kind! Fancy bothering about such trifles *now!* And they actually say he is not honest and takes bribes. What nonsense! Besides, why shouldn't he take bribes? That's the way he has been brought up. And they all do it. But such a pleasant, good-tempered face, and he smiles when he looks at me.'

Pierre went to Princess Maria's to dinner.

As he drove through the streets past the charred remains of houses he was surprised at the beauty of the ruins. The picturesqueness of the chimney-stacks and fallen walls in the burned-out quarters of the town, stretching in long rows and hiding one another, reminded him of the Rhine and the Colosseum. The hack-drivers he met and their passengers, the carpenters at work squaring timber for new houses, the women hawkers and shopkeepers all looked at Pierre with cheerful, beaming eyes that seemed to say: 'Ah, there he is! We shall see what comes of it.'

When he reached Princess Maria's house Pierre was beset by a sudden doubt whether he really had been there the night before and really had seen Natasha and talked to her. 'Perhaps I imagined it: perhaps I shall go in and find no one.' But he had hardly entered the room before an instantaneous feeling of loss of freedom made him aware with his whole being of her presence. She was wearing the same black dress that hung in soft folds, and her hair was done in the same way as the night before, yet she was quite different. Had she looked like this when he came in the day before he could not for a second have failed to recognize her.

She was just as he had known her almost as a child, and later on as Prince Andrei's betrothed. A bright, questioning light shone in her eyes; there was a friendly and strangely roguish expression on her face.

Pierre dined and would have spent the whole evening there; but Princess Maria was going to vespers and Pierre went with them.

Next day he arrived early, had dinner with them and stayed on. Although Princess Maria and Natasha were obviously glad to see their visitor, and although all the interest of Pierre's life was now centred in that house, by the evening they had said all they had to say and the conversation passed from one trivial topic to another and often broke off altogether. Pierre stayed so late that Princess Maria and Natasha exchanged glances, evidently wondering when he would go. Pierre noticed, and yet could not tear himself away. He began to feel uncomfortable and awkward but sat on because he simply *could not* get up and take his departure.

Princess Maria, foreseeing no end to the situation, was the first to rise, and complaining of a sick headache began to say good-night.

'So tomorrow you are off to Petersburg?' she asked.

'No, I am not going,' Pierre replied hastily, in a surprised and what sounded an offended tone. 'To Petersburg, you say? Tomorrow – only I won't say good-bye now. I'll call round in case you have any commissions for me,' he added, standing in front of Princess Maria and turning red but not leaving.

Natasha gave him her hand and retired. Princess Maria, on the contrary, instead of going away sank into an arm-chair and looked sternly and intently at him with her deep, luminous eyes. The weariness she had unmistakably betrayed just before had now quite passed off. She drew a deep, prolonged sigh, as though she were preparing for a lengthy talk.

The moment Natasha left the room all Pierre's confusion and awkwardness vanished, to be replaced by eager excitement. He quickly moved up an arm-chair close to Princess Maria.

'Yes, I wanted to tell you,' said he, replying to her look as though she had spoken. 'Princess, help me! What am I to do? Can I hope? Princess, my dear friend, listen! I know it all. I know I am not worthy of her; I know this is not the time to speak. But I want to be a brother to her. No, not that. ... I don't want, I can't ...'

He paused and passed his hands over his face and eyes.

'It's like this,' he went on, with an evident effort to control himself and speak coherently, 'I don't know when I first began to love her. But my whole life long I have loved her, and her alone, and I love her so that I cannot imagine life without her. I cannot ask for her hand at present, but the thought that she might be mine and that I may be letting the opportunity slip ... the opportunity ... is awful. Tell me, can I hope? Tell me, what shall I do? Dear princess!' he added, after a little silence, touching her hand when she did not answer.

'I am thinking of what you have told me,' returned Princess Maria. 'This is what I think. You are right – to speak to her of love just at present ...' Princess Maria stopped. She had been going to say that to speak of love now was impossible; but she stopped because she had seen by the sudden change in Natasha that her friend would not only not be upset if Pierre were to confess his love but that this was the very thing she was longing for.

'To speak to her now ... wouldn't do,' said the princess all the same.

'But what am I to do?'

'Leave it to me,' said Princess Maria. 'I know ...'

Pierre was looking into Princess Maria's eyes.

'Well? ... Well? ...' he said.

'I know that she loves ... will love you,' Princess Maria corrected herself.

Before her words were out Pierre had sprung up and, with a startled face, clutched at Princess Maria's hand.

'What makes you think so? You think I may hope? You really ...?'

'Yes, I believe so,' said Princess Maria with a smile. 'Write to her parents. And leave it to me. I will tell her when the moment comes. I hope for it. And I feel in my heart that it will be.'

'No, it can't! How happy I am! But it can't be. ... How happy I am – no, it's not possible!' Pierre kept saying, kissing Princess Maria's hands.

'You go to Petersburg, that will be best. And I will write to you,' she said.

'To Petersburg? Go away? Very well, I'll go. But may I come and see you again tomorrow?'

Next day Pierre came to say good bye. Natasha was less animated than on the preceding occasions; but that day when he now and again looked into her eyes Pierre felt that he was vanishing away, that neither he nor she existed any more, that nothing existed but happiness. 'Is it possible? No, it can't be,' he told himself at every glance she gave, every gesture, every word of hers, that filled his heart with bliss.

When he took her thin slender hand and was saying good-bye he could not help holding it somewhat longer in his own.

'Is it possible that this hand, this face, these eyes, all this treasure of womanly charm, so far from me now – is it possible that one day it may all be mine for ever, as familiar to me as I am to myself? ... No, surely not! ...'

'Good-bye, count,' she said to him, and then added in a whisper: 'I shall look forward very much to your return.'

And those simple words, with the look in her eyes and the expression on her face that accompanied them, for two whole months formed the subject of inexhaustible memories, interpretations and exquisite day-dreams for Pierre. '*I shall look forward very much to your return.* ... Yes, yes, how did she say it? I remember – *I shall look forward very much to your return.* Oh, how happy I am! What is happening – how can I be so happy?' said Pierre to himself.

19

PIERRE'S soul knew nothing this time of what had troubled it in similar circumstances during his courtship of Hélène.

He did not go over, as he had then, with a sickening sense of shame the words he had uttered, or ask himself: 'Oh, why did I not say that?' and 'Whatever made me say "*Je vous aime*"?' Now, on the contrary, every word Natasha had said, every word of his own, he went over in his imagination and pictured every detail of her look and smile, and had no wish to add or take away anything but only to have it repeated again and again. As for doubts – whether what he contemplated doing was right or wrong – there was never a trace of them now. Only one terrible anxiety sometimes assailed his mind: 'Wasn't it all a dream? Isn't Princess Maria mistaken? Am I not too conceited and self-confident? I believe in it – but isn't this what is bound to happen: Princess Maria will tell her, and she will smile and say: "How strange! He is certainly deluding himself. Doesn't he know that he is just an ordinary mortal, a man like any other man, while I – I am something altogether different, and far superior"?'

This was Pierre's only doubt, and it frequently recurred to him. And he made no plans of any sort now. The happiness before him appeared so incredible that if only he could attain it anything more would be a matter of supererogation. Everything ended with it.

A joyous, unexpected frenzy, which Pierre had not believed himself capable of feeling, possessed him. The whole meaning of life – not for him alone but for all the world – seemed to him centred in his love and the possibility of her loving him. At times he thought that everybody was occupied by one thing only – his future happiness. At times it seemed to him that other people were all rejoicing as he himself was, and only tried to conceal their gladness by pretending to be busy with other interests. In every word and gesture he saw intimations of his own happiness. He often surprised those he met by his momentous, blissful looks and smiles, which they fancied expressed some secret understanding between him and them. But when he realized that people could not be aware of his happiness he pitied them from the bottom of his heart and longed somehow to explain to them that they were wasting their time on fiddlesticks and nonsense not worthy of attention.

When it was suggested to him that he should take some official post, or when the war or public affairs in general were discussed with the assumption that the welfare of the human race depended on this or that issue of a certain event, he would listen with a gentle smile of commiseration and astound those who were conversing with him by his odd observations. But at this period he saw everybody – both those who seemed to him to grasp the true significance of life (that is, what he was feeling) and those unfortunates who obviously had no notion of his state – in the brilliant light of the emotion that radiated within him, so that without the slightest effort he immediately saw in who-ever came his way everything that was good and deserving of love.

As he went through the papers and belongings of his dead wife her memory aroused no feeling in him but pity that she had not known the bliss which was now his. Prince Vasili, particularly puffed up at that time, having obtained some new office and a decoration, struck him as a pathetic, kindly, pitiful old man.

Often in after life Pierre recalled this period of blissful insanity. All the opinions he had then formed for himself of men and circum-stances remained true for him always. He not only did not renounce them subsequently, but when he was in doubt or inwardly at variance he flew back to the view he had held at this time of his madness, and that view always turned out to be a true one.

'I may have appeared strange and queer then,' he thought, 'but I was not so mad as I seemed. On the contrary, I was wiser and had more insight than at any other time; and I understood all that is worth understanding in life, because … I was so happy.'

Pierre's insanity consisted in not waiting, as he used to do, to dis-cover personal grounds, which he called 'good qualities', in people before loving them: love filled his heart to overflowing and in loving his fellow-men without cause he never failed to discover incontestable reasons that made them worth loving.

20

FROM that first evening after Pierre had left them, when Natasha had said to Princess Maria with a gay, mischievous smile that he looked exactly – yes, exactly – as if he had just come out of a bath, with his short jacket and cropped hair – from that moment something hidden and unrecognized by herself, yet irresistible, awoke in Natasha's soul. Everything: her face, the way she walked, her expression and her voice, underwent a sudden change. To her own surprise the sap of life and hopes of happiness rose to the surface and clamoured to be satisfied. From that first evening Natasha seemed to have forgotten all that had happened to her. From that time she never once bewailed her state or said a single word about the past, and no longer feared to make light-hearted plans for the future. She spoke little of Pierre, but when Princess Maria mentioned him a light that had long been dimmed kindled in her eyes and her lips curved into an odd smile.

The change that took place in Natasha at first surprised Princess Maria; but when she understood its meaning she felt grieved. 'Can she have loved my brother so little that she can so soon forget him?' she thought when she brooded over the transformation. But when she was with Natasha she was not vexed with her and did not blame her. Natasha's reawakening to life was obviously so overwhelming, so unexpected for the girl herself, that in her presence Princess Maria felt that she had no right to reproach her even in her heart.

Natasha gave herself up so fully and frankly to this new feeling that she made no attempt to mask the fact that sorrow had given way to gladness.

When Princess Maria returned to her room that night after her talk with Pierre, Natasha met her on the threshold.

'Has he spoken? Yes? He has?' she repeated. And a joyful and at the same time piteous expression, which seemed to plead forgiveness for her joy, settled on Natasha's face.

'I wanted to listen at the door but I knew you would tell me.'

Understandable and touching as was the look Natasha fastened on Princess Maria, and sorry as Princess Maria was for her friend's agitation, the words wounded her for a moment. She remembered her brother and his love.

'But what's to be done? She can't help it,' thought Princess Maria.

And with a sad and rather stern face she told Natasha all that Pierre had said. When she heard that he was going to Petersburg Natasha was shattered.

'To Petersburg?' she repeated, as though unable to take it in.

But noticing the mournful expression of Princess Maria's face she surmised the reason for her melancholy and suddenly burst into tears.

'Marie,' she said, 'tell me what to do. I am so afraid of behaving badly. I'll do whatever you say. Tell me. ...'

'You love him?'

'Yes,' whispered Natasha.

'What are you crying for, then? I am glad for you,' said Princess Maria, moved by those tears to complete forgiveness of Natasha's joy.

'It won't be just yet ... some day. Only think how happy we'll be when I am his wife and you marry Nicolas.'

'Natasha, I asked you not to speak of that. Let us talk about you.'

They were silent.

'But why must he go to Petersburg?' cried Natasha suddenly, and hastened to answer herself. 'Well, well, it is best so. ... Eh, Marie? It is best so. ...'

WAR AND PEACE

★

EPILOGUE

PART ONE

I

SEVEN years had passed. The storm-tossed sea of European history had sunk to rest upon its shores. The sea appeared to be calm; but the mysterious forces that move humanity (mysterious because the laws that govern their action are unknown to us) were still at work.

Though the surface of the ocean of history seemed motionless, the movement of humanity continued as uninterrupted as the flow of time. Coalitions of men came together and separated again; the causes that would bring about the formation and the dissolution of empires and the displacement of peoples were in course of preparation.

The ocean of history was no longer, as before, swept from shore to shore by squalls: it seethed in its depths. The personages of history were not borne by the waves from coast to coast as before; now they seemed to revolve in stationary eddies. Historical personages who had lately been leading armies and reflecting the movement of the masses by decreeing wars, campaigns and battles now reflected the turbulent flux by political and diplomatic combinations, statutes, treaties, and so on.

This activity of the figures of history the historians call *reaction*.

In dealing with the part played by these historical personages the historians are severe in their criticism, supposing them to be the cause of what they describe as *reaction*. All the famous people of that period, from Alexander and Napoleon to Madame de Staël, Photius, Schelling, Fichte, Chateaubriand, and the rest, are arraigned before their stern tribunal and acquitted or condemned according to whether they conduced to *progress* or *reaction*.

Russia too is described by the historians as the scene at this time of reaction, and for this they throw the chief responsibility on Alexander I – the same Alexander I to whom they also give the credit for the liberal enterprises at the beginning of his reign, and for the saving of Russia.

There is no one in Russian literature today, from schoolboy essay-writer to learned historian, who does not throw his little stone at Alexander I for one or another ill-considered measure at this later period of his sovereignty.

'He ought to have acted in such and such a way. In this case he did well, on that occasion badly. He conducted himself admirably at the beginning of his reign and during 1812; but he erred in granting a constitution to Poland, in establishing the Holy Alliance, in entrusting power to Arakcheyev, in encouraging first Golitsyn and his mysticism and afterwards Shishkov and Photius. He did wrong in interfering with the army on active service, did wrong in disbanding the Semeonovsk regiment, and so on.'

It would take a dozen pages to enumerate all the faults the historians find in him on the strength of the knowledge they possess of what is for the good of humanity.

What do these strictures signify?

Do not the very actions for which the historians applaud Alexander I – the attempts at liberalism at the beginning of his reign, his struggle with Napoleon, the firmness he displayed in 1812 and the campaign of 1813 – proceed from those very sources – the circumstances of birth, breeding and life that made his personality what it was – from which also flowed the actions for which they censure him, like the Holy Alliance, the restoration of Poland and the reaction of the 1820s?

What is the substance of these strictures?

In this – that an historical character like Alexander I, standing on the highest possible pinnacle of human power with the blinding light of history focused upon him; a character exposed to those most potent of influences – the intrigues, flatteries and self-delusion inseparable from power; a character who at every moment of his life felt a responsibility for all that was being done in Europe; and a character, not from fiction but as much alive as any other man, with his own personal bent, passions, and impulses towards goodness, beauty and truth – that this character, though not lacking in virtue (the historians do not accuse him on that score), living fifty years ago,* had not the same conception concerning the welfare of humanity as a present-day professor who from his youth up has been engaged in study, i.e. in reading, listening to lectures and making notes on those books and lectures in a note-book.

* *War and Peace* was written between 1864 and 1869. — [Tr.]

But if we are going to assume that Alexander I, fifty years ago, was mistaken in his view of what was good for the peoples we can hardly help considering that the historian who criticizes Alexander may, after a certain lapse of time, prove to be equally incorrect in his idea of what is for the good of humanity. This assumption is all the more natural and inevitable because, watching the development of history, we see that every year, with each new writer, opinion as to what constitutes the welfare of humanity changes; so that what once seemed good, ten years later seems bad, and vice versa. That is not all: we even find in history, at one and the same time, quite contradictory views as to what was good and what was bad. Some people place the giving of a constitution to Poland, and the Holy Alliance, to Alexander's credit, while others censure him for them.

The activity of Alexander or of Napoleon cannot be termed beneficial or harmful, since we cannot say for what it was beneficial or harmful. If that activity fails to please someone, this is only because it does not coincide with his restricted conception of what constitutes good. I may regard the preservation of my father's house in Moscow in 1812, or the glory of Russian arms, or the prosperity of Petersburg and other universities, or the independence of Poland, or the might of Russia, or the balance of power in Europe, or a certain kind of European enlightenment called 'progress' – I may regard all these as good but I am still bound to admit that, besides these ends and aims, the action of every historic character has other more general purposes beyond my grasp.

But let us suppose that what we call science has the power of reconciling all contradictions and possesses an invariable standard of right and wrong by which to try historical persons and events.

Let us say that Alexander could have done everything differently. Let us assume that he might – in accordance with the prescriptions of those who accuse him and who profess to know the ultimate goal of the movement of humanity – have arranged matters in harmony with the programme of nationalism, freedom, equality and progress (for there would seem to be no other) with which his present-day critics would have provided him. Let us assume that this programme could have been possible and had actually been formulated at the time, and that Alexander could have acted in accordance with it. What then would become of the activity of all those who opposed the tendency of the government of the day – of the activity which in the opinion of the historians was good and beneficial? Their activity would not have existed: there would have been no life, nothing.

Once say that human life can be controlled by reason, and all possibility of life is annihilated.

2

IF we assume, as the historians do, that great men lead humanity towards the attainment of certain ends – such as the majesty of Russia or of France, the balance of power in Europe, the propagation of the ideas of the Revolution, progress in general, or anything else you like – it becomes impossible to explain the phenomena of history without intruding the concepts of *chance* and *genius*.

If the object of the European wars of the beginning of this century had been the aggrandizement of Russia, that object might have been attained without any of the preceding wars and without the invasion. If the object was the aggrandizement of France, that might have been attained without either the Revolution or the Empire. If the object was the propagation of ideas, the printing-press could have accomplished that much more effectually than soldiers. If the object was the progress of civilization, one may very readily suppose that there are other more expedient means of diffusing civilization than by slaughtering people and destroying their wealth.

Why then did things happen thus and not otherwise?

Because they did so happen. 'Chance created the situation; *genius* made use of it,' says history.

But what is *chance*? What is *genius*?

The words *chance* and *genius* do not denote anything that actually exists, and therefore they cannot be defined. These two words merely indicate a certain degree of comprehension of phenomena. I do not know why a certain event occurs; I suppose that I cannot know: therefore I do not try to know, and I talk about *chance*. I see a force producing effects beyond the scope of ordinary human agencies; I do not understand why this occurs, and I cry *genius*.

To a flock of sheep, the one the shepherd drives into a separate enclosure every night to feed, and that becomes twice as fat as the others, must seem to be a genius. And the circumstance that every evening this particular sheep, instead of coming into the common fold, chances into a special pen with extra oats, and that this sheep, this particular one, fattens up and is killed for mutton, doubtless im-

1342

presses the rest of the flock as a remarkable conjunction of genius with a whole series of fortuitous chances.

But the sheep need only rid themselves of the idea that all that is done to them is done solely for the furtherance of their sheepish ends; they have only to concede that what happens to them may also have purposes beyond their ken, and they will immediately perceive a unity and coherence in what happens with their brother that is being fattened. Although it may not be given to them to know to what end he was being fattened, they will at least know that all that happened to him did not occur accidentally, and will no longer need to resort to conceptions of *chance* or *genius*.

It is only by renouncing our claim to discern a purpose immediately intelligible to us, and admitting the ultimate purpose to be beyond our ken, that we shall see a logical connexion in the lives of historical personages, and perceive the why and wherefore of what they do which so transcends the ordinary powers of humanity. We shall then find that the words *chance* and *genius* have become superfluous.

We have only to admit that we do not know the purpose of the convulsions among the European nations, and that we know only the hard facts – the butchery, first in France, then in Italy, in Africa, in Prussia, in Austria, in Spain and in Russia – and that the movements from west to east and from east to west constitute the essence and end of those events, and we shall not only find it no longer necessary to see some exceptional ability – *genius* – in Napoleon and Alexander; we shall be unable to regard them as being anything but men like other men. And far from having to turn to *chance* to explain the little incidents which made those men what they were, it will be clear to us that all those little incidents were inevitable.

If we give up all claim to a knowledge of the ultimate purpose we shall realize that, just as it is impossible to imagine for any given plant other more appropriate blossom or seed than those it produces, so it is impossible to imagine any two persons, with all their antecedents, more completely adapted, down to the smallest detail, to the mission which Napoleon and Alexander were called upon to fulfil.

3

THE fundamental and essential point of European events at the beginning of the present century is the militant mass movement of the

European peoples from west to east and then from east to west. The first impulse to this flux was given by the movement from west to east. For the peoples of the west to be able to achieve their militant advance as far as Moscow they had to (1) form themselves into a military group of sufficient magnitude to sustain a collision with the military group of the east; (2) renounce all established traditions and customs; and (3) have at their head, during their military movement, a man able to justify to himself and to them the guile, robbery and murder which must be the concomitants of their progress.

So, beginning with the French Revolution, the old group which is not large enough is destroyed; old habits and traditions are abolished; and step by step a group of new dimensions is elaborated, new customs and traditions are developed, and a man is prepared who is to stand at the head of the coming movement and bear the whole responsibility for what has to be done.

A man of no convictions, no habits, no traditions, no name, not even a Frenchman, emerges – by what seems the strangest freak of chance – from among all the seething parties of France, and, without attaching himself to any one of them, is borne forward to a prominent position.

The incompetence of his colleagues, the weakness and inanity of his rivals, the frankness of his falsehoods and his brilliant and self-confident mediocrity raise him to the head of the army. The brilliant quality of the soldiers of the army sent to Italy, his opponents' reluctance to fight and his own childish insolence and conceit secure him military glory. Innumerable so-called *chance* circumstances attend him everywhere. The disfavour into which he falls with the French Directorate turns to his advantage. His attempts to avoid his pre-destined path are unsuccessful: Russia refused to receive him into her service and the appointment he seeks in Turkey comes to nothing. During the wars in Italy he more than once finds himself on the brink of disaster and each time is saved in some unexpected manner. Owing to various diplomatic considerations the Russian armies – the very armies which have the power to extinguish his glory – do not appear upon the European scene while he is there.

On his return from Italy he finds the government in Paris in the process of dissolution in which all those who are in that government are doomed to erasure and extinction. And by chance an escape from this dangerous situation offers itself to him in the nonsensical, gratuitous expedition to Africa. Again so-called *chance* accompanies him. Malta the impregnable surrenders without a shot; his most reckless schemes are crowned with success. The enemy's fleet, which later on does not let a single row-boat through, now suffers a whole army to elude it. In Africa a whole series of outrages is perpetrated against the practically defenceless inhabitants. And the men committing these atrocities, and their leader most of all, persuade themselves that this is admirable, this is glory, this is like Caesar and Alexander the Great, and is fine.

This ideal of *glory* and *greatness* – which consists not merely in the assurance that nothing one does is to be considered wrong but in glorying in one's every crime and ascribing to it an incomprehensible, supernatural significance – this ideal, destined to guide this man and his associates, is provided with fertile ground for its development in Africa. Whatever he does succeeds. The plague does not touch him. Responsibility for the cruel massacring of prisoners is not laid at his door. His childishly incautious, unreasoning and ignoble departure from Africa, leaving his comrades in distress, is accounted to his credit, and again the enemy's fleet twice lets him slip past. Completely intoxicated by the success of his crimes and ready for his new rôle, though without any plan, he arrives in Paris just when the disintegration of the Republican government, which a year before might have made an end of him, has reached its utmost limit and his presence there now, as a newcomer free from party entanglements, can only lift him to the heights.

He has no plan of any kind; he is afraid of everything; but the parties hold out their hands to him and insist on his participation.

He alone – with the ideal of glory and grandeur built up in Italy and Egypt, his insane self-adulation, his insolence in crime and frankness in lying – he alone can justify what has to be done.

He is needed for the place that awaits him and so, almost apart from his own volition and in spite of his indecision, his lack of a plan and all the blunders he makes, he is drawn into a conspiracy that aims at seizing power, and the conspiracy is crowned with success.

He is dragged into a meeting of the legislature. In alarm he tries to flee, believing himself in danger; pretends to be falling into a faint; says the most senseless things which should have meant his ruin. But the once proud and discerning rulers of France, feeling their part is over, are even more panic-stricken than he, and fail to pronounce the word they should have spoken to preserve their power and crush him.

Chance, millions of chances, invest him with authority, and all men everywhere, as if by agreement together, co-operate to confirm that power. Chance forms the characters of the rulers of France who cringe before him; chance forms the character of Paul I of Russia who recognizes his power; chance contrives a plot against him which not only fails to injure him but strengthens his position. Chance throws the duc d'Enghien into his hands and unexpectedly impels him to assassinate him – thereby convincing the mob by the most potent of all arguments that he has right on his side since he has might. Chance sees to it that though he strains every nerve to prepare an expedition against England (which would undoubtedly have been his downfall) he never carries this enterprise into execution but abruptly falls upon Mack and the Austrians, who surrender without a battle. Chance and genius give him the victory at Austerlitz; and by chance it comes to pass that all men, not only the French but all Europe – except England, who takes no part in the events about to happen – forget their former horror and detestation of his crimes and now recognize his consequent authority, the title he has bestowed upon himself and his ideal of grandeur and glory, which seems to one and all something excellent and reasonable.

As though measuring and making ready for the movement to come, the forces of the West several times – in 1805, 1806, 1807, 1809 – sally eastwards, gaining strength and growing. In 1811 the body of men that had formed in France unites into one enormous body with the peoples of Central Europe. Every increase in the size of this group adds further justification for Napoleon's power. During the ten-year preparatory period before the great push this man forms relations with all the crowned heads of Europe. The discredited rulers of the world have no rational ideal to oppose to the meaningless Napoleonic mystique of glory and grandeur. One after another they rush to display to him their insignificance. The King of Prussia sends his wife to curry favour with the great man; the Emperor of Austria is gratified that this man should take the daughter of the Kaisers to his bed; the Pope, guardian of all that the nations hold sacred, utilizes religion to raise the great man higher. It is less that Napoleon prepares himself for the performance of his rôle than that all about him lead him on to acceptance of entire responsibility for what is happening and has to happen. There is no act, no crime, no petty deceit he might commit, which would not immediately be proclaimed by those about him as a great deed. The most suitable fête the Teutons can think of to observe in his honour is a celebration of Jena and Auerstädt. Not only is he great but so are his forefathers, his brothers, his stepsons and his brothers-in-law. Everything is done to deprive him of the last vestige of his reason and to prepare him for his terrible part. And when he is ready so too are the forces.

The invasion streams eastwards and reaches its final goal – Moscow. The capital is taken: the Russian army suffers heavier losses than the enemy ever suffered in previous wars from Austerlitz to Wagram. But all at once, instead of the *chance* happenings and the *genius* which hitherto had so consistently led him by an uninterrupted series of successes to the predestined goal, an innumerable sequence of reverse *chances* occur – from the cold in his head at Borodino to the frosts and the spark which set Moscow on fire – and, instead of *genius*, folly and baseness without parallel appear.

The invaders run, turn back, run again, and all the *chances* are now not for Napoleon but always against him.

A counter-movement follows, from east to west, bearing a remarkable resemblance to the preceding movement from west to east. There are similar tentative drives westward as had in 1805, 1807 and 1809 preceded the great eastward movement; there is the same coalescence into a group of colossal proportions; the same adhesion of the peoples of Central Europe to the movement; the same hesitation midway and the same increased velocity as the goal is approached.

Paris, the ultimate goal, is reached. The Napoleonic government and army are overthrown. Napoleon himself is no longer of any account; all his actions are manifestly pitiful and mean; but again inexplicable chance steps in: the allies detest Napoleon whom they regard as the cause of their troubles. Stripped of his power and authority, his crimes and his treacheries exposed, he should have appeared to them what he had appeared ten years previously and was to appear a year later – a bandit and an outlaw. But by some strange freak of chance no one perceives this. His rôle is not yet played to a finish. The man who ten years before and a year later was looked on as a miscreant outside the law is sent to an island a couple of days' journey from France, which is given to him as his domain, with guards and millions of money, as though to pay him for some service rendered.

1347

4

THE flood of nations begins to subside into its normal channels. The waves of the great movement abate, leaving a calm surface ruffled by eddies where the diplomatists busy themselves (in the belief that the calm is the result of their work).

But suddenly the smooth sea is convulsed again. The diplomats imagine that their dissensions are the cause of this new upheaval of the elements; they anticipate war between their sovereigns; the position seems to them insoluble. But the wave they feel to be gathering does not come from the quarter expected. It is the same wave as before, and its source the same point as before – Paris. The last backwash of the movement from the west occurs – a backwash which serves to solve the apparently insuperable diplomatic difficulties and put an end to the militant flux of the period.

The man who has devastated France returns to France alone, without any conspiracy and without soldiers. Any gendarme might apprehend him; but by a strange chance not only does no one touch him – they all rapturously acclaim the man they had cursed the day before and will be cursing again within a month.

This man is still needed to justify the final collective act.

The act is performed. The last part is played. The actor is bidden to disrobe and wash off his powder and paint: he will not be wanted any more.

And several years pass during which, in solitude on his island, this man plays his pitiful farce to himself, pettily intriguing and lying to justify his conduct when justification is no longer needed, and revealing to the world at large what it was that people had mistaken for strength so long as an unseen hand directed his actions.

The stage manager, having brought the drama to a close and stripped the puppet of his motley, shows him to us.

'Look – this is what you believed in! Here he stands! Do you see now that it was not he but I who moved you?'

But, dazed by the violence of the movement, it was long before people understood this.

A still more striking example of logical sequence and inevitability is to be seen in the life of Alexander I, the figure who stood at the head of the counter-movement from east to west.

What qualities should the man possess if he were to overshadow everyone else and head the counter-movement westwards?

He must have a sense of justice and a sympathy with European affairs, but a detached sympathy not obscured by petty interests; a moral superiority over his peers – the other sovereigns of the day; a gentle and attractive personality; and a personal grievance against Napoleon. And all this is found in Alexander I; all this has been prepared by countless so-called *chance* circumstances in his life: his upbringing and early liberalism, the advisers who surrounded him; by Austerlitz and Tilsit and Erfurt.

So long as the war is a national one he remains inactive because he is not needed. But as soon as the necessity for a general European war becomes apparent, at the given moment he is in his place and, uniting the nations of Europe, leads them to the goal.

The goal is reached. After the final war of 1815 Alexander finds himself at the summit of human power. How does he use it?

Alexander I, the peacemaker of Europe, the man who from his youth up had striven only for the welfare of his peoples, the first champion of liberal reforms in his country, now when it seems that he possesses the utmost power and therefore the possibility of achieving the welfare of his peoples (while Napoleon in exile is drawing up childish and mendacious plans of how he would have made mankind happy had he retained power) – Alexander I, having fulfilled his mission and feeling the hand of God upon him, suddenly recognizes the nothingness of the supposed power that is his, turns away from it and hands it over to contemptible men whom he despises, saying only:

'"Not unto us, not unto us, but unto Thy Name!" I too am a man like the rest of you. Let me live like a man, and think of my soul and of God.'

*

Just as the sun and every particle of the ether is a sphere complete in itself and at the same time only a part of a whole too immense for the comprehension of man, so every individual bears within himself his own aims and yet bears them so as to serve a general purpose unfathomable by man.

A bee poised on a flower has stung a child. And so the child is afraid of bees and declares that bees are there to sting people. A poet delights in the bee sipping honey from the calyx of a flower and says the bee exists to suck the nectar of flowers. A bee-keeper, seeing the bee collect pollen and carry it to the hive, says that the object of bees is to gather honey. Another bee-keeper, who has studied the life of the swarm more closely, declares that the bee gathers pollen-dust to feed the young bees and rear a queen, and that it exists for the propagation of its species. The botanist, observing that a bee flying with pollen from one dioecious plant to the pistil of another fertilizes the latter, sees in this the purpose of the bee's existence. Another, remarking the hybridization of plants and seeing that the bee assists in this work, may say that herein lies the purpose of the bee. But the ultimate purpose of the bee is not exhausted by the first or the second or the third of the processes the human mind can discern. The higher the human intellect soars in the discovery of possible purposes, the more obvious it becomes that the ultimate purpose is beyond our comprehension.

Man cannot achieve more than a certain insight into the correlation between the life of the bee and other manifestations of life. And the same is true with regard to the final purpose of historical characters and nations.

5

NATASHA's marriage to Bezuhov, which took place in 1813, was the last happy event for the older generation of the Rostov family. Count Ilya Rostov died that same year and, as is always the case, with the father's death the family was broken up.

The events of the previous year – the burning of Moscow and the flight from the capital, the death of Prince Andrei and Natasha's despair, Petya's death and the old countess's grief – rained, blow upon blow, on the old count's head. He seemed not to understand, and to feel that he lacked the strength to understand, the meaning of all these events and, figuratively speaking, bowed his old head as though expecting and inviting further blows to make an end of him. He would appear alternately frightened and distraught or alert and active.

The arrangements for Natasha's wedding occupied him for a while. He ordered dinners and suppers and obviously tried to give the impression of being cheerful; but his cheerfulness was not infectious as it used to be: on the contrary, it evoked the compassion of those who knew and were fond of him.

After Pierre and his bride had taken their departure he grew very quiet and began to complain of depression. A few days later he fell ill and took to his bed. Despite the doctors' assurances, he realized from the first that he would never get up again. For two weeks the countess did not take her clothes off, sitting in a low chair by his bedside. Every time she gave him his medicine he sobbed and mutely kissed her hand. On the closing day of his life, sobbing, he begged forgiveness of his wife and his absent son for having squandered their property – the chief sin that lay on his conscience. Having received communion and the last anointing, he quietly died; and next day a throng of acquaintances, come to pay their final respects to the deceased, filled the house rented by the Rostovs. All these acquaintances, who had so often dined and danced at his house, and had so often made fun of him, now said, with a unanimous feeling of self-reproach and emotion, as though seeking to justify themselves: 'Well, anyhow, he was a most worthy man. One doesn't meet his like nowadays. ... And we all have our failings, have we not? ...'

It was precisely when the count's fortunes had become so entangled that it was impossible to conceive what would happen if he lived another year that he unexpectedly died.

Nikolai was with the Russian army in Paris when the news of his father's death reached him. He at once resigned his commission and without waiting for his discharge took leave of absence and went to Moscow. The position of the count's finances became quite obvious within a month of his death, astounding everyone by the immense total of various petty debts, the existence of which no one had suspected. The debts amounted to double the value of the estate.

Friends and relations advised Nikolai to decline the inheritance. But Nikolai saw in such a course a slur on his father's memory, which he held sacred, and therefore would not hear of refusing, and so accepted the inheritance together with the obligation to pay the debts.

The creditors, who had so long been silent, kept in check while the old count was alive by the vague but powerful influence which his easy-going good-nature exerted upon them, all beset Nikolai at once. As always happens, rivalry sprang up as to which of them should get paid first, and the very people who, like Mitenka, held promissory notes given them as presents, now showed themselves the most exacting of creditors. Nikolai was allowed no respite and no peace, and those who had apparently had pity on the old man – the cause of their

1351

losses (if they really had lost money by him) – now remorselessly pursued the innocent young heir who had voluntarily assumed responsibility for payment.

Not one of the plans that Nikolai resorted to was successful: the estate was sold by auction for half its value, leaving half the debts still unpaid. Nikolai took thirty thousand roubles offered him by his brother-in-law, Bezuhov, to settle what he regarded as genuine monetary obligations. And to avoid being thrown into prison for the remaining debts, as creditors threatened, he re-entered government service.

To return to the army, where he would have been made colonel at the next vacancy, was out of the question, for his mother now clung to him as her last hold on life; and so, despite his reluctance to remain in Moscow among people who had known him in former days, and in spite of his distaste for the civil service, he accepted an official post in Moscow, doffed his beloved uniform and moved with his mother and Sonya to a small house in one of the poorer quarters.

Natasha and Pierre were living in Petersburg at the time and had no very distinct idea of Nikolai's circumstances. Having borrowed money from his brother-in-law, Nikolai did his utmost to conceal his poverty-stricken state from him. His situation was rendered the more difficult because on his salary of twelve hundred roubles he had not only to keep himself, his mother and Sonya but had to support his mother in such a way that she would not be sensible of their poverty. The countess could not conceive of life without the conditions of luxury to which she had been accustomed from her childhood and, without realizing how hard it was for her son, was continually requiring, now a carriage (which they did not have) to send for a friend, now some expensive delicacy for herself, or wine for her son, or money to buy a surprise-present for Natasha, for Sonya or for Nikolai himself.

Sonya kept house, waited on her aunt, read to her, bore with her caprices and secret ill-will, and helped Nikolai to conceal their poverty from the old countess. Nikolai felt himself irredeemably indebted to Sonya for all she was doing for his mother; he admired her patience and devotion but tried to keep aloof from her.

In his heart of hearts he seemed to harbour a sort of grudge against her for being too perfect, and because there was nothing to reproach her with. She had all the qualities for which people are prized, but little that could have made him love her. And he felt that the more he appreciated her the less he loved her. He had taken her at her word when she wrote giving him his freedom, and now behaved as though all that had passed between them had been forgotten ages ago and could never in any circumstances be renewed.

Nikolai's position was growing worse and worse. His hope of putting something aside out of his salary proved an idle dream. Far from saving anything, he was even running up small debts to satisfy his mother's exigencies. He could see no way out of his difficulties. The idea of marrying some rich woman, which his female relatives suggested, was repugnant to him. The only other solution – his mother's death – never entered his head. He wished for nothing and hoped for nothing, and deep in his heart experienced a grim, melancholy enjoyment in enduring his position with resignation. He tried to avoid his old acquaintances with their commiseration and mortifying offers of assistance, shunned every sort of entertainment and recreation, and even at home did nothing but play patience with his mother or pace silently up and down the room, smoking one pipe after another. He seemed bent on preserving in himself the gloomy frame of mind which alone enabled him to bear his position.

6

A T the beginning of the winter Princess Maria came to Moscow. From the gossip of the town she heard of the Rostovs' situation, of how 'the son was sacrificing himself for his mother', as people were saying. 'It is just what I should have expected him to do,' said Princess Maria to herself, finding in it a delightful confirmation of her love for him. Remembering her friendly relations with the whole household – which made her almost one of the family – she decided that it was her duty to go and see them. But when she thought of her contact with Nikolai in Voronezh she felt timid about doing so. A few weeks after her arrival in Moscow she did however nerve herself to the effort and went to call on the Rostovs.

Nikolai was the first to meet her, since it was impossible to reach the countess's room without passing through his. But instead of the delight Princess Maria had expected to see on his face, after a first glance at her his features assumed a cold, stiff, haughty expression she had never seen in him before. He inquired after her health, conducted her to his mother's room, where he sat with them for five or six minutes and then departed.

When the princess left the countess Nikolai met her again and with marked formality and reserve accompanied her to the hall. To her remarks about his mother's health he made no reply. 'What's that to you? Leave me in peace,' his look seemed to say.

'Why should she come prowling about here? What does she want? I can't stand these *mesdames* and all this sweet amiableness!' he said aloud in Sonya's presence, evidently unable to repress his vexation, after the princess's carriage had rolled away from the house.

'Oh, Nicolas, how can you talk like that!' exclaimed Sonya, scarcely concealing her delight. 'She is so kind, and *maman* likes her so much!'

Nikolai made no reply and would have preferred not to mention the princess again. But after her visit the old countess spoke of her several times a day.

She sang her praises, insisted that her son must call on her, expressed a wish to see more of her, and yet was always out of temper when she had been talking of her.

Nikolai tried to hold his tongue when his mother spoke of the princess, but his silence irritated her.

'She is a very admirable and excellent young woman,' she would say, 'and you must go and call on her. You would at least be seeing somebody; I am sure it is dull for you here with only us.'

'But I don't in the least want to see people, mamma.'

'You used to be keen enough but now it's all "I don't want to". Really, my dear, I don't understand you. One minute you are bored and the next you suddenly don't care to see anyone.'

'Why, I never said I was bored.'

'Well, at all events you've just said you didn't wish even to see her. She is a very praiseworthy girl, and you always liked her; but now all of a sudden you have got some notion or other into your head. I am always kept in the dark.'

'Not at all, mamma.'

'If I were asking you to do something disagreeable now – but all I ask of you is to return a call. Why, one would think mere politeness required that. ... Well, I have asked you, and now I shall not interfere any more, since you choose to have secrets from your mother.'

'All right, I'll go if you wish it.'

'It doesn't matter to me. I only wish it for your own sake.'

Nikolai sighed, bit his moustache and laid out the cards for patience, trying to divert his mother's attention to something else.

Next day and the day after and the day after that the same conversation was repeated.

After her visit to the Rostovs and the unexpectedly chilly reception she had met with from Nikolai, Princess Maria confessed to herself that she had been right in not wanting to be the first to call.

'I wasn't expecting anything else,' she told herself, summoning pride to her aid. 'I have no concern with him and I only wanted to see the old lady, who has always been kind to me and to whom I am under many obligations.'

But she could not soothe herself with these reflections: a feeling akin to remorse fretted her whenever she thought of her visit. Although she was firmly resolved not to call on the Rostovs again and to forget the matter altogether, she felt uncomfortable all the time. And when she asked herself what it was that was worrying her she was obliged to admit that it was her encounter with Rostov. His frigid, formal manner did not proceed from his feeling for her (she knew that) but it was a cover for something. What that something was she must find out; and until she did so she felt she would never have any peace.

One day in midwinter she was sitting in the schoolroom superintending her nephew's lessons when she was informed that Rostov was below. With the firm resolve not to betray herself or evince any sign of her agitation she sent for Mademoiselle Bourienne and went with her to the drawing-room.

Her first glance at Nikolai's face told her that he had only come to fulfil the obligations of civility, and she resolutely determined to keep to the tone he adopted towards her.

They talked of the countess's health, of mutual acquaintances, of the latest news of the war, and when the ten minutes demanded by etiquette had elapsed, after which the visitor may rise, Nikolai got up to say good-bye.

With Mademoiselle Bourienne's help the princess had maintained the conversation very well; but at the very last moment, just when he had risen to his feet, she was so weary of talking of what did not interest her, and she was so absorbed in wondering why she alone was granted so little happiness in life, that in a fit of absent-mindedness she sat still, her luminous eyes staring straight before her, oblivious of the fact that he had risen.

Nikolai glanced at her, and anxious to appear not to notice her abstraction made some remark to Mademoiselle Bourienne and then glanced at the princess again. She still sat motionless with a look of suffering on her gentle face. He suddenly felt sorry for her and a dim idea came to him that perhaps he might be the cause of the sadness in her face. He longed to help her, say something nice to her, but he could not think what to say.

'Good-bye, princess,' he said.

She started, flushed and sighed heavily.

'Oh, I beg your pardon!' she murmured, as though waking from a dream. 'You are going already, count: well, good-bye! Oh, but the cushion for the countess!'

'Wait, I'll fetch it,' said Mademoiselle Bourienne, and she left the room.

Both sat in silence, with an occasional glance at one another.

'Yes, princess,' said Nikolai at last, with a mournful smile, 'it doesn't seem so long ago since we first met at Bogucharovo, but how much water has flowed under the bridges since then! We all seemed to be in trouble enough then, but I would give a great deal to have that time back ... but there's no bringing it back.'

Princess Maria gazed intently at him with her luminous eyes as he said this. She seemed to be trying to fathom the secret import of his words which would make clear his feelings towards her.

'Yes, yes,' she replied, 'but you have no reason to regret the past, count. As I conceive of your life now, I think you will always recall it with satisfaction, because the self-sacrifice that fills it today ...'

'I cannot accept your praise,' he interrupted her hurriedly; 'on the contrary, I am always reproaching myself. ... But this is not at all an interesting or cheerful subject.'

And again the stiff and cold expression came back into his face. But the princess had caught a glimpse of the man she had known and loved and it was to him that she spoke now.

'I thought you would allow me to say that,' she told him. 'You and I ... your family and I have been brought so near together that I thought you would not feel my sympathy out of season; but I was mistaken.' Her voice suddenly shook. 'I don't know why,' she went on, recovering herself, 'but you used to be different, and ...'

'There are a thousand reasons *why*' – he laid special emphasis on the word *why*. 'Thank you, princess,' he added softly. 'Sometimes it is hard.'

'So that's why! That's why!' cried a voice in Princess Maria's heart. 'No, it was not only that gay, kind, frank look, not only that handsome exterior, that I loved in him: I divined his noble, indomitable, self-sacrificing spirit too,' she said to herself. 'Yes, he is poor now, and I am rich. ... Yes, that is the only reason. ... Yes, if it were not for that ...' And remembering his former tenderness, and looking now at his kind, sorrowful face, she suddenly understood the cause of his coldness.

'But why, count, why?' she almost cried, unconsciously moving closer to him. 'Why? Tell me. You must tell me!'

He was silent.

'I don't understand your *why*,' she continued. 'But I am heavy-hearted, I ... I do not mind confessing to you. For some reason you wish to deprive me of our old friendship. And that hurts.' There were tears in her eyes and in her voice. 'I have had so little happiness in my life that every loss is hard for me. ... Excuse me, good-bye!' and suddenly she burst into tears and was hurrying from the room.

'Princess, wait, for God's sake!' he called, trying to detain her. 'Princess!'

She looked round. For a few seconds they gazed dumbly into one another's eyes, and all at once what had seemed impossible and remote became possible, near at hand and inevitable. ...

7

IN the autumn of 1814 Nikolai married Princess Maria and moved to Bald Hills with his wife, his mother and Sonya.

Within four years he had settled his remaining debts, without selling any of his wife's property, and having come into a small legacy on the death of a cousin he repaid what he had borrowed from Pierre too.

In another three years, by 1820, Nikolai had managed his pecuniary affairs so successfully that he was able to purchase a modest estate adjoining Bald Hills and was negotiating to buy back his ancestral home of Otradnoe – that being his pet dream.

At first his own steward of necessity, he soon grew so passionately interested in farming that it came to be his favourite and almost his sole occupation.

Nikolai was a plain farmer: he did not like innovations, especially the English ones then coming into fashion. He laughed at theoretical treatises on estate management, did not care for home refineries and expensive processes, or for sowing costly grain, and as a general thing did not confine himself to one department of agriculture alone: he always kept before his eye the welfare of the *estate* as a whole, and not one particular part of it. The chief thing to his mind was not the nitrogen in the soil or the oxygen in the air, nor manures or special ploughs, but the principal agent by which nitrogen, oxygen, manure and plough were made effective – the peasant labourer. When Nikolai first took up farming and began to go into its different branches it was the peasant who especially attracted his attention: the peasant seemed to him not merely a tool but also an end in himself and his critic. At first he studied the peasants attentively, trying to understand what they were after, what they considered good and bad, and only made a pretence of supervising and giving orders while in reality he was learning from them their methods, their manner of speech and their judgement of what was good and bad. And it was only when he had gained an insight into the peasants' tastes and aspirations, had learnt to talk their language, to grasp the inner meaning of their sayings and felt akin to them, that he began boldly giving them orders – in other words, fulfilling towards them the duties expected of him. And Nikolai's management produced the most brilliant results.

On taking over the control of the property Nikolai had at once by some unerring instinct appointed as bailiff, village elder and peasant representative the very men the peasants would have elected themselves had the choice been theirs, and these posts never changed hands. Before analysing the properties of manure, before entering into 'debits and credits' (his ironic term for book-keeping), he found out how many cattle the peasants possessed and did his utmost to increase the number. He kept the peasant families together in the largest possible groups and would not allow them to split up into separate households. The lazy, the dissolute and the feeble he pursued and tried to banish from the community.

He was as careful of the sowing and reaping of the peasants' hay and corn as of his own, and few landowners had their crops sown and harvested so early and so well as Nikolai.

He disliked having anything to do with the domestic serfs – the *parasites*, as he called them – and everybody said that he demoralized and spoilt them. When a decision had to be taken regarding a house-serf, especially if one had to be punished, he could never make up his mind and consulted the opinion of all in the house: only whenever it was possible to have a domestic serf conscripted in place of a peasant he did so without the smallest hesitation. In all his dealings with the peasants he never experienced the slightest diffidence. Every order he gave would, he knew, be approved by the great majority with very few exceptions.

He never allowed himself either to be hard on or punish a man just because he felt like it, or to make things easy for or reward anyone because that happened to be his own wish. He could not have advanced any definition of this standard of his, of what he should or should not do, but the standard lived firm and inflexible inside him.

Often in vexation at some failure or irregularity he would complain hopelessly of 'these Russian peasants of ours', and imagine that he could not bear them.

But heart and soul he loved 'these Russian peasants of ours' and their way of life, and so he understood and was able to adopt the one method of managing the land which could produce good results.

Countess Maria was jealous of this passion of her husband's and regretted that she could not share it, but the joys and heart-aches he met with in that world, to her so remote and alien, were beyond her comprehension. She could not understand why it should make him so brisk and cheerful to rise at dawn, to spend a whole morning in the fields or on the threshing-floor before he returned from the sowing or mowing or reaping to have tea with her. She did not understand why he was delighted and enthusiastic about the thrifty and well-to-do peasant Matvey Yermishin, who had been up all night with his family, carting his sheaves, and had got his corn stacked before anyone else had so much as reaped their fields. She did not understand why he chuckled under his moustaches and winked when he stepped out of the window on to the balcony and saw a warm, fine rain falling on the dry and thirsty shoots of the young oats, or why, when the wind carried away a threatening cloud during the hay harvest, he would come in from the barn, flushed, sunburnt and perspiring, with a smell of wormwood and gentian in his hair, and, gleefully rubbing his hands together, exclaim: 'Well, another day of this and my stuff and the peasants' will all be under cover.'

Still less could she understand how it was that with his kind heart and never-failing readiness to anticipate her wishes he should be driven almost frantic when she brought him a petition from a peasant or his woman who had appealed to her for relief from some drudgery or other – why it was that he, her good-natured Nikolai, should obstinately refuse her and angrily request her not to interfere in what was not her business. She felt he had a world apart, which he loved passionately, governed by laws she had not fathomed.

Sometimes, in her endeavours to understand him, she would talk to him of the good work he was doing for his serfs, but he would only grow vexed and reply: 'Not in the least! Such an idea never even enters my head; and I wouldn't lift my little finger for their good! That's all romantic nonsense and old wives' cackle – all that doing-good-to-one's-neighbour business. What I want is that our children should not have to go begging: I want to build up our fortunes in my lifetime, that's all. And to do that, order and discipline are necessary. ... That's all about it!' he would declare, clenching a confident fist. 'And fairness too, of course,' he would add. 'Because if the peasant is naked and starving, and has only one wretched horse, he can do no good for himself or me.'

And doubtless because Nikolai did not allow himself to entertain the idea that he was doing anything for others, for the sake of virtue, everything he touched was fruitful. His fortune rapidly increased; serfs from neighbouring estates came to beg him to buy them, and long after he was dead and gone the peasantry cherished a pious memory of his rule. 'He was a proper master ... the peasants' welfare first and then his own. And of course he allowed no liberties. Yes, a real good master he was!'

8

THE one thing which troubled Nikolai in connexion with the administration of his affairs was his hasty temper and his old habit, acquired in the hussars, of making free use of his fists. At first he saw nothing reprehensible in this, but in the second year of his marriage his views on that form of correction underwent a sudden change.

One summer day he had sent for the village elder from Bogucha-rovo, a man who had succeeded to the post when Dron died and who now stood accused of various instances of fraud and negligence. Nikolai went out to him on the porch and the man had scarcely opened his mouth to reply before the sound of shouts and blows was heard. Going indoors later on for lunch, Nikolai joined his wife, who was sitting with her head bent low over her embroidery frame. As usual, he began to tell her what he had been doing that morning and among other things mentioned the Bogucharovo elder. Countess Maria, turning first red and then white, continued to sit with bowed head and compressed lips, offering no rejoinder to her husband.

'The insolent scoundrel!' he cried, growing hot again at the mere recollection. 'Well, he should have told me he was drunk and did not see. ... Why, what is it, Marie?' he asked suddenly.

Countess Maria raised her head and tried to say something but hastily looked down again and her lips gathered.

'Why, whatever is the matter, my dearest?'

Tears always improved the plain looks of Countess Maria. She never cried from pain or vexation: it was always from sorrow or pity. And when she wept her luminous eyes acquired an irresistible charm.

The moment Nikolai took her hand she could restrain herself no longer and burst into tears.

'Nicolas, I saw you ... he was in the wrong but you, why did you...? Oh, Nicolas!...' and she hid her face in her hands.

Nikolai said nothing. He flushed crimson, left her side and began pacing up and down the room in silence. He understood why she was weeping but he could not all at once agree with her in his heart that what he had been used to from childhood, what he took as a matter of course, was wrong. 'Is it just sentimentality, a feminine foible, or is she right?' he asked himself. Before he had decided the point he glanced again at her suffering, loving face and suddenly realized that she was right and that he had been sinning against himself.

'Marie,' he said softly, going up to her, 'it shall never happen again: I give you my word. Never,' he repeated in a trembling voice, like a boy begging for forgiveness.

The tears flowed faster still from the countess's eyes. She took her husband's hand and kissed it.

'Nikolai, when did you break your cameo?' she asked to change

1361

the subject, examining the finger on which he wore a ring with a cameo representing the head of Laocoön.

'This morning – at the same time. Oh, Marie, don't remind me of it!' and he flushed again. 'I give you my word of honour it shan't occur any more. And let this always be a reminder to me.' And he pointed to the broken ring.

After that, whenever he was having it out with village elders and foremen and the blood rushed to his face and his fists began to clench, Nikolai would twist the broken ring on his finger and look away from the man who was making him angry. But he did forget himself once or twice within a twelvemonth and then he would go and confess to his wife and promise her again that this should really be the very last time.

'Marie, you must despise me, don't you ?' he would say. 'I deserve it.'

'You should walk away, walk away as fast as you can if you don't feel strong enough to control yourself,' she would tell him sadly, trying to comfort him.

Among the gentry of the province Nikolai was respected but not liked. The local politics of the Nobility did not interest him and so some thought him stuck up and others a fool. In summer, from spring-sowing to harvest, he spent his every minute on the land. In the autumn he gave himself up with the same business-like earnestness to sport, going out for a month or two at a time with his hunt. During the winter he rode off to visit his other villages, or occupied himself with reading. The books he read were mainly historical works on which he spent a certain sum every year. He was building up for himself, as he said, a 'serious library', and he made it a principle to read through every book he bought. He would sit in his study with a grave air for this reading which at first he imposed on himself as a duty but which afterwards became a habit affording him a special kind of gratification to think that he was engaging in a 'serious' pursuit. Except for business excursions he passed most of the winter at home, entering into the domestic life of his family and interesting himself in all the details of his children's relations with their mother. He grew steadily closer to his wife, every day discovering fresh spiritual treasures in her.

Sonya had lived with them since their marriage. Before that, however, Nikolai had told his betrothed all that had happened between him and Sonya, blaming himself and extolling her. He had begged Princess Maria to be kind and affectionate to his cousin. The princess was fully sensible of the wrong he had done Sonya and felt guilty herself, fancying that her wealth had influenced Nikolai's choice. She had no fault to find with Sonya and tried to be fond of her but simply could not: indeed, she often found herself cherishing uncharitable feelings towards her which she could not overcome.

Once she had a talk with her friend Natasha about Sonya and her own unfairness towards her.

'You know,' said Natasha, 'you are always reading the Gospels. There's a passage in them that just fits Sonya.'

'Is there?' Countess Maria asked in surprise.

'"To him that hath shall be given, but from him that hath not shall be taken away" – remember? She is one that hath not: why, I don't know. Perhaps she lacks egoism – I don't know, but from her is taken away, and everything has been taken away. Sometimes I am dreadfully sorry for her. I used to be awfully anxious for Nicolas to marry her but I always had a sort of presentiment that it would not happen. She is a *barren flower* – you know, like one of those unfertilized flowers one finds on a strawberry plant. Sometimes I am sorry for her and sometimes I think she doesn't feel it as you or I would.'

And although Countess Maria explained to Natasha that those words in the Gospel were meant in a different sense, still, looking at Sonya, she could not help agreeing with her friend's interpretation. It did really seem that Sonya was not fretted by her position and was quite reconciled to her lot as a *barren flower*. She appeared to be fond not so much of individuals as of the family as a whole. Like a cat, she had attached herself not to people but to the house. She waited on the old countess, petted and spoiled the children, was always ready to perform the small services for which she had a gift – but all this was unconsciously accepted from her with a less than adequate measure of gratitude.

The manor-house at Bald Hills had been restored, though not on the same scale as under the old prince.

The structure, begun in the days of straitened circumstances, was more than simple. The huge house on the old stone foundations was of wood, plastered only on the inside. The great rambling mansion had bare deal floors, was furnished with the plainest hard sofas, armchairs, tables and chairs made from their own birch-trees by their own serf-carpenters. The house was very roomy, with quarters for the domestic-serfs and apartments for visitors. Sometimes whole families of Rostov and Bolkonsky relations would come to Bald Hills with almost a score of horses and dozens of servants, and stay for months. And four times a year, on the name-days and birthdays of the master and mistress, as many as a hundred visitors would gather there for a day or two. The rest of the year life pursued its unbroken routine with its ordinary occupations, with breakfasts, lunches, dinners and suppers provided out of the produce of the estate.

9

IT was the eve of St Nikolai, the fifth of December, 1820. That year Natasha had been staying at her brother's with her husband and children since early autumn. Pierre had gone to Petersburg on business of his own for three weeks, as he said, but had remained nearly seven and was expected back every minute.

On this 5th of December, besides the Bezuhov family, Nikolai's old friend, the retired General Vasili Fiodorovich Denisov, was staying with the Rostovs.

On the 6th, which was his name-day, when the house would be full of visitors, Nikolai knew he would have to exchange his Tartar tunic for a frock-coat, and put on narrow boots with pointed toes and drive to the new church he had built; after which he would be expected to receive congratulations, offer refreshments to his guests and talk about the elections of the Nobility and the year's crops. But the eve of that day he considered he had a right to spend as usual. By dinner-time Nikolai had gone over the bailiff's accounts from the Ryazan estate, the property of his wife's nephew, written two business letters and walked through the granaries, the cattle-yards and the stables. Having taken precautions against the general drunkenness to be expected on the morrow because it was a great saint's day, he returned to dinner and without having time for a private talk with his wife sat down to the long table laid with twenty covers, at which all the household were assembled. At the table were his mother, his mother's old companion Mademoiselle Byelov, his wife, their three children with their governess and tutor, his wife's nephew with his tutor, Sonya, Denisov, Natasha, her three children, their governess, and old Mihail Ivanych, the late prince's architect, who was living in retirement at Bald Hills.

Countess Maria was sitting at the opposite end of the table. As soon as her husband took his place she knew by the gesture with which he picked up his table-napkin and quickly pushed back the tumbler and wine-glass set before him that he was out of humour, as he sometimes was – especially before the soup, and when he came in to dinner straight from the farm. Countess Maria was thoroughly familiar with this mood of his, and when she herself was in a good temper she would wait quietly till he had swallowed his soup and only then begin to talk to him and make him admit that there was no cause for his ill-humour. But today she quite forgot, and was hurt and felt miserable that he should be angry with her for no reason. She asked him where he had been. He told her. Then she inquired whether everything was going well on the estate. He scowled disagreeably at her unnatural tone and made a curt reply.

'So I was not mistaken,' thought Countess Maria. 'Now, why is he vexed with me?' In the tone in which he answered her she detected ill-will towards herself and a desire to cut short the conversation. She was aware that her remarks sounded artificial but could not refrain from asking several other questions.

Thanks to Denisov, talk round the table soon became general and lively and she did not say any more to her husband. When they rose and came round to thank the old countess, Countess Maria held out her hand and kissed her husband and asked him why he was angry with her.

'You always have such strange fancies. I had no thought of being angry with you,' he replied.

But the word *always* seemed to her to imply: 'Yes, I am angry and I don't choose to say why.'

Nikolai and his wife lived on such excellent terms that even Sonya and the old countess, who felt jealous and would have been pleased to see them disagree, could find nothing to reproach them with; but even they had their moments of mutual antagonism. At times, and particularly after a more than usually happy period, a feeling of estrangement and hostility assailed them both. This feeling occurred most frequently when Countess Maria was with child. Such was her condition now.

'Well, *messieurs et mesdames*,' said Nikolai loudly and with a show of cheerfulness (it seemed to his wife that this was on purpose to wound her), 'I have been on my feet since six o'clock this morning.

Tomorrow I shall have to be a victim and suffer, but today I'm off to have a rest.'

And without a word to his wife he disappeared into the little sitting-room and lay down on the sofa.

'That's always the way,' thought Countess Maria. 'He talks to everyone except me. I see ... I see that I am repulsive to him, especially when I am in this condition.' She looked down at her swollen figure and then into the glass at her pale, sallow, sunken face in which the eyes appeared bigger than ever.

And everything jarred on her: Denisov's clamour and boisterous laughter, Natasha's chatter and, above all, the hasty glance Sonya stole at her.

Sonya was always the first excuse Countess Maria found for feeling irritated.

After sitting a little while with her guests and not taking in a word of what they were saying, she slipped out and went to the nursery.

The children were perched on chairs playing at driving to Moscow, and invited her to join them. She sat down and played with them a little but the thought of her husband and his unreasonable crossness worried her all the time. She got up and with difficulty walking on tiptoe went to the small sitting-room.

'Perhaps he is not asleep and I can have it out with him,' she said to herself. Andrusha, her eldest boy, tiptoed behind her, imitating her, but she did not notice him.

'*Chère Marie*, I think he is asleep – he was so tired,' said Sonya, meeting her in the larger divan-room (it seemed to Countess Maria that Sonya was everywhere). 'Mind Andrusha doesn't wake him.'

Countess Maria looked round, saw Andrusha behind her, felt that Sonya was right, and for that very reason flushed angrily and with obvious difficulty refrained from a harsh retort. She said nothing but, to avoid heeding Sonya, beckoned to Andrusha to follow her without making a noise, and went to the door. Sonya moved towards the other door. From the room where Nikolai was asleep came the sound of even breathing, every tone of which was familiar to his wife. As she listened to it she could see before her mind's eye his smooth handsome forehead, his moustaches, the whole face she had so often gazed at in the stillness of the night when he slept. Suddenly Nikolai stirred and cleared his throat. And at the same instant Andrusha called from the other side of the door: 'Mamma's here, papa!'

Countess Maria turned pale with dismay and made signs to the boy. He was quiet at once and for a moment or two there ensued what seemed to Countess Maria a dreadful silence. She knew how Nikolai hated being waked. Then through the door she heard him clear his throat again and move, and his voice said crossly:

'I'm never given a moment's peace. Maria, is that you? Why did you bring him here?'

'I only came to see if – I did not notice ... forgive me. ...'

Nikolai coughed and said no more. His wife stepped away from the door and took the boy back to the nursery. Five minutes later little black-eyed, three-year-old Natasha, her father's favourite, hearing from her brother that papa was asleep in the sitting-room, ran in to her father without her mother seeing. The dark-eyed little girl rattled boldly at the door, scampered energetically up to the sofa on her sturdy little legs and, having taken stock of the attitude her father was lying in – he was asleep with his back to her – rose on tiptoe and kissed the hand which lay under his head. Nikolai turned round with a smile of tenderness on his face.

'Natasha, Natasha!' came Countess Maria's frightened whisper from the door. 'Papa is trying to have a nap.'

'No, he isn't, mamma,' answered little Natasha with conviction. 'He's laughing.'

Nikolai lowered his legs, sat up and took his daughter in his arms. 'Come in, Marie,' he called to his wife.

She went in and sat down beside her husband.

'I did not notice him following me,' she said timidly. 'I just glanced in.'

Holding his little girl on one arm, Nikolai looked at his wife and, perceiving the apologetic expression on her face, put his other arm round her and kissed her hair.

'May I kiss mamma?' he asked Natasha.

Natasha smiled demurely.

'Again!' she commanded, pointing with an imperious gesture to the spot where Nikolai had kissed her mother.

'I don't know why you should think I am in a bad temper,' said Nikolai, replying to the question he knew was in his wife's mind.

'You have no idea how unhappy, how lonely I feel when you are like that. It always seems to me ...'

'Marie, stop! What nonsense! Aren't you ashamed of yourself?' he asked gaily.

'I always think you can't care for me, that I am so plain ... always ... and now ... in this condi ...'

'Oh, how absurd you are! "Handsome is, as handsome does," you know – not the other way about. It's only the Malvinas who are loved because they are beautiful; but do I love my wife? I don't love her but ... I don't know how to put it. Without you, or when something comes between us like this, I feel quite lost and can't do anything. Do I love my own finger? No, but just try cutting it off. ...'

'No, I am not like that myself, but I understand. So you're not vexed with me?'

'Horribly vexed!' he said, smiling and getting up. And smoothing his hair he began walking about the room.

'Do you know, Marie, what I've been thinking?' he began, immediately starting to think aloud to his wife now that they had made it up. He did not inquire whether she were disposed to listen: he took it for granted. An idea occurred to him and so it must to her, too. Accordingly he told her of his intention to persuade Pierre to stay with them till spring.

Countess Maria listened till he had finished, made some comment and then in her turn began thinking aloud. Her thoughts ran on about the children.

'One can see the woman in her already,' she said in French, pointing to little Natasha. 'You reproach us women with being illogical. There's an example of our logic. I say: "Papa is trying to have a nap!" but she answers, "No, he's laughing." And she was right,' said Countess Maria with a contented smile.

'Yes, yes!' And Nikolai picked his little daughter up with a powerful grip, set her on his shoulder, held her by the legs and paced the room with her. The faces of father and daughter shone with light-hearted happiness.

'But, you know, you may be unfair. You are too fond of this one,' his wife whispered in French.

'Yes, but what can I do? ... I try not to show it. ...'

At that moment they heard the sound of the door-pulley and footsteps in the hall and ante-room, as if someone had arrived.

'Somebody has come.'

'I am sure it's Pierre. I'll go and find out,' said Countess Maria.

While she was gone Nikolai allowed himself to give his little daughter a gallop round the room. Panting for breath, he took the laughing child quickly from his shoulder and pressed her to his heart. His capers reminded him of dancing, and looking at the little mite's round happy face he wondered what she would be like when he was an old man, taking her into society and dancing the mazurka with her as his old father had danced the *Daniel Cooper* with his daughter.

'Yes, it *is* he, Nicolas,' said Countess Maria, returning a few minutes later. 'Now our Natasha has come to life again. You should have seen her delight, and what a scolding he got for having stayed away longer than he said he would! Well, come along now, quick, make haste! It's time you two were parted,' she added, looking smilingly at the little girl nestling close to her father.

Nikolai went out, holding his daughter by the hand.

Countess Maria lingered behind in the sitting-room.

'Never, never would I have believed that one could be so happy,' she whispered to herself. Her face broke into a smile; but at the same time she sighed and a gentle melancholy showed itself in the depths of her eyes, as though over and above the happiness she was feeling there existed another sort of happiness, unattainable in this life, which she had involuntarily thought of at that instant.

10

NATASHA had married early in the spring of 1813, and by 1820 had three daughters and the son she had longed for passionately and was now nursing herself. She had filled out and grown broader, so that it was difficult to recognize in the buxom young mother the slim, vivacious Natasha of old. Her features were more defined and wore a sedate expression of quiet serenity. Her face had lost the ever flashing, eager light which had once constituted its charm. Now one often saw only her face and physical presence, without anything of the animating soul. The impression one had was of fine, vigorous maternity. Very seldom now was the old fire kindled. That happened only when, as today, her husband returned after absence, or a sick child recovered, or when she and Countess Maria spoke of Prince Andrei (she never mentioned him to her husband, fancying he might be jealous of Prince Andrei's memory), or when some unusual occasion induced her to sing – a practice which she had quite abandoned since her marriage. And at such times as these the revival of the old fire in her ample, comely form made her more attractive than she had ever been in the past.

Since their marriage Natasha and her husband had lived in Moscow, in Petersburg, on their estate near Moscow, or with her mother – that is to say, at Nikolai's. Society saw little of the young Countess Bezuhov, and those who did see her found her unsatisfactory, since she was neither sociable nor ingratiating. It was not that Natasha liked solitude – she hardly knew whether she liked it or not: indeed, she rather supposed that she did not – but with her pregnancies, her confinements, the nursing of her children, and sharing every moment of her husband's life, she had demands enough, which could only be fulfilled by renouncing society. Everyone who had known Natasha before her marriage marvelled at the change in her, as though it were something extraordinary. Only the old countess, whose maternal instinct had always told her that Natasha's waywardness proceeded solely from the need of children and a husband – as Natasha herself had cried more in earnest than in jest at Otradnoe – was surprised at the wonder of people who had never understood her daughter, and kept saying that she had always known Natasha would make an exemplary wife and mother.

'Only,' the old countess would add, 'she carries her love for her husband and children to extremes; so much so that it becomes positively absurd.'

Natasha did not follow the golden rule preached by so many clever folk, especially the French, which lays down that a girl should not let herself go when she marries, should not neglect her accomplishments, should be even more careful of her appearance than when she was single, and should try to captivate her man as much as she had before he became her husband. Natasha, on the contrary, had instantly dropped all her witchery, in the armoury of which she had one extraordinarily powerful weapon – her singing. She gave up even her singing just because it was such a great attraction. As they say, she let go. Natasha bothered no more about charm of manner or graceful speech, or her clothes; nor did she think of striking attractive attitudes before her husband, or to avoid wearying him with her demands. In fact, she contravened every one of these rules. She felt that the allurements instinct had taught her to use before would now seem merely ridiculous in the eyes of her husband, to whom she had from the first moment surrendered herself entirely – that is, with her whole soul, leaving no corner of it hidden from his sight. She felt that the bond between them rested not on the romantic feelings which had attracted him to her but on something else, as indefinable but as firm as the bond between her own body and soul.

To fluff out her curls, put on a fashionable gown and sing sentimental songs in order to fascinate her husband would have seemed as strange as to adorn herself so as to attract herself. To adorn herself for others might perhaps have given her pleasure now – she did not know – but she simply had not the time. The chief reason she neglected her singing, her wardrobe and pretty turns of speech was that there was absolutely not a moment to spare for such things.

It is a well-known fact that man has the faculty of becoming completely absorbed in one subject, however trivial that subject may appear to be. And it is well known that no subject is so trivial as to be incapable of boundless development if one's entire attention is devoted to it.

The subject in which Natasha was completely absorbed was her family, that is, her husband, whom she had to keep so that he should belong entirely to her and to the home, and the children whom she had to carry, to bear, to nurse, to bring up.

And the more she put, not her mind only but her whole soul, her whole being, into the subject that absorbed her the more that subject seemed to enlarge under her eyes and the feebler and more inadequate did her own powers appear, so that she concentrated them all on that one thing and still had not the time to do all that she considered necessary.

In those days, just as now, there were arguments and discussions on the rights of women, the relations of husband and wife, their freedoms and rights – only people did not then call them *questions*, as we do today. But it was not that Natasha was not interested in them: she had absolutely no comprehension of them.

Those questions, then as now, existed only for those who see nothing in marriage but the pleasure married people may derive from one another – who see only the first beginnings of a marriage and not its whole significance, the family.

Such discussions and arguments, which are like the question of how to get the utmost possible gratification out of one's dinner, did not then, and do not now, exist for those for whom the object of dinner is the nourishment it affords and the object of wedlock is – the family.

If the purpose of dinner is to nourish the body the man who eats two dinners at a sitting may perhaps attain greater enjoyment but not his object, since the stomach will not digest two dinners.

If the purpose of marriage is the family the person who seeks to have a number of wives or husbands may possibly obtain much pleasure therefrom, but will not in any case have a family.

If the purpose of food is nourishment and the purpose of marriage is the family the whole question resolves itself into not eating more than the stomach can digest and not having more wives or husbands than are needed for the family – that is, one wife or one husband. Natasha needed a husband. A husband was given her. And her husband gave her a family. And she not only saw no need of any other or better husband but as all her spiritual energies were devoted to serving that husband and family she could not imagine, and found no interest in imagining, how it would be if things were different.

Natasha did not care for society in general but this made her all the fonder of being with her relatives – with Countess Maria, her brother, her mother and Sonya. She took delight in the society of those to whom she could come striding dishevelled from the nursery in her dressing-gown and with joyful face show a diaper stained yellow instead of green, and from whom she could hear reassuring words to the effect that baby was much better.

Natasha was so neglectful of herself that her dresses, the way she did her hair, her untimely remarks, her jealousy – she was jealous of Sonya, of the governess, of every woman, pretty or plain – were stock jests among her friends. The general opinion was that Pierre was tied to his wife's apron strings, which really was the case. From the very earliest days of their married life Natasha had intimated her claims. Pierre had been greatly surprised at his wife's view, to him a totally novel idea, that every moment of his life belonged to her and the home. His wife's demands astonished him but they also flattered him and he submitted.

Pierre's subjection entailed not daring not only to flirt but even to speak smilingly to another woman; not daring to dine at the club without good reason, *merely* as a pastime, not daring to spend money on a whim or to absent himself for any length of time, except on business – in which category his wife included his scientific pursuits, to which, although not in the least understanding them, she attributed great importance. To make up for this, Pierre had full licence to regulate life at home as he chose, for himself and his family. Natasha in her own home placed herself on the footing of a slave to her husband, and the whole household went on tiptoe when he was occupied – that is, was reading or writing in his study. Pierre had only to manifest a leaning, to find his desire instantly being fulfilled. He had only to express a wish and Natasha would jump up and perform it.

The entire household was governed according to the imaginary injunctions of the master, in other words in accordance with Pierre's wishes which Natasha tried to anticipate. Their manner of life and place of residence, their acquaintance and ties, Natasha's occupations, the children's upbringing – all followed not only Pierre's expressed wishes but what Natasha supposed his wishes to be from the ideas he gave voice to in conversation. And she deduced the essentials of his wishes quite correctly and, having once arrived at them, clung to them tenaciously. When Pierre himself showed signs of wanting to change his mind she would meet him with his own arguments.

Thus in the anxious time, which Pierre would never forget, after the birth of their first child, when they tried three different wet-nurses for the delicate baby and Natasha fell ill with worry, Pierre one day told her of Rousseau's views (with which he was in complete agreement) of how unnatural and deleterious it was to have wet-nurses at all. When the next baby was born, in spite of vigorous opposition from her mother, the doctors and even from her husband himself – who were all against her nursing the baby, which to them was something unheard of and pernicious – she insisted on having her own way, and after that nursed all her children herself.

It very often happened that in a moment of irritation husband and wife would quarrel, but for a long while after the dispute Pierre, to his delight and surprise, would discover his wife reflecting, not only in theory but in practice, the very idea of his against which she had rebelled – and not the idea alone but the idea purged of any personal element which he had imported into it in the heat of argument.

After seven years of married life Pierre was able to feel a comforting and assured conviction that he was not a bad fellow after all. This he could do because he saw himself mirrored in his wife. In himself he felt the good and bad inextricably mixed and overlapping. But in his wife he saw reflected only what was really good in him, since everything else she rejected. And this reflection was not the result of a logical process of thought but came from some other mysterious, direct source.

Two months previously, when Pierre was already staying with the Rostovs, he had received a letter from a certain Prince Fiodr asking him to come to Petersburg to discuss various important questions that were agitating the members of a society of which Pierre had been one of the principal founders.

As soon as she had read the letter (she read all her husband's letters) Natasha had urged him to go to Petersburg, acutely though she would feel his absence. She attributed immense weight to all her husband's intellectual and abstract interests, though she did not understand them, and was always in dread of being a hindrance to him in such matters. To Pierre's timid look of inquiry after reading the letter she replied by begging him to go, but to fix a definite date for his return. And leave of absence was given him for four weeks.

This term had expired a fortnight ago, and Natasha had since been in a constant state of alarm, depression and irritability.

Denisov, now a general on the retired list and much dissatisfied with the present progress of public affairs, had arrived during that fortnight, and gazed at Natasha with pained amazement, as at a bad likeness of a once dear one. Dejected, melancholy looks, random replies and talk about the nursery were all he saw and heard from his former enchantress.

Natasha was mournful and bad-tempered the whole of this time, but never more so than when her mother, her brother or Countess Maria sought to comfort her, and tried to excuse Pierre and suggest reasons for his delay in returning.

'It's all nonsense, all rubbish – those discussions which never lead to anything, and all those stupid societies!' Natasha would declare of the very affairs in the immense importance of which she firmly believed. And she would march off to the nursery to feed Petya, her only boy.

No one could give her such soothing and sensible consolation as this little three-months-old creature when he lay at her breast and she felt the movement of his lips and the snuffling of his tiny nose. The diminutive being said to her: 'You are angry, you are jealous, you would like to pay him out, you are afraid – but he is here in me, he is here in me! ...' And to that there was no answer. It was more than true.

During those two weeks of restlessness Natasha resorted to the infant for comfort so often, and fussed over him so much, that she overfed him and he fell ill. She was terrified by his illness, and at the same time it was just what she needed. In caring for him she found it easier to bear her uneasiness about her husband.

She was nursing the baby when the sound of Pierre's sledge was heard at the front door, and the old nurse, knowing how to please her mistress, hurried noiselessly into the room with a beaming face.

'Has he come?' asked Natasha quickly in a whisper, afraid to stir for fear of waking the baby who was dropping off to sleep.

'The master's here, ma'am,' whispered the nurse.

The blood rushed to Natasha's face and her feet involuntarily moved; but to jump up and run was out of the question. The baby opened his eyes and glanced at her as much as to say, 'You are here?', and again lazily smacked his lips.

Cautiously withdrawing her breast, Natasha rocked her son a little, handed him to the nurse and went with swift steps towards the door. But at the door she stopped as though her conscience pricked her for letting her joy take her away from the child so soon, and she looked back. The nurse, with her elbows raised, was lifting the infant over the rail of the cot.

'Yes, you go, ma'am, you go. Don't worry, run along,' she whispered, smiling, with the sort of familiarity that grows up between nurse and mistress.

And Natasha fled on light feet to the ante-room.

Denisov, issuing pipe in hand from the library into the hall, now recognized the old Natasha again for the first time. A flood of radiant, joyous light streamed from her transfigured face.

'He's come!' she exclaimed as she flew past, and Denisov felt that he was delighted that Pierre, whom he did not much care for, had returned.

Running into the vestibule, Natasha saw a tall figure in a fur coat unwinding his scarf. 'It's he! It's really he! He's here!' she said to herself, and darting up to him she hugged him, pressing his head to her breast and then pushing him away and gazing into his red, happy face which was all over hoar-frost. 'Yes, it's he, happy and contented....'

And all at once she remembered the tortures of suspense she had gone through during the last two weeks: the joy that had lit up her face vanished; she frowned and a torrent of reproaches and bitter words broke over Pierre.

'Yes, it's all very well for you! You are pleased – you have been having a good time. ... But what about me? You might at least have shown some consideration for your children. I am nursing, my milk went wrong. Petya was at death's door. But you were enjoying yourself. Yes, you were enjoying yourself.'

Pierre knew he was not in the wrong, for he could not have come sooner; he knew this outburst was unseemly and would blow over in a minute or two; above all, he knew that he himself was glad and happy. He wanted to smile but did not even dare think of doing so. He put on a piteous, frightened face and bowed before the storm.

'I swear I could not get away sooner. But how is Petya?'

'All right now. Come along! I wonder you aren't ashamed! If only you could see what a state I am in without you, how wretched I was. ...'

'You are well?'

'Come along, come along!' she said, not letting go of his arm. And they went off to the suite of rooms they were occupying.

When Nikolai and his wife came to look for Pierre they found him in the nursery dandling his baby son, who was awake again, on the great palm of his right hand. There was a fixed and gleeful smile on the baby's broad face with its open toothless mouth. The storm had spent itself long since and Natasha's face was all sunshine as she gazed tenderly at her husband and son.

'And did you manage to say all you wanted to to Prince Fiodr?' Natasha was saying.

'Yes, indeed.'

'You see, he can hold his head up.' (Natasha meant the baby.) 'But what a fright I've had with him! ... And you saw the princess? Is it true she's in love with that —'

'Yes, just fancy ...'

At that moment Nikolai and Countess Maria came in. Pierre, still with the baby in his arms, stooped down, kissed them and replied to their inquiries. But it was obvious that in spite of the many interesting things they had to discuss the baby with its little wobbling night-capped head was absorbing all Pierre's attention.

'What a pet!' said Countess Maria, looking at the baby and beginning to play with it. 'That's a thing I can't understand, Nicolas,' she went on, turning to her husband. 'I can't understand how it is you don't appreciate the charm of these exquisite little marvels.'

'I don't, I can't,' replied Nikolai, looking at the baby with indifferent eyes. 'Just a lump of flesh, that's all. Come along, Pierre.'

'And yet really he's such an affectionate father,' said Countess Maria in defence of her husband, 'but only after they are a year or fifteen months old. ...'

'Now Pierre makes a capital nurse,' said Natasha. 'He says his hand is just made for a baby's seat. Look there!'

'Well, only not for this ...' Pierre suddenly exclaimed with a laugh, and shifting the baby he handed him back to the nurse.

12

As is the way with every large household, several quite separate microcosms lived together at Bald Hills and, while each preserved its own individuality but made concessions to the rest, merged into one harmonious whole. Every event that happened in the house was important, joyful or sad for all these microcosms, though each circle had its own private grounds for independent rejoicing or mourning over a given event.

Thus Pierre's return was a happy and important occurrence affecting them all.

The servants (always the most reliable judges of their masters since they assess not on words or expressions of sentiment but on actions and manner of life) were glad when Pierre came back because they knew that when he was there their count would cease his daily round of the estate and would be in better spirits and temper, and also because they knew there would be handsome presents for them all for the fête day.

The children and their governesses rejoiced to see him back because there was no one like Pierre for drawing them into the social life of the household. He alone could play on the harpsichord that écossaise – his one piece! – which, as he said, would do for every sort of dance, and he was sure to have brought presents for everyone.

Young Nikolai Bolkonsky, now a slim, delicate, intelligent lad of fifteen with curly light-brown hair and beautiful eyes, was delighted:

'Uncle Pierre,' as he called him, was the object of his passionate adoration and affection. No one had tried to instil into Nikolai any special love for Pierre, whom he only saw occasionally. His aunt and guardian, Countess Maria, had done her utmost to induce the boy to love her husband as she loved him, and Nikolai did like his uncle, but with just a shade of contempt in his liking. Pierre, however, he worshipped. He had no ambitions to be a hussar or a Knight of St George like his uncle Nikolai: he wanted to be learned, wise and good like Pierre. In Pierre's presence his face was always beaming, and he blushed and choked whenever Pierre addressed him. He never missed anything Pierre said, and afterwards, with Dessalles or on his own, he would recall and ponder the meaning of his every word. Pierre's past life and his unhappiness before 1812 (of which young Nikolai had formed a vague, romantic picture from fragmentary phrases he had overheard), his adventures in Moscow, his captivity, Platon Karata)ev (whom he knew about from Pierre), his love for Natasha (to whom the boy himself was particularly devoted) and, above all, Pierre's friendship with the father Nikolai did not remember, all made Pierre in his eyes a hero and a being apart.

From stray references to his father and Natasha, from the emotion with which Pierre spoke of the dead man, and the thoughtful reverent tenderness with which Natasha spoke of him too, the boy, who was only just beginning to guess at love, conceived for himself the idea that his father had been in love with Natasha and had bequeathed her to his friend when he was dying. This father of his, whom the boy did not remember, seemed to him a divinity who could not even be imagined, and of whom he never thought without an aching heart and tears of grief and rapture.

And so the boy too was happy at Pierre's return.

The guests in the house were glad to see Pierre because he always helped to enliven and unite any company he was in.

The grown-up members of the family, to say nothing of his wife, were pleased to have back a friend whose presence made life run more smoothly and tranquilly.

The old ladies were pleased both at the presents he brought them and, above all, because Natasha would now be herself again.

Pierre sensed these attitudes towards him of the different sections of the household and hastened to satisfy the expectations of each.

Though he was the most absent-minded and forgetful of men, with the aid of a list his wife drew up he had bought everything, not forgetting his mother- and brother-in-law's commissions, nor the presents of a dress for Mademoiselle Byelov and toys for his nephews. In the early days of marriage it had seemed strange to him that his wife should expect him to remember all the items he had undertaken to buy, and he had been taken aback by her serious annoyance when he returned after his first absence, having forgotten everything. But in time he had grown used to this. Knowing that Natasha never asked him to get anything for herself, and only gave him commissions for others when he himself volunteered, he now found an unforeseen and childlike pleasure in this purchase of presents for the whole household, and never forgot anything. If he incurred Natasha's censure now, it was only for buying and spending too much. To her other defects (as most people thought them but which to Pierre were virtues) of untidiness and neglect of herself Natasha certainly added that of thriftiness.

From the time that Pierre set up as a family man on a scale entailing heavy expenditure he had noticed to his astonishment that he spent only half as much as in the past, and that his circumstances, somewhat straitened latterly (mainly owing to his first wife's debts) were beginning to improve.

Living was cheaper because it was circumscribed: that most expensive of luxuries, the sort of life which allows of going somewhere else or doing something different at a moment's notice, was his no longer, nor did he have any desire for it. He felt that his manner of life was determined now, once and for all, till death, and that to alter it was not in his power, and so that order of life proved economical.

With a jovial, smiling face Pierre was unpacking his purchases.

'What do you think of this?' he cried, unrolling a length of printed cotton like a shopman.

Natasha, who was sitting opposite him with her eldest daughter on her knee, turned her sparkling eyes from her husband to the things he was showing her.

'Is that for Mademoiselle Byelov? Splendid!' She felt the quality of the material. 'A rouble a yard, I suppose?'

Pierre told her the price.

'Very dear,' remarked Natasha. 'However, how pleased the children and *maman* will be! Only you shouldn't have bought me this,' she added, unable to suppress a smile as she admired the gold comb set with pearls, in a style just then coming into fashion.

'Adèle tempted me – she kept on at me to buy it,' said Pierre.

'When am I to wear it?' and Natasha stuck it in her coil of hair. 'It will do when I have to bring little Masha out; perhaps they will be fashionable again by then. Well, let's go now.'

And collecting the presents they went first to the nursery and then to see the old countess.

The countess was sitting with her companion, Mademoiselle Byelov, playing grand-patience as usual, when Pierre and Natasha came into the drawing-room with parcels under their arms.

The countess was now turned sixty. Her hair was quite grey and she wore a cap with a frill which framed her whole face. Her face was shrivelled, her upper lip had sunk in and her eyes were misted.

After the deaths in such rapid succession of her son and husband she felt herself a being accidentally forgotten in this world, with no object and no interest in life. She ate and drank, slept and lay awake, but did not live. Life made no impression on her. She wanted nothing from life but peace, and that peace only death could give her. But until death came she had to go on living, that is, employ her time, her vital forces. She evinced to a remarkable degree a trait noticeable in the very young and the very old. Her existence had no manifest aim but was merely, so far as could be seen, occupied by the need to exercise her various functions and proclivities. She had to eat, have a little sleep, ruminate and reminisce, shed a few tears, do some hand-work, lose her temper occasionally, and so forth, simply because she had a stomach, brains, muscles, nerves and a liver. She did all these things not at the promptings of any external impulse, like people in the full vigour of life when the aim towards which they strive screens from our view that other aim of exercising their functions. She spoke only because it was a physical necessity to her to use her tongue and lungs. She cried as a child cries, because its nose is stuffed up, and so on. What to people possessed of full health and strength appears as a final aim for her was merely a pretext.

Thus in the morning – especially if she had eaten anything too rich the day before – she was apt to feel a need to be cross, and would select the handiest excuse – Mademoiselle Byelov's deafness.

From the other end of the room she would begin to say something in a low voice.

'I fancy it is a little warmer today, my dear,' she would murmur. And when Mademoiselle Byelov replied: 'Yes, they've come to be sure,' she would mutter angrily: 'Mercy on us, how deaf and stupid she is!'

Another excuse would be her snuff, which was either too dry or too damp or not rubbed fine enough. After these outbursts of irritability her face would grow yellow, and her maids knew by infallible tokens when Mademoiselle Byelov would be deaf again, and the snuff damp, and the countess look bilious. Just as she needed to work off her spleen, so she had sometimes to exercise another of her remaining faculties – namely, the one of thinking, and for this the pretext was her game of patience. When she needed to cry, the late count would be the pretext. When she needed anxiety, there was Nikolai and his health. When she felt a need to say something spiteful, Countess Maria provided the excuse. When her vocal organs required exercise, which usually happened towards seven o'clock, after her after-dinner rest in a darkened room, the pretext would be the re-telling of the same stories over and over again to the same audience.

The old lady's condition was understood by the whole household, though no one ever spoke of it, and they all made every possible effort to satisfy her needs. Only a rare glance exchanged with a sad half-smile between Nikolai, Pierre, Natasha and Countess Maria expressed their common realization of her condition.

But those glances said something more: they said that she had played her part in life, that what they now saw was not her whole self, that we must all come to the same extremity one day, and that they were glad to give way to her, to forbear for the sake of this poor creature, once so dear, once as full of life as ourselves, now so pitiful. 'Memento mori,' said those glances.

Only the really heartless and stupid members of the household, and the little ones, failed to understand this, and kept away from her.

13

WHEN Pierre and his wife entered the drawing-room the countess was in her recurring condition of needing the mental exercise of a game of patience, and so – though by force of habit she repeated the formula she always employed when Pierre or her son returned after an absence: 'High time, my dear boy, high time! We got tired of waiting for you. Well, thanks be to God you are home again!' and received her presents with another stock phrase: 'It's not the gift that counts, my dear. ... Thank you for thinking of an old woman like me. ...' – it was clear that Pierre's arrival at that moment was unwelcome, since it distracted her in dealing out the cards. She finished her game and only then turned her attention to the presents. They consisted of a beautifully worked card-case, a bright blue Sèvres cup with a lid and shepherdesses painted on it, and a gold snuff-box with the late count's portrait in the lid which Pierre had had executed by a miniature-painter in Petersburg. The countess had long wished for such a box; but just now she had no inclination to weep and so she glanced indifferently at the portrait and took more notice of the card-case.

'Thank you, my dear, you have cheered me up,' said she, as she always did. 'But best of all you have brought yourself back. Why, I never saw anything like it – you really must give your wife a good scolding! Would you believe it: she is like a crazed creature when you are not there. No eyes for anything, forgets everything,' she said, going on in her usual strain. 'Look, Anna Timofeyevna,' she added to her companion, 'see what a beautiful case for cards my son has brought us!'

Mademoiselle Byelov duly admired the presents and was in raptures over her printed cotton.

Though Pierre, Natasha, Nikolai, Countess Maria and Denisov had much to talk about that they could not discuss before the old countess – not because anything was concealed from her but simply because she had dropped so far out of things that had they started on any topic in her presence they would have had to answer so many random questions and repeat for her benefit what had already been repeated over and over again: that this person was dead and that one married, which she would not be able to remember this time any more than the last – yet they sat at tea round the samovar in the drawing-room as usual, and Pierre answered the countess's questions as to whether Prince Vasili had aged, and whether Countess Maria Alexeyevna sent greetings and still thought of them, and other matters that interested none of them and to which she herself was indifferent.

Conversation of this kind, which entertained no one but could not be avoided, lasted all through tea-time. All the adult members of the family were gathered about the round table at which Sonya presided beside the samovar. The children with their tutors and governesses had had tea and their voices could be heard in the next room. In the drawing-room everyone sat in his accustomed place: Nikolai by the stove at a small table where his tea was handed to him, while Milka, the old borzoi bitch (daughter of the first Milka), with her large black eyes looking more prominent than ever in her now completely grey muzzle, lay on an arm-chair beside him. Denisov, whose curly hair, moustaches and whiskers were liberally streaked with grey, sat next to Countess Maria with his general's tunic unbuttoned. Pierre sat between his wife and the old countess, talking of things he knew might interest the old lady and be intelligible to her. He was telling her of the superficial events of society and of the people who had once made up the circle of her contemporaries and in the days gone by had been an active, lively, distinct coterie but who were now for the most part scattered here and there, like herself living out their remnant of life, garnering the last ears of the crop they had sown in earlier years. But to the old countess those contemporaries of hers seemed to make up the only real world that was worth considering. Natasha saw by Pierre's animation that his visit had been full of interest and that he had much to talk about which he could not say before the countess. Denisov, who was not a member of the family, did not understand Pierre's reserve and, being a malcontent, was concerned to hear what was going on in Petersburg. He kept urging Pierre to tell them about the recent scandal in the Semeonovsk regiment, or about Arakcheyev, or about the Bible Society. Once or twice Pierre let himself be drawn into discussing these subjects but Nikolai and Natasha always brought him back to the health of Prince Ivan and Countess Maria Antonovna.

'Now what about all this idiocy – Gossner and Madame Tatawinov?' asked Denisov. 'Is that weally still going on?'

'Going on!' Pierre exclaimed. 'It's worse than ever! The Bible Society has absorbed the whole government!'

'What is that, *mon cher ami*?' inquired the countess, who had finished her tea and was evidently casting about for some excuse for a little peevishness after her meal. 'What were you saying about the government? I don't understand.'

'Why, you see, *maman*,' put in Nikolai, who knew how to translate things into his mother's language, 'Prince Alexander Golitsyn has founded a society, so he has great influence, they say.'

'Arakcheyev and Golitsyn,' remarked Pierre incautiously, 'are practically the government now. And what a government! They see conspiracy everywhere and are afraid of everything.'

1383

'Oh, but what fault could anyone find with Prince Golitsyn, I should like to know?' demanded the old countess in an offended tone. 'He is a most estimable man. I used to meet him in the old days at Maria Antonovna's.' And still more aggrieved by the general silence she went on: 'Nowadays people find fault with everyone. A Gospel Society – what harm is there in that?' and she got up (everybody else rose too) and with a forbidding air sailed back to her table in the sitting-room.

The rather glum silence that followed was broken by the sound of children's voices and laughter from the next room. Evidently some joyful excitement was afoot there.

'Finished, finished!' little Natasha's gleeful shriek rose above all the rest.

Pierre exchanged glances with Countess Maria and Nikolai (Natasha he never lost sight of) and smiled happily.

'That's delightful music!' he said.

'Anna Makarovna must have finished her stocking,' said Countess Maria.

'Oh, I'm going to have a look,' said Pierre, jumping up. 'You know,' he added, stopping at the door, 'why it is I'm so particularly fond of that music? It is always the first thing to tell me that everything is all right. When I was driving back today the nearer I got to the house the more nervous I grew. Then as I entered the ante-room I heard Andrusha in peals of laughter, and I knew all was well. ...'

'I know. I know that feeling,' Nikolai chimed in. 'But I mustn't come – those stockings are to be a surprise for me.'

Pierre went in to the children, and the shrieks and laughter were louder than ever.

'Now then, Anna Makarovna,' Pierre's voice was heard saying, 'step into the middle of the room and at the word of command – one, two, and when I say three. ... (That's right, you stand there. And you I'll have in my arms.) Now – one, two ...' said Pierre; there was dead silence. 'Three!' – and children's voices filled the room with a rapturous shout.

'There *are* two, there *are* two!' they roared.

There were two stockings which by a secret method known only to herself Anna Makarovna used to knit at the same time on the same needles and produce one out of the other in the children's presence, when the pair was done.

14

SOON after this the children came in to say good-night. The children kissed everyone; the tutors and governesses made their bows and went away. Only Dessalles and his charge remained. Dessalles whispered to the boy to come downstairs.

'No, Monsieur Dessalles, I shall ask my aunt to let me stay,' young Nikolai Bolkonsky replied, also in a whisper.

'*Ma tante*, please let me stay,' he pleaded, going up to his aunt. His face was full of entreaty, agitation and excitement. Countess Maria glanced at him and turned to Pierre.

'When you are here he can't tear himself away ...' she said.

'I will bring him to you directly, Monsieur Dessalles. Good-night,' said Pierre, giving his hand to the Swiss tutor, and he turned to young Nikolai with a smile. 'You and I haven't seen anything of one another yet. ... Marie, how like he is growing!' he added, addressing Countess Maria.

'Like my father?' asked the boy, flushing crimson and looking up at Pierre with rapturous, shining eyes.

Pierre nodded, and went on with what he had been saying when the children interrupted. Countess Maria had some canvas embroidery in her hands; Natasha sat with her eyes fixed on her husband. Nikolai and Denisov got up, asked for pipes, smoked and went to fetch more tea from Sonya, still sitting with weary pertinacity at the samovar, as they plied Pierre with questions. The curly-haired, delicate boy sat with shining eyes unnoticed in a corner, starting every now and then and murmuring something to himself, evidently thrilling to a new and violent emotion as he turned his curly head with the slender neck showing above the folded-down collar in Pierre's direction.

The conversation ran on the scandals of the day in the higher administrative circles, a subject in which most people see the chief interest of home politics. Denisov, who bore a grudge against the government because of his own disappointments in the Service, rejoiced to hear of the follies (so he deemed them) being committed in Petersburg, and commented in harsh, cutting terms.

'In the old days one had to be a German to be anybody – now you must dance with Mesdames Tatawinov and Kwüdner, and wead Ecka'tshausen and the bwethwen. Ugh, I would let good old Bonaparte loose again! He'd knock all the nonsense out of 'em. Fancy giving the command of the Semeonovsk wegiment to a fellow like that Schwa'tz!' he cried.

Nikolai, though he had not Denisov's disposition to find everything amiss, also thought it dignified and becoming to criticize the government, and believed that the fact that *A* had been appointed minister of this department and *B* governor-general of that province, and that the Emperor had said this and this minister had said that, were all matters of the greatest importance. And so he thought it incumbent upon him to take an interest in these things and interrogate Pierre. Hence the questions put by Nikolai and Denisov kept the discussion from ranging beyond the ordinary lines of gossip about the upper spheres of the administration.

But Natasha, who knew her husband's every manner and thought, saw that Pierre had long been trying, though in vain, to divert the conversation into another channel and open his heart on another idea – the idea concerning which he had gone to Petersburg to consult his new friend, Prince Fiodr, and she came to the rescue with the query: How had he settled things with Prince Fiodr?

'What was that?' asked Nikolai.

'Oh, the same old thing over again,' said Pierre, looking about him. 'Everybody perceives that matters are going so badly that they cannot be allowed to continue so, and that it's the duty of all honest men to counteract it as far as they can.'

'Why, what can honest men do?' Nikolai inquired, frowning slightly. 'What can be done?'

'Well, this ...'

'Let us go into the study,' said Nikolai.

Natasha, who had for some time been expecting to be fetched to her baby, now heard the nurse calling and went off to the nursery. Countess Maria accompanied her. The men adjourned to the study and young Nikolai Bolkonsky stole in, unnoticed by his uncle, and sat down at the writing-table in a dark corner by the window.

'Well, what would you suggest doing?' asked Denisov.

'Still another hare-brained scheme!' said Nikolai.

'Why this,' Pierre began, not sitting down but pacing the room, occasionally stopping short, and lisping and gesticulating rapidly as he talked. 'The position in Petersburg is this: the Emperor lets everything go. He is entirely wrapped up in this mysticism.' (Pierre could not tolerate mysticism in anyone now.) 'All he asks for is peace, and he can only get peace through these men of no faith and no conscience, who recklessly hack at and strangle everything – I mean men like Magnitsky, Arakcheyev and *tutti quanti.* ... You will agree that if you did not look after your estates yourself, and only asked for peace and quiet, the more savage your bailiff was the more readily your object might be attained,' he said, turning to Nikolai.

'Well, but what is the drift of all this?' inquired Nikolai.

'Why, everything's going to pieces. Larceny in the law-courts, in the army nothing but flogging, drill and forced labour in military settlements. Civilization is being crushed. Anything that is youthful and honourable is persecuted! Everybody sees that it can't go on like this. The strain is too great, something's bound to snap,' said Pierre (as men examining the performance of any government have always said since governments began). 'One thing I told them in Petersburg.'

'Told whom?' asked Denisov.

'Oh, you know whom,' said Pierre, with a meaning glance from under his brows. 'Prince Fiodr and all of them. Zeal in the encouragement of culture and philanthropy is all very well of course. The aim is excellent, but in present circumstances something else is needed.'

At that moment Nikolai noticed the presence of his nephew. His face darkened and he went up to the boy.

'Why are you here?'

'Why not? Let him be,' said Pierre, taking hold of Nikolai's arm and continuing. 'That is not enough, I told them: something else is needed now. While you stand expecting the overstrained cord to snap at any moment; while everyone waits for the inevitable upheaval, as many people as possible should join hands as closely as they can to withstand the general calamity. All that is young and strong in the nation is being enticed away and corrupted. One is lured by women, another by honours, a third by ambition or money, and over they go to the other camp. As for independent, free men such as you or me – there are none left. What I say is, widen the scope of our Society, let the *mot d'ordre* be not virtue alone but independence and action!'

Nikolai, moving away from his nephew, irritably pushed up an arm-chair, sat down in it and listened to Pierre, uttering the while an occasional grunt of dissatisfaction and frowning more and more.

'Yes, but what action to what end?' he cried. 'And what attitude will you adopt towards the government?'

'Why, the attitude of supporters. The Society need not be a secret one if the government will sanction it. So far from being hostile to the government, we are the true conservatives – a Society of *gentlemen* in the full meaning of the word. Our object: to prevent another Pugachov from coming tomorrow to cut the throats of your children and mine, to prevent Arakcheyev from dispatching me to a military settlement. We band together exclusively for the common weal and general security.'

'Yes, but a secret society must necessarily be an inimical and mischievous one, which can only breed evil,' said Nikolai, raising his voice.

'Why? Was the *Tugendbund* which saved Europe' (people did not then venture to suggest that Russia had saved Europe) 'productive of anything harmful? The *League of Virtue* is an alliance of virtue: it means love, mutual help ... it is what Christ preached on the Cross ...'

Natasha, who had come into the room in the middle of the conversation, looked joyfully at her husband. It was not what he was saying that pleased her – that did not even interest her because it all seemed so perfectly simple, and something she had known long ago. It appeared so to her because she knew so well the source from which it all sprang – Pierre's heart and soul. She was glad, looking at his eager, enthusiastic face.

Pierre was watched with even more passionate joy by the boy with the thin neck sticking out from the turn-down collar, whom everyone had forgotten. Every word of Pierre's burned into his heart, and with nervous movements of his fingers he unconsciously picked up and snapped the sealing-wax and quill pens on his uncle's table.

'It's not at all what you imagine; but that is what the German *Tugendbund* was and that is what I am proposing.'

'No, my fwiend! A *Tugendbund* is all vewy well for the sausage-eaters. But I don't understand it and can't even pwonounce it,' interposed Denisov in a loud, positive voice. 'Evewything is wotten and cowwupt, I agwee, but I still do not fathom that *Tugendbund* of yours, nor do I care about it. A pwoper wevolt now, and I'm your man!'

Pierre smiled, Natasha laughed, but Nikolai only scowled the more and began arguing with Pierre that no revolution was to be expected, and that the danger he talked of existed only in his imagination. Pierre maintained the contrary, and as his intellectual faculties were keener and more resourceful Nikolai soon found himself nonplussed. This made him still angrier, for in his heart he knew – not by reasoning but by something stronger than reason – that his opinion was the right one.

'Let me tell you this,' he said, rising and trying with nervously twitching fingers to prop up his pipe in a corner, and finally letting it fall. 'I can't prove it to you. You say everything is all rotten in Russia and a revolution is coming. I don't see it. But you also say that our oath of allegiance is a conditional matter, and to that I reply: "You are my best friend, as you know, but if you formed a secret society and began working against the government – whatever government – I know it would be my duty to obey the government. And if Arakcheyev bid me lead a squadron against you and mow you down, I shouldn't hesitate for a second, I should do it! Now make what you like of that." '

An awkward silence followed. Natasha was the first to speak, taking her husband's side and attacking her brother. Her defence was weak and clumsy but she attained her object. The discussion began again, and no longer in the unpleasantly hostile tone in which Nikolai's last words had been spoken.

When they all got up to go in to supper young Nikolai Bolkonsky went up to Pierre, pale and with shining luminous eyes.

'Uncle Pierre ... you ... no . If Papa were alive ... he would agree with you, wouldn't he ?' he asked.

In a flash Pierre realized what an extraordinary, independent, complex and strenuous travail of thought and feeling must have been going on in this boy during the conversation, and remembering all he had been saying he regretted that the lad should have heard him. He had to give him an answer, however.

'Yes, I believe he would,' he said reluctantly, and left the study.

The boy looked down and then for the first time seemed to become aware of the havoc he had wrought with the things on the writing-table. He flushed and went up to Nikolai.

'Uncle, forgive me, I did that ... but not on purpose,' he said, pointing to the broken sealing-wax and pens.

Nikolai started angrily.

'Very well, very well,' he said, throwing the pieces under the table. And, evidently suppressing his fury with difficulty, he turned away from the boy.

'You ought not to have been here at all,' he said.

15

A T supper no more was said about politics or societies, and conversation turned on the subject Nikolai liked best – reminiscences of 1812, which Denisov started and over which Pierre was particularly genial and amusing. And the family separated on the friendliest terms.

After supper Nikolai, having undressed in his study and given instructions to the steward who had been waiting for him, went in his dressing-gown to the bedroom, where he found his wife still at her writing-table.

'What are you writing, Marie?' Nikolai asked.

Countess Maria reddened. She was afraid that what she was writing would not be understood or approved of by her husband.

She would have liked to conceal what she was writing from him, but at the same time was glad that he had caught her and that she would now have to tell him.

'It's my diary, Nicolas,' she replied, handing him a blue exercise-book filled with her firm, bold script.

'Diary?...' echoed Nikolai with a shade of irony, and he took up the book. It was in French.

December 4th

Today when Andrusha [the eldest boy] woke up he did not want to dress, and Mademoiselle Louise sent for me. He was naughty and obstinate. I tried threatening him but it only made him more wilful. Then I took things in hand: I left him alone and helped nurse to get the other children up, declaring that I did not love him. For a long while he was quiet, as though wondering, then he jumped up out of bed and rushed to me in his night-shirt, sobbing so that I could not soothe him for a long time. It was plain that what troubled him most was having grieved me. Then when I gave him his report in the evening he cried again most pitifully as he kissed me. One can do anything with him by tenderness.

'What does his "report" mean?' asked Nikolai.

'I have begun giving the elder ones little marks every evening, showing how they have behaved.'

Nikolai looked into the brilliant eyes that were watching him, and continued to turn over the pages and read. The diary recorded everything in the children's lives which seemed to the mother of interest as indicative of their characters, or suggesting general reflections on educational methods. The entries consisted mainly of the most trifling details but they did not seem so to the mother or the father now reading this journal about his children for the first time.

On the 5th of December there was the note:

Mitya was naughty at table. Papa said he was to have no pudding. He had none, but looked so miserably and greedily at the others while they were eating. To my mind punishing a child by not letting him have any sweet only encourages his greediness. Must tell Nicolas.

Nikolai put down the book and looked at his wife. The radiant eyes gazed at him questioningly: would he approve or disapprove of her diary? There could be no doubt not only of Nikolai's approval but also of his admiration of his wife.

Perhaps it need not be done so pedantically, Nikolai thought, perhaps it need not be done at all; but this constant, tireless spiritual application, the sole aim of which was the children's moral welfare, enchanted him. If Nikolai could have analysed his feelings he would have found that his proud, tender, assured love for his wife rested on this very feeling of awe at her spirituality, at the lofty moral world, almost beyond his reach, in which she had her being.

He was proud that she was so wise and good, and recognizing his own insignificance beside her in the spiritual world rejoiced all the more that a soul like that not only belonged to him but was part of his very self.

'I quite, quite approve, my dearest!' he said, with an expressive look. And after a short pause he added: 'And I behaved badly today. You weren't in the study. Pierre and I began arguing, and I lost my temper. But he is impossible – such a child! I don't know what would become of him if Natasha didn't keep him in hand. Can you imagine what he went to Petersburg about? ... They have formed ...'

'Yes, I heard,' said Countess Maria. 'Natasha told me.'

'Well, then, you know,' pursued Nikolai, growing hot at the mere recollection of the discussion, 'he wants to convince me that it's the duty of every honest man to go against the government, and that the oath of allegiance and duty ... I am sorry you weren't there. As it was, they all fell on me – Denisov and Natasha too. ... Natasha is too absurd. We know she can twist him round her little finger, but when it comes to an argument she hasn't an idea to call her own – she simply repeats what he says,' added Nikolai, succumbing to the irresistible inclination which tempts one into criticism of one's nearest and dearest. He forgot that what he was saying of Natasha could apply word for word to himself in relation to his wife.

'Yes, I have noticed that,' said Countess Maria.

'When I told him that duty and sworn allegiance come before everything, he began trying to prove the Lord knows what. A pity you were not there – what would you have said?'

'To my way of thinking, you were absolutely right. I told Natasha so. Pierre says everybody is wretched, and being persecuted and corrupted, and that it is our duty to help our neighbour. Of course he is right there,' said Countess Maria, 'but he forgets that we have other duties nearer home, which God Himself has marked out for us, and that we may run risks for ourselves but not for our children.'

'Yes, yes, that's just what I told him!' cried Nikolai, who fancied he actually had said just that. 'But they kept on about love for one's neighbour and Christianity and all the rest of it in front of young Nikolai, who slipped into the study and sat breaking all my things.'

'Ah, do you know, Nicolas, I often worry about young Nikolai. He is such a curious boy. And I am afraid I neglect him for my own. We all have children and parents, but he has no one. He is always alone with his thoughts.'

'Well, I don't think you have anything to reproach yourself with on his account. All that the fondest mother could do for her son you have done, and are doing, for him. And of course I am glad you do. He is a fine lad, a fine lad! This evening he listened to Pierre in a sort of trance. And only fancy – we got up to go in to supper and I looked, and he had broken everything on my table to bits, and he told me of it at once. I have never known him tell an untruth. A fine lad, a fine lad!' repeated Nikolai, who at heart was not fond of Nikolai Bolkonsky but always felt moved to acknowledge he was a fine lad.

'Still, I am not the same as a mother,' said Countess Maria. 'I feel I am not the same and it distresses me. He's a wonderful boy, but I am dreadfully afraid for him. It would be a good thing for him to have companionship.'

'Oh well, it won't be long now. Next summer I'll take him to Petersburg,' said Nikolai. 'Yes, Pierre always was a dreamer, and always will be,' he went on, returning to the discussion in the study, which had evidently stirred him deeply. 'Why, what can I care what goes on there – whether Arakcheyev is a villain, and so forth? How could I have cared at the time of our marriage when I had so many debts that they were going to put me in prison, and a mother who couldn't see or understand the situation? And then there are you and the children and our affairs. Is it for my own pleasure that I work on the estate or in the office from morning till night? No, I know I must work to be a comfort to my mother, to repay you, and not to leave the children such paupers as I was left myself.'

Countess Maria wanted to tell him that man does not live by bread alone; that he attached too much importance to this *work*; but she knew that it would be better not, and useless. She only took his hand and kissed it. He accepted this as a sign of approval and a confirmation of his ideas, and after a few minutes' silent reflection he continued to think aloud.

'Do you know, Marie,' he said, 'Ilya Mitrofanych' (this was one of their overseers) 'was here today from the Tambov estate, and he tells me they are already offering eighty thousand for the forest.' And with an eager face Nikolai began talking of the possibility of buying back Otradnoe before long. 'Given another ten years of life,' he said, 'and I shall leave the children ... well provided for.'

Countess Maria listened to her husband and took in all that he said. She knew that when he was thinking aloud he would sometimes ask her what he had been saying, and be vexed if he noticed that she had been thinking of something else. But she had to force herself to attend, for what he was saying in no way interested her. She looked at him and though she was not exactly thinking of other things her feelings were elsewhere. She felt a submissive, tender love for this man who would never understand all that she understood – and this seemed to make her love him the more, and added a touch of passionate tenderness. Besides this feeling which absorbed her entirely and prevented her from following the details of her husband's plans, thoughts that had no connexion with what he was saying kept flitting through her brain. She thought of her nephew (her husband's account of the boy's excitement over Pierre's discourse struck her forcibly) and various traits of his gentle, sensitive nature recurred to her. Thinking of her nephew led her to her own children. She did not compare him with them, but compared her feeling for him with her feeling for them, and was sadly conscious of something lacking in her feeling for young Nikolai.

Sometimes the idea had occurred to her that this difference arose from the difference in their ages, but she felt guilty towards him and vowed deep down in her heart to do better and to accomplish the impossible – in this life to love her husband, and her children, and young Nikolai, and all her fellow-creatures, as Christ loved mankind. Countess Maria's spirit was always striving towards the infinite, the eternal and the absolute, and could therefore never be at peace. An austere expression born of hidden, lofty suffering of spirit burdened by the flesh appeared on her face. Nikolai gazed at her. 'My God, what would become of us if she were to die, which is what I dread when she looks like that!' he thought, and placing himself before the icon he began to say his evening prayers.

16

As soon as Natasha and Pierre were alone they too began to talk as only husband and wife can talk – that is, exchanging ideas with extraordinary swiftness and perspicuity, by a method contrary to all the rules of logic, without the aid of premisses, deductions or conclusions, and in a quite peculiar way. Natasha was so used to talking to her husband in this fashion that a logical sequence of thought on Pierre's part was to her an infallible sign of something being wrong between them. When he began proving anything or calmly arguing, and she, led on by his example, began to do the same, she knew that they were on the verge of a quarrel.

From the moment they were alone together and Natasha, with wide-open happy eyes, crept up to him and all at once, quickly seizing his head, pressed it to her bosom, saying, 'Now you are all mine, mine! You shan't escape!' – from that moment the conversation began that contravened every law of logic in that it turned at one and the same time upon entirely different topics. This simultaneous discussion of all sorts of subjects, far from being an obstacle to understanding, was the surest token that they understood one another fully.

Just as in a dream everything may be unreal, incoherent and contradictory except the feeling behind the dream, so in this communion of ideas, so contrary to all the laws of logic, the words that passed between husband and wife were not logical and clear, but the feeling that prompted them was.

Natasha was telling Pierre of the daily round of existence at her brother's; of how miserable and half-alive she had been without him; and of how she was fonder than ever of Marie, and how Marie was in every respect a better person than herself. In saying this Natasha was quite sincere in acknowledging Marie's superiority but at the same time she implied that she meant Pierre to prefer herself to Marie or any other woman, and that now, when he had just been seeing so many other women in Petersburg, was the moment for him to tell her so anew.

Accordingly Pierre told her how intolerable he had found the evening parties and dinners in the company of ladies in Petersburg.

'I have quite lost the art of small talk with ladies,' said he. 'It was horribly tedious. Especially as I was so busy.'

Natasha looked intently at him and went on:

'Marie, now she is wonderful!' she said. 'The way she understands children! She seems to see into their very souls. Yesterday, for instance, Mitya was naughty ...'

'How like his father he is,' Pierre interpolated.

Natasha knew why he made this remark about Mitya's likeness to Nikolai: he felt uncomfortable at the memory of his dispute with his brother-in-law and was longing to hear what she thought about it.

'It's a weakness of Nikolai's that unless a thing is generally accepted he will never agree with it. But I know you set great store on what opens up a fresh field,' said she, repeating words Pierre had once uttered.

'No, the truth of the matter is,' said Pierre, 'that to Nikolai ideas and discussions are only an amusement – almost a waste of time. There he is, collecting a library, and has made it a rule for himself not to buy a new book until he has read the last one – Sismondi and Rousseau and Montesquieu,' he added with a smile. 'You know how I ...' he began, to soften his criticism; but Natasha interrupted to show that this was unnecessary.

'So you say that ideas are just a pastime to him. ...'

'Yes, and for me everything else is pastime. All the while in Petersburg I saw everyone as in a dream. When an idea takes hold of me everything else seems waste of time.'

'Oh, what a pity I missed your meeting with the children!' remarked Natasha. 'Which was the most delighted? Liza, I'm sure.'

'Yes,' Pierre replied, and went on with what was in his mind.

'Nikolai says we have no business to reason. But I can't help it. Not to mention the fact that when I was in Petersburg I felt (I can say this to you) that without me the whole affair would go to pieces – every one was pulling his own way. But I succeeded in uniting them all; and then my idea is so clear and simple. You see, I don't say that we ought to oppose this and that. We may be mistaken. What I say is: Let those who love what is right join hands, and let us have but one banner – the banner of action and virtue. Prince Sergei is a capital fellow, and intelligent.'

Natasha would have had no doubt about Pierre's idea being a grand idea but that one thing disconcerted her. It was his being her husband. 'Could anyone so important and necessary to society also be my husband? How can it have happened?' She wanted to express this misgiving to him. 'Now who could decide whether he is really cleverer than all the others?' she wondered, and she passed in review all the people Pierre most respected. There was nobody whom, to judge by his account, he had held in higher regard than Platon Karatayev.

'Do you know what I'm thinking about?' she asked. 'About Platon Karatayev. What would he have said? Would he have approved of you now?'

Pierre was not at all surprised at this question. He understood the drift of his wife's thoughts.

'Platon Karatayev?' he said, and pondered, evidently sincerely trying to imagine what Karatayev's judgement would have been on the point. 'He would not have understood ... and yet, I think he would.'

'I love you awfully!' said Natasha suddenly. 'Awfully, awfully!'

'No, he wouldn't have approved,' said Pierre, after reflection. 'What he would have approved of is our family life. He was always so anxious to find seemliness, happiness, peace in everything, and I could have pointed with pride to ourselves. You know, you talk about when we are parted, but you wouldn't believe what a special feeling I have for you after a time of separation ...'

'Yes, I was going to say ...' Natasha began.

'No, it's not that. I never leave off loving you. And no one could love more; but this is something special ... Oh well, you know ...' he did not finish because their eyes meeting said the rest.

'What nonsense it is,' Natasha exclaimed suddenly, 'about honeymoons, and that the greatest happiness is at the beginning. On the contrary, now is much the best. If only you wouldn't go away. Do you remember how we used to quarrel? And it was always my fault. Always. And what it was we quarrelled about – I don't remember even.'

'It was always the same thing,' said Pierre with a smile. 'Jealo ...'

'Don't say it! I can't bear it!' cried Natasha, and a cold, vindictive light glittered in her eyes. 'Did you see her?' she added, after a pause.

'No, and if I had I shouldn't have recognized her.'

They were silent.

'Oh, do you know? While you were talking in the study I was looking at you,' Natasha began, obviously anxious to disperse the cloud that had overtaken them. 'You are as like as two peas – you and the boy.' (She meant her baby son.) 'Ah, it's time I went to him ... my milk. ... But I'm sorry to go away.'

They were silent for a few seconds. Then suddenly turning to each other they both started to speak, Pierre with self-satisfaction and enthusiasm, Natasha with a quiet, happy smile. Immediately, they both stopped to let the other continue.

'No, what were you saying? Go on, go on.'

'No, you go on, mine was only nonsense,' said Natasha.

Pierre finished what he had been about to say. It was the sequel to his complacent reflections on his success in Petersburg. At that moment it seemed to him that he was chosen to give a new direction to the whole Russian community and the world at large.

'I only wanted to say,' he explained, 'that all ideas which have great results are always simple. My idea is just that if vicious people unite together into a power, then honest folk must do the same. That's simple enough, isn't it?'

'Yes.'

'Now what were you going to say?'

'Oh, nothing – only nonsense.'

'Say it, though.'

'Oh, nothing, only silly nonsense,' said Natasha, beaming with a still more radiant smile. 'I was only going to tell you about Petya: today nurse was coming to take him from me, and he laughed and shut his eyes and snuggled up to me – I'm sure he thought he was hiding. He's terribly sweet! There he is crying. Well, good-bye!' and she went out of the room.

Meanwhile, downstairs in young Nikolai Bolkonsky's bedroom a lamp was burning as usual. (The boy was afraid of the dark and could not be cured of his fear.) Dessalles was asleep propped up on four pillows, his Roman nose emitting rhythmic snores. Young Nikolai, who had just woken in a cold perspiration, sat up in bed and stared before him with wide-open eyes. He had awoken from a fearful dream. He had been dreaming that he and Uncle Pierre, wearing helmets like the helmets in his illustrated edition of Plutarch, were marching at the head of a huge army. The army was composed of slanting white threads, filling the air like the cobwebs which float about in autumn and which Dessalles called *le fil de la Vierge*. In front of them lay glory, also exactly like those threads, only somewhat stouter. They – he and Pierre – were being borne along lightly and joyously, nearer and nearer to their goal. Suddenly the threads that moved them began to slacken and become entangled, and everything was dark and confused. And Uncle Nikolai stood before them in a stern and menacing attitude.

'Is this your work?' he said, pointing to some broken pens and sticks of sealing-wax. 'I loved you once but Arakcheyev has given me orders and I shall kill the first of you to advance a step further.' The boy Nikolai looked round for Pierre but Pierre was no longer there. In his place stood his father – Prince Andrei – and his father had neither shape nor form but there he was, and seeing him young Nikolai grew faint with love: he felt himself without strength, without bones or marrow. His father caressed and was sorry for him. But Uncle Nikolai was moving down upon them, coming closer and closer. Horror seized Nikolai and he awoke.

'My father!' he thought. (Though there were two very good portraits of Prince Andrei in the house, Nikolai never imagined him in human form.) 'My father has been with me and made much of me. He was pleased with me; he approved of Uncle Pierre. Whatever Uncle Pierre says I will do. Mucius Scaevola burnt his hand. And why shouldn't the same sort of thing happen in my life? I know they want me to study. And I will. But one day I shall have finished learning, and then I will do something. I only ask one thing of God: that it may be with me as it was with Plutarch's men, and I will do as they did. I will do better. Everyone shall know of me, shall love and applaud me.' And all at once Nikolai felt his breast heaving with sobs, and he burst into tears.

'*Êtes-vous indisposé?*' he heard Dessalles' voice asking.

'*Non*,' answered Nikolai, and lay back on his pillow. 'He is good and kind and I am fond of him,' he said to himself, thinking of Dessalles. 'But Uncle Pierre! Oh, what a wonderful person he is! And my father? Oh, Father, Father! Yes, I will do something that even *he* would be content with....'

PART TWO

I

HISTORY has for its subject the life of nations and of humanity. To catch hold of and encompass in words – to describe exactly – the life of a single people, much less of humanity, would appear impossible.

The ancient historians all employed one and the same method for seizing the seemingly elusive and depicting the life of a people. They wrote of the parts played by the individuals who stood in authority over that people, and regarded their activity as an expression of the activity of the nation as a whole.

To the twofold question of how individuals could oblige nations to act as they wished, and by what the will of those individuals themselves was guided, the historians of old replied by recognizing a Divinity which, in the first case, made the nation subject to the will of one chosen person, and, in the second, guided the will of that chosen person to the accomplishment of predestined ends.

For the old historians the question was thus resolved by belief in the direct participation of the Deity in human affairs.

Neither proposition finds a place in the theory of the new school of history.

It would seem that, having rejected the belief of the ancients in man's subjection to the Deity and in a predetermined aim towards which nations are led, the new school ought to be studying not the manifestations of power but the causes which create power. But modern history has not done this. Though it has repudiated the theory of the older historians it still follows their practice.

In place of men endowed with divine authority and governed directly by the will of God modern history has set up either heroes possessed of extraordinary, superhuman ability, or simply men of any and every degree, from monarchs to journalists, who dominate the masses. Instead of the former divinely appointed purposes of nations –

of the Jews, the Greeks, the Romans – which the old historians saw at the back of movements of humanity, the new school postulates aims of its own – such as the welfare of the French, German or English people, or, in its highest flights, the welfare and civilization of humanity in general, by which is usually meant the peoples inhabiting a small, north-western corner of a large continent.

Modern history has rejected the beliefs of the ancients without establishing any new conviction in place of them, and the logic of the situation has obliged the historians, who were under the impression that they had dismissed the hypothesis of the divine authority of kings and the *Fatum* of the ancients, to arrive at the same conclusion by another route – that is, to recognize that (1) nations are guided by individuals, and (2) there exists a certain goal towards which the nations and humanity are moving.

In the works of all the modern historians, from Gibbon to Buckle, in spite of their seeming differences of outlook and the apparent novelty of their opinions, these two time-honoured, unavoidable premisses lie at the basis of the argument.

In the first place the historian describes the activity of separate persons who in his opinion have dictated to humanity (one historian accepts only monarchs, military generals and ministers of state in this category, while another will also include orators, scholars, reformers, philosophers and poets). Secondly, the historians assume that they know the goal towards which humanity is being led: to one this goal is the majesty of the Roman or the Spanish or the French empire; for another it is liberty, equality and the kind of civilization that obtains in the little corner of the globe called Europe.

In 1789 fermentation starts in Paris: it develops and spreads, and finds expression in a movement of peoples from west to east. Several times this movement is directed towards the east and comes into collision with a counter-movement from the east westwards. In the year 1812 it reaches its extreme limit – Moscow – and then, with remarkable symmetry, the counter-movement follows from east to west, attracting to it, as the original movement had done, the peoples of middle Europe. The counter-movement reaches the departure-point in the west of the first movement – Paris – and subsides.

During this period of twenty years an immense number of fields are left untilled; houses are burned; trade changes its orientation; millions of people grow poor, grow rich, move from place to place;

and millions of Christian men professing the law of love for their neighbour murder one another.

What does all this mean? Why did it happen? What induced these people to burn houses and kill their fellow-creatures? What were the causes of these events? What force compelled men to act in this fashion? These are the instinctive, guileless and supremely legitimate questions humanity propounds to itself when it encounters the monuments and traditions of that bygone period of turmoil.

For an answer to these questions mankind in commonsense looks to the science of history, whose purpose is to teach nations and humanity to know themselves.

Had history adhered to the ideas of the ancients it would have said that the Deity, to reward or punish His people, gave Napoleon power and guided his will for the attainment of His own divine ends. And this reply would have been complete and lucid. One might or might not believe in the divine significance of Napoleon; but for anyone who believed in it all the history of that period would be intelligible and free from contradictions.

But modern history cannot answer in that way. Science does not admit the conception of the ancients as to the direct participation of the Deity in human affairs, and must therefore give other answers.

Replying to these questions the new school of history says: 'You want to know what this movement means, what caused it, and what force produced these events? Listen:

'Louis XIV was a very proud and self-confident man; he had such and such mistresses and such and such ministers, and he ruled France vilely. Louis' successors, too, were weak men and they, too, ruled France vilely. And they had such and such favourites and such and such mistresses. Furthermore, certain people were at this time writing books. At the end of the eighteenth century there had gathered in Paris a couple of dozen persons who began talking about all men being equal and free. Because of this, over the length and breadth of France men fell to slaughtering and destroying one another. They killed the king and a good many others. At this time there was in France a man of genius – Napoleon. He got the upper hand of everybody everywhere – that is to say, he killed numbers of his fellows because he was a great genius. And for some reason he went to kill Africans, and killed them so well and was so cunning and clever that when he returned to France he ordered everyone to obey him. And they all did. Having made himself an Emperor he again went off to kill people in Italy, Austria and Prussia. There, too, he killed a great many. Now in Russia there was an Emperor, Alexander, who decided to restore order in Europe, and so he fought wars against Napoleon. But in '07 he suddenly made friends with him, until in 1811 they quarrelled again, and again began killing a lot of people. And Napoleon brought six hundred thousand men to Russia and captured Moscow; but afterwards he suddenly ran away from Moscow, and then the Emperor Alexander, aided by the counsels of Stein and others, united Europe into a coalition to march against the disturber of her peace. All Napoleon's allies suddenly turned into enemies; and their forces advanced against the fresh forces which he raised. The allies defeated Napoleon, entered Paris, forced Napoleon to abdicate, and exiled him to the island of Elba, not depriving him of the dignity of Emperor or failing to show him every respect, though five years before and one year later they all regarded him as a bandit and an outlaw. Thereupon Louis XVIII, who till then had been a laughing-stock both to the French and the allies, began to reign. As for Napoleon, after shedding tears before the Old Guard he renounced his throne and went into exile. Next, astute statesmen and diplomats (in particular Talleyrand, who had managed to sit down before anyone else in the famous arm-chair and thereby to extend the frontiers of France) proceeded to hold conversations in Vienna, and by this means make the nations happy or unhappy. All at once the diplomats and monarchs almost came to blows: they were on the point of ordering their armies to massacre one another again; but at this point Napoleon arrived in France with a battalion, and the French, who had been abhorring him, immediately all submitted to him. But the allied monarchs got very annoyed at this and again went to war with the French. And they defeated the genius Napoleon and, suddenly confirming that he was a bandit, removed him to St Helena. And there the exile, parted from his dear ones and his beloved France, died a lingering death on the rocky island, and bequeathed his great deeds to posterity. As for Europe, reaction set in, and the sovereigns all took to outraging their subjects again.'

It would be a mistake to think this mere irony – a caricature of historical descriptions. On the contrary, it is a very mild expression of the incongruous answers which fail to answer given by *all* historians, from the compilers of memoirs and of histories of individual countries to the 'universal histories' and the new sort of histories of the *culture* of that period.

The grotesqueness of these answers arises from the fact that modern history is like a deaf man answering questions no one has put to him.

If the purpose of history is the description of the flux of humanity and of peoples, the first question to be answered, unless all the rest is to remain unintelligible, will be: What is the power that moves nations? To this the new school laboriously replies either that Napoleon was a great genius or that Louis XIV was very arrogant, or else that certain writers wrote certain books.

All that may well be so, and mankind is quite ready to say Amen; but it is not what was asked. All that might be very interesting if we recognized a divine power, self-subsisting and consistent, governing the nations by means of Napoleons, Louises and philosophical writers; but we acknowledge no such power, and therefore, before any talk of Napoleons, Louises and philosophical writers, we ought to be shown the relation obtaining between these persons and the movement of nations.

If divine power is to be replaced by some other force, then it should be explained what this new force consists of, in which the whole interest of history is contained.

History seems to take it for granted that this force is self-evident and known to everyone. But in spite of every desire to regard it as known the frequent reader of historical works will find himself doubting whether this new force, so variously understood by the historians themselves, is really quite so familiar to all and sundry.

2

WHAT is the force that moves nations?

Biographical historians and historians of individual peoples understand this force as a power inherent in heroes and rulers. According to their chronicles events occur solely at the will of a Napoleon, an Alexander or in general the personages of whom they treat. The answers which historians of this *genre* return to the question of what force causes events to happen are satisfactory only so long as there is but one historian to each event. But as soon as historians of different nationalities and views begin describing one and the same event, the replies they give immediately lose all meaning, since this force is understood by them not only differently but often in absolutely opposite ways. One historian will maintain that a given event owed its origin to Napoleon's power; another that it was Alexander's power; while a third ascribes the event to the influence of some other person. Moreover, historians of this type contradict one another even in their interpretation of the force on which the authority of one and the same figure was based. Thiers, a Bonapartist, says that Napoleon's power was based on his virtue and his genius; Lanfrey, a Republican, declares that it rested on his rascality and skill in deceiving the people. So that the historians of this class, by mutually destroying one another's position, destroy the conception of the force which produces events, and furnish no reply to history's essential question.

Universal historians, who deal with all the nations, appear to recognize the erroneousness of the specialist historians' view of the force that produces events. They do not recognize it as a power pertaining to heroes and rulers but regard it as the resultant of a multiplicity of variously directed forces. In describing a war, or the subjugation of a people, the general historian looks for the cause of the event not in the power of any one individual but in the interaction of many persons connected with the event.

According to this view, the power of historical personages conceived as the product of several different forces can hardly, it would seem, be regarded as the force which in itself produces events. Yet general historians do almost invariably make use of the concept of power as a force which itself produces events and stands to events in the relation of cause to effect. We find them (the historians) saying at one minute that an historical personage is the product of his time and his power only the outcome of various forces; and at the next that his power is itself a force producing events. Gervinus, Schlosser and others, for instance, in one place argue that Napoleon was the product of the Revolution, of the ideas of 1789 and so forth, and in another plainly state that the campaign of 1812 and other incidents not to their liking were simply the outcome of Napoleon's misdirected will, and that the very ideas of 1789 were arrested in their development by Napoleon's caprice. The ideas of the Revolution and the general temper of the age produced Napoleon's power. But Napoleon's power stifled the ideas of the Revolution and the general temper of the age.

This curious contradiction is no chance occurrence. It not only confronts us at every turn but volume upon volume of universal history is made up of a chain of such contradictions – which spring from the fact that after taking a few steps along the road of analysis the universal historians stop short half-way.

For component forces to give rise to a certain composite or resultant force the sum of the components must equal the resultant. This condition is never observed by the universal historians. Hence, to explain the resultant force they are obliged to admit, in addition to inadequate components, a further, unexplained, force affecting the resultant.

The specialist historian describing the campaign of 1813, or the restoration of the Bourbons, asserts in so many words that these events were brought about by the will of Alexander. But the general historian, Gervinus, refuting this opinion of the specialist historian, seeks to prove that the campaign of 1813 and the restoration of the Bourbons were due not only to Alexander but to the activity of Stein, Metternich, Madame de Staël, Talleyrand, Fichte, Chateaubriand and others. He evidently decomposes Alexander's power into its component factors – Talleyrand, Chateaubriand and the rest – but the sum of these components, that is, the interaction of Chateaubriand, Talleyrand, Madame de Staël and the others, obviously does not equal the resultant, namely, the phenomenon of millions of Frenchmen submitting to the Bourbons. And therefore to explain how the submission of millions resulted from these components – that is, how component forces equal to a given quantity A gave a resultant equal to a thousand times A – he is obliged to fall back on the same force – power – which he has been denying inasmuch as he was regarding it as the resultant of the given forces; that is, he has to concede an unexplained force acting on the resultant. And this is just what the universal historians do. And consequently contradict not only the sectional historian but themselves too.

Country people having no clear idea of the cause of rain say, 'The wind has blown away the rain,' or 'The wind is blowing up for rain,' according to whether they want rain or fine weather. In the same way the universal historians at times when they want it to be so, when it fits in with their theory, say that power is the result of events; and at others, when it is necessary to prove the opposite, say that power produces the events.

A third class of historians – the so-called historians of *culture*, following on the lines laid down by the writers of universal history who sometimes accept *littérateurs* and *grandes dames* as forces producing events – interpret this force still differently. They see it in what is termed *culture*, in intellectual activity.

The historians of culture from first to last take after their progenitors, the writers of universal histories, for if historical events may be explained by the fact that certain persons treated one another in certain ways, why not explain them by the fact that certain people wrote certain books? Out of all the immense number of tokens that accompany every vital phenomenon these historians select the manifestation of intellectual activity, and declare that this manifestation is the cause. But, despite their endeavours to prove that the cause of events lies in intellectual activity, only by a great stretch can one agree that there is any connexion between intellectual activity and the movement of peoples, and it is altogether impossible to agree that intellectual activity has controlled the actions of mankind, for such phenomena as the brutal murders of the French Revolution, which were the outcome of the doctrine of the equality of man, and the most wicked wars and executions resulting from the Gospel of Love belie this hypothesis.

But even admitting that all the cunningly devised arguments with which these histories abound are correct: admitting that nations are governed by some undefined force called an *idea*, the essential question of history either still remains unanswered or else to the power of monarchs and the influence of counsellors and other persons introduced by the universal historians we must add another, new force – the *idea*, the relation of which to the masses requires explanation. One can understand that Napoleon had power and so an event came to pass; with some effort one may even grant that Napoleon together with other influences was the cause of an event; but how a book, *Le Contrat social*, had the effect of making Frenchmen destroy one another is unintelligible without some explanation of the causal nexus of this new force with the event.

There undoubtedly exists a connexion between all the people alive at one time, and so it is possible to discover some sort of connexion between the intellectual activity of men and their historical movements, just as such a connexion may be discovered between the movements of humanity and commerce, handicrafts, horticulture, or anything else you please. But why intellectual activity should appear to the historians of culture to be the cause or expression of the whole historical movement is hard to understand. Only the following considerations can have led the historians to such a conclusion: (1) that history is written by learned men and so it is natural and agreeable for them to believe that the pursuit of their calling supplies the ruling element in the movement of all humanity, just as a similar belief is natural and agreeable to merchants, agriculturists or soldiers (only it does not find expression because merchants and soldiers do not write history); and (2) that spiritual activity, enlightenment, civilization, culture, ideas are all vague, indefinite conceptions under whose banner they can very conveniently employ words having a still less definite meaning and which can therefore be readily adapted to any theory.

But leaving aside the question of the intrinsic worth of histories of this kind (which may possibly even be of use to someone for something), the histories of culture, to which all general histories tend more and more to approximate, are remarkable for the fact that after examining seriously and in detail various religious, philosophic and political doctrines as causes of events, so soon as they have to describe an actual historical event, such as the campaign of 1812 for instance, they involuntarily describe it as resulting from an exercise of power – roundly declaring that that campaign was the result of Napoleon's will. In saying this, the historians of culture unconsciously contradict themselves; they show that the new force they have invented does not account for what happens in history, and that history can only be explained by introducing the power which they apparently do not recognize.

3

A LOCOMOTIVE is moving. Someone asks: 'What makes it move?' The peasant answers, ''Tis the devil moves it.' Another man says the locomotive moves because its wheels are going round. A third maintains that the cause of the motion lies in the smoke being carried away by the wind.

The peasant's contention is irrefutable: he has devised a complete explanation. To refute him someone would have to prove to him that there is no devil, or another peasant would have to tell him that it is not a devil but a German who makes the locomotive go. Only then, because of the contradiction, will they see that they are both wrong. But the man who argues that the movement of the wheels is the cause confounds himself, for having once started on analysis he ought to proceed further and explain why the wheels go round. And until he has reached the ultimate cause of the movement of the locomotive in the pressure of steam in the boiler he has no right to stop in his search for the cause. Finally, the man who explained the movement of the locomotive by the smoke that is borne back has noticed that the theory about the wheels does not furnish a satisfactory explanation, and has seized upon the first feature to attract his attention, and in his turn produces that as an explanation.

The only conception capable of explaining the movement of the locomotive is that of a force commensurate with the movement observed.

The only conception capable of explaining the movement of peoples is that of some force commensurate with the whole movement of the peoples.

Yet to supply this conception various historians assume forces of entirely different kinds, all of which are incommensurate with the movement observed. Some see it as a force directly inherent in heroes, as the peasant sees the devil in the steam-engine; others, as a force resulting from several other forces, like the movement of the wheels; others again, as an intellectual influence, like the smoke that is blown away.

So long as histories are written of separate individuals, whether Caesars, Alexanders, Luthers or Voltaires, and not the histories of *all* – absolutely *all* – those who take part in an event, it is impossible not to ascribe to individual men a force which can compel other men to direct their activity towards a certain end. And the only conception of such a kind known to historians is the idea of power.

This conception is the sole handle by means of which the material of history, as at present expounded, can be dealt with; and anyone who breaks that handle off, as Buckle did, without finding some other method of treating historical material, merely deprives himself of the last possible way of dealing with it. The necessity for the conception of power as an explanation of the phenomena of history is most strikingly illustrated by the universal historians and historians of culture themselves, who, after professedly rejecting the conception of power, inevitably have recourse to it at every step.

Up to now historical science in its relation to humanity's inquiry is like money in circulation – bank-notes and coin. The biographies and national histories are the paper money. They may pass and circulate and fulfil their function without mischief to anyone, and even to advantage, so long as no question arises as to the security behind them. One has only to forget to ask how the will of heroes produces events, and the histories of Thiers and his fellows will be interesting, instructive and not without their touch of poetry. But in exactly the same way as doubts of the real value of bank-notes arise either because, being easy to manufacture, too many of them get made, or because people try to exchange them for gold, so doubts concerning the real value of histories of this kind arise either because too many of them are written or because someone in the simplicity of his heart inquires: What force enabled Napoleon to do that? – that is, wants to exchange the current paper money for the pure gold of true understanding.

The writers of universal histories and the history of culture are like people who, recognizing the defects of paper money, decide to substitute for it coin of some metal inferior to gold. Their money will be 'hard coin', no doubt; but while paper money may deceive, the ignorant coin of inferior metal will deceive no one. Just as gold is gold only where it is employable not merely for barter but also for the real use of gold, so too the universal historians will only rank as gold when they are able to answer the cardinal question of history: What constitutes power? The universal historians give contradictory replies to this question, while the historians of culture thrust it aside altogether and answer something quite different. And as imitation gold counters can only be used among a community of persons who agree to accept them for gold or who are ignorant of the nature of gold, so the universal historians and historians of culture who fail to answer the essential questions of humanity only serve as currency for sundry purposes of their own – in the universities and among the legions who go in for 'serious' reading, as they are pleased to call it.

4

HAVING dismissed the conviction of the ancients as to the divinely ordained subjection of the will of a nation to the one chosen vessel and the subjection of the will of that chosen vessel to the Deity, history cannot take a single step without being involved in contradictions. It must choose one of two alternatives: either to return to its old belief in the direct intervention of the Deity in human affairs, or to find a definite explanation of the meaning of the force producing historical events which is termed 'power'.

A return to the first is impossible: the old belief has been shattered, and so an explanation must be found of what is meant by power.

'Napoleon commanded an army to be raised and to march forth to war.' Such a statement is so familiar, we are so entirely at home with such a point of view, that the question why six hundred thousand men go out to fight when Napoleon utters certain words seems to us foolish. He had the power and so what he ordered was done.

This solution is perfectly satisfactory if we believe that the power was given him by God. But, as soon as we discountenance that, it becomes essential to determine what this power is that one man has over others.

It cannot be the direct physical ascendancy of a strong creature over a weak one – an ascendancy based on the application or threat of physical force, like the power of Hercules; nor can it be founded on the possession of moral force, as in the innocence of their hearts some historians suppose, who say that the leading figures in history are cast in heroic mould, that is, are endowed with an extra-ordinary strength of soul and mind called genius. This power cannot be based on any preponderance of moral strength seeing that, not to mention heroes such as Napoleon concerning whose moral qualities opinions differ widely, history shows us that neither a Louis XI nor a Metternich, who ruled over millions of their fellows, had any particular moral qualities but on the contrary in most respects were morally weaker than any of the millions they ruled over.

If the source of power lies neither in the physical nor the moral qualities of the individual who possesses it, it is obvious that it must be looked for elsewhere – in the relation to the masses of the man who wields the power.

And that is how power is understood by the science of jurisprudence, that *bureau d'échange* of history, which undertakes to exchange history's concept of power for true gold.

Power is the collective will of the masses, transferred by their expressed or tacit consent to their chosen rulers.

In the domain of jurisprudence, deliberating as it does on how the State and its power ought to be constructed were it possible to do so *a priori*, all this is very clear; but when applied to actual history this definition of power calls for elucidation.

The science of jurisprudence regards the State and its power much as the ancients regarded fire – namely, as something existing absolutely. For history the State and its power are merely phenomena, in the same way as for modern physics fire is not an element but a phenomenon.

From this fundamental difference in the points of view of history and jurisprudence it follows that jurisprudence can discuss in detail how, in its opinion, power should be constituted and what power is in its immutable essence, outside the conditions of time; but to history's questions about the meaning of the mutations of power in time it can return no answer.

If power is the collective will of the masses transferred to their ruler, was Pugachov a representative of the will of the people? If not, then why was Napoleon I? Why was Napoleon III a criminal when he was apprehended at Boulogne, and why were those whom he afterwards apprehended criminals?

Do palace revolutions – in which sometimes only two or three people take part – transfer the will of the people to a new ruler? In international relations is the will of the people also transferred to their conqueror? Was the will of the Confederation of the Rhine transferred to Napoleon in 1808? Was the will of the Russian people transferred to Napoleon in 1809 when our army in alliance with the French made war upon Austria?

These questions may be answered in three different ways:

(1) by maintaining that the will of the people is always unconditionally transferred to the ruler or rulers whom they have chosen, and that therefore every emergence of a new power, every struggle against the power once delegated, must be regarded as a contravention of the real power; or

(2) by maintaining that the will of the masses is delegated to the rulers on certain definite and known conditions, and by showing that all restrictions on, conflicts with and even abolitions of power proceed from non-observance by the rulers of the conditions upon which their power was entrusted to them; or

(3) by maintaining that the will of the masses is delegated to the rulers conditionally but that the conditions are uncertain and undefined, and that the appearance of several authorities, their struggles

and their falls result solely from the greater or lesser fulfilment by the rulers of the uncertain conditions upon which the will of the people is transferred from one set of persons to another.

These are the three ways in which the historians explain the relation of the masses to their rulers.

Some historians, failing in their simplicity to understand the question of the meaning of power – those sectional and biographical historians already referred to – seem to believe that the collective will of the people is delegated to historical leaders unconditionally, and therefore in writing about some particular State they assume that Power to be the one absolute and real power, and that any other force opposing it is not a power but a violation of power – mere violence.

This theory of theirs, though convenient for covering primitive and peaceful periods of history, has the disadvantage when applied to complex and stormy periods in the life of nations, during which various powers arise simultaneously and come into collision, that the legitimist historian will try to prove that the Convention, the Directory and Bonaparte were only infringers of the true power, while the Republican and Bonapartist will argue, the one that the Convention and the other that the Empire was the true authority and all the rest a violation of authority. It is evident that the interpretations furnished by these historians, being mutually contradictory, can satisfy none but children of the tenderest age.

Recognizing the falsity of this view of history, another class of historians assert that power rests on a conditional delegation of the collective will of the people to their rulers, and that historical leaders possess power only conditionally on their carrying out the programme which the will of the people has by tacit agreement prescribed to them. But what this programme consists of, these historians do not tell us, or if they do they continually contradict one another.

Each historian, according to his view of what constitutes the goal of a nation's progress, conceives of this programme as, for instance, the greatness, the wealth, the freedom or the enlightenment of the citizens of France or some other country. But ignoring the mutual contradictions of the historians as to the nature of this programme – even granted the existence of some one general programme – we find that the facts of history almost always gainsay this theory. If the conditions on which power is vested in rulers consist in the wealth, freedom and enlightenment of the people, how is it that Louis XIV and Ivan the Terrible live out their reigns in peace, while Louis XVI and Charles I are put to death by their peoples? To this question such historians reply that the actions of Louis XIV, which ran counter to the programme, were visited on Louis XVI. But why did they not react on Louis XIV or Louis XV? – why expressly on Louis XVI? And what is the term for such reactions? To these questions there is and can be no reply. Equally little does this view explain why for several centuries the collective will remains vested in certain rulers and their heirs, and then suddenly in the course of fifty years is transferred to a Convention, to a Directory, to a Napoleon, to an Alexander, to a Louis XVIII, to a Napoleon again, to a Charles X, to a Louis Philippe, to a Republican government and to a Napoleon III. To explain these swift transferences of the people's will from one individual to another, especially when complicated by international relations, conquests and alliances, the historians are reluctantly obliged to allow that a proportion of these phenomena are not normal delegations of the popular will but accidents proceeding from the cunning or the craft, the blundering or the weakness, of a diplomatist, a monarch or a party leader. So that most of the phenomena of history – civil wars, revolutions, conquests – are presented by these historians not as the results of free transferences of the people's will but as the products of the ill-directed will of one or more individuals, that is, once again, as usurpations of power. And so these historians too see historical events as exceptions to their theory.

These historians are like a botanist who, having observed that some plants germinate with two cotyledons, should insist that every growing thing grows by dividing into a pair of leaflets; and that the palm-tree, therefore, and the mushroom, nay, even the oak – which in its full-grown ramification loses all resemblance to the twin-leaflet, dicotyledonous form – are departures from theory.

Historians of the third class assume that the will of the people is vested in historical personages conditionally, but that the conditions are not known to us. They say that historical leaders have powers only because they are carrying out the will of the people which has been delegated to them.

But in that case, if the force that moves nations lies not in their historical leaders but in the peoples themselves, where is the significance of those leaders?

Historical personages, so these historians tell us, are the expression of the will of the masses: the activity of the historical leader represents the activity of the people.

But in that case the question arises, Does all the activity of the leaders serve as an expression of the people's will, or only a certain side of it? If the whole activity of the leaders serves as the expression of the people's will, as some historians suppose, then all the *minutiae* of court scandal contained in the biographies of the Napoleons and the Catherines serve to express the life of the nation, which is obvious nonsense; but if it is only one side of the activity of an historical leader which serves to express the life of a people, as other so-called 'philosophical' historians believe, then in order to determine what side of the activity of the historical personage expresses the nation's life we have first of all to know in what the nation's life consists.

Confronted by this difficulty, historians of the kind I am speaking of will invent some most obscure and impalpable, generalized abstraction to cover the greatest possible number of occurrences, and then declare this abstraction to be the aim of mankind's movement. The most usual generalizations adopted by almost all historians are: freedom, equality, enlightenment, progress, civilization and culture. Having postulated some such generalization as the goal of the movements of humanity, the historians go on to study those personages in history who have left the greatest number of memorials behind them: kings, ministers, generals, authors, reformers, popes and journalists – according as these personages, in their judgement, have contributed to or hindered the abstraction in question. But as it is nowhere proven that the aim of humanity does consist in freedom, equality, enlightenment or civilization, and as the connexion of the masses with the rulers and enlighteners of humanity only rests on the arbitrary assumption that the collective will of the masses is always vested in these figures which attract our attention, it happens that the activity of the millions who migrate, burn their houses, abandon tilling the soil, and butcher one another, never does find expression in descriptions of the activity of some dozen persons who do not burn houses, have nothing to do with agriculture or killing their fellow-creatures.

History proves this at every turn. Is the ferment of the peoples of the west at the end of the last century and their drive eastwards explained by the activity of Louis XIV, XV and XVI, their mistresses and ministers, or by the lives of Napoleon, Rousseau, Diderot, Beaumarchais and others?

Is the movement of the Russian people eastwards to Kazan and Siberia expressed in the details of the morbid character of Ivan the Terrible and his correspondence with Kurbsky?

Is the movement of the peoples at the time of the Crusades explained by the life and activity of the Godfreys and the Louises and their ladies? For us that movement of the peoples from west to east, without any object, without leadership – a crowd of vagrants following Peter the Hermit – remains incomprehensible. And still more incomprehensible is the cessation of that movement when a rational and sacred aim for the Crusades – the deliverance of Jerusalem – had been clearly proclaimed by historical leaders. Popes, kings and knights urged the people to free the Holy Land; but the people did not move, for the unknown cause which had previously impelled them existed no longer. The history of the Godfreys and the Minnesingers evidently cannot be taken as an epitome of the life of the people. And the history of the Godfreys and Minnesingers has remained the history of Godfreys and Minnesingers, while the history of the life of the people and their incentives has remained unknown.

Even less explanatory of the life of the people is the history of writers and reformers.

The history of culture will explain to us the impelling motives and circumstances of the life and thoughts of a writer or a reformer. We may learn that Luther had a hasty temper and delivered such and such orations; we may learn that Rousseau was of a suspicious nature and wrote such and such books; but we shall not learn why the nations flew at one another's throats after the Reformation, or why men guillotined one another during the French Revolution.

If we unite both these kinds of history, as is done by the most modern historians, we shall get histories of monarchs and writers but not history of the lives of nations.

5

THE life of nations cannot be summarized in the lives of a few men, for the connexion between those men and the nations has not been discovered. The theory that this connexion is based on the transference of the collective will of a people to certain historical personages is a hypothesis not supported by the experience of history.

The theory of the transference of the collective will of the people to historical personages may perhaps explain much in the domain of jurisprudence and be essential for its purposes, but in its application to history, as soon as revolutions, conquests or civil wars make their appearance – as soon as history begins, in fact – this theory explains nothing.

The theory seems to be irrefutable just because the act of transference of the people's will cannot be verified.

No matter what event takes place, nor who directs it, the theory can always claim that such and such a person took the lead because the collective will was vested in him.

The replies this theory gives to historical questions are like the replies of a man who, watching the movements of a herd of cattle, and paying no attention to the varying quality of the pasturage in different parts of the field, or to the drover's stick, should attribute the direction the herd takes to what animal happens to be at its head.

'The herd goes in that direction because the animal in front leads it there and the collective will of all the other cattle is vested in that leader.' That is what historians in our first category say – those who assume an unconditional transference of power.

'If the animals leading the herd change, this happens because the collective will of all the cattle is transferred from one leader to another, according to whether the leader leads them in the direction selected by the whole herd.' Such is the reply of the historians who assume that the collective will of the masses is delegated to rulers on terms which they regard as known. (With this method of observation it very often happens that the observer, influenced by the direction he himself prefers, reckons as leaders those who, owing to the people's change of direction, are no longer in front but on one side or even in the rear.)

'If the beasts in front are continually changing and the direction of the whole herd constantly alters, this is because, in order to follow a given direction, the cattle transfer their will to those beasts which attract our attention, and to study the movements of the herd we must watch the movements of all the prominent animals moving on all sides of the herd.' So say the third class of historians who accept all historical characters, from monarchs to journalists, as the expression of their age.

The theory of the transference of the will of the masses to historical persons is merely a paraphrase – a re-statement of the question in other words.

What causes historical events? Power.

What is power? Power is the collective will of the masses vested in one person.

On what condition is the will of the people delegated to one person? On condition that that person expresses the will of the whole people.

That is, power is power. That is, power is a word the meaning of which we do not understand.

*

If the domain of human knowledge were confined to abstract thinking, then humanity, having subjected to criticism the explanation of power that *juridical science* gives us, would conclude that power is merely a word and has no existence in reality. But for the knowledge of phenomena man has, besides abstract reasoning, another instrument – experience – by which he verifies the results of his reasoning. And experience tells him that power is not merely a word but an actually existing phenomenon.

Not to speak of the fact that no description of the collective activity of men can dispense with the concept of power, the existence of power is proved both by history and by observation of contemporary events.

Whenever an event occurs one man or several men make their appearance, by whose will the event seems to take place. Napoleon III issues a decree and the French go to Mexico. The King of Prussia and Bismarck issue decrees and an army enters Bohemia. Napoleon I gives a command and soldiers march into Russia. Alexander I gives a command and the French submit to the Bourbons. Experience shows us that whatever event occurs it is always related to the will of one or of several men who decreed it should be so.

The historians, from the old habit of recognizing divine intervention in human affairs, are inclined to look for the cause of events in the exercise of the will of the person endowed with power, but this supposition is not confirmed either by reason or by experience.

On the one hand reflection shows that the expression of man's will – his words – are only part of the general activity expressed in an event, as for instance, in a war or a revolution; and so without assuming an incomprehensible, supernatural force – a miracle – it is impossible to admit that words can be the immediate cause of the movements of millions of men. On the other hand, even if we admitted that words could be the cause of events, history shows that the expression of the will of historical personages in the majority of cases does not produce any effect – that is, their commands are often not executed and sometimes the very opposite of what they order is done.

Without admitting divine intervention in the affairs of humanity we cannot accept 'power' as the cause of events.

Power, from the standpoint of experience, is merely the relation that exists between the expression of the will of a person and the execution of that will by others.

To explain the conditions of that relationship we must first of all establish a concept of the expression of will, referring it to man and not to the Deity.

If it were the Deity giving commands and expressing His will (as history written by the older school assures us), the expression of that will could never be dependent upon time nor evoked by temporal things, seeing that the Deity is in no way bound to the event. But when we speak of commands that are the expression of the will of men, functioning in time and having a relation to one another, we must, if we are to understand the connexion of commands with events, restore two conditions: (1) the uninterrupted connexion in the time process both of the events themselves and of the person issuing commands – a condition to which all that occurs is subject; and (2) the indispensable connexion between the person issuing commands and those who execute them.

6

ONLY the expression of the will of the Deity, not affected by time, can relate to a whole series of events that have to take place over a period of years or centuries; and only the Deity, who is stirred to action by no temporal agency, can by His sole will determine the direction of humanity's movement. Man is subject to time and himself takes part in the event.

Reinstating the first condition neglected – that of time – we perceive that no single command can be executed without some preceding command making the execution of the last command possible.

No command ever appears spontaneously (i.e. without any external stimulus), or itself covers a whole series of occurrences; but each command follows from another, and never refers to a whole series of events but always to one moment only of an event.

When we say, for instance, that Napoleon ordered armies to go to war we combine in one single expression a series of consecutive commands dependent one on another. Napoleon could not have commanded an invasion of Russia and never did so. One day he ordered certain documents to be dispatched to Vienna, to Berlin and to Petersburg; the following day saw such and such decrees and orders issued to the army, the fleet, the commissariat, and so on and so on – millions of separate commands making up a series of commands corresponding to a series of events which brought the French armies into Russia.

If throughout his reign Napoleon continues to issue commands concerning an invasion of England and expends on no other undertaking so much time and effort, and yet during his whole reign never once attempts to execute his design but undertakes an expedition into Russia, with which country, according to his repeatedly expressed conviction, he considers it to his advantage to be in alliance – then this results from the fact that his commands did not correspond to the course of events in the first case but did so in the latter.

For a command to be carried out to the letter it must be a command actually capable of fulfilment. But to know what can and what cannot be carried out is impossible, not only in the case of Napoleon's invasion of Russia, in which millions participated, but even in the case of the simplest event, seeing that both the one and the other are liable at any moment to find themselves confronted by millions of obstacles. Every command executed is always one of an immense number unexecuted. All the impossible commands are inconsistent with the course of events and do not get carried out. Only the possible ones link up into a consecutive series of commands corresponding to a series of events, and are carried out.

Our erroneous idea that the command which precedes the event causes the event is due to the fact that when the event has taken place and out of thousands of commands those few which were consistent with that event have been executed we forget about the others that were not executed because they could not be. Apart from that, the chief source of our error in this regard arises from the fact that in the historical account a whole series of innumerable, diverse and petty events, such, for example, as all those which led the French soldiers into Russia, is generalized into a single event in accord with the result produced by that series of events; and by a corresponding generalization a whole series of commands is also summed up into a single expression of will.

We say: Napoleon chose to invade Russia and he did so. In reality we never find in all Napoleon's career anything resembling an expression of that design. What we do find is a series of commands or expressions of his will of the most varied and indefinite tenor possible. Out of a countless series of unexecuted commands of Napoleon's one series, for the campaign of 1812, was carried out – not because they differed in any way from other commands that were *not* executed but because they coincided with the course of events which brought the French army into Russia; just as in stencil-work a certain figure comes out, not because the colour was laid on from this side or in a particular way but because colour was smeared all over the figure cut out in the stencil.

So that examining the relation in time of commands to events we find that a command can never in any case be the cause of the event but that a definite interdependence none the less exists between the two.

To understand what this interdependence is, it is necessary to reinstate the second of our two conditions governing every command which emanates from man and not from the Deity – the condition that the man who issues the command must also be a participator in the event.

It is this relation of commander to commanded which is called 'power'. This relation may be analysed as follows:

For the purpose of common action men always unite in certain combinations in which, regardless of the difference of the aims set for their common action, the relation between those taking part in it always remains the same.

Men uniting in these combinations always assume among themselves such a relationship that the larger number take a more direct part, and the smaller number a less direct part, in the collective action for which they have combined.

Of all such combinations in which men unite for joint action one of the most striking and precise is an army.

Every army is composed of men of the lowest service grades – the rank and file – who always form the majority; then of those of a slightly higher military standing – corporals and non-commissioned officers, fewer in number than the privates; and of still higher officers, of whom there are still fewer, and so on up to the highest military command, which is concentrated in one person.

A military organization may very truly be likened to a cone, the base of which, with the largest diameter, consists of the rank and file; the next higher and smaller section of the cone consists of the next higher grades of the army, and so on to the apex, the point of which will represent the commander-in-chief.

The soldiers forming the majority constitute the lower section of the cone and its base. The soldier himself does the stabbing and hacking, the burning and pillaging, and always receives orders for these actions from the men above him: he himself never gives an order. The non-commissioned officer (there are not so many of him) does less of the immediate work of war than the private, but he gives commands. An officer takes an active part more rarely still but issues commands the more frequently. A general does nothing but command the army, indicates the objective and hardly ever uses a weapon himself. Finally the commander-in-chief: he never takes a direct part in the actual work of war but only makes general dispositions for the movement of the masses under him. A similar mutual relationship of individuals obtains in every combination of men for joint activity – in agriculture, commerce and every administrative department.

Thus, without exaggeratedly separating all the contiguous sections of the cone – all the ranks of an army, or the ranks and positions in any administrative or public body, from lowest to highest – we discern a law by which men concerned to take common action combine in such relations that the more directly they participate in performing the action the less they can command and the more numerous they are, while the less they take any direct part in the work itself the more they command and the fewer they are in number; rising in this way from the lowest strata to a single man at the top, who takes the least direct share in the action and devotes his energy to a greater extent than all the others to the giving of commands.

It is this relationship between commander and commanded which constitutes the essence of the concept called power.

Having restored the conditions of time under which all events take place, we find that a command is executed only when it is related to a corresponding course of events. Likewise restoring the essential condition of connexion between those who command and those who execute, we have seen that by the very nature of the case those who command take the smallest part in the action itself, and that their activity is exclusively directed to commanding.

7

WHEN some event takes place people express their various opinions and hopes in regard to it, and inasmuch as the event proceeds from the collective activity of many some one of the opinions or hopes expressed is sure to be fulfilled, if only approximately. When one of the opinions expressed is fulfilled that opinion gets connected with the event as the command preceding it.

Men are hauling a log. Each of them may be expressing opinion as to how and where it should be hauled. They haul the log to its destination, and it turns out that it has been done in accordance with what one of them said. He gave the command. This is commanding and power in their primary form. The man who laboured hardest with his arms was the least able to think what he was doing, or reflect on what would be the result of the common activity, or give a command; while the man who was doing the most commanding was obviously the least able of the party, by reason of his greater verbal activity, to perform direct manual labour. In a larger aggregate of men directing their efforts to a common end the category of those who, because their activity is devoted to giving commands, take less part in the joint enterprise stands out still more prominently.

When a man is acting alone he always keeps before him a certain set of considerations which, so he believes, have regulated his action in the past, justify his action in the present and guide him in planning future activity.

In exactly the same way amalgamations of people leave those who do not take a direct part in the activity to devise considerations, justifications and projects concerning their collective activity.

For reasons known or unknown to us the French began to shipwreck and butcher each other. And corresponding to and accompanying this phenomenon we have the justification of the people's expressed determination that this was necessary for the welfare of France, for liberty and for equality. The French cease to murder one another, and justify that on the ground of the necessity of a centralization of power, of resistance to Europe, and so on. Men march from west to east, slaying their fellow-men, and this proceeding is accompanied by figures of speech about the glory of France, the baseness of England, and so on. History shows us that these justifications of events have no general sense and are self-contradictory – like, for instance, killing a man pursuant to recognition of his rights, or the slaughter of millions in Russia for the humiliation of England. But these justifications have a very necessary significance in their own day.

These justifications relieve those who produce the events from moral responsibility. At the time they do the work of the brooms that are fixed in front of a locomotive to clear the snow from the rails ahead: they clear men's moral responsibilities from their path. Without such justifications there would be no reply to the exceedingly simple question which presents itself when we examine any historical event: How do millions of men come to combine to commit crimes, wars, massacres and so forth?

Under the present complex forms of political and social life in Europe can any event be imagined that is not prescribed, decreed or ordered by monarchs, ministers, parliaments or newspapers? Is there any collective action which cannot find its justification in political unity, in patriotism, in the balance of power or in civilization? So that every event that occurs inevitably coincides with some expressed desire and, having found justification for itself, appears as the product of the will of one or more persons.

In whatever direction a ship is moving the surge where the prow cuts the waves will always be noticeable ahead. To those on board the ship the movement of this wave-form will be the only movement they see.

Only by watching closely, moment by moment, the movement of this wave-form and comparing it with that of the ship shall we convince ourselves that it is entirely conditioned by the forward movement of the ship and that we were deluded by the fact that we ourselves are imperceptibly moving.

We see the same thing if we observe, moment by moment, the movement of historical personages (that is, restoring the inevitable condition of all that occurs – continuity in the flow of time) and do not lose sight of the essential connexion of historical figures with the masses.

When the ship keeps on in one direction the surge ahead of her stays constant; if she tacks about, it too will change. But wherever the ship may turn there will always be the surge ahead, anticipating her movement.

Whatever happens it will always appear that precisely this had been foreseen and decreed. Whichever way the ship turns, the surge which neither directs nor accelerates her movement will always foam ahead of her and at a distance seem to us not merely to be moving on its own account but to be governing the ship's movement also.

*

Examining only those expressions of the will of historical personages which may be considered to have borne to events the relation of commands, historians have assumed that events depend on commands. But examining the events themselves and the connexion in which the historical characters stand to the masses, we have found that historical characters and their commands are dependent on the event. An incontestable proof of this deduction lies in the fact that, however many commands may be given, the event does not take place unless there are other causes for it; but as soon as an event does take place – whatever it may be – then out of all the incessantly expressed wishes of different people some will always be found which in meaning and time of utterance will bear to the event the relation of commands.

Arriving at this conclusion, we are able to give a direct and positive reply to those two essential questions of history:

(1) What is power?

(2) What force produces the movement of nations?

(1) Power is the relation of a given person to other persons, in which the more this person expresses opinions, theories and justifications of the collective action the less is his participation in that action.

(2) The movement of nations is caused not by power, nor by intellectual activity, nor even by a combination of the two, as historians have supposed, but by the activity of *all* the people who participate in the event, and who always combine in such a way that those who take the largest direct share in the event assume the least responsibility, and *vice versa*.

Morally, power appears to cause the event; physically, it is those who are subordinate to that power. But, inasmuch as moral activity is inconceivable without physical activity, the cause of the event is found neither in the one nor the other but in the conjunction of the two.

Or, in other words, the concept of a cause is not applicable to the phenomenon we are examining.

In the last analysis we reach an endless circle – that uttermost limit to which in every domain of thought the human intellect must come if it is not playing with its subject. Electricity produces heat; heat produces electricity. Atoms attract and atoms repel one another.

Speaking of the interaction of heat and electricity and of atoms we cannot say why this occurs, and we say that such is the nature of these phenomena, such is their law. The same applies to historical phenomena. Why do wars or revolutions happen? We do not know. We only know that to produce the one or the other men form themselves into a certain combination in which all take part; and we say that this is the nature of men, that this is a law.

8

If history had to do with external phenomena the establishment of this simple and obvious law would suffice and we might end our discussion. But the law of history relates to man. A particle of matter cannot tell us that it is unconscious of the law of attraction and repulsion and that that law is not true; but man, who is the subject of history, says bluntly: I am free, and am therefore not subject to laws.

The presence of the problem of man's freewill, though unexpressed, is felt at every step in history.

All seriously thinking historians are involuntarily led to this question. All the contradictions and obscurities of history, and the false path historical science has followed, are due solely to the lack of a solution of this question.

If the will of every man were free, that is, if every man could act as he pleased, all history would be a series of disconnected accidents.

If one man only out of millions once in a thousand years had the power of acting freely, i.e. as he chose, it is obvious that one single free act of that man in violation of the laws would be enough to prove that laws governing all human action cannot possibly exist.

Again, if there is a single law controlling the actions of men, free-will cannot exist, for man's will will then be subject to that law.

In this contradiction lies the problem of freewill, which from earliest times has occupied the best intellects of mankind and has from earliest times appeared in all its colossal significance.

The problem lies in the fact that if we regard man as a subject for observation from whatever point of view – theological, historical, ethical or philosophic – we find the universal law of necessity to which he (like everything else that exists) is subject. But looking upon man from within ourselves – man as the object of our own inner consciousness of self – we feel ourselves to be free.

This inner consciousness is a source of self-cognition distinct from and independent of reason. With his reason man observes himself, but only through self-consciousness does he know himself.

Now without consciousness of self no observation or application of reason is conceivable.

In order to understand, to observe, to draw conclusions, man must first of all be conscious of himself as living. A man is only conscious of himself as a living being by the fact that he wills: he is conscious of his volition. And his own will – which is the very essence of his life – he is and cannot but be conscious of as being free.

If on submitting himself to observation man perceives that his will is directed by a constant law (say he observes the imperative need of taking food, or the way the brain works, or whatsoever it may be) he cannot regard this consistent direction of his will otherwise than as a limitation of it. But a thing can only be limited if it is free to begin with. Man sees his will to be limited just because he is conscious of it in no other way than as being free.

You tell me I am not free. But I have just lifted my arm and let it fall. Everyone understands that this reply, however illogical, is an irrefutable demonstration of freedom.

The reply is the expression of a consciousness that is not subject to reason.

If the consciousness of freedom were not a separate and independent source of self-knowledge it would be subject to reasoning and experience; but in fact it is not, and it is unthinkable that it could be so.

Man learns from a succession of experiments and reflections that he, as the object under observation, is subject to certain laws, to which he submits, and never, once he has become acquainted with them, will he resist the laws of gravitation or impermeability. But the same series of experiments and reflections proves to him that the complete freedom of which he is conscious in himself is impossible; that every action of his depends on his particular organism, on his character and the motives inspiring him; yet he never submits to the deductions of these experiments and arguments.

Having learned from experience and by reasoning that a stone falls downwards, man is convinced beyond doubt and in all cases expects to find this law operating which he has discovered.

But having learned just as surely that his will is subject to laws, he does not and cannot believe it.

However often experience and deliberation may show a man that in the same circumstances and with the same character he will do the same thing as before, he will feel none the less assured of being able to act as he pleases when in the same circumstances and with the same character, and for, perhaps, the thousandth time, he approaches the action which always ends in the same way. Every man, savage and sage alike, however incontestably reason and experience may prove to him that it is impossible to imagine two different courses of action in precisely identical circumstances, feels that without this nonsensical conception (which constitutes the essence of freedom) he cannot conceive of life. He feels that, however impossible it may be, it is so, for without this conception of freedom not only would he be unable to understand life but he would be unable to live for a single moment.

Life would be intolerable because all man's aspirations, all the interest that life holds for him, are so many aspirations and strivings after greater freedom. Wealth and poverty, fame and obscurity, power and subjection, strength and weakness, health and disease, culture and ignorance, work and leisure, repletion and hunger, virtue and vice are only greater or lesser degrees of freedom.

To imagine a man wholly destitute of freedom is the same thing as to imagine a man destitute of life.

If the concept of freedom appears to the reason as a senseless contradiction, like the possibility of performing two actions at one and the same instant of time, or the possibility of an effect without a cause, that only proves that consciousness is not subject to reason.

It is this unwavering, certain consciousness of freedom – a consciousness indifferent to experience or reason, recognized by all thinkers and felt by everybody without exception – it is this consciousness without which there is no imagining man at all, which forms the other side of the question.

Man is the creation of an almighty, infinitely good and omniscient God. What is sin, the conception of which springs from man's consciousness of freedom? That is the question for theology.

The actions of man are subject to general and immutable laws which can be expressed in statistics. What is man's responsibility to society, the conception of which follows from his consciousness of freedom? That is the question for jurisprudence.

Man's actions proceed from his natural character and the motives influencing him. What is conscience and the sense of right and wrong behaviour that follow from the consciousness of freedom? That is the question for ethics.

Man in connexion with the common life of humanity conceives himself as subject to the laws which determine that life. But the same man apart from this connexion conceives of himself as free. How is the past life of nations and of humanity to be regarded – as the product of the free or the unfree activity of man? That is the question for history.

Only in our conceited age of the popularization of knowledge – thanks to that most powerful engine of ignorance, the diffusion of printed matter – has the question of freedom of will been put on a level on which the question itself cannot exist. In our day the majority of so-called 'advanced' people – that is, a mob of ignoramuses – have accepted the result of the researches of natural science, which is occupied with one side only of the question, for a solution of the whole problem.

They say and they write and they print that the soul and freedom do not exist, since the life of man is expressed by muscular movements and muscular movements are conditioned by the working of the nervous system: soul and freewill do not exist because at some unknown period of time we sprang from the apes. They say this with no inkling that thousands of years ago that same law of necessity which they are now so strenuously trying to prove by physiology and comparative zoology was not merely acknowledged by all religions and all thinkers but has never been denied. They do not see that the rôle of the natural sciences in this matter is merely to illumine one side of it. For even if, from the point of view of observation, reason and the will are but secretions of the brain, and if man following the general law

1429

of evolution developed from lower animals at some unknown period of time, all this will only elucidate from a fresh angle the truth admitted thousands of years ago by all religious and philosophic theories – that from the standpoint of reason man is subject to the laws of necessity; but it does not advance by a hair's breadth the solution of the question, which has another, opposite, side, founded on the consciousness of freedom.

If men descended from apes at an unknown period of time, that is as intelligible as that they were made from a handful of dust at a known period of time (in the first case the unknown quantity is the date, in the second it is the origin); and the question of how man's consciousness of freedom is to be reconciled with the law of necessity to which he is subject cannot be solved by comparative physiology and zoology, seeing that in the frog, the rabbit and the ape we can observe only muscular and nervous activity, whereas in man we find muscular and nervous activity plus consciousness.

The naturalists and their disciples who suppose they are solving this question are like plasterers set to stucco one side of a church wall. In an access of zeal, in the absence of their foreman, they plaster over windows, icons, woodwork and still unbuttressed walls, and rejoice that from their plasterers' point of view everything is now so smooth and even.

9

In this matter of freewill versus necessity history has the advantage over other branches of knowledge which have attempted a solution in that, so far as history is concerned, the question relates not to the essential nature of man's freewill but to our presentation of how this freewill actually manifested in the past and under certain conditions.

In this respect history stands to the other sciences in the same relation as empirical to speculative science.

The subject of history is not the will of man as such but our presentation of it.

And so for history the insoluble mystery presented by the union of freewill and necessity does not exist as it does for theology, ethics and philosophy. History deals with a presentation of the life of man in which the union of those two antinomies has already taken place.

In actual life every historical event, every human action, can be quite clearly and specifically comprehended without any sense of the contradictory, even though each event will be seen to be in part free and in part necessitated.

To solve the question of how freedom and necessity amalgamate and what constitutes the essence of these two concepts the philosophy of history can and must pursue a route contrary to that followed by other sciences. Instead of first defining the concepts of freedom and necessity *per se*, and then ranging the phenomena of life under those definitions, history must form her definitions of the concepts of free-will and necessity from the immense quantity of phenomena of which she is cognizant, and that are always dependent on those two elements.

Whatever presentation of the activity either of many men or of one man we may consider we always regard it as the product partly of freewill and partly of the law of necessity.

Whether we speak of the migration of peoples and the incursions of the barbarians, or the decrees of Napoleon III, or someone's action an hour ago in choosing one direction out of several for his walk, we are unconscious of the presence of any contradiction. The measure of freedom and necessity governing the actions of these men is clearly defined for us.

Very often indeed our conception of the degree of freedom varies with the point of view from which we examine the phenomenon; but every human action always appears to us alike as a certain combination of freedom and necessity. In every action we investigate we see a certain measure of freedom and a certain measure of necessity. And always, the more freedom we see in any action the less necessity do we perceive, and the more necessity the less freedom.

The ratio of freedom to necessity decreases and increases according to the point of view from which the action is regarded; but their relation is always one of inverse proportion.

A drowning man who clutches at another and drags him under; or a hungry mother exhausted by feeding her baby who steals food; or a well-disciplined soldier who slays a defenceless fellow-creature because he is ordered to do so – seem less guilty, that is less free and more subject to the law of necessity, to one who knows the circumstances in which they were placed, and more free to an observer unaware that the man was drowning, the mother starving, and the soldier under orders, and so on. Similarly a man who committed a murder twenty years ago and has since lived peaceably and harmlessly in society seems less guilty, and his deed more subject to the law of necessity, to someone who considers what he did after a lapse of twenty years than to one looking at the same act the day after it was committed. And in the same way every act of a madman, a drunkard or a man labouring under violent excitement appears less free and more inevitable to one who knows the mental condition of the person who performed the action, and more free and less inevitable to the one who does not know it. In all such cases the conception of freedom is increased or diminished, and that of compulsion is correspondingly diminished or increased, according to the point of view from which the action is regarded. So that the greater the estimate of necessity the smaller the estimate of freedom, and *vice versa*.

Religion, ordinary common sense, the science of jurisprudence and history itself appreciate alike this relation between necessity and freedom.

In every case, without exception, where our impression concerning the ratio of freewill to necessity may vary there are three points only to be taken into consideration.

(1) The relation to the external world of the man who commits the deed;

(2) his relation to time; and

(3) his relation to the causes leading to the deed.

In consideration (1) our judgement will be affected by the degree to which we realize the man's relation to the external world – by the more or less clear idea we form of the definite position occupied by the man generally in relation to everything co-existing with him. It is this sort of consideration which makes it evident that a drowning man is less free and more subject to necessity than a man standing on dry ground; and that makes the actions of a man living in close connexion with others in a thickly populated district, bound by family, official or business duties, seem undoubtedly less free and more subject to necessity than those of a man living in solitude and seclusion.

If we study one man by himself, if we isolate him from his environment, every action of his seems free to us. But if we see any relation of his whatever to what surrounds him, if we see any connexion with anything whatever – with another man talking to him, a book read by him, the work in which he is engaged, even with the air he breathes or the light that falls on the objects about him – we see that each of these circumstances has its influence on him and orders at least one side of his activity. And the more we perceive of these influences the less free does he seem to us and the greater the impression we have of the necessity to which he is subject.

(2) Here our conclusion will be affected by how far the man's relation in time to the world is apparent – by the degree to which we perceive the specific place of his action in the course of time. It is this consideration which causes the fall of the first man, resulting in the emergence of the human race, to appear obviously less free than a man's entry into wedlock today. It is this consideration which accounts for the fact that the life and activity of people who lived centuries ago and are connected with me in time cannot seem to me as free as the life of a contemporary, the consequences of which are as yet unknown to me.

Our scale of judgement as to the greater or lesser degrees of freedom and necessity will here depend on the greater or lesser interval of time between the performance of the action and our appraisal of it.

If I examine an act I performed a moment ago in circumstances approximately identical with those I am in now my action appears to me to have been wholly free. But if I examine an act performed a month ago, being now in different circumstances I cannot help recognizing that if that act had not been committed much that resulted from it – useful, agreeable and even indispensable – could never have taken place. If I reflect on a more remote action of ten or more years ago the consequences of my action are still plainer to me and I shall find it hard to imagine what would have been had that action not been performed. The farther I go back in memory or – which is the same thing – the longer I postpone my appraisal the more uncertain becomes my belief in the freedom of my action.

Precisely the same process operates in history, too, so that we find our convictions varying as to the part played by freewill in the general affairs of humanity. A contemporary event seems to us indubitably the doing of all the men we know of concerned in it; but in the case of a more remote event we have had time to observe its inevitable consequences, which prevent our conceiving of anything else as possible. And the farther back we go in our investigation of events the less arbitrary do they appear.

The Austro-Prussian war looks to us to be the undoubted consequence of the crafty conduct of Bismarck, and so on.

The Napoleonic wars, though less positively this time, seem to us the outcome of their heroes' will. But when we get to the Crusades we see an event occupying its definite place in history as an occurrence without which the modern history of Europe is unimaginable, although to the chroniclers of the Crusades that event appeared simply due to the will of certain individuals. In the migration of peoples it never enters anyone's head today to suppose that the renovation of the European world depended on a caprice of Attila's. The more remote in history the object of our observation the more doubtful we feel of the freewill of those concerned in the event and the more manifest becomes the law of necessity.

(3) The third element influencing our judgement is the degree to which we can apprehend that endless chain of causation demanded by reason, in which every phenomenon capable of being understood (and therefore every human action) must have its definite place as a result of what has gone before and as a cause of what will follow.

It is in virtue of this principle that the better we are acquainted with the physiological, psychological and historical laws deduced from observation and by which man is controlled, and the more correctly we discern the physiological, psychological and historical causes of the action, and the simpler the action we are investigating and the less complex the character and mind of the individual whose action it is, the more subject to necessity and the less free do our actions and those of others appear.

When we have absolutely no understanding of the cause of an action – whether it be a crime, a virtuous act or even one that is neither – we ascribe a greater element of freewill to it. In the case of a crime we are more urgent in demanding punishment for the deed; in the case of a virtuous act we are warmer in our appreciation of its merits. In cases of no moral bearing we recognize the maximum of individuality, originality and independence. Yet let but *one* of the countless causes of the act become known to us and we at once recognize a certain element of necessity and are less insistent on punishment for the crime, less ready to acknowledge merit in the virtuous act or freedom in the apparently original performance. The fact that the criminal was reared in vicious surroundings mitigates his fault in our eyes. The self-sacrifice of a father or a mother, or self-sacrifice in the hope of gain, is more intelligible than gratuitous self-sacrifice and therefore appears less deserving of sympathy and less the work of freewill. The founder of a sect or a party, or an inventor, impresses us less when we know how and by what the way was paved for him beforehand. If we have a large range of examples, if our observation is continually directed to seeking the correlation between cause and effect in people's actions, their actions appear to us more subject to compulsion and less free the more accurately we connect effects with causes. If the actions investigated are simple, and we have a vast number of such actions under observation, our conception of their inevitability will be still more complete. The dishonest conduct of the son of a dishonest father, the misbehaviour of a woman who has fallen into bad company, a reformed drunkard's relapse into drunkenness, and so on, are cases that seem to us less free the better we understand their cause. If, again, the human being whose conduct we are considering stands on a very low plane of mental development, like a child or a lunatic or an imbecile, we who know the causes of the act and the simplicity of the character and intelligence in question see forthwith so great a measure of necessity and so little freewill that as soon as we know the cause compelling the action we can foretell what will happen.

The concepts of legal disability, admitted by all legislative codes, and that of extenuating circumstances rest entirely on these three considerations. Responsibility appears greater or less according to our greater or lesser knowledge of the conditions in which the individual was placed whose action is under judgement, and according to the longer or shorter interval of time between the perpetration of the action and its investigation, and according to our greater or lesser understanding of the causes that led to the action.

10

THUS our impression of freewill and necessity is gradually diminished or increased according to the degree of connexion with the external world, the greater or lesser degree of remoteness in time and the degree of dependence on causes which we see in the phenomenon of a man's life that we examine.

So that if we select for observation a point in the life of a man at which his connexion with the external world is best known, where the interval of time between the action and our appraisal of it is as long as possible, and the causes of the action are as easy as possible to arrive at, we form the idea of a maximum of necessity and a minimum of freewill. On the other hand, if we select for observation a man in the least possible dependence on external conditions, and observe a given act of his which was accomplished at the nearest possible moment to the present time, and of which the causes are beyond our ken, we form the idea of a minimum of necessity and a maximum of freewill.

But in neither case – and however we shift our point of view – however clear we may make to ourselves the connexion between our man and the external world or however hopelessly we fail to trace any such connexion, however much we lengthen or shorten the period of time involved, however intelligible or incomprehensible the causes of the action may be to us, we can never conceive of either complete freedom or complete necessity of action.

(1) However hard we try to imagine a man exempt from the influence of the external world we never arrive at a conception of freedom in space. Every human action is inevitably conditioned by what surrounds him and by his own body. I raise my arm and let it fall. My action seems to me free; but on asking myself whether I could raise my arm in any direction I see that I raised it in the direction in which there was least resistance to the action either from things around me or from the construction of my own body. I chose one out of all the possible directions because in that direction I met with the least hindrance. For my action to be wholly free it would have to meet with no obstacles at all. To conceive of a man being absolutely free we must imagine him outside space, which is obviously impossible.

(2) However much we approximate the time of appraisal to the time of the deed we can never arrive at a conception of freedom in time. For if I examine an action committed a second ago I must still recognize it as not being free, since it is irrevocably linked to the moment at which it was committed. Can I lift my arm ? I lift it; but I ask myself: Could I have refrained from lifting my arm at that moment which is already in the past ? To satisfy myself on this score I do not lift it the next moment. But I am not now refraining from doing so at the first moment when I asked myself the question. Time has gone by which it was not in my power to detain, and the arm which I then raised and the air in which I raised it are no longer the same air which now surrounds me or the same arm which I now refrain from

lifting. The moment at which the first movement was made is irrevocable and at that moment I could perform one movement and no other and whatever movement I made it could have been the only one. The fact that I did not lift my arm a moment later does not prove that I could not have raised it. And since I could only make one movement at one moment of time it could not have been any other. To imagine it as free one would have to imagine it in the present, on the boundary between the past and the future – i.e. outside time, which is impossible.

(3) However much the difficulty of apprehending the causes of an act may be enlarged we never reach a conception of complete freewill – i.e. of absolute absence of cause. However much we may fail to see the cause of a given expression of will (as manifested in any act of our own or another) the first demand of the intellect is to assume and seek out a cause, without which no phenomenon is conceivable. I raise my arm in order to perform an action independent of any cause, but my wish to perform an action without a cause is the cause of my action.

But even if, imagining a man entirely exempt from all influences and examining a momentaneous act of his in the present which we assume to have had no cause, we were to reduce the element of necessity to an infinitesimal minimum equivalent to zero we should still not have arrived at a conception of complete freedom in man, for a being uninfluenced by the external world, standing outside of time and independent of causes would not be a human being at all.

In the same way we can never conceive of a human action quite devoid of freedom and entirely subject to the law of necessity.

(1) However we may increase our knowledge of the spatial conditions in which a man is situated this knowledge can never be complete, since the number of those conditions is as infinite as the infinity of space. And therefore so long as not *all* the conditions that may influence man are defined the circle of necessity is not complete and a certain measure of freedom enters in.

(2) However we may prolong the period of time between the action we are examining and our appraisal of it that period will be finite, while time is infinite, and so in this respect too there can never be absolute inevitability.

(3) However accessible may be the chain of causation of any action we shall never know the whole chain, since it is endless, and so again we never get a conception of absolute necessity.

Moreover, even if, having reduced the residuum of freedom to a minimum equalling zero, we were to assume in some given case – as, for instance, that of a dying man, an unborn babe or an idiot – a complete absence of freedom, by so doing we should destroy the very conception of man in the case we are examining, for as soon as there is no freedom there is no man either. And so the conception of the action of a man subject solely to the law of necessity, devoid of any particle of freedom, is just as impossible as the conception of a completely free human action.

Thus to imagine a human action subject only to the law of necessity, without any freedom, we must assume a knowledge of an *infinite* number of spatial conditions, an *infinitely* long period of time and an *infinite* chain of causation.

To imagine a man perfectly free and not subject to the law of necessity we must imagine him alone, *outside space, outside time* and *outside dependence on cause.*

In the first case, supposing necessity were possible without freewill, we should be brought to a definition of necessity by the law of necessity itself, i.e. mere form without content.

In the second case, if freewill were possible without necessity, we should come to unconditioned freewill outside space, time and cause, which by the fact of its being unconditioned and unlimited would be nothing, or mere content without form.

In general, then, we should have arrived at the two fundamentals on which man's whole cosmic philosophy is constructed – the incomprehensible essence of life and the laws defining that essence.

Reason says: (1) Space with all the forms of matter that give it visibility is infinite, and cannot be imagined otherwise. (2) Time is infinite progression without a moment's pause, and cannot be imagined otherwise. (3) The connexion between cause and effect has no beginning and can have no end.

Consciousness says: (1) I alone am, and all that exists is only I; consequently I include space. (2) I measure flowing time by the fixed moment of the present, in which moment alone I am conscious of myself as living; consequently I stand outside of time. (3) I am independent of cause, since I feel myself to be the cause of every manifestation of my life.

Reason gives expression to the laws of necessity. Consciousness gives expression to the reality of freewill.

Freedom not limited by anything is the essence of life in man's consciousness. Necessity without content is man's reason with its three forms of approach.

Freedom is the thing examined. Necessity is the examiner. Freedom is the content. Necessity is the form.

Only by separating the two sources of cognition, related to one another as form is to content, do we get the mutually exclusive and separately inapprehensible concepts of freedom and necessity.

Only by uniting them do we get a clear conception of the life of man.

Apart from these two concepts which in their synthesis mutually define one another as form and content no conception of life is possible.

All that we know of the life of man is merely a certain relation of freewill to necessity, that is, of consciousness to the laws of reason.

All that we know of the external world of nature is only a certain relation of the forces of nature to necessity, or of the essence of life to the laws of reason.

The great natural forces lie outside us and are not objects of our consciousness; we call these forces gravitation, inertia, electricity, vital force, and so on; but the force of life in man is an object of our consciousness and we call it freewill.

But just as the force of gravitation, inconceptible in itself but realized by every man, can only be understood by us to the extent to which we know the laws of necessity to which it is subject (from the initial fact that all bodies have weight and down to Newton's law), so too the force of freewill, inconceptible in itself but recognized by the consciousness of every human being, is only intelligible to us in so far as we know the laws of necessity to which it is subject (beginning with the fact that every man dies and continuing to the knowledge of the most complex laws of political economy and history).

All knowledge is but the bringing of the essence of life under the laws of reason.

Man's freewill differs from every other force in that man is directly conscious of it: but in the eyes of reason it in no way differs from any other force. The forces of gravitation, electricity or chemical affinity are only distinguished from one another in that they are differently defined by reason. Similarly the force of man's freewill is distinguished by reason from the other forces of nature only by the definition reason gives it. Freewill apart from necessity, that is, apart from the laws of reason that define it, differs in no way from gravitation or heat or the force that makes things grow – for reason it is only a momentary, undefinable sensation of life.

And as the undefinable essence of the force moving the heavenly bodies, the undefinable essence of the forces of heat and electricity, or of chemical resources, or of the vital force, forms the subject-matter of astronomy, physics, chemistry, botany, zoology and so on, so the essence of the force of freewill constitutes the subject-matter of history. But just as the subject of every science is the manifestation of this unknown essence of life, while the essence itself can only be the subject of metaphysics, so too the manifestation of the force of freewill in space, in time and in dependence on cause forms the subject of history, while freewill itself is the subject of metaphysics.

In the biological sciences what we know we call the laws of necessity; what is unknown to us we call vital force. Vital force is only an expression for what remains unexplained by what we know of the essence of life.

So too in history: what is known to us we call the laws of necessity; what is unknown we call freewill. Freewill is for history only an expression connoting what we do not know about the laws of human life.

II

HISTORY examines the manifestations of man's freewill in connexion with the external world in time and in dependence on cause; that is, it defines this freedom by the laws of reason. And so history is a science only in so far as this freewill is defined by those laws.

The recognition of man's freewill as a force capable of influencing historical events, that is, as not subject to laws, is the same for history as the recognition of a free force moving the heavenly bodies would be for astronomy.

Such an assumption would destroy the possibility of the existence of laws, that is, of any science whatever. If there is even one heavenly body moving freely then the laws of Kepler and Newton are negated and no conception of the movement of the heavenly bodies any longer exists. If there is a single human action due to freewill then not a single historical law can exist, nor any conception of historical events.

History is concerned with the lines of movement of human wills, one extremity of which is hidden in the unknown while at the other end men's consciousness of freewill in the present moment moves on through space and time and causation.

The more this field of movement opens out before our eyes the more evident do the laws of the movement become. To discover and define those laws is the problem of history.

From the standpoint from which the science of history now regards its subject, by the method it now follows – seeking the causes of phenomena in the freewill of man – a scientific statement of those laws is impossible, for, whatever limits we may set to man's freewill, as soon as we recognize it as a force not subject to law the existence of law becomes impossible.

Only by reducing this element of freewill to the infinitesimal, that is, by regarding it as an infinitely small quantity, can we convince ourselves of the absolute inaccessibility of causes, and then instead of seeking causes history will adopt for its task the investigation of historical laws.

Research into those laws was begun long ago and the new methods of thought which history must adopt are being worked out simultaneously with the self-destroying process towards which the old kind of history with its perpetual dividing and dissecting of the causes of events is tending.

All human sciences have gone along this path. Reaching the infinitesimal or infinitely small, mathematics – the most exact of the sciences – leaves off dividing and sets out upon the new process of integrating the infinitesimal unknown. Abandoning the concept of causation, mathematics looks for laws, i.e. the properties common to all the infinitely small unknown elements.

The other sciences, too, have proceeded along the same path in their thinking, though it has taken another form. When Newton formulated the law of gravitation he did not say that the sun or the earth had a property of attraction. What he said was that all bodies, from the largest to the smallest, have the property of attracting one another; that is, leaving on one side the question of the cause of the movement of bodies, he expressed the property common to all bodies, from the infinitely large to the infinitely small. The natural sciences do the same thing: putting aside the question of cause, they seek for laws. History, too, is entered on the same course. And if the subject of history is to be the study of the movements of the nations and humanity, and not descriptions of episodes in the lives of individuals, it too is bound to lay aside the notion of cause and seek the laws common to all the equal and indissolubly interconnected infinitesimal elements of freewill.

12

IMMEDIATELY the law of Copernicus was discovered and demonstrated the mere recognition of the fact that it was not the sun but the earth that moves destroyed the whole cosmography of the ancients. It might have been possible by refuting that law to retain the old conception of the movements of the heavenly bodies; but without refuting it it would seem impossible to continue studying the Ptolemaic worlds. Yet long after the discovery of the law of Copernicus the Ptolemaic worlds continued to be a subject of study.

From the time the first person said and proved that the number of births or of crimes is subject to mathematical laws, and that this or that form of government is determined by certain geographical and politico-economic conditions, and that certain relations of population to soil lead to migrations of peoples – from that moment the foundations on which history had been built were destroyed in their essence.

By refuting the newer laws history's former approach might have been retained, but unless they were rejected it would appear impossible to continue studying historical events as though they were the arbitrary product of man's freewill. For if such and such a form of government was established or such and such a migration of peoples took place in consequence of certain geographical, ethnographical or economic conditions, then the freewill of those persons who are represented to us as having established that form of government or evoked the migrations can no longer be regarded as the cause of those phenomena.

And yet the old style of history continues to be studied *pari passu* with the laws of statistics, geography, political economy, comparative philology and geology, which flatly contradict its tenets.

The struggle between the old views and the new was long and stubborn in physical philosophy. Theology stood on guard over the old views and accused the new of violating revelation. But when truth emerged victorious theology rebuilt its house as firmly as before on the new ground.

Equally prolonged and obstinate is the conflict today between the old and the new conception of history, and in the same way theology mounts guard before the old view and accuses the new of subverting revelation.

In both cases and on both sides the struggle rouses passion and stifles truth. On the one side there is fear and regret at the loss of the whole edifice constructed through the centuries; on the other, the passion for destruction.

To the men who fought against the dawning truths of physical philosophy it seemed that if they were to admit those truths their belief in God, in the creation of the universe and in the miracle of Joshua the son of Nun would be shattered. To the defenders of the laws of Copernicus and Newton – to Voltaire, for example – it seemed that the laws of astronomy put an end to religion, and he made use of the law of gravitation as a weapon against religion.

In exactly the same way now it seems that we have only to admit the law of necessity in order to destroy the conception of the soul, of good and evil, and of all the institutions of State and Church that have been built up on those conceptions.

So too, like Voltaire in his day, uninvited defenders of the law of necessity use the law as a weapon against religion, though the law of necessity in history, like the law of Copernicus in astronomy, far from destroying, even strengthens the foundations on which the institutions of State and Church are erected.

As in the question of astronomy then, so in the question of history now, the whole difference of opinion rests on the recognition or non-recognition of some absolute unit serving as the measure of visible phenomena. In astronomy the standard measure was the immovability of the earth; in history it is the independence of the individual – freewill.

As with astronomy the difficulty in the way of recognizing that the earth moves consisted in having to rid oneself of the immediate sensation that the earth was stationary accompanied by a similar sense of the planets' motion, so in history the obstacle in the way of recognizing the subjection of the individual to the laws of space and time and causality lies in the difficulty of renouncing one's personal impression of being independent of those laws. But as in astronomy the new view said: 'True, we are not conscious of the movement of the earth but if we were to allow that it is stationary we should arrive at an absurdity, whereas if we admit the motion (which we do not feel) we arrive at laws,' likewise in history the new theory says: 'True, we are not conscious of our dependence but if we were to allow that we are free we arrive at an absurdity, whereas by admitting our dependence on the external world, on time and on causality we arrive at laws.'

In the first case it was necessary to surmount the sensation of an unreal immobility in space and to recognize a motion we did not feel. In the present case it is similarly necessary to renounce a freedom that does not exist and to recognize a dependence of which we are not personally conscious.